WAR OF
LANKA

Amish is a 1974-born, IIM (Kolkata)-educated banker-turned-author. The success of his debut book, *The Immortals of Meluha* (Book 1 of the Shiva Trilogy), encouraged him to give up his career in financial services to focus on writing. Besides being an author, he is also an Indian-government diplomat, a host for TV documentaries, and a film producer.

Amish is passionate about history, mythology and philosophy, finding beauty and meaning in all world religions. His books have sold more than six million copies and have been translated into over twenty languages. His Shiva Trilogy is the fastest-selling and his Ram Chandra Series the second fastest-selling book series in Indian publishing history. You can connect with Amish here:

- www.facebook.com/authoramish
- www.instagram.com/authoramish
- www.twitter.com/authoramish

CW00923126

Other Titles by Amish

SHIVA TRILOGY

The fastest-selling book series in the history of Indian publishing

The Immortals of Meluha (Book 1 of the Trilogy)

The Secret of the Nagas (Book 2 of the Trilogy)

The Oath of the Vayuputras (Book 3 of the Trilogy)

RAM CHANDRA SERIES

The second fastest-selling book series in the history of Indian publishing

Ram – Scion of Ikshvaku (Book 1 of the Series)

Sita – Warrior of Mithila (Book 2 of the Series)

Raavan – Enemy of Aryavarta (Book 3 of the Series)

INDIC CHRONICLES

Legend of Suheldev

NON-FICTION

Immortal India: Young Country, Timeless Civilisation

Dharma: Decoding the Epics for a Meaningful Life

'[Amish's] writings have generated immense curiosity about India's rich past and culture.'

*– **Narendra Modi***
(Honourable Prime Minister of India)

'[Amish's] writing introduces the youth to ancient value systems while pricking and satisfying their curiosity…'

*– **Sri Sri Ravi Shankar***
(Spiritual Leader and Founder, Art of Living Foundation)

'{Amish's writing is} riveting, absorbing and informative.'

*– **Amitabh Bachchan***
(Actor and Living Legend)

'[Amish's writing is] a fine blend of history and myth … gripping and unputdownable.'

*– **BBC***

'Thoughtful and deep, Amish, more than any author, represents the New India.'

*– **Vir Sanghvi***
(Senior Journalist and Columnist)

'Amish's mythical imagination mines the past and taps into the possibilities of the future. His book series, archetypal and stirring, unfolds the deepest recesses of the soul as well as our collective consciousness.'

*– **Deepak Chopra***
(World-renowned Spiritual Guru and Bestselling Author)

'[Amish is] one of the most original thinkers of his generation.'

*– **Arnab Goswami***
(Senior Journalist and MD, Republic TV)

'Amish has a fine eye for detail and a compelling narrative style.'
— **Dr Shashi Tharoor**
(Member of Parliament and Author)

'[Amish has] a deeply thoughtful mind with an unusual, original and fascinating view of the past.'
— **Shekhar Gupta**
(Senior Journalist and Columnist)

'To understand the New India, you need to read Amish.'
— **Swapan Dasgupta**
(Member of Parliament and Senior Journalist)

'Through all of Amish's books flows a current of liberal, progressive ideology: about gender, about caste, about discrimination of any kind... He is the only Indian bestselling writer with true philosophical depth – his books are all backed by tremendous research and deep thought.'
— **Sandipan Deb**
(Senior Journalist and Editorial Director, Swarajya)

'Amish's influence goes beyond his books, his books go beyond literature, his literature is steeped in philosophy, which is anchored in bhakti, which powers his love for India.'
— **Gautam Chikermane**
(Senior Journalist and Author)

'Amish is a literary phenomenon.'
— **Anil Dharker**
(Senior Journalist and Author)

————◆ RAM CHANDRA SERIES BOOK 4 ◆————

WAR OF
LANKA

AMISH

HarperCollins *Publishers* India

First published in India by HarperCollins *Publishers* 2022
Building No 10, Tower A, 4th Floor, DLF Cyber City, Phase II,
Gurugram – 122002
www.harpercollins.co.in

2 4 6 8 10 9 7 5 3 1

P-ISBN: 978-93-5629-152-2
E-ISBN: 978-93-5629-154-6

Typeset in 11/13.7 Adobe Caslon Pro at
Manipal Technologies Limited, Manipal

Printed and bound at
Thomson Press (India) Ltd

Om Namah Shivāya
The Universe bows to Lord Shiva
I bow to Lord Shiva

To my father, the late V.K. Tripathi,
And to my young son, Neel.

I used to reach up and hold his hand, to learn how to walk,
I reach down to embrace him, for it makes my heart soar.
I used to ask him questions, for he schooled me best,
I give him books to read, to expand his horizons.
I strove to make my father proud of me,
I strive to be worthy of emulation to my son.
Blessed am I,
With among the most sacred of bonds,
Which stretches across generations.
The one with my father, the one with my son.
And the soul will forever reverberate with these beautiful words.
When a father told his son:
I am proud of you, my boy. Always was, always will be.
And a son told his father:
I love you, dad. Always have, and always will.

Death may be the greatest of all human blessings…
—*Socrates*

In fact, the greatest blessing is when you never have to die again.
When you attain Moksha or Nirvana,
Liberation from the unrelenting cycle of rebirths.

Do good.
Help others.
Perform positive karma.
Lead a worthy life.
And earn that greatest blessing for yourself:
A death to end all deaths.

List of Characters and Important Tribes
(In Alphabetical Order)

Akampana: A smuggler; one of Raavan's closest aides

Arishtanemi: Military chief of the Malayaputras; right-hand man of Vishwamitra

Annapoorna Devi: A brilliant musician who lived in Agastyakootam, the capital of the Malayaputras.

Ashwapati: King of the northwestern kingdom of Kekaya; father of Kaikeyi and a loyal ally of Dashrath

Bharat: Ram's half-brother; son of Dashrath and Kaikeyi

Dashrath: Chakravarti king of Kosala and emperor of the Sapt Sindhu; father of Ram, Bharat, Lakshman and Shatrughan

Hanuman: A Naga and a member of the Vayuputra tribe

Indrajit: Son of Raavan and Mandodari

Janak: King of Mithila; father of Sita

Jatayu: A captain of the Malayaputra tribe; Naga friend of Sita and Ram

Kaikesi: Rishi Vishrava's first wife; mother of Raavan and Kumbhakarna

Kanyakumari: Literally, the Virgin Goddess. It was believed that the Mother Goddess Herself temporarily resided in the bodies of carefully chosen young girls, who were then worshipped as living Goddesses.

Khara: A captain in the Lankan army; Samichi's lover

Krakachabahu: The governor of Chilika

Kubaer: The chief-trader of Lanka

Kumbhakarna: Raavan's brother; also a Naga

Kushadhwaj: King of Sankashya; younger brother of Janak

Lakshman: One of the twin sons of Dashrath; Ram's halfbrother

Malayaputras: The tribe left behind by Lord Parshu Ram, the sixth Vishnu

Mandodari: Wife of Raavan

Mara: An independent assassin for hire

Mareech: Kaikesi's brother; Raavan and Kumbhakarna's uncle; one of Raavan's closest aides

Nagas: Human beings born with deformities

Nandini: A good friend of Vishwamitra and Vashishtha from their days in the Gurukul. She was from the land of Branga.

Prithvi: A businessman in the village of Todee

Raavan: Son of Rishi Vishrava; brother of Kumbhakarna; half-brother of Vibhishan and Shurpanakha

Ram: Son of Emperor Dashrath and his eldest wife

Kaushalya; eldest of four brothers; later married to Sita

Samichi: Police and protocol chief of Mithila; Khara's lover

Shatrughan: Twin brother of Lakshman; son of Dashrath and Sumitra; Ram's half-brother

Shochikesh: The landlord of Todee village

Shurpanakha: Half-sister of Raavan

Sita: Daughter of King Janak and Queen Sunaina of Mithila; also the prime minister of Mithila; later married to Ram

Sukarman: A resident of Todee village; Shochikesh's son

Sursa: An employee of the trader Naarad. She was passionately in love with Hanuman, despite his vow of celibacy.

Suryavanshis: The descendants of the Sun God. This dynasty of kings and queens was founded by Emperor Ikshvaku.

Vaanars: The Vaanars were the powerful dynasty that ruled the land of Kishkindha along the Tungabhadra River.

Vali: The king of Kishkindha

Vashishtha: *Raj guru*, the *royal priest* of Ayodhya; teacher of the four Ayodhya princes

Vayuputras: The tribe left behind by Lord Rudra, the previous Mahadev

Vedavati: A resident of Todee village; Prithvi's wife

Vibhishan: Half-brother of Raavan

Vishrava: A revered rishi; the father of Raavan, Kumbhakarna, Vibhishan and Shurpanakha

Vishwamitra: Chief of the Malayaputras; also temporary guru of Ram and Lakshman

Note on the Narrative Structure

If you have picked up this book, then in all probability you have read the three earlier books of the Ram Chandra Series. And hopefully, have liked them!

Thank you for your continued love and support.

More so, thank you for that most precious gift to an artist: your time. I hope this book lives up to your expectations.

As some of you may know, I have been inspired by a storytelling technique called hyperlink. It has also been called the multilinear narrative, in which a connection brings many characters together. The three main characters in the Ram Chandra Series are Ram, Sita and Raavan. Each has life experiences which mould their characters. Each life in this story is an adventure with a riveting backstory. And finally, their stories converge with the kidnapping of Sita.

The first book explores the tale of Ram, the second the story of Sita, and the third burrows deep into the life of Raavan. And the three stories merge from the fourth book onwards into a single narrative. You hold in your hand this combined narrative: the fourth book of the Ram Chandra Series.

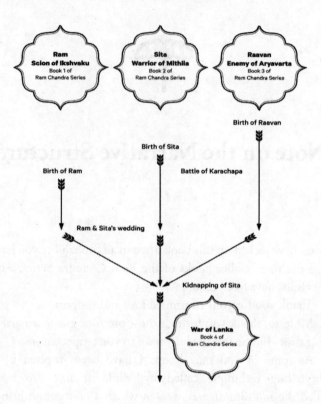

I knew that writing three books in a multilinear narrative would be a complicated and time-consuming affair, but I must confess, it was thoroughly exciting. I hope it is as rewarding and thrilling an experience for you as it was for me. Understanding Ram, Sita and Raavan as characters helped me inhabit their worlds and explore the maze of plots and stories that illuminate this great epic. I feel truly blessed for this.

Since I was following a multilinear narrative, I left clues in the first (Ram–*Scion of Ikshvaku*), the second (Sita–*Warrior of Mithila*), and the third books (Raavan–*Enemy of Aryavarta*), and most of them are unveiled in the fourth, *War of Lanka*.

I hope that you enjoy reading *War of Lanka*. Do tell me what you think of it, by sending me messages on my Facebook, Instagram or Twitter accounts given on the first page.

Love,
Amish

Acknowledgements

Life is what happens when you are planning other things. And it has led me to now having 4 jobs, simultaneously. Firstly, I work with the Indian government cultural diplomacy corps. Secondly, I also host TV documentaries, and am, in addition, co-producing a movie based on one of my books. Notwithstanding, writing remains the core pursuit. Truly, it keeps me going, even when life is difficult and hard. I'd like to thank all those who help me in my writing, for they are the buttresses to my core.

The three men I look up to: My father, the late Vinay Kumar Tripathi; my father-in-law, the late Dr Manoj Vyas; and my brother-in-law, the late Himanshu Roy. They look upon me from *pitralok* now. I strive to make them proud of me.

Neel, my young son. The purpose of my soul, my supreme joy, my greatest achievement, my deepest love. I strive to be worthy-of-emulation to him.

Usha, Bhavna, Anish, Meeta, Ashish, and Donetta - my mother, my siblings and my sisters-in-law, for all that they do.

They read the first draft, usually as each chapter is written. More importantly, we all know that we will always be there for one another. We have each other's back. Always.

The rest of my family: Shernaz, Preeti, Smita, Anuj, Ruta, Mitansh, Daniel, Aiden, Keya, Anika and Ashna. For their consistent faith and love.

Aman and Shivani, who run all my work and life. They are family to me.

The team at HarperCollins. My editor Swati, the marketing team Shabnam and Akriti, the sales team Gokul, Vikas, and Rahul, and my publisher Udayan, led by the brilliant CEO of HarperCollins India Ananth. This is my first published book with them. And I am enjoying this new journey immensely. Looking forward to many more.

The CEO of my previous publisher Gautam, my editors Karthika and Deepthi (who edited the first draft of this book), the marketing manager Neha, and the rest of the Westland team. We may have parted ways in unfortunate circumstances, but they will always be family to me.

Vijay, Shubhangi, Padma, Divya, Anuj, Yukta and the rest of my office colleagues. They look after my business work which frees up my time to write.

Hemal, Neha, Rohan, Hitesh, Shikha, Shriram, Vinit, Harsh, Akshata, Sarah, Prakash, Sujit and Team OktoBuzz. They have produced most of the marketing material for the book, including the awesome cover, and much of the digital activities. I have worked with them for many years. Like fine wine, they age well!

Mayank, Deepika, Sneha, Naresh, Vishaal, Paridhi, Gunjan, and the Moe's Art team, who have supported media relations for the book. Calm and wise, they are among the best media managers I have ever seen.

Ashish Mankad, a brilliant designer, and more importantly, a thinker, who helps guide and drive the art for my books. He also designed the new website.

Satya and his team who have shot the author photos that have been used on the inside cover of this book. He made a rather ordinary subject appear easy on the eyes.

Preeti, a publishing industry wizard, who works on the international deals for my books.

Caleb, Kshitij, Sandeep, Akhil, and their respective teams, who support my work with their business and legal advice.

Mrunalini, a diligent Sanskrit scholar, who works with me on research.

Aditya, a passionate reader of my books, who has now become a friend and a fact-checker.

Sanjay, Archana, Olivier, Pranjulaa, Sandeep, Ravichandran, Vineet, Somnath, Kanwarpreet, Jaseena, and Naseema - my team at Nehru Centre, London, for their love and support. And I want to acknowledge a former Nehru Centre team member we lost recently, the late BV Narayana, a gem of a man who is sorely missed.

And last and most eminently, you, the reader. Your consistent affection, support, understanding and encouragement keeps me going. Thank you so much. May Lord Shiva bless you all.

Chapter 1

3400 BCE, India

Raavan, the king of Lanka, was bleeding profusely from wounds all over his body.

He was running hard. Calling out the name of the woman he loved. The only woman he had ever loved.

'Vedavati! Vedavati!'

He was finding it difficult to breathe. The ever-present dull pain in his navel had suddenly become excruciating. Tears streamed down his eyes. He could hear wild animals – the howling of wolves; vultures screaming; bats screeching. He could not see them, though. It was pitch dark as Raavan sprinted through the deserted streets of Todee village.

'Vedavati!'

He saw a torch flaming bright at a distance.

Raavan raced towards it.

'*Vedavati!*'

A sudden explosion of light from a hundred torches lit simultaneously. Raavan screamed in agony as he stopped and covered his eyes with one hand. As his irises adjusted to the brightness, he removed his hand to see a mob gathered under the blinding light of the torches.

Raavan ran towards the light, lithe and swift.

'*Vedavati!*'

In the crowd were his men. Kumbhakarna. Indrajit. Mareech. Akampana. And his soldiers.

Something wasn't right.

Kumbhakarna looked old. Haggard. He was crying. He raised his arms towards his elder brother. 'Dada ...'

Raavan looked over the shoulders of his beloved younger brother. Towards the hut he recognized only too well.

Her house.

He heard a scream. A loud wail of pain. Of terror. He knew the voice. He loved that voice. He worshipped that voice.

'*Vedavati!*'

Kumbhakarna tried to stop Raavan. 'Dada ... don't ...'

Raavan pushed Kumbhakarna aside as he ran towards the hut. To the door that stood ajar like the hungry mouth of a demon.

Vedavati's husband, Prithvi, lay on the floor. On his back. Lifeless. Eyes open wide in shock and terror. Brutal knife wounds all over his body still oozing blood. A blade was buried in his heart. The kill wound.

Raavan looked up.

His Vedavati.

Sukarman, the wayward son of the local landlord, was holding her up by her neck. His face was twisted with anger. His hands were squeezing her throat brutally. His biceps bursting with malevolent strength. Her body was sliced all over by a knife gone mad. Muscle and sinew were weeping red tears. Her clothes were bloodied, her beautiful face swollen and covered by wounds. A pool of blood collected at her pristine, unblemished, uninjured feet.

NOOO!

No sound escaped Raavan's mouth. It was as if he had been paralysed by a great demonic force. He could do nothing. He just stood there and watched.

'Where is the money?' screamed Sukarman. His voice was like thunder. Monstrous.

Despite the pain she was in, Vedavati's face was calm. Gentle. Like the Virgin Goddess, *the Kanyakumari that she was. She answered softly, 'It's Raavan's money. He has given it to me as charity. It's his chance to discover the God within him. I will not give it to you. I will not part with it.'*

Give it to him, Vedavati! Give it to him! I don't care about the money! I care about you!

'Give me the money!' growled Sukarman. He increased the pressure on her throat with his left hand. A slow squeeze. He raised his right hand, the one that held the bloodied knife, and brought it close to her face. 'Or I'll run this through your eye!'

Give him the money, Vedavati! Give it to him!

Vedavati's answer was simple and calm. 'No.'

Sukarman grunted like a beast as he brutally stabbed Vedavati's left eye, leaving the knife buried. Blood burst forth, spraying Sukarman's face. He brought his right hand back, opened his palm, and banged the back of the scabbard. Hard. The knife dug through her eye socket and pushed into her brain.

NOOOOO!

Raavan was crying. Shouting. But only he could hear himself. His voice remained buried in his throat, echoing miserably within him.

He could not move.

Suddenly, he heard the cries of a baby. Wailing loudly.

And the fiendish paralysing hold on his body was released. He looked down.

The baby was lying on the ground. Wrapped in a rich red cloth with prominent black stripes.

'Raavan ...'

He looked up.

It was her.

His obsession. His great love. The Kanyakumari. Vedavati.

Sukarman was no longer there. But she remained.

Her right arm was twisted at a strange angle. Broken. She had been knifed at least twenty times. Most of the wounds were on her abdomen and her left hand was on her belly, blood gushing through the gaps between her fingers. It flowed down her body and congealed around her, on the ground. A knife was buried deep in her left eye.

But her face was still and serene. Like it had always been. Like it always would be.

'She's my little girl, Raavan. Promise me that you will protect her. Promise me.'

Raavan looked down again. At Vedavati and Prithvi's baby. Sita.

He looked back up. At Vedavati. He was crying helplessly.

'She's my little girl, Raavan.'

'Dada ...'

Raavan realized he was being shaken. He opened his eyes groggily and stumbled out of his dream to see Kumbhakarna peering down at him.

The king of Lanka was strapped to his chair in the *Pushpak Vimaan, the legendary Lankan flying vehicle.* He was clutching his pendant in a tight grip—the pendant that always hung from a gold chain around his neck. Created from the bones of Vedavati's two fingers, the phalanges carefully fastened with gold links. They had survived the cremation of her body. They now served as crutches, supporting him through his tormented life.

He looked around, still unsteady from his disturbing dream. The ever-present pain in his navel was much stronger. Throbbing.

The *Pushpak Vimaan* was shaped like a cone that gently tapered upwards. The portholes at the base were sealed with thick glass but the metallic window shades had been drawn down. The sound of the rotors winding down reverberated in the air. The *vimaan* had just landed in the grand Lankan capital of Sigiriya. Around ninety Lankan soldiers stood at attention inside the craft, waiting for their liege to disembark.

Kumbhakarna unstrapped Raavan and helped him to his feet.

And then Raavan saw her.

Sita.

She had been untied, and was being held tight by four Lankan women soldiers. She strained furiously against their vice-like grip.

Raavan stared at the warrior princess of Mithila. The wife of Ram, the king-in-absentia of Ayodhya. The Lankans had succeeded in kidnapping her.

Sita. Thirty-eight years of age. Born a short while before her mother and father were killed. She was the spitting image of the woman who had given her life.

Raavan couldn't tear his eyes away from her face. The face of Vedavati.

Sita was unusually tall for a Mithilan woman. Her lean, muscular physique gave her the appearance of a warrior in the army of the Mother Goddess. Battle scars stood out proudly on her wheat-complexioned body. She wore a cream dhoti and a white single-cloth blouse. A saffron *angvastram* hung from her right shoulder.

A shade lighter than the rest of her body, her face had high cheekbones and a sharp, small nose. Her lips were neither thin nor full. Her wide-set eyes were neither small nor large. Strong brows arched in a perfect curve above creaseless eyelids. Her long, lustrous black hair had come undone and fell in a disorderly manner around her face. She had the look of the mountain people from the Himalayas.

Her face was thinner than her mother's. Tougher. Less tender. But it was still almost a perfect replica of the original.

'You may as well kill me now,' growled Sita. 'I will never allow Ram or the Malayaputras to negotiate with you for my release. You have nothing to gain.'

Raavan remained silent. His eyes brimmed with tears of grief and misery.

'Kill me now!' shouted Sita.

She's my little girl, Raavan. Promise me that you will protect her. Promise me.

And Raavan whispered his answer to that noble soul he had loved his entire life. An answer that travelled across the wide chasm of time. A chasm that can only be crossed by the relief that is death.

A whispered answer, audible only to him. And Vedavati's soul.

'I promise.'

— J+ ɹ˩ꟼ⊃ —

The Sun God had begun his journey across the horizon and a new dawn was breaking. A new day. A tragically melancholic new day.

Ram stood silently, looking at the conflagrations as they rose high above the funeral pyres. Unblinking. The quivering flames reflected in his pupils. Sixteen pyres. Consuming the bodies of the brave Jatayu and his Malayaputra soldiers. Brave men who had made the ultimate sacrifice while battling to protect his wife Sita from being kidnapped by Raavan.

His younger brother Lakshman stood beside him, his gigantic, muscular body hunched by a sagging spirit. They looked at Lord Agni, the God of Fire, resolutely devouring the bodies of their noble friends. The brothers drew tortured comfort by repeating the powerful chants from the sacred *Isha Vasya Upanishad* that filled the air.

Vayur anilam amritam; Athedam bhasmantam shariram.
This temporary body may burn to ashes; But the breath of life belongs elsewhere. May it find its way back to the Immortal Breath.

Ram's face was blank. Devoid of expression, as it always was when he was enraged. And right now, he was beyond furious.

He looked at the rising sun.

Ram was a *Suryavanshi*, from the *clan of Surya*. As had been the tradition in their family for centuries, the day began with a prayer to Surya, the Sun God. But Ram was in no mood to pray. Not today.

His ragged breath and clenched fists were the only sign of the furious storm that raged within. The rest of him – his body and his face – was eerily calm.

He stared at the sun.

Return my wife to me. Return Sita to me. Or I swear upon the blood of my ancestors, I will burn the world down! I will burn the entire world down!

Suddenly his instincts awoke with a warning. He was being watched.

Ram was instantly alert, unclenching his fists that had been compressed into tight balls just moments ago. He regulated his breath. The steely training of a warrior kicked in.

Ram glanced at his brother without turning his head. Lakshman was staring at the funeral pyres, tears streaming down his face. He was clearly unaware of any threat.

Ram looked down. His bow and quiver were a few feet away. Not close enough.

He looked at the pyres, and beyond them. Into the forest, behind the treeline. Into the darkness.

Someone was there. He could sense it. Clearly, whoever it was, was a very good tracker, for they had made no sound; no mistakes which would send out a warning.

Why haven't they shot us yet?

And then it hit him.

He spoke loudly. 'Lord Hanuman?'

Hanuman, the Naga Vayuputra, emerged from the darkness behind the trees. Gargantuan, yet moving as weightlessly as a feather, sure as a shadow. He was dressed in a saffron *dhoti* and *angvastram*. The outgrowth from his lower back, almost like a tail, followed behind him like a silent companion. It swished in constant rhythm, as though it watched his path. Hanuman was massively built, with a sturdy musculature, and was unnaturally hirsute. His awe-inspiring presence radiated a godly aura, and his facial features were distinctive. His flat nose pressed against his face and his beard and facial hair encircled its periphery with neat precision; the skin above and below his mouth was silken smooth and hairless; it had a puffed appearance and was light pink in colour. His lips were a thin, barely noticeable line.

It almost seemed as if the Almighty had placed the head of a monkey on a man's body.

Thirty Vayuputra soldiers followed him with soldierly discipline. Their complexion, features and attire made it clear that they were from Pariha, a land beyond the western borders of India. The homeland of the previous Mahadev, Lord Rudra.

Parihan Vayuputras.

Hanuman walked with his mouth slightly open, the fingers of his right hand pressed against his lips. Tears fell freely from his grief-stricken eyes. He stared at the two brothers from Ayodhya and then at the funeral pyres.

Lord Rudra have mercy.

Ram and Sita had often met Hanuman during their exile in the forest. Sita had known Hanuman since she was a child, and treasured him as an *elder brother.* She called him Hanu *bhaiya.* She was the one who had introduced him to Ram.

Lakshman had never met Hanuman formally. He had seen the Naga Vayuputra twice when he was a child. When Hanuman had come in secret to meet their Guru Vashishtha in their *gurukul.* Little Lakshman had been suspicious. To this day, he harboured the same prejudice that almost every Indian felt against the Nagas. 'Naga' was the term Indians used to describe those born with deformities. Now, his long-held suspicions were instantly triggered again.

Lakshman quickly picked up the bow lying at his feet and nocked an arrow.

Ram leaned across, pushed Lakshman's hands down and shook his head.

Lakshman growled, 'Dada …'

Ram whispered, 'He's a friend.'

Ram walked around the funeral pyres and towards Hanuman.

The mighty Vayuputra sank to his knees and covered his face with his hands as Ram approached. He was crying now, his body shaking with misery.

Ram immediately understood. Hanuman had assumed that Sita had been killed and her body was being consumed by fire now, in one of the funeral pyres. Hanuman had cherished Sita as his younger sister.

Ram went down on his knees and hugged Hanuman. He whispered, 'Raavan has kidnapped her ...'

Hanuman looked up immediately, stunned but relieved. He turned to the pyres. His gaze had altered. He now beheld the warriors who had met a most glorious end.

Jatayu. And his fifteen Malayaputras.

Hanuman was a Vayuputra, the tribe left behind by the previous Mahadev, Lord *Rudra*, the *Destroyer-of-Evil*. The Malayaputras were the tribe left behind by the previous *Vishnu*, the *Propagator-of-Good*, Lord Parshu Ram. These two tribes worked in partnership with each other, even if differences cropped up on rare occasions, for they represented the Gods that had once walked this earth.

Hanuman slowly balled his fists with resolve. 'Jatayu and his Malayaputras will be avenged. And we will bring Queen Sita back.'

Chapter 2

'Dada!'

Shatrughan rushed into the training hall. Many Ayodhyan soldiers had gathered, as they often did, to watch their regent Bharat practise with his spear. On his deathbed, Emperor Dashrath, their father, had proclaimed Bharat the crown prince. But Bharat had spurned the coronation and instead placed his elder brother Ram's slippers on the throne of Ayodhya, and announced that he would administer the empire as Ram's regent, till such time that his elder brother returned to rule his kingdom. The youngest among the four brothers, Shatrughan, had opted to stay with Bharat in Ayodhya. Shatrughan's twin brother Lakshman had accompanied Ram on his fourteen-year banishment to the forest, a punishment for the unauthorised use of a *daivi astra*, a *divine weapon*, in the Battle of Mithila.

Bharat ignored his brother's voice. No distraction. He remained focused on his battle practice.

The spear he held was normally used as a projectile, to hit enemies from a distance. Or by the cavalry to mow down the opposing army. But Bharat was reviving the ancient tradition of using the spear as a weapon of close combat. It increased a warrior's reach dramatically as compared to a sword. It was a two-in-one weapon, and the wooden shaft at its gripping end could be used as a stick-bludgeon, while the knife-edged metallic end was a sharp blade. It was a fearsome weapon that was difficult to wield, but Bharat was good with it. Very good.

'Dada!'

Bharat didn't stop as he smoothly transferred his weight to his back foot and swung the shaft-side of the spear, smacking his adversary on the head. Before his opponent could steady himself, Bharat went down on one knee and swung with the other side of the spear, pulling back just in time so as not to cause actual damage. But the message was clear. Bharat could have disembowelled the soldier duelling him.

The audience of battle-hardened soldiers broke into loud applause.

'Dada!'

Bharat finally turned to look at Shatrughan. He did not express his surprise at finding his diminutive, intellectual brother in the battle-training gymnasium, a place he rarely visited.

One look at Shatrughan, and Bharat knew that something was disastrously wrong.

— JF ꓘꙄD —

'I have sent the message to Hanuman, Guruji,' said Arishtanemi. 'But …'

Arishtanemi, the military chief of the tribe of Malayaputra, was with Vishwamitra, the formidable chief of the Malayaputras, in their capital city, Agastyakootam. The previous day, Arishtanemi had given Vishwamitra the shocking news that Sita had been kidnapped by the villainous king of Lanka, Raavan. She had been recognised as the seventh Vishnu—the *Propagator-of-Good*—by the Malayaputras. Vishwamitra had not seemed at all perturbed at all by the news. In fact, he had expressed joy.

'But what?' asked Vishwamitra.

'I mean, Guruji ... Who am I to question you? And you know everything.' Arishtanemi was not being facetious. Just the previous day, he had discovered that Vishwamitra had known for more than two decades that Sita was the daughter of Vedavati, the love of Raavan's life. Raavan would never hurt Sita and therefore, the Malayaputra plan was still plausible. Raavan – villainous and evil according to most Indians – would be destroyed by Sita, which would cement Sita's image as the saviour of the land. That Vishwamitra had envisaged and plotted this over such a long period of time seemed inconceivable to Arishtanemi. 'But Hanuman ... I mean ...'

'Speak it,' growled Vishwamitra. 'Speak your mind.'

'Well, Hanuman is a friend of Guru ... I mean the other ...' Arishtanemi knew better than to utter the name of Vashishtha, once Vishwamitra's closest friend and now his arch-enemy. Very few knew the details of how the antagonism had begun, but almost everyone knew the toxicity of it.

Vishwamitra softened his voice to an ominous whisper. 'Say it.'

'I mean ... Hanuman is loyal to Guru Vashishtha ... Will he listen to us?' Arishtanemi blurted.

Vishwamitra leaned back and took a deep breath. He closed his eyes and composed himself. Hearing that name always had a strange effect on him. His friend-turned-foe. A flurry of emotions flooded his heart. Hatred. Anger. Resentment. Melancholy. Pain … Love.

Nandini.

When he opened his eyes, Vishwamitra was calm again. Unruffled. As someone who believes he carries the fate of Mother India on his shoulders must be.

'Why do you think I did what I did with Annapoorna Devi?' Vishwamitra answered the query with another question.

Arishtanemi knew that Vishwamitra had used Annapoorna Devi and her strained relationship with her estranged husband, Surya, to leak the information to Kumbhakarna that the Malayaputras had recognised Sita as the seventh Vishnu. Vishwamitra had bet that it would only be a matter of time before Kumbhakarna's elder brother, Raavan, would think of kidnapping the Vishnu to exercise leverage over the Malayaputras for the medicines that both he and Kumbhakarna needed to stay alive. And his bet had paid off.

'Because, for all your love and respect for Annapoorna Devi,' answered Arishtanemi, 'you love and respect Mother India more.'

'Exactly,' said Vishwamitra. 'I will do what must be done for what I love and respect most. Hanuman may be loyal to that snake Vashishtha. But he is more loyal to Sita. He loves her like a sister. He thinks that Sita's life is in danger while she's in Lanka. Hanuman will do what we tell him to do, because he will think it is the only way to save Sita.'

Arishtanemi nodded. 'Yes, Guruji.'

— Jꟼ ꟼꞀꝹ —

Sita had been imprisoned in the famed Ashok *Vatika*. A stunning and massive *garden* citadel, it was built five kilometres from the Lankan capital city of Sigiriya. The plush garden was atop a tabletop hill, surrounded by thick, well-bastioned fort walls. Two parallel walls, each twenty-five metres high and four metres thick, stretched outwards from Sigiriya. Both walls were dotted with watch towers that allowed for easy scouting and defence. The path nestled between them opened into the citadel of Ashok Vatika. The garden spread over one hundred acres and contained trees sourced from all corners of the world. Floral beds spread their aroma and attracted life around them, from colourful butterflies to elegant ladybirds. Peacocks danced in splendid isolation on verdant flats and rolling grass-covered, man-made hillocks. Their preening vanity snatched pride of place in this effusion of life. Known as the favourite of Lord Rudra, the peacock added a touch of elegance and grace to this place of extravagant beauty. Luxurious cottages in the centre of the garden were well equipped for comfortable living. The grand cottage in the heart of the garden had been allocated to Sita.

The name, Ashok Vatika, was itself resonant with both fact and symbolism. A profusion of Ashok trees, especially around the cottages in the centre, established the literal intent of the nomenclature. But there was more. The old Sanskrit word for *grief* was *shok*. Hence, *ashok* meant *no grief*. This garden, this Ashok Vatika, was an oasis of happiness, joy, even bliss. But Indians are philosophical by nature; therefore, naturally, they also have a penchant for digging deeper. And *ashok* can also mean 'to not feel grief'. Some are cursed by fate to experience misery that becomes the foundation of their very being. They are inured to the vicissitudes of life. Nothing can hurt them any more, for they have already been hurt beyond endurance. Fresh drops of grief cause no ripples in their ocean of anguish.

It was an *ashok* Kumbhakarna who walked into the Ashok Vatika, having left his horse at the citadel gate.

Raavan had decided that Sita would be kept in protective custody in the garden, away from Sigiriya. A mysterious plague had ripped through the city over the last too-many years. He would not have Sita put at risk. Well-trained women soldiers had been stationed in the garden and at the citadel walls to ensure that Sita did not escape. Food, books, musical instruments and anything that Sita might need to keep herself occupied had been provided. But Sita was not in the mood to distract herself with any of these pretences at normalcy.

'I know you are only following orders,' she said politely. 'But I will not eat this food.'

She was sitting on the veranda outside her cottage. Soldiers had placed before her bowls filled with the finest gourmet food in Sigiriya, cooked by the royal chefs in Raavan's personal kitchen.

A soldier officiously opened a lid. 'This food is not poisoned, great Vishnu,' she said, confused but still deferential. 'If you so order, I will taste each dish right now and dispel your concerns.'

Sita laughed. 'Why would Raavan poison my food? He could have killed me several times over by now. With complete ease. I know it is not poisoned. But I will not eat.'

'But …'

'I will not allow Raavan to negotiate with my husband or the Malayaputras for my life.' She pointed with her thumb at the cottage behind her. 'In there, and around here, you have removed every possible means for me to kill myself. All I can do is refuse to eat. I understand you are only following orders, and I hold nothing against you. But I will not eat.'

The nervous soldier began pleading. 'But, My Lady… Please listen to me. We cannot let you die. We will be forced to make you eat.'

Sita smiled. 'Try it.'

Kumbhakarna had been hiding behind an Ashok tree, watching the interaction. He stepped into her line of vision now. Instantly, the polite Sita was gone. She stood up, fury stiffening every muscle in her body.

The soldiers turned around and, upon seeing Kumbhakarna, went down on one knee in respect to the Lankan royal. He dismissed them and they left immediately.

Kumbhakarna stared at Sita. It was beyond astonishing. She was almost a replica of Vedavati. Almost, but not entirely. For Vedavati was calm and gentle while Sita clearly could be aggressive and combative. It was time to check if she possessed her mother's compassion and sense of fairness.

'You don't have to eat if you don't want to, great Vishnu,' said Kumbhakarna politely as he walked up to Sita. 'But may I request you to look at this?'

Sita looked suspiciously at the rolled-up painting that Kumbhakarna was holding out.

'Why?' snarled Sita, wary.

'What harm can it cause, looking at a painting, Queen Sita?'

Sita stepped back from the giant Kumbhakarna, raised her hands in combat position, and said, 'You unroll the painting.'

Kumbhakarna nodded gently, stepped back to increase the distance between Sita and him, held up the rolled-up canvas horizontally, and slowly, deliberately, unrolled it.

Sita was stunned.

It was her. It was a portrait of her. But younger, around twenty-one or twenty-two years of age. Her clothes were a soft violet: the most expensive dye in the world and the colour favoured by royalty. The face, the body, the hair, everything was exactly like her. To be fair, *almost* exactly. For there were subtle differences. In the portrait she was calm and gentle, almost like a *rishika*. She was curvaceous, full and voluptuous, unlike Sita in real life. She was more feminine. Less muscular. Less lean. None of Sita's proud battle scars found expression in the painting.

It wasn't as if a thirty-eight-year-old Sita had been altered into a much younger version in the painting. Instead, a warrior Mother Goddess had been transformed into an achingly attractive celestial nymph.

There was something ethereal about the painted lady's beauty. Her face. Her eyes. Her serenity. Sita had never imagined herself so full of beauty.

And then it hit her. This painting was a labour of love. Every brushstroke was a caress. It was prayer. Devotion. The passion, the longing was palpable. This painter was deeply, madly and heartbreakingly in love with the object of the painting.

Bizarre.

She took a step back and growled in anger. 'What the bloody hell is this? What are you trying to do? Who painted this?'

Kumbhakarna's answer was simple. 'My brother Raavan.'

'Why in Lord Indra's name would Raavan paint this? I had never met him before the day you kidnapped me. And certainly not when I was that age!'

'I didn't say that he's met you before.'

'Then what the hell are you two trying to do? What mind games are these? Some stupid good policeman–bad policeman routine? Do you really think I'll fall for this nonsense?'

'We are not trying to make you fall for anything.'

'Tell that demon brother of yours that he can keep painting me for as long as he wishes, but he will not sway me! I will starve to death! I swear on the holiest of them all, Lord Rudra!'

Kumbhakarna's eyes were moist as he said softly, 'This is not you. This is not your portrait.'

Sita was silenced. For only a moment. And then she gasped as her expression changed dramatically. From anger to shock. Almost like she knew what the next sentence would be. But it couldn't be ... It could *not* be ...

Kumbhakarna continued, 'This is your mother. Your birthmother.'

Chapter 3

'Ram,' said Vashishtha, 'I don't think you understand.'

'No, Guruji,' said Ram, unfailingly polite. 'I do understand. And I am not changing my mind.'

The *rajguru* of the Ayodhya royal family tried hard to control his irritation. Ram could be extremely stubborn once he made up his mind. Almost nothing could sway him. Not even the *guru* whom he respected as a father.

Hanuman, Ram and Lakshman had quickly marched northwards to the sacred Tapti River, along with thirty Vayuputra soldiers. Tapti was one of the only two major rivers in India that flowed from east to west along its entire course; the other one being the holy Narmada River. Indians, who saw a divine plan in everything, deeply loved this river, which moved in the same direction as the sun. Hence the name: *Tap* means *heat*, especially that of ascetism and meditation. The *Tapti* River, the *one fired with the heat of ascetism*, was dotted with *ashrams* along its banks, which had been established by great *rishis* and *rishikas* for people who sought ascetic knowledge. Vashishtha had waited for Ram, Lakshman, Hanuman and the Vayuputras at one such *ashram* – the abode of the pious saint Changdev.

The convoy had left the *ashram* after seeking the blessings of Rishi Changdev. They now sailed down the Tapti River towards the Gulf of Cambay – which was a part of the Western Sea – from where they intended to head northwards. The Gulf of Cambay was an inverse-funnel shaped inlet of the Western Sea, sandwiched between the Deccan peninsula to the right and Saurashtra to the left. They would sail through this funnel towards their ultimate destination, the port city of Lothal, a few hours away.

'Listen to me, Ram,' said Vashishtha, deeply troubled by Ram's decision. 'I don't think this will work. I don't think Hanuman can do it alone.'

'I disagree with you, Guruji,' cut in Hanuman. 'It can be done. And I will not be alone. The Malayaputras know Lanka, they know the secret entrances into the Sigiriya fort. And I know the Malayaputras. We will do it.'

The plan was simple. Hanuman would steal into Sigiriya along with some Malayaputras whom he knew well. They would find Sita and escape with her, making a quiet getaway. A surgical strike. It would be far more effective than open war. Many lives could be saved.

'Do you really think he will just let this happen? So easily?' asked Vashishtha. 'You don't …'

'My sincere apologies for interrupting you, Guruji,' said Hanuman, his hands folded together in contrition. 'But you needn't worry about Raavan. Kumbhakarna, you know, owes me his life. And he is an honourable man. He will not deny the debt he owes me. I will get Sita out of Lanka, alive and unhurt.'

Vashishtha took a long breath and then let it out in a rush. With frustration. 'I am not talking about Raavan. He is not in control of this situation.'

Ram and Hanuman understood who he was talking about.

His friend-turned-mortal-enemy. Vishwamitra.

They remained silent.

'Guruji,' Ram said finally, with polite boldness, 'I request you to not allow your prejudice ...'

Vashishtha interrupted him with a raised voice. 'Ram, are you calling me prejudiced? I assure you I know that ... that ... man. I know him better than anyone else. Better than even he knows himself.' Vashishtha paused and composed himself. 'He wants this war. It serves his purpose. He has built an image of Raavan as the perfect villain, like a butcher feeding a sacrificial goat. And now that man wants the ritual sacrifice of Raavan. He wants the war. The Malayaputras will not help Hanuman on this mission. Trust me. I know.'

Ram didn't say anything, shocked at this public display of anger by his *guru*. He had never heard him raise his voice in this manner. Or lose his poise.

Hanuman spoke quietly. 'Guruji, not all the Malayaputras want war. I know some who don't. You too were a Malayaputra once. You know that they can be as divided internally as we Vayuputras are. Some of them will help me, I'm sure. Shouldn't we at least try to avoid a war and save countless lives?'

'I want you to steer clear of Vishwamitra and Arishtanemi,' said Vashishtha sternly. 'You will not take any help from them. You will ensure that they are not even aware of your plans.'

'Yes, Guruji. I will take care,' said Hanuman.

Hanuman thought that Vashishtha was insisting on this because of his enmity with Vishwamitra, the chief of the

Malayaputras. But Hanuman was wrong. Vashishtha had a deeper reason.

Tacticians focus on tomorrow, intent on winning the immediate battle. Strategists obsess about the day after tomorrow. They must win the war. The *rajguru* of Ayodhya, Vashishtha, was thinking about the day after.

Vashishtha looked unconvinced and troubled. And then surrendered. He might disagree with Ram and Hanuman, but he had faith in Sita.

Ram doesn't understand. But Sita will. She will not come back with Hanuman. She will not. She knows she cannot. Even if that means risking her life.

But Vashishtha too was in the dark. He did not know what Vishwamitra knew. He did not know what Sita meant to Raavan.

—ᒍᖴ ᒎᔕᗪ—

The next day, early in the morning, Raavan ambled into the Ashok Vatika. A regal sixty-year-old with a commanding presence. A hint of a stoop suggested the backbone's reduced ability to bear the load of the massive body. Stretch lines on the shoulders and arms, that had once been mighty and infused with vigour, indicated reduced muscle mass. His forehead was furrowed with deep lines and crow's feet had formed around the corners of his eyes. His cheeks were marked by faded pockmarks, the legacy of a bout of smallpox when he was a baby. The once-thick crop of black hair was now a sparse patch of grey with a receding hairline. The beard remained thick, although white had replaced the virile black of youth.

An ageing, partly enfeebled tiger. But a tiger with renewed purpose. A tiger who had been gifted a second chance.

Beside him walked his brother, Kumbhakarna. He dwarfed even the tall Raavan. His hirsute body made him look more like a giant bear than a human being. The strange outgrowths from his ears and shoulders marked him out as a Naga.

A trail of palace maids and attendants followed the two brothers, carrying trays full of food.

Sita was seated on the veranda outside her cottage, her comfortable cane chair starkly contrasting with her obvious unease. Kumbhakarna's revelations the previous day had robbed her of sleep. She knew she couldn't kill herself now. Not until she knew more about her birth-mother. Also, truth be told, her mother's relationship with Raavan. So Sita had eaten the previous night. Her first meal in Lanka.

She turned her head towards the commotion. Raavan and Kumbhakarna had stepped into the open courtyard and left the treeline behind. The sun arose behind them.

Sita straightened up. And shivered.

Maids ran ahead of the Lankan royals and quickly brought out a cane table from Sita's cottage. They placed it in front of her. Others pulled two cane chairs which were placed around the table. Just in time for Raavan and Kumbhakarna to seat themselves in one fluid motion.

Raavan stared at Sita, a sense of wonder on his face. He had not imagined he would ever behold that face in the flesh again. His heart was racing.

Kumbhakarna spoke. 'May we join you for breakfast, princess?'

Sita remained quiet. Unmoving and silent. But her eyes spoke aloud. *It's your kingdom. It's your city. It's your garden. Who's going to stop you?*

'Thank you,' Kumbhakarna replied politely to that challenging look.

The brothers relaxed in their seats. Enthusiastic maids quickly brought the food to the table. Three silver plates were placed in front of them. A delectable aroma rose up from a large silver bowl and wafted through the air as the chief maid took away its lid. It made even the disinterested Sita look at the food. Processed, softened and flattened rice had been lightly sautéed with mustard, cumin seeds, curry leaves, onion and green chillies. Roasted peanuts added a rich source of plant-based protein to the dish. It was a delicacy from the land of Godavari, called *poha*. The royal chef had assumed that Sita would like it, having spent many years in Panchavati. A maid poured buttermilk into three silver glasses and placed them beside the plates.

Raavan smiled and rubbed his hands together in anticipation. 'Mmm ... Smells delicious.'

He was trying really hard. Awkwardly friendly. He did not mention that the rice had been especially imported from Gokarna for this meal. Practically everyone in Sigiriya ate wheat and almost no one ate rice. This was an expensive meal.

Kumbhakarna looked at his brother and smiled softly. He thought about the life they could have lived. If only ...

Two maids circled them with a pitcher of water and a large bowl each, enabling the three seated royals to wash their hands.

A third was about to serve the *poha* when Raavan halted her with a raised hand.

'That's all right,' said Raavan. 'We'll serve ourselves.'

The maid was shocked. But she had learnt, like almost everyone in Lanka, that they must never question Raavan. Ever.

She placed the bowl on the table and the assemblage retreated, walking backwards deferentially. They did not dare turn their backs to their king.

Raavan looked at them distractedly and smiled. 'Thank you.'

Kumbhakarna raised his eyebrows, pleasantly surprised by this display of uncharacteristic courtesy. The maids, though, were taken aback. They halted mid-step in confusion, then quickly recovered and disappeared post-haste.

Raavan turned towards Sita. 'Please ... eat.'

Sita did not respond. She was staring intently at the floor.

Raavan stood up, reached over and picked up Sita's plate, served some *poha* onto it, and gently placed it in front of her.

Sita did not raise her eyes.

Raavan frowned.

Perhaps she suspects that the food is poisoned.

He briskly served himself and then picked up a small amount with the tips of his fingers. Good manners. He placed the *poha* in his mouth.

'Mmm ... wow. It's delicious,' cooed Raavan.

Kumbhakarna too began to eat.

But Sita just sat there. Silent. Unmoving.

Staring at her veins. In disgust.

They carried her blood. She could almost feel her appalled heart rejecting the blood it was receiving from her veins.

My blood ...

His blood ...

Lord Rudra ... No ... Have mercy ...

How can you test me like this?

Not this demon ... Not this monster ...

Kumbhakarna suddenly understood what was going on in her mind. His gaze flew towards his brother.

The king of Lanka was staring at Sita and frowning. 'Why aren't you eati—'

Then Raavan got it too. His eyes flashed with anger as he reached for the finger-bone pendant hanging from a chain on his neck. He held Vedavati's hand.

Kumbhakarna almost sprang to his feet and then sat down again as he saw his brother's expression transform.

A rueful smile spread across Raavan's face. She had calmed him down. She had focused him. His Goddess ... helping him from the beyond.

Some people say that focus requires a mind with a fearsome intellect. They are wrong. What it needs most, in fact, is a calmly breathing heart. For a fearsome intellect without the curb of a calm heart is like an unguided missile. It can blow up and destroy anyone, even itself.

'Sita ...' whispered Raavan.

Sita did not stir.

'Queen Sita!' said Raavan, louder this time.

Sita looked up. And pierced him with her unblinking eyes.

'Your mother's name was Vedavati. She was a Goddess. I loved and worshipped her. I still love and worship her.' Raavan paused before he continued pointedly. 'And your *father's* name was Prithvi.' Raavan laid particular emphasis on the word 'father'. 'Your father was a good man. Weak, but a good man.'

Sita's eyes widened with surprise. Her shoulders sagged with relief as a sigh escaped her lips. Raavan almost heard her thoughts.

Oh, thank God! I don't have his blood!

Sita suddenly realised how rude she had been. 'I ... I didn't mean to ...'

Raavan began to laugh. 'It's all right. You are Vedavati's daughter. I cannot be angry with you.'

Kumbhakarna stared at his brother with surprise. And regret. Regret for the man Raavan could have been. For the life they could have had. If only ...

Raavan smiled as he pointed at Sita's plate. 'There will be time to talk. For now, let's eat.'

Chapter 4

'What does Dada say?' asked Shatrughan.

Bharat and Shatrughan sat in the family room of the Ayodhya royal palace. They had just received a bird courier from their eldest brother, Ram.

'He's asking us to not mobilise the army,' answered Bharat. 'They are trying to find a way to rescue Sita *bhabhi* from Lanka without triggering a war. Something about using a delicate surgical scalpel rather than a mighty war sword.'

Shatrughan frowned. 'I hope it works. But I wouldn't count on it.'

'Ram dada is trying to save the lives of soldiers.'

'Which is the right thing to do ... But what if he fails? And we take too long to mobilise? What do you think our subordinate kingdoms will make of it? Some demon kidnaps the queen of Ayodhya and we don't even mobilise our army? We may end up encouraging rebellions all over the land.'

Bharat stared at Shatrughan. 'Is that the strategic mind of the prince of Ayodhya speaking? Or is it the righteous anger of a brother-in-law?'

'Aren't you angry, Dada? She is our *bhabhi*,' said Shatrughan, his fists clenched tight. 'How dare that demon of Lanka do this? Fight as warriors, that is fair. But this … this is *adharma*.'

Bharat nodded.

'Both the *dharma* of the empire and the *dharma* of the family dictate that we mobilise our army and navy,' continued Shatrughan. 'We'll need a few weeks in any case. Let's hope Ram dada succeeds at whatever he's planning. If he fails, we should leave for Lanka within the day.'

'Yes,' said Bharat. 'Issue the orders.'

—Jᖴ Ɉ5D—

'So good to see you, my friend,' said Naarad as he embraced Hanuman.

Ram, Lakshman, Vashishtha, Hanuman and the Vayuputras had reached Lothal, an important port city of the Sapt Sindhu. Leaving the bulk of the party in the guest house, Vashishtha, Ram and Hanuman had left immediately to meet Naarad, a friend of Hanuman.

Naarad was a brilliant trader, but also a lover of art, poetry and the latest gossip. Hanuman had informed them that he was a better source of information than the intelligence services of the most powerful kingdoms in the Sapt Sindhu.

'It's been too long!' said Hanuman.

'Yeah,' Naarad said with a smile. 'I thought you were avoiding me!'

Naarad turned to the two men who had accompanied his friend.

Hanuman indicated Vashishtha. 'This is …'

'Of course, I know Guru Vashishtha,' said Naarad, bending to touch the sage's feet.

'*Ayushman bhav*,' said Vashishtha, placing his right hand on Naarad's head and *blessing him with a long life*.

'Aah, Guruji …' said Naarad. 'I think a life that burns bright with passion, even for a short while, is better than one that flickers and struggles for a long time.'

Vashishtha did not know what to make of the strange response to what was, after all, a standard blessing. He remained silent.

With a naughty twinkle in his eye, Naarad continued, 'So, speaking of burning bright, why do Guru Vishwamitra and you hate each other so much? And speaking of passion, who's Nandini?'

Vashishtha had been warned by Hanuman that Naarad had a bizarre sense of humour. Despite this, he was taken aback. He hadn't expected the trader from Lothal to be so forward. In a flash, though, he understood what Naarad was doing. He was using humour to gaslight and then gather information. This was the secret behind his talent!

Vashishtha smiled and turned to Hanuman. 'You are right.' Pointing at Naarad, Vashishtha continued, 'This gentleman is a very useful ally.' He smiled at Naarad and said, 'An irritating but useful ally.'

Naarad laughed, appreciating the way Vashishtha had smoothly avoided answering his questions. 'I'm impressed, Guruji.' Turning to Ram, Naarad said, 'So you are the Vishnu, eh?'

Ram was direct, honest to a fault, and transparent like the pure waters of a freshly formed river. Not for him the verbal jousting of men focused on their agendas; he was focused only on the truth and law, even if the truth and law worked against him. His answer was straight. 'My wife Sita has been recognised as a Vishnu by the only ones with the authority to recognise the Vishnu – the Malayaputras. We need to save her, not just because she is my life, but because she is important to Mother India. Are you going to help us or not?'

Naarad did a double-take. Innocence and truthfulness were so rare among adults. Life had a way of torturing those characteristics out of people, leaving resentment or cynicism in their place. Some adults gave their bitterness another word – maturity. A gracious word to hide their selfishness and cowardice. It was a delight to see this rare combination of fierce courage, quiet truthfulness and pure innocence … and in one who had suffered so much. *This man, this king of Ayodhya, is special.*

Naarad smiled. 'It will be my honour to help.'

Hanuman spoke up. 'Will you come with us, my friend?'

'Yes, I will,' answered Naarad. 'But you will also have to tolerate someone else. A former Malayaputra. She has visited Lanka often and is the only one I know who can get us into Sigiriya.'

Hanuman frowned.

Naarad turned to the door and shouted, 'Sursa!'

Hanuman froze. Sursa was an employee of Naarad. Wilful, beautiful and aggressive, she was passionately in love with Hanuman – much to the dismay of the Naga Vayuputra, who had taken a vow of lifelong celibacy.

'Hans!' squealed Sursa, sashaying into the room.

Hanuman winced. He did not fancy that name at all.

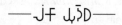

Early the next morning, Raavan and Kumbhakarna visited Sita's cottage in the Ashok Vatika.

They had broken the ice the previous day, ably assisted by what Indians are most passionate about – food. Yesterday it was *poha*. Today, the royal cooks had rustled up something different. Rice and *udad* dal had been fermented and ground into a thick batter. Small portions of this batter were wrapped in banana leaves and steamed into cylindrical roundels. They were served wrapped in the banana leaf, accompanied by coconut chutney and a stew made with lentils, tamarind and a unique blend of spices. Dunked in it were well-known immunity-boosters – moringa sticks. They called the food *idli-sambar*.

Rice had been imported from Gokarna once again for this meal.

Raavan ate his breakfast messily, not feeling the need to impress Sita any longer with put-on manners as he had done the previous day. The genuinely refined Kumbhakarna however, continued to eat slowly, delicately.

Sita looked at Raavan and said, 'Tell me about my mother …'

Raavan paused and glanced at her. He picked up a napkin and wiped his hand clean. A wistful smile spread across his face. 'Where do I begin? How do I describe a Goddess?'

'Start at the beginning. A good place, always.'

'I met her when I was four years old.'

'And how old was she?'

'Probably eight or nine years old, I think … I've been in love with her ever since.'

'How can you fall in love at four?'

'You can, if the object of your affection is the *Kanyakumari*.'

'My mother was a *Kanyakumari*?' asked Sita, surprised.

'Yes,' answered Raavan.

An ancient tradition of worshipping the *Kanyakumari*, *the Virgin Goddess*, prevailed in many parts of India. The *Kanyakumari* was believed to be an incarnation of the Mother Goddess Herself. It was held that She resided temporarily in the bodies of carefully chosen young girls. These girls were then worshipped as living Goddesses. People approached them for advice and prophecies – even kings and queens often became their devotees. When they reached puberty, the Goddess moved into the body of another pre-pubescent girl. India was dotted with temples dedicated to Kanyakumaris.

'Which temple was she the *Kanyakumari* of?'

'Vaidyanath temple in eastern India. But she was beyond comparison. No *Kanyakumari*, who has ever existed or ever will, can match her. She was peerless. Noble. Kind. Generous. Righteous. She did not ever stop being a Goddess. To me she wasn't a Goddess because the Mother Goddess chose her. It was her character that made her divine. Perfect in every way. Perfect …'

Sita had caught on to something. 'She was from Vaidyanath? How old would she have been when I was born?'

'Perhaps twenty-six or twenty-seven years of age …' answered Raavan.

Many former Kanyakumaris returned to their temple to live out their remaining years.

'I was found close to Trikut Hills by my adoptive parents. Not far from Vaidyanath.'

Raavan and Kumbhakarna could guess what was coming next. The obvious question. The most obvious question from any adopted child.

'Why did my parents abandon me?' asked Sita. 'Why did they not come back for me? Where are they now? Here in *Lanka?*'

Raavan looked down. His eyes had clouded with tears. It had been so many years, and yet the memory of that horrible day made his heart crumble into a million pieces.

Sita turned to Kumbhakarna. 'Why did they abandon me, Kumbhakarnaji? And why did they continue to reject me? Did my mother not want to see her child even once in thirty-eight long years? Is this expected from a noble Goddess and her husband? You say you know them. You must know why ...'

'Brave Vishnu ...' whispered Kumbhakarna, his voice shaking in misery. 'They did not ... The *Kanyakumari* ... She ...'

'Where is she now? Is she here?'

Raavan looked up at Sita, his hand tightly clutching the finger-bone pendant. 'She is here.'

Sita's eyes fell on the pendant hanging around Raavan's neck. Two human finger bones – the phalanges carefully fastened with gold links. Tears clouded her eyes as she understood.

Raavan murmured, as if from a distant land, 'Shortly after you were born, Vedavati and Prithvi died while ...' Raavan stopped. He drew a deep breath and corrected himself. 'Vedavati and Prithvi were *killed* ...'

Sita's hand shot up and covered her mouth as tears flowed down her cheeks.

Raavan wanted to stop. But the words tumbled from his mouth of their own volition. He knew he had to go on. Vedavati's daughter deserved the truth. 'Some ... I ...' He was shivering in misery now. 'I had given her some money as charity. The *basta* ... the *son of the local landlord* ... He came with his gang ... He threatened ... He ... they ... knives ...'

Sita was crying helplessly now.

Raavan couldn't go on any more.

His devoted brother, Kumbhakarna, had to step in. 'Vedavatiji was convinced that she had redeemed Raavan dada. That she had put him on the right path. And she had. He … Both he and I … had done some terrible things. The noble Vedavatiji reformed us … Gave us direction … And the money … It was Dada's first step towards redemption … His first act of charity … It would have been used to build a hospital … When those criminals demanded the money, she refused to hand it over … She offered her own meagre savings instead … All of it… But she would not part with Dada's money … his charity … That was holy, she apparently said … she would not surrender Raavan dada's chance to discover the God within himself …'

An agonised moan escaped Sita's lips. She wept for the virtuous mother she had never met. For the magnificent woman whose blood flowed in her veins.

'They killed Prithvi … They killed her … And stole …'

Sita suddenly felt rage course through her veins. Blinding rage. 'What did you do to those men? What did …'

'We tortured them. We made them beg for death …'

'Every single scoundrel,' said Raavan. Despite the passage of so many years, he still seethed with fury. 'We cut them alive, bit by bit. We burnt them even as they breathed. We cooked them to the bone …'

Sita's body eased with satisfaction.

'And then we massacred the entire village. Coward rascals who stood by while their living Goddess was brutally murdered for a few measly coins! We killed them all! And left them there to be eaten by wild animals.'

Sita stared at the king of Lanka, the same frenzied anger reflecting in her eyes.

Raavan closed his eyes and breathed in deeply. Trying to slow his heart down.

Sita too closed her eyes. She wiped away her tears. But more took their place, moistening her face again. She opened her eyes as she heard Raavan speak.

'Even from the beyond, she reached out to help me,' said Raavan.

Sita looked at Raavan. *How?*

Raavan looked at his right hand, remembering what had been – what would always be – the high point of his tormented life. 'I had touched the Ka ... Ka ... *Kanyakumari* just once in my life ... She had held this hand for a moment ... for a lifetime ... for a moment ... Touched me just that one time.'

Kumbhakarna's tears flowed as he reached out and gently touched his brother's arm.

'Do you know what survives a cremation pyre conducted according to full Vedic rituals?' asked Raavan, before he answered the question himself. 'Almost nothing ... A few pieces of the skull ... Maybe parts of the spine ... Nothing else ... But the *Kanyakumari* ... Vedavati ... she ... left me her hand. The hand with which she had touched me once ... Two fingers ... So that whenever I am lost and alone, I can hold her hand ...'

Sita stared at the pendant hanging around Raavan's neck.

'I always wondered ...' cried Raavan, 'Why ... why did she leave me two fingers? Why two? Now I know ...'

He unclipped the chain and pulled out the pendant. He kept one finger for himself. 'I am not the only one who needs her ... I'm not the only one who craves her hand ...'

Raavan leaned across and handed Vedavati's finger-relic to Sita.

Sita felt an electric current pass through her body as she felt her mother's caress. She brought the finger to her forehead in reverence. It was a profoundly holy icon. She kissed it softly and then held it in a tight grip. She looked up at Raavan.

They were both crying.

For what they had lost. And what they had found again.

Their Goddess.

The *Kanyakumari*.

Vedavati.

Chapter 5

'I had ordered him not to mobilise the army,' said Ram, an unhappy expression spreading across his face.

Ram, Vashishtha, Lakshman, Hanuman and Naarad were on a mid-sized seafaring ship sailing down the Western Sea. They had gathered on the upper deck. Sursa was asleep in her cabin. They had left the Konkan coast behind and were now cruising along the Malabar coast – the lower half of the western Indian peninsular coastline. They were accompanied by forty soldiers, thirty among them being Parihan Vayuputras.

'Hmmm … I heard that's what you expressly ordered,' said Naarad, in a droll voice. 'But your younger brother has disregarded you. He is going ahead and mobilising his army.'

'Perhaps he believes that your mission to Lanka will not be a success, Hanuman,' said Vashishtha, looking at the Naga Vayuputra.

'But that is not for Bharat to decide,' said Ram, cutting in.

'A good brother will not just blindly follow his elder brother's orders,' said Naarad. 'He will do what he thinks is in the best interest of his brother, even if it means disobeying him.'

'If you expect our mission to fail, why have you asked Sursa to take me to Lanka?' asked Hanuman.

'We cannot be certain of anything, Hanuman,' said Naarad, 'least of all this delicate operation. We must try, of course. If there's the slightest chance of saving innocent lives, then we must at least try. But I think the odds are long. Bharat is right. If your mission fails, we will need to move in an army quickly. We don't want to waste months mobilising at that time.'

Naarad looked at Ram as he said this. Ram had a strange expression on his face, a mix of disquiet that his brother had disobeyed the legal order of the king-in-exile of Ayodhya, but also affection for a brother who loved him dearly and would do all that was possible to fight for him and Sita.

'Anyway,' said Hanuman. 'You all can wait at Shabarimalaji temple while Sursa and I steal into Sigiriya with a few soldiers and rescue Sita. The ship will dock at Alappuzha. You can disembark and my Vayuputra soldiers will guide you to the temple hamlet. The Lady of the Forest will give you refuge. Sursa and I will head onwards from Alappuzha with our soldiers.'

The famous Shabarimala temple was dedicated to Lord Ayyappa, son of the previous Mahadev, Lord Rudra, and the Vishnu, Lady Mohini. Devotees from across India visited it during the pilgrimage season after taking the temporary vow of *sanyas, renunciation*. The temple was maintained by a small forest-dwelling community from the region, led by Shabari, the Lady of the Forest. They also managed the affairs of the community that lived around the temple.

'I would love to pay my respects at the Shabarimalaji temple, but I can't,' said Ram. 'I am coming to Lanka.'

Hanuman shot a look at Ram and then Vashishtha.

It was Vashishtha who spoke first. 'You cannot go, Ram.'

Ram's answer was simple and direct. 'Sita is my wife. She is mine to protect.'

'That's noble of you, Ram. But we cannot allow you to put yourself at risk.'

'With respect, Guruji, that is not your choice to make.'

'With respect, King Ram,' said Hanuman. 'It's not your choice to make either.'

Ram was steadily getting upset. But his face and his voice were, characteristically, very calm. 'It's my life. She is my wife. I don't see—'

Hanuman cut in. 'You are not just a husband, King Ram. You are not just an Ayodhya royal either. You have been recognised as a Vishnu by the Vayuputras. We cannot—'

It was Ram's turn to interrupt Hanuman. 'Please accept my gratitude towards the Vayuputras for thinking so highly of me. But the only ones who have the authority to recognise the Vishnu are the Malayaputras. And they have recognised Sita as a Vishnu. So even if your goal is to protect the Vishnu, you should go along with my idea. It is a wise choice.'

'King Ram,' said Hanuman, 'this cannot be argued any further. You too have been recognised as a Vishnu.'

'You might think that this is a wise decision, but it's not,' said Vashishtha to Ram.

Long ago, in the *gurukul*, Vashishtha had taught Ram the three drivers of decision-making: Desire, Emotions and Intelligence. They arrange themselves in a hierarchy, with Desire at the bottom and Intelligence at the top. Desire and Emotions can be allowed to drive decisions at times. But Desire must never be allowed to override Emotions in decision-making. And Emotions must never overpower Intelligence. When we allow our behaviour and decisions to be primarily driven by Intelligence, then we have the opportunity to live wisely. 'You are being driven by your emotions, Ram. Think calmly, with your intelligence, factoring in all the knowledge at our disposal. And then decide.'

'Also,' said Hanuman, 'this may be Raavan's precise plan. If he kills both the Vishnus, or worse, makes both the Vishnus his prisoners, then Mother India is doomed. Not only will he have destroyed our motherland's past, he will also destroy her future. Don't you have a duty to Mother India as well? You said to me once that Mother and Motherland are greater than heaven!'

Ram was quiet. He had no answer for Hanuman.

Vashishtha gently touched his shoulder. 'Ram, it's not in Raavan's interest to kill Sita for as long as you are alive. Raavan is a cold and calculating trader. I know he needs medicines from the Malayaputras. He will blackmail them for it. It is actually Vishwamitra who wants to trigger a war. We want to get Sita out of Lanka quietly to avoid that war. But if you rush into Lanka now, and both Sita and you are captured and thrown into Raavan's dungeons, a war would be inevitable. Think rationally. Decide wisely. Let Hanuman and Sursa go.'

Ram slowly looked down. A shadow pulled over his eyes.

He surrendered.

—JƗ J5D—

The sun came up over Ashok Vatika. It was a beautiful morning. The air was warm. The wind was soft. Purple, pink, orange and white flowers swayed in unison, as if to shake the dew off their beaming faces. Squirrels skittered about, chasing each other in frenzy. Raavan, Kumbhakarna and Sita were seated at breakfast.

It was slowly becoming a daily ritual now. Anticipated by them all.

They had almost finished eating. And what was most important had begun.

Conversation.

'It was ...' Raavan leaned back and stopped speaking. He looked up at the sky and took a deep breath. As if to compose himself. 'Yesterday was cathartic, Sita ... Speaking of Vedavati ... Grief that had been buried so deep inside me ... For so long ... Speaking of it ... Crying ... Letting it out ... It helped. I feel ... I feel lighter.'

Raavan looked at Sita. 'Thank you.'

Sita smiled and held his gaze, her eyes moist.

Kumbhakarna exhaled deeply and patted his brother's knee. 'Dada, it helped. It helped me as well. I can't say that I have felt anything remotely like your grief ... But I've carried the scars too from that terrible day.' Kumbhakarna turned to Sita. 'I have tried to speak to Dada often about it. To pull him out of his misery. But what I couldn't do in decades, you have accomplished in a few days, Queen Sita.'

Sita smiled. 'I haven't done anything. It's my face. My mother's face.'

'No,' said Kumbhakarna. 'You carry her within your soul. She had a magical ability to make things better just by her presence. You have that ability too ... The Malayaputras have chosen well.'

Sita laughed softly, but didn't say anything.

'I can see the greatness in you, Queen Sita,' continued Kumbhakarna. 'You will make an excellent Vishnu. You have strength, courage, wisdom and empathy. You have the grit and determination.'

Raavan looked at Kumbhakarna and smiled, then turned to Sita. 'And most importantly, you have known grief ... The most powerful emotion. The source of true greatness.'

Sita frowned. *What?*

'I read this in a book once,' continued Raavan, 'that grief and suffering can serve as engines that move life forward. Happiness is overrated. Hatred, of course, is destructive.'

'What sense does that make?' asked Sita. 'Though I agree that hatred is destructive. But grief? Really?'

'Yes, really. It makes sense. Think of the great people you know today.' Raavan widened his chest and almost preened, throwing his head back in challenge.

Sita narrowed her eyes and stared at Raavan. None of the politeness of her birth-mother in her. No hesitation in being brutally honest. She was communicating her thoughts clearly with her eyes. *Great? You think you are great? Really?*

Raavan answered her look. 'Great does not mean good, Sita. Great only means the person makes a real impact on the world. Ordinary people do not impact the world, they are only impacted by it. Now, with great people, the impact can be good or bad. But know this: Happy people can never be great.'

Sita did not agree. 'Come on, Raavanji. Do you actually believe that? My adoptive mother Sunaina was a great woman. She reformed Mithila. Brought peace and prosperity to it, as much as she could. She helped so many. Brought me up. Gave me direction. Gave me strength and motivation.'

'But was she happy?'

'She was always smiling. She was—'

Raavan interrupted Sita. 'That's not an answer to my question. People assume that depressed people *look like* they are in depression. That they cry all the time. Or mope. No. Most people who are depressed, smile. In fact, they smile more than necessary. Because they hide their grief from the world.'

Sita didn't respond.

'What were your last moments with Queen Sunaina like? I know she died a long time back, when you were very young. Yes?'

Sita nodded. 'Yes.'

'So, what did she say to you on her deathbed?' asked Raavan. 'Did she tell you to be happy? Peaceful? Calm? Joyful?'

Sita remembered her mother's words only too well. *You will not waste your life mourning me. You will live wisely and make me proud.*

'She told me that she wanted me to make her proud,' said Sita.

Raavan pointed his index finger at her. 'Aha! That's the difference between great people and happy people. Great people always keep striving, keep achieving, as if they have a monster living inside them that will not let them rest. It is so strong, this monster, that it makes them want to keep growing and achieving even after they die. So, they want others around them, especially the ones they love, to also be great. Happiness as an accidental by-product is acceptable, but it is not the purpose of their lives. Happy people, on the other hand, are satisfied people. Satisfied with what they have. Their smiles are genuine, the kind of smile that reaches the eyes. Their hearts are light. They are warm to everyone around them. And they want others, especially the ones they love, to be joyful, to accept what life has blessed or cursed them with, and be satisfied with it. Basically, their *mantra* is: Be happy by managing your mind rather than changing the world. Great people, on the other hand, want to change the world. Happy people just want to make their minds accept whatever the world throws at them, so that, in their little cocoon, they can be joyful. Like people who are drugged.'

'Oh, come on!'

'No, I mean it,' said Raavan. 'Happiness is like a drug. The ultimate drug. It makes you accept life as it is. Just inject the drug into your mind, be blissed out and don't achieve anything, don't change anything. Just be a joyful idiot.'

'Listen—'

Raavan interrupted Sita. 'But grief, on the other hand, drives you insane. You are not satisfied with anything. Anything. How do you banish that grief from your life? How? By changing the world, or so you think … For no matter how much you change the world, you will not find happiness. Why? Because the only way to be happy is by being drugged; by managing your own mind, rather than changing the world. That is why the only people who bring about change are the ones who are *not* happy, the ones who are grief-stricken.'

Sita narrowed her eyes. 'I have been joyful for the last thirteen years with Ram. These years in banishment have been the happiest of my life. Ram tells me exactly the same thing.'

'And what exactly have both of you achieved in these thirteen years?'

Sita didn't say anything. But the answer was obvious. *Not much.*

Raavan continued. 'There's nothing wrong with wanting to be happy. Many people make that choice. But you must realise what you are giving up – you are giving up any chance of becoming great.'

Sita had a slight smile on her face. She was thinking of her friend Radhika, who had chosen happiness.

'Think of the sun,' said Raavan. 'It is, after all, a gigantic, radioactive ball of fire. No life is possible close to it. And within it is only death. But a mere eight minutes of light-speed away is Mother Earth, teeming with life made possible by the sun. The sun is like a grievously hurting man, burning himself up with his suffering. But his suffering makes life possible some distance away. That is greatness.'

'Yes, but like you say, some distance away. Not alongside the sun.'

'True. The sun can never find happiness. But he is great. It is said that the fate of truly great people is to suffer, but they confuse correlation with causality. It is actually the other way around. Because they suffer, they become great.'

Sita shielded her eyes as she looked up at the brilliant radiance of the sun. She smiled as a thought reinforced her understanding of her husband. *Ram* ...

'Do you agree with me?' asked Raavan.

Sita turned to Raavan. 'Maybe. There is something to it, I admit. But the thing is, it's only if the sun keeps its grief to itself that it can make good happen. When it cannot, it will erupt in solar flares, which will damage and hurt life, even from a distance. Grief can provide the fuel for greatness, but it can also be the trigger for evil.'

Raavan nodded. 'Yes. I have damaged the world a lot.'

Kumbhakarna cut in. 'No no, Dada. You have done some good too. It's not that—'

'Kumbha!' boomed Raavan, admonishing his brother. His eyes, though, twinkled with good humour. 'Love me, but don't lie so much that it is a sin to even listen to you!'

Kumbhakarna laughed, as did Sita.

'I have been a terrible person,' said Raavan. 'I have suffered all my life, and I have, in turn, inflicted that suffering on the whole world. But you,' continued Raavan, pointing at Sita. 'You are different. You are good and perfect.'

Sita shook her head. 'You are once again projecting my mother on to me. Maybe you inflicted ALL your suffering on the world. But it's not that I never did. Often, I absorbed my grief, but sometimes, when it became too much, I lashed out. And those with power in their hands do not have the luxury of lashing out. If I am a Vishnu, I will have that power.'

Raavan looked at Kumbhakarna and then back at Sita.

'Yesterday, when you told me what happened to my mother, and what you did to the people who killed her, for a moment I felt the rage you felt. I thought what you did, torturing those murderers, was justified. But I know a man who would not have felt this way; who, even at such a moment of intense grief, would have been lawful. I know a man who never loses his focus, no matter how much suffering he undergoes. The greater the grief, the more righteous his response. I always thought that he would make a better Vishnu than I would. Now I know for sure.'

Raavan smiled slightly.

Sita looked away for a moment, remembering something. 'You know,' she said, 'I once read that winning wars is different from winning peace. You need anger to win a war. Anger in the moment. And that is why the Mahadevs have always been those with immense anger. But to win peace... that requires something different. You and I can win wars. But war can only take away an injustice. It cannot create justice. War can only take away Evil. It cannot create Good. To create Justice and Good, you need peace. And to win peace, you need a leader who will stay the course, no matter what comes along – grief, suffering – to sway him from his path.'

'True.'

'Ram is that leader,' said Sita.

Chapter 6

The ship docked at Alappuzha in the region of Kerala, the land of Lord Parshu Ram. The party was going to ride over eighty kilometres to the holy land of Shabarimala, which cradled the great Ayyappa temple deep in the forests.

Kerala was blessed by the Gods. It had an excess of everything: deep-water lakes, backwaters and rivers bisected almost every path; dense forests made the road ahead almost unmappable; tall and craggy mountains tested the spirit of even the most devout devotee; and wild animals sometimes brought an unwelcome and sudden end to travel. It made the journey to Shabarimala not an easy one.

But the ancestors had designed pilgrimages to be difficult. The journey must be a penance. It must prepare you for the destination.

The old Sanskrit word for a place of pilgrimage was *teerth sthan*. The root of this word was '*the point of crossing over*'. So, a pilgrimage place was where one's soul could cross over and touch the divine. Which is why, often, pilgrimage temples were built in inhospitable terrain, arduous and difficult to reach; the journey would serve as a preparation, purging the body to prepare the soul.

But Ram was occupied with another journey. The one that Hanuman was about to undertake.

Hanuman and Sursa, along with ten soldiers, were setting out on a cutter boat. They intended to sail farther down to the southern tip of mainland India, and then on to the island of Lanka, where they would beach on the relatively uninhabited western coast. Then they would march towards the centre of the island, towards Sigiriya.

'Please give her this letter, Lord Hanuman,' said Ram, as he handed a rolled and sealed parchment to the Naga Vayuputra. He removed one of his rings. 'And please give her this as well.'

Hanuman looked at the letter and then at Ram, a wan smile on his face. 'You think so too?'

Ram nodded. 'Yes. She will resist coming back.'

Hanuman took a deep breath. 'I will try my best to convince her.'

'Yes, I know. But I am the reason she will not want to escape. I think she will want me to battle Raavan and rescue her. So that my name is indisputably cemented as the Vishnu. But she is wrong. I am not the Vishnu, she is. She has to return.'

Hanuman held Ram's forearms tightly. 'I will bring her back, Great One.'

— J干 ﻝ5D —

'Where in Lord Parshu Ram's name is Hanuman?' asked an angry Vishwamitra.

A message had been sent by the Malayaputras to Hanuman a few days ago. To Lothal, where it was believed he was to arrive. But they had not received any reply.

'Guruji,' said Arishtanemi, 'it's unlike Hanuman to not respond to us. Perhaps he didn't receive the message.'

'I have heard that… that infernal man was also seen in the area.'

Arishtanemi knew Vishwamitra was referring to Vashishtha. He had heard the news as well. But he didn't want to speculate about what may have happened.

'You go,' said Vishwamitra suddenly.

Arishtanemi was surprised. 'To Lanka, Guruji?'

'Yes.'

'But… but I am not sure that Sita will listen to me, Guruji.'

'Make her listen!'

Arishtanemi remained silent.

Vishwamitra continued. 'We have made so many sacrifices for Mother India. She cannot be stupid now. We are mobilising our own army. We will get them across to Lanka. The Vayuputras will also have to join us … they will have no choice. Armed with our *daivi astras*, Sita can lead us all into battle and easily kill Raavan. But first, she must arrange a dramatic escape. It will build her image across India. The entire chessboard is set, everything is ready, she just needs to move in for the kill.'

'But Guruji …'

'She has to listen. She has nothing in her hands now, no cards left. She must be imagining that Raavan will kill her. She doesn't know where Ram is. She has no support. We are her only hope. The Malayaputras have used a *daivi astra* to save her, during the Battle of Mithila. She knows we are loyal to her. We are her only hope. She has to take on her role as the Vishnu.'

'But she is stubborn, Guruji. She doesn't—'

Vishwamitra leaned forward and interrupted Arishtanemi. 'Go to Lanka and make her understand. Do not disappoint me.'

—JF ꓷꙄD—

Raavan shielded his eyes and looked up at the sun. And smiled.

'What's so funny?' asked Kumbhakarna.

Raavan and Kumbhakarna were standing on the veranda of Sita's cottage, waiting for her to emerge. They had just finished breakfast. Sita had gone back into the cottage for her after-breakfast *puja*.

'Just ... the grief-stricken sun,' answered Raavan.

Kumbhakarna grinned mischievously. 'I don't know which version of you tortures me more, Dada. The older version who never listened to me, or this new philosophical version who talks in circles!'

Raavan boxed Kumbhakarna on his stomach. 'Bloody dog!'

Kumbhakarna laughed even more loudly, enclosing his brother in a bear hug. They held each other tightly, laughing till the tears rolled down their cheeks. And then they shed some more tears. This time, tears of sadness. Sadness at the years wasted.

They disengaged when they heard the sound of someone clearing their throat. Sita stood a short distance away, an amused grin on her face.

The brothers wiped their eyes and sat down. Sita sat down as well.

'Are you both all right?' asked Sita.

Kumbhakarna answered for the brothers. 'Never been better.'

Raavan laughed and punched his gargantuan brother on his shoulder.

'So, what are we going to talk about today?'

Raavan leaned forward. 'No more philosophical discussions!'

'By the great Lord Rudra, yes! Enough philosophical discussions!' said Kumbhakarna, laughing.

'Hey!' said Raavan, chortling.

Kumbhakarna leaned back and laughed. Even Sita joined in the inane laughter.

It took a few moments for everyone to settle down, and then Raavan spoke. 'We must decide our next step.'

'Yes,' said Sita.

Raavan continued. 'Guru Vishwamitra will send someone to rescue you.'

'He probably will.'

'And your husband is alive. He will come too.'

'Yes, he will.'

'And what will you do? Will you escape with them?'

Sita knew she couldn't tell them what she really wanted to do. 'Umm…'

'Speak honestly. You are Vedavati's daughter.'

'Well … I mean …'

'All right,' said Raavan, interrupting Sita. 'Let me answer for you then.'

An embarrassed smile played on Sita's face. For she could guess what was to follow.

'Somewhere in the back of my mind I knew what Guru Vishwamitra was thinking,' said Raavan. 'He needed to build someone up into a villain, who could then be destroyed by the Vishnu, so that the rebellious and uncontrollable people of India would follow that Vishnu.'

'Umm …'

'Let me continue,' said Raavan, raising his hand. 'Indians are the most difficult people to manage in the world. Constantly rebelling. They love breaking the law, even if there is nothing to be gained by it. We don't like following orders from any leader. Unless it is that rare leader whom we look up to like a God. We would follow that leader to the ends of the Earth, and beyond. But how do you transform a human being into a God? Even a perfect human being is not enough. People have to want to follow him. He has to earn their admiration and loyalty. And nothing quite like delivering the head of the villain that people hate, right?'

'Raavanji … I don't know what to say … But what Guru Vishwamitra … His plans …'

Raavan smiled. 'No, it's all right… I understand. My life has not amounted to much. Maybe my death can mean something.'

Sita was silent. So was Kumbhakarna.

'But your husband Ram coming here and rescuing you will not set the Indian imagination alight. There must be a great war.'

'But…'

'Hear me out. You and your husband will be making a lot of changes to India. You will be asking people to make a lot of sacrifices. All for the motherland. So that Mother India's future is secure. They will not follow you and make those sacrifices unless they worship you. And to worship you both, they need a spectacle.'

Raavan paused before continuing.

'What will actually help India,' said Raavan, 'is what you two will do later. The reforms that you will make. I suggest you study Lankan administration. There is a lot you can learn from what we've done in Lanka. Roads, infrastructure …' Raavan looked at Kumbhakarna before continuing. 'Though our health facilities could do with some improving… We still haven't been able to figure out how to stop the plague ravaging Sigiriya. But do you think that my Lankans sing songs in praise of the roads

I've built for them? Or the water pipes I've constructed? Or the parks? The schools? Oh no... They celebrate stories of my military victory at Karachapa! It will be the same for the both of you. If you succeed, maybe they will call the perfect Vishnu-created times Ram Rajya or Sita Rajya. And it will be a time of order, comfort, peace and convenience; roads, canal irrigation, hospitals, schools. Most importantly, institutional systems. But trust me, when Ram and Sita's story is written – maybe they will call it the Ramayana or Sitayana, who knows – there will be scant mention of this Ram Rajya we are talking about. No storyteller's imagination is fired by the prospect of writing twenty pages on how a great canal was constructed. Which reader would be interested in that story? What will get the storytellers excited is your adventures. Your love story, your struggles, your time in the jungle, and crucially, your war against me in Lanka. Because that is all that the common folk will want to hear. That's what you will be remembered for. That's what people will follow you for. Because most people are stupid ...'

Kumbhakarna stirred uncomfortably.

'Okay, okay, Kumbhakarna, stop frowning,' Raavan said. 'People don't consciously register the things that truly make their life better. Like schools and hospitals. They take these things for granted once they have them. Instead, they focus on the magic of the stories that beguile them, like great battles between a hero and a villain. The common people are, fundamentally, idiots.'

'Come on, Raavanji,' said Sita. 'You can't say that ...'

Raavan interrupted Sita. 'You can say whatever politically correct thing you want to say to make yourself feel morally superior. But you know that I am speaking the truth.'

Sita remained silent.

'So, if we have to give them a war, let's give them one. And a good one.'

'Um …'

'That would serve another purpose too. It would destroy my army.'

'What?'

'The Lankan army must be destroyed. For the good of India.'

Kumbhakarna nodded, in agreement with his elder brother this time.

'Why?' asked Sita. 'Why would you want your own loyal soldiers to be massacred? They would only be following your orders.'

'No. You do not know my army. They don't just follow orders. They enjoy the violence. Those are the kind of soldiers I collected; angry people with tortured, damaged souls, who hate the world and want to see it burn. My Lankan people, the ordinary citizens, are good. And we have an efficient police force here to protect them. But my army … Well, they are a reflection of what I was … They are ruthless monsters. And without me to restrain them, they can cause chaos. They are barbarians who will burn alive unarmed people, even children, just to collect some loot, as they did in Mumbadevi. Thugs who will rape any non-Lankan woman who falls into their hands. Butchers who will carry out public beheadings because they enjoy the spectacle. Fiends who will sell people into slavery, even though dharma bans it, because it's profitable. Terrific killers with oodles of courage, no doubt. But without the restraint of *dharma*. I collected such soldiers. I was a connoisseur of such men and women. You know one of them. Samichi. You thought you knew her intimately, but you did not know her at all. Why did I recruit her? Because she is damaged in the core of her being. She has her reasons. Horrific childhood suffering. Her rage against her cruel father deflected into an unfocused anger against the entire world; an unquenchable fury. It makes every living moment a miserable torture for her; and the same fury makes her a killer beyond compare. A killer completely under my control. I have two hundred thousand such soldiers, Sita. They are a threat to any society. Not just to India, but also to my Lanka. They are a threat to *dharma*, since they are an army of *adharma*. They are not strong enough to conquer India right now, because of the plague afflicting us. But they will create decades of chaos in India and Lanka. How will you build a better India then? The Lankan army must be destroyed. And the best way to do that is a war. A war to the very end.'

Sita didn't say anything. What Raavan had said sounded cold, ruthless, but logical.

'Will your husband fight to the very end?' asked Raavan.

'Oh yes, he will… But only if he believes that you are fighting to the end as well. If he suspects that you are not fighting to win, he will stop the battle. Because it's *adharma* to fight an enemy who is holding back. That is the way he thinks.'

Raavan frowned. 'How will he know? Who will tell him?'

He looked at Kumbhakarna and Sita. Neither would speak about this with anyone else.

'But I will genuinely not hold myself back,' said Raavan. 'I will battle hard. Will your husband win?'

Sita smiled. A smile of supreme confidence. 'The only one who can defeat Ram is Ram himself. He will defeat you, Raavanji.'

Raavan grinned. 'It will be a glorious war then.'

'But …' Sita fell silent, hesitating to voice her question.

Raavan understood. But he waited for her to ask.

'But why do this to yourself?'

Raavan smiled. 'Have you heard that statement, "They buried us, but they did not know that we were seeds"?'

Sita nodded. 'Yes, I have. Beautiful. Evocative and rebellious. Who said that?'

'Someone from the Greek islands to our west. I think his name was Konstantinos. But, in my honest opinion, it covers only half the journey towards wisdom.'

'How so?'

'It assumes that the seed itself rises. But we know that is not what happens. The seed will remain dead like a stone if it is not buried in fertile ground. The seed *has* to be buried. And allow itself to be destroyed. So that a glorious tree emerges from its shattered chest. That is the *purpose*, the *swadharma*, of the seed. For as long as the tree lives, songs will be sung of the seed that experienced death – even though it was already dead – to allow the tree to emerge. The seed is either lifeless above ground, or wrecked below ground. But when it rips open to allow a tree to emerge, it becomes immortal. Through the only way any living thing can become immortal: in the memory of others who live on after them. Its sacrifice makes the seed immortal.'

Sita remained silent.

'I died the day Vedavati died. I have been dragging my carcass around all this time. It is time to let my corpse itself die. The right time. I can allow myself to be destroyed so that the legend of Ram and Sita may rise. And as long as the world remembers the two of you, it will remember me. I will be immortal too.'

Sita looked down, her eyes moist with sentiment.

Raavan looked at Kumbhakarna, whose eyes glistened with unshed tears. He looked back at Sita. 'There are three good men in my army. My only request is that they be kept out of this. Kumbhakarna, my uncle Mareech, and my son, Indrajit.'

Kumbhakarna's response was instantaneous. 'No. I am staying. I am fighting.'

'Kumbha … you should …'

'No.'

'Listen to me … Escape with Mareech uncle and Indrajeet and then—'

'No, Dada.'

'Kumbha … please.'

'NO, DADA!'

Raavan fell silent. Kumbhakarna stared at his brother. His eyes conveyed a mixture of love, anger and pride. Then Raavan got up and embraced his younger brother.

Chapter 7

Nations that do not have a coastline can be forgiven for thinking that reaching an island is a challenge: they imagine the island as a fortress and the sea as a moat. Which is not true. With good ships and fast boats, the sea can be a highway rather than an obstacle. The real challenge lies in marching inland, especially if the terrain is densely forested and marked by deep rivers and lofty mountains. So, while Ram and his band marched towards Shabarimala, Hanuman, Sursa and ten Vayuputra soldiers had already sailed into the north-western coast of Lanka on a quick cutter boat.

This region of Lanka did not have good harbours. In fact, these were treacherous waters for large sea-faring ships to sail on, due to the massive sandbanks, many of which rose above water level during low tide. It was why Hanuman had decided to use a much smaller cutter boat.

But the sandbanks, and the resultant absence of good harbours, gave this coast an immeasurable advantage for

Hanuman's secret mission: this part of Lanka was largely deserted.

Late in the night, the cutter boat passed the long and not-too-broad Mannar island. It lay south-east to north-west, stretching like a yearning lover towards the Pamban island off the mainland Indian coast a mere twenty-five kilometres away. They sailed farther southwards from the island, deep into the sea. They needed to do this because of the celebrated Ketheeswaram temple on the Lankan mainland, to the east of Mannar. It was the only place in this region that would have some crowds, which they wanted to avoid. For obvious reasons.

As they passed, Hanuman turned towards the Lankan mainland with folded hands in the direction of the lights, and bowed to the Mahadev, Lord Rudra, whose idol was consecrated at the Ketheeswaram temple.

'*Jai Shri Rudra*,' he whispered.

Glory to Lord Rudra.

'*Jai Shri Rudra*,' repeated everyone on the boat.

Around twenty kilometres farther south, the Aruvi Aru River flowed into the sea. The headwaters of the second longest river in Lanka were close to the Lankan capital city of Sigiriya. This should have made the river an important waterway for travelling into the Lankan interior. Theoretically, ships could easily come in from the sea and sail up the river towards Sigiriya. But this had been made impossible due to the insidious sandbanks in the sea around this region. Seafaring ships normally avoided this route for fear of being grounded. As a result, ship traffic towards the hinterland of Sigiriya was captured by the Mahaweli Ganga, the longest river in Lanka, which joined the sea on the eastern coast, on the other side of the island.

It was perfect for Hanuman's mission.

For this north-western coastline of Lanka was almost completely deserted. They could simply sail up the river in their smaller boat, undetected, to reach very close to Sigiriya. This was crucial, because the biggest risk in marching within Lanka was getting lost in the dense jungle hinterland. The river would serve as a guide. There was another possible route: the road from Ketheeswaram temple leading to the Lankan capital. But it was dotted with military barricades, making it a risky proposition.

'There's just one problem,' whispered Sursa.

'What?' asked Hanuman, leaning closer, keeping his voice low.

'There is a lighthouse close to the river mouth. It serves as a warning to seafaring ships to not sail farther north, due to the sandbanks.'

'And it's manned?'

'Yes, it is. Around ten men.'

Hanuman looked back at the ten Vayuputra soldiers behind them. 'I think we can take them.'

'We must do it quickly.'

'Why?'

'There is a full battalion posted just twenty kilometres from the lighthouse, at the Ketheeswaram temple. It protects the royal road from the temple to Sigiriya. It's a mere thirty-minute ride on horseback. If even one soldier escapes, we'll have an entire battalion upon us in no time at all.'

'Hmm. All right. So, we'll have to kill them all. Quickly.'

'Yes.'

'How frequent is the changeover?'

'This unit is largely self-sufficient. And a completely unimportant post where nothing happens. Relief comes once in four weeks. It will be a while before the battalion even knows that these lighthouse soldiers have been killed. By which time we will have finished our work in Sigiriya and be back in mainland India.'

Hanuman nodded and quickly gave orders to his soldiers. Check weapons and shields. Tighten armour. Stretch muscles.

He then sat tall on the thwart, bringing his ridiculously muscular left arm overhead and dropping the forearm behind his back, resting his left hand between his brawny shoulder blades. With his right hand, Hanuman grabbed his left bent elbow and pulled gently. He sighed as he felt a stretch in his powerful left deltoid and triceps muscles.

Almost immediately, he felt someone's eyes upon him. He turned to see Sursa staring at him with open admiration. Hanuman's cheeks turned bright red with embarrassment and he quickly looked away. Sursa laughed and began stretching her own shoulders.

— Ꝓ Ꝓ —

Hanuman and Sursa were hiding in the trees along with the Vayuputra soldiers. They had beached their boat a good distance north and then noiselessly made their way south, racing behind the dense treeline. They stood in the shadows, observing the lighthouse across the broad beach. The tall, five-storey structure had a massive fire lit on its top storey, spreading its light and signalling a warning to ships far into the sea. A simple warning: *Stay away.*

'There are ten of them,' confirmed Hanuman, counting the Lankan soldiers who had gathered at the beach and were looking towards the expanse of water. It may have been late at night, but the light of the full moon made them clearly visible. They were only a short distance away.

'But Hans, we should check for men within the lighthouse too,' said Sursa.

Hanuman ignored the fond but inappropriate mangling of his name. 'I agree. But let's get rid of these soldiers first.'

Sursa nodded.

Hanuman turned to his fellow Vayuputras. 'They have spears. Bear that in mind.'

Hanuman and the Vayuputras were armed with swords and knives. The Lankans had these weapons too, but they also had spears, which dramatically increased their reach.

Hanuman drew his sword, went down on one knee, and dug the tip of the blade into the soft, sandy ground. His band followed.

Hanuman closed his eyes, bowed his head and whispered, 'Everything I do, I do for Rudra.'

The words were softly echoed by the warriors behind him. 'Everything I do, I do for Rudra.'

Hanuman rose, his huge frame crouched low, his sword held away from his body. He began to move forward on light feet.

Fast as a cheetah, nimble as a panther.

Hanuman and his platoon were in the open now. On the beach. Racing towards the Lankans, who sat facing the other way. Towards the sea.

A Lankan soldier turned a few moments before the Vayuputras would have been upon them. An ancient animal instinct, from when humans protected themselves from great predators in the grasslands of Africa; an instinct that warns those who remain attuned to their gut reaction.

'WHO GOES THERE?'

In one fluid motion, the superbly trained soldiers of Raavan were on their feet and had whirled around, their spears thrust forward, shields held together with perfect discipline.

This was one of the most potent defensive tactics in open battles. The soldiers held their shields together, each one overlapping partly with the next, forming an impenetrable wall. And through a curved opening on the right edge of each shield emerged a threatening long spear.

The dreaded shield wall.

It was natural for any attacking force to slow down when confronted with a shield wall. For it was almost impossible to penetrate. The attacker would run into the forest of spear blades if he charged, and run himself through.

But Hanuman was no ordinary attacker.

No defensive hesitation in this mighty son of Vayu Kesari.

Hanuman raised his huge frame to its full height. No need to crouch or be silent any more. He did not slow down. His sword was still held to his side.

His platoon fell slightly behind as he raced ahead.

When he was almost upon the forest of spears, Hanuman roared, '*Kalagni Rudra!*'

Kalagni was the *mythical end-of-time fire*; the conflagration that marked the end of an age. And the beginning of a new one. It was the fire of Lord Rudra that signalled the end of time for those who stood against the mighty Mahadev.

'*Kalagni Rudra!*' bellowed the Vayuputras.

Hanuman ran straight towards the spear in the centre of the shield wall. When it almost seemed like the Naga Vayuputra would run into the blade, Hanuman twisted his torso to one side and raised his left arm. Bypassing the spear's blade, he brought his left arm down with force, trapping the spear shaft between his left arm and the side of his chest. Now the Lankan was locked in position for as long as he held on to the spear. Hanuman had not slowed down. His left shoulder rammed into the shield and the Lankan staggered back. Hanuman raised his sword and brutally thrust it into the man's throat. Yanking his sword out almost immediately, he swung his blade to the side in the same smooth movement, slicing the throat of the Lankan next to him.

Within a few seconds Hanuman had killed two Lankans. And, most crucially, the shield wall had broken.

The shield wall is impenetrable when held together. But a single breach can make the entire structure collapse shockingly quickly. The Vayuputra platoon smashed into the opening provided by Hanuman. They cut down the rest of the Lankans with rapid efficiency.

Except for one Lankan, who had dropped his spear and was scurrying away towards his horse. As Hanuman killed the man confronting him, he noticed the Lankan mounting his horse a short distance away.

'Stop that man!' hollered Hanuman as he raced towards him.

The Lankan spurred his horse viciously. It looked like he would escape. And soon warn the battalion at Ketheeswaram temple.

This mission could fail even before it began.

And then Hanuman saw a most exquisite kill.

Sursa thundered down the sandy ground, from the right of the Lankan on horseback. The unfortunate man did not notice death racing towards him. His eyes were fixed on the fearsome Hanuman, on the opposite side. As she neared the horse, Sursa sprang from her feet and vaulted high into the air, bending her knees, perfectly timed, to get maximum lift.

Hanuman felt like he was seeing it in slow motion.

Splendid.

Sursa flying through the air, her back arched, right hand raised high, knife ready. She crashed into the mounted Lankan and brought her right hand down simultaneously. Ramming her blade into the Lankan's left eye. The metal tip tore through the eye socket and sank into the brain. The Lankan and Sursa rolled off the horse as one. The Lankan was dead before he hit the ground.

The horse kept running for a few seconds and then stopped in confusion.

Hanuman could not take his eyes off Sursa, his expression one of awe.

Sursa rolled over one more time and rose in the same smooth movement. She looked around. A jungle cat on the prowl.

All the Lankans were dead.

Her steely eyes settled on Hanuman. 'Let's check the lighthouse quickly.'

Hanuman nodded. He turned towards his soldiers. 'Pick up the bodies and get them into the lighthouse. Tie up the horses.'

'Yes, Lord Hanuman,' they replied in unison.

Hanuman and Sursa moved quickly towards the lighthouse.

— J+ ⅃ᴐD —

'Father, I deserve to know what is going on,' said Indrajit, politely but firmly.

Raavan's twenty-seven-year-old son had walked into his private chambers unannounced while the king of Lanka was in discussion with Kumbhakarna. Indrajit had the same intimidating physical presence as his father. Tall and muscular, his baritone voice was naturally commanding. But also beguiling. He had inherited his mother Mandodari's high cheekbones and thick brown hair, a leonine mane which he styled with two side partings and a knot at the crown of his head. An oiled handlebar moustache sat well on his smooth-complexioned face. His clothes were sober, as always. He wore no jewellery but for the ear studs that most warriors in India favoured. A *janau*, the *sacred thread*, hung diagonally from his left shoulder, across his chest.

Raavan stopped speaking and turned towards his pride and joy. 'What are you talking about, Indrajit?'

Indrajit stared at his father. And then turned to his uncle. 'Uncle, are you going to talk?'

Kumbhakarna looked away wordlessly.

'Father,' said Indrajit, turning his gaze back to Raavan, 'the last I heard, the plan was to kidnap the Vishnu and then negotiate with the Malayaputras for the medicines that you both need. It has been days since we kidnapped her. Many days. But nobody has been sent to the Malayaputras, nor has any message gone to them. And I keep seeing the two of you trotting off to Ashok Vatika for long conversations with Queen Sita. What is going on?'

'Indrajit, there are things to be considered.'

Indrajit stood silently, waiting for his father to explain. Since no explanation was offered, he took a deep breath and spoke with steely calm. 'Father, do I still have your trust?'

'Of course, you do, my son.'

'Then why are you not telling me the whole truth?'

'My son, there are bigger issues that your uncle and I need to deliberate upon before taking any step.'

'Bigger issues? Father, Ayodhya is mobilising its army. We thought they wouldn't do that if we didn't harm Queen Sita. We were wrong. And if even *I* know what Ayodhya is doing, there is no way that you don't know. If Ayodhya is able to rally all the armies of the Sapt Sindhu kingdoms, we will lose. We will give them a tough fight, but we will lose. You know that. What can be a bigger issue than that?'

Raavan remained silent.

'Father …'

Raavan picked up a scroll from the side table. 'There is this problem.'

'What problem?'

'I need you to go to Bali.'

Bali was an island far to the east of India, an extremely important entrepot for trade with South-east Asia and China. One that Lanka controlled.

Indrajit was shocked, but managed to keep his expression stoic. 'Bali?'

'Yes.'

'Why in Lord Rudra's name should I go to Bali?'

'There are some major trade disputes that need immediate attention. And it can only be sorted out by one of us. Someone from the royal family.'

Indrajit narrowed his eyes in exasperation. 'Trade disputes?'

'Yes.'

Indrajit's fists were clenched tight, his knuckles white. 'Father, I will come back when you are in a mood to trust me.'

Saying this, Indrajit turned and marched calmly out of the chamber.

Chapter 8

It took more than a week to cover the little less than one-hundred-kilometre distance from the coastal city of Alappuzha to Shabarimala. On the last night, Ram and his companions camped beside the Pampa River in the valley below. Early the next morning, they began their march to the mountain top. The temple was at a height of over one thousand five hundred feet above sea level.

They were still some distance from the main temple when they met Shabari, the Lady of the Forest. She had walked up to meet them at the entrance to the complex.

'Lady Shabari,' said Vashishtha, bringing his palms together in a respectful namaste and bowing his head.

Shabari was not a name but a title for the head of the Shabarimala temple. Her formal title was Tantri Shabari. As is the Indian way, a deep symbolism was woven into it. The word *Tantri* in old Sanskrit was gender-agnostic and could be used for a male or a female. The root of the word was *string* or *cord*. The name Shabarimala translated as the Hill of Shabari in the local language. But in old Sanskrit, *mala* meant *garland*. Thus, the *Shabarimala, garland of Shabari*, was held together by a *tantri*, the string.

The present *tantri* was an old woman, at least one hundred years old. Nobody knew her original birth-name. She herself had forgotten her old identity and had committed her entire being to the service of the great warrior-God, Lord Ayyappa, represented in this particular temple in his celibate form.

The wizened old woman had a fair-skinned face and warm, motherly eyes. She brought her calloused and forest-roughened hands together in a namaste. 'Maharishi Vashishtha. What an honour to have you grace our land. *Swamiye Sharanam Ayyappa.*'

We find refuge at the feet of Lord Ayyappa.

'The honour is all mine, great Shabariji,' answered Vashishtha. '*Swamiye Sharanam Ayyappa.*' Then the *rajguru* of Ayodhya turned to Ram and Lakshman. 'Please allow me to introduce—'

'Who does not know the great Ram,' said Shabari, with a smile that began in her heart and extended unbidden to her eyes. 'Welcome, great Vishnu.'

Ram smiled with embarrassment at being addressed as Vishnu. He whispered '*Swamiye Sharanam Ayyappa*' and bent his lean frame to touch Shabari's feet.

She touched Ram's head and whispered, 'May you have the greatest blessing of all: May you be of service to our motherland, India.'

Vashishtha smiled, for he had given this very blessing to Ram's wife, Sita, many years ago.

Ram arose, his hands folded together in a namaste.

Lakshman stepped forward, said '*Swamiye Sharanam Ayyappa*,' bent his massive frame, and touched Shabari's feet as well. He stepped back as soon as he received her blessing.

'Come with me, King Ram,' said Shabari, taking his hand and leading him along the side of the entrance. Most referred to Ram as king, even though he had not been officially coronated as yet. For Bharat had clearly declared that he ruled in the name of Ram.

Ram looked back. Vashishtha and Lakshman were following. Within a few minutes they arrived at a massive stepwell. It had a surface area of nearly five hundred square metres. Shabarimala received plentiful rain during the monsoon season, but the mountain was steep and there were no lakes. They were inundated with water during the rainy season but ran short the rest of the year, especially during the dry summer months. The stepwell was ingeniously designed in the shape of a horseshoe that descended into seven steep levels, the last of which was almost fifty feet deep. Smaller steps from its narrower ends led into the water. The stepwell's massive capacity ensured that it trapped enough water during the monsoon season to serve the needs of the temple complex all round the year.

Shabari skirted the stepwell, her hand still holding Ram's, and walked towards the mountain side.

Vashishtha smiled. For he knew where she was headed. A test. The test of Shabari. A test that no one had passed.

But Vashishtha was supremely confident of his student.

Shabari led Ram up to an installation at the edge of the mountain, just inside the perimeter wall of the complex. The view from here, of the valley below, was breathtaking. But Ram's attention was occupied elsewhere. He was transfixed by two sculptures.

Shabari turned to Ram. 'Tell me, great prince, what do these two sculptures say to you? What is their message?'

Shabari had posed this question to every important visitor to the temple. And none had got it right.

The two sculptures faced each other, a short distance separating them.

A rampaging bull.

A fearless little girl standing right in front of the beast.

The bull was life-sized, an awe-inspiring symbol of aggressive masculinity. Its head was lowered, its nostrils flared, its teeth bared. Its long, sharp horns curved threateningly. As though about to gore the little girl. The ridiculously muscled body was twisted to the right as it charged forward. Its forefeet dug into the ground. Its tail was raised, curling like a terrifying whip.

A livid, fearsome, dangerous beast.

And then there was the fearless little girl.

Petite. No older than five or six years. Hands on her hips, her shoulders thrown back in defiance. Her feet were spread apart and firmly planted for balance. Eyes rebellious. Chin up. Her hair flying back in disarray. Her clothes whipped against her body, as if a great wind was striking her. Unafraid of the beast that was about to run her down. Strong. Heroic.

Ram stared, unblinking.

Lakshman spoke first. He had the same thought as every other person who had seen these figures. 'What a magnificent girl! Powerful! Brave! Fearless! She tells us it is not the size of the person in the fight but the size of the fight in the person that matters!'

Shabari didn't acknowledge Lakshman or his answer. She didn't even turn to look at him. Her eyes were fixed on Ram.

Ram smiled slightly and murmured. 'What a magnificent beast ...'

Shabari cast a glance at Vashishtha and smiled. And then turned her attention back to Ram.

Ram was staring at the sculptures.

'Explain, great king,' said Shabari.

'The little girl is outmatched,' said Ram. 'She may be brave, but somewhere in the back of her mind she would know that she doesn't stand a chance. Had she been confronting a beast of this size and ferocity who was genuinely ruthless and cruel, she would have been trampled to death in moments. There is no way she cannot know that. The emotion with which she is standing, fearless and strong, means that she knows the truth … Not just knows, she has absolute faith in the truth: that the bull will not harm her. That the bull is reined in by *dharma*. The bull will not do any wrong. To my mind, the beast is the Bull of *Dharma*.'

Vashishtha beamed with pride. Since ancient times, *dharma* – all that is right, balanced and perfectly aligned with the universe – had been represented by a bull. All life must aim to live in consonance with *dharma*. And one of the key principles of a *dharmic* life is that the strong must protect the weak.

'The horns of the bull … look at them,' continued Ram. 'There is a thin string tied to the horns and going through the bull's mouth, like a bit. Like a nearly invisible bridle, with the reins attached to the horns. It may appear that the bull is baring its teeth, but actually the bit of the bridle is pulling its cheeks back. It's symbolic. What we do with *dharma* is in *our* control. It is our choice. Only our choice. The bull was charging, but immediately began reining himself in upon seeing the little girl, who is far weaker than him. Look at the body twisting away, almost like the beast is trying to avoid the child. The forefeet are digging into the ground, trying to slow down. Its tail is raised in an instinctive attempt to balance itself as it evades the little girl ... *Paripalaya durbalam ...*'

Shabari nodded. An old Sanskrit phrase. *Protect the weak.*

Ram folded his hands together and bowed to the bull.

Shabari looked at Vashishtha in approval, communicating her thoughts with her eyes. *You've chosen well.*

Then she stepped up to Ram. 'Among the most important components of a strong society is the spirit of aggressive masculinity. Without it, society would be weak and vulnerable. It would be conquered by outsiders. It would fall apart. But aggressive masculinity without the control of *dharma* transforms into toxic masculinity. It leads to chaos, even more than that caused by conquerors from elsewhere. Remember the last days of the *Asuras* ... the violence, rape, pillage and oppression they unleashed upon the entire land. Aggressive masculinity is needed, sorely needed. But it must be restrained by *dharma*. So that the power and strength of the bull are put to use for the greater good.'

Ram nodded.

Shabari touched Ram's shoulder. 'There is no sight more magnificent than a dangerous and powerful man, with complete control over his own base desires, who also has an innate yearning for justice and a deep, abiding love for his land and his people.'

Ram stood silent.

'You will fight,' said Shabari. 'You will fight that man from Lanka who has committed *adharma*. But you will also remember that Raavan is only your opponent. Your true enemies, the enemies of your people, are back home in your own land. That will be your final battle. You will win it. And then you will work hard to rebuild Mother India's greatness. Once you have done all that, you can rest. And I can die in peace.'

—⅃⊦ ⅃⅂⊃—

Having finished her morning *puja* and breakfast, Sita stepped out of her cottage. She had been informed that Raavan and Kumbhakarna would not be visiting today and had decided, therefore, to explore Ashok Vatika. Until now she had spent most of her time in the cottages in the centre of the vast gardens.

As she descended the steps, she saw a young man standing a short distance away. He was tall and muscular. Fair-complexioned. With high cheekbones and a smoothly oiled handlebar moustache. Long hair with two side-partings and a knot tied at the crown of his head. He had a lot of his mother in him, no doubt. But enough of his father as well for Sita to guess who he was.

The son of Raavan.

'Prince Indrajit?' asked Sita.

Indrajit was staring at her face. A face he was seeing for the first time. And yet, the son of Raavan was stunned.

'What can I do for you, prince?'

Indrajit seemed to be at a loss for words.

'What is it, great prince?'

Indrajit didn't speak. Rooted to the spot, as if turned to stone.

Sita pointed to the chairs in the veranda. 'Would you like to sit and talk?'

Indrajit moved. He walked up and past her. He sat on the chair. Not once taking his eyes off her face.

Sita sat across from the prince of Lanka, sympathy writ large on her face. She could guess what Indrajit was thinking. 'I guess you've seen the paintings.'

Indrajit nodded.

'They're of my mother, Vedavati.'

'I know …' answered Indrajit, finally speaking. 'I know the lady in those paintings … I know every single thing about my father … At least I thought I did. But I didn't know about you.'

'Your father did not know about me either.'

'Are you … I mean … Do I call you *didi*?' asked Indrajit incredulously, using the respected word for an *elder sister*.

Sita reacted immediately. 'No, I am not your sister. Your father may have loved my mother. But he never more than touched her hand once. I am the daughter of Vedavati and her husband Prithvi.'

Indrajit smiled slightly. 'So, I remain the only child of Raavan.'

Sita smiled. 'Apparently so.'

Indrajit looked down.

'You don't hate me?' asked Sita.

'Why would I hate you? I've just met you.'

'I mean … I am the daughter of Vedavati …'

She was the daughter of the woman Indrajit's father had loved all his life. And Indrajit was the son of Mandodari, Raavan's legal wife. His mother must have suffered, for his father's heart was never hers. It had always been with another woman, a long-dead woman.

Indrajit had a complicated relationship with Raavan. He loved and admired his father deeply. But he also despised him. He respected Raavan's intellect, his strength, his warrior spirit, his head for business, his artistic abilities. The Gods had blessed his father with all the talents possible. And then had cursed him with an infantile, insecure heart with no control over his desires. In his younger days, Indrajit had detested his father, his cruelty, his temper. But he had especially hated the way Raavan treated his mother. Even more, the way his father surrounded himself with 'flaky dumb bimbos', as he called the women around Raavan; for how could they even hold a candle to his intelligent, calm and wise mother? And then he found out about Vedavati ... the *Kanyakumari* ...

Indrajit whispered, almost to himself, 'The *Kanyakumari* changed my relationship with my father ...'

Sita frowned slightly, but chose silence as a response.

Indrajit had investigated. He had discovered what a great woman Vedavati was. A woman of rare nobility. A *Kanyakumari*. A Goddess. And perhaps, in some ways, better than his own mother. Strangely, knowing that his father ignored his mother Mandodari, for the *Kanyakumari* brought him peace of mind. His father wasn't just a lecherous philanderer. There was, actually, some depth in his heart. And with that realisation, he started seeing his father more clearly. He still saw Raavan's weaknesses. But he didn't judge him as much. Over time, he drew closer to his father.

'I think I understand what is going on ...' whispered Indrajit.

Indrajit didn't let the rest of his thoughts escape his mind. *You have the Kanyakumari's face. And just like the Kanyakumari, you will make my father want to be a better man.*

'I don't understand what you mean, great prince,' said Sita.

'A Greek philosopher once said that "Death may be the greatest of all human blessings".'

Sita's expression changed ever so slightly.

'One should not pray for one's own death. For it should happen when it's meant to happen. But one should contemplate it, plan for it, even design it ... to the extent possible. For is there anything more beautiful in this entire benighted earth than a good death?'

Sita remained silent.

'His life may have been meaningless, but his death will have a purpose. Having said that ...'

Indrajit didn't say anything more. The conflict was clear in his mind. Should he do that which was in the interest of his father's soul or in the interest of his country? Should he be a good son or a good prince?

Sita read the conflict on Indrajit's face. She spoke up. 'Prince Indrajit—'

Indrajit interrupted her. 'No words are necessary, great Vishnu ... Don't say anything more. If we don't speak of it further, there is nothing you need to hide.'

Sita didn't speak any further.

Chapter 9

'No ships?' asked Ram, surprised.

Ram, Vashishtha, Shabari, Lakshman and Naarad were sitting a short distance from the main temple base at Shabarimala. The legendary eighteen steps, built from solid granite rock, were visible in the distance. Ram had not climbed the sacred steps, nor done his darshan of Lord Ayyappa, for he had not performed the forty-one-day *vratham*, the *holy vow*, that a devotee who seeks to pray to Lord Ayyappa at this temple must undertake. And Ram was very clear: the laws applied to everyone, including him. He had sworn to return someday, after completing the ritual, to offer his prayers.

Ram had just finished explaining his plan in the event that Hanuman's mission failed. 'Our army will board ships, navigate to Gokarna, then sail up the Mahaweli Ganga River and its tributary – the Amban Ganga – to the point where it is closest to Sigiriya. And then we will march the rest of the distance over land.'

The Mahaweli Ganga was the longest river in Lanka. It disgorged its waters into the Indian Ocean at the sea port of Gokarna on the eastern coast of the island. This river was, in effect, the highway into the heartland of Lanka.

But the Mahaweli Ganga had a choke point at Onguiaahra, where the great river crashed through a narrow opening between some hills before embracing its main tributary, the Amban Ganga River. In a remarkable feat of engineering, the Lankans had converted the hilly chokepoint into a gigantic fort. They had also built well-designed barricades and dams at this point to release water at will, in order to destroy unauthorised ships that sailed up the river. Never in human history had Onguiaahra been conquered.

Ram had been evaluating the various options to breach this citadel, so they could sail farther up the river towards Sigiriya. For there was no other way to reach the Lankan capital. No other navigable river went anywhere close to the city. And marching a large army through the dense forests of Lanka, without the guidance of a road, was fraught with risk. One could easily get lost; these forests were even more dense than those in the Indian mainland.

When Ram was done, Shabari had made a suggestion, that they refrain from using ships to move their main army to the island of Lanka.

'How is that possible, Lady Shabari?' asked Vashishtha.

'Yes, how can one attack Lanka without ships?' Ram asked.

'Oh, I didn't mean that you should not use ships at all, great Ram,' said Shabhari. 'I know your brothers Bharat and Shatrughan are planning to sail down the east coast of India with the Ayodhyan army. I think you should hold the bulk of the army on the Tamil lands to our east. And make those other, lightly manned ships travel the path you've just described. Make them sail up the Mahaweli Ganga River to Onguiaahra. And give the Lankans a fierce battle over there. But this battle will be a feint. For your main army will march across.'

Lakshman did a double take. 'March across? To an island!'

Shabari glanced at Lakshman and smiled. And then she looked at Ram. 'I'm sure you are aware that, in ancient times, Lanka was a part of mainland India. This was before the end of the last great Ice Age, when the sea levels were a lot lower. The human bonds may have frayed, but the sea and the land remember that relationship.'

Ram frowned.

Shabari pulled a map from the folds of her *angvastram*. She spread it out and continued, indicating the various points on it, 'This is the region of the Tamil lands to the south of Vaigai River. Look at the lay of the land here. Mother India is reaching out to her long-lost kin. And the sibling Lanka, in turn, reaches back to her elder sister.'

Ram, Vashishtha, Lakshman and Naarad leaned over to look at the map closely. The mainland Indian territory extended out in a promontory, jutting into the sea, a mere kilometre and a half of shallow waters separating it from Pamban Island. Pamban Island itself stretched north-west to south-east, pointing towards Lanka. Beyond the south-east coast of Pamban, separated by some twenty-five kilometres of sea water, was the island of Mannar, which too spanned north-west to south-east. It almost touched the mainland of Lanka, separated by a few metres of shallow waters.

Shabari looked at Ram. 'It is possible to build some boat bridges from the Indian mainland to Pamban Island, and also cover the very short distance from Mannar to Lanka very easily. But the key problem …'

'… is the twenty-five-kilometre distance between Pamban Island and Mannar Island,' said Ram, completing Shabari's sentence. 'It's too long to bridge. And that too, over a treacherous sea with the tides pulling in and out regularly.'

'That twenty-five-kilometre gap between Pamban and Mannar has sandflats, King Ram. They are so high up from the seabed that during low tide they are actually visible.'

Ram leaned forward and looked at the map again. Intrigued. He took a deep breath and sighed. 'But it will still be very difficult.'

'Of course it will be difficult. But let us imagine that you manage to bridge this gap and march across with the bulk of your army. When you cross Mannar and land in Lanka, you will arrive at the Ketheeswaram temple, which is dedicated to Lord Rudra. Being a royal temple, it is connected by a broad road that leads all the way to Sigiriya.'

Naarad drew in a quick, excited breath. 'Just a day's march to Sigiriya!'

'Less than a day,' corrected Shabari. She turned to Ram. 'You would take the Lankans by surprise. Nobody expects an attack from the western side of Lanka. All the defences are built on the eastern side. You can beat them before they even get their act together.'

Ram held his chin thoughtfully. 'The entire plan hinges on building a bridge. And that seems almost impossible.'

'Wars are not won by great warriors only, noble Vishnu,' said Shabari. 'They are also won by brilliant engineers who can forge into reality that which most ordinary people consider impossible.'

Ram looked at Lakshman. Both the brothers had had the same thought. Only one genius could pull off such an incredible feat of engineering. Their youngest brother, Shatrughan.

—J+ J̱5D—

'Brilliant …' said Lakshman. *But …*

Ram looked at Lakshman and smiled, then turned back to Vashishtha. 'You are right, Guruji. This can work.'

Vashishtha had just suggested a battle strategy to Ram. Elephants had been used by Indian armies for decades; even a small number of well-trained tuskers could be devastating to enemy cavalry. They could also break the enemy infantry lines. Elephants often led the charge. They hammered and broke enemy barricades, creating openings for the cavalry and the infantry to swoop in and complete the task.

Vashishtha nodded. 'Lanka has wild elephants too, but they have not been trained for war. The Lankans have never bothered to tame and harness the power of elephants.'

'And why would they?' asked Ram. 'Lanka is an island. They don't need to defend against land attacks. Naval threats are their main worry. And nobody has thought of building ships that can carry elephants across the seas.'

'And nobody has ever marched an army across to Lanka either,' said Vashishtha, smiling slightly. 'We will simply make our elephants walk across to Lanka. We can destroy their cavalry with just a hundred, or even fifty, war elephants.'

'Just one minor, tiny, insignificant, little problem,' said Lakshman. 'The Lankans don't have war elephants. Neither do we. Marching elephants all the way from Ayodhya will take too many months. We don't have that much time to rescue Sita *bhabhi*.'

'We don't need our own elephants,' said Vashishtha. 'We'll get them from our allies.'

'Who? The Malayaputras?' asked Ram. 'But why would Guru Vishwamitra help us attack Lanka? He might want to attack Lanka himself!'

Only the Malayaputras had trained war elephants in the region. Or so Ram thought. The Malayaputra capital, Agastyakootam, was a mere hundred kilometres to the south of Shabarimala. But it was obvious that he could expect very little help from the Malayaputras.

'Not them,' answered Vashishtha.

'Then who?' asked Ram.

'The Vaanars.'

The Vaanars were the legendary dynasty that ruled the land of Kishkindha along the Tungabhadra River, around six hundred and fifty kilometres north of Shabarimala. A fabulously wealthy people, they were known to be allies of Lanka. They were ruled by the warrior king Vali.

'They have war elephants?' asked Lakshman.

'Exceptionally well-trained ones,' said Vashishtha.

'But I have been hearing strange reports of King Vali,' said Ram. 'Lakshman, Sita and I met him briefly many years ago. During a Jallikattu tournament. He was brave but foolhardy. Almost like he *wanted* to die. I have heard he was, and still is, very noble. A good ruler. But for the last decade or so, he has been exceptionally aggressive. He has attacked many kingdoms around his domain and then, inexplicably, not annexed the lands of his defeated enemies. It's almost like he craves the bloodlust of battle.'

'Hmm,' said Vashishtha. 'I don't know what the reason for that is. I'll find out.'

'But these repeated wars would have made his army battle-tested,' said Lakshman. 'An army that has been blooded is an army that knows how to make the enemy bleed. The Lankan army – and let's be honest, the Ayodhya army too – has not fought a real battle in a long time. The Vaanar army would be a formidable partner for us to have.'

'So how do we ally with him, Guruji?' asked Ram.

'Lanka has been taking away a significant part of the trade earnings of Kishkindha for a long time. King Vali has honoured that treaty. He isn't strong enough to take on Lanka, even in its present weakened state. But the combined armies of Ayodhya and Kishkindha can certainly defeat Lanka. He can then renegotiate the treaty and have more money to spare for his own people.'

'We will have the army of Kekaya as well,' said Ram.

Kekaya was ruled by Bharat's grandfather, Ashwapati. It was well-known that King Ashwapati, who had been a loyal ally of Ayodhya while Emperor Dashrath was alive, had tried to increase his influence when Bharat became the surrogate ruler. The king of Kekaya must have assumed that his grandson, the son of his daughter Kaikeyi, could be easily boxed into a subordinate role. But Bharat, loyal to his elder brother Ram, had pushed back. Ashwapati and his allied clan of the Anunnaki had not taken this well.

'Kekaya will not come, Dada,' said Lakshman. 'Not according to the information Naaradji has collected from his extensive spy network.'

Ram suffered from a shortcoming found in many honourable people. They assume that others – or at least, most people – are also honourable. 'King Ashwapati will come, I am sure. Whatever be his differences with us, he will support a *dharmic* war against one who has hurt India.'

'Dada,' said Lakshman, sighing, 'I hate to tell you this, but you are wrong about Kekaya.'

'Anyway,' interrupted Vashishtha, 'let's save this conversation for later. We'll know soon enough if Kekaya and the Anunnaki are coming or not. Let's focus on the Vaanars. King Vali is a devotee of Lord Ayyappa. He'll be arriving in Shabarimala in a few days. Let's ask him then.'

'All right,' said Ram.

Chapter 10

'No killings,' whispered Hanuman.

Hanuman, Sursa and the Vayuputra soldiers had reached Sigiriya without incident. Late in the night, they made their way quietly to the gates of *Ashok Vatika*. Sursa had found out, from her spies within Sigiriya, that Sita had been imprisoned in the *Garden of No Grief*. Leaving the soldiers behind, Hanuman and Sursa scoped out the security at the fabled garden complex. They were now contemplating how to enter the citadel, which was protected by an alert and well-trained platoon of women soldiers.

'You didn't hesitate to kill the soldiers at the lighthouse,' hissed Sursa. 'Are you trying to be "sensitive" because the guards here are women?'

'No, that's not what—'

Sursa interrupted Hanuman, anger bubbling within her like molten lava. 'I thought you were better than that, Hans

... Bloody patriarchy! Women are never given the respect of equality, even when they are warriors!'

Hanuman kept his irritation at bay. 'There's nothing patriarchal about this. A soldier is a soldier. It doesn't matter if they are male or female. I don't want any killing here for a different reason. Nobody will notice for some time that the soldiers at the lighthouse have been killed. Out here, people will.'

'What difference does that make? By the time they realise it, we would have escaped with Queen Sita.'

Hanuman did not respond.

Sursa took a moment to understand. 'Goddamit! You expect Sita to refuse to come with us?'

Hanuman nodded. *Yes.*

'What the hell is wrong with her? Why would she want to remain in this hellhole?' Sursa was clearly exasperated.

'Because she doesn't just think about tomorrow. Queen Sita also tends to think about the day after tomorrow.'

Sursa rolled her eyes. 'I haven't put my life at risk and come all the way here for philosophical lessons. Either we are saving her or we are not.'

'For now, I have to get in without killing or hurting these guards. Let's concentrate on the task at hand.'

'I suppose you wouldn't want the guards to even know that someone has entered Ashok Vatika.'

'Correct,' said Hanuman. He knew that Sursa had spent time in Lanka negotiating Naarad's trade deals. Maybe she could come up with a scheme. 'Do you have any ideas?'

Sursa took a deep breath. She looked up, towards the high walls of the garden, and said softly, 'I may have one. But there will be a cost.'

'What cost?'

She turned towards Hanuman. A wicked smile played on her face. 'You will have to kiss me.'

Hanuman stared back at her, his face deadpan. 'Madam, I have told you so many times, please desist from such talk.'

'Why do you have to suddenly get so formal?'

'I … Madam, please, can we focus on the task at hand? I mean no insult to you and your beauty, but …'

'My beauty? You noticed?'

Hanuman hissed softly in anger, conscious that they were in enemy territory and should remain undetected. 'Madam, please understand what I'm trying—'

Sursa waved her hand to get him to stop. 'All right, all right. You could have just said no, Hans.'

Hanuman kept quiet.

'I'll figure something out,' said Sursa. 'Let's rejoin the rest of the group.'

— J+ J5D —

'Something is not right,' whispered Sursa.

She had just returned from a recce of Ashok Vatika, having crept close to the main gates and all the secret entrances she knew of already. Hanuman and the Vayuputra soldiers had waited deep in the forest. They were surprised at how quickly she had returned. She couldn't have done a thorough job so quickly.

'What happened?' asked Hanuman.

'All the guards are asleep,' said Sursa.

'Maybe they are tired, Lady Sursa,' suggested a Vayuputra soldier, the youngest of the lot.

Sursa sneered. 'These are Lankan soldiers. Their training is better than what the Vayuputras receive.' She turned to Hanuman. 'What do you think?'

Hanuman observed her thoughtfully. 'I know it would have been very difficult, but did you manage—'

'Yes, I did,' interrupted Sursa. 'I actually tiptoed up to one of the sleeping guards and held a finger under her nose. Deep asleep. Very fast breathing. Abnormally fast. Shallow and irregular. Her nose was slightly blueish. I noticed the slight discolouration of a few other noses too.'

'They've been drugged,' said Hanuman.

'Yes.'

Hanuman frowned. And then it struck him. 'The Malayaputras have arrived.'

'Precisely what I was thinking,' Sursa said.

'Guru Vishwamitra would only trust one man with this job.'

Sursa nodded. 'Arishtanemi.'

Hanuman smiled.

Sursa frowned. 'So, Arishtanemi likes you, does he?'

'Of course he does.' And then, seeing Sursa's expression, Hanuman asked the obvious question. 'Are you telling me he doesn't like you?'

'He hates me.'

'Why?'

Sursa smiled. 'I can be … difficult.'

Hanuman laughed softly.

'It's best that I stay out of the way,' said Sursa. 'I'll go inside Ashok Vatika with you. I'll guide you to the cottages in the centre, which is the only place where Queen Sita could be held prisoner. But I'll ensure that Arishtanemi does not see me. He too must be here to convince Queen Sita to leave with him. How you persuade her to leave with you instead is up to you.'

Hanuman nodded.

'But I am not going to wait very long,' continued Sursa. 'Finish this quickly. We must leave Ashok Vatika before first light.'

'All right.'

—JF J͞D—

Guided by Sursa, Hanuman slipped into the clearing in the centre of the legendary garden, in sight of the cottages. Sursa and the Vayuputra soldiers remained behind the treeline. The night was faintly illuminated by a crescent moon; it was *Chaturthi* in *Shukla paksh*, the fourth day of the waxing moon cycle of the month.

Hanuman could hear some voices.

'Queen Sita, you cannot be so stubborn,' he heard an obviously exasperated Arishtanemi say.

'I've made my decision already, Arishtanemiji,' said Sita, with utmost politeness. 'My sincere apologies, but nothing you say can change my mind. Please—'

'I have something that may change your mind,' interrupted Hanuman, speaking from where he stood in the darkness.

Arishtanemi instinctively reached for his sword. Upon seeing Hanuman, he relaxed.

'Hanu *bhaiya*!' cried Sita, her face lighting up. She arose and embraced her brother warmly.

'How are you doing, Sita?' asked Hanuman.

Sita smiled as she stepped back and looked at Arishtanemi. 'Not very well right now. Struggling to explain to Arishtanemiji that I cannot come with him.'

'While I, on the other hand, am struggling for another explanation,' said Arishtanemi, bemused. 'How in Lord Parshu Ram's name did you come this far without my soldiers stopping you? They're just behind the treeline. I need to fire them all.'

'Don't blame them,' said Hanuman, laughing softly. 'They know me. They are chatting with my Vayuputras even as we speak.'

Arishtanemi looked at the treeline in the darkness beyond. Imagining wistfully the bonhomie between his Malayaputra soldiers – the followers of the sixth Vishnu, Lord Parshu Ram – and their friends from the Vayuputra tribe – the followers of the Mahadev, Lord Rudra. The companionable banter.

'If only we could work together,' said Arishtanemi to Hanuman. 'We could solve all these problems so easily.'

Hanuman smiled. 'True. But that's not possible unless Guru Vashishtha and Guru Vishwamitra sort out their problems.'

Arishtanemi shook his head and sighed. 'Anyway, since you are here, Hanuman, please try to convince your sister to come with us.'

'There is no argument that can convince me,' said Sita.

'You are not safe here, my sister,' said Hanuman.

'I am.'

'But Raavan is a mercurial monster,' said Arishtanemi. 'He could turn on you any instant.'

'No, he won't,' said Sita. She hid her astonishment as she watched Arishtanemi's expression change ever so slightly. *Does he know who my birth-mother was? Does he know why Raavan will never hurt me?*

Hanuman, on the other hand, knew nothing about Vedavati. 'Sita, Arishtanemi is correct. We cannot trust Raavan. You are not safe here. We have to leave now.'

'No. I know I am safe here.'

'What makes you so sure?' Hanuman asked, exasperated.

Sita had a simple answer. 'Kumbhakarnaji.'

Sita was aware that both Arishtanemi and Hanuman thought highly of Raavan's younger brother.

'But Kumbhakarna cannot control Raavan all the time,' said Hanuman.

Sita answered immediately. 'He has till now, Hanu *bhaiya*.'

'What are their demands?' asked Arishtanemi. His mind raced to consider what it might mean if Sita knew about Raavan's love for her birth-mother, Vedavati.

'You know that already, Arishtanemiji,' answered Sita. 'And their demands are legitimate.'

'I don't know what they want – we haven't received any letter.'

'I am sure you will receive one soon, then,' said Sita. She had already suggested to Raavan and Kumbhakarna that a letter be sent to the Malayaputras. 'They want the medicines that keep Raavan and Kumbhakarna alive.'

'Why are you so interested in keeping them alive?'

'Because the Vishnu has to come and defeat them in battle,' said Sita. 'A great battle. That's when the common folk in India will learn to trust and follow the Vishnu.'

Arishtanemi's heart flickered with hope. 'So you do agree with Guru Vishwamitra's plans?'

'Oh, yes, I do,' answered Sita. 'Except that the Vishnu who will defeat Raavan will not be me. It will be Ram.'

Arishtanemi drew in a sharp breath, irritated. 'You are the Vishnu.'

Hanuman cut in. 'And Sita, you should know that Ram himself does not believe he should be a Vishnu. I'm carrying a letter from him,' he said, holding it out.

Sita smiled as she grabbed the letter from Hanuman. She could guess what was written in it. But she wasn't interested in the words. She needed to touch it because her Ram had touched it.

Sita smelled the letter, her eyes moistening. She caressed the paper lovingly, as if it were Ram's hand. A faint, wistful smile played on her lips.

Hanuman also smiled as he continued, 'I have something else from him as well.'

Sita looked up.

Hanuman reached into the pouch tied to his cummerbund and fished out Ram's ring. Sita reached for it with a longing that was indescribable. She kissed the jewelled ring made from the finest gold. She slid it onto her index finger and gazed at it lovingly. She let out a long breath and then reached for her earrings. She took them off and gave them to Hanuman. 'Give these to my Ram.'

'Why don't you give them yourself? Come with me,' said Hanuman.

'No,' said Sita firmly.

Arishtanemi spoke. 'Queen Sita, even a blind man can see the love you feel for your husband. Return to him. Allow us to take you to your husband.'

'No.'

'In the name of all that is good and holy, why?'

'Because he is not only my husband. He is also the Vishnu.'

Arishtanemi turned to Hanuman and shook his head with annoyance. His hand went to his forehead, rubbing it slightly to control his rising anger.

Sita ignored the duo and turned her attention to Ram's letter. She broke the seal and unrolled the papyrus. The message from her husband was clear.

'Come back with Lord Hanuman. You are the Vishnu. The Vishnu has no right to unnecessarily put her own person at risk. We will return to Lanka with an army later. We will teach Raavan a lesson in dharma.*'*

Sita smiled and kissed the letter, leaving traces of her fragrance on it. Then she picked up a writing stylus fashioned from graphite and wrote her reply on the same papyrus.

'No. I will not return. You will come here. You are my Vishnu. I am your wife. It is your dharma *to fight for me. So, fight for me.'*

'Give this to him, Hanu *bhaiya*,' said Sita, handing the letter to Hanuman. Then she turned to Arishtanemi. 'Arishtanemiji, regardless of what Guru Vishwamitra may say, I expect you, and those loyal to the Vishnu, to join the battle on the rightful side. You will stand behind Ram when he fights Raavan. This is a *dharmayudh*, a *war for dharma*. There are no bystanders in a *dharmayudh*.'

Arishtanemi remained silent.

Sita continued, 'Please go back now. Go with Lord Rudra and Lord Parshu Ram.'

—— Jᖴ ᒑꓱD ——

'Goddammit,' whispered Arishtanemi.

Hanuman and Arishtanemi were walking back towards the gates of Ashok Vatika, having left Sita behind at her cottage.

Hanuman looked at his friend and smiled. 'What are you going to say to Guru Vishwamitra?'

'What can I say? I failed. It's as simple as that.'

'Guruji doesn't react well to bad news. Or failure.'

'I know. Hence the "Goddammit"!'

Hanuman laughed softly. 'And what are you going to do?'

Arishtanemi stopped in his tracks and looked back towards the trees and into the darkness. Beyond lay the many cottages, with the main one in the centre. In which she sat, the one he respected as the Vishnu. Arishtanemi turned towards Hanuman. 'She would make such a fantastic Vishnu.'

Hanuman nodded and smiled. 'Yes, she would.'

'Ram would make a wonderful Vishnu as well.'

'Yes, that's also true.'

Arishtanemi laughed. 'This is not going according to plan.'

'When has the story arc of any Vishnu or Mahadev in the past gone according to plan?'

Arishtanemi smiled and nodded. 'True.'

Hanuman started walking again towards the gates. 'So, what will you do?'

Arishtanemi walked alongside his friend. 'What else can I do? I have orders from my Vishnu. I will fight in King Ram's army.'

'And Guruji?'

Arishtanemi shrugged his shoulders and sighed. 'That … That will be a difficult conversation. But it's not for today. Let's—'

Arishtanemi's words were interrupted by a loud feminine voice.

'So, two great champions couldn't convince a young queen to accompany them!'

Arishtanemi stopped in his tracks. His eyes closed, his shoulders drooped. He released a long sigh. *Sursa.*

'How much worse will this day get?' he mumbled.

Sursa burst into laughter as she punched Arishtanemi on his shoulder. 'Arishtanemi, you useless wastrel, it will get much, much worse. We are travelling back together.'

Arishtanemi looked at Hanuman, his expression blank.

'It makes sense to travel back together, Arishtanemi,' said Hanuman. 'There is strength in numbers. We will be able to leave Lanka safely.'

Sursa sniggered. 'And Arishtanemi could certainly use some strength. He once lost a duel with me.'

'That was because …' Arishtanemi stopped himself in time. He composed himself and said in a low voice, 'Let's get moving. The sun will be rising soon.'

Chapter 11

'Hmm,' said Vali, thoughtfully rubbing his chin.

The king of Kishkindha had arrived in Shabarimala the previous day, after completing the forty-one-day *vratham*. He had performed his *darshan* and worshipped at the temple. Since the *puja* was completed, he was not dressed in black now. He was also free of the vow of non-violence, a very strict part of the *vratham*.

'What do you say, King Vali?' asked Ram. 'Will you support us in this battle against *adharma*?'

Ram, accompanied by his *guru* Vashishtha and brother Lakshman, had come to the guest house that King Vali was staying in. Vali had readily agreed to meet Ram, for he was, after all, the king-in-absentia of Ayodhya and, technically, the overlord of the Sapt Sindhu. Ram had informed Vali about the kidnapping of Sita by the king of Lanka. He had requested the use of the Kishkindha elephant corps in the imminent battle against Raavan.

'But how will you take my elephants to Lanka?' asked Vali, intrigued.

'We have a plan,' said Vashishtha. He was still not sure if he could trust Vali, despite all the assurances he had received from Shabari. She had said unequivocally that the king of Kishkindha was an honourable man. But Vashishtha did not want to take even the smallest chance of their battle plans reaching the ubiquitous spies of Lanka.

'Hmm,' said Vali again, apparently non-committal.

Vashishtha felt that this was the time to offer the carrot to convince Vali. 'Once we defeat Lanka, the Sapt Sindhu will be happy to revise the trade agreements and double Kishkindha's share in the business with Lanka. The share of the wealth that Lanka corners from the land trade will thereafter go to the rightful owner, the noble kingdom of Kishkindha.'

'Hmm,' repeated Vali.

Vashishtha looked at Ram, not sure what more could be said.

Vali looked at Lakshman. 'I do remember you.'

'And I remember you, Your Highness,' said Lakshman, bringing his hands together in a respectful *namaste*.

Lakshman was usually a tactless man. So, it was surprising that he did not immediately mention that he had saved Vali's life once. This was during a Jallikattu tournament many years ago in a small town called Indrapur. A gargantuan bull would have gored the king of Kishkindha to death had the massive Lakshman not jumped into the fray and waylaid the bull temporarily. Vali had survived. The massive scar running along his left arm was a reminder of that incident. It was a remnant from the many surgeries that had been carried out to repair his shattered left arm. It would have been rude to remind the great king of that day, though. You never reminded a true Kshatriya that you had saved his life. Instead, a true Kshatriya's duty was to remember that he had been saved. And Vali was one of the finest Kshatriyas ever.

Vali turned to Ram. 'But why do you want *only* my elephant corps? Why not take my entire army?'

Ram was surprised. Pleasantly surprised. 'Umm, thank you so much, great king.'

'But there is one condition,' added Vali.

And here we go, thought Vashishtha, expecting some further haggling on the trade deal. But even he couldn't have guessed what came next.

'I demand a duel.'

'What?' asked Ram, stunned.

'You heard me,' said Vali. 'I want a duel. With you.'

'Why?'

'Why not?' asked Vali. 'My terms are very simple. If I win, you don't get my elephant corps. If you win, you not only get my elephant corps, but also my entire army.' Then Vali turned to Vashishtha. 'And I don't want that silly trade deal, Guruji. I am happy with the terms of trade as they are. If Ayodhya defeats Lanka, you can keep all the extra gold from the Lanka overland business. All I want is my duel with the king of Ayodhya.'

Ram and Vashishtha were stunned.

'I hear that Sugreev is here – that indolent cretin of a brother I have been cursed with. Ask that halfwit to come and watch how two real men fight.'

Lakshman was aghast. 'But ...'

Vali turned to Lakshman. 'I understand your shock, mighty Lakshman. For you must be thinking that I am ungrateful. You imagine that you saved my life that day.'

Lakshman glared with thinly concealed anger. Vali was breaking the unwritten code of the Kshatriyas: The debt owed to the one who saves your life is the greatest debt of all. It must be repaid.

'A tiger always fights alone, Prince Lakshman,' said Vali. 'It doesn't matter if he wins or loses, lives or dies. That is the tiger's fate. But receiving help from one weaker than him? A tiger would rather die.'

Ram finally cut in. 'King Vali, I am not sure that this is the best—'

'This is the only deal on the table, king of Ayodhya,' said Vali. 'Take it or leave it. It's up to you. I am here for a week. And I am ready whenever you are.'

Vali stood up, signifying that the meeting was over.

— J+ ⅃‚ᛝD —

Rivers are the best passageways in the world. A quick and efficient path to get from the coast to the hinterland, or vice versa. A cutter boat on a river can accommodate many more travellers than a horse on a road. You don't need to stop during mealtimes; you can eat on the boat itself. Most importantly, if you are sailing downriver, a river is a road that moves; it carries you to your destination much quicker.

A few hours later, two cutter boats were navigating the river waters of the Aruvi Aru, having rowed from near Sigiriya to almost the edge of the north-western coast of the island.

One of the boats carried Hanuman, Arishtanemi and Sursa, accompanied by seven soldiers. Ten others were in the boat to the left of it. The Malayaputras and Vayuputras were travelling as a team.

'In a few minutes we will reach the mouth of the river,' whispered Sursa. It was the fifth hour of the first *prahar* of the day, just before dawn. At this time of the year, the sun's rays would break through in an hour and a half at the most. They would be out at sea well before that. 'We have made good time.'

'Yes, we have,' agreed Arishtanemi.

Hanuman was quiet. He was listening intently. His instincts had picked up a warning.

'What's the matter, Hanuman?' asked Arishtanemi softly.

Hanuman looked at him and said, keeping his voice low, 'It's too quiet.'

Good warriors pick up signals from the slightest of sounds. Exceptional ones pick up cues even from silence.

'The brown fish owls are silent,' whispered Hanuman.

Owls are nocturnal creatures. And most owls are silent as they go about their nightly business: flying, hunting, eating. But the brown fish owls, especially common in these parts, were not the quiet type. They made loud hooting sounds: the typical *tu-whoo-hu*, but also the deep hollow *boom-boom* of the exhibitionist male of the species. The most distinctive sound indicating a brown fish owl's presence was its loud, singing wingbeat.

Tonight, there was no sound of wingbeats. Which meant the birds were stationary. Not hunting for food on the seashore, as would be usual at this time of night.

Odd.

Unless they were scared by the presence of another predator.

Perhaps the greatest predator of them all.

Man.

'Do you think we have been detected?' asked Sursa.

'Only one way to find out,' whispered Arishtanemi. 'Let's bank on the right. I'll send two guards out to do a quick reconnaissance.'

Hanuman nodded.

—JF JꝪD—

'Almost half a battalion, Lord Arishtanemi,' said the Malayaputra soldier.

The two guards had just returned from their reconnaissance. They reported that around one hundred and fifty Lankans, armed to the teeth, were lying in ambush at the mouth of the Aruvi Aru River. The place where the sweet waters of the second longest river on the island of Lanka merged into the salty sea waters of the Gulf of Mannar.

They had also seen burning cremation pyres, perhaps of the soldiers killed by Hanuman and the Malayaputras.

'How did they discover the bodies? And our presence?' asked Sursa.

'I don't know,' said Arishtanemi. 'But no point dwelling on that now. If they have sent so many soldiers, they must suspect a big enemy contingent is sailing downriver.'

'Chances are they have sent this information to Sigiriya already,' said Hanuman. 'The Lankans may send more soldiers downriver.'

'We will be stuck in a pincer attack,' said Sursa. 'Lankans behind us, and more Lankans blocking our way at the mouth of the river.'

'There are one hundred and fifty of them, my lady,' said the Malayaputra guard who had returned with the information. 'We are only twenty. We cannot fight our way out of this.'

Hanuman, Arishtanemi and Sursa did not respond. They knew they had very little time. They had to move fast. And there was only one way out of their predicament.

A diversion.

'I'll do it,' said Hanuman. 'I'll take two soldiers with me. Maybe three. You guys wait for my signal and then rush through to the sea at top oar-speed. Pick me up farther north, at the beach. But don't be late. Or else I will be Lankan toast on the Lankan coast.'

Humour among warriors, in the face of death, is a sure sign of courage. And manhood.

Arishtanemi laughed softly. 'The plan is perfect. But it will be *me* creating the diversion. You two make sure that—'

Sursa interrupted Arishtanemi. 'Enough of this testosterone match-up. I'll cause the diversion.'

Hanuman and Arishtanemi looked at her as if she had said something incredibly stupid.

'Really?!' Sursa snapped in response. 'You're going to pull some patriarchal nonsense on me?'

Hanuman showed his irritation. 'Sursa, please stop getting hysterical. This has nothing to do with patriarchy. But it's better if—'

'Why is it better if you two do it? You are big. You move slower than I do. You do not have the skills to create a diversion. I do.'

Arishtanemi made an attempt. 'Sursa …'

'I have spoken, Arishtanemi. You know I will be better at this than either you or Hanuman. If I was a man, you wouldn't be wasting time arguing with me.'

'Sursa …' pleaded Hanuman.

'What does a woman have to do to get respect around here?' asked Sursa.

'It's not about that …'

'It is! You both want to protect me. Protect me? *Me*? I'm one of the finest warriors in the land! You wouldn't think this way if I wasn't a woman. Your job as a warrior is to protect those who are not warriors, be they men or women. And your duty is to take the help of other warriors when you need it, be they men or women.'

Hanuman and Arishtanemi remained silent.

Sursa turned to look at the three guards who had gone on the reconnaissance. They were short. Slim. Lithe.

Perfect. They'll be fast and soundless.

'You three are coming with me,' said Sursa. 'Arm yourselves. Carry as many blades as you can. Bow and arrows too. Short bow. Make sure your leather armour is tight, both front and back. Keep the thighs clear. We will be running fast and hard.'

The guards nodded and rushed to obey.

Sursa turned to Hanuman and Arishtanemi. 'When you hear loud noises from up north, that will be your cue to sail out. Row fast. Get to the sea quickly. Then turn north.'

'Yes,' said Arishtanemi. He held Sursa's arms, just below the elbow. 'Go with Lord Parshu Ram, brave Sursa.'

Sursa nodded, and then looked at Hanuman.

Hanuman drew his knife from his side scabbard. He slid the blade across his thumb, drawing blood. He smeared the blood on Sursa's forehead in a firm stroke. In the tradition of the great brother-warriors of yore, it sealed the pact that his blood would protect her.

'Go with Lord Rudra, noble Sursa,' whispered Hanuman.

Sursa smiled. 'One day I will force you do that with something other than blood. And maybe not my brow but a little higher, on the parting of my hair.'

Hanuman laughed softly.

Humour among warriors, in the face of death, was a sure sign of warriorhood.

'Pick me up north of the lighthouse,' said Sursa. 'The spot where we beached our boat while coming in.'

Hanuman nodded. *Yes.*

'And we'll be coming with the Lankans in hot pursuit. Be ready.'

'We will,' answered Hanuman. 'You make sure you get there alive.'

'That I will,' said Sursa.

—— J⫟ Ɪ˘⫟Ɗ ——

Sursa had read the Lankans right. She knew their standard tactics.

Lankans never trusted animals completely. Or more accurately, they didn't trust the trainers who trained their war animals. Therefore, unless it was absolutely necessary, they kept their war animals at a distance when setting up an ambush. An ambush required stealth. They didn't trust their animals to be stealthy and quiet.

Sursa and the three soldiers moved through the jungles, quick-footed and silent. They raced along a long arc, avoiding any unnecessary encounters with the enemy soldiers. Soon they were up north, far beyond the point where the Lankan soldiers lay in ambush.

Sursa held up her right hand. Fists closed. The men came to a halt.

They were behind the enemy lines now. Every unnecessary word must be avoided. Quietude was their best shield.

In the dark skies, the moonlight was faint.

Sursa whispered, pointing, 'There.'

About a hundred metres ahead of them, over one hundred and fifty horses were confined. Some were, unwisely, tied to thin trees that they had wound themselves around, so that the beasts had become entangled in their ropes. Others were, wisely, tied to stakes hammered into the ground and had swivel room. But none had wind breaks. The animals were restive.

A thick line of trees obfuscated the path to the animals.

Four Lankan soldiers guarded the horses.

Just four.

'Here's the plan,' said Sursa softly, turning to the soldiers. 'We'll get the four Lankans with arrows. Aim for their throats. All at the same time. Into their throats. No screams. No warning to the others. Then we rush forward and release as many horses as we can. As silently as possible. Once that is done, we mount four horses and ride up north, making a lot of noise as we do so. That will be the signal for our comrades in the river to start rowing towards the sea. Hearing the noise we make, the Lankans will rush back to the beach. They will give us chase. But most of them will be on foot. They will be slow. We must stay ahead. Ride hard. Our friends will meet us farther north. We will ride into the sea. Into the sea, boys. As far as the horses will carry us. And then we jump off and swim to the boats. And from there, we row our way out. Clear?'

The soldiers nodded. *Clear.*

'Remember, they must see as many horses as possible, racing around on the beach. In this dim light they will assume that most of them are mounted. And that all of us are here—their foes. If they see just four, they'll guess that it's a diversion.'

'Yes, Lady Sursa.'

Sursa nodded. She brought her short bow forward and tightened the string on it. Then, like any good archer, she pulled the string and released it close to her ear. To check the cord tension.

Perfect.

Standard warrior rules. Always check the equipment before *battle*.

Her soldiers did the same.

Bows ready. Arrows nocked.

'Let's go,' whispered Sursa.

They moved forward stealthily. And came to a halt some forty metres from the four Lankans. They were clearly not the best, these Lankans that had been left behind to guard the horses. Clustered together, they were engaged in banter.

The first two rules on guard duty. Do not cluster. Do not gossip. You make yourself an easy target. And you are distracted.

Sloppy.

'One arrow, one kill,' whispered Sursa. 'Mark your target. We'll shoot together on my count. That's the plan.'

It's a cliché that most battle plans don't survive the first contact with the enemy. And most clichés have some measure of truth to them.

Sursa began to count down.

'Three ... two ... one!'

Four arrows were released simultaneously. Three of them found their mark, slamming into the throats of three Lankans. They collapsed almost immediately. Soundless. But one arrow missed by just a bit. It sank into the mid clavicle of the unfortunate Lankan. Between the shoulder and the neck. Painful. Very painful. But not fatal.

The Lankan screamed in agony. It was not loud enough to alert his Lankan comrades at the Aruvi Aru River mouth. But it frightened the horses. And the dumb beasts began to neigh and whinny in alarm.

Sursa cursed. She drew another arrow and fired quickly. Straight at the man's throat. Severing his life, and all sound, immediately.

But the horses were panic-stricken by now. They were straining against the ropes that held them, neighing and bucking.

'Follow me!' roared Sursa. 'Quick!'

She raced ahead, throwing her bow aside. It was of no use now. She drew her short sword. Her soldiers followed. Sprinting hard.

'Release as many horses as you can. Quickly! And drive them towards the beach!'

The soldiers rushed to obey. Unhobbled some of the horses. Cut the reins of those tied to stakes and trees. They had to move fast while avoiding the panicky beasts stomping around.

Some twenty-five to thirty horses had been freed when Sursa ordered, 'Enough! Mount a horse! Ride north! We don't have much time!'

Sursa could hear the Lankan battalion running north. Making loud noises. War cries.

'Ride!' ordered Sursa.

Along with her soldiers, Sursa rode out. Onto the beach. They left the treeline behind.

Too many horses had been left back. Sursa knew that. Horses that would be used by their Lankan enemies. She knew that too.

They had little time.

'Fast!'

She looked back. She could see the flame-torches in the distance. The Lankans were far behind. But not far enough. And they would soon mount their horses.

'Ride hard!' shouted Sursa.

They had to optimise this temporary advantage of being on horseback while the Lankans were still on foot. They had to build as much distance as possible.

It was too dark to see far out to sea. To check if Hanuman and Arishtanemi had managed to row out from the mouth of the river into the sea.

She had to trust that they had done so. She had to.

The alternative was terrifying. For ahead of them, a mere thirty-minute ride on horseback, was the rest of the battalion stationed at the Ketheeswaram temple. There was no other way to escape, except into the sea.

'Ride!' Sursa roared.

Her soldiers kept pace with her.

She looked back. The first Lankans on horseback were in sight. The chase had begun.

Some were riding out from behind the treeline on to the beach. Some had begun shooting arrows. From too far though. They were out of range. For now.

'Here!'

Sursa recognised the place where they had tied their cutter boat earlier.

'Ride into the sea.'

Galloping into the choppy waters would slow down their horses, reducing the distance between the Lankans and Sursa. While the Lankans could never catch up with them, they would come within range of the Lankan arrows soon.

'Ride hard! Push your horses!'

The horses panicked at being led into the sea. Their pace slowed, but, admirably, the magnificent animals did not stop.

'Keep going!' screamed Sursa.

The Lankan arrows were close.

In Lord Rudra's name, be there, Hanuman.

Sursa heard a shout from the distance. She recognised that voice. She loved that voice.

'Sursaaaa …'

'They're here! Ride on!'

Sursa and her brave soldiers pushed their horses farther into the sea. The ground sloped gently here, so they could ride farther in than they would have been able to in most other parts along the shore. But they knew it was a matter of time before the horses turned back in panic. When their feet could not touch the ground any more. And Sursa could sense that the moment was close.

'Push!'

The horses were neighing loudly now, in protest. But they still kept moving ahead. The Lankan arrows were coming thick and fast, but still falling short. Just out of range.

'Sursaaa!' It was Arishtanemi this time. 'We are coming! Swim out!'

Sursa sensed that the time had come. The horses were about to surrender.

She slid her feet out of the stirrups. And shouted over the din of the waves and the Lankan war cries behind. 'Feet out of stirrups! Prepare to jump!'

Her soldiers obeyed.

'Now! Jump!'

They dived into the sea. And began to swim. Tearing valiantly through the waves which were aggressively pushing them back.

Through the dim moonlight, Sursa saw the two cutter boats rushing towards them.

They swam hard.

Towards their rendezvous.

Towards the boats.

The Lankans pushed their horses into the sea, continuing to fire their arrows.

They were now in range.

The arrows fell all around Sursa and her soldiers. They continued to swim. Hard.

The Lankans were shooting blind in the dim moonlight. They were hoping for sheer numbers to make up for the lack of accuracy.

And make up it did.

One of her soldiers screamed in agony as an arrow pierced his thigh. But he kept swimming.

Sursa looked back. He was falling behind.

The two others had already reached the cutter boats and were clambering on.

'Sursa!' screamed Hanuman, stretching his hand out.

But Sursa turned around and swam towards the injured soldier. Arrows were falling all around them like torrid rain. She reached him and began to pull him towards the boats. One more arrow hit the poor soldier. This time on the shoulder. Sursa pushed him towards the boat and he was speedily pulled in.

An arrow sailed in and slammed into Sursa's shoulder. She roared in agony. Arishtanemi jumped into the water, picked her up, and almost threw her into the boat. He climbed back up.

All the Malayaputras and Vayuputras were safely on board.

'Row back!'

Arrows were raining all around them.

The Malayaputras and the Vayuputras began to row.

'Row back! Hard!'

Hanuman looked at Sursa, his brow creased with concern. He tried to break the shaft of the arrow buried in her shoulder. But, in pulling the soldier along, Sursa's leather armour had come loose. It was making it difficult to break the shaft of the arrow.

'Let it ... be ...' whispered Sursa, still out of breath.

'Sursa ...' Hanuman moaned. He recognised the arrow. It was one of the specially created ones. Expensive. The serrated reversed-edges made it difficult for them to be pulled out. And they were, usually, poisoned.

Sursa smiled. 'I'm okay ... Just a scratch ...'

Humour among warriors, in the face of death, was a sure sign of true warriorhood.

Hanuman smiled. It was a serious injury, but not too serious. The poisoned arrow was worrisome, but it had only embedded itself in the shoulder, not a major organ. She had not lost consciousness. They would reach the Indian coast in an hour or two. They would rush to the closest village from the landing point and pull the arrow out. And stitch up and medicate the wound.

The wound was bad, but not too bad.

As the soldiers continued rowing hard, the boats began to move rapidly, out of range of the arrows. Or so it seemed.

The ancients say that even the best foreteller cannot beat female intuition. Sursa suddenly had a sense of foreboding. Without a thought, she thrust Hanuman aside and turned around, covering him with her own body.

The arrow came in hard. With demonic precision. And timing. It pounded into Sursa's abdomen. If only her leather armour had not come undone earlier. If only.

The cruel arrow rammed deep inside her, slicing through her major organs. The kidney, the liver, even the intestines.

Sursa collapsed backwards onto Hanuman as Arishtanemi rushed towards her.

Hanuman held Sursa in his arms. 'SURSAAA …'

The soldiers did not stop. They kept rowing. Moving the boats deep into the sea. Away from the Lankan arrows.

Sursa struggled to breathe as she looked down at the arrow buried deep in her abdomen. She recognised the arrow now. She knew her time had come.

Hanuman turned towards the rowers. 'Faster! Get us to the mainland! Quick!'

Sursa held Hanuman's hand. 'It's okay … It's okay …'

Arishtanemi was crying inconsolably. 'Sursa …'

Sursa didn't look at him. Her eyes were pinned on Hanuman.

Hanuman was sobbing. 'It should have been me ... It should have been me ...'

'It's all right ... It's all right ...' said Sursa, struggling against the darkness. Refusing to fall into the deep sleep. Not yet. Not yet. She had things to say. 'I had three dreams, Hans ...'

Hanuman could not meet her eyes. He looked at the arrow. The flood of blood bursting forth. It was over. No hope.

He finally looked at Sursa's face. His eyes were clouded with tears.

'One dream ...' said Sursa softly, 'was to win your love ... Another, to die in your arms ... And the third ... to see you cry when I die ...'

'Sursa ...' Hanuman whispered.

Sursa smiled. The darkness was closing in. 'Two out of three is not bad ... Two out of three ... not bad ...'

Hanuman closed his eyes, tears streaming down his face.

'Look at ... me,' whispered Sursa.

Hanuman opened his eyes.

'I love you, Hans ...' murmured Sursa. She looked into the eyes she loved, and then allowed herself to slip into unconsciousness. Into the darkness.

Arishtanemi reached out and held Sursa's hand. He sobbed like a child. He knew this was the last time he was hearing Sursa's voice.

Chapter 12

'This is truly bizarre,' said Vashishtha.

Vashishtha was sitting on a mat in Shabari's simply appointed hut. He had visited the wise woman right after the strange meeting with the king of Kishkindha. He needed her sage advice. The meeting hadn't panned out the way Vashishtha had imagined. Not by a long shot.

Shabari raised her chin and looked out of the window. Towards the temple of Lord Ayyappa in the distance. She held back her words.

'What kind of an outlandish demand is this?' asked Vashishtha. 'A duel with the emperor of Sapt Sindhu as a condition to support him with the Kishkindha army! And only doing so if he loses. Bizarre.'

Shabari said softly, 'Perhaps the rumours are true …'

Vashishtha narrowed his eyes. 'Rumours? What rumours?'

'I have been hearing them for some time,' said Shabari. 'But I did not give them much credence.'

'What rumours, Shabariji?' repeated Vashishtha.

Shabari looked at Vashishtha. 'Guruji, it seems that Angad was conceived through *niyoga*.'

'What?' asked a stunned Vashishtha.

Niyoga was an ancient tradition in India that stretched back to the hoary past. According to its tenets, a woman married to a man who was incapable of fathering a child could request another man to impregnate her. Usually, she would turn to a *rishi*. For one, the intellectual prowess of the *rishi* could pass on, genetically, to the offspring. More importantly, *rishis* were wandering mendicants and would not lay claim to the child. A child born of a union sanctioned by *niyoga* would, for all practical and societal purposes, be the legitimate child of the woman and her legal husband; the biological father would ideally remain anonymous.

'I have heard that Vali was once grievously injured while saving the cowardly Sugreev. It happened a long time ago during a hunt. As a result of the injuries, and the medicines administered at the time, Vali can't father children.'

'Sugreev has always been a burden on the royal family of Kishkindha,' said Vashishtha. 'But what does this have to do with Vali challenging Ram to a duel?'

'His anger.'

'But why is Vali angry? I don't understand. Our traditions allow *niyoga*. Nothing wrong with it. His wife Tara's child is his child. I understand his anger with his idiot brother, Sugreev. But I don't see the connection. And why is this unfocused anger directed at everyone? Towards Ram? That makes no sense. Not for one as noble as Vali.'

'It's a lot more complex ...' said Shabari. 'I have heard that Queen Mother Aruni decided to ...'

Shabari hesitated.

'Decided to … what?' asked Vashishtha.

'You know what Aruni was like.'

'Yes … She was … headstrong and stubborn. So, what did she do?'

'Well, apparently she wanted to ensure that it was her bloodline on the throne. So, she …'

Vashishtha understood. 'Lord Rudra have mercy!'

Queen Mother Aruni's other son. Sugreev.

Vashishtha held his head with both hands. He was dumbstruck. The *niyoga* ritual had been performed by Sugreev. Angad was the biological son of Sugreev.

'This is beyond belief!'

'I know,' agreed Shabari.

Vashishtha now understood Vali's anger and pain. And then something else struck him. 'But this would have been a secret. The *niyoga* would have happened in the Himalayas, according to tradition. How did King Vali discover the truth?'

'There are rumours that Queen Mother Aruni told him herself. On her deathbed.'

Vashishtha's mouth fell open in shock. 'Why did she do that? Why didn't she just keep quiet? Why inflict the truth on someone if it does him no good and only causes pain?'

'Guilt, perhaps? She had wronged Vali. Perhaps she thought that speaking the truth would ease her conscience. Cleanse her soul of the sin.'

'No. You cannot cleanse your soul with selfishness. By telling Vali the truth, she condemned him to a lifetime of torment. And all this just to alleviate her own feeling of guilt before dying. It was a most selfish act.'

Shabari nodded in agreement.

'But Vali loves his son, Angad. That is so obvious.'

'He does love him,' agreed Shabari.

'Angad doesn't know, I hope.'

'I don't think so,' answered Shabari. 'And I don't think the lay public does either. Or even the royals in the Sapt Sindhu. It's only our *rishi* and *rishika* circles that seem to have some inkling of it.'

'Why didn't you tell me about this?'

'I don't indulge in unsubstantiated rumour-mongering, Vashishthaji. But Vali's conduct makes me suspect it's true. I thought his frequent military expeditions were a quest for glory. Now, I understand… he was swinging between his innately noble character and furious rage at what life has done to him.'

Vashishtha let out a long breath. 'Oh, Lord Agni …'

Shabari stared ahead, unblinking.

Vashishtha, single-mindedly committed to what he thought was good for India, saw the situation clearly. Beyond the human emotions at play.

'We cannot defeat Raavan without the elephant corps,' said Vashishtha. 'We need it.'

'True.'

'Perhaps I should advise Ram to go ahead with the duel.'

'Perhaps you should,' agreed Shabari.

Neither of them verbalised the obvious truth. *Vali's unchecked emotions and rage would make him easier to defeat.*

—JF J5D—

'A longsword?' muttered Lakshman, surprised.

Naarad frowned and shrugged.

It was Ram who had been challenged, making it his right to select the type of weapon for the duel. The gallant Ram, though, had offered the choice of weapon to Vali. And Vali had, inexplicably, chosen the longsword. It was odd. Very odd. Vali was muscular and strong, but of medium height. Ram was leaner but much taller, touching six feet in height. A sword master would have advised Vali to pick a short sword. And keep close during the duel, giving Ram as little room as possible, reducing his advantage of a longer reach. By choosing a longsword that was normally held with both hands while fighting, Vali had handed Ram an obvious edge.

'What is King Vali thinking?' asked Lakshman.

Almost all the denizens of the temple complex had gathered to watch the duel. It could obviously not be staged within the temple complex. That would be *adharma*. So, they had gathered at an open training ground, with amphitheatre-style stands built around it, at the base of the hill. The temple was clearly visible in the distance.

Two thousand people stood in the stands. To watch a duel the likes of which they knew they would probably not see again in their lives. Shabari and Vashishtha stood together, their eyes grimly pinned to the centre. The duellists were stretching their bodies on one side of the ground. They had chosen to duel without any seconds to help them.

Vali walked to the centre of the ground. Fair and hirsute, he strode with his chest out and shoulders back. He began to swing his arms, making wide arcs with his sword. Imperious and cocky. Exhilarated. Ram, dark-skinned, tall and sinewy, walked alongside. Head raised. Measured footsteps. Swinging his arms and loosening his limbs in a controlled manner. Focused and deliberate.

Vali thrust his sword into the soft ground, went down on his knees, and faced the great Shabarimala temple in the distance. Ram gently placed his sword on the ground, touched it and brought his hands to his brow in reverence. Offering respect to his weapon. Then he too went down on his knees and faced the temple.

Both the warriors folded their hands in unison and prayed to Lord Ayyappa – among the greatest warriors who had ever walked the holy land of India.

They ended their prayer with a chant familiar to all who are loyal to the Lord.

'*Swamiye Sharanam Ayyappa.*'

We find refuge at the feet of Lord Ayyappa.

The entire assemblage echoed the prayer. '*Swamiye Sharanam Ayyappa.*'

Ram picked up his sword, rose and held it out. Vali tapped Ram's blade with his own. Tradition before the duel.

The swords are supposed to tap each other and whisper before the murderous argument begins.

Ram looked at Vali and smiled. Vali responded with a curt nod. And they walked to their respective starting lines. Vali looked at his son, Angad. He stood at the edge of the combat circle, a short distance from Shabari and Vashishtha.

Angad. A little less than twenty years of age, he was the spitting image of Vali, his legal father. Fair-skinned. Hirsute. Ridiculously muscled. Gladdening the hearts of all those who looked upon the likeness between father and son. But Vali knew better. For his brother, Sugreev, was also his exact replica.

Vali breathed in deeply and shook his head. Then glanced at Ram. The contestants turned to Shabari and bowed low.

Shabari announced, 'May Lord Ayyappa grant victory to the most worthy.'

And with that the duel began.

Ram, ever the orthodox swordsman, abided strictly by his training. He held the longsword with both hands and angled his body sidewards, offering less target room to his opponent. His sword pointed straight ahead.

Vali held the sword in his right hand, pointing to one side. His body fully exposed. Reckless. As if with a death wish.

Suddenly, the king of Kishkindha roared and charged. As he came close, he pirouetted with abandon, swinging his right arm viciously as he turned. But with no control. Ram bent backwards and effortlessly blocked the blow.

This was rash beyond measure. Pivoting and swinging from a distance while charging in can be a wildly riveting sight in theatrical plays. It always drew applause and loud gasps from audiences who knew no better. But it was unwise. It meant that you turned your back to your opponent for an instant. Ridiculously stupid against a skilled adversary in an actual sword fight. He could simply stab you in the back with ease.

But Ram's integrity was above reproach. He would never stab in the back. He blocked Vali and pushed him away.

Vali turned in the same movement and thrust his longsword forward. Ram had expected this expert manoeuvre. He blocked and pushed Vali's blade aside and swivelled his body. Moving his abdomen out of the way.

And then Vali did something completely unexpected.

He flicked his sword up rapidly, using Ram's sword that was held against his own, as a slide. Vali's strong wrist made the movement so quick that it was difficult to see. Instinctively, Ram threw his head back, avoiding the glancing cut by a microsecond.

Ram stepped back immediately and smiled. Nodding at Vali.

Good one.

Vali, a cocky grin on his face, nodded back slightly.

Ram raised his sword again. Ready.

Vali charged in, dancing on his feet, swinging the sword from the right and then from the left with machine-like precision. Ram took a step back with each defensive stroke, both hands firmly on the grip. The pommel below and cross-guard above kept the sword in place, not allowing Vali to deflect it with his repeated strikes. Ram moved back slowly. Completely orthodox. Or so it seemed.

Vali held the aggressive charge, yelling wildly as he swung his blade hard. It didn't strike him until almost too late. He was walking into a trap.

Ram moved backwards, each step measured and slow. Towards the combat-circle perimeter. Intending to move to the side at the boundary. Vali was now committed to his aggressive forward charge. He would not be able to avoid the deep cut on the elbow that would incapacitate his sword arm.

But Vali pulled back just in time, whirled around, extending his elbows up, with both hands behind his shoulders and holding the sword downwards vertically behind his back. Protecting his back from a blow as he retreated.

As Vali turned around, he found Ram staring at him with narrowed eyes. Forehead furrowed. A severe expression on his face.

Vali understood. Ram's honour had been injured. How could he entertain the thought that Ram would strike him from the back? That would be *adharma*.

Ram was the scion of Ikshvaku. The noble descendant of Raghu. He would rather die than win with *adharma*.

Vali held Ram's glare for an instant. A strange expression crossed his face. As if he was now certain.

Shabari saw that look from the distance. And she recognised it instantly. She had seen that look on a man she had loved, many many decades ago. An honourable warrior with a noble Kshatriya desire: death at the hands of a worthy enemy.

Shabari's mouth fell open in shock. She finally understood what Vali wanted. What he was hankering for.

Vali yelled loudly and charged again.

This time, Ram did not just defend. He pushed back hard. Brutally countering each strike of Vali with one of his own. Their blades clashed repeatedly. Vicious swinging strikes. Sparks flew from the steel. He would not just push back now. He began to use Vali's blows as a spring for his own. This was poetry in motion. A warrior's poem, written by the sword, with the ink of courage.

And then ... the masterstroke.

As Vali struck Ram's blade down, Ram flicked his sword up.

An expert strike. An unreal combination of fierce brutality and exquisite precision.

The return swing converted into a jab, splitting the skin above the right brow.

Vali pulled back, roaring in frustration.

Ram spoke loudly. 'Yield!'

'Never!' was the booming answer.

If one did not understand sword fighting, one would be forgiven for wondering why Ram had demanded surrender after a tiny wound on his opponent's forehead. But a bleeding brow would blind one eye with dripping blood. A serious impediment in a sword fight.

Ram only had to wait it out now. Vali would be severely impaired in a few minutes.

The duellists circled each other. Each waiting for the other to strike.

Vali grinned. He roared as he charged again.

He held his sword with both hands this time. Swinging hard repeatedly. The sound of clashing steel echoed all over the ground. The people knew. They felt it in their bones. In their blood. They were watching history in the making. Poets would write verses in homage to this encounter. Singers would sing paeans. Years from now. Millenia from now. This story would defeat time.

Vali swung hard from a low angle, seeking to disembowel Ram. The king of Ayodhya danced back, letting the blow strike the air. He did not block it. Using Vali's momentum, Ram stabbed forward. A low, brutal strike.

He had expected Vali to bring his sword back in time to deflect the weapon and swivel out of the way. What Vali did, instead, was perform a half action. With precision.

He swung his sword down, but not fast enough. Nor did he swivel. His body remained upright.

It was time.

Ram's blade entered the Kishkindha king's abdomen. Unhindered.

It happened so fast that, for a moment, even the audience did not realise what had occurred. Vali did not cry out. Not in agony. Not in anger. Not in shock. He just let out a long-held breath. His sword dropped from his hand. His body slumped. Shabari could see his eyes. They didn't show the shock of pain, but the peace of release.

Ram stood rooted to the spot. Stunned. *Why didn't Vali swivel out of the way?*

Ram released his hold on his sword.

It was lodged too deep inside; it had pierced the vital organs. Stillness in the air.

A kill wound. It was over for the valiant Vali.

The king of Kishkindha fell back, his strength ebbing. Ram reached forward and held him, gently easing him to the ground.

'Father!' screamed Angad, running towards Vali.

Ram looked at Angad, and then at Vali. Shocked. Helpless. *Why did he not move out of the way?*

Vali's eyes rested on Angad. Finding the strength to pull his reginal ring from his finger, he slid the bloodied symbol on to Angad's forefinger.

His son. His heir.

Vali was publicly acknowledging him as the next rightful ruler of his people. 'You will be king now… Angad…'

Angad was crying inconsolably. For a father he loved and admired. A father whose approval he had always sought. A father who had strangely, since his grandmother's demise, swung between extremes, sometimes full of deep affection, and at other times, aloof and cold.

Vali held Angad's arm and then pointed to Ram. 'I have promised the king of Ayodhya that our army … You will … join him … Treat him as you would treat me … Stay with him … Till the time that Raavan is defeated… Then you will be your own man …'

Angad wept. 'Father …'

Ram looked at Vali. At this noble man he had pushed into the arms of death.

'Angad!' said Vali, raising his voice. 'Promise me … Promise me that you will honour my word …'

'I will, father …' whispered Angad through his tears. 'I promise …'

Vali let out a long sigh. He knew that Angad would never break his promise. Never.

He looked at the Suryavanshi sword buried deep in his abdomen. And then at Ram, kneeling on one knee beside him.

Silent. Respectful. The honourable man who had gifted him death.

He looked around. At his people. Many of them crying. Everyone looking at him with reverence.

Then he turned his eyes towards the temple in the distance. His Lord, his God, Ayyappa.

He finally looked at his son. Angad. Holding his hand in his own.

Perfect.

A worthy death.

Just one thing missing.

The truth.

He understood his mother now. As it prepares to leave the body it is caged in, the soul craves to speak the most important truth. To the most important one in this life.

His mother had to tell him the truth.

He understood her now.

He looked at his son. His boy. He had to tell him the truth. He understood now.

The truth … The only truth that mattered.

'Angad …'

Angad was crying.

'Listen … to me …'

Angad looked at his father, holding his hand tight.

The truth. The only truth that mattered. It must be spoken.

'I love you, my boy …' whispered Vali.

'I love you, Father,' cried Angad, pressing his father's hand to his heart.

The blood from the wounded brow was clouding Vali's eyes. And through his blood, he saw his own blood. His son. A man does not become a father merely through his body. A man earns the privilege of fatherhood with his protection, his care, his ability to provide. A man earns fatherhood by being worthy of emulation. A man earns fatherhood through love.

The truth must be spoken. And the only truth that matters is love.

'I love you … my son …'

And, having spoken the truth that mattered, Vali's soul left his mortal body. Ready for its next life.

Chapter 13

'I had told you to stay put in Ayodhya,' said Ram, gently admonishing his brother Bharat. With a smile.

Two weeks after the duel with Vali, Ram had received word that Bharat and Shatrughan had sailed into the Vaigai River which cut across the Tamil lands to the east of Shabarimala. They brought with them a four-hundred-ship-strong navy, each a large vessel that could carry almost two hundred and fifty soldiers. One hundred thousand soldiers had left Ayodhya on these four hundred ships. They had sailed down the Sarayu River till it joined the Ganga, and the great Mother river had safely deposited them in the Eastern Sea. The orderly fleet had then sailed down the east coast of India, right to the mouth of the Vaigai River. At any other time of the year, the Vaigai would not have been able to accommodate such a large fleet. But the south-west monsoon had been particularly bountiful this year. And the Ashwin month had brought the north-east winds, which usually also brought more rain to the Tamil and

Andhra lands. The Vaigai was swollen with floodwaters. It was ready for the task at hand.

Angad had returned to the Kishkindha capital to mobilise his army, as his father had commanded. Ram, Lakshman and Vashishtha had sailed down the Vaigai River with their entourage, to meet Bharat and the Ayodhya navy at the river mouth. They were now on the deck of Bharat's ship. Vashishtha and Naarad had followed Ram and Lakshman aboard.

'I am your younger brother, Dada.' Bharat laughed. 'My job is to do what is in your best interests, not what you order me to do.'

Ram laughed softly and embraced Bharat. Emotions ran high in the two men of strong will. It had been too long. Too long.

'And in any case, Dada,' said Shatrughan, grinning, 'we haven't come for you. We have come for Sita *bhabhi*.'

Ram laughed and extended his left arm. Shatrughan joined the brothers in a bear hug.

'Hey! What about me?' asked Lakshman, raising his hands in the air in mock protest.

'Nobody is interested in you, bro!' Shatrughan laughed.

And Lakshman, with a heart as big as his gigantic body, found tears springing to his eyes. He rushed into the group hug.

Some men don't express love in words but in their actions. And the more love they so express, the more the cutting banter they indulge in.

The four brothers held each other. In a huddle.

Brothers in arms. A fort. Nobody could break them. Nobody.

Vashishtha stood at a distance and smiled.

Naarad turned to Vashishtha and also smiled. 'The brothers truly love each other. That's rare in a royal family. You have done a good job, Guruji.'

'No, no,' said Vashishtha. 'Parents have a greater influence than a mere teacher.'

Naarad looked at Vashishtha with a sly smile on his face. 'If you say so.'

Vashishtha was not a man for unnecessary rejoinders. He smiled.

'They will need this togetherness,' said Naarad. 'Defeating Lanka will be easy. Raavan is merely an opponent. Their actual enemies are in their own land, among their own people. That is when their unity will be truly tested.'

Vashishtha looked at the brothers and spoke with confidence. 'They will never lose this unity.'

— JF Jɔ̃D —

'Elephants?' asked Bharat, startled. 'Dada, our ships are big ... But no ship can carry elephants, to the best of my knowledge.'

The four brothers were supping in the captain's cabin on the royal ship. Vashishtha had wisely left them alone. Allowing them time to reconnect.

Ram smiled. 'Not on the ships. We will march across.'

'March? Walk on water?' asked Bharat.

'Yes,' answered Ram, turning to Shatrughan, who seemed to have cottoned on to the plan already.

Lakshman and Bharat too followed Ram's gaze. Three pairs of eyes rested on the youngest brother. The most intelligent and well-read of them all. The genius.

Shatrughan leaned back and smiled.

'Brilliant ...' he whispered. Almost like he was talking to himself.

'Will someone tell me what the hell is going on?' growled Bharat, irritated at being the only one who didn't seem to have a clue.

Shatrughan looked at Ram. 'The sand flats of Dhanushkodi ...'

'Bingo!' said Ram, pointing his index finger at Shatrughan.

Shatrughan laughed softly. 'Brilliant ... Brilliant ... The Lankans will not expect this at all ... We'll catch them by surprise.'

'Precisely,' said Lakshman.

Bharat seemed to have also caught on by now. He knew the topography of this part of India. He had occasionally paid attention to the geography lessons conducted by their *guru* Vashishtha all those years ago in the *gurukul*.

South of the Vaigai River mouth, the peninsular part of mainland India extended out into a promontory, jutting into the sea. A mere kilometre and a half of shallow waters separated it from an island called Pamban. Pamban island itself stretched north-west to south-east in the direction of Lanka. Beyond the south-east coast of Pamban island lay Mannar island, separated by around twenty-five kilometres of sea. It also spanned north-west to south-east, almost touching the mother island of Lanka, from which it was separated by a few stray metres of shallow waters.

Bharat had the same thought as Ram had had when Shabari suggested the idea to him. 'I have sailed in these parts before. It might be possible to build some pontoon bridges from the Indian mainland to Pamban Island. The elephants could even swim the short distance. Yes. We can also simply wade across the very tiny distance from Mannar Island to Lanka. Easy. But what about the twenty-five kilometres separating the Pamban and Mannar islands? Fording it is impossible. The waters are too high. And pontoon bridges will not survive the strong high tides. There is no way we can march an army across.'

'We can, if we build a bridge,' said Shatrughan.

'A *bridge* bridge?' asked Bharat. 'As in, a proper bridge?'

'Why would anyone build an improper bridge?'

Bharat burst out laughing and slapped Shatrughan on his shoulder.

'But no, seriously,' said Lakshman, 'do you really think it's possible to build a proper bridge?'

Bharat added with a flourish, 'Yeah… Tell us. For this will be the longest bridge in human history. And it will have to be built even as treacherous tides pull the sea water out and then back in with clockwork precision. We will have a window of no more than six hours from low tide to the next high tide, and then another six hours in reverse. And we have to build this entire bridge in two months flat, for you, Dada, intend to attack just as the north-east monsoon ends.'

Shatrughan nodded. 'It's a bit of a challenge, I admit.'

Ram smiled and patted Shatrughan on the back.

Bharat was not convinced. 'A bit of a challenge? This is impossible! No engineer can pull this off!'

'Correct, no engineer in the world can pull this off,' said Shatrughan, before pointing at himself. 'Except this one!'

Bharat sighed. 'Shatrughan, you know I love you. But this is—'

'Dada,' said Shatrughan, interrupting Bharat. 'You didn't bring me here for my warrior skills, did you?'

Everyone laughed. As far as fighting skills were concerned, Shatrughan had lost the gene pool to the invincible Lakshman. As for intellect, however …

'Are you sure you can do it, Shatrughan?' asked Ram.

'Do we have a choice, Dada?' Shatrughan countered. 'It's about Bhabhi. I have to get this done.'

Ram, Bharat and Lakshman smiled at their youngest brother.

'Dhanushkodi Setu, the world will call it,' said Lakshman. In the local language, *dhanush* was the *bow*, and *kodi* was the *string of the bow.* 'A bridge across the string of the bow. The greatest bridge ever. The greatest architectural wonder. The greatest monument to what man can do.'

Shatrughan shook his head. 'No. It will be called *Ram Setu*, the *bridge of Ram*. The greatest monument to what man can do, *for love*. And as Lord Rudra is my witness, we will build that bridge.'

— J╪ ↓⅝D —

'We don't have a choice, Guruji,' said Arishtanemi, his head bowed politely. But his voice was firm.

Arishtanemi was with Vishwamitra in the Malayaputra capital of Agastyakootam. Earlier in the day, Hanuman and Arishtanemi had performed the funeral ceremony of Sursa with full Vedic honours. Hanuman had then left, along the Vaigai, to rendezvous with the Ayodhya royals, while Arishtanemi had returned to Agastyakootam.

Vishwamitra nodded in response to Arishtanemi, but did not utter a word.

Vishwamitra knew that Arishtanemi was right. Despite his frustration with Sita for refusing to take up the mantle of the Vishnu, he could not allow for the slightest possibility of Raavan defeating Ram in a battle. That would make it impossible to get Sita to follow his plans. He had only one move left in the game for now: lend support to Ram in this conflict. Which, with the support of the Malayaputras and the Vayuputras, would end in the death of Raavan. Once that was done, he fully intended to bring his plan back on track.

'So, what are our orders, Guruji?'

Vishwamitra smiled wanly. 'The Malayaputras are being forced to support that Vashishtha's candidate. Just because of Sita's obstinacy.'

'True, Guruji. What would you have us do?'

Vishwamitra shook his head and sighed. 'However much I may hate that … that treacherous man, I will always love Mother India more …' Then, almost as if the words were being prised out of him, he announced his decision: 'Take our soldiers. Take our elephant corps. Go join the war.'

'As you say, Guruji,' said Arishtanemi, bowing low with his hands joined in a *namaste*.

As he turned to leave, Vishwamitra raised his hand. 'And Arishtanemi … I am …' Vishwamitra seemed to hesitate. 'I am sorry for your loss.'

Arishtanemi did not utter a sound. He understood. His *guru* was talking about her. The woman he loved. The woman he had always loved. Who had died in the arms of the man she loved. Saving him. Protecting him … His pain was deeper than that of unrequited love. For with unrequited love, there is always hope that the man may someday be able to win the woman's affection. Hope keeps the heart alive. But Arishtanemi's heart had died with his beloved.

He stood rooted to the spot. No crying.

'You will want vengeance. Against the faceless warriors of that battalion at Ketheeswaram,' said Vishwamitra. 'It's fair.'

The general of the Malayaputras gazed back at him.

'You have my permission, Arishtanemi,' said the chief of the Malayaputras. 'When you cross over with our Malayputra soldiers, you may wreak your vengeance upon them. Hand out justice.'

Arishtanemi bowed low with gratitude towards his *guru*. He did not utter a word, afraid that the tears would escape. Saluting his chief, he walked out of the chamber.

Suddenly, an idea struck Vishwamitra. He held his breath.

There is a way. Ram. His obsession with rules. Another daivi astra. *And the punishment would be ...*

Vishwamitra allowed himself a slight smile. Maybe he could still make Sita the Vishnu.

There is a way.

Chapter 14

'The next wave …' said Bharat.

The four brothers, accompanied by their *guru* Vashishtha, stood next to their cutter boat on the beach of Dhanushkodi on the south-eastern tip of Pamban Island. They, or more specifically Shatrughan, intended to survey the area to begin designing a bridge across the sea. Something that had never been attempted in the history of humanity. They were dressed in simple clothes, like the fishermen of the area, and unaccompanied by soldiers or guards. For that would have attracted the attention of the lookouts at Ketheeswaram, in Lanka, on the other side of the straits. No news of their plans must travel to Sigiriya.

The brothers held the gunwale of the beached cutter boat. Vashishtha was seated on the central thwart. They would not have their *guru* help them push the boat into the sea.

'This is a good one, Dada,' said Lakshman, standing at the rear end where maximum thrust was required. He was the strongest of the four brothers.

The wave crested high and then broke in a fierce curve, washing the Ayodhya princes with its embrace.

'Now!' ordered Ram.

The brothers began to push hard, helped along by the backwash of the wave. The boat lifted off the wet sand and careened gently into the waters, helped along forcefully by the princes.

'Push through!' screamed Shatrughan, bringing his limited muscular strength into play.

Another wave crested over and crashed into the boat. The brothers kept running with the vessel. Into the sea. Their feet dug into the sand as they raced forward, propelling the craft.

'Shatrughan, jump on board!' shouted Bharat over the roar of the waves.

Shatrughan was the shortest among them. He would soon run out of ground to run on. One cannot float and push a boat at the same time. Shatrughan did as ordered. On board, he immediately rushed to the centre thwart, picked up an oar and began pulling hard against the waters. Vashishtha was working the oar as hard as his aged body permitted on the other side.

'Another wave!' yelled Ram.

The three brothers kept pushing. Shatrughan and Vashishtha, within the boat, continued to row. They tore past this wave as well.

They were through.

'Come on board!' ordered Vashishtha.

Ram, Bharat and Lakshman jumped into the boat as it headed deeper into the sea, farther south from Pamban Island, towards Mannar Island.

Lakshman laughed as he shook the water from his long leonine mane. 'What a rush! I love the sea!'

Ram and Bharat laughed as well. They relieved Shatrughan and Vashishtha of the oars, and began rowing.

As the boat settled into a steady rhythm, Ram and Bharat turned towards their youngest brother. Shatrughan had already moved to the forward thwart, his sight pinned beyond the bow of the vessel, looking at Mannar in the distance. There was no time to stop and stare at the power and beauty of the sea. No time to allow his soul to enjoy the pleasure of the moment. He had already begun to analyse and survey.

'How long will you need, Shatrughan?' asked Bharat.

Shatrughan did not answer. He was looking down into the water, at the sandy seabed, six to seven feet below.

'It will probably take the entire day, Bharat,' said Vashishtha, answering on Shatrughan's behalf.

Lakshman sighed and leaned against the stern thwart. *The entire day?!*

The rush was forgotten. Boredom was already setting in. Lakshman looked at Bharat, his shoulders stooped and face deadpan. Bharat smiled at his brother and gestured with his hand. *Patience.*

—— ⅃Ⅎ ⅃⁵Ⅾ ——

'What do you think, Shatrughan?' asked Ram.

Shatrughan turned to his elder brother, a confident look in his eyes. 'It can be done, Dada. It will take a week to ten days.'

The four brothers and their *guru* had spent the entire day at sea, between the Pamban and Mannar islands, surveying the area in detail. Dressed as fishermen, they did not attract too much attention. It also helped that much of the land around here was thinly populated. At times Shatrughan had asked his brothers to stop rowing and had dived into the sea to check some features underwater. He touched the corals and dug his hands into the sand flats to understand the nature of the material. The grains of sand were finer than gravel, but coarser than silt. Perfect. He had thoroughly scoped out the northern part of Mannar Island and decided where the bridge would end. The sun had almost set and they were now back on Pamban beach. It had begun to drizzle; the God of Rain and Thunder, Indra, had kindly held back the rain all day.

Vashishtha had discussed the finer points of the topography and oceanography with Shatrughan through the day. But even he, who had taught Shatrughan almost all he knew, was amazed at his former student's confidence. 'A week to ten days, Shatrughan? That's it?! We are talking about a bridge across the sea. The longest bridge built in human history.'

Shatrughan's face was calm, focused and self-assured. 'Can be done, Guruji.'

'How?' asked Bharat, incredulous.

'We will need to ensure a few things first.'

'Anything you say, Shatrughan,' said Ram.

Shatrughan turned to Bharat. 'Dada, I understand the overall battle strategy you have in mind. You would lead a feinting naval attack up the Mahaweli Ganga River. The attack will be brutal. It will need a lot of soldiers. We only have one hundred and thirty thousand men. The hundred thousand Ayodhyans and thirty thousand Vaanars of Prince Angad. But—'

Ram interrupted Shatrughan. 'We will have more men, Shatrughan. Rest assured. We will not be launching any attack for another three months, till the end of the north-east monsoons. Angad and his thirty-thousand-strong Vaanar army will of course be here soon ... But by the end of the north-east monsoons, the Anunnaki of Kekaya will also be here with their allies from the lands of the sacred River Indus. They will have another fifty to sixty thousand men, at the least.'

Shatrughan looked at Lakshman and Bharat.

Bharat spoke up. 'They are not coming, Dada. I am close to Yudhaajit uncle, not so much to *Nanaji*.' He was referring to the king of Kekaya, Ashwapati. Also, his *maternal grandfather*. 'I'm aware that uncle Yudhaajit is trying his best to help us, but *Nanaji* has decided to stay out of this battle.'

Ram remained still. But his body had tensed in anger. A noble person expects nobility from his close relations and friends. All of them. Such a person is frequently disappointed.

'But there is some good news as well,' cut in Vashishtha. 'From most unexpected quarters.'

The brothers turned to their *guru*.

'The Malayaputras are joining us.'

'What?' Ram was shocked.

'I just received word from Arishtanemi,' said Vashishtha. 'Fifteen thousand Malayaputras will be joining us in battle, including, most crucially, their elephant corps. Combine that with the fifteen thousand Vayuputras who should reach soon, and our army will be at least one hundred and sixty thousand strong – the Ayodhya troops and Vaanar military, coupled with the Malayaputra and Vayuputra soldiers. I was hoping the Vayuputras would give us permission to threaten Lanka with *daivi astras*, so that the war would be over quickly. But they have refused. Their soldiers are coming, but no *daivi astras* will be allowed.'

Ram was not concerned with the *daivi astras*. He couldn't use them in any case, as the punishment for a second unauthorised use of divine weapons was death. But his transparent eyes held a question. For his *guru*. *The Malayaputras are joining us? Why?*

'It's not about you,' clarified Vashishtha. 'And, honestly, it's not about Sita either. I know my ... my friend ... Vishwamitra. I know his faults. But I also know his strengths. His anger is uncontrollable and he has a mighty ego. But I also know this – however much he may hate me, he loves Mother India more.'

Ram looked at Bharat, smiled slightly and shook his head. A noble man is frequently surprised. Sometimes by the lack of nobility in those he expects it from. At other times, by a display of nobility in those he did not expect it from.

'When all is said and done, he is a good man, this friend of yours, Guruji,' said Bharat.

Vashishtha let out a long breath, his expression stoic. Even remote. Just a trace of moisture danced within his eyes. It did not slip out.

Ram looked at the sky and folded his hands together in gratitude. 'Praise be to Lord Indra for this blessing.'

'Praise be to Lord Indra,' everyone repeated.

Bharat turned to Shatrughan. 'So, I can guess what you want, Shatrughan. You want to keep a majority of the men here.'

'Yes,' answered Shatrughan.

'How many?'

'Around one hundred and twenty-five thousand.'

'One hundred and twenty-five thousand?!'

'Yes, Dada. I will need that many to build the bridge. This will not be an easy task.'

'You want me to conduct a combined naval and land assault on the main Lankan defensive formations of the Mahaweli Ganga River with only thirty-five thousand soldiers?'

'You don't need to win that battle, Dada,' said Shatrughan with a hint of a smile. 'Just keep them busy till we cross over from here. Our main attack will come from here.'

Bharat laughed softly.

'And if I come along with you to the Mahaweli Ganga, Bharat Dada,' said Lakshman, 'we might just win the battle. Even with only thirty-five thousand soldiers.'

'That we will, brother!' said Bharat. 'We will win.'

Lakshman looked at Ram for confirmation. Ram nodded his assent. Lakshman would go with Bharat.

'Anything else?' Bharat asked Shatrughan.

'Yes,' said Shatrughan. 'We can gather the material for the bridge in secret. But once we move it to Pamban Island and start preparing for construction, there is no way that it can be kept quiet.'

'True.'

'And therefore, the Lankan battalion at Ketheeswaram …'

Shatrughan didn't complete his statement. But it was obvious what he was saying. The Lankan soldiers stationed in and around the Ketheeswaram temple had to be neutralised. Either imprisoned or killed. Not a single one of them could escape to warn the Lankans in Sigiriya of the goings-on in this part of the island.

Bharat looked at Ram and nodded.

'It will be done,' said Ram.

'Now, enough already!' said Bharat. 'Tell us how you will build the bridge.'

'All right, all right.' Shatrughan laughed. 'But first you need to understand something about the Eastern Sea. Something that makes it different not just from the Western Sea, but all the other seas in the world.'

'What?' asked Lakshman.

'Do you know the difference between sea water and river water?' asked Shatrughan with a gleam in his eyes. He was clearly enjoying this. This was his domain. His realm. Knowledge.

Vashishtha leaned back and smiled. He thought he understood where Shatrughan was going with this. *Genius.*

'Sea water is salty, while river water is fresh and sweet,' answered Ram.

'That is true of every sea in the world,' said Shatrughan. 'But only partially true of the Eastern Sea. Most of the Eastern Sea has a thin layer of fresh water on top of the sea water. The depth of this fresh water varies, at different times of the year, from a few inches to substantially more. It is also not uniform across the entire stretch of the Eastern Sea.'

'No way!'

'Yes way!'

'How? Why?' asked Lakshman, who had paid very little attention in school. He threw an apologetic glance at his teacher Vashishtha and then looked back at his twin brother.

'Mother India has been abundantly blessed with rivers. More than any other land. Egypt is called the Gift of the Nile River System. Mesopotamia exists because of the Tigris–Euphrates river system. They are lucky lands since they have a large river system. That's what makes civilisation possible. Some really, really fortunate lands have two, or maybe even three large river systems. Our Mother India has seven!' Shatrughan began to name the great river systems, counting them off on his fingertips. 'The Indus river system, the Saraswati river system, the Ganga–Brahmaputra river system, the Narmada river system, the Mahanadi river system, the Godavari–Krishna river system, the Kaveri river system. And then there are many smaller ones, like the Tapti and Penna, which we don't even count among the seven, but they each carry as much water as the Euphrates River! Even the Mahanadi, which is the smallest of the seven major river systems, often carries as much water as the Nile River!'

'Woah!' said Lakshman.

'No wonder our ancestors insisted that India is the land most blessed by the Gods.'

'*Jai Maa Bhaarati*,' said Vashishtha. *Glory to Mother India.*

The brothers repeated his words. '*Jai Maa Bhaarati.*'

'So, we have these mighty river systems in India. And a majority of them empty gigantic quantities of fresh water into the Eastern Sea. Even the massive Irrawaddy and Salween from the foreign lands to the east – Myanmar and Thailand – pour into the Eastern Sea. And not just this, the south-west monsoon releases huge quantities of rain into the Eastern Sea as well. But by far the biggest infusion of fresh water into the Eastern Sea is from the Ganga–Brahmaputra river system. All this creates the layer of fresh water on the Eastern Sea. And this layer is deepest in the northern parts close to the mouth of the Ganga–Brahmaputra river system.'

Bharat nodded his understanding.

'And we are in the Bhadra month.'

'So?'

'So, this is the time when the East Indian coastal current starts flowing down south, bringing even more fresh water from the northern parts of the Eastern Sea, close to the Ganga–Brahmaputra river system, to the south Indian coast.'

'How in Lord Indra's name does that help us?' asked Ram.

'It helps us with wood.'

'What?'

Shatrughan explained. 'To build this bridge, we need wood that sinks in water and stone that floats on water. Lots and lots of such wood and stone.'

Shatrughan had now left everyone even more befuddled. Including Vashishtha.

'Let me explain,' said Shatrughan.

'Please do!' said Bharat, grinning delightedly.

'We cannot build a traditional bridge, with piers and a roadway on top. We don't have time to plant pillars in the sea.'

'Correct.'

'So,' said Shatrughan, 'we will build a causeway across the Dhanushkodi straits. In effect, blocking the flow of water …'

Vashishtha spoke up immediately. 'But that will—'

Shatrughan interrupted his *guru*. 'No, Guruji. It will not weaken the bridge. We need the piers in traditional bridges because they allow the flowing water to pass under them. That is not a problem here. This is the sea. Water doesn't constantly flow here.'

'But there is the tide,' said Vashishtha. 'Coming in and out, changing direction every six hours and a bit. The tidal currents may not be as strong as flowing river water. But—'

'Guruji, look at the sea here,' said Shatrughan, interrupting his teacher again. 'We can call it Palk Bay and Gulf of Mannar if we want. But it's essentially the waters of the Eastern Sea in Palk Bay and the Indian Ocean waters in Gulf of Mannar. Both the waters crash into each other here – at Dhanushkodi – and dissipate each other's energy. Therefore, the sea is relatively calm here. If there is any place in this entire region which is perfect to build a bridge across the sea, it is this.'

'But no matter how relatively calm the waters, it is still the sea. It has tides and waves that are strong enough to weaken a bridge.'

'Not my bridge.'

'Why not your bridge?'

'It's in the design, Guruji. And the material.'

'The wood that sinks and the stones that float?' whispered Bharat.

Shatrughan nodded, grinning. 'Yeeesss, Dada! I know what you are thinking. But this is not a fantasy.'

'I believe you, brother. Now, what is this magical wood that sinks?'

'The wood of the *ebony* tree,' said Shatrughan. 'It's called *kupilu* in old Sanskrit.'

Vashishtha rocked back, holding his head, his mouth open with awe at the sheer audacity of innovation. He understood it now. Ebony wood. Fresh water. The tidal current. The sandbanks. The season. It all came together finally. He had not heard, seen or read about such brilliance since the *greatest scientist of them all, who lived many millennia ago*. 'By the great *Lord Brahma* himself, you are a genius, Shatrughan! But I still don't understand the thing about the floating stones.'

'Guruji,' said Lakshman, folding his hands together in an apologetic *namaste*. 'I am still stuck at trying to understand the sinking wood. So are my *dadas*. Can you please wait for your turn?'

Vashishtha laughed and gestured for Shatrughan to continue. 'Carry on, wise Nalatardak,' he said, calling him by his *gurukul* name.

Shatrughan resumed, 'So, ebony is one of the hardest woods in the world. It is native to this region of south India and Lanka. The strangest thing about it is that it is stronger when it is wet.'

'But I thought,' said Ram, 'that wood swells and weakens when wet. Isn't that true?'

'That's right, Dada,' said Shatrughan, smiling, 'but only up to a point. The wood fibres expand with a little moisture, and contract when the moisture disappears. And the wood weakens due to this. But when the moisture content goes above a certain limit – I think for ebony it should be around thirty to forty per cent – wood fibres actually become more stable. The wood becomes harder.'

'So let me get this,' said Bharat. 'If we subject wood to some moisture, it swells, but when you subject it to excessive moisture, it hardens.'

'And we will not just be "subjecting it to moisture". We'll be drowning the damn thing!'

'Woah …' said Lakshman. 'This is next level, brother.'

'But what about the fresh water?' asked Ram. 'Why did you tell us that long story about the fresh water layer in the Eastern Sea?'

'That is the true genius of the man!' said Vashishtha, looking at Shatrughan with fatherly pride. 'Go on, explain it.'

'What do you think happens when you leave something in salt water, as compared to fresh water?' asked Shatrughan.

'It erodes,' answered Bharat.

'Precisely. The wooden logs will be the foundation of the bridge. If they erode, the bridge will not last for very long. But since the sea floor is not more than six to seven feet deep in this region, most of the water here is fresh water. The logs will not erode and the bridge will stand strong for a long time.'

'But,' said Lakshman to Shatrughan, 'we don't need this bridge to last very long. We need just two or three days to march the army across. So long as it holds for those many days, we are set.'

'And what about our return?' asked Shatrughan. 'How will we bring the elephants back? We do have to return them to Kishkindha and to the Malayaputras. And we don't know how long the campaign will last. It could be a month. It could even be a year. An engineer must prepare for the worst-case scenario.'

'So, what are you saying?' asked Lakshman. 'That this bridge will last for a year?'

Shatrughan leaned forward. 'It's my bridge, Lakshman. It will last for at least one thousand years. If not more.'

'No bridge can last that long, Shatrughan!' said Bharat. 'You know I love you and respect your intelligence, but this is stretching it.'

'It's not,' said Vashishtha. 'That is his genius. The way he is designing it, or at least the way I think he is designing it, it will become almost like a natural feature. It will last a really, really long time.'

'But why use wood as the foundation?' asked Lakshman. 'Why not big boulders and rocks? Won't that be harder and better?'

'Many reasons,' answered Shatrughan. 'First, not every soldier in our army is as massive as you are, Lakshman. Quarrying, carrying and placing large boulders in the sea will be very difficult for average-sized men. But logs of ebony wood can be easily carried. They are lighter. And once placed in the sea they will slowly harden and become heavy, as water works its magic on the wood. This will make them sink gently, so the wet sand underneath is not displaced. Not too much at least. A heavy boulder, with its sharp edges, might shift the sand too much. That would be disastrous. We need the foundation to settle gently into the wet sand, with the grains surrounding it. That will hold the logs in place, a little like how our gums hold our teeth in place. We will also pour more sand in between the logs, filling up the open spaces, thus giving solidity to the foundation. And remember, the sand we pour in will moisten from the sea water here, thus becoming harder and more adhesive.'

'And that's what makes his design superlative,' said Vashishtha. 'There is a lot of sand in the area. So much that both high tide and low tide move it in from the sandbanks. Since this bridge, with its log foundation, will be the strongest structure in the vicinity, wet sand will naturally collect around it with the tidal movements. It will make the foundations stronger and stronger.'

'Brilliant!' said Ram. 'You intend to use the forces of nature to reinforce the bridge.'

'Thanks, Dada. There's more, though. We will place small stones atop the wooden foundation, which will serve as a secondary base and help keep the logs below in place.'

'I have a question,' said Vashishtha.

'I'm coming to the floating stones, Guruji.'

'No, no. You explain that later. I have one more question on the matter of the tides. I have no doubt you have thought about this, but if the bridge is built in a straight line from Pamban to Mannar, the tidal current could wear out the centre. The bridge will still hold for a year, I think. But there is a risk that, over time, it may crack in the middle. How do we mitigate that?'

'I've thought of that, Guruji. Have you studied aerodynamics?'

Vashishtha let out a loud laugh. 'I know you are very smart, Shatrughan, but I am your teacher. Do not forget that. Yes, I understand aerodynamics.'

Aerodynamics had been studied by ancient Indians in the fields of defence technology and ship-building. Essentially, they studied the motion of air and its interaction with solid bodies that moved either with or against it. Less wind resistance aids the trajectory of an arrow or a spear, for instance. It moves faster and farther.

'Sorry, Guruji,' said Shatrughan, smiling and folding his hands together into a *namaste*. 'It struck me that aerodynamics is the study of the movement of air. But even water is a bit like air in its movements. Fluid movements. It's just a lot denser. So, I thought, why not apply aerodynamic principles to the bridge?'

'Oh, brilliant!' said Vashishtha.

'Oh, what?' asked Bharat. 'I don't understand.'

'Basically, Dada,' said Shatrughan, 'we will not build a straight causeway across Pamban and Mannar. Guruji is right. The force of the tides will be stronger on a straight wall. But if we curve the bridge in a great arc, this force will get distributed. Simple principles of aerodynamics. There will be less erosion. The bridge causeway will curve like a bow. That will make it longer, yes. But it will make it more stable.'

'So how long will the bridge be?' asked Ram. 'The straight-line distance between Pamban and Mannar is around twenty-five kilometres.'

'By my calculations, it should be around thirty-five kilometres in length,' said Shatrughan. 'And I'm thinking we will make it around three and a half kilometres broad.'

'That broad?' asked Ram. 'That will require a lot of material and men.'

'We have enough men. And we have three months to gather the material. We can begin construction only after the north-east monsoons. Remember, Dada, the broader the bridge, the more stable it will be. The principles of this particular bridge are very different from those that work in the case of a normal bridge.'

The three brothers nodded. Understanding … somewhat.

'My main question has still not been answered, though,' said Vashishtha.

'The floating stones,' said Shatrughan, smiling.

'Yes, the floating stones. Why? Why not just use normal rocks?'

Lakshman cut in. 'And even more importantly, where will we find these floating stones?'

'We'll find them right here,' answered Shatrughan. 'The floating rocks are Platygyra coral stone.'

'What?' asked Bharat. 'Corals aren't stone. They are plants … or maybe animals … or …'

'Corals look like plants, Dada. But they are actually animals.'

'Whatever … They are beautiful things that live in the sea. They're certainly not stone.'

'They are not stone when they are alive, Dada. But once they die, they turn into stone.' Shatrughan pointed at a huge rock next to them. 'Can you lift that rock, Dada?'

'Are you crazy, Shatrughan?' asked Bharat. 'Even Lakshman will find it difficult to pick that up without risking a slipped disc.'

The diminutive Shatrughan took a few quick steps and picked up the rock. With one hand.

Lakshman was dumbfounded. 'What the …'

'Coral stones are very light. Very easy to carve and flatten. And yet, they have tremendous load-bearing strength. We can even construct small buildings with them. They are perfect architectural material. And they abound in this region. We will use Platygyra coral stone for the top layer, and bind it with wet sand. On which our army will march.'

'So, we will not be actually walking on floating stones?' asked Lakshman, disappointed.

'Of course not,' answered Shatrughan. 'But all the stones we use for the bridge, the small ones in the foundation and the flat ones on top, will be coral stones.'

'What is the advantage? Why not use harder rocks as a top layer?' asked Vashishtha. 'Won't hard rocks give the bridge stability?'

'They will be more difficult to carve into flat stones. It will take too much time. And I fear that the top surface may not be completely flat otherwise.'

'Our soldiers are tough.' Bharat laughed. 'They can survive a few pricks on the foot if the surface isn't completely flat.'

'Yes, they will be all right, but it is the elephants I'm thinking about,' said Shatrughan. 'Panicky elephants will be a disaster on the march.'

'Fair enough.'

'More importantly, no matter how well we stack and bond the top surface bricks, some of them will get displaced during the march. After all, elephants will be walking on it. And many of those stones will fall into the sea.'

'So?'

'Heavier stones will sink,' said Shatrughan. 'And then they will be moved around by the tidal currents. They will bang against the bridge foundations. Hard stones hitting the bridge repeatedly with incoming and outgoing tides … Not good for the bridge.'

Vashishtha nodded. 'Hence the floating stones … Even if some of the stones get displaced, they will float on the sea surface and not damage the bridge foundation. And being very light, their impact on the top level will be minimal.'

'Precisely.'

Vashishtha's face broke into a massive smile. 'You've thought of everything!'

Shatrughan preened with mock pride. 'I am Nalatardak!'

He had used his *gurukul* name from when the brothers studied, many years ago, in Vashishtha's *school*.

'Our genius brother!' said Bharat fondly.

'Forget the earlier name!' said Ram. 'This bridge will be called Nala Setu, after the one who will build it!'

Chapter 15

'*Namaste*, Raavanji and Kumbhakarnaji,' said Sita. 'Where have you been all these days? It's been a long time.'

It had been two weeks since Raavan and Kumbhakarna had last visited the Ashok Vatika. However, they were aware of Hanuman and Arishtanemi's rendezvous with Sita. They also were aware of the attack on the Ketheeswaram battalion by a small band of foreigners who escaped down the Aruvi Aru River that night. There were a few casualties, but the skirmish was not too serious. Clearly, whatever message Hanuman and Arishtanemi had for Sita had been delivered, and they had gone back. Raavan and Kumbhakarna were considering leaving a skeletal staff of soldiers at Ketheeswaram and recalling the rest. For the main attack would come from the east. They knew that the Ayodhyan navy had sailed down to south India and was waiting in the Vaigai River. Once the north-east monsoon ended, it would sail out and then move up the Mahaweli Ganga River into the hinterland of Lanka. The first battle would be fought at the great river fort of Onguiaahra that protected the waterway of Amban Ganga to Sigiriya, the Lankan capital.

'The battle will begin soon, queen,' said Raavan. 'Any time after the north-east monsoon. Just a few more weeks. A few weeks left to enjoy all there is to life, before war destroys us. So, I have been busy with that which is most important.'

'The battle plans?' asked Sita.

'Oh, that too!' said Kumbhakarna. 'Dada and I have been strategising on how to make it difficult for the Ayodhyan navy. But Dada has also been busy with things he considers more important!'

'What can be more important than battle preparations before a battle?' asked Sita.

'Art,' answered Raavan.

'Art?'

'Yes. I will never again be able to paint or sculpt or play instruments or sing. So, I have been enjoying as much of that as I can. But mostly painting and sculpting.'

Sita smiled and shook her head. 'You never fail to surprise me.'

'Yes ... I either surprise or disappoint. I never seem to meet expectations!'

'What paintings and sculptures have you created? What will you do with it?'

'Well, there's some for my brother, some for my son, some for my wife and even some for that useless mother of mine.'

Sita frowned with disapproval.

'Yeah, yeah. I know you don't like my speaking about my mother like this,' said Raavan. 'But not every mother is like your mother. Some mothers are a burden that children carry.'

'No mother is a burden.'

'Only someone who has had not one but two perfect mothers can say something so breathtakingly broad-brush and erroneous.'

'Big words!' laughed Sita, raising her eyebrows. 'You have been reading!'

'I always read. I read a lot. But lately I have been reading the works of those who think big words replace deep thoughts. There is a comforting pleasure in reading their supercilious nonsense.'

Sita looked at Kumbhakarna. 'Is he always like this?'

'Usually worse,' said Kumbhakarna, laughing softly.

'Aaaanywaaay,' said Raavan, laughing, 'I have made some stuff for you as well.'

Sita smiled. 'More paintings of my birth-mother?'

Raavan shook his head. 'No. Of you and your husband.'

Sita was surprised. This, she hadn't expected.

'And I'll have you know, my art is bewitching,' said Raavan. 'History will remember Ram and Sita the way *I* painted and sculpted them.'

Sita smiled, used by now to Raavan's bombastic words and almighty ego.

Raavan clapped his hands and a retinue of attendants apparated in a flurry, carrying large packages. Raavan got up with a flourish and summoned one over.

Sita's heart began to thud in anticipation. She had seen Raavan's work. His talent. But her mind pulled back in judgement. She said to herself that she would politely appreciate the painting to an appropriate measure. Not less. Not more. *This is the way history will remember the seventh Vishnu, Ram? I don't think so…*

Raavan theatrically removed the cloth covering and revealed the painting like a magician. Sita gasped. It was her. And yet she could never have imagined that she looked like this. This … divine.

This was she, not her mother. The body was lean, more muscular. The face and arms carried faded battle scars. She was seated alone in the Ashok Vatika. Everything looked exquisite. The sky radiated the beauty of the early morning sun. The trees painted so realistically that they created an optical illusion of swaying in the breeze, watching the wondrous Goddess seated amidst them. Deer and peacocks danced in devotion, craving her attention. At the heart, in the centre, was Sita. Dressed in a *dhoti*, a blouse and an *angvastram* that fell from her right shoulder. Virginal white. A pendant made from the bones of a single finger—a relic of her mother Vedavati's body—with the phalanges carefully fastened with gold links, hung from a black string tied around her neck.

Sita was depicted sitting on a large rock. In the Ashok Vatika. Her legs rested on the ground, crossed at the feet. Her hands clasped together, with fingers interlocked, resting on her thighs. Her back was slightly slouched. She gazed into the distance. A picture of contemplation and repose.

What was passing through her mind? Was she thinking of Ram? Pining for him? Longing for a reunion? Or was she just melancholic? Lonely?

Distant. Divine. Like a Goddess.

Sita was both fascinated and dispirited by the painting, if that was possible. 'Where is Ram?'

Raavan smiled. 'I'm sorry I took you away from him. But it won't be too long now. You will meet him again soon.'

Sita smiled slightly and gazed again at the painting. She couldn't have imagined that a painting could conquer time. A copy of it would hang in a secret temple, in a city that was yet to be built, a city that would be named after the five banyan trees in that area. In future, Sita would expressly order that her image not be recorded anywhere. But some would still keep copies of this painting. They would worship her in this form. They would call her Bhoomidevi, the Goddess of the Earth.

'Thank you,' said Sita. And then she added, without knowing why she said it, 'I will try and be worthy of this painting.'

'You already are, princess,' said Kumbhakarna gently.

'And now,' said Raavan, 'the next one …'

Another painting was brought to them by the attendants. Raavan removed the cloth covering with some more drama. Always the showman. He made the staff hold the painting aloft. Sita blushed and broke into a delighted smile. For it was her, along with the object of her deepest affection. Ram.

Ram and Sita were dressed simply, with no royal ornaments or crowns. They wore plain hand-spun cotton, the clothes of the poorest of the poor. Their eyes rested on each other. Oblivious to the world. It was a look of love, trust and, most importantly, respect. A man and woman made for each other. Sita held Ram's right hand from below, as if supporting him.

Again, Sita could not have known the future. How could she? But this image would serve as model for the main gargantuan *murti* in a great temple dedicated to the Vishnu himself, in the noble city of Ujjain. Many, many centuries later, a rough-hewn saviour from Tibet would look up and behold the idol in that great temple. In a meeting with a tribe that was yet to be created – the Vasudevs. In the effort to fulfil his mission – removing Evil.

'Ram will become the Vishnu,' said Raavan, 'because of you. And he will be a great Vishnu.'

Sita shook her head. 'He will become the Vishnu on his own. The best one. My task is to assist him.'

Raavan smiled and did not contradict her. He signalled for the next piece of art. This was not a painting but a sculpture. A small work of exquisite art. He removed the cloth covering to reveal a bust. Sita's eyes welled up with emotion. A soft smile played on her lips.

She looked at Raavan, smiled broadly and applauded. 'Your talent is unique.'

'I know.'

Sita laughed and shifted her attention back to the sculpture. It was Ram. Ram, the way he would be decades later. For Raavan's special ability was to age a person in his mind's eye and capture it in a work of art.

'This is Ram,' said Raavan, 'after he has achieved all that he will as a Vishnu. When he has established a new empire. When people are happy and prosperous. When there will be order and beauty. When our beloved Mother India will lead the world once again. This is how he will look after fulfilling his role. This is how he will be remembered.'

Sita murmured, 'We will call the empire *Meluha*.'

Raavan smiled. '*The Land of Pure Life* … A nice name.'

'He has the look of a *rajrishi*,' said Sita.

Raavan nodded. 'This is the way he came to me. A *priest-king*.'

Rajrishi, an old Sanskrit word, was a conjoint of *raja* and *rishi*. *King* and *sage*. It was sometimes used for kings who walked away from kingship and became sages. But more often, it referred to kings who ruled like sages. Who dedicated their energy, emotions, mind and their very soul to one purpose alone: the good of their people.

Sita was hypnotised by the sculpture. Flawless in its beauty and form, it was the head and upper torso of Ram. He was bare-chested and wore a simple patterned *angvastram* that was wrapped around his right armpit and his left shoulder, covering his left arm completely but leaving the right sword-arm and right shoulder bare. The *angvastram* was delicately decorated with trefoil embroidery: overlapping ring patterns filled with red pigment. Simple and elegant. He wore no jewellery save for modest gold-stud earrings. Raavan had drilled holes in the exquisitely sculpted ears and adorned them with gold studs. Ram wore a fillet or ribbon headband, etched with astounding detail. The headband held an inlay ornament in the centre that dangled high on his forehead. It was the Sun, with its rays streaming out. The symbol of a *Suryavanshi*, the *Solar Dynasty*. The simplest of crowns for one who was, after all, a *rajrishi*. A similar, smaller amulet was tied to his right upper arm with a silky gold thread.

Sita looked closer. 'What are those symbols on the amulet?'

'Random symbols for now,' said Raavan. 'But you had once told me that Ram is obsessed with merit. I remember your exact words: that people's status and regard in society should be defined by their *karma* and not their birth. I thought he would like a system in which people display that acquired status … Perhaps a chosen-tribe instead of a birth-tribe … that they have earned with their merit … And wear with pride on their arm bands.'

Sita smiled. *That would be so Ram …*

Raavan smiled with rare embarrassment. 'Just a thought …'

She walked around the sculpture. She looked at the back. The two ends of the fillet-crown were neatly tied behind the head. His hair was punctiliously combed and gathered into a large neat bun at the crown of his head. The moustache and beard were neatly trimmed. Everything about the figure was immaculate, sober and modest.

So very Ram …

But what captivated her were the eyes. Deep and incisive. Half-closed. Like a monk in meditation. Calm. Gentle.

'Wow …' whispered Sita. Mesmerised. 'This is how people will remember Ram.'

'This is how people will remember Ram,' repeated Raavan.

Raavan was right. The people would remember this image. For millennia.

They would remember their *rajrishi*.

They would remember their *priest-king*.

They would remember their Vishnu, Ram.

For as long as the land of India breathed, it would sing the name of Ram.

—JᚠᏌ5D—

'All preparations over?' asked Ram.

Bharat nodded. 'Yes, Dada.'

The north-east monsoon had been extremely intense in the first month this year, but had inexplicably died down almost completely after that. Ram and his brothers had decided to bring forward their planned attack on Lanka. They were ready. Shatrughan and his assigned soldiers had worked double quick in gathering the material needed for the construction of the bridge. In just one month. The Malayaputras had arrived with their fifteen thousand troops and their elephant corps. So had the Vayuputras, with another fifteen thousand warriors. And Angad too had marched in, with his Vaanar soldiers and elephants. Provisioning this massive army for another two months would prove unnecessarily expensive when the opportunity to launch the war had already presented itself. Furthermore, as all good generals know, a bored army is a dangerous thing. Testosterone-laden men, held back from battle with the enemy, can instead turn on each other.

It made perfect sense to launch the attack without delay.

The invasion of Raavan's Lanka would begin the following day. The first day of the month of Ashwin.

Ram boxed his younger brother's shoulder. 'I missed you, you stupid oaf!'

Ram and Bharat were alone together. A rare occurrence in the hectic frenzy of war preparation. They sat on the beach next to the mouth of the great Vaigai River. Their armies visible in the distance.

'Who told you to banish yourself?' said Bharat gruffly, laughing also, as he put his arm around his brother's shoulder.

Ram smiled quietly. He stared into the distance. At the point where the night sky touched the calm waters of the Eastern Sea at the horizon.

The brothers sat in silence. Bharat knew that Ram was troubled. He also knew that however close Ram was to Lakshman, he could not express his apprehensions to their hot-headed brother.

So, he waited for Ram to speak.

'Bharat …'

'Yes, Dada …'

Ram sighed.

Bharat waited again. In silence.

'I don't even …'

Bharat held Ram's shoulder. 'Raavan wouldn't kill her, Dada. He needs Bhabhi alive. We know that.'

Ram looked at the sea, averting his eyes from his brother. Kshatriyas hide their tears, even from their own.

'He won't kill her,' repeated Bharat. 'You know that.'

'Yes. But he could hurt her. He's a monster.'

'If he has dared to do that, Dada, then I swear we will make him suffer. We will be more monstrous than that monster.'

Ram continued to look into the distance. Soft tears fell in a steady flow now. And then it slipped out. The thought in his head. That had not escaped his lips. For who could he speak to besides Bharat?

'I failed,' Ram whispered in an agonised voice.

'No! No, you didn't, Dada …'

'She's my wife. It is my duty to protect her from harm. It is my duty to die for her. I was not there … And she was kidnapped … I failed in my duty …'

Bharat allowed his elder brother to speak.

'She's the love of my life. She's my woman. And I let some monster … to my …'

Bharat held Ram's hand. No words.

'I shouldn't have gone after that deer … I could have run faster … I could have …' Ram halted as the tears overwhelmed him.

Bharat reached over and embraced his brother. Ram held him tight. He allowed the tears to flow. He let the agony of the months of separation from her seep out.

Bharat silently held his brother. He straightened when he felt Ram relax.

'You know, Dada,' said Bharat, 'most women can do everything that a man can, except fight physically with men. The average man is bigger and stronger than the average woman.'

Ram looked at Bharat quizzically. For this had nothing to do with what he was troubled by.

'But,' continued Bharat, 'Sita *bhabhi* is not an average woman. She can fight. She can hold her own in battle.'

Ram smiled.

'If you ask me, honestly,' said Bharat, 'I am not worried about what harm Raavan could do to Sita *bhabhi*. I would worry more about what harm she can do to him!'

Ram smiled fully.

Bharat held Ram's hand. 'Dada, you haven't failed. Fate is testing Sita *bhabhi* and you. But even if you do believe that you have failed, remember that it isn't as if great men never fall. Everyone falls some time or the other. Great are those who rise after they fall, dust themselves off and get right back into the battle of life.'

Ram nodded.

'And you are not just a great man. You are the Vishnu.'

Ram rolled his eyes. 'It's Sita who is the Vishnu.'

Bharat sighed. 'You settle that between the two of you. All I know is that you are a tough, powerful man. And you have your brothers and your people standing right behind you. Raavan has stirred up a hornets' nest by taking us on. We will teach him a lesson that the world will remember forever.'

Chapter 16

Bharat, Lakshman and the Ayodhyan navy sailed out from the Vaigai in the morning. The sun was setting behind them as the lead ship sailed into the Gokarna Bay. By the time the last ship anchored it was well past sundown. The Ayodhyan navy was massive.

Gokarna – literally, the cow's ear – was the main port of Lanka. Located in the north-east of the island, its natural harbour was endowed with a deep bay. The land extended into the sea, serving as a natural breakwater. It received and safely anchored the seafaring Ayodhyan navy ships. A majority of Bharat's ships remained outside the bay, safe from any surprise attacks.

The *Mahaweli* Ganga flowed into the Gokarna Bay at its southern end. Named the *Great Sandy* Ganga, it was the longest river in Lanka and had a navigable channel with a deep watercourse, which allowed ships to sail into the heart of the island. Much farther upriver, ships sailed into the Amban

Ganga – a tributary of the Mahaweli Ganga –which allowed a craft to reach very close to the Lankan capital, Sigiriya. The capital lay around one hundred kilometres to the south-west of Gokarna, and the journey to it was mostly navigated through water.

One would have predicted some military resistance to the expected attack from the Ayodhyans at Gokarna. But one would have been wrong to do so.

Lanka focused all its energies on two fronts: trade, and warfare which supported that trade. Not much else. Most Lankans were either warriors or businessmen, or those who served these two groups. There were almost no farmers, Lanka producing very little of its own food requirements. This made sense for an island that thrived on free trade. Food was expensive to grow in Lanka and they had the Sapt Sindhu next door – the territory with the largest proportion of arable land in the world. Lanka could import cheap and high-quality agricultural produce from the Sapt Sindhu, and devote all its energy towards trade and warfare to abet that trade.

While this state of affairs made sense from a free trade perspective, it was disastrous militarily. An enemy could easily blockade the Gokarna port and starve people there into surrendering in a short time. Gokarna was the import hub for Sigiriya, which made the Lankan capital itself vulnerable to such a siege.

Kumbhakarna had understood the military disadvantage of importing all their food and had, over the years, encouraged farming in and around Sigiriya. But Gokarna had remained stubbornly addicted to imported food. Few Gokarnans wanted to shift from profitable trade to low-income farming. And how does one farm without farmers?!

So Raavan had made his soldiers retreat from Gokarna and set vigil in Sigiriya when he received news of the Ayodhyan navy preparing to set sail from Vaigai. It made sense to prepare for the siege in Sigiriya and not waste precious resources in defending a city like Gokarna that was so vulnerable to a blockade.

True to its mercantile spirit, senior officials from the Gokarna trading guilds had gathered at the main port quay to welcome the Ayodhyan navy. Businessmen in this Lankan port city were determined to remain pragmatic. To business-focused minds, everything is negotiable. They chose to surrender to the invaders instead of putting up resistance bound to be ineffective. They would allow the soldiers free passage to Sigiriya in return for their safety and security. Whoever won the battle in Sigiriya would later become their administrators and overlords, they had calculated.

Logical.

Bharat and Lakshman looked on bemused as their ship captain expertly navigated into the quay.

Musicians, singers, priests with *puja* thalis, top businessmen dressed in their finery ...

'They have lined up a welcoming party!' exclaimed Lakshman. 'You were right about them, Dada.'

Bharat nodded. 'Hmm ... Let's hope I am right about what they will do later on as well.'

Bharat's ship docked at the quay and the gangway plank was quickly fixed. The Ayodhya sailors began to lower the sails and pack them in as Bharat and Lakshman disembarked, preceded and followed by fierce bodyguards.

As they stepped on land, they were besieged by smiling businessmen rushing in with garlands and *laddoos*. Musicians injected renewed energy into their sonorous musical *ragas*, welcoming the brothers to Lanka. The city's artistic elite lined the road, gently showering rose petals on the brothers.

'Lord Bharat,' said an obviously eminent citizen, having confidently walked up to the prince of Ayodhya. 'Has Emperor Ram not accompanied you?'

Bharat cast a quick glance towards their grandest ship, farther back in the middle of the bay. And then he turned his attention to the businessman. 'Why don't we speak first?'

The businessman bowed low with his hands folded in a namaste. 'Of course, of course, Prince Bharat. Greetings to you as well, Prince Lakshman. Please do follow me.'

Bharat was pleased to note that Lakshman was following instructions. He was keeping his mouth shut. He had faithfully followed his brother's gaze and also glanced at the grand ship that had not come up to the quay.

Bharat was not sure of the businessmen's motives. They might also be spying on them for Raavan. He had warned Lakshman that under no circumstances were they to give the impression that Ram and Shatrughan were not with them. That would make the Lankans suspect that this naval assault up the Mahaweli Ganga River was a ruse, and that the actual attack would come from elsewhere.

The Lankan merchants were now convinced that Ram and Shatrughan were in the grand ship that had stayed back.

Bharat nodded to Lakshman and they both began to walk alongside the merchant. The brothers' bodyguards moved with them in a discreet semi-circle of protection.

— J⌐ ⊍⌐⊃ —

'Remember our orders, Arishtanemi,' said Hanuman.

It was late in the night. A thin sliver of moon was struggling to illuminate the dark. Hanuman and Arishtanemi pushed their cutter boat out to sea, accompanied by twenty able soldiers. They moved past the second wave, jumped into their boat and swiftly rowed deep into the Dhanushkodi straits. A few hours would bring them to the Lankan mainland.

Arishtanemi was as silent as a meditating monk. After some time, he looked to the right. Cutter boats sailed behind, faintly visible in the distance, almost noiseless. It was dark, but streaks of white foam in the inky black sea brought them occasionally into view. The small boats were valiantly battling the sea as they moved towards their target. He could not hear his deathly silent comrades. But the rhythmic sounds of the rowing made it known to him that they accompanied him.

A hundred cutter boats. Two thousand Vayuputras and Malayaputras. More than enough.

The enemy was outnumbered. Arishtanemi and Hanuman knew that the bulk of the Ketheeswaram battalion had been recalled to Sigiriya a few weeks ago. The few that remained would not number more than a hundred. They had rarely been sighted in the last few weeks by the Ayodhya scouts. Perhaps they remained confined to their quarters, fearful of attacks from the Ayodhyans just a few hours away by boat. They would also be under the impression that most of Ram's army was on its way to engage in battle from the eastern front of Lanka. No, they would not be expecting soldiers rowing silently towards them.

Two thousand soldiers. Against one hundred enemy ones. More than enough.

Hanuman's orders from his commander Lord Ram were clear. They should try and arrest the Lankans at Ketheeswaram. Only kill if necessary. None would be allowed to escape. News of the bridge-building at Dhanushkodi could not reach Sigiriya before the Ayodhyans did. That would be an unmitigated disaster.

So, Hanuman had been given two thousand soldiers for this mission. One needs more soldiers to capture the enemy alive, much fewer to simply kill them.

'Arishtanemi?' Hanuman said again.

Hanuman knew that they must arrest the Lankans. Not kill. But he also knew what Arishtanemi would want to do. Kill.

Arishtanemi did not answer. He held the gunwale tight and stared straight ahead.

Hanuman fell silent.

— JF JᵗD —

An hour before dawn, the waves swept the Ayodhyans on to the beach, two kilometres south of the Ketheeswaram battalion quarters. The soldiers quickly jumped off and pushed their boats high above the waterline.

They had timed their arrival well. It was peak high tide. The boats had landed high on the beach, pushed by the natural thrust of the waves. The waters would slowly recede now and rise to these levels again after twelve-and-a-half hours. They did not need the usual animal-powered pulleys to pull their boats to higher ground, for fear that they could be dragged out to sea.

Twelve hours. Ample time. To overwhelm the Lankans at Ketheeswaram and get back. Shatrughan's bridge construction could then begin.

'Landing report,' Hanuman addressed a soldier.

The soldier saluted Hanuman and rushed to tally the boats that had beached.

Hanuman pulled Arishtanemi to the side.

'Arishtanemi, let's avoid the killing if we can,' whispered Hanuman.

Arishtanemi looked blankly at Hanuman.

'Listen to me …'

'You did not love her,' said Arishtanemi. 'I did.'

'Brother …'

'You did not love her,' repeated Arishtanemi. 'I did.'

'Those Lankan soldiers were only doing their duty.'

'And I will do mine.'

'Sursa would not have wanted you to do this.'

'You know that's not true. Had you been killed, Sursa would have roasted them alive.'

Hanuman remained silent.

'One who doesn't feel love cannot know how love feels. One who doesn't know love will feel no need for vengeance.'

'Arishtanemi, listen to me …' pleaded Hanuman.

'Do not come between my vengeance and me,' said Arishtanemi. He walked away from Hanuman.

—— ⅃⊦ ⅃Ɔ⊃ ——

'This is strange …' whispered Hanuman.

Hanuman and Arishtanemi were hiding behind the treeline, two hundred metres from the Lankan battalion quarters. The light of dawn had begun to dispel the darkness. Vague shadows could be discerned. With effort.

The battalion quarters were a mess. Scattered leaves. Animal droppings. Stale puddles of water. Two horses had escaped from the stables, their restraints having come loose. They were aimlessly roaming around the elaborate flowerbeds and trees at the entrance. Chomping at the leaves.

Arishtanemi looked at Hanuman. 'I know Lankan traditions. Their army is brutal but very well-trained. Their quarters are always well ordered. Spick and span. Those trees are not just for show, their leaves are medicinal. Why are the horses eating them? What's going on?'

Hanuman considered sending in a small team to investigate. He turned back to his men.

'Don't send in anyone just yet,' said Arishtanemi in a soft voice, almost as if he had read Hanuman's mind.

'What do you suggest?'

Arishtanemi, the besotted lover seeking vengeance, was gone. Arishtanemi, the feared warrior with legendary tactical brilliance, had come to the fore.

'Give me a minute,' he whispered as he stealthily crept forward.

— Jᖴᖷᒲᗡ —

Arishtanemi rushed back to Hanuman fifteen minutes later. Alarm writ large upon his face.

'What's the matter?'

'The plague ...'

'Plague?'

'Sigiriya has been afflicted by a plague for many years. For some reason it hadn't spread to Gokarna. Nor to Ketheeswaram. It appears that it has now.'

Hanuman instinctively stepped back.

'I didn't go too close. It was clear from a distance ...' said Arishtanemi. 'Typical symptoms are severe pain, sluggishness, fatigue, etc. But there is a new addition recently ... of relentless spells of coughing and loss of breath. Don't worry – the Malayaputras have the medicine for this disease and we are carrying enough, even for our army.'

'All right then. We will arrest these men and take them back with us. They can be taken care of in our field hospitals. The Malayaputra medicines can be used to ...'

Hanuman stopped speaking as Arishtanemi turned towards his Malayaputra lieutenant at the back, giving quick hand-signal commands.

Hanuman instantly understood. 'Arishtanemi … no …'

Arishtanemi looked at Hanuman. A silent rage flashed in his eyes.

'They are incapacitated … They cannot fight back … This is *adharma*.'

Arishtanemi loosened the scabbard-hold on his sword and checked the assorted knives tied all over his body in different sheaths.

Hanuman held his friend's arm. 'You are better than this, Arishtanemi. Don't … Come on … Don't force me to …'

Arishtanemi glared at Hanuman. 'You will do nothing. You will wait here.'

'Don't do this … You're better than this …'

In a flash, some two hundred Malayaputras had lined up behind Arishtanemi, whose loyal lieutenants briskly briefed them. Hanuman knew that the Malayaputra soldiers were not merely following orders from their revered leader. Sursa was a former Malayaputra as well. This was personal. For all of them.

'Arishtanemi …' whispered Hanuman. Beseeching his friend.

'Stay here. Don't get involved.'

Arishtanemi drew his sword and turned to his men. And nodded.

The Malayaputras pulled their blades out and began moving forward.

Sursa would be avenged.

Blood would be answered with blood.

Chapter 17

'Where is your militia?' asked Bharat.

Bharat, Lakshman and their bodyguards had awoken early from a restful night's sleep in their comfortable quarters. A section of Raavan's mansion in Gokarna had been allotted to the Ayodhyan princes. Late into the second *prahar*, senior partners of the trade guilds of Gokarna had trooped in to meet the brothers.

The businessmen had begun their negotiations with a flow of flattery. Bharat and Lakshman were the rays of sunshine in their bleak horizon, they had said. The brothers – the true rulers of the Indian subcontinent – would liberate them, they had said. Bharat speedily brought the pantomime to an end and they had gotten down to work.

Time was of the essence. He would not waste a second.

Manigramaa was the senior managing partner of the Cotton and Silk Guild. It was the richest guild in Gokarna.

She responded cautiously to Bharat's question. 'Militia, great prince?'

Most manufacturers, merchants and traders across the Indian subcontinent were organized into guilds: essentially corporations composed of members pursuing a common craft or trade. Aspiring individuals entered a trade guild as apprentices and climbed the ladder based on the profits they earned for the guild – becoming managers, then ship captains and then partners. Five managing partners were elected by the members on a biannual basis. No managing partner could hold office for more than two consecutive terms.

Each member of the guild received a portion of the annual profits. All accounts were kept open at the guild offices and, manager upwards, members could inspect the accounts at any time of their choosing. Systematically, then, all members could focus on guild profits. For these profits directly determined the profit-shares of the members.

Pirates attacking trading ships in the Indian ocean were bad for profits. It made sense then for the guilds to either maintain their in-house militia to guard their ships, or hire the services of the Lankan army.

'Yes, Manigramaaji,' said Bharat. 'I am certain your guild has an in-house militia. You wouldn't waste money on the expensive Lankan army. Your guild is big enough.' Reverse flattery proves useful sometimes. 'Where are the militia soldiers?'

Manigramaa looked at her co-managing partner, and then at the managing partners of the other guilds. All nodded imperceptibly. Lying to the Ayodhyans would be bad for business.

'Great prince,' said Manigramaa. 'Our militia has been commandeered by emperor ... I mean the ... the evil kidnapper, Raavan. We do not have any soldiers here with us.'

Bharat looked into Manigramaa's eyes. She was not lying. But he did not want to trust her.

'Your boats …' said Bharat.

'Yes, Lord Bharat?'

'I need your boats.'

'But …' said Manigramaa softly. 'Great prince, the Mahaweli Ganga is in flood. Your own seafaring ships can go up the Mahaweli Ganga since there is enough water in the river channel. You do not really need our small riverboats. Your bigger seafaring ships can ram into and destroy the riverboats of the Sigiriya navy.'

Bharat was impressed by the trader's knowledge of warfare. She was right. But only partially so. His seafaring ships could go up river, yes. But they would prove too bulky at the Onguiaahra River fort. The smaller riverboats of the guilds would be useful at that crucial point. Once the fort was breached, his ships could sail through.

There was one other reason why he intended to commandeer the guild ships. He didn't want to leave vessels behind, which could be used to attack his navy from the rear when he sailed onward into the Mahaweli Ganga River. Some of the guilds could be loyal to Raavan. Abundant caution would dictate that he destroy the guild ships he could not use.

In war, one hopes for the best and prepares for the worst.

'Thank you for the wise military advice,' said Bharat. 'All the same, I want those ships. *All* your vessels. The seafaring ones as well as the riverboats.'

'Um …'

Manigramaa looked at her companions, all shifting uncomfortably in their seats. Some were looking at her. Others were staring fixedly at the floor.

Bharat understood. Ayodhya and the Sapt Sindhu held businessmen in great contempt. Unlike Raavan, who was at heart a trader, most Sapt Sindhu kings did not understand the concept of property rights of businessmen. Bharat guessed that the Gokarna guilds suspected they would not be compensated for the loss of their ships.

'I will pay a fair price for all your ships,' he said.

Manigramaa brightened up. She did not need to look at the others in the delegation before responding. 'Then we will be very happy to hand over our ships to you.'

Bharat nodded. 'Thank you.'

'In fact,' continued Manigramaa, sensing an opportunity for further profit, 'if the Ayodhya treasury is short of funds for this purchase, or any other supplies you may need, our Cotton and Silk Guild would be very happy to lend you the money. Our interest rates are quite competitive. Far lower than what is charged in the Sapt Sindhu.'

Bharat smiled ruefully. The Lankan guilds were legendarily profitable, and he knew that many were sitting on huge amounts of excess money that they had now deployed in banking. In effect, they were muscling into the market of the traditional moneylenders. And since they were flush with cash, they happily charged lower interest rates. But Bharat had already raised money in Ayodhya. At high interest rates, yes. The rates would be unnaturally high in a land that resented its traders and business houses, and loans would be difficult to come by. But the task was done. It was too late now.

He politely declined. 'Thank you, Manigramaaji. But no thank you.'

Manigramaa smiled genially. 'All right, then. I guess our business here is done.'

'Yes, I would think so.'

'Thank you, great prince,' said Manigramaa rising. 'You are a fair and just man. I did not expect this from a Sapt Sindhu royal.'

'We are not all bigoted,' Bharat said with a smile, standing too in respect. 'Or foolish. I understand that traders generate wealth for our land.'

Manigramaa held back her emotions with restraint. She was unaccustomed to receiving respect from the royals of the Sapt Sindhu. She smiled and folded her hands into a *namaste*. 'May Goddess Lakshmi bless you with victory and success, great prince.'

'Thank you,' said Bharat, folding his hands into a respectful *namaste*.

She seemed to hesitate a bit before adding, 'You can trust us, Prince Bharat … I don't think Emperor Ram and Prince Shatrughan need to remain in the royal ship. They can be brought on shore.'

Bharat smiled genially. 'It is an Ayodhya royal ship, Manigramaaji. Trust me, it's very comfortable.'

Manigramaa smiled with understanding. Bharat had, in effect, told her he couldn't afford to risk his king's life. It was a pragmatic choice. But he had implied this with grace. Without insulting her honour. *A good man.*

'I will take your leave then,' said Manigramaa, bowing low.

Bharat nodded his head slightly, his hands folded together into a *namaste*.

Manigramaa, followed by the rest of her delegation, walked out of the chamber.

Bharat waited for the Lankans to leave and then looked at Lakshman. 'And now we must meet that traitor.'

'Are you sure, Dada?' asked Lakshman. 'Can we trust a man who is betraying his own elder brother?'

'We certainly cannot trust him,' said Bharat. 'But we can use him. Have you sent our soldiers to man the peaks on the hills surrounding the city?'

'Yes, Dada. Done already. I have also set up a courier system from the heights to warn us of any sneak Lankan land attacks. Our ship is not too far from here. We can make a quick getaway if Raavan tries anything underhand.'

Bharat nodded. He was a careful commander. 'All right, then. Send a messenger and get the Lankan turncoat here.'

— JF J5D —

'We have come to take your leave, princess. It is time,' said Raavan.

Raavan and Kumbhakarna had arrived in Ashok Vatika dressed in the uniforms the Lankans wore when they went to war: black *dhotis* and *angvastrams*. The *angvastram* was wrapped around their nose and mouth, like a mask. They stood at a distance from Sita, who had just finished her breakfast.

She frowned. She hadn't heard the news. It was only a day since the disease had been discovered.

Kumbhakarna turned to a lady physician standing behind him. She too had her *angvastram* wrapped around her nose and mouth. She bowed low, holding in place a bag slung over her shoulder.

Sita stepped back instinctively. 'What's going on?'

Raavan looked at the doctor. 'Step back.'

The physician took a few steps backwards.

'Out of earshot,' hissed Raavan.

The doctor turned around and ran back a few more steps.

Raavan looked at Sita. 'It's for your protection, princess.'

'From what?' asked Sita.

'Princess, we have been struck by another flu pandemic,' said Kumbhakarna. 'This one is dangerous. It seems to be hitting the older ones hard.'

'We have enough Malayaputra medicine for now,' said Raavan. 'But we need to prioritise its use for the army. And for you. My army cannot fight if it is difficult for them to even breathe. And I cannot meet Vedavati in the land of the ancestors if I allow you to die before your time.'

Sita stepped back in horror. 'Your primary duty is towards your citizens.'

'We have enough for the first round of medicine for them,' answered Raavan, expecting this objection from Sita. 'The next round for the citizens will be needed two weeks later. I am hoping you will convince Guru Vishwamitra to send some more medicine by then. But to convince him, you need to remain alive.'

'Why does this plague keep hitting Lanka? It doesn't occur in the rest of India so much.'

'Perhaps I will do research on that in my next life. For now, we need to ensure that you are safe. Please take the medicine.'

Sita smiled and nodded.

Kumbhakarna turned towards the physician in the distance. And gestured for her to come forward.

The doctor began to walk towards them.

Raavan snapped. 'Move. Move. Move!' he boomed.

The physician broke into a run. As she came close, Raavan sneered, 'Are we waiting for the next monsoon season?'

'My apologies, Your Highness,' said the doctor.

'Give the medicine to the princess.'

The doctor had made the medicine paste already. She quickly opened her cloth bag, unlocked the container and, using a fresh spoon, offered the medicine to Sita. Sita swallowed the bitter medicine and the doctor quickly locked the container. The medicine could not be exposed to the elements.

'*Jai Rishi Chyawan*,' whispered the doctor.

Glory to Rishi Chyawan.

It was well-known that this Malayaputra medicine had been formulated by the great Rishi Chyawan in ancient times. In his honour, the medicine was sometimes called *Chyawanprash*, the *medicine of Chyawan*.

'*Jai Rishi Chyawan*,' repeated everyone.

'Leave the medicine here please, respected doctor,' said Kumbhakarna.

The doctor immediately placed it on the table and turned towards Sita. 'You have to take this medicine once a—'

Sita bowed low in respect, folded her hands into a *namaste* and said softly, 'I know the dosage, respected physician. Thank you so much for all your help.'

The doctor smiled and stepped back.

Raavan pinned his eyes on the doctor. She immediately twirled around and retreated to a safe distance. Out of earshot.

'Be sure to get a lot more of this medicine for the entire city, princess,' said Kumbhakarna. 'Guru Vishwamitra will not deny you.'

'I will,' promised Sita. 'Your citizens will not die from this disease.'

Kumbhakarna smiled. 'I know you will honour your word.'

'I have another request,' said Raavan.

'Tell me,' said Sita.

'I have packed off my son Indrajit to Bali, along with my uncle Mareech. To sort a trade dispute, they have been told ...' Raavan smiled as he said this, impressed that he had managed to fool his son and uncle to save their lives. 'They will return in a few weeks. Everything will be over by then. Please ensure that your husband Ram does not oppose Indrajit's ascension to the throne of Lanka. He will be a good king.'

Sita thought it unlikely that Indrajit had left for Bali. She suspected that he would fight alongside Raavan. And he would not aspire for a noble death, but victory in battle. However, if Indrajit survived the battle, she would ensure that the capable and *dharmic* son of Raavan became king of Lanka.

'I promise, Raavanji,' said Sita.

'Give my son this letter from me,' said Raavan, handing over a sealed scroll to Sita.

'I will,' said Sita, accepting the letter.

Raavan smiled. There was nothing more to be said. Except goodbye. The final goodbye.

'Are you leaving today?' asked Sita.

'Within a few hours, actually,' said Raavan. 'Your husband and his army have reached Gokarna. They should be within sight of Onguiaahra in a few days.'

Sita nodded. In all probability this was her last meeting with Raavan and Kumbhakarna. She had enjoyed her conversations with them, discovering so much about her mother, learning so many things. They had forged a bond of friendship.

She folded her hands together into a *namaste* and bowed low towards Raavan, showing respect to the man he was becoming. Instead of the monster he had been.

Raavan smiled and raised his right hand from a distance. '*Akhand saubhagyavati bhav*,' said Raavan, blessing Sita with the traditional invocation. *May her husband always be alive and by her side.*

A generous blessing, from one who was about to battle her husband.

He may have lived badly. But he will die well.

—ᒍᖴ ᒐ⁵ᗡ—

'*Namaste*, great prince,' said Vibhishan, as he sauntered in with cultivated confidence into the chamber. Bharat and Lakshman were waiting for him.

'*Namaste*, noble Vibhishan,' said Bharat with a winsome smile.

Bharat gestured to his soldiers to wait outside. They saluted the prince of Ayodhya and left. Vibhishan was alone with the brothers.

Vibhishan looked at Lakshman with a friendly smile, folding his hands into a *namaste*. 'This meeting is taking place in much more fortuitous circumstances than the earlier one, Prince Lakshman.'

They had last met in Panchavati, where things had speedily devolved into a knife fight. Lakshman was convinced that that particular series of events had in fact triggered this war. He could not have fathomed that the war was inevitable, regardless of what had transpired in Panchavati.

Lakshman grunted and perfunctorily brought his hands together.

Vibhishan let the insult pass. He turned to Bharat. 'Will not the virtuous King Ram join us, Prince Bharat?'

'Why don't you speak with us first?' Bharat spoke in a dulcet voice. 'And then we will decide what to do next.'

'I do not intend to assassinate your commander, Prince Bharat,' said Vibhishan, attempting a feeble joke as he preened with self-delight.

Bharat suppressed an amused grin. This joker actually thought he could kill Ram.

Never confront a fool with his stupidity, though. It only incites a cycle of ego-driven, unproductive counter-reactions. Praising the 'intelligence' and leveraging the self-satisfaction helps further one's cause.

'We trust you completely, Prince Vibhishan,' said Bharat. 'But we also know your fearsome valour. I'm sure you will understand that it's wise for us to err on the side of caution. The king must be protected in a game of chess.'

'I understand, Prince Bharat. Perhaps I would have done the same in your position.'

'Thank you, Prince Vibhishan,' said Bharat. 'Now, you had sent a message that you have some information to share.'

Vibhishan smiled, clearly thrilled by his own brilliance. 'Not just information … I have come to provide assistance.'

Lakshman could barely suppress his mirth. *This imbecile will help us against his formidable brother, Raavan, is it?!*

But he had been given strict instructions by Bharat to keep quiet. So, he kept quiet.

'Assistance, brave prince?' asked Bharat, feigning intrigue.

'Perhaps the better word would be a trade-off.'

'Yes, yes, a trade-off between equals.'

'Yes, of course,' said Vibhishan, preening some more. 'A fair trade-off. Victory for your brother, Emperor Ram, and the throne of Lanka for me.'

Bharat smiled. 'Sounds fair. Courageous even. But what are you offering? Besides yourself, of course …'

Vibhishan looked at Lakshman, a proud smile spread across his face. He looked back at Bharat. 'I bring the keys to Onguiaahra.'

Bharat leaned forward. Genuinely interested now. And hence, silent.

'You do know of the great river fort of Onguiaahra,' said Vibhishan.

Bharat nodded. *Yes.*

'It has never been conquered. It is impossible to conquer. And without control over Onguiaahra, your ships cannot sail farther up the Amban Ganga – the tributary of Mahaweli Ganga – and get close to the port of Sigiriya. And your army cannot march through the dense forests of Lanka. They will be hopelessly lost. They will die. The Amban Ganga River is the only path. And Onguiaahra blocks it resolutely.'

'I am aware of this, Prince Vibhishan,' said Bharat. 'What are you offering?'

'Onguiaahra cannot be taken with a direct assault. It is impossible. I will share the maps and designs of the fort with you.'

Bharat had already procured the maps of Onguiaahra through his spies. He knew that a direct assault was pointless. Siege specialists hold that every fort has some flaws, some weaknesses. But try as he might, Bharat could not divine any flaws in Onguiaahra's design. The topography around the citadel, and its skilful use by the fort builders, made it impregnable. No invader had ever breached it.

'Are you saying that your elder brother made a mistake in the fort design?' asked Bharat.

'No,' answered Vibhishan. 'My elder brother made a different mistake. He trusted the wrong person.'

Bharat maintained a deadpan expression. 'Carry on.'

'My brother is an extremely suspicious man. He distrusts even his own army. And he understands the importance of Onguiaahra. As long as Onguiaahra holds, Sigiriya is safe. So, he didn't leave Onguiaahra in the hands of the local commander.'

'And have you brought over the commander?'

Vibhishan shook his head. 'No. The commander – Dhumraksha – is loyal to Lanka. He is a ruthless and fierce warrior. But since Raavan dada didn't trust him completely, he instructed that a secret underground passage be built without the knowledge of Dhumraksha, leading into the fort's rear embankments. In fact, two secret underground passages. One which opens downriver in the direction of Gokarna, and another upriver, towards Sigiriya.'

Bharat kept the excitement off his face. 'I guess he wanted to ensure that if Dhumraksha turned, Raavan could quickly enter the fort in secret and regain control.'

Vibhishan nodded.

'And how do you know about these passages?'

'I built them,' said Vibhishan.

Bharat nodded. 'Take us into Onguiaahra and the throne of Lanka is yours.'

Vibhishan smiled. 'I know you will honour your word, great prince. But can I also hear this from the emperor of Ayodhya, Ram?'

Lakshman burst out in anger, 'Do you doubt the words of a prince of Ayodhya? Don't you know that we Ayodhyans would rather die than break our promise?'

Bharat glanced at his brother. 'Relax, Lakshman. I understand why Prince Vibhishan wants reassurance.' Bharat looked at Vibhishan. 'I will issue a proclamation, sealed by my brother Ram himself, acknowledging you as the rightful king of Lanka. Good enough?'

Vibhishan folded his hands together into a *namaste*. 'More than good enough, Prince Bharat. You are fair and just.'

'And you will stay with us as our honoured guest till we enter Onguiaahra,' continued Bharat.

Bharat did not trust this man.

Vibhishan frowned. 'But I am used to comfort.'

'And you shall be very comfortable, I assure you.'

'All right,' said Vibhishan. 'I shall be your guest till we take Onguiaahra.'

The deal had been sealed.

Vibhishan looked out the window, at the Ayodhyan ships anchored in the Gokarna Bay. He was also aware of the many vessels stationed outside the bay, in the open ocean. He turned to Bharat.

'I hope you have enough soldiers, Prince Bharat,' said Vibhishan.

'The Lankan army may not be what it was, but my brother Raavan will feel no fear. For he knows that two hundred thousand soldiers stand between him and defeat.'

Bharat smiled. 'We have one hundred and sixty thousand soldiers. And they will feel no fear. For they know that Ram stands between them and defeat.'

Chapter 18

'You may need to wait, Lord Hanuman and Lord Arishtanemi,' said Angad.

It was the day after the massacre of the leftover Lankan battalion at Ketheeswaram. Ram had been extremely angry about the attack; they were incapacitated soldiers and this was against the rules of honourable warfare, he had said. But he also knew he could not punish the Malayaputras. Not only was it their right to seek vengeance, he also knew that he needed the fifteen thousand Malayaputra soldiers; more so, their elephant corps. Sometimes, a general must tolerate the excesses of his men for the greater good of the war. Ram had swallowed this bitter pill.

Arishtanemi and Hanuman had settled near a beachhead at the Lankan mainland, planning stockades as protection for Ram's army when it would land. Leaving their men to complete this work, the duo had rowed across the Dhanushkodi straits and returned to the Pamban island, where Shatrughan was supervising final preparations to build the bridge between Mannar and Pamban. The building material was being transported from the Indian mainland by the Ayodhya army. They forded the shallow sea flats on foot. Over three hundred elephants from the Malayaputra and Vaanar corps made the task easier and quicker than had been originally envisaged.

'How much longer will the *puja* take?' asked Arishtanemi.

Hanuman, Arishtanemi, Angad and Naarad stood a short distance from the spot where Ram and Shatrughan had begun a Rudraabhishek *prayer and worship ceremony*, conducted by their *guru* Vashishtha. The *puja*, dedicated to the previous Mahadev Lord Rudra, was usually conducted to ward off negative energy. There was one other reason. Lord Rudra was one of the greatest warriors the world has ever seen, and they sought his blessings before a war. The *puja* was being conducted on a flat promontory-type sandy patch of land that extended in a north-easterly direction on Pamban Island. The bridge would begin from the south-east end of the island, two kilometres from here. Years from now, a great temple to Lord Rudra would be built on this spot. It would be known as the temple of *Ram's God* or *Rameshwaram*.

'This is not the standard Rudraabhishek *puja*, Arishtanemiji,' answered Naarad. 'Guru Vashishtha began it two hours back. It should be ending soon.'

'Hmm,' answered Hanuman.

'Yes, we have had our medicine,' said Vashishtha, in answer to Arishtanemi.

'Good,' said Arishtanemi. 'This disease is dangerous.'

The Malayaputra medicine had been administered to the Ayodhyans, Vayuputras, Malayaputras and Vaanars within the day. The benefit of disciplined armies: soldiers follow orders and do not question.

'Do we have enough medicine for the next few months?' asked Shatrughan. 'This campaign may last a long time. Or should we delay the bridge construction till we have enough medicine?'

Ram shook his head. 'We cannot delay the construction. Bharat is already at Gokarna. He has to start sailing up the Mahaweli Ganga soon, or else he risks making Raavan suspicious. We cannot assume that the king of Lanka is a fool. Raavan's army is already marching towards the Amban Ganga. He is preparing for a traditional naval battle. We need to distract his army at Onguiaahra in the east, so that no Lankan expects our main army to be marching in from the west.'

'I agree,' said Vashishtha, who had also read the coded message from Bharat that had arrived by bird courier. 'Bharat has made an alliance with Vibhishan. Raavan's younger brother will guide Bharat's army through a secret passage into the Onguiaahra citadel. Once Bharat controls Onguiaahra, he can easily inflict severe damage on Raavan's navy. The king of Lanka will be forced to retreat. Then Bharat can move his army up the Amban Ganga River and march to Sigiriya from the east, while we move in from the west. Having said that, Vibhishan could be a double agent. Or he might ultimately help whoever he thinks is winning. If Bharat delays his advance, Vibhishan is likely to think we have run into problems with our invasion, and he may switch sides again.'

'So, net-net, we must start building the bridge tomorrow,' said Shatrughan.

'Precisely,' agreed Hanuman.

Angad spoke up. 'Prince Vibhishan reminds me of that ancient code for a king. Avoid both trustworthy fools and untrustworthy experts. Raavan has trustworthy counsel in Kumbhakarna and Indrajit. But he doesn't listen to them.'

'Vibhishan is neither a trustworthy fool nor an untrustworthy expert,' said Naarad. 'He is the worst combination: an untrustworthy fool. Why Raavan even allowed that imbecile to stay with him in Lanka is a mystery.'

'That's not our problem,' said Shatrughan. 'Our problem is that we will soon need more medicine. This could be a long campaign. Can it be arranged, Arishtanemiji?'

'I'm conscious of this need, Shatrughan,' said Arishtanemi. 'I have already asked a group of Malayaputras to travel to Agastyakootam. They are leaving tomorrow morning. I've asked them to row down south along the coast, and then up the River Thamiravaruni. They should be back in a week, at most.'

'That's good news,' said Vashishtha.

'Can we get a month's supply for the city of Sigiriya as well?' asked Ram. 'Ayodhya will pay for those medicines.'

Arishtanemi's eyes widened in shock. 'You want to help the enemy?!'

'Just the citizens,' answered Ram. 'They have done nothing wrong.'

Ram was upset enough over having been forced to countenance the killing of incapacitated Lankan soldiers at Ketheeswaram. He would not allow ordinary non-combatant citizens to suffer.

'Don't do that, great Vishnu,' said Naarad. 'Know that the ends justify the means. Raavan must be destroyed for the good of India. Let's not lose sight of that goal.'

'The end exists only in our minds,' said Ram. 'Time never stops. So, there is no real end, is there? There is only the path. All of us are stuck with the means, for we will never reach the real end. Therefore, we have to think very carefully about the means. Innocent non-combatants cannot be killed, even if it is by omission and not commission. That is *adharma*.'

'But you just spoke of laying siege to Sigiriya, even stopping their food supply,' said Vashishtha. 'Isn't that against the citizens? Aren't those questionable means?'

'I'm hoping the siege and blockade will encourage the citizens to revolt against King Raavan. We'll go slow. The citizens won't die. They will be given every opportunity to help themselves by rebelling against their ruler. But if we don't give them the medicine for this disease, they will die. And soon. There is a difference between squeezing enemy citizens to incite a rebellion and directly pushing them into the jaws of death. The first is a legitimate means of war. The second is a war crime.'

'But Raavan could divert the medicine to his army. It would sustain his soldiers longer,' countered Hanuman.

'We will catapult messages into Sigiriya, informing the citizens that we have given the Malayaputra medicine for their use. And that Raavan is diverting it to his soldiers. That, too, will encourage disaffection. A siege works well when the citizens of a besieged city rebel against their own lords and army. We must get Sigiriya to rebel.'

Everyone kept quiet. Only Naarad sported a hint of a smile.

'I know what you are thinking,' said Ram. 'That I am naïve. But I am not. We will follow *dharma* by giving medicine to the citizens of Sigiriya. And our generosity towards King Raavan's citizens will raise agitators in his city. This is *dharma* as well as good battle strategy.'

'Do you remember what Raavan's army did in Mumbadevi?' asked Naarad. 'Let me remind you. The peaceful Devendrars were burnt to the last man, woman and child. The commander who led that brutal invasion – Prahast – wasn't punished. Instead, he was promoted. This is what you are facing. This is what your enemy is like. Raavan may just allow his entire citizenry to die. You are rationalising your need to be ethical by convincing yourself that it's also good battle strategy. But your enemy has no ethics. Raavan only wants to win. That is the difference between you and him. Between us and them.'

'Yes. That is the difference,' said Ram. 'And that difference must be maintained. We will win. But we will win the right way. We must set an example for a better India.'

Naarad smiled, keeping his thoughts to himself. *I may just be on the side of Good this time ... Let's hope we win ...*

'All right,' said Arishtanemi. 'I will tell my soldiers to get more medicine from Agastyakootam. Enough for the citizens of Sigiriya as well.'

—◁⊦ ◁⸍⸝D—

The day finally dawned.

Vishwakarma, the God of the Architects and Engineers, was propitiated in a solemn ceremony. Lord Varun, the God of Water and the Seas, was also ritually invoked. The former was to bestow diligence and expertise, the latter to allow their work to flow unhindered through His realm. The material for the first phase of construction had reached the south-eastern part of Pamban Island. The nadir of the low tide would soon be upon them. Perfect timing.

The initial batch of elephants and soldiers had been trained and deployed; the workers would be rotated in short shifts of four hours each, for this was hard work.

Four mahouts on elephants had been tasked with marking the northern and southern boundaries of the bridge that was being built west to east. It was a low-tech, effective method designed by Shatrughan.

Two elephants stood in line in the shallow water while their mahouts held a rope at two ends, which served to represent the northern edge of the starting point of the bridge. Ram and Shatrughan stood some distance away, observing man and animal working in tandem. Another set of two elephants with their mahouts had been placed in an exact mirror formation, three and a half kilometres to the south. The ropes held by the two sets of mahouts represented the northernmost and southernmost edge of the breadth of the bridge. All building activities would be conducted within the rope boundaries which curved gently, creating the aerodynamic – rather, hydrodynamic – bridge that Shatrughan had envisioned.

'Dada,' said Shatrughan, handing a Platygyra coral stone brick to his elder brother. Ram looked at the brick. His name had been carved into it on one side. On the other side was engraved the number '1'. 'Drop this into the water and let the construction begin. This will be our first offering to Lord Varun.'

Ram looked at the brick and then at Shatrughan. He took a few steps, bent and picked up a sharp stone. He began carving a few more words on the Platygyra brick. Shatrughan leaned over to see what his brother had written.

Ram had added the names of his brothers. Bharat, next to his own. And Lakshman and Shatrughan below.

'I don't work alone,' said Ram. 'I am nothing without my brothers.'

Shatrughan smiled and touched his brother's arm.

Ram flipped the stone over. 1 became 4.

'Hold the stone with me,' said Ram.

Shatrughan reached out and held the brick. Then the brothers walked into the sea.

They whispered the chant of ancient Indian mariners.

Sham No Varunah.

May Varun, the God of Water and the Seas, be auspicious unto us.

They bent low and dropped the brick into the water. It floated on the surface, swaying gently with the waves.

The waves did not push the stone back to the beach.

Lord Varun had accepted the offering.

Ram nodded. 'Let's begin.'

'Tell him to wait,' Bharat ordered his attendant.

The attendant saluted and left the room.

The construction of the bridge had begun off the western coast of the island of Lanka two days back. Of course, no Lankan on the eastern part of the island had an inkling of this.

Bharat and Lakshman were at their temporary palace quarters in Gokarna. They had spent the previous night in the Ayodhya royal ship. Gokarna was still convinced that Ram and Shatrughan were on board. The Ayodhya ships had moved in the night from Gokarna Bay and had anchored themselves, along with the rest of their fleet, in the open ocean. Bharat and Lakshman had returned in the morning with a fresh set of orders for their soldiers. And information to gather.

Vibhishan had arrived unannounced. Bharat had decided he could wait.

'Any news, Dada?' asked Lakshman.

Two days back, Bharat had ordered a few soldiers to take a quick cutter boat and row up the Mahaweli Ganga to the Onguiaahra River citadel. They had been told to strictly avoid all confrontation and being seen. Their job was to check if the Lankan army and river-navy were on the other side of the choke point at Onguiaahra.

Bharat looked at Lakshman and nodded. 'Raavan has taken the bait. He has brought almost his entire army to Onguiaahra. They are all aboard ships on the Amban Ganga, at the place before it meets the Mahaweli Ganga.'

Lakshman clenched his right fist and banged it into his open left palm. 'Fantastic. We've pulled them here. Ram dada and Shatrughan have a clear field on their side.'

'Hmm. And we'll have to keep them here.'

'We'll not just keep them here, Dada. We'll destroy them here. Ram dada will not waste his time battling. He can just march triumphant into Sigiriya.'

Bharat smiled fondly. It had been so long. He had almost forgotten what Lakshman was like, having spent close to fourteen years with Shatrughan. Lakshman and Shatrughan were like chalk and cheese despite being twins. Shatrughan was calm, cerebral and pragmatic, while Lakshman was aggressive, impulsive and short-tempered. But both had hearts of gold.

Fierce confidence is highly effective in a warrior but oftentimes, it is counter-productive in a general, who must be realistic. He must think two steps ahead of his enemy, and fight only when he knows he can win.

A good general does not let his soldiers die in vain.

Bharat was a good general.

'Let's see, Lakshman,' said Bharat. 'Our main aim is to hold Raavan here as long as possible. If we can give his army some body-blows, all the better.'

Their attention was suddenly diverted by some loud explosive sounds. Lakshman looked out of the window. 'It's begun, Dada.'

Bharat walked over to the window. From the high perch of their palace, he had a clear view of Gokarna Bay.

'Lakshman, did you deliver the *hundi* to the guilds? To purchase the Gokarna merchant ships?' asked Bharat.

'Yes, Dada, just as you ordered.'

The Gokarna merchant ships now belonged to Ayodhya. And all them were lashed together and anchored at the bay centre. Fire raged through the fleet now, aided by some wax and oil that had been liberally poured onto the decks. Many ships had the secondary square-rigged masts open to half height – cloth with oil would catch fire quicker. Bharat had carefully planned the details. A combination of charcoal and saltpetre – used in fireworks – had been placed in the cargo holds of some of the bigger merchant ships in the knotted fleet. One of those explosive mixes had just erupted.

A spectacle of hellish flames. For the benefit of Raavan's spies.

Bharat could guess at the kind of reports that would travel to the Lankan high command. The Ayodhya commanders were covering their backs. Preventing any likelihood of merchant ships launching a surprise attack on the Ayodhyan navy from the rear. The inference was obvious: the attack via the Mahaweli Ganga River was imminent.

'You don't think it's a little too obvious? The very public burning?' asked Lakshman. 'We could have just sunk the ships. Raavan could become suspicious.'

Bharat opened his eyes wide in amusement. 'Lakshman, my darling brother, are *you* talking about subtlety?'

Lakshman laughed and slapped his elder brother on the back.

'I want Raavan to think that we are angry. Fire of vengeance and all that sort of thing,' continued Bharat. 'I want him to think that we have allowed emotions to cloud our judgement. It's best that the enemy underestimates you in battle.'

'Hmm ...'

'So, when Vibhishan comes in this time, let loose a bit. Let him see that you are angry. Hint that so is Ram dada. And I am the only one holding you people back with some dose of realism.'

Lakshman nodded. 'Do you think our conversations with Vibhishan are reaching Raavan?'

'I have no doubt they are. Maybe not through Vibhishan himself. But through others here. Vibhishan just needs to be a little loose-tongued with someone he thinks is a friend in this city. The heart of an efficient government is a good spy network that keeps the ruler one step ahead of everyone else. And Raavan is an efficient ruler. He has built all this from scratch. We may hate the guy, but we must respect his abilities.' Bharat turned towards the door and spoke loudly to the doorman on the other side. 'Let Prince Vibhishan in.'

Vibhishan sauntered in with affected nonchalance. Arms stretched out to accommodate non-existent biceps in a reed-thin body. *'Boils under his armpits, apparently ...'* Bharat remembered Lakshman's laconic remark and smiled.

Vibhishan had raised his game with his clothes, though. He wore a purple silk dhoti and *angvastram*. Purple was the most expensive dye in the world, the colour of royalty. His jewellery, too, was no longer understated; extravagant gold and ruby-encrusted earrings, a delicately filigreed necklace and a diamond line bracelet encased in gold.

Clearly, he was already seeing himself as a king.

'Welcome, Your Highness,' said Bharat, leaning into Vibhishan's weak character with the term of address.

Vibhishan preened pretentiously. 'What a pleasure to meet you again, Prince Bharat.' Vibhishan turned to Lakshman and executed an elaborately extravagant *namaste*. Lakshman nodded cursorily. Vibhishan, as always, ignored the insult. 'So, when do we sail, Prince Bharat? Now that you have covered your rear flanks by making a bonfire of the merchant ships ... Which is a brilliant move, might I add.'

Bharat's answer was simple and pithy. 'Soon, Your Highness.'

'We should burn this entire city down, Dada,' said Lakshman suddenly, anger blazing in his eyes, 'and not just the ships. Lanka will pay for messing with the Sapt Sindhu royals.'

Vibhishan looked at Lakshman, alarmed. Sigiriya may be the resplendent capital of Lanka, but the port city of Gokarna was the engine that drove Lankan prosperity. Sigiriya may well be destroyed, but a ravaged Gokarna would be the end of Lanka.

Bharat raised his palm as if advocating calm. 'Lakshman …'

'Ram dada is right, Bharat dada,' said Lakshman, his face red with rage. 'We need to teach them a lesson. I don't know why you—'

'Enough!' said Bharat loudly and firmly.

Lakshman fell silent.

'Leave me alone with Prince Vibhishan,' said Bharat.

'Dada …'

'Which part of my order did you not understand, Lakshman?' growled Bharat.

Lakshman glared at Bharat for a few seconds and then stormed out of the chamber.

'I'm sorry that you had to see that, Your Highness,' said Bharat to Vibhishan.

Vibhishan was too stunned to say anything. He had witnessed Lakshman's temper once, in Panchavati. But it was shocking to discover that even the serene Ram was enraged; angry enough to want to destroy an innocent city like Gokarna, it would seem. Perhaps it was understandable. Sita was his wife, after all. For a brief moment, Vibhishan wondered if he had made a mistake in seeking Ayodhya's help. But Raavan probably knew about his treachery by now. His boat, too, had burned. There was no going back; not for him. He would either sink or swim with Bharat now.

'We must keep our alliance strong, Prince Bharat,' said Vibhishan, his voice almost a whine. The earlier insouciance had disappeared. 'Otherwise too many innocents will die.'

'I know,' said Bharat. 'I am a practical man. I want to win the war with as few casualties as possible among my soldiers. Our friendship can ensure that.'

'Yes, Prince Bharat, it certainly can.'

Bharat reached over to his table and handed a rolled-up scroll to Vibhishan. 'And as a token of our friendship ...'

Vibhishan guessed what the scroll was, but he still couldn't contain his excitement as he rolled it open. A royal Ayodhyan decree, marked with the seal of the emperor of the Sapt Sindhu, Ram. It formally acknowledged Vibhishan as the king of Lanka and committed Ayodhya through all means, including military, to placing Vibhishan upon the Sigiriya throne.

His heart skipped a beat. *I'll show that ... that monster ... I'm unworthy, he said ... I'll show ...*

Vibhishan's train of thought was interrupted by Bharat. 'Now ... I will need a token of friendship from you in return, Your Highness.'

'Anything,' said a grateful Vibhishan.

'I'd initially thought that you could accompany Lakshman and guide him through the secret tunnel into the Onguiaahra fort.'

Vibhishan visibly recoiled at the thought of being stuck in the thick of battle, not least of all with the hot-tempered Lakshman.

'But,' continued Bharat, 'seeing the emotions that are coursing through my brother's veins – all my brothers, really – I would much rather send Lakshman and his battalion without you.'

'That may be wise, Prince Bharat,' said Vibhishan, his shoulders sinking with visible relief. 'The conquest of Onguiaahra is a job for butchers, not for kings.'

Bharat struggled to keep the contempt off his face. 'Yes, of course, Your Highness.' He pulled up a detailed map of the course of the Mahaweli Ganga and the Amban Ganga on which Sigiriya and Gokarna were clearly marked. Then he picked up some sheaves of papyrus and a graphite pencil. 'I will need you to mark the entire secret passage.'

'Of course,' said Vibhishan. He took the map, the papyrus leaves and the graphite pencil from Bharat.

'Please mark all indicators and cues to identify the entrance to the passage as well. And also put down all the features of the tunnels that Lakshman would need to know to march quickly through it. The length, breadth, height, airflow holes, lighting holes, floor construction and evenness, and so on. I want him to "see" the passage in his mind before he enters it. You can make separate notes on the papyrus sheets.'

Vibhishan was already at work. 'I designed and built the tunnels, Prince Bharat. Mind you, I'm a trained architect and cartographer. I'll make the map and instructions foolproof.'

'I have no doubt you will.' Bharat smiled.

Chapter 19

'You missed your true calling, bro!' Bharat laughed.

'I put up a good show, didn't I?' gloated Lakshman, with a proud half-smile.

After Vibhishan had left the royal chamber, Bharat had sent for Lakshman and ordered that dinner be served.

'Actually, I take back the compliment,' teased Bharat. 'You were not acting. You were just being yourself!'

Lakshman guffawed as he tore a piece of *roti* and used it to gather the vegetable on the plate. 'Has he given you proper maps?' asked Lakshman.

'Hmm,' said Bharat, chewing his food slowly.

'Awesome.'

'But he is a sly one, this Vibhishan.'

'That I've always told you. But what brought on this sudden epiphany?'

Bharat stopped mid-action, leaving his piece of *roti* on the vegetable, his eyes opening wide in mock shock. 'Epiphany?! Where in Lord Indra's name did you learn this word?'

'From Shatrughan, of course?!' Lakshman laughed. 'Why? Did I use the word wrong?'

'No, no … Epiphany is a sudden and great revelation or realisation. And you used it sarcastically. So, you used it right, my brother …'

Lakshman smiled beatifically, extended his left arm above his head, bent his elbow and patted himself on the back. 'Well done, Lakshman. Well done.' He laughed uproariously.

Bharat laughed along. 'I've missed your antics, you clown! We've been apart too long.'

'Yes, we've been apart too long …' Lakshman echoed.

'Getting back to the tunnels,' said Bharat. 'Apparently no one in the Onguiaahra citadel is aware of them. Neither is the Lanka administration nor, of course, the ordinary people. Only Raavan, Kumbhakarna, their maternal uncle Mareech, Raavan's son Indrajit, Vibhishan and the workers who worked on the tunnels.'

'The workers did not talk about it with anyone? Strange.'

'Dead men don't talk. The workers were killed after the construction. To the last man.'

'Woah … That is …'

'… ruthless, and paranoid,' Bharat completed Lakshman's words. 'But also efficient. Very Raavan. That's why almost no one knows about these tunnels.'

'But why did Raavan use Vibhishan? That man is shifty, clearly a sneaky weasel.'

'Apparently, Vibhishan has the best architecture and engineering skills in the Lankan royal family. Or so he professes.

He claims to have designed the tunnels and supervised the construction.'

'Then he can give us the best information on the tunnels.'

'It gets better. We have to assume that Raavan knows that Vibhishan has joined us. His spy network in Gokarna is very good. He would logically deduce that Vibhishan has revealed the existence of the tunnels to us. Obviously, then, Raavan will ambush us in those passages or he will collapse the tunnel at the Gokarna side so that we cannot use it.'

Lakshman nodded. It was the most logical line of reasoning.

'But,' continued Bharat, 'we have another route open to us.'

'Which one?'

'Vibhishan must have planned his betrayal over a long time. He built yet another hidden passage into Onguiaahra from downriver, as a back-up to the back-up.'

Lakshman started laughing. 'How many bloody tunnels go into that citadel?! Is it a fort or a waystation?!'

Bharat laughed.

'So, anyway,' said Lakshman, pulling himself together, 'there is one more tunnel leading into Onguiaahra ... which Raavan, Kumbhakarna and Indrajit are not aware of. Only Vibhishan knows of it.'

'Vibhishan and the workers who built the tunnel.'

'The workers that are dead.'

'Yes.'

'We really got lucky when we snared this Lankan traitor.'

'Vibhishan would have gone to any credible enemy of his brother,' said Bharat. 'When he built this tunnel, Ayodhya had no reason to declare war on Lanka. Vibhishan was waiting for anyone who would pick a fight with King Raavan.'

'I guess Raavan sealed his fate the day he decided to trust Vibhishan.'

'Actually, he sealed his fate the day he decided to not trust his battalion in Onguiaahra. And in trying to cover that risk, he opened the possibility for us finding an easy route to defeating him.'

'Hmm.'

'Shatrughan told me something once. Something a writer from the far west, beyond Greece – someone called Fontaine – had said. "A person often meets his fate on the road he took to avoid it".'

Lakshman smiled. 'Yeah ... And we'll lead Raavan to the end of his road.'

—J∓ ⅃⁊Ɔ—

Four days had passed since the bridge construction on the north-western side of the island of Lanka had begun. On the north-eastern side of the island, at the southern end of Gokarna Bay, Lakshman and Bharat stood on their lead ship, ready to sail up the Mahaweli Ganga River. They had received a messenger bird informing them that Shatrughan had constructed more than half the bridge. Three days from now the main contingent of the Ayodhyan army would march on to Lankan ground, and rush towards Sigiriya.

'Shouldn't we meet Emperor Ram before we sail out?' asked Vibhishan.

Vibhishan stood alongside the brothers. They were on the bow upper deck, hands on the balustrade, looking at the river extending endlessly ahead. The vessel was poised at the mouth of the Mahaweli Ganga, where the river emptied into the Gokarna Bay. Bharat had organised the fleet in a convoy of two abreast, extending behind them in a long double line. Four hundred ships in two hundred rows of two vessels each, one behind the other. The ships extended way beyond the bay into the Indian Ocean. An onlooker on the banks at the mouth of the river could spend four hours watching the entire convoy of the Ayodhyan navy from the first ship to the last sail by; the fleet formation was that long. It was a show of strength from the Sapt Sindhu military. A shock-and-awe campaign to cow down the Lankans into submission.

'Bharat dada and I met him this morning,' said Lakshman in answer to Vibhishan. 'Why do you want to meet him? What do you want to tell him that you cannot tell us?'

'It's nothing like that, Prince Lakshman,' said Vibhishan. He was smiling, his standard response to the constant hostility from Lakshman. 'I just thought that, since I am an ally, I should meet the leader of our army before we begin our invasion of Lanka.'

Lakshman's face exhibited intense hostility. 'You are not an ally. You are a collaborator. It is a trading relationship between us. We get Onguiaahra. You get the Lanka throne. Don't try to be something you are not.'

'Lakshman …' said Bharat, pretending exasperation.

'Dada, I am listening to you and following your directions,' said Lakshman. 'So is Ram dada. But tell your friend to know his limits.'

'Lakshman,' growled Bharat. 'Leave me alone with King Vibhishan. Leave.'

'He's not a king yet,' sneered Lakshman.

Bharat stepped towards Lakshman. 'Are you suggesting that we Suryavanshis break our word of honour?'

Lakshman fell silent.

'Leave us alone,' ordered Bharat. 'And that's an order. Go, do your job. Let's start sailing up the Mahaweli Ganga.'

Lakshman saluted like a subordinate following an order from his general and not a loving brother, and left. Bharat made a mental note to compliment Lakshman on his histrionics later. Lakshman was clearly enjoying this.

Bharat turned to Vibhishan. 'I'm sorry, Your Highness. Not all my siblings are happy about taking your help. They would much rather win without subterfuge. They want to win like warriors of the old school. But I understand that war is nasty business. We must win, with all the means at our disposal.'

'But—' began Vibhishan.

He was interrupted by a loud noise. Both turned. The lead ship horn had blasted a long hoot, which was followed by three short bursts. And the flags were raised. The convoy was too massive for orders to be conveyed through verbal commands. And sending row boats with written instructions would take too long. So, Bharat had instituted a system in which commands could be conveyed through blasts of a ship horn, accompanied by various flags atop the mainmast. Each combination of coloured flags broadcast a specific simple instruction in a code understandable only to the ship captains. The instruction being communicated right now was clear: Set sail.

Bharat looked at Vibhishan. He guessed what was transpiring in the mind of Raavan's younger brother.

'King Vibhishan,' said Bharat softly, 'I can understand what you must be thinking … *Can I trust an emperor who hates me? Will he honour his word and make me king?*'

Vibhishan remained quiet.

'My brother Ram sticks to the path of honour even if it hurts him personally. Which is why he does not want your help right now. Do you think such a man will refuse to keep his word to establish you as king? Something that he has committed in writing to you?'

Vibhishan let out a long breath. The logic was irrefutable.

'But, yes, he doesn't like you,' continued Bharat. 'He will not meet you.'

The conversation stopped as the ship began to move. The sails had been raised and the rhythmic drumbeats of the ship count-masters could be heard. A drumbeat to which the rowers synchronised their rowing. Six battalions—three each on the western and eastern banks of the Mahaweli Ganga—marched alongside the navy in lines of four abreast on the banks of the river. Their shields raised towards the forest side. Spears and swords ready. In case of surprise attacks by the Lankans.

Bharat was a careful general.

The marching soldiers served one other purpose. They provided a credible excuse for the slow movement of the Ayodhya navy up the Mahaweli Ganga River. A half-day journey would now take two days, since the boats would need to slow down and remain in alignment with the soldiers on the banks. Guarding against possible ambush attacks would not arouse suspicion. The real reason was to delay the battle at Onguiaahra as much as possible, to give Ram and Shatrughan time to build the bridge and march across.

'I'm sure Emperor Ram will like me once he knows how I have helped weaken his enemy's capacity to battle,' said Vibhishan.

'What do you mean?' asked Bharat, intrigued.

'Do you know that Sigiriya has been weakened by a plague?'

'I've heard of the flu pandemic.' Bharat did not reveal that he had received this information from a bird courier sent by Ram. He had also been sent medicines through Arishtanemi's fast cutter boats. 'And we have enough Malayaputra medicines with us. You needn't worry.'

'Oh that—I know you can manage that. There is another plague that they have been suffering from for a long time. Many years, actually. It has weakened Sigiriya and their army.'

'What is it? I don't know about this plague.'

'Most people outside Lanka don't. My brother Raavan has kept it secret for obvious reasons. And the strange thing about the plague is that it has not travelled to Gokarna. Many believe that Sigiriya is cursed. And all who live there will suffer.'

'What is it?' Bharat repeated.

'This plague is not an infection, or a curse of the Gods,' said Vibhishan, laughing softly. 'It is something that Sigiriya brought on itself.'

'What?'

'My brother wanted to supply water to people's homes.'

'So, what's the problem? I have had wells dug across Ayodhya, close to every home so that people have easy access to water.'

'No, no!' laughed Vibhishan. 'He wanted to make it even more convenient for citizens. If you dig wells, people need to maintain them. Which is inconvenient. And Raavan dada didn't want the hardened brick-type pipes you have in some Sapt Sindhu areas for obvious reasons. So, he designed what he thought was a brilliant thing: metal lead pipes. They would be easy to make. Easy to build right into homes. No leakages. Minimal maintenance required. And he could deliver water to his people. They all blessed him for it. Of course, he had me do all the hard work. I designed and built it.'

'I still don't see what the problem is.'

'Well, I discovered later that lead is not good for you.'

'What? We use lead in the Sapt Sindhu too!'

'Yes, but the Sapt Sindhu doesn't use lead in large quantities. You primarily use copper vessels and pipes. Copper is good. You use lead very sparingly. In excessive quantities, lead begins to poison and weaken you. You see, lead dissolves in water, especially the kind of water we have in Sigiriya. And everyone who drinks that water slowly starts showing signs of illness. It seems like the plague. But it is not the plague. The illness spreads gradually, over many years. Net-net, Raavan dada has been slowly poisoning himself and his beloved city.'

Vibhishan sniggered as he said this.

Bharat was shocked. 'Why didn't you save the—'

Vibhishan interrupted Bharat. 'I saved my immediate family and my mother and sister. They live in Gokarna now. But Raavan's army, which is largely based in Sigiriya, has been slowly poisoned over the years. The lead poisoning is also why they suffer more from the flu pandemic than your soldiers will. They are much much weaker than you think.'

'But … but what about the citizens of Sigiriya?'

'Collateral damage, Prince Bharat,' said Vibhishan. 'As you said, war is nasty business. So, as you can see, I have been weakening Lanka for a while. All for Emperor Ram and you. You will win easily. I have been helping you even before I met you! Once I become emperor, I will replace the lead pipes with copper pipes or some other metal. I will save the people and they will thank me for it.'

Bharat turned away and stared at the river. Trying to keep the disgust he felt for Vibhishan off his face.

Chapter 20

'Guruji?' questioned Matikaya, surprised.

Vishwamitra suppressed his irritation. *The idiot believes that his understanding is critical for solving a problem. He thinks he can improve upon a solution that I myself have conceptualised. FOOL!* Vishwamitra preferred Arishtanemi to Matikaya. Arishtanemi was intelligent enough to know when not to ask questions. Matikaya was constantly hungry for more information.

Vishwamitra had been laying out the plan for a few months now. Communicating in secret code. Through bird couriers. But now he had to send something. A large box, almost a trunk. With precious merchandise in it. Very precious. In the trunk was a weapon. A bird could obviously not carry it. And, therefore, he needed this idiot Matikaya. He could not trust anyone else. Matikaya would keep on with his questions, but he knew how to stay silent about the instructions he received from Vishwamitra. This, the formidable *guru* knew.

'Just carry this, Matikaya. And leave it at the Devagiri *ashram*. It will be picked up from there.'

'But … but the Devagiri *ashram* has been abandoned, Guruji. Nobody there. I mean …'

'Do you think it is possible that I don't know something that even you know?'

'My apologies, Guruji,' said Matikaya, folding his hands together into a penitent *namaste*.

The Saraswati was the holiest river in India. Therefore, it was held as neutral ground. It was not under any king's jurisdiction. No forts along its banks. The place was left to the sages, intellectuals, monks and mostly to Mother Nature Herself. Everyone passed these lands without let or hindrance. It was considered *adharmic* by many to even fight alongside the banks of the Saraswati.

And since nobody fought wars along the Saraswati, these lands had not been surveyed from a martial perspective. Therefore, no one understood the military significance of Devagiri. *Almost* no one.

'Just do what I tell you to do,' ordered Vishwamitra.

'Of course, Guruji,' said Matikaya, saluting smartly.

Vishwamitra turned his head. Towards the grand ParshuRamEshwar temple, the heart of the Malayaputra capital, Agastyakootam. The heart of his being.

Lord Parshu Ram, I beg you … Bless that descendant of Yayati and Sharmishtha. His sacrifice will not be in vain. It's all for Mother India.

Of course, the descendant of Yayati and Sharmishtha did not know that he was being readied as a sacrifice.

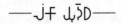

It had been six days since Shatrughan had begun constructing the bridge. They expected to touch Mannar island in a day. Thereafter, a day's march would get them to Sigiriya via the Ketheeswaram road.

The sky was an ethereal mix of a strikingly vibrant red and an unusual, melancholic purple. It was early evening and the sun was sinking into the horizon. The Sun God, Surya, had painted a stunning picture on the canvas of the sky. A parting gift to his devotees who looked up in wonder. Till he would meet them again. Next morn.

Vashishtha, Ram and Shatrughan sat on the edge of the bridge, mesmerised by the gorgeous sky.

'Rarely have I seen a construction project move exactly to plan,' Vashishtha said with a smile, looking at Shatrughan.

'Thank you, Guruji,' said Shatrughan, folding his hands together into a *namaste*.

'Have you measured—'

Shatrughan interrupted Ram. 'Yes, Dada. We have already built a little more than thirty kilometres of the bridge length. Just five kilometres more, which we will finish tomorrow. And then we will be on Mannar island. The army can cross over the day after tomorrow.'

Ram smiled. 'We will be in Sigiriya within three days.'

'Bharat and Lakshman?' asked Vashishtha.

'They are reaching Onguiaahra tonight, Guruji,' said Ram. 'They have to keep the Lankan army busy for only three more days. By then we will reach Sigiriya and the battle will be over.'

'I have been studying the plans of the Sigiriya fort system, Dada,' said Shatrughan. 'Arishtanemiji and Hanumanji shared it with me. A siege will be long and difficult. It truly is a well-designed fort. I can't see any weakness.'

'Every fort has a weakness,' said Ram.

'It appears that this one doesn't.'

'Every fort has a weakness. And do you know what Sigiriya fort's is?'

Shatrughan shook his head. *No.*

'That the defending army will be away in Onguiaahra when we arrive. That is its weakness!'

—— ⅃Ⅎ Ⴑ,ℶⅅ ——

The Lanka countryside was an unending jungle. Denser and thicker than any forest that the Ayodhyans had ever seen, including the famed Dandakaranya of peninsular India.

Lanka was a tear-drop shaped island in the Indian Ocean. Highlands and mountains ran in a north-south direction down its central spine. Placed thus, both the south-west and north-east monsoon winds precipitated plentiful rain on Lanka. Most of the Indian subcontinental mainland had six seasons, one of them being the monsoon. But Lanka had two full-blown monsoon seasons, with two inter-monsoon seasons separating them. And it rained even in the inter-monsoon period due to Lanka's proximity to the equator.

Their yearly climate was simple: Rain. Very heavy rain. Rain. Exceptionally heavy rain. And heat all year round. All dispensed upon an extraordinarily fertile land.

Perfect conditions for dense rain forests.

The forests were so impenetrable that the marching soldiers had no visibility beyond fifteen to twenty feet from the river banks into the jungles. They kept their shields raised at all times. At night, they retired to the ships and the vessels simply anchored mid-river.

Progress was slow.

Finally, they approached the enemy stronghold. They were now about two kilometres downriver from the great citadel of Onguiaahra.

Lakshman had disembarked in the morning and marched alongside the battalions advancing along the eastern banks of the north-flowing Mahaweli Ganga River. Bharat did not want a Lankan spy to see an Ayodhya battalion disembarking from the ships at night. So, he had decided that some soldiers from the eastern banks would simply disappear into the jungles when the sun set. And sneak quickly into the secret tunnel.

Bharat was a careful general. And a careful general does not underestimate the opponent or his spy network.

The sun was close to the horizon. It was twilight. Time for the Ayodhyan ships to anchor mid-river and the marching soldiers to board the ship. Bharat made no attempts to keep the morning disembarking and evening embarking operations quiet. He wanted the Lankans to know that he was being careful, following standard protocols for military movements.

Amidst the noise of the soldiers boarding the ships, no one noticed that some – almost a mid-sized battalion of elite special forces – had melted into the half-light. Lakshman, along with five hundred soldiers, soon assembled two hundred metres inside the jungles. Not visible from the river.

Their shoes were coated with extra leather to smother the sounds of their footsteps. Their blades were wrapped in cotton cloth, muffling the soft din of the steel rubbing against the scabbard. The cotton cloth would tear away when the sword was drawn. Their *dhotis* were tied tight, military style. Their armour was made from leather, instead of metal. Less protection but also less noise. These were Ayodhya special forces. Accomplishing the mission was more important than protecting their lives. No verbal orders were to be given; only hand signals. They quickly fell into double file. A thin rope was tied from the waist of one to the one behind, all down the line. Each soldier had a buddy to the side and was literally tied to the entire group, through the man in front and behind.

Lakshman identified the marker to the covert pathway that would lead them to the secret tunnel. Vibhishan's maps were easy to decipher.

It was a simple marker. A Fiji dwarf coconut tree. A very pretty small coconut palm with long fronds and leaflets, midget coconuts and pronounced bronze-coloured leaf-ring scars on its trunk. The fruit of this tree was not high up, and coconuts could be removed without the need to climb it. Its name was a true descriptor: dwarf coconut tree.

Lakshman smiled.

Smart.

Obviously, Vibhishan couldn't leave a signpost at this place with the legend 'This Way to Secret Tunnel' inscribed on it. But even a blank marker could easily have aroused suspicion, for there was no reason for the presence of a manmade sign in this part of the jungle. It was best to hide the marker in plain sight. This place had a remarkable abundance of trees. So, why not use a tree itself as a marker? But to distinguish the marker, this was a tree that had no natural reason to be here. The Fiji dwarf coconut tree was not native to the region. And this would be missed by most casual observers. Only someone specifically looking for this tree would have found it.

Hidden in plain sight.

Lakshman had already memorised the map. He pulled out his compass to orient his direction, then touched the tree, being careful to hold the south side of the trunk. Then he turned to the right and walked five foot-length steps, then three steps to the left and another step to the right.

He looked down. He felt the pointy end of a stone underneath the thin upper layer of soil, poking into his shoe. The pointy stone. The starting point. The other stones, buried lightly underground, would mark the way.

That Vibhishan may be a sneaky weasel, but he is a smart sneaky weasel.

Lakshman turned to his soldiers and raised his right hand, palm open and at a right angle to his face, fingers together and pointing at the sky. And then he flicked his wrist, the fingers now pointing east.

A clear hand signal: march east.

The signal was quickly relayed down the line. And the battalion began to march. Together. In step. Guided by the rope that tied them into one mass and the buried stones that lay under their feet.

— ᒍᖴ ᒪ5ᗞ —

'Do you think your father knows that we did not leave for Bali, grand-nephew?' Mareech asked Indrajit. 'And that we are here in Onguiaahra?'

Onguiaahra was not just a fort, it was also a dam. One with an ingenious design. Originally conceptualised as a barrage, Kubaer, the previous ruler, had begun its construction many decades ago. The obvious place for a barrage was the cataracts between the hills of Onguiaahra. These hills on both sides of the great Mahaweli Ganga naturally constricted the river, thus quickening the water flow. The cataracts made it impossible to sail farther up the Mahaweli Ganga, with boulders and small rocky islets sticking out of the riverbed. Therefore, ships would naturally divert into the calmer Amban Ganga, the tributary which merged into the Mahaweli Ganga downriver from the cataracts. The barrage across the cataracts of Mahaweli Ganga would, then, not impact shipping and its trading profits. The supporters of the project saw many benefits as well. The barrage would divert the floodwaters from the Mahaweli Ganga to the Amban Ganga and increase its flow size. This would ease the passage of even seafaring ships up this tributary. An aqueduct from the river would also provide ample drinking water for the rapidly expanding population of Sigiriya. One barrage, so many benefits.

But what about the costs of construction?

The Mahaweli Ganga was squeezed between the hills of Onguiaahra. So, the barrage would be relatively narrow for the scale of the massive river that was being barricaded. And the rocky cataracts meant that the foundations did not need to extend too deep into the earth. All this significantly lowered the construction costs, a very important factor for the profit-conscious Kubaer.

'I don't think so, grand-uncle,' said Indrajit, to his grandmother's brother. Indrajit wasn't sure how old Mareech was, but he was certainly more than seventy. The man could still pack a warrior punch, though. 'But I am not about to go to Bali for some silly trade dispute. We need to defeat the Ayodhyans and protect Lanka. And this is the best place to beat back Emperor Ram and his army.'

'True,' agreed Mareech. 'I would much rather not face them in Sigiriya. I don't know how much grit our citizens have to live through a long siege. The plague has weakened many.'

Indrajit nodded and looked over the fort wall railings, at the artificial lake behind the dam.

Raavan had realised the military significance of the barrage at Onguiaahra. Around thirty years ago, he deposed Kubaer and took over as the ruler of Lanka. And immediately ordered that the under-construction barrage be redesigned as a dam. The dam reservoir would hold back the waters of the Mahaweli Ganga and create a massive artificial lake. The change in design significantly increased the cost and complexity of the project. But Raavan was not lacking in wealth or boldness.

As compared to a barrage, the benefits of a dam were even greater. The huge artificial lake gave the citadel defenders access to massive quantities of water. They could release it at will, through multiple sluice gates, into the river below. They could release small quantities of water as well, through delicate control of the smaller sluices, and fill up the control-steps downriver. This naturally regulated the number of ships allowed to or prevented from sailing up the Amban Ganga.

Opening all the sluice gates simultaneously and releasing the massive hold of the artificial reservoir would push all the ships downriver. But the floodwaters would travel all the way to Gokarna at the mouth of the Mahaweli Ganga and destroy the city, of course. Therefore, this was a desperate measure, a nuclear option. Not one to be exercised lightly.

The sluice gates were resolutely shut at this moment. As were the floodwater spillway gates far away at the back of the artificial lake, which allowed water from the reservoir to flow, via a canal, into the Amban Ganga upriver. This reduced the flow of water at the control-steps and made it impossible for a ship to sail farther up beyond the steps of Onguiaahra.

All sides are in defensive positions just before the onset of battle. That's natural.

'But, nephew, do you really need so many men stationed at the tunnel entrance? One hundred?'

This was a substantial number for the Onguiaahra defence forces. All in all, it was a small team of only five hundred soldiers. Every soldier was a legend in his own right. Commanding the

Onguiaahra battalion, or even being a part of it, was among the highest honours for a Lankan soldier. For they protected that which was most precious: their capital city. And being small made the Onguiaahra battalion an exclusive club. What is easily available is not often desirable. What was true among lovers is also true among warriors. It requires great wisdom and discernment to differentiate unavailability from desirability. But there is something about love and bloodlust which diminishes the ability to be wise.

Having said that, the size of the Onguiaahra battalion was not dictated by the needs of exclusivity but the limited capacity of the citadel itself. The Onguiaahra fort was originally designed as a barrage and later converted into a dam. By design, the heart of the fort was a strong wall across the breadth of the Mahaweli Ganga River. An engineer cannot make a dam wall too thick. The costs, for one, would escalate prohibitively. But structural issues were more important. The thicker the wall, the farther away the toe of the dam would need to be on the downstream side, to stabilise the wall. This would create space constraints. Also, the sluice way from the upstream to downstream side, for the dammed reservoir water, would need to lengthen. That would create its own instabilities. Onguiaahra was primarily a dam and not a fort: so Raavan had done the next best thing, and created small bastions at both ends of the wall, which dug into the hillsides.

It was at the secret tunnel entrance within the bastion on the eastern side of the wall that Indrajit had placed these one hundred soldiers.

'Yes, we do,' said Indrajit. 'The Ayodhyans will come from there. Trust me. I am absolutely sure that Vibhishan uncle has betrayed us.'

Raavan had designed the Onguiaahra fort in the shape of a dumb-bell. The 'barbel bar' was the dam wall that blocked the Mahaweli Ganga River. The 'handles' and 'weights' at both ends of the dam wall were the bastions built on top of the hills into which the dam wall foundations were extended. The two bastions on the eastern and western ends of the dam wall were round-shaped with double walls, towers and two gates. Within the inner wall boundary were quarters, armouries, a kitchen, a training ground, an exercise hall, a medical bay, toilets and all else required by a healthy and effective battalion. Steps ran down the inner gates of the bastions, leading to the sluice gate controls on the dam wall. The hills near the bastions had been scarped and the slopes were steep, almost perpendicular. An attacking army would encounter cliff-like hillsides. And charging up the dam wall was impossible. Onguiaahra was unconquerable. A limited battalion of five hundred was enough. More than enough, the son of Raavan knew.

Except if the invaders slipped into the bastion through a secret tunnel.

'My child, I am not sure,' said Mareech. 'I know Vibhishan is weak. But I think he has only escaped to Gokarna to the safety of your grandmother and aunt, since the Ayodhyans will not attack non-combatant women and children. I agree with Raavan. Vibhishan is a coward, not a traitor. It's unlikely that he will betray us.'

'He will. Trust me.'

'I do trust you, even if I disagree with you on this. I proved it by allowing you to reveal the secret entrance to Dhumraksha, didn't I?'

'General Dhumraksha was not happy,' said Indrajit.

'Dhumraksha has a right to be angry. He may be an aggressive warmonger but he has been loyal to us for decades, and Raavan did not trust him enough to tell him about the secret tunnel.'

'Hmm.'

'But he remains here. I give him credit for that. He's still willing to battle for Lanka.'

'This will not be a battle, grand-uncle. It will be a massacre. When we pounce upon the Ayodhyans skulking up the tunnel that they think is the secret to destroying us!'

Chapter 21

'Ram is very slow and very careful,' said Raavan, as he and Kumbhakarna headed out on to the deck of their lead ship. They were anchored mid-river on the Amban Ganga River, safely behind the control-steps of Onguiaahra. They knew that the Ayodhyans had arrived downriver on the Amban Ganga. But no attempt had been made to sail closer to the control-steps that loomed just after the Amban Ganga merged into the Mahaweli Ganga. The control-steps were like an inverse amphitheatre; the highest 'step' was on the eastern banks of the Mahaweli Ganga, and each successive step progressively lowered towards the western banks. Each step width was massive, large enough to accommodate even sea-faring ships. Low water levels covered just the last step close to the western banks, allowing one ship to sail through. Increasing the water levels covered more steps, allowing more ships to row through. And if the water levels were very low, no ships could pass. The steps were built from granite, the hardest rock known to man, and could destroy ship hulls.

All in all, the Lankans had built an artificial cataract, which was regulated by the reservoir waters held back by the dam-fort of Onguiaahra. A simple idea brought to life by brilliant engineering.

'Right,' said Kumbhakarna. 'King Ram is staying put where the spillway canal merges into the Mahaweli Ganga. Well behind.'

An additional spillway canal moved the waters of the Mahaweli Ganga from the dam-fort of Onguiaahra in a long arc, bypassing the control-steps. The waters merged into the same river farther down. It ensured that flood waters did not overwhelm the control-steps with water. Therefore, despite the present flood in the river, resulting in excess water behind the dam-fort of Onguiaahra and downriver at the merge-point of the spillway canal and the Mahaweli Ganga, the great river had regulated water at the control-steps midway.

'Ram has made a mistake by bringing seafaring ships up the Mahaweli Ganga,' said Raavan. 'He probably thought he would have an advantage over our much smaller riverine ships. My spies tell me that the front bow sections of his ships are reinforced with metal. He can ram our smaller ships to oblivion. The problem for him is, there isn't enough water for his big ships to sail upriver!' Raavan laughed softly as he said this.

'He is not stupid. He wouldn't have brought his seafaring ships all the way here without a plan. Do you think that Vibhishan …'

'No,' said Raavan, shaking his head. 'Vibhishan is a coward. He doesn't have the guts to be a traitor.'

Kumbhakarna kept quiet.

'Let's see what Ram does now. He can't remain anchored forever.'

—— ⅃Ⅎ ⅃⸲ЗD——

Lakshman and his troops had marched for over an hour, following the zig-zag path marked by the buried stones. They now stood near the tree marking the entrance to the tunnel. The next rung in their expedition.

Lakshman smiled again. He was beginning to like Vibhishan. Just a bit.

Sneaky weasel. But a very smart sneaky weasel.

The map had instructed Lakshman on what to expect; despite this, he was impressed. Sheer genius. The entrance had been made to look completely natural. A small rocky cave was quite organic in these highlands.

The thick tree-cover and fading twilight made for poor visibility, but Lakshman could discern a shallow cave, extending inwards not more than five or ten feet. His eyes fell on a jagged rocky outcrop from among the rock edges. The lever that would open the secret door.

Brilliant. Looks so bloody natural. That Vibhishan fellow is a good architect.

Notwithstanding Vibhishan's engineering skills, though, Lakshman still did not trust the man.

He held up his right hand and raised three fingers, separating each from the other. He paused for a moment and then raised all his fingers, this time sticking together, palm facing outward. He flicked his wrist and the fingers now pointed east. Then he raised the fingers skywards again and closed his fist into a ball. He stuck his thumb out horizontally.

A clear message. Three men. Go east, around and behind the cave entrance. Check and come back and report.

Three men untied the linking rope from their waist, broke away and followed the orders.

Lakshman repeated similar hand signals, this time pointing west. Three more soldiers stepped away from the formation and moved stealthily away.

The soldiers soon returned and silently conveyed their reports. Nothing. No threats. All clear.

Lakshman then pulled his *angvastram* loose, wrapped it around his nose, and secured it behind his head. Vibhishan's notes were clear and detailed.

His five hundred soldiers followed their commander and did the same with their *angvastrams*.

They were ready.

Lakshman took one step into the cave and halted, drawing his sword. The four soldiers who followed him also drew their blades.

Lakshman closed his eyes and allowed his pupils to expand and adapt. The cones within the retina rested, the rods kicked into work mode and his dark vision improved. He blinked a couple of times and took a few quick steps forward. Just a few feet; it was a shallow cave. Seeing clearly in the dark now, he moved unerringly to the stony jagged sprout. Nobody would have divined it was man-made. With his left hand, he gently pushed the sprout backwards. The stone depressed with a hydraulic hiss.

The stony sprout fell into a hollow and the back wall of the cave appeared to loosen.

Lakshman held out his sword. Ready for surprises.

Though warned earlier via Vibhishan's instructions, the shock of the assault was devastating.

An assault on his nose.

As the back wall slid sideways, a feral stench hurtled out from within the cave, smacking the olfactory nerves of the soldiers standing in the hollows. Lakshman struggled to hold in the vomit. He pressed his *angvastram* against his nose. He did not step back. Admirably, neither did his soldiers.

The back wall had revealed itself as a sliding door. It was surprisingly smooth and silent as it moved slickly aside.

There was no sound. Except for the almost-noiseless attempts of Lakshman and the four men behind him to not gag.

By all that is good and holy! This is beyond tolerance!

Lakshman held out his sword and pointed at the dark passage that had opened up behind the cave back-wall. He stepped back and walked away from the cave mouth. As did his relieved soldiers.

— JF J5D —

The men sat outside the cave. Not directly in line with the cave opening, but to the side, for the malodour still infected the air. In disciplined lines of two abreast. Quiet. Patient.

This was the key difference between special forces and ordinary soldiers. Of course, the quality of training was better. Physical fitness was superior. The military equipment sanctioned to special forces was high grade. But the key difference was patience. Ordinary soldiers lack patience. Special forces can hold still, without sound and movement, disciplined and focused, for hours on end. And can spring to action at a moment's notice.

Eight soldiers remained at the entrance with drawn swords. In readiness for untoward incidents. Changeover provided relief every fifteen minutes. This was necessary. The horrific odour was unbearable.

Lakshman stared at the cave.

To be fair, Vibhishan had warned him in the notes. The stench collected from fifteen years of the fort's drainage—that was how long the tunnel had remained shut. While the drainage had a separate exit leading directly into the river, one end of the tunnel, at the top of the fort, was close to the barracks toilets. A smart place to end the tunnel. The drainage would not be checked unless clogged. And the sheer incline from the fort to the river ensured that the drainage never blocked. Vibhishan's design was faultless.

Vibhishan had advised that they wait for an hour after opening the cave door. The stench would dissipate, he'd said. He had built hidden ventilation ducts which allowed airflow once the cave door opened.

Lakshman had thought he was being ridiculous at the time, asking them to wait for an hour to clear the air. Now he wondered if an hour would suffice. He decided they would wait for two hours.

He looked up at the sky. It was the fifth day of the fortnight of the waxing moon, and moonlight was faint. They were more than halfway into the fourth and last prahar of the day. Midnight was approximately three hours away. Enough time. They would attack in the morning.

He signalled his lieutenant, Kshiraj. An Ayodhyan. *We'll wait for two hours.*

Kshiraj smiled with relief.

— JF JᴣD —

Shatrughan shook his head. 'Bloody hell!'

'This is sheer bad luck, Shatrughan,' said Ram. 'What can we do.'

The end of the fourth hour of the fourth *prahar* was drawing near. Midnight was two hours away. The Ayodhya war camp, spread over the Mannar island and the Indian mainland, was mostly asleep. Armed guards patrolled the thirty-kilometre length of the under-construction bridge. They had planned to complete the remaining five kilometres of the bridge the following day. But an unexpected problem had presented itself.

'I am sorry. I think it was my black tongue,' said Vashishtha guiltily. A few hours earlier he had commented that he had never seen a construction project go exactly to plan.

'No, Guruji,' said Naarad, always ready with a clever one-liner. 'I'm afraid it wasn't your black tongue, but the black *maansaudan* that did this!'

Vashishtha looked at a grinning Naarad and rolled his eyes.

Maansaudan. Meat rice. Mentioned in the Shatapatha Braahmana, this meal was a particular favourite with the soldiers. Fine rice is first rinsed, soaked and drained. Tender meat of the quail bird, minced to the same size as the grains of rice, is then added. The European quail, being a migratory bird, visited southern India in the winter months like clockwork. Its fresh meat was readily available this time of the year. Freshly made ghee and coconut milk is blended into the rice and meat. Musk and camphor are added for fragrance, for the ancients strongly believed that food must appeal not only to the senses of taste and vision, but also to the olfactory sense. The vessel is closed with a heavy lid and the mixture is cooked on a low flame for hours. The contents are periodically stirred till it becomes a smoothly amalgamated gooey mass. The cooked musk gives this delicacy a distinctively deep red colour.

When the *maansaudan* is ready to serve, it is garnished with petals from the *ketaki* flower. The Parihans, Lord Rudra's people, took this simple gastronomical delight from India to their own land, and named it *biryani*. Sinfully decadent and nourishing, no meal could please the tastebuds of warriors more. Regrettably, stale meat could sometimes cause a stomach upset. The *maansaudan* that evening was almost black instead of deep red, which should have triggered a warning. But, as the Parihans often said, any red-blooded man would merrily die for the taste of *biryani*. What's a tiny stomach upset in comparison? An infinitesimal health problem.

Health problems frequently occur in battle. Too many men, travelling and living in proximity out in the open, absence of civilised drainage facilities and assured, nutritious food. Soldiers fall ill. Animals fall ill. These things happen.

A good general not only divines brilliant war strategies and tactics, but also manages logistics efficiently.

And Ram, ably assisted by Vashishtha, Shatrughan, Hanuman, Arishtanemi, Angad and Naarad, had managed logistics exceedingly well.

Ram had insisted on one thing though: that all units eat together and not just with their own communities. A spirit of comradeship had been subtly built across the entire army. Over the last few months, it had helped forge disparate forces into one united army under the stewardship of King Ram.

The elephant mahouts were either Malayaputras or Vaanars. They had never interacted with each other till they became a part of Ram's army. Now they were eating together on a regular basis. But as luck would have it, it was the food for the mahouts that turned out to be bad that evening. They were stricken with diarrhoea. This is not a serious physical hazard in a battlefield. Diseases and injuries can get much worse. Most mahouts would recover within a day, at most two.

But the elephants were critical to build the last five kilometres of the bridge the following day. And while elephants are docile and obedient animals in the able hands of their mahouts, they are unmanageably fearsome with strangers.

Work on the bridge seemed impossible the next day, or even the day after. Which would delay the army's arrival at Sigiriya.

'What now?' asked Arishtanemi.

'We'll wait till the mahouts are healthy again.'

Shatrughan looked at Ram. 'Bharat dada and Lakshman will need to drag out their battle for three more days at least. We must reach Sigiriya before the Lankan army returns from Onguiaahra if we want this war to end quickly. It may be best if Bharat dada delays his attack.'

'He was planning to attack tonight. He may have launched it already. There's nothing we can do.'

Naarad spoke up. 'You are right, there is nothing we can do now.'

Everyone looked at Naarad. Waiting for him to say something sarcastic or inappropriate.

And Naarad obliged. 'The wise have always said that if you find yourself awake and troubled in the late hours of the night, when there is nothing that you can do about what troubles you, then the best idea is to simply go to sleep. That is what *dharma* dictates.'

Nobody said anything.

'Well, at least I'll follow my own advice. You all can stay up and worry. Goodnight.'

—JF ᒍ5D—

It was an hour to midnight.

Lakshman had led his soldiers into the tunnel. As mentioned in Vibhishan's notes, many torches—numbering over two hundred and made from limestone—were fixed into nooks on the wall. Every second soldier carried a piece of cloth doused with sulphur and lime. Over the last hour, they had wrapped the cloth around the top of the torches and lit them. While Vibhishan had said that they needn't close the cave door as the rocky overhang and dense tree cover would prevent the lights from being seen from the hill fort in the distance, Lakshman erred on the side of caution. After the last man stepped into the tunnel, the sliding cave door had been shut. Almost completely. It had been left open just a smidgen to allow for airflow. Faint traces of the malodour remained.

Lakshman and his troops moved silently. The tunnel entrance was a kilometre and half from the hill upon which the east wing of the Onguiaahra citadel stood. Lakshman planned to move slowly and cover the distance in an hour. There was no rush. They could attack in the morning. He did not want to risk his men getting injured in a dimly lit tunnel.

Even as he marched, Lakshman's regard for Vibhishan's prowess increased. The floor was packed earth, and reasonably flat. It was covered with cobblestones, giving it solidity. Easy to march on. Small drainage lines ran on both sides of the path, which would allow water seeping in from the regular heavy rains of Lanka to drain out of the tunnel without causing structural damage. The tunnel was bigger than he had expected. Broad enough for two soldiers to walk abreast, and tall enough for even him to not have to bend his gargantuan frame. In fact, a soldier could walk his horse through the tunnel without any difficulty. Riding would not be possible, of course. Not enough headroom. But even this much was amazing in a secret tunnel. The walls had been reinforced with rock, making them solid and impregnable. They did not come across any cave-ins, which was surprising, given that the tunnel was fifteen years old and had had absolutely no maintenance work in that time. Vibhishan's work had been thorough. A straight excavation with almost no twists and turns. High-quality planimetry while digging underground, along with exceptional structural strength, called for rare design and architectural skill.

Sneaky weasel. But a very, very smart sneaky weasel.

An hour later, Lakshman and his five hundred men reached the end of the tunnel at the base of the hill. Or more specifically, in the innards of the rocky hill, as Lakshman guessed by observing the changes in the floor and sidewall patterns.

And now he was truly in awe.

Vibhishan and his workers had burrowed their way up the inner bowels of the hill. The path rose steeply in a westerly direction for around twenty metres and then took a hairpin bend, turning and rising in an easterly direction. At the next hairpin bend, the tunnel turned again, towards the west. Essentially, a giant staircase excavated *inside* a hill. A spectacular piece of engineering.

A large cavity was dug out at the nose-end of each hairpin bend: an extension of the staircase landing, deep into the hill.

Lakshman mused, *What is this for? Why this cavity?*

Those climbing the staircase would use the landing and turn towards the next set of steps. Why was a cavity needed? Then it struck him. It had been built to collect and store loose stones or cave-in material that rolled down the steps. A back-up that would ensure the staircase landings remained clear.

Wow. This is next level, man.

A complex tunnelled-staircase built inside a hill. Directly from the flat tunnel under the jungle ground. The flat part of the tunnel would have required sound planimetry and the tunnelled-staircase, altimetry of a divine order. And he did all this in secret. Without anyone finding out about the goings-on. While also building two other secret tunnels.

Bloody smart sneaky weasel!

Lakshman turned to his men and signalled, slowly. He raised his hand high, ensuring that everyone received the order in the dim light of the torches.

The message was clear: Start climbing. Quietly. And wait at the top.

Chapter 22

'Go to sleep, prince,' said Dhumraksha. 'It's close to midnight. I'm on guard. As are the hundred soldiers, awake and alert.'

Dhumraksha had appointed a rotating strength of one hundred soldiers in shifts of six hours each. They guarded the opening to the secret tunnel in the eastern wing of the citadel, swords drawn. The entrance to the tunnel was unopened and unlit. The Ayodhyans would not suspect that they were walking into a trap.

Indrajit shook his head in response to Dhumraksha's suggestion. *No.*

Dhumraksha, the name, meant *smoky eyes*. And his eyes did rage with aggressive fire. His parents had named him well. Of massive build and fierce temperament, he was born to be a warrior. As the commander of the Onguiaahra battalion, he headed the Lankan special forces. Being a good warrior, he respected fellow warriors. Indrajit had come all the way to the citadel to face a possible attack from enemy special forces. The royal had put himself in harm's way. It was worthy of respect. And old smoky eyes treated the respect-worthy with very obvious, ostentatious regard.

Dhumraksha looked at Mareech. 'Lord Mareech, one of us must remain awake all the time and be ready for the attack. We must take turns to sleep.' Pointing at the commander's quarters, which were at a height, above where the youngest Lankan soldiers in the battalion lived, Dhumraksha continued, 'You both can sleep for now. In my quarters.'

Indrajit looked to where Dhumraksha was pointing. 'That's too far. I have a strong feeling they will attack tonight. We'll stay here.'

'Prince Indrajit,' said Dhumraksha, 'I will blast the war-horn the moment the enemy arrives. They can only emerge in twos from the tunnel. We will hold them here. And keep enough of them alive for you to kill.'

Indrajit laughed softly.

Mareech spoke up. 'General Dhumraksha is speaking wisely, Indrajit. Let's take his advice. Join the next watch, and get a few hours of sleep at least.'

Indrajit relented and got up, adjusting the scabbard sideways.

Mareech leaned towards Indrajit as he began to walk. 'But first…'

'Yes, grand-uncle?'

—— JF J,5D ——

Lakshman and his soldiers had reached the top of the staircase and were standing before the exit.

Vibhishan's work quality had been such that Lakshman was assured that the light from the torches would not slip out through the sealed door in front of them. Unless he opened it, of course.

Using hand signals, Lakshman warned his soldiers to stay away from the clearly marked lever at a height on the wall. The lever that would open the door. He did not want it opened by mistake.

Lakshman rested his ear against a specific spot on the rocky door. He had been informed that, from here, he could hear the goings-on outside.

He heard … nothing.

He looked at his troops.

Suddenly a loud bell rang out. His ears reverberated painfully. *Bloody…*

Stunned by the clarity of the sound, and despite the aural discomfort, Lakshman did not move from the spot. He had to hear this.

Another bell.

And then silence.

Lakshman turned to his soldiers and made hand signals.

Second hour of the watch has begun.

Lakshman calculated. The standard shift in Onguiaahra was six hours. Four hours from now, the sixth hour of the watch would begin.

That would be the best time for attack. The soldiers on guard would be tired as they approached the end of their shift.

He made hand signals again.

We wait. Four hours more.

The message was relayed down the line.

Lakshman placed his ear against the little patch on the wall. He wondered at the technology Vibhishan must have used to make sound travel with such clarity through a thick rocky wall.

Not for the first time did the same thought run through his mind. *Vibhishan. Genius sneaky weasel.*

He listened for voices. But there were none.

Maybe there is nobody on the other side of this door.

He looked at his soldiers. Stationary. Deathly silent. Patient. Just like soldiers in the special forces should be.

No reason to assume that the Lankan special forces would be less well-trained. They could be right outside. Quiet, as discipline dictated.

We'll know in four hours.

Lakshman assigned a soldier to man the sounding post. He then sat on the floor, rested his back against a wall, and decided to get some sleep.

— ⅃Ⅎ ⅃⸴⊃—

Lakshman opened his eyes as he felt a light touch. The hand signal from his soldier was clear.

The sixth hour of the watch had begun.

Lakshman rose quickly and gave orders through hand signals.

Prepare.

The soldiers stretched their arms, shoulders, back and legs. Loosening them.

They speedily drank from the water carriers. Then reached into their bags and quickly wolfed down dry fruits and gram. Having emptied their food and water containers, they left the bags in the tunnel; they wouldn't need them anymore. Quickly checking their weapons, they loosened the hold covers on their scabbards. They unhooked their shields and held them in position.

Ready.

It had taken them ten minutes. They were special forces soldiers.

Lakshman looked at them. Satisfied. He carefully gave hand signal orders.

Remain quiet outside. We assemble first. Then attack.

The soldiers had been briefed earlier. They knew the tunnel exited into a space hidden from view by a colonnaded passageway with a low ceiling. At least one hundred from among them could assemble before charging. The rest would follow in unceasing waves.

Lakshman drew his sword, as did the others. He nodded at the soldier standing near the lever and edged towards the door. Kshiraj darted ahead, putting himself at risk as the door opened. Lakshman hissed softly in annoyance. Kshiraj looked at Lakshman and smiled. But refused to yield the vanguard position.

Lakshman surrendered to Kshiraj's valour and remained behind in the line. He raised his left hand and closed his fist abruptly. All the torches were put out and the tunnel plunged into darkness. And the lever was pressed.

The feral smell assaulted them again. But it wasn't as intense as when they had opened the tunnel entrance earlier in the night. They were prepared. They expected it. They knew they would exit near the drainage. So, none reacted.

But Lakshman frowned. Something was not right.

No sound. None at all. In a camp full of testosterone-laden soldiers.

Strange. Eerie.

Are the Lankans expecting us?

The faint light of dawn filtered into the tunnel.

Kshiraj crept out of the tunnel and, as had been planned, advanced quickly to the right. Lakshman stepped out and moved to the centre. Very soon a hundred soldiers had manoeuvred into formation outside the tunnel.

There was a sinister silence.

They were in a colonnaded passage which had been carved into the black stone of the hill. It was built such that, while Lakshman and his soldiers were hidden in the dark, the rest of the compound was visible. To the right, the passage led to the common toilets. To the left, it led to the rookies' dormitory, where the youngest Lankan soldiers in the battalion lived. Ahead of them were steps that descended to the common ground in the eastern wing of the fort. To the far right of the common ground was the east-wing gate to the central dam wall. Lakshman remembered this from the map.

Couldn't have exited the tunnel at a better place. Lakshman silently thanked the Lankan traitor Vibhishan again.

Their pupils slowly contracted and they began to see more clearly in the dawn light. Lakshman raised his left hand and flicked his wrist to the left. Fifty soldiers padded in the direction of the rookies' dormitory, knives drawn.

Fifty others stealthily moved out of the tunnel to take their place.

Lakshman wondered where the Lankan guards were.

And then he saw them.

Oh Lord Rudra!

He made hand signals and pointed. The signals were relayed down the line.

A hundred Lankan soldiers stood at the other end of the courtyard, some distance away. They huddled silently against a wall next to the small fort temple. Lakshman saw that they stood with their swords drawn.

He suppressed a soft laugh.

They are expecting an attack from the other tunnel! They have no idea about this tunnel.

Yet again, Lakshman silently thanked Vibhishan.

Lord Indra bless that sneaky weasel!

None of the Lankans looked in their direction. They had some more time.

He gave another order through hand signals. Ten soldiers broke formation. And slunk silently up the railing-protected stairs on the edge of the fort wall. Towards the commander's quarters at the height. If they got lucky and found the commander, the battle would be over before it could begin.

Ten more soldiers emerged from the tunnel and replaced those who had stepped away.

Lakshman looked to the right. In the distance he saw the east wing's gates to the central dam of Onguiaahra. They were open. He had been briefed by Vibhishan to take control of those gates immediately. If the Lankans succeeded in locking the gates from outside, the Ayodhyans would be trapped inside. The Lankans could then destroy the sluice controls, thus compromising Lakshman's ability to release water into the control-steps downriver. That would make the conquest of Onguiaahra pointless. However, Bharat had repeatedly emphasised that Lakshman should gain complete control of the eastern wing first, and only then move towards the central dam. Bharat didn't want unnecessary Ayodhyan casualties while facing attacks from the rear.

In any case, Lakshman couldn't order his soldiers to take the gate. Not yet. For it was clearly visible to the Lankans who were next to the fort temple.

Enough time for that.

He looked to the left. One of his soldiers stepped out of the rookies' quarters. He was wiping his knife on his arm band. He looked towards Lakshman and signalled.

Fifty Lankans. All dead now.

Lakshman ordered them to remain where they were.

Fifty gone. Another hundred at the other tunnel entrance. The rest would be asleep. The main dormitory to the left had a capacity of two hundred, according to Vibhishan. So, there were at most three hundred and fifty Lankans here, fifty of whom were dead. The other one hundred and fifty would be at the western-wing of the Onguiaahra fort, far away at the other end of the central dam. They would play little role in this battle here.

My five hundred versus their three hundred. Good odds. Especially since we have the element of surprise as well.

He looked at the commander's quarters. His soldiers were still inside. He would ideally want that quarter covered as well to prevent any attacks from the rear when he charged.

He raised his hand and gave orders to the soldiers who were still in the tunnel.

Go towards the main dormitory. When I say so. Kill all there.

The command was relayed down the line.

Lakshman looked up at the commander's quarters again. A soldier stepped out and signalled: *Nobody here.*

No problem, Lakshman whispered to himself. The Lankan commander Dhumraksha must be with his soldiers at the other tunnel entrance. *We'll kill him there.*

All he had to do now was silently creep ahead with the men who had already emerged from the tunnel, get as close as possible to the Lankans at the other tunnel entrance, and surprise them before they turned around and made formations again. It would be an easy massacre.

He was about to relay his order when he stopped dead in his tracks.

Goddammit!

Lakshman looked towards the courtyard and groaned soundlessly.

As history had been witness, Lakshman was not an early riser. He was fond of his sleep. Only war or the express command of his elder brothers could awaken him early. And, like most late risers, he despised those who woke up early for no good reason.

Two such specimens walked out of the main dormitory now. Lankan soldiers. Muscled and fit. Bare-chested, wearing only loose lungis. One of them scratched his backside and the other yawned loudly.

Don't come here. Don't come here.

They began to head in Lakshman's direction. Holding mugs. Indians, like most civilised people, washed rather than wiped.

Lakshman looked to his right. His soldiers stood exactly in front of the toilets.

Dammit. There goes the surprise element.

If that advantage was gone, Lakshman thought, he may as well use his favourite weapon. He pushed his sword back into its scabbard, carefully.

The blade made a soft noise as it slipped back into its sheath. Most would have missed it. But it was a sound that a good soldier would recognise anywhere, especially in the quiet of an early daybreak. The two Lankans froze. They could not see anything, as the Ayodhyans were hidden in the colonnaded passageway. The dim light of the dawn did not reach that corner. They glanced at each other briefly, confirming that they had both heard it. They strained their eyes to get a better look.

Lakshman reached behind and unhooked his favourite weapon. The war mace.

A typical mace is a type of club with a heavy head on one end, which can deliver powerful strikes. But Lakshman's weapon had been specially engineered for him. It had a strong, heavy metal shaft, and a head made of metal as well. The head and handle were forged from one piece, giving the mace a fearsome solidity. Moreover, the head contained sharp metallic flanges from top to bottom and along the left and right axes. They helped penetrate leather armour. There was more. The head was covered with sharp metallic spikes all around. Forget leather, even metallic armour would give way with a strong blow from this head. Normally a mace measures two to three feet in length, about the same as a sword. But this weapon had been stretched and lengthened for Lakshman. It was a little over three and a half feet; longer than a longsword.

This formidable and heavy weapon would be difficult for most ordinary warriors to hold, let alone wield. But Lakshman was six feet ten inches tall and built like a bull. In his hands, this mace was terrifying beyond measure.

Lakshman untied the thick leather cover from the mace head and cast it aside. He would retrieve it in good time.

No point in remaining silent now.

'Kshiraj,' he whispered, 'cover the gates.'

And then Lakshman stepped out of the passageway onto the landing. In the open. One hundred soldiers followed him.

The two Lankans immediately dropped their mugs, which clattered noisily, breaking the silence all around. They ran back to their quarters for their weapons, screaming at the top of their lungs. 'ENEMY AT PASSAGEWAY! ENEMY AT PASSAGEWAY!'

The Lankans at the other tunnel whirled around and stood rooted to the spot. Shocked into momentary paralysis. Meanwhile, Kshiraj and his ten soldiers were sprinting towards the gates.

'Charge!' roared Lakshman. *'Ayodhyatah Vijetaarah!'*

The conquerors from the unconquerable city!

'*Ayodhyatah Vijetaarah!*' shouted Lakshman's men.

Lakshman and his first line of soldiers stormed towards the Lankans at the other tunnel entrance. The rest of the Ayodhyans began pouring out of the secret tunnel. Some ran behind Lakshman, but most rushed to the main dormitory. As they had been ordered to.

To his credit, the stunned Dhumraksha immediately rallied. His loud commanding voice instilled instantaneous purpose into his soldiers.

'Upon me!' thundered Dhumraksha. 'Charge! *Bhaarat Bhartri Lanka!*'

Lanka, owner of India!

'*Bhaarat Bhartri Lanka!*' the Lankans bellowed loudly as they charged towards the Ayodhyans.

One Lankan ran towards the Ayodhya prince; he was tall, and yet dwarfed by the gargantuan Lakshman. It was a brave and smart tactic. Take down the opposing commander; his soldiers would surrender. Unfortunately for the Lankan, the opposing commander was Lakshman.

The Lankan held his shield high, intending to block the standard downward strike from Lakshman's mace. After which he would aim to draw close with the same move and turn the long reach of the mace into a disadvantage. Then, with an upward movement of his shorter sword, he would stab Lakshman's abdomen. That was the plan.

Bad plan.

Disposed of at first contact with the enemy.

The mace is a fearsome weapon on its own. When wielded by Lakshman, with his unbeatable combination of colossal size, bull-like strength and swashbuckling skill, it is invincible. The club ripped through the leather and wooden shield. It struck the Lankan's left arm. Lakshman's mace didn't just break bones, it shattered them to powder. The Lankan's elbow joint, parts of the humerus bone above, and the radius and ulna bones below almost instantaneously crumbled into fragmented bits of calcium and collagen. The Lankan looked down, stunned. His mangled left arm was hanging limp by his side, connected by stray strands of sinew at what had been the elbow. His brain had blocked the pain, which was beyond endurance. The sword dropped from his other hand. Soon thereafter he was put out of his misery as Lakshman swung brutally from his left and his mace crushed the right half of the Lankan's head so that it sunk into the other half.

Lakshman continued the same swing onwards, and the spikes in the head of the mace buried themselves in another Lankan's head. The unfortunate soul was fighting an Ayodhyan. A Suryavanshi blade had ripped into his heart as Lakshman had smashed his mace in. It was difficult to tell what killed the Lankan – his crushed head or the steel through his heart.

Even as Lakshman was swinging at the next Lankan charging towards him, his soldiers in the main dormitory were massacring the enemy. Lakshman had given his soldiers clear orders: No mercy. Kill all Lankans who resist. And all of them were resisting.

The situation wasn't any better for the defenders of Onguiaahra in the courtyard. Lakshman's soldiers were scything through most of the battalion, killing all who stood in their path.

To Lakshman's admiration, not a single Lankan surrendered. With the odds clearly stacked against them, they kept on fighting.

Worthy enemies.

The bloodletting continued. Mostly with the blood of the Lankans.

'Wait!' roared Lakshman.

Almost all the Lankans were dead. The rest were injured so badly that survival was difficult.

One Lankan was still standing. Injured. Bloodied. But proud and unbowed.

General Dhumraksha.

'Hold,' ordered Lakshman. 'And disarm the Lankans.'

The Ayodhyans immediately began to follow Lakshman's orders. But none approached Dhumraksha. Those who had been fighting him a moment ago stepped back.

Lakshman stared at the Lankan commander.

Dhumraksha was a physically intimidating man, but not as big as Lakshman was. The Lankan general was six and a half feet in height. Muscular. Fair-skinned. He sported a long handle-bar moustache and was clad in sleeveless leather armour. He wore black arm bands and a black *dhoti*, tied in military style. His body was covered in blood, most of it his own.

He breathed heavily, trying to regain his strength and composure. He stared back at Lakshman with unblinking eyes. Defiant.

Lakshman noticed the weapon in Dhumraksha's hand. A war mace.

Lakshman recognised it immediately. 'Kodumanal?'

Dhumraksha smiled and nodded his head slowly. 'The best will only use the best.'

Lakshman smiled.

A worthy enemy.

Kodumanal was the great city of the Cheras on the Kanchinadi, a tributary of the sacred Kaveri River. It was widely acknowledged to be the best place in the world for manufacturing swords and maces. Dhumraksha's war mace was crafted by the hands of the finest metallurgists and blacksmiths of Kodumanal. As was Lakshman's.

Dhumraksha raised his mace. One last duel.

Lakshman raised his mace as well. Challenge accepted.

Lakshman gave due respect to a soldier of Dhumraksha's calibre by holding his mace with both hands. No imprudent swinging with one hand against a skilled warrior. The prince of Ayodhya held his position. No careless charging against the Lankan general either.

The two warriors began to circle one another. Gauging each other.

Dhumraksha moved first. He took a quick step forward and swung his mace hard. Lakshman stayed rooted but leaned backwards, easily avoiding the blow like a deft boxer. His back sprung forward with the same velocity and he swung his mace from the left. Aiming at Dhumraksha's shoulder. But the Lankan flicked his wrist and his mace deflected the blow.

Lakshman stepped back, smiling and nodding.

As did Dhumraksha.

They had crucial information about each other now. Most bulky, muscular men possess strength and power, but not speed and agility. However, these apparently contradictory qualities mingled comfortably in both these men.

This will be interesting, thought Lakshman.

Dhumraksha charged again and Lakshman parried the blow.

A voice boomed from behind Lakshman. 'My Lord, finish this! We have a lot to do!'

Lakshman ignored it.

Dhumraksha charged again. Lakshman sidestepped and jabbed his mace forward with force. The sharp point at the top edge of the mace head poked Dhumraksha's chest. Not deep enough. It had sliced through the leather armour though.

Lakshman had drawn first blood. Dhumraksha stepped back and darted suddenly to his right. Lakshman had expected that. He swung in quickly from the left. Dhumraksha's mace hit first. It collided with Lakshman's shoulder. A micro second later Lakshman's mace head struck Dhumraksha's left shoulder, but it was a weak blow. Lakshman had just been hit.

A direct hit from a large Kodumanal mace head would have shattered, or at least broken a bone, in most warriors. But when the bone is protected by layers of bull-like muscle, as in the case of Lakshman and Dhumraksha, it would not be so. Blood burst steadily from wounds on both the warriors. But they still had use of their shoulders.

The voice was heard again, from behind Lakshman, this time laced with impatience. 'My Lord!'

Dhumraksha charged, swinging his mace from left to right and right to left, as if it was a sword. Lakshman parried each blow, stepping back slowly. As if retreating. But he was drawing Dhumraksha into a trap.

As Dhumraksha swung hard from the right, Lakshman's parry became more rigid. He held the mace in place as Dhumraksha pushed forward. The Lankan realised only too late what he had done. Moving quick like lightning, Lakshman pressed a lever on his mace handle with his right thumb. His left hand slipped down, just as a knife, hidden within the mace handle, ejected quickly. Lakshman grabbed the knife and stabbed. Before Dhumraksha could disengage, the knife had sunk into the heart.

It all happened within the blink of an eye.

Lakshman had done what Dhumraksha had intended in the very next strike.

The prince of Ayodhya pushed the knife in deeper, and felt a thump. A reverberation. Dhumraksha had dropped his mace.

Lakshman held the knife and felt another thump on the blade. It was Dhumraksha's mighty heart, still beating, transmitting its muscular vibration onto the metal, which carried the pulse into the handle of the blade that Lakshman held.

Dhumraksha collapsed backwards. Lakshman dropped his mace and eased him to the ground.

The Lankan commander was smiling with satisfaction. As if he was thanking his enemy. He had been accorded an honourable death. No warrior wishes to be killed by inferior hands, like hyenas surrounding a lion. If he must die, then it must be in a duel with a worthy adversary. Another lion.

Lakshman gently touched Dhumraksha's forehead. 'May Lord Yama guide you across the sacred Vaitarni, brave Dhumraksha.' The next world, the land of the ancestors, lay beyond the mythical river, Vaitarni. Yama, the Lord of Death, guided souls into that stopover land. After some time, the souls either returned to this earth reincarnated, or moved onwards towards moksha, liberation from the cycle of rebirths.

Dhumraksha raised his weakened hand and touched Lakshman's forehead. 'I will ... see you ... on the other side ...'

'I will see you on the other side, brother.'

Dhumraksha's hand fell to the ground and his soul slipped away.

Lakshman took a deep breath and bowed his head low. Having paid his respects, he rose and looked at his men. 'Well done, boys.'

'Thank you, Lord.'

Lakshman then glanced at the gates in the distance.

And cursed loudly.

Chapter 23

As luck would have it, Indrajit and Mareech had been awake when Lakshman and his troops emerged from the secret tunnel. They had woken up an hour earlier and had gone down to the guards' room next to the east-wing gate. They were with the guards, making small talk, when Lakshman had ordered his soldiers to charge.

Indrajit, Mareech and the fifteen Lankan soldiers in the guards' cabin were completely out of sight for Lakshman and his Ayodhyans.

Kshiraj and his Ayodhyan soldiers had not seen the Lankans emerge from behind as they had raced to the gates. Many Ayodhyans were killed before they had even turned around to face the enemy.

Mareech had bellowed an order as his guards had rushed towards Kshiraj. 'Don't kill him! Drag him out! I want him alive!'

Indrajit had wanted to move farther into the courtyard and attack the Ayodhyans as they charged into Dhumraksha and his men close to the fort temple. But Mareech had pulled his nephew back. 'This is not the time to be a hero. This is the time to be a leader!' Mareech had implored Indrajit.

Sometimes the hero and the leader can fuse in the same individual. But often this does not happen. A hero does not need followers, a leader cannot be imagined without those he leads. A hero sacrifices himself, while a leader may not succumb to this magnificent impulse. A hero must be courageous, a leader does what must be done, even risk being perceived as cowardly sometimes. A hero inspires the storytellers, a leader lives on in the hearts of his followers. A hero is concerned with what the gods will think of him, a leader is concerned with protecting and nurturing his people and his land. A hero will not leave the moral high ground, even if it hurts his people, while a leader will step down from the moral high ground if need be, and even sacrifice his own soul for the good of the people he leads.

A hero will fight the enemy against insurmountable odds and embrace death with a flourish.

A leader will respond calmly and deny the enemy a key strategic advantage in a battle.

Indrajit had listened to Mareech, and behaved like a leader.

They had retreated from the gate to the central dam area along with fifteen soldiers. The fighting continued to rage at the other end of the courtyard of the east-wing. They had found some hammers in the guards' cabin, to be used for repairs. Now they would be used for destruction.

Kshiraj had tried to warn his fellow Ayodhyans who were battling Dhumraksha and his men at the other end of the courtyard. But a soldier from Indrajit's tight band had knocked him on the head and carried the unconscious Ayodhyan out. The gate had been quickly barred from the outside and barricaded.

They had then set to work.

The levers of the sluice gates were destroyed. The loss of even a few major sluice gate controls would have hampered Ayodhya's ability to manage water-outflow. Nevertheless, Indrajit had insisted that every sluice control, even the minor ones, be smashed. The spillways were already closed. It would take the Ayodhyans at least a week to repair the controls. Their ships would be stuck downriver on the Mahaweli Ganga till then.

The Lankans had bought a week for themselves. To evaluate and formulate new strategies to take on the Ayodhyans.

As Lakshman had killed Dhumraksha, the last of the sluice controls had been destroyed by Indrajit's men. This was when the Ayodhyan prince had noticed the barricaded gates of the eastern-wing.

He immediately ordered that they be broken. But that would take some time. It was a high-quality Lankan construction, designed by Vibhishan.

Indrajit looked back. He could hear the battering ram pounding at the gates. He looked at Mareech and smiled. 'That will take them half an hour, almost forty-five minutes, in fact. Unless they burn the gate.' Indrajit turned to two soldiers. 'Race to the western-wing.. Gather our soldiers and horses in the courtyard there. Move!'

The Ayodhyan attack on the eastern wing of the Onguiaahra citadel had begun just fifteen minutes ago. Those fifteen minutes had changed the war dynamic drastically.

As the two soldiers sprinted across the central dam wall, Indrajit and Mareech walked briskly towards the western-wing. The rest of the soldiers followed.

'What do you plan to do?' asked Mareech. 'Will you defend the western-wing?'

Indrajit shook his head. 'No. That's pointless. We will lock the western-wing gate from the inside; that will make it difficult for the Ayodhyans to enter from the dam side. Then we will salvage what we can and burn the rest of the stores; we will not make it easy for them to survive here. Then we will ride out and warn our ships below.'

Mareech smiled. 'There is no dishonour in retreating when it is the best course available. Now you are thinking like a leader, not a hero.'

Indrajit smiled slightly. 'I am sorry. I became emotional earlier.'

Mareech patted Indrajit's shoulder as he walked beside his grand-nephew. 'You are young. And young people like to be heroes. It takes wisdom to do adulting.'

Indrajit raised his eyebrows. 'Are you learning our words, grand-uncle?'

Mareech laughed softly. 'I must learn at least a bit if I want to get through to you people.'

They passed the gates at the western-wing. Indrajit turned around and gave precise orders. 'Bar the dam-side gates from the inside. Lock and barricade them thoroughly. Then gather our horses and the provisions that you can carry. We ride out from the main hillside gate.'

His lieutenant saluted.

'And one more thing,' continued Indrajit. 'Burn all the provisions that we cannot carry with us.'

'Lord?' asked the lieutenant, hesitating.

'You heard me.'

'Yes, My Lord.'

The lieutenant and the soldiers saluted, and rushed to obey.

'And what do we do when we ride out?' asked Mareech.

'Grand-uncle, you should go to father and update him on all that has happened. Tell him that I will come within a day, and then we can decide on our subsequent battle strategy.'

'What do I say when Raavan asks me why you are here and not in Bali?'

Indrajit laughed. 'Tell him that I am the son of Raavan. Breaking rules and disobeying orders are a part of my genetic makeup!'

Mareech laughed and patted Indrajit on the back. 'But where are you headed? Where are you planning to go for a day?'

'I'm taking these men to the flood-water spillway gates far away at the back of the reservoir,' said Indrajit. 'The one that allows water from the reservoir to flow via a canal into the Amban Ganga upriver. I will block that spillway and break the controls.'

Mareech frowned. 'How will that help?'

'Jiujitsu.'

'What?!'

Indrajit didn't answer immediately, as his attention was diverted by the sound of the western-wing gate being shut and the wooden barricade being laid. He turned back to Mareech. 'Jiujitsu is a form of martial art from the Far East, grand-uncle. In it, we use our opponent's strength against him.'

Mareech frowned, confused. 'What does that have to do with the flood-water spillway, Indrajit?'

'Think about it. What is the Ayodhyan navy's main strength over our own?' asked Indrajit.

Mareech curled his lips in a snarl, exposing his upper teeth. 'Their ships are bigger than ours. Much bigger.'

'Precisely. They have used the floods on the Mahaweli Ganga and sailed their larger seafaring ships upriver. They assumed, logically, that our seafaring ships would be in Gokarna, and only the river navy would be here in Onguiaahra. My spies told me that their larger ships have metal-reinforced bow sections. They planned to ram our riverine ships with their seafaring ones and sink them. And with uncle Vibhishan—that traitor—in their camp, they expected to take control of Onguiaahra, flood the chokehold control-steps, and sail their bigger ships upriver. A smart strategy.'

'So what's your point?' asked Mareech, confused. 'Their seafaring ships are here. They will soon have control over Onguiaahra. It will take them a week at most to repair the sluice controls. They still have Vibhishan, and he is a brilliant engineer. Once the sluice controls are repaired, they can sail their seafaring ships here and ram us into oblivion.'

Indrajit smiled. 'What do seafaring ships need, grand-uncle, that riverine ships don't?'

And then it hit Mareech. 'Greater draught ... water displacement ...'

'Precisely. Much, much greater.'

Mareech smiled. *Brilliant!*

A ship displaces some amount of water in a river or sea, to take its place. The ship floats if the weight of the displaced water is more than the weight of the ship. Being bigger and heavier, a seafaring ship needs to displace more water. Obviously. Draught is the depth of the bottom-most part of the ship below the water line. Usually, the greater the water displacement, the greater the draught. The riverine Lankan ships had a draught of about one metre. If the Amban Ganga River retained a depth of more than one metre, they would float.

'So, what's the draught of the Ayodhyan ships?' asked Mareech.

'Skilful ship designers inscribe the draught across the ship hull. It's good product design. My spies tell me that seafaring Ayodhyan ships have a draught of five metres.'

Mareech could tell that Indrajit had some greater insight. 'And?'

'See, grand-uncle, the thing is that ship designers calculate the draught for seafaring ships only with sea water. Obviously. Not with river water ...'

Mareech smiled. 'River water is less dense.'

'Precisely. A ship that floats on the sea at a particular draught needs much greater draught in river water. Simple science.'

Mareech laughed.

'Like I said, the seafaring ships of Ayodhya have a draught of five metres in the sea. But they would need five and a half metres in river water. Which is good enough for the flooded Mahaweli Ganga. It would be fine in the Amban Ganga as well, if the flood-control spillway gates remained open and more water flowed into that river. However, if they were closed, then the Ayodhya ships would cross the control-steps but not be able to enter the Amban Ganga and confront the Lanka ships. They would get grounded.'

'Had they been conservative, they would have brought riverine ships and been able to sail up the Amban Ganga,' said Mareech.

'Exactly. But it's too late for that now.'

'Brilliant. Their strength – the bigger ships – has turned into a weakness. Jiujitsu.'

Indrajit nodded. 'They will eventually understand the reason behind the water shortfall and attack us on the reservoir as well. That's open ground, difficult to defend. And the extension walls from the Onguiaahra citadel cover the reservoir too, almost completely. They will ultimately take the flood-water spillway as well. But we will delay them by another week, maybe more.'

'That will frustrate them and bog them down. And they are far away from their supply chain. We are not. We may not defeat them, but we can drag this on and tire them in a battle of attrition.'

'Exactly.'

'Go do it, my boy. I'll handle Raavan.' Mareech looked at the unconscious Kshiraj. 'And what do you want to do with him?'

'I want to ask him some questions. I have a gut feeling that we are missing something. Something big. Maybe he can throw some light on what that is.'

'Do you want me to …' Mareech didn't go too deep into the indelicate manner in which Kshiraj could be made to talk.

'No, grand-uncle. Let me handle this. You go to father.'

'All right, my boy.'

— J≠ J͵ϽD —

'He's taken the eastern wing,' said Vibhishan, looking through his telescope.

As the early morning sun shone through, Bharat and Vibhishan stood at the poop deck of the lead ship of the Ayodhyan navy. The elevated deck was ideal for observation. Bharat could see the standard flag of Ayodhya on the eastern wing of the Onguiaahra citadel through his telescope. The regulation mark of the Ayodhyans was a white cloth with a red circular sun in the centre, its rays streaming out in all directions. At the bottom half of the standard, suffused by the bright rays of the sun, was a magnificent leaping tiger. Bharat saw their flag had been raised. But not on the western-wing. The Lankan flag continued to flutter in the air on that side. It was a black flag in which the head of a roaring lion emerged from a profusion of fiery flames. Bharat couldn't see the details in the flags, but the white and the black stood out in stark contrast.

'The western-wing is still under Lankan control,' said Bharat.

'Are those flames?' asked Vibhishan.

'Looks like it.'

'Dammit. They are burning up the stores. I hope Prince Lakshman isn't boxed in within the eastern wing. If the Lankans destroy the sluice controls on the dam, it will delay us by many days.'

Bharat remained silent.

Vibhishan turned to Bharat. 'Do you know, Prince Bharat, that the nerve fibre length in the human brain, when stretched end-to-end, is over eight hundred and fifty thousand kilometres long? That is more than twice the distance between our earth and the moon.'

Bharat tried not to reveal his perplexed irritation as he looked at Vibhishan. *What in Lord Indra's name is this fool talking about now? What does this have to do with Onguiaahra?*

Vibhishan spoke again. 'There is no instrument as powerful as the human brain. And it is time to use my brain over your brother's brawn.'

Bharat kept quiet.

'The sluice controls have most probably been destroyed,' continued Vibhishan. 'That's what I would do if I was Dhumraksha. That is why I had asked your brother to make quick work of it. I will need to go and start repairing the sluice controls. Conquering Onguiaahra is useless unless we control the dam waters.'

'You are right,' Bharat was constrained to admit. 'If Lakshman doesn't control the dam, that is.'

'I fear I might be right. For I don't see our flag fluttering over the central dam.'

Bharat continued to stare at Onguiaahra in the distance.

'Let me go,' continued Vibhishan. 'I can ride quickly up the main road to the eastern wing now. It's in our control. Send one hundred men with me. I will have the sluice controls ready for you in a few days.'

'I'll send three hundred men with you.'

Vibhishan bowed low, theatrically. 'Thank you, good prince.'

'But I want you to first bring the western-wing fires under control, make sure the tunnel to the western-wing is destroyed, and the main gate is effectively barricaded.'

'You are being too conservative, Prince Bharat. Doing all you ask will take a day or two. It will delay the repair of the sluices. I know the Lankans. They will not return. We need to be aggressive and move fast so that—'

'No,' said Bharat firmly. 'I will not risk unnecessary casualties.'

'But—'

Bharat moved close to Vibhishan and dropped his voice menacingly low. 'You will do as I tell you. Is that clear?'

Vibhishan surrendered. 'Yes of course, Prince Bharat.'

—JF Ɉ϶D—

'They now control Onguiaahra,' said Vashishtha. 'But it's a half-victory, says Lakshman.'

A messenger bird had arrived from the battlefront at the Mahaweli Ganga River. Bharat and Lakshman had taken some Indian peregrine falcons along with them; these fast-flying birds delivered messages across the island of Lanka in just a few hours. Well before lunch then, Vashishtha, Ram and members on the war council discussed the contents of the message.

'Half-victory?' asked Hanuman.

'They conquered the eastern wing in fifteen minutes, early this morning.'

'And the west wing?' asked Arishtanemi.

'They had control over it three hours later. The Lankans retreated to that wing and held off Lakshman's soldiers behind barricaded gates. They then set fire to their own stores. Lakshman had to get his soldiers to scale the wall and put out the fires. There were no Lankans around to offer any resistance by that time. They had all escaped through the open main gates of the fort.'

'So, we have control over both the wings of the citadel,' said Arishtanemi. 'We control all Onguiaahra. How is that a half-victory?'

'Did the Lankans destroy the sluice gate controls?' asked Shatrughan, immediately guessing what it meant.

'Yes,' said Vashishtha. 'So, we have won the prize basket. But the prize itself has been stolen.'

'Not stolen, just broken, Guruji,' said Shatrughan. 'A good engineering team can repair those sluice gates within a week, maybe even sooner.'

'True,' said Vashishtha. 'But we will not be able to flood the control-steps for one more week. Bharat's ships are stuck till then.'

'But this is perfect,' said Ram. 'I wouldn't call it a half-victory. I would call it a two-fold victory!'

Everyone turned to Ram.

Ram continued. 'Lakshman sees it as a half-victory because he is driven by bravery, not strategy. Bharat's daily message usually arrives by nightfall. I'm sure he will see it the way I do.'

'And how do you see it?'

'It is the perfect outcome. Had Bharat made no attempt to attack the Lankans, they would have gotten suspicious. Bharat knows that he is desperately undermanned, with only thirty-five thousand soldiers. Yesterday, his report stated that the Lankans have brought almost their entire army to Mahaweli Ganga. That is around one hundred and eighty thousand soldiers. The Lankans have the advantage of numbers and the additional advantage of being upriver. This is the reason why Bharat took the big seafaring ships with him. It isn't about attacking better, but defending better.'

'Fair point,' said Naarad.

'Attacking the Lankans against these odds is unwise. And not attacking them will make them suspect that our entire army is not there as yet. This is perfect. See this from the Lankan perspective. Bharat launched an audacious attack on Onguiaahra, with the help of the traitor Vibhishan, simply because Bharat is eager to cross over with his larger ships. But the brave Onguiaahra battalion has delayed him by smartly destroying the sluice controls. The Lankans will wait patiently at the river till Bharat's engineers repair the Onguiaahra sluice controls. And by the time it is repaired, we will move in from the west and be in Sigiriya.'

'Hmm,' said Hanuman. 'If Bharat's numbers are correct, then only twenty thousand soldiers are left in Sigiriya. We can simply march in. The battle will be over even before it begins.'

'Precisely,' said Ram. 'This is perfect.'

Chapter 24

Indrajit stared in frustration at Kshiraj, the captured Ayodhyan soldier.

It was late evening and Indrajit and his soldiers had blocked the flood-control spillways at the back of the reservoir to prevent deluge water from flowing into the Amban Ganga. After this they had destroyed the spillway sluice controls. Then they had retreated to the positions held by the Lankan navy on the western banks of the Amban Ganga. Deeper into the forest.

He looked at his soldiers, annoyance writ large on his face. 'Where the hell is she?'

Kshiraj bent forward, limp. His arms were stretched back and tied around a tree with a strong hemp rope. His legs were similarly stretched and tied. The rope was rough and hard, precisely as intended by the Lankans. It had made vicious cuts into his wrists and ankles as he had struggled. Of course, these were the least of the injuries on the unfortunate Ayodhyan.

Blood dripped from the open wounds where his finger nails had been pulled out. His eyelids had been pulled back and snipped off. Some toes were missing. His knees had been smashed with a hammer. A nail had been hammered into the crook of his right arm. It had dug into the anconeus muscle and cut the ulnar nerve. That had been particularly painful.

Kshiraj had screamed in pain, pleaded for mercy, cried out for his mother.

But he had not talked. He did not divulge any secret of the Ayodhyan army.

Indrajit was beginning to suspect that maybe what they knew was all there was to Ram's strategy: an overwhelming attack from the Mahaweli Ganga River and using the captured Onguiaahra citadel to open the floodgates. Maybe there was no secret to unearth. But a deep instinct continued to nag him that there was more. Like an itch he couldn't reach. And so, he was reluctant to give up on Kshiraj.

But he also understood that this method was not delivering results. He needed to tweak the torment. He needed a better torturer. And he had sent for one.

'Where is Brigadier Samichi, dammit? It's been two hours since I sent for her!'

Samichi, in an earlier life, had been the police and protocol chief of Mithila, working under the direct supervision of Princess Sita, the prime minister of the kingdom. Unknown to Sita, however, Samichi was a Raavan loyalist. When she was a child, the king of Lanka had saved her from her abusive father. It was this loyalty that had driven Samichi to betray her princess. Indrajit was aware that Samichi, along with her lover Khara, had extracted critical information from a Malayaputra soldier; an extremely tough warrior to break. The information was on the whereabouts of Sita, her husband Ram, his brother

Lakshman, and sixteen Malayaputra soldiers who were hiding in the forests of Dandak, close to the Godavari River. It was why Raavan had been able to kidnap Sita so easily, and with minimal loss of life.

Maybe Samichi would succeed with this obdurate man.

'My Lord!' said a relieved soldier. 'Brigadier Samichi has arrived.'

Indrajit turned around.

Samichi immediately went down on one knee and brought her clenched right fist up to her chest. 'My prince, I'm honoured to be called to your service.'

Samichi had been removed from her post by Raavan when she had tried to injure Sita in the Pushpak Vimaan, immediately after the princess had been kidnapped. Samichi's attempted assault was a natural reaction – Sita had killed Samichi's lover, Khara. Raavan had granted Samichi pardon in recognition of past services. However, to be discarded by her liege was a punishment worse than death for a warrior. She was, therefore, delighted to be called back to service by the Lankan royal family. Even if it was by the prince and not the king.

'Brigadier Samichi,' said Indrajit. She had been briefed already. But he wanted her to hear it from him directly. 'I fear that this Ayodhyan soldier has very little life left in him. I also have a suspicion that we are missing something – there is some part of King Ram's strategy that we are not aware of. I need this man to talk. And to live till he does so. Can you strike that fine balance?'

'Of course, My Lord!' exclaimed Samichi, smiling, eager to please. She turned to a Lankan soldier and said, her tenor radically different with a subordinate, 'You! Don't stand around staring like an idiot. I want you to tie the Ayodhyan scum's forehead to the tree. Keep it tight. He shouldn't be able to move

his head.' Then she turned to some other Lankans standing to
the side. 'You five, come with me! On the double!'

And Samichi raced into the forests, followed by the five
Lankans she had picked.

Within less than half an hour, Samichi was back.

Each of the five soldiers carried large banana leaves, with
nests perched on them. They weren't traditional nests made of
sticks, grass and leaves. These nests were made from the bodies
of the animals that they were carrying.

Indrajit looked bewildered. *Ants?*

Human beings labour under the delusion that they are the
most successful species on earth. It is a highly questionable
assumption.

Ants have been on earth for nearly one hundred million
years, well before human beings made their appearance. They
were around when dinosaurs walked the earth, and survived
whatever it was that destroyed those massive beasts. And then
their population exploded a few million years later. The ant
population is large, some estimates placing it in many thousands
of trillions. They constitute between fifteen to twenty per cent
of the terrestrial animal biomass; more than all humans and
mammals combined!

They build large, complex colonies and organise themselves
efficiently along job specialisation: some are worker ants, others
are soldiers, and most importantly there is the queen who
founds a colony of ants and dedicates herself to laying eggs
and producing the next generation. Ants, like human beings,
conduct wars and exhibit complicated battle strategies. Enmities
last generations. Their main competitive advantage is that an
entire colony, comprising perhaps a million to twenty million
ants, has a hive mind. Millions in one colony can self-organise
and work together, like an eerily coordinated superorganism.

When moving together, this 'superorganism' stretches many hundreds of metres.

These details about ants did not interest Samichi. What did interest her was their immense strength relative to their small size. It allowed them to deliver pain to the most unusual places.

'Place the nests over there,' said Samichi to the five soldiers, pointing to a spot in the distance but in full view. 'And make a small moat of water around the banana leaves, so that the ants cannot escape.'

'Yes, Brigadier,' said one of the soldiers, saluting.

Indrajit couldn't contain himself anymore. He wondered if he had made a mistake in summoning Samichi. 'Ants? Really?'

'They are not ordinary ants, great prince,' said Samichi. 'These are driver ants. More specifically, the soldiers of a driver ant colony.'

Driver ants are carnivorous; they feed on the flesh of other insects. When they attack in swarms, led by their soldier ants, they have been known to dismember and carry away far bigger creatures, such as chickens and goats. Even pigs, if they are injured or are unable to escape the marauding ants.

'Build a fire quickly,' Samichi brusquely ordered a soldier. And turned to Indrajit with an ingratiating smile. 'They are females ants, noble prince. Much more vicious.'

Indrajit wanted to ask how Samichi knew that the ants were female, but thought better of it. If he had asked, she would have told him: practically, the entire driver ant colonies are female; the males live for only a week and they either die or are killed after procreation.

Indrajit walked over to see the soldier ants. They were smaller than the queen ant but bigger than worker ants. The queen only delivers babies; she does little else. The worker ants only, well, work. The soldier ants are the warriors in the colony.

Fiercely protective of their own and aggressively combative with foreigners. They carry vicious weapons built into their body in the form of serrated claws and mandibles.

Samichi picked up a twig from the fire, brought it close to one of the nests on a banana leaf and blew smoke on to it. The temporary 'nests' of the soldiers among driver ants are not like those of other ants; they are made of the ants themselves. They cluster together to form walls and fasten onto each other using their mandibles and the claws on their legs, assembling what is in effect a living bivouac. As the smoke disturbed them, the bivouac began to dissolve and the ants scattered themselves across and beyond the banana leaf. A few of them drowned in the tiny watery moat around the leaf.

Samichi turned to a soldier and barked, 'Make a few hollow straws from the river reeds. Keep them ready.'

She then carefully picked up an ant with a pair of pincers. Watchful not to injure the tiny beast. The ant was a little less than one centimetre long; a good size for a driver ant. It had massive jaws; in fact, the jaws of soldier ants are so big that they are unable to feed and must rely on worker ants to give them all the nourishment they need. The soldier ant had a pale orange head, dark orange legs, and large, dark mandibles that were sharp and poisonous. It had fearsome claws on its legs. Its antennae jut out aggressively as Samichi carried it. Its serrated, poison-tipped mandibles clawing the air.

Indrajit watched. Captivated.

Samichi stared coldly at Kshiraj and said in a low, cruel whisper, 'Look at this soldier ant, Kshiraj.'

Kshiraj returned her stare, grim determination writ upon his face. He had survived everything they had done to him. What could an ant do? What could be worse?

But torture was a fine art for Samichi. Constant, gnawing pain can break the spirit. But only if it is carefully calibrated to a level of tolerance that the brain does not shut out.

Samichi gestured to one of the soldiers, who rushed forward and pushed a soft bit between Kshiraj's teeth. Samichi turned to Indrajit with an eerie smile. 'We don't want him biting off his tongue in pain. Otherwise, how will he talk?'

Indrajit stared at Samichi, a smidgen of cold fear gripping his heart. *She actually enjoys this...*

'I know what you are thinking, Kshiraj,' said Samichi to her prey, her tone soft and creepy. 'What can an ant do, right?'

Kshiraj did not respond.

Samichi continued. 'But an ant can do a lot. The venom of its sting will make even the true king of the jungle, the mighty elephant, holler for mercy.'

Samichi turned to another soldier, who ran up with a hollow reed straw that he had fashioned. Samichi took the straw from him.

'But it is crucial to ensure that the ant is in the right place.' Samichi laughed softly as she said this. 'It can do little on an elephant's back, which it will simply not penetrate. But deep inside an elephant's trunk ... aah, well.'

Samichi came close to Kshiraj's ear and whispered, 'I wonder if you know that your ear canal extends nearly three centimetres into your head.'

Kshiraj shrank with terror, not fearful of the ant but the freakishly monstrous aura that this woman exuded. But he could not move. His head had been tied tight.

Samichi continued to murmur, her face hideously excited with the prospect of inflicting pain. 'Do you know that we have very sensitive nerves on the other side of the eardrum? I have often wondered how to get deep enough inside the ear canal with something small and deadly.'

Samichi carefully pushed one end of the hollow reed deep inside Kshiraj's ear. As far as it would go. 'The obstacle, as I am sure you understand, is the structure of the ear canal. It's just too small. And not straight. But if we can get something sharp and deadly, deep enough in there ... Mmmm.' Samichi stepped back to admire her handiwork. 'Do you know that the nerves on the other side of your eardrum take all sensations from the ear directly to the brain? No filtration at the spinal cord. You will know soon enough. It took me some time to perfect this technique ... Some interesting experiments. You will find it ... memorable.'

Kshiraj's agitated eyes swivelled and stared at the wriggling insect. A drop of venom dribbled out of the soldier ant's serrated mandibles.

Samichi brought the soldier ant up to the hollow reed. And dropped it in. Then she covered the open end of the reed with some clay. And stepped back.

'Listen to it coming towards you.'

Kshiraj writhed in fear as he heard the footsteps of the ant, amplified by the hollow reed pushed almost up to his eardrum. It sounded like the distant thumping of elephant feet.

'Feel it coming ... hear it coming ...' Samichi whispered.

He made desperate attempts to drive the ant out. He tried to shake his head, his eyes rolling with possessed madness. But his entire body, including his head, had been tied securely to the tree, restricting his movements. And the hollow reed was lodged too deep inside.

He could feel it now. The ant had stepped out of the reed hollow and was in his ear canal. Scurrying around in anger, its body had released a piercing chemical stench, a natural reaction to perceived threat. The odour drove the ant into greater frenzy. It turned back into the hollow reed and rushed forward. It hit the soft clay covering the opening, turned around in a furious rage and charged.

Kshiraj was screaming inaudibly now, the sounds muffled by the bit in his mouth.

The soldier ant reached Kshiraj's eardrum, tested the tissue with its antenna, threw its head back, spread its poison-tipped mandibles and bit hard.

Kshiraj shrieked in agony. The bit could not hold back the sound. His eyes rolled into his head, the whites of his eyeballs staring blindly at the sky. His rigid and tense body strained against the unforgiving ropes that bound him in a vice-like grip. Desperate tears streamed out like a tiny river in spate. He was bathed in sweat. He lost control of his bowels. The contents of his intestines burst through and ran down his legs.

He screamed repeatedly. Howling for his God. Screeching for his *guru*. Wailing for the most powerful benefactor of all, his mother. His mouth cramped with the bit, it all emerged as a mash of indistinguishable blubber.

Indrajit looked at Samichi with horrified awe. 'Just an ant …?'

'It's all about putting it in the right place, great prince. The vestibular and cochlear nerves are very close to the eardrum. But wait … The real fun will begin if the ant manages to tear the eardrum. But that's up to the ant, of course. I cannot control that.'

Indrajit looked at Kshiraj.

The Ayodhyan was twisted with spasms of unbearable pain. The ant had caused a minor tear in the eardrum and the man was bawling with agonised desperation. He lost control of his bladder. Thick yellow urine dribbled down his legs to mix with his excreta. He was straining miserably against the ropes. The veins in his neck threatened to burst with his repeated attempts to shake his head.

'He'll break his neck,' said a worried Indrajit.

'No, he won't, My Lord,' insisted Samichi.

'He is no good to me if he dies.'

Samichi sighed inaudibly and walked up to Kshiraj. She took a swig of water from her bottle, removed the clay cover from one end of the hollow reed and spat the liquid through the reed into Kshiraj's ear. The water drowned the ant and its carcass emerged from the ear, flowing out and then sticking to Kshiraj's neck.

The Ayodhyan hung limp against the tree, his eyes swivelling wildly, his head and body shivering violently within the constraints of the tight ropes.

Indrajit flicked his fingers. A Lankan soldier rushed up to Kshiraj and removed the bit from his mouth. He loosened the bonds around the Ayodhyan's arms. He did not move. A thin dribble of vomit fell like droplets from the side of his mouth.

Indrajit walked up to Kshiraj, holding his angvastram against his nose to block the stench of the Ayodhyan's faeces and urine. 'Talk. And you shall have mercy.'

'You will have to wait for a bit, noble prince,' said Samichi. 'The inner ear is also the centre of the sense of balance. He is deeply disoriented right now.'

Indrajit waited for a few seconds and then spoke again. 'Talk … What is King Ram's secret strategy?'

Kshiraj's head moved infinitesimally, indicating response. A faint will to talk.

'Was that a nod, Prince Indrajit?' asked Samichi.

Indrajit looked at Samichi. 'Loosen the restraints around his head. But only a little.'

Samichi did as ordered. Kshiraj moved his head. He was shivering, his eyes wild and disoriented.

Indrajit stepped up close. 'Talk.'

Kshiraj's plea was frantic. 'Please … please … kill me …' His voice broke.

'Talk.'

'Please …'

'TALK!'

Kshiraj was silent for a few seconds, and then he spoke the words. Almost like they were prised out of him. 'Main army … not here …'

Indrajit glanced at Samichi and then back at Kshiraj.

'Main army … coming … from west …'

'From the west?' asked Samichi. 'That's not possible. There are no ports there. He's lying!'

Indrajit looked into Kshiraj's eyes. 'No, he is not.'

'But—'

Indrajit raised his hand and Samichi fell silent. What Kshiraj was saying sounded ludicrous, but some instinct in Indrajit made him believe it.

Indrajit asked Kshiraj again. 'From where in the west?'

Kshiraj remained silent.

'Do you want another ant?'

'Please … no …'

'From where in the west?'

'Dhanushkodi …'

'Dhanushkodi?! The sand flats are too high. Their ships will get grounded. They will not reach Lanka.'

'Crossing … to Lanka … on bridge …'

Indrajit's mouth fell open in shock. *A bridge? Across the sea?*

Dhanushkodi is right next to the Ketheeswaram temple. If they did manage to build a bridge and arrive in Lanka in that region, they would get to Sigiriya within a day via the royal road. He turned his head and looked at the river, towards the Lankan ships. *While we are stuck here, we will lose our capital.*

He looked at Kshiraj. *There's more. I know it …*

'What else?' asked Indrajit.

Kshiraj shook his head.

'Talk, Goddammit,' growled Indrajit.

Kshiraj refused to open his mouth.

Indrajit turned to Samichi. 'Another ant.'

Samichi carefully picked up another specimen from the banana leaf with her pincers. But before she could take her first step towards the Ayodhyan, he jerked his head forward and pushed his body against the ropes with sudden violence. The ropes held his head, legs and feet in an iron grip. But the binds around his arms had been loosened, allowing his torso some movement. Enough for his neck to snap as he jerked forward.

'Son of a …' Indrajit cursed in frustration, his hands flying to his head.

Samichi rushed forward and pulled Kshiraj's limp head up. He was dead. She looked at the ant she was holding, a deeply disappointed expression on her face.

Indrajit turned to a soldier. 'Get a rowboat. Quick. I must meet my father immediately.' As the soldiers rushed to obey, the Prince of Lanka turned to Samichi. 'You have done well, Brigadier. Thank you.'

Samichi had a half-smile on her face. She looked again at the ant and then crushed it between her fingers.

Chapter 25

'Go back to Sigiriya?!' asked Raavan, flabbergasted. 'Are you crazy?'

Raavan, Kumbhakarna, Mareech and Indrajit had gathered in the Lankan Emperor's sumptuous private cabin in the navy's main ship. Indrajit had reached the vessel late in the night. He had interrupted his father's dinner, insisting on meeting him immediately.

'Yes, father,' said Indrajit, his voice calm and confident. 'They have only sent a small diversionary force here.'

'Small diversionary force? Have you counted the number of ships?'

'Yes, I have! Perhaps they want to give us the impression that they have many soldiers. These ships are probably manned by skeletal staff. We cannot know for sure till we actually enter their ships, isn't it?'

'Perhaps? Probably? You want me to change my entire battle strategy on your "perhaps" and "probably"?'

'Father, I feel it in my guts – the information is correct. Their main army will come in from the west. They will conquer Sigiriya easily if we all remain here.'

'And what if you are wrong? What if we leave this river post and give the Ayodhyans an easy victory? And then they march all the way up to Sigiriya?'

'Even if that happens, we will be safely ensconced in our fort. Well-stocked and defended. They will be stranded outside with stretched supply lines. Trust me, it will be far worse if the Ayodhyans actually come from the west and take our capital. Then they will be inside our fort, well-stocked and defended, while we will be stuck outside. They will wear us down.'

Kumbhakarna spoke up. 'And how will they come from the west? What is your information on that?'

Indrajit looked at Mareech. He knew his father and uncle would find it difficult to believe what he had to say. Mareech nodded. *Tell them.*

Indrajit turned to Kumbhakarna. 'They are crossing over at Dhanushkodi, uncle. And then they will march up the Ketheeswaram temple road. It's less than a day's march to Sigiriya.'

'And how exactly will they cross over from the Indian mainland to Lanka?' asked Raavan, an incredulous look on his face. 'You know that area. Many sandflats are actually above the water level during low tide. No ship can safely anchor there.'

Indrajit took a deep breath. 'I believe they are building a bridge.'

Raavan and Kumbhakarna burst out laughing.

'Father ...' growled Indrajit, upset and angry.

Mareech cut in. 'Raavan, Kumbhakarna. Listen to Indrajit. I believe the information he has is true.'

Raavan turned to Mareech. 'Uncle, do you believe this nonsense? A bridge across the sea?! Really?!'

Mareech kept quiet.

'I think that the youngest among the brothers—Prince Shatrughan—could do it,' said Indrajit. 'He is brilliant.'

'Shatrughan may be brilliant, my boy,' said Raavan. 'But he's not a wizard. Nobody can build a bridge across the sea.'

'Father, trust me. I can feel it in my bones. The information I have is right.'

'Indrajit, don't be childish. You want me to retreat from here, based on something you extracted from a person you tortured. Do you realise how this will appear to our soldiers? They will see me as a coward! I'd much rather die here. Fighting.'

Mareech cut in once again. 'How about sending a few quick riders to Ketheeswaram to check this out? If it's nothing, then it's nothing. But if the Ayodhyans are actually crossing, then we can …'

'All right,' surrendered Raavan. He turned to Kumbhakarna. 'Send some riders tomorrow morning.'

'No, father,' said Indrajit. 'If you send them tomorrow morning, they will only return the day after. It may already be too late by then. Send them right away.'

Raavan was clearly irritated. 'My boy …'

'Father! Please! Just trust me!'

Raavan closed his eyes and shook his head. 'Fine! Send them now, Kumbha.'

—⅃Ⅎ ⅃�̄⁵D—

'Overproduction of elites? That's your big theory?' asked Vashishtha.

Vishwamitra, Vashishtha and Nandini were sitting on a large rock outside their gurukul, on the banks of the Kaveri River. The three friends were teachers at the gurukul of Maharishi Kashyap, the celebrated Saptrishi Uttradhikari, successor to the seven legendary seers. The three were in their early forties. Vishwamitra and Vashishtha had been students of the gurukul in their early years. Upon graduation, they had gone their separate ways. Vashishtha had shone as a celebrated teacher while Vishwamitra became a distinguished and feared Kshatriya royal. Two decades later, they had joined the prestigious institution again, this time as teachers. They had instantly rekindled their childhood friendship. In private, they still referred to each other by the gurukul names of their student days: Kaushik for Vishwamitra and Divodas for Vashishtha. There had been another student at the gurukul: Nandini. A brilliant girl from the land of Branga, the lush, rich, fertile delta that the confluence of the Brahmaputra and Ganga rivers watered. She was now a stunningly beautiful woman. Nandini had been just an acquaintance during their childhood, but had now become a good friend. She had not just converted the duo to a trio, but had dramatically improved the quality of the group. For not only was she as intellectually luminous as the formidable Vishwamitra and Vashishtha, she was more attractive than the two men could ever have hoped to be!

'Not just overproduction of elites, Divodas,' said Vishwamitra to Vashishtha. 'That is only one half of the theory. The other half is the immiseration of the masses.'

'Immise-what?' asked Nandini.

'It means economic impoverishment. Making someone poorer.'

'So why not just say "impoverishment of the masses" then?' Nandini joked. 'Using big words doesn't make you sound more intelligent, Vishwamitra.'

Vishwamitra narrowed his eyes and mock-glared at Nandini. The love he felt for her made him control the irritation that yearned to express itself on his face.

'You are intelligent enough as it is, Vishwa,' said Nandini. 'All of us know that.'

Vishwamitra smiled. He loved it when Nandini called him by that nickname.

'So,' continued Vashishtha. 'The immiseration of the masses and overproduction of elites ...'

'Yes,' continued Vishwamitra, looking pointedly at Nandini with a smile, 'the impoverishment of the masses and overproduction of elites. This theory only applies to large, complex civilisations, obviously. Not to small groups. The key ingredient that makes large and complex civilisations possible is cooperation among massive numbers of people. At the biggest scale, even millions of people can cooperate and live together, like in our India. And this entire societal structure among humans works on a social contract between an elite which leads, and the masses that follow.'

'But some New Age people say that this entire concept of elite and masses is a social construct,' said Nandini. 'It's artificial and should be broken. We should go back to the natural way.'

'The "natural way" means an average lifespan of thirty years, many women and infants dying in childbirth, even a small cut on a finger probably leading to death, violence and hunger every few days. Because in the brilliant "natural way", we would be living like animals. Of course, the concept of an elite and the masses living together in large societies is artificial. The entire idea of millions of individuals cooperating is artificial. But just because it's not "natural" doesn't mean that it's not good.'

'But I think the point they make is about the difference between the elite and the masses. It is not inclusive.'

'I agree that too much power concentrated in the hands of the elite is not good. We must have balance. But swinging to the other extreme is also not good. Also, this thing about being inclusive ... Look, by its very nature, excellence is not inclusive. It cannot be inclusive. It has to be exclusive. You can either have inclusiveness, where everyone feels involved, or you can have excellence, where those who are good at a certain thing are given the freedom and encouragement to achieve, with the hope that society at large will also benefit. But you have to pick one, either inclusivity or excellence. You cannot have both. And without excellence, civilised life is not possible. But I'll say it again, we need balance. The elite should not be too powerful.'

'And, hence, the social contract. Which is a balance between the elite and the masses. Neither side becoming too powerful.'

'Precisely. If the social contract works, then both the elite and the masses are happy, and the society is successful. If the social contract breaks down, the society collapses into political violence and chaos.'

'So, why do the social contracts within societies break down?' asked Nandini. 'And what does your theory say about how it can be prevented?'

'I should clarify,' said Vishwamitra, 'it's not my theory. At least not originally. I have built on it, but I heard the basics of this theory from a man I met in the Yamnaya steppelands, a man called Turchin.'

'The Yamnaya?!' Vashishtha was shocked. The Yamnaya were one of the tribes that lived on the vast steppes that stretched over eight thousand kilometres from Europe through Central Asia to Eastern Asia. These fertile, undulating grasslands were perfect for breeding the best horses in the world, far superior to the smaller equus found in India. They also produced hardy, tough, nomadic humans, among whom the males were usually raised from childhood for one profession alone: the fine art of killing and plundering. And among the most brutal and genocidal of these steppe tribes were the Yamnaya. 'They are just brutal killers. There cannot be any intellectuals among those barbarians.'

'Well, Lord Turchin is the exception that proves the rule.'

'*Actually, it makes sense,*' said Nandini. '*The entire way of life of the people of the steppes is to attack and plunder the settled civilisations. Those civilisations that exist along the Mediterranean Sea, the Middle East, the Indian subcontinent and China. If they want to attack and plunder us, they need to understand us. They need to know when and where to attack so that they get the maximum loot for every person they kill.*'

'*Correct,*' said Vishwamitra. '*The hunter must understand the prey.*'

'*We are hardly the prey!*' exclaimed Vashishtha.

'*Well, we are not the prey when we are strong. But when we are weak, yes, we do become the prey to the killers of the steppes. The best defence against external enemies is our own strength and unity.*'

'*Hmm …*'

'*So, the theory …*' said Nandini. '*Why do civilisations weaken and collapse?*'

'*The theory states that this is a natural corollary to success. Some call it catastrophic success. The seeds of failure of some complex societies are sown in their journey towards success.*'

'*How so?*'

Vishwamitra continued, '*When a society is on the path of success, it gets richer steadily. And if the elite is efficient and just, as it would be in a successful society, they would share the rewards fairly with the masses. So, the masses also get richer and healthier steadily. But resultantly, the masses multiply. They grow in numbers. And as their numbers increase, the labour supply also grows. This is not a problem if the elite continuously finds new ways to grow the economy and absorb the increased labour into jobs. But if they fail to do that, and the supply of labour keeps growing, then the price of labour—wages—will steadily fall. And as wages for the masses fall, they get poorer and angrier, creating the conditions for rebellion, even revolution.*'

'But wages can fall for other reasons, right?' asked Nandini. 'Like the elite allowing in a massive number of immigrants, without creating enough jobs to absorb those immigrants. Or the elite importing goods from other lands where the masses earn less.'

'True,' said Vashishtha. 'And I guess we can call that elite selfish. But they write their own long-term doom. The main point is that, if the masses become poorer or unhealthier as compared to before, they are unhappy and this creates the conditions for a revolution. A smart elite, with basic survival instincts, should want to control this and ensure that the masses don't become too unhappy.'

'Absolutely,' said Vishwamitra. 'Every member of the elite should realise that he or she needs to help the poor masses constantly. It is in their own selfish interest. If they don't do that, they will need to spend more and more money on a bigger security and military set-up to keep the masses suppressed and under control. And even that has limits. At some point or another the military will get overwhelmed. But a revolution won't be triggered just by the masses getting impoverished. The masses, by definition, don't lead. They follow. Their unhappiness creates a necessary condition for rebellion, political violence and social breakdown. But it is not sufficient. This discontentment must be accompanied by another phenomenon.'

'What phenomenon is that?' asked Vashishtha.

'The rise of a counter-elite,' said Vishwamitra.

'Those who will lead the rebellion and revolution?' asked Nandini.

'Exactly,' said Vishwamitra. 'And the conditions for the emergence of a counter-elite are created by the impoverishment of the masses. As the masses become poorer, their wages fall, and those who consume the labour of the masses – the elite – become wealthier. As the gap between the two increases, the aspirations of the masses become focused and acute. The talented among them are

desperate to enter the elite ranks. In fact, more and more people from the masses try ever harder to join the elite, because the rewards appear so attractive. This is especially true if the elite is ostentatious, showing off their wealth rather than being conservative and understated.

'Some among the masses gradually become a part of the elite. They work hard, educate themselves and rise. But the problem is that the elite cannot keep expanding. There are only so many elite positions. There can only be one king. There can only be one chief general of the army. There can only be one chief priest of a religion. A big lie told to children today in civilised societies is that all of them are special, all of them can aspire to reach the top. This is nonsense. The top does not have endless space. The nature of a complex society makes the elite a small class. And if there are more and more aspirants for the elite class, logically more and more people will be denied their ambitions and psychological space under the sun. And these aspirants then get frustrated and become the counter-elite.'

'Since, usually, the counter-elite has risen from the masses by the dint of their hard work, are they more capable than the children of the old elite?' asked Vashishtha.

'Precisely,' agreed Vishwamitra. 'The elite aspirants who have risen from the masses have fire in their belly. This is why they have risen. And the children of the old elite are born with a silver spoon in the mouth. Most of them have very little appetite for hard work and the sacrifices necessary for success. They think they are entitled to be the elite and that mommy and daddy will ensure it for them.'

'True,' said Nandini, smiling wickedly. She and Vashishtha were both self-made.

'Hey!' said Vishwamitra, laughing softly. For he was the son of a king, clearly a progeny of the old elite. 'Not every kid born with a silver spoon is fat and lazy.'

'*I agree with you on lazy,*' *said Vashishtha, sniggering.* '*But fat? I don't know …*'

Vishwamitra looked at his massive belly and laughed aloud. He playfully punched his friend Vashishtha on the shoulder. Vashishtha leaned over and hugged his friend, both laughing in unison now.

Nandini also laughed. '*All right, all right. Settle down, you two.*'

'*Yeah, okay,*' *said Vishwamitra, patting Vashishtha and leaning back.*

'*So … these changes in society, they take place over long periods of time, right?*' *asked Nandini.*

'*Yeah, of course. These changes take place over decades. So those who are in charge of the long-term health of a society should keep a check on some parameters, so they have enough advance warning of oncoming societal chaos. What should those parameters be? Like these… How much inequality exists between the masses and the elite? What should its limit be, beyond which some intervention must be made? Is there an overproduction of elites? How many aspirants compete for each elite position? Is a counter-elite rising?*'

'*One clarification, please. When you say elite, you don't only mean Brahmins, Kshatriyas and Vaishyas, right?*'

'*Of course not,*' *said Vishwamitra.* '*There are many Brahmins, Kshatriyas and Vaishyas who are not part of the elite. For example, teachers in small schools, or soldiers, or sub-traders in a trading guild. And many Shudras are a part of the elite: for example, Shudra artistes, like storytellers and painters with big followings, are part of the ideological elite. So, this is not about the varna that people belong to. It is about power; those who have it and those who don't. The elite class is defined by one thing alone: power. Those who exercise power over others in their society are members of the elite.*'

'*Okay,*' *said Nandini.*

'So, how do we control this process?' asked Vashishtha. 'A smart elite should be able to anticipate these problems and avoid or control them, before they blow their society up.'

'Right,' said Vishwamitra. 'The first and foremost way is ensuring that the material life of the masses steadily improves. Whatever varna the masses belong to, their life must continuously improve, even if in small measures. Remember, the masses don't evaluate their state in comparison to people from other countries. They compare it to their own past. India is the richest country on earth. So, the Indian masses are far richer than the Greek masses, for instance. If the Indian masses become worse off, they will move towards dissatisfaction, protests and rebellions, even if, in their poorer state, they remain economically better off than the Greeks.'

'Yeah,' said Vashishtha. 'That's true.'

'So, it is in the interest of the elite to help the poor. Be mindful of them. When in doubt, help the poor. When you have nothing else to occupy yourself with, help the poor. The default position of a smart elite must always be: help the poor.'

'And the problem of overproduction of elites?'

'It's different for the elite. I don't think their material life should be on an ever-improving spiral. In fact, I do think that for the sake of stability in a society, there must be a periodic culling of the elite. So that the old elite, which has become fat and lazy, is replaced by a new rising elite, with more energy and drive.'

'Culling?' asked Nandini. 'Isn't that cruel? Really, Vishwa, I wish you would measure your words. Words have energy, my friend!'

'Look, I speak my mind, using the most descriptive and not necessarily appropriate words. In any case, that's what happens with political civil violence, doesn't it? Many elite members are killed, and then there is less internal competition in that class. In fact, often, elite overproduction leads to some of the old elite or even the counter-elite, inviting foreign intervention. Garnering additional *support and validation. This is the point that Turchin from the Yamnaya tribe was making to me. He said that Yamnaya warriors are on the lookout for countries with too many people in the elite class. Some among them are open to inviting these warriors of the steppes to assist them in their internal battles with the other elite in their own nation. Like a flock of sheep inviting wolves to kill the sheep they don't like. This normally doesn't end well for the sheep that sends out the invitation as well. Intra-elite civil war is disastrous for a society.'*

'So, competition between different elite groups must be reduced before it reaches this stage, I suppose.'

'Precisely. There are many ways to achieve this, if we want to avoid intra-elite civil wars and the incumbent chaos. The simplest is to expel specific elite groups from the country. Subtly, of course, by creating conditions for their departure. Let them compete in some foreign land, not in India. Then there will be less intra-elite competition within India. But there is one other way.'

'Your Maika system ...' said Vashishtha.

'Maika system?' asked Nandini. 'What is that?'

'Kaushik had expanded upon this once,' Vashishtha took over, using Vishwamitra's gurukul name. 'Quite a radical idea. He suggested that children must be compulsorily adopted by the State at the time of birth. The birth parents would surrender their children to the kingdom. The State would feed, educate and nurture the innate talents and capabilities of these children. At fifteen years of age, they would be tested on their physical, psychological and mental abilities in a rigorous examination. Based on the results, appropriate castes would be allocated to them. Subsequent training would further polish their natural skills. Eventually, they would be adopted by citizens of the same caste as the one assigned to the adolescents through the examination process. The children would

not know their birth parents, only their adoptive caste-parents. The birth parents, too, would not know the fate of their birth children.'

Nandini raised her eyebrows. 'Only someone who has not had children will think that parents will willingly hand over their child to the State.'

'But this system will be perfect for society, Nandini,' said Vishwamitra. 'Think about it with an open mind. In a sense, we are reducing the status of those who are incapable among the old elite's descendants every generation. They will become a part of the masses. And those from the masses, who are capable, will join the elite. In an open and fair way. Even those descendants of the old elite who are capable can rejoin the elite club, but without any special boosts that a doting mummy and daddy may give them. The elite will remain efficient and capable for much longer. It will keep the society stable. It will also keep it competitive.'

'But you're envisioning a society built exclusively around duty and efficiency. What about love? What are we human beings without love?'

'Love is the greatest illusion, Kaushik believes,' said Vashishtha, smiling. 'Or at least, that's what he believed many years ago.'

'Really?' asked Nandini, looking at Vishwamitra, eyes twinkling.

Vishwamitra didn't say anything.

Nandini turned to Vashishtha. 'Maybe love is an illusion, maybe it isn't. But even so, there is no reason we should not enjoy it while we feel it. Illusion or not. Only those who have not suffered the dreary desert of grief will deny the ethereal, even if temporary, comfort of love.'

Vashishtha seemed uncomfortable. He went back to the subject at hand. 'Well, I don't know if such a society is even possible. Where can the Maika system be implemented? I admit, though – it would be a very interesting experiment.'

Nandini smiled and looked away from Vashishtha, almost imperceptibly shaking her head.

'I am sure I can convince the next Vishnu to implement this system,' said Vishwamitra.

Nandini laughed softly. 'You have to become the chief of the Malayaputras first.'

'That will happen …'

'That certainly will,' said Vashishtha. 'My friend will make it.'

Vishwamitra looked at Vashishtha, smiled, and patted his friend's hand.

Nandini looked at both of them as a shadow of pain briefly crossed her face. And then it lifted. 'I have one more question.'

'Shoot,' said Vishwamitra.

'Many Kshatriya royals attack Vaishya businessmen these days. I think there may come a time when they will start appropriating Vaishya wealth. Would you call that a culling of a segment of the elite, in a manner of speaking?'

'No, I would call it bigotry and stupidity.'

'Why? You just said that there must not be too many elite members.'

'It's like this. There are four kinds of power: military, economic, political and ideological. Military power is based on the ability to use violence. This could be the army or police or any other such agency. Economic power is not about just wealth, but the ability to use that wealth. For example, a wealthy businessman may have more personal wealth than the managing partner of a large trade guild, but the managing partner can wield power derived from the guild's money. So, this hypothetical managing partner of ours may have less money than the businessman, but she is more powerful. Therefore, she is elite. Political power is exercised by politicians and administrators; basically, the king, top bureaucrats, the judges, et al., who use the administrative machinery of the State to enforce

their will upon the people. Lastly, ideological power is the ability to make the masses buy into ideas and memes that are supportive of the elite group's grip on power. The ideological elite could include storytellers, academics, reporters, artistes and such others. Now, a coherent elite group will have ALL four power sources. They must have intra sub-groups with the ability to deploy all these four sources of power. Therefore, one sub-group attacking another sub-group in its own elite group is stupidity and, frankly, long-term suicide.'

'Interesting …' said Vashishtha. 'So, which are the elite groups in India today, you think?'

'I think the groups aren't as obvious as you might imagine. I believe there are three elite groups in India. The holy Saraswati River divides …'

Vashishtha suddenly awakened from the dream. A dream that recalled a memory that was more than a century old. 'Oh Lord Brahma!'

It was late in the morning. Vashishtha knew that Shatrughan was planning to restart construction a day earlier than planned. Half the mahouts had recovered. The pace of work would be slower, but it was better than nothing. Vashishtha had dozed off again after breakfast. A short nap on the beachside of Pamban island. And this dream had come to him. For a reason.

I know what he will do …

Vashishtha looked at the sky. Remembering his friend turned foe.

Kaushik … I know what you will do … the Anunnaki …

Chapter 26

The Lankan lay on the ground, struggling with surprising strength given the knife buried deep in his abdomen. The Ayodhyan sat astride him, beating his face repeatedly with his right fist. He had covered the Lankan's mouth with his left hand and was straining to get to his throat. Strangulate and finish the scuffle. The Lankan kept shifting, not giving the Ayodhyan clear punches. He boxed the Ayodhyan's chest, slapped his head. But each successive Lankan blow was weaker. He was losing too much blood from the wound in his abdomen.

The Ayodhyan held his grip on the Lankan's mouth. He had to. If the Lankan screamed, they would be discovered. There could be others.

The Lankan had locked his chin into his chest. Protecting his neck. At last, the Ayodhyan managed to prise his head away, while continuing to keep his mouth covered. He quickly gripped the Lankan's neck with his right hand. A vice-like grip. The Lankan was bucking desperately. Trying to push the

Ayodhyan off. The Ayodhyan's thumb found the bony cartilage of his larynx. And he pressed. Hard. Now he could safely release his left hand from the Lankan's mouth. No sound was possible anymore. He quickly brought both his hands into play and squeezed brutally. The Lankan's hands and legs thrashed the soft muddy ground. His eyes bulged from the vicious pressure on his throat.

'Just die, dammit,' whispered the Ayodhyan.

The Lankan was twitching weakly now. The Ayodhyan increased the pressure mercilessly. Harder and harder, he squeezed. Finally, the Lankan lay still, his limp tongue protruding from his mouth. The Ayodhyan picked a stone from the ground and banged it repeatedly on the Lankan's head, breaking it. Just in case.

He got up. Exhausted. And looked around.

Five Lankans lay dead around him. And four Ayodhyans; his comrades.

The Ayodhyan was a member of a small squad, a hunter-gatherer band that had spread out into the Lankan heartland to rummage for food. To provision the massive Ayodhyan army that was on the verge of crossing over. This particular band were early-morning scouts who hunted nocturnal animals just as they prepared to turn in. None of the Ayodhyan bands had run into Lankans until now. They believed that the Lankans had retreated to Sigiriya.

Hence, they had been momentarily stunned when they ran into the small band of Lankans. The Lankans were clearly shocked too. The clash had been swift and brutal.

The Ayodhyan slowly got his breathing back to normal. He had to rush back and report. To the commander of the landing brigades, Arishtanemi.

The Lankans are here!

As his breathing returned to normal and the adrenaline eased up, he looked at the scene around him with fresh eyes. He knew that Arishtanemi would ask him probing questions.

What the hell were these Lankans doing here by themselves? So far from their base?

He looked at the Lankan horses that they had ridden on. They had probably come from far. The Ayodhyans had no horses, for they foraged on foot.

The Lankan horses were tied to stumps. *These men were waiting here. Why? Lying in ambush for us? But our path was not pre-determined. They were waiting here for some other reason.*

And then he noticed something he should have seen earlier. There were six horses. And only five dead Lankans.

Oh Lord Ru—

The Ayodhyan didn't have the time to complete his thought. A knife flew in and pierced his throat. He fell back on the ground. Right next to the Lankan he had just killed. Through blurring eyes, he saw a man descending from the tree branches. The man came up close, pulled out another knife, and savagely stabbed the Ayodhyan in the heart.

Having silenced the enemy, the man, a Lankan, rose to his feet and rushed to his horse.

He had seen all he needed to see. He had climbed up the tree earlier to get a better look. From his vantage point at the top of the tree on the dense forested hill, he had seen a lot. Far into the distance, towards the beach of Ketheeswaram. It was early morning but there was enough light. He saw at least two thousand Ayodhyans at work; cutting trees, building stockades and generally preparing for the arrival of an army.

By the size of the stockade, it would be a formidable army.

He could also see the Ketheeswaram battalion quarters, the local base for Lankan soldiers. Or what was supposed to have been the base. For the building was burned down.

The Ketheeswaram temple remained untouched. Of course. No civilised man would damage a temple to the Gods. He had, in fact, seen some Ayodhyans enter the temple with garlands made from flowers. Perhaps for the morning prayers.

He couldn't see beyond the south-east coast of Mannar island, so he couldn't be sure whether a bridge was being built or not. When he had been specifically tasked with checking that, he had been incredulous.

A bridge across the sea? Ridiculous!

But one thing was certain. Whatever method the Ayodhyans were using to cross over to Lanka, clearly they were preparing for it.

I must rush back. To warn the king.

—— J∓ ⅃⅃𐌃 ——

'I will not go back to the land of the Indus, Guruji,' said Naarad firmly. 'The battle is here.'

Vashishtha was speaking with Naarad in one corner of Pamban island. They were alone. And yet, Vashishtha was whispering. He knew that Arishtanemi's Malayaputras were all around.

'Listen to me, Naarad,' Vashishtha said softly. 'This is critical. Please. You needn't go yourself. But you must send a message to your best spy. I need this information.'

'But the other day you said that the Anu were not coming. That they will not support King Ram.'

'I am not talking about this battle, Naarad. I am talking about the battle that will follow this one.'

Naarad remained silent.

'I am not thinking about tomorrow,' whispered Vashishtha. 'It is the day after tomorrow that I worry about. You have one of the best intelligence-gathering networks in the land. Do this for me. Do this for the good of Mother India. Please.'

Naarad nodded. 'All right, Guruji.'

— JF J5D —

'My son ...'

Raavan was clearly moved. A rare display of emotion. He held Indrajit's head, bent over, and touched his forehead to that of his son. His eyes closed. His breathing was ragged.

Late in the evening, the Lankan royal council had received word that the Ayodhyan army had gathered on the north-west coast of Lanka, close to the Ketheeswaram temple. After the initial shock, the decision to be taken was obvious to all. The bulk of the Lankan army would disembark from their ships and be taken on a forced march to Sigiriya to reach their capital before the Ayodhyans did. And prepare for siege.

A small contingent of the Lankan forces would remain on the ships at Onguiaahra. And hold these Ayodhyans here as long as possible. If the Lankans abandoned this area completely, the Ayodhyans would lower their cutter boats from the massive seafaring ships, quickly row to the landing point for Sigiriya, march up the road and attack the Lankan army from the rear. But if a part of the Lankan river navy remained, the Ayodhyans would be wary of taking them on in their tiny cutter boats.

Net-net, the Lankan army needed a rear-guard to protect its retreat from the Ayodhyan navy at the Mahaweli Ganga. And Indrajit had offered to lead that rear-guard.

'Father,' grinned Indrajit. 'Don't worry. I'm not going to die. I'll see you in Sigiriya.'

Raavan laughed softly. 'You remind me of me sometimes.'

'I am better than you, dad. I can defeat you in a one-on-one.'

Raavan laughed loudly now. 'You are the only one who can say that and remain alive!'

'A man never gets defeated by his son,' Mareech said. 'He just sees a better version of himself.'

Raavan and Indrajit smiled and hugged each other.

Kumbhakarna stepped forward and patted Indrajit on his back. 'I'll see you in Sigiriya, my boy.'

Indrajit hugged Kumbhakarna. 'I'll see you soon, uncle. Prepare for the siege.'

'Yes, we will.'

'Are you sure about this, uncle?' Raavan asked Mareech.

Mareech had offered to stay back with Indrajit. To fight the Ayodhyans at Onguiaahra.

Mareech smiled. 'Well, there has to be some adult supervision!'

All four burst out laughing.

—JF JꞱꓘD—

Seafaring ships have many strategic advantages in battles. They have many sails, so they can catch even the slightest wind and harness it to power the ship. They have many decks, one above the other, to allow for offensive attacks from many levels. Some well-designed vessels have reinforced bows, to ram other ships. But it is the massive mainmast that provides the key edge in a riverine naval battle.

If the sails are big, the mainmast must be very tall. And on Bharat's lead ship, it soared to almost a hundred and fifty feet. This was very useful for gathering information.

High-quality information is as valuable as tonnes of gold in a war.

All seafaring ships have a lookout point at the top of the mainmast. It is essentially a barrel with a reinforced bottom and railing, rigged up high on the mainmast. The barrel-man is usually one of the youngest in the crew and with the best eyesight. He mans the lookout points and reports his findings below.

Bharat was speaking with the barrel-man.

'What do you see?' asked Bharat, speaking loudly into the speaking-trumpet.

Through out the night, the Ayodhyans had heard distant sounds of trees being hacked with axes from beyond the control-steps of Onguiaahra. Bharat had wanted this checked at first light of dawn. The answer was not a surprise to the crew.

'They are cutting trees, My Lord,' the barrel-man hollered into the speaking-trumpet. 'Some of the tree trunks have been dropped into the river.'

Bharat looked at Lakshman. The latter had returned to Bharat's lead ship after securing both wings of the Onguiaahra citadel. The sluice-gate controls were being repaired by Vibhishan and his engineers.

'Dada,' said Lakshman. 'It's a simple idea … They will clog up the Mahaweli Ganga with wooden logs. Making it difficult for us to sail up the river, even after we repair the Onguiaahra dam sluice controls. These are delaying tactics. It can slow us down but it will not stop us.'

Bharat frowned. Something didn't feel right. *This is too defensive. Not like Raavan at all, whose aggressive proclivities are well known. As it is, we are delayed due to the repair work at Onguiaahra. How much will the wooden logs help them? They will be useless against seafaring ships. We can just break through. Such logs are effective only against small riverine ships and cutter boats … How will this move help the Lankans?*

And then it struck him.

Dammit!

He looked at the barrel-man and thundered into the speaking-trumpet. 'Come down! Now!'

'Yes, My Lord,' replied the barrel-man.

Bharat fixed the speaking-trumpet back on its mainmast hold. He removed his angvastram from his shoulder and handed it to Lakshman.

'Dada?'

Bharat looked at Lakshman.

'Dada …' said Lakshman. 'You are thirty-three years old. Not as young as you used to be. Are you sure that you—?'

Lakshman stopped mid-sentence as Bharat glared at him. He immediately raised both his hands in surrender and grabbed the angvastram.

Bharat bent and gathered the mid-pleats of his dhoti. He tucked them into his waistband, both front and back. The ends were well above the knees now and tightened around his thighs.

Meanwhile, the barrel-man had descended onto the deck.

Bharat grabbed the climbing rope with both hands, swung his knees and ankles around it, grinned at Lakshman, and began climbing. Smooth, fluid motions. Just like he had learnt in the *gurukul*. Using the hands to haul himself up, and the ankles and knees for support and stabilisation. He used the rigging to rest briefly when necessary, for Lakshman was right; Bharat was getting on in age. But he made it above the windless sails in almost the same time as the much-younger barrel-man had.

Bharat dropped into the barrel of the lookout point. Or crow's nest, as it was called in naval lingo. He was a little short of breath.

Lakshman is right. I am getting old.

He took a moment to catch his breath and allow his heart to slow down. He was well above the treeline. Well above the stale odour of the perpetually moist sail canvas. Well above the dank, constant smell of human refuse and sweat of sailors who lived, slept, ate and abluted on the ship. Well above the tangy fragrance of soggy Lankan soil. Well above the dense tropical trees and vegetation.

Fresh clean open air.

Bharat breathed it in deeply. It calmed his heart and at the same time energised him.

He looked upriver. Into the distance.

Along the curve of the Mahaweli Ganga, beyond the Onguiaahra control-steps, he saw the trees being cut. Some logs were already floating in the river. Others were piling up at the control-steps that were above water. The clogging would spread.

Some lead Lankan ships had pulled back. Logical. To create space in the water for the logs of wood.

Where is Raavan's ship?

The chief admiral led from the front in Indian naval battles. It was a tradition. He wouldn't hide behind the cover of lead ships. That would be pusillanimous. More importantly, his pennant flapped proudly from the top of the mainmast. It was a challenge to his enemies: here I am. Come and get me.

That is how real men fought.

So ... where is Raavan's ship?

It had been spotted earlier. It had definitely been there. True to tradition and valour, right at the head of the Lankan command. Bharat had a sinking feeling in the pit of his stomach that his suspicion was right.

He looked upriver.

Legends hold that the term 'crow's nest' was coined by the Asura navigators. They were the first to travel deep into the oceans. Most seafarers preceding them always kept land in sight while sailing, their shipping lanes hugging the coast lines. This imposed longer routes and, hence, prolonged travel times. The Asura ships travelled straight, as 'the crow flies'. They were able to do this due to better navigation equipment that helped them venture far into the oceans. There were rumours about a peculiar element: that they always travelled with a cage filled with crows, secured to the lookout point on the mast. In poor visibility, a crow was released and the navigator plotted a course corresponding to the bird's flight path. As the crow would invariably head towards the nearest land mass.

The Asura Divine, it was believed, had imposed one strict diktat: that the crow's nest must *not* be placed at the absolute top-point of the mainmast. For the top of the ship was the seat of their God, who guided the sailors of the ship. And, it was believed, their God did not like crows. Not beside him.

Was it true, this legend? Only the Asura God knew.

But the tradition passed down with fidelity. The lookout point barrel was always fixed a little below the mainmast's top point. There was, therefore, a point at least seven to eight feet higher than the crow's nest.

A better view. If Bharat could climb it.

And he made the choice. He began to climb.

'Dada …' whispered a worried Lakshman from the deck, over one hundred and fifty feet below.

The climb was fraught with risk. The top of the mainmast wasn't designed for climbing. It was slippery wood. There were no safety nets below. A fall from that height to hard wood below would not lead to serious injury—it would mean death.

Bharat made quick work of it.

And looked deep upriver into the Lankan naval positions.

Lord Rudra, have mercy!

Chapter 27

It was late in the morning, the second hour of the second prahar. The Lankans were relentlessly cutting trees – more and more and more – and pushing them into the river, ahead of their positions. Between them and the Ayodhya navy. The cutting and chucking had begun the previous night, almost immediately after Raavan, Kumbhakarna and most of the Lankan navy had retreated. Indrajit had stayed behind with a skeletal convoy of twenty riverine ships. Arrayed against a massive naval armada of four hundred Ayodhyan ships.

The son of Raavan intended to conduct a rear-guard defensive action for as long as possible, to allow the rest of the Lankans to retreat behind the fort walls of Sigiriya, safe and sound. After which he would retreat as well, along with his remaining soldiers.

'King Ram – or whoever is in charge, if King Ram is on the western front – would have been informed by his lookouts at first light that the bulk of the Lankan navy was retreating,' said Indrajit. 'The Ayodhyans would know that they cannot get their seafaring ships past the control-steps and up the Amban Ganga River. But their seafaring ships would be loaded with multiple cutter boats. Hundreds of these boats could set sail, each loaded with soldiers. These smaller cutter boats could easily get past the control-steps, and then attack and overwhelm us with their sheer numbers. We have only twenty ships now. They could then give chase to our Lankan comrades who are on their way back to Sigiriya. These logs are good enough to stop their cutter boats.'

Both Indrajit and Mareech were on the top deck, in the bow section of the lead riverine ship of the Lankan convoy. They saw the logs of wood slowly clogging up the entire breadth of the river. Right ahead of them.

Mareech smiled. 'This is such a brilliant idea. Brilliant in its sheer simplicity. Sometimes, not offering battle is the best way to win that battle.'

Indrajit laughed softly. He raised his head. And looked far ahead. To the Onguiaahra control-steps. And whispered softly to the Ayodhyan ships he couldn't directly see, which were far downriver. To the Ayodhyan commander of that navy, whose identity he did not know, he said, 'Your move.'

—— JF J5D ——

Arishtanemi quickly scanned the concise letter, turning increasingly aghast as he read each word. 'Goddammit!'

He handed the letter to Hanuman, who read it almost as rapidly as Arishtanemi. 'Lord Rudra, have mercy!'

Naarad grabbed the letter from Hanuman. He raced through the words. 'By the cursed balls of a diseased dog! This destroys our battle plans!'

Naarad finally handed the letter to Vashishtha. The great *rajguru* of Ayodhya read the contents. Even he was constrained to admit it, though only within the quiet confines of his mind: *this is a disaster.*

The Lankans were retreating from Onguiaahra. It could be safely assumed that they had somehow found out about the impending Ayodhyan invasion from the west. And would be secure behind the walls of Sigiriya by the time Ram and his army arrived. The Ayodhyan military council had suspected as much when the corpses of a few Ayodhyan hunter-gatherer scouts were found deep in the forests that morning. Along with the bodies of some Lankan soldiers. This letter confirmed their worst fears.

Vashishtha looked at Ram. The only one in the assemblage whose face was calm and eyes still. But Vashishtha knew Ram; the angrier or more troubled he was, the calmer he appeared. He would force the stillness upon himself. To allow himself to focus and solve the problem at hand.

A troubled mind cannot solve a problem. It only makes it worse.

'What now, Ram?' asked Vashishtha. 'Do we tell Shatrughan to speed up?'

'Don't trouble Shatrughan at this moment, Guruji,' said Ram. 'The mahouts are back in action. The elephants are at work. He will finish the bridge by evening. Telling him now will only make him nervous. He is brilliant, but is easily shaken.'

'So then?' asked Hanuman.

'We prepare to cross over this evening itself. Along with our special forces. As soon as the bridge is ready.'

The original plan had been to prepare for the march over the next few days, with a conservative marching speed. This way, the troops would be fresh when they approached Sigiriya.

They had intended to rush into Sigiriya when they reached within viewing distance of the Lankan scouts. And overwhelm the defenders with speed. But that plan would be abandoned now. Obviously.

'So, we march to Sigiriya tonight?' asked Arishtanemi.

'No,' answered Ram. 'I cannot predict King Raavan's actions. He may choose to be conservative and secure himself behind the walls of Sigiriya. Or he may aggressively send out a few brigades to attack us here, even as we cross over. He may decide to not give us the opportunity to get entrenched with a strong beachhead in Lanka.'

'What are your orders?' asked Hanuman.

'A few. Firstly, I'd like you and Lord Arishtanemi to cross over with as many soldiers as will fit on our boats. Begin expanding our stockade along the landing point at Ketheeswaram immediately. This will provide cover for Lankan attacks. Secondly, I want our elephants kept back. Hidden. The secret of the bridge may have been revealed. No reason to believe that they also know about the presence of our elephants. That can be an element of surprise at Sigiriya. Thirdly, we leave for Sigiriya tomorrow morning in a standard secure formation, with flank protection. It'll be slow, but will protect against any Lankan attacks. Fourthly, I will write to Bharat to cross over the Onguiaahra control-steps as quickly as he can, and meet us outside Sigiriya. But he should leave around five thousand men manning his seafaring ships at the Amban Ganga wharf, and also patrolling downriver. We want control of the river, all the way to Gokarna.'

'So, we lay siege on Sigiriya?' asked Naarad.

'We have no other choice,' answered Ram.

'Ram, you understand war tactics better than I do,' said Vashishtha, 'but a siege is a war of attrition. Raavan will be comfortable in his well-stocked city. We will be outside, deep in the hinterland of Lanka, with no major villages or cities close by. How will we supply our massive army?'

An army marches on its stomach, it is said. A competent general focuses on good battle tactics alone. A great general has his eye on supply lines as well.

'Hence the control of the river route, Guruji,' said Ram. 'There are no resource installations outside Sigiriya. But we can easily keep ourselves supplied from Gokarna, if we control the river route. Which Bharat can readily ensure with the men he leaves on his ships. It's a good thing that Bharat was kind and accommodating with the traders at Gokarna. They will continue to supply us with provisions. Raavan will be holed in, while we will have an open supply line. We will outlast him.'

'This will not be a short battle then,' Naarad said, sighing.

'What's the rush?' asked Arishtanemi, laughing. 'Do you have a party to attend?'

Everyone laughed.

— J+ J,5D —

It had been a week since the Lankans had retreated from Onguiaahra.

Ram had marched his army into the large plateau that nestled the capital of the Lankans: Sigiriya. They were at the outskirts of a city that was protected by sturdy fort walls and moats all around.

Ram had set up camp and besieged all the four gates of the Sigiriya fort: the Bull Gate, Elephant Gate, Boar Gate and the Outer Lion Gate. They were marked by huge petroglyphs of the animals they were named after, chiselled into the rocky stone surfaces of the central archways. The Outer Lion Gate at the northern end was prefixed with 'Outer', as the road it protected stretched seven kilometres in, winding through the city into the heart of the Lankan capital. At the other end of the road was an archway called the Lion Gate.

The Lion Gate was the entrance to a much smaller path that was a steep climb up a massive monolith, called Lion's Rock. It rose, sharp, edgy and sheer, to a height of two hundred metres from the surrounding flatland and towered over the city, spreading over two square kilometres at its summit. In fact, the city was named after this rock, Sigiriya being a local-dialect adaptation of the Sanskrit *Sinhagiri* or *Lion's Hill*. At the top of the monolith was the enormous palace complex belonging to Raavan. It had multiple pools, verdant gardens, luxurious private chambers, courts, offices, and a parking bay for his Pushpak Vimaan. No gainsaying, it contained the best luxuries the world offered, for the richest man in the world.

Two fort walls encompassed the entire city in concentric circles, with no man's land between the outer and inner walls. Beyond the outer fort wall lay open land that was lined with multiple boulder-strewn hills. The flat tops of these towering boulders served as secure foundations for small structures that housed soldiers who provided protection from an unassailable height. These buildings lay abandoned as the Lankans had retreated rapidly into the fort, en masse. Ram had moved quickly and stationed his soldiers on these heights. They could now track any Lankan attempt to escape the siege, even in small numbers. And arrest it.

A siege is effective only when it is utterly absolute.

'Nobody can escape, right?' asked Ram.

'Not a chance,' said Bharat. 'Nobody will escape or enter Sigiriya.'

Vibhishan had surprised Bharat by speedily repairing the sluice gates of Onguiaahra. It had taken him three days. He had also opened up some of the sluice gates at the back of the reservoir, thus allowing the excess flood waters to flow into the Amban Ganga. Both the Onguiaahra control-steps and the Amban Ganga now had enough water to allow Bharat's seafaring ships to sail upriver. He had ordered thirty thousand soldiers to disembark as soon as the Ayodhya navy ported on the Amban Ganga wharf. Five thousand soldiers remained on the four hundred ships. These five thousand, under the command of a rear admiral, were tasked with protecting the Amban Ganga wharf and patrolling the river route, all the way to Gokarna at the mouth of the Mahaweli Ganga. They would secure the Ayodhyan supply lines. Meanwhile, Bharat, Lakshman and the thirty thousand men who had disembarked had marched on in standard secure formations. They had converged with Ram and his troops outside Sigiriya.

Bharat and Ram sat on top of a boulder rock and looked at the fort walls of Sigiriya in the distance.

'Good,' said Ram.

'The siege will be long and hard, Dada,' said Bharat. 'Sigiriya is too well-stocked. There is a massive lake within the city itself. And the twice-a-year monsoon in this island ensures that that wretched lake is perpetually full. They will never run out of water. They are well-stocked with food as well. These people grow their own crops on the open land between the inner and outer fort walls. They have almost everything that their citizens would need to handle a long siege. Even medicines. Except for that one …'

'Bharat,' said Ram, interrupting his younger brother, for he knew where he was going with this. 'We will give them the Malayaputra medicines.'

'Dada …'

'We are *Suryavanshis*, brother. We are the descendants of the finest among men, the greatest among the greats. We have the blood of Ikshvaku and Raghu running in our veins. We will not bring dishonour to the name of our clan. We will fight hard. But we will fight fair. With *dharma*. Not *adharma*.'

Bharat sighed and kept quiet.

Everyone in the Ayodhyan army knew that Sigiriya was suffering from a flu pandemic. It had affected the Ayodhyan army too, but stocked as they were with enough Malayaputra medicines – the only known cure for the illness – they had remained unfazed. Many among the Ayodhyans believed that to deny the medicines to the Sigiriyans was a legitimate war tactic. It would force them to surrender.

But Ram had been clear from the beginning. Siege tactics – even slowly squeezing food supplies – were legitimate in war. The enemy could respond without hurting civilians. But a pandemic which spread and killed rapidly in the absence of medicine, and to which the elderly were particularly vulnerable, could not be used as a tool of war. That was *adharma*. Ram's decision was unambiguous and inviolable. The Ayodhyans would give the Malayaputra medicine to the Lankans.

'I believe many among our men think that I am naïve about this,' said Ram.

Bharat didn't respond.

'Bharat, I am thinking about the period after we win the war,' Ram continued. 'I am thinking about winning the peace. There may be two hundred thousand Lankan soldiers. But there are over eight hundred thousand citizens here. They could become unmanageable if they believe that we could have saved their elders but did not. If, on the other hand, they perceive us as honourable, they will be easier to handle when we win.'

Bharat did not say anything. At least not out loud. *But first we have to win.*

'You handled the businesspersons of Gokarna with even-handedness and grace. They were not combatants. Did it not stand us in good stead? Our supply lines are open and secure.'

Bharat nodded. He was constrained to agree. 'Yes, you are right.'

'Will you go tomorrow?' asked Ram.

Bharat looked at his brother. 'I will oppose you when I disagree with you, Dada. That is my right. But I will only do it in private. Once a decision has been made, I will always support it in public. That is my duty.'

Bharat left another thing unsaid. He was widely seen as Ram's second-in-command in the Ayodhyan army. And many common soldiers had misgivings about giving the medicine to the Lankans. Fate had handed them an easy path to victory. The enemy was on the ropes. Why let them escape? Bharat, and all other commanders in the army, had to unequivocally support the decision to ensure that everyone fell in line. And the most effective way to establish that was for Bharat to lead the delegation that handed the medicine to the Lankans. The following day.

Ram smiled, reached over, and held Bharat's hand. 'Brotherrrrr ...'

Bharat grinned and squeezed Ram's hand hard. 'Brotherrrrr ...'

They both sat silently. Looking at Sigiriya in the distance.

'She's in there ...' whispered Ram.

Bharat patted Ram on the back. 'She'll be back with you soon.'

Ram looked at Bharat. 'We have to get her out of there for Mother India. She has to be the Vishnu.'

Bharat smiled. Ram was almost trying to justify the war. Convincing himself that it wasn't just about the love of a husband. There was a larger purpose.

'That is also true. But there is nothing wrong with you wanting her back as a husband. Great leaders are also human beings.'

Ram laughed softly. 'It's difficult for me to pretend to keep secrets from you.'

'So don't even try.'

The brothers laughed.

'Wars are usually a messy business,' said Bharat. 'But here we have a war that will be good for Mother India and for you. So, it has my full endorsement!'

Ram smiled.

'But you *are* lucky that you have someone like her,' said Bharat. 'She truly is a remarkable woman.'

Ram smiled dreamily. '*Mritaih praapyah svargo yadiha kathayati etad anritam.*

Paraksho na svargo bahugunamihaiva phalati.'

Ram had recited a couplet from an ancient Sanskrit play: *They say that only the dead are allowed to reach heaven. But that is false. True heaven is not beyond us in this life. It is right here on earth. With the one you love.*

Bharat cast a surprised look at his elder brother, eyebrows raised. 'Wow ... Quoting Bhasa himself?'

Bhasa was acknowledged across India as the greatest Sanskrit playwright ever. But Ram was not known to be interested in poetry. Or plays.

'Impressed?'

'Not by you. Impressed with love, actually. It can make even someone like you a lover of poetry!'

Ram laughed. 'She is the morning to my night. She is the destination to my travels. She is the rain to my cloud. Whatever be the questions of my life, she is the answer.'

Bharat laughed softly. 'You have really enjoyed the last fourteen years, haven't you?'

'This exile has been the best time in my life. Who would have imagined that? I only missed Shatrughan and you. If you both had also been there, my world would have been complete. My wife, my brothers. I don't need anything else.'

Bharat laughed. 'Who would have imagined this? I was the romantic one in the *gurukul*. You were the straight and sober one.'

'Hey, I am still straight and sober!' said Ram, laughing.

Bharat laughed too.

'But Bharat,' said Ram. 'It has been so long. Over sixteen years. You have to move on.'

Bharat took a deep breath. 'Dada … I can't … I can't forget her …'

'Bharat …'

'Let it be, Dada … Let it be. Let's talk about the war.'

'No, let's not.'

Bharat looked at his brother.

'I wish I could help you, Bharat. You have a good heart. You deserve to experience the indescribable beauty of loving a woman who loves you back.'

'Life is long, Dada. There are still many years left. You've travelled a long way. Maybe I will travel back too.'

Ram smiled and put his arm around Bharat's shoulders.

Bharat grinned and said, 'Of course, that is assuming we survive this war! Life is simultaneously long and short!'

Ram laughed. 'We will live. And we will win.'

Chapter 28

More than half way into the second prahar the next day, Bharat, Hanuman and Naarad marched in through the Elephant Gate of the outer wall of Sigiriya. They were accompanied by twenty soldiers.

Kumbhakarna, Indrajit and Akampana waited for them in the open ground between the inner and outer wall. Twenty Lankan soldiers stood behind them.

One Lankan soldier carried a white flag. Emblazoned on it was the image of Shantidevi, the Goddess of Peace. She was seated on a lotus, wearing a serene and compassionate expression on her face. One of her four hands held a *kamandalu*, while another held a water pot. The third held a *rudraksh mala*, and the fourth stretched gently in the *varada* posture. It was a mirror image of the flag carried by the Ayodhyans.

As the Ayodhyans approached, Kumbhakarna held out his hands and received a small water pot from a soldier. He stretched his right hand in the *varada* posture and poured water on it, allowing it to fall to the ground. He ensured that the Ayodhyans saw the ritual.

'*Om Shanti*,' said Kumbhakarna.

Let there be peace. For now.

Bharat repeated the exact ritual. With this ancient custom, both the parties committed themselves to a peaceful conversation by sacred oath.

The Goddess watched. No one in this gathering would draw their weapons. The karmic consequences on the soul would be dire.

Kumbhakarna spoke first, folding his hands together in a namaste. 'Prince Bharat, Lord Hanuman and I'm afraid I don't know who you are …'

'No need to be afraid. I am Naarad,' said Naarad.

Kumbhakarna raised his eyebrows and laughed softly.

'Prince Kumbhakarna, Prince Indrajit and Lord Akampana,' said Bharat, folding his hands into a *namaste*. 'It's a pleasure indeed.'

Akampana was surprised that Bharat knew his name. *Perhaps that traitor Vibhishan has told them.*

'To what do we owe the honour of your presence?' asked Kumbhakarna.

The Ayodhyans had asked for the meeting.

Hanuman spoke up. 'Kumbhakarna, old friend, the crop fields outside the city have been burnt, the wells have been poisoned with the carcasses of dead animals, storehouses at the Amban Ganga wharf have been destroyed.'

Hanuman the Vayuputra had saved the life of the Lankan prince once. Since then, they had been friends.

'Scorched earth policy, Lord Hanuman,' said Kumbhakarna courteously, referring to the tradition of destroying all means of sustenance for the enemy, like food and water sources, in the area that they camped in. 'With utmost respect, you do not expect us to make it easy for you, do you?'

'In any case, you have secured a supply line through the river route all the way from Gokarna,' said Indrajit. 'A more expensive supply route, but one that works.'

'And a supply route that you won with the help of a traitor,' said Akampana, his aged body shaking with fury. 'That ... that viper Vibhishan helped you take the Onguiaahra citadel through deceit.'

'Are you simply repeating old news?' asked Naarad, grinning at Akampana. 'Or offering your services as well?'

'Enough,' said Bharat firmly, raising his hand.

All fell silent.

'Prince Kumbhakarna,' said Bharat, 'many tactics are fair in battle. We don't hold a grudge against you. But one tactic is never fair; knowingly hurting innocent civilians. That is *adharma*.'

Kumbhakarna frowned. The Lankans had done nothing of the sort in this war. At least as far as he knew.

'We know that your city is suffering from a flu epidemic,' continued Bharat. 'We have the Malayaputras with us. And, hence, we have their medicine.'

Kumbhakarna was even more confused now.

'Bring it,' ordered Bharat.

The twenty Ayodhyan soldiers immediately marched up, carrying large sacks. Indrajit reached for his sword.

'Prince Indrajit,' said Bharat, a disapproving tone in his voice, 'we have taken the Shantidevi oath.'

Indrajit moved his hand away from his sword.

'Bring one sack here,' ordered Bharat.

An Ayodhyan soldier marched up to Bharat with a sack. He placed it on the ground, between Kumbhakarna and the

Ayodhyan prince. Bharat opened the sack, revealing a dark brown powder. He picked up a pinch with his thumb and index finger, and placed it on his tongue. And then looked at Kumbhakarna. Kumbhakarna nodded, acknowledging the safety of the powder.

'You know how to convert this powder into the medicine that can be distributed, right?' asked Bharat.

'Yes,' said Kumbhakarna. 'Our doctors can do it.'

'This should be enough for a week for all your citizens. We'll speak again after that.'

Kumbhakarna nodded at his soldiers. They briskly walked up and took custody of the sacks. Kumbhakarna looked at Bharat, a puzzled look on his face. 'Why? Why help our citizens?'

Bharat's chest swelled and his eyes narrowed with pride. 'Because our commander is a man called Ram.'

Kumbhakarna smiled slightly. *Queen Sita was right. Her husband is special.*

'I will see you on the battlefield, Prince Kumbhakarna,' said Bharat. 'We will not be so kind to your soldiers.'

Kumbhakarna bowed his head with respect. 'I look forward to it, noble prince.'

Bharat turned around. As did the others accompanying him. Hanuman looked at the fields of crop as they walked out. An idea had just struck him.

—JƩ J⌐D—

The Ayodhyan war council had gathered in Ram's tent. They sat around a round table, placed on which was a scale model of the city of Sigiriya: its fort walls, moats and the surrounding plateau. The talented model builders had worked fast, aided by the detailed information provided by Vibhishan.

Ram looked at the others. 'I am open to ideas.'

Vashishtha, Bharat, Hanuman and Lakshman sat to the left of Ram, while Shatrughan, Arishtanemi, Angad and Naarad sat to his right. All remained silent. None verbalised what appeared to be abundantly clear.

It had been a truism among soldiers for millennia: every fort had a weakness. Every single fort. Well, Sigiriya proved it a fallacy. It was without a chink. None could divine a way for Ayodhyan soldiers to slip into the fort. And the problem was compounded by the fact that the Ayodhyans did not have a numerical advantage over the Lankans. Numerical superiority can help an attacking force against an enemy safely ensconced behind impregnable walls. There was another stumbling block: the Sigiriyans were comfortably stocked with provisions that would last for months, if not a couple of years.

'There are no weaknesses,' Vibhishan said with a sigh. 'The fort walls of Sigiriya are impregnable. We should have defeated them on the river, or got here early enough to secure ourselves inside the fort. We lost both chances.'

Bharat was finding Vibhishan increasingly irritating. This defeatist attitude could cast a pall of gloom over the soldiers.

'Prince Vibhishan,' said Lakshman, 'have you not built any astutely-designed tunnels here as well? Like the ones you built at Onguiaahra?'

Always susceptible to flattery, Vibhishan smiled happily. 'I didn't get the opportunity, Prince Lakshman.'

'More's the pity.'

'I could have built something glorious. For most agree that I am the best engineer in the world.' Vibhishan pointedly glanced at Shatrughan as he said this.

Shatrughan raised his eyebrows in disdain and smiled. But did not rise to the bait. There were more important tasks at hand. A silly royal dolt's insecurities deserved a hard pass.

Ram repeated himself. 'Any ideas? I am open to anything. Even if unconventional.'

'I have an idea,' said Hanuman.

Everyone turned to the great Vayuputra.

'If the mountain will not come to Verulam, then the Verulam must go the mountain,' said Hanuman.

'What?' asked Arishtanemi.

'I heard this idiom during my travels in the West. Basically, if we can't enter the fort, then we must force the Lankan army to come out.'

'Hmm,' said Naarad. 'Good idea. I think they might well do it too, if we ask them nicely enough.'

'Naaradji,' said Angad, 'let's hear him out. Lord Hanuman is one of the finest battle strategists ever.'

'Lord Hanuman,' said Bharat, 'why will the Lankans leave the walls of Sigiriya?'

'Food,' answered Hanuman.

'But they have enough food for months,' protested Vibhishan. 'Their crops are ready for harvest.'

'Which crops?' asked Hanuman.

'What difference does that make?' asked Vibhishan. 'It will be edible grain, I assure you. My brother Raavan learnt this tactic from Mithila, actually; the idea of two concentric walls. He got the outer wall built to enclose the inner wall, a few years after the Battle of Mithila. And used the land in between the walls to grow crops. That stretch of land is at least one kilometre wide and runs a circumference of fifty kilometres all around the city. It is a massive area. Lush with food crops. The city cannot go hungry. It is impossible.'

'Woah ...' whispered Bharat. He had zoned out the harangue from Vibhishan and had just realised what Hanuman was thinking of. For he had seen the land. *Awesome.*

'What?' asked Ram.

'I think Lord Hanuman should have the honour of explaining it,' said Bharat. 'It's his terrific idea.'

Ram, and everyone else in the war council, turned to Hanuman.

'What is the most popular grain across the Indian subcontinent?' asked Hanuman. 'What do most of us eat?'

The answer was obvious. 'Rice.'

'Yes, most of us eat rice. Many eat wheat too. But we mostly eat rice.'

'And?' asked Ram.

'Which is the only region of India that doesn't eat rice? But only eats wheat.'

'Only the north-west,' answered Vashishtha. 'From Indraprastha westwards, including Punjab.'

'Especially the land of the Anu,' said Naarad. 'They only eat rotis made from wheat. No rice.'

Naarad glanced at Vashishtha with a slight grin as he said this. But Vashishtha did not look at Naarad.

'Again, so what?' asked Vibhishan. 'To answer your question, yes, Raavan and my family mostly eat rotis. We rarely eat rice. We are from the land close to Indraprastha. And the Sigiriyans, in their slavish devotion to my brother, also shifted to wheat en masse. We're perhaps the only city outside the north-western region of the Indian subcontinent that exclusively eats wheat. Almost no rice.'

'Hang on, hang on,' said Shatrughan. 'Are you telling me that wheat crop has been planted between the inner and outer walls of Sigiriya? And only wheat? And nothing else but wheat?'

Vibhishan turned to Shatrughan with an expression of utter scorn. 'Yes, obviously!'

'Woah ...' said Shatrughan, holding his head. He looked at Hanuman and smiled. And nodded his head in agreement. 'Brilliant. Brilliant. This will certainly work.'

'What will work?' asked Naarad.

This war council had the finest warriors, but they were warriors from urban lands. They weren't farmers. Agricultural affairs did not strike them immediately. Unless they had experienced it, like Bharat. Or had read about it, like Shatrughan.

'Rice crop needs a lot of water,' said Hanuman. 'From its initial planting phase until its transplantation. The soil remains wet even during harvest. But wheat ... wheat is different. It requires much less water. It requires much less care.' Hanuman leaned forward and whispered, 'And during harvest time, wheat is dry as bone.'

'Woah,' whispered Ram, understanding Hanuman's plan now.

'What?' asked Angad. 'I don't understand.'

'We burn their fields?' asked Lakshman.

'Precisely,' answered Hanuman. 'We don't need oil. We don't need paraffin. We don't need anything inflammable. The entire field of about-to-be-harvested wheat is highly combustible right now. All we need to do is to light a fire ...'

Everyone leaned over the table and peered at the model of Sigiriya city, the fort walls and the surrounding land. And, the no man's land between the outer and inner fort walls that surrounded the entire city. It would be a massive wall of flames, over one kilometre thick and fifty kilometres long, all around the city.

'Not only will it drastically reduce their food supplies,' said Vashishtha, 'the sheer heat and smoke from the flames wafting in will severely hit the morale of their citizenry.'

'They used a scorched earth policy to reduce our food supplies,' said Bharat, looking at Ram. 'We are only paying back in kind. This is not *adharma*. This is legitimate siege tactics.'

Ram nodded.

The decision was obvious. There was no need for debate. Just one thing was left to be decided.

'When?' asked Hanuman.

'Is it absolutely ready to be harvested?' asked Ram.

'I am surprised they haven't harvested it yet,' said Hanuman. 'They will probably do it any day now.'

'Then we need to attack right away,' answered Ram briskly. 'Tonight.'

Chapter 29

'Halt,' whispered Hanuman, raising his right hand. It was balled into a fist.

The eleven Vayuputra men behind him immediately came to a halt.

They were behind the treeline and at least two kilometres of open space stretched ahead of them. At the other end loomed the outer fort wall of Sigiriya – a massive twenty-five metres in height. It was the night of *amavasya*, the *new moon*. The darkness hid the Ayodhyans deftly. The distinct nip in the air helped them as well. For the Lankan guards had lit bonfires atop the broad wall-walks on the fort ramparts to warm themselves. But the fires also gave away their locations to the intruders.

Stupid.

Hanuman turned his head and spoke softly. 'Vibhishan's information seems correct. Most Lankan soldiers are trained for naval warfare. They are not adept at siege tactics for land battles. King Raavan has posted his better soldiers on the inner wall.

And the less-trained ones on the outer wall. Logical. They don't mind a trespasser jumping over the outer wall. They want us to make a dash across the one-kilometre kill zone between the two walls. The expert soldiers atop the inner wall will then shoot us like fish in a barrel.'

The veteran Vayuputra soldiers nodded. That would be the Lankan strategy.

'We don't want to fight the better soldiers on the inner wall tonight,' said Hanuman. 'They are ruthless monsters. And they have a huge strategic advantage over us, high up on their walls. So, we don't want them to notice anything. We must take care of the relatively amateur soldiers on the outer wall. Kill them. Quietly. No noise.'

'Yes, Lord Hanuman,' was the quiet chorus.

'We stick to our plan,' said Hanuman. 'No changes.'

'Yes, Lord Hanuman.'

'Last weapons check.'

The soldiers silently checked their blades. Each had seven knives and one long sword. They loosened the leather-strap holds, freeing the weapons slightly. Each soldier then checked the leather armour strings on his buddy soldier. Each armour, coloured deep black, was fitted well. The dhotis were also black and tied in military style. Their faces, arms and legs were camouflaged with black polish. It made them meld into the black moonless night. Eight soldiers were carrying bows. They strung them and fixed the weapon on the band-hold across the torso. For ease of running. They carefully checked the fletching and the resin-cloth-wrap on the head of each arrow. This was their most crucial weapon. Then, they slipped the arrows back within the separate niches in the quiver. Long black climbing ropes were rolled up, clipped together, and slung over their shoulders.

Two groups of two soldiers each, who did not carry bows, checked two sets of slim wooden logs. They were from the sheesham tree, one of the hardest Indian woods. They too were painted black. The two sets of logs, more than twenty-five metres long, had been innovatively designed and built rapidly by Shatrughan for this operation: a collapsible, easily portable ladder.

All this checking of equipment was done in less time than you took to read the two paragraphs above. These were trained Vayuputra soldiers. Among the finest in the world.

The soldiers turned to Hanuman. Ready. Waiting.

'Half of you, follow me. We move east for four hundred metres,' whispered Hanuman. 'The other half remains here. On the bird call signal, both teams start running towards the moat surrounding the wall. Slow-speed. Don't tire yourselves. Both teams must reach at the same time. You know what we have to do then.'

Ram had put the soldiers through rigorous marching drills as they waited for the monsoon to end. They had been trained to run at the same pace and stick to formation even when out of each other's line of sight. They had been trained to follow three levels of pace: slow, fast and charge-speed.

'Any questions?'

'None, Lord Hanuman.'

Hanuman stretched his arm forward. The soldiers stepped up and one by one, and placed their hands on top of Hanuman's.

'*Kalagni* Rudra.' Hanuman whispered the Vayuputra war cry.

Kalagni is the mythical end-of-time fire; the conflagration that marks the end of an age. And the beginning of a new one. The Vayuputras also believed it to be the fire of Lord Rudra and it signalled end-of-time for those who stood against the mighty Mahadev.

The fire was about to be lit.

'Kalagni Rudra,' repeated the soldiers.

Hanuman nodded, turned east and began to trot. Five soldiers followed in step. Two carried one logs-ladder between them. They moved on light feet. Easy smooth breathing.

Six soldiers stayed behind at the original location. The other ladder with them.

In a few minutes, Hanuman and his soldiers reached their destination. He looked up at the campfire atop the wall-walk on the fort ramparts. An imaginary straight line from the fire would bisect almost exactly halfway between the platoon of soldiers with Hanuman, and the other that was four hundred metres to the west.

Perfect.

The Lankan guards would be attacked from both sides.

Hanuman pursed his lips together and made a near-perfect bird call. Almost instantaneously, they heard an answering bird call.

Hanuman nodded at his men. 'Now.'

The six began running towards the outer fort wall of Sigiriya. At the standard slow-speed. Completely out in the open now. But almost completely invisible in the dark.

In just short of ten minutes, they crossed the two-kilometre distance and drew near the moat that surrounded the outer fort wall. A relatively leisurely pace, to conserve energy. For they would need it now.

The moat was around ten metres wide.

Hanuman looked up. The campfire burned some two hundred metres to the west, on top of the wall. The light was starkly visible in the dark night.

He sniffed softly. No talking from now. Too risky in the silent, dark night, so close to the wall.

He conveyed his instructions in coded bird calls. *Ladder.*

Three soldiers placed the wooden logs on the ground. Then slowly extended them over the entire moat. Keeping it steady. Noiseless.

The ladder had had to be twenty-five metres long. They would use it to scale the twenty-five-metre-high fort wall later. The moat was only ten-metres-wide. The ladder's length was more than enough for the moat.

For the moment, though, the wooden logs had not been prised open into a ladder. They were folded together. Compressed and strong.

The logs soon found purchase on the strip of flat land on the inner side of the moat, close to the fort wall. Then, the biggest soldier in the half-platoon, Obuli, put his entire weight on the end of the logs, anchoring them to the ground. Thereafter, Deepankar, the lightest soldier, got down on all fours and began crawling across the logs.

This was the riskiest part of the operation.

Though not as wide as most, the moat was deep. At some points, the width had been reduced, as the boundary of the outer wall had been extended to increase the land under cultivation within the city walls. The moat was usually populated with crocodiles and alligators – aggressive amphibious creatures with a powerful bite strength. You wouldn't want anyone's body trapped between their jaws. Fortunately for the Vayuputras, many of the animals had been infected by the plague virus and succumbed to it.

But Deepankar wasn't worried about slipping and becoming food for the few surviving crocodiles. Dying was an ever-present risk for the special forces. He was more worried about the noise of the splash if he fell into the water. It would alert the Lankans, thus compromising the entire mission.

He needn't have worried. He was across in quick time.

Deepankar sat on the logs, anchoring them to the ground on the inner side of the moat. And then he whistled a bird call.

The four remaining soldiers, including Hanuman, crossed over to the other side. Once there, Hanuman whistled. Oboli immediately stepped off the logs and began pushing the ladder up. The five on the other side leveraged it from the other end. Soon the logs were leaning against the fort wall, the top end extending beyond the embrasures of the wall ramparts; in fact, reaching the merlons. Hanuman sniffed twice. Two soldiers held one log, while the mighty Naga Vayuputra and two soldiers held the other. They prised the logs apart; the leather treads stretched in between. The ladder had opened. The treads were fabricated from chemically-treated and extremely strong leather, supported by a folding cross metal strut that opened out. It made the ladder lighter to carry, and surprisingly sturdier than those that were traditionally designed.

Good soldiers win wars. But so do good engineers.

Deepankar held the bottom of the ladder steady, ensuring that the base didn't slip back.

Hanuman began to climb and three soldiers from his half-platoon followed. Deepankar remained below.

Hanuman reached the top, climbed through the embrasure and dropped lightly onto the rampart wall-walk. The three others followed, landing silently. Hanuman blew out air from his nose. A soft hiss; a command. The soldiers unclipped the black ropes from their shoulders, slipped the pre-tied large loop across the merlon, checked the slack on the knot to ensure that the rope didn't slip, and then flung the other end of the rope down on the outer side of the wall.

This was a precaution. For a quick getaway if they were discovered by the enemy. They would rappel down the rope instead of using the ladder. Such measures saved lives in emergencies. A special forces soldier was expensive to train. No army would want to lose these lives cheaply.

Deepankar had begun to drop the ladder back over the moat, slowly, for Obuli to catch it on the other side. It would be ready and available, when Hanuman and his soldiers returned.

Hanuman softly blew out some more air from his nose. The four soldiers of Ram's army drew their short knives and moved stealthily westwards. Still hidden by the dark night, they moved towards the small bonfire. Towards the Lankans.

Rapidly drawing close, they saw the enemy clearly in the light of the flames. Six Lankans sat around the fire, lulled by the comforting warmth; three on the eastern side from where Hanuman and his soldiers approached, and three on the western side from where the other Ayodhyan half-platoon were, no doubt, drawing near. Hanuman could hear them gossiping; something about Lankan businessmen that were profiteering from the siege; and some about the illicit relations of a few noble women. One Lankan sighed and asked in a murmur why ordinary soldiers like them should die to protect these corrupt, selfish, supercilious elites.

This was a common complaint among frontline soldiers of all armies. Who were they dying for? Who were they killing for? Was it worth it? Ordinary citizens sometimes value soldiers, who protect them. But warriors make the ultimate sacrifice even for unworthy countrymen, who do not appreciate their valour. Why? Because that is what heroes do.

Hidden by the darkness, Hanuman whistled a perfect Asian koel bird call.

A Lankan soldier immediately turned his head. He stared into the darkness. Hanuman was a few metres away, but the Lankan saw nothing.

'Stop trying to birdwatch in the dark, Jormuyu,' said one of the Lankans. 'Wait until the first light of day.'

Another Lankan laughed. 'Jormuyu is in the wrong line of work! He should have been an ornithologist!'

Jormuyu continued to stare into the darkness. Hanuman almost felt as if the Lankan had seen him. Jormuyu suddenly smiled wistfully, convinced he had seen the Asian koel bird, and then turned away.

A veteran's instinct would have warned him. These guys are truly amateurs.

There was the sound of another Asian koel. This time from the westward side.

It was time.

Hanuman rushed forward, covering the distance in little over a second. His soldiers drew in from both sides.

Sorry, Jormuyu.

Before Jormuyu could react to the sudden appearance of the hulking warrior, Hanuman covered his mouth and slashed his neck with his long knife. Right across. Deep. The knife sliced extensively through the sternomastoid muscles, the jugular vein, and also a part of the deeply embedded carotid arteries, both on the left and right side of the Lankan's neck. Blood squirted out like a child's holi water jet. Hanuman immediately stepped back and melded back into the shadows.

Hanuman's soldiers had done the same to their marked men.

It was all over under four seconds. Vayuputras had emerged from the shadows noiselessly, covered six Lankan mouths, sliced their throats and retreated into the shadows.

The Lankans now lay prone on the wall-walkway. Bleeding to death. Out of the line of sight of Lankans on the inner wall, as their bodies were hidden by the three-foot-high stone parapet.

Jormuyu was dead in ten seconds. Hanuman's cut had been mercifully deep. Some of the other Lankans suffered silently for a while longer. But they were all dead in two minutes. And no Lankan on the inner or outer wall was any the wiser.

Travel safely to the other side of the sacred Vaitarni, gentle Jormuyu. I am sorry I had to do what I had to do.

Having ascertained that the Lankans were dead, Hanuman made a bird call again. He continued to desist from voicing commands.

An Ayodhyan soldier from the westward side quietly moved forward. He was careful not to slip on the floor, slick with fresh Lankan blood. He had drawn his bow and the arrow was nocked. He held the resin-cloth-wrapped arrowhead to the Lankan bonfire. Instantly, the resin was aflame. The Ayodhyan leaned over the parapet and shot the arrow straight down into the gold-coloured wheat fields.

A mistake.

The arrow whizzed down and buried itself into the earth, between the wheat stalks. The flame snuffed out instantly.

The soldier stepped back into the shadows with a chagrined expression on his face. He looked in the direction of his commander.

Hanuman made two short bird calls.

The Vayuputras came to a dead stop.

Hanuman unclipped his bow, held it aloft, carefully pulled out an arrow from the quiver and nocked it on the string.

He stepped forward. As he reached the bonfire, he quickly looked east and west. Towards his soldiers. The message was clear: *Watch and learn. For this is how it's done.*

Hanuman held the arrowhead over the fire. It sprang to life. Aflame. He stepped close to the parapet, and bent forward from his hip. He held the bow horizontally and arched his torso over it. His head bent sideways, his right eye aligned to the line of the arrow. He flexed his mighty shoulders and upper back, and pulled the string, almost to his ear. As he released the arrow, he flicked the fletching. The arrow sailed. Almost horizontally, gliding at a gentle angle towards the wheat fields. Very different from the sharp-angled quick descent of the previous arrow.

The arrow kissed the top of some wheat stalks. And then bounced over successive stalks. Like a flat pebble chucked horizontally over a still pond. The arrow travelled over a long distance, setting fire to several wheat stalks over a fifty-metre distance. It bounced four times before it fell to the ground. Almost all the wheat stalks in its path were ablaze. The fire rapidly spread to the neighbouring stalks.

Hanuman looked at his soldiers and stepped back.

It had seemed beguilingly simple, his shot. A wheat stalk is driest at the top, slowly becoming humid down the kernel. The simple lesson: if you want to burn wheat, start at the top.

Hanuman's soldiers stepped up. One by one. Six arrows were fired. And almost the entire wheat field in the area was soon alight. The fire travelled with the wind. It bounced from stalk to stalk. The flames began to stretch frighteningly high.

It all happened under three minutes.

They heard the panicked cries of the Lankans from the outer wall now, and even some parts of the better-staffed inner wall.

'FIRE!'

'FIRE!'

'GET WATER!'

'FIRE!'

Loud noises everywhere. No need for silent signals now.

'Enough!' ordered Hanuman. 'Retreat!'

The Vayuputra soldiers took flight. Half to the east, half to the west. Back to the climbing point. They grabbed the ropes and rappelled down the outer wall rapidly, and then crossed over the moat to the other side. They abandoned the ladders and sprinted back at charge-speed. Racing back to the safety of the treeline.

Hanuman's platoon was one of six that tore back at almost the same time. The other five were led by Ram, Bharat, Lakshman, Arishtanemi and Angad.

Fifty kilometres of crop land, one-kilometre wide, encircled Sigiriya in a giant arc. It was covered with precious about-to-be-harvested wheat crop. All of it was aflame.

— JF J5D —

'My husband is brilliant, no doubt about it,' said Sita, her eyes shining with pride. 'But I suspect the genius in this particular project was Shatrughan's.'

Raavan and Kumbhakarna were visiting Sita in Ashok Vatika. They had walked through a protected path between two extensions of the fort walls. The path was lined by towers for easy defence and led from Sigiriya to the citadel of Ashok Vatika, over eight kilometres away. It was the first night of relative calm. The siege seemed to have settled into a stalemate, Raavan believed. This would last for a few weeks. Having not met Sita in many days, he had decided to dine with her and his brother. Of course, Sita and the brothers had made their goodbyes before the Lankans had marched to Onguiaahra a few weeks earlier, but that battle had been a feint, and the Lankans had rushed back to Sigiriya when they found out about the Ayodhyans marching in from the west.

'All the same,' said Raavan, respectfully, 'the very idea of building a bridge across the sea ... Brilliant. I expected Ram to be courageous. I expected him to be a man of integrity; he provided medicine for our citizens. But I did not expect this innovative brilliance ... whether it was his own or that of his brother, does not matter. This war will be magnificent.'

'Why do men enjoy battle so much?'

'And you don't?'

'No, I don't.'

'Don't lie so much that it's a sin to even listen to you!' joked Raavan. 'Of course, you enjoy war. That is why you fight so well.'

'I may fight well, but I don't enjoy it. I'd much rather avoid war if I—'

Sita stopped speaking as she noticed a flock of birds flying above them. As if they were fleeing. *Weird ...*

But Raavan was continuing the conversation. 'Some men do enjoy it. That is a fact. And, like I told you once, many such men are in my army! But without war we human beings would not have become civilised, I think. It forces societies to organise and learn to work together. An external enemy can make fractious men in a society find common ground. It leads to the birth of new technology, whose products help ordinary non-warriors as well. War has a purpose. War is at the heart of civilisation.'

'I don't know if—'

Sita stopped speaking again. A much larger flock of birds were now flying past above their heads. It seemed as if they were escaping from Sigiriya.

'What's going on?' asked Kumbhakarna, looking up. 'This is bizarre ...'

'There's some kind of glow from the direction of Sigiriya,' said Sita.

Raavan and Kumbhakarna stood up and looked into the distance. And detected a faint, flickering glare.

Raavan turned to a lady guard standing near them. 'Go up to the watch tower and report.'

The guard sprinted towards the watch tower built atop a cluster of tall eucalyptus trees. The trees were over three hundred feet tall, but the guard raced up the wooden winding staircase built around the tree, and reached the platform built at the top in less than a minute. She looked in the direction of Sigiriya. And was locked into paralysis.

'What the hell is going on?' shouted Raavan from below, impatient.

The voice of her liege pulled the guard out of her shocked state. She unclipped the speaking-trumpet fixed to the parapet of the platform, and spoke into it, loudly. 'Your Highness, please come up and see this!'

Raavan began climbing the stairs. Kumbhakarna and Sita followed. Raavan was getting on in age, so it took them two minutes to reach the top. On reaching, their eyes turned towards Sigiriya.

'What the hell?!' roared Raavan, aghast.

It looked like Sigiriya, the capital city of Lanka, was on fire.

Sita's mouth was open in awe. *Woah ... How did you pull this off, Ram?*

Chapter 30

'Thank you,' said Ram, bringing his hands together into a namaste and bowing his head. It had been two days since the burning of the wheat crops of Sigiriya.

Gajaraj, the chief of the village, also folded his hands together into a respectful namaste, and bowed his head much lower. He was meeting Ram for the first time. 'Please do not thank me, great king. It is my village's honour to help you.'

Gajaraj's village – twenty-five kilometres north of Sigiriya – was almost completely populated by Naga refugees from the Sapt Sindhu. The Ayodhya war camp had been erected midway between the Lankan capital and Gajaraj's village. Being Nagas, the villagers faced universal discrimination and persecution. Ordinary people had a superstitious dread of them. Raavan and Kumbhakarna were also Nagas, but they were too powerful to face the same prejudice.

Around twenty-five years ago, Kumbhakarna had convinced his brother to allow Naga refugees to live close to Sigiriya. They had been settled in this village. Over the years, as the Lankan royals became busy with their dreams and ambitions, the village administration passed into the hands of local Sigiriyan bureaucracy. And this bureaucracy was as bigoted as the ordinary people. Administration soon turned into exploitation. The Nagas in Gajaraj's village did not complain. They were grateful for a village of their own, close to a rich city like Sigiriya, which offered many opportunities for livelihood. They built their lives. Slowly. They offered impeccable elephant management skills to the citizens of Sigiriya. Elephants were commonly used in Lanka for transportation, construction projects and even for temple rituals. They made reasonable money from renting the elephants they reared. But their entire model of living, built over twenty-five years, had been destroyed in a few hours. Lankan soldiers had burnt their crops, poisoned their wells and demolished their homes.

Scorched earth policy.

To prevent the Ayodhyans from procuring local supplies.

Those who depended on the earth that had been scorched, were collateral damage.

'Please accept my apologies for disturbing you so late at night,' said Ram politely.

'Of course not, Your Highness,' said Gajaraj. 'I understand that you could not have risked exposure by coming here during the day. Lankan spies may recognise you.'

Ram nodded.

'Would you like to see them, Lord Ram?' asked Gajaraj.

'Yes, I would. If it's not too much trouble.'

Gajaraj smiled. 'No trouble at all, Your Highness. It is your right.'

Gajaraj led the way. Ram was accompanied by Bharat, Hanuman, Arishtanemi and Angad. A small bodyguard platoon of ten soldiers followed them discreetly.

'We saw the flames, Your Highness,' said Gajaraj. 'Burning the crops – it was a brilliant war tactic.'

Ram gestured towards Hanuman as he walked. 'All credit is due to Lord Hanuman. He came up with the idea. And planned the entire operation.'

Ram was ever-willing to share glory. He was not a jealous leader who cornered all credit for himself. It's amazing how much can be achieved when one gives people the recognition they deserve.

Hanuman folded his hands together in a namaste and smiled.

Gajaraj continued. 'The granaries will run out of stock in a few weeks. They were counting on the new harvest from within their walls. The price of essentials has shot up in the city. I have heard that the morale of the citizens has collapsed. King Raavan's army cannot remain behind the walls of Sigiriya much longer. They will have to step out and battle you in the open. Which is what you wanted, I guess, Lord Ram. Their numerical superiority will count for less when they are not perched high up on the impregnable fort walls of Sigiriya.'

Ram smiled warmly and kept pace with Gajaraj.

They soon reached their destination.

Ram walked up and smoothly jumped over the low fence. He stepped up confidently to the mighty beast and touched its trunk.

Gajaraj took a deep nervous breath, but didn't say anything. War elephants can only be handled by their mahouts. They are extremely volatile and hostile with anyone other than their mahouts. Usually.

War elephants are usually male. And there are multiple reasons for this. Testosterone gives male elephants robust bone density, substantial muscle mass and strength and, most importantly, fierce aggression. Critical for war. Male elephants have long tusks as well, whose tips can be sharpened and used like spears by adept mahouts in battle. Favourable for war. Also, crucially, male elephants are generally used to being abandoned. In popular imagination, elephant herds are believed to be kind, nurturing and protective of each other. They are. But only the female elephants, led by the matriarch, are a part of this idyllic set-up; the chief of an elephant herd, incidentally, is always female. Male elephants are ordinarily expelled from the herd when they reach adolescence. Thereafter, they either fend for themselves or join nomadic and unstable male herds. The male elephants are allowed into the much larger, more stable female herd only during mating season, and after their job is done, they are kicked out again. Most of the time.

The male of the species, over generations, has made peace with this unfairness and loneliness. But the survival instinct has simultaneously increased their aggression. When in captivity, these abandoned male elephants bond deeply with their human mahouts, who are the only ones who treat them like family. Like good soldiers, they do whatever the mahout orders them to do. Without a second thought.

Very useful for war.

Abandoned and lonely male elephants, just like abandoned and lonely men, can make for efficient killers.

Giriraj was surprised, therefore, when the elephant bobbed its head warmly when it sniffed Ram. It extended its trunk out and embraced the king of Ayodhya. Ram patted the elephant's trunk affectionately.

The biggest challenge for Ram had been to hide his three hundred war elephants till the battle began. They were the main element of surprise in his strategy. Effective use of the elephants at the beginning of the battle could dramatically rebalance the numerical superiority of the Lankan infantry.

But how does one hide three hundred massive elephants from Lankan spies, whose eyes were pinned on the Ayodhyan war camp? In plain sight, it would seem.

Gajaraj's village was forced to abandon their elephants when their lands were ravaged by the Lankan army. Running out of food and water to feed themselves, it was impossible now to look after their elephants. They had driven the animals into the jungles farther north, where they hoped the beasts would be able to fend for themselves. The village sanctuary was empty. And Ram's soldiers had managed to convince Gajaraj to accommodate the Ayodhyan army's elephants there. In return for money and, more critically, supplies of food and water, which the Ayodhyans were getting from Gokarna. A Lankan spy would believe the pachyderms in the village were the in-house beasts.

Ram's main strategic battle weapon – his elephants – were hidden in plain sight. And no Lankan was any the wiser.

'He likes you, my lord,' murmured Gajaraj.

Ram patted the elephant's trunk once more and smiled at Gajaraj.

'I need to explain why I did what I did,' said Gajaraj.

Ram looked at Gajaraj with surprise. He stepped out of the low fencing. Hanuman, Arishtanemi and Angad were checking on the other elephants. Only Bharat remained.

'You don't need to explain anything, my friend,' said Ram.

'I do,' said Gajaraj. 'For I am sure you must be thinking that if I betrayed Lanka, would I not betray you as well?'

'If I thought that, then I wouldn't be keeping my elephants with you.'

'Even so… Please allow me to explain.'

'Go ahead, noble Gajaraj,' said Ram. He saw that this was important to the village chieftain.

'I will always be grateful to King Raavan, and even more to Prince Kumbhakarna, for offering us refuge twenty-five years ago. We built our lives here, away from the non-Nagas, who dislike us. Both of them were good to us, but their bureaucrats, their soldiers ... They are monsters. We tolerated it for so long, only out of loyalty to King Raavan and Prince Kumbhakarna. But when they attacked us ten days back ... They ... they could have ordered us to burn our crops and poison our wells and leave. We would have done it. They know us now. But they wanted to do it themselves. They beat us, killed some of us, assaulted some of our women ...'

Tears sprang in Gajaraj's eyes. Ram drew near and placed his hand on the village chief's shoulder.

'But it isn't desire for vengeance that is making us help you,' continued Gajaraj. 'Your soldiers ... They were different ... They were polite. Calm. They requested us ... didn't order us. They gave us food and water before we had agreed to help them. Your soldiers are as strong, well-armed and powerful as the Lankan soldiers. But they behaved with grace. They conducted themselves with *dharma* ...'

Ram kept silent. Allowing Gajaraj to speak.

'A soldier's conduct is a reflection of the general, King Ram. All soldiers are aggressive. It's the nature of their job. They have a monstrously violent side to them. A leader like King Raavan gives free reign to this side, letting them rape, loot, plunder, till it's almost second nature to them. They behave this way even if a decent option is available. On the other hand, a leader like you, Lord Ram, teaches these soldiers to harness their monstrous side for the greater good, to protect the weak, to use their strength in the service of *dharma*. No soldier of yours would kill non-combatant women or children, because they know, I have heard, that you will punish them severely for that.'

Ram remained quiet.

'You are a better leader, King Ram. You will be good for Mother India. That is why we are helping you.' Gajaraj gestured towards the elephants. 'These wild elephants were lucky to find their mahouts, who, with their kindness and firmness, gave them purpose. You are the mahout of men, King Ram. You are our mahout.'

Gajaraj bent to touch Ram's feet, but Ram stopped him and pulled him into a bear hug.

'I am no mahout of men,' said Ram. 'I am just a devotee of Mother India. As are you. We will fight for our mother. And restore her glory together.'

—— ⅃⅂ ⅃⌐⌐ ——

'Yes, I agree with you,' said Ram.

Ram and Bharat had just returned from Gajaraj's village. They were sitting around a small bonfire, outside the royal tent. It was dinner time.

'Hmm ...' said Bharat. 'I managed to change your mind, right, Dada?'

'No.' Ram laughed. 'You didn't change my mind. You just read my mind.'

Bharat laughed. He scooped some vegetables with a piece of roti and placed it in his mouth. Bharat had just told Ram that Shatrughan should not be put to active service in the army. Their youngest brother was brilliant and had already contributed immensely to the war effort by building the bridge across the sea. But unlike the other three siblings, Shatrughan was not warlike. It served little purpose to risk his life by making him fight in the battle. Ram had agreed with Bharat's suggestion instantly.

Lakshman and Shatrughan walked in. They had checked on the horses and gone over the preparations for the cavalry. It was in order. They could not know when the Lankans would step out of the city and offer battle. They had to be battle-ready at all times.

'Come, brothers,' said Ram. 'Eat.'

'Yes, Dada,' was the chorus from the twins.

Lakshman and Shatrughan washed their hands and sat around the bonfire. Attendants brought in their food as well, on banana-leaf plates.

'Horses okay, Lakshman?' asked Bharat.

'Yes, Dada,' said Lakshman, even as he began eating. 'No influenza, no diseases. But they are getting skittish. They haven't been taken for a run for a week.'

'The Lankans will give them some cause for action soon, we hope,' said Ram. Then he turned to Shatrughan. 'Shatrughan ...'

'Yes, Dada?' asked Shatrughan, looking up from his plate.

'Listen, Bharat and I were just talking ... and we think ... about you and the battle ...'

'I know,' said Shatrughan. 'Lakshman was thinking the same thing. He spoke to me while we were inspecting the horses. I agree. It makes sense. I am certainly no warrior.'

Ram smiled, relieved that he would not need to have what he thought would be a difficult conversation. 'I had forgotten how practical you were, Shatrughan. You don't let ego get in your way.'

'Why should there be any ego, Dada? I know my strengths. I also know my weaknesses. Every person should know these things. With honesty and without any self-delusions. For that is the only way to be the best you can be.'

'True,' said Ram. 'But while most find it easy to celebrate their strengths, they find it difficult to even acknowledge their weaknesses. Usually, they see only their strengths and in others, only their weaknesses. *I am perfect, everyone else is imperfect!*'

'Freedom comes from understanding that there is no perfection. Nothing in this universe can ever be perfect. Nothing can have all qualities. Gold has no fragrance; sugarcane has no fruit; and sandalwood has no flowers. But that doesn't take away their beauty, does it?'

'Absolutely,' said Bharat.

'And your intellectual strengths are glorious, Shatrughan,' said Lakshman. 'For as long as the story of this war will be told, no one will forget your building a bridge across the sea. And that we actually marched war elephants into Lanka!'

Shatrughan smiled and continued eating.

'Also,' said Bharat, 'only the gods know who among the three of us will survive the war. If we all die, then Shatrughan will carry forward our line.'

'Dada,' said Shatrughan. 'Don't say such things before a battle. It invites bad fate.'

'This is war, Shatrughan. People will die.'

'Yes, but—'

'Anyway, forget all this,' said Lakshman, putting his plate down. He was done with his food. As were his brothers.

Attendants ran up with a water pitcher and a large receptacle. They poured water for each of the royal brothers as they washed their hands in the bowl. Ram, Bharat and Shatrughan took the small towels offered and wiped their hands. Lakshman, however, wiped his hands on his dhoti.

'Lakshmannnn …' said Ram disapprovingly.

'Dadaaa …' said Lakshman jocularly.

The four brothers laughed. And then stood up and moved close, into a circle. Next to the bonfire. As they always did before going to their respective tents. They locked their arms on each other's shoulders and came into a huddle.

Brothers in arms.

Together.

Stronger together.

Nothing could break them. Not the poison of life. Not even the sweet release of death.

'Aaah … others may see four, but I see one.'

The brothers turned to see Naarad standing a short distance away.

'We *are* one,' said Lakshman.

Naarad walked in with a mischievous smile hovering on his face. 'It is interesting how one hears what one wants to hear, regardless of the words spoken.'

'What?!' asked Ram, confused.

'You brothers assumed my meaning; that the four brothers are together, as one. For all you know, maybe I meant that three of you will not survive the war. Only one will. Hence, I see only one.'

'Naaradji,' said Shatrughan, 'your joke is not really appropriate.'

'Appropriate jokes are often not funny.'

'Your joke wasn't funny either,' said Shatrughan.

Naarad laughed. 'Ouch … that was a good one.'

'Naaradji,' said Ram politely, 'is there anything particular you wanted to discuss? Because we were all going to retire to our tents.'

'I have some news.'

'What is it?' asked Bharat.

'I've just received the latest spy report. The Lankans are mobilising. Raavan is performing an astra *puja* in his private temple as well. We should expect them to march out of their fort tomorrow.'

The four brothers glanced at each other, and then back at Naarad.

'It's time.'

Chapter 31

The Outer Lion Gate, at the northern end of the fort, had been flung open two hours after the break of dawn. The massive Lankan army had been marching out for an hour now – over two hundred thousand warriors, comprising the infantry, archers and cavalry. There was a smaller contingent of two hundred warriors in chariots. Powered by two horses, smooth and manoeuvrable on two wheels, large enough to accommodate two people and a mini horde of weapons, with a charioteer to drive it, a chariot afforded a warrior tremendous ability to command the battlefield. Of course, provided the battlefield was suitable for chariots. The smooth and flat field immediately outside Sigiriya was very suitable.

'We will probably take another hour to march out,' said Kumbhakarna. 'And then, one more hour to assemble. We will be ready for battle by the end of the third hour of the second prahar.'

Raavan and Kumbhakarna were mounted on two separate chariots, on the raised plinth at the side of the Outer Lion gate. They were clearly visible to the soldiers marching out. They had no charioteer with them as yet and held the reins of the horses themselves. This was so they could talk freely. Each regiment saluted the Lankan royals as they passed. The two brothers returned the salute.

'Good,' said Raavan, taking a deep breath.

'You seem excited, Dada.'

Raavan turned to Kumbhakarna and smiled. 'Yes. This will be a glorious day.'

Kumbhakarna laughed. 'The gods must be dumbfounded to see someone so eager to die.'

'We are all going to die in any case, Kumbha. What makes life worth living is figuring out what is worth dying for. And then dying for it. Mark my words. This war will be remembered forever. You and I will be remembered forever.'

Another regiment marched past, with perfect military discipline. All the soldiers turned their heads to the right, towards their liege. And roared the Lankan war cry. '*Bhaarat Bhartri Lanka!*'

Lanka, Owner of India!

Raavan and Kumbhakarna raised their right hands high, and repeated the war cry. '*Bhaarat Bhartri Lanka!*'

This had been going on for an hour. But Raavan and Kumbhakarna's enthusiasm had not wavered even once. The mounted soldiers positioned behind Raavan – just out of earshot – had keenly noticed the commitment of their leaders. It inspired them. Soldiers must see their leaders raring to battle. If you have no exposure to military life, you might imagine that soldiers die for abstract ideas like their country, or religion, or simply because it is their job. There is a measure of truth in that, no doubt. But it is not the whole truth. The primary reason why a soldier marches to his death is his faith in his leader. A leader who knows that, ensures that he behaves appropriately.

Raavan turned to Kumbhakarna. 'So, what surprises are you expecting from Ram today?'

'I don't know,' said Kumbhakarna. 'Our spies have reported nothing out of the ordinary. He has the same divisions in his army as us, though he has around forty thousand lesser infantry. And he has far fewer chariots as well. At least on paper, we are stronger. I suspect we will see some unexpected innovations in the tactics.'

Raavan nodded.

Indrajit and Mareech rode up to the brothers.

'Father,' said Indrajit.

Raavan smiled broadly and his chest puffed up in pride. He looked at his son, the saviour of the Lankan army, who had pre-empted the would-be surprise enemy attack from the west. 'My son …'

'The Ayodhyans are coming into formation on the open grounds outside. Parallel to our walls. So, when we come into formation opposing them, we will have the Sigiriya walls to our back.'

Raavan frowned. 'Our lines will remain strong. We cannot break.'

'Precisely,' said Indrajit. 'We had hoped to march out early in the day and make our formations, to counter the risk of the Ayodhyans coming into formation perpendicular to our walls. Otherwise, in opposing them, one of our flanks would get hemmed in. But they began getting into their formation earlier than anticipated. And have done exactly what we wanted them to do.'

Mareech made clear the implication. 'Both our flanks remain open. And, our army is much larger. We can outflank and surround them. What is Ram thinking? Why is he playing to our strengths?'

'What do you think he is planning?' asked Raavan.

'I don't know,' Kumbhakarna said. 'But I would expect him to have some trick up his sleeve. He has demonstrated his tactical inventiveness over and over again.' Kumbhakarna turned to Mareech. 'Uncle, you command the right flank. And I will command the left.'

The initial battle plan had put the Lankan royals in the centre. In the thick of battle. And, to direct the war efforts efficiently.

'Are you sure, uncle?' asked Indrajit. 'I could man the left flank. You can stay with father.'

'No,' said Kumbhakarna. 'Let me do it.'

The next regiment passed the Lankan royals and bellowed the Lankan war cry. '*Bhaarat Bhartri Lanka!*'

Raavan, Kumbhakarna, Mareech and Indrajit raised their right hands high and repeated, '*Bhaarat Bhartri Lanka!*'

—— J̵F ⫝̸�⊃D ——

Raavan's battle formation was in the traditional chaturanga arrangement and the divisions were organised separately. The infantry was in the centre, in tight and disciplined lines. The archers were in rows running along the entire front line. They would shoot the initial volleys and then move aside for the infantry charge. The cavalry was at the flanks, ably supported by the fearsome chariot corps. It was a logical formation for a numerically superior army against an opponent with not only fewer infantry soldiers, but a smaller cavalry and chariot corps as well.

They intended to keep the centre stable while building fearsome flanks, with which Raavan's army could surround Ram's forces and decimate them from both sides.

Astute and sensible.

Apparently.

Ram's army was arranged, on the other hand, in a manner that was anything but logical.

A traditional military general would have advised Ram to buttress both his flanks with his cavalry and chariots. And keep the centre strong with a tight infantry configuration. While his flanks would hold against the superior Lankan numbers, the compact central infantry could try to break through the Lankan middle.

That would be the only hope against superior Lankan numbers, especially the advantage of their cavalry and chariot corps.

Hold the flanks, and fight hard to break the centre.

Logical.

Apparently.

Ram's formation did not suggest this strategy at all.

It was a strange formation, and Raavan couldn't understand the rationale behind it.

For the Ayodhyan army had not been arranged by divisions. Instead, the formation was in an unprecedented joint command. Ram's army of one hundred and sixty thousand had been divided into eighty regiments. Each regiment comprised one thousand five hundred infantry soldiers arranged tightly in a phalanx; they had archers embedded within the ranks, and cavalry both in the front and sides. The few phalanxes at the lead had chariots in front. It was evident that each of these regiment commanders had the freedom to attack and defend independently. They had been trained to do so. Ram had, in effect, divided his army into eighty decentralised smaller armies, with a complete complement of divisions within, to mount an attack or even defend independently.

This decentralised formation in an era of set piece battles could be called brave, if one were being polite, and foolhardy, if one were being honest.

Small Ayodhyan cavalries had been placed at the far left and right flanks. But they were clearly not enough to defend against the massive Lankan divisions on the sides.

Quick math would also have revealed that over thirty thousand of Ram's troops had not been arranged on the battlefield. Perhaps they were being held in reserve. At their rear. Within the jungles.

By holding so many soldiers in reserve, Ram had worsened his numerical disadvantage in the battle.

Bizarre.

'What is he doing?' asked Indrajit. 'It is almost as if he is inviting an attack on his flanks.'

Raavan did not speak. He had learnt to not underestimate Ram's strategic brilliance.

'I think he plans to use a flexible charging strategy with this decentralised army. To break through some of our lines in the centre,' continued Indrajit. 'And then pour into the breaches with the rest of his troops. But we will decimate his flanks long before that happens. He has made a mistake. We will nail him for sure.'

'You cannot nail down the sea,' said Raavan. 'Some instinct tells me that attacking his flanks would be a mistake.'

Raavan's instinct was right. Ram's intention *was* to entice the enemy to attack his flanks. For then he would unleash his secret weapons. Weapons hidden in the darkness of the jungle behind his formations. Ram's war elephants.

'But we cannot attack the centre either, father,' said Indrajit. 'His flexible lines will hurt us. Some of those regiments would attack, others would stay behind. And that would break our lines as they charge forward, disturbing our formations. We will get massacred by them in the breaches. It's better for us to keep our infantry stationary and hold off their charge.'

Raavan breathed deeply. A good general is always wary of doing exactly what the enemy wanted.

'We must charge from the flanks,' continued Indrajit. 'That is our only play.'

'No. Send a message to Mareech and Kumbhakarna to hold back. They must not make the first move.'

'Father, we have the advantage. We *must* make the first move.'

Raavan turned to Indrajit. 'The only thing all of you *must* do is follow my orders. Send a message to the flanks. We will not charge. Let Ram make the first move.'

'As you command, father.' Indrajit gestured to his flagbearer to come close. He relayed the order.

Raavan was suddenly distracted by a loud roar from the Ayodhyan ranks in the distance.

Clad in war armour and mounted on his horse, Ram had just ridden to the head of his troops. He was followed by Bharat, Arishtanemi and Lakshman. Hanuman and Angad were hidden in the jungles, in command of the two elephant corps.

Ram raised his right arm high, hand closed in a fist. Acknowledging the wild cheering from the soldiers. Over the last couple of months, Ram had successfully forged the four different armies – the Ayodhyans, Vaanars, Malayaputras and Vayuputras – into one united, disciplined and well-aligned fighting unit.

'Ram!'

'Ram!'

'Ram!'

The cheering was loud and insistent.

'Ram!'

'Ram!'

'Ram!'

'My friends!' roared Ram, his voice ringing in all directions. His arm still raised, he opened his right hand as a signal for silence. 'Hear me, my friends!'

A hushed silence descended upon his army. His followers.

'I have walked with you. I have lived with you. I have spoken with you.' Ram's voice rose now. 'And I have listened to you.'

Bharat looked at the troops. All eyes were pinned in admiration upon his elder brother.

'Many of you have spoken about the reasons for fighting this battle!' Ram's voice was loud and booming. 'Almost all of you think we fight for my wife, Sita!'

Arishtanemi stared at Ram. And smiled a bit. For he guessed what was coming.

'All of you are wrong!' thundered Ram. 'Sita is great beyond measure! She is the Vishnu! I will proudly fight for her! I will willingly die for her!' And then his voice dropped low. 'But I cannot ask that sacrifice of you …'

The soldiers looked at each other. Confused.

Ram held the pommel horn on his saddle with his left hand, and leaned over from his horse. Bending low. Down to the ground. He picked up some soil in his hand. And then reared up high on his horse. He held the sacred earth aloft. 'We fight for one much greater than my wife! We fight for the greatest Lady we will ever know! We fight for the one that has cradled us from birth! We fight for the one who will cherish our ashes in her bosom when we pass on to the next life! We fight for the mightiest Goddess of them All. We fight for This Land, Our Mother!'

The soldiers bellowed loudly. For one thing united them all. Love. Fierce love. For the one who was Mother to them all.

India.

'Raavan and his army dare to say that they own India! Can a child own his Mother?!'

The soldiers roared in fury, remembering the Lankan war cry.

'Our land was rich once! Our land was peaceful once! But since the Battle of Karachapa, Raavan has ravaged our land!'

Pointing at the Lankans with the fist that held the sacred earth of India, Ram bellowed, 'Those children of Mother India have insulted her! Devastated her! Looted her! We will defeat them! We will restore our precious Mother's glory! For that which is most precious can survive only if there are men willing to die to protect it! Our sacrifice will be a new beginning for This Land, Our Mother!'

Kicking his horse, Ram rode up and down the line, holding his fist high.

'We fight ... for This Land, Our Mother!'

Ram's soldiers yelled loudly. A patriotic gush surging through them.

'We will free ... This Land, Our Mother!'

The fierce Ayodhyan, Vayuputra, Malayaputra and Vaanar cries reverberated far, beyond the walls of Sigiriya, into the vitals of the city.

'We will honour with our blood ... This Land, Our Mother!'

Ram placed the consecrated earth of the motherland in his left palm, pinched some of it with three fingers of his other hand and marked his forehead. From left to right. In three lines. It was the sign of those who were loyal to the Mahadev, Lord

Rudra; a deeply symbolic act. The mark of the Mahadev, made with the sacred earth of the Motherland.

He raised his hand high and roared. *'Jai Maa Bhaarati!'*
Glory to Mother India!

'Jai Maa Bhaarati!' repeated his soldiers.

'Jai Maa Bhaarati!' bellowed Arishtanemi, Bharat and Lakshman.

'Jai Maa Bhaarati!'

Ram, followed by his deputies, rode up and down the line. They repeated the war cry.

'Jai Maa Bhaarati!'

'Jai Maa Bhaarati!'

As the soldiers chanted the war cry, Bharat spurred his horse close to Ram. His face flushed with admiration. 'Not bad, Dada, not bad at all. That was … inspirational.'

Ram looked at his younger brother. And whispered with a smile, *'Janani Janmabhumishcha Swargaadapi Gariyasi.'*
Mother and Motherland are superior to heaven.

Bharat smiled. Leaders delivered speeches to charge and motivate troops. But only a few truly meant the words they uttered. Ram was one of those few. A unique leader of men.

'Now?' asked Arishtanemi.

'Now, we wait for the Lankans to act.'

'Back to positions, Dada?' asked Lakshman.

'Yes,' said Ram. 'Back to positions.'

Arishtanemi saluted Ram and steered his horse towards the left flank of the army. Bharat spurred his horse and galloped to the right flank, while Ram and Lakshman rode to the centre.

And waited.

For the first move from the Lankans.

It would be a long wait.

Chapter 32

'What the hell!' growled an agitated Lakshman, pulling the reins of his horse and turning towards his elder brother.

Thirty minutes had passed since Ram's rousing speech. Raavan had also delivered his address to his soldiers. The Ayodhyan royals had not been able to hear the Lankan king's words from where they were, but they had heard its impact in the loud roars and cheers from the Lankan troops. And after that ... absolutely nothing.

The Lankans had simply lingered. Waiting for the Ayodhyans to make the first move.

The line of Lankan archers had fired a few volleys, but they were way out of range. The arrows had fallen harmlessly in the open ground between the two armies.

'Charge, you bloody cowards!' thundered Lakshman.

'Lakshman ...' whispered Ram, suggesting calm in his tone rather than words.

Lakshman took a long breath in, and turned to Ram. Not saying anything.

'They are wary,' said Ram. 'They think we have some trick up our angvastram. Which will get triggered the moment they attack our flanks.'

'Should we attack from the centre then?'

Ram paused to think. 'Sometimes a tiny pinprick works better than a mighty cut.'

Lakshman nodded, understanding his brother's mind. Somewhat.

'Send four regiments …'

'Just four regiments? We have eighty!' said Lakshman, incredulous.

'The idea is to deliver a pinprick, Lakshman,' said Ram. 'Maybe two from Arishtanemiji's flank. And two from Bharat's command.' Ram looked at the sky. And then at the flags tied high on flagpoles at the fort walls behind the Lankan lines. 'The winds are strong. Arrows will not stay on course. Good for us …'

Lakshman nodded. He turned to his flag bearer, and relayed the orders.

Two regiments each from two ends of the Ayodhya formation marched out simultaneously. One thousand five hundred soldiers in each regiment. Archers embedded within. Chariots at the lead. And cavalry protecting the sides.

It was the slow advance of an orderly army and not the raucous charge of savage rabble. Ram had trained them well. A disciplined march forward was better than wildly tearing ahead and wasting energy. Further, maintaining formation while running at breakneck speed was almost impossible. This army's battle was about maintaining formation and keeping the line. The Ayodhya regiments soon reached midpoint between the two armies. Within the range of arrows. Having reached, they were ordered to halt. The infantry soldiers provided room and the archers nocked arrows onto their bows. As did the chariot-mounted warriors.

'Fire,' the regiment commanders ordered. The arrows were shot. They flew in a high, irregular arc as the strong winds swayed them eastwards. But the Lankan ranks were dense with soldiers. Almost every arrow fell on a Lankan. Many blocked the missiles with their shields. But some got through. Another volley was fired. Same result. And then another volley.

The damage wasn't significant. At most, a little over a hundred from the over two hundred thousand Lankan soldiers were hit. A tiny pinprick. But the Lankan commanders were finding it difficult to control their soldiers from not responding, for the fiery men were straining to charge and wipe out the few Ayodhyans in the middle of the field. Lankan archers did shoot volleys in reply to the Ayodhyans. But there were only two enemy regiments on this flank. A very small target. And the strong winds sent the arrows splaying in all directions. Most Lankan arrows fell on open ground, causing little damage. And the few that did fall on the Ayodhyan regiments were easily blocked by shields.

A bugle was sounded.

The Ayodhyan regiments, both from Arishtanemi's and Bharat's flanks, began retreating. Slowly. Deliberately.

And four other Ayodhyan regiments marched out. The same tactic. The same result. Absolutely no Ayodhyan casualties. A few Lankan casualties.

Another pinprick.

The impact of these repeated pinpricks on the Lankan soldiers was becoming increasingly visible. They were getting provoked. Angry. They wanted to charge. Their Lankan commanders were struggling to hold them back.

The bugle was sounded again. And the Ayodhyan regiments marched back to safety.

And finally, the commander of the Ayodhyan left flank, Arishtanemi, himself rode out, leading two fresh regiments to midfield. The time was right. The two regiments were composed almost entirely of Vayuputra soldiers, and were led by the Malayaputra Arishtanemi. Symbolic of Ram's organisational principle: mix soldiers from different backgrounds and make one united army. And it was poetic that Arishtanemi should lead this final pinprick, for the idea of multiple regiments with joint commands was his.

Arishtanemi positioned his mounted warriors and chariots, along with his infantry regiment, close to the right cavalry and chariot flanks of the Lankan army. This Lankan flank was commanded by Mareech. And this is where Ram's tactics would, at last, bear fruit.

Some Lankan cavalrymen finally lost their patience and thundered out. They knew they could easily wipe out the small Ayodhyan regiment in the middle of the battlefield. The Ayodhyan infantry turned and ran back on spotting the mounted Lankan warriors. At charge-speed. They maintained formation as they ran. The Ayodhyan cavalry and chariots also retreated. But Arishtanemi ensured that they remained behind the running soldiers. As a rear guard to their infantry. Shooting arrows backwards.

More Lankan cavalrymen from Mareech's end broke ranks and galloped. Enticed into the web by the 'cowardly' Ayodhyans who were retreating.

'What the hell are they doing?!' bellowed Raavan at the centre of the Lankan army, when he saw what was happening at the right flank. 'They are thinning out the flanks! Order them to stay back! Send a rider to Mareech immediately!'

But the mounted Lankans at the right flank had committed themselves to the attack. Some more Lankan cavalrymen dashed out. And, most critically, all the Lankan charioteers raced forward. Charging towards the retreating Ayodhyan regiment.

Ram smiled. 'Perfect.' He turned to Lakshman. 'Order the charge of the elephants. From both flanks. Full attack.'

'And what about the twenty reserve infantry regiments?'

'Bring in fifteen. Keep five in reserve, back in the jungle.'

'Okay. I'll order them to follow Angad's elephant corps, and attack from our left flank onto the right flank of the Lankans. That's where we will get maximum impact.'

Ram nodded. *Yes.*

Lakshman quickly relayed the orders, which speedily went down the line through flag signals and bugles.

Even as this played out, more Lankan cavalrymen from Mareech's end hurtled out. Blood lust had overpowered discipline.

At the other end, Kumbhakarna had managed to keep his cavalry in formation. Stationary.

And then came the reverberations.

Like the menacing thunder of oncoming doom.

Boom.

Boom.

Boom.

Boom.

Mareech looked around. As did Kumbhakarna.

The charging Lankan cavalry slowed down. Confused.

Boom.

Boom.

Boom.

Boom.

Like the grim footsteps of death.

Like the very earth was trembling in fear.

Like the menacing voice of wrathful Gods.

It was Raavan who decoded the sounds first. But he couldn't believe it. *Impossible!*

And suddenly, the impossible made itself visible.

The Lankans were stunned into paralysis.

From beyond the edges of the Ayodhyan flanks, war elephants were storming out of the jungle. A corps of one hundred and fifty elephants from the left. And another corps of one hundred and fifty from the right. Charging ahead. Guided expertly by their mahouts in disciplined lines. Trumpeting loudly with their trunks aggressively pointing forward.

Like the messengers of annihilation.

Announcing. Brazenly. That they were coming to kill. And there was nothing anyone could do about it.

A shocked Mareech stared in fear. 'Lord Rudra have mercy …' But the old warhorse quickly took control. Or at least, tried to. 'Fall in line! Fall in line!'

The few Lankan cavalrymen who had stayed behind tried to rapidly get into formation and fill the gaps. Many of those who had charged recklessly ahead had begun to race back. To reinforce their threatened flanks.

But it was already too late.

'Turn!' roared Angad, from atop the lead elephant, his flag bearer raising the flag to convey the orders clearly.

The Ayodhyan elephants had already charged to the outer edge of the Lankan flank. They traced a gentle curve and turned slowly. With awe-inspiring discipline. Each elephant within its own imaginary lane. No bumping into other elephants. No slowing down. No break in rhythm. It was a manoeuvre they had been trained for repeatedly. And expertly. Under Ram's personal supervision. And then, the gargantuan beasts charged headlong into the Lankan flank cavalry. Not from the front, where stronger resistance was possible. But from the side.

The thinned-out cavalry lines ensured there was little resistance; the chariots that could have slowed them down were gone. The elephants exploded through the Lankan flanks. Barely slowing down, they cut through the formations like hot knife through butter. Crushing the horses and the mounted riders.

Each Ayodhyan elephant was guided by its mahout. Through foot signals on its temples. And three mounted warriors balanced themselves on the howdah tied high on the beast's back. These warriors shot arrows and spears continuously. Their elevated positions ensuring that not a single missile missed its target.

It was carnage.

Within a few minutes, the massive Lankan flank cavalry had been breached. Their formations lay in tatters.

The elephants barely slowed down. They charged on relentlessly. Obliterating all in their paths. Their tusks, sharpened like long swords, slashed soldiers and horses. Viciously. Their trunks flung enemies high in the air. Savagely. Their feet crushed all in their path. Mercilessly.

Arishtanemi ordered the retreating Vayuputra regiments to stop and turn around. The time had come. Time to move in for the kill. They charged towards the Lankans. With Arishtanemi in the lead. Bellowing the war cry of his Vayuputra troops. '*Kalagni Rudra!*'

'*Kalagni Rudra!*' roared many more regiments, and raced down the field. Shooting arrows and thrusting spears at the Lankan cavalrymen who were rushing back to reinforce their decimated flanks.

Caught between the pincer attack of Angad's elephant corps from the side and the charging Ayodhyan regiments of Arishtanemi from the enemy-front, the right cavalry and chariot flank of the Lankan army collapsed completely.

Leaving the field open for the elephants to charge into the infantry ranks. Not from the front from where a modicum of defence would have been possible. But, once again, from the side.

The fifteen reserve regiments of the Ayodhyan army, consisting of over twenty thousand soldiers, charged into the ravages left behind by the elephants corps. Killing all who may have survived.

To the credit of the Lankan infantry, no soldier retreated. Those that weren't crushed to death by the elephants fought the charging Ayodhyans till the end. But it was a lost cause.

They were being massacred. Being thrown into a meat grinder.

And yet, they fought. They died. But not with wounds on their backs, like retreating cowards. They died with their swords in their hands. Like the valiant do.

While Lankans in the right flank were being butchered, on the left flank, with Kumbhakarna in command, the cavalry and chariots held on. Brave and grim. He had already sent a message to his brother Raavan in the centre. A simple message: Retreat before we are all exterminated.

Meanwhile, Kumbhakarna held on.

In a courageous flank-guard struggle.

Refusing to let the elephants pass.

'Their infantry lines are breaking from their right,' said Ram, standing up on his saddle to get a better view.

'We should let loose our infantry, Dada,' suggested Lakshman.

Ram nodded. 'Yes. All in! Full attack!'

Orders were efficiently relayed out.

Bharat ordered all the infantry regiments from the Ayodhyan right flank to charge. While Ram and Lakshman led the regiments from the centre.

All in! Full attack!

The Ayodhyan infantry formations blitzed ahead.

The Lankan infantry ranks were now breaking. And they were falling back. For they had been ordered to do so. Facing two adversary war-elephant corps boring ruthlessly into the sides of their dense formation. Unprepared. It was almost impossible to resist.

Retreat was the only option.

But withdrawing tens of thousands of soldiers through a gate in a fort, while fighting a flank-guard action, presented a massive logistical challenge. Emerging from the fort had taken two hours. They didn't have two hours to pull back. They'd all be dead by then.

It was the bottleneck of all bottlenecks.

Indrajit personally directed the retreat at the gate. The army had to be saved if they hoped to offer battle the next day. Raavan held the front, fighting a brave vanguard action to protect the passage for his retreating troops. But the bravest, most ferocious battle was being fought on the Lankan left flank.

For if that flank broke, it would all be over for the Lankans.

The mercilessly fearsome pachyderms had simply not been able to plough through this flank.

The terrifying war-elephant corps, led by the formidable Hanuman, was fighting a grim and brutal battle here.

No inch was being lost with any ease; every fingerbreadth was being acquired by the Ayodhyans with a king's ransom of blood.

For here, the Ayodhyans faced the most dogged defiance of the day.

For here, the irresistible force of the elephant corps had crashed into an immovable object.

For here, stood the mighty Kumbhakarna.

Chapter 33

'Aim for their eyes!' thundered Kumbhakarna.

An ironical barricade now blocked the Ayodhyan elephant corps led by Hanuman. It was a long, thick line of decimated Lankan chariots, dead horses and the corpses of the massacred charioteers. The elephants couldn't crash through the sharp and mangled metal, mortared together with the gore, flesh and bones of horses and men. The Lankan cavalry, positioned behind the barrier of the battered chariots, was unreachable.

It had been magnificent. The Lankan charioteers had embraced defiant deaths, fighting to the last man and last weapon. And with their sacrifice, they had saved the Lankan cavalry and infantry. It was a resistance that had refused to yield. Even after the end.

The elephants were no longer weapons of war. They were blocked. From ramming with their massive bodies, stabbing with their tusks and thrashing with their trunks. They were now merely carriers of the warriors atop their howdahs. Yes, the mounted Ayodhyans had the advantage of elevation and were shooting arrows and hurling spears. But the distance from the Lankan cavalry made their missiles less effective.

All due to the insurmountable barricade of wrecked chariots.

The Lankan cavalry had not wasted the supreme sacrifice of the charioteers. The horses were held in control behind the safety of the barricades. And rotated regularly in the *Anavarata Taranga Vyuha;* the *strategy of unceasing waves.* Mounted riders shot arrows at the Ayodhyan warriors perched upon the elephant howdahs. On exhausting their missiles or peak strength from the exertions of shooting, the front row of riders slipped back and made room for a fresh line of warriors to ride in and take position. And the assault of arrows would continue. In unceasing waves.

The arrows of the Lankan cavalry were even less effective than that of the Ayodhyans. They were shooting from a lower level and the few arrows that did reach their target mostly injured and did not kill. But the Lankans were not trying to defeat the elephant corps. There were fighting a desperate rear-guard battle to delay the charge of the elephants. Till such time that their infantry had safely retreated behind the Sigiriya walls.

They were not fighting for victory. They were fighting for time.

Having said that, the sheer advantage of height was extracting a bloodied price. Slowly but surely. Kumbhakarna was losing more and more of his cavalrymen to the missiles from the elephant-mounted Ayodhyans. He looked back. Still many infantrymen waiting to retreat through the gates. He had to hold on for some more time. The current strategy was not enough.

And so Kumbhakarna had made a bold decision.

Offence was the best defence.

He would take the battle to the enemy. Not by charging at the elephants. Kumbhakarna was brave. Not stupid.

Instead, he decided to shoot at the elephants and not the Ayodhyans atop them. Target the beasts at their only vulnerable part, if using arrows …

'Shoot in the eyes of the elephants!' roared Kumbhakarna. Messengers behind him immediately dashed out, rode up and down the Lankan mounted warrior line, and relayed the order in the noise of war.

The Lankan cavalry soldiers changed tack. They began shooting at the elephants now. But the eyes weren't an easy target. The elephants kept moving their heads and flapping their ears. The distance increased the difficulty. The eyes were a tiny target.

Most of the arrows missed.

Then Kumbhakarna decided to show them how it needed to be done.

He steadied his horse, pulled his short-recurved bow forward and nocked an arrow, aiming at an elephant. Focusing on the beast's eye. The cavalry soldiers on both sides provided covering fire. Ensuring that the enemy would not shoot their commander. Kumbhakarna calibrated for the elephant's moving head. He needed to shoot at the spot where the eye would be a split second later. He arched his bow a little higher and gave the arrow the parabolic path to adjust for the height and distance. He pulled the bowstring back to his ear and released the arrow, flicking the fletching as the arrow launched.

The missile flew in a shallow parabolic path – just as Kumbhakarna had planned – and rammed into the left eye of the beast. It cut through the cornea and sank deep into the soft tissue of the vitreous sac. The elephant hollered in agony, jerked its head and stepped back. One Ayodhyan soldier fell off the howdah due to the sudden movement and was crushed underneath his elephant's foot. A deafening roar went up from the Lankans, for they had finally killed one Ayodhyan despite the odds. But it speedily died down. For the elephant did not retreat.

An arrow in the eye of a massive pachyderm is not a fatal wound at all. The Lankans knew this, of course, but had expected the beast to at least pull back. However, the superbly trained war elephant did not. It came back into battle. It picked up the corpse of a Lankan charioteer lying at its feet, with its trunk, and flung it at Kumbhakarna. The body projectile missed Kumbhakarna by a hairbreadth and hit the rider beside him.

And then the elephant held itself back, having received orders from the mahout above. It was stable and stationary again. Letting the warriors atop its howdah do their job: shoot arrows.

Kumbhakarna cursed, clipped his bow on his back and pulled his horse back. These war elephants were unbeatable. They could only be held back, not defeated. He stood on his saddle stirrups and looked at his rear formations. The infantry behind the Lankan cavalry was beginning to move back to safety. The retreat march was finally reaching this end of the Lankan infantry lines. Indrajit was managing the gates well.

Half an hour more ... We'll save them. We'll fight again tomorrow.

'A little while more, lads!' roared Kumbhakarna, keeping up the spirit of his men. 'We'll save our boys. Hang in there! Keep shooting!'

The order for the next change was relayed out. The front line of the Lankan cavalry retreated, to be replaced by the next batch of mounted warriors. And the fresh soldiers began firing arrows once again.

Kumbhakarna looked towards the Ayodhyan command. Towards Hanuman. And was surprised to find his opponent missing.

Where is Lord Hanuman?

The Ayodhyans were also following the Anavarata Taranga Vyuha. Like the Lankans. Moving back the front line of war elephants every ten minutes and replacing them with a fresh line of warriors. But Hanuman, just like Kumbhakarna, had never retreated. Through the last hour of pitched battle, he had remained unmoving. Up in front.

A good field commander should always be right up front. Where he is needed: to direct the war effort, to rally his troops and inspire them.

He would never retreat. Unless he is seriously injured. Or if he is—

And it suddenly struck Kumbhakarna.

He pulled his horse farther back, stood up on the saddle stirrups and stared into the distance. Far to the left. Towards the Sigiriyan walls. At the gap in the lines. For, obviously, when the Lankans had formed for battle, they had kept some space between themselves and the fort walls. To allow for the movement of medical corps and relief supplies.

Oh Lord Rudra!

No soldier ever attacked the medical corps and relief supply regiments. They were not armed. Assaulting them was against the rules of war. It was *adharma*. Neither the Lankans nor the Ayodhyans would break this rule.

But the medical corps and relief supplies regiments had already retreated. That land was empty. Nothing there to stop the adversary.

The Ayodhyan war elephants could smash through from that point, outflank the Lankan cavalry, and go straight for the infantry behind them. If they made it through, hundreds, maybe thousands of Lankan infantry soldiers would be killed within a very short while. It would be like the massacre at the right flank.

'Upon me!' thundered Kumbhakarna to the mounted warriors behind him.

He turned his horse and raced towards the walls. A squadron of fifty cavalrymen galloped after him. Riding hard.

'Faster!'

Kumbhakarna feared the worst.

'Faster!'

They rode at breakneck speed and soon arrived at the end of the cavalry lines. Kumbhakarna circled the warriors and turned his horse. Towards the front line.

And he saw them.

A boundary line of twenty horses to his right, one in front of the other, facing away from Kumbhakarna. Each horse marked the ground like a stake at the left end of the line and stretched to the right. It was a part of the Lankan cavalry formation fighting the Ayodhyans. Beyond the horses in the distance was the barricade of destroyed Lankan chariots. And farther still, a long way off, was a thick border of five war elephants, one in front of the other, all facing in the direction of Kumbhakarna, each war elephant manning the left-most edge of the elephantry formations that stretched to the right. And beyond that boundary line of the elephantry formation, far into the distance, Kumbhakarna saw some elephants turn in.

Lord Hanuman.

It was too far. It was only a silhouette. But Kumbhakarna knew in his heart. It was Hanuman.

This was it.

This was the end.

Kumbhakarna took a deep breath.

This was a channel of death.

With the Sigiriya walls to the left of him. And a boundary defined by the Lankan cavalry, destroyed chariots and Ayodhyan war elephants to the right, stretching into the distance.

At the end of the channel, seven hundred metres away, a contingent of Malayaputra war elephants, led by Hanuman. Taking formation for a charge.

Nothing between the two opposing forces. Just open land. Broad enough for two elephants to charge abreast from the Ayodhyan side. And three horses, abreast, from the Lankan side.

Kumbhakarna instinctively knew he couldn't allow the enemy elephants to cross the line of mangled and destroyed chariots. For they would plough through his cavalry from the side.

Only one thing would hold the elephants back – if one of them lay on the ground. Elephants never step on corpses of their own. Everyone knew that.

A seven-hundred-metre-long open-ground channel.

Fort walls to the left. Beasts and destroyed chariots to the right.

The mission was clear.

The elephants had to be stopped.

The first few elephants had to be killed.

Quickly.

The mission was clear.

For it was a suicide mission.

And Kumbhakarna, valiant Kumbhakarna, did not hesitate. Not for a moment.

He drew his sword and held it high. His brave cavalry and experienced warriors, all knew exactly what they were charging into. They took formation behind Kumbhakarna. Three abreast.

Stretching back to sixteen lines. Two riders took position on either side of Kumbhakarna.

The rider to the left of the Lankan prince spoke. 'Fighting alongside you has been my life's honour, Lord Kumbhakarna.'

Kumbhakarna looked at him and smiled. 'I'll see you on the other side, my friend.'

The soldier smiled and nodded.

Kumbhakarna looked at his courageous fifty and thundered, 'We must kill the first two elephants! More, if we can! We have to!'

'Yes, Lord!' roared his soldiers.

Kumbhakarna faced the Malayaputra elephants. He swung his sword down and pointed forward, towards his adversaries. And roared, '*Bhaarat Bhartri Lanka!*'

'*Bhaarat Bhartri Lanka!*'

And the valiant Lankans charged. Galloping hard. Galloping strong. Galloping to their deaths.

At the other end of the channel, Hanuman was atop the lead elephant. Even from that distance, he could see the giant form of Kumbhakarna, on his massive steed, charging towards them in a storm of dust. He should have been surprised that the Lankan prince had deduced the Ayodhyan tactic. But he wasn't. He knew Kumbhakarna's genius at battle. He also knew – oh, he knew so well – Kumbhakarna's raw courage. For Hanuman had once saved his life. And, now, it had fallen upon him to take it away.

Fate.

So, there he was, the mighty Vayuputra, beholding his Lankan friend charging bravely towards him. To what was certain death.

Magnificent …

He turned to his warriors. They knew what had to be done. What they had to do. They had been briefed.

Hanuman raised his spear high above his head. And bellowed the war cry of his Malayaputra soldiers. A Vayuputra, honouring the Malayaputra ways. *'Jai Parshu Ram!'*

Glory to Lord Parshu Ram.

'Jai Parshu Ram!' roared the Malayaputras behind him.

'Attack!'

The elephants charged, the very earth beneath their feet trembling with their mighty strides.

The elephants were stronger. But the horses were quicker. They passed the Lankan cavalrymen to the right faster than the time it took for the elephants to pass the Ayodhyan elephantry formations.

Soon the adversaries were sandwiched between the Sigiriya walls and the battered chariot barricades. They raced towards each other.

The Malayaputras atop the elephants began to fire arrows. Three warriors on each elephant. With the advantage of height. A lot of arrows were fired. Too many Lankan cavalrymen were hit. But no slowing down. They kept coming. Riding hard.

'For Lanka!' roared Kumbhakarna as he neared the charging elephants, spurring his horse to a manic speed.

'For Mother India!' bellowed Hanuman from the other end. He hurled his spear at the Lankan next to Kumbhakarna. The missile rammed into the Lankan with brutal force, propelling him backwards off his horse and under the feet of the horse behind. But no horse slowed down. Including the one that raced without its rider now.

Hanuman's elephant swung its mighty trunk at Kumbhakarna; an immense whip moving at a fearsome speed. The prince of Lanka ducked and swerved to the right. The trunk lashed into the Lankan soldier riding to left of Kumbhakarna, flinging the rider towards the fort walls. His head bludgeoned into the wall and shattered like a melon, giving him the blessing of instant death. The horse came under the feet of the charging elephant, neighing desperately even as it was crushed.

Meanwhile, Kumbhakarna had swerved between the first two elephants at the Ayodhyan front line. He held his sword out in his right hand. Gripping it strong and steady, his muscled arm flexing fiercely as he passed the elephant to the right of the one carrying Hanuman. The elephant's trunk whizzed above Kumbhakarna's head. A miss. Kumbhakarna's sword viciously slashed into the right front leg of the beast. From the side. It sliced through the gargantuan digitorum lateralis and digitorum communis muscles. Amazingly, Kumbhakarna did not lose his hold on the sword; it dug farther into the elephant's front leg, cutting the carpi ulnaris muscles, both the extensor and the flexor. It was but a micro-moment. Kumbhakarna passed by as blood burst out in a shower of red. But he wasn't done. He slashed again, savagely, as he passed the right rear leg, cleaving the massive digitorum, peroneus and soleus muscles.

The beast was roaring in pain now. It collapsed, its front and rear right legs rendered useless. Blood was spraying in a flood. The howdah toppled over and the three Malayaputra archers crashed into the mangled chariots to the left of them. The mahout was crushed under his own elephant. Kumbhakarna immediately pulled the reins of his horse and turned around, barely missing the tusk of an elephant charging on the second line.

As Kumbhakarna charged back towards the elephant that he had just felled, the warriors on the elephants behind him began shooting arrows at him. Kumbhakarna swerved his body to the left and right as he rode, avoiding the missiles by a whisker. But only just. He was flirting with his fate ... And the law of numbers always overrides fate … There were just too many arrows … Three of them finally hit. Kumbhakarna's body arched forward as the arrows slammed into his back with brutal force. But he did not slow down. He swerved to his right. Towards Hanuman's elephant. It was charging towards the second line of Lankan cavalrymen ahead. Kumbhakarna stretched out his sword hand and attempted to slice the left rear leg of Hanuman's elephant.

But the elephant he had attacked earlier, grievously wounded and lying on the ground, had fight left in him. You can bring a good elephant down, but it is not easy to kill it. The beast lay on the ground, blood jetting out of the massive wounds on its legs, roaring in fury. It swung its massive trunk. Weak, and yet, it carried punch. It brushed Kumbhakarna's horse. The stallion lost its footing momentarily, and Kumbhakarna's strike on Hanuman's elephant lost its bite. The sword sliced into the elephant's rear left leg and got buried in the flesh as Kumbhakarna lost his grip on the blade.

The prince of Lanka immediately reached to his side and pulled out another sword. Simultaneously, two more Malayaputra arrows hit him from behind; one punched into his thigh, and the other pierced his left shoulder. He roared with rage, ignoring the searing pain. He extended his sword arm again. Hanuman's elephant slowed a bit, turned its head and swung its trunk out viciously. The prince of Lanka ducked and lashed out with his sword, cutting into the elephant's front left leg. But it was a weaker strike. Though it cut through the thick hide and drew blood from the muscles and tissue, it was not incapacitating.

The Lankans on the other side were raining arrows at the Malayaputras in a high loop, hoping to slow down the unstoppable elephants.

Kumbhakarna's horse had galloped ahead. He pulled the reins and turned it around again. He was bang in front of Hanuman's elephant now. Hanuman hurled a spear at Kumbhakarna. He ducked again. But the missile hit the outgrowth, that was like an extra arm, on his left shoulder. This was a spear flung by the mighty Hanuman himself. Robust and strong, it sliced through, severing the small extra arm cleanly.

Arrow wounds all over. Spears buried into limbs. This was agony beyond endurance for an ordinary human being. But Kumbhakarna was no ordinary human being. He barely flinched and swung at the elephant's trunk with his sword.

The elephant smoothly moved its trunk aside and stabbed with its mighty tusks, which were the size of long-swords. They were sharpened at the point-edge. One tusk gored Kumbhakarna's horse, ramming into its viscera. The horse hollered in desperate pain even as Kumbhakarna quickly pulled his feet out of the stirrup. The elephant trumpeted ferociously as it swung its head, carrying the horse with its mighty tusk and flinging it away. Like a rag doll. Kumbhakarna had, meanwhile, jumped off his horse, rolled on the ground and come to his feet. Right in front of the now almost stationary elephant.

'Come on!' hollered Kumbhakarna at the elephant. 'Do your worst!'

Arrows were shot from atop the elephant, but the Lankans behind gave covering fire. Only two hit Kumbhakarna. One slammed into his left arm. The other pounded into his chest. But he was beyond noticing, or even caring about his numerous wounds.

The elephant swung its tusks but the nimble-footed Kumbhakarna, despite his massive size and his wounds, dodged the blow.

Or at least it appeared that he had.

For elephants are not like horses. They are not dumb beasts. They are menacingly intelligent.

The stab with the tusks was just a feint. The actual blow was with the trunk.

As Kumbhakarna sprang to the side, the elephant's trunk veered in and wrapped around the Lankan's legs.

The trunk of an elephant has no bones. Instead, it has forty thousand powerful muscles, more than sixty times the entire count of muscles in a human body. An elephant's trunk has the power to crush, swing hard, thrash and bang down. And yet, it also has the delicate dexterity to lift a feather from the ground.

The beast swung its trunk high, carrying the gargantuan Kumbhakarna up. Hanging upside down. It was planning to pound the prince of Lanka down into the ground, smack on his head. And it would all be over.

A feint, followed by the main blow.

The elephant is a menacingly intelligent animal.

But there is one animal even more menacingly intelligent: man.

The strength of an elephant's trunk is also its weakness. So many muscles. It also means much more vascularity. And more vascularity means much more blood flow.

Kumbhakarna roared loudly and crunched his massive stomach, swinging his shoulders up as he swivelled high. Dangling off the elephant's trunk. He flexed his mighty shoulders and slashed hard with his long sword. Hacking through the trunk of the pachyderm, severing it cleanly.

The elephant howled in frenzied agony as blood burst from its sundered trunk. Moving with the motion of the trunk that had been swinging him rapidly higher, Kumbhakarna flew in the air and crashed to the ground, landing on his right shoulder. The shoulder joint smashed to smithereens. As the Lankan prince bounced onto his back, the buried arrows burst through and emerged from his chest, slicing his vital organs. Blood pumped out of the gashing wound on his shoulder where the small extra arm had been severed and from the numerous arrow wounds on his body.

Meanwhile, the elephant collapsed. It had lost too much blood from its severed trunk. But its descent was slow. Deliberate. Ensuring that its mahout remained unharmed. Hanuman and the warriors dismounted quickly from the howdah atop the grievously injured elephant.

Arrows were still falling like missile showers. From both the Ayodhyan and Lankan ends. Two arrows walloped into the prone Kumbhakarna. Inflicting two more punctures. Piercing his massive abdomen.

'STOP!' Hanuman commanded, raising his hand. 'Ceasefire!'

The fight was over. The Lankan infantry behind the cavalry had escaped to safety behind the walls of Sigiriya. Kumbhakarna's courageous last stand had saved a significant portion of the Lankan army.

The Malayaputras immediately followed the order of their commander. Putting their weapons down. Within a flash, the Lankan arrows also stopped.

Hanuman looked at the prince of Lanka. His friend. Lying on the ground. A few short steps away.

Kumbhakarna's broken body was twisted into inhuman angles. He struggled to lift his head. He saw one elephant on the right, bleeding from its severely injured legs, thrashing about in pain with its mahout crushed underneath. Another elephant lay to the left, blood spurting like a fountain from its severed trunk; in its dying throes, its mahout holding the pachyderm's head, crying. Like a man mourning the imminent death of his brother.

Two elephants. On the ground. The charge had been stopped. He rolled his eyes and looked at the back. Practically the entire Lankan cavalry contingent that had followed him into this courageous charge had been decimated. They lay on the ground, felled by the arrows and spears of the Ayodhyan elephantry division.

They had died, but they had fulfilled their mission.

They had died. And saved the lives of their comrades behind them.

I will see you soon, my brothers.

'My friend …'

Kumbhakarna turned. And saw Hanuman standing over him. Tears in his eyes.

The mighty Kumbhakarna smiled. Weakly. 'Lord … Hanuman …'

Hanuman went down on one knee and held Kumbhakarna's hand gently. 'I'm sorry … I'm so sorry …'

Kumbhakarna shook his head slightly and laughed. 'You did your duty … my friend … And I did mine …'

Hanuman's tears flowed.

'You saved … my life once … you had the right … to take it now … the accounts are settled … As they should be …'

'You are a noble man, Prince Kumbhakarna. A good man …' Hanuman sensitively did not complete his statement. *A good man on the wrong side.*

Kumbhakarna tried to lift his head again. Hanuman helped him and placed his head on his lap.

Kumbhakarna looked at the heroic elephant. His last battle. The beast was bleeding slowly to death from the massive gaping wound on its cleanly hacked trunk. 'That beast … is noble … Put him down with grace … Lord Hanuman … put him down … with me …'

'We will …'

Hanuman looked at the elephant. And then back at his friend, Kumbhakarna.

A beast. And a human. But common in their fate.

Tragic males. Both.

The beast. That had been abandoned by its mother, its sisters, its lovers ... when the matriarchal clan had no further use of it.

The man. Hated by the world simply because of the way he looked. And for the crimes of his elder brother.

Both lonely. Both angry. Suppressed anger. Both courageous. Both ... noble.

Both deeply in love with their brothers.

The elephant with its brother, the mahout. And Kumbhakarna with his brother, Raavan.

Both saved by their brothers.

The elephant by the mahout, who gave it purpose when it was alone. Kumbhakarna by Raavan, who saved his brother's life at birth.

Both used by their brothers.

The elephant, used by its mahout for his own glory in war. Kumbhakarna, forced into a lifetime of managing his brother's actions.

Hanuman looked at the mahout, leaning against the elephant's head. Desperately crying. The elephant was bending its head. Almost as though, even in its dying throes, it was trying to console its mahout.

Love beyond measure.

'He loved me ... the most ...' whispered Kumbhakarna.

Hanuman looked down at his friend.

'Give him ... nobility in his death ...'

Hanuman's heart felt heavy. Even in his last moments, Kumbhakarna was thinking about his *elder brother,* Raavan.

His *dada*. His blessing. His curse.

'I fight under the banner of Ram,' said Hanuman. 'We will be noble, my friend. You know that.'

Kumbhakarna nodded. 'Goodbye ... my friend ...'

'I will see you soon on the other side, my brother,' whispered Hanuman.

Kumbhakarna's eyes twinkled. 'Take your time ...'

Hanuman laughed softly.

Kumbhakarna smiled. He then looked at the elephant again; the beast was bleeding to death. Slowly. He bowed his head with respect towards the magnificent fighter, a worthy adversary. And then, Kumbhakarna allowed his last breath to slip out softly.

Hanuman's tears spilled out in a stronger flood now. He embraced his friend. And then gently put his head back on the ground.

The mighty Vayuputra stood up tall, drawing his sword and holding it high. So that all, both friend and foe, could see him clearly. He then swung the sword down and pushed it, tip first, into the ground. And then went down on one knee. And bowed his head.

Showing respect to an extraordinary enemy.

And all the soldiers present, both Lankans and Ayodhyans, went down on one knee.

As good soldiers do. When a noble warrior dies.

A great warrior is neither an enemy nor a friend. He is just a great warrior.

The elephant and Kumbhakarna.

Both lonely and tragic.

Both had been blessed with what such males deeply hanker for.

A good death.

Chapter 34

A little after noon, during the third prahar, Ram stood quietly at the feet of Kumbhakarna's body.

The day's battle had been called to a close, though the sun remained high in the sky. There had been a little over two hours of fighting. It had devastated a majority of the Lankan army.

Lankan corpses were being carried back by tearful relatives. The funeral ceremonies would be conducted in the no man's land between the outer and inner fort walls of Sigiriya. There was enough open land to conduct the mass cremations that would be required. The rituals would be conducted in accordance with Vedic precepts. The injured were being cared for by Lankan doctors. Ram had offered his army's doctors as well. They were working in tandem with Lankans, tending to the their wounded. A proper count of the casualties had not been conducted as yet. But the figures would run into many tens of thousands for the Lankans. And perhaps a few hundreds, for the Ayodhyans.

The Ayodhyan elephants had wrecked the Lankan battle plans.

'What a man ...' said Ram, looking down at the corpse of Kumbhakarna. 'I wish that fate had blessed him with a different family ...'

Standing next to Ram, Hanuman had just described the entire battle that had taken place there, and the way Kumbhakarna had saved this section of the Lankan army.

Ram went down on one knee, pulled his *angvastram* off his shoulder and placed it across the body of Kumbhakarna. Covering his torso, up to his knees. His face was left uncovered. The Suryavanshi symbol of the sun, with its rays streaming out in all directions, was emblazoned on the cloth.

Ram's angvastram covering Kumbhakarna's corpse.

A mark of respect.

Marking Kumbhakarna as one of his own.

There was some noise behind them. Ram turned to see Raavan and Indrajit. On a single chariot. Both injured in battle. Raavan injured more than his son. For he had led the gritty vanguard action to stop the Ayodhyan infantry from breaking through till his own infantry had retreated.

Raavan had not taken off his leather-coated metallic battle armour. His left arm was in a makeshift sling made of cloth. Two arrow-stumps lay buried in his left biceps. The shafts had been broken off and some herbal paste was packed around the wound. Quick battlefield first aid. The blood around his numerous wounds had congealed, leaving thick red streaks that ran down the side of his head and both his arms. He limped, favouring his right side. Clearly his right leg had suffered a serious injury, but it wasn't an open wound. No remnants of blood on his dhoti. His right eye had been pierced with shrapnel. It was evident that he would not be able to use that eye anymore, no matter how talented the surgeon.

Raavan cut a grisly figure.

But the indescribable pain on his face was not caused by any of these wounds.

The weapons could not have done what the sight of the corpse of his younger brother had achieved.

Raavan did not let a tear escape. No show of weakness in the presence of the enemy. Not in front of Ram. Never.

Six Lankan soldiers rushed forward. Quickly, but gently, they lifted Kumbhakarna's mangled body and placed it on a stretcher. They carried him to Raavan. The king of Lanka stared unblinkingly at his brother's face. Kumbhakarna's last expression, the one that his immortal soul would record as the residue of this life's final thought, was not the agony of immense pain but the smile of happiness. Like he had shared an easy moment with a friend.

The king of Lanka turned and cast a look at Hanuman. For Hanuman would have been the last man Kumbhakarna saw. Without saying anything, Raavan looked away.

Hanuman also remained silent. He brought his hands together into a namaste and bowed his head low in respect to the corpse of Kumbhakarna.

The king of Lanka tenderly touched his younger brother's face. He ran his hand along the cheeks, then up the forehead and through the hair. Staring at Kumbhakarna. A forlorn expression on his face.

But he did not cry. He kept his sorrow bottled up within his soul. There would be time to release it. Later.

He took a deep breath, and composed himself.

He looked at the Suryavanshi-inscribed angvastram of Ram on his brother's body. And then turned to the king of Ayodhya.

Raavan whispered, 'Thank you.'

Ram bowed his head and said, politely, 'Your brother was a brave warrior. He has earned the respect of his adversaries. May Lord Yama guide him across the Vaitarni. May his songs be sung forever.'

Raavan smiled slightly, though with his wounds it appeared more like a grimace. *You don't measure your worth only with the love in the eyes of your friends. You also measure it with the admiration in the eyes of your enemies.*

Raavan glanced at the gates and then back at Ram. He repeated. 'Thank you.'

Raavan had just thanked Ram for not chasing his army into the city. Which he could have done through the open gates, while the Lankans had retreated. Had Ram done that, he could have finished the war today itself. But a good general knows that once an enemy army enters a city during battle, there is no telling what will happen. It is very difficult for the general to control the troops. There are no formations. Chains of command can break down. Street battles between adversary forces cause a lot of collateral damage. Fighting could have broken out between the Ayodhyan army and the Sigiriya citizens, and many thousands of unarmed civilians could have been killed. An enemy army should enter a city only as a last resort; only if the defender army is not coming out to offer battle.

Ram had behaved with *dharma*. And Raavan had had the grace to recognise it.

The king of Ayodhya nodded once, acknowledging Raavan's gratitude.

'We ...' Raavan hesitated.

'Yes, King Raavan?' asked Ram.

'Lord Ram, we have different traditions in our community of Brahmins. We do two separate funerals. We make a straw replica of the body with a facial death mask made in the exact likeness to the last expression of the deceased. It is then cremated. The body itself is not cremated, but buried. Close to the birthplace, where the umbilical cord of the individual was once buried. We bury the body along with a few objects that were important to the passed soul in this life. And, if he died in battle, we keep some remnant of the enemy or weapon that caused his death, within the burial chamber.'

'I know the tradition,' said Ram. 'Lord Hanuman told me about your community's rituals. We will send a tusk of the elephant he battled at the end to you. Bury the tusk of the noble beast with your brother. It will honour our brave elephant as well.'

Queen Sita was right about this man … He will make a good Vishnu …

Raavan couldn't move his left arm freely, with the arrow shafts buried in his biceps. So, he pulled his right hand to his chest and bowed his head. 'Thank you.'

Ram brought his hands together into a *namaste*.

Raavan turned around and limped back to his chariot, followed by Indrajit. Kumbhakarna's body was placed in the chariot next to Raavan's. The king of Lanka glanced back at Ram, and then turned, to be driven away from the battlefield.

'Do you think he will surrender now?' asked Hanuman.

Ram shrugged. 'I don't know.'

'I estimate that he's lost at least half his army. And most of his cavalry and chariot corps. Two of his best commanders, Kumbhakarna and Mareech, are dead. He cannot carry on the fight. He should see that for his own good. The battle is as good as over.'

But a battle is never over till it's over.
Raavan's son Indrajit was not one to surrender easily.
He had a plan. And he had given the orders already.

—JᶧF JᴐD—

'They should be cremated with full honours,' said Ram. 'Just like our soldiers.'

The two elephants that had died in the battle had been moved on giant rollers, pulled by elephants, to the outskirts of the Ayodhyan camp. Once there, all the elephants, even those not part of this particular corps, had come up and paid their respects. One by one, the elephants had slowly walked up to the two corpses, stretched their trunks and, with deep deference, gently touched the foreheads of their fallen comrades. They had walked around the corpses reverentially and then trudged away. Without looking back. The Ayodhyans waited patiently till the last elephant completed the ceremony. Animals have as much right to their rituals as humans have to theirs. Funeral pyres glowed in the distance, where the Ayodhyan departed were being consigned to the great God Agni, the messenger between human and divine orders. Priests were softly chanting Sanskrit hymns from the Garuda Purana. The sounds wafted in the air, infusing the atmosphere with poignant dignity.

'Yes, of course, Dada,' said Bharat. 'But first, the tusks.'

Ram nodded.

Removing tusks from a dead elephant is painstaking work. Stripped to the waist, men had been working for some time, methodically prying the skin and flesh around the base of the tusks. And cutting it out.

Hanuman stood on the other side of Ram. He turned as he heard footsteps. As did Lakshman and Shatrughan.

Arishtanemi, Vibhishan and Naarad walked up.

'We just received the spy reports,' said Arishtanemi. 'I'm afraid there is bad news.'

'Bad news?!' asked Bharat, surprised. 'Are they not surrendering?'

The casualties had been tallied. Three hundred and six Ayodhyan soldiers had died in action. The fatalities on the Lankan side brooked no comparison. Over seventy thousand infantrymen were dead. Another forty thousand seriously injured, unlikely to be fit for battle the next day. The cavalry and chariot corps were practically wiped out. Those that had survived owed their lives to the lionhearted last stand of Kumbhakarna and his cavalry. The Lankans were down to ninety thousand soldiers now, with almost no cavalry to reinforce their flanks. The Ayodhyans, on the other hand, still had nearly one hundred and sixty thousand soldiers and almost all of their cavalry and elephantry.

'No, they are not,' answered Arishtanemi. 'But that is not the bad news we bring.'

'Careful …' Naarad suddenly called out to the soldiers working on removing the tusks.

Everyone turned to look.

The soldiers were now at the most delicate part of the operation. Through meticulous and careful axe strokes, they were chipping away at the bone around the roots of the tusks. One careless tap could damage or crack the tusks. But they clearly knew what they were doing. They didn't deign to reply to Naarad.

'How can there be bad news?' asked Lakshman, bringing the conversation back on track. 'Half their army is destroyed, thanks to our elephants. And we will destroy the other half tomorrow. Our elephants will finish the job.'

'The bad news is that our elephants cannot fly,' said Naarad.

Shatrughan frowned. 'What?! Please be clear, Naaradji.'

'Indrajit is loading the Pushpak Vimaan with fuel. And weapons. I have heard that he intends to use it in the battle tomorrow.'

Bharat frowned. 'That's ridiculous. The Pushpak Vimaan is not a weapon of war.'

'Indrajit did not receive that memo,' said Naarad, sardonic as usual. 'He plans to fly low over our army tomorrow, raining arrows, spears and burning oil upon our troops. The only good news is that the vimaan has a very small door; the rest of it is tightly sealed. So, they will not have more than two warriors shooting at us at a time.'

Ram looked up at the sky. 'A flying ship, firing weapons … That's a formidable adversary. They can break our infantry formations. They can also wear our elephantry and cavalry down.'

'Precisely,' said Naarad.

They heard loud grunts from the soldiers and turned to look once again. The bones around the base of a tusk had been chipped away now. Four soldiers carefully pulled the tusk out of its bony canal and lay it on the ground. Clearly, it was extremely heavy. One man squatted over the tusk and skilfully sliced and freed the long strobile nerves and tissue from the hollow base of the tusk. The white viscous fibres slithered out with a plop. Two soldiers walked up with jars of water and began to wash the tusk, cleaning it thoroughly of blood and tissue; both, of enemies stabbed with that tusk by the elephant, and of the elephant itself.

'Vibhishan,' said Naarad, as he turned to the Lankan prince, 'I'm sure you have given some thought to the solution.'

'The same thought that must have occurred to you, I think.'

'Akampana?'

Vibhishan nodded.

'Who is Akampana?' asked Shatrughan.

'One of Raavan dada's oldest allies,' answered Vibhishan. 'Raavan Dada began his career in piracy on Akampana's ship. Now, Akampana looks after the royal finances and accounts.'

'How can he help us with the Pushpak Vimaan?' asked Lakshman. 'Will he refuse to clear the bills for the vimaan's fuel?'

Naarad laughed. 'You are finally learning the art of humour, Prince Lakshman.'

Bharat laughed too. 'Coming back to the point,' he said, 'how can Lord Akampana help us?'

'The vimaan is very difficult to fly,' said Vibhishan. 'They have very few pilots. And the pilots were also soldiers. They fought in the battle today. They didn't survive.'

'And Akampana can fly the vimaan?'

'Yes. Among the senior officers and royalty, only Kumbhakarna Dada and Akampana knew how to fly the vimaan. So, now, there is only Akampana ...'

Bharat observed Vibhishan keenly. The Lankan prince was least perturbed by the fact that his elder brother had been killed today. *Strange family ...*

He looked at Ram. Who was probably thinking the same thing.

Ram spoke up. 'And if Minister Akampana is on our side, he can, at the right time ...'

'Precisely.'

The soldiers were now packing the massive ivory tusk in a large cloth. They knew it was to be sent to Raavan, inside Sigiriya.

'But why will he help us?' Bharat asked Vibhishan. 'What is his angle in this?'

It was Naarad who answered. 'The thing with Akampana is this: he was born crying. And he never stopped.'

Bharat laughed. 'That's a good one, Naaradji. But it's not an answer to my question.'

'Akampana is always worried about what can go wrong,' said Vibhishan. 'I have never known a more pessimistic man. And the mood in the Lankan camp today would be that everything has gone wrong. That they will almost certainly lose it all tomorrow. Even an honourable defeat may be difficult. Akampana would want to keep his options open.'

'Hmm, then let's contact him,' said Ram. 'Prince Vibhishan, what do you need from us?'

'What can I offer him?'

'Whatever you feel appropriate. I trust you. Naaradji can also go with you to help in the negotiations.'

Vibhishan nodded. 'I will bring him to our side, King Ram.'

—J+ J5D—

'We need a back-up plan,' said Ram.

The four brothers were sitting together for a late lunch in Ram's tent. Their wounds had been washed and dressed. Their bodies freshly bathed and oiled.

'Yes,' said Lakshman. 'I'm not sure Vibhishan will succeed.'

'I think Dada doesn't trust Prince Vibhishan completely,' said Bharat. He knew that Ram's conduct suggested that he trusted his followers completely. But both of them had also set up a very efficient and discreet spy system within the army. To ensure that they were aware of the exact goings-on among their troops. They wouldn't allow anyone to do to them what

Vibhishan had done to Lanka. Don't just look at your enemies without, also focus on the traitors within, Ram had told Bharat once.

'I don't trust him completely either,' said Shatrughan. 'A traitor to his family will also be a traitor to his friends if it suits him.'

'Anyway,' said Ram, 'this is not about Prince Vibhishan. This is about the Pushpak Vimaan. If Prince Indrajit uses the vimaan well, he will devastate and scatter our infantry formations. Imagine arrows and fire raining down on us from the skies. Imagine the tremendous roar of the vimaan rotors, and the impact it will have on our elephants. They might run in panic, causing devastation among our own soldiers. Hanumanji and Angad are sure that the mahouts will be able to control the elephants, but the risk to the infantry remains. It's critical that we have a back-up plan, just in case Minister Akampana doesn't deliver.'

Bharat nodded. 'Agreed.'

'So, this is what we will do …' said Ram, leaning close to his brothers.

— J� —

The massively muscled Lakshman stood tall atop the elephant howdah, his feet shoulder-width apart. He gripped the triceps muscle of his left arm above the elbow with his right hand. Holding the grip, he pulled the left arm across his chest. He felt the stretch on his left shoulder and sighed in pleasure as his muscles relaxed, stimulating increased blood flow. Better circulation would aid oxygen availability and rid the muscles of lactic acid accumulation, reducing the likelihood of cramping.

He then reversed the hold and stretched his right shoulder. Sighing once again.

'Enough, already!' grumbled Bharat, from atop another elephant howdah to the side of Lakshman's pachyderm. 'I've finished my stretches.'

Lakshman turned to Bharat, and with complete insouciance, answered, 'Dada, please understand … More muscles. Longer stretches.'

Bharat raised an eyebrow, a crooked smile playing on his face. He had a pretty impressive physique as well. By most standards. At five feet, ten inches tall, he was well built through regular exercise and a good diet. But Lakshman was a good one foot taller at six feet, ten inches, and built like a bull. Some battles are best left unfought. 'All right, all right … Let's get started now.'

Lakshman grinned and picked up a spear from the weapons hold. He held it high above his right shoulder. His grip, perfect; the spear shaft flat on the palm of his hand, between the index and middle finger, the thumb pointing backward, while the rest of the fingers faced the other direction. He placed his right leg back, his foot perpendicular to his body. The left leg was up front, the foot pointing forward. Left arm raised high, elbow straight and rigid, palm facing down. The body was twisted slightly to the right, to give the required momentum to the throw. Back arched. Eyes towards the sky.

'Release!' ordered Lakshman loudly.

A captured white-throated needletail bird was released from a treetop. The bird was perfect for the task. Bred in Central Asia, it wintered in the Indian subcontinent and was among the fastest flying creatures. The needletail had a length of just twenty centimetres and a wingspan of forty-five. It provided a very small, fast-moving target.

Perfect.

Throw ... thought Bharat.

But Lakshman waited. Letting the bird soar higher. Farther away. Raising the challenge. Literally.

Throw, Lakshman ...

Just when it appeared that the bird was getting away, Lakshman whipped his body to the left, putting the fearsome power of his formidable shoulder and back into the throw. He flung the spear, spurring its momentum with a flick of his wrist and fingers. The spear shot up high with awe-inspiring force and speed. It appeared headed slightly ahead of the flight path of the bird. But Lakshman's instincts had calculated the increasing acceleration of the swift bird with precision.

The missile walloped ferociously into the needletail, its sharp metallic head slicing the bird into two. The spear soared farther ahead, barely slowing down. Blood sprayed like a cosmic jet and coloured the sky with a speck of red as the bisected body of the bird fell to the earth in two neatly cleaved halves.

Lakshman pulled his hands together into a namaste and bowed to the bird, seeking forgiveness for what had to be done.

'Woah ...' said Bharat.

Lakshman looked at his brother and smiled jauntily.

Bharat nodded, his lip curled up on one side as if an acknowledgement was being prised out. But a compliment was due. 'Not bad ... Not bad at all ...'

Lakshman laughed. 'Not bad? That was awesome, Dada ...'

'Yes, it was,' laughed Bharat. 'That was awesome.'

'Your turn.'

Bharat stretched again. And prepared himself. The next bird was released. Bharat flung his spear with perfect timing. Earlier. At a lower height. Less flashy. But it hit the bird and killed it instantly.

'That too was awesome, Dada!' said Lakshman.

'Only twenty more birds to practice on,' said Bharat.

Ram had suggested that they not overdo it. It was important that they not strain their muscles. But the brothers had decided that 'practice makes perfect'.

Picking up another spear, Lakshman called out, 'Next ...'

Ram and Shatrughan were busy with other things. Ram was training his infantry on new formations, preparing for the Pushpak Vimaan attacks. And Shatrughan was designing and fabricating some extra-protective gear for the elephants and horses. Gear that Ram believed would be critical for battle the next day.

Chapter 35

'If only he had listened to me, none of this would have happened …' cried Kaikesi, Raavan's mother. She was with her half-daughter Shurpanakha, standing in one corner of the royal hospital chamber.

Kaikesi had come back to Sigiriya from Gokarna and had been provided safe passage through the Ayodhyan siege, as per Ram's orders. She was in the hospital now, mourning the passing of her favourite son, Kumbhakarna, and her brother, Mareech.

The ostensible reason for her return was her desire to morally support her sons in this war. But Raavan knew better. She was here to torture him. One last time.

He overheard his mother's apparently whispered words and ignored them. He knew in his heart that she had deliberately ensured that he heard her.

She lived the good life, feeding off his success. And yet, she ill-treated him the most.

But he didn't want to waste his time on her. His attention was focused on the one who he knew he had ill-treated.

Kumbhakarna's body lay on top of the operation table in the centre. It was already exhibiting signs of rigor mortis. Raavan held his brother's right hand, the fingers stiff and unbending. The extremities of the body become rigid first.

The royal physician was making the death mask, even though this was not, technically, a medical process. To start with, the physician had applied grease to the face and facial hair. This was to prevent the hair from sticking to the plaster. Then plaster was carefully layered upon the face to capture every single detail.

As the plaster was applied, Kumbhakarna's face was progressively hidden behind a white gooey cover. Kaikesi began to wail even more loudly, beating her chest and tearing out her hair. 'I can't even see my son anymore! I can't even see my son anymore!' Kaikesi lamented theatrically, apparently losing her ability to breathe as well. She was panting desperately now.

The physician stopped and turned to his attendant, signalling him to go check on the queen mother. Raavan stopped them with a slight hand gesture. 'Focus on my brother,' growled Raavan softly, straining to control the expletives that he wanted to hurl at his mother. His navel had been hurting excruciatingly for the last few hours. It was unbearable now.

The physician got back to work on Kumbhakarna. He smeared more and more layers of plaster. The more the layers, the stronger the cast. While it normally took an hour or two for the plaster to dry into a cast mould, the Lankan physicians had developed a new formulation that dried in fifteen to twenty minutes.

For Raavan, it was fifteen to twenty minutes with his mother's howling lamentations in the background. Finally, he turned to her. 'Why don't you ... Why don't you wait with Mareech uncle's body? His death mask has already been prepared. And the physicians are—'

'You want to make me see my brother's body again?' screeched Kaikesi. 'Have you even seen what the elephants did to his body?! There was almost nothing left after they trampled him to death! Just the head and some parts of the torso!' Kaikesi took a break from her screaming and began to sob loudly again. And in between her wailing and bawling, she managed to shriek some more. 'I will ... I will die if I have to ... have to ... see Mareech Dada again! Are you trying to ... kill me, Raavan?! Why do you ... hate me so much?! I am your mother!!'

Kaikesi dramatically began beating her chest. Banging her hands against the wall. Cursing her fate.

Raavan tried to control himself. His navel ached desperately. 'Then why don't you wait in your chambers, mother? I will call you when Kumbhakarna's death mask is ready.'

'I am not leaving!' hollered Kaikesi angrily.

'Please ...' said Raavan, holding his head. 'I have just lost ... Please ... Don't irritate me.'

'It was because of you that he died! You caused this war! I have lost my good son because of you!'

Raavan would have so loved to draw his sword on his mother. But he knew that Kumbhakarna's soul was around. His brother wouldn't approve of even a rude word thrown at their mother. Raavan turned to Shurpanakha. Normally, she would have rushed to obey an order, even an implied and silent one. But she just stood there. Disdain on her face.

Perhaps she thinks Vibhishan is already king in my stead.

Raavan turned to his guards. 'Please escort the queen mother to her chambers.'

Kaikesi did not fight the guards. But she did keep muttering loudly as she walked out. Complaining that her good son was gone because of the curse that had afflicted her womb sixty-one years ago. Shurpanakha followed her half-mother out of the room, glaring at Raavan.

The royal physician looked down. Too embarrassed to glance at his king.

Raavan looked at the gooey white plaster that concealed his brother's face. He clung to Kumbhakarna's hand.

There was nothing to do now but wait.

His left arm was cramping. It was in a sling. The arrow heads had been removed, antiseptic ointment applied and *guduchi* stitches sown. The shrapnel from his right eye had been removed and the wound had been cleaned and bandaged. Numerous other wounds all over his body had also been medicated and bandaged. And he had been given herbal infusions to rebuild his strength. The battle would, after all, resume the next day.

The doctors had advised some rest. Raavan couldn't do that. He had to be there for his brother. He had often ill-treated Kumbhakarna when he was alive. He had to make up for it now.

'It's time, my lord,' said the physician.

Raavan looked at the prahar lamp clock. And realised that twenty minutes had passed. 'All right. Go ahead.'

The mould had hardened well. It simply came off Kumbhakarna's face with a pop. The physician cleaned the inner side of the mould with a soft felt cloth, while an assistant cleaned Kumbhakarna's face. All traces of plaster and grease were removed. The physician, meanwhile, started pouring liquid molten wax into the mould.

Raavan looked at him, puzzled.

'This is just for back-up, my lord,' explained the physician. 'A copy of the mould in wax. In case, we need to use it later. We will use the same mould to make a bronze death mask of Prince Kumbhakarna. It will be ready by late tonight.'

'Please make two bronze death masks,' said Raavan.

This was against the standard rituals. Only one death mask was supposed to be made. But the physician wasn't about to argue with his liege. 'Of course, my lord.'

Raavan continued to hold his brother's hand.

'Do we ...' asked the physician carefully. 'I mean the body.'

'Not here,' said Raavan. 'We will not bury Kumbhakarna here. We will bury him back in my homeland. Close to where we both were born.'

'All right, my lord. Then what do we do with ...'

'You will create a freezing room. You will preserve my brother's body.'

'Yes, my lord.'

'And ...'

The physician waited. Surprised at Raavan's hesitation.

'And,' continued Raavan, 'if either Indrajit or I die, you will keep our bodies here in frozen condition. They will be taken home for burial when appropriate. You will also create two bronze death masks for each of us. You will receive your orders from one who will understand my desire.'

The physician suddenly straightened up. 'You will win tomorrow, my lord! We will mutilate the corpses of your deplorable enemies and then—'

'Just shut up and do what I am telling you to do,' growled Raavan, irritated.

'Yes, my lord.'

— JF JꞫD —

Sita looked up as she heard the rustle of the leaves.

It was late in the evening, and she was sitting in the veranda of her cottage within the Ashok Vatika. Chanting to the

Mother Goddess, with a rosary of one hundred and eight beads. Chanting for the protection of her husband and his army.

She saw Raavan at the edge of the clearing. On a wheelchair, being pushed by a soldier. His left arm was in a sling. A bandage was tied across his right eye, and also around multiple other wounds on his body. He was followed by a bodyguard platoon of twenty soldiers. Sita looked behind Raavan. No Kumbhakarna.

Oh Lord Rudra … Have mercy …

Despite knowing that he fought on the side of her husband's enemies, despite knowing that this day would come, her heart felt burdened with grief. She mourned for the gentle giant.

Kumbhakarna.

He was a hero. A hero on the wrong side. A hero who fought for *adharma*. But a hero, nonetheless.

In a war, no one side has a monopoly on heroes.

Raavan was wheeled to Sita's presence. With a wave of his hand, he dismissed his guards. They walked back to the treeline, well out of ear shot.

'I'm so sorry …' said Sita, her eyes moist, her hands folded together into a namaste in honour of the departed soul.

'I should have died before him …' said Raavan. 'He was a better man than me …'

'Perhaps this, too, is your burden to bear.'

Raavan shook his head. 'No … Truthfully, I was a burden on him … Always … He is free of me now …'

Sita didn't respond. But she knew in her heart that Raavan was right.

Raavan looked around him. 'I still feel his presence … As if his soul watches over me.'

'How did he go?' asked Sita.

'Like the courageous warrior that he was …'

And Sita listened as Raavan described the Battle of the Left Flank. She was awestruck by the astounding courage of Kumbhakarna. At the same time, though, she was also amazed by her husband's brilliant strategy and Hanuman's battle tactics.

'Kumbhakarnaji died a warrior's death,' said Sita, once Raavan completed the tale. 'He will be honoured by the ancestors in *pitralok* when his soul crosses the Vaitarni River.'

Vedic people believed that, after death, the soul of the deceased remained on earth for thirteen days, till the funeral rites of the body it inhabited were completed. And then the soul crossed the mythical Vaitarni River to the *land of the ancestors, pitralok. Pitralok* was beyond the constraints of time and space. Three generations of ancestors remained in *pitralok*. And generations beyond either came back to earth for their next life, or attained *moksha, liberation from the cycle of rebirths.*

'I'll be with him soon …'

Sita looked at Raavan's wheelchair, a quizzical expression on her face.

'I will fight tomorrow,' said Raavan, clarifying. 'My right leg is injured, but I am able to walk. This is only a precaution my doctors insisted upon. So that my legs have a chance to recuperate.'

Sita nodded. Still quiet.

'You were right,' said Raavan. 'Your husband is a brilliant general.'

'He is.'

'And a good leader. He has forged four disparate armies into one tight fighting unit.'

'Hmm.'

'My son, Indrajit, is trying his best. He does not surrender easily. He has had a brilliant idea. Let's see …'

Sita nodded. 'Let's see …'

Raavan took a deep breath. He reached into a side pocket in his wheelchair and pulled out Kumbhakarna's death mask. Sita arose and accepted the death mask from Raavan. With both hands. Respectfully.

She stared at the mask. It had recorded for posterity the final moment of Kumbhakarna's life. Suffused not by pain but happiness.

Many incarnations go by before one is blessed with a death that makes a soul smile.

'It was Hanuman …' said Raavan. 'He was there … At the final moment … With Kumbha … Whatever they said to each other – I don't know, but my brother left with peace. And happiness.'

Sita bowed her head in respect to the death mask.

'We have distinct ceremonies in our sub-community of Brahmins,' said Raavan.

'Yes. I am aware of that. Kumbhakarnaji had told me.'

'The …' Raavan struggled with his words.

Sita waited. Silently.

'The straw replica of Kumbha's body is ready for cremation. And his corpse remains in the Sigiriya royal hospital … In frozen condition.'

Sita knew what she would have to do. But she waited for Raavan to spell it out.

'I've given instructions that my body should also be treated the same way … Hopefully, Indrajit will live … But if not, his body will also … Once I am dead, and if Indrajit also dies, can you ensure that all our bodies are buried in the land where we were born? It's a village close to Yamunaji. Far to the north. It's called—'

'Sinauli,' said Sita, completing Raavan's sentence. 'I know. Kumbhakarnaji told me.'

'Also, my uncle Mareech … He was a good man … His corpse remains in refrigeration in the royal hospital as well. If his body can also be …'

'I will ensure it.'

'Thank you. I don't care what is done with the rest of the royal family.'

'We fight under the banner of Ram. All non-combatants will be treated well.'

Raavan laughed softly. 'Feel free to treat the rest of my royal family well. But don't trust them. Except my wife, Mandodari. She's a hard nut, but she is a good woman.'

Sita nodded.

Just then it began to drizzle. Some soldiers silently ran up and fixed an umbrella into a cupped cavity on Raavan's wheelchair. They gave an umbrella to Sita as well. And then, just as silently, they retreated to the treeline.

Raavan tilted the umbrella with his left hand and turned his face up. He let the rain drops moisten his face. He looked down and readjusted the umbrella before the bandage over his right eye could become wet.

'I will be with her soon,' said Raavan, smiling slightly, rubbing his face.

Sita smiled too.

It was time to go. Just one last thing left to do. Raavan took a deep breath and touched his gold chain. He unclipped the clasp and removed his pendant. The pendant made from Vedavati's finger-bones.

'What are you doing?' asked Sita, raising her hands in a gesture of denial.

Raavan stared at Sita. He held the pendant in his hands. 'To you and me, these are the relics of a Goddess. To anyone else, they are just bones. You should keep it.'

'I have one already,' said Sita, holding her mother's bone pendant. It hung on a black thread around her neck. 'You still need her.'

'I am going to her in any case,' smiled Raavan.

'Don't just go to her. Go with her.'

Raavan smiled.

'Whenever you pass to the other side—'

Raavan interrupted Sita. 'It will probably be tomorrow.'

Sita ignored Raavan's interruption. 'Whenever you pass to the other side, it will be my personal responsibility to ensure that this finger pendant is with you in your burial chamber.'

Raavan took a deep breath, his eyes moistening. Only a little.

'Tears can fester inside the body,' said Sita. 'There is no dishonour in letting them flow.'

'The tears will, anyway, get hidden in the rain …' Raavan smiled, wiping his left, good eye. 'My grief and anger will die with my death. I will be free. I will be healed.'

The pain in Raavan's navel had reduced. The thought of the release of death helped.

'You are healed when you remember rather than relive. For then you can smile with your heart…'

'Hmm … Then I can smile with my heart …' Raavan fixed Vedavati's pendant back on his gold chain. 'Don't forget your promise to me. I need her help in my burial chamber.'

'I will not forget.'

'Well, then … there is nothing more to be said,' said Raavan.

'Except, farewell …'

'Farewell, noble princess. You will always be a Vishnu to me.'

'Farewell, brave king.'

'It's not over,' said Akampana firmly. 'Prince Indrajit can turn things around.'

'Then why have you agreed to meet us here?' asked Naarad. 'There is nothing to talk about.'

Vibhishan and Naarad had made their way stealthily to Sigiriya's outskirts on the southern side, far from the Ayodhya war camp. Akampana had joined them there, using one of the tiny secret tunnels through the walls; the tunnels that smugglers normally utilised during peace time to avoid customs duties at the city gates. The trio had met beyond the open land surrounding the outer walls, within the forest treeline, far from prying eyes. Though the moonless night ensured that even if prying eyes were on the lookout, there was little they would see.

'Then I should leave,' said Akampana, always on edge.

'Calm down, my friend,' said Vibhishan, reaching out and holding Akampana by the shoulders.

Vibhishan cast a stern, reproachful look at Naarad, apparently admonishing him. Only apparently though. They were playing the traditional good cop–bad cop routine. A nervous Akampana had to be cajoled into this.

'What do you want, Vibhishan?' asked Akampana.

'You are intelligent enough to know what we want,' said Vibhishan. 'I don't need to spell it out.'

'If I refuse to fly the vimaan, I will be executed.'

'But we are not asking you to not fly it.'

Akampana frowned. Then his eyes opened wide as he understood what they were planning. 'Are you mad? That is impossible.'

'You don't worry about what is impossible and what is not,' said Naarad. 'Leave that to us. Are you in or are you out?'

'There is no way you will succeed. Do you know how fast the Pushpak Vimaan moves? It is impossible for any of you to—'

'Good for you then,' interrupted Naarad. 'You will become the hero who helped Indrajit defeat the Ayodhyans. The rewards will be great.'

Akampana didn't say anything, but his indecision was writ large on his face.

Vibhishan said, 'My friend, you face no risk. You have been given the greatest privilege that anyone caught between two warring sides can receive. You can play both sides. And whichever side wins, you will be their hero.'

'But this is impossible, I tell you,' said Akampana. 'The vimaan moves too fast. And the door is too small. Arrows will be useless, due to the distance as well as the solid armour of Prince Indrajit. It has to be a—'

'Leave that to us, my friend,' interrupted Vibhishan, as he pointed to a spot on the map he was holding. 'Just fly the vimaan close to the treeline at this point. With the door facing the forest. Do that once. Just once.'

Akampana remained silent. Staring at the map. Shaking his head.

'Akampana?' asked Vibhishan.

Akampana looked at Vibhishan and Naarad. 'This is impossible. No one can fling a spear that far into the distance with accuracy. You can either get accuracy or distance. You cannot get both.'

'Thank you for the spear-throwing lesson,' said Naarad. 'Now, are we doing this or not?'

'Akampana,' said Vibhishan, his voice calm and gentle. 'You know that, even with the Pushpak Vimaan, Indrajit can only delay the inevitable. We have the elephants, Lanka doesn't. We have a large cavalry, Lanka doesn't any more. And we have more infantry than Lanka. We will win. It's a matter of time. And I will become the king of Lanka when the war is over. It's not a question of if, but when. It's just about cutting Lanka's losses now. The longer the war takes, the more Lanka will lose. You know that. You support us now, and I will remember what you did for us.'

'So, what will it be, Akampana?' asked Naarad.

Akampana nodded briefly. And then turned and ran. Quickly. Towards the outer wall of Sigiriya.

Chapter 36

Indrajit was waiting patiently. Sitting on the ground. He knew his mother. She could not be disturbed during her meditation. Never.

Mandodari sat in the lotus position on the terrace outside her simple hut. Mandodari's simple hut, made of wood and stone. A home for an ascetic. It was a short distance away from the monolith, Lion's Rock, upon which stood Raavan's fabulously opulent palace complex. It was within the garden complex that surrounded Lion's Rock, guarded by fierce Lankan soldiers. Except for that tiny surrender to the requirements of security, Mandodari had refused to compromise on her choice of life. She had steadfastly spurned the life of luxuries that, she said, had been paid for by crimes and piracy. By *adharma*.

She was very clear: if I live a life of luxuries provided by my husband's life of crime, then I am a partner in his crime. If the tree is poisonous, the fruit of that tree will be poisonous as well.

A simple maxim. But it took a woman of Mandodari's clear conscience to put it into practice.

She wore a simple, saffron coloured cotton *dhoti*, blouse and angvastram. Saffron, the colour of *sanyasins, women hermits,* who had detached themselves from the world. A woman of average height, she was fair-skinned and slightly overweight. Her straight brown hair was combed back fastidiously and tied into a plait. Her nails were cut short and her hands were hard and calloused as she had refused all personal staff, preferring to look after her home by herself. A gentle smile played on her face always, hinting at a life lived in consonance with dharma. Nothing about her physical appearance conveyed her steely character. Except her eyes. Her dark, strong-willed, captivating eyes that revealed her unbending, righteous spirit.

The eyes were closed right now.

Indrajit recalled a conversation with his mother. He was sixteen at the time.

'Life, at its core, is very simple, my son,' Mandodari had said. 'We build complicated nonsense around it to avoid looking at the simple truth. Maybe because the truth troubles us. Maybe because the truth makes us unhappy. And so, we waste our lives living a lie.'

Indrajit had said nothing. Just listened quietly. He had recently found out about Vedavati, the Kanyakumari; apparently, the love of his father's life. It had redeemed his father in his eyes, somehow. A father he had despised earlier for his debauchery and life of excess.

He was shocked to discover that his mother already knew about Vedavati.

'You live in the fond hope, my son, that there is some good in your father. Like your uncle Kumbhakarna does. You uncle is a good man, who is wasting his life living a lie. The lie that your father could ever have been a good man. Do you think your father would have been different had the Kanyakumari lived here with us in Lanka, rather than in the Land of our Ancestors?'

Indrajit had nodded. 'I think he could have been a better man, Maa.'

'No,' Mandodari had answered. 'It's the nature of the beast. Your father would have behaved himself for a while. A short while ... to impress the Kanyakumari. But his innate nature would have ultimately prevailed. The Kanyakumari, Vedavatiji, was lucky that she passed away before she could be disappointed by Raavan. Otherwise disappointment would have been inevitable. The true nature of the beast, ultimately, always prevails.'

Indrajit had shifted uncomfortably. Like any good son, he wished to love his father. Even if his father gave him no cause for it. And he was clinging, with fond hope, to the one thing that indicated to him that his father was more than just a cruel, selfish, debauched pirate. An extremely capable pirate, with fearsome intelligence and extraordinary talent. But a pirate, nonetheless.

'My son,' Mandodari had continued, 'it is said that power corrupts, and absolute power corrupts absolutely. It is not so simple. Power doesn't corrupt, it simply unveils. The hidden character of a man remains what it is. Whether in power or not. Power just brings it all out in the open. Why? Because a powerful man thinks he can get away with it. You will be a king someday. And a king must always see things for what they are, in all their ugly truth, rather than what he would like them to be. The delusional view should be left to fools in universities; let them formulate air-headed theories. Kings and administrators need to live in the real world. That is the only way they can actually do their jobs. So many silly fallacies and maxims float in this world. Like 'All people are decent at their core'. Or 'All religions are the same and none of them preach hatred'. Or 'All cultures are worthy of respect'. The truth is ugly. All people are not fundamentally decent. Some are actually good, and some are actually bad. All religions are not the same, and some do preach hatred. Just read their scriptures. Some cultures are better than others. That is reality. Strip the nonsense away and have the

courage to see the simple truth. Remember, life is not complicated. It is simple. We make it complicated to avoid seeing the simple truths that trouble us. Don't we?'

'Yes, Maa.'

'And you have to understand the truth about your father and yourself. You will be a warrior when you grow up. In many aspects you already are.'

'Yes, Maa.'

'Warriors are so male. With all their masculine glory and also its hideousness. Some willing to sacrifice their lives to protect the weak. And others willing to kill and rob to get what they desire. We – the ordinary people – we cannot have a normal relationship with warriors. We either admire them beyond limits or despise them so much that we cannot even bear to see them exist. We either worship them like Warrior-Gods or despise them like Warrior-Devils. There is no middle ground.'

Indrajit remained silent.

'You will be a God, my son. You will not be like your father. You will conduct yourself in a manner that is worthy of admiration.'

'Yes, Maa,' said Indrajit, out loud.

Mandodari opened her eyes. And smiled, seeing her son. 'When did you come, my child? Have you been waiting long?'

Indrajit shook his head. 'Not too long, Maa.'

Mandodari patted Indrajit's hand gently.

'Maa, Kumbhakarna uncle ...'

'I know. I was praying for him ...' said Mandodari. 'He was a good man. A dharmic man. I prayed that the wheel of *dharma* would bless him with an easier life the next time. He deserves it.'

Indrajit nodded. 'And also ...'

'Yes, I prayed for your Mareech grand-uncle as well. He was loyal to the family. Always. He saved your father's and Kumbhakarna uncle's lives many times. Om *Shanti*.'

The Vedic Indians acknowledged a soul's journey as it leaves a body with two words: Om *Shanti*. Thereby wishing for *peace*, and, hopefully, moksha for the departed soul.

'Om *Shanti*,' repeated Indrajit.

Mandodari waited silently for her son to bring up what he wanted to speak about.

'Maa …'

Mandodari waited.

'Tomorrow is a difficult day. We have lost most of our commanders today. Practically, all our cavalry. More than half our infantry. Our army is, I think, almost permanently broken.'

Mandodari continued to wait for Indrajit to arrive at his question.

'I am attempting something unorthodox tomorrow,' said Indrajit. 'I don't know if it will succeed.'

'The Pushpak Vimaan?'

'Yes.'

'I think you could succeed.'

'Really?!' Indrajit was surprised.

'What is your definition of success in this battle?'

'Defeating the Ayodhyans.'

Mandodari remained silent. But her eyes clearly conveyed that she didn't think that was likely.

'What would you call success?' asked Indrajit.

'Peace.'

'Why will the Ayodhyans give us the option of peace? They have us outmanoeuvred.'

'King Ram will … once your father is dead.'

'Maaaa …' Indrajit knew that his mother detested his father. But to speak so casually of his death, in the middle of a battle.

'I am only speaking the truth to you, my child.'

Indrajit didn't respond.

'Once your father dies, only you will be left. Offer peace to King Ram then. He will accept.'

'Why would he?'

'Do you remember that we had spoken about two types of warriors? Many years ago?'

'Yes, Maa. The Warrior-God and the Warrior-Devil.'

'Yes. The Warrior-Gods fight to protect that which is precious. And the Warrior-Devils kill to loot that which is precious. You are a Warrior-God. As is King Ram, from what I have heard. There is much that Lanka can learn from him. How to mould an army, for instance, into one that fights for Good, rather than one that plunders kingdoms, rapes women and murders innocents. But, also, there is much that King Ram can learn from Lanka. How to not destroy their *trader* class, for example; for destroying your *Vaishya* community only guarantees poverty for everyone, as the Sapt Sindhu kings have done. Once your father is gone, King Ram will accept peace. Trust me.'

'But Maa, what I have ...'

'But peace must be attained from a position of strength, Indrajit,' interrupted Mandodari. 'Not from weakness. The Lankans have lost too much today. You can balance that by causing some losses in the Ayodhyan forces with your Pushpak Vimaan. And hope that your father dies tomorrow. No peace is possible till he is alive.'

'Maaaaa ...' Indrajit's eyes conveyed his disapproval.

'I will only think of what is good for our land, not what is good for your father. Only the nation matters, Indrajit. Only the nation is *most precious. Desh sarvopari.*'

Indrajit didn't say anything.

'Also, don't waste time trying to kill their infantry soldiers tomorrow,' Mandodari continued. 'You cannot kill that many by firing arrows and throwing spears from the narrow door of the Pushpak Vimaan.'

'Then what should I do?'

'Go for their main strength.'

'Their elephants?' asked Indrajit, flummoxed.

'Yes.'

'What can I do to armoured elephants with spears and arrows? I will not cause enough damage.'

'You cannot do much to elephants, sure,' said Mandodari. 'But you can do a lot to those who control the elephants.'

Indrajit smiled at the simple brilliance of the idea.

'I have always wondered, Maa,' said Indrajit. 'How come you know so much about everything? Including even the art of war?'

Mandodari smiled. 'Life is all about learning how to live, my son. As Seneca – the great intellectual living far to our west – once said, *As long as you live, keep learning how to live.*''

Indrajit smiled. 'Only the Gods know what role you may yet play for the good of others and for our motherland, Maa.'

Mandodari leaned over and kissed her son's forehead. 'The only role that I wish to play, my child, is that of a proud mother. The proud mother of a magnificent man.'

—JF JˌʒD—

'Is it hurting?' asked Shatrughan.

Lakshman and Shatrughan were sitting outside Shatrughan's tent. They were eating together. A camp doctor had massaged Lakshman's strained shoulder with a mixture of mahanarayan and ashwagandha oil. And then wrapped it tight with a warm cloth.

'No,' answered Lakshman. 'It's not hurting. Just a bit strained with the practice this afternoon. I want it to remain strong tomorrow.'

'Hmm … Do you think the battle will end tomorrow?'

'Let's see … I will be surprised if it does. The Lankans won't surrender so easily. Where are the dadas?'

'Both have gone towards the city walls. Some war strategy, I guess.'

—— JF J5D ——

'I think the war will end tomorrow if we can neutralise the Pushpak Vimaan,' said Ram.

'I agree,' said Bharat. 'They will have no other move left.'

'Either Lakshman or you must get him.'

'We will, Dada.'

'They will be better prepared for our elephants tomorrow,' said Ram. 'Shatrughan has quickly got some extra armour manufactured for our elephants.'

'I have seen that. I've asked both Hanumanji and Angad to ensure that all our elephants are covered with the extra armour.'

'Hmm …'

'This is hardly a reason to delay dinner, Dada,' said Bharat. 'Why have you brought me here?'

'Because if the war ends tomorrow, we need to be clear on how we intend to manage the peace. Especially how our army will enter the city. We cannot allow even a single instance of looting or random killing.'

'I agree. For we may need Lanka as an ally for our future battles.'

'Correct.'

'So, what's your plan?' asked Bharat.

Chapter 37

The second day of the Battle of Sigiriya dawned.

The Lankan troops had made their formations outside the walls again. The militias belonging to the Gokarna business guilds had slipped away the previous evening, using an old contractual clause, which stated that the guilds have the right to recall their soldiers if their own security was at risk. The result was that the Lankan infantry numbers were further reduced from ninety thousand to only sixty-five thousand.

An army built on promises of plunder and wealth suffers desertions at the first sign of serious trouble. On the other hand, an army built on the far more precious emotion of patriotism will fight to the last man.

Ideas are more powerful than wealth and weapons. Few get this. And those who do, rule the world.

Most of Raavan's great generals, along with the cavalry and chariot corps, had been killed in battle the previous day. And his best general still alive, Indrajit, was in the city. With the

Pushpak Vimaan. Raavan had one other good general, the ruthless but efficient Prahast. And his brigade-level officers were also still available. Supported by them, he was supervising the infantry formations now. He had a plan for the Ayodhyan elephant corps. It wasn't about killing the elephants, for that was almost impossible now. This was a survival plan. While Indrajit carried out his aerial attack and damage the heart of the Ayodhyan lines.

Raavan's left bicep had been washed with ointments and then wrapped tight with a thick cloth bandage. It allowed for some movement of the damaged muscles. The left arm had been tied to the shield. He would use it as defence. He wore an eye patch to cover his surgically removed right eye; it had had to be removed or it would have turned septic. And he rode on his horse, to avoid putting weight on his injured right leg. The talented physicians of Lanka had given Raavan energy-enhancing infusions. They lent him the vigour he required to fight hard, and more importantly, to supervise the battle. Raavan had refused the painkillers. They would have dulled his faculties.

Physical pain can break a weak mind. But it has value to a mind that is strong. For it can bring focus.

While Raavan was readying his troop formation, at the other end of the field Ram, aided ably by his generals, was supervising the arrangement of his army divisions.

'When do you think Indrajit will fly in?' asked Arishtanemi, who by now had enormous respect for Ram's brilliant battle tactics.

'I am assuming he is unaware that we know about his plans with the vimaan,' said Ram, 'so, I think he'll come in late. When we have committed our infantry and are charging ahead.

Which is why our infantry must not move. We must draw Indrajit towards us. For only then will our trap work.'

'Only elephants, cavalry and chariots then,' said Angad, who was on the other side of Ram.

'Yes,' confirmed Ram. 'And, Lord Hanuman …'

'Yes, King Ram,' answered Hanuman.

'You know what you have to do.'

Hanuman looked towards the jungles. Behind the right flank. Where Bharat and Lakshman waited. In hiding. On two elephants. Hanuman had to lead Indrajit into the trap. His role was the riskiest in the battle plan. And, hence, the most glorious.

'I'll handle it,' said Hanuman. 'I'll draw Prince Indrajit towards the jungles.'

'And my brothers won't miss.'

'I know they won't.'

Ram nodded and reached out with both his hands. Hanuman held Ram at the forearms.

'Go with Lord Rudra,' said Ram.

'Go with Lord Parshu Ram,' answered Hanuman.

Then Ram extended his hands towards Angad. But Angad stepped forward and embraced Ram. The king of Ayodhya smiled and warmly hugged Angad. 'You destroyed many Lankans yesterday. Today is the day we end it all.'

'We will, Lord Ram,' Angad said, smiling.

Hanuman and Angad saluted Ram and left to take up position at the head of their respective elephant corps.

Arishtanemi and Ram mounted their horses. And rode to the front lines.

'Oh hell,' whispered Arishtanemi, pulling his horse up.

Ram looked at Arishtanemi. And then up towards the sky.

'Oh man …'

It had started raining close to the city walls. Upon the Lankan formation. But the clouds were moving. It was only a matter of time ...

'This island gets rain practically all year round,' said Arishtanemi. 'How the hell do they plan proper battles?'

And, just then, the rain began pelting down over the Ayodhyan formations as well.

Rain – especially the heavy rain that fell on the Indian subcontinent – made war exceptionally difficult. It drenched the ground, which made the movement of chariot wheels arduous. Chariots were all about speed and manoeuvrability. They had little role to play if they were bogged down in wet mud.

Raavan had no chariot corps left. Ram did.

Rain also made bowstrings soggy. It was difficult to shoot arrows using a dank string. And even if a talented archer managed to do so, the range was heavily compromised.

Raavan had a much smaller archer corps left with him. Ram had a full complement of archer corps.

Rain would mitigate some of Raavan's main weaknesses, and weaken some of Ram's key strengths.

Apparently.

'This is bad news,' said Arishtanemi.

'No ... I think the rain is good news,' answered Ram.

Arishtanemi turned to Ram. Confused. 'Are you thinking of our elephant corps?'

Rain or sunshine made no difference to the elephants. They could move even through marshy terrain. Elephants were known to swim when needed. Damp ground would not slow them down.

The rain would not notably diminish the effectiveness of Ram's elephant corps.

'No … Not our elephants. Though they can still cause some serious devastation. The real benefit of the rain lies somewhere else.'

'Tell me.' Arishtanemi was really confused now.

'We need the rains to help us make them commit to the Pushpak Vimaan strategy,' said Ram.

Arishtanemi waited for Ram to explain.

'King Raavan and Prince Indrajit are talented generals. We must not underestimate them. They know that we have one hundred and sixty thousand troops and that they have only sixty-five thousand. We have a full chariot and cavalry corps. They have practically none. And we also have the elephant corps. And if, despite all this, we do not launch a full-scale attack, it would make them suspicious. They would suspect that we know about their plans with the Pushpak Vimaan. And they may then change their strategy.'

Arishtanemi smiled. The hallmark of a great general is the ability to read the mind of his enemy. 'So, we now have an apparently good reason to not charge in a full-scale attack? Without raising their suspicions. It is the rains after all!'

'Precisely,' said Ram. 'And if we don't charge with all our troops, then we are not vulnerable to the vimaan. Remember, this battle ends only when we take away the Pushpak Vimaan factor.'

'Do you think they will retreat behind their walls and wait for tomorrow?'

'No. King Raavan will lose even more men to desertion tonight. It will end today. Either way.'

Arishtanemi looked at the Lankan formations. They were ready. And waiting. The rain had slowed down a bit. It wasn't raining cats and dogs anymore. Just kittens and puppies.

'So, what are your orders?' asked Arishtanemi.

Ram touched his chin thoughtfully. 'Only our elephants. The rest will hold back.'

Arishtanemi turned to relay the orders.

'Just an echelon, Arishtanemiji,' added Ram.

An echelon would mean fifty elephants. A third of a single elephant corp.

A light attack. Not meant to cause serious damage. Just to provoke a response.

'Yes, my lord,' answered Arishtanemi.

In no time, fifty elephants thundered out from the Ayodhya ranks. The elephants were trumpeting loudly, their trunks thrust forward. Some archers atop the elephant howdahs began firing arrows as they neared the Lankan infantry lines. But the distance and their soggy bowstrings ensured that they did not cause too much damage.

The inadequacy in the arrows could be more than adequately compensated by the rumbling mass of elephant feet, though. For soldiers could be crushed to death under their weight.

Or so was the plan.

But Raavan was not out of tricks yet.

'Break formations!' ordered Raavan.

And, at an unbelievable speed, the Lankan lines reformed. Across the formations, soldiers moved quickly sidewards and five lines merged into one. This was done within a few minutes. Rapid speed. It had been practised repeatedly the previous evening, within the city walls.

The result was spectacular. A dense traditional *chaturanga* formation of Lankan infantry in two hundred lines seamlessly recoalesced to just forty lines, with massive open lanes in between.

A dense formation of soldiers would have been perfect for the elephants. A target-rich environment. Like the previous day.

Just crash through and stamp the Lankans in massive numbers. The resultant stampede would add to the mayhem.

Now, there was empty ground in thirty-nine broad lanes, with soldiers lined up in single-file on either side. All of a sudden.

The mahouts could have attempted to crash into the single files of Lankan soldiers, in a zig-zag manner. But that was risky. A golden rule in elephant charges: keep the elephants in their lane. For there is only one thing that can bring down an elephant quickly. Another elephant.

The risk of elephants running zigzag was that they would crash into each other. The entire Ayodhyan elephantry charge could collapse.

The elephant mahouts had no choice. They had to rush into the open lanes. And hope that the Ayodhyan soldiers atop the howdahs would kill as many Lankans on-ground as possible. With their spears and arrows.

But the bowstrings were wet. The arrows were not effective.

The elements seemed to be helping Raavan today.

The Ayodhyan warriors flung spears at the Lankans. They killed a few. But the bigger hope was to get them to break formation in panic. The Lankans though, in an awesome display of discipline, and despite the great fear of elephants stampeding so close to them, remained in formation. They stood firm.

And then Raavan unleashed his secret weapon.

Long axes.

Essentially, they were spears, with the pointed blade at the top edge replaced with an axe head. An axe head with a wickedly sharp metallic bit.

Raavan had learnt from the Battle of the Left Flank the previous day. Kumbhakarna had brought down two elephants. By slicing the legs and incapacitating the beasts.

The Lankan soldiers along the lines lifted the long axes which had been lying on the ground, undetected. And simply held them up. Intending to slice through as many elephant legs as possible. And bring them down.

But if Raavan had a secret weapon, then Ram had a secret shield!

Unfortunately for Raavan, Ram too had studied Kumbhakarna's tactics. And had quickly put Shatrughan to work, designing and fabricating a leather armour which ran down the outer side of the elephants' legs.

Most of the axe thrusts were ineffective.

Two struck through and drew blood. But not enough to bring down the pachyderms. The elephants swung their trunks in rage and swatted the axes away.

'There is no damage being caused, my lord,' said Arishtanemi. 'To them or to us. It's a stalemate.'

'We wait,' answered Ram.

'Why don't we send out a few infantry battalions?'

'No. We wait.'

'But ...'

Arishtanemi stopped speaking when he heard the sound. The unmistakeable sound.

Whump! Whump!

Whump! Whump!

He looked at Ram.

Ram nodded. 'Finally ...' He turned to his flagbearer. 'Message for Hanumanji ... The Pushpak Vimaan is coming ...'

The message was relayed quickly to the right flank.

Meanwhile, all the faces of the Ayodhyan infantry were turned towards the sky.

Whump! Whump!

A roar went up from the Lankans. Their champion was coming!

War elephants, like most beasts of war, are trained for loud battle noise. Even so, the thundering blast of the flying machine was alarming. Some elephants charging down the Lankan ranks stopped in their tracks. The expert mahouts started turning the elephants around. To get them to retreat, even as they whispered calming messages to them, through signals from their feet on the beasts' temples.

And then …

The vimaan swiftly emerged from high above the fort walls. Like the sudden appearance of a demonic monster. Colossal. Shaped like an inverted cone that gently tapered upwards. The massive main rotor at the top of the cone rotating rhythmically, like the giant slices of a mammoth sword. There were many small manoeuvring rotors close to the broad base, which controlled directional movement. They were whirring smoothly. The portholes at the base of the vimaan were sealed with thick glass, soldiers clearly visible behind them. The main door was ajar. Two warriors plainly outlined against the opening. One of them was the prince of Lanka. Indrajit. Dressed in black dhoti, tied tight in the military style. A sleeveless armour covered his torso. A bow in his left hand. A rope tied around his waist, which was hooked farther inside the vimaan; to ensure that he did not topple out with any sudden movement.

He turned around and shouted an order to the pilot. Akampana.

The vimaan dipped lower. Bearing down quickly upon the enemy.

Whump!

Whump!

Whump!

Whump!

Raavan looked at the vimaan. 'Go get them, son!'

Across the battlefield, Ram bellowed his order. 'Cover!'

Orders were rapidly relayed out through flag signals,

The infantry had been trained well, the previous day. They quickly held up their massive shields. Laid them flat above their heads. Each soldier's shield partially covered the soldier ahead and behind him. Within seconds, the Ayodhyan infantry regiments looked, from the air, like massive turtles: the hard shell made from many shields. Protecting the soldiers from assaults from the sky. They were metallic shields, coated with leather. Strong. Waterproof. Providing protection against arrows, spears and even burning oil.

Indrajit looked at the Lankan standing beside him and laughed. 'The Ayodhyans expect us to attack their infantry!'

The Lankan laughed along with his prince.

Ram had prepared for an attack that wasn't coming.

Indrajit was not about to have his soldiers pour burning oil on the infantry. That would have efficiently killed many hundreds of Ayodhyan soldiers. But it was fraught with risk for the Lankan soldiers within the vimaan as well. A flying vehicle making sudden movements *and* woodfires with tubs of boiling oil within ... Not a good combination. The oil could very easily spill on the Lankans within the vimaan. The fire itself could spread within the flying vehicle.

No. Not burning oil. Instead, Indrajit had listened to his smartest advisor. His mother.

He wasn't going for his enemy's weakest link. He was going for their strongest.

Jiujitsu.

The vimaan turned suddenly. Away from the infantry at the centre. Towards the left flank.

It took but a moment for Ram to understand what his enemy planned to do.

'Lord Rudra have mercy ...'

'What do we do, Lord?' asked Arishtanemi.

The vimaan was approaching the left-flank elephant corps, commanded by Angad, the hero of the previous day.

'You have the command, Arishtanemiji!' roared Ram.

'What?!' asked Aristhanemi. And then he understood. 'No, Lord Ram! Don't!'

But Ram was already riding towards the left flank. Galloping hard. Into the mouth of danger.

Arishtanemi immediately controlled his emotions. Ram had to do what he must. And he had to do the same. He turned towards his flagbearer with brisk commands for the infantry. 'Hold formations! We don't break!'

Arishtanemi's job was to hold the infantry and prevent panic. If it came down to it, they would fight the Lankan infantry soldiers to the finish. But Ram had to stop the vimaan before that. Or contain the damage it would wreak.

Ram was riding hard. Spurring his horse forward. Followed closely by his personal bodyguard.

But the vimaan was a demonic machine of fearsome ability. No horse could match it for speed. It was already hovering over the left-flank elephant corps. Indrajit and the Lankan beside him had begun their attack. Spears. And poisoned arrows shot from bows with strings that had remained dry within the vimaan. Other soldiers were showering stones from behind Indrajit. Stones falling from that height, powered by vicious warriors and the pull of gravity, were lethal missiles that killed on impact.

Spears. Arrows. Stones.

Targeted. Surgical. Brutally effective.

He had listened to his brilliant mother.

Strike the enemy's strength. Strike the elephants. Not directly. But through their mahouts.

It was very difficult to target mahouts from the ground, because of their elevation and heavy armour. But from the altitude of the flying Pushpak Vimaan, they were sitting ducks. And without the mahouts, the elephants were as good as useless; like the Pushpak Vimaan would be without any rotors to guide it. The elephants would either be paralysed without instructions from a trusted source, or run amuck with grief for their slain mahouts.

'Prince Angad!' thundered Ram from a distance. 'Hold!'

But Angad had already been struck. A stone had fallen on him, hard. On his head. His metal helmet had prevented a head injury that would have killed him. But it had rendered him unconscious. Twenty mahouts had already been killed or knocked out cold. Most elephants were standing still. Not knowing what to do, as the instructions, conveyed through the feet of the mahouts on their temples, had suddenly stopped. It was only a matter of time before some elephant lost his self-control and reacted angrily to the death of his mahout. For most elephants looked up to mahouts like their elder brothers.

If even one elephant reacted with rage and rampaged, the others would follow suit. And the only ones who would die in this melee would be the soldiers around them. Ayodhyans.

This would be fratricide.

The elephants that had destroyed the Lankans the previous day could very well hurt the Ayodhyans today.

Jiujitsu.

Using your opponent's strength against him.

Indrajit was turning the battle single-handedly. Or so it seemed.

The strategy intrinsic to Jiujitsu can be countered in only one way. The opponent steps back and does not strike. If your strength is going to be used against you, then you stand down and don't use your strength.

Ram was galloping hard. And as he reached the elephantry corps, finally, an elephant became hysterical.

It was Angad's elephant. The lead elephant. As it saw its mahout fall to the ground, two arrows buried deep in his throat, the beast bellowed in rage. Emotions had clouded the thinking of an intelligent animal. It raised its trunk and trumpeted ferociously at the Pushpak Vimaan. And charged towards its shadow. Other elephants followed. Frenzied. Incensed.

Some Ayodhyan soldiers on the elephant's path were trampled to death.

This would very soon turn into a stampede.

'No, my lord!' screamed a worried bodyguard, as he saw Ram racing towards the lead elephant, not slowing down at all.

Meanwhile, Indrajit turned and shouted to Akampana at the flight controls, making sure his voice carried over the roar of the vimaan motors. 'Towards the other flank! Quickly!'

As Akampana worked the controls to turn the vehicle, Indrajit looked at the Lankan beside him. 'Our task here is done. The elephants will do our job for us. We have to get to the elephants on the right flank before they retreat.'

The Ayodhyan infantry formations next to the left-flank elephantry were breaking, as soldiers tried to avoid getting trampled. Ram raced towards the lead elephant. If he managed to control it, the other beasts behind would also calm down.

Ram pulled his feet out of the stirrups, jumped up and crouched on top of the saddle. He transferred the reins, placing them between his teeth. Still expertly guiding the horse towards the rampaging elephant. As he neared, he swerved the horse to the side, leveraged himself with his upper limbs and stood up on the saddle. The elephant was chasing the vimaan, its eyes pinned on the object in the sky. It did not notice the horse galloping up to it. Ram guided the horse close to the elephant's right, and, in an awe-inspiring feat of athleticism, coupled with a super-human sense of timing, sprung from the saddle. He landed on the elephant's massive tusk, used it as leverage, and vaulted up. Onto the top of the elephant's head. All in a moment. The elephant sensed a presence on itself. It raised its trunk in fury, but stopped as the scent of the human being was familiar. And dear.

There was trust.

Suddenly the elephant felt a gentle and controlled pressure on its temples. From Ram's feet.

Calm down.

I'm here.

Slow down.

And the beast listened. It started slowing down.

Calm down ...

The elephant listened to the familiar.

It listened to its elder brother.

Ram had spent the last many months not just acquainting himself with most of his soldiers but also with each elephant. They trusted him. They listened to him.

Calm down ...

Slow down ...

After a few seconds, the lead elephant came to a halt. And so did the elephants behind it.

The Ayodhyan infantry soldiers roared in triumph. Their king had saved them. But their king was not roaring. He was staring into the distance. Towards the right flank.

'Hanumanji …' Ram whispered. 'Take them towards the jungle …'

On the right flank, Hanuman and his elephant corps were in full retreat. Hurtling back towards the forest.

'Lower!' roared Indrajit, shouting at Akampana. He knew that the vimaan was still too high for their missiles to be effective.

The elephants of the right flank were racing hard. Towards the trees. Most of them would enter the jungle soon. And would then be protected from arrows and spears by the tree tops.

'Lower, Akampanaji!'

Akampana turned to look at Indrajit. At the door. And took a deep breath.

I am only following orders. The other soldiers will back me up.

He expertly lowered the vimaan. Much lower than he should have. And boosted the rear directional motors. Turning the doorway towards the jungle. Slowly.

Just a few moments more, and the target would be presented. Perfectly.

Now, you Ayodhyans do your thing …

And the main Ayodhyan, who had to do his thing, was ready.

Lakshman was not wearing his armour. It would hamper his ability to fling the spear to his farthest limit. He saw the vimaan nearing and ordered his mahout to move his elephant forward. Out of the tree cover.

'Lakshman! Wait!' shouted Bharat, who was on an elephant to the left of Lakshman's.

The vimaan still wasn't in perfect position. But the deafening din of the vimaan's motors meant that Lakshman didn't hear his brother. He held his spear up and took position. Feet spread apart. Backfoot perpendicular. Left arm raised high. The spear shaft flat on the palm of his right hand, between the index and middle finger, the thumb pointing back, and the rest of the fingers facing the other direction. Breathing steady and rhythmic. Eyes pinned on the vimaan door.

Meanwhile, within the vimaan, the Lankan beside Indrajit spoke loudly, pointing with his left hand, 'My lord! That is the prince of Ayodhya, Lakshman! Kill him!'

Indrajit whipped his body to the right, changing the planned direction of his shot, and released his arrow.

At that same moment, Lakshman flung the spear high. With all his might. Aiming unerringly for Indrajit.

A sudden gust of air turbulence made the vimaan shift a degree.

'Lakshman!' roared Bharat, as he saw the arrow swooping in.

Lakshman's spear missed. Due to the slight movement of the vimaan. But Indrajit's arrow did not miss. It slammed into Lakshman's chest. Brutally. Cutting through knotted layers of bull-like muscle, piercing through a rib, puncturing the right lung. Striking deep into the body of the mighty Lakshman. He fell back in the howdah. Blood burst forth from his chest.

'Lakshmaaaaan!' howled Bharat. 'Noooo!'

The vimaan continued turning slightly. And began to rise.

Bharat already had a spear in his hand. He looked up and hurled it hard. His instinct guiding the aim.

The vimaan was moving higher. It was already beyond the limit of Bharat's throwing range. But this thrust of the spear was not just powered by muscle, bone and training. It was also powered by the furious rage of a protective elder brother.

The spear sped high, piercing through the air like lightning.

Indrajit was exulting at the sight of Lakshman lying prone in his howdah. He knew how close the four royal brothers were. This would devastate them all. As the vimaan turned, another elephant came into view. The prince of Lanka reached for an arrow from his quiver. But the warrior atop the howdah was bent forward, his arm hanging down, as if he had just flung a spear. Before Indrajit could piece together this information, the missile flung by Bharat pounded into his chest. The spear had serrated edges along a ridiculously sharp blade point. And it was propelled to a manic speed. It crashed through his armour, tore through his ribs, and burst out from his back. Slicing his right lung asunder. Indrajit swayed for a moment. The pain had immobilised him. And then he fell forward. Out, from the open vimaan door. He fell like a stone, the descent picking up force, powered by gravity. Till the rope that had been tied around his waist and hooked to the vimaan halted his fall mid-air. But the sudden jerk also broke his back and neck. Killing him instantly.

Hanuman, farther out to right, at the edge of the jungle line, looked at the vimaan. Indrajit's body was dangling below it. The rope was tied around his waist, his torso twisted at an odd angle from his legs. His head hung askew from his broken neck. His body was skewered by the spear.

'Lakshmaannn!' cried Bharat, as his elephant rushed towards Lakshman's mount.

Meanwhile, the vimaan had begun its descent onto the open ground. Akampana was bringing it down. Slowly. Careful to ensure that the vimaan did not land on the swinging corpse of Indrajit.

The prince of Lanka was a true warrior. He deserved not to have his corpse crushed under a machine.

'Dismount!' Hanuman ordered his elephant corps soldiers. 'Rush into the vimaan. Arrest them all! No killing!'

Chapter 38

'Dada ...' whispered Bharat, tears flooding his eyes.

The white flag of Shantidevi, the Goddess of Peace, had been raised as soon as the Pushpak Vimaan had landed on the ground. A temporary truce had been declared.

Messengers had been sent to Raavan, carrying news of his son's death.

Ram had rushed to the right flank. Close to the jungle edge, where the vimaan had been forced to land. Hanuman and his troops had already disarmed and arrested the Lankan soldiers inside the Pushpak Vimaan. Akampana stood in front, his hands tied behind him. Indrajit's body had been freed from the rope tied around his waist, and his corpse had been laid, sideways, on a piece of cloth on the ground. With respect.

This was Ram's army. Their conduct was dharmic, even with their enemies.

Ram and Bharat were down on their knees. Bharat cradled Lakshman's head on his lap. Their giant young brother lay unconscious. His torso was smeared with congealed blood. Some quick battlefield first aid had been performed. The shaft of the arrow had been broken. But the arrowhead and point remained buried deep in Lakshman's right lung. The physician had put ointments around the wound to stem the bleeding. And an apparatus on Lakshman's nose to help him breathe.

Ram placed his hand on Bharat's shoulder and turned to the physician. His face was lined with pain, but he held himself strong. An emotionally devastated elder brother is of no use during a younger brother's crisis. Only someone who remains calm and focused can pull his brother out of an emergency situation.

'What can you do, doctor?' asked Ram.

'He is breathing, great king,' said the doctor. 'He is alive. I can perform a surgery and remove the arrow. But the surgery itself ...'

'What about the surgery?' asked Bharat.

'My lords, this is a poisoned arrow. A very specific poison. It temporarily paralyses the muscles around the wound. Even more, surgically removing the arrowhead can trigger the worst effects of the poison. It will kill Prince Lakshman within a few minutes ... But if we don't do anything, then ...'

The doctor was sensitive enough not to complete the statement. For they truly were in the horns of a dilemma. If the doctor left the arrowhead inside, the wound would turn septic and Lakshman would die a slow, excruciatingly painful death over a few days. But if the doctor surgically removed the arrow, then the poison would get triggered and the Ayodhyan prince would die within a few minutes. In simple terms, a surgery would be merciful and spare him the pain.

But Ram and Bharat were not the kind of brothers who would give up.

'There must be something you can do, doctor,' said Bharat, for he knew the miracles that were possible in the traditional Indian form of medicine. '*Ayurveda* has an answer to everything.'

'There is something that can help, my lords. But it is almost impossible to get the medicine.'

'Nothing is impossible,' said Ram. 'What do you need?'

'I will need three particular herbs. Vishalyakarani, Saavarnyakarani and Samdhaani. And the branches of the Sanjeevani tree.'

'Oh no ...' whispered Bharat. He knew that these herbs and tree were found in the Himalayas. Far to the north. Too far.

'It's not as far as you think, Lord Bharat. They have been transplanted in very limited quantities in the southern mountains. The closest hillside where these herbs are available is the Dronagiri mountain, in the campus of the Mahodayapuram university, in the land of Kerala. But even that is too far. For it is impossible to transport Lord Lakshman there without triggering the poison. We cannot move him too much, and we certainly cannot transport him over a long distance.'

'But why do you need to move him? I don't understand. Don't you have the medicines here?'

'We have the branches of the Sanjeevani tree. But the three herbs of Vishalyakarani, Saavarnyakarani and Samdhaani must be used within half an hour of being plucked from the soil. So, the surgery has to be done at Mahodayapuram itself. That is the conundrum. It is impossible to bring the medicine here. And we cannot move him. We are stuck between a rock and a hard place. There are no options.'

Ram and Bharat looked at each other. They both had the same thought.

If Lakshman cannot go to the mountain, then the mountain's treasures must be brought to Lakshman.

'The Pushpak Vimaan …' said Bharat.

Ram looked at Akampana, standing in the distance.

—— J⌐ ⅃⌐⁷D ——

The vimaan was commandeered by Ram. Akampana had agreed to fly it. The Lankan minister was happy to curry favour with the Ayodhyan royals, as the war was as good as over. Hanuman was to lead the mission, accompanied by Shatrughan and one hundred Ayodhyan soldiers. Three doctors were a part of the team as well. Their role was to ensure that the right herbs were collected in the proper manner. The Dronagiri mountain was only a half-hour flight away. So, they hoped to be back very soon.

A makeshift bed had been made on the battleground itself and Lakshman had been placed on it. Prince Angad, who had recovered substantially but was still weak, also rested on a bed nearby, the doctors carefully monitoring for signs of concussion. The medicine men hovered around the two royals, ensuring that no further harm came to them.

Meanwhile, physicians had set up a field hospital behind the Ayodhyan lines and were taking care of the wounded.

There was a sudden commotion at the thunderous sound of galloping horses approaching in a storm of dust. Ram and Bharat turned to look while Arishtanemi closed in, next to them, protectively.

It was Raavan.

He swayed over the saddle and a bodyguard helped him dismount. His haggard face had aged a decade within a few hours. There were only two men that he had truly loved. Ever. The first had died the previous day. And he was about to see the corpse of the second.

There was a time when he would have gruffly pushed aside a helping hand. But now, he allowed his bodyguard to hold his elbow, as he stumbled towards the king of Ayodhya.

'King Raavan,' said Ram as he came to his feet, politely folding his hands into a namaste. 'My sincere condolences. Your son fought fiercely. Like the warrior that he was. He made his ancestors proud today.'

Raavan folded his hands into a namaste. 'Lord Ram ... Where ...'

Ram took Raavan by the arm and gently led him forward. They were enemies, but Ram was a follower of the Vedic code of conduct. The path of *dharma*. There is a protocol to be honoured, a grace to be maintained, even in enmity.

Ram led Raavan to where Indrajit's body lay, guarded by Ayodhyan soldiers. They were followed by Raavan's bodyguards.

The king of Ayodhya nodded to his soldiers. They saluted smartly and stepped aside.

A strangled cry escaped from Raavan's mouth as he saw the broken body of his son. He fell to his knees. Tears streamed down his face. His soul was crushed. He couldn't take it anymore. If the Gods had to bear witness, they would think that this was the final tragedy that would break Raavan's dogged, pig-headed spirit. This was the straw that would finally break the beast's back.

Indrajit was lying on his side. He was placed with honour on a large piece of cloth bearing the Suryavanshi symbol. The shaft of the spear, buried deep in Indrajit's chest, had been cut with care. The main foreshaft remained buried in his lungs and heart. The pointed, serrated blade that had run through him and burst from his back, remained where it was. Thick blood had congealed around the blade and hardwood support. His head had been carefully put back in place, but it was obvious that the neck was broken. The skull was clearly detached from the cervical vertebrae. The Ayodhyans had placed Indrajit's legs back in position as well. The rope that was tied around his waist had been cut and removed. But it was still apparent that the base of the torso and the legs were at an unnatural angle to each other. The pelvic girdle, which held the torso in place, had not just fractured when the rope had broken Indrajit's fall, it had cleaved apart, shattering into four pieces.

No father should have to see his son this way. No father should see his son this way.

There is no glory in war. Only pain and devastation. Bhasa – the greatest Sanskrit playwright of antiquity – had written, this war-ground is actually a sacrificial ground, where dead warriors are the sacrificial victims, war cries are the mantras, dead elephants are the altar, arrows are the sacrificial grass, and hatred and enmity are the burning fire.

But one among them was willing to give up hatred and enmity.

Ram walked up to the kneeling Raavan and gently touched his shoulder. 'I am so sorry, King Raavan. He was a brave man ... your son.'

Raavan was staring at his son's beautiful face. Indrajit had inherited his looks. And without the pockmarks that had ravaged Raavan's visage, he was handsome. Raavan knew his son represented the best that he could ever have been. For Indrajit was a combination of his father's physical appearance and fearsome capability, and his wife's unblemished character. Raavan was being forced to witness the death of someone who embodied the best he could have been.

'I will have my men help you take Prince Indrajit's body back into Sigiriya,' said Ram. 'To carry out the funeral ceremonies that you must. We honour him. We will continue to honour him.'

Raavan didn't turn to look at Ram. He was frozen, his eyes pinned unblinkingly on his son. Tears surged down his face. Squeezing out the remains of his soul, to be burned in the heat of the sun.

Honour … Knowledge … Wealth … Dignity … Dharma … All nonsense…

Raavan stopped crying. He wiped the tears off his face. And looked up. The rain clouds had retreated. Revealing a sullen sun. Burning bright. Scorching all below it. Proud of its immense power. The clouds, swollen with their droplets of tear-like rain, may hide it at times. But the sun will, ultimately, emerge. It will. It will conquer the clouds. And burn those who challenge it. Why? Because that is what the sun does.

Power … That is all there is … Power … Demonstrating your power … Crushing others with your power … Making them cower with your power …

Raavan stared at the sun. Still a few hours away from its highest point for the day. There was life left in the sun. More life for today. It hadn't begun its descent. Not yet. Not yet.

The sun still had more to burn of itself. It still had more to burn of others.

Raavan brushed Ram's gentle hand off his shoulder and stood up abruptly. The pain in his right leg was forgotten. He turned around and looked at his enemy. Proud unbending face. Defiant reckless eye.

'Duel of Indra,' whispered Raavan.

'What?' asked a flummoxed Ram. He thought he hadn't heard right.

'I challenge you to the Duel of Indra!' barked Raavan. Loudly, so that all around could hear him.

Ram stared at Raavan. Eyes steady. Face calm. But Bharat could feel his brother's rage in the slightly clenched muscles of his arms.

Ram had been decent. Ram had been gracious. Ram had been dharmic.

But Ram had made the cardinal mistake of most gracious people. They expect grace in return.

'Dada ...' whispered Bharat.

He knew what his elder brother would do. What his brother would be honour-bound to do. He had to dissuade Ram. There was no need for this duel. They had won already. The Lankans were defeated. Pragmatic Bharat understood this. But before he could say anything more, Ram raised his hand for quiet.

And then, staring at Raavan, in a voice that was eerily calm, Ram said, 'I accept. Duel of Indra. In the centre of the battlefield. Fourth hour of the third prahar, today.'

Duel of Indra. Fight to the death.

—— JF J5D ——

Raavan stood quietly. Holding Indrajit's hand. Just like he had held Kumbhakarna's the previous day. Letting the physician do his work. Making the death mask. An image of Indrajit's last expression, the one that would be recorded for posterity in a bronze mask.

It was an expression of *veera ras*. The *emotion of courage and triumph*. He had nearly turned the battle single-handedly. Stopped only by the courage and brilliance of Ram and Bharat. History would record, in glowing words, Indrajit's lionhearted defence of his land and his father. A brave last stand in the face of defeat.

'My lord…' whispered the physician. He knew that Raavan would be fighting a duel in a few hours. He wanted his lord and master to rest. 'Do you need a chair? Should I ask for some herbal infusions for you?'

'Just do your job,' growled Raavan. 'Make sure my son's death mask is perfect.'

'Yes, my lord.'

Ram had not allowed the Lankan army to return to Sigiriya. He had insisted that Raavan order his troops to disarm and remain outside the fort walls, in the open ground. They were detained and surrounded by the Ayodhyan army. Raavan had been allowed to go back into the city with the corpse of his son and a hundred bodyguards. Not one warrior more.

Ram had ensured that, if he won the duel and ordered a victory march into Sigiriya to take control of the city, there would be no street-by-street resistance. He would restore order in Sigiriya immediately and cleanly.

Ram had accepted the challenge of the Duel of Indra. But he was putting only himself in harm's way. He was not about to make a move that would damage his army later.

There is a difference between being noble and being stupid. Ram was certainly not stupid.

'My lord?' The physician asked for permission to pour the plaster on Indrajit's face. Raavan would not then be able to see his son's visage anymore.

Raavan remained quiet. He could not tear his eyes away from his son's warrior countenance. *I'll be with you soon, my boy.*

He ran his fingers through his son's hair. *But I will leave this world like you did … In a blaze of glory … I will go like the sun …*

For the sun does not go quietly into the night. As he sets, he rages. He turns the sky into vivid colours of orange and purple as he burns everything around him with his fury.

I will not go quietly. I will go in a blaze of glory …

'My lord?' asked the physician once again.

Raavan was about to answer when he stopped. A sound at the door. Someone had entered the royal hospital chamber. Raavan turned and looked.

Mandodari.

'Please wait,' said Mandodari, politely and softly.

This was the first time she had entered the palace complex in nearly two decades. The ever-present, sage-like gentle smile on her face was missing. Her dark, captivating eyes normally revealed her unbending and righteous spirit; now, it was a window into a person who was broken and bereft.

She stood there.

Looking at her son.

Her pride and joy.

Her finest accomplishment.

Her sun and moon.

Her refuge from the misery caused by the husband she had been cursed with.

Gone.

Mandodari staggered to the corpse of Indrajit as Raavan stepped back quietly.

The one woman – besides Vedavati – whose moral force Raavan acknowledged, was his wife Mandodari. But he had never loved Mandodari. There was space in his heart only for Vedavati. If he was honest with himself, though, he would accept that in the dark suppressed corners of his heart, he was afraid of Mandodari.

The queen of Lanka reached Indrajit and gently touched her son's face. She did not utter a sound. No crying. She did not allow the tears to slip past. Her eyes had imprisoned grief which ached to burst forth from her soul now.

She would not cry. Not in front of Raavan. Not in front of her husband.

'I'm so sorry, Mandodari ...' whispered Raavan, speaking to her for the first time in many years. 'He died like a hero ... He was one of the finest ever ... A better man than me ...'

Mandodari did not look at Raavan. She had eyes only for her son.

'I ...'

Mandodari ignored her husband.

'I am fighting a duel with King Ram in a few hours. I will ... This will probably be the last time that you and I ...'

Mandodari did not say anything.

'I am sorry for everything ...'

Mandodari remained silent. Focused on her son. Only on her son. Gently running her hands over his face.

'I will be with our son soon ... I will go with my head held high.'

Mandodari looked at Raavan. And whispered, 'The only thing you will be holding high is what you have always held high – your ego.'

Raavan took a sharp short breath. Anger coursed through his veins. He wanted to shout curses and expletives at his wife. But he could not. Not in front of his son. For he knew ... He knew that his son had worshipped Mandodari like a Goddess.

Raavan bent down, kissed Indrajit's forehead, turned around and stormed out of the chamber.

Mandodari held her son's hands. And finally allowed her tears to pour out in a flood. Crying bitterly.

A mother who had lost her son. Her magnificent son.

A mother who had lost everything. All that she was left with was her life.

Life. Vicious life. Lucky are those who escape early. The others are kept around long enough to suffer more.

I am sorry that I couldn't protect you from him, my son. I am sorry that I couldn't protect you from your father.

Chapter 39

The ground for the duel was prepared strictly according to the rules prescribed by Lord Indra himself. A circle had been carefully drawn, with the field shaped into a circular net made of the ground's clay, the chords stretching wide and half buried into the ground. The Indrajal. The net of Indra. The ground for the Duel of Indra.

All the measurements within Indra's net were deeply symbolic. The radius of the circular ground was exactly 10.185 metres. The circumference then was sixty-four metres, a number sacred to Lord Indra. At the vertexes of the 'chords of the circular net' at the boundary, along the perimeter of the circle, were bows of the colour of a rainbow. The *Indradhanush*. Literally, *Indra's bow*. But, also, a word that meant *rainbow*.

The symbolic meaning of the ground's design was steeped in esoteric mystique.

The Atharva Veda describes Indra's Net as a deeply philosophical metaphor representing the universe as a web of interconnectedness and interdependence. The entire universe as a whole remains in balance and all the vertexes of the universe are either positive or negative reflections. All the positives and negatives combine to make the *zero principle* or *shunyata*. It's not exactly zero, for the universe is not actually in complete balance, but that is not important here. And, the logical corollary to shunyata is *pratityasamutpada*, or *dependent origination*, like the seven colours of the rainbow, the *Indradhanush*, originating from white light.

In the simple words of the warrior, it can be stated that in order to remove the effect we must first remove the cause. To remove the seven colours we must remove white light. To end the enmity, one of the foes must die.

So, when soldiers say that entering Indra's Net ends enmities, they are correct. Without the enemy, there is no enmity.

Ram and Raavan waited on opposite ends of the circle. Facing each other. Their seconds stood behind them. Bharat with Ram. Prahast with Raavan.

Hanuman and Shatrughan had returned with the Vishalyakarani, Saavarnyakarani and Samdhaani herbs, carefully carried in large pots filled with the soil of Dronagiri mountain. The herbs were alive when plucked off the plants by doctors at the battleground outside Sigiriya. Lakshman's surgery had been conducted and he was on his way to recovery. The herbs had helped Angad's recovery from concussion as well. They had also helped heal Angad's fractured leg.

Ram's mind was at rest. His brothers were safe. He was free to put his own life at risk. He was ready for the duel.

The priestess of the temple dedicated to Lord Indra emerged from the gates of the city of Sigiriya. She was followed by an assistant carrying a large plate. They moved ceremonially to the centre of the ground. The heart of Indra's Net. The assistant's plate held a conch shell, a small seven-coloured bow, a tiny net, a hook, and the vajra – a thunderbolt-shaped knife. Symbols of Lord Indra, the great conqueror.

No one knew the original name or antecedents of the priestess of Lord Indra. As tradition dictated, she had come from the sacred mountain valley of Kashmir. Like all the priestesses before her. The Lankans knew her only by her title: Indrani.

The priestess picked up the *shankh – conch shell –* from the plate and brought it to her lips. She took a deep breath and blew into it strongly. The deep resonance of the conch shell reverberated like streams of sonic consciousness over the teeming audience that had gathered to witness this duel. A duel that people knew would be the greatest in the century, if not the millennium. A hush descended like an invisible cloak on all.

The Indrani delicately picked up a copper ewer with her left hand. She poured water from it and washed the conch shell, nestled in the palm of her right hand. After placing the shankh back on the plate, she poured the rest of the water, via the palm of her right hand, onto the ground. She performed the ritual three times.

She then spoke in a loud, clear voice. 'May the heroic Indra, the wielder of the mighty vajra, the slayer of the heinous dragon Vritra, the splitter of immortal mountains, bless the soul of the two duellists.'

'*Om Indraya Namah!*' chorused Ram and Raavan.

I bow to Lord Indra.

'*Om Indraya Namah!*' repeated all who stood there.

The Indrani turned to Bharat. 'You second the duellist who was thrown the challenge. By the immutable laws of Lord Indra, he has the right to choose the weapon of combat. What say you?'

Bharat stepped up to Ram. 'Dada?'

Ram didn't hesitate for a second. He whispered, 'The sword. No armour.'

Bharat hesitated. He expected nothing less than honourable behaviour from his brother but had hoped nevertheless that Ram would be practical. Nope. His brother had chosen honour over pragmatism. Ram's favourite weapon was the bow. He was the most skilled archer alive. But Raavan's left arm was injured. Everyone knew that. The king of Lanka would not be able to wield a bow well. It would not be a fair fight.

Dharma dictates that a warrior must defeat his enemy fair and square. Ram had chosen *dharma*.

But Ram was enraged as well. A righteous rage. For his hand of grace and dharma had been rejected by Raavan. Hence, no armour.

The battle would be brutal.

Dharmic goodness, without the power of righteous indignation, can be weak. Ram had chosen goodness, but he had rejected weakness.

Bharat looked at the priestess and announced, in a loud clear voice, 'My warrior brother Ram has chosen. With Lord Indra's permission, he chooses a sword as a weapon. With one condition. No armour.'

The audience audibly gasped with surprise. Ram had given away his tactical advantage by not choosing bow and arrow. The soldiers, men among men, warriors all, acknowledged the honour in Ram's choice. Even the Lankan soldiers were constrained to admit within their hearts: Ram is a warrior of the noble code.

The Indrani smiled slightly. Impressed. She understood well what the weapon of choice meant. She turned to Prahast, the second of Raavan. 'What say you?'

Prahast was a warrior of the ignoble code. He could not believe his master's luck. Without even checking with Raavan, he answered. 'My warrior brother Raavan has chosen. With Lord Indra's permission, he accepts the choice of a sword as the weapon. And also accepts the condition of no armour.'

The Indrani turned to the audience. 'So let it be recorded.'

Prahast meanwhile edged up to Raavan and whispered, 'What luck, my king! Your opponent is a moralising moron! You will defeat him easily!'

Raavan did not say anything. He continued to stare at Ram. But his mind was haunted by Mandodari. And her last words.

The Indrani glanced at Ram and Raavan. 'Enter the Indra's Net.'

The warriors bent and touched the boundary with their right hands, and then brought their hands to their foreheads in reverence. Offering respect and obeisance to the ground on which the duel would take place. Then they entered in unison, whispering the words, *'Om Indraya Namah.'*

Raavan looked at the sun, still thinking of Mandodari as he walked to the centre. Towards the priestess of Lord Indra. Ram was looking directly at Raavan as he walked with calm self-assuredness, as if to defeat and bend the very earth under his gait. They stood on either side of the Indrani, and waited.

The priestess of Lord Indra announced in a thunderous voice, 'Dying wishes!'

This was a tradition of the Duel of Indra. Both warriors handed a written list of dying wishes to the opponent. The champion who won and lived was duty-bound to honour and fulfil the dying wishes of the duellist he had killed.

This was the law.

Raavan pulled out his list from his cummerbund and handed it over with his right hand to the Indrani. Respectfully.

As did Ram. The priestess of Lord Indra studied the dying wishes. None broke the rules and conventions of what could be demanded. She handed over Raavan's dying wish list to Ram. And Ram's to Raavan.

The warriors read the demands.

Ram had asked Raavan to not hurt his wife, his brothers, any soldier in his army, or the people of his land. Raavan must honour all these wishes if Ram died. That was it. A simple list. Simple direct men place simple direct demands.

Complicated men, on the other hand, place complicated demands. The first in a long list from Raavan: that Vibhishan would not be made king of all Lanka. The second in the list: the corpses of Raavan, Kumbhakarna and Indrajit would be given full royal burials by Ram, near the ground where the umbilical cords of the three Lankans were buried. Helpfully, Raavan had named the place. Sinauli. Third in the list: that the straw bodies of the three Lankan royals, along with the death mask, would be cremated in Lanka, again by Ram. Fourth in the list: that Ram personally fund and maintain a hospital in Vaidyanath. He had written the address of the hospital. And, fifth in the list: that his pendant be handed to the Vishnu, Sita.

Ram looked up from the list and saw the single finger-bone pendant that hung on a gold chain around Raavan's neck.

Strange request.

But Ram set all deeper thought of the requests aside. A warrior should not allow himself to be distracted before a battle. He looked back at the list. And read on.

Sixth in the list: hand over his musical instruments to Annapoorna Devi. Ram knew of Annapoorna Devi, the brilliant musician who lived in Agastyakootam, the capital of the Malayaputras. Seventh in the list: Raavan's books should be handed over to Ram's youngest brother, Shatrughan.

Ram felt a lump in his throat. Genuinely surprised by this demand. But he did not allow a change of expression. He read on.

The eighth in the list of demands: that if and when the story of Ram and Sita was ever written, Raavan would not be erased from the tale.

And finally, the ninth in the list, clearly added later, in a fast scrawl: Mandodari, wife of Raavan, would not be allowed to live in Sigiriya.

Ram had no choice. He had to agree to carry out all the demands. It was the rule of the Duel of Indra.

He looked at the Indrani and nodded.

'Now, the blood oath,' said the Indrani.

The priestess of Lord Indra picked up the thunderbolt-shaped knife – the vajra – and handed it to Ram. He pricked his thumb and let a few drops of blood fall on the bow of Indra. He then smeared the bow with his blood in one strong action. The Indrani took the knife from Ram and handed it to Raavan. He repeated the blood oath.

The Indrani raised the tiny, delicate replica of Indra's bow, smeared now with the blood of Ram and Raavan, and spoke in a booming voice belying her petite stature. 'The duellists have taken the blood oath of Indra's Net. They will honour the dying wishes of their defeated opponent.'

This oath was not to be taken lightly. For the thunderbolt of Lord Indra strikes dead the one who breaks this blood oath. There was a more practical reason to not break this pledge as well: a true disciple of Lord Indra, from any corner of the world, was honour-bound to kill the winner who broke the blood oath of Indra's Net.

The seconds briskly walked up and took the pieces of paper from the two duellists.

The opening rituals concluded, the Indrani, accompanied by her assistant, walked out ceremonially from the field. Ram and Raavan stood with their heads bowed in her direction.

Then the duellists turned to each other. Ram drew his sword and held it out, straight. He waited for Raavan to tap it with his sword.

A tradition. Before the duel began.

The swords should tap each other and whisper, before the murderous argument began.

Ram believed in tradition. This was an honourable one.

Raavan drew his sword and sneered at Ram. He stepped back jauntily. Without tapping his opponent's blade.

Ram drew a short angry breath and also stepped back. He walked a short distance away, turned around and stood in the orthodox sword-fighter stance. Feet spread out shoulder width. Left leg slightly forward, right slightly back. Body twisted sideways, offering a narrower target to the opponent.

Ram wore a coarse white dhoti and saffron cummerbund, tied tight in the military style. It offered his legs ease of movement. His left hand held the shield close to the body, angled towards the opponent. His right hand gripped the sword and was held high. The blade rested on top of the shield. He did not intend to tire the right, killer arm. Not yet.

Raavan stood at a distance. He wore a violet-coloured silk dhoti, a colour-dye only royalty could afford. He had on a pink cummerbund. Tied tight in military style. His right eye was covered by an eye patch. His right leg seemed to be moving smoothly; the magic of talented Lankan doctors.

He stood straight, his full body confronting his opponent. Both shield and sword were held low. Raavan was arrogantly offering his entire body as target. Challenging his opponent: Come and get me, if you dare.

Raavan's navel though, covered by the cummerbund, was throbbing with the familiar dull pain again. There was nothing that the doctors could do about it. Ever present, it was often forgotten and in the background. But sometimes it surged in intensity. To remind Raavan of its existence. A mark of his *Nagahood*. A recorder and reminder of the tragedy that his life had been. A signal that told him he had suffered yet another blow.

Mandodari.

She always hated me.

'Let the duel begin!' ordered the Indrani loudly from outside the circle.

Ram waited. Breathing smoothly. Focused.

Raavan seemed distracted. He glanced at the sun and stretched his shoulder.

Ram was too experienced a swordsman to be deceived by this schoolboy trick. His attention was directed on Raavan's eye. The eye moves before the body does.

Suddenly Raavan darted forward, leading with his left leg. Using a powerful pumping action from his right calf muscles to spring ahead. At a speed and pace that seemed preternatural, especially for one over sixty years old!

A flicker of surprise flashed on Ram's face as Raavan was suddenly upon him. The king of Lanka violently swung a standard up-down blow, using his great height and bulk to effective advantage. Ram swiftly raised his shield high and blocked the blow. The sound of hard metallic blade striking shield echoed through the air. The blow had jarred Ram's defensive shield arm. He ducked low, avoiding Raavan's follow-up slash from high on the left, and darted forward. He turned around after a couple of steps. In position again.

Raavan whirled around to face Ram.

Grinning. Eyes gleaming.

Not so old after all ...

I've still got it, young man ...

Raavan was bulky in musculature and a good three inches taller than Ram. He remained in situ. Hips bent slightly, letting more of his weight fall on his left leg. Shield down. Sword held to the side. Haughty and cocky. Daring the younger, leaner, shorter man to charge.

Ram also remained in situ. He would not be triggered. Shield held up. Close to the body. In the orthodox standard position. Sword resting on top of the shield. Elbow high. No strain on the fighting right arm. Breathing calmly.

Raavan charged. Swinging hard from the right, and then from the left. Ram kept his shield up, but at an angle, deflecting Raavan's blows rather than arresting them head-on. Letting Raavan complete his swings. One more blow from Raavan. Ram deflected it easily. The force of Raavan's strike kept his sword in motion, heading away from his body. And Ram found an opening. He stabbed forward.

But Raavan, too, was an experienced warrior.

He swerved to the side and deftly avoided the blow. And then thrust his shield forward, like a boxer jabbing with his left arm. It hit Ram's face. Hard.

Ram stepped back. Holding his shield up in defence.

Raavan grinned broadly. He was enjoying this. The sun had more to rise. The sun had more to burn.

An ugly blue splotch rapidly formed on Ram's right cheek. He did not flinch. He did not reach up to touch the bruise with his hand.

Never show your pain. Not to an enemy. That is the way of warriors.

Raavan paced around. Staring at Ram. Swinging his sword in small circles. Taunting the king of Ayodhya to charge.

Ram remained steady. In the standard fighting stance.

Raavan charged again, swinging his sword with frenzied aggression. From the left. Then the right. Ram moved back, step by step. Defending against the strokes with his shield and then his sword. Ram knew what was coming. But he could not predict the when.

And then it came. Earlier than Ram had expected.

Raavan should have waited till Ram had been pushed to the edge of Indra's Net. Stepping out of the boundary would have nullified the duel and called for the execution of the loser. Ram's freedom of movement would have been constrained at the boundary.

But Raavan moved early.

The king of Lanka had been pushing the king of Ayodhya back with his ferociously brutal blows. Repeatedly. And Ram's shield and sword were held high to defend himself. Raavan suddenly pushed his shield forward in a jab, intending to block Ram's field of vision and swiftly stab with his sword. Aiming low. Going for the abdomen. Using the monstrous power of his bulk for what would have been a devastating strike.

But Ram was no amateur. He was expecting this. And with a body that was leaner and more flexible, he had options that Raavan did not possess. For the bulkier a body, the less flexible it is. A biological fact.

Ram twisted his body and pirouetted sidewards, letting Raavan's sword glance the side of his torso, inflicting a minor cut. But Ram was a genius swordsman. In the same movement he swung his sword from behind, extending his flexible shoulder more than one would have assumed possible. With the added momentum of the pirouette that he had just executed, the sword careened out from behind him in a savage swinging cut. Raavan was focused on his forward stab, his shield held high. He did not notice the brutal slash coming towards his abdomen.

The blade cut deep, tearing across Raavan's abdomen. In the same smooth movement, Ram moved a few steps ahead and then whirled around. Steady. His shield held high. His sword, stained now with Raavan's blood, resting on top of his shield. Left foot forward. Right foot at the back. Breathing calm and rhythmic. Standard orthodox fighting position.

The audience – men of war – held their breath. This was awe-inspiring sword skills on display.

Raavan shifted weight and faced Ram. His gaze fell on the insignificant snip he had inflicted on Ram's torso. And then he looked down. At the savage cut across his abdomen. Blood dripped freely from the wound.

Raavan looked at Ram, raised his eyebrows cockily and smiled. He nodded. Acknowledging a strike of exceptional skill by his enemy.

Ram's eyes remained steady. No loss of focus. No acknowledgment of Raavan's appreciation. He did not glance once at the wound he had inflicted. Or, the ugly purple outgrowth on Raavan's navel, which now lay exposed as the cummerbund had come loose. Most people had a morbid fascination with Naga deformities and couldn't help but look. Again and again. But not Ram. His eyes were fixed upon Raavan's eye.

Raavan began moving to the right, edging slowly towards the centre. Staring at Ram with menace.

Ram followed. Moving slowly. Deliberately. Never off balance. He kept pace with his opponent.

Raavan suddenly charged again. Ram was in mid-step, moving to the left to keep pace with Raavan. He dug his right foot into the ground, flexed his muscles and held his shield and sword in readiness to tackle Raavan's assault. Swords brutally thumped on shields. The warriors held each other in a tackle. Their swords and shields pushed into each other. Raavan was bulkier. He should have pushed the leaner Ram back. But he was also older. And, more importantly, injured. The cut on his abdomen was deep.

A few moments in this stalemate and then Raavan disengaged and stepped back. To a safe distance. He held his shield high. Defensively. And rested his sword blade on top of the shield. In the classic sword-fighter pose for the first time in the duel. Staring at Ram. Breathing deeply and hurriedly.

Ram instantly knew. Now was the time. Now was the time to charge.

'*Ayodhyatah Vijetaarah!*' roared Ram, and charged forward.

The conquerors from the unconquerable city.

Ram swung his sword in pitilessly. Incessantly. From the left and right. He kept his brutal strikes at mid-body level. He used his shield like a battering weapon. He forced Raavan to step back. The Lankan's shield was held high as he tottered at an unnatural angle. And then steadied. Ram kept advancing. Subtly moving to his left. He was forcing Raavan to put more weight on his injured right leg. And, also, moving in the direction in which the Lankan's vision was impaired by his patch-covered right eye.

Raavan knew he was being pushed to the edge of Indra's Net. He could not continue to step back. He suddenly swung in hard from the right. It was the rage of the cornered. As Ram was also committed to charging forward, Raavan pushed back hard with his shield. Ram thumped back brutally and appeared to slip. Raavan saw a golden opportunity. He roared triumphantly, dropped his shield, held his sword with both his hands and swung in viciously. A back-hand strike. From an unexpected angle.

And the trap was shut. The victim ensnared.

Ram had feinted the slip. It was a bluff. With his left foot dug in deep, he now expertly angled his shield, allowing Raavan's blade to glide off without aggressively blocking it. Raavan's fearsome momentum from the brutal strike made his body turn. Ram moved like lightning. The opening emerged precisely as Ram had expected and the king of Ayodhya did not lose the moment. He stabbed forward ferociously.

The sword tore into Raavan's abdomen remorselessly. It encountered no resistance. It sliced his Naga purple-coloured outgrowth into half and then cut deep inside, cleaving the intestines, liver and kidney. Ram gave no quarter. He rammed forward, using the full weight of his shoulder and back. The blade burst forth from Raavan's back, having ripped through all in its path.

Ram the warrior was ruthless when the need arose. But he was not cruel. He pulled out his sword instantly. But moved it to the right as he did so. The sharp edge of the sword transversely cut through the ganglia near Raavan's spinal cord. Ensuring no further pain.

Raavan's sword dropped from his hands as he fell on his knees. He looked down. Blood was pouring out of the massive wound on his abdomen, almost like a small fountain. But he felt no pain. He looked at his gaping injury with detached wonder. Was this his body? Shouldn't he be feeling some pain?

He fell on the ground. Down on his back.

Vedavati … I'm coming …

Ram stepped up, bent over and straightened Raavan's legs. With the severed spinal cord, Raavan had no control over his lower body anymore.

A small gesture. But one that was noticed by all who had gathered. And a single thought passed through the many minds. *Ram is a noble warrior.*

Ram went down on a knee, dug his sword into the soft ground and waited next to Raavan's head. 'Tell me when ...'

Raavan was breathing slowly. Eyes drooping.

'Not yet ...' whispered Raavan.

Ram waited.

Raavan reached up to his neck, yanked at the gold chain and removed Vedavati's finger. He held it tight in his bloodied right hand. He took a few long, gentle breaths. Firing energy into his body. He looked at Ram. 'I ... I never touched your wife ...'

Ram's eyes were expressionless. No pity. No anger either. 'She wouldn't let you touch her. She is Sita. She is the Vishnu. She is too powerful for you.'

Raavan smiled slightly. 'No ... You don't understand ... I loved her mother ...'

Ram frowned. Genuinely confused now.

Raavan opened his palm, letting Ram see the finger bone, the phalanges carefully fastened with gold links. 'I return to this Goddess now ...'

Raavan paused for breath and then continued. 'After I am gone ... give this finger to Vedavati's daughter ... Sita ... She will know what to do with it...'

Ram nodded.

'My death will give rise to the legend of Ram ... Maybe that was my purpose ... For Light is the child of Darkness ...'

Ram chose to keep quiet again. He didn't agree with Raavan. But he had the grace to not argue with a dying man.

Raavan took a deep breath. 'I am ready ...'

Ram looked at Raavan's sword. It lay in the distance. Warriors that worshipped Lord Indra believed they should die holding their weapon in their fighting hand. 'Would you like to hold your sword?'

Raavan smiled. 'Your wife is right ... You are a good man ...'

Ram paused. He appreciated this first sign of grace from Raavan. He repeated his question, softer this time. 'King Raavan, do you want to hold your sword?'

'No ... I am holding what I want. The only thing I ever truly needed ... Vedavati's hand ....

Ram held his breath for a moment. A man who loved a woman so magnificently could not have been all bad. Maybe there was some good in him ... Maybe ...

'Go in peace, King Raavan,' whispered Ram.

Ram picked up his sword and held it vertically. He brought the tip of the sword to Raavan's chest. Just above his heart. He looked at Raavan's eye for confirmation. And Raavan smiled. For he was about to see her again.

Vedavati ...

Ram pushed the sword in swiftly. It sliced easily through the sheath and muscles, gliding between the bones of the rib cage, finding the heart and cleaving through it. In one quick merciful strike. Ram was a skilled warrior.

Raavan's heart ripped apart and blood burst forth, offering his soul the path to escape. And the love that had been caged inside, till it had turned malignant, was released. Into the cosmos beyond this petty world. Where malignancy does not survive in the radiant sheen of the spirit.

His soul rushed out. Carrying the memory that was important. The only memory that was important.

Vedavati.

Chapter 40

Late in the evening, Ram stood in the Ashok Vatika. At the edge of the clearing. Staring at the central hut.

She was inside. His Sita was inside.

Events had moved quickly after Raavan's death. Ram had ordered that Raavan's corpse be treated with utmost respect. Along with his brothers and key generals, he had carried Raavan's body to his palace. The death mask was being made. Some in Ram's army felt this was unnecessary and according excessive respect to an enemy. But Ram had silenced them by quoting Lord Indra himself: *Maranaantaani Vairani. Enmity ends with death.*

The disarmed Lankan army had been stationed outside the city, with Ayodhyan soldiers standing guard. A contingent of Ram's army had entered Sigiriya and flag-marched along the main streets, to ensure that there was no lawlessness. The Lankan citizens remained orderly, though fearful of their fate.

Having rapidly ensured that there was no chaos in the city, Ram had rushed to Ashok Vatika. He had fulfilled what his head had dictated were the duties of a victorious commander. Now, finally, he was listening to the insistent calls of his forlorn heart. A husband had arrived to meet his beloved wife. After a separation that had been too long.

'Wait here, please,' whispered Ram to the men with him, and then he walked towards the hut.

Ram's bodyguard soldiers stood silent at the edge of the clearing. Bharat and Shatrughan, his brothers, followed at a discreet distance. Lakshman was still recuperating from his surgery. He had been transferred to the royal hospital of Sigiriya.

Ram stopped just outside the hut. He looked at the cane chairs and table on the veranda. Beyond the furniture was the open door that led into the simple dwelling that had been his wife's prison for many months.

He breathed in deeply. Slowing his wildly beating heart.

Sita.

He climbed up the three stairs and walked towards the door.

'Sita …'

And then he stopped.

For his life, his Sita, had just appeared at the doorway of the hut. Clad in a white dhoti and a white blouse, a saffron-coloured angvastram hung from her right shoulder. She held a golden *puja thali* with both her hands. On it was placed a small earthen-lamp, some grains of rice, a pinch of saffron powder and a small bowl of water. She beheld her victorious husband, eyes brimming with pride, a smile infused with love.

Ram remained where he was standing. That was the tradition.

Sita walked up to him and circled the *puja* plate, clock-wise, around Ram's face. Three times. Lord Agni, the God of Fire, bore witness that her husband had come back to her in triumph.

The conquering hero from the unconquerable city.

She dipped her fingers in the small bowl of water and then the grains of rice. They stuck to her fingers. She pressed the grains on Ram's forehead. The rice grains plastered themselves between his eyes. She then pressed the saffron powder with her moistened ring finger and smeared it on Ram's forehead. In a neat vertical line.

Following ancient tradition then, she repeated the proud words of Ayodhyan queens as they welcomed their conquering husbands back home. 'May the news of your great victory travel on the back of every single ray of the mighty Sun God and reach every corner of the universe that they fall upon.'

'*Jai Surya Dev*,' said Ram, hailing the patron God of his dynasty, the Suryavanshis.

Glory to the Sun God.

'*Jai Surya Dev*,' repeated Sita.

Ram took the *puja* plate from his wife's hands and placed it on the table. And he reached for her. She melted into his arms. As he melted into hers.

It had been many months. It had been a lifetime.

Dhyaus, the Sky God, had no reason to be blue anymore. And had taken on a saintly saffron hue. Surya, the Sun God, was still emanating strong light, but had gently reduced his heat at this late evening hour. Chandra, the Moon God, had come in early, despite the night sky being some time away... For Chandra, the amorous divinity, is forever enchanted by passion. Vayu, the Wind God, blew tenderly across the verdant gardens, spreading the fragrance of love. And Prithvee, the Earth Goddess, serenely cradled her warrior daughter Sita and the victorious descendant of the solar dynasty, Ram. As they held each other.

It had been many months. It had been a lifetime.

The ancients say that young love is like coal. It burns brightly and with passion. Alas, it does not last often. But when subjected to pressure – immense pressure – it transforms into a diamond. A love that is strong – strongest – in this world. Ram and Sita ... Their love had been strengthened by the heat and pressure of grief. By the burden of separation. Nothing could break it now. Nothing.

If the universe spreads to infinity in every direction, then where is the centre? Is it even possible to find a centre within infinity? Wise men say that your centre is where you stand. Spiritually wise men say that the true centre is where your true love stands.

Ram and Sita had found their true centres. Once again.

'I love you, my princess,' whispered Ram.

'I love you, my heart,' said Sita.

Ashok Vatika, the garden with *No Grief,* had truly, become Ashok.

─── ⅃Ⅎ ℲℲⅅ ───

It was well into the next day. The third hour of the second prahar. And the sun was nearing its daily peak.

Ram and Sita had attended to pressing matters of city administration. And then had visited the Lankan queen, Mandodari. As they had been advised to do by Vashishtha. For Mandodari was not just a queen. Respected by rishis and rishikas around the Indian subcontinent, she was one of the foremost scholars of the Vedic path.

Ram and Sita waited outside the open door of the simple hut that was home to the queen of Lanka. Vashishtha walked in alone.

Bharat had wisely not accompanied his brother and sister-in-law on this visit. He had killed Mandodari's son. It would not be proper for her to see him. Not so soon.

'Mandodariji,' said Vashishtha, holding his hands together in a namaste. He went down on his knees by her side and said, gently, 'You have a lot to do in life. Much more to give to Mother India. You cannot ... You cannot go ...'

Mandodari lay on a simple straw mat on the ground. She had made the decision to undertake the ancient Dharmic tradition of *Praayopaveshan*; *lying down until death*. In the colloquial Prakrit tongue of the masses, *Praayopaveshan* was known as *Santhara*. Having undertaken this vow, one voluntarily fasted to death by gradually reducing the intake of food and liquids. Spiritually, it represents thinning the human body and its passions when a soul decides that its karma in this life is over and it must move on.

Mandodari had decided that there was nothing more for her to do in this life. Vashishtha disagreed with her.

'Vashishthaji,' said Mandodari, with her ever-present soft smile, and also the radiant spirit of one moving on the noble path of *Santhara*. 'I have given all that I had. Now it falls upon you to guide those who must lead Mother India to a purposeful path. My time is done. My karma is done.'

Sita walked quietly into the hut. She went down on her knees, touched Mandodari's feet and spoke. 'I am too small to open my mouth in the presence of masters such as you and Guru Vashishtha. But, Guru Mandodari, if I may say something ...'

'Of course, my child,' said Mandodari.

'The paralysis caused by grief does not mean that one's karma is over,' said Sita. 'All it means is that one is paralysed by grief. Which is perfectly understandable. But this paralysis will end. For change and movement are the very essences of life. We must not give in to grief.'

Mandodari smiled. 'No, my child. Do not devalue grief. It can bring clarity to the mind. My mind is clear. Remember the words of Sikhi Buddha: Grief is the ultimate reality of the universe.'

'That is true, Mandodariji,' said Sita, 'but only from the prism of the universe. From a different prism, that of human beings, grief is merely love that is aching to be expressed. Grief is dammed up love. It arises when love is blocked, like the waters of a dam. Grief is made of feelings that have nowhere to go; because the one you ache to express your love to, is gone ...'

Mandodari remained silent. Her eyes were moist. With dammed up love.

Sita continued, her fingers clutching the pendant hanging around her neck. Her mother's finger. 'I know what you are going through, Guru Mandodari. Love needs to flow, for it is the energy of youth and life in a soul. Love should not be static, for then it becomes disconsolate. When you lose the one you love, when there is nobody to give love to, then love ripens into grief. Grief is disheartened love, Guru Mandodari. Grief is love that has been bound by depression. Grief is not having the one you want to give love to. Not having the one who will accept your love ... I did not get to meet the one I wanted to give love to ... My birth mother ... I lost the one I had given love to ... My adoptive mother ... But I have someone else now. Someone who makes me complete.' Sita looked at Ram, who stood silently in the doorway. 'I waited, I opened my heart, and my grief did go ...'

Mandodari took a deep breath. She struggled to hold back tears that insistently begged to flow from her soul. For she had so much more love to give. So much more love to give to her son. Indrajit.

'Give your love to me, my mother,' said Ram.

Mandodari looked at Ram. And the tears burst forth. She sobbed aloud.

Ram walked up to the queen of Lanka and went down on his knees. 'Give your love to me, Maa. I promise you, I will be a good son. I vow that me and my brothers – all my followers – will honour Indrajit and Kumbhakarnaji every year. Till the end of time. That is my Dashrath vow.'

The Dashrath vow. An open-ended promise that could never be broken. No matter what the circumstances. No matter what the time. No matter what the space.

Mandodari reached out and gently stroked Ram's cheek. Like a mother soothing her child. Her tears fell strong. They cleansed.

'Everyone suffers, Mandodariji,' said Vashishtha. 'Nobody escapes suffering. That is the reality of life. But the suffering of the selfish is different from the suffering of the noble. The selfish wallow in their misery, they whine, want attention, want others to empathise and console. They are convinced of their sense of victimhood. The noble, on the other hand, do not view themselves as victims. They make it their life's mission to reduce the suffering of others. The noble want that nobody else should suffer the way they suffered. The way the one they loved, suffered. The suffering of the selfish harms the world. The suffering of the noble makes the world a better place.'

Mandodari was quiet. But her eyes reflected a new understanding. Vashishtha's words were getting through.

'Stay in this world, Mandodariji. Make it a better place.'

— JF ມ̄ˌɔ̄D —

Three of the four brothers and Sita were glued to the glass-encased porthole windows, gazing at their home. Their lovely home. Shatrughan, the fourth brother, was reading a book.

The Pushpak Vimaan hovered over the vast Grand Canal that encircled the mighty fort walls of Ayodhya. It had been built a few centuries ago, during the reign of Emperor Ayutayus. Engineered by efficiently drawing in the waters of the Sarayu River, the Grand Canal's dimensions were almost other worldly. It stretched for over fifty kilometres and circumnavigated the third and outermost wall of the city of Ayodhya. Enormous in breadth as well, it extended to about two-and-a-half kilometres across the banks. It was breathtaking. And for Ram, Sita and Lakshman, the view was ethereal. Indescribable. They had last set eyes upon this magnificent view over fourteen years ago.

Surya, the Sun God, was slowly calling it a day. It was late in the evening. The citizens of Ayodhya, though, were celebrating with verve. Every home was lined with lamps—inside, on the thresholds, the verandas, and also their roofs and terrace edges. The ramparts of the three fort walls had been meticulously skirted with lamps, alight and ablaze. The air was rife with the sound and light of fireworks, firing without a break in all the various gardens of the city.

Their king and queen were returning. Ram and Sita were coming home.

It was a special day in an auspicious period. The third of a traditional five-day celebration that commemorated events for most dharmic paths: the Mother Goddess, the Mahadevs, the Vishnus, Jain Tirthankaras, Sikhi Buddha; all celebrated since ancient times. Now onwards, there would be one more. Forever. The legend of Ram and Sita was grafted on to this bouquet. The Ayodhyans did not know it then, but they had established a resplendent tradition for their people, their land, their culture.

For all time to come. For this was the day of the first Diwali. And as long as India would breathe, it would mark this day with pomp and pageantry.

Ram held Sita's hand as they both looked at their city. With awe and wonder. And hearts bursting with love.

'Urmila is waiting for you at the palace, Lakshman,' said Bharat.

Lakshman looked at his brother and smiled warmly. He hadn't seen his wife in fourteen years. He couldn't wait to see her again.

Ram had ensured that he had honoured all the vows he had made to Raavan on the day of the Duel of Indra.

The straw body-replicas of Raavan, Kumbhakarna and Indrajit were embellished with their death masks and consigned to the holy flames on cremation pyres by Ram. Their corpses were buried with full royal honours at the site where their umbilical cords had been laid to rest upon their births: Sinauli. Ram had handed over Vedavati's finger relic – given to him by Raavan before he died – to Sita. Sita had interred the relic with Raavan's body in his burial chamber. The king of Lanka did go into pitralok holding Vedavati's hand. Mareech, Raavan's uncle, had also been buried in Sinauli.

Ram had made a promise: that he would repeat the ritual of cremating the bodies of his three enemies on the anniversary of Indrajit's death; the tenth day of Shukla paksh in the month of Ashwin. Year after year. His brothers reminded him that he had given his word to Mandodari for only honouring Kumbhakarna and Indrajit thus. Why include Raavan? With his typical grace, Ram had repeated: *Maranaantaani Vairani*.

Ram had used his personal funds to create an endowment for the hospital in Vadiyanath, named after Vedavati. It met all the expenses of the hospital.

Raavan's musical instruments were taken to Agastyakootam by Arishtanemi and handed over to Annapoorna Devi. The collection of instruments included the Raavanhatha, invented by the talented Raavan. All his books were given to the one who would appreciate them the most: Shatrughan. In fact, he was reading one right now, immune to the commotion all around.

One dying wish of Raavan's had been particularly difficult to implement. For he had demanded that Vibhishan not be made the king of Lanka. However, Ram had already given his word of honour to Vibhishan that he would be enthroned. Ram would never break his promise. But what do you do when two promises stand in contradiction to each other?

The ever-pragmatic Bharat had found a solution. With the creative verbal skill of a lawyer, he had pointed out that Raavan had only demanded that Vibhishan not be made the king of *all* Lanka. So, they had partitioned Lanka. The coastal city of Gokarna and its surrounding regions were made an independent republic, to be administered by its entrepreneurial guilds and citizens in the democratic traditions established by the Shakyas, Vajjis and others in the Sapt Sindhu. Lanka was reduced to Sigiriya and the island's west coast. And Vibhishan was crowned the king of this truncated region. Hence, with Bharat's ingenuity, Ram had kept his word of honour given to Vibhishan, while also upholding the vow made to Raavan at the Duel of Indra.

Raavan's hastily written last dying wish, too, had been honoured. Mandodari did not wish to stay in Lanka anymore. She sat now in the Pushpak Vimaan, in deep conversation with Vashishtha at the back.

'The only dying wish of Raavan that you have not honoured yet, Dada,' said Bharat, 'is ensuring that he is woven into the story of Bhabhi and you!'

Sita laughed. 'Trust Raavanji and his ego, to even demand something like this.'

Ram looked at Sita, the daughter of Vedavati. His eyes fell upon the finger bone pendant hanging around her neck. The mark of Vedavati, Sita's birth mother. He smiled. 'It was his right to demand anything. But this is not in my hands. It's up to the storytellers.'

'Then he will certainly be woven in!' said Bharat, grinning. 'Flawed, doomed characters are terrible to live with. But are wonderful to read about. Storytellers hunt for such characters with the ardency of a lost ship searching for land!'

Ram, Sita, Bharat and Lakshman laughed.

An announcement informed them that the vimaan would soon be landing. The brothers and Sita got back to their seats and clasped their seat belts.

'Who do you think will attack us first?' Bharat asked Ram and Sita.

'Why will anyone attack us now?' asked Lakshman.

'Raavan was not the real enemy, Lakshman,' said Bharat. 'He was just a stepping stone. His defeat gave the Vishnu …' Bharat stopped, and then pointed at both Ram and Sita, before continuing, 'the *Vishnus*, the aura they need, to do the more important task.'

'What more important task?'

'Their real mission: reviving Mother India. They are not just the Vishnus for Ayodhya, but for India. The whole of India. And it will be a long struggle. We will hurt many vested interests among the ruling classes.'

'I'm sure we can build allies among the nobility,' said Ram.

'I'm sure we can,' said Sita. 'But even the allies will turn against us when we work for the people. Old feudal interests are rarely aligned with those of the common people.'

'It will be a struggle,' said Ram. 'Maybe a long struggle. But we will prevail. For the good of Mother India.'

'Hmm,' said Sita. 'There's so much more that we have to do.'

'And there will be a lot more for the storytellers to record!' Bharat laughed.

Shatrughan smiled and quoted from the book he was reading. '*Kathaa adyaapi avashishtaa re vayasya.*'

It was old Sanskrit. *The story is not yet over, my friend!*

There was laughter all around.

'Well said, Shatrughan!' said Ram. 'The story is not yet over.'

'But for now, we rest,' said Sita. 'This may not be the climactic end, but it certainly is a good penultimate end!'

— Jꟼ ꞀꝪD —

Annapoorna put the Raavanhatha aside.

Vishwamitra blinked away his tears. The raga had touched his heart and then plunged deep into his soul, bringing to life emotions from lifetimes ago. Annapoorna had played the complex Raga *Malkauns* on as modest an instrument as the Raavanhatha. 'Only someone with your divine skill can play the *Malkauns* on this simple instrument, Annapoornaji. You truly have Goddess Saraswati's blessings.'

Vishwamitra and Annapoorna were at the Hall of Hundred Pillars at the ParshuRamEshwar temple in Agastyakootam. She had stepped out of her house. For, with the death of Raavan, her vow had expired as well. She could leave her home now. And Vishwamitra had delighted her with the gifts that Arishtanemi had come bearing: the musical instruments of Raavan himself.

'It is the magic of the instrument, Guruji,' said Annapoorna. 'It may look simple, but the Raavanhatha has the musical cadence of Raavan's divine talents. He was the one truly blessed by *Goddess Saraswati*, not me.'

Vishwamitra smiled and brought his hands together into a namaste. 'Well, whoever may have been blessed by the great *Goddess of Knowledge*, it is I who have truly felt bliss listening to this raga on the Raavanhatha.'

Annapoorna folded her hands into a *namaste* and smiled. She looked to her right, towards the citizens of Agastyakootam who waited outside the temple. Arishtanemi stood among them. They too had heard the loud timbre of her instrument clearly. And enjoyed the raga she had just played. But they did not hear the words that were exchanged between Vishwamitra and her. They were spoken softly. She looked at the Malayaputra chief. 'What are you planning, Guruji?'

'I don't understand your question, Annapoornaji.'

'I am well aware of the manner in which news of Sita reached Raavan's ears, Guruji,' said Annapoorna, smiling. 'And I did play along. For I do owe you for giving me refuge when I had nowhere else to go. Among the foremost rules of *dharma* is to remember the debt we owe to those who help us.'

Vishwamitra paused for a moment, almost as if he was evaluating how much he could trust Annapoorna. Having made a decision, he spoke. 'What did you think of Raavan?'

'A talented fool. The Almighty gave awesome capabilities to one whose character was incapable of handling it. His talents were not a blessing to him; they were his curse. But all said and done, I believe there was some good in him.'

'Hmm ... And what do you think of Ram?'

'A good man. He is noble. So noble, that it's difficult to believe he is real.'

Vishwamitra's expression remained deadpan. 'Hmm.'

'And Raavan is dead.'

'Yes, Raavan is dead.'

'So, what are you planning, Guruji?'

'Divodas thinks he is in control now.'

Annapoorna knew enough about Vishwamitra's life to know that Divodas was the *gurukul* name of his childhood friend who was now his greatest foe, Vashishtha. 'And he's not?'

'No, he's not.'

'Why do you say that?' asked Annapoorna, intrigued.

'Firstly, I have planted someone right in the heart of Ayodhya. Mrigasya of the Bheda family.'

Annapoorna was shocked. She didn't know this. 'Is Mrigasya a Bheda?'

'Yes. And, more importantly, Divodas only has his precious Ram and the kingdom of Ayodhya. I have ten kings with me.'

Annapoorna leaned forward and listened keenly to Vishwamitra's plan.

——— J⫪ ⫪⌐5D ———

'There will be a period of peace, I suspect,' said Mandodari. 'But it won't be long-lasting.'

'No, it will not be a long peace,' agreed Vashishtha. 'A long peace only happens after a war to end all wars ... After a war that settles issues in such a comprehensive manner that the losing elite accepts their fate.'

It was early in the morning after the first Diwali and Vashishtha and Mandodari had walked to the Grand Canal for their morning *puja*. Having completed the ritual, they asked their bodyguards to wait at a distance and strolled along the majestic terrace that ran along the inner banks of the Grand Canal.

'A war to end all wars,' said Mandodari. 'Yes, there lies the difference between wars and wealth.'

Vashishtha looked at her, intrigued.

'I had read this statement in a book, long ago,' said Mandodari. 'Written by a philosopher far to our west, called Schopenhauer. "Wealth is like sea water; the more we drink, the thirstier we become," he had written.'

Vashishtha laughed softly. 'That is truc.'

'And that's where war is different. The more war there is, the more people grow tired of it. Excessive warring creates conditions for a long period of peace. Peace that will last at least a few generations.'

'True …'

'And, a new social order emerges only when the elite of the old social order surrenders completely.'

'And that has not happened … The old elite is still strong in India. They have to be defeated comprehensively. They have to be afraid of the new elite. Only then will they accept the new order. For fear is the mother of love. But we are not there yet.'

'Yes … we are not there yet. But once they are defeated completely, and accept the new ways, we have two fine leaders who will create that new social order.'

'Three, come to think of it.'

'Three?'

'Yes. Ram, Sita and Bharat … Sudas, Bhoomi and Vasu.'

'Those were their *gurukul* names?' asked Mandodari.

'Yes,' answered Vashishtha. 'We have our trinity. Our new trinity.'

'Hmm. And they will create a new order. They will restore Mother India's glory.' Mandodari looked at Vashishtha and smiled, her eyes twinkling. 'Though we still have to win the war to end all wars.'

'Oh, we will. The Gods are with us. And our three heroes will certainly create a *Land of Pure Life*.'

'*Meluha* is the name they have decided upon, haven't they?'

'Yes, that's the name. And to help them build that perfect empire is the last goal and purpose of my life. That will be my final journey. The last story to be written. Once it is recorded, my life's purpose will be complete. I can go in peace … I will go in peace … The last story in this long chain … The story of the Rise of Meluha.'

… to be continued.

Other Titles by Amish

The Shiva Trilogy

The fastest-selling book series in the history of Indian publishing

THE IMMORTALS OF MELUHA

(Book 1 of the Trilogy)

1900 BC. What modern Indians mistakenly call the Indus Valley Civilisation, the inhabitants of that period knew as the land of Meluha – a near perfect empire created many centuries earlier by Lord Ram. Now their primary river Saraswati is drying, and they face terrorist attacks from their enemies from the east. Will their prophesied hero, the Neelkanth, emerge to destroy evil?

THE SECRET OF THE NAGAS

(Book 2 of the Trilogy)

The sinister Naga warrior has killed his friend Brahaspati and now stalks his wife Sati. Shiva, who is the prophesied destroyer of evil, will not rest till he finds his demonic adversary. His thirst for revenge will lead him to the door of the Nagas, the serpent people. Fierce battles will be fought and unbelievable secrets revealed in the second part of the Shiva trilogy.

THE OATH OF THE VAYUPUTRAS

(Book 3 of the Trilogy)

Shiva reaches the Naga capital, Panchavati, and prepares for a holy war against his true enemy. The Neelkanth must not fail, no matter what the cost. In his desperation, he reaches out to the Vayuputras. Will he succeed? And what will be the real cost of battling Evil? Read the concluding part of this bestselling series to find out.

The Ram Chandra Series

The second fastest-selling book series in the history of Indian publishing

RAM – SCION OF IKSHVAKU
(Book 1 of the Series)

He loves his country and he stands alone for the law. His band of brothers, his wife, Sita and the fight against the darkness of chaos. He is Prince Ram. Will he rise above the taint that others heap on him? Will his love for Sita sustain him through his struggle? Will he defeat the demon Raavan who destroyed his childhood? Will he fulfil the destiny of the Vishnu? Begin an epic journey with Amish's latest: the Ram Chandra Series.

SITA – WARRIOR OF MITHILA
(Book 2 of the Series)

An abandoned baby is found in a field. She is adopted by the ruler of Mithila, a powerless kingdom, ignored by all. Nobody believes this child will amount to much. But they are wrong. For she is no ordinary girl. She is Sita. Through an innovative multi-linear narrative, Amish takes you deeper into the epic world of the Ram Chandra Series.

RAAVAN – ENEMY OF ARYAVARTA
(Book 3 of the Series)

Raavan is determined to be a giant among men, to conquer, plunder, and seize the greatness that he thinks is his right. He is a man of contrasts, of brutal violence and scholarly knowledge. A man who will love without reward and kill without remorse. In this, the third book in the Ram Chandra series, Amish sheds light on Raavan, the king of Lanka. Is he the greatest villain in history or just a man in a dark place, all the time?

Indic Chronicles

LEGEND OF SUHELDEV

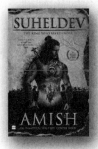

Repeated attacks by Mahmud of Ghazni have weakened India's northern regions. Then the Turks raid and destroy one of the holiest temples in the land: the magnificent Lord Shiva temple at Somnath. At this most desperate of times, a warrior rises to defend the nation. King Suheldev—fierce rebel, charismatic leader, inclusive patriot. Read this epic adventure of courage and heroism that recounts the story of that lionhearted warrior and the magnificent Battle of Bahraich.

Non-fiction

IMMORTAL INDIA

Explore India with the country's storyteller, Amish, who helps you understand it like never before, through a series of sharp articles, nuanced speeches and intelligent debates. In *Immortal India*, Amish lays out the vast landscape of an ancient culture with a fascinatingly modern outlook.

DHARMA – DECODING THE EIP ICS FOR A MEANINGFUL LIFE

In this genre-bending book, the first of a series, Amish and Bhavna dive into the priceless treasure trove of the ancient Indian epics, as well as the vast and complex universe of Amish's Meluha, to explore some of the key concepts of Indian philosophy. Within this book are answers to our many philosophical questions, offered through simple and wise interpretations of our favourite stories.

Ram – Scion of Ikshvaku

Amish is a 1974-born, IIM (Kolkata)-educated banker-turned-author. The success of his debut book, *The Immortals of Meluha* (Book 1 of the Shiva Trilogy), encouraged him to give up his career in financial services to focus on writing. Besides being an author, he is also an Indian-government diplomat, a host for TV documentaries, and a film producer.

Amish is passionate about history, mythology and philosophy, finding beauty and meaning in all world religions. His books have sold more than 6 million copies and have been translated into over 20 languages. His Shiva Trilogy is the fastest selling and his Ram Chandra Series the second fastest selling book series in Indian publishing history. You can connect with Amish here:

- www.facebook.com/authoramish
- www.instagram.com/authoramish
- www.twitter.com/authoramish

Other Titles by Amish

SHIVA TRILOGY

The fastest-selling book series in the history of Indian publishing

The Immortals of Meluha (Book 1 of the Trilogy)

The Secret of the Nagas (Book 2 of the Trilogy)

The Oath of the Vayuputras (Book 3 of the Trilogy)

RAM CHANDRA SERIES

The second fastest-selling book series in the history of Indian publishing

Sita – Warrior of Mithila (Book 2 of the Series)

Raavan – Enemy of Aryavarta (Book 3 of the Series)

War of Lanka (Book 4 in the Series)

INDIC CHRONICLES

Legend of Suheldev

NON-FICTION

Immortal India: Young Country, Timeless Civilisation

Dharma: Decoding the Epics for a Meaningful Life

'{Amish's} writings have generated immense curiosity about India's rich past and culture.'
— ***Narendra Modi***
(Honourable Prime Minister, India)

'{Amish's} writing introduces the youth to ancient value systems while pricking and satisfying their curiosity…'
— ***Sri Sri Ravi Shankar***
(Spiritual Leader & Founder, Art of Living Foundation)

'{Amish's writing is} riveting, absorbing and informative.'
— ***Amitabh Bachchan***
(Actor & Living Legend)

'{Amish's writing is} a fine blend of history and myth…gripping and unputdownable.'
— ***BBC***

'Thoughtful and deep, Amish, more than any author, represents the New India.'
— ***Vir Sanghvi***
(Senior Journalist & Columnist)

'Amish's mythical imagination mines the past and taps into the possibilities of the future. His book series, archetypal and stirring, unfolds the deepest recesses of the soul as well as our collective consciousness.'
— ***Deepak Chopra***
(World-renowned spiritual guru and bestselling author)

'{Amish is} one of the most original thinkers of his generation.'
— *__Arnab Goswami__*
(Senior Journalist & MD, Republic TV)

'Amish has a fine eye for detail and a compelling narrative style.'
— *__Dr. Shashi Tharoor__*
(Member of Parliament & Author)

'{Amish has} a deeply thoughtful mind with an unusual, original, and fascinating view of the past.'
— *__Shekhar Gupta__*
(Senior Journalist & Columnist)

'To understand the New India, you need to read Amish.'
— *__Swapan Dasgupta__*
(Member of Parliament & Senior Journalist)

'Through all of Amish's books flows a current of liberal progressive ideology: about gender, about caste, about discrimination of any kind… He is the only Indian bestselling writer with true philosophical depth – his books are all backed by tremendous research and deep thought.'
— *__Sandipan Deb__*
(Senior Journalist & Editorial Director, Swarajya)

'Amish's influence goes beyond his books, his books go beyond literature, his literature is steeped in philosophy, which is anchored in bhakti, which powers his love for India.'
— *__Gautam Chikermane__*
(Senior Journalist & Author)

'Amish is a literary phenomenon.'

— *__Anil Dharker__*
(Senior Journalist & Author)

Ram – Scion of Ikshvaku

Book 1
of the
Ram Chandra Series

Amish

HarperCollins *Publishers* India

www.authoramish.com

First published in 2015

This edition published in India by HarperCollins *Publishers* 2022
4th Floor, Tower A, Building No. 10, Phase II, DLF Cyber City,
Gurugram, Haryana – 122002
www.harpercollins.co.in

2 4 6 8 10 9 7 5 3 1

P-ISBN: 978-93-5629-079-2
E-ISBN: 978-93-5629-090-7

Typeset by PrePSol Enterprises Pvt. Ltd.

Printed and bound at
Thomson Press (India) Ltd

MIX
Paper
FSC® C010615

This book is produced from independently certified FSC® paper
to ensure responsible forest management.

To my father, Vinay Kumar Tripathi,
and my mother, Usha Tripathi

Khalil Gibran said that parents are like a bow,
And children like arrows.
The more the bow bends and stretches, the farther the arrow flies.
I fly, not because I am special, but because they stretched for me.

Om Namah Shivāya
The universe bows to Lord Shiva.
I bow to Lord Shiva.

Rāmarājyavāsī tvam, procchrayasva te śiram
Nyāyārthaṁ yudhyasva, sarveṣu samaṁ cara
Paripālaya durbalam, viddhi dharmaṁ varam
Procchrayasva te śiram,
Rāmarājyavāsī tvam.

You live in Ram's kingdom, hold your head high.
Fight for justice. Treat all as equal.
Protect the weak. Know that dharma is above all.
Hold your head high,
You live in the kingdom of Ram.

List of Characters and Important Tribes
(In Alphabetical Order)

Arishtanemi: Military chief of the Malayaputras; right-hand man of Vishwamitra

Ashwapati: King of the north-western kingdom of Kekaya; a loyal ally of Dashrath; father of Kaikeyi

Bharat: Ram's half-brother; son of Dashrath and Kaikeyi

Dashrath: The Chakravarti king of Kosala and emperor of Sapt Sindhu; husband of Kaushalya, Kaikeyi and Sumitra; father of Ram, Bharat, Lakshman, and Shatrughan

Janak: King of Mithila; father of Sita and Urmila

Jatayu: A captain of the Malayaputra tribe; a Naga friend of Sita and Ram

Kaikeyi: Daughter of King Ashwapati of Kekaya; second and the favourite wife of Dashrath; mother of Bharat

Kaushalya: Daughter of King Bhanuman of South Kosala and his wife Maheshwari; the eldest queen of Dashrath; mother of Ram

Kubaer: Trader and ruler of Lanka before Raavan

Kumbhakarna: Raavan's brother; he is also a Naga (a human being born with deformities)

Kushadhwaj: King of Sankashya; younger brother of Janak

Lakshman: One of the twin sons of Dashrath; born to Sumitra; faithful to Ram; later married to Urmila

Malayaputras: The tribe left behind by Lord Parshu Ram, the sixth Vishnu

Manthara: The richest merchant of Sapt Sindhu; an ally of Kaikeyi

Mrigasya: General of Dashrath's army; one of the nobles of Ayodhya

Nagas: A feared race of human beings born with deformities

Nilanjana: Lady doctor attending to members of the royal family of Ayodhya, she hails from South Kosala

Raavan: King of Lanka; brother of Vibhishan, Shurpanakha and Kumbhakarna

Ram: Eldest of four brothers, son of Emperor Dashrath of Ayodhya (the capital city of Kosala kingdom) and his eldest wife Kaushalya; later married to Sita

Roshni: Daughter of Manthara; a committed doctor and *rakhi*-sister to the four sons of Dashrath

Samichi: Police and protocol chief of Mithila

Shatrughan: Twin brother of Lakshman; son of Dashrath and Sumitra

Shurpanakha: Half-sister of Raavan

Sita: Adopted daughter of King Janak of Mithila; also the prime minister of Mithila; later married to Ram

Sumitra: Daughter of the king of Kashi; the third wife of Dashrath; mother of the twins Lakshman and Shatrughan

Vashishtha: Raj guru, the royal priest of Ayodhya; teacher of the four princes

Vayuputras: The tribe left behind by Lord Rudra, the previous Mahadev

Vibhishan: Half-brother of Raavan

Vishwamitra: Chief of the Malayaputras, the tribe left behind by Lord Parshu Ram, the sixth Vishnu; also temporary guru of Ram and Lakshman

Urmila: Younger sister of Sita; the blood-daughter of Janak; she is later married to Lakshman

Refer to inside back cover for map of India in 3400 BCE

Note on the Narrative Structure

Thank you for picking up this book and giving me the most important thing you can share: your time. The Ram Chandra Series, of which *Ram – Scion of Ikshvaku* is the first book, has an intricate narrative structure. This note is my attempt to explain it.

I have been inspired by a storytelling technique called hyperlink, which some call the multilinear narrative. In such a narrative, there are many characters; and a connection brings them all together. The three main characters in the Ram Chandra Series are Ram, Sita, and Raavan. Each character has life experiences which mould who they are and their stories converge with the kidnapping of Sita. And each has their own adventure and riveting back-story.

So, while the first book explores the tale of Ram, the second and third will offer a glimpse into the adventures of Sita and then Raavan respectively, before all three stories merge from the fourth book onwards into a single story.

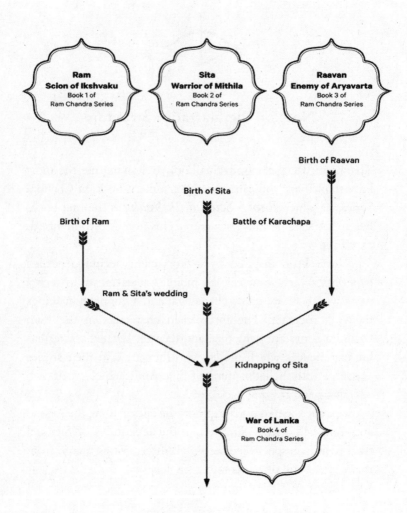

I knew it would be a complicated and time consuming affair, but I must confess, it was thoroughly exciting. I hope this will be as rewarding and thrilling an experience for you as it was for me. Understanding Ram, Sita and Raavan as characters helped me inhabit their worlds and explore the maze of plots and stories that make this epic come alive. I feel truly blessed for this.

There are clues in this book (***Ram – Scion of Ikshvaku***) which will tie up with the stories in the second and third books. Needless to say, there are surprises and twists in store for you in all the books of the series!

I hope you like reading ***Ram – Scion of Ikshvaku***. Do tell me what you think of it, by sending me messages on my Facebook or Twitter accounts listed below.

Love,

Amish

www.facebook.com/authoramish
www.instagram.com/authoramish
www.twitter.com/authoramish

Acknowledgements

The acknowledgements written above were composed when the book was published in 2015. I must also acknowledge those that are publishing this edition of **Ram-Scion of Ikshvaku**. *The team at HarperCollins: Swati, Shabnam, Akriti, Gokul, Vikas, Rahul, and Udayan, led by the brilliant Ananth. Looking forward to this new journey with them.*

***

I don't agree with everything that John Donne wrote, but he was right on one count: 'No man is an island'. I am lucky to be connected to many others who keep me from being 'rifted'. For creativity has no greater sustenance than the love and support of others. I'd like to acknowledge some of them. Lord Shiva, my God, for blessing me with this life and all there is in it. Also, for bringing Lord Ram (who my grandfather, Pandit Babulal Tripathi, was a great devotee of) back into my life.

Neel, my son, my blessing, my pride, my joy. He gives me happiness by simply being who he is.

Preeti, my wife; Bhavna, my sister; Himanshu, my brother-in-law; Anish and Ashish, my brothers, for all their inputs to the story. My sister Bhavna deserves special mention for her dedication and the time she gave while advising me on the philosophies in the book. My wife Preeti deserves my eternal gratefulness, as always, for her brilliant marketing advice.

My family: Usha, Vinay, Meeta, Donetta, Shernaz, Smita, Anuj, Ruta. For their consistent faith and love.

Sharvani, my editor. We have a strange relationship. Fun and laughter in normal times; we fight with each other passionately when we edit. It's a match made in heaven!

Gautam, Krishnakumar, Preeti, Deepthi, Satish, Varsha, Jayanthi, Vipin, Senthil, Shatrughan, Sarita, Avani, Sanyog, Naveen, Jaisankar, Gururaj, Sateesh and the fantastic team at Westland, my publishers. They have been partners from the beginning.

Anuj, my agent. Big man with an even bigger heart! The best friend an author could have.

Hemal, Neha, Hitesh, Natashaa, Parth, Vinit and the Oktobuzz team, the social media agency for the book. They made the new cover, which I think is truly exceptional! It looks very good and has a lot of hidden symbology! Oktobuzz is hardworking, super smart and intensely committed. They are an asset to any team.

Sangram, Shalini, Parag, Shaista, Rekha, Hrishikesh, Richa, Prasad and the team at Think WhyNot, the advertising agency for the book. They have made most of the marketing material for the book, including the trailer. They are among the best ad agencies in the country.

Jaaved, Parthasarthy, Rohit and the rest of the production team of the trailer film. Brilliant guys. Trust me, the world will soon be their oyster.

Mohan, a friend, whose advice on communication matters is something I always treasure.

Vinod, Toral, Nimisha and the great team at Clea PR for the work that they did on the PR efforts for the book.

Mrunalini, a Sanskrit scholar, who works with me. My discussions with her are stimulating and enlightening. I learn a lot from her.

Nitin, Vishal, Avani and Mayuri for their hospitality in Nashik where I wrote parts of this book.

And last, but certainly not the least, you, the reader. Thank you from the depths of my being for the support you've given to the Shiva Trilogy. I hope I don't disappoint you with this book, the first in a new series. Har Har Mahadev!

Chapter 1

3400 BCE, somewhere near the Godavari River, India

Ram crouched low as he bent his tall, lean and muscular frame. He rested his weight on his right knee as he held the bow steady. The arrow was fixed in place, but he knew that the bowstring should not be pulled too early. He didn't want his muscles to tire out. He had to wait for the perfect moment. *It must be a clean strike.*

'It's moving, *Dada*,' whispered Lakshman to his *elder brother*.

Ram didn't reply. His eyes were fixed on the target. A light breeze played with the few strands of hair that had escaped the practical bun atop his head. His shaggy, unkempt beard and his white *dhoti* gently fluttered in the breeze. Ram corrected his angle as he factored in the strength and direction of the wind. He quietly cast his white *angvastram* aside to reveal a battle-scarred, dark-skinned torso. *The cloth should not interfere with the release of the arrow.*

The deer suddenly came to a standstill as it looked up; perhaps instinct had kicked in with some warning signals. Ram could hear its low snort as it stomped its feet uneasily. Within a few seconds it went back to chewing leaves as silence prevailed. The rest of the herd was a short distance away, hidden from view by the dense foliage of the forest.

'By the great Lord Parshu Ram, it ignored its instincts,' said Lakshman softly. 'Thank the Lord. We need some real food.'

'Quiet…'

Lakshman fell silent. Ram knew they needed this kill. Lakshman and he, accompanied by his wife Sita, had been on the run for the last thirty days. A few members of the *Malayaputra* tribe, the *sons of Malaya*, led by their captain, Jatayu, were also with them.

Jatayu had urged flight well before the inevitable retaliation came. The botched meeting with Shurpanakha and Vibhishan would certainly have consequences. They were, after all, the siblings of Raavan, the wrathful demon-king of Lanka. Raavan was sure to seek vengeance. Lankan royal blood had been shed.

Racing east through the *Dandakaranya*, the dense *forest of Dandak*, they had travelled a reasonable distance parallel to the Godavari. They were fairly reassured now that they wouldn't be easily spotted or tracked. Straying too far from the tributary rivers or other water bodies would mean losing out on the best chance of hunting animals. Ram and Lakshman were princes of Ayodhya, inheritors of the proud Kshatriya tradition of the *Raghukul*, the *descendants of Raghu*. They would not survive on a diet of herbs, fruit and leaves alone.

The deer remained stationary, lost in the pleasure of grazing on tender shoots. Ram knew this was the moment. He held the composite bow steady in his left hand as he pulled the string back with his right, till it almost touched his lips. His elbow was held high, almost perfectly parallel to the ground, exactly the way his guru, Maharishi Vashishtha, had taught him.

The elbow is weak. Hold it high. Let the effort come from the back muscles. The back is strong.

Ram pulled the string a notch further and then released the arrow. The missile whizzed past the trees and slammed into the deer's neck. It collapsed immediately, unable to even utter a bleat as blood flooded its lungs. Despite his muscular bulk, Lakshman rushed forward stealthily. Even as he moved, he pulled out a knife from the horizontal scabbard tied to the small of his back. Within moments he reached the deer and quickly plunged the blade deep in between the animal's ribs, right through to its heart.

'Forgive me for killing you, O noble beast,' he whispered the ancient apology that all hunters offered, as he gently touched the deer's head. 'May your soul find purpose again, while your body sustains my soul.'

Ram caught up with Lakshman as his brother pulled the arrow out, wiped it clean and returned it to its rightful owner. 'Still usable,' he murmured.

Ram slipped the arrow back into his quiver as he looked up at the sky. Birds chirped playfully and the deer's own herd displayed no alarm. They had not sensed the killing of one of their own. Ram whispered a short prayer to Lord Rudra, thanking him for what had been a perfect hunt. The last thing they needed was for their position to be given away.

Ram and Lakshman made their way through the dense jungle. Ram walked in front, carrying one end of a long staff on his shoulder, while Lakshman walked behind, holding up the other end. The deer's carcass dangled in the middle, its feet having been secured to the staff with a sturdy rope.

'Aah, a decent meal after so many days,' said Lakshman.

Ram's face broke into a hint of a smile, but he remained silent.

'We can't cook this properly though, right *Dada*?'

'No, we can't. The continuous line of smoke will give our position away.'

'Do we really need to be so careful? There have been no attacks. Maybe they have lost track of us. We haven't encountered any assassins, have we? How would they know where we are? The forests of Dandak are impenetrable.'

'Maybe you're right, but I'm not taking any chances. I'd rather be safe.'

Lakshman held his peace even as his shoulders drooped.

'It's better than eating leaves and herbs,' said Ram, without turning to look at his brother.

'That it certainly is,' agreed Lakshman.

The brothers walked on in silence.

'There is some conspiracy afoot, *Dada*. I'm unable to pin down what it is. But there's something going on. Perhaps Bharat *Dada*...'

'Lakshman!' rebuked Ram sternly.

Bharat was the second oldest after Ram, and had been anointed crown prince of Ayodhya by their father Dashrath following Ram's banishment. The youngest, Shatrughan and Lakshman, were twins separated by differing loyalties. While Shatrughan remained in Ayodhya with Bharat, Lakshman unhesitatingly chose a life of hardship with Ram. The impulsive Lakshman was sceptical of Ram's blind trust in Bharat. He considered it his duty to warn his excessively ethical eldest brother about what appeared to him as Bharat's underhand dealings.

'I know you don't like hearing this, *Dada*,' Lakshman persisted. 'But I'm certain that he's hatched a plot against—'

'We'll get to the bottom of it,' reassured Ram, interrupting Lakshman. 'But we first need allies. Jatayu is right. We need to find the local Malayaputra camp. At least they can be trusted to help us.'

'I don't know whom to trust anymore, *Dada*. Maybe the vulture-man is helping our enemies.'

Jatayu was a Naga, a class of people born with deformities. Ram had come around to trusting Jatayu despite the fact that the Nagas were a hated, feared and ostracised people in the *Sapt Sindhu, the Land of the Seven Rivers,* which lay north of the Narmada River.

Jatayu, like all Nagas, had been born with inevitable deformities. He had a hard and bony mouth that extended out of his face in a beak-like protrusion. His head was bare, but his face was covered with fine, downy hair. Although he was human, his appearance was like that of a vulture.

'Sita trusts Jatayu,' said Ram, as though that explained it all. 'I trust Jatayu. And so will you.'

Lakshman fell silent. And the brothers walked on.

—— 大 🐟 ☼ ——

'But why do you think it's irrational to think Bharat *Dada* could—'

'Shhh,' said Ram, holding his hand up to silence Lakshman. 'Listen.'

Lakshman strained his ears. A chill ran down his spine. Ram turned towards Lakshman with terror writ large on his face. They had both heard it. *A forceful scream!* It was Sita. The distance made faint her frantic struggle. But it was clearly Sita. She was calling out to her husband.

Ram and Lakshman dropped the deer and dashed forward desperately. They were still some distance away from their temporary camp.

Sita's voice could be heard above the din of the disturbed birds.

'… Raaam!'

They were close enough now to hear the sounds of battle as metal clashed with metal.

Ram screamed as he ran frantically through the forest. 'Sitaaaa!'

Lakshman drew his sword, ready for battle.

'… Raaaam!'

'Leave her alone!' shouted Ram, cutting through the dense foliage, racing ahead.

'… Raaam!'

Ram gripped his bow tight. They were just a few minutes from their camp. 'Sitaaa!'

'… Raa…'

Sita's voice stopped mid-syllable. Trying not to imagine the worst, Ram kept running, his heart pounding desperately, his mind clouded with worry.

They heard the loud whump, whump of rotor blades. It was a sound he clearly remembered from an earlier occasion. This was Raavan's legendary *Pushpak Vimaan*, his *flying vehicle*.

'Nooo!' screamed Ram, wrenching his bow forward as he ran. Tears were streaming down his face.

The brothers broke through to the clearing that was their temporary camp. It stood completely destroyed. There was blood everywhere.

'Sitaaa!'

Ram looked up and shot an arrow at the *Pushpak Vimaan,* which was rapidly ascending into the sky. It was a shot of impotent rage, for the flying vehicle was already soaring high above.

'Sitaaa!'

Lakshman frantically searched the camp. Bodies of dead soldiers were strewn all over. But there was no Sita.

'Pri… nce… Ram…'

Ram recognised that feeble voice. He rushed forward to find the bloodied and mutilated body of the Naga.

'Jatayu!'

The badly wounded Jatayu struggled to speak. 'He's…'

'What?'

'Raavan's… kidnapped… her.'

Ram looked up enraged at the speck moving rapidly away from them. He screamed in anger, 'SITAAAA!'

Chapter 2

Thirty-three years earlier, Port of Karachapa, Western Sea, India

'Lord Parshu Ram, be merciful,' whispered Dashrath, the forty-year-old king of Kosala, the overlord kingdom of the Sapt Sindhu.

The emperor of the Sapt Sindhu had marched right across his sprawling empire from Ayodhya, its capital, to finally arrive at the western coast. Some rebellious traders sorely needed a lesson in royal justice. The combative Dashrath had built on the powerful empire he had inherited from his father Aja. Rulers from various parts of India had either been deposed or made to pay tribute and accept his suzerainty, thus making Dashrath the *Chakravarti Samrat*, or the *Universal Emperor*.

'Yes, My Lord,' said Mrigasya, the general of Dashrath's army. 'This is not the only village that has been laid to waste. The enemy has destroyed all the villages in a fifty-kilometre radius from where we stand. The wells have been poisoned with the carcasses of dead animals. Crops have been burned down ruthlessly. The entire countryside has been ravaged.'

'Scorched earth policy...' said Ashwapati, the king of Kekaya, a loyal ally of Dashrath, and the father of the emperor's second and favourite wife, Kaikeyi.

'Yes,' said another king. 'We cannot feed our army of five hundred thousand soldiers here. Our supply lines are already stretched.'

'How the hell did that barbarian trader Kubaer acquire the intellect for military strategy?' asked Dashrath.

Dashrath could scarcely conceal his Kshatriyan disdain for the trading class, the Vaishyas. For the Sapt Sindhu royalty, wealth was the conqueror's right when acquired as the spoils of war, but inappropriate when earned through mere profiteering. The Vaishyas' 'lack of class' invited scorn. They were subjected to heavy regulation and a draconian system of licences and controls. The children of the Sapt Sindhu aristocracy were encouraged to become warriors or intellectuals, not traders. Resultantly, the trading class in these kingdoms was depleted over the years. With not enough money pouring in from wars, the royal coffers quickly emptied.

Ever sensing an opportunity to profit, Kubaer, the trader king of the island of Lanka, offered his services and expertise to carry out trading activities for all the Sapt Sindhu kingdoms. The then king of Ayodhya, Aja, granted the monopoly to Kubaer in return for a huge annual compensation, which was then distributed to each subordinate kingdom within the Sapt Sindhu Empire. Ayodhya's power soared for it became the source of funds for other kingdoms within the empire. And yet, they could continue to hold on to their old contempt towards trade. Recently, however, Kubaer had unilaterally reduced the commissions that Dashrath rightfully believed were Ayodhya's due. This impertinence of a mere trader certainly deserved punishment. Dashrath directed his vassal kings to merge their troops with his own, and led them to Karachapa to remind Kubaer of his place in the power hierarchy.

'Apparently, My Lord,' said Mrigasya, 'it is not Kubaer who is calling the shots.'

'Then who is?' asked Dashrath.

'We do not know much about him. I have heard that he is no more than thirty years of age. He joined Kubaer some years ago as the head of his trading security force. Over time, he recruited more people and transformed the unit into a proper army. I believe he is the one who convinced Kubaer to rebel against us.'

'I'm not surprised,' said Ashwapati. 'I can't imagine that obese and indolent Kubaer having the nerve to challenge the power of the Sapt Sindhu!'

'Who is this man?' asked Dashrath. 'Where is he from?'

'We really don't know much about him, My Lord,' said Mrigasya.

'Do you at least know his name?'

'Yes, we do. His name is Raavan.'

—— |大| ⦷ ☼ ——

Nilanjana, the royal physician, rushed down the hallway of the palace of Ayodhya. She had received an urgent summons late in the evening from the personal staff of Queen Kaushalya, the first wife of King Dashrath.

The gentle and restrained Kaushalya, the daughter of the king of South Kosala, had been married to Dashrath for more than fifteen years now. Her inability to provide the emperor with an heir had been a source of constant dismay to her. Frustrated by the absence of a successor, Dashrath had finally married Kaikeyi, the tall, fair and statuesque princess of the powerful western Indian kingdom of Kekaya, which was ruled by his close ally Ashwapati. That too was of no avail. He finally married Sumitra, the steely but unobtrusive princess of the holy city of Kashi, the city that housed the spirit of Lord Rudra and was famous for non-violence. Even so, the great Emperor Dashrath remained without an heir.

No wonder then that when Kaushalya finally became pregnant, it was an occasion marked by both joy and trepidation. The queen was understandably desperate to ensure that the child was delivered safely. Her entire staff, most of whom were loyal retainers from her father's household, understood the political implications of the birth of an heir. Abundant caution was the norm. This was not the first time that Nilanjana had been summoned, many a times over frivolous reasons and false alarms. However, since the doctor too was from Queen Kaushalya's parental home, her loyalty forbade any overt signs of irritability.

This time, though, it appeared to be the real thing. The queen had gone into labour.

Even as she ran, Nilanjana's lips fervently appealed to Lord Parshu Ram for a smooth delivery, and yes, a male child.

—— 𝚰𝚱𝚰 🐟 ☼ ——

'I order you to restore our commission to the very fair nine-tenths of your profits and, in return, I assure you I will let you live,' growled Dashrath.

In keeping with the rules of engagement, Dashrath had sent a messenger in advance to Kubaer for a negotiated settlement as a last resort. The adversaries had decided to meet in person on neutral ground. The chosen site was a beach midway between Dashrath's military camp and the Karachapa fort. Dashrath was accompanied by Ashwapati, Mrigasya, and a bodyguard platoon of twenty soldiers.

Kubaer had arrived along with his army's general, Raavan, and twenty bodyguards.

The Sapt Sindhu warriors could scarcely conceal their contempt as the obese Kubaer had waddled laboriously into the tent. A round, cherubic face with thinning hair was balanced on the humongous body of the seventy-year-old fabulously wealthy trader from Lanka. His smooth complexion and fair skin belied his age. He wore a bright green *dhoti* and pink *angvastram* and was bedecked with extravagant jewellery. A life of excess which, when added to his girth and effeminate manner, summed up in the mind of Dashrath what Kubaer was: the classic effete Vaishya.

Dashrath restrained his thoughts as they struggled to escape through words. *Does this ridiculous peacock actually think he can take me on?!*

'Your Highness…' said Kubaer nervously, 'I think it might be a little difficult to keep the commissions fixed at that level. Our costs have gone up and the trading margins are not what they—'

'Don't try your disgusting negotiating tactics with me!' barked Dashrath as he banged his hand on the table for effect. 'I am not a trader! I am an emperor! Civilised people understand the difference.'

It had not escaped Dashrath's notice that Kubaer seemed ill at ease. Perhaps the trader had not intended for events to reach this stage. The massive troop movement to Karachapa had evidently unnerved him. Dashrath presumed that a few harsh words would effectively dissuade Kubaer from persisting with his foolhardy quest. After which, to be fair, he had decided that he would let Kubaer keep an extra two percent. Dashrath understood that, sometimes, a little magnanimity quelled discontent.

Dashrath leaned forward as he lowered his voice to a menacing whisper. 'I can be merciful. I can forgive mistakes. But you really need to stop this nonsense and do as I say.'

With a nervous gulp, Kubaer glanced at the impassive Raavan who sat to his right. Even sitting, Raavan's great height and rippling musculature was intimidating. His battle-worn, swarthy skin was pock-marked, probably by a childhood disease. A thick beard valiantly attempted to cover his ugly marks while a handlebar moustache set off his menacing features. His attire was unremarkable though, consisting of a white *dhoti* and a cream *angvastram*. His headgear was singular, with two threatening six-inch-long horns reaching out from the top on either side.

Kubaer helplessly turned back to Dashrath as his general remained deathly still. 'But Your Highness, we are facing many problems and our invested capital is—'

'You are trying my patience now, Kubaer!' growled Dashrath as he ignored Raavan and focused his attention on the chief trader. 'You are irritating the emperor of the Sapt Sindhu!'

'But My Lord…'

'Look, if you do not continue to pay our rightful commissions, believe me you will all be dead by this time tomorrow. I will first defeat your miserable army, then travel all the way to that cursed island of yours and burn your city to the ground.'

'But there are problems with our ships and labour costs have—'

'I don't care about your problems!' shouted Dashrath, his legendary temper at boiling point now.

'You will, after tomorrow,' said Raavan softly.

Dashrath swung sharply towards Raavan, riled that Kubaer's deputy had had the audacity to interrupt the conversation.

'How dare you speak out of—'

'How dare *you*, Dashrath?' asked Raavan, an octave higher this time.

Dashrath, Ashwapati and Mrigasya sat in stunned silence, shocked that the mere head of a protection force had had the temerity to address the emperor of the Sapt Sindhu by his name.

'How dare you imagine that you can even come close to defeating an army that I lead?' asked Raavan with an eerie sense of calm.

Dashrath stood up angrily and his chair went flying back with a loud clutter. He thrust his finger in Raavan's direction. 'I'll be looking for you on the battlefield tomorrow, you upstart!'

Slowly and menacingly, Raavan rose from his chair, all the while his closed right fist covering a pendant that hung from a gold chain around his neck. As Raavan's fist unclenched, Dashrath was horrified by what he saw. The pendant was actually the bones of two human fingers — the phalanges of which were carefully fastened with gold links. Clenching this macabre souvenir again, Raavan appeared to derive enormous power from it.

Dashrath stared in disbelief. He had heard of demons that drank blood and wine from the skulls of their enemies and even kept their body parts as trophies. But here was a warrior who wore the relics of his enemy! *Who is this monster?*

'I assure you, I'll be waiting,' said Raavan, with a hint of wry humour lacing his voice, as he watched Dashrath gape at him with horror. 'I look forward to drinking your blood.'

Raavan turned around and strode out of the tent. Kubaer hurriedly wobbled out behind him, followed by the Lankan bodyguards.

Dashrath's anger bubbled over. 'Tomorrow we annihilate these scum. But no one will touch that man,' he growled pointing towards the retreating figure of Raavan. 'He will be killed by me! Only me!'

Dashrath was bristling with fury even as the day drew to a close. 'I will personally chop up his body and throw it to the dogs!' he shouted.

Kaikeyi sat impassively as her seething husband paced up and down the royal tent of the Ayodhya camp. She always accompanied him on his military campaigns.

'How dare he speak to me like that?'

Kaikeyi scrutinised Dashrath languidly. He was tall, dark and handsome, the quintessential Kshatriya. A well-manicured moustache only added to his attractiveness. Though muscular and strong, age had begun to take its toll on his well-built physique. Stray streaks of white in his hair were accompanied by a faint hint of a sag in the muscles. Even the Somras, the mysterious anti-ageing drink reserved for the royals by their sages, had not been able to adequately counter a lifetime of ceaseless warring and hard drinking.

'I am the emperor of the Sapt Sindhu!' shouted Dashrath, striking his chest with unconcealed rage. 'How dare he?'

Even though alone with her husband, Kaikeyi maintained the demure demeanour normally reserved for her public interactions with him. She had never seen him so angry.

'My love,' said Kaikeyi, 'save the anger for tomorrow. Have your dinner. You will need your strength for the battle that lies ahead.'

'Does that outcaste mercenary even have a clue as to who he has challenged? I have never lost a battle in my life!' Dashrath continued as though Kaikeyi hadn't spoken.

'And you will win tomorrow as well.'

Dashrath turned towards Kaikeyi. 'Yes, I will win tomorrow. Then I will cut him to pieces and feed his corpse to mongrel dogs and gutter pigs!'

'Of course you will, my love. You have determined that already.'

Dashrath snorted angrily and turned around, ready to storm out of the tent. But Kaikeyi could no longer contain herself.

'Dashrath!' she said harshly.

Dashrath stopped in his tracks. His favourite wife used that tone with him only when necessary. Kaikeyi walked up to him, held his hand and led him to the dinner table. She held his shoulders and roughly pushed him into the chair. Then she tore a piece of the *roti*, scooped up some vegetables and meat with it, and offered it to him. 'You cannot defeat that demon tomorrow if you don't eat and sleep tonight,' she barely whispered.

Dashrath opened his mouth. Kaikeyi stuffed the morsel of food into it.

Chapter 3

Lying in her bed, Queen Kaushalya of Ayodhya appeared frail and worn. All of forty, her prematurely grey hair seemed incongruous against her dark, still gleaming skin. Though short in stature, she'd once been strong. In a culture that valued women for their ability to produce heirs, being childless had broken her spirit. Despite being the senior-most wife, King Dashrath acknowledged her only on ceremonial occasions. At most other times, she was relegated to obscurity, a fact that ate away at her. All she desired was a fraction of the time and attention that Dashrath lavished on his favourite wife, Kaikeyi.

She was keenly aware that giving birth to an heir, hopefully Dashrath's first son, had the potential to dramatically alter her status. No wonder then that today her spirit was all fired up, even though her body was weak. She had been in labour for more than sixteen hours but she barely felt the pain. She soldiered on determinedly, refusing the doctor her permission to perform a surgical procedure to extract her baby from her womb.

'My son will be born naturally,' announced Kaushalya firmly.

A natural birth was considered more auspicious. She had no intention of putting the future prospects of her child at risk.

'He will be king one day,' continued Kaushalya. 'He will be born with good fortune.'

Nilanjana sighed. She wasn't even sure if the child would be a boy. But she wouldn't risk the merest flagging of her mistress' spirits. She administered some herbal pain relievers to the queen and bided her time. Ideally, the doctor wanted the birth to take place before midday. The royal astrologer had warned her that if the child was born later, he would suffer great hardships throughout his life. On the other hand, if the child was born before the sun reached its zenith, he would be remembered as one of the greatest among men and would be celebrated for millennia.

Nilanjana cast a quick glance at the *prahar* lamp, which measured time in six-hour intervals. The sun had already risen and it was the third hour of the second *prahar*. In another three hours it would be midday. Nilanjana had decided to wait till a half hour before noon and, if the baby was still not born, she would go ahead with the surgery.

Kaushalya was stricken with another bout of dilatory pain. She pursed her lips together and began chanting in her mind the name she had chosen for her child. This gave her strength for it wasn't an ordinary name. The name she had picked was that of the sixth Vishnu.

'Vishnu' was a title given to the greatest of leaders who were remembered as the Propagators of Good. The sixth man to have achieved this title was Lord Parshu Ram. That is how he was remembered by the common folk. *Parshu* means *axe*, and the word had been added to the name of the sixth Vishnu because the mighty battle axe had been his favourite weapon. His birth name was Ram. That was the name that reverberated in Kaushalya's mind.

Ram... Ram... Ram... Ram...

The fourth hour of the second *prahar* saw Dashrath battle-ready. He had hardly slept the previous night, his self-righteous rage having refused to dissipate. He had never lost a battle in his life, but this time it was not mere victory that he sought. Redemption now lay in his vanquishing that mercenary trader and squeezing the life out of him.

The Ayodhyan emperor had arranged his army in a *suchi vyuha*, the *needle formation*. This was because Kubaer's hordes had planted dense thorny bushes all around the Karachapa fort. It was almost impossible to charge from the landward side of the port city. Dashrath's army could have cleared the bushes and created a path to charge the fort, but that would have taken weeks. Kubaer's army had scorched the earth around Karachapa, and the absence of local food and water ensured that Dashrath's army did not possess the luxury of time. They had to attack before they ran out of rations.

More importantly, Dashrath was too angry to be patient. Therefore he had decided to launch his attack from the only strip of open land that had access to the fort of Karachapa: its beach.

The beach was broad by usual standards, but not enough for a large army. Hence, Dashrath's tactical decision to form a *suchi vyuha*. The best troops, along with the emperor, would man the front of the formation, while the rest of the army would fall in a long column behind. They intended a rolling charge, where the first lines would strike the Lankan ranks, and after twenty minutes of battle slip back, allowing the next line of warriors to charge in. It would be an unrelenting surge of brave Sapt Sindhu soldiers aiming to scatter and decimate the enemy troops of Kubaer.

Ashwapati nudged his horse a few steps ahead and halted next to Dashrath.

'Your Highness,' he said, 'are you sure about this tactic?'

'Don't tell me you're having second thoughts, King Ashwapati!' remarked Dashrath, surprised by the words of caution from his normally aggressive father-in-law. He had been a worthy ally in most of Dashrath's conquering expeditions throughout the realms of India.

'I was just thinking we will not be using our numerical superiority in full strength. The bulk of our soldiers will be behind the ones charging upfront. They will not be fighting at the same time. Is that wise?'

'It is the only way, believe me,' asserted Dashrath confidently. 'Even if our first charge is unsuccessful, the soldiers at the back will keep coming in waves. We can sustain our onslaught on Kubaer's eunuch forces till they all die to the last man. I do not see it coming to that though. I will annihilate them with our first charge!'

Ashwapati looked to his left where Kubaer's ships lay at anchor more than two kilometres into the sea. There was something strange about their structure. The front section, the bow, was unusually broad. 'What role will those ships play in the battle?'

'Nothing!' dismissed Dashrath, smiling fondly at his father-in-law; while Dashrath had had experience of a few naval battles, Ashwapati hadn't. 'Those fools haven't even lowered their row-boats from the vessels. Even if they have a reserve force on those ships, they cannot be brought into battle quickly enough. It will take them at least a few hours to lower their row-boats, load their soldiers, and then ferry them to the beach to join the battle. By then, we would've wiped out the soldiers who are inside the fort.'

'Outside the fort,' corrected Ashwapati, pointing towards Karachapa.

Raavan had, strangely, abandoned the immense advantage of being safe within the walls of the well-designed fort. Instead of lining them up along the ramparts, he had chosen to arrange his army of probably fifty thousand soldiers in a standard formation *outside* the city, on the beach.

'It is the strangest tactic I have ever seen,' said Ashwapati warily. 'Why is he giving up his strategic advantage? With the fort walls being right behind his army, he does not even have room to retreat. Why has Raavan done this?'

Dashrath sniggered. 'Because he is a reactionary idiot. He wants to prove a point to me. Well, I will make the final point when I dig my sword into his heart.'

Ashwapati turned his head towards the fort walls again as he surveyed Raavan's soldiers. Even from this distance he could see Raavan, wearing his hideous horned helmet, leading his troops from the front.

Ashwapati cast a look at his own army. The soldiers were roaring loudly, hurling obscenities at their enemy, as warriors are wont to do before the commencement of war. He turned his gaze to Raavan's army once again. In sharp contrast, they emanated no sound. There was no movement either. They stood quietly in rigid formation, a brilliant tribute to soldierly discipline.

A shiver ran down Ashwapati's spine.

He couldn't get it out of his mind that those soldiers were bait that Dashrath had chosen to take.

If you are a fish charging at bait, then it usually doesn't end well.

Ashwapati turned towards Dashrath to voice his fears, but the emperor of the Sapt Sindhu had already ridden away.

Dashrath was on horseback at the head of his troops. He ran his eyes over his men confidently. They were a rowdy, raucous bunch with swords drawn, eager for battle. The horses, too, seemed to have succumbed to the excitement of the moment, for the soldiers were pulling hard at their reins, holding them in check. Dashrath and his army could almost smell the blood that would soon be shed; the magnificent killings! They believed, as usual, that the Goddess of Victory was poised to bless them. *Let the war drums roll!*

Dashrath squinted his eyes as he observed the Lankans and their commander Raavan up ahead in the distance. Molten rage was coursing through him. He drew his sword and held it aloft, and then bellowed the unmistakable war cry of his kingdom, Kosala and its capital city, Ayodhya. *'Ayodhyatah Vijetaarah!'*

The conquerors from the unconquerable city!

Not all in his army were citizens of Ayodhya, and yet they were proud to fight under the great Kosala banner. They echoed the war cry, *'Ayodhyatah Vijetaarah!'*

Dashrath roared as he brought his sword down and spurred his horse. 'Kill them all! No mercy!'

'No mercy!' shouted the riders of the first charge, kicking their horses and taking off behind their fearless lord.

But then it all began to unravel.

Dashrath and his finest warriors comprised the sturdy tip of the Sapt Sindhu needle formation. As they charged down the beach towards the Lankans, Raavan's troops remained stationary. When the enemy cavalry was just a few hundred metres away, Raavan unexpectedly turned his horse around and retreated from the front lines, even as his soldiers held firm. This further infuriated Dashrath. He screamed loudly as he kicked his horse to gather speed, intending to mow down the Lankan front line and quickly reach Raavan.

This was exactly what Raavan had envisaged. The Lankan front line roared stridently as the soldiers suddenly dropped their swords, bent, and picked up unnaturally long spears, almost twenty feet in length, that had been hitherto lying at their feet. Made of wood and metal, the spears were so heavy that it took two soldiers to pick each one up. The soldiers pointed these spears, tipped with sharp copper heads, directly at Dashrath's oncoming cavalry. The pointed heads tore into the unprepared horses and their mounted soldiers. Even as the charge of Dashrath's cavalry was halted in its tracks and the mounted soldiers thrown forward as their horses suddenly collapsed under them, Lankan archers emerged, high on the walls of the Karachapa fort. They shot a continuous stream of arrows in a long arc from the fort ramparts, right into the dense formation of Dashrath's troops at the back, ripping through the Sapt Sindhu lines.

Many of Dashrath's warriors, who had been flung off their impaled horses, broke into a fierce hand-to-hand battle with their enemies. Their liege Dashrath led the way as he swung his sword ferociously, killing all who dared to come in his path. But the Ayodhyan king was alive to the devastation being wrought upon his fellow soldiers who rapidly fell under the barrage of Lankan arrows and superbly-trained swordsmen. Dashrath ordered his flag bearer, who was beside him, to raise the flag as a signal for the Sapt Sindhu soldiers at the back to also break into a charge immediately and support the first line.

But things continued to deteriorate.

The troops on the Lankan ships in the distance abruptly weighed anchor, extended the oars, and began to row rapidly to the beach, with their sails up at full mast to help them catch the wind. Within moments, arrows were being fired from the ships into the densely packed forces under Dashrath's command. The Lankan archers on the ships tore through the ranks of the Sapt Sindhus.

No brigadier in Dashrath's army had factored in the possibility of the enemy ships beaching; it would have cracked their hulls. Unbeknownst to them, though, these were amphibious crafts, built by Kubaer's ingenious ship-designers, with specially constructed hulls that could absorb the shock of landing. Even as these landing crafts stormed onto the beach with tremendous force, the broad bows of the hulls rolled out from the top. These were no ordinary bows of a standard hull. They were attached to the bottom of the hull by huge hinges which simply rolled out onto the sand like a landing ramp. This opened a gangway straight onto the beach, disgorging cavalrymen of the Lankan army mounted on disproportionately large horses imported from the west. The cavalry rode out of the ships and straight onto the beach, mercilessly slicing into all who lay in their path.

Even as he watched the destruction unleashed upon his forces near the fort, Dashrath's instincts warned him that something terrible was ensuing at the rear guard. As the emperor stretched to gaze beyond the sea of frenzied battling humanity, he detected a quick movement to his left and raised his shield in time to block a vicious blow from a Lankan soldier. Screaming ferociously, the king of Ayodhya brutally swung low at his attacker, his sword slicing through a chink in the armour. The Lankan fell back as his abdomen ripped open with a massive spurt of blood, accompanied by slick pink intestines that tumbled out in a rush. Dashrath knew no mercy as he turned away from the poor sod even as he bled to his miserable end.

'NO!' he yelled. What he saw was enough to break his mighty warrior's heart.

Caught between the vicious pincer attack of the brutal Lankan archers and infantry at the Karachapa walls from the front, and the fierce Lankan cavalry at the back, the spirit of his all-conquering army had all but collapsed. Dashrath stared at a scene he'd never imagined he would as the supreme commander of his glorious army. His men had broken rank and were in retreat.

'NO!' thundered Dashrath. 'FIGHT! FIGHT! WE ARE AYODHYA! THE UNCONQUERABLES!'

Dashrath swung hard and decapitated a giant Lankan in one mighty blow. As he turned to face another of the seemingly never-ending waves of Raavan's hordes, his gaze fell upon the monster who was the mastermind of this devastation. Raavan, on horseback, was leading his cavalry down the beach on the left, skirting the sea. It was the only flank of the Lankans that was open to counter-attack from the Ayodhya infantry. Accompanied by his well-trained cavalry, Raavan was shrieking maniacally and hacking his way brutally through the Ayodhya outer infantry lines before they could regroup. This was not a war anymore. It was a massacre.

Dashrath knew that he'd lost the battle. He also knew that he'd rather die than face defeat. But he had one last wish. Redemption lay in his spitting on the decapitated head of that ogre from Lanka.

'YAAAAAHH!' screamed Dashrath, as he hacked at the arm of a Lankan who jumped at him, severing the limb cleanly just above the wrist. Pushing his enemy out of the way, Dashrath lunged forward as he desperately tried to reach Raavan. He felt a shield crash into his calf and heard the crack of a bone above the din.

The mighty emperor of the Sapt Sindhu screamed as he spun around and swung his sword at the Lankan who had broken the rules of combat, decapitating him cleanly. He felt a hard knock on his back. He turned right back with a parry, but his broken leg gave way. As he fell forward, he felt a sharp thrust into his chest. *Someone had stabbed him.* He didn't feel the blade go in too deep. *Or had it gone in deeper than he thought? Maybe his body was shutting the pain out...* Dashrath felt darkness enveloping him. His fall was cushioned by another soldier from among the heaving mass of warriors battling in close combat. As his eyes slowly closed, he whispered his last prayers within the confines of his mind; to the God he revered the most: the sustainer of the world, the mighty Sun God Surya himself.

Don't let me live to bear this, Lord Surya. Let me die. Let me die...

This is a disaster!

A panic-stricken Ashwapati rounded up his bravest mounted soldiers and raced across the battlefield on horseback. He negotiated his way through the clutter of bodies to quickly reach the kill zone right outside Karachapa fort, where Dashrath lay, probably seriously injured, if not dead.

Ashwapati knew the war had been lost. Vast numbers of the Sapt Sindhu soldiers were being massacred before his very eyes. All he wanted now was to save Emperor Dashrath, who was also his son-in-law. His Kaikeyi would not be widowed.

They rode hard through the battle zone, even as they held their shields high to protect themselves from the unrelenting barrage of arrows raining down from the Karachapa walls.

'There!' screamed a soldier.

Ashwapati saw Dashrath's motionless form wedged between the corpses of two soldiers. His son-in-law lay there firmly clutching his sword. The king of Kekaya leapt off his horse even as two soldiers rushed forward to offer him protection. Ashwapati dragged Dashrath towards his own horse, lifted him, and laid the emperor's severely injured body across the saddle. He then jumped astride and rode off towards the field of thorny bushes even as his soldiers struggled to keep up with him.

Kaikeyi stood resolute in her chariot near the clearing along the line of bushes, her demeanour admirably calm. As her father's horse drew near, she reached across and dragged Dashrath's prone body into the chariot. She didn't turn to look at her father, who had also been pierced by many arrows. She picked up the reins and whipped the four horses tethered to her chariot.

'Hyaah!' screamed Kaikeyi, as she charged into the bushes. Thorns tore mercilessly into the sides of the horses, ripping skin and even some flesh off the hapless animals. But Kaikeyi only kept whipping them harder and harder. Bloodied and tired, the horses soon broke through to the other side, onto clear land.

Kaikeyi finally pulled the reins and looked back. Riding furiously on the other side of the field of thorns, her father and his bodyguards were being chased by a group of mounted soldiers from Raavan's army. Kaikeyi understood immediately what her father was trying to do. He was leading Raavan's soldiers away from her.

The sun had nearly reached its zenith now. It was close to midday.

Kaikeyi cursed. *Damn you, Lord Surya! How could you allow this to happen to your most fervent devotee?*

She kneeled beside her unconscious husband, ripped off a large piece of her *angvastram,* and tied it firmly around a deep wound on his chest, which was losing blood at an alarming rate. Having staunched the blood flow somewhat, she stood and picked up the reins. She desperately wanted to cry but this was not the time. She had to save her husband first. She needed her wits about her.

She looked at the horses. Blood was pouring down their sides in torrents, and specks of flesh hung limply where the skin had been ripped off. They were panting frantically, exhausted by the effort of having pulled the chariot through the dense field of thorns. But she couldn't allow them any respite. Not yet.

'Forgive me,' whispered Kaikeyi, as she raised her whip.

The leather hummed through the air and lashed the horses cruelly. Neighing for mercy, they refused to move. Kaikeyi cracked her whip again and the horses edged forward.

'MOVE!' screamed Kaikeyi as she whipped the horses ruthlessly, again and again, forcing them to pick up a desperate but fearsome momentum.

She had to save her husband.

Suddenly an arrow whizzed past her and crashed into the front board of the chariot with frightening intensity. Kaikeyi spun around in alarm. One of Raavan's cavalrymen had broken off from his group and was in pursuit.

Kaikeyi turned back and whipped her horses harder. 'FASTER! FASTER!'

Even as she whipped her horses into delirious frenzy, Kaikeyi had the presence of mind to shift slightly and use her body to shield her husband.

Even Raavan's demons would be chivalrous enough not to attack an unarmed woman.

She was wrong.

She heard the arrow's threatening hum before it slammed into her back with vicious force. Its shock was so massive that it threw her forward as her head flung back. Her eyes beheld the sky as Kaikeyi screamed in agony. But she recovered immediately, the adrenaline pumping furiously through her body, compelling her to focus.

'FASTER!' she screamed, as she whipped the horses ferociously.

Another arrow whizzed by her ears, missing the back of her head by a tiny whisker. Kaikeyi cast a quick look at her husband's immobile body bouncing furiously as the chariot tore through the uneven countryside.

'FASTER!'

She heard another arrow approach, and within a flash it slammed into her right hand, slicing through the forefinger cleanly; it bounced away like a pebble thrown to the side. The whip fell from her suddenly-loosened grip. Her mind was ready for further injuries now, her body equipped for pain. She didn't scream. She didn't cry.

She bent quickly and picked up the whip with her left hand, transferring the reins to her bloodied right hand. She resumed the whipping with mechanical precision.

'MOVE! YOUR EMPEROR'S LIFE IS AT STAKE!'

She heard the dreaded whizz of another arrow. She steeled herself for another hit; instead, she now heard a scream of agony from behind her. A quick side glance revealed her injured foe; the arrow had buried itself deep into his right eye. What she also perceived was a band of horsemen moving in; her father and his faithful bodyguards. A flurry of arrows ensured that the Lankan attacker toppled off his animal, even as his leg got entangled in the stirrup. Raavan's soldier was dragged for many metres by his still galloping horse, his head smashing repeatedly against the rocks strewn on the path.

Kaikeyi looked ahead once again. She did not have the time to savour the brutal death of the man who'd injured her. *Dashrath must be saved.*

The rhythmic whipping continued ceaselessly.

'FASTER! FASTER!'

Nilanjana was patting the baby's back insistently. He still wasn't breathing.

'Come on! Breathe!'

Kaushalya watched anxiously as she lay exhausted from the abnormally long labour. She tried to prop herself up on her elbows. 'What's wrong? What's the matter with my boy?'

'Get the queen to rest, will you?' Nilanjana admonished the attendant who was peering over her shoulder.

Rushing over, the attendant put her hand on the queen's shoulder and attempted to coax her to lie down. A severely weakened Kaushalya, however, refused to submit. 'Give him to me!'

'Your Highness…' whispered Nilanjana as tears welled up in her eyes.

'Give him to me!'

'I don't think that…'

'GIVE HIM TO ME!'

Nilanjana hurried over to her side and placed the lifeless baby next to Kaushalya. The queen held her motionless son close to her bosom. Almost instantly the baby moved and intuitively gripped Kaushalya's long hair.

'Ram!' said Kaushalya loudly.

With a loud and vigorous cry, Ram sucked in his first breath in this, his current worldly life.

'Ram!' cried Kaushalya once again, as tears streamed down her cheeks.

Ram continued to bawl with robust gusto, holding on to his mother's hair as firmly as his tiny hands would permit. He opened his mouth and suckled reflexively.

Nilanjana felt as if a dam had burst and began to bawl like a child. Her mistress had given birth to a beautiful baby boy. The prince had been born!

Despite her evident delirium, Nilanjana did not forget her training. She looked to the far corner of the room at the *prahar* lamp to record the exact time of birth. She knew that the royal astrologer would need that information.

She held her breath as she noticed the time.

Lord Rudra, be merciful!

It was exactly midday.

'What does this mean?' asked Nilanjana.

The astrologer sat still.

The sun was poised to sink into the horizon and both Kaushalya and Ram were sound asleep. Nilanjana had finally walked into the chamber of the royal astrologer to discuss Ram's future.

'You'd said that if he was born before midday then history would remember him as one of the greatest,' said Nilanjana. 'And that if he was born after midday, he'd suffer misfortune and not know personal happiness.'

'Are you sure he was born exactly at midday?' asked the astrologer. 'Not before? Not after?'

'Of course I'm sure! Exactly at noon.'

The astrologer inhaled deeply and became contemplative once again.

'What does this mean?' asked Nilanjana. 'What will his future be like? Will he be great or will he suffer misfortune?'

'I don't know.'

'What do you mean you don't know?'

'I mean I don't know!' said the astrologer, unable to contain his irritation.

Nilanjana looked out of the window, towards the exquisite royal gardens that rolled endlessly over many acres. The palace was perched atop a hill which also was the highest point in Ayodhya. As she gazed vacantly at the waters beyond the city walls, she knew what needed to be done. It was really up to her to record the time of birth, and she didn't *have* to record it as midday. How would anyone be any the wiser? She'd made her decision: Ram was born a minute *before* midday.

She turned to the astrologer. 'You will remain quiet about the actual time of birth.'

She needn't have exercised any caution. The astrologer, who also belonged to Kaushalya's parental kingdom, didn't need any convincing. His loyalties were as clear as Nilanjana's.

'Of course.'

Chapter 4

Maharishi Vashishtha approached the fort gates of Ayodhya, followed by his bodyguards at a respectful distance. As the guards on duty sprang to attention, they wondered where the great *raj guru*, the *royal sage* of Ayodhya, was headed early in the morning.

The chief of the guards bowed low, folded his hands into a namaste and addressed the *great man of knowledge* respectfully, '*Maharishiji*.'

Vashishtha did not break a step as he nodded in acknowledgement with a polite namaste.

He was thin to a fault and towering in height, despite which his gait was composed and self-assured. His *dhoti* and *angvastram* were white, the colour of purity. His head was shaven bare, but for a knotted tuft of hair at the top of his head which announced his Brahmin status. A flowing, snowy beard, calm, gentle eyes, and a wizened face conveyed the impression of a soul at peace with itself.

Yet, Vashishtha was brooding as he walked slowly towards the massive Grand Canal that encircled the ramparts of *Ayodhya*, the *impregnable city*. His thoughts were consumed by what he knew he must do.

Six years ago, Raavan's barbaric hordes had decimated the Sapt Sindhu army. Though its prestige had depleted, Ayodhya's suzerainty had not thus far been challenged by other kingdoms of North India, for every subordinate kingdom of the empire had bled heavily on that fateful day. Wounded themselves, none had the strength to confront even a weakened Ayodhya. Dashrath remained the emperor of the Sapt Sindhu, albeit a poorer and less powerful one.

The pitiless Raavan had extracted his pound of flesh from Ayodhya. Trade commissions paid by Lanka were unilaterally reduced to a tenth of what they had been before the humiliating defeat. In addition, the purchase of goods from the Sapt Sindhu was now at a reduced price. Inevitably, even as Lanka's wealth soared, Ayodhya and the other kingdoms of North India slipped into penury. Why, rumours even abounded that the streets of the demon city were paved with gold!

Vashishtha raised his hand to signal his bodyguards to fall behind. He walked up to the shaded terrace that overlooked the Grand Canal. He raised his eyes towards the exquisite ceiling that ran along the canal's entire length. He then ran his gaze along the almost limitless expanse of water that lay ahead. It had once symbolised Ayodhya's immense wealth but had begun to exhibit signs of decay and poverty.

The canal had been built a few centuries ago, during the reign of Emperor Ayutayus, by drawing in the waters of the feisty Sarayu River. Its dimensions were almost celestial. It stretched for over fifty kilometres as it circumnavigated the third and outermost wall of the city of Ayodhya. It was enormous in breadth as well, extending to about two-and-a-half kilometres across the banks. Its storage capacity was so massive that for the first few years of its construction, many of the kingdoms downriver had complained of water shortages. Their objections had been crushed by the brute force of the powerful Ayodhyan warriors.

One of the main purposes of this canal was militaristic. It was, in a sense, a moat. To be fair, it could be called the Moat of Moats, protecting the city from all sides. Prospective attackers would have to row across a moat that had river-like dimensions. The adventurous fools would be out in the open, vulnerable to an unending barrage of missiles from the high walls of the unconquerable city. Four bridges spanned the canal in the four cardinal directions. The roads that emerged from these bridges led into the city through four massive gates in the outermost wall: the North Gate, East Gate, South Gate and West Gate. Each bridge was divided into two sections. Each section had its own tower and drawbridge, thus offering two levels of defence at the canal itself.

Even so, to consider this Grand Canal a mere defensive structure was to do it a disservice. The Ayodhyans also looked upon the canal as a religious symbol. To them, the massive canal, with its dark, impenetrable and eerily calm waters, was reminiscent of the sea; similar to the mythic, primeval ocean of nothingness that was the source of creation. It was believed that at the centre of this primeval ocean, billions of years ago, the universe was born when *The One*, *Ekam*, split into many in a great big bang, thus activating the cycle of creation.

The impenetrable city, Ayodhya, viewed itself as a representative on earth of that most supreme of Gods, the *One God*, the formless *Ekam*, popularly known in modern times as the *Brahman* or *Parmatma*. It was believed that the *Parmatma* inhabited every single being, animate and inanimate. Some men and women were able to awaken the *Parmatma* within, and thus become Gods. These Gods among men had been immortalised in great temples across Ayodhya. Small islands had been constructed within the Grand Canal as well, on which temples had been built in honour of these Gods.

Vashishtha, however, knew that despite all the symbolism and romance, the canal had, in fact, been built for more prosaic purposes. It worked as an effective flood-control mechanism, as water from the tempestuous Sarayu could be led in through control-gates. Floods were a recurrent problem in North India.

Furthermore, its placid surface made drawing water relatively easy, as compared to taking it directly from the Sarayu. Smaller canals radiated out of the Grand Canal into the hinterland of Ayodhya, increasing the productivity of farming dramatically. The increase in agricultural yield allowed many farmers to free themselves from the toil of tilling the land. Only a few were enough to feed the massive population of the entire kingdom of Kosala. This surplus labour transformed into a large army, trained by talented generals into a brilliant fighting unit. The army conquered more and more of the surrounding lands, till the great Lord Raghu, the grandfather of the present Emperor Dashrath, finally subjugated the entire Sapt Sindhu, thus becoming the *Chakravarti Samrat*.

Wealth pouring into Kosala sparked a construction spree: massive temples, palaces, public baths, theatres and market places were built. Sheer poetry in stone, these buildings were a testament to the power and glory of Ayodhya. One among them was the grand terrace that overhung the inner banks of the Grand Canal. It was a continuous colonnaded structure built of red sandstone mined from beyond the river Ganga; the terrace was entirely covered by a majestic vaulted ceiling, providing shade to the constant stream of visitors.

Every square inch of the ceiling had been painted in vivid colours, chronicling the stories of ancient Gods such as Indra, and the ancestors of kings who ruled Ayodhya, all the way up to the first, the noble Ikshvaku. The ceiling was divided into separate sections and, at the centre of each was a massive sun, with its rays streaming boldly out in all directions. This was significant, for the kings of Ayodhya were Suryavanshis, the descendants of the Sun God, and just like the sun, their power boldly extended out in all directions. Or so it had been before the demon from Lanka destroyed their prestige in one fell swoop.

Vashishtha looked into the distance at one of the numerous artificial islands that dotted the canal. This island, unlike the others, did not have a temple but three gigantic statues, placed back to back, facing different directions. One was of Lord Brahma, the Creator, one of the greatest scientists ever. He was credited with many inventions upon which the Vedic way of life had been built. His disciples lived by the code he'd established: relentless pursuit of knowledge and selfless service to society. They had, over the years, evolved into the tribe of Brahma, or Brahmins.

To its right was the statue of Lord Parshu Ram, worshipped as the sixth Vishnu. Periodically, when a way of life became inefficient, corrupt or fanatical, a new leader emerged, who guided his people to an improved social order. Vishnu was an ancient title accorded to the greatest of leaders, idolised as the Propagators of Good. The Vishnus were worshipped like Gods. Lord Parshu Ram, the previous Vishnu, had many centuries ago guided India out of its Age of Kshatriya, which had degenerated into vicious violence. He'd ushered in the Age of Brahmin, an age of knowledge.

Next to Lord Parshu Ram, and to the left of Lord Brahma, completing the circle of trinity was the statue of Lord Rudra, the previous Mahadev. This was an ancient title accorded to those who were the Destroyers of Evil. The Mahadev's was not the task to guide humanity to a new way of life;

this was reserved for the Vishnu. His task was restricted to finding and destroying Evil. Once Evil had been destroyed, Good would burst through with renewed vigour. Unlike the Vishnu, the Mahadev could not be a native of India, for that would predispose him towards one or the other side within this great land. He had to be an outsider to enable him to clearly see Evil for what it was, when it arose. Lord Rudra belonged to a land beyond the western borders of India: Pariha.

Vashishtha went down on his knees and touched the ground with his forehead, in reverence to the glorious trinity who were the bedrock of the present Vedic way of life. He raised his head and folded his hands in a namaste.

'Guide me, O Holy Trinity,' whispered Vashishtha. 'For I intend to rebel.'

A sudden gust of wind echoed around his ears as he gazed at the triumvirate. The marble was not what it used to be. The Ayodhya royalty wasn't able to maintain the outer surface anymore. The gold leafing on the crowns of Lords Brahma, Parshu Ram and Rudra had begun to peel off. The ceiling of the terrace had paint flaking off its beautiful images, and the sandstone floor was chipped in many places. The Grand Canal itself had begun to silt and dry up, with no repairs undertaken; the Ayodhya royal administration was probably unable to budget for such tasks.

However, it was clear to Vashishtha that not only was the administration short of funds for adequate governance, it had also lost the will for it. As the canal water receded, the exposed dry land had been encroached upon with impunity. The Ayodhyan population had grown till the city almost seemed to burst at its seams. Even a few years ago it would have been unthinkable that the canal would be defiled thus;

that new housing would not be constructed for the poor. But, alas, many improbables had now become habitual.

We need a new way of life, Lord Parshu Ram. My great country must be rejuvenated with the blood and sweat of patriots. What I want is revolutionary, and patriots are often called traitors by the very people they choose to serve, till history passes the final judgement.

Vashishtha scooped some mud from the canal that was deposited on the steps of the terrace, and used his thumb to apply it on his forehead in a vertical line.

This soil is worth more than my life to me. I love my country. I love my India. I swear I will do what must be done. Give me courage, My Lord.

The soft rhythm of liturgical chanting wafted through the breeze, making him turn to his right. A small group of people walked solemnly in the distance, wearing robes of blue, the holy colour of the divine. It was an unusual sight these days. Along with wealth and power, the citizens of the Sapt Sindhu had also lost their spiritual ardour. Many believed their Gods had abandoned them. Why else would they suffer so?

The worshippers chanted the name of the sixth Vishnu, Lord Parshu Ram.

'Ram, Ram, Ram bolo; Ram, Ram, Ram. Ram, Ram, Ram bolo; Ram, Ram, Ram.'

It was a simple chant: 'Speak the name of Ram.'

Vashishtha smiled; to him, this was a sign.

Thank you, Lord Parshu Ram. Thank you for your blessings.

Vashishtha had pinned his hopes on the namesake of the sixth Vishnu: the six-year-old eldest prince of Ayodhya, Ram. The sage had insisted that Queen Kaushalya's chosen name, Ram, be expanded to Ram Chandra. Kaushalya's father, King Bhanuman of South Kosala, and mother, Queen Maheshwari of the Kurus, were *Chandravanshis,* the *descendants of the moon.* Vashishtha thought it would be wise to show fealty towards

Ram's maternal home as well. Furthermore, Ram Chandra meant 'pleasant face of the moon', and it was well known that the moon shone with the reflected light of the sun. Poetically, the sun was the face and the moon its reflection; who, then, was responsible for the pleasant face of the moon? *The sun!* It was appropriate thus: Ram Chandra was also a Suryavanshi name, for Dashrath, his father, was a Suryavanshi.

That names guided destiny was an ancient belief. Parents chose the names of their children with care. A name, in a sense, became an aspiration, *swadharma, individual dharma*, for the child. Having been named after the sixth Vishnu himself, the aspirations for this child could not have been set higher!

There was another name that Vashishtha had placed his hopes on: Bharat, Ram's brother, younger to him by seven months. His mother, Kaikeyi, did not know at the time of the great battle with Raavan that she was carrying Dashrath's child in her womb. Vashishtha was aware that Kaikeyi was a passionate, wilful woman. She was ambitious for herself and those she viewed as her own. She had not settled for the eldest queen, Kaushalya, being one up on her by choosing a great name for her son. Her son, then, was the namesake of the legendary Chandravanshi emperor, Bharat, who had ruled millennia ago.

The ancient Emperor Bharat had united the warring Suryavanshis and Chandravanshis under one banner. Notwithstanding the occasional skirmishes, they had learnt to live in relative peace; a peace that held. It was exemplified today by the Emperor Dashrath, a Suryavanshi, having two queens who traced their lineage to Chandravanshi royalty, Kaushalya and Kaikeyi. Ashwapati, the father of Kaikeyi and the Chandravanshi king of Kekaya, was in fact the emperor's closest advisor.

One of the two names will surely serve my purpose.

He looked at Lord Parshu Ram again, drawing strength from the image.

I know they will think I'm wrong. They may even curse my soul. But you were the one who had said, My Lord, that a leader must love his country more than he loves his own soul.

Vashishtha reached for his scabbard, hidden within the folds of his *angvastram*. He pulled out the knife and beheld the name that had been inscribed on the hilt in an ancient script: Parshu Ram.

ᚌ ᚈ ᚖ

Inhaling deeply, he shifted the knife to his left hand and pricked his forefinger, puncturing deep to draw out blood. He pressed the finger with his thumb, just under the drop of blood, and let some droplets drip into the canal.

By this blood oath, I swear on all my knowledge, I will make my rebellion succeed, or I will die trying.

Vashishtha took one last look at Lord Parshu Ram, bowed his head as he brought his hands together in a respectful namaste, and softly whispered the cry of the followers of the great Vishnu. *'Jai Parshu Ram!'*

Glory to Parshu Ram!

Chapter 5

Kaushalya, the queen, was happy; Kaushalya, the mother, was not. She understood that Ram should leave the Ayodhya palace. Emperor Dashrath had blamed him for the horrific defeat he'd suffered at the hands of Raavan, on the day that Ram was born. Till that fateful day, he had never lost a battle; in fact, he'd been the only unbeaten ruler in all of India. Dashrath was convinced that Ram was born with bad karma and his birth was the undoing of the noble lineage of Raghu. There was little the powerless Kaushalya could do to change this.

Kaikeyi had always been the favourite wife, and saving the emperor's life in the Battle of Karachapa had only made her hold over Dashrath absolute. Kaikeyi and her coterie had speedily let it be known that Dashrath believed Ram's birth was inauspicious. Soon the city of Ayodhya shared its emperor's belief. It was widely held that all the good deeds of Ram's life would not succeed in washing away the 'taint of 7,032', the year that, according to the calendar of Lord Manu, Dashrath was defeated and Ram was born.

It would be best if Ram left the palace with Raj Guru Vashishtha, Kaushalya knew. He would be away from the Ayodhya nobility, which had never accepted him anyway. Furthermore, he would stand to gain from the education he'd receive at Vashishtha's *gurukul. Gurukul* meant the *guru's family,* but in practice it was the *residential school* of gurus. He would learn philosophy, science, mathematics, ethics, warfare and the arts. He would return, years later, a man in charge of his destiny.

The queen understood this, but the doting mother was unable to let go. She held on to her child and wept. Ram stood stoic as he held his mother, who hugged and smothered him with kisses; even at this tender age, he was an unusually calm boy.

Bharat, unlike Ram, was crying hysterically, refusing to let his mother go. Kaikeyi glared at her son with exasperation. 'You are my son! Don't be such a sissy! Behave like the king you will be one day! Go, make your mother proud!'

Vashishtha watched the proceedings and smiled.

Passionate children have strong emotions that insist on finding expression. They laugh loudly. They cry even more loudly.

He observed the brothers as he wondered whether his goal would be met through stoic duty or passionate feeling. The twins, Lakshman and Shatrughan, the youngest of the four sons of Dashrath, stood at the back with their mother, Sumitra. The poor three-year-olds seemed lost, not quite understanding what was going on. Vashishtha knew it was too soon for them, but he couldn't leave them behind. Ram and Bharat's training would take a long time, maybe even a decade, if not more. He could not risk the twins being in the palace during this period, for the political intrigue among the nobility would lead to the younger princes being co-opted into camps. This malicious nobility was already bleeding Ayodhya dry with its scheming and plotting to enrich itself; the emperor was weak and distracted.

The princes would return home for two *nine-day* holidays, twice a year, during the summer and winter solstices. The ancient *navratra* festival, which commemorated the six-monthly change in the direction of the Sun God's north-south journey across the horizon, was celebrated with great vigour. Vashishtha believed those eighteen days would suffice to console the bereft mothers and sons. The autumn and spring *navratras*, aligned with the two equinoxes, would be commemorated at the *gurukul*.

The raj guru turned his attention to Dashrath.

The last six years had taken their toll on the emperor. Parchment-like skin stretched thinly over a face that was worn out by grief, his eyes sunken, his hair grey. The grievous battle wound on his leg had long since turned into a permanent deformity, depriving him of the hunting and exercising that he so loved. Seeking refuge in drink, his bent body gave little indication of the strong and handsome warrior he'd once been. Raavan had not just defeated him on that terrible day. He continued to defeat him every single day.

'Your Highness,' said Vashishtha, loudly. 'With your permission.'

A distracted Dashrath waved his hand, confirming his order.

—— 内 🐚 ☼ ——

It was a day after the winter solstice and the princes were in Ayodhya on their half-yearly holiday. It had been three years since they first left for the *gurukul*. *Uttaraayan*, the northward movement of the sun across the horizon, had begun. Six months later, in peak summer, Lord Surya would reverse his direction and *Dakshinaayan*, the southward movement of the sun, would begin.

Ram spent most of his time, even on holiday, with Guru Vashishtha, who had moved back to the palace with the boys;

Kaushalya could not do much besides complain. Bharat, on the other hand, was strictly confined to Kaikeyi's chambers, subjected to incessant tutoring and interrogation by his forceful mother. Lakshman had already started riding small ponies, and he loved it. Shatrughan … just read books!

Lakshman was rushing to his mother Sumitra after one such riding lesson when he stopped short, hearing voices outside her chamber. He peeped in from behind the curtains.

'You must understand, Shatrughan, that your brother Bharat may make fun of you, but he loves you the most. You should always stay by his side.'

Shatrughan was holding a palm-leaf booklet in his hand, desperately trying to read as he pretended to pay attention to his mother.

'Are you listening to me, Shatrughan?' asked Sumitra, sharply.

'Yes Mother,' Shatrughan said, looking up, sincerity dripping from his voice.

'I don't think so.'

Shatrughan repeated his mother's last sentence. His diction was remarkably clear and crisp for his age. Sumitra knew that her son hadn't been paying attention, and yet she couldn't do anything about the fact that he'd not been genuinely listening to her at all!

Lakshman smiled as he ran up to his mother, yelping with delight as he leapt onto her lap.

'I will li*th*en to you, *Maa*!' he said with his childish lisp.

Sumitra smiled as she wrapped her arms around Lakshman. 'Yes, I know you will always listen to me. You are my good son!'

Shatrughan glanced briefly at his mother before going back to his palm-leaf booklet.

'I will do whatever you tell me to do,' said Lakshman, his earnest eyes filled with love. 'Alway*th*.'

'Then listen to me,' said Sumitra, leaning in with a clownish, conspiratorial expression, the kind she knew Lakshman loved. 'Your elder brother Ram needs you.' Her expression changed to compassionate wistfulness as she continued. 'He is a simple and innocent soul. He needs someone who can be his eyes and ears. No one really likes him.' She focused on Lakshman once again and murmured, 'You have to protect him from harm. People always say mean things about him behind his back, but he sees the best in them. He has too many enemies. His life may depend on you…'

'Really?' asked Lakshman, his eyes widening with barely-understood dread.

'Yes! And believe me, I can only count on you to protect him. Ram has a good heart, but he's too trusting of others.'

'Don't worry, *Maa*,' said Lakshman, stiffening his back and pursing his lips, his eyes gleaming like a soldier honoured with a most important undertaking. 'I will alway*th* take care of Ram *Dada*.'

Sumitra hugged Lakshman again and smiled fondly. 'I know you will.'

'*Dada*!' shouted Lakshman, banging his little heels against the pony's sides, willing it to run faster. But the pony, specially trained for children, refused to oblige.

Nine-year-old Ram rode ahead of Lakshman on a taller, faster pony. True to his training, he rose gracefully in his saddle at every alternate step of the canter, in perfect unison with the animal. On this vacant afternoon, they'd decided to practise by themselves the art of horsemanship, at the royal Ayodhya riding grounds.

'*Dada*! *Th*op!' screamed Lakshman desperately, having abandoned by now any pretence at following vaguely-learnt instructions. He kicked and whipped his pony to the best of his ability.

Ram looked back at the enthusiastic Lakshman and smiled as he cautioned his little brother, 'Lakshman, slow down. Ride properly.'

'*Th*op!' yelled Lakshman.

Ram immediately understood Lakshman's frantic cry and pulled his reins as Lakshman caught up and dismounted rapidly. '*Dada*, get off!'

'What?'

'Get off!' shouted an agitated Lakshman as he grabbed Ram's hand, trying to drag him down.

Ram frowned as he got off the horse. 'What is it, Lakshman?'

'Look!' Lakshman exclaimed, as he pointed at the billet strap that went through the buckle on the girth strap; the girth, in turn, kept the saddle in place. The buckle had almost come undone.

'By the great Lord Rudra!' whispered Ram. Had the buckle released while he was riding, he would have been thrown off the dislodged saddle, resulting in serious injury. Lakshman had saved him from a terrible accident.

Lakshman looked around furtively, his mother's words echoing in his brain. '*Th*omeone tried to kill you, *Dada*.'

Ram carefully examined the girth strap and the attached buckle. It simply looked worn out; there were no signs of tampering. Lakshman had certainly saved him from an injury, though, and possibly even death.

Ram embraced Lakshman gently. 'Thank you, my brother.'

'Don't worry about any con*th*pira*thieth*,' said Lakshman, wearing a solemn expression. He was now certain about his mother's warnings. 'I will protect you, *Dada*. Alway*th*.'

Ram tried hard to prevent himself from smiling. 'Conspiracies, huh? Who taught you such a big word?'

'*Th*atrughan,' said Lakshman, looking around again, scanning the area for threats.

'Shatrughan, *hmm*?'

'Ye*th*. Don't worry, *Dada*. Lakh*th*man will protect you.'

Ram kissed his brother's forehead and reassured his little protector. 'I feel safe already.'

— 大 🐟 ☼ —

The brothers were all set to go back to the *gurukul* two days after the horse saddle incident. Ram visited the royal stable the night before their departure to groom his horse; both of them had a long day ahead. There were stable hands, of course, but Ram enjoyed this work; it soothed him. The animals were among the handful in Ayodhya who did not judge him. He liked to spend time with them occasionally. He looked back at the sound of the clip-clop of hooves.

'Lakshman!' cried Ram in alarm, as little Lakshman trooped in atop his pony, obviously injured. Ram rushed forward and helped him dismount. Lakshman's chin had split open, deep enough to urgently need stitches. His face was covered with blood, but with typical bravado, he did not flinch at all when Ram examined his wound.

'You are not supposed to go horseback riding in the night, you know that, don't you?' Ram admonished him gently.

Lakshman shrugged. '*Th*orry... The hor*the th*uddenly...'

'Don't talk,' interrupted Ram, as the blood flow increased.

'Come with me.'

Ram hastily sped towards Nilanjana's chambers along with his injured brother. En route, they were accosted by Sumitra and her maids who had been frantically searching for her missing son.

'What happened?' shouted Sumitra, as her eyes fell upon the profusely bleeding Lakshman.

Lakshman stood stoic and tight-lipped. He knew he was in for trouble as his *dada* never lied; there was no scope for creative storytelling. He would have to confess, and then come up with strategies to escape the inevitable punishment.

'It's nothing serious, *Chhoti Maa*,' said Ram to his *younger stepmother*, Sumitra. 'But we should get him to Nilanja*ji* immediately.'

'What happened?' Sumitra persisted.

Ram instinctively felt compelled to protect Lakshman from his mother's wrath. After all, Lakshman had saved his life just the other day. He did what his conscience demanded at the time; shift the blame on himself. '*Chhoti Maa*, it's my fault. I'd gone to the stable with Lakshman to groom my horse. It's a little high-spirited and suddenly reared and kicked Lakshman. I should have ensured that Lakshman stood behind me.'

Sumitra immediately stepped aside. 'Quickly, take him to Nilanjana.'

She knows Ram Dada *never lies,* Lakshman thought, filled with guilt.

Ram and Lakshman rushed off, as a maid attempted to follow them. Sumitra raised her hand to stop her as she watched the boys moving down the corridor. Ram held his brother's hand firmly. She smiled with satisfaction.

Lakshman brought Ram's hand to his heart, and whispered, 'Together alway*th*, *Dada*. Alway*th*.'

'Don't talk, Lakshman. The blood will…'

—— 大 🐚 ☼ ——

The Ayodhyan princes had been in the *gurukul* for five years now. Vashishtha watched with pride as the eleven-year-old Ram practised with his full-grown opponent. Combat training had commenced for Ram and Bharat this year; Lakshman and Shatrughan would have to wait for two more years. For now, they had to remain content with lessons in philosophy, mathematics and science.

'Come on, *Dada*!' shouted Lakshman. 'Move in and hit him!'

Vashishtha observed Lakshman with an indulgent smile. He sometimes missed the cute lisp that Lakshman had now lost; but the eight-year-old had not lost his headstrong spirit. He also remained immensely loyal to Ram, whom he loved dearly. Perhaps Ram would eventually be able to channel Lakshman's wild streak.

The soft-spoken and intellect-oriented Shatrughan sat beside Lakshman, reading a palm-leaf manuscript of the *Isha Vasya Upanishad*. He read a Sanskrit verse.

'*Pushannekarshe yama surya praajaapatya vyuha rashmeen samuha tejah;*

Yatte roopam kalyaanatamam tatte pashyaami yo'saavasau purushah so'hamasmi.'

O Lord Surya, nurturing Son of Prajapati, solitary Traveller, celestial Controller; Diffuse Your rays, Diminish your light;

Let me see your gracious Self beyond the luminosity; And realise that the God in You is Me.

Shatrughan smiled to himself, lost in the philosophical beauty of the words. Bharat, who sat behind him, bent over and tapped Shatrughan on his head, then pointed at Ram. Shatrughan looked at Bharat, protest writ large in his eyes. Bharat glared at his younger brother. Shatrughan put his manuscript aside and looked at Ram.

The opposing swordsman Vashishtha had selected for Ram belonged to the forest people who lived close to Vashishtha's *gurukul*. It had been built deep in the untamed forests far south of the river Ganga, close to the western-most point of the course of the river Shon. The river took a sharp eastward turn thereafter, and flowed north-east to merge with the Ganga. This area had been used by many gurus for thousands of years. The forest people maintained the premises and gave it on rent to gurus.

The solitary approach to the *gurukul* was camouflaged first by dense foliage and then by the overhanging roots of a giant banyan. A small glade lay beyond, at the centre of which descending steps had been carved out of the earth, leading to a long, deep trench covered by vegetation. The trench then became a tunnel as it made its way under a steep hill. Light flooded the other end of this tunnel as it emerged at the banks of a stream which was spanned by a wooden bridge. Across lay the *gurukul*, a simple monolithic structure hewn into a rocky hillside.

The hill face had been neatly cut as though a huge, cube-shaped block of stone had been removed. Twenty small temples carved into the surface faced the entrance to the structure, some with deities in them, others empty. Six of these were adorned with an idol each of the previous Vishnus, one housed Lord Rudra, the previous Mahadev, and in yet another sat Lord Brahma, the brilliant scientist. The king of the *Devas*, the *Gods*, Lord Indra, who was also the God of Thunder and the Sky, occupied his rightful place in the central temple, surrounded by the other Gods. Of the two rock surfaces that faced each other, one had been cut to comprise the kitchen and store rooms, and the other, alcove-like sleeping quarters for the guru and his students.

Within the *ashram*, the princes of Ayodhya lived not as nobility, but as children of working-class parents; their royal background, in fact, was not public knowledge at the *gurukul*. In keeping with tradition, the princes had been accorded *gurukul* names: Ram was called Sudas, Bharat became Vasu, Lakshman was Paurav, and Shatrughan, Nalatardak. All reminders of their royal lineage were proscribed. Over and above their academic pursuits, they cleaned the *gurukul*, cooked food and served the guru. Scholastic mastery would help them achieve their life goals; the other activities would ingrain humility, with which they'd choose the *right* life goals.

'Looks like you're warmed up, Sudas,' Vashishtha addressed Ram, one of his two star pupils. The guru then turned to the chief of the tribe, who sat beside him. 'Chief Varun, time to see some combat?'

The local people, besides being good hosts, were also brilliant warriors. Vashishtha had hired their services to help train his wards in the fine art of warfare. They also served as combat opponents during examination, like right now.

Varun addressed the tribal warrior who had been practising with Ram. 'Matsya…'

Matsya and Ram immediately turned to the spectator stand and bowed to Vashishtha and Varun. They walked over to the edge of the platform, picked up a paintbrush broom each, dipped it in a paint can filled with red dye, and painted the sides and tips of their wooden practice swords. It would leave marks on the body when struck, thus indicating how lethal the strike was.

Ram stepped on the platform and moved to the centre, followed by Matsya. Face-to-face, they bowed low with respect for their opponent.

'Truth. Duty. Honour,' said Ram, repeating a slogan he'd heard from his guru, Vashishtha, which had made a deep impact on him.

Matsya, almost a foot taller than the boy, smiled. 'Victory at all costs.'

Ram took position: his back erect, his body turned sideways, his eyes looking over his right shoulder, just as Guru Vashishtha had trained him to do. This position exposed the least amount of his body surface to his opponent. His breathing was steady and relaxed, just as he had been taught. His left hand held firmly by his side, extended a little away from the body to maintain balance. His sword hand was extended out, a few degrees above the horizontal position, bended slightly at the elbow. He adjusted his arm position till the weight of the sword was borne by his trapezius and triceps muscles. His knees were bent and his weight was on the ball of his feet, affording quick movement in any direction. Matsya was impressed. This young boy followed every rule to perfection.

The remarkable feature in the young boy was his eyes. With steely focus, they were fixed on those of his opponent, Matsya. *Guru Vashishtha has taught the boy well. The eye moves before the hand does.*

Matsya's eyes fractionally widened. Ram knew an attack

was imminent. Matsya lunged forward and thrust his sword at Ram's chest, using his superior reach. It could have been a kill-wound, but Ram shifted swiftly to his right, avoiding the blow as he flicked his right hand forward, nicking Matsya's neck.

Matsya stepped back immediately.

'Why didn't you slash hard, *Dada*!' screamed Lakshman. 'That should have been a kill-wound!'

Matsya smiled appreciatively. He understood what Lakshman hadn't. Ram was probing him. Being a cautious fighter, he would move into kill strikes only after he knew his opponent's psyche. Ram didn't respond to Matsya's smile of approval. His eyes remained focused, his breathing normal. He had to discern his opponent's weaknesses. Waiting for the kill.

Matsya charged at him aggressively, bringing in his sword with force from the right. Ram stepped back and fended off the blow with as much strength as his smaller frame could muster. Matsya bent towards the right and brought in his sword from Ram's left now, belligerently swinging in close to the boy's head. Ram stepped back again, raising his sword up to block. Matsya kept moving forward, striking repeatedly, hoping to pin Ram against the wall and then deliver a kill-wound. Ram kept retreating as he fended off the blows. Suddenly he jumped to the right, avoiding Matsya's slash and in the same smooth movement, swung hard, hitting Matsya on the arm, leaving a splash of red paint. It was a 'wound' again, but not the one that would finally stop the duel.

Matsya stepped back without losing eye contact with Ram. *Perhaps he's too cautious.*

'Don't you have the guts to charge?'

Ram didn't respond. He took position once again, bending his knees a little, keeping his left hand lightly on his hips with the right hand extended out, his sword held steady.

'You cannot win the game if you don't play the game,' teased Matsya. 'Are you simply trying to avoid losing or do you actually want to win?'

Ram remained calm, focused and steady. Silent. He was conserving his energy.

This kid is unflappable, Matsya mused. He charged once again, repeatedly striking from above, using his height to try and knock Ram down. Ram bent sideways as he parried, stepping backwards steadily.

Vashishtha smiled for he knew what Ram was attempting.

Matsya did not notice the small rocky outcrop that Ram smoothly sidestepped as he slowly moved backwards. Within moments, Matsya stumbled and lost his balance. Not wasting a moment, Ram went down on one knee and struck hard, right across the groin of the tribal warrior. A kill-wound!

Matsya looked down at the red paint smeared across his groin. The wooden sword had not drawn blood but had caused tremendous pain; he was too proud to let it show.

Impressed by the young student, Matsya stepped forward and patted Ram on his shoulder. 'One must check the layout of the battlefield before a fight; know every nook and cranny. You remembered this basic rule. I didn't. Well done, my boy.'

Ram put the sword down, clasped his right elbow with his left hand and touched his forehead with the clenched right fist, in the traditional salute typical of the tribe of Matsya, showing respect to the *noble* forest-dweller. 'It was an honour to battle with you, great *Arya.*'

Matsya smiled and folded his hands into a namaste. 'No, young man, the honour was mine. I look forward to seeing what you do with your life.'

Varun turned to Vashishtha. 'You have a good student here, Guru*ji*. Not only is he a fine swordsman, he is also noble in his conduct. Who is he?'

Vashishtha smiled. 'You know I'm not going to reveal that, Chief.'

Meanwhile, Matsya and Ram had walked to the edge of the platform. They chucked their swords into a water tank, allowing the paint to wash off. The swords would then be dried, oiled and hammered, ready to be used again.

Varun turned to another warrior of his tribe. 'Gouda, you are next.'

Vashishtha signalled Bharat, addressing him by his *gurukul* name. 'Vasu!'

Gouda touched the ground with reverence, seeking its blessings before stepping onto the platform. Bharat did no such thing. He simply sprang up and sprinted towards the box that contained the swords. He'd marked a sword for himself already; the longest. It negated the advantage of reach that his opponent, a fully grown man, had.

Gouda smiled indulgently; his opponent was a child after all. The warrior picked up a wooden sword and marched to the centre, surprised to not find Bharat there. The intrepid child was already at the far end of the platform where the red dye and paintbrush brooms were stored. He was painting the edges and point of his sword.

'No practice?' asked a surprised Gouda.

Bharat turned around. 'Let's not waste time.'

Gouda raised his eyebrows in amusement; he walked up and painted his sword edges as well.

The combatants walked to the centre of the platform.

Keeping with tradition, they bowed to each other. Gouda waited for Bharat to state his personal credo, expecting a repeat of that of his elder brother's.

'Live free or die,' said Bharat, thumping his chest with gusto.

Gouda couldn't contain himself now, and burst into laughter. 'Live free or die? *That* is your slogan?'

Bharat glared at him with unvarnished hostility. Still smiling broadly, the tribal warrior bowed his head and announced his credo. 'Victory at all costs.'

Gouda was again taken aback, now by Bharat's stance. Unlike his brother, he faced his enemy boldly, offering his entire body as target. His sword arm remained casually by his side, his weapon held loose. He wore a look of utter defiance.

'Aren't you going to take position?' asked Gouda, worried now that he might actually injure this reckless boy.

'I am always battle ready,' whispered Bharat, smiling with nonchalance.

Gouda shrugged and got into position.

Bharat waited for Gouda to make the first move as he observed the tribal warrior lazily.

Gouda suddenly lunged forward and thrust his sword into Bharat's abdomen. Bharat smoothly twirled around and brought his sword in from a height, landing a sharp blow at Gouda's right shoulder. Gouda smiled and retreated, careful not to reveal any pain.

'I could have disembowelled you,' said Gouda, drawing the boy's attention to the red mark smeared across his abdomen.

'Your arm would be lying on the floor before that,' said Bharat, pointing at the red mark his wooden sword had made on Gouda's shoulder.

Gouda laughed and charged in again. To his surprise, Bharat

suddenly leapt high to his right, bringing his sword down from a height once again. It was an exquisite manoeuvre. Gouda could not have parried that strike from such height, especially since the attack was not on the side of the sword-arm. It could only have been blocked by a shield. However, Bharat was not tall enough to successfully pull off this ingenious manoeuvre. Gouda leaned back and struck hard, using his superior reach.

Gouda's sword brutally hit the airborne Bharat's chest, throwing him backwards. Bharat fell on his back, a kill-wound clearly marking his chest, right where his heart lay encased within.

Bharat immediately got back on his feet. The blood capillaries below the skin had burst, forming a red blotch on his bare chest. Even with a wooden sword, the blow must have hurt. To Gouda's admiration, Bharat disregarded the pain. He stood his ground, staring defiantly at his opponent.

'That was a good move,' said Gouda. 'I haven't seen it before. But you need to be taller to pull it off.'

Bharat glared at Gouda, his eyes flashing with anger. 'I will be taller one day. We will fight again.'

Gouda smiled. 'We certainly will, boy. I look forward to it.'

Varun turned to Vashishtha. 'Guru*ji*, both are talented. I can't wait for them to grow up.'

Vashishtha smiled with satisfaction. 'Neither can I.'

——— 大 🐟 ☀ ———

Dusk had fallen as a contemplative Ram sat by the stream, which flowed a little away from the *ashram*. Spotting him from a distance as he set out for his evening walk, the guru walked up to his student.

Hearing the quick footsteps of his guru, Ram rose

immediately with a namaste. 'Guru*ji.*'

'Sit, sit,' said Vashishtha, and then lowered himself beside Ram. 'What are you thinking about?'

'I was wondering why you did not reveal our identity to Chief Varun,' said Ram. 'He seems like a good man. Why do we withhold the truth from him? Why do we lie?'

'Withholding the truth is different from lying!' Vashishtha remarked with a twinkle in his eye.

'Not revealing the truth is lying, isn't it, Guru*ji*?'

'No, it isn't. Sometimes, truth causes pain and suffering. At such times, silence is preferred. In fact, there may be times when a white lie, or even an outright lie, could actually lead to a good outcome.'

'But lying has consequences, Guru*ji*. It's bad karma.'

'Sometimes, the truth may also have consequences that are bad. Lying may save someone's life. Lying may bring one into a position of authority, which in turn may result in an opportunity to do good. Would you still advocate not lying? It may well be said that a true leader loves his people more than he loves his own soul. There would be no doubt in the mind of such a leader. He would lie for the good of his people.'

Ram frowned. 'But Guru*ji*, people who compel their leaders to lie aren't worth fighting for…'

'That's simplistic, Ram. You lied for Lakshman once, didn't you?'

'It was instinct. I felt I had to protect him. But I've always felt uneasy about it. That's the reason why I needed to talk to you about it, Guru*ji*.'

'And, I am repeating what I said then. You needn't feel guilty. Wisdom lies in moderation, in balance. If you lie to save an innocent person from some bandits, is that wrong?'

'One odd example, out of context, doesn't justify lying,

Guru*ji*,' Ram wouldn't give up. 'Mother lied once to save me from Father's anger; Father soon discovered the truth. There was a time when he would visit my mother regularly. But after that incident, he stopped seeing her completely. He cut her off.'

The guru observed his student with sadness. *Truth be told, Emperor Dashrath blamed Ram for his defeat at the hands of Raavan. He would have found some excuse or the other to stop visiting Kaushalya, regardless of the incident.*

Vashishtha measured his words carefully. 'I am not suggesting that lying is good. But sometimes, just like a tiny dose of a poison can prove medicinal, a small lie may actually help. Your habit of speaking the truth is good. But what is your reason for it? Is it because you believe it's the lawful thing to do? Or, is it because this incident has made you fear lying?'

Ram remained silent, almost thoughtful.

'Now, I am sure you are wondering what this has to do with Chief Varun.'

'Yes, Guru*ji*.'

'Do you remember our visit to the chief's village?'

'Of course, I do.'

The boys had once accompanied their guru to Varun's village. With a population of fifty thousand, it was practically a small town. The princes were enchanted by what they saw. Streets were laid out in a semi-urban, well-organised living area in the form of a square grid. The houses were made of bamboo, but were strong and sturdy; they were exactly the same, from the chief's to the ordinary villager's. Houses were without doors, each with an open entrance, simply because there was no crime. The children were raised communally by the elders, not just by their own parents.

During their visit, the princes had had a most interesting

conversation with an assistant to the chief. They had wanted to know who the houses belonged to: the individual living in that unit, or to the chief, or to the community as a whole. The assistant had answered with the most quizzical response: *'How can the land belong to any of us? We belong to the land!'*

'What did you think about the village?' asked Vashishtha, bringing Ram back to the present.

'What a wonderful way to live. They lead a more civilised life than we city-dwellers do. We could learn so much from them.'

'Hmm, and what do you think is the foundation of their way of life? Why is Chief Varun's village so idyllic? Why have they not changed for centuries?'

'They live selflessly for each other, Guru*ji*. They don't have a grain of selfishness in them.'

Vashishtha shook his head. 'No, Sudas, it is because at the heart of their society are simple laws. These laws can never be broken, and must be followed, come what may.'

Ram's eyes opened wide, like he had discovered the secret to life. 'Laws…'

'Yes, Ram. Laws! Laws are the foundation on which a fulfilling life is built for a community. Laws are the answer.'

'Laws…'

'One might believe that there's no harm in occasionally breaking a minor law, right? Especially if it's for the Greater Good? Truth be told, I too have occasionally broken some rules for a laudable purpose. But Chief Varun thinks differently. Their commitment to the law is not based on traditions alone. Or the conviction that it is the right thing to do. It's based on one of the most powerful impressions in a human being: the childhood memory of guilt. The first time a child breaks a law in their society, however minor and inconsequential it may be, he's made to suffer; every child. Any recurrent breach of the law results in further shaming. Just like you find it difficult to lie even when it benefits someone because of what your mother suffered, Varun finds it impossible to do the same.'

'So, not revealing our identity is in some way linked to their laws? Will knowing who we are mean that they're breaking their laws?'

'Yes!'

'What law?'

'Their law prevents them from coming to the aid of the Ayodhya royalty. I don't know why. I'm not sure if even they know why. But this law has held for centuries. It serves no purpose now but they follow it strictly. They don't know where I'm from; I sometimes think they do not want to know. All they know is that my name is Vashishtha.'

Ram seemed troubled. 'Are we safe here?'

'They are duty-bound to protect those who are accepted into this *gurukul*. That is also their law. Now that they've accepted us, they cannot harm us. However, they might expel us if they discover who the four of you are. We're safe here, though, from other more powerful enemies who are a threat to our cause.'

Ram fell into deep contemplation.

'So, I haven't lied, Sudas. I've just not revealed the truth. There's a difference.'

Chapter 6

Dawn broke over the *gurukul* at the fifth hour of the first *prahar*, to the chirping of birds. Even as the nocturnal forest creatures returned to their daytime shelters, others emerged to face the rigours of another day. The four Ayodhyan princes though, had been up and about for a while. Having swept the *gurukul*, they had bathed, cooked and completed their morning prayers. Hands folded in respect, they sat composed and cross-legged in a semi-circle around Guru Vashishtha. The teacher himself sat in *padmaasan*, the *lotus position*, on a raised platform under a large banyan tree.

In keeping with tradition, they were reciting the *Guru Stotram*, the *hymn in praise of the teacher*, before the class commenced.

As the hymn ended, the students rose and ceremoniously touched the feet of their guru, Vashishtha. He gave them all the same blessing: 'May my knowledge grow within you, and may you, one day, become my teacher.'

Ram, Bharat, Lakshman and Shatrughan took their allotted seats. Thirteen years had passed since the terrible battle with Raavan. Ram was thirteen years old, and both Bharat and he were showing signs of adolescence. Their voices had begun to break and drop in pitch. Faint signs of moustaches had made an appearance on their upper lips. They'd suddenly shot up in height, even as their boyish bodies had begun to develop lean muscle.

Lakshman and Shatrughan had now begun combat practice, though their pre-adolescent bodies made fighting a little difficult for them. They'd all learnt the basics of philosophy, science and mathematics. They had mastered the divine language, Sanskrit. The ground work had been done. The guru knew it was time to sow the seed.

'Do you know the origins of our civilisation?' asked Vashishtha.

Lakshman, always eager to answer but not well read, raised his hand and began to speak. 'The universe itself began with—'

'No, Paurav,' said Vashishtha, using Lakshman's *gurukul* name. 'My question was not about the universe but about us, the Vedic people of this *yug*.'

Ram and Bharat turned to Shatrughan in unison.

'Guru*ji*,' began Shatrughan, 'it goes back to Lord Manu, a prince of the Pandya dynasty, thousands of years ago.'

'Teacher's pet,' whispered Bharat, indulgently. While he teased Shatrughan mercilessly for his bookish ways, he appreciated the fearsome intellect of his youngest brother.

Vashishtha looked at Bharat. 'Do you have something to add?'

'No, Guru*ji*,' said Bharat, immediately contrite.

'Yes, Nalatardak,' said Vashishtha, turning his attention back to Shatrughan and using his *gurukul* name. 'Please continue.'

'It is believed that thousands of years ago, swathes of land were covered in great sheets of ice. Since large quantities of water were frozen in solid form, sea levels were a lot lower than they are today.'

'You are correct,' said Vashishtha, 'except for one point. It is not a belief, Nalatardak. The "Ice Age" is not a theory. It is fact.'

'Yes, Guru*ji*,' said Shatrughan. 'Since sea levels were a lot lower, the Indian landmass extended a lot farther into the sea. The island of Lanka, the demon-king Raavan's kingdom, was joined to the Indian landmass. Gujarat and Konkan also reached out into the sea.'

'And?'

'And, I believe, there were—'

Shatrughan stopped short as Vashishtha cast him a stern look. He smiled and folded his hands into a namaste. 'My apologies, Guru*ji*. Not belief, but fact.'

Vashishtha smiled.

'Two great civilisations existed in India during the Ice Age. One in south-eastern India called the Sangamtamil, which included a small portion of the Lankan landmass, along with large tracts of land that are now underwater. The course of the river Kaveri was much broader and longer at the time. This rich and powerful empire was ruled by the Pandya dynasty.'

'And?'

'The other civilisation, Dwarka, spread across large parts of the landmass, off the coast of modern Gujarat and Konkan. It now lies submerged. It was ruled by the Yadav dynasty, the descendants of Yadu.'

'Carry on.'

'Sea levels rose dramatically at the end of the Ice Age. The Sangamtamil and Dwarka civilisations were destroyed, their heartland now lying under the sea. The survivors, led by Lord Manu, the father of our nation, escaped up north and began life once again. They called themselves the people of *vidya*, *knowledge*; the Vedic people. We are their proud descendants.'

'Very good, Nalatardak,' said Vashishtha. 'Just one more point. The Ice Age came to an abrupt end in the time-scale that Mother Earth operates in. But in human terms, it wasn't abrupt at all. We had decades, even centuries, of warning. And yet, we did nothing.'

The children listened with rapt attention.

'Why did the Sangamtamil and Dwarka, clearly very advanced civilisations, not take timely corrective actions? Evidence suggests that they were aware of the impending calamity. Mother Earth had given them enough warning signs. They were intelligent enough to either possess or invent the technology required to save themselves. And yet, they did nothing. Only a few survived, under the able leadership of Lord Manu. Why?'

'They were lazy,' said Lakshman, as usual jumping to conclusions.

Vashishtha sighed. 'Paurav, if only you'd think before answering.'

A chagrined Lakshman fell silent.

'You have the ability to think, Paurav,' said Vashishtha, 'but you're always in a hurry. Remember, it's more important to be right than to be first.'

'Yes, Guru*ji*,' said Lakshman, his eyes downcast. But he raised his hand again. 'Were the people debauched and careless?'

'Now you're guessing, Paurav. Don't try to pry open the door with your fingernails. Use the key.'

Lakshman seemed nonplussed.

'Do not rush to the "right answer",' clarified Vashishtha. 'The key, always, is to ask the "right question".'

'Guru*ji*,' said Ram. 'May I ask a question?'

'Of course, Sudas,' said Vashishtha.

'You said earlier that they had decades, even centuries of warning. I assume their scientists had decoded these warnings?'

'Yes, they had.'

'And had they communicated these warnings to everyone, including the royalty?'

'Yes, they had.'

'Was Lord Manu the Pandyan king or a prince, at the time? I have heard conflicting accounts.'

Vashishtha smiled approvingly. 'Lord Manu was one of the younger princes.'

'And yet, it was he and not the king who saved his people.'

'Yes.'

'If anyone other than the king was required to lead the people to safety, then the answer is obvious. The king wasn't doing his job. Bad leadership, then, was responsible for the downfall of Sangamtamil and Dwarka.'

'Do you think a bad king is also a bad man?' asked Vashishtha.

'No,' said Bharat. 'Even honourable men sometimes prove to be terrible leaders. Conversely, men of questionable character can occasionally be exactly what a nation requires.'

'Absolutely! A king need be judged solely on the basis of what he achieves for his people. His personal life is of no consequence. His public life, though, has one singular purpose: to provide for his people and improve their lives.'

'True,' said Bharat.

Vashishtha took a deep breath. The time was ripe. 'So, does that make Raavan a good king for his people?'

There was stunned silence.

Ram wouldn't answer. He hated Raavan viscerally. Not only had the Lankan devastated Ayodhya, he had also ruined Ram's future. His birth was permanently associated with the 'taint' of Raavan's victory. No matter what he did, Ram would always remain inauspicious for his father and the people of Ayodhya.

Bharat finally spoke. 'We may not want to admit it, but

Raavan is a good king, loved by his people. He is an able administrator who has brought prosperity through maritime trade, and he even runs the seaports under his control efficiently. It is fabled that the streets of his capital are paved with gold, thus earning his kingdom the name "Golden Lanka". Yes, he is a good king.'

'And what would you say about a very good man, a king, who has fallen into depression? He has converted his personal loss to that of his people. They suffer because he does. Is he, then, a good king?'

It was obvious whom Vashishtha was referring to. The students were quiet for a long time, afraid to answer.

It had to be Bharat who raised his hand. 'No, he is not a good king.'

Vashishtha nodded. *Trust the boldness of a born rebel.*

'That's it for today,' Vashishtha brought the class to an abrupt end, leaving a lot unsaid. 'As always, your homework is to mull over our discussion.'

— |太| 🐟 ☼ —

'My turn, *Dada,*' whispered Bharat as he softly tapped Ram's shoulder.

Ram immediately tied his pouch to his waistband. 'Sorry.'

Bharat turned to the injured rabbit lying on the ground. He first anesthetised the animal and then quickly pulled out the splinter of wood buried in its paw. The wound was almost septic, but the medicine he applied would prevent further infection. The animal would awaken a few minutes later, on the road to recovery, if not immediately ready to face the world.

As Bharat cleaned his hands with medicinal herbs, Ram gently picked up the rabbit and wedged it into a nook in a tree to keep it away from predators. He glanced at Bharat. 'It will wake up soon. It'll live.'

Bharat smiled. 'By the grace of Lord Rudra.'

Ram, Bharat, Lakshman and Shatrughan were on one of their fortnightly expeditions into the jungle, where they tended to injured animals. They did not interfere in a predator's hunt; it was only its natural behaviour. But, if they came upon an injured animal, they assisted it to the best of their abilities.

'*Dada*,' said Shatrughan, standing at a distance, watching his elder brothers with keen concentration.

Ram and Bharat turned around. A dishevelled Lakshman was even farther away, behind Shatrughan. He was distractedly throwing stones at a tree.

'Lakshman, don't linger at the back,' said Ram. 'We are not in the *ashram*. This is the jungle. There is danger in being alone.'

Lakshman sighed in irritation and walked up to the group.

'Yes, what is it, Shatrughan?' asked Ram, turning to his youngest brother.

'Bharat *Dada* put *jatyadi tel* on the rabbit's wound. Unless you cover it with neem leaves, the medicine will not be effective.'

'Of course,' exclaimed Ram, tapping his forehead. 'You're right, Shatrughan.'

Ram picked up the rabbit as Bharat pulled out some neem leaves from his leather pouch.

Bharat looked at Shatrughan, grinning broadly. 'Is there anything in the world that you do not know, Shatrughan?'

Shatrughan smiled. 'Not much.'

Bharat applied the neem leaves on the rabbit's wound, tied the bandage again, and placed him back in the nook.

Ram said, 'I wonder if we actually help these animals on our bi-weekly medical tour or are we just assuaging our conscience?'

'We are assuaging our conscience,' said Bharat, with a

wry smile. 'Nothing more, but at least we aren't ignoring our conscience.'

Ram shook his head. 'Why are you so cynical?'

'Why are you not cynical at all?'

Ram raised his eyebrows resignedly and began to walk. Bharat caught up with him. Lakshman and Shatrughan fell in line, a few steps behind.

'Knowing the human race, how can you not be cynical?' Bharat asked.

'Come on,' said Ram. 'We're capable of greatness, Bharat. All we need is an inspirational leader.'

'*Dada*,' said Bharat, 'I'm not suggesting that there is no goodness in human beings. There is, and it is worth fighting for. But there is also so much viciousness that sometimes I think it would have been better for the planet if the human species simply did not exist.'

'That's too much! We're not so bad.'

Bharat laughed softly. 'All I'm suggesting is that greatness and goodness is a potential in a majority of humans, not a reality.'

'What do you mean?'

'Expecting people to follow rules just because they should is being too hopeful. Rules must be designed to dovetail with selfish interest because people are primarily driven by it. They need to be shepherded into good behaviour through this proclivity.'

'People also respond to calls for greatness.'

'No, they don't, *Dada*. There may be a few who will answer that call. Most won't.'

'Lord Rudra led people selflessly, didn't he?'

'Yes,' said Bharat. 'But many who followed him had their own selfish interests in mind. That is a fact.'

Ram shook his head. 'We'll never agree on this.'

Bharat smiled. 'Yes, we won't. But I still love you!'

Ram smiled as well, changing the topic. 'How was your holiday? I never get to speak with you when we are there…'

'You know why,' muttered Bharat. 'But I must admit it was not too bad this time.'

Bharat loved to have his maternal relatives visit Ayodhya. It was an opportunity for him to escape his stern mother. Kaikeyi did not like his spending too much time with his brothers. In fact, if she could have her way, she would keep him to herself exclusively during the times when they were home. To make matters worse, she would insist on endless conversations about the need for him to be great and fulfil his mother's destiny. The only people Kaikeyi did not mind sharing her son with were her own blood-family. The presence of his maternal grandparents and uncle on this holiday ensured that Bharat was free of his mother. He had spent practically the entire vacation in their indulgent company.

Ram punched Bharat playfully in his stomach. 'She's your mother, Bharat. She only wants what is best for you.'

'I could do with some love instead, *Dada.* You know, I remember when I was three, I once dropped a glass of milk and she slapped me! She slapped me so hard, in the presence of her maids.'

'You remember stuff from when you were three? I thought I was the only one who did.'

'How can I forget? I was a little boy. The glass was too big for my hands. It was heavy; it slipped! That's it! Why did she have to slap me?'

Ram understood his stepmother, Kaikeyi. She had her share of frustrations. She'd been the brightest child in her family. Unfortunately, her brilliance did not make her father proud. Quite the contrary, Ashwapati was unhappy that Kaikeyi outshone his son, Yudhaajit. It appalled Ram that society did not value capable women. And now, the intelligent yet frustrated Kaikeyi sought vicarious recognition through Bharat, her son. She aimed to realise her ambitions through him.

Ram held his counsel though.

Bharat continued, wistfully, 'If only I had a mother like yours. She would have loved me unconditionally and not chewed my brains.'

Ram did not respond, but he got the feeling that something was playing on Bharat's mind.

'What is it, Bharat?' asked Ram, without turning to look at his younger brother.

Bharat lowered his voice so that Lakshman and Shatrughan wouldn't overhear. 'Ram *Dada*, have you thought about what Guru*ji* said today?'

Ram held his breath.

'*Dada*?' asked Bharat.

Ram stiffened. 'This is treason. I refuse to entertain such thoughts.'

'Treason? To think about the good of your country?'

'He is our father! There are duties that we have—'

'Do you think he's a good king?' Bharat interrupted.

'There's a law in the *Manu Smriti* that clearly states a son must—'

'Don't tell me what the law says, *Dada*,' said Bharat, dismissing with a wave of his hand the laws recorded in the *Book of Manu*. 'I have read the *Manu Smriti* too. I want to know what *you* think.'

'I think the law must be obeyed.'

'Really? Is that all you have to say?'

'I can add to that.'

'Please do!'

'The law must *always* be obeyed.'

Bharat rolled his eyes in exasperation.

'I understand that this might not work under a few exceptional circumstances,' said Ram. 'But if the law is obeyed diligently, come what may, then over a period of time a better society *has* to emerge.'

'Nobody in Ayodhya gives two hoots about the law, *Dada*! We are a civilisation in an advanced state of decay. We're the most hypocritical people on earth. We criticise corruption in others, but are blind to our own dishonesty. We hate others who do wrong and commit crimes, blithely ignoring our own misdeeds, big and small. We vehemently blame Raavan for all our ills, refusing to acknowledge that we created the mess we find ourselves in.'

'And how will this change?'

'This attitude is basic human nature. We'd rather look outward and blame others for the ills that befall us than point the finger at ourselves. I've said it before and I'll say it again. We need a king who can create systems with which one can harness even selfish human nature for the betterment of society.'

'*Nonsense.* We need a great leader, one who will lead by example. A leader who will inspire his people to discover their godhood within! We don't need a leader who will leave his people free to do whatever they desire.'

'No, *Dada*. Freedom is an ally, if used with wisdom.'

'Freedom is never the ally of the law. You can have freedom to choose whether you want to join or leave a society based on the rule of law. But so long as you live in such a society, you must obey the law.'

'The law is and always will be an ass. It's a tool, a means to an end,' said Bharat.

Ram brought the exchange to an end with a convivial laugh. Bharat grinned and patted his brother on his back.

'So, all these things you say about a great leader being inspirational and enabling the discovery of the God within and other such noble things…' said Bharat. 'You think Father lives up to that ideal?'

Ram cast a reproachful look at his brother, refusing to rise to the bait.

Bharat grinned, playfully boxing Ram on his shoulder. 'Let it be, *Dada*. Let it be.'

Ram was genuinely conflicted. But, as a dutiful son, he would not allow himself, even in his own mind, to entertain rebellious thoughts against his father.

Lakshman, walking a few steps behind, was engrossed in the frenetic activities of the jungle.

Shatrughan, however, was listening in on the conversation with keen interest. *Ram* Dada *is too idealistic. Bharat* Dada *is practical and real.*

Chapter 7

Another one? Ram refrained from voicing his thoughts, trying to control his surprise. *This is his fifth girlfriend.*

Seventeen years had gone by since Dashrath lost the Battle of Karachapa. At the age of sixteen, Bharat had discovered the pleasures of love. Charismatic and flamboyant as he was, girls liked Bharat as much as he liked them. Tribal traditions being liberal, the empowered women of the tribe of Chief Varun, the local hosts of the *gurukul*, were free to form relationships with whomever they pleased. And Bharat was especially popular.

He walked up to Ram now, holding hands with an ethereally beautiful maiden who was clearly older than him, perhaps twenty years of age.

'How are you, Vasu?' asked Ram, using Bharat's gurukul name as there was an outsider present.

'Never been better, *Dada*,' grinned Bharat. 'Any better and it would be downright sinful.'

Ram smiled politely and turned to the girl with grace.

'*Dada*,' said Bharat, 'allow me to introduce Radhika, the daughter of Chief Varun.'

'Honoured to make your acquaintance,' said Ram, formally bringing his hands together in a polite namaste and bowing his head.

Radhika raised her eyebrows, amused. 'Vasu was right. You are ridiculously formal.'

Ram's eyes widened at her forthrightness.

'I did not use the word "ridiculous",' protested Bharat, as he let her hand go. 'How can I use a word like that for *Dada*?'

Radhika ruffled Bharat's hair affectionately. 'All right, "ridiculous" was my own addition. But I find your formality charming. So does Vasu, actually. But I'm sure you know that already.'

'Thank you,' said Ram, straightening his *angvastram* stiffly.

Radhika giggled at Ram's obvious discomfort. Even Ram, relatively immune to feminine wiles, was forced to acknowledge that her laughter had a pleasing lilt, like that of the *apsaras, celestial nymphs*.

Ram said to Bharat, careful to speak in old Sanskrit so that Radhika wouldn't understand, '*Saa Vartate Lavanyavati.*'

Though Bharat's understanding of archaic Sanskrit was not as good as Ram's, he understood the simple compliment. Ram had said, '*She is exquisitely beautiful.*'

Before Bharat could respond, Radhika spoke. '*Aham Jaanaami.*'

'*I know.*'

An embarrassed Ram retorted, 'By the great Lord Brahma! Your old Sanskrit is perfect.'

Radhika smiled. 'We may speak new Sanskrit these days, but the ancient scriptures can only be understood in the old language.'

Bharat felt the need to cut in. 'Don't be fooled by her intelligence, *Dada*. She is also very beautiful!'

Ram smiled and brought his hands together once again, in a respectful namaste. 'My apologies if I offended you in any way, Radhika.'

Radhika smiled, shaking her head. 'No, you didn't. Why would a girl not enjoy an elegant compliment to her beauty?'

'My little brother is lucky.'

'I'm not so unlucky myself,' assured Radhika, ruffling Bharat's hair once again.

Ram could see that his brother was besotted. Clearly, this time it was different; Radhika meant a lot more to him than his previous girlfriends. But he was also aware of the traditions of the forest people. Their girls, no doubt, were liberated, but they did not marry outside their community. Their law simply forbade it. Ram did not understand the reason for this. It could be an effort to retain the sense of purity of the forest people, or it might even be that they considered city dwellers inferior for having moved away from Mother Nature. He hoped his brother's heart would not be broken in the process.

'How much butter will you eat?!' Ram could never quite understand Bharat's addiction.

Evening time, the last hour of the third *prahar,* found Ram and Bharat relaxing under a tree at the *gurukul.* Lakshman and Shatrughan were using their free time for some riding practice; in fact, they were competing fiercely in the open ground. Lakshman, by far the best rider among the four, was beating Shatrughan hollow.

'I like it, *Dada,*' shrugged Bharat, butter smeared around his mouth.

'But it's unhealthy. It's fattening!'

Bharat flexed his biceps as he sucked in his breath and puffed up his chest, displaying his muscular and well-toned physique. 'Do I look fat to you?'

Ram smiled. 'Girls certainly do not find you unappealing. So my opinion really is of no consequence.'

'Exactly!' Bharat chuckled, digging his hand into the clay pot and spooning some more butter into his mouth.

Ram gently put his hand on Bharat's shoulder. Bharat stopped eating as he read the concerned look on his brother's face.

Ram spoke softly. 'Bharat, you do know—'

Bharat interrupted him immediately. 'It won't happen, *Dada*.'

'But Bharat…'

'*Dada*, trust me. I know girls better than you do.'

'You're aware that Chief Varun's people do not…'

'*Dada*, she loves me as much as I love her. Radhika will break the law for me. She will not leave me. Trust me.'

'How can you be so sure?'

'*I am!*'

'But Bharat…'

'*Dada*, stop worrying about me. Just be happy for me.'

Ram gave up and patted him on his shoulder. 'Well then, congratulations!'

Bharat bowed his head theatrically, 'Thank you, kind sir!'

Ram's face broke into a broad smile.

'When will I get the opportunity to congratulate *you*, *Dada*?' asked Bharat.

Ram looked at Bharat and frowned.

'Aren't you attracted to any girl? Here or in Ayodhya? We have met so many on our annual holidays…'

'Nobody is worth it.'

'Nobody?'

'No.'

'What are you looking for?'

Ram looked into the distance at the forest line. 'I want a woman, not a girl.'

'Aha! I always knew there was a naughty devil behind that serious exterior!'

Ram rolled his eyes and punched Bharat playfully on his abdomen. 'That's not what I meant. You know that.'

'Then what did you mean?'

'I don't want an immature girl. Love is secondary. It's not important. I want someone whom I can respect.'

'Respect?' frowned Bharat. 'Sounds boring.'

'A relationship is not just for fun, it is also about trust and the knowledge that you can depend on your partner. Relationships based on passion and excitement do not last.'

'Really?'

Ram quickly corrected himself. 'Of course, Radhika and you will be different.'

'Of course,' grinned Bharat.

'I guess what I'm trying to say is that I want a woman who is better than I am; a woman who will compel me to bow my head in admiration.'

'You bow to elders and parents, *Dada*. A wife is the one you share your life and passions with,' said Bharat, a crooked grin on his face, brows arched suggestively. 'By the great Lord Brahma, I pity the woman you will marry. Your relationship will go down in history as the most boring of them all!'

Ram laughed aloud as he pushed Bharat playfully. Bharat dropped the pot and pushed Ram back, then sprang to his feet and sprinted away from Ram.

'You can't outrun me, Bharat!' laughed Ram, quickly rising to his feet and taking off after his brother.

'Whom do you favour?' asked the visitor.

A mysterious stranger had made a quiet entry into the *gurukul*. In keeping with Vashishtha's desire to maintain the secrecy of this visit, he'd arrived late in the night. As luck would have it, the intrepid Lakshman was out riding at the same time, having broken the rule of being in the sleeping quarters at this time of the night. As he traced his way back, he came upon an unknown horse tied discreetly to a tree far from the *ashram* premises.

He led his own animal quietly back into the stable. The Ayodhyan prince then decided to inform his guru of a possible intruder. On finding Vashishtha's room empty, Lakshman grew suspicious. Unable to contain himself, he decided to investigate the goings-on. He finally spotted the sage under the bridge, conversing softly with the mysterious visitor. Lakshman crept close, hid behind the bushes, and eavesdropped on the conversation. 'I haven't made up my mind as yet,' answered Vashishtha.

'You need to decide quickly, Guru*ji*.'

'Why?'

Though unable to see the visitor clearly, Lakshman was barely able to contain the panic rising within him. Even the failing light couldn't conceal the stranger's unnaturally fair skin, giant size and rippling musculature. His body was covered with fur-like hair, and a peculiar outgrowth emerged from his lower back. Clearly he was a dangerous Naga, the mysterious race of the deformed, which was feared in all of the Sapt Sindhu. He made no attempt to conceal his identity, like most Nagas did, with a face mask or a hooded robe. Notably, his lower body was draped in a *dhoti*, in keeping with traditional Indian custom.

'Because *they* are on to you,' said the Naga, with a meaningful look.

'So?'

'Are you not afraid?'

Vashishtha shrugged. 'Why should I be?'

The Naga laughed softly. 'There's a thin line that separates courage from stupidity.'

'And that line is only visible in retrospect, my friend. If I'm successful, people will call me brave. If I fail, I will be called foolish. Let me do what I think is right. I'll leave the verdict to the future.'

The Naga thrust his chin forward in a show of disagreement, but gave up the argument. 'What would you have me do?'

'Nothing for now. Just wait,' answered Vashishtha.

'Are you aware that Raavan is—'

'Yes, I know.'

'And you still choose to remain here and not do anything?'

'Raavan...' murmured Vashishtha, choosing his words carefully, 'well, he has his uses.'

Lakshman could barely control his shock. Yet, the teenager had the presence of mind to stay silent.

'There are some who are convinced you are preparing for a rebellion against Emperor Dashrath,' said the Naga, his tone clearly indicating his disbelief.

Vashishtha laughed softly. 'There is no need to rebel against him. The kingdom is practically out of his hands anyway. He's a good man, but he has sunk into the depths of depression and defeatism. My goal is bigger.'

'Our goal,' corrected the Naga.

'Of course,' smiled Vashishtha, patting him on his shoulder. 'Forgive me. It is our collective goal. But if people insist on thinking that our ambitions are limited to Ayodhya, I suggest we let them be.'

'Yes, that's true.'

'Come with me,' said Vashishtha. 'I have something to show you.'

Lakshman let out a deep breath as the two men walked away. His heart was pounding desperately.

What is Guruji up to? Are we safe here?

Checking carefully that the coast was clear, Lakshman slipped away and rushed to Ram's quarters.

— 大 🐟 ☼ —

'Lakshman, go back to sleep,' admonished an irritated Ram. He had been woken up by a hysterical Lakshman. He'd heard the panic-stricken report, and groggily decided that his brother was once again indulging his love for conspiracy.

'*Dada*, I'm telling you, there's something going on. It concerns Ayodhya, and Guru*ji* is involved,' insisted Lakshman.

'Have you told Bharat?'

'Of course not! He could be in on it too.'

Ram glared at Lakshman. 'He too is your *dada*, Lakshman!'

'*Dada*, you are too simple. You refuse to see the den of conspiracies that Ayodhya is. Guru*ji* is in on it. Others could be too. I trust only you. You are supposed to protect us all. I have done my duty by letting you know. Now, it is up to you to investigate this.'

'There is nothing to investigate, Lakshman. Go back to your room and sleep.'

'*Dada*…'

'Back to your room, Lakshman! Now!'

Chapter 8

'What is the ideal way of life?' asked Vashishtha.

In the early hours of the morning, the four Ayodhyan princes sat facing their guru, having just completed the *Guru Stotram*.

'Well?' prompted Vashishtha, having been met with silence.

He looked at Lakshman, expecting him to take the first shot. However, to Vashishtha's surprise, the boy sat tense, barely able to conceal his hostility.

'Is there a problem, Paurav?' enquired Vashishtha.

Lakshman cast an accusatory glance at Ram, then stared at the ground. 'No, Guru*ji*. There is no problem.'

'Do you want to attempt an answer?'

'I don't know the answer, Guru*ji*.'

Vashishtha frowned. Ignorance had never deterred Lakshman from attempting a response before. He spoke to Bharat. 'Vasu, can you try and answer?'

'An ideal way of life, Guru*ji*,' said Bharat, 'is one where everyone is healthy, wealthy, happy, and working in consonance with his purpose in life.'

'And, how does a society achieve this?'

'It's probably impossible! But if it were possible at all, it would only be through freedom. Allow people the freedom to forge their own path. They will find their way.'

'But will freedom help each person realise his dreams? What if one person's dream is in conflict with that of another's?'

Bharat gave that question some careful thought before replying. 'You are right. A strong man's effort will always overwhelm that of a weak man.'

'So?'

'So the government has to ensure that it protects the weak. We cannot allow the strong to keep winning. It would create discontent among the masses.'

'Why, *Dada*?' asked Shatrughan. 'I would say, allow the strong to win. Will that not be better for the society as a whole?'

'But isn't that the law of the jungle?' asked Vashishtha. 'The weak would die out.'

'If you call it the law of the jungle, then I say that this is the law of nature, Guru*ji*,' said Shatrughan. 'Who are we to judge nature? If the weakest deer are not killed by tigers, the population of deer will explode. They will eat prodigious amounts of greens and the jungle itself may die out, in the long run. It is better for the jungle if only the strong survive — it is nature's way of maintaining balance. The government should not interfere with this natural process. It should merely establish systems that ensure the protection of the weak, giving them a fair chance at survival. Beyond that, it must get out of the way and let society find its own path. It's not the government's job to ensure that all achieve their dreams.'

'Then why even bother with a government?'

'It's needed for a few essentials that individuals cannot provide: an army to protect the borders from external attack, a system of basic education for all. One of the things that differentiates us from animals is that we do not kill our weak. But if the government interferes to such an extent that the weak thrive and the strong are oppressed, society itself will collapse over time. A society should not forget that it thrives on the ideas and performance of the talented among its citizens. If you compromise the prospects of the strong, and lean too much towards the interests of the weak, then your society itself goes into decline.'

Vashishtha smiled. 'You have carefully studied the reasons for the decline of India under the successors of Emperor Bharat, haven't you?'

Shatrughan nodded. Bharat was a legendary Chandravanshi emperor who lived thousands of years ago. He was one of the greatest rulers since the great Indra of the Devas. He brought all of India under his rule and his government had been the most compassionate and nurturing of all times.

'Why, then, did Bharat's successors not change their ways when they could see that it wasn't working anymore?' asked Vashishtha.

'I don't know,' said Shatrughan.

'It was because the philosophy that guided Emperor Bharat's empire was itself a reaction to an equally successful, but radically different one which determined how society was organised earlier. Emperor Bharat's empire could be described as the apogee of the feminine way of life — of freedom, passion and beauty. At its best, it is compassionate, creative and especially nurturing towards the weak. But as feminine civilisations decline, they tend to become corrupt, irresponsible and decadent.'

'Guru*ji*,' said Ram, 'are you saying there is another way of life? The masculine way?'

'Yes. The masculine way of life is defined by truth, duty and honour. At its peak, masculine civilisations are efficient, just and egalitarian. But as they decline, they become fanatical, rigid and especially harsh towards the weak.'

'So when feminine civilisations decline, the masculine way is the answer,' said Ram. 'And, as masculine civilisations decline, the feminine way should take over.'

'Yes,' said the teacher. 'Life is cyclical.'

'Can it be safely said that today's India is a feminine nation in decline?' asked Bharat.

Vashishtha looked at Bharat. 'Actually, India is a confused nation today. It does not understand its nature, which seems to be a hotchpotch of the masculine and feminine way. But if you force me to choose, then I would state that, at this point in time, we're a feminine culture in decline.'

'Then the question is: is it time to move towards a masculine way of life or a revived feminine culture?' argued Bharat. 'I'm not sure India can live without freedom. We're a nation of rebels. We argue and fight about everything. We can only succeed by walking down the path of femininity, of freedom. The masculine way may work for a short span of time, but it cannot last. We are simply not obedient enough to follow the masculine way for too long.'

'So it seems today,' said Vashishtha. 'But it wasn't always so. There was a time when the masculine way of life characterised India.'

Bharat was silenced into contemplation.

But Ram was intrigued. 'Guru*ji*, you said that the feminine way of life established by Emperor Bharat was unable to change even when it needed to, because it was a reaction to the ills that an earlier masculine culture had degenerated into. Possibly, to them, the earlier way of life was stamped as evil.'

'You're right, Sudas,' said Vashishtha, using Ram's *gurukul* name.

'Can you tell us about this earlier masculine way of life? What was this empire like?' asked Ram. 'Could we find answers in it, to our present-day ills?'

'It was an empire that arose many millennia ago, and conquered practically all of India with stunning swiftness. It had a radically different way of life and, at its peak, it scaled the heights of greatness.'

'Who were these people?'

'Their foundations were laid right here, where we are. It was so long ago that most have forgotten the significance of this *ashram*.'

'Here?'

'Yes. It was here that the progenitors of that empire received their education from their great guru. He taught them the essentials of an enlightened masculine way of life. This was his *ashram*.'

'Who was this great sage?' asked Ram in awe.

Vashishtha took a deep breath. He knew that the answer would evoke shock. The name of that ancient *great rishi* was feared today; so much so that it was not even uttered aloud, ever. Keeping his eyes fixed on Ram, he answered, '*Maharishi* Shukracharya.'

Bharat, Lakshman and Shatrughan froze. Shukracharya was the guru of the Asuras, and the Asuras were demonic fanatics who had controlled almost the entire Indian landmass thousands of years ago. They were finally defeated by the *Devas*, respected today as *Gods*, in brutal battles fought over a protracted period of time. Although the Asura Empire was eventually destroyed, the wars took a heavy toll on India. Millions died, and rebuilding civilisation took a very long time. Indra, the leader of the Devas, ensured the expulsion of the Asuras from India. Shukracharya's name was reduced to mud, his memory violated by righteous indignation and irrational fear.

The students were too stunned to react. Ram's eyes, though, conveyed curiosity, unlike the others.

Vashishtha stepped out late in the night, expecting a tumult among his students; the conversation about Guru Shukracharya had been meant to provoke. Lakshman and Shatrughan were sound asleep in their rooms, but Ram and Bharat were missing. Vashishtha decided to walk around the premises in search of them, the moonlight providing adequate illumination. Hearing soft voices ahead, he soon came upon the silhouette of an animated Bharat in the company of a girl.

Bharat seemed to be pleading. 'But why…'

'I'm sorry, Vasu,' the girl said calmly. 'I will not break the laws of my people.'

'But I love you, Radhika … I know you love me… Why should we care about what others think?'

Vashishtha quickly turned around and began to walk in the other direction. It was inappropriate to intrude on a private and painful moment.

Where is Ram?

On a whim, he changed course once again and walked up the stone pathway that led to the small temples built into the central facade of the rock face. He entered the temple of Lord Indra, the king of the Devas; the one who defeated the Asuras. The symbolism of Indra's temple being in the centre was powerful, for Indra had led the army that obliterated Shukracharya's legacy.

Vashishtha heard a soft sound from behind the massive idol, and instinctively moved towards it. The space at the back was large enough to comfortably accommodate four or five people. The shadows of Vashishtha and the idol seemed to dance on the floor as flames leapt from a torch on the wall.

As his gaze travelled beyond the idol, he could vaguely make out the figure of Ram on his knees, prising open with a metal bar a heavy stone that covered an ancient inscription on the floor. Just as he succeeded, Ram sensed Vashishtha's presence.

'Guru*ji*,' said Ram, as he dropped the tool and stood up immediately.

Vashishtha walked up to him, put his arm around his shoulder and gently sat him down again as he bent down to examine the inscription that Ram had uncovered.

'Can you read what it says?' asked Vashishtha.

It was an ancient, long-forgotten script.

'I have not seen this script before,' said Ram.

'It is particularly ancient, banned in India because the Asuras used it.'

'The Asuras were the great masculine empire you mentioned today, isn't it?'

'That's obvious!'

Ram gestured towards the inscription. 'What does it say, Guru*ji*?'

Vashishtha ran his forefinger along the words of the inscription. '"How can the universe speak the name of Shukracharya? For the universe is so small. And Shukracharya is so big."'

Ram touched the inscription lightly.

'Legend holds that this was his *aasan*, the *seat* that he sat upon as he taught,' said Vashishtha.

Ram looked up at Vashishtha. 'Tell me about him, Guru*ji*.'

'A very small minority still maintains that he probably was

one of the greatest Indians that trod the earth. I don't know much about his childhood; apocryphal accounts suggest that he was born to a slave family in Egypt that abandoned him when he was but an infant. He was then adopted by a visiting Asura princess, who raised him as her own, in India. However, records of his works were deliberately obliterated and the ones that remained were heavily doctored by the powerful and wealthy elite of that time. He was a brilliant, charismatic soul who transformed marginalised Indian royals into the greatest conquering force of his time.'

'Marginalised *Indian* royals? But the Asuras were foreigners, weren't they?'

'Nonsense. This is propaganda spread by those with an agenda. Most Asuras were actually related to the Devas. In fact, the Devas and Asuras descended from common ancestors, known as the Manaskul. But the Asuras were the poorer, weaker cousins, scorned and half-forgotten members of an extended family. Shukracharya remoulded them with a powerful philosophy of hard work, discipline, unity and fierce loyalty for fellow Asuras.'

'But that would not add up to a recipe for victory and dominance. So how did they succeed so spectacularly?'

'The ones who hate them say they succeeded because they were barbaric warriors.'

'But you obviously disagree with them.'

'Well, the Devas weren't cowards either. It was the Age of Kshatriya, warrior-like qualities were highly sought after. They were probably as good as the Asuras in the art of warfare, if not better. The Asuras succeeded because they were united by a common purpose, unlike the Devas who had too many divisions.'

'Then why did the Asuras eventually decline? Did they

become soft? How were the Devas able to defeat them?'

'As it often happens, the very reason for your success, over a prolonged period of time, can lead to your downfall. Shukracharya united the Asuras with the concept of the *Ekam*, the *One God*. All who worshipped the One God were equal in His eyes.'

Ram frowned. 'But that was hardly a new idea! Even the *Rig Veda* refers to *Ekam*, the *One Absolute*. To this day we call him the *Sum of all Souls*, the *Parmatma*. Even the followers of the feminine principle, like the Devas, believed in the *Ekam*.'

'There is a nuance that you're missing, Sudas. The *Rig Veda* states clearly that while the *Ekam* is the One God, He comes to us in many forms, as many Gods, to help us grow spiritually, in the hope that we will eventually understand Him in His original form. After all, variety is what surrounds us in nature; it is what we relate to. Shukracharya was different. He said that all other manifestations of the *Ekam* were false, leading us into *maya*, the *illusion*. The *Ekam* was the only True God, the only Reality, so to speak. It was a radical thought for that period. Suddenly, there was no hierarchy in the spiritual journey of both, the one who knew no scripture, as well as the one who was an expert on them, simply because they both believed in the *Ekam*.'

'This would make all human beings equal.'

'True. And, it worked well for some time for it obliterated all divisions within the Asuras. Furthermore, the dispossessed and oppressed among other groups like the Devas began to join the Asuras; it suddenly raised their social status. But like I've said many times, every idea has a positive and a negative. The Asuras thought that everyone who believed in their *Ekam* was equal. And what did they think of those who did not believe in their *Ekam*?'

'That they were not equal to them?' asked Ram, tentatively.

'Yes. All efforts to impose the concept of the One God upon minds that do not respect diversity will only result in intolerance. The *Upanishads* contain this warning.'

'Yes, I remember the hymn. Especially this couplet: *Giving a sharp sword to a child is not an act of generosity, but irresponsibility.* Is that what happened with the Asuras?'

'Yes. Shukracharya's immediate students, having been chosen by him, were intellectually and spiritually equipped to understand the seemingly radical concept of the *Ekam*. But the Asura Empire inevitably expanded, including within its folds increasing multitudes of people. As time went by, these believers held on to their faith in the *Ekam* but became exclusionist, demanding undivided devotion; their God was true, the other Gods were false. They grew to hate those who didn't believe in their One God, and ultimately began to kill them.'

'What?' Ram asked flabbergasted. 'That's preposterous! Doesn't the hymn on the *Ekam* also state that the only marker as to whether one truly understands the One God is that it becomes impossible to hate anyone? The *Ekam* exists in everybody and everything; if you feel any hatred at all towards anything or anyone, then you hate the *Ekam* Himself!'

'Yes, that's true. Unfortunately, the Asuras genuinely believed they were doing the right thing. As their numbers grew, their storm troopers let loose a reign of terror, tearing down temples, smashing idols and shrines, slaughtering those who persisted with the practice of worshipping other Gods.'

Ram shook his head. 'They must have turned everyone against them.'

'Exactly! And when circumstances changed, as they invariably do, the Asuras had no allies. The Devas, on the other hand, were always divided and hence did not attempt to force their ways on others. How could they? They could not even agree among themselves on what their own way of life was! Fortuitously then, they were spoilt for choice when it came to allies. All the non-Asuras were tired of the constant provocation and violence from the Asuras. They joined forces with their enemies, the Devas. Ironically, many Asuras themselves had begun to question this over-reliance on violence. They too changed allegiance and moved over to the other side. Is it any surprise that the Asuras lost?'

Ram shook his head. 'That is a major risk with the masculine way, isn't it? Exclusivist thought can easily lapse into intolerance and rigidity, especially in times of trouble. The feminine way will not face this problem.'

'Yes, rigid intolerance creates mortal enemies with whom negotiation is impossible. But the feminine way has other problems; most importantly, of how to unite their own behind a larger cause. The followers of the feminine way are usually so divided that it takes a miracle for them to come together for any one purpose, under a single banner.'

Ram, who had seen the worst of the divisions and inefficiencies of the feminine way of life in the India of today, appeared genuinely curious about the masculine order. 'The masculine way needs to be revived. The way of the Asuras is a possible answer to India's current problems. But the Asura way cannot and should not be replicated. Some improvements and adjustments are necessary. Questioning must be encouraged. And, it has to be tailored to suit our current circumstances.'

'Why not the feminine way?' asked the guru.

'I believe leaders of the feminine way tend to shirk responsibilities. Their message to their followers is: "It's your decision". When things go wrong, there's no one who can be held accountable. In the masculine way, the leader has to assume all the responsibility. And only when leaders assume responsibility can society actually function. There is clear direction and purpose for society as a whole. Otherwise, there is endless debate, analysis and paralysis.'

Vashishtha smiled. 'You are oversimplifying things. But I will not deny that if you want quick improvements, the masculine way works better. The feminine route takes time, but in the long run, it can be more stable and durable.'

'The masculine way can also prove to be stable, if we learn lessons from the past.'

'Are you willing to forge such a new path?'

'I will certainly try,' said Ram with disarming honesty. 'It is my duty to my motherland; to this great country of ours.'

'Well, you are welcome to revive the masculine way. But I suggest you don't name it Asura. It is such a reviled name today that your ideas will be doomed from the very beginning.'

'Then what do you suggest?'

'Names don't matter. What matters is the philosophy underlying them. There was a time when the Asuras represented the masculine way and the Devas, the feminine. Then, the Asuras were destroyed and only the Devas survived. The Suryavanshis and Chandravanshis are descendants of the Devas; both representatives of the feminine. But, for all you know, if you achieve what I think you can, the Suryavanshis could end up representing the masculine way of life and the Chandravanshis could carry forward the legacy of their ancestors, the Devas. Like I said, names don't matter.'

Ram looked down again at the inscription as he pondered over the unknown person who had carved this message long ago. It seemed like an act of impotent rebellion. Shukracharya's name had been banned across the land. His loyal followers were not even allowed to speak his name. Perhaps this was their way of applying a salve to their conscience at not being able to publicly honour their guru.

Vashishtha put his hand on Ram's shoulder. 'I will tell you more about Shukracharya, his life and his philosophy. He was a genius. You can learn from him and create a great empire. But you must remember that while you can certainly learn from the successes of great men, you can learn even more from their failures and mistakes.'

'Yes, Guru*ji*.'

Chapter 9

'We will not be meeting for a long time after this, Guru*ji*,' said
the Naga.

A few months had elapsed since Ram and Vashishtha's
conversation on Shukracharya in the temple of Lord Indra.
The formal education of the princes in the *gurukul* was
complete, and the boys would be returning home for good
the following day. Lakshman had decided to go riding one last
time, late in the night. While trying to return undetected, he
came upon a replay of the meeting between his guru and the
suspicious Naga.

They had met under the bridge, once again.

'Yes, it will be difficult,' agreed Vashishtha. 'People in
Ayodhya do not know about my other life. But I will find ways
to communicate.'

The outgrowth from his lower back flicked like a tail as the
Naga spoke. 'I have heard that your former friend's alliance
with Raavan grows stronger.'

Vashishtha closed his eyes and took a deep breath before
speaking softly. 'He will always remain my friend. He helped
me when I was alone.'

The Naga narrowed his eyes, his interest piqued. 'You have
to tell me this story sometime, Guru*ji*. What happened?'

Vashishtha gave the hint of a wry smile. 'Some stories are best left untold.'

The Naga realised he had ventured into painful territory and decided not to pry any further.

'But I know what you've come for,' said Vashishtha, changing the topic.

The Naga smiled. 'I have to know…'

'Ram,' said Vashishtha, simply.

The Naga seemed surprised. 'I thought it would be Prince Bharat…'

'No. It's Ram. It has to be.'

The Naga nodded. 'Then, Prince Ram it is. You know you can count on our support.'

'Yes, I know.'

Lakshman felt his heartbeat quicken as he continued to listen, soundlessly.

— 🧍 🐟 ☀ —

'*Dada*, you really do not understand the world,' cried Lakshman.

'In the name of Lord Ikshvaku, just go back to sleep,' mumbled an exasperated Ram. 'You see conspiracies everywhere.'

'But…'

'Lakshman!'

'They have decided to kill you, *Dada*! I know it.'

'When will you believe that nobody is trying to kill me? Why would Guru*ji* want me dead? Why would *anyone* want me dead, for crying out loud?!' exclaimed Ram. 'Nobody was trying to kill me then, when we were out riding. And, nobody is trying to kill me now. I am not so important, you know. Now go to sleep!'

'*Dada*, you're just so clueless! At this rate, I don't know how I'm supposed to protect you.'

'You will protect me forever, somehow,' said Ram, softening and smiling indulgently as he pulled his brother's cheek. 'Go back to sleep now.'

'*Dada…*'

'Lakshman!'

'Welcome home, my son,' cried Kaushalya.

Unable to suppress her tears of joy, the queen looked proudly at her son as he held her awkwardly, slightly embarrassed by her open display of emotion. Like his mother, the eighteen-year-old eldest prince of the Raghu clan of Ayodhya had a dark, flawless complexion, which perfectly set off his sober white *dhoti* and *angvastram*. His broad shoulders, lean body and powerful back were a testimony to his archery skills. Long hair tied neatly in an unassuming bun, he wore simple ear studs and a string of Rudraaksh beads around his neck. The studs were shaped like the sun with streaming rays, which was symbolic of the Suryavanshi rulers, descendants of the sun. The Rudraaksh, brown, elliptical beads derived from the tree of the same name, represented Lord Rudra, who had saved India from Evil some millennia ago.

He stepped away from his mother as she finally stopped crying. He went down on one knee, bowing his head with respect towards his father. A hushed silence descended on the court, in full attendance during this ceremonial occasion. The impressive Great Hall of the Unconquerable hadn't seen a gathering like this in nearly two decades. This royal court hall, along with the palace, had been built by the charismatic warrior-king Raghu, the great-grandfather of Ram. He had famously restored the power of the Ayodhya royalty through stunning conquests, so much so that the title of the House of Ayodhya had been changed from the 'Clan of Ikshvaku', to the 'Clan of Raghu'. Ram did not approve of this change, for to him it was a betrayal of his lineage. Howsoever great one's achievements were, they could not overshadow those of one's ancestors. He would have preferred the use of 'Clan of Ikshvaku' for his family; after all, Ikshvaku was the founder of the dynasty. But few were interested in Ram's opinions.

Ram continued to kneel, but the official acknowledgment was not forthcoming. Vashishtha, the raj guru, sat to the right of the emperor, looking at him with silent disapproval.

Dashrath seemed lost in thought as he stared blankly into space. His hands rested on golden armrests shaped like lions. A gold-coloured canopy, embedded with priceless jewels, was suspended over the throne. The magnificent court hall and the throne were symbolic of the power and might of the Ayodhyans; or at least, they had been so, once upon a time. Peeling paint and fraying edges spoke volumes of the decline of this once-great kingdom. Precious stones from the throne had been pulled out, probably to pay the bills. The thousand-pillared hall still appeared grand, but an old eye would know that it had seen better days in years past, when vibrant silk pennants hung from the walls, separating engraved figures of ancient *rishis* — *seers* and *men of knowledge*. The figures could have certainly done with a thorough cleaning.

Palpable embarrassment spread in the hall as Ram waited. A murmur among the courtiers reaffirmed what was well known: Ram was not the favoured son.

The son remained still and unmoved. Truth be told, he was not the least bit surprised. Used to disdain and calumny, he had learnt to ignore it. Every trip back home from the *gurukul* had been torture. Almost by design, most people found some way to constantly remind him of the misfortune of his birth. The 'taint of 7,032', the year of his birth according to the calendar of Manu, would not be forgotten. It had troubled him in his childhood, but he found himself wryly recalling what the man he admired as a father, Guru Vashishtha, had said to him once.

Kimapi Nu Janaahaa Vadishyanti. Tadeva Kaaryam Janaanaam.
People will talk nonsense. It is, after all, their job.

Kaikeyi walked up to her husband, went down on her knees and placed Dashrath's partially paralysed right leg on the foot stand. Carefully displaying the dutiful and submissive gesture for public consumption, she brought her aggression into full play in private, as she hissed her command. 'Acknowledge Ram. Remember, descendant, not protector.'

A flicker of life flashed across the emperor's face. He raised his chin imperiously as he spoke. 'Rise, Ram Chandra, descendant of the Raghu clan.'

Vashishtha narrowed his eyes with disapproval and cast a glance at Ram.

Adorned in rich finery and heavy gold ornaments, prominent among the first row of nobility, was a fair-skinned woman with a bent back. Her face was scarred by an old disease, and along with the hunched back, she had a menacing presence. Turning slightly to the man standing beside her, she whispered, 'Hmm, did you understand, Druhyu? Descendant, not protector.'

Druhyu bowed his head in deference as he addressed the wealthiest and most powerful merchant of the Sapt Sindhu, 'Yes, Manthara*ji*.'

That Dashrath had avoided the word 'protector' was a clear indication to all who were present that Ram would not be accorded what was the birthright of the first-born. Ram did not show disappointment as he rose to his feet with stoic decorum. Folding his hands together in a namaste, he bowed his head and spoke with crisp solemnity, 'May all the Gods of our great land continue to protect you, my father.' He then stepped back to take his position in single file along with his brothers.

Standing beside Ram, Bharat, though shorter, was heavier in build. Years of hard work showed in his musculature, while the scars he bore gave him a fearsome yet attractive look. He'd inherited his mother's fair complexion and had set it off with a bright blue *dhoti* and *angvastram*. The headband that held his long hair in place was embellished with an intricate, embroidered golden peacock feather. His charisma, though, lay in his eyes and face; a sharp nose, strong chin and eyes that danced with mischief. At this moment though, they displayed sadness. He cast a concerned look at his brother Ram before turning to Dashrath, visibly angry.

Bharat marched forward with studied nonchalance and went down on one knee. Shockingly for the assemblage, he refused to bow his head. He stared at his father with open hostility.

Kaikeyi had remained standing next to Dashrath. She glared at her son, willing him into submission. But Bharat was too old for such efforts at intimidation. Imperceptibly, unnoticed by anyone, Kaikeyi bowed her head and whispered to her husband. Dashrath repeated what was told to him.

'Rise, Bharat, descendant of the Raghu clan.'

Bharat smiled delightedly at not being accorded the title of the 'protector' either. He stood up and spoke with casual aplomb, 'May Lord Indra and Lord Varun grant you wisdom, my father.'

He winked at Ram as he quickly walked back to where his brothers stood. Ram was impassive.

It was then Lakshman's turn. As he stepped forward, those assembled were struck by his gigantic frame and towering height. Though usually dishevelled, his mother Sumitra had ensured that the fair-complexioned Lakshman had turned up dressed neatly for the ceremony. Much like his beloved brother Ram, Lakshman too avoided wearing jewellery, save for the ear studs and the threaded Rudraaksh beads around his neck. His ceremony was completed without fuss, and he was soon followed by Shatrughan. The diminutive youngest prince was meticulously attired as always, his hair precisely tied, his *dhoti* and *angvastram* neatly pressed, his jewellery sober and minimal. The completion of his ceremony marked his acknowledgement, too, as a descendant of Raghu.

The court crier brought the proceedings of the court to an end. Kaikeyi stepped up to assist Dashrath, signalling an aide who stood next to the emperor. Dashrath placed his hand on the attendant's shoulder as his eyes fell on Vashishtha, who had also risen from his seat. Dashrath folded his hands together into a namaste. 'Guru*ji*.'

Vashishtha raised his right hand and blessed the king. 'May Lord Indra bless you with a long life, Your Majesty.'

Dashrath nodded and cast a cursory look towards his sons, standing firmly together. His eyes rested on Ram; he coughed irritably, turned and hobbled away with assistance. Kaikeyi followed Dashrath out of the court.

The crier then announced that the emperor had left the court and the courtiers immediately began filing out of the hall.

Manthara remained rooted to her spot, staring intently at the four princes in the distance.

'What is it, My Lady?' whispered Druhyu.

The man's submissive demeanour was a clear indication of the dread he felt for the lady. It was rumoured that Manthara was even wealthier than the emperor. Added to this, she was believed to be a close confidante of the most powerful person in the empire, Queen Kaikeyi. The mischievous even suggested that the demon-king Raavan of Lanka was an ally; the reasonable, however, dismissed the last as fanciful.

'The brothers are close to each other,' whispered Manthara.

'Yes, they appear to be…'

'Interesting… Unexpected, but interesting…'

Druhyu cast a furtive glance over his shoulder, and then murmured. 'What are you thinking, My Lady?'

'I have been thinking about this for some time. I'm not sure we can write Ram off. If, after all the hatred and vilification that he has been subjected to for eighteen years, he is still standing strong, we must assume that he is made of sterner stuff. And Bharat, very obviously, is spirited and devoted to his brother.'

'So, what should we do?'

'They are both worthy. It's difficult to decide which one to bet on.'

'But Bharat is Queen Kaikeyi's—'

'I think,' said Manthara, cutting off her aide mid-sentence, 'I will find some way to make Roshni increase her interaction with them. I need to know more about the character of these princes.'

Druhyu was taken aback. 'My Lady, please accept my sincere apologies, but your daughter is very innocent, almost like *Kanyakumari*, the *Virgin Goddess*. She may not be able to—'

'Her innocence is exactly what we need, you fool. Nothing disarms strong men like a genuinely innocent and decent woman. It's the fascination that all strong men have for the Virgin Goddess, who must always be honoured and protected.'

Chapter 10

'Thank you,' smiled Bharat, as he held up his right hand and admired the exquisite golden-thread *rakhi* tied around his wrist. A petite young woman stood by his side; she answered to the name of Roshni.

A few weeks had lapsed since the recognition ceremony of the Ayodhya princes. Lakshman and Shatrughan already wore the *rakhi* thread, signifying a promise of protection made by a brother to his sister. In a break from tradition, Roshni had chosen to tie the *rakhi* threads first to the youngest and then move on, age-wise, towards the eldest. They sat together in the magnificent royal garden of the main Ayodhya palace. Situated high on a hill, the palace afforded a breathtaking view of the city, its walls and the Grand Canal beyond. The garden had been laid out in the style of a botanical reserve, filled with flowering trees from not only the Sapt Sindhu but other great empires around the world as well. Its splendid diversity was also the source of its beauty, reflecting the composite character of the people of the Sapt Sindhu. Winding paths bordered what should have been a carefully laid out lush carpet of dense grass in geometric symmetry. Alas, the depleting resources of Ayodhya had taken a toll on the maintenance of the garden, and ugly bald patches dotted the expanse.

Roshni applied the ceremonial sandalwood paste on Bharat's forehead. Manthara's daughter had inherited her mother's fair complexion, but in all other ways the dissimilarity could not be more obvious. Dainty and small-boned, she was soft-spoken, gentle and childlike. The simplicity of her attire was a subtle rejection of the opulence afforded by her family's wealth: a white upper garment coupled with a cream-coloured *dhoti*. Tiny studs and a bracelet made from Rudraaksh beads gave a hint of festive gaiety to a solemn face framed by long, wavy hair that was tied, as usual, in a neat ponytail. Her most magical attribute, though, was her eyes: overflowing with innocent tenderness and the unconditional, compassionate love of a true *yogini; one who had discovered union with God.*

Bharat pulled out a pouch full of gold coins from his waistband and held it out to Roshni. 'Here you go, my sister.'

Roshni gave the slightest of frowns. It had become fashionable of late for brothers to offer money or a gift to sisters during the *rakhi* ceremony. Women like Roshni did not approve of this trend. They believed that they were capable of doing the work of Brahmins, Vaishyas and Shudras: disseminating knowledge, trading or performing physical labour. The only task that sometimes proved challenging for them was that of a Kshatriya. They simply did not possess the physical strength and proclivity for violence. Nature had blessed them with other attributes. They believed that accepting anything besides the promise of physical protection during the *rakhi* ceremony was an admission of the inferiority of women. Equally, though, Roshni didn't want to be rude.

'Bharat, I'm elder to you,' smiled Roshni. 'I don't think it's appropriate for you to give me money. But I most willingly accept your promise of protection.'

'Of course,' said Bharat, quickly tucking the pouch back into his waistband. 'You are Manthara*ji's* daughter. Why would you need any money?'

Roshni immediately fell silent. Ram could see that she was hurt. He knew she was uncomfortable about the fabulous wealth that her mother possessed. It pained her that many in her country were mired in poverty. Roshni was known to avoid, if possible, the legendary parties that her mother frequently threw. Nor did she move around with an escort. She gave money and time to many charitable causes, especially the education and health of children, considered the worthiest of all by the great law book, *Maitreyi Smriti*. She also frequently used her medical skills as a doctor to help the needy.

'It's a wonder Bharat *Dada* allowed you to tie a *rakhi*, Roshni *Didi*,' Shatrughan broke the awkward silence even as he teased his elder brother.

'Yes,' said Lakshman. 'Our dear *dada* certainly loves women, but not necessarily as a brother.'

'And, from what I have heard, women love him in return,' said Roshni, as she gazed fondly at Bharat. 'Haven't you come across any dream lover yet, someone who will sweep you off your feet and make you want to settle down?'

'I do have a dream lover,' quipped Bharat. 'The problem is, she disappears when I wake up.'

Shatrughan, Lakshman and Roshni laughed heartily, but Ram could not bring himself to join in. He knew Bharat was assiduously hiding the pain in his heart with his jest. He had still not gotten over Radhika. Ram hoped his sensitive brother would not pine for her forever.

'My turn now,' said Ram, as he stepped forward and held out his right hand.

Lakshman spotted Vashishtha walking by in the distance. He immediately scanned the area for possible threats, as he had not completely set aside his suspicions regarding their guru.

'I promise to protect you forever, my sister,' said Ram, looking solemnly at the golden *rakhi* tied to his wrist, and then equally, at Roshni.

Roshni smiled and applied some sandalwood paste on Ram's forehead. She turned around and walked towards a bench to put away the *aarti thali*.

'*DADA!*' screamed Lakshman, as he lunged forward and pushed Ram aside.

Lakshman's tremendous strength threw Ram back. In the same instant, a heavy branch landed with a loud thud at the very spot that Ram had been standing a moment ago. It had first smashed into Lakshman's shoulder, cracking his collar bone in two. Shards of bone jut out as blood gushed in a horrifying flow.

'Lakshman!' screamed his brothers as they rushed towards him.

'He'll be all right,' said Roshni, as she stepped out of the operation theatre. Vashishtha, Ram, Bharat and Shatrughan stood anxiously in the lobby of the *ayuralay*. Sumitra sat still on a chair against the wall of the *hospital*, her eyes clouded with tears. She immediately rose and embraced Roshni.

'There will be no permanent damage, Your Highness,' assured Roshni. 'His bone has been set. Your son will recover fully. We are very lucky that the branch missed his head.'

'We're also lucky that Lakshman is built like a bull,' said Vashishtha. 'A lesser man would not have survived that hit.'

Lakshman opened his eyes in a large room, meant for nobility. His bed was big but not too soft, providing the support needed for his injured shoulder. He couldn't see too well in the dark but he detected a soft sound. Within moments, he found a red-eyed Ram standing by his bedside.

I woke Dada *up,* thought Lakshman.

Three nurses rushed towards the bed. Lakshman shook his head slowly and they stepped back.

Ram touched Lakshman's head gently. 'My brother…'

'*Dada*… the tree…'

'The branch was rotten, Lakshman. That's why it fell. It was bad luck. You saved my life once again…'

'*Dada*… Guru*ji*…'

'You took the hit for me, my brother… You took the hit that fate had meant for me…' said Ram, as he bent over and ran his hand over Lakshman's forehead.

Lakshman felt a tear fall on his face. '*Dada*…'

'Don't talk. Try to sleep. Relax,' said Ram, turning his face away.

Roshni entered the *ayuralay* room with some medicines for the prince. A week had elapsed since the accident. Lakshman was stronger now, and restless.

'Where is everyone?'

'The nurses are still here,' said Roshni with a smile, mixing the medicines into a paste in a bowl and handing it over to Lakshman. 'Your brothers have gone to the palace to bathe and change into fresh clothes. They'll be back soon.'

Lakshman's face contorted involuntarily as he ingested the medicine. 'Yuck!'

'The yuckier it is, the more effective the medicine!'

'Why do you doctors torture patients like this?'

'Thank you,' Roshni smiled as she handed the bowl to a nurse. Turning her attention back to Lakshman, she asked, 'How are you feeling now?'

'There is still a lot of numbness in my left shoulder.'

'That's because of the pain-killers.'

'I don't need them.'

'I know you can tolerate any amount of pain. But, for as long as you are my patient, you won't.'

Lakshman smiled. 'Spoken like an older sister.'

'Spoken like a doctor,' scolded Roshni, as her kindly gaze fell upon the golden *rakhi* still tied around Lakshman's right wrist. She turned to leave and then stopped.

'What is it?' asked Lakshman.

Roshni requested the nurses to leave. She then walked back to his bedside. 'Your brothers were here for most of the time. Your mother too was here; so were your stepmothers. They came to see you every day, remained here for most of the time and only went back to the palace to sleep. I'd expected that.

But you must know that Ram refused to leave for one full week. He slept here in this room. He did a lot of the work that our nurses should have rightfully done.'

'I know. He's my *dada*…'

Roshni smiled. 'I came in late one night to check on you and I heard him talking in his sleep: "Don't punish my brother for my sins; punish me, punish me".'

'He blames himself for everything,' said Lakshman. 'Everyone has made his life a living hell.'

Roshni knew what Lakshman was talking about.

'How can anyone blame *Dada* for our defeat? *Dada* was just born on that day. We lost to Lanka because they fought better than us.'

'Lakshman, you don't have to…'

'Inauspicious! Cursed! Unholy! Is there any insult that has not been heaped upon him? And yet, he stands strong and steadfast. He doesn't hate, or even resent, anyone. He could have spent a lifetime being angry with the entire world. But he chooses to live a life of honour. He never lies. Did you know that? He never lies!' Lakshman was crying now. 'And yet, he lied once, just for me! I was out riding in the night, despite knowing that it wasn't allowed. I fell and hurt myself pretty badly. My mother was so angry. But *Dada* lied to save me. He said I was in the stable with him and that the horse kicked me. My mother instantly believed him, for *Dada* never lies. In his mind, he tainted his soul, but he did it to save me from my mother's wrath. And yet, people call him…'

Roshni stepped forward and gently touched Lakshman's face, wiping away some of his tears.

He continued with fervent vigour, tears streaming down his cheeks, 'There will come a time when the world will know what a great man he is. Dark clouds cannot hide the sun forever. One day, they will clear and true light will shine through. Everyone will know then, how great my *dada* is.'

'I already know that,' said Roshni, softly.

Manthara stood by the window in her office room, built at the far end of the official wing of her palatial residence. The exquisitely symmetrical garden, along with the estate, was appropriately smaller when compared to the emperor's; a conscious choice. It was also perched on a hill, though lower than the one on which the royal palace stood. Her residence adequately reflected her social status.

She was a brilliant businesswoman, no doubt, and she was no fool. The anti-mercantile atmosphere of the Sapt Sindhu accorded her a low stature, notwithstanding her wealth. None had the courage to say it to her face, but she knew what she was called: a 'profiteering lackey of the foreign-demon Raavan'. Truth was, all businessmen had no choice but to trade with Raavan's Lankan traders as the demon-king held a monopoly over external trade with the Sapt Sindhu. This was not a treaty signed by the Sapt Sindhu traders but their kings. Yet, it was the traders who were reviled for playing by the rules of this agreement. Being the most successful businesswoman, Manthara was the prime recipient of the anti-trader prejudice.

But she had suffered enough abuse in her childhood to inure her from bigotry for many a lifetime. Born into a poor family, she was afflicted with smallpox when young, leaving her pallid face scarred for life. As if that wasn't enough, she contracted polio at the age of eleven. The symptoms gradually abated but her right foot remained partially paralysed, giving her an odd limp. At age twenty, owing to her awkward gait, she slipped from the balcony at a friend's house, leaving her back hideously disfigured. She was teased wretchedly when young, and looked at with disdain even today, except that nobody dared to say anything to her face. Her wealth could have easily financed the entire royal expenditure of Kosala, along with a few other kingdoms, without even having to draw on her credit. Needless to say, it brought her immense power and influence.

'My Lady, what did you want to talk about?' asked Druhyu, standing deferentially a few feet away from her.

Manthara limped to her desk and sat on the specially designed padded chair. Druhyu stood at the other end of the desk.

She crooked her finger and he immediately shuffled around the desk, going down on his knees as he reached her. They were alone in the office, and no one would have heard a word of what was exchanged between them. The assistants were on the ground floor in the secretarial annexe. But he understood her silences. And, he didn't dare argue. So he waited.

'I know all there is to know,' declared Manthara. 'My sweet Roshni has unwittingly revealed the character of the princes to me. I've thought hard about this and I've made up my mind. Bharat will be in charge of diplomatic affairs and Ram will look after the city police.'

Druhyu was surprised. 'I thought you had begun to like Prince Ram, My Lady.'

Diplomatic affairs were a perfect opportunity for an Ayodhyan prince to build relations with other kingdoms; and thus, build his base for a future strong empire. Although Ayodhya was still the overlord of the Sapt Sindhu confederacy, it was nowhere near as powerful as it had once been. Building relations with other kings would prove to be advantageous.

The role of the city police chief, on the other hand, would not serve as a suitable training ground for a prince. Crime rates were high, law and order was abysmal, and most rich people maintained their own personal security set-up. The poor suffered terribly as a result. Simplistic explanations would not do justice to the complex picture, though. The people were, to a fairly large extent, themselves responsible for the chaotic state of affairs. Guru Vashishtha had once remarked that it was possible for the system to maintain order if a small percentage of the people disobeyed the law, but no system could prevent upheaval and disruption if practically all the citizens had no respect for the law. And Ayodhyans broke every law with impunity.

If Bharat managed diplomatic relations well, he would be in a strong position to succeed Dashrath eventually, whereas Ram would be left with a thankless job. If he was tough and managed to control crime, people would resent him for his ruthlessness. If he was kind, crime rates would continue to soar and he would be blamed for it. Even if, by some miracle, he managed to control crime and be popular at the same time, then too it would not prove beneficial for him, for the opinion of the people did not matter in the selection of the next king.

'Oh, I like Ram,' said Manthara dismissively. 'I just like profits more. It'll be good for business if we back the right horse. This is not about choosing between Ram and Bharat, but Kaushalya and Kaikeyi. And, rest assured, Kaikeyi will win. That is a certainty. Ram may well be capable, but he does not have the ability to take on Kaikeyi.'

'Yes, My Lady.'

'Also, don't forget, the nobility hates Ram. They blame him

for the defeat at the Battle of Karachapa. So it would cost us more in bribes to secure a good position for Ram. We won't have to pay that much to the nobility to get them to accept Bharat as the chief of diplomatic affairs.'

'Our costs go down as well,' said Druhyu, smiling.

'Yes. That too is good for business.'

'And, I think, Queen Kaikeyi will be grateful.'

'Which will not hurt us either.'

'I will take care of it, My Lady. Raj Guru Vashishtha is away from Ayodhya, and that will make our task easier. He has been a strong supporter of Prince Ram.'

Druhyu regretted mentioning the raj guru as soon as the words escaped his lips.

'You still haven't discovered where Guru*ji* is, have you?' asked an irritated Manthara. 'Where has he gone for such a long period? When is he returning? You know nothing!'

'No, My Lady,' said Druhyu, keeping his head bowed. 'I'm sorry.'

'Sometimes I wonder why I pay you so much.'

Druhyu remained still, afraid of uttering another sound. Manthara dismissed him from her presence with a wave of the hand.

Chapter 11

'You will make an excellent chief of police,' said Roshni, her eyes glittering with childlike excitement. 'Crime will decrease and that will be good for our beleaguered people.'

Roshni sat in the palace garden with a restrained but disappointed Ram, who'd been hoping for a greater responsibility, like the deputy chief of the army. But he wasn't about to reveal this to her.

'I'm not sure if I'll be able to handle it,' said Ram. 'A good chief of police needs the support of the people.'

'And, you imagine that you don't have it?'

Ram smiled wanly. 'Roshni, I know you don't lie; do you really think the people will support me? Everyone blames me for the defeat at the hands of Lanka. I am tainted by 7,032.'

Roshni leaned forward and spoke earnestly. 'You have only interacted with the elite, the ones who were "born-right", people like us. Yes, they do not like you. But there is another Ayodhya, Ram, where people who were "not born-right" exist. There's no love lost between them and the elite. And remember, they will be sympathetic towards anyone the elite ostracise, even one from the nobility itself. The common folk will like you simply because the elite don't like you. They might even follow you for the same reason.'

Ram had lived in the bubble of the royal experience. He was intrigued by this possibility.

'People like us don't step out into the real world. We don't know what's going on out there. I have interacted with the common people and I think I understand them to some extent. The elite have done you a favour by hating you. They have made it possible for you to endear yourself to the common man. I'm sure you can make them listen to you. I know you can bring crime under control in this city; dramatically so. You can do a lot of good. Believe in yourself as much as I believe in you, my brother.'

— 仈 ⚷ ☼ —

Within a year the reforms that Ram instituted began to have a visible effect. He tackled the main problem head on: most people were unaware of the laws. Some did not even know the names of the law books, called *Smritis*. This was because there were too many of them, containing contradictory laws that had accumulated over centuries. The *Manu Smriti* was well known, but most people were unaware that there were versions of it as well, for instance the *BrihadManu Smriti*. There were other popular ones too — the *Yajnavalkya Smriti, Narad Smriti, Aapastamb Smriti, Atri Smriti, Yam Smriti* and *Vyas Smriti*, to name a few. The police applied sections from the law that they were familiar with, in an ad hoc fashion. The court judges were sometimes aware of other *Smritis*, depending on the communities they were born into. Confusion was exacerbated when the police would arrest under a law of one *Smriti*, while the judge would base his judgement on a law from another *Smriti*. The result was almighty chaos. The guilty would escape by exploiting the loopholes and contradictions among the *Smritis*. Many innocents, however, languished in prisons due to ignorance, leading to horrific overcrowding.

Ram understood that he had to simplify and unify the law. He studied the *Smritis* and carefully selected laws that he felt were fair, coherent, simple and relevant to the times. Henceforth, this law code would govern Ayodhya; all the other *Smritis* would be rendered obsolete. The laws were inscribed on stone tablets and put up at all the temples in Ayodhya; the most important among them being engraved at the end: Ignorance of the law is not a legitimate excuse. Town criers were assigned the task of reading the code aloud every morning. It was only a matter of time before the laws were known to all.

Ram was soon given a respectful title by the common people: Ram, the Law Giver.

His second reform was even more revolutionary. He gave the police force the power to implement the law without any fear or favour. Ram understood a simple fact: policemen desired respect from society. They hadn't been given the opportunity to earn it earlier. If they unhesitatingly took action against any law-breaker, high and mighty though he may be, they would be feared and respected. Ram himself repeatedly demonstrated that the law applied equally to him.

In an oft-quoted incident, Ram returned to the city after dusk, when the fort gates had been shut. The gatekeeper opened the gates for the prince. Ram upbraided him for breaking the law: the gates were not to be opened for anyone at night time. Ram slept outside the city walls that night and entered the city the next morning. The ordinary people of Ayodhya talked about it for months, though it was studiously ignored by the nobles.

What did get the elite into a tizzy was Ram's intervention in cases where members of the nobility attempted to browbeat the police when the law caught up with them. They were aghast that they were being brought to book, but soon understood there would be no leniency. Their hatred of Ram increased manifold; they began to call him dictatorial and dangerous. But the people loved him more, this eldest prince of Ayodhya. Crime rates collapsed as criminals were either thrown in jail or speedily executed. Innocents were increasingly spared in a city that steadily became safer. Women began to venture out alone at night. Ram was rightfully credited with this dramatic improvement in their lives.

It would be decades before the name of Ram would transform into a splendid legend. But the journey had begun, for among the common folk, a star was slowly sputtering to life.

—— 人 ▮ ☼ ——

'You are making too many enemies, my son,' said Kaushalya. 'You should not be so rigid about enforcing the law.'

Kaushalya had finally summoned Ram to her private chamber, having received too many complaints from nobles. She was worried that, in his zeal, her son was losing the few allies he still had in court.

'The rule of law cannot be selective, *Maa*,' said Ram. 'The same law has to apply to everyone. If the nobles don't like it, they should not break the law.'

'I'm not discussing the law, Ram. If you think that penalising one of General Mrigasya's key aides will please your father, you're wrong. He's completely under Kaikeyi's spell.'

Mrigasya, the army chief, had become increasingly powerful as Dashrath sank into depression. He was the magnet around whom all those who opposed the powerful Queen Kaikeyi had coalesced. His reputation of fiercely defending his loyalists, even if they committed crimes or were thoroughly incompetent, ensured ferocious allegiance. Kaikeyi intensely disliked him for his wilful disregard of her wishes, which influenced Dashrath's attitude towards the general.

Recently, Ram had used the law to recover land that one of Mrigasya's aides had illegally appropriated from poor villagers. Ram had even had the temerity to enforce a penalty on the aide, something nobody had dared to do with the men who surrounded the powerful general.

'General Mrigasya and Kaikeyi *Maa*'s politics do not interest me. His aide broke the law. That's all there is to it.'

'The nobility will do as they please, Ram.'

'Not if I can help it!'

'Ram…'

'Nobility is about being *noble*, Maa. It's about the way of the *Arya*. It's not about your birth, but how you conduct yourself. Being a noble is a great responsibility, not a birthright.'

'Ram, why don't you understand?! General Mrigasya is our only ally. All the other powerful nobles are in Kaikeyi's camp. He's the only one who can stand up to her. We are safe for as long as we have Mrigasya and his coterie on our side.'

'What does this have to do with the law?'

Kaushalya consciously made an effort to contain her irritation. 'Do you know how difficult it is for me to build support for you? Everyone blames you for Lanka.'

When her comment was met with a stony silence, Kaushalya turned placatory. 'I'm not suggesting that it was your fault, my child. But this is the reality. We must be pragmatic. Do you want to be king or not?'

'I want to be a good king. Or else, believe me, I'd rather not be one.'

Kaushalya closed her eyes in exasperation. 'Ram, you seem to live in your own theoretical world. You have to learn to be practical. Know that I love you and I'm only trying to help you.'

'If you love me, *Maa*, then understand what I'm made of.' Ram spoke calmly but there was steely determination in his eyes. 'This is my *janmabhoomi*, my *land of birth*. I have to serve it by leaving it better than I found it. I can fulfil my karma as a king, a police chief or even a simple villager.'

'Ram, you don't—'

Kaushalya was interrupted by a loud announcement. 'Her Highness Kaikeyi, queen of Ayodhya!'

Ram immediately got to his feet, as did Kaushalya. He discreetly glanced at his mother, noting the impotent anger in her eyes. Kaikeyi approached her with a smile on her lips, her hands folded in a namaste. 'Namaste, *Didi*. Please accept my sincere apologies for disturbing you during your private time with your son.'

'That's quite all right, Kaikeyi,' remarked Kaushalya with studied affability. 'I'm sure it's something important.'

'Yes, it is, actually,' said Kaikeyi, turning to Ram. 'Your father has decided to go on a hunting trip, Ram.'

'A hunting trip?' asked a surprised Ram.

Dashrath had not gone big game hunting in Ram's living memory. His battle injury had precluded even such simple pleasures from the life of the once great hunter.

'Yes. I would have sent Bharat along with him. I could do with some of my favourite deer meat. But as you know, Bharat is in Branga on a diplomatic mission. I was wondering if I could lay this onerous responsibility on your able shoulders.'

Ram smiled slightly. He knew Kaikeyi wanted him to accompany Dashrath in order to protect him, and not for any choice meats. But Kaikeyi never said anything derogatory about Dashrath in public; and the royal family was 'public' for her. Ram folded his hands into a namaste. 'It will be my honour to serve you, *Chhoti Maa.*'

Kaikeyi smiled. 'Thank you.'

Kaushalya looked at Ram quietly, her face inscrutable.

'What is she doing here?' asked Dashrath gruffly.

Kaushalya had just been announced by the doorman in Kaikeyi's wing of the royal palace. Dashrath and Kaikeyi lay in bed. She reached out and tucked Dashrath's long hair behind his ear. 'Just finish whatever it is and come back quickly.'

'You will also have to get up, my love,' said Dashrath.

Kaikeyi sighed in irritation and rolled off the bed. She quickly picked up her *angvastram* and placed it across her shoulder, rolling the other end around her right wrist. She walked over to Dashrath and helped him off the bed. She went down on her knees and straightened his *dhoti*. Finally, she picked up Dashrath's *angvastram* and placed it across his shoulder. She then helped him walk into the reception room and bade him wait.

'Let Her Majesty in,' ordered Kaikeyi.

Kaushalya entered the room with two attendants in tow. One of them carried a large golden plate on which was placed Dashrath's battle sword. The other attendant carried a small *puja thali*. Kaikeyi straightened up in surprise. Dashrath seemed lost as usual.

'*Didi*,' said Kaikeyi, folding her hands together in a namaste. 'What a pleasure to see you twice in the same day.'

'The pleasure is all mine, Kaikeyi,' replied Kaushalya. 'You mentioned that His Majesty is going on a hunt. I thought I should perform the proper ceremony.'

The ritual of the chief wife of a warrior ceremonially handing the sword to her departing husband had come down through the ancient times.

'Things have not gone too well whenever I have not presented His Majesty with the sword,' said Kaushalya.

Dashrath's vacant expression changed suddenly. He frowned, as if he was struck by the enormity of the not-so-subtle implication. Kaushalya had not handed him the sword when he had set out for Karachapa, and that had been his first defeat. He slowly took a step towards his first wife.

Kaushalya took the small *puja thali* from her attendant and looped it in small circles around Dashrath's face seven times. Then she took a pinch of vermillion from the plate and smeared it across Dashrath's forehead in a vertical *tilak*. 'Come back victorious…'

Kaikeyi sniggered, interrupting the ceremony. 'He's not going to war, *Didi*.'

Dashrath ignored Kaikeyi. 'Complete the line, Kaushalya.'

Kaushalya swallowed nervously, half convinced now that this was a big mistake; that she should not have listened to Sumitra. But she completed the ritual statement. 'Come back victorious, or do not come back at all.'

Kaushalya thought she detected a flicker of fire in her husband's eyes, reminiscent of the young Dashrath, who lived for thrill and glory. 'Where's my sword?' Dashrath demanded, as he extended his arms solemnly.

Kaushalya immediately turned and handed the *puja thali* back to her attendant. She then picked up the sword with both her hands, faced her husband, bowed ceremonially and handed him the sword. Dashrath held it firmly, as if drawing energy from it.

Kaikeyi looked at Dashrath and then at Kaushalya as she narrowed her eyes, deep in thought.

This must be Sumitra's doing. Kaushalya couldn't have planned this by herself. Perhaps I've made a mistake in asking Ram to accompany Dashrath.

Royal hunts were grand affairs that lasted many weeks. A large entourage accompanied the emperor on the expedition, moving the headquarters of the court to a hunting lodge built deep in the great forest to the far north of Ayodhya.

Action commenced on the day after their arrival. The technique involved numerous soldiers spreading out in a giant circle, circumscribing almost fifty kilometres sometimes. They beat loud drums ceaselessly as they slowly moved to the centre, steadily drawing the animals into an increasingly restricted area, at times a watering hole. The animals would then be attacked in the kill-zone, where the emperor and his hunting party would indulge in this royal sport.

Dashrath stood on a howdah atop the royal elephant. Ram and Lakshman were seated behind him. The emperor thought he heard the soft chuff of an unsuspecting tiger; he ordered the mahout to charge forward. Within no time, Dashrath's elephant had separated from the rest of the hunting party. He was alone with his sons.

They were surrounded on all sides by dense vegetation. Many trees were so tall that they towered over the elephant, blocking out much of the sunlight. It was almost impossible to see beyond the first few lines of trees into the impenetrable darkness.

Lakshman leaned in and whispered to Ram, '*Dada*, I don't think there is any tiger here.'

Ram gestured for Lakshman to remain quiet as he observed his father, standing in front. Dashrath was barely able to contain his enthusiasm. His body weight was on his strong left foot. His inert right foot was stabilised with an innovative mechanism built into the howdah platform: a swivelling circular base with a sturdy column fixed in the centre. Boot straps attached to the base secured his foot as it leaned on the column, the leather support extending all the way to his knee. The circular base allowed him swift movement for shooting his arrows in all directions. Nevertheless, his back showed signs of visible strain as he held the bow aloft with the arrow nocked on the bowstring.

Ram would have preferred it if his father did not exert his weakened body so. But he also admired the spirit that drove him to push his corporeal frame beyond its natural limits.

'There's nothing there, I tell you,' whispered Lakshman.

'Shh,' said Ram.

Lakshman fell silent. Suddenly, Dashrath flexed his right shoulder and pulled the bowstring back. Ram winced as he watched the technique. Dashrath's elbow was not in line with the arrow, which would put greater pressure on his shoulder and triceps. Sweat beads formed on the emperor's forehead, but he held position. A moment later he released the arrow, and a loud roar confirmed that it had found its mark. Ram revelled in the spirit of the all-conquering hero that his father had once been.

Dashrath swivelled awkwardly on the howdah and looked at Lakshman with a sneer. 'Don't underestimate me, young man.'

Lakshman immediately bowed his head. 'I'm sorry, Father. I didn't mean to…'

'Order some soldiers to fetch the carcass of that tiger. They will find it with an arrow pierced through its eye and buried in its brain.'

'Yes, Father, I'll—'

'Father!' screamed Ram as he lunged forward, drawing a knife quickly from the scabbard tied around his waist.

There was a loud rustle of leaves as a leopard emerged on a branch overhanging the howdah. The sly beast had planned its attack meticulously. Dashrath was distracted as the leopard leapt from the branch. Ram's timing, however, was perfect. He jumped up and plunged his knife into the airborne animal's chest. But the suddenness of the charge made Ram miss his mark. The knife didn't find the leopard's heart. The beast was injured, but not dead. It roared in fury and slashed with its claws. Ram wrestled with the leopard as he tried to pull the knife out so he could take another stab; but it was stuck. The animal pulled back and sank his teeth into the prince's left triceps. Ram yelled in pain as he attempted to push the animal out of the howdah. The leopard pulled back its head, ripping out flesh and drawing large spurts of blood. It instinctively struggled to move to Ram's neck, to asphyxiate the prince. Ram pulled back his right fist and hit the leopard hard across its head.

Lakshman, in the meantime, was desperately trying to reach Ram even as Dashrath blocked his way, tied as he was to the stationary column. Lakshman jumped high, caught an overhanging branch and swung out of the howdah in an arc. He propelled himself forward and landed in front of the howdah, right behind the leopard. He drew his knife as the leopard pulled back again to bite into Ram. Lakshman thrust brutally and, by good fortune, the blade sank into the leopard's eye. The animal howled in pain as a shower of blood sprang out of its shattered eye-socket. Lakshman strained his mighty shoulder and jammed hard, pushing the knife deep into the animal's brain. The beast struggled for a brief moment and then fell, lifeless.

Lakshman picked up the leopard's body with his bare hands, and threw it to the ground. Ram had collapsed in a pool of blood.

'Ram!' screamed Dashrath, twisting desperately as his right leg remained fixed to the column.

Lakshman turned to the mahout. 'Back to the camp!'

The mahout sat paralysed, shaken by the sudden turn of events. Dashrath bellowed his imperial command. 'Back to the camp! Now!'

— |大| ▮ ☼ —

Torches were lit across a hunting camp seized with frenetic activity late into the night. The injured prince of Ayodhya lay in the massive and luxurious tent of the emperor. He should have been in the medical tent, but Dashrath had insisted that his son be tended to in the comfort of the emperor's living quarters. Ram's pallid body was covered in bandages, weak from tremendous loss of blood.

'Prince Ram,' whispered the doctor as he touched the prince gently.

'Do you *have* to wake him up?' demanded Dashrath, sitting on a comfortable chair placed to the left of the bed.

'Yes, Your Majesty,' said the doctor. 'He must take this medicine now.'

As the doctor repeated Ram's name, the prince opened his eyes, blinking slowly to adjust to the light. He saw the doctor holding the bowl of medicine. He opened his mouth and swallowed the paste, wincing at the bitter taste. The doctor turned, bowed towards the emperor and left the room. Ram was about to slip back into sleep when he noticed the ceremonial gold umbrella on top of the bed. At its centre was a massive sun in intricate embroidery, with rays streaming boldly out in all directions; the Suryavanshi symbol. Ram's eyes flew open as he struggled to get up. He wasn't supposed to be sleeping on the emperor's bed.

'Lie down,' commanded Dashrath, raising his hand.

Lakshman rushed over to the bed and gently tried to calm his brother down.

'In the name of Lord Surya, lie down, Ram!' said Dashrath.

Ram fell back on the bed as he looked towards Dashrath. 'Father, I'm sorry. I shouldn't be on your—'

Dashrath cut him off mid-sentence with a wave of his hand. Ram couldn't help but notice a subtle change in his father's appearance. A spark in the eyes, steel in the voice, and an alertness that brought back stories his mother would constantly repeat, about the kind of man Dashrath had once been. Here sat a powerful man who wouldn't take kindly to his orders being disregarded. Ram had never seen him like this.

Dashrath turned to his attendants. 'Leave us.'

Lakshman rose to join the attendants.

'Not you, Lakshman,' said Dashrath.

Lakshman stopped in his tracks and waited for further orders. Dashrath stared at the tiger and leopard skins spread out in the corner of the tent; trophies of the animals he and his sons had hunted.

'Why?' asked Dashrath.

'Father?' asked Ram, confused.

'Why did you risk your life for me?'

Ram did not utter a word.

Dashrath continued, 'I blamed you for my defeat. My entire kingdom blamed you; cursed you. You've suffered all your life, and yet you never rebelled. I thought it was because you were weak. But weak people celebrate when twists of fate hurt their tormentors. And yet, you risked your life trying to protect me. Why?'

Ram answered with one simple statement. 'Because that is my *dharma*, Father.'

Dashrath looked quizzically at Ram. This was the first real conversation he was having with his eldest son. 'Is that the only reason?'

'What other reason can there be?'

'Oh, I don't know,' said Dashrath, snorting with disbelief. 'How about angling for the position of crown prince?'

Ram couldn't help smiling at the irony. 'The nobility will never accept me, Father, even if I'm able to convince you. It is not in my scheme of things. What I did today, is what I must always do: be true to my *dharma*. Nothing is more important than *dharma*.'

'So, you don't believe that you are to blame for my defeat at the hands of Raavan, is it?'

'It doesn't matter what I think, Father.'

'You didn't answer my question.'

Ram remained silent.

Dashrath leaned forward. 'Answer me, prince.'

'I don't understand how the universe keeps track of our karma across many births, Father. I know I could not have done anything in this birth to make you lose the battle. Maybe it was something to do with my previous birth?'

Dashrath laughed softly, amazed at his son's equanimity.

'Do you know whom I blame?' asked Dashrath. 'If I were truly honest, if I had had the courage to look deep into my heart, the answer would have been obvious. It was my fault; only my fault. I was reckless and foolhardy. I attacked without a plan, driven only by anger. I paid the price, didn't I? My first defeat ever... And, my last battle, forever.'

'Father, there are many—'

'Do not interrupt me, Ram. I'm not finished.' Ram fell silent and Dashrath continued. 'It was my fault. And I blamed the infant that you were. It was so easy. I just had to say it, and everyone agreed with me. I made your life hell from the day you were born. You should hate me. You should hate Ayodhya.'

'I don't hate anyone, Father.'

Dashrath stared hard at his son. After what seemed like eternity, his face broke into a peculiar smile. 'I don't know whether you've suppressed your true feelings completely or you genuinely don't care about the ignominy that people have heaped on you. Whatever be the truth, you have held strong. The entire universe conspired to break you, and here you are, still unbowed. What metal have you been forged in, my son?'

Ram's eyes moistened as emotion welled within him. He could handle disdain and apathy from his father; he was used to it. Respect was difficult to deal with. 'I was forged from your metal, my father.'

Dashrath laughed softly. He was discovering his son.

'What are your differences with Mrigasya?' asked Dashrath.

Ram was surprised to discover that his father kept track of court matters. 'None at all, Father.'

'Then why did you penalise one of his men?'

'He broke the law.'

'Don't you know how powerful Mrigasya is? Aren't you afraid of him?'

'Nobody is above the law, Father. None can be more powerful than *dharma*.'

Dashrath laughed. 'Not even me?'

'A great emperor said something beautiful once: *Dharma* is above all, even the king. *Dharma* is above the Gods themselves.'

Dashrath frowned. 'Who said this?'

'You did, Father, when you took your oath at your coronation, decades ago. I was told that you had paraphrased our great ancestor Lord Ikshvaku himself.'

Dashrath stared at Ram as he jogged his memory to remember the powerful man he had once been.

'Go to sleep, my son,' said Dashrath. 'You need the rest.'

Chapter 12

Ram was awakened by the doctor at the beginning of the second *prahar* for his next dose of medicine. As he looked around the room, his eyes fell on a visibly delighted Lakshman, standing by his bedside bedecked in a formal *dhoti* and *angvastram*. The saffron *angvastram* had a Suryavanshi sun emblazoned across its length.

'Son?'

Ram turned his head to the left and saw his father attired in regal finery. The emperor sat on his travel-throne; the Suryavanshi crown was placed on his head.

'Father,' said Ram. 'Good morning.'

Dashrath nodded crisply. 'It will be a fine morning, no doubt.'

The emperor turned towards the entrance of his tent. 'Is anyone there?'

A guard pulled the curtain aside and rushed in, saluting rapidly.

'Let the nobles in.'

The guard saluted once again and retraced his steps. Within minutes, the nobles entered the tent in single file. They gathered in a semicircle around the emperor, waiting with a solemn air of ceremony.

'Let me see my son,' said Dashrath.

The nobles parted immediately, surprised at the voice of authority emerging from their emperor.

Dashrath looked directly at Ram. 'Rise.'

Lakshman rushed over to help Ram, but Dashrath raised his hand firmly to stop him from doing so. The assemblage stood rooted as it watched a severely weakened Ram struggle to raise himself, stand on his feet and hobble towards his father. He saluted slowly once he reached the emperor.

Dashrath locked eyes with his son, inhaled deeply and spoke clearly, 'Kneel.'

Ram was unable to move, overwhelmed by a sense of shocked disbelief. Tears welled up in his eyes, despite his willing them not to do so.

Dashrath's voice softened slightly. 'Kneel, my son.'

Ram struggled with emotions as he sought the support of a table close at hand. Laboriously, he went down on one knee, bowed his head and awaited the call of destiny.

Dashrath spoke evenly, his voice reverberating even outside the royal tent. 'Rise, Ram Chandra, *protector* of the Raghu clan.'

A collective gasp resounded through the tent.

Dashrath raised his head and the courtiers fell into a taut silence.

Ram still had his head bowed, lest his enemies see the tears in his eyes. He stared at the floor till he regained absolute control. Then he looked up at his father and spoke in a calm voice. 'May all the Gods of our great land continue to protect you, my father.'

Dashrath's eyes seemed to penetrate the soul of his eldest son. A hint of a smile appeared on his face as he looked towards his nobles. 'Leave us.'

General Mrigasya attempted to say something. 'Your Majesty, but—'

Dashrath interrupted him with a glare. 'What part of "leave us" did you not understand, Mrigasya?'

'My apologies, Your Majesty,' said Mrigasya, as he saluted and led the nobles out.

Dashrath, Ram and Lakshman were soon alone in the tent. Dashrath leaned heavily to his left as he made an effort to get up, resisting Lakshman's offer of help with a brusque grunt. Once on his feet, he beckoned Lakshman, placed his hand on his son's massive shoulders and hobbled over to Ram. Ram, too, had risen slowly to his feet and stood erect. His face was inscrutable, his eyes awash with emotion, though coupled with surprising tranquillity.

Dashrath placed his hands on Ram's shoulders. 'Become the man that I could have become; the man that I did not become.'

Ram whispered softly, his vision clouded, 'Father…'

'Make me proud,' said Dashrath, with tears finally welling up in his eyes.

'Father…'

'Make me proud, my son.'

—— 𖣔 ⬮ ☼ ——

All doubts about the tectonic shifts that had taken place in the royal family were laid to rest when Dashrath moved out of Kaikeyi's wing of the Ayodhya palace. He had been unable to convincingly answer Kaikeyi's repeated and forceful questions as to why he had suddenly made Ram the crown prince. Dashrath moved in, along with his personal staff, to Kaushalya's wing. The bewildered chief queen of Ayodhya had suddenly regained her status. But the timid Kaushalya was careful with her new-found elevation. No changes were attempted, though it was difficult to say whether this was because of her diffidence or fear that the good fortune might not last.

Ram's brothers were delighted. Bharat and Shatrughan had rushed to his chambers on their return from Branga, word having reached them even as they travelled back home. Roshni had decided to join them.

'Congratulations, *Dada*!' said Bharat, embracing his elder brother with obvious delight.

'You deserve it,' said Shatrughan.

'He surely does,' said Roshni, her face suffused with joy. 'I ran into Guru Vashishtha on my way here. He mentioned that the reduction in the crime rate in Ayodhya is only a tiny example of what Ram can truly achieve.'

'You bet!' said Lakshman, enthusiastically.

'All right, all right,' said Ram, 'you're embarrassing me now!'

'Aaah,' grinned Bharat, 'that's the point of it all, *Dada*!'

'As far as I know, speaking the truth has not been banned in any scripture,' said Shatrughan.

'And we'd better believe him, *Dada*,' said Lakshman, laughing heartily. 'Shatrughan is the only man I know who can recite every single *Veda, Upanishad, Brahmana, Aranyaka, Vedanga, Smriti,* and everything else communicated or known to man!'

'The weight of his formidable brain pressed so hard upon his body that it arrested his vertical growth!' Bharat joined in.

Shatrughan boxed Lakshman playfully on his well-toned abdomen, chuckling along good-naturedly.

Lakshman laughed boisterously. 'Do you really think I can feel your feeble hits, Shatrughan? You may have got all the brain cells created in *Maa's* womb, but I got all the brawn!'

The brothers laughed even louder. Roshni was happy that, despite all the political intrigue in the Ayodhyan court, the princes shared a healthy camaraderie with each other. Clearly the Gods were looking out for the future of the kingdom.

She patted Ram on his shoulder. 'I have to go.'

'Go where?' asked Ram.

'Saraiya. You're aware that I hold a medical camp in our surrounding villages once a month, right? It's Saraiya's turn this month.'

Ram looked a little worried. 'I will send some bodyguards with you. The villages around Saraiya are not safe.'

Roshni smiled. 'Thanks to you, criminal activity is at an all-time low. Your law enforcement has ensured that. There is nothing to worry about.'

'I have not been able to achieve that completely, and you know it. Look, there's no harm in being safe.'

Roshni noticed that Ram was still wearing the *rakhi* she had tied on his wrist a long time ago. She smiled. 'Don't worry, Ram. It's a day trip, I'll be back before nightfall. And I will not be alone. My assistants will be accompanying me. We will give the villagers free medicines and treatment, if required. Nobody will hurt me. Why would they want to?'

Bharat, who had been listening in on the conversation, stepped up and put his arm around Roshni's shoulder. 'You are a good woman, Roshni.'

Roshni smiled in a childlike manner. 'That I am.'

The blazing afternoon sun did not deter Lakshman, Ayodhya's finest rider, from honing his skills. He knew that the ability of horse and horseman to come to a sudden halt was of critical advantage in battle. To practise this art he chose a spot some distance away from the city, where sheer cliffs descended into the rapids of the Sarayu deep below.

'Come on!' shouted Lakshman, spurring his horse on as it galloped towards the cliff edge.

As his horse thundered dangerously near the edge of the precipice, Lakshman waited till the last moment, leaned forward in his saddle, and wrapped his left arm around the horse's neck even as he pulled the reins hard with his right. The magnificent beast responded instantly by rearing up on its hind legs. The rear hooves left a mark on the ground as the horse stopped a few feet away from certain death. Gracefully dismounting, Lakshman stroked its mane in appreciation.

'Well done … well done.'

The horse's tail swished in acknowledgment of the praise.

'Once again?'

The animal had had enough and snorted its refusal with a vigorous shake of its head. Lakshman laughed softly as he patted the horse, remounted and steered the reins in the opposite direction. 'All right. Let's go home.'

As he rode through the woods, a meeting was in progress a short distance away; one he may have liked to eavesdrop on, had he been aware of it. Guru Vashishtha was engrossed in deep discussion with the same mysterious Naga.

'That said, I'm sorry you…'

'…failed?' Vashishtha completed his sentence. The guru had returned to Ayodhya after a long and unexplained absence.

'That is not the word I would have used, Guru*ji*.'

'It's appropriate, though. But it's not just our failure. It's a failure of—'

Vashishtha stopped mid-sentence as he thought he heard a sound.

'What is it?' asked the Naga.

'Did you hear something?' asked Vashishtha.

The Naga looked around, listened carefully for a few seconds, and then shook his head.

'What about Prince Ram?' asked the Naga, resuming the conversation. 'Are you aware that your friend is on his way here, seeking him?'

'I know that.'

'What do you intend to do?'

'What can I do?' asked Vashishtha, raising his hands helplessly. 'Ram will have to handle this himself.'

They heard the unmistakable sound of a twig snapping. Perhaps it was an animal. The Naga murmured cautiously, 'I had better go.'

'Yes,' agreed Vashishtha.

He quickly mounted his horse and looked at Vashishtha. 'With your permission.'

Vashishtha smiled and folded his hands into a namaste. 'Go with Lord Rudra, my friend.'

The Naga returned his namaste. 'Have faith in Lord Rudra, Guru*ji*.'

The Naga gently tapped his horse into motion and rode away.

—— 𝍐 🐚 ☼ ——

'It's only a sprain,' Roshni reassured the child as she wrapped a bandage around his ankle. 'It will heal in a day or two.'

'Are you sure?' asked the worried mother.

Numerous villagers from the surrounding settlements had gathered at the Saraiya village square. Roshni had patiently attended to them all. This was the last patient.

'Yes,' said Roshni, as she patted the child on his head. 'Now, listen to me,' she cupped the child's face with her hands. 'No climbing trees or running around for the next few days. You have to take it easy till your ankle heals.'

The mother cut in. 'I will ensure that he stays at home.'

'Good,' said Roshni.

'Hey, Roshni *Didi!*' said the child, pouting with pretend annoyance. 'Where is my sweet?'

Roshni laughed as she beckoned one of her assistants. She pulled out a sweet from his bag and handed it to the delighted child. She ruffled his hair and then rose from her stool. Stretching her back, she turned to the village chief. 'If you will excuse me, I should be leaving now.'

'Are you sure, My Lady?' asked the chief. 'It's late and you may not be able to reach Ayodhya before nightfall. The city gates will be shut.'

'No, I think I'll make it in time,' said a determined Roshni. 'I have to. My mother wants me back in Ayodhya tonight. She has planned a celebration and I need to be there for it.'

'All right, My Lady, as you wish,' said the chief. 'Thank you so much, once again. I don't know what we would do without you.'

'The one you must truly thank is Lord Brahma, for he has given me the skills to be of use to you.'

The chief, as always, bent down respectfully to touch her feet. Roshni, as always, stepped back. 'Please, don't embarrass me by touching my feet. I am younger than you.'

The chief folded his hands together in a namaste. 'May Lord Rudra bless you, My Lady.'

'May he bless us all!' said Roshni. She walked up to her horse and mounted swiftly. Her assistants had already gathered all their medical material and had mounted their horses. At a signal from Roshni, the trio rode out of the village.

Moments later, eight horse-mounted men appeared at the chief's front door. They were from a nearby village called Isla, and had taken some medicines from Roshni earlier in the day. Their village had been struck by an epidemic of viral fever. One of the riders was an adolescent called Dhenuka, the son of the Isla village chief.

'Brothers,' said the chief. 'Have you got everything you need?'

'Yes,' said Dhenuka. 'But where is Lady Roshni? I wanted to thank her.'

The village chief was surprised. Dhenuka was famous for his rude, uncouth behaviour. But then he had met Roshni for the first time today. She must have impressed even this rowdy youth with her decency and goodness. 'She has ridden out already. She needed to get to Ayodhya before nightfall.'

'Right,' said Dhenuka, scanning the road leading out of the village. He smiled and spurred his horse into action.

'Can I help you, My Lady?' asked Dhenuka.

Roshni turned around, surprised at the intrusion. They had made good time and she had stopped for some rest near the banks of the Sarayu River. They were an hour's ride from Ayodhya.

At first she didn't recognise him, but soon smiled in acknowledgment.

'That's all right, Dhenuka,' said Roshni. 'Our horses needed some rest. I hope one of my assistants explained how the medicine should be administered to your people.'

'Yes, they have,' said Dhenuka, smiling strangely.

Roshni suddenly felt uneasy. Her gut instinct told her that she must leave. 'Well, I hope everyone in your village gets better soon.'

She walked up to her horse and reached for the reins. Dhenuka immediately jumped off his horse and held Roshni's hand, pulling her back. 'What's the rush, My Lady?'

Roshni shoved him back and retreated slowly. The other members of Dhenuka's gang had dismounted by then. Three of them moved towards her assistants.

A terrifying chill went up Roshni's spine. 'I… I helped your people…'

Dhenuka grinned ominously. 'Oh, I know. I'm hoping you can help me too…'

Roshni suddenly turned around and ran. Three men took off after her and caught up in no time. One of them slapped her hard. As blood burst forth from Roshni's injured lips, the second man twisted her hand brutally behind her back.

Dhenuka ambled up slowly, reached out and caressed her face. 'A noble woman… Mmm… This is going to be fun.'

His gang burst out laughing.

— 大 🐟 ☼ —

'*Dada*!' screamed Lakshman as he rushed into Ram's office.

Ram did not raise his eyes as he continued to pore over the documents on his desk. It was the first hour of the second *prahar* and he had expected some peace and quiet.

Ram spoke with casual detachment, continuing to read the document in his hand, 'What's the matter now, Lakshman?'

'*Dada*…' Lakshman was choked with emotion.

'Laksh...' Ram stopped mid-sentence as he looked up and saw the tears streaming down Lakshman's face. 'What happened?'

'*Dada*... Roshni *Didi*...'

Ram immediately stood up, and his chair hurtled back. 'What happened to Roshni?'

'*Dada*...'

'Where is she?'

Chapter 13

A stunned Bharat stood immobile. Lakshman and Shatrughan were bent over, crying inconsolably. Manthara held her daughter's head in her lap, looking into the distance with a vacant expression, her eyes swollen but dry. She was drained of tears. Roshni's body was covered with a white cloth. She had been found lying next to the Sarayu River by Manthara's men, violated and bare. The corpse of one of her assistants lay a short distance away. He had been brutally bludgeoned to death. The other assistant was found by the side of the road, severely injured but still alive. Doctors tended to him as Ram stood by their side; his face was impassive but his hands shook with fury. He had questions for Roshni's assistant.

When Roshni had not returned by the next morning, Manthara had sent out her men to Saraiya to find and bring back her daughter. They had ridden out at dawn as soon as the city gates were unlocked. An hour's ride away from the city, they had chanced upon Roshni's body. She had been brutally gang-raped. Her head had been banged repeatedly against a flat surface. The marks on her wrist and her back suggested that she had been tied to a tree. Her body was covered with bruises and vicious bite marks. The monsters had ripped off some of her skin with their teeth, around her abdomen and bare arms. She had been beaten with a blunt object all over her body, probably in a sick, sadistic ritual. Her face was torn on one side, from her mouth to the cheekbone, the injuries and blood clots in her mouth suggesting that she was probably alive through this torture. There were semen stains all over her body. She had died in a most gruesome manner, as one of the assailants had poured acid down her throat.

The assistant opened his eyes painfully. Ram bent over him and growled. 'Who were they?'

'I don't think he can speak, My Lord,' said the doctor.

Ram ignored the man as he knelt next to the injured assistant. 'Who were they?' he repeated.

Roshni's assistant barely found the strength to whisper a name before he passed out once again.

Roshni was a rare figure who was popular among the masses as well as the classes. She had devoted her life to charity. She was a woman of impeccable character, a picture of grace and dignity. Many compared her to the fabled *Kanyakumari*, the *Virgin Goddess*. The rage that this brutal crime generated was unprecedented. The city demanded retribution.

The criminals were rounded up quickly from Isla village just as they were planning to escape. The chief of Isla was beaten black and blue by the women of his village when he made vain attempts to protect his son. They had suffered Dhenuka's bestiality in silence for too long. Even by the standards of Ram's vastly improved police force, the investigations were completed, the case presented in front of judges, and sentences delivered in record time. Within a week, preparations were on to mete out punishment to the perpetrators. They had all been sentenced to death; all except one; all except Dhenuka.

Ram was devastated that Dhenuka, the main perpetrator of the heinous gang rape and murder, had been exempted from maximum punishment on a legal technicality: he was underage. But the law could not be broken. Not on Ram's watch. Ram, the Law Giver, had to do what he had to do. But Ram, the *rakhi*-brother of Roshni, was drowning in guilt, for he was unable to avenge the horrifying death of his sister. He had to punish himself. And he was doing so by inflicting pain on himself.

He sat alone on a chair in the balcony of his private study, gazing out towards the garden where Roshni had tied a *rakhi* on his wrist. He looked down at the golden thread, eyes brimming with tears. The heat of the mid-day sun bore down mercilessly on his bare torso. He shaded his eyes as he looked up at the sun, and inhaled deeply before turning his attention back to his injured right hand. He picked up the wedge of wood placed on the table by his side. Its tip was smouldering.

He looked up at the sky and whispered, 'I'm sorry, Roshni.'

He pressed the burning wood on the inner side of his right arm, the one that still had the sacred thread which represented his solemn promise to protect his sister. He didn't make a sound, his eyes did not flicker. The acrid smell of burning flesh spread through the air.

'I'm sorry…'

Ram closed his eyes as tears flowed freely down his face.

Hours later, Ram sat in his office with a vacant air of misery. His injured arm was covered by his archer's arm band.

'This is wrong, *Dada*!'

Lakshman entered Ram's office, visibly seething with fury. Ram looked up from his desk, the grief in his eyes concealing the rage within.

'It is the law, Lakshman,' said Ram calmly. 'The law cannot be broken. It is supreme, more important than you or me. Even more important than…'

Ram choked on his words as he could not bring himself to take her name.

'Complete your sentence, *Dada*!' Bharat lashed out harshly from near the door.

Ram looked up. He raised his hand towards Bharat, wincing in pain. 'Bharat…'

Bharat strode into the room, his eyes clouded with sorrow, his body taut, his fingers trembling, yet unable to adequately convey the storm that raged within. 'Finish what you were saying, *Dada*. Say it!'

'Bharat, my brother, listen to me…'

'Let it out! Tell us that your damned law is more important than Roshni!' Fierce tears were flowing in a torrent from Bharat's eyes now. 'Say that it matters more to you than that *rakhi* around your wrist.' He leaned over and grabbed Ram's right arm. Ram did not flinch. 'Say that the law is more important to you than our promise to protect our Roshni forever.'

'Bharat,' said Ram, as he gently freed his arm from his brother's vice-like grip. 'The law is clear: minors cannot be executed. Dhenuka is underage and, according to the law, will not be executed.'

'The hell with the law!' shouted Bharat. 'This is not about the law! This is about justice! Don't you understand the difference, *Dada*? That monster deserves to die!'

'Yes, he does,' said Ram, tormented by the guilt that wracked his soul. 'But a juvenile will not be killed by Ayodhya. That is the law.'

'Dammit, *Dada*!' shouted Bharat, banging his hand on the table.

A loud voice boomed from behind them. 'Bharat!'

The three brothers looked up to find Raj Guru Vashishtha standing at the door. Bharat immediately straightened and folded his hands together in a respectful namaste. Lakshman refused to react, his untrammelled anger now focused on his guru.

Vashishtha walked in with deliberate, slow-paced footsteps. 'Bharat, Lakshman, your elder brother is right. The law must be respected and obeyed, whatever the circumstances.'

'And what about the promise we made to Roshni, Guru*ji*? Doesn't that count?' asked Bharat. 'We gave our word that we would protect her. We had a duty towards her too, and we failed in that. Now, we must avenge her.'

'Your word is not above the law.'

'Guru*ji*, the descendants of Raghu never break their word,' said Bharat, repeating an ancient family code.

'If your word of honour is in conflict with the law, then you must break your word and take dishonour upon your name,' said Vashishtha. 'That is *dharma*.'

'Guru*ji*!' shouted Lakshman, on the brink of losing all semblance of propriety and control.

'Look at this!' said Vashishtha, as he walked up to Ram, tore his archer's band off and raised his arm for all to see. Ram tried to pull it away but Vashishtha held firm.

Bharat and Lakshman were shocked. Ram's right inner arm was badly burnt. The skin around the wound was charred and discoloured.

'He has been doing this again and again, every single day, ever since the judge announced that Dhenuka will escape death on a legal technicality,' said Vashishtha. 'I have been trying to get him to stop. But this is his way of punishing himself for having broken his word to Roshni. However, he will not break the law.'

—— |木| 🐚 ☼ ——

Ram did not attend the execution of the seven rapists.

The judges, in their anger at not being able to put the main accused to death, had, in an act of judicial overreach, prescribed in detail the manner of punishment to be meted out to the seven other accused. Ram's new law on execution had laid out a quick procedure: to be hanged by the neck till the person is dead. Furthermore, he had decreed that the execution be carried out in a designated area of the prison premises, the clause ending with giving the judge discretion in matters of procedure. Using this clause, the fuming judges had pronounced a detailed, exceptional procedure for the execution: that it would be carried out in public, that they would be made to bleed to death, and that it would be as painful as can be; they justified their impropriety by asserting that it would serve as a lesson for all time to come. In private they argued that this would also allow people to adequately give vent to their righteous rage. The police had no choice but to obey the ruling.

The execution platform was constructed outside the city walls, built to a height of four feet to enable an adequate view from even a distance. Thousands gathered outside the city walls from early morning to witness the spectacle. Many were armed with eggs and rotten fruit, to be used as missiles.

An angry roar erupted from the crowds as the seven convicts were led out of the mobile prison carts that they had been transported in. It was clear from the injuries on their body that they had already been beaten mercilessly in the prison; despite his best efforts, Ram had not been able to control the moral outrage of not only the prison guards, but also the other prisoners. Without exception, they had all been the recipients, in some form or the other, of Roshni's benevolence. The desire for retribution was strong.

The criminals walked up the steps of the platform. They were first led to wooden pillories erected on a post, with holes where the head and hands were inserted, exposed to the people for ritual public abuse. Having secured the prisoners, the guards marched off the platform.

That was the cue for the crowd. Missiles began to fly with unerring accuracy, accompanied by vehement cursing and spitting. At this distance, even eggs and fruit drew blood, causing tremendous pain. The crowd had been strictly forbidden from hurling any sharp objects or big stones. No one wanted the convicts to die too quickly. They had to suffer. They had to pay.

This lasted for almost a half hour. The executioner finally called the mass attack to an end when the people began to slow down, probably with exhaustion. He stepped onto the platform and walked up to the first convict, whose wild eyes were frantic with terror. With the help of two assistants, he stretched the convict's legs to the maximum, making him almost choke on the pillory. Then the executioner picked up a large nail and a metalsmith's hammer from the floor, with slow, deliberate movements. As his assistants held the splayed legs apart, the executioner calmly nailed the foot into the wooden platform, hammering with rhythmic precision. The convict screamed desperately as the crowd roared its approval. The executioner carefully examined his handiwork before giving it a few more hits. He stepped back with satisfaction. The convict had just about stopped shrieking in agony when the executioner walked up to his other leg.

He then repeated the horror, one by one, with each of the six other miserable convicts, nailing their feet to the wooden platform. The crowd was delirious and roared with each desperate cry of pain that the criminals let out. When finally finished, the executioner moved to the edge of the platform and waved at the crowd as it cheered him on.

He walked up to the first convict he had nailed. The criminal had fainted by now. Some medicine was forced down his throat and he was slapped till he was awake once again.

'You need to be awake to enjoy this,' hissed the executioner.

'Kill ... me,' pleaded the convict. 'Please ... mercy...'

The executioner's face turned to stone. Roshni had helped deliver his baby girl four months back; all she had accepted in return was a meal in his humble abode. 'Did you have mercy on Lady Roshni, you son of a rabid dog?'

'Sorry ... sorry ... please ... kill me.' The criminal burst into tears.

The executioner walked away nonchalantly.

After three hours of brutal, public torture, the executioner pulled out a small, sharp knife from a scabbard tied to his waist. He loosened the pillory hold on the first convict's right hand and pulled the arm farther out. He examined the wrist closely; he needed to pick the right artery, one that would not bleed out too quickly. He smiled as he found one.

'Perfect,' said the executioner, as he brought his knife close and cut delicately, letting the blood spurt out in small bursts. The convict groaned in agony. Death was at least a painful couple of hours away. The executioner moved quickly, slitting the same artery on the wrists of the remaining criminals. The crowd roared and hurled obscenities each time the knife cut.

The executioner gestured to the crowd that he was done for the day, before stepping down from the platform. They began hurling missiles again, only to be interrupted periodically by an official who would check on the flow of blood. It took two-and-a half more hours for the last of the criminals to finally die, all having suffered a slow and painful death that would scar their soul for many rebirths.

As the criminals were declared dead, the crowd roared loudly: 'Glory to Lady Roshni!'

Manthara sat hunched on an elevated chair, close to the platform. Her eyes still blazed with hatred and fury. She had no doubt the executioner would have tortured the monsters of his own accord; her Roshni was so well loved. Notwithstanding that, she had paid him handsomely to not hold back on the brutality of the execution. She had barely blinked throughout the long and tortuous proceeding, keenly observing each twitch of pain that they had been made to suffer. It was over now, and yet, there was no sense of release, no satisfaction. Her heart had turned to stone.

She clutched an urn close to her chest as she sat. It contained her Roshni's ashes. She looked down as a tear slipped from one eye. It fell on the urn. 'I promise you my child, even the last one will be made to pay for what he did to you. Dhenuka too will face the wrath of justice.'

Chapter 14

'This is barbaric,' said Ram. 'It is against everything Roshni stood for.'

Ram and Vashishtha were in the prince's private office.

'Why is it barbaric?' asked Vashishtha. 'Do you think the rapists should not have been killed?'

'They should have been executed. That is the law. But the way it was done … at least judges should not give in to anger. It was savage, violent and inhumane.'

'Really? Is there such a thing as humane killing?'

'Are you justifying this behaviour, Guru*ji*?'

'Tell me, will rapists and murderers be terrified of breaking the law now?'

Ram was forced to concede. 'Yes…'

'Then, the punishment has served its purpose.'

'But Roshni wouldn't have…'

'There is a school of thought which states that brute force can only be met with equal brute force. One fights fire with fire, Ram.'

'But Roshni would have said that an eye for an eye will only make the whole world blind.'

'There is virtue in non-violence, no doubt, but only when you're not living in the Age of Kshatriya, of violence. If in the Age of Kshatriya, you are among the very few who believe that "an eye for an eye makes the whole world blind", while everyone else believes otherwise, then you will be the one who is blinded. Universal principles too need to adjust themselves to a changing universe.'

Ram shook his head. 'Sometimes I wonder if my people are even worth fighting for.'

'A real leader doesn't choose to lead only the deserving. He will, instead, inspire his people into becoming the best that they are capable of. A real leader will not defend a monster, but convert that demon into a God; tap into the God that dwells within even him. He takes upon himself the burden of *dharma sankat*, but he ensures that his people become better human beings.'

'You are contradicting yourself, Guru*ji*. Was this brutal punishment justified, in that case?'

'According to me, no. But society is not made up of people like you and me. There are all kinds of people with all shades of opinion. A good ruler must prod his people gently in the direction of *dharma,* which lies in the centre, in balance. If there is too much anger in society, leading to chaos and disruptive violence, then the leader needs to move it towards stability and calm. If, on the other hand, a society is passive and uncomplaining, then the leader needs to incite active participation and outrage, even anger, among the people. Every emotion in the universe exists for a purpose; nothing is superfluous in nature's design. Every emotion also has an opposite: like anger and calm. Society ultimately needs balance. But is this display of anger towards Roshni's rapists and murderers the answer to injustice? Maybe, maybe not. We will know for sure in a few decades. For now, it serves as a pressure-release mechanism.'

Ram looked out of the window, deeply unsettled.

Vashishtha knew he couldn't afford any further delay. He didn't have much time on his hands. 'Ram, listen to me.'

'Yes, Guru*ji*,' said Ram.

'Someone is on his way here, he's coming for you. He's a great man, and he's going to take you away. I cannot stop it. It is beyond me.'

'Who is this—'

Vashishtha cut in. 'I assure you, you will not be in danger. But you may be told things about me. I want you to remember that you are like my son. I want to see you fulfil your *swadharma*, your *true purpose*. My actions have been defined by that goal.'

'Guru*ji*, I don't understand what…'

'Do not believe what you hear about me. You are like my son. That is all I will say for now.'

A confused Ram folded his hands together into a namaste. 'Yes, Guru*ji*.'

— 大 🐟 ☼ —

'Manthara, please understand, I can do nothing,' said Kaikeyi. 'It is the law.'

Manthara had not wasted any time in seeking an audience with Ayodhya's second queen. Kaikeyi had a determined visitor early the next morning. The queen continued with her breakfast, Manthara having refused the repast; all she sought was her personal brand of justice. But Kaikeyi would never admit to anyone that she had little influence over Dashrath now, much less on Ram. She resorted to blaming the law. To the proud, the pretence of noble compliance is better than admittance of failure.

But Manthara would not be denied. She was aware that Dhenuka was incarcerated in a high-security prison within the city. She also knew that only a member of the royal family could pull off what she had in mind. 'My Lady, I have enough money to buy every nobleman in the kingdom. You know that. It will all be put at your disposal. I promise.'

Kaikeyi's heart skipped a beat. She knew that with Manthara's immense resources on her side, she might even be able to force Bharat onto the throne. She was careful to remain non-committal. 'Thank you for the promise. But it is a promise for tomorrow. And, who has seen tomorrow?'

Manthara reached into the folds of her *angvastram* and pulled out a *hundi*, a *document bearing her official seal*. It promised to honour the debt of a stated sum of money. Kaikeyi was keenly aware that what she was receiving was, for all practical purposes, cash. Anyone in the Sapt Sindhu would give her money against a *hundi* signed by Manthara; her reputation in such matters was unquestionable. Kaikeyi accepted the *hundi* and scanned it quickly as she did so. The queen was shocked. The staggering amount that was neatly inscribed in the document was the equivalent of more than ten years of Ayodhya's royal revenue. In a flash, she had made Kaikeyi richer than the king! The extent of this woman's fabulous wealth was beyond even the queen's imagination.

'I understand that encashing a *hundi* of this large an amount of money might prove difficult for most merchants, My Lady,' said Manthara. 'Whenever you need the money, I will reimburse this *hundi* myself and pay the amount in gold coins.'

Kaikeyi was well aware of another exemplary law: refusal to honour a *hundi* led to many years of imprisonment in a debtor's prison.

Manthara drove her advantage home. 'I have a lot more where this came from. It is all at your disposal.'

Kaikeyi held the *hundi* tight. She knew that it was her ticket to realising all her dreams for her son; ones that had started looking distant due to recent events.

Manthara struggled out of her chair, hobbled to Kaikeyi, and leaned over as she hissed, 'I want him to suffer. I want him to suffer as much as he made my daughter suffer. I am not interested in a speedy death.'

Kaikeyi gripped Manthara's hands firmly. 'I swear by the great Lord Indra, that monster shall know what justice means.'

Manthara stared at the queen in stony silence. Her body quivered with cold rage.

'He will suffer,' promised Kaikeyi. 'Roshni will be avenged. That is the word of the queen of Ayodhya.'

—— 𣸧 ◉ ☼ ——

'*Maa*, believe me, I would love to kill that monster with my bare hands,' said Bharat, earnestly. 'I know I would be serving the cause of justice if I were to do so. But Ram *Dada's* new law forbids it.'

Kaikeyi had left for Bharat's quarters as soon as Manthara exited the palace. She knew exactly what she had to do, and how to go about it. Appealing to her son's ambition would be a waste of time; he was more loyal to his half-brother than he was to his own mother. She had to appeal to his sense of justice, his righteous anger, his love for Roshni.

'I fail to understand this new law, Bharat. What kind of justice did it serve?' asked Kaikeyi passionately. 'Doesn't the *Manu Smriti* clearly state that the Gods abandon the land where women are not respected?'

'Yes, *Maa*, but this is the law! Minors cannot be given the death sentence.'

'Do you know that Dhenuka is not even underage anymore? He was a minor only when the crime was committed.'

'I'm aware of that, *Maa*. I've had a massive fight with *Dada* over it. I agree with you, justice is far more important than the technicalities of a law. But *Dada* doesn't understand that.'

'Yes, he doesn't,' fumed Kaikeyi.

'*Dada* lives in a world that should be, not the world as it is. He wants to enforce the values of an ideal society, but he forgets that Ayodhya is not an ideal society. We are very far from it. And monsters like Dhenuka will always exploit the loopholes in the law and escape. Others will learn from him. A leader has to first make the society worthy of enlightened laws before implementing them.'

'Then, why don't you…'

'I can't. If I break, or even question *Dada*'s law, I will hurt his credibility. Why will anyone else take him seriously if his own brother doesn't?'

'You are missing the point. Criminals who were afraid of Ram's laws thus far, will now know that there are ways to exploit and work around them. Juveniles will be made to commit crimes planned by adults. There are enough poor, frustrated, underage youths who can easily be influenced into a life of crime for a handful of coins.'

'It's possible.'

'An example must be made of Dhenuka. That will serve as a lesson to others.'

Bharat looked at Kaikeyi quizzically. 'Why are you so interested in this, *Maa*?'

'I just want justice for our Roshni.'

'Really?'

'She was a noblewoman, Bharat. Your *rakhi*-sister was raped by a bloody villager,' Kaikeyi drove the point home.

'I'm curious; would you be thinking differently had it been the other way round? Had a nobleman raped a village woman, would you still be clamouring for justice?'

Kaikeyi remained silent. She knew that if she said yes, Bharat would not believe her.

'I would want a rapist-murderer from the nobility to be killed as well,' growled Bharat. 'Just like I want Dhenuka to be killed. That is true justice.'

'Then why is Dhenuka still alive?'

'The other rapists *have* been punished.'

'This is a first! Partial justice! Disingenuous, isn't it? There is no such thing as partial justice, son! You either get justice or you don't!'

'*Maa...*'

'The most brutal among them is still alive! What's more, he's a guest of Ayodhya! His board and lodging are being financed by the royal treasury; from your coffers. You are personally feeding the man who brutalised your *rakhi*-sister.'

Bharat remained quiet.

'Maybe Ram did not love Roshni enough,' ventured Kaikeyi.

'In the name of Lord Rudra, how can you say that, *Maa*? Ram *Dada* has been punishing himself because...'

'How does that make any sense?! How does that get her justice?'

Bharat fell silent.

'You have Kekaya blood in you. You have the blood of Ashwapati coursing through your veins. Have you forgotten our ancient motto? "Blood shall always be answered with blood!" Only then do others learn to be afraid of you.'

'Of course, I remember that, *Maa*! But I will not hurt Ram *Dada's* credibility.'

'I know a way...'

Bharat looked at Kaikeyi, puzzled.

'You should leave Ayodhya on a diplomatic visit. I will publicise your absence. Double back to Ayodhya incognito; get some of your trusted men to break into prison and escape with Dhenuka. You know what you have to do with him. Resume your foreign visit after the deed is done. Nobody will be any the wiser. Practically the whole city will come under suspicion for the killing, for there is no one in Ayodhya who doesn't want Dhenuka dead. It will be impossible for Ram to discover who did it. Ram will escape the stigma of being seen as shielding his brother, for no one will connect you to it. It will just be seen as the one time that Ram was unable to catch the so-called killer. Most importantly, justice will be served.'

'You have really thought this through,' said Bharat. 'And, how do I leave the city without a diplomatic invitation? If I ask for royal permission to leave without one, it will raise suspicion.'

'There is already an invitation for you from Kekaya for a diplomatic visit.'

'No, there isn't.'

'Yes, there is,' said Kaikeyi. 'It did not come to anyone's notice in the chaos and confusion following Roshni's death.' What she did not reveal to Bharat was that she had used some of her newly-acquired wealth to get a back-dated invitation from Kekaya inserted into the Ayodhya diplomatic files. 'Accept the invitation. And then get justice for your sister's soul.'

Bharat sat still, cold as ice, as he contemplated what his mother had just said.

'Bharat?'

He looked at his mother, as if startled by her presence.

'Will you or won't you?'

Bharat murmured, almost to himself, 'Sometimes you have to break the law to do justice.'

Kaikeyi pulled out a piece of bloodied white cloth from the folds of her *angvastram*; it was from the one that had been used to cover Roshni's brutalised body. 'Help her get justice.'

Bharat took the cloth gently from his mother, gazed at it and then at his *rakhi*. He closed his eyes as a tear slid down his cheek.

Kaikeyi came up to her son and held him tight. 'Shakti *Maa* has her eyes on you, my son. You cannot allow the one who has committed such a heinous crime on a woman to go unpunished. Remember that.'

Shakti Maa, the *Mother Goddess*, was a deity that all Indians looked upon with love. And fear.

Blood shall always be answered with blood.

Dhenuka was awoken by the sound of a door creaking open in his solitary cell at the royal prison.

There was no light streaming in, even from the high window on this dark, moonless night. He sensed danger. He turned his body towards the door, pretending to be asleep as he clenched his fists tight, ready for attack. He opened his eyes slightly, but it was impossible to see anything in the dark.

He heard a soft whistle above his head. Dhenuka sprang up as he hit out hard. There was nobody there. But the sound *had* come from above. A confused Dhenuka's eyes darted in all directions, desperately trying to see what was going on. The blow came unexpectedly.

He felt a sharp blow on the back of his head and he was thrown to the front. A hand yanked him by the hair and shoved a wet cloth against his nose. Dhenuka instantly recognised the odour of the sweet-smelling liquid. He himself had used it on his victims on many an occasion. He knew he couldn't fight it. He fell unconscious in a matter of seconds.

Dhenuka awoke to the gentle rolling of wheels on a dirt road. He seemed unhurt, except for the blow to his head, which made it throb unbearably. His kidnappers hadn't injured him. He wondered who they were. Could they be his father's men, helping him escape? Where was he? Now, bumps on the road were making the wheels bounce, and the steady sound of crickets seemed to indicate that they were in a jungle, already outside the city. He tried to raise his head to get a better sense of his whereabouts, but the wet cloth made an appearance again. He fell unconscious.

A splash of water woke Dhenuka up with a start. He shook his head, cursing loudly.

A surprisingly gentle voice was heard. 'Come, now.'

An astonished but wary Dhenuka tried to sit upright. He realised that he was in a covered bullock cart, the kind used to transport hay. He brushed some that was still lying around off his body. He was assisted as he stepped down. It was still pitch dark but some torches had been lit, which allowed him to look around to find his bearings. He still felt groggy and unsteady on his feet; perhaps the after-effects of the sedative that had been administered. He reached out and grabbed the cart to steady himself.

'Drink this,' said a man who silently materialised beside him, holding a cup.

Dhenuka took the cup from his hand but hesitated as he examined the contents warily.

'If I had wanted to kill you, I would have done so already,' said the man. 'This will clear your head. You will need your wits about you for what is to follow.'

Dhenuka drank the contents without a protest. The effect was almost instantaneous. His head cleared and his mind became alert. As his senses stabilised, Dhenuka heard the sound of flowing water.

Perhaps I'm near the river. The moment the sun rises, I will swim across to safety. But where is Father? Only he could have bribed the officials to engineer my escape.

'Thank you,' said Dhenuka, as he returned the cup to the man. 'But where is my father?'

The man silently took the cup and melted into the darkness. Dhenuka was left alone. 'Hey! Where are you going?'

A well-built figure emerged from where the man had disappeared. His fair skin shone in the light of the fire torches, as did his bright green *dhoti* and *angvastram*. He wore a small head band that held his long hair in place; it had an intricately-built, golden peacock feather attached to it. His eyes, normally mischievous, were like shards of ice.

'Prince Bharat!' exclaimed Dhenuka, as he quickly went down on one knee.

Bharat walked up to Dhenuka without replying.

Dhenuka had heard of Bharat's popularity with the women of Kosala. 'I knew you would understand me. I didn't expect any better from your strait-laced elder brother.'

Bharat stood still, breathing evenly.

'I knew you would understand that women have been created for our enjoyment, My Lord. Women are meant to be used by men!' Dhenuka laughed softly, bowed his head, and reached out to hold Bharat's *angvastram* in a gesture of humble gratitude.

Bharat moved suddenly, flung Dhenuka's hand aside, and grabbed his throat, a menacing voice emerging through his gritted teeth. 'Women are not meant to be used. They are meant to be loved.'

Dhenuka's expression changed to one of unadulterated terror. Like a trapped animal, he stood rooted to the spot as twenty powerfully-built men emerged, seemingly from nowhere. He struggled to break free of Bharat as the prince began to slowly squeeze his throat.

'My Lord,' interrupted a man from behind.

Bharat caught his breath and abruptly released Dhenuka. 'You will not die so quickly.'

Dhenuka coughed desperately as he strained to recover his breath. All of a sudden he straightened, whirled around and tried to make a dash for it. Two men grabbed him roughly and dragged him back to the cart, kicking and screaming.

'The law!' screeched Dhenuka. 'The law! I cannot be touched. I was a juvenile!'

A third man stepped forward and punched Dhenuka in the jaw, breaking a tooth and drawing blood. 'You are not a juvenile anymore.'

'But Prince Ram's laws—'

Dhenuka's words were cut short as the man boxed him again in the face, this time breaking his nose. 'Do you see Prince Ram anywhere?'

'Tie him up,' said Bharat.

Some men picked up the torches as two others dragged Dhenuka backwards, to a large tree. They spread his arms wide and tied them around the tree trunk with a rope. They spread his legs apart and repeated the process with his feet. One of them turned around. 'It is done, My Lord.'

Bharat turned to his side. 'I'm saying this for the last time, Shatrughan. Leave. You don't have to be here. Stay away from this…'

Shatrughan cut in. 'I will always be by your side, *Dada*.'

Bharat stared at Shatrughan with expressionless eyes.

Shatrughan continued. 'This may be against the law, but it is just.'

Bharat nodded and began to walk forward. As he approached Dhenuka, he pulled out a piece of bloodied white cloth from under his waistband, touched it to his head reverentially, and tied it around his right wrist, above the *rakhi*.

Dhenuka was as desperate as a tethered goat surrounded by a pride of lions. He bleated, 'My Lord, please, let me go. I swear, I will never touch a woman again.'

Bharat slapped him hard across his face. 'Do you recognise this place?'

Dhenuka looked around and realisation dawned. This was where he and his gang had raped and murdered Roshni.

Bharat held out his hand. One of his soldiers immediately stepped up and handed him a metallic bottle. Bharat opened the lid and held it close to Dhenuka's nose. 'You will soon know what pain really means.'

Dhenuka burst into tears as he recognised the acidic smell. 'My Lord, I'm sorry… I'm so sorry… Forgive me… Let me go… Please…'

'Remember Roshni *Didi's* cries, you filthy dog,' growled Shatrughan.

Dhenuka pleaded desperately, 'Lady Roshni was a good woman, My Lord… I was a monster… I'm sorry… But she wouldn't want you to do this…'

Bharat returned the bottle to the soldier while another soldier handed him a large twisted drill. Bharat placed the sharp end of the drill on Dhenuka's shoulder. 'Maybe you are right. She was so good that she would have forgiven even a monster like you. But I am not as good as she was.'

Dhenuka began wailing in a loud, high-pitched voice as a soldier stepped up and handed Bharat a hammer.

'Scream all you want, you demented bastard,' said the soldier. 'Nobody will hear you.'

'*Nooooo! Please…*'

Bharat raised his arm and held the hammer high. He positioned the twisted drill on Dhenuka's shoulder. He just wanted a hole large enough to pour some acid into. A quick death would end the suffering and pain too soon.

'Blood shall always be answered with blood…' whispered Bharat.

The hammer came down, the drill penetrated perfectly. Desperate screams rang out loud and clear, above the noise of the raging Sarayu.

Chapter 15

As the first rays of the sun hesitantly nudged at the darkness, Kaikeyi set off for a rendezvous with Bharat and Shatrughan across the Sarayu River, beyond the northernmost tip of Ayodhya; it was at least a two-hour ride from the southern side, where Dhenuka's corpse lay.

The brothers had assiduously washed off the blood and other signs of the events of the night before. Their blood-stained clothes had been burnt after they donned fresh garments. Kaikeyi was accompanied by Bharat's bodyguards.

She stepped down from her chariot and embraced the two. 'You have served justice, my boys.'

Bharat and Shatrughan did not say anything, their faces a mask that hid the storm still raging within; anger still coursing through them. Sometimes wrath is required to deliver justice. But the strange thing about anger is that it is like fire; the more you feed it, the more it grows. It takes a lot of wisdom to know when to let anger go. The princes, still young, had not yet mastered this.

'And now, you must leave,' said Kaikeyi.

Bharat held out the piece from the blood-stained cloth that had covered Roshni's body.

'I will return this to Manthara personally,' said Kaikeyi, as she took the cloth from Bharat.

Bharat bent down to touch his mother's feet. 'Bye, *Maa.*'
Shatrughan followed suit wordlessly.

Dhenuka's body was found by a group of villagers walking by,
as they heard the cawing of a murder of crows, fighting over
his entrails.

The villagers cut the ropes that still held the body and
laid it on the ground. Numerous holes had been viciously
hammered into him while he was still alive, judging by the clot
formation around the wounds. The burn marks around the
holes indicated that something acidic had been poured into
each of these wounds.

Death had become inevitable once a sword was rammed
into Dhenuka's abdomen, right through to the tree trunk. He
must have slowly bled to death; he was probably still alive
when the crows had swooped down for a feast.

One of the villagers recognised Dhenuka. 'Why don't we
just leave?' he asked.

'No, we'll wait,' said the leader of the group, wiping a tear
from his eye as he asked one of his men to walk to Ayodhya
and convey the news. He too had known Roshni's kindness.
His anger had known no bounds when he had discovered that
Dhenuka would be let off on a legal technicality. He wished
that he'd been the one who killed this monster. He turned to
the Sarayu and thanked the River Goddess, for justice had
been served.

He looked down and spat on the corpse.

Manthara rode out of the North Gate on a horse-drawn carriage, accompanied by Druhyu, her man Friday, and some bodyguards. They crossed the Grand Canal, moving steadily till they reached the cremation ground by the river in half an hour. At the far end of the ghats was the temple of the mythical first mortal, Lord Yama. Interestingly, Lord Yama was revered as both the God of Death as well as the God of Dharma. The ancients believed that *dharma* and death were interlinked. In a sense, a tally sheet was drawn at the end of one's mortal life; if there was an imbalance, the soul would have to return to physical form in another mortal body; if the accounts were in balance and karma was in alignment with *dharma*, then the soul would attain ultimate salvation: release from the cycle of rebirth, and reunification with the universal soul, the *Parmatma*, the *Ekam*, the *Brahman*.

Seven pandits conducted the rites in the temple of Lord Yama as Manthara held the urn, within which lay the ashes of her most beauteous creation. In a second urn was the bloodied white cloth that Kaikeyi had handed to her in the morning.

Druhyu sat by the river, quietly contemplating the tumultuous changes that had occurred within a brief span of time. His mistress had changed forever. He had never seen her do the things she had done in the past few days; actions that could directly harm her business and even her personal well-being. She had staked her life's work at the altar of vengeance. Druhyu suspected that his true lord would be incensed by the amount of money that had been thrown away of late. A large portion of it was not Manthara's to do with as she pleased. He was afraid for his own well-being. A movement at the temple door distracted him.

As Manthara walked towards the ghats, her limp seemed more pronounced, her hunched back more bent. Her guards walked silently behind her, followed by the chanting *pandits*. She slowly descended to the river, one step at a time. She sat on the final step, the water from the river edge gently lapping around her feet. She waved the guards away. The *pandits* stood a step above, diligently reciting Sanskrit mantras to help the soul on its journey into the next world, beyond the mythical river Vaitarni. They concluded their prayers by repeating a hymn from the *Isha Vasya Upanishad,* one that had also been recited during the cremation ceremony.

Vayur anilam amritam; Athedam bhasmantam shariram

Let this temporary body be burned to ashes. But the breath of life belongs elsewhere. May it find its way back to the Immortal Breath.

Druhyu observed the proceedings from a distance, his attention focused on the pathetic shadow of the calculating, sharp woman that Manthara had once been. A single thought kept running in his mind, as if on a loop.

The old woman has lost it. She is no longer useful to the true lord. I need to take care of myself now.

Manthara held the urn close to her bosom. Inhaling deeply, she finally mustered the strength to do what had to be done. She opened the lid and turned the urn upside down, allowing her daughter's ashes to drift away in the river waters. She held the bloodied white cloth close to her face and whispered, 'Don't come back to this ugly world, my child; it has not been created for one as pure as you.'

Manthara stared at her daughter's remains moving steadily away from her. She looked up at the sky, her chest bursting with anger.

Ram…

Manthara squeezed her eyes shut, her breath emerging in erratic rasps.

You protected that monster… You protected Dhenuka… I will remember…

— 𝝢 🐟 ☀ —

'Who's responsible for this?' growled Ram, his body taut with tension. He was surrounded by police officials.

Ram had rushed to the scene of the crime as soon as he received intimation of the grisly murder of Dhenuka. The officers were silent, taken aback by the fury of a man who was defined by his composure.

'This is a travesty of the law, a perversion of justice,' said Ram. 'Who did this?'

'I … I don't know, My Lord,' said one of the officers nervously.

Ram leaned towards the frightened man, stepping closer. 'Do you really expect me to believe that?'

A loud shout was heard from behind. '*Dada!*'

Ram looked up to see Lakshman galloping furiously towards them.

'*Dada*,' said Lakshman, as he pulled up close. 'You need to come with me right away.'

'Not now, Lakshman,' said Ram, waving his hand in dismissal. 'I'm busy.'

'*Dada*,' said Lakshman, 'Guru Vashishtha has asked for you.'

Ram looked at Lakshman with irritation. 'I will be back soon. Please tell Guru*ji* that I have to—'

Lakshman interrupted his elder brother. '*Dada*, Maharishi Vishwamitra is here! He is asking for you; *specifically* for you.'

Ram stared at Lakshman, stunned.

Vishwamitra was the chief of the Malayaputras, the mysterious tribe left behind by the previous Vishnu, Lord

Parshu Ram. They represented the sixth Vishnu, tasked with carrying forward his mission on earth. The legendary powers of the Malayaputras instilled a sense of awe among the people of the Sapt Sindhu. This effect was further enhanced by Vishwamitra's fearsome reputation. Born as Kaushik, a Kshatriya, he was the son of the great King Gaadhi. Despite being a brave warrior in his youth, his nature drove him towards becoming a *rishi*. Against all odds, he succeeded. Thereafter, he reached the pinnacle of Brahmin ascension when he became the chief of the Malayaputras. After taking over as the chief, he had changed his name to Vishwamitra. The Malayaputras were tasked with assisting the next Mahadev, when he appeared. They believed their primary reason for existing, however, was to give rise to the next Vishnu when the time came.

Ram looked down at Dhenuka's body and then at his brother, torn between the two calls of duty. Lakshman dismounted and caught him by his elbow.

'*Dada*, you can come back to this,' insisted Lakshman, 'but Maharishi Vishwamitra should not be kept waiting. We have all heard about his legendary temper.'

Ram relented. 'My horse,' he ordered.

One of the officers quickly fetched his horse. Ram mounted and swiftly tapped the animal into action; Lakshman followed him. As the horses galloped towards the city, Ram recalled the odd conversation he had had with Vashishtha a few days earlier.

Someone is on his way here… I cannot stop it…

'What can Maharishi Vishwamitra possibly want from me?' whispered Ram to himself.

…you serve a purpose for him too…

Ram brought his attention back to the present and made a clicking noise, urging the horse to move quicker.

—— |大| 🐚 ☼ ——

'Are you saying no to me, Your Highness?' asked Vishwamitra in a mellifluous voice. But the underlying threat was unmistakable.

As if his position and reputation were not fearsome enough, Maharishi Vishwamitra's towering persona added to his indomitable aura. He was almost seven feet in height, of gigantic proportions, with a large belly offset by a sturdy, muscular chest, shoulders and arms. His flowing white beard, Brahmin knotted tuft of hair on an otherwise shaven head, large limpid eyes and the holy *janau, sacred thread*, tied over his shoulder, stood in startling contrast to the numerous battle scars that lined his face and body. His dark complexion was enhanced by his saffron *dhoti* and *angvastram*.

Emperor Dashrath and his three queens had received the maharishi in the king's private office. The maharishi had come straight to the point. One of his *ashrams* was under attack and he needed Ram's help to defend it; that was it. No explanations were offered as to the nature of the attack, and how exactly the young prince would defend the mighty Malayaputras, who were reputed to have one of the most feared militias in India within their ranks. The great chief of the Malayaputras would not be questioned or denied.

Dashrath swallowed nervously. Even at the peak of his powers, he would have been afraid to take on Vishwamitra; he was frankly terrified now, though thoroughly confused. He had grown increasingly fond of Ram over the last few months and he did not want to part with him. 'My Lord, I'm not suggesting that I do not want to send him with you. It's just that, I feel General Mrigasya should be equal to the task. My entire army is at your disposal and...'

'I want Ram,' said Vishwamitra, his eyes boring into

Dashrath's, unnerving the emperor of the Sapt Sindhu. 'And, I also want Lakshman.'

Kaushalya did not know what to make of the offer from Vishwamitra. While, on the one hand, she was delighted with the possibility that Ram would have a chance to get closer to the great sage, on the other, she was concerned that Vishwamitra would simply use Ram's martial skills for his own ends and then discard him. Moreover, Kaikeyi could easily grab the opportunity presented by Ram's absence to have Bharat installed as the crown prince. Kaushalya responded the only way she could when faced with such situations: she shed silent tears.

Kaikeyi felt no such conflict. She already found herself regretting having agreed to Manthara's plotting, and wished her son was here. 'Maharishi*ji*,' said Kaikeyi, 'I would be honoured to send Bharat to accompany you. We may just have to—'

'But Bharat is not in Ayodhya,' said Vishwamitra. It seemed that there was nothing he did not know.

'You are right, Maharishi*ji*,' said Kaikeyi. 'That's what I was about to say. We may have to wait for a few weeks. I can send a message immediately to have Bharat recalled.'

Vishwamitra stared into Kaikeyi's eyes. A nervous Kaikeyi looked down, feeling inexplicably as if her secrets had been suddenly exposed. There was an uncomfortable silence. Then Vishwamitra's booming voice filled the room. 'I want Ram, Your Highness; and Lakshman, of course. I don't need anyone else. Now, are you sending them with me or not?'

'Guru*ji*,' said Sumitra, 'I offer my sincere apologies for interrupting the conversation. But I think that there has been a big protocol blunder. You have already been with us for a while, but our venerated raj guru, Maharishi Vashishtha, has still not had the pleasure of meeting you. Should we send word to him to grace us with his presence? We will carry on our discussion once he's here.'

Vishwamitra laughed. 'Hmm! What I've heard is true, after all. The third and junior-most queen is the smartest of them all.'

'Of course I'm not the smartest, Maharishi*ji*,' said Sumitra, feeling her face redden with embarrassment. 'I was just suggesting that protocol…'

'Yes. Yes, of course,' said Vishwamitra. 'Follow your protocol. Bring your raj guru. We shall then talk about Ram.'

The king and his wives rushed out of the room, leaving the maharishi alone with some petrified attendants.

— 大 ⬮ ☀ —

Vashishtha entered the private royal office alone and dismissed the attendants. No sooner did they leave than Vishwamitra stood up with a sneer, 'So what arguments will you use to keep him away from me, Divodas?'

Vishwamitra had purposely used the *gurukul* name of Vashishtha, a name that the sage had had when he was a child in school.

'I am not a child anymore, Maharishi Vishwamitra,' said Vashishtha, with deliberate politeness. 'My name is Vashishtha. And I would prefer it if you addressed me as Maharishi Vashishtha.'

Vishwamitra stepped close. 'Divodas, what are your arguments? Your royal family is a divided house, in any case. Dashrath does not want to part with his sons. Kaushalya is confused, while Kaikeyi definitely wants Bharat to be the one who accompanies me. And Sumitra, smart Sumitra, is happy come what may, for one of her sons will be aligned to whoever wins. You have done quite a job here, haven't you, *Raj Guru*?'

Vashishtha ignored the barb. It was clear to him that there was little he could do. Ram and Lakshman would have to go with Vishwamitra, regardless of the arguments he could make.

'Kaushik,' said Vashishtha, using Vishwamitra's childhood name, 'it looks like you will force your way once again; no matter how unfair it is.'

Vishwamitra took one more step towards Vashishtha, looming large over the raj guru. 'And it looks like you will run away, once again. Still scared of a fight, eh, Divodas?'

Vashishtha closed his fist tight, but his face remained deadpan. 'You will never understand why I did what I did. It was for—'

'For the greater good?' sniggered Vishwamitra, stopping him mid-sentence. 'Do you really expect me to believe that? There is nothing more pathetic than people hiding their cowardice behind seemingly noble intentions.'

'You haven't lost any of your haughty Kshatriya ways, have you? It's amazing that you actually have the temerity to imagine that you represent the great Lord Parshu Ram, the one who destroyed Kshatriya arrogance!'

'Everyone is aware of my background, Divodas. At least I don't hide anything.' Vishwamitra glared at the shorter man. 'Should I reveal your true origin to your precious little boy? Tell him what I did to—'

'You didn't do me any favour!' shouted Vashishtha, finally losing control.

'I may just do one now,' smiled Vishwamitra.

Vashishtha turned around and stormed out of the room. Despite the passage of time, he felt he still owed the arrogant Vishwamitra a modicum of courtesy for the memory of the friendship they once had.

Chapter 16

A week later, Ram and Lakshman stood at the balustrade of the ship of the chief of Malayaputras as it sailed down the Sarayu. They were on their way to one of Vishwamitra's several *ashrams* on the banks of the Ganga River.

'*Dada*, this massive ship belongs to Maharishi Vishwamitra, as do the two that are following us,' whispered Lakshman. 'There are at least three hundred trained and battle-hardened warriors aboard. I have heard stories about thousands more at his secret capital, wherever that is. What in Lord Parshu Ram's name does he need us for?'

'I don't know,' said Ram, as he looked into the dark expanse of water. Everyone aboard kept a safe distance from them. 'This makes no sense. But Father has ordered us to treat Maharishi Vishwamitra as our guru and that is—'

'*Dada*, I don't think Father had a choice.'

'And neither do we.'

A few days later, Vishwamitra ordered the ships to drop anchor. Boats were quickly lowered and fifty people rowed across to the shore, Ram and Lakshman included.

As the boats banked, the Malayaputras jumped ashore onto the narrow beach and began to prepare the ground for a *puja*.

'What are we planning to do here, Guru*ji*?' asked Ram politely as he folded his hands into a namaste.

'Hasn't your raj guru taught you anything about this place?' asked Vishwamitra, his eyebrows furrowed together, a sardonic smile on his face.

Ram would not say anything uncomplimentary about his guru, Vashishtha. But Lakshman had no such compunctions.

'No Guru*ji*, he hasn't,' said Lakshman, shaking his head vigorously.

'Well, this is where Lord Parshu Ram offered a prayer to the fifth Vishnu, Lord Vaaman, before he set out to battle Kaartaveerya Arjun.'

'Wow,' said Lakshman, as he looked around with newfound respect.

'He also performed the *Bal-Atibal puja* here,' continued Vishwamitra, 'which bestowed upon him health, and freedom from hunger and thirst.'

'May I request you, Guru*ji*,' said Ram, his hands held together in respect before Vishwamitra, 'to teach us as well.'

Lakshman became distinctly uncomfortable. He had no desire to be free of hunger and thirst. He quite liked his food and drink.

'Of course,' said Vishwamitra. 'Both of you can sit beside me as I conduct the *puja*. The effect of the *puja* reduces your hunger and thirst for at least one week. The impact on your health is life-long.'

Within a few weeks, the convoy of ships reached the confluence of the Sarayu and the Ganga, after which they steered westwards up the Ganga. They dropped anchor a few days later and secured the vessels to a makeshift jetty. Leaving a skeletal staff behind, Vishwamitra, Ram and Lakshman set off on foot along with two hundred warriors. The entourage finally reached the local *ashram* of the Malayaputras after a four-hour march in a south-easterly direction.

Ram and Lakshman had been told that they were being brought to the *ashram* to bolster the efforts to protect it from enemy attacks. But what they saw was a complete surprise to the brothers. The *ashram* was not designed for any kind of serious defence. A rudimentary fence of hedge and thorny creepers would probably suffice to keep out some animals, but was certainly not enough to stave off well-armed soldiers. The shallow stream near the *ashram* had not been adequately barricaded to prevent a determined attack on the camp. There was no area cleared, either outside or inside the fence, to afford a line of sight. The mud-walled, thatch-roofed huts in the *ashram* were clustered together; a serious fire hazard. All one needed to do was set fire to a single hut, and the blaze would quickly spread through the *ashram*. Even the animals had been housed in the innermost circle of the camp, instead of near the boundary, from where their instinct would provide a timely warning of an attack.

'Something is not right, *Dada*,' Lakshman spoke under his breath. 'This camp looks like it's a new settlement; recent, in fact. The defences are, quite frankly, useless and…'

Ram signalled him with his eyes to keep quiet. Lakshman stopped talking and turned around to find Vishwamitra walking up to them. The maharishi was slightly taller than even the gigantic Lakshman.

'Have your lunch, princes of Ayodhya,' said Vishwamitra. 'Then we will talk.'

The Ayodhyan princes sat by themselves, ignored by the denizens of the camp who scurried about, implementing the instructions of Arishtanemi, the legendary military chief of the Malayaputras and Vishwamitra's right-hand man. Vishwamitra sat in *sukhaasan* under a banyan tree: his legs folded in a simple cross-legged position, with each foot tucked beneath the opposite knee. His hands lay on his knees, palms down; his eyes were closed; the relaxed yogic *aasan* for non-rigorous meditation.

Lakshman observed Arishtanemi speaking to an aide as he pointed towards the princes. Within moments, a woman dressed in a saffron *dhoti* and blouse approached Ram and Lakshman with two plantain leaves. She spread them out in front of the princes and sprinkled ritual water on them. She was followed by a couple of young students bearing food bowls. Food was served under the able supervision of the woman.

She smiled, folded her hands together into a namaste and said, 'Please eat, princes of Ayodhya.'

Lakshman looked suspiciously at the food and then at Vishwamitra in the distance. A banana leaf had been placed in front of the maharishi as well, on which was placed a solitary *jambu* fruit: the fruit that had been consecrated with the ancient name of India, *Jambudweep*.

'I think they are trying to poison us, *Dada*,' said Lakshman. 'As guests we have been served all this food, while Maharishi Vishwamitra is eating just one *jambu* fruit.'

'That fruit is not for eating, Lakshman,' said Ram, as he tore a piece of the *roti* and scooped some vegetables with it.

'*Dada!*' said Lakshman, as he grabbed Ram's hand, preventing him from eating.

Ram smiled. 'If they wanted to kill us, they had better opportunities on the ship. This food is not poisoned. Eat!'

'*Dada*, you trust every—'

'Just eat, Lakshman.'

—— 𝗂𝗑𝗂 🐟 ☼ ——

'This is where they attacked,' said Vishwamitra, pointing to the partially-burnt hedge fencing.

'Here, Guru*ji*?' asked Ram, astonished as he cast a quick look at Lakshman before turning his attention back to Vishwamitra.

'Yes, here,' said Vishwamitra.

Arishtanemi stood behind Vishwamitra in silence.

Ram's incredulity was well founded. It didn't look like much of an attack. A two-metre wide strip of the hedge fencing had been partially burnt. Some miscreants seemed to have poured paraffin and set it on fire; they must not have had sufficient quantities of it, for practically the whole fence was still intact. The vandals must have struck at night time, when dew formation on the hedge had thwarted their amateur attempts at arson.

These were clearly not professionals.

Ram stepped out of the boundary through the small breach in the fencing and picked up a partially burnt piece of cloth.

Lakshman quickly followed his brother, took the cloth from Ram and sniffed it, but detected no flammable substance. 'It's a piece of cloth from an *angvastram*. One of them must have accidentally set his own clothes on fire. Idiot!'

Lakshman's eyes fell on a knife; he examined it closely before handing it to his brother. It was old and rusty, though well sharpened; it clearly did not belong to a professional soldier.

Ram looked at Vishwamitra. 'What are your orders, Guru*ji*?'

'I need you to find these attackers who disrupt our rituals and other *ashram* activities,' said Vishwamitra. 'They must be destroyed.'

An irritated Lakshman butted in. 'But these people are not even…'

Ram signalled for silence. 'I will follow your orders, Guru*ji*, because that is what my father has asked me to do. But you need to be honest with me. Why have you brought us here when you have so many soldiers at your command?'

'Because you have something that my soldiers do not possess,' answered Vishwamitra.

'What is that?'

'Ayodhya blood.'

'What difference does that make?'

'The attackers are the Asuras of the old code.'

'They're Asuras?!' exclaimed Lakshman. 'But there are no more Asuras left in India. Those demons were killed by Lord Rudra a long time ago.'

Vishwamitra looked at Lakshman with exasperation. 'I'm talking to your elder brother.' Turning back to Ram, he said, 'The Asuras of the old code would not dream of attacking an Ayodhyan.'

'Why, Guru*ji*?'

'Have you heard of Shukracharya?'

'Yes, he was the guru of the Asuras. He is, or was, worshipped by the Asuras.'

'And do you know where Shukracharya was from?'

'Egypt.'

Vishwamitra smiled. 'Yes, that is technically true. But India has a big heart. If a foreigner comes here and accepts our land as his motherland, he is a foreigner no more. He becomes Indian. Shukracharya was brought up here. Can you guess which Indian city was his home town?'

Ram's eyes widened with amazement. 'Ayodhya?!'

'Yes, Ayodhya. The Asuras of the old code will not attack any Ayodhyan, for that land is sacred to them.'

—— 冭 ⬤ ☼ ——

Ram, Lakshman and Arishtanemi rode out of the *ashram* the following day, at the first hour of the second *prahar*. Accompanied by fifty soldiers, they moved in a southward direction. The local Asura settlement was believed to be a little more than a day's ride away.

'Tell me about their leaders, Arishtanemi*ji*,' Ram respectfully asked the military chief of the Malayaputras.

Arishtanemi was equal in height to Lakshman, but unlike the young prince, was lean, almost lanky. He wore a saffron *dhoti* with an *angvastram* slung over his right shoulder, one end of which was wrapped around his right arm. He wore a *janau* thread; his shaven head and a knotted tuft of hair at the crown were signs of his Brahmin antecedents. Unlike most Brahmins, though, Arishtanemi's wheat-complexioned body had a profusion of battle scars. It was rumoured that he was more than seventy years of age, although he did not look a day older than twenty. Perhaps Maharishi Vishwamitra had revealed to him the secret of the mysterious Somras, the drink of the Gods. Its anti-ageing properties could keep one healthy till the astounding age of two hundred.

'The Asura horde is led by a woman called Tadaka, the wife of their deceased chieftain, Sumali,' said Arishtanemi. 'Tadaka belongs to a Rakshasa clan.'

Ram frowned. 'I thought the Rakshasas were aligned with the Devas, and by extension, their descendants: us.'

'The Rakshasas are warriors, Prince Ram. Do you know what the word "Rakshasa" means? It's derived from the old Sanskrit word for protection, *Raksha*. It is said that the word Rakshasa emerged from their victims asking to "be protected from them". They were the finest mercenaries of ancient times. Some had allied with the Devas, while others joined the Asuras. Raavan himself is half Rakshasa.'

'Oh!' Ram exclaimed, as his eyebrows rose.

Arishtanemi continued. 'Tadaka maintains a militia of fifteen soldiers, led by her son, Subahu. Along with women, children and the old, the settlement must be made up of not more than fifty people.'

Ram frowned. *Just fifteen soldiers?*

Early next morning, the party left the temporary camp they'd set up the previous night.

'The Asura camp is an hour's ride from here,' said Arishtanemi. 'I have asked our soldiers to be on the lookout for scouts and possible traps.'

As they rode on, Ram steered his horse towards Arishtanemi's, clearly intending to impose further conversation on the taciturn soldier. 'Arishtanemi*ji*,' said Ram, 'Maharishi Vishwamitra mentioned the Asuras of the old code. It can't possibly comprise only this band of fifty. Fifty people cannot keep an ancient code alive. Where are the others?'

Arishtanemi smiled but did not proffer a response. *This boy is smart. I should warn Guruji to be careful with his words.*

Ram persisted with his questioning. 'Had they been in India, the Asuras would have launched an attack on us, the descendants of the Devas. This suggests that they must not be here. Where are they?'

Arishtanemi sighed imperceptibly and looked up at the dense canopy of trees preventing light from shining through. He decided to oblige the prince with the truth. 'Have you heard about the Vayuputras?'

'Of course, I have,' said Ram. 'Who hasn't? They are the tribe left behind by the previous Mahadev, Lord Rudra, just as your people are the ones left behind by the previous Vishnu, Lord Parshu Ram. The Vayuputras are tasked with protecting India from Evil whenever it arises. They believe that one among them will rise and become the next Mahadev when the time comes.'

Arishtanemi smiled enigmatically.

'But what does this have to do with the Asuras?' asked Ram.

Arishtanemi's expression did not change.

'By the great Lord Rudra, are the Vayuputras giving shelter to the Asuras, to India's enemies?'

Arishtanemi's smile broadened.

And then, the truth hit Ram. 'The Asuras have joined the Vayuputras…'

'Yes, they have.'

Ram was perplexed. 'But, why? Our ancestors went to great lengths to destroy the Asura Empire in India. They should hate all the Devas and their descendants. And here they are, having joined a group whose sole purpose is to protect India from Evil; why are they protecting the descendants of their mortal enemies?'

'Yes, they are, aren't they?'

Ram was stunned. 'But, why?'

'Because Lord Rudra ordered them to do so.'

This made no sense anymore! Ram was shocked beyond belief, but more importantly, intellectually provoked. He looked towards the sky with a bemused expression. *The people of the masculine are very strange, no doubt; but also magnificent!* He was on his way now to meet some of these quixotic creatures.

But why should they be destroyed? What law have they broken? I'm sure Arishtanemiji knows. But he will not tell me. He is loyal to Maharishi Vishwamitra. I need to get some more information about the Asuras, instead of blindly attacking them.

Ram frowned as he suddenly became aware that Arishtanemi was keenly observing him, almost as if he was attempting to read his mind.

— 𝙸𝚡 𝟅 ☼ —

The mounted platoon had ridden for half an hour when Ram silently signalled for them to halt. Everyone immediately pulled their reins. Lakshman and Arishtanemi steered their horses gently towards Ram.

'Up ahead,' whispered Ram, 'high up that tree.'

Around fifty metres ahead, an enemy soldier sat on a *machan* built on a fig tree, around twenty metres from the ground. Some branches had been pulled in front, in a vain attempt to conceal it.

'The idiot is not even camouflaged properly,' whispered Lakshman with disgust.

The Asura soldier was dressed in a red *dhoti;* if the intention was to serve as a spy or a lookout, the effect was disastrous, for the colour screamed his presence; like a parrot in a parade of crows.

'Red is their holy colour,' said Arishtanemi. 'They wear it whenever they go into battle.'

Lakshman was incredulous. 'But he is supposed to be a spy, not a warrior! Amateurs!'

Ram removed the bow slung over his shoulder and tested the pull of the string. He bent forward and rubbed his horse's neck as he crooned a soft tune; the animal became completely still. Ram pulled an arrow from the quiver tied to his back, nocked it and pulled the string back, aiming quickly. He flicked his releasing thumb and fired the arrow. The missile spun ferociously as it sped to its target, hitting its mark with precision: the thick rope that held the *machan* in place. It immediately gave way and the Asura came crashing down, hitting the branches on his downward journey. This effectively broke his fall and he landed on the ground, reasonably uninjured.

Arishtanemi stared in wonder at Ram's exquisite archery. *This boy is talented.*

'Surrender immediately and you will not be harmed,' Ram reassured. 'We only need some answers from you.'

The Asura quickly rose to his feet. He was, really, a youth, no more than fifteen years of age. His face was twisted with anger and disgust. He spat loudly and tried to draw his sword. Since he had not held the scabbard with his other hand to steady it, he only succeeded in getting the sword stuck. He cursed and yanked hard and the blade finally came free. Arishtanemi jumped off his horse and casually drew his sword.

'We don't want to kill you,' said Ram. 'Please surrender.'

Lakshman noticed that the poor boy's grip on the sword hilt was all wrong; it was vice-like, which would quickly tire him out. Also, the weight of the sword was taken by his forearm, instead of his shoulder and triceps, the way it should be. He held the weapon from the farthest edge of the hilt; it would just get knocked out of his hand!

The Asura spat again, before screaming loudly. 'You excreta of vermin! Do you think you can defeat us? The True Lord is with us. Your false Gods cannot protect you! You will all die! Die! Die!'

'Why are we here, hunting these imbeciles?' Lakshman threw up his hands.

Ram ignored Lakshman and spoke to the young warrior again, politely. 'I'm requesting you. Throw down your weapon. We don't want to kill you. Please.'

Arishtanemi began to move forward slowly, intending to intimidate the Asura. The effect, however, was quite the opposite.

The Asura screamed loudly. *'Satyam Ekam!'*
The True One!

He charged at Arishtanemi. It all happened so quickly that Ram had no time to intervene. The Asura tried to strike Arishtanemi with a standard downward slice, in what was intended to be a kill-strike. But he was not close enough to his opponent. The tall Arishtanemi deftly avoided the blow by swaying back.

'Stop!' warned Arishtanemi.

The young soldier, however, screamed loudly, moved his sword arm, and swung from the left. He should have used both his hands for this backhand attempt. Even then, it would have been a mistake against a man of Arishtanemi's strength. The Malayaputra swung hard, his blow so powerful that the Asura's sword flew out of his hand. Without losing momentum, Arishtanemi sliced from a high angle and nicked the Asura's chest. Perhaps hoping to scare him into surrendering.

Arishtanemi stepped back and drove his sword tip into the soft ground in a gesture that conveyed he meant no harm.

He said loudly, 'Just step back. I don't want to kill you. I am a Malayaputra.' Then, under his breath, low enough for only the Asura to hear, Arishtanemi whispered, 'Shukracharya's pig.'

The enraged Asura suddenly pulled out a knife from a scabbard tied to the small of his back and charged forward, screaming, 'Malayaputra dog!'

Arishtanemi instinctively stepped back, bringing his hands up in defence. The sword, held in his right hand, came up horizontal. The Asura simply ran into Arishtanemi's sword, the blade cutting through his abdomen cleanly.

'Dammit!' cursed Arishtanemi as he stepped back and pulled his sword out. He turned towards Ram, eyes filled with remorse.

The stunned Asura dropped his knife and looked down at his abdomen, at the blood that began as a trickle and, within moments, burst forth with steadily increasing intensity. The shock of the trauma had blocked out the pain, and he stared at his body as though it was another's. He collapsed on the ground when it became too much for his brain to handle. He screamed, more with fright than in pain.

Arishtanemi threw his shield to the ground in frustration. 'I told you to stop, Asura!'

Ram held his head. 'Lord Rudra, be merciful…'

The Asura was bawling helplessly. There was no saving him, now. The force of the blood flow was a clear indication that the sword had pierced many vital organs and arteries. It was only a matter of time before he bled to death.

The Malayaputra turned to Ram. 'I warned him… You warned him… He just ran into…'

Ram closed his eyes and shook his head in frustration. 'Put this poor fool out of his misery.'

Arishtanemi looked at the Asura lying prone at his feet. He went down on one knee. He bent close, so that his expression was visible only to the Asura, and sneered slightly before he carried out Ram's order.

Chapter 17

Ram signalled for the party to halt once again.

'These people are beyond all limits of incompetence,' said Lakshman, as he steered his horse close to his brother.

Ram, Lakshman and Arishtanemi looked into the distance, at what appeared to be the Asura camp. They had barricaded themselves for a veritable siege, but it was not exactly a sterling example of military genius. The entire camp was surrounded by high wooden palisade fencing, held together with hemp rope. Whereas this provided an adequate defence against arrows, spears and other missiles, a good fire would wreak havoc with this barricade. A stream flowing by the camp had been left unfenced. It was too deep for warriors to wade through on foot, but mounted soldiers could easily ride across.

'I'm sure they imagine that the unguarded opening at the stream will serve as bait for the unsuspecting,' laughed Arishtanemi.

As if expecting the enemy cavalry to attempt an attack by riding across the shallow stream, the Asuras had dug a small trench on the far side, just short of the bank, which had been crudely camouflaged. Asura archers, hidden within the trench, could rain a shower of arrows on enemy riders once they were mid-stream. In theory, it was an effective military tactic. The execution, however, was shoddy and amateurish.

A dull splash had sounded from the ground nearby alerting Ram to the possibility of the trench. Owing to its proximity to the stream, water had seeped through, making the trench slippery; it had not been adequately waterproofed. A soldier must have slipped.

In what seemed like another stroke of amateur brilliance, the Asuras had built a *machan* atop a tree, seemingly overlooking the trench. The *machan* had been built with the same idea in mind, to man it with archers who would fire at enemy soldiers crossing the stream. However, the *machan* was empty. This gave Ram an easy solution to the matter of the Asura soldiers hidden in the trench.

Ram crooned gently in the horse's ear; as the animal became still, he reached for an arrow, nocked it in one fluid movement and took aim.

'The arrow cannot curve in flight and fall into the trench with force, prince,' objected Arishtanemi. 'They are positioned deep in the ground. You cannot hit them this time.'

As Ram adjusted for the wind, he whispered, 'I'm not aiming for the trench, Arishtanemi*ji*.'

He pulled the string back and released the missile as he flicked the fletching, making the arrow spin furiously as it sped forward. The missile hit the main rope that tethered the *machan,* slashing it cleanly. As the rope snapped, the logs came loose and thundered down, many falling right into the trench.

'Brilliant!' Arishtanemi laughed.

These were logs with which a *machan* had been built: good enough to injure, not to kill. Frantic shouts emanated from the trench.

Lakshman looked at Ram. 'Should we—'

'No,' he interrupted Lakshman. 'We'll wait and watch. I don't want to trigger a battle. I hope to take them alive.'

A faint smile played on Arishtanemi's lips.

Yells of distress and anger continued to emerge from the trench. Perhaps the Asuras were clearing the logs that had landed on them. Soon enough, an Asura popped up, followed by others who dragged themselves out. The tallest, obviously the leader, surveyed his men. He turned around defiantly and stared at his opponents.

'That is Subahu,' offered Arishtanemi. 'Tadaka's son and their military chief.'

Subahu's left arm had been dislocated by a fallen log, but the rest of him appeared unharmed. He pulled out his sword; it took some effort to do so, for his left arm was disabled with the injury, and he was unable to hold his scabbard. He held his sword aloft and roared in defiance. His soldiers followed his cue.

Ram was thoroughly bemused now. He did not know whether to laugh at, or applaud, this foolhardy heroism that bordered on unheard-of stupidity.

'Oh, for Lord Parshu Ram's sake,' groaned Lakshman. 'Are these people mad? Can't they see that we have fifty mounted soldiers on our side?'

'*Satyam Ekam!*' bellowed Subahu.

'*Satyam Ekam!*' shouted the other Asuras.

Ram was astonished that the Asuras still persisted with what seemed like foolishness, despite what Guru Vishwamitra had said. He turned around and was annoyed at what he saw. 'Lakshman, where is the Ayodhya standard? Why haven't you raised it?'

'What?' asked Lakshman. He quickly looked back and realised that the soldiers behind him had raised the banner of the Malayaputras. The mission had been tasked by Vishwamitra, after all.

'Do it now!' shouted Ram, not taking his eyes off the Asuras, who appeared to be preparing to charge.

Lakshman pulled out the flag lying folded in the bag attached to the horse saddle. He unfurled it and held high the standard under which the Ayodhyans marched to battle. It was a white cloth with a red circular sun in the centre, its rays streaming out in all directions. At the bottom of the standard, suffused in the brightness of the rays of the sun, was a magnificent tiger appearing to leap out.

'Charge!' shouted Subahu.

'*Satyam Ekam!*' cried the Asuras as they took off.

Ram raised a balled fist and shouted aloud, '*Ayodhyatah Vijetaarah!*'

It was the war cry of the Ayodhyans. *The conquerors from the unconquerable city!*

Lakshman held the standard high and roared. '*Ayodhyatah Vijetaarah!*'

The Asuras stopped in their tracks as they gaped at the two princes and the Ayodhya flag. They had come to a halt a mere fifty feet from where Ram's horse stood still.

Subahu edged forward slowly, holding his sword low, non-threateningly.

'Are you from Ayodhya?' asked Subahu, as he reached close enough to be heard.

'I am the crown prince of Ayodhya,' said Ram. 'Surrender and I swear by the honour of Ayodhya, you will not be harmed.'

Subahu's sword fell from his suddenly limp hand as he went down on his knees. As did the other Asuras. Some of them were whispering to each other. But it was loud enough to reach Ram's ears.

'Shukracharya…'

'Ayodhya…'

'The voice of *Ekam*...'

— 𝕀𝕏𝕀 🐚 ☼ —

Ram, Lakshman and the Malayaputras were ceremoniously led into the Asura camp. The fourteen Asura soldiers were received by Tadaka; the women quickly got down to tending to the injuries of their men, who had been disarmed by the Malayaputras.

The hosts and the guests eventually settled down in the central square. After a quick round of meagre refreshments, Ram addressed the Malayaputra military chief. 'Arishtanemi*ji*, please leave me alone with the Asuras.'

'Why?' asked Arishtanemi.

'I would like to speak with them alone.'

Lakshman objected vehemently. '*Dada*, when I said that we shouldn't attack these people, I didn't mean that they are good and we should talk to them. I just meant that it is beneath us to attack these morons. Now that they have surrendered, we're done with them. Let's leave them to the Malayaputras and return to Ayodhya.'

'Lakshman,' said Ram. 'I said I would like to speak with them.'

'What will you talk about, *Dada*?' persisted Lakshman, beyond caring that he was within earshot of the Asuras. 'These people are savages. They are animals. They are the remnants of those who survived the wrath of Lord Rudra. Don't waste your time on them.'

Ram's breathing slowed down as his body stiffened imperceptibly. His face acquired an expression of forbidding calm. Lakshman immediately recognised it for what it was: a sign of deep anger welling up beneath the still waters of his brother's essentially cool personality. He also knew that this anger was coupled with unrelenting stubbornness. He threw up his hands in a gesture of frustrated surrender.

Arishtanemi shrugged. 'All right, you can talk to them. But it is not advisable that you do it in our absence.'

'I have taken note of your advice. Thank you! But I trust them,' said Ram.

Tadaka and Subahu heard Ram's words. It took them by surprise because they had been considered the enemy for so long.

Arishtanemi gave in. However, he also made sure the Asuras heard him loud and clear. 'Fine, we'll move away. But we will be battle-ready, mounted on horseback. At the slightest sign of trouble, we'll ride in and kill them all.'

As Arishtanemi turned to leave, Ram repeated his directive, this time to his protective brother. 'I would like to speak to them *alone*, Lakshman.'

'I'm not leaving you alone with them, *Dada*.'

'Lakshman...'

'I am not leaving you alone, *Dada*!'

'Listen, brother, I need...'

Lakshman raised his voice. 'I am not leaving you alone, *Dada*!'

'All right,' said Ram, giving in.

Arishtanemi and the Malayaputra warriors lined up at the border of the camp with the stream behind them, mounted on horses, ready to ride to Ram and Lakshman's rescue at the first hint of trouble. The brothers were seated on a raised platform in the central square, with the Asuras gathered around them. Subahu wore an arm sling; he sat in front, beside his mother, Tadaka.

'You are committing slow suicide,' said Ram.

'We are only following our law,' said Tadaka.

Ram frowned. 'What do you intend to achieve by continually attacking the Malayaputras?'

'We hope to save them. If they come to our side, reject their false beliefs and listen to the call of the *Ekam*, they will save their own souls.'

'So, you think you are saving them by persistently harassing them, interfering in their rituals, and even trying to kill them.'

'Yes,' said Tadaka, making it obvious that her strange logic was irrefutable to her. 'And, really, it is not we who are trying to save the Malayaputras. It is, in fact, the True One, the *Ekam* himself! We are mere instruments.'

'But if the *Ekam* is on your side, how come the Malayaputras have been thriving for centuries? How do you explain that the people of the Sapt Sindhu, almost all of whom reject your interpretation of the *Ekam*, have been dominant for so long? Why haven't you Asuras conquered India once again? Why isn't the *Ekam* helping you?'

'The Lord is testing us. We haven't been sufficiently true to his path.'

'Testing you?' asked Ram. 'Is the *Ekam* making the Asuras lose every single major battle they have fought for centuries, for millennia actually, just so he can test you?'

Tadaka did not respond.

'Have you considered that he may not be testing you at all?' asked Ram. 'Maybe he is trying to teach you something? Maybe he is trying to tell you that you have to change with the times? Didn't Shukracharya himself say that if a tactic has led to failure, then persisting with it unquestioningly, in the wild hope of a different outcome, is nothing short of insanity?'

'But how can we live by the rules of these disgusting, decadent Devas who worship everything in theory but nothing in practice?' asked Tadaka.

'These "disgusting, decadent Devas" and their descendants have been in power for centuries,' said Lakshman aggressively. 'They have created magnificent cities and a sparkling civilisation, while you have been living in a run-down pathetic camp in the middle of nowhere. Maybe it is you people who need to change your theory *and* practice, whatever it may be!'

'Lakshman…' said Ram, raising a hand to silence him.

'This is nonsense, *Dada*.' Lakshman would not relent. 'How delusional can these people be? Don't they see reality?'

'Their only reality is their law, Lakshman. Change is difficult for the people of the masculine way of life. They are only guided by their law and, if that is out of sync with the times, it is very difficult for them to accept and initiate change; instead, more often than not, they will cling more strongly to the certainties of their law. We don't see the attitude of the feminine civilisations towards change as open-minded and liberal; instead, to us, it appears fickle, corrupt and debauched.'

'*We? Us?*' asked Lakshman, frowning at Ram identifying himself with the masculine way.

Tadaka and Subahu keenly watched the exchange between the brothers. Subahu raised his balled fist to his heart, in an ancient Asura salute.

Ram asked Lakshman. 'Do you think what was done to Dhenuka was wrong?'

'I think the way the Asuras randomly kill people who do not agree with their interpretation of the *Ekam* is even more wrong.'

'On that I agree with you. The Asura actions were not just wrong, they were evil,' said Ram. 'But I was talking about Dhenuka. Do you think what was done to him was wrong?'

Lakshman refused to respond.

'Answer me, my brother,' said Ram. 'Was it wrong?'

'You know I will not oppose you, *Dada…*'

'I'm not asking what you will do. What do you *think*, Lakshman?'

Lakshman remained silent. But his answer was obvious.

'Who is Dhenuka?' asked Subahu.

'A hardened criminal, a blot on society whose soul will atone for his deed for at least a million births,' said Ram. 'But the law did not allow for his execution. Had Shukracharya's law not permitted it, no matter how heinous the crime, should he have been executed?'

Subahu didn't need a moment to think. 'No.'

Ram smiled ever so slightly as he turned to Lakshman. 'The law applies equally to all. No exceptions. And the law cannot be broken. Except when…'

Lakshman turned away from him. He remained convinced that in Dhenuka's case, justice had been served.

Ram turned to address the small band of Asuras. 'Try to understand what I am saying to you. You are law-abiding people; you follow the masculine way. But your laws are not working anymore. They haven't been for centuries, because the world has changed. That is what karma is trying to teach you, again and again. If karma is giving you a negative signal repeatedly, then it is not testing you, it is trying to teach you. You need to tap into the disciple in you and find a new Shukracharya. You need a new masculine way. You need new laws.'

Tadaka spoke up. 'Guru Shukracharya had said that he would reincarnate when the time was ripe, to lead us to a new way…'

There was a long silence in the assemblage.

Tadaka and Subahu suddenly stood up in unison. They brought their balled right fists to their heart, as they bowed low to Ram; the traditional full Asura salute. Their soldiers sprang to their feet and followed suit, as did the women, children and the old.

Ram felt as if a crushing weight was suddenly placed on his chest and the wind knocked out of him. Guru Vashishtha's words entered his mind of their own volition. *Your responsibility is great; your mission is all-important. Stay true to it. Stay humble, but not so humble that you don't accept your responsibilities.*

Lakshman glared at the Asuras, and then at Ram, scarcely believing what was going on.

'What would you have us do, My Lord?' asked Tadaka.

'Most Asuras live with the Vayuputras today, far beyond the western borders of India, in a land called Pariha,' said Ram. 'I want you to seek refuge there, with the help of the Malayaputras.'

'But why would the Malayaputras help us?'

'I will request them.'

'What will we do there?'

'Honour the promise that your ancestors made to Lord Rudra. You will work with the Vayuputras to protect India.'

'But protecting India today means protecting the Devas…'

'Yes, it does.'

'Why should we protect them? They are our enemies. They are…'

'You will protect them because that is what Lord Rudra ordered you to do.'

Subahu held his mother's hand to restrain her. 'We will do as you order, My Lord.'

Uncertain, Tadaka yanked her wrist out of her son's grip. 'But this is our holy land. We want to live in India. We cannot be happy outside of its sacred embrace.'

'You will return eventually. But you cannot come back as Asuras. That way of life is over. You will return in a new form. This is my promise to you.'

Chapter 18

Lakshman had expected anger from the volatile Vishwamitra, instead he looked intrigued; even impressed. Lakshman did not know what to make of it.

The maharishi sat in *padmaasan* on the platform built around a banyan tree. His feet were placed on opposite thighs, facing upwards; the knotted tuft of hair at the back of his shaven head fluttered in the strong breeze. His white *angvastram* had been placed on the side.

'Sit,' commanded Vishwamitra. 'This will probably take some time.'

Ram, Lakshman and Arishtanemi took their seats around him. Vishwamitra observed the Asuras standing quietly in the distance. They had not been tied up; Ram had insisted on that, to the consternation of the camp denizens. But it appeared that shackling them was not required, after all. They stood in a disciplined line, not moving from their positions. Arishtanemi had nevertheless kept thirty guards stationed around them, just in case.

Vishwamitra addressed Ram. 'You have surprised me, prince of Ayodhya. Why did you disobey my direct order to kill all the Asuras? And what did you tell them to bring about this dramatic transformation? Is there some secret mantra that can suddenly civilise the uncivilised?'

'I know even you don't believe what you have just said, Guru*ji*,' said Ram in a calm voice. 'You don't really think the Asuras are uncivilised; you cannot, for I have seen you worship Lord Rudra, and I know that the Asuras have joined the Vayuputras, the tribe that he left behind. The Vayuputras are your *partners in deed*, your *karmasaathis*. So, my suspicion is that you were trying to provoke me with what you just said. I find myself wondering, why?'

Vishwamitra's eyes widened fractionally as they focused on Ram, to the exclusion of all others. But he did not give him an answer. 'Do you really think these imbeciles are worth the effort of rescuing?'

'But that question is immaterial, Guru*ji*. The question really is: why should they be wiped out? What law have they broken?'

'They attacked my camp repeatedly.'

'But they didn't kill anyone. All they did the last time was burn a small portion of the hedge fencing. And they broke some of your mining equipment. Do these crimes deserve the death sentence under the laws of any *Smriti*? No. The laws of Ayodhya, which I always obey, clearly state that if the weak have not broken any law, then it is the duty of the strong to protect them.'

'But my orders were explicit.'

'Forgive me for being explicit too, Guru*ji*, but if you genuinely intended to kill these Asuras, then Arishtanemi*ji* would have easily done it for you. Your warriors are trained professionals. These Asuras are amateurs. I believe you brought us here because you knew that they would listen to the princes of Ayodhya, and no one else. You wanted to find a practical, non-confrontational solution to the problem they posed. Not only have I followed the law, but I've also delivered on what you truly wanted. What I fail to understand is why you did not want to reveal your true intentions to me.'

Vishwamitra wore an expression that was rare for this great Brahmin: one of bemused respect. He also felt outfoxed. He smiled. 'Do you always question your guru like this?'

Ram remained silent. The unspoken answer was obvious. Vashishtha, not Vishwamitra, was his guru. Ram was merely following the orders of his father in according Vishwamitra that stature.

'You are right,' Vishwamitra continued, ignoring the subtle slight. 'The Asuras are not bad people; they just have an understanding of *dharma* that is not valid for today's world. Sometimes, the followers are good but the leaders let them down. Sending them to Pariha is a good idea. They will find some purpose. We'll arrange for their departure.'

'Thank you, Guru*ji*,' said Ram.

'As for your original question, I'm not going to give you an answer right now. Maybe later.'

Within two weeks, a small group of Malayaputras had been readied, along with the Asuras, to undertake the journey to the hidden city of the Vayuputras, beyond the western borders of India. The Asuras had recovered completely from their injuries.

Vishwamitra stood at the gate of the Malayaputra camp, giving last-minute instructions to his men. Arishtanemi, Ram and Lakshman stood beside him. As the Malayaputra group walked away to mount their horses, Tadaka and Subahu approached Vishwamitra.

'Thank you for this,' said Tadaka, bowing her head low and folding her hands together into a namaste.

As Vishwamitra broke into a smile at the surprising display of manners from the Asura woman, Tadaka turned to Ram, her eyes seeking approval. Ram smiled his gentle appreciation.

'Your fellow Asuras live in the west,' said Vishwamitra. 'They will keep you safe. Follow the setting sun and it will guide you home.'

Tadaka stiffened. 'Pariha is not our home. This is our home, right here, in India. We have lived here for as long as the Devas have. We've lived here from the very beginning.'

Ram cut in. 'And you will return when the time is right. For now, follow the path of the sun.'

Vishwamitra looked at Ram with surprise, but remained silent.

—— 𝍖 🐚 ☼ ——

'It didn't work out the way we had planned, Guru*ji*,' said Arishtanemi.

Vishwamitra was sitting by a lake, not far from the Malayaputra camp. Arishtanemi, as was his practice whenever he was alone with his master, had kept his sword close at hand, unsheathed and ready. He would need to move fast if anyone dared attack Vishwamitra.

'You don't seem particularly unhappy,' said Vishwamitra.

Arishtanemi looked into the distance, avoiding eye contact with his leader. He was hesitant. 'Honestly, Guru*ji*... I like the boy... I think he has...'

Vishwamitra narrowed his eyes and glared at Arishtanemi. 'Don't forget the one we have committed ourselves to.'

Arishtanemi bowed his head. 'Of course, Guru*ji*. Can I ever go against your wishes?'

There was an uncomfortable silence. Vishwamitra took a deep breath and looked across the vast expanse of water. 'Had the Asuras been killed in their camp by him, it would have proved ... useful.'

Arishtanemi, wisely, did not contradict him.

Vishwamitra laughed ruefully, shaking his head. 'Outwitted by a boy who wasn't even trying to outwit me. He was just following his "rules".'

'What do we do?'

'We follow plan B,' said Vishwamitra. 'Obvious, isn't it?'

'I have never been too sure about the other plan, Guru*ji*. It's not like we have complete control over matters of—'

Vishwamitra did not allow him to complete his statement. 'You are wrong.'

Arishtanemi remained silent.

'That traitor Vashishtha is Ram's guru. I can never trust Ram as long as he continues to trust Vashishtha.'

Arishtanemi had his misgivings, but kept quiet. He knew any discussion on the subject of Vashishtha was one that was fraught with danger.

'We will go ahead with the other plan,' said Vishwamitra, with finality.

'But will he do what we expect him to?'

'We will have to use his beloved "rules" on him. Once it is done, I will have complete control over what will follow. The Vayuputras are wrong. I will show them that I am right.'

Two days after the Asuras left for Pariha, Ram and Lakshman woke up to feverish activity in the camp. Keeping to themselves, they stepped out of their hut and set out for the lake to offer early morning prayers to the Sun God and Lord Rudra.

Arishtanemi fell into step alongside them. 'We'll be leaving soon.'

'Thank you for letting us know, Arishtanemi*ji*,' said Ram.

Ram noticed an unusually large trunk being carried out with great care. It evidently contained something heavy, for it was placed on a metallic palanquin which was being carried on the shoulders of twelve men.

'What is that?' asked Lakshman, frowning and instantly suspicious.

'Something that is both Good and Evil,' said Arishtanemi mysteriously, as he placed his hand on Ram's shoulder. 'Where are you going?'

'For our morning prayers.'

'I'll come with you.'

— 𑀓 𑀖 ☼ —

Arishtanemi normally prayed to Lord Parshu Ram every morning. In the company of Ram and Lakshman, he also decided to pray to the great Mahadev, Lord Rudra. All Gods trace their divinity to the same source, after all.

They sat together on a large boulder on the banks of the lake, once the prayers were done.

'I wonder whether Tadaka and her tribe will be able to cope with Pariha,' said Arishtanemi.

'I'm sure they will,' said Ram. 'They are easy to manage if they see you as one of their own.'

'That appears to be the only way to handle them: keep them among their own. They find it impossible to get along with outsiders.'

'I have been giving their ideas a lot of thought. The problem lies in the way they look upon the *Ekam*.'

'The One God…?'

'Yes,' Ram said. 'We've been told repeatedly that the *Ekam* lives beyond our world of illusion. He is beyond *gunas*, the *characteristics* of created things. For isn't it *gunas* that create this world of illusion, of temporary existence, illusive because no moment in time lasts? Isn't that why he is not only called *niraakaar, formless*; but also *nirguna, beyond characteristics*?'

'Exactly,' said Arishtanemi.

'And if the *Ekam* is beyond all this, how can He pick a side?' asked Ram. 'If He is beyond *form* then how can He have a preference for any one form? He can, therefore, never belong to any one specific group. He belongs to all, and at the same time, to none. And this is not just applicable to human beings but to every created entity in the universe: animals, plants, water, earth, energy, stars, space, everything. Regardless of what they do or think or believe, all created entities belong to, and are drawn from, the *Ekam*.'

Arishtanemi nodded. 'This fundamental misunderstanding between our world of forms, and the *Ekam's* formless world, makes them believe in the lie that my God is the true God and your God is a false God. Just like a wise human will have no preference for his kidneys over his liver, the One God will not pick one group over another. It's stupid to even think otherwise.'

'*Exactly!*' said Ram. 'If He is *my* God, if He picks my side over someone else's, He is *not* the *One God*. The only true One God is the one who picks no sides, who belongs to everything, who doesn't demand loyalty or fear; in fact, who doesn't demand anything at all. Because the *Ekam* just exists; and His existence allows for the existence of all else.'

Arishtanemi was beginning to respect this wise young prince of Ayodhya. But he was afraid to admit this to Vishwamitra.

Ram continued. 'Shukracharya was right in wanting to create a perfect masculine society. Such a society is efficient, just, and honourable. The mistake he made was that he based it on faith. He should have built it purely on laws, keeping the spiritual separate from the material. When times change, as they inevitably do, one finds it impossible to give up on one's faith; in fact, one clings to it with renewed vigour. Difficult times make men cling to their faith even more strongly. But if you base a masculine way of life on laws, then, possibly, when needed, the laws can be changed. The masculine way of life should be built on laws, not faith.'

'Do you actually believe that it is possible to save the Asuras? There are many of them in India. Hidden in small groups, but they are there.'

'I think they will make disciplined followers. Certainly better than the rebellious, law-breaking people I call my own. The problem with the Asuras is that their laws are obsolete. The people are good; what they need is enlightened and effective leadership.'

'Do you think you can be that leader? Can you create a new way of life for them?'

Ram inhaled deeply. 'I don't know what role fate has in store for me but—'

Lakshman cut in. 'Guru Vashishtha believes Ram *Dada* can be the next Vishnu. He will not just provide leadership for the Asuras, but everyone; all of India. I believe that too. There is nobody like Ram *Dada*.'

Ram looked at Lakshman, his face inscrutable.

Arishtanemi leaned back, sucking in a deep breath. 'You are a good man; in fact, a special man. And I can certainly see that you will play an important role in history. Though what exactly, I do not know.'

Ram's face remained expressionless.

'My suggestion to you is to listen to Maharishi Vishwamitra,' said Arishtanemi. 'He is the wisest and most powerful among the *rishis* today, bar none.'

Ram didn't react, though his face hardened imperceptibly.

'Bar none,' repeated Arishtanemi for emphasis, clearly referring to Vashishtha.

———— 𐤀 𐤀 ☼ ————

The group rode unhurriedly through the jungle. Vishwamitra and Arishtanemi rode in front, at the head of the caravan, right behind the cart cradling the heavy trunk. Ram and Lakshman had been asked to ride at the back, with the rest of the Malayaputras marching on foot. It would take a few hours for them to reach the ships anchored on the Ganga.

Vishwamitra beckoned Arishtanemi with a nod. He immediately pulled the reins to the right and drew close.

'So?' asked Vishwamitra.

'He knows,' said Arishtanemi. 'Maharishi Vashishtha has told him.'

'Why, that conniving two-faced upstart; that rootless piece of…'

Arishtanemi kept his gaze pinned to the distance as Vishwamitra vented his fury. It was followed by a charged silence. Finally the disciple gathered the courage to ask, 'So, what do we do now, Guru*ji*?'

'We will do what we have to do.'

Chapter 19

Ram and Lakshman stood on the deck of the lead vessel as the three-ship convoy sailed smoothly down the Ganga. Vishwamitra chose to stay ensconced in his cabin for most of the trip. Arishtanemi made the most of this opportunity; the Ayodhya princes aroused inordinate interest in this Malayaputra.

'How are the princes doing today?' asked Arishtanemi, as he approached them.

Ram had washed his long hair and left it loose, struggling to dry it in the sultry air.

'Suffering in this oppressive heat,' said Lakshman.

Arishtanemi smiled. 'It has only just begun. The rains are months away. It'll get worse before it gets better.'

'Which is why we are on the open deck; any draught is a gift from the Gods!' said Lakshman, as he dramatically fanned his face with his hands. Many had gathered on the deck, seeking a brief, post-lunch break before descending to the lower deck and on to their assigned tasks.

Arishtanemi stepped closer to Ram. 'I was surprised by what you said about our ancestors. Are you against the Devas?'

'I was wondering when you were going to bring that up,' said Ram, with a sense of wry inevitability.

'Well, you can stop wondering now.'

Ram laughed. 'I'm not against the Devas. We are their descendants, after all. But I am an admirer of the way of the masculine, a life of laws, obedience, honour and justice. I prefer and advocate it as opposed to a life of freedom without end.'

'There is more to the way of the feminine than just passion and freedom, prince,' Arishtanemi said. 'There is unbridled creativity as well.'

'That, I concede; but when civilisation goes into decline, the people of the feminine are prone to divisiveness and victim-mongering. In the middle ages of the Devas, the caste system, which was originally based on karma and not birth, became rigid, sectarian and politicised. This allowed the Asuras to easily defeat them. When the later Devas reformed and made the caste system flexible again, they regained their strength and defeated the Asuras.'

'Yes, but the masculine way can also become rigid and fanatical when such a society goes into a decline. That the Asuras relentlessly attacked the Devas, just because the Devas had a different interpretation of the *Ekam*, was inexcusable.'

'I agree. But didn't these attacks unite the Devas? Maybe the Devas should acknowledge the few positives that emerged from that horrific violence. They were forced to confront the evil that the caste system had descended into; they needed unity. In my opinion, the most important reform that Lord Indra was able to carry out was making the caste system flexible once again. The united later-age Devas finally defeated the Asuras, who lost because of their fanatical rigidity.'

'Are you suggesting that the Devas should be grateful to the Asuras for all that brutal violence?'

'No, I'm not,' said Ram. 'What I'm suggesting is that some good can emerge from the most horrific of events. There is something positive hidden in every negative, and something negative hidden in every positive. Life is complicated, and a balanced person can see both sides. For instance, can you deny that, with the Asura experience long forgotten, the caste system has become rigid once again? A man's status in society today is determined by his birth and not his karma. Will you deny that this evil is ravaging the vitals of the modern Sapt Sindhu?'

'All right!' said Lakshman. 'Enough of this philosophical stuff; you will make my head explode!'

Arishtanemi laughed uproariously, while Ram gazed indulgently at Lakshman.

'Thankfully, this will all end as soon as we disembark at Ayodhya,' said Lakshman.

'*Uhh*,' said Arishtanemi. 'There may be a little delay, prince.'

'What do you mean?' asked Ram.

'Guru Vishwamitra intends to visit Mithila en route to Ayodhya. He has an important mission there as well.'

'When were you planning to tell us about this?' asked Lakshman, irritated.

'I'm telling you now,' said Arishtanemi.

Signalling Lakshman to be patient, Ram said, 'It's all right, Arishtanemi*ji*. Our father commanded us to remain with Guru Vishwamitra till he sees fit. A delay of a few months will not harm us in any way.'

'Mithila…' groaned Lakshman. 'It's the back of beyond!'

Unlike most big cities of the Sapt Sindhu, *Mithila*, the *city for the sons of the soil* or the *city founded by King Mithi*, was not a river-town; at least not after the Gandaki River had changed course westwards a few decades ago. This altered the fate of Mithila dramatically. From being counted among the great cities of the Sapt Sindhu, it speedily declined. Most trade in India was conducted through riverine ports. With Gandaki turning its face away, Mithila's fortunes collapsed overnight. Raavan's nifty traders withdrew the appointed sub-traders from Mithila; the miniscule volume of trade simply didn't justify their presence anymore.

The city was ruled by King Janak, a devout, decent and spiritual man. He was a classic example of a good man, albeit not for the job at hand. Had Janak chosen to be a spiritual guru, he would have been among the finest in the world. However, fate had decreed that he would be king. Even as a monarch, he assiduously guided the spiritual growth of his people through his *dharma sabhas*, or *spiritual gatherings*. Material growth and security, though, had been severely neglected.

To add to Mithila's woes, power within the royal family had decidedly shifted to Janak's younger brother, Kushadhwaj. The Gandaki River's new course skirted the border of Sankashya, whose ruler was Kushadhwaj. Mithila's loss was Sankashya's gain. Easy availability of water led to a boom in trade as well as a dramatic increase in the population of Sankashya. Armed with the heft of both money and numbers, Kushadhwaj made moves to establish himself as the representative of his royal family within the Sapt Sindhu. Careful to maintain appearances, he remained outwardly deferential towards his saintly elder brother. Despite this, rumours abounded that this was just a charade; that Kushadhwaj plotted to absorb Mithila and bring it under his own rule.

'That's where we're headed, Lakshman, if that is what Guru*ji* wants,' said Ram. 'We will need an escort from Sankashya, right? I have heard that there are no proper roads that lead to Mithila from Sankashya.'

'There used to be one,' said Arishtanemi. 'It was washed away when the river changed course. There were no efforts made to rebuild it. Mithila is ... short of funds. But their prime minister has been informed and she has arranged for an escort party.'

'Is it true that King Janak's daughter is his prime minister?' asked Lakshman. 'We found that hard to believe. Is her name Urmila?'

'Why is it hard to believe that a woman could be prime minister, Lakshman?' Ram asked, before Arishtanemi could reply. 'Women are equal to men in mental abilities.'

'I know, *Dada*,' said Lakshman. 'It's unusual, that's all.'

'Lady Mohini was a woman,' continued Ram. 'And she was a Vishnu. Remember that.'

Lakshman fell silent.

Arishtanemi touched Lakshman's shoulder in a kindly way as he said, 'You are right, Prince Lakshman. King Janak's daughter is his prime minister. But it's not Princess Urmila, who incidentally is his biological daughter. It's his adopted daughter who is the prime minister.'

'Adopted daughter?' asked Ram, surprised. Adopted children were rarely given equal rights in India these days. He had it in mind to set this right by changing the law.

'Yes,' said Arishtanemi.

'I wasn't aware of that. What's her name?'

'Her name is Sita.'

—— |人| 🐟 ☼ ——

'Are we not going to meet the king of Sankashya?' asked Ram.

Vishwamitra's ships had docked at the port of Sankashya, a few kilometres from the city. They were met by officials from Mithila, led by Samichi, the police and protocol chief of the city. Samichi and her team would lead a small band of one hundred Malayaputras to Mithila. The others would remain aboard the anchored ships.

'No,' said Arishtanemi, as he mounted his horse. 'Guru Vishwamitra would prefer to pass this town incognito. In any case, King Kushadhwaj is travelling right now.'

Lakshman surveyed the simple white garments that Ram and he had been asked to wear. Clearly, the princes were supposed to pass off as commoners.

'Incognito?' asked Lakshman, his suspicions immediately aroused as he sceptically gazed upon the Malayaputra party. 'You could have fooled me.'

Arishtanemi smiled and squeezed his knees; his horse began to move. Ram and Lakshman mounted their horses and followed him. Vishwamitra had already left, at the head of the convoy, accompanied by Samichi.

—— 大 ⚲ ☼ ——

The pathway through the jungle was so narrow that only three horses could ride abreast. At some spots glimpses of an old cobble-stoned road would emerge where the pathway suddenly got broader. For the most part though, the jungle had aggressively reclaimed the land. Often, the convoy rode single file for long stretches.

'You have not visited Mithila, have you?' asked Arishtanemi.

'There was never any need to go there,' answered Ram.

'Your brother Bharat did visit Sankashya a few months ago.'

'He is in charge of diplomatic relations for Ayodhya. It's natural that he would meet with kings from across the Sapt Sindhu.'

'Oh? I thought he may have visited King Kushadhwaj for a marriage alliance.'

Lakshman frowned. 'Marriage alliance? If Ayodhya wanted a marriage alliance, it would be with one of the more powerful kingdoms. Why ally with Sankashya?'

'Nothing prevents you from forming multiple marriage alliances. After all, some say marriages are a way to build political alliances by strengthening personal ties.'

Lakshman cast a furtive glance at Ram.

'What is it?' asked Arishtanemi, following Lakshman's gaze. 'You disagree?'

Lakshman butted in. 'Ram *Dada* believes marriage is sacred. It should not be treated as a political alliance.'

Arishtanemi raised his eyebrows. 'That was the way it was in the ancient world, yes. Nobody really believes in those values anymore.'

'I'm not a fan of everything that our ancestors did,' said Ram. 'But some practices are worth reviving. One of them is looking upon marriage as a sacred partnership between two souls; not as a political alliance between two power centres.'

'You are, perhaps, among the very few people who think this way.'

'That doesn't mean that I am wrong.'

Lakshman interrupted the conversation again. '*Dada* also believes that a man must marry only one woman. He believes that polygamy is unfair to women and must be banned.'

'That's not exactly what I believe, Lakshman,' said Ram. 'I say that the law must be equal for all. If you allow a man to marry many women, then you should also allow a woman to marry many men if she so chooses. What is wrong is that the current law favours men. Polygamy is allowed but polyandry is not. That is simply wrong. Having said that, my personal preference is for a man to find one woman, and remain loyal to her for the rest of his life.'

'I thank Lord Brahma that your preference doesn't extend to a man being loyal to the same woman for many lifetimes!' Arishtanemi chuckled.

Ram smiled.

'But Prince Ram,' said Arishtanemi, 'I'm sure you must be aware that polygamy as a practice rose a few centuries ago with good reason. We had survived the fifty-year war between the Suryavanshis and the Chandravanshis. Millions of men died. There were simply not enough bridegrooms left, which is why men were encouraged to marry more than one woman. Quite frankly, we also needed to repopulate our country. Thereafter, more and more people began to practice polygamy.'

'Yes, but we don't have that problem now, do we?' asked Ram. 'So why should men continue to be allowed this privilege?'

Arishtanemi fell silent. After a few moments, he asked Ram, 'Do you intend to marry only one woman?'

'Yes. And I will remain loyal to her for the rest of my life. I will not look at another woman.'

'*Dada*,' said Lakshman, grinning slyly, 'how can you avoid looking at other women? They're everywhere! Are you going to shut your eyes every time a woman passes by?'

Ram laughed. 'You know what I mean. I will not look at other women the way I would look at my wife.'

'So, what are you looking for in a woman?' asked Arishtanemi, intrigued.

Ram was about to start speaking when Lakshman promptly jumped in. 'No. No. No. I have to answer this.'

Arishtanemi looked at Lakshman with an amused grin.

'*Dada* had once said,' continued Lakshman, 'that he wants a woman who can make him bow his head in admiration.'

Lakshman smiled proudly as he said this. Proud that he knew something so personal about his elder brother.

Arishtanemi cast a bemused look at Ram and smiled. 'Bow your head in admiration?'

Ram had nothing to say.

Arishtanemi looked ahead. He knew a woman who Ram would almost certainly admire.

Chapter 20

Vishwamitra and his entourage reached Mithila a week later. Being a fertile, marshy plain that received plentiful monsoonal rain, the land around Mithila was productive beyond measure. It was said that all a Mithila farmer needed to do was fling some seeds and return a few months later to harvest the crop. The land of Mithila would do the rest. But since the farmers of Mithila had not cleared too much land or flung too many seeds, the forest had used the bounty of nature and created a dense barrier all around the city. The absence of a major river added to its isolation. Mithila was cut off from most other Indian cities, which were usually accessed by river.

'Why are we so dependent on rivers?' Ram asked. 'Why don't we build roads? A city like Mithila need not be cut off.'

'We did have good roads once upon a time,' said Arishtanemi. 'Maybe you can rebuild them.'

As the convoy broke through the forest line, they came upon what must have served as a defensive moat once, but had now been converted into a lake to draw water from. The lake circumscribed the entire city within itself so effectively that Mithila was like an island. There were no animals, like crocodiles, in the lake, for it no longer served a military purpose. Steps had been built on the banks for easy access to water. Giant wheels drew water from the lake, which was carried into the city through pipes.

'It is incredibly dim-witted to use the moat as your main water supply,' said Lakshman. 'The first thing a besieging army would do is to cut it off. Or worse; they may even poison the water.'

'You are right,' said Arishtanemi. 'The prime minister of Mithila realised this. That is why she had a small, but very deep lake constructed, within the city walls.'

Ram, Lakshman and Arishtanemi dismounted at the outer banks of the lake. They had to cross a pontoon bridge to enter the city. Because a pontoon bridge is essentially a floating platform supported by parallel lines of barges or boats, making the structure shaky and unstable, it was wiser to walk across on foot, leading your horse.

Arishtanemi explained enthusiastically, 'Not only is it cheaper than a conventional bridge, it can also be destroyed easily if the city is attacked. And, of course, be rebuilt just as easily.'

Ram nodded politely, wondering why Arishtanemi felt the need to talk up Mithila. In any case, the city was obviously not wealthy enough to convert the temporary bridge into a more permanent structure.

But then, which kingdom in India, besides Lanka, is wealthy today? The Lankans have taken away all our wealth.

After they crossed over, they came upon the gates of Mithila's fort walls. Interestingly, there were no slogans or military symbols of royal pride emblazoned across the gate. Instead, there was a large image of Lady Saraswati, the Goddess of Knowledge, which had been carved into the top half of the gate. Below it was a simple couplet:

Swagruhe Pujyate Murkhaha; Swagraame Pujyate Prabhuhu

Swadeshe Pujyate Raja; Vidvaansarvatra Pujyate.

A fool is worshipped in his home.

A chief is worshipped in his village.

A king is worshipped in his kingdom.

A knowledgeable person is worshipped everywhere.

Ram smiled. *A city dedicated to knowledge.*

'Shall we enter?' asked Arishtanemi, pulling his horse's lead rope and clicking as he stepped forward.

Ram nodded to Lakshman, and they led their horses behind Arishtanemi as he entered the city. Behind the gates, a simple road led to another fort wall, at a distance of a kilometre from the outer wall. The rest of the area between the two walls was neatly partitioned into plots of agricultural land. Food crops were ready for harvest.

'Smart,' said Ram.

'Yes *Dada*, growing crops within the fort walls secures their food supply,' said Lakshman.

'More importantly, there's no human habitation here. This area would be a killing field for an enemy who manages to breach the outer fort wall. An attacking force will lose too many men in the effort to reach the second wall, without any hope of a quick retreat. It's militarily brilliant — two fort walls with uninhabited land in between. We should replicate this in Ayodhya as well.'

Arishtanemi quickened his footsteps as they approached the inner fort wall.

'Are those windows I see?' asked Lakshman, pointing towards the top section of the inner fort wall.

'Yes,' said Arishtanemi.

'Do people use the fort wall as a part of their accommodation?' asked Lakshman, surprised.

'Yes, they do,' said Arishtanemi.

'Oh,' said Lakshman, shrugging.

Arishtanemi smiled as he looked ahead again.

'What the hell!' said Lakshman, stopping short as soon as he passed the gates of the inner city walls of Mithila. He reached for his sword, instinctively. 'We've been led into a trap!'

'Calm down, prince,' said Arishtanemi, with a broad smile. 'This is not a trap. This is just the way Mithila is.'

They had walked into a large, single-walled structure that lay on the other side of the gate; it was a continuous line of homes that shared a huge wall. All the houses were built against each other, like a honeycomb, with absolutely no divisions or space in between. There was a window high on the wall for each individual home, but no doors existed at the street level. It was no surprise that Lakshman thought they had been led into a dead end, a perfect trap or ambush. The fact that most of Vishwamitra's convoy was missing only added to his suspicions.

'Where are the streets?' asked Ram.

Since all the houses were packed against each other in one continuous line, there was no room for streets or even small paths.

'Follow me,' said Arishtanemi, enjoying the obvious befuddlement of his fellow travellers. He led his horse to a stone stairway built into the structure of a house.

'Why on earth are you climbing up to the roof?! And that too, with your horse!' Lakshman exclaimed.

'Just follow me, prince,' said Arishtanemi calmly.

Ram patted Lakshman, as though to soothe him, and started walking up the steps. Lakshman reluctantly followed, leading his horse. They reached the rooftop to confront a scene that was simply unimaginable.

The 'rooftops' of all the houses was in fact a single smooth platform; a 'ground' above the 'ground'. 'Streets' had been demarcated with paint, and they could see people headed in different directions, purposefully or otherwise. Vishwamitra's convoy could be seen far ahead.

'My God! Where are we? And where are those people headed?' asked Lakshman, who had never seen anything like this.

'But how do these people enter their houses?' asked Ram.

As if in answer, a man pulled open a flat door on what evidently was the 'sidewalk' on the roof, and then stepped down, into his house, shutting the door behind him. Ram could now see that, at regular intervals on the sidewalks, where no traffic was allowed, were trapdoors to allow residents access to their homes. Small vertical gaps between some lines of houses exposed grilled windows on the side walls, which allowed sunlight and air into some of the homes.

'What do they do during the monsoon?' asked Lakshman.

'They keep the doors and windows closed when it rains,' said Arishtanemi.

'But what about light, air?'

Arishtanemi pointed to ducts that had been drilled at regular intervals. 'Ducts have been built for a group of four houses each. Windows from inside the houses open up into these ducts to allow in air and light. Rainwater run-off collects in drains below the duct. The drains run under the "Bees Quarter" and lead into either the moat outside the walls, or the lake inside the city. Some of it is used for agriculture.'

'By the great Lord Parshu Ram,' said Lakshman. 'Underground drains. What a brilliant idea! It's the perfect way to control disease.'

But Ram had caught on to something else. 'Bees Quarter? Is that what this area is called?'

'Yes,' answered Arishtanemi.

'Why? Because it is built like a honeycomb?'

'Yes,' smiled Arishtanemi.

'Someone obviously has a sense of humour.'

'I hope you have one as well, because this is where we will be living.'

'What?' asked Lakshman.

'Prince,' said Arishtanemi apologetically, 'the Bees Quarter is where the workers of Mithila live. As we move inwards, beyond the gardens, streets, temples and mercantile areas, we arrive at the abodes and palaces of the rich, including the royalty. But, as you're aware, Guru Vishwamitra wants you to travel incognito.'

'How exactly do we do that if the prime minister knows we are here?' asked Lakshman.

'The prime minister only knows that Guru Vishwamitra has arrived with his companions. She doesn't know about the princes of Ayodhya. At least, not as yet.'

'We're the princes of Ayodhya,' said Lakshman, his fists clenched tight. 'A kingdom that is the overlord of the Sapt Sindhu. Is this how we will be treated here?'

'We're only here for a week,' said Arishtanemi. 'Please…'

'It's all right,' said Ram, cutting in. 'We'll stay here.'

Lakshman turned to Ram. 'But *Dada*…'

'We have stayed in simpler quarters before, Lakshman; it's just for a short while. Then we can go home. We have to honour our father's wishes.'

'I hope you both are comfortable,' said Vishwamitra, as he stepped down into the apartment through the roof door.

In the afternoon, the third hour of the third *prahar,* Vishwamitra had finally visited the Bees Quarter. The brothers had been given accommodation in an apartment at the inner extreme end, beyond which lay a garden; one of the many that proliferated the inner, more upmarket parts of the city. Being at one end of the massive Bees Quarter structure, they were lucky to have a window on the outer wall, which overlooked the garden. Ram and Lakshman had not visited the inner city as yet.

Vishwamitra had been housed in the royal palace, within the heart of the city. It used to be a massive structure once upon a time, but the kindly King Janak had gradually given away parts of the palace to be used as residences and classrooms for *rishis* and their students. The philosopher-king wanted Mithila to serve as a magnet for men of knowledge from across the land. He showered gifts from his meagre treasury upon these great teachers.

'Well, certainly less comfortable than you must be, Guru*ji*,' said Lakshman, a sneer on his face. 'I guess only my brother and I need to remain incognito.'

Vishwamitra ignored Lakshman.

'We are all right, Guru*ji*,' said Ram. 'Perhaps the time has come for you to guide us on the mission we have to complete in Mithila. We are eager to return to Ayodhya.'

'Right,' said Vishwamitra. 'Let me get to the point straight away. The king of Mithila has organised a *swayamvar* for his eldest daughter, Sita.'

A *swayamvar* was an ancient tradition in India. The father of the bride organised a gathering of prospective bridegrooms, from whom his daughter was free to either select her husband, or mandate a competition. The victor would win her hand.

Mithila did not figure in the list of powerful kingdoms of the Sapt Sindhu. The prospect of the overlord kingdom of Ayodhya making a marriage alliance with Mithila was remote at best. Even Ram was at a loss for words. But Lakshman had had enough by now.

'Have we been brought here to provide security for the *swayamvar*?' asked Lakshman. 'This is even more bizarre than making us fight with those imbecile Asuras.'

Vishwamitra turned towards Lakshman and glared, but before he could say anything Ram spoke up.

'Guru*ji*,' said Ram politely, although even his legendary patience was running thin, 'I do not think that Father would want a marriage alliance with Mithila. I, too, have sworn that I will not marry for politics but for—'

Vishwamitra interrupted Ram. 'It may be a little late to refuse participation in the *swayamvar*, prince.'

Ram immediately understood what had been implied. With superhuman effort, he maintained his polite tone. 'How could you have nominated me as a suitor without checking with my father or me?'

'Your father designated me your guru. You're aware of the tradition, prince; a father, a mother or a guru can make the decision on a child's marriage. Do you want to break this law?'

A stunned Ram stood rooted to the spot, his eyes blazing with anger.

'Furthermore, if you refuse to attend the *swayamvar* despite your name being listed among the suitors, then you will be breaking the laws in *Ushna Smriti* and *Haarit Smriti*. Are you sure you want to do that?'

Ram did not utter a word. His body shook with fury. He had been cleverly trapped by Vishwamitra.

'Excuse me,' said Ram, abruptly, as he walked up the steps, lifted the roof door and climbed out. Lakshman followed his elder brother, banging the door shut behind him.

Vishwamitra laughed with satisfaction. 'He'll come around. He has no choice. The law is clear.'

Arishtanemi looked at the door sadly and then back at his guru, choosing silence.

Chapter 21

Ram walked down the stairway and reached the lower 'ground' level. He entered a public garden and sat on the first available bench, alive only to his inner turmoil. To the casual passer-by, his eyes seemed focused on the ground, his breathing slow and even, as though he was meditating deeply. But Lakshman knew his brother and his signs of anger. The deeper *Dada's* anger, the calmer he appeared. Lakshman felt the pain acutely, for his brother became distant and shut him out on such occasions.

'The hell with this, *Dada*!' Lakshman lashed out. 'Tell that pompous guru to take a hike and let's just leave.'

Ram did not react. Not a muscle twitched to suggest that he had even heard his brother's rant.

'*Dada*,' continued Lakshman, 'it's not as if you and I are particularly popular among the royal families in the Sapt Sindhu. Let Bharat *Dada* handle them. One of the few advantages of being disliked is that you don't need to fret over what others think about you.'

'I don't care what others think of me,' said Ram, his voice startlingly calm. 'But it is the law.'

'It's not your law. It's not our law. Forget it!'

Ram turned to look into the distance.

'*Dada*…' said Lakshman, placing his hand on Ram's shoulder.

Ram's body tensed in protest.

'*Dada*, whatever you decide, I am with you.'

His shoulder relaxed. Ram finally looked at his woebegone brother. He smiled. 'Let's take a walk into the city. I need to clear my head.'

Beyond the Bees Quarter, the city of Mithila was relatively more organised, with well-laid out streets lined by luxurious buildings; luxurious in a manner of speaking, for it would be unfair to compare them to the grand architecture of Ayodhya. Dressed in the coarse, un-dyed garments of the common class, the brothers did not attract any attention.

Their aimless wandering led them into the main market area, built in a large, open square. It was lined by *pucca* stone-structured expensive shops, with temporary stalls occupying the centre, offering a low-cost option. The neatly numbered stalls were covered by colourful cloth awnings held up by upright bamboo poles. They were organised in a grid layout, marked by chalk lines with adequate lanes for people to walk around.

'*Dada*,' said Lakshman as he picked up a mango. He knew his brother loved the fruit. 'These must be among the early harvests of the season. It may not be the best, but it's still a mango!'

Ram smiled faintly. Lakshman immediately purchased two mangoes, handed one to Ram and set about devouring the other, biting and sucking the succulent pulp with gusto. It made Ram laugh.

Lakshman looked at him. 'What's the point of eating mangoes if you cannot make a mess of it?'

Ram set upon his own mango, joining his brother as he slurped noisily. Lakshman finished first and his brother stopped him in time from casually chucking the mango stone by the sidewalk. 'Lakshman…'

Lakshman pretended as if nothing was amiss and, equally casually, walked up to a garbage collection pit dug next to a stall and dropped the mango stone in the rightful place. Ram followed suit. As they turned around to retrace their steps to the apartment, they heard a loud commotion from farther ahead in the same lane. They quickened their pace as they walked towards the hubbub.

They heard a loud, belligerent voice. 'Princess Sita! Leave this boy alone!'

A firm feminine voice was heard in reply. 'I will not!'

Ram looked at Lakshman, surprised.

'Let's see what's going on,' said Lakshman.

Ram and Lakshman pushed forward through the crowd that had gathered in a flash. As they broke through the first line of the throng, they came upon an open space, probably the centre of the square. They stood at the rear of a corner stall, beyond which their eyes fell on a little boy's back, probably seven or eight years of age. He held a fruit in his hand, as he cowered behind a woman, also facing the other way. The woman confronted a large and visibly angry mob.

'That's Princess Sita?' asked Lakshman, his eyes widening as he turned to look at Ram. His brother's visage knocked the breath out of him. Time seemed to inexplicably slow down, as if Lakshman was witnessing a cosmic event.

Ram stood still as he looked intently, his face calm. Lakshman detected the flush on his brother's dark-skinned face; his heart had clearly picked up pace. Sita stood with her back towards them, but Ram could see that she was unusually tall for a Mithilan woman, almost as tall as he was. She looked like a warrior in the army of the Mother Goddess, with her lean and muscular physique. She was wheatish-complexioned; she wore a cream-coloured *dhoti* and a white single-cloth blouse. Her *angvastram* was draped over her right shoulder, with one end tucked into her *dhoti* and the other tied around her left hand. Ram noticed a small knife scabbard tied horizontally to the small of her back. It was empty. He had been told that Sita was a little older than he was—she was twenty-five years of age.

Ram felt a strange restlessness; he felt a strong urge to behold her face.

'Princess Sita!' screamed a man, possibly the leader of the mob. Their elaborate attire suggested that this crowd was made up of the well-to-do. 'Enough of protecting these scum from the Bees Quarter! Hand him over!'

'He will be punished by the law!' said Sita. 'Not by you!'

Ram smiled slightly.

'He is a thief! That's all we understand. We all know whom your laws favour. Hand him over!' The man inched closer, breaking away from the crowd. The air was rife with tension; nobody knew what would happen next. It could spiral out of control any moment. Crazed mobs can lend a dangerous courage to even the faint-hearted.

Sita slowly reached for her scabbard, where her knife should have been. Her hand tensed. Ram watched with keen interest: no sudden movements, not a twitch of nervous energy when she realised she carried no weapon.

Sita spoke evenly. 'The law does not make any distinction. The boy will be punished. But if you try to interfere, so will you.'

Ram was spellbound. *She's a follower of the law…*

Lakshman smiled. He had never thought he would find another as obsessed with the law as his brother.

'Enough already!' shouted the man. He looked at the mob and screamed as he swung his hand. 'She's just one! There are hundreds of us! Come on!'

'But she's a princess!' Someone from the back tried to reason weakly.

'No, she's not!' shouted the man. 'She is not King Janak's real daughter. She's adopted!'

Sita suddenly pushed the boy out of the way, stepped back and dislodged with her foot an upright bamboo stick that held the awning of a shop in place. It fell to the ground. She flicked the stick with her foot, catching it with her right hand in one fluid motion. She swung the stick expertly in her hand, twirling it around with such fearsome speed that it whipped up a loud, humming sound. The leader of the mob remained stationary, out of reach.

'*Dada*,' whispered Lakshman. 'We should step in.'

'She has it under control.'

Sita stopped swinging and held the stick to her side, one end tucked under her armpit, ready to strike. 'Go back quietly to your houses, nobody will get hurt. The boy will be punished according to the law; nothing more, nothing less.'

The mob leader pulled out a knife and swiftly moved forward. Sita swerved back as he swung the blade wildly. In the same movement, she steadied herself by going back one step and then down on one knee, swinging her stick with both her hands. The weapon hit the man behind his knee. Even before his knee buckled, she transferred her weight to her other foot and yanked the stick upwards, using his own legs as leverage as his feet went up in the air. His legs flew upwards and he fell hard, flat on his back. Sita instantly rose, held the stick high above her head with both her hands, and struck his chest hard; one brutal strike. Ram heard the sound of the rib cage cracking with the fierce blow.

Sita twirled the stick and held it out, one end tucked under her armpit again; her left hand stretched out, her feet spread wide, offering her the balance she needed to move to either side swiftly. 'Anyone else?'

The crowd took one step back. The swift and brutal downing of their leader seemed to have driven some sense into them. Sita forced the point home. 'Anyone else wants a cracked rib, free of charge?'

They began to move backwards, even as the people in the back melted away.

Sita summoned a man who stood to the right of Ram, pointing towards the one who lay prone on the ground. 'Kaustav! Round up a few men and take Vijay to the *ayuralay.* I will check on him later.'

Kaustav and his friends rushed forward. As she turned, Ram finally beheld her visage.

Had the entire universe garnered all its talents into creating a perfect feminine face — of delicate beauty and ferocious will — this would be it. Her round face was a shade lighter than the rest of her body, with high cheekbones and a sharp, small nose; her lips were neither thin nor full; her wide-set eyes were neither small nor large; strong brows arched in a perfect curve above creaseless eyelids, and a limpid fire shone in her eyes, enhanced right now by what she had unleashed. A faint birthmark on her right temple made real a face that to Ram was both flawless and magnificent. She had the look of the mountain people from the Himalayas; Ram had fond memories of them from his short visit to the valley of Kathmandu, when he was young. Her straight, jet-black hair was braided and tied into a neat bun. Her warrior's body carried the proud scars from battle wounds.

'*Dada…*' Lakshman's voice seemed to have travelled from a distant land. It was, quite simply, almost inaudible to him.

Ram stood as if he was carved from marble. Lakshman knew his brother so well; the more transfixed his face, the deeper the tumult of emotions within.

Lakshman touched Ram's shoulder. '*Dada…*'

Ram still could not respond. He was mesmerised. Lakshman turned his attention back to Sita.

She threw the stick away and caught hold of the boy-thief. 'Come on.'

'My Lady,' pleaded the boy. 'I'm sorry. This will be the last time. I'm really sorry.'

Sita tugged at the boy's hand and began to walk briskly towards Ram and Lakshman. Lakshman took hold of Ram's elbow and attempted to step aside. But Ram seemed to be in the grip of a higher power. His face was expressionless, his body still, his eyes almost unblinking, his breathing even and regular. The only movement was his *angvastram* fluttering in the breeze; exaggerated by his immobility.

Almost as if it was beyond his control, Ram bowed his head.

Lakshman held his breath as his mouth fell open. He had never thought he'd see this day; after all, which woman would inspire the admiration of a man such as his brother? That love would slam into a heart that had only known obedience to, and strict control of, his mind? That a man whose mission was to raise every person's head with pride and purpose would find comfort in bowing to another?

A line from an ancient poem came floating into his mind; one that his romantic heart had found ethereal. But he had never thought his staid elder brother would find meaning in that line before he did.

She has that something, like the thread in a crystal-bead necklace. She holds it all together.

Lakshman could see that his brother had found the thread that would hold the disparate beads of his life together.

Ram's heart, despite the fact that it had never been given free rein due to his immense self-control, was probably aware that it had just found its greatest ally. It had found Sita.

She came to a standstill, surprised by these two strangers blocking her path; one looked like a giant but loveable ruffian, and the other was too dignified for the coarse clothes he wore. Strangely, for some reason, he was bowing to her.

'Out of my way!' snapped Sita, as she pushed past Ram.

Ram stepped aside, but she had already whizzed past, dragging the boy-thief along.

Lakshman immediately stepped up and touched Ram on his back. '*Dada*…'

Ram hadn't turned to see Sita walking away. He stood mystified, almost as if his disciplined mind was trying to analyse what had just happened; what his heart had just done to him. He seemed surprised beyond measure; by himself.

'Umm, *Dada*…' said Lakshman, smiling broadly now.

'Hmm?'

'*Dada*, she's gone. I think you can raise your head now.'

Ram finally looked at Lakshman, a hint of a smile on his face.

'*Dada!*' Lakshman gave a loud laugh, stepped forward and embraced his brother. Ram patted him on his back. But his mind was preoccupied.

Lakshman stepped back and said, 'She'll make a great *bhabhi!*'

Ram frowned, refusing to acknowledge his brother's unbridled enthusiasm in referring to the princess as his *sister-in-law*.

'I guess we will be going to the *swayamvar* now,' said Lakshman, winking.

'Let's go back to our room for now,' said Ram, his expression calm again.

'Right!' said Lakshman, still laughing. 'Of course, we should behave maturely about this! Mature! Calm! Stoic! Controlled! Have I forgotten any word, *Dada*?!'

Ram tried to keep his face expressionless but it was obviously a bigger struggle than usual. He finally surrendered to his inner joy and his face lit up with a dazzling smile.

The brothers began to walk back to the Bees Quarter.

'We must tell Arishtanemi*ji* that you will, after all, be participating in the *swayamvar* willingly!' said Lakshman.

As Ram fell a few steps behind Lakshman, he allowed himself another full smile. His mind had probably begun to understand what had just happened to him. What his heart had done to him.

—— 𝕂 𓆟 ☼ ——

'This is good news,' said Arishtanemi. 'I'm delighted that you have decided to obey the law.'

Ram maintained a calm demeanour. Lakshman couldn't seem to control his smile.

'Yes, of course, Arishtanemi*ji*,' said Lakshman. 'How can we disregard the law? Especially one that has been recorded in two *Smritis*!'

Arishtanemi frowned, not really understanding Lakshman's sudden about-turn. He shrugged and turned to address Ram. 'I will inform Guru*ji* right away that you are willing to participate in the *swayamvar*.'

—— 𝕂 𓆟 ☼ ——

'*Dada!*' said Lakshman, rushing into their room.

It had been just five days since Ram had seen Sita. And there were less than two days to go for the *swayamvar*.

'What's the matter?' asked Ram, putting down the palm-leaf book he had been reading.

'Just come with me, *Dada*,' insisted Lakshman, as he grabbed Ram by the hand.

'What is it, Lakshman?' asked Ram once again.

They were on top of the Bees Quarter, walking down the streets. They moved in the direction away from the city. This section of the Bees Quarter actually merged with the inner fort wall, making it a fantastic lookout point to see the fields up to the outer wall and beyond at the land outside the city. A massive crowd had gathered, many of them pointing and gesticulating wildly as they spoke to each other.

'Lakshman… Where are you taking me?'

He did not get an answer.

'Move aside,' said Lakshman harshly as he pushed his way through the throng, leading Ram by the hand. People got out of the way at the sight of the muscular giant, and soon the brothers were at the wall.

As soon as they reached the edge, Ram's attention was caught by what he saw. Beyond the second wall and the lake-moat, in the clearing ahead of the forest line, a small army seemed to be gathering with devastating precision and discipline. There were ten standard bearers at regular intervals, holding their flags high. Waves of soldiers emerged from the forest in neat rows and, within a few minutes, they were all in formation, approximately a thousand behind each standard.

Intriguingly, they had left a large area clear, right in the centre of their formation.

Ram noticed that the colour of the *dhotis* that the soldiers wore was the same as their standards. He estimated that there must be ten thousand soldiers. Not a very large number, but enough to cause serious trouble to a city like Mithila, which was not a garrison city.

'Which kingdom has sent this army?' asked Ram.

'It's apparently not an army,' remarked the man standing next to Lakshman. 'It's a bodyguard corps.'

Ram was about to pose another question to the man when they were all distracted by the reverberating sounds of conch shells being blown by the soldiers in the clearing. A moment later, even this sound was drowned out by one that Ram had not heard before. It almost seemed like a giant demon was slicing through the air with quick strokes from a gigantic sword.

Lakshman looked up, tracing the source of the sound. 'What the...'

The crowd watched in awe. It must be the legendary flying vehicle that was the proud possession of Lanka, the *Pushpak Vimaan*. It was a giant conical craft, made of some strange, unknown metal. Massive rotors attached to the top of the vehicle, right at its pointed end, were swinging with a powerful force in a right to left, circular motion. A few smaller rotors were attached close to the base, on all sides. The body of the craft had many portholes, each of which was covered with thick glass.

The vehicle made a noise that could overpower that of trumpeting elephants in hot pursuit. It appeared to intensify as it hovered above the trees for a bit. As it did so, small circular metal screens descended over the portholes, covering them completely, blocking any view of the insides of the

Vimaan. The crowd gaped in unison at this outlandish sight as they covered their ears. So did Lakshman. But Ram did not. He stared at the craft with a visceral anger welling up deep inside him. He knew whom it belonged to. He knew who was in there. The man responsible for having destroyed all possibilities of a happy childhood before Ram was even born. He stood amidst the throng as if he was alone. His eyes burned with fearsome intensity.

The sound of the rotors suddenly dipped as the craft began its descent. The *Pushpak Vimaan* landed perfectly in the clearing designated for it, in the centre of the formations of the Lankan soldiers. The Mithilans of the Bees Quarter spontaneously broke into applause. For the soldiers of Lanka though, they may not have existed at all. They stood absolutely straight, rooted to their positions, in a remarkable display of raw discipline.

A few minutes later, a section of the conical *Vimaan* swung open, revealing a perfectly concealed door. The door slid aside and a giant of a man filled the doorway. He stepped out and surveyed the ground before him. A Lankan officer ran up to him and gave him a crisp salute. They exchanged some quick words and the giant looked intently towards the wall, at the avid spectators. He abruptly turned around and walked back into the *Vimaan.* After a while, he appeared again, this time walking out, followed by another man.

The second man was distinctly shorter than the first, and yet taller than the average Mithilan; probably of the same height as Ram. But unlike Ram's lean muscular physique, this Lankan was of gigantic proportions. His swarthy skin, handlebar moustache, thick beard and pock-marked face lent him an intimidating air. He wore a violet *dhoti* and *angvastram*, a colour-dye that was among the most expensive in the Sapt

Sindhu. He wore a large headgear with two threatening six-inch curved horns stretching out from either side. He stooped a bit as he walked.

'Raavan…' whispered Lakshman.

Ram did not respond.

Lakshman looked at Ram. *'Dada…'*

Ram remained silent, looking intently at the king of Lanka in the distance.

'Dada,' said Lakshman. 'We should leave.'

Ram looked at Lakshman. There was fire in his eyes. He then turned back to look at the Lankans beyond the second wall of Mithila; to *the* Lankan beyond the second wall of Mithila.

Chapter 22

'Please don't leave,' pleaded Arishtanemi. 'Guru*ji* is as troubled as you are. We don't know how or why Raavan landed up here. But Guru*ji* thinks it's safer for the two of you to remain within the fort walls.'

Ram and Lakshman sat in their room in the Bees Quarter. Arishtanemi had returned with a plea from Vishwamitra to the princes of Ayodhya: *please do not leave*. Raavan had set up camp outside the walls of Mithila. He had not entered the city, though a few of his emissaries had. They had gone straight to the main palace to speak to King Janak and his younger brother King Kushadhwaj; the latter had newly arrived in the city to attend the *swayamvar*.

'Why should I bother about what Guru Vishwamitra thinks?' asked Lakshman aggressively. 'I only care about my elder brother! Nobody can guess what this demon from Lanka will do! We have to leave! *Now!*'

'Please think about this with a calm mind. How will you be safe all alone in the jungle? You are better off within the walls of the city. The Malayaputras are here for your defence.'

'We cannot just sit here, waiting for events to unfold. I am leaving with my brother. You Malayaputras can do whatever the hell you want to!'

'Prince Ram,' Arishtanemi turned to Ram, 'please, trust me. What I am advising is the best course of action. Do not withdraw from the *swayamvar*. Do not leave the city.'

Ram's external demeanour was calm as usual, and yet Arishtanemi sensed a different energy; the inner serenity, so typical of Ram, was missing.

Had Ram been truly honest with himself, he would admit that there were many who had hurt him, who he should have at least resented, if not hated, with equal ferocity. Raavan, after all, had simply done his job; he had won a battle that he had fought. However, the child that Ram had once been was incapable of such rationalisation. That lonely and hurt child had focused all his frustration and anger at the injustices that he had faced on the iconic, invisible demon who had wrought such a devastating change in his father, turning him into a bitter man who constantly put his eldest son down and neglected him. As a child, he had convinced himself that Raavan had triggered all his misfortunes; that if Raavan had not won that battle on that terrible day in Karachapa, Ram would not have suffered so.

The anger that Ram reserved for Raavan stemmed from that childhood memory — it was overwhelming and beyond reason.

Arishtanemi had left for Vishwamitra's guest quarters, leaving Ram and Lakshman to themselves.

'*Dada*, trust me, let's just escape from here,' said Lakshman. 'There are ten thousand Lankans; we're only two. I'm telling you, if push comes to shove, even the Mithilans and Malayaputras will side with Raavan.'

Ram stared at the garden beyond, through the only window in the room.

'*Dada*,' said Lakshman, insistent. 'We need to make a run for it. I've been told there's a second gate at the other end of the city-wall. Nobody, except for the Malayaputras, knows who we are. We can escape quietly and return with the Ayodhya army. We will teach the damned Lankans a lesson, but for now, we need to run.'

Ram turned to Lakshman and spoke with eerie calm. 'We are the descendants of Ikshvaku, the descendants of Raghu. We will not run away.'

'*Dada*…'

He was interrupted by a knock on the door. He cast a quick look at Ram and drew his sword. Ram frowned. 'Lakshman, if someone wanted to assassinate us, he wouldn't knock. He would just barge in. There is no place to hide in here.'

Lakshman continued to stare at the door, unsure whether he should sheath his sword.

'Just open the door, Lakshman,' said Ram.

Lakshman crept up the stairs to the horizontal door on the roof. He held his sword to his side, ready to strike if the need so arose. There was another knock, more insistent this time. Lakshman pushed the door open to find Samichi, the police and protocol chief of Mithila, peering down at him. She was a short-haired, tall, dark-skinned and muscular woman, and her soldier's body bore scars of honour from battles well fought. She wore a blouse and *dhoti* made from the same green cloth. She had on leather armbands and a leather under-blouse; a sheathed long sword hung by her waist.

Lakshman gripped his sword tight. 'Namaste, Chief Samichi. To what do we owe this visit?' he asked gruffly.

Samichi grinned disarmingly. 'Put your sword back in the scabbard, young man.'

'Let me decide what I should or should not do. What is your business here?'

'The prime minister wants to meet your elder brother.'

Lakshman was taken aback. He turned to Ram, who signalled his brother to let them in. He immediately slipped his sword in its scabbard and backed up against the wall, making room for the party to enter. Samichi stepped in and descended the stairs, followed by Sita. As Sita stepped down through the door hole, she gestured behind her. 'Stay there, Urmila.'

Lakshman instinctively looked up to see Urmila, even as Ram stood up to receive the prime minister of Mithila. The two women climbed down swiftly but Lakshman remained rooted, entranced by the vision above. Urmila was shorter than her elder sister Sita, much shorter. She was also fairer; so fair that she was almost the colour of milk. She probably remained indoors most of the time, keeping away from the sun. Her round, baby face was dominated by her large eyes, which betrayed a sweet, childlike innocence. Unlike her warrior-like elder sister, Urmila was clearly a very delicate creature, aware of her beauty, yet childlike in her ways. Her hair was arranged in a bun with every strand neatly in place. The *kaajal* in her eyes accentuated their exquisiteness; the lips were enhanced with some beet extract. Her clothes were fashionable, yet demure: a bright pink blouse was complemented by a deep red *dhoti* which was longer than usual — it reached below her knees. A neatly pressed *angvastram* hung from her shoulders. Anklets and toe-rings drew attention to her lovely feet, while rings and bracelets decorated her delicate hands. Lakshman was mesmerised. The lady sensed it, smiled genially, and looked away with shy confusion.

Sita turned and saw Lakshman looking at Urmila. She had noticed something that Ram had missed.

'Shut the door, Lakshman,' said Ram.

Lakshman reluctantly did as ordered.

Ram turned towards Sita. 'How may I help you, princess?'

Sita smiled. 'Excuse me for a minute, prince.' She looked at Samichi. 'I'd like to speak to the prince alone.'

'Of course,' said Samichi, immediately climbing out of the room.

Ram was surprised by Sita's knowledge of their identity. He revealed nothing as he nodded at Lakshman, who turned to leave with alacrity. Ram and Sita were alone in no time.

Sita smiled and pointed towards a chair in the room. 'Please sit, Prince Ram.'

'I'm all right.'

Is it Guru Vishwamitra himself who revealed my identity to her? Why is he so hell-bent on this alliance?

'I insist,' said Sita, as she sat down herself.

Ram sat on a chair facing Sita. There was an awkward silence for some time before Sita spoke up. 'I believe you were tricked into coming here.'

Ram remained silent, but his eyes gave the answer away.

'Then why haven't you left?' asked Sita.

'Because it would be against the law.'

Sita smiled. 'And is it the law that will make you participate in the *swayamvar* day after tomorrow?'

Ram chose silence, for he would not lie.

'You are Ayodhya, the overlord of Sapt Sindhu. I am only Mithila, a small kingdom with little power. What purpose can possibly be served by this alliance?'

'Marriage has a higher purpose; it can be more than just a political alliance.'

Sita smiled enigmatically. Ram felt like he was being interviewed; this, strangely enough, did not stop him from noticing that an impertinent strand had slipped out of Sita's neatly braided hair. The gentle breeze wafting in from the window lifted the wisp of hair playfully. His attention shifted seamlessly to the perfect curve of her neck. He noticed his heart begin to race. He smiled to himself ruefully and tried to restore his inner calm as he admonished himself. *What is wrong with me? Why can't I control myself?!*

'Prince Ram?'

'Excuse me?' asked Ram, bringing his focus back to what she was saying.

'I asked, if marriage is not a political alliance, then what is it?'

'Well, to begin with, it is not a necessity; there should be no compulsion to get married. There's nothing worse than being married to the wrong person. You should only get married if you find someone you admire, who will help you understand and fulfil your life's purpose. And you, in turn, can help her fulfil her life's purpose. If you're able to find that one person, then marry her.'

Sita raised her eyebrows. 'Are you advocating just one wife? Not many? Most people think differently.'

'Even if *all* people think polygamy is right, it doesn't make it so.'

'But most men take many wives; especially the nobility.'

'I won't. You insult your wife by taking another.'

Sita drew back her head, raising her chin in contemplation; as though she was assessing him. Her eyes softened in admiration. A charged silence filled the room. As she gazed at him, her expression changed with sudden recognition.

'Wasn't it you at the market place the other day?' she asked.

'Yes.'

'Why didn't you step in to help me?'

'You had the situation under control.'

Sita smiled slightly.

It was Ram's turn to ask questions. 'What is Raavan doing here?'

'I don't know. But it makes the *swayamvar* more personal for me.'

Ram was shocked, but his expression remained impassive. 'Has he come to participate in your *swayamvar*?'

'So I have been told.'

'And?'

'And, I have come here.'

Ram waited for her to continue.

'How good are you with a bow and arrow?' asked Sita.

Ram allowed himself a faint smile.

Sita raised her eyebrows. 'That good?'

Sita arose from her chair, as did Ram. The prime minister of Mithila folded her hands into a namaste. 'May Lord Rudra continue to bless you, prince.'

Ram returned Sita's namaste. 'And may He bless you, princess.'

Ram's eyes fell on the bracelet made of Rudraaksh beads that Sita wore on her wrists; she was a fellow Lord Rudra devotee. His eyes involuntarily strayed from the beads to her perfectly formed, artistically long fingers. They could have belonged to a surgeon. The battle scar on her left hand suggested, though, that Sita's hands used tools other than scalpels.

'Prince Ram,' said Sita, 'I asked—'

'I'm sorry, can you repeat that?' asked Ram, refocusing on the here and now, on what Sita was saying.

'Can I meet with you and your brother in the private royal garden tomorrow?'

'Yes, of course.'

'Good,' said Sita, as she turned to leave. Then she stopped, as if remembering something. She reached into the pouch tied to her waistband and pulled out a red thread. 'It would be nice if you could wear this. It's for good luck. It is a representation of...'

But Ram's attention was seized by another thought; his mind wandering once again, drowning out what Sita was saying. He remembered a couplet; one he had heard at a wedding ceremony long ago.

Maangalyatantunaanena bhava jeevanahetuh may. A line from old Sanskrit, it translated into: *With this holy thread that I offer to you, please become the purpose of my life...*

'Prince Ram...' said Sita, loudly.

Ram suddenly straightened up as the wedding hymn playing in his mind went silent. 'I'm sorry. What?'

Sita smiled politely, 'I was saying...' She stopped just as suddenly. 'Never mind. I'll leave the thread here. Please wear it if it pleases you.'

Placing the thread on the table, Sita began to climb up the stairs. As she reached the door, she turned around for a last look. Ram was holding the thread in the palm of his right hand, gazing at it reverentially, as if it was the most sacred thing in the world.

—— 大 🐟 ☼ ——

The city of Mithila became increasingly more visually appealing as one moved beyond the main market to the enclaves of the upper classes. This was where Ram and Lakshman had decided to walk, late the following evening.

'It's pretty, isn't it, *Dada*?' remarked Lakshman, as he looked around in appreciation.

Ram had been noting the sudden change in Lakshman's attitude towards Mithila since the previous day. The road they were on was relatively broad but meandering, much like village roads. Trees and flower beds lined dividers made of stone and mortar, around three to four feet in height. Beyond the road edge were an array of trees, gardens and the stately mansions of the wealthy. Idols of various personal and family deities were placed above the boundary walls of the mansions. Incense sticks and fresh flowers were placed as offerings to the deities, indicating the spiritual inclinations of the citizens; Mithila was a bastion of the devout.

'Here we are,' pointed Lakshman.

Ram followed his brother into a narrow, circuitous lane on the right. The sidewalls being higher, it was difficult to see what lay beyond.

'Should we just jump over?' asked Lakshman, grinning mischievously.

Ram frowned at him and continued walking. A few metres ahead lay an ornate metal gate. Two soldiers stood at the entrance.

'We have come to meet the prime minister,' said Lakshman, handing over a ring that had been given to him by Samichi.

The guard examined the ring, was seemingly satisfied, and signalled to the other to help him open the gates.

Ram and Lakshman quickly walked into the resplendent garden. Unlike the royal gardens of Ayodhya, this one was less variegated; it only contained local trees, plants and flower beds. It was a garden whose beauty could be attributed more to the ministrations of talented gardeners than to the impressive infusion of funds. The layout was symmetrical and well-manicured. The thick green carpet of grass was thrown into visual relief by the profusion of flowers and trees of all shapes and colours. Nature expressed itself in ordered harmony.

'Prince Ram,' Samichi walked up to them from the shadows behind a tree. She bowed low with a respectful namaste.

'Namaste,' said Ram, as he folded his hands together.

Lakshman too returned Samichi's greeting and then handed the ring back to her. 'The guards recognise your mark.'

'As they should,' said the police chief, before turning to Ram. 'Princesses Sita and Urmila await you. Follow me, princes.'

Lakshman beamed with delight as he followed Ram and Samichi.

— 大 🐟 ☼ —

Ram and Lakshman were led into a clearing at the back of the garden; below their feet was plush grass, above them the open evening sky.

'Namaste, princess,' said Ram to Sita.

'Namaste, prince,' replied Sita, before turning to her sister. 'May I introduce my younger sister, Urmila?' Gesturing towards Ram and Lakshman, Sita continued, 'Urmila, meet Prince Ram and Prince Lakshman of Ayodhya.'

'I had occasion to meet her yesterday,' said Lakshman, grinning from ear to ear.

Urmila smiled politely at Lakshman, with her hands folded in a namaste, then turned towards Ram and greeted him.

'I would like to speak with the prince privately, once again,' said Sita.

'Of course,' said Samichi immediately. 'May I have a private word before that?'

Samichi took Sita aside and whispered in her ear. Then she cast a quick look at Ram before walking away, leading Urmila by the hand. Lakshman followed Urmila.

Ram felt as if his interview from yesterday would proceed from where they had left off. 'Why did you want to meet me, princess?'

Sita made sure that Samichi and the rest had indeed left. She was about to begin when her eyes fell on the red thread tied around Ram's right wrist. She smiled. 'Please give me a minute, prince.'

Sita went behind a tree, bent and picked up a very long package covered in cloth. She walked back to Ram. He frowned, intrigued. Sita pulled the cloth back to reveal an intricately carved, unusually long bow. An exquisite piece of weaponry, it was a composite bow with recurved ends, which must give it a very long range. Ram carefully examined the carvings on the inside face of the limbs, both above and below the grip of the bow. It was the image of a flame, representative of Agni, the God of Fire. The first hymn of the first chapter of the *Rig Veda* was dedicated to the deeply revered deity. However, the shape of this particular flame seemed familiar to Ram, in the way its edges leapt out.

Sita pulled a flat wooden base platform out of the cloth bag and placed it on the ground ceremonially. She looked up at Ram. 'This bow cannot be allowed to touch the ground.'

Ram frowned, wondering what made it so important. Sita placed the lower limb of the bow on the platform, steadying it with her foot. She used her right hand to pull down the other end with force. Judging by the strain on her shoulder and biceps, Ram knew it was a very strong bow with tremendous resistance. With her left hand, Sita pulled the bowstring up and quickly strung it. She let the upper limb extend up and relaxed as she let out a long breath. The mighty bow adjusted to the constraints of the potent bowstring. She held the bow with her left hand and pulled the bowstring with her fingers, letting it go with a loud twang.

Ram knew from the sound of the string that this bow was special. It was the strongest he had ever heard. 'Wow. That's a good bow.'

'It's the best.'

'Is it yours?'

'I cannot own a bow like this. I am only its caretaker, for now. When I die, someone else will be deputed to take care of it.'

Ram narrowed his eyes as he closely examined the image of the flames around the grip of the bow. 'These flames look a little like—'

Sita interrupted him. 'This bow once belonged to the one whom we both worship. It still belongs to him.'

Ram stared at the bow with a mixture of shock and awe, his suspicion confirmed.

Sita smiled. 'Yes, it is the *Pinaka*.'

The *Pinaka* was the legendary bow of the previous Mahadev, Lord Rudra, considered the strongest bow ever made. Legend held that it was a composite, a mix of many materials, which had been given a succession of specific treatments to arrest its degeneration. It was also believed that maintaining this bow was not an easy task. The grip, the limbs and the recurved ends needed regular lubrication with special oil. Sita was obviously up to the task, for the bow was as good as new.

'How did Mithila come into the possession of the *Pinaka*?' asked Ram, unable to take his eyes off the beautiful weapon.

'It's a long story,' said Sita, 'but I want you to practice with it. This is the bow which will be used for the *swayamvar* competition tomorrow.'

Ram took an involuntary step back. There were many ways in which a *swayamvar* was conducted, two of them being: either the bride could directly select her groom; or she could mandate a competition. The winner would marry the bride. But this was unorthodox, to say the least: for a groom to be given advance notice and help. In fact, it was against the rules.

Ram shook his head. 'It would be an honour to even touch the *Pinaka,* much less hold the bow that Lord Rudra himself graced with his touch. But I will only do so tomorrow. Not today.'

Sita frowned. 'I thought you intended to win my hand.'

'I do. But I will win it the right way. I will win according to the rules.'

Sita smiled, shaking her head as she experienced a peculiar sense of fear mixed with elation.

'Do you disagree?' asked Ram, seeming a bit disappointed.

'No, I don't. I'm just impressed. You are a special man, Prince Ram.'

Ram blushed. His heart, despite his mental admonishments, picked up pace once again.

'I look forward to seeing you fire an arrow tomorrow morning,' said Sita.

Chapter 23

The *swayamvar* was held in the Hall of *Dharma* instead of the royal court. This was simply because the royal court was not the biggest hall in Mithila. The main building in the palace complex, which housed the Hall of *Dharma*, had been donated by King Janak to the Mithila University. The hall hosted regular debates and discussions on various esoteric topics: the nature of *dharma*, karma's interaction with *dharma*, the nature of the divine, the purpose of the human journey... King Janak was a philosopher-king who focused all his kingdom's resources on matters that were spiritual and intellectual.

The Hall of *Dharma* was in a circular building, built of stone and mortar, with a massive dome; quite rare in India. The delicate elegance of the dome was believed to represent the feminine, while the typical temple spire represented the masculine. The Hall of *Dharma* embodied King Janak's approach to governance: an intellectual love of wisdom and respectful equality accorded to all points of view. The hall, therefore, was circular. All *rishis* sat as equals, without a moderating 'head', debating issues openly and without fear; freedom of expression at its zenith.

However, today was different. There were no manuscripts lying on low tables, or *rishis* moving to the centre in a disciplined sequence, to deliver speeches or debate their points. The Hall of *Dharma* was set to host a *swayamvar*.

Temporary three-tiered spectator stands stood near the entrance. At the other end, on a wooden platform, was placed the king's throne. A statue of the great King Mithi, the founder of Mithila, stood on a raised pedestal behind the throne. Two thrones, only marginally less grand, were placed to the left and right of the king's throne. A circle of comfortable seats lined the middle section of the great hall, where kings and princes, the potential suitors, would sit.

The spectator stands were already packed when Ram and Lakshman were led in by Arishtanemi. Most contestants too had taken their seats. Not many recognised the two princes of Ayodhya, dressed as they were as hermits. A guard gestured for them to move towards the base platform of a three-tiered stand, occupied by the nobility and rich merchants of Mithila. Arishtanemi informed the guard that he accompanied a competitor. The guard was surprised but he did recognise Arishtanemi, the lieutenant of the great Vishwamitra, and stepped aside to let them proceed. After all, it would not be unusual for the devout King Janak to invite even Brahmin *rishis*, not just Kshatriya kings, for his daughter's *swayamvar*.

The walls of the Hall of *Dharma* were decorated by portraits of the greatest *rishis* and *rishikas* of times past: Maharishi Satyakam, Maharishi Yajnavalkya, Maharishika Gargi, and Maharishika Maitreyi, among others. Ram mused: *How unworthy are we, the descendants of these great ancestors. Maharishikas Gargi and Maitreyi were rishikas, and today there are fools who claim that women are not to be allowed to study the scriptures or to write new ones. Maharishi Satyakam was the son of a Shudra single mother. His profound knowledge and wisdom is recorded in our greatest Upanishads; and today there are bigots who claim that the Shudra-born cannot become rishis.*

Ram bowed his head and brought his hands together, paying obeisance to the great sages of yore. *A person becomes a Brahmin by karma, not by birth.*

'*Dada,*' said Lakshman, touching Ram's back.

Ram followed Arishtanemi to the allotted seat.

He seated himself as Lakshman and Arishtanemi stood behind him. All eyes turned to them. The contestants wondered who these simple mendicants were, who hoped to compete with them for Princess Sita's hand. A few, though, recognised the princes of Ayodhya. A conspiratorial buzz was heard from a section of the contestants.

'Ayodhya…'

'Why does Ayodhya want an alliance with Mithila?'

Ram, however, was oblivious to the stares and whispers of the assembly. He had eyes only for the centre of the hall; placed ceremonially on a table top was the bow. Next to the table, at ground level, was a large copper-plated basin.

Ram's eyes first lingered on the *Pinaka*. It was unstrung. An array of arrows was placed by the side of the bow.

Competitors were first required to pick up the bow and string it, which itself was no mean task. But it was then that the challenge truly began. The contestant would move to the copper-plated basin. It was filled with water, with additional drops trickling in steadily from the rim of the basin, attached to which was a thin tube. Excess water was drained out of the basin by another thin tube, attached to the other side. This created subtle ripples within the bowl, which spread out from the centre towards the edge. Agonisingly, the drops of water were released at irregular intervals, making the ripples, in turn, unpredictable.

A hilsa fish was nailed to a wheel, fixed to an axle that was suspended from the top of the dome, a hundred metres above the ground. The wheel, thankfully, revolved at a constant speed. The contestants were required to look at the reflection of the fish in the unstill water below, disturbed by ripples generated at irregular intervals, and use the *Pinaka* bow to fire an arrow into the eye of the fish, fixed on the revolving wheel high above them. The first to succeed would win the hand of the bride.

'This is too simple for you, *Dada*,' said Lakshman, mischievously. 'Should I ask them to make the wheel revolve at irregular intervals, too? Or twist the feather-fletching on the arrow? What do you think?'

Ram looked up at Lakshman, narrowed his eyes and glared at his brother.

Lakshman grinned. 'Sorry, *Dada*.'

He stepped back as the king was announced.

'The Lord of the Mithi clan, the wisest of the wise, beloved of the *rishis*, King Janak!'

The court arose to welcome their host, Janak, the king of Mithila. He walked in from the far end of the hall. Interestingly, in a deviation from tradition, he followed Vishwamitra, who was in the lead. Behind Janak was his younger brother, Kushadhwaj, the king of Sankashya. Even more interestingly, Janak requested Vishwamitra to occupy the throne of Mithila, as he moved towards the smaller throne to the right. Kushadhwaj walked towards the seat on the left of the great maharishi. A flurry of officials scuttled all over the place, for this was an unexpected breach of protocol.

A loud buzz ran through the hall at this unorthodox seating arrangement, but Ram was intrigued by something else. He turned towards Lakshman, seated behind him. His younger brother verbalised Ram's thought. 'Where is Raavan?'

The court crier banged his staff against the large bell at the entrance of the hall, signalling a call for silence.

Vishwamitra cleared his throat and spoke loudly. The superb acoustics of the Hall of *Dharma* carried his voice clearly to all those present. 'Welcome to this august gathering called by the wisest and most spiritual of rulers in India, King Janak.'

Janak smiled genially.

Vishwamitra continued. 'The princess of Mithila, Sita, has decided to make this a *gupt swayamvar*. She will not join us in the hall. The great kings and princes will, on her bidding, compete—'

The maharishi was interrupted by the ear-splitting sounds of numerous conch shells; surprising, for conch shells were usually melodious and pleasant. Everyone turned to the source of the sound: the entrance of the great hall. Fifteen tall, muscular warriors strode into the room bearing black flags, with the image of the head of a roaring lion emerging from a profusion of fiery flames. The warriors marched with splendid discipline. Behind them were two formidable men. One was a giant, even taller than Lakshman. He was corpulent but muscular, with a massive potbelly that jiggled with every step. His whole body was unusually hirsute — he looked more like a giant bear than human. Most troubling, for all those present, were the strange outgrowths on his ears and shoulders. He was a Naga. Ram recognised him as the first to have emerged from the *Pushpak Vimaan*.

Walking proudly beside him was Raavan, his head held high. He moved with a minor stoop; perhaps a sign of increasing age.

The two men were followed by fifteen more warriors, or more correctly, bodyguards.

Raavan's entourage moved to the centre and halted next to the bow of Lord Rudra. The lead bodyguard made a loud announcement. 'The king of kings, the emperor of emperors, the ruler of the three worlds, the beloved of the Gods, Lord Raavan!'

Raavan turned towards a minor king who sat closest to the *Pinaka*. He made a soft grunting sound and flicked his head to the right, a casual gesture which clearly communicated what he expected. The king immediately rose and scurried away, coming to a standstill behind another competitor. Raavan walked to the chair, but did not sit. He placed his right foot on the seat and rested his hand on his knee. His bodyguards, including the giant bear-man, fell in line behind him. Raavan finally cast a casual glance at Vishwamitra. 'Continue, great Malayaputra.'

Vishwamitra, the chief of the Malayaputras, was furious. He had never been treated so disrespectfully. 'Raavan...' he growled.

Raavan stared at Vishwamitra with lazy arrogance.

Vishwamitra managed to rein in his temper; he had an important task at hand. He would deal with Raavan later. 'Princess Sita has decreed the sequence in which the great kings and princes will compete.'

Raavan began to walk towards the *Pinaka* while Vishwamitra was still speaking. The chief of the Malayaputras completed his announcement just as Raavan was about to reach for the bow. 'The first man to compete is not you, Raavan. It is Ram, the prince of Ayodhya.'

Raavan's hand stopped a few inches from the bow. He looked at Vishwamitra, and then turned around to see who had responded to the sage. He saw a young man, dressed in the simple white clothes of a hermit. Behind him stood another young, though gigantic man, next to whom was Arishtanemi. Raavan glared first at Arishtanemi, and then at Ram. If looks could kill, Raavan would have certainly felled a few today. He turned towards Vishwamitra, Janak and Kushadhwaj, his fingers wrapped around the macabre, finger-bone pendant that hung around his neck. He growled in a loud and booming voice, 'I have been insulted!'

Ram noticed that the giant bear-man, who stood behind Raavan's chair, was shaking his head imperceptibly; seemingly rueing being there.

'Why was I invited at all if you planned to make unskilled boys compete ahead of me?!' Raavan's body shook with fury.

Janak looked at Kushadhwaj with irritation before turning to Raavan and interjecting weakly, 'These are the rules of the *swayamvar*, Great King of Lanka…'

A voice that sounded more like the rumble of thunder was finally heard; it was the giant bear-man. 'Enough of this nonsense!' He turned towards Raavan. '*Dada*, let's go.'

Raavan suddenly bent and picked up the *Pinaka*. Before anyone could react, he had strung it and nocked an arrow on the string. Everyone sat paralysed as Raavan pointed the arrow directly at Vishwamitra. Lakshman was forced to acknowledge the strength as well as the skill of this man.

The crowd gasped collectively in horror as Vishwamitra stood up, threw his *angvastram* aside, and banged his chest with his closed fist. 'Shoot, Raavan!'

Ram was stunned by the warrior-like behaviour of this *rishi*. Raw courage in a man of knowledge was a rarity. But then, Vishwamitra had been a warrior once.

The sage's voice resounded in the great hall. 'Come on! Shoot, if you have the guts!'

Raavan released the arrow. It slammed into the statue of Mithi behind Vishwamitra, breaking off the nose of the ancient king. Ram stared at Raavan; his fists were, uncharacteristically, clenched. This insult to the founder of the city was not challenged by a single Mithilan.

Raavan dismissed King Janak with a wave of his hand as he glared at King Kushadhwaj. He threw the bow on the table and began to walk towards the door, followed by his

guards. In all this commotion, the giant bear-man stepped up
to the table, unstrung the *Pinaka,* and reverentially brought it
to his head as he held it with both hands; almost like he was
apologising to the bow. He turned around and briskly walked
out of the room, behind Raavan. Ram's eyes remained pinned
on him till he left the room.

As the last of the Lankans exited, the people within the
hall turned in unison from the doorway to those seated at the
other end of the room: Vishwamitra, Janak and Kushadhwaj.

What are they going to do now?

Vishwamitra spoke as if nothing had happened. 'Let the
competition begin.'

The people in the room sat still, as if they had turned to
stone, en masse. Vishwamitra spoke once again, louder this
time. 'Let the competition begin. Prince Ram, please step up.'

Ram rose from his chair and walked up to the *Pinaka.*
He bowed with reverence, folded his hands together into a
namaste, and softly repeated an ancient chant: '*Om Rudrāya
Namah.*' *The universe bows to Lord Rudra. I bow to Lord Rudra.*

He raised his right wrist and touched both his eyes with
the red thread tied around it. He felt a charge run through
his body as he touched the bow. Was this his devotion
towards Lord Rudra, or did the bow unselfishly transmit its
accumulated power to the prince of Ayodhya? Those seeking
only factual knowledge would analyse what happened. Those
in love with wisdom would simply enjoy the moment. Ram
savoured the moment as he touched the bow again. He then
brought his head down and placed it on the bow; he asked to
be blessed.

He breathed steadily as he lifted the bow with ease. Sita,
hidden behind a latticed window next to Kushadhwaj, looked
at Ram intently with bated breath.

Ram placed one arm of the bow on a wooden stand placed on the ground. His shoulders, back and arms strained visibly as he pulled down the upper limb of the *Pinaka*, simultaneously pulling up the bowstring. His body laboured at the task, but his face remained serene. He bent the upper limb farther with a slight increase in effort as he tied the bowstring. His muscles relaxed as he let go of the upper limb and held the bow at the grip. He brought the bowstring close to his ear and plucked; the twang was perfect.

He picked up an arrow and walked to the copper-plated basin with deliberate, unhurried footsteps. He went down on one knee, held the bow horizontally above his head and looked down at the water; at the reflection of the fish that moved in a circle above him. The rippling water in the basin danced as if to tantalise his mind. Ram focused on the image of the fish to the exclusion of all else. He nocked the arrow on the string of the bow and pulled slowly with his right hand, his back erect, the core muscles activated with ideal tension. His breathing was steady and rhythmic. As was his consciousness, so was the response from the universe. He handed himself over to a higher force as he pulled the string all the way back and released the arrow. It shot up, as did the vision of each person in the room. The unmistakable sound of a furiously speeding arrow crashing into wood reverberated in the great hall. It had pierced the right eye of the fish, and lodged itself into the wooden wheel. The wheel swirled rhythmically as the shaft of the arrow drew circles in the air. Ram's mind reclaimed its awareness of the surroundings as his eyes continued to study the rippling water; he smiled. Not because he had hit the target. He had, in fact, earned a sense of completion of his being, with that shot. From this moment on, he was no longer alone.

He whispered, in the confines of his mind, a tribute to the woman he admired; Lord Rudra had said the same words to Lady Mohini, the woman he loved, many many centuries ago.

I have become alive. You have made me alive.

Chapter 24

The wedding was a simple set of solemn rituals, observed in the afternoon of the day that Ram won the *swayamvar*. To Ram's surprise, Sita had suggested that Lakshman and Urmila get married in the same auspicious hour of the day. To Ram's further disbelief, Lakshman had enthusiastically agreed. It was decided that while both the couples would be married in Mithila — to allow Sita and Urmila to travel with Ram and Lakshman to Ayodhya — a set of grand ceremonies would be held in Ayodhya as well; ones befitting the scions of the clan of Raghu.

Sita and Ram were alone at last. They sat on floor cushions in the dining hall, their dinner placed on a low stool. It was late in the evening, the sixth hour of the third *prahar*. Despite the fact that their relationship had been sanctified by *dharma* a few hours earlier, there was an awkwardness that underlined their ignorance of each other's personalities.

'Umm,' said Ram, as he stared at his plate.

'Yes, Ram?' asked Sita. 'Is there a problem?'

'I'm sorry, but … the food…'

'Is it not to your liking?'

'No, no, it's good. It's very good. But…'

'Yes?'

'It needs a bit of salt.'

Sita immediately pushed her plate aside, rose and clapped her hands. An attendant came rushing in.

'Get some salt for the prince, please.' As the attendant turned, Sita ordered with emphasis, 'Quickly!'

The attendant broke into a run.

Ram cleaned his hand with a napkin as he waited for the salt. 'I'm sorry to trouble you.'

Sita frowned as she resumed her seat. 'I'm your wife, Ram. It's my duty to take care of you.'

Ram smiled. 'Umm, may I ask you something?'

'Of course.'

'Tell me something about your childhood.'

'You mean, before I was adopted? You do know that I was adopted, right?'

'Yes... I mean, you don't have to talk about it if it troubles you.'

Sita smiled. 'No, it doesn't trouble me, but I don't remember anything. I was too young when I was found by my adoptive parents.'

Ram nodded.

Sita answered the question that she thought was on his mind. 'So, if you ask me who my birth-parents are, the short answer is that I don't know. But the one I prefer is that I am a daughter of the earth.'

'Birth is completely unimportant. It is just a means of entry into this *world of action*, into this *karmabhoomi*. Karma is all that matters. And your karma is divine.'

Sita smiled. Ram was about to say something when the attendant came rushing in with the salt. Ram added some to his food and resumed eating as the attendant retreated from the room.

'You were saying something,' said Sita.

'Yes,' said Ram, 'I think that…'

Ram was interrupted again, this time by the doorkeeper announcing loudly, 'The chief of the Malayaputras, the *Saptrishi Uttradhikari*, the protector of the way of the Vishnus, Maharishi Vishwamitra.'

Sita frowned and looked at Ram. Ram shrugged, clearly conveying he did not know what this visit was about.

Ram and Sita rose as Vishwamitra entered the room, followed by Arishtanemi. Sita gestured to her attendant to get some washing bowls for Ram and herself.

'We have a problem,' said Vishwamitra, not feeling the need to exchange pleasantries.

'What happened, Guru*ji*?' asked Ram.

'Raavan is mobilising for an attack.'

Ram frowned. 'But he doesn't have an army. What's he going to do with ten thousand bodyguards? He can't hold a city of even Mithila's size with that number. All he'll achieve is getting his men killed in battle.'

'Raavan is not a logical man,' proffered Vishwamitra. 'His ego is hurt. He may lose his bodyguard corps, but he will wreak havoc on Mithila.'

Ram looked at Sita, who shook her head with irritation and addressed Vishwamitra. 'Who in Lord Rudra's name invited that demon for the *swayamvar*? I know it was not my father.'

Vishwamitra took a deep breath as his eyes softened. 'That's water under the bridge, Sita. The question is, what are we going to do now?'

'What is your plan, Guru*ji*?'

'I have with me some important material that was mined at my *ashram* by the Ganga. I needed it to conduct a few science experiments at Agastyakootam. This was why I had visited my *ashram*.'

Agastyakootam was the capital of the Malayaputras, deep in the south of India, beyond the Narmada River. In fact, it was very close to Lanka itself.

'Science experiments?' asked Ram.

'Yes, experiments with the *daivi astras*.'

Sita drew a sharp breath for she knew the power and ferocity of the *divine weapons*. 'Guru*ji*, are you suggesting that we use *daivi astras*?'

Vishwamitra nodded in confirmation as Ram spoke up. 'But that will destroy Mithila as well.'

'No, it won't. This is not a traditional *daivi astra*. What I have is the *Asuraastra*.'

'Isn't that a biological weapon?' asked Ram, deeply troubled now.

'Yes. Poisonous gas and a blast wave from the *Asuraastra* will incapacitate the Lankans, paralysing them for days on end. We can easily imprison them in that state and end this problem.'

'Just paralyse, Guru*ji*?' asked Ram. 'I have learnt that, in large quantities, the *Asuraastra* can kill as well.'

Vishwamitra knew that only one man could have possibly taught this to Ram. None of the other *daivi astra* experts had ever met this young man. He was immediately irritated. 'Do you have any better ideas?'

Ram fell silent.

'But what about Lord Rudra's law?' asked Sita.

Lord Rudra, the previous Mahadev who was the Destroyer of Evil, had banned the unauthorised use of *daivi astras* many centuries ago. Practically everyone obeyed this diktat from the fearsome Lord Rudra. Those who broke the law he had decreed would be punished with banishment for fourteen years. Breaking the law for the second time would be punishable by death.

'I don't think that law applies to the use of the *Asuraastra*,' said Vishwamitra. 'It is not a weapon of mass destruction, just mass incapacitation.'

Sita narrowed her eyes. Clearly, she wasn't convinced. 'I disagree. A *daivi astra* is a *daivi astra*. We cannot use it without the authorisation of the Vayuputras, Lord Rudra's tribe. I am a Lord Rudra devotee. I will not break his law.'

'Do you want to surrender, then?'

'Of course not! We will fight!'

Vishwamitra laughed derisively. 'Fight, is it? And who, please explain, will fight Raavan's hordes? The namby-pamby intellectuals of Mithila? What is the plan? Debate the Lankans to death?'

'We have our police force,' said Sita quietly.

'They're not trained or equipped to fight the troops of Raavan.'

'We are not fighting his troops. We are fighting his bodyguard platoons. My police force is enough for them.'

'They are not. And you know that.'

'We will not use the *daivi astras*, Guru*ji*,' said Sita firmly, her face hardening.

Ram spoke up. 'Samichi's police force is not alone. Lakshman and I are here, and so are the Malayaputras. We're inside the fort, we have the double walls; we have the lake surrounding the city. We can hold Mithila. We can fight.'

Vishwamitra turned to Ram with a sneer. '*Nonsense!* We are vastly outnumbered. The double walls...' He snorted with disgust. 'It seems clever. But how long do you think it will take a warrior of Raavan's calibre to figure out a strategy that works around that obstacle?'

'We will not use the *daivi astras*, Guru*ji*,' said Sita, raising her voice. 'Now, if you will excuse me, I have a battle to prepare for.'

——— |大| 🐟 ☼ ———

It was late at night; the fourth hour of the fourth *prahar*. Ram and Sita had been joined by Lakshman and Samichi on top of the Bees Quarter, close to the inner wall edge. The entire Bees Quarter complex had been evacuated as a precautionary step. The pontoon bridge that spanned the moat-lake had been destroyed.

Mithila had a force of four thousand policemen and policewomen, enough to maintain law and order for the hundred thousand citizens of the small kingdom. Notwithstanding the strategic advantage of the double walls, would they be able to thwart an attack from the Lankan bodyguards of Raavan? They were outnumbered five to two.

Ram and Sita had abandoned any plans of securing the outer wall. They wanted Raavan and his soldiers to scale it and launch an assault on the inner walls; the Lankans would, then, be trapped between the two walls, which the Mithilan arrows would convert into a killing field. They expected a volley of arrows from the other side, in preparation for which the police had been asked to carry their wooden shields, normally used for crowd control within Mithila. Lakshman had taught them some basic manoeuvres with which they could protect themselves from the arrows.

'Where are the Malayaputras?' Lakshman asked Ram.

The Malayaputras had, much to Ram's surprise, not come to the battle-front. Ram whispered, 'I think it's just us.'

Lakshman shook his head and spat. 'Cowards.'

'Look!' said Samichi.

Sita and Lakshman looked in the direction that Samichi had pointed. Ram, on the other hand, was drawn to something else: a hint of nervousness in Samichi's voice. Unlike Sita, she appeared troubled. Perhaps she was not as brave as Sita believed her to be. Ram turned his attention to the enemy.

Torches lined the other side of the moat-lake that surrounded the outer wall of Mithila. Raavan's bodyguards had worked feverishly through the evening, chopping down trees from the forest and building rowboats to carry them across the lake.

Even as they watched, the Lankans began to push their boats into the moat-lake. The assault on Mithila was being launched.

'It's time,' said Sita.

'Yes,' said Ram. 'We have maybe another half hour before they hit our outer wall.'

— 大 ▮ ☼ —

Conch shells resounded through the night, by now recognised as the signature sound of Raavan and his men. As they watched in the light of the flickering flames of torches, the Lankans propped giant ladders against the outer walls of Mithila.

'They are here,' said Ram. Messages were relayed quickly down the line to the Mithila police-soldiers. Ram expected a shower of arrows now from Raavan's archers. The Lankans would fire their arrows only as long as their soldiers were outside the outer wall. The shooting would stop the moment the Lankans climbed over. The archers would not risk hitting their own men.

A loud whoosh, like the sudden onrush of a gale, heralded the release of the arrows.

'Shields!' shouted Sita.

The Mithilans immediately raised their shields, ready for the Lankan arrows that were about to rain down on them. But Ram was perturbed. Something about the sound troubled him. It was much stronger than the sound of a thousand arrows being fired. It sounded like something much bigger. He was right.

Huge missiles rammed through the Mithilan defences with massive force. Desperate cries of agony mixed with sickening thuds as shields were ripped through and many in the Mithilan ranks were brought down in a flash.

'What is that?' screamed Lakshman, hiding behind his shield.

Ram's wooden shield snapped into two pieces as a missile tore through it like a knife through butter. It missed him by a hair's breadth. Ram looked at the fallen missile.

Spears!

Their wooden shields were a protection against arrows, not large spears.

How in Lord Rudra's name are they throwing spears over this distance? It's impossible!

The first volley was over and Ram knew they had but a few minutes of respite before the next. He looked around him.

'Lord Rudra, be merciful…'

The destruction was severe. At least a quarter of the Mithilans were either dead or severely injured, impaled on massive spears that had brutally ripped through their shields and bodies.

Ram looked at Sita as he commanded, 'Another volley will be fired any moment! Into the houses!'

'Into the houses!' shouted Sita.

'Into the houses!' repeated the lieutenants, as everybody ran towards the doors, lifted them and jumped in. It was one of the most disorganised retreats ever seen, but it was effective. In a few minutes, practically every surviving Mithilan police-soldier had jumped to safety within the houses. As the doors closed, the volley of spears resumed on the roofs of the Bees Quarter. A few stragglers were killed as the rest made it to safety; for now.

Lakshman did not say anything as he looked at Ram. But his eyes sent out a clear message. *This is a disaster.*

'What now?' Ram asked Sita. 'Raavan's soldiers must be scaling the outer walls. They will be upon us soon. There's no one to stop them.'

Sita was breathing hard, her eyes flitting like that of a cornered tigress, anger bursting through every pore. Samichi stood behind her princess, helplessly rubbing her forehead.

'Sita?' prompted Ram.

Sita's eyes suddenly opened wide. 'The windows!'

'What?' asked Samichi, surprised by her prime minister.

Sita immediately gathered her lieutenants around her. She ordered them to get the surviving Mithilans to break the wood-panel-sealed windows of the houses in the Bees Quarter; the ones that shared the inner wall, or opened into the narrow gaps between some of the houses; like the one they were in. Their window overlooked the ground between the two fort walls. Arrows would be fired at the charging Lankans, after all.

'Brilliant!' shouted Lakshman, as he rushed to a barricaded window. He pulled back his arm, flexed his muscles, and punched hard at the wood, smashing the barricade with one mighty blow.

All the houses in this section of the Bees Quarter were internally connected through corridors. The message travelled rapidly. Within moments, the Mithilans smashed open the sealed windows and fired arrows at the Lankans, caught between the outer and inner wall. The Lankans had expected no resistance. They were effectively caught off-guard and arrows shredded through their lines. The losses were heavy. The Mithilans fired arrows without respite, killing as many of the Lankans as they could, slowing the charge dramatically.

Suddenly, the conch shells sounded; but this time, they played a different tune. The Lankans immediately turned and ran, retreating as rapidly as they had arrived.

A loud cheer went up from the Mithilan quarters. They had beaten back the first attack.

Ram, Sita and Lakshman stood on the roof of the Bees Quarter as dawn broke through. The gentle rays of the sun threw into poignant contrast the harsh devastation of the Lankan spears. The damage was heart-rending.

Sita stared at the mutilated bodies of the Mithilans strewn all around her: heads hanging by a sinew to bodies, some with their guts spilled out, many simply impaled on spears, having bled to death. 'At least a thousand of my soldiers...'

'We too have hit them hard, *Bhabhi*,' said Lakshman to his *sister-in-law*. 'There are at least a thousand dead Lankans lying between the inner and the outer wall.'

Sita looked at Lakshman, her usually limpid eyes now brimming with tears. 'Yes, but they have nine thousand left. We have only three thousand.'

Ram surveyed the Lankan camp on the other side of the moat-lake. Hospital-tents had been set up to tend to the injured. Many Lankans, though, were furiously at work: hacking trees and pushing the forest line farther with mathematical precision. Clearly they did not intend to retreat.

'They will be better prepared next time,' said Ram. 'If they manage to scale the inner wall … it's over.'

Sita placed her hand on Ram's shoulder and sighed as she stared at the ground. Ram found himself being momentarily distracted by her nearness. He looked at Sita's hand on his shoulder, then closed his eyes. He had to focus, teach his mind to re-learn the art of mastering his emotions.

Sita turned around and looked towards her city. Her eyes rested on the steeple of the massive temple dedicated to Lord Rudra, which loomed beyond the garden of the Bees Quarter. Fierce determination blazed from her eyes, resolve pouring steel into her veins. 'It's not over yet. I'll call upon the citizens to join me. Even if my people stand here with kitchen knives, we will outnumber the Lankan scum ten to one. We can fight them.'

Ram could not bring himself to share her confidence.

Sita nodded, like she had made up her mind, and rushed away, signalling other Mithilans to follow her.

Chapter 25

'Where have you been, Guru*ji*?' asked Ram, in a polite voice that belied the fury that defined his stony face and rigid body.

Vishwamitra had finally arrived in the fifth hour of the first *prahar*. The early morning light sharply outlined the frenetic activity in the Lankan camp. Sita was still trying to rally a citizen-army. Arishtanemi stood at a distance, strangely choosing to remain out of earshot.

'Where were the Malayaputra cowards, actually?' growled Lakshman, who did not feel the need for any attempt at politeness.

Vishwamitra cast Lakshman a withering look before addressing Ram. 'Someone has to be the adult here and do what must be done.'

Ram frowned.

'Come with me,' said Vishwamitra.

In a hidden section of the roof of the Bees Quarter, far from the scene of the Lankan attack, Ram finally confronted what the Malayaputras had been busy with all night: the *Asuraastra*.

A simple weapon to configure, it had still taken a long time to set up. Vishwamitra and his Malayaputras had worked through the night, in minimal light. The missile and its launch stand were finally assembled and ready. The stand was a little taller than Lakshman and was made of wood. The outer body of the missile was made of lead. Its components, along with the core material that had been mined at the Ganga *ashram*, had been brought along by Vishwamitra and his party to Mithila. The core material was now loaded in the detonation chamber.

The missile was ready but Ram was unsure.

He looked across the outer wall.

The Lankans were hard at work, clearing the forest. They were building something.

'What are those people doing at the far end of the forest line?' asked Lakshman.

'Look closely,' said Vishwamitra.

A group of Lankans were working with planks fashioned from the trees that had been cut. At first Lakshman thought they were building boats, but a careful examination proved him wrong. They were linking these planks into giant rectangular shields with sturdy handles on the sides as well as at the base end. Each shield was capable of protecting twenty men, if they were lined up two abreast.

'Tortoise shields,' said Ram.

'Yes,' said Vishwamitra. 'They will return once they build enough of these. They will break the outer wall without any resistance from us; why scale it? They will move towards our inner wall, protected by their tortoise shields. Successive waves of attacks will breach our walls. You know what will be done to the city. Even the rats will not be spared.'

Ram stood quietly. He knew that Vishwamitra was right. They could see that fifteen or twenty of these massive shields were already ready. The Lankans had worked at a prodigious pace. An attack was imminent, probably as early as tonight. Mithila would certainly not be ready.

'You need to understand that firing the *Asuraastra* is the only solution available,' said Vishwamitra. 'Fire it right now, when they're still not ready, and are farthest away from the city. Once they launch the attack and breach the outer wall, we will not be able to do even this, without risking Mithila; the detonation would be too close.'

Ram stared at the Lankans.

This is the only way!

'Why don't *you* fire the weapon, Guru*ji*?' asked Lakshman, sarcasm dripping from his voice.

'I am a Malayaputra; the leader of the Malayaputras,' said Vishwamitra. 'The Vayuputras and the Malayaputras work in partnership, just as the Vishnus and the Mahadevs did over millennia. I cannot break the Vayuputra law.'

'But my brother choosing to do so is okay?'

'You can also choose to die. That option is always available,' Vishwamitra said caustically. Then he turned and spoke to Ram directly, 'So, what will it be, Ram?'

Ram turned around and looked in the direction of the Mithila palace, where Sita was probably trying desperately to convince her reluctant citizens to fight.

Vishwamitra stepped close to the prince of Ayodhya. 'Ram, Raavan will probably torture and kill every single person in this city. The lives of a hundred thousand Mithilans are at stake. Your wife's life is at stake. Will you, as a husband, protect your wife or not? Will you take a sin upon your soul for the good of others? What does your *dharma* say?'

I will do it for Sita.

'We will warn them first,' said Ram. 'Give them a chance to retreat. I have been told that even the Asuras followed this protocol before firing any *daivi astra*.'

'Fine.'

'And if they don't heed our warning,' said Ram, his fingers wrapping themselves around his Rudraaksh pendant, as if for strength, 'then I will fire the *Asuraastra*.'

Vishwamitra smiled with satisfaction, as though Ram's compliance was a trophy he had just earned.

— 大 🐟 ☼ —

The giant bear-man moved among the men, checking the tortoise shields. He heard the arrow a second before it slammed into the plank of wood close to his feet. He looked up in surprise.

Who in Mithila can fire an arrow that could travel this distance with such unerring accuracy?

He stared at the walls. All he could make out were two very tall men standing close to the inner wall, and a third, a trifle shorter. The third man held a bow; he seemed to be staring directly at him.

The bear-man immediately stepped forward to examine the arrow that had buried itself into the tortoise shield. It had a piece of parchment tied around its shaft. He yanked it out and untied the note.

— 大 🐟 ☼ —

'You actually believe they will do this, Kumbhakarna?' asked Raavan, snorting with disgust as he threw the note away.

'*Dada*,' said the bear-man, his voice booming even at its lowest amplitude, due to his massive vocal chords. 'If they fire an *Asuraastra*, it could be—'

'They don't have an *Asuraastra*,' interrupted Raavan. 'They're bluffing.'

'But *Dada*, the Malayaputras do have—'

'Vishwamitra is bluffing, Kumbhakarna!'

Kumbhakarna fell silent.

—— |灻 ▯ ☀ ——

'They haven't retreated an inch,' said Vishwamitra, with urgency. 'We need to fire the weapon.'

By the end of the third hour of the second *prahar*, the sun had risen high enough to afford good visibility. Three hours earlier, Ram had shot the warning message to the Lankans. It had clearly made no impact.

The Malayaputras had already rolled the missile tower to the section of the rooftop that faced the main body of the Lankan troops.

'We gave them a warning of one hour,' continued Vishwamitra. 'We have waited for three. They probably think we are bluffing by now.'

Lakshman looked at Vishwamitra. 'Don't you think we should check with Sita *Bhabhi*, first? She had clearly said that—'

Vishwamitra suddenly interrupted Lakshman. 'Look!'

Lakshman and Ram immediately turned in the direction Vishwamitra had pointed.

'Are they boarding their boats?' asked Ram.

'They could be testing them,' said Lakshman, hoping against hope. 'In which case, we still have some time.'

'Do you think we should take that chance, Ram?' asked Vishwamitra.

Ram did not move a muscle.

'We need to fire now!' said Vishwamitra, forcefully.

Ram lifted his bow from his shoulders, brought it close to his ear, and plucked the bowstring. *Perfect.*

'Bravo!' said Vishwamitra.

Lakshman glared at the maharishi. He touched his brother's shoulder. '*Dada…*'

Ram turned around and began walking away. Everyone followed him. Most *daivi astras* were fired from a distance by shooting a flaming arrow into a target on the launch pad. This protected the people igniting the weapon from getting incinerated in the initial launch explosion of the missile. Only a skilled archer could fire an arrow from a great distance and hit a target that was no larger than a fruit.

Vishwamitra halted Ram when they reached a distance of over five hundred metres from the *Asuraastra* stand. 'That's enough, Prince of Ayodhya.'

Arishtanemi handed him an arrow. Ram sniffed its tip; it had been coated with a combustible paste. He examined the fletching and was momentarily surprised. Arishtanemi had, clearly, used one of Ram's own arrows. He didn't stop to think too deeply if Arishtanemi had learnt Ram's secret of the spinning arrow. This was not the time. He nodded to Arishtanemi and faced the missile launch tower.

'*Dada…*' murmured Lakshman. He was visibly distressed at what he knew would take an immense toll on his law-abiding brother.

'Step back, Lakshman,' said Ram, as he flexed forward to stretch his back. Lakshman, Vishwamitra and Arishtanemi moved away. Ram slowed down his breathing without forcing the process; it reduced his heart rate in tandem. He stared at the missile launch tower as his mind drowned out the sounds around him. He squeezed his eyes as the rhythm of time slowed down, as if to keep pace with his heart beats; everything around him seemed to shift into slow motion. A crow flew over the *Asuraastra* tower, flapping its wings as it attempted to fly higher. Ram followed the movement of the crow's wings. It seemed to require less effort for the bird to gain height; it had wind beneath its wings.

Ram's mind processed this new information: the wind was blowing leftwards close to the tower. He flicked his thumb on the arrow tip and the flames burst through. He shifted his hand to hold the arrow by its fletching. He nocked it on the bowstring, allowing the shaft to rest between his left thumb and forefinger as his hand gripped the bow firmly. Ram tipped the bow slightly upwards, factoring in the parabolic movement that the arrow would need. Arishtanemi knew this was unorthodox; the angle of the arrow was a lot lower than he would have kept. But he was also aware of Ram's immense talent with the bow and arrow; and, of course, of the brilliant design of the arrow fletching. He did not say a word.

Ram took aim and focused on the target; it was a pineapple-sized red square, over five hundred metres away. The waving windsock next to the target was within his concentration zone; all else faded into nothingness. The sock had been pointing left, but it suddenly drooped completely. The wind had stopped.

Ram pulled the string back in that instant, but held steady. His forearm was at a slight angle upwards from the ground, his elbow aligned with the arrow, the weight of the bow transferred to the back muscle. His forearm was rigid, the bowstring touching his lips. The bow was stretched to its maximum capacity, the flaming arrowhead now touching his left hand. The windsock remained slumped. Ram released the arrow, flicking the fletching as he did, making the arrow spin rapidly as it sped forward. The spin made it face less wind resistance. Arishtanemi savoured the archery skill on display; it was almost poetic. This was why Ram could fire the arrow at a lower height despite the distance. The parabola was sharper as the arrow moved at a faster pace, the spin maintaining its fearsome speed as it tore through the air.

— 𝝹 🎐 ☼ —

Kumbhakarna saw the flaming arrow being released by the archer. His instincts kicked in as he turned around, screaming loudly. '*Dada!*'

He charged towards his brother; Raavan stood at the massive door of the *Pushpak Vimaan*.

— 𝝹 🎐 ☼ —

The arrow slammed into the small red square on the *Asuraastra* tower, pushing it backwards instantly. The fire from the arrow was captured in a receptacle behind the red square, and then it spread rapidly into the fuel chamber that powered the missile. In a flash, the initial launch explosions of the *Asuraastra* were heard. A few seconds later, heavy flames gathered near the base of the missile and then rose, steadily picking up pace.

Kumbhakarna threw his weight on his brother, who went flying backwards into the *Pushpak Vimaan*.

The *Asuraastra* flew in a mighty arc, covering the distance across the walls of Mithila in a few short seconds. None on the roof of the Mithila Bees Quarter could tear their eyes away from the spectacle. As the missile flew high above the moat-lake, there was a small, almost inaudible explosion, like that of a fire cracker meant for a child.

Lakshman's awe was quickly replaced by disappointment. He frowned. 'That's it? Is that the famed *Asuraastra*?'

Vishwamitra answered laconically. 'Cover your ears.'

Kumbhakarna, meanwhile, rose from the floor of the *Pushpak Vimaan* even as Raavan lay sprawled inside. He rushed to the door and hit the metallic button on the sidewall with his full body weight. The door of the *Pushpak Vimaan* began to slide as the bear-man watched, straining his muscles as if to lend it speed.

The *Asuraastra* hovered above the Lankans and exploded with an ear-shattering boom that shook the very walls of Mithila. Many Lankan soldiers felt their eardrums burst, sucking the air from their mouths. But this was only a prelude to the devastation that would follow.

Even as an eerie silence followed the explosion, the spectators on the Mithila rooftop saw a bright green flash of light emerge from where the missile had splintered. It burst with furious intensity as it hit the Lankans below like a flash of lightning. They stayed rooted, stunned into a temporary paralytic immobility. Fragments of the exploded missile showered on them mercilessly.

Kumbhakarna saw the flash of green light as the door of the *Pushpak Vimaan* slid shut. Even as the door sealed and locked automatically, saving those inside the flying vehicle from any further damage by the *Asuraastra*, Kumbhakarna collapsed, unconscious. Raavan rushed to his younger brother, screaming loudly.

'By the great Lord Rudra,' whispered Lakshman, cold fear having gripped his heart. He looked at his brother, similarly staggered by what he was witnessing.

'It's not over,' warned Vishwamitra.

A dreadful hissing sound became suddenly audible, like the battle-cry of a gigantic snake. Simultaneously, the fragments of the *Asuraastra* missile that had fallen to the ground emitted demonic clouds of green gas, which spread like a shroud over the stupefied Lankans.

'What is that?' asked Ram.

'That gas,' said Vishwamitra, 'is the *Asuraastra*.'

The deathly, thick gas gently enveloped the Lankans. It would put them in a coma that would last for days, if not weeks. It would possibly kill some of them. But there were no screams, no cries for mercy. None made an attempt to escape. They simply lay on the ground, motionless, waiting for the fiendish *Asuraastra* to push them into oblivion. The only sound in the otherwise grim silence was the hiss…

Ram touched his Rudraaksh pendant, his heart benumbed.

An agonising fifteen minutes later, Vishwamitra turned to Ram. 'It's done.'

Sita bounded up the stairway of the Bees Quarter, three steps at a time. She had been passionately conversing with the citizens of Mithila in the market square when she heard the explosion and saw the sudden flash in the sky. She had immediately known that the *Asuraastra* had been fired. She knew she had to rush back.

She first encountered Arishtanemi and the Malayaputras, standing in a huddle, away from Vishwamitra, Ram and Lakshman. A grim-faced Samichi followed Sita.

'Who shot it?' demanded Sita.

Arishtanemi just stepped aside, and Ram came into Sita's view, the only one holding a bow.

Sita cursed loudly as she ran towards her husband; she knew that he must be shattered. Ram, with his moral clarity and obsession with the law, would have been hurting inside at the sin he had been forced to commit. Forced by his sense of duty towards his wife and her people.

Vishwamitra smiled as he saw her approach. 'Sita, it is all taken care of! Raavan's forces are destroyed. Mithila is safe.'

Sita glared at Vishwamitra, too furious to say anything. She ran right up to her husband and embraced him. A shocked Ram dropped his bow. He had never been embraced by Sita. He knew that she was trying to comfort him. Yet, as he held his hands to the side, his heartbeat started picking up. The emotional overload drained him of energy as he felt a solitary tear trickle down his face.

Sita pulled her head back as she held Ram and looked deep into his empty eyes. Her face was creased with concern. 'I am with you, Ram.'

Ram remained silent. Strangely, a long-forgotten image entered his mind: of the *arya* concept of Emperor Prithu; Prithvi, the earth, had been named after him. Prithu had spoken of the ideal human archetype of the *aryaputra*, a 'gentleman', and the *aryaputri*, a 'lady', a prototypical human partnership of two strong individuals, who didn't compete for exact equality but were complementary, completing each other. Two souls that were dependent on each other, giving each other purpose; two halves of a whole.

Ram felt like an *aryaputra*, being held, being supported, by his lady.

Sita continued to hold Ram in a tight embrace. 'I am with you, Ram. We will handle this together.'

Ram closed his eyes. He wrapped his arms around his wife. He rested his head on her shoulder. *Paradise.*

Sita looked over her husband's shoulder and glared at Vishwamitra. It was a fearsome look, like the wrathful fury of the Mother Goddess.

Vishwamitra glared right back, unrepentant.

A loud sound disturbed them all. They looked beyond the walls of Mithila. Raavan's *Pushpak Vimaan* was sputtering to life. Its giant rotor blades had begun to spin. Within moments they picked up speed and the flying vehicle rose from the earth, hovering just a few feet above the ground. Then, with a great burst of sound and energy, it soared into the sky; away from Mithila, and the devastation of the *Asuraastra*.

Chapter 26

Sita cast an eye over her husband as he rode beside her. Lakshman and Urmila rode behind them. Lakshman was talking non-stop with his wife as she gazed at him earnestly. Urmila's thumb kept playing with the massive diamond ring on her left forefinger; an expensive gift from her husband. Behind them were a hundred Mithilan soldiers. Another hundred soldiers rode ahead of Ram and Sita. The convoy was on its way to Sankashya, from where it would sail to Ayodhya.

Ram, Sita, Lakshman and Urmila had set off from Mithila two weeks after the *Asuraastra* laid waste the Lankan camp. King Janak and his brother, King Kushadhwaj, had authorised the imprisonment of the Lankan prisoners-of-war left behind by Raavan. Vishwamitra and his Malayaputras left for their own capital, Agastyakootam, taking the Lankan prisoners with them. The sage intended to negotiate with Raavan on Mithila's behalf, guaranteeing the kingdom's safety in return for the release of the prisoners-of-war. It was a difficult decision for Sita to leave her friend Samichi behind, but the police force of Mithila could not afford a change in leadership at this vulnerable moment of time.

'Ram…'

Ram turned to his wife with a smile as he pulled his horse close to hers. 'Yes?'

'Are you sure about this?'

Ram nodded. There was no doubt in his mind.

'But you are the first in a generation to defeat Raavan. And, it wasn't really a *daivi astra*. If you—'

Ram frowned. 'That's a technicality. And you know it.'

Sita took a deep breath and continued. 'Sometimes, to create a perfect world, a leader has to do what is necessary at the time; even if it may not appear to be the "right" thing to do in the short term. In the long run, a leader who has the capacity to uplift the masses must not deny himself that opportunity. He has a duty to not make himself unavailable. A true leader will even take a sin upon his soul for the good of his people.'

Ram looked at Sita. He seemed disappointed. 'I have done that already, haven't I? The question is, should I be punished for it or not? Should I do penance for it? If I expect my people to follow the law, so must I. A leader is not just one who leads. He must also be a role model. He must practise what he preaches, Sita.'

Sita smiled. 'Well, Lord Rudra had said: "A leader is not just one who gives his people what they want. He must also be the one who teaches his people to be better than they imagined themselves to be".'

Ram smiled too. 'And I'm sure you will tell me Lady Mohini's response to this as well.'

Sita laughed. 'Yes. Lady Mohini said that people have their limitations. A leader should not expect more from them than what they are capable of. If you stretch them beyond their capacity, they will break.'

Ram shook his head. He did not really agree with the great Lady Mohini, respected by many as a Vishnu; though many others believed that she should not be called a Vishnu. Ram expected people to rise above their limitations and better themselves; for only then is an ideal society possible. But he didn't voice his disagreement aloud.

'Are you sure? Fourteen years outside the boundaries of the Sapt Sindhu?' Sita looked at Ram seriously, returning to the original discussion.

Ram nodded. He had already made his decision. He would go to Ayodhya and seek permission from his father to go on his self-imposed exile. 'I broke Lord Rudra's law. And this is his stated punishment. It doesn't matter whether the Vayuputras pass the order to punish me or not. It doesn't matter whether my people support me or not. I must serve my sentence.'

Sita leaned towards him and whispered, 'We … not I.'

Ram frowned.

Sita reached out and placed her palm on Ram's hand. 'You share my fate and I share yours. That is what a true marriage is.' She entwined her fingers through his. 'Ram, I am your wife. We will always be together; in good times and bad; through thick and thin.'

Ram squeezed her hand as he straightened his back. His horse snorted and quickened its pace. Ram pulled back the reins gently, keeping his horse in step with his wife's steed.

'I'm not sure this will work,' said Ram.

The newly-wed couples, Ram-Sita and Lakshman-Urmila, were on the royal ship of Ayodhya, sailing up the Sarayu, on their way home. They would probably reach Ayodhya within a week.

Ram and Sita sat on the deck discussing what an ideal society meant, and the manner in which a perfect empire must be governed. For Ram, an ideal state was one which treated everyone as equal before the law.

Sita had thought long and hard about the meaning of equality. She felt that just promoting equality before the law would not solve society's problems. She believed that true equality existed only at the level of the soul. But in this material world, everyone was, in fact, not equal. No two created entities were exactly the same. Among humans, some were better at knowledge, others at warfare, some at trading and others offered their manual skills and hard work. However, the problem, according to Sita, was that in the present society, a person's path in life was determined by his birth, not by his karma. She believed that a society would be perfect only if people were free to do what they actually wanted to, based on their karma, rather than following the diktats of the caste they were born into.

And where did these diktats come from? They came from parents, who forced their values and ways on their children. Brahmin parents would encourage and push their child towards the pursuit of knowledge. The child, on the other hand, may have a passion for trade. These mismatches led to unhappiness and chaos within society. Furthermore, the society itself suffered as its people were forced to work at jobs they didn't want to do. The worst end of this stick was reserved for the poor Shudras. Many of them could have been capable Brahmins, Kshatriyas or Vaishyas, but the rigid and unfair birth-based caste system forced them to remain skill-workers. In an earlier era, the caste system had been flexible. The best example of that was from many centuries ago: Maharishi Shakti, now known as Ved Vyas, a title used through successive ages for those who compiled, edited or differentiated the Vedas. He was born a Shudra, but his karma turned him into not just a Brahmin, but a *rishi*. A *rishi* was the highest status, below Godhood, that any person could achieve. However, today, due to the rigid birth-based caste system, a Maharishi Shakti emerging from among the Shudras was almost impossible.

'You may think this is unworkable; you may even consider it harsh. I concede your point that all should be equal before the law and equally deserving of respect. But just that is not enough. We need to be harsh to destroy this birth-based caste system,' said Sita. 'It has weakened our *dharma* and our country. It must be destroyed for the good of India. If we don't destroy the caste system as it exists today, we will open ourselves to attacks from foreigners. They will use our divisions to conquer us.'

Sita's solution, which indeed seemed harsh to Ram, would be complicated to implement. She proposed that all the children of a kingdom must be compulsorily adopted by the state at the time of birth. The birth-parents would have to surrender their children to the kingdom. The kingdom would raise these children, educate and hone the natural skills that they were born with. At the age of fifteen, they would appear for an examination that would test them on their physical, psychological and mental skills. Based on the result, appropriate castes would be allocated to the children. Subsequent training would further polish their natural talent, after which the children would be put up for adoption by citizens from the same caste as the ones assigned to the adolescents through the examination process. The children would never know their birth-parents, only their caste-parents.

'I agree that this system would be exceedingly fair,' conceded Ram. 'But I can't imagine parents willingly giving up their birth-children to the kingdom permanently, making the decision never to meet them again, or even know them. Is it even natural?'

'Humans moved away from the "natural way" when we began to wear clothes, cook our food and embraced cultural norms over instinctive urges. This is what civilisation does. Among the "civilised", right and wrong is determined by cultural conventions and rules. There were times when polygamy was considered abhorrent, and other times when it was considered a solution when there was a shortage of men due to war. And now, for all you know, you may succeed in bringing monogamy back in fashion!'

Ram laughed. 'I'm not trying to start a trend. I don't want to marry another woman because I will be insulting you by doing so.'

Sita smiled as she pushed her long, straight hair away from her face as it dried in the breeze. 'But polygamy is unfair only according to you; others may disagree. Remember, justice in terms of "right" or "wrong" is a man-made concept. It is entirely up to us to define justice in new terms of what is fair or unfair. It will be for the greater good.'

'Hmm, but it will be very difficult to implement, Sita.'

'No more difficult than getting the people of India to actually respect laws!' laughed Sita, for she knew that was Ram's pet obsession.

Ram laughed loudly. *'Touché!'*

Sita moved close to Ram and held his hand. Ram bent forward and kissed her, a slow, gentle kiss that filled their souls with deep happiness. Ram held his wife as they observed the Sarayu waters flowing by and the green riverbanks in the distance.

'We didn't finish that Somras conversation... What were

you thinking?' asked Sita.

'I think it should either be made available to all or to none. It's not fair that a few chosen ones from the nobility get to live so much longer, and be healthier, than most others.'

'But how would you ever be able to produce enough Somras for everyone?'

'Guru Vashishtha has invented a technology that can mass-produce it. If I rule Ayodhya—'

'When,' interrupted Sita.

'Sorry?'

'*When* you rule Ayodhya,' said Sita. 'Not "if". It will happen, even if it is fourteen years from now.'

Ram smiled. 'All right, *when* I rule Ayodhya, I intend to build this factory that Guru Vashishtha has designed. We will offer the Somras to all.'

'If you are going to create an entirely new way of life, then you must have a new name for it as well. Why carry the karma of the old?'

'Something tells me you have thought of a name already!'

'A land of pure life.'

'That's the name?'

'No. That is simply what the name will mean.'

'So, what will be the new name of my kingdom?'

Sita smiled. 'It will be Meluha.'

— 大 ● ☼ —

'Are you insane?' shouted Dashrath.

The emperor was in his new private office in Kaushalya's palace. Ram had just informed Dashrath about his decision to banish himself from the Sapt Sindhu to atone for the sin of firing a *daivi astra* without the permission of the Vayuputras; a decision that had not gone down too well with Dashrath, to say the least.

A worried Kaushalya hurried to her husband and tried to get him to remain seated. His health had been deteriorating rapidly of late. 'Please calm down, Your Majesty.'

Kaushalya, still unsure of the influence that Kaikeyi exercised over Dashrath, had remained careful in her dealings with her husband. She wasn't sure how long she would remain Dashrath's favourite queen. To her, he was still 'His Majesty'. But this kid-glove treatment only agitated Dashrath further.

'In Lord Parshu Ram's name, Kaushalya, stop mollycoddling me and knock some sense into your son,' screamed Dashrath. 'What do you think will happen if he is gone for fourteen years? Do you think the nobles will just wait around patiently for his return?'

'Ram,' said Kaushalya. 'Your father is right. Nobody has asked for you to be punished. The Vayuputras have not made any demands.'

'They will,' said Ram in a steady voice. 'It's only a matter of time.'

'But we don't have to listen to them. We do not follow their laws!'

'If I expect others to follow the law, then so should I.'

'Are you trying to be suicidal, Ram?' asked Dashrath, his face flushed, his hands trembling in anger.

'I am only following the law, Father.'

'Can't you see what my health is like? I will be gone soon. If you are not here, Bharat will become king. And, if you are out of the Sapt Sindhu for fourteen years, by the time you return Bharat will have consolidated his rule. You will not even get a village to govern.'

'Firstly, Father, if you pronounce Bharat crown prince when I am gone, then it is his right to become king. And I think Bharat will make a good ruler. Ayodhya will not suffer. But if you continue with me as the crown prince even while I'm in exile, I am sure that Bharat will give back the throne to me when I return. I trust him completely.'

Dashrath laughed harshly. 'You actually think it will be Bharat ruling Ayodhya once you're gone? *No!* It will be his mother. And Kaikeyi will have you killed in exile, son.'

'I will not allow myself to be killed, Father. But if I am killed, maybe that is what fate has in store for me.'

Dashrath banged his fist on his head, his frustration ringing loudly through the angry grunt he let out.

'Father, my mind is made up,' said Ram with finality. 'But if I leave without your permission, it will be an insult to you; and an insult to Ayodhya. How can a crown prince disobey the king's orders? That's why I am asking you to please banish me.'

Dashrath turned to Kaushalya, throwing up his hands in frustration.

'This is going to happen, Father, whether you like it or not,' said Ram. 'Your banishing me will keep Ayodhya's honour intact. So, please do it.'

Dashrath's shoulders drooped in resignation. 'At least agree with my other suggestion.'

Ram stood resolute, but with an apologetic expression on his face. *No.*

'But Ram, if you marry a princess from a powerful kingdom, then you will have a strong ally when you return to claim your inheritance. Kekaya will never side with you. Ashwapati is Kaikeyi's father after all. But if you marry a princess from another powerful kingdom, then—'

'My apologies for interrupting you, Father. But I have always maintained that I will marry only one woman. And I have. I will not insult her by marrying another.'

Dashrath stared at him helplessly.

Ram felt he needed to clarify further. 'And if my wife dies, I will mourn her for the rest of my life. But I will never ever marry again.'

Kaushalya finally lost her temper. 'What do you mean by that, Ram? Are you trying to imply that your own father will get your wife killed?'

'I didn't say that, Mother,' said Ram, calmly.

'Ram, please understand,' pleaded Dashrath, desperately trying to keep his temper in check. 'She is the princess of Mithila, a minor kingdom. She will not prove to be of any use in the struggle you will face ahead.'

Ram stiffened, but kept his voice polite. 'She is my wife, Father. Please speak of her with respect.'

'She is a lovely girl, Ram,' said Dashrath. 'I have been observing her for the last few days. She is a good wife. She will keep you happy. And you can remain married to her. But if you marry another princess, then—'

'Forgive me, Father. But no.'

'Dammit!' screamed Dashrath. 'Get out of here before I burst a blood vessel!'

'Yes, Father,' said Ram, and calmly turned to leave.

'And you are not leaving this city without my order!' yelled Dashrath at Ram's retreating form.

Ram looked back, his face inscrutable. With deliberate movements, he bowed his head, folded his hands into a namaste, and said, 'May all the Gods of our great land continue to bless you, Father.' And then, with equal lack of haste, he turned and walked out.

Dashrath glared at Kaushalya, rage pouring out of his eyes. His wife cowered with an apologetic expression on her face, as though she had somehow failed him in this show of will by Ram.

Chapter 27

On returning to his section of the palace, Ram was told that his wife was out, visiting the royal garden. He decided to join her, and found her in conversation with Bharat. Just like everyone else, his brother had initially been shocked when he heard about Ram's marriage to an adopted princess from a small kingdom. However, within a short span of time, Bharat had grown to respect Sita, her intelligence and strength of character. The two had spent a lot of time with each other, finding a deep sense of appreciation for the qualities they discovered in the other.

'...Which is why I think freedom is the most important attribute of life, *Bhabhi*,' said Bharat.

'More important than the law?' asked Sita.

'Yes. I believe there should be as few laws as possible; enough just to provide a framework within which human creativity can express itself in all its glory. Freedom is the natural way of life.'

Sita laughed softly. 'And what does your elder brother have to say about your views?'

Ram walked up to them from behind and placed his hands on his wife's shoulders. 'His elder brother thinks that Bharat is a dangerous influence!'

Bharat burst out laughing as he rose to embrace his brother. '*Dada…*'

'Should I be thanking you for entertaining your *bhabhi* with your libertarian views?!'

Bharat smiled as he shrugged. 'At least I won't convert the citizens of Ayodhya into a bunch of bores!'

Ram laughed and said, tongue in cheek, 'That's good then!'

Bharat's expression instantly transformed and became sombre. 'Father is not going to let you go, *Dada*. Even *you* know that. You're not going anywhere.'

'Father doesn't have a choice. And neither do you. You will rule Ayodhya. And you will rule it well.'

'I will not ascend the throne this way,' said Bharat, shaking his head. 'No, I will not.'

Ram knew that there was nothing he could say that would ease Bharat's pain.

'*Dada*, why are you insisting on this?' asked Bharat.

'It's the law, Bharat,' said Ram. 'I fired a *daivi astra*.'

'The hell with the law, *Dada*! Do you actually think your leaving will be in the best interests of Ayodhya? Imagine what the two of us can achieve together; your emphasis on rules and mine on freedom and creativity. Do you think either you or I can be as effective alone?'

Ram shook his head. 'I'll be back in fourteen years, Bharat. Even you just conceded that rules have a significant place in a society. How can I convince others to follow the law if I don't do so myself? The law must apply equally and fairly to every single person. It is as simple as that.' Then Ram stared directly into Bharat's eyes. 'Even if it helps a heinous criminal escape death, the law should not be broken.'

Bharat stared right back, his expression inscrutable.

Sita, sensing that the brothers were talking about something else and that things were getting decidedly uncomfortable, rose from the bench and said to Ram, 'You have a meeting with General Mrigasya.'

'I don't mean to be rude, but are you sure that your wife should be here?' asked Mrigasya, the general of the Ayodhyan army.

Ram and Sita had received the general in their private office.

'There are no secrets between us,' said Ram. 'In any case, I would tell her what has been discussed. She may as well hear it directly from you.'

Mrigasya cast an enigmatic look at Sita, and let out a long breath before addressing Ram. 'You can be emperor right away.'

The king of Ayodhya automatically became the emperor of the Sapt Sindhu; this had been the privilege of the Suryavanshi clan that ruled Kosala, since the days of Raghu. Mrigasya was offering to smoothen the path for Ram to ascend the throne of Ayodhya.

Sita was stunned, but kept her face deadpan. Ram frowned.

Mrigasya misunderstood what was going through Ram's mind. He assumed that Ram was wondering why the general would help him, when one of his officials had been penalised on the orders of the prince, for what Mrigasya thought was a minor crime of land-grabbing.

'I am willing to forget what you did to me,' said Mrigasya, 'if you are willing to remember what I am doing for you right now.'

Ram remained silent.

'Look, Prince Ram,' continued Mrigasya, 'the people love you for your police reforms. There is the matter of Dhenuka, for which you became unpopular for a while, but that has been forgotten in the glow of your victory over Raavan in Mithila. In fact, you may not know this, but you have become popular among the common people across India, not just Kosala. Nobody is hated more in the Sapt Sindhu than Raavan, and you defeated him. I can bring the nobles of Ayodhya to your side. Most of the major kingdoms in the Sapt Sindhu will swing towards the eventual winner. The only one we need to worry about is Kekaya and the kingdoms under its influence. But even those kingdoms, the descendants of King Anu, have differences among themselves that we could easily exploit. In short, what I'm telling you is that the throne is yours for the taking.'

'What about the law?' asked Ram.

Mrigasya looked baffled, like someone had spoken in an unknown language. 'The law?'

'I have fired the *Asuraastra* and I have to serve my sentence.'

Mrigasya laughed. 'Who will dare punish the future emperor of the Sapt Sindhu?'

'Maybe the present emperor of the Sapt Sindhu?'

'Emperor Dashrath wants you to ascend the throne. Trust me. He will not send you off on some ludicrous exile.'

Ram's expression did not change but Sita could sense that her husband was getting deeply irritated as he closed his eyes.

'Prince?' asked Mrigasya.

Ram ran his hand across his face. His fingers rested on his chin as he opened his eyes and stared into Mrigasya's; he whispered, 'My father is an honourable man. He is a descendant of Ikshvaku. He will do the honourable thing; as will I.'

'Prince, I don't think you understand—'

Ram interrupted Mrigasya. 'I don't think *you* understand, General Mrigasya. I am a descendant of Ikshvaku. I am a descendant of Raghu. My family would rather die than bring disrepute to our clan's honour.'

'Those are mere words…'

'No. It is a code; a code that we live by.'

Mrigasya leaned forward, adopting a manner as if he was speaking to a child not familiar with the ways of the world. 'Listen to me, Prince Ram. I have seen a lot more of this world than you have. Honour is for the textbooks. In the real world…'

'I think we are done, General,' said Ram, rising with a polite namaste.

'What?' asked Kaikeyi. 'Are you sure?'

Manthara had rushed to Kaikeyi's chamber, secure in the knowledge that neither Dashrath nor any of his personal staff would be present. Kaikeyi's staff was not a concern; originally from her parental home in Kekaya, they were fiercely loyal to her. Seating herself beside the queen, she nevertheless exercised abundant caution and commanded the queen's maids to leave the room, ordering them to shut the door on their way out.

'I wouldn't be here if I wasn't sure,' said Manthara, as she shifted in her chair to ease the discomfort to her back. The royal furniture was a travesty compared to the well-designed, ergonomic furniture in Manthara's opulent home. 'Money opens all mouths; everyone has a price. The emperor is all set to announce in court tomorrow that Ram will be king in his stead, and that he will take *Vanvaas* in the forests. *Vanvaas* with all his queens, I might add. You too may have to live in some jungle hut, from now on.'

Kaikeyi scowled at her, as she gritted her teeth.

'Gritting your teeth will only wear out the enamel,' said Manthara. 'If you think you should do something more practical, then today is the day. The time is right now. You will never get an opportunity like this again.'

Kaikeyi was annoyed at Manthara's tone; her demeanour had changed from the day she had given her that money to carry out her vengeance. But she needed the powerful trader for now, so she exercised restraint. 'What do you suggest?'

'You once mentioned the promise that Dashrath made to you after you saved him at the Battle of Karachapa.'

Kaikeyi leaned back in her chair as she remembered the long-forgotten promise, a debt she never really believed she would need to collect. She had saved his life in that disastrous battle with Raavan, losing a finger and getting seriously injured herself. When Dashrath had regained consciousness, he had, in his gratitude, made an open-ended promise to Kaikeyi that he would honour any two wishes she made, anytime in life. 'The two boons! I can ask for anything!'

'And he has to honour it. *Raghukul reet sadaa chali aayi, praan jaaye par vachan naa jaaye.*'

Manthara had recited the motto of the Suryavanshi clan that ruled Ayodhya; or at least, what had been their motto since the days of the great Emperor Raghu. It translated as: The clan of Raghu has always followed a tradition; they would much rather die than dishonour their word.

'He cannot say no...' whispered Kaikeyi, a glint in her eye. Manthara nodded.

'Ram should be banished for fourteen years,' said Kaikeyi. 'I'll tell him to say publicly that he is doing so to punish him according to the rules of Lord Rudra.'

'Very wise. That will make the public accept it. Ram is popular with the people now, but nobody will want to break Lord Rudra's rule.'

'And he has to declare Bharat the crown prince.'

'Perfect! Two boons; the solution to all problems.'

'Yes…'

———— 𝙸𝗑𝙸 🗿 ☼ ————

As she rode over the bridge that spanned the Grand Canal, Sita looked around to check that she was not being followed. She had covered her face and upper body with a long *angvastram*, as if protecting herself from the cold, late evening breeze.

The road stretched into the distance, heading east towards lands that Kosala controlled directly. A few metres ahead, she looked back again, and steered the reins to the left, off the road. She rode into the jungle and immediately made a clicking sound, making her horse break into a swift gallop. She had to cover an hour's distance in just half the time.

———— 𝙸𝗑𝙸 🗿 ☼ ————

'But what will your husband say?' asked the Naga.

Sita stood in a small clearing in the jungle, her hand on the hilt of her knife, encased within a small scabbard; a precaution against wild animals.

She did not need any protection from the man she had just met, though. He was a Malayaputra, and she trusted him like an elder brother. The Naga had a hard and bony mouth, extending out of his face like a beak. His head was bare but his face was covered with fine downy hair. He looked like a man with the face of a vulture.

'Jatayu*ji*,' said Sita, respectfully, 'my husband is not just unusual, he's the kind of man who comes along once in a millennium. Sadly, he doesn't realise how important he is. As far as he is concerned, he simply thinks he's doing the right thing by asking to be exiled. But in doing so, he is also putting himself in serious danger. The moment we cross the Narmada, I suspect we will face repeated attacks. They will try every trick in the book to kill him off.'

'You have tied a *rakhi* on my hand, my sister,' said Jatayu. 'Nothing will happen to you or the one you love, for as long as I am alive.'

Sita smiled.

'But you should tell your husband about me, about what you are asking me to do. I don't know if he dislikes the Malayaputras. But if he does, it would not be completely unfair. He may harbour some ill-will about what happened at Mithila.'

'Let me worry about how to handle my husband.'

'Are you sure?'

'I know him quite well by now. He won't understand at present that we might need some protection in the forest; maybe later. For now, I just need your soldiers to keep a constant but discreet watch on our positions and prevent any attacks.'

Jatayu thought he heard a sound. He pulled out his knife and stared into the darkness beyond the trees. A few seconds later he relaxed and turned his attention back to Sita.

'It's nothing,' said Sita.

'Why is your husband insisting on being punished?' asked Jatayu. 'It can be argued against. The *Asuraastra* is not really a weapon of mass destruction. He can get away on a technicality, if he chooses to.'

'He is insisting on being punished because that is the law.'

'He can't be so…' Jatayu didn't complete his statement. But it was obvious what he wanted to say.

'People see my husband as a naive and blind follower of the law. But a day will come when the entire world will see him as one of the greatest leaders ever. It is my duty to protect him and keep him alive till then.'

Jatayu smiled.

Sita was embarrassed by her next request, as it seemed selfish. But she had to be sure. 'And the…'

'The Somras will be arranged. I agree that you and your husband will need it, especially if you have to be strong enough to complete your mission when you return fourteen years later.'

'But won't you face difficulties in getting the Somras out? What about…'

Jatayu laughed. 'Let me worry about that.'

Sita had heard all that she needed to. She knew that Jatayu would come through.

'Goodbye. Go with Lord Parshu Ram, my brother.'

'Go with Lord Rudra, my sister.'

Jatayu lingered for a bit after Sita mounted her horse and rode away. Once sure that she was gone, he touched the ground she had been standing on, picked up some of the dust that had been touched by her sandals, and then brought it reverentially to his forehead; a mark of respect for a great leader.

—— 大 🐟 ☼ ——

'*Chhoti Maa* is in the *kopa bhavan*!' exclaimed a surprised Ram, referring to his stepmother, Kaikeyi.

'Yes,' said Vashishtha.

Ram had earlier been informed that his father would announce the ascension of the prince to the throne the next day. He had determined his next course of action. He was planning to abdicate the throne and install Bharat as king instead. He would then leave for the forest. But Ram had misgivings about this plan as it would, in effect, mean publicly dishonouring his father's wishes.

Therefore, when Vashishtha came in and told Ram about his stepmother's move, his first reaction was not negative.

Kaikeyi had lodged herself in the *kopa bhavan*, the *house of anger*. This was an institutionalised chamber created in royal palaces many centuries ago, once polygamy became a common practice among the royalty. Having multiple wives, a king was naturally unable to spend enough time with all of them. A *kopa bhavan* was the assigned chamber a wife would go to if angry or upset with her husband. This would be a signal for the king that the queen needed redressal for a complaint. It was believed to be inauspicious for a husband to allow his wife to stay overnight in the *kopa bhavan*.

Dashrath had no choice but to visit his aggrieved spouse.

'Even if her influence has reduced, if there's one person who can force my father to change his mind, it would be *Chhoti Maa*,' said Ram.

'It looks like your wish will come true after all.'

'Yes. And, if ordered so, Sita and I will leave immediately.'

Vashishtha frowned. 'Isn't Lakshman going with you?'

'He wants to, but I don't think that's necessary. He needs to stay here, with his wife, Urmila. She is delicate. We should not impose a harsh forest-life on her.'

Vashishtha nodded in agreement. Then he leaned over and spoke earnestly. 'I will spend the next fourteen years preparing the ground for you.'

Ram smiled at his guru.

'Remember your destiny. You will be the next Vishnu, regardless of what anyone else says. You have to rewrite the future of our nation. I will work towards that goal and make sure that we are ready for you when you return. But you have to ensure that you remain alive.'

'I will certainly try my best.'

Chapter 28

Dashrath stepped out of the palanquin with assistance and hobbled into the *kopa bhavan*. He seemed to have aged a decade; the stress of the last few days had been immense. He sat on his usual rocking chair and dismissed the attendant with a wave of his hand.

He raised his eyes and observed his wife; Kaikeyi had not acknowledged his entry into the room. She sat on a divan, her hair undone, unkempt. Not a speck of jewellery on her person, her *angvastram* lay on the ground. She wore a white *dhoti* and blouse, and sat with an appearance of calm that belied the fury that raged within; he knew her well; he also knew what was going to happen and that he couldn't say no.

'Speak,' said Dashrath.

Kaikeyi looked at him with sorrow-filled eyes. 'You may not love me anymore, Dashrath, but I still love you.'

'Oh, I know you love me. But you love yourself more.'

Kaikeyi stiffened. 'And are you any different? Are you going to teach me about selflessness? Seriously?'

Dashrath smiled ruefully. '*Touché.*'

Kaikeyi seethed with the anger of a woman scorned.

'You were always the smartest of all my wives. I enjoyed my verbal battles with you the way I enjoyed duelling with a warrior.

I miss those sharp, acerbic words that could even draw blood.'

'I can bleed you with a sword, too.'

Dashrath laughed. 'I know.'

Kaikeyi leaned back on the divan, trying to slow down her breathing, trying to control herself. But the hurt still showed through. 'I dedicated my life to you. I nearly died for you. I disfigured myself in saving your life. I never ever humiliated you in public, unlike your precious Ram.'

'Ram has never—'

Kaikeyi interrupted Dashrath. 'He has, now! You know that he will not follow your order tomorrow. He will dishonour you. And Bharat would never—'

It was Dashrath's turn to interrupt. 'I am not choosing between Bharat and Ram. You know they have no problems with each other.'

Kaikeyi leaned forward and hissed, 'This is not about Ram and Bharat. This is about Ram and me. You have to choose between Ram and me. What has he ever done for you? He saved your life once. That's it. I have saved your life every day, for the last so many years! Do my sacrifices count for nothing?'

Dashrath refused to succumb to her emotional blackmail.

Kaikeyi laughed contemptuously. 'Of course! When you don't have any counter argument, all you do is clam up!'

'I do have an answer, but you will not like it.'

Kaikeyi laughed harshly. 'All my life, I have tolerated things that I don't like. I submit to the insults of my father. I tolerate your selfishness. I live with my son's disdain for me. I can tolerate a few words. Tell me!'

'Ram offers me immortality.'

Kaikeyi was confused. And it showed on her face. She had always managed to get large quantities of Somras for Dashrath, repeatedly haranguing Raj Guru Vashishtha for the legendary drink of the Gods. It dramatically increased the life-spans of those who consumed it. For some reason, it had not worked its wonders on Dashrath.

Dashrath explained. 'Not immortality for my body. The last few days have made me fully aware of my mortality. I'm talking about immortality for my name. I know that I have wasted my life and my potential. People compare me to my great ancestors and find me wanting. But Ram... He will go down in history as one of the greatest ever. And he will redeem my name. I will be remembered as Ram's father for all time to come. Ram's greatness will rub off on me. He has already defeated Raavan!'

Kaikeyi burst out laughing. 'That was pure luck, you fool. It was sheer chance that Guru Vishwamitra happened to be there with the *Asuraastra*!'

'Yes, he got lucky. That means the Gods favour him.'

Kaikeyi cast him a dark look. This was getting nowhere. 'The hell with this. Let's get this over with. You know you cannot refuse me.'

Dashrath sat back and smiled sadly. 'Just when I was beginning to enjoy our conversation...'

'I want my two boons.'

'Both of them?' asked Dashrath, surprised. He had expected only one of them to be called.

'I want Ram banished from the Sapt Sindhu for fourteen years. You can announce at court that this is because he broke Lord Rudra's law. You will be praised for it. Even the Vayuputras will applaud you.'

'Yes, I know how concerned you are about my prestige!' said Dashrath caustically.

'You cannot say no!'

Dashrath sighed. 'And the second?'

'You will declare Bharat the crown prince tomorrow.'

Dashrath was shocked. This was unexpected. The implication was obvious. He growled softly, 'If Ram is killed in exile, people will lynch you.'

Kaikeyi was aghast. She shouted, 'Do you really think I could shed royal blood? The blood of Raghu?'

'Yes, I think you could. But I know that Bharat won't. I will warn him about you.'

'You do what you want. Just honour my two boons.'

Dashrath stared at Kaikeyi with anger. He suddenly looked towards the door. 'Guards!'

Four guards rushed in with Dashrath's attendant.

'Order my palanquin,' said Dashrath, brusquely.

'Yes, Your Highness,' said his attendant, as they all scurried out.

As soon as they were alone, Dashrath said. 'You can leave the *kopa bhavan*. You will get your two boons. But I am warning you, if you do anything to Ram, I will…'

'I will not do anything to your precious Ram!' screamed Kaikeyi.

———— 肀 ▲ ☼ ————

The royal court assembled in the massive Great Hall of the Unconquerable in the second hour of the second *prahar*. Dashrath sat on his throne, visibly tired and unhappy, but dignified. Not one of the queens was present. Vashishtha, the raj guru, sat on the throne to the right of the emperor. The court was packed with not just the nobility, but also as many of the common people as could be accommodated in the hall.

Except for a few, most were unaware of what was to transpire that morning. They simply couldn't understand why Ram should be punished for defeating Raavan. In fact, the crown prince deserved to be commended for restoring Ayodhya's glory and washing away the taint on his birth.

'Silence!' announced the court crier.

Dashrath sat with heartbreaking majesty upon the throne, as if seeking honour from his son. Ram stood in the middle of the great hall, directly in his line of sight. The emperor coughed softly as his eyes fell on the lion-shaped armrest. He tightened his hold around it as he felt an overpowering temptation to change his mind. Realising the futility of the sentiment, he closed his eyes in resignation.

How do you save someone who thinks that doing so is an act of dishonour?

Dashrath looked straight into the eyes of his insanely virtuous son. 'The law of Lord Rudra has been broken. Some good did come of it, for Raavan's bodyguard corps was destroyed. By all accounts, he is licking his wounds in Lanka!'

The audience broke into a loud cheer. Everybody hated Raavan; almost everybody.

'Mithila, the kingdom of our Princess Sita, the wife of my beloved son Ram, was saved from annihilation.'

The crowd cheered once again, but it was more muted this time. Very few knew Sita, and most did not understand why their crown prince had forged an alliance with a deeply spiritual but powerless kingdom.

Dashrath's voice shook as he continued. 'But the law has been broken. And Lord Rudra's word has to be honoured. His tribe, the Vayuputras, have not yet asked for Ram to be punished. But that will not stop the Raghuvanshis from doing the right thing.'

A hushed silence descended on the hall. The people felt a dread as they steeled themselves to hear what they now feared their king would say to them.

'Ram has accepted the punishment that must be his. He will leave Ayodhya, for I banish him from the Sapt Sindhu for fourteen years. He will return to us after cleansing himself with the fire of penance. He is a true follower of Lord Rudra. Honour him!'

A loud cry rent the air: of dismay from the commoners and shock from the nobility.

Dashrath raised his hands and the crowds fell silent. 'My other beloved son, Bharat, will now be the crown prince of Ayodhya, the kingdom of Kosala and the Sapt Sindhu Empire.'

Silence. The mood in the hall had turned sombre.

Ram held his hands together in a formal namaste as he spoke in a loud and clear voice. 'Father, even the Gods in the sky marvel at your wisdom and justice today!'

Many among the common folk were openly crying now.

'The golden spirit of the greatest Suryavanshi, Ikshvaku himself, lives strong in you, my father!' said Ram loudly. 'Sita and I will leave Ayodhya within a day.'

In the far corner of the hall, standing unobtrusively behind a pillar, was a tall, unusually fair-skinned man. He wore a white *dhoti* and *angvastram*; he seemed visibly uncomfortable in the *dhoti,* though — perhaps it wasn't his normal attire. His most distinguishing features were his hooked nose, beaded full beard, and drooping moustache. His wizened face creased into a smile as he heard Ram's words.

Guru Vashishtha has chosen well.

— 𝝟 ⚱ ☼ —

'I must say that I am surprised by the emperor,' said the fair-skinned man with the hooked nose, adjusting his uncomfortable *dhoti*.

He sat with Vashishtha in the raj guru's private chamber.

'Do not forget where the real credit lies,' said Vashishtha.

'I think that's obvious. I must say you have chosen well.'

'And will you play your role?'

The fair-skinned man sighed. 'You know we cannot get involved too deeply, Guru*ji*. It is not our decision to make.'

'But…'

'But we will do all that we can. That is our promise. And you know that we don't break our promises.'

Vashishtha nodded. 'Thank you, my friend. That is all I ask. Glory to Lord Rudra.'

'Glory to Lord Parshu Ram.'

—— 𑀓 ☘ ☀ ——

Bharat walked into Ram and Sita's sitting room even as he was being announced. They had already changed into the garb of hermits, made from rough cotton and bark. It made Bharat wince.

'We have to dress the way forest people do, Bharat,' said Sita.

Tears sprang into his eyes. He looked at Ram as he shook his head. '*Dada*, I don't know whether to applaud you or try and knock some sense into you.'

'You needn't do either,' said Ram, smiling. 'Just embrace me and wish me goodbye.'

Bharat rushed towards his brother and gathered him in his arms as a torrent of tears ran down his face. Ram held him tight.

As Bharat stepped back, Ram said, 'Don't worry. Sweet are the fruits of adversity. I will return with more sense knocked into me, I assure you.'

Bharat laughed softly. 'One of these days, I'll stop speaking to you for the fear of being understood.'

Ram laughed as well. 'Rule well, my brother.'

There were some who believed that Bharat's emphasis on liberty was more suited to the temperament of Ayodhya citizens, indeed the people of the Sapt Sindhu.

'I won't lie that I did not want it,' said Bharat. 'But not this way ... not this way...'

Ram put his hands on Bharat's strong muscular shoulders. 'You will rule well. I know that. Make our ancestors proud.'

'I don't care what our ancestors think.'

'Then make *me* proud,' said Ram.

Bharat's face fell, along with a fresh stream of tears. He embraced his brother again and they held each other for a long time. Ram overcame his natural reserve as he held on to Bharat. He knew his brother needed this.

'Enough,' said Bharat, pulling back, wiping his tears and shaking his head. He turned to Sita. 'Take care of my brother, *Bhabhi*. He does not know how unethical this world is.'

Sita smiled. 'He knows. But he still tries to change things.'

Bharat sighed. Then he turned towards Ram as an idea struck him. 'Give me your slippers, *Dada*.'

Ram frowned as he looked down at his simple hermit slippers.

'Not these,' said Bharat. 'Your royal slippers.'

'Why?'

'Just give them to me, *Dada*.'

Ram walked to the side of the bed, where his recently discarded royal garments lay. On the floor was a pair of gold-coloured slippers, with exquisite silver and brown embroidery. Ram picked them up and handed them to Bharat.

'What are you going to do with these?' asked Ram.

'When the time comes, I will place these rather than myself on the throne,' said Bharat.

Ram and Sita immediately understood the implication. With this one gesture, Bharat would effectively declare that Ram was the king of Ayodhya and that he, Bharat, was only a caretaker in his elder brother's absence. Any attempts to murder the king of Ayodhya would invite the wrath of the mighty empire of the Sapt Sindhu. This was mandated by the treaties between the various kingdoms of the Sapt Sindhu. Added to the cold reality of treaty obligations was the superstition that it was bad karma to kill kings and crown princes, except in battle or open combat. It would offer a powerful shield of protection to Ram, though it would severely undercut Bharat's own authority and power.

Ram embraced his Bharat again. 'My brother…'

'Lakshman?' said Sita. 'I thought I'd told you…'

Lakshman had just entered Ram and Sita's sitting room. He wore the same attire that his elder brother and sister-in-law did: one of a forest hermit.

Lakshman dared Sita with determination blazing in his eyes. 'I'm coming, *Bhabhi*.'

'Lakshman…' pleaded Ram.

'You will not survive without me, *Dada*,' said Lakshman. 'I'm not letting you go without me.'

Ram laughed. 'It's touching to see the faith my family has in me. No one seems to trust me to be able to keep myself alive.'

Lakshman laughed too, but turned serious in a flash. 'You're free to laugh or cry about it, *Dada*. But I am coming with you.'

— |大| 🐟 ☼ —

An excited Urmila greeted Lakshman as he entered his private chamber. She was dressed in simple, yet fashionable attire. Her *dhoti* and blouse were dyed in the common colour brown, but an elegant gold border ran along its edges. She wore simple, modest gold jewellery, unlike what she normally favoured.

'Come, my darling,' said Urmila, smiling with childlike enthusiasm. 'You must see this. I have single-handedly supervised the packing and most of it is done already.'

'Packing?' asked a surprised Lakshman, with a fond smile.

'Yes,' said Urmila, taking his hand and pulling him into the wardrobe room. Two massive trunks made of teak were placed in the centre. Urmila quickly opened both. 'This one has my clothes and that one has yours.'

Lakshman stood nonplussed, not knowing how to react to his innocent Urmila.

She pulled him into their bed chamber, where lay another trunk, packed and ready. It was full of utensils. A small container in one corner caught her attention. Urmila opened it to reveal small packets of spices. 'See, the way I understand it, we should be able to get meat and vegetables easily in the jungle. But spices and utensils will be difficult. So...'

Lakshman stared at her, bemused and a trifle dismayed.

Urmila moved towards him and embraced her husband, smiling fondly. 'I will cook the most divine meals for you. And for Sita *Didi* and Ram *Jijaji* also, of course. We will return fat and healthy from our fourteen-year holiday!'

Lakshman returned his wife's embrace gently; her head reached his muscular barrel-chest. *Holiday?*

He looked down at his excited wife, who was obviously trying very hard to make the best of what was a bewildering situation for her. *She has been a princess all her life. She assumed that she would be living in an even more luxurious palace in Ayodhya. She is not a bad soul. She just wants to be a good wife. But is it right of me, her husband, to agree to her following me into the jungle, even if she wants to do so? Isn't it my duty to protect her, just like it is my duty to protect my Ram Dada?*

She will not last a day in the jungle. She won't.

A heavy weight settled on Lakshman's heart as it became obvious what he had to do. But he knew he must do so gently so it would not break his Urmila's tender heart.

Keeping one arm around her, he raised her chin with his other hand. Urmila gazed at him lovingly with her childlike innocence. He spoke tenderly, 'I'm worried, Urmila.'

'Don't be. We'll handle it together. The forest will be…'

'It's not about the forest. I'm worried about what will happen here, in the palace.'

Urmila arched her spine and threw her head back so she could get a better look at her extremely tall husband. 'In the palace?'

'Yes! Father's not keeping too well. *Chhoti Maa* Kaikeyi will be controlling everything now. And, frankly, I don't think Bharat *Dada* can stand up to her. My mother will at least have Shatrughan to look after her. But who will look after *Badi Maa* Kaushalya? What will happen to her?'

Urmila nodded. 'True…'

'And if *Chhoti Maa* Kaikeyi can do this to Ram *Dada*, can you imagine what she will do to *Badi Maa*?'

Urmila's open face was guileless.

'Someone has to protect *Badi Maa*,' Lakshman repeated, as if to drive home his point.

'Yes, that's true, but there are so many people in the palace. Hasn't Ram *Dada* made any arrangements?' asked Urmila.

Lakshman smiled sadly. 'Ram *Dada* is not the most practical of men. He thinks everyone in the world is as ethical as he is. Why do you think I'm going with him? I need to protect him.'

Urmila's face fell as she finally understood what Lakshman was trying to say. 'I'm not living here without you, Lakshman.'

He pulled his wife close. 'It will be for a short time, Urmila.'

'*Fourteen years?* No, I'm not...' Urmila burst into helpless tears as she hugged him tight.

Lakshman eased his hold as he gently raised her chin again. He wiped away her tears. 'You are a Raghuvanshi now. We hold duty above love; we uphold honour, even at the cost of happiness. This is not a matter of choice, Urmila.'

'Don't do this, Lakshman. Please. I love you. Don't leave me.'

'I love you too, Urmila. And I cannot force you to do anything you don't want to do. I am only requesting you. But before you give me your answer, I want you to think of Kaushalya *Maa*. Think of the love she has showered upon you over the last few days. Didn't you tell me that after a long time, you felt as if you had a mother again, in Kaushalya *Maa*? Doesn't she deserve something in return?'

Urmila burst out crying and embraced Lakshman tightly again.

— 🛐 ☀ —

A cool evening breeze blew through the palace at the fifth hour of the third *prahar*, as Sita walked towards Lakshman and Urmila's private chambers. The guards immediately stood at attention. As they turned to announce her, they were halted by a pensive Lakshman emerging from the chambers. Sita felt a lump in her throat as she looked at his face.

'I'll sort this out,' said Sita sternly, as she attempted to walk past him and enter her sister's chambers.

Lakshman stopped her, holding her hand with a pleading expression in his eyes. 'No, *Bhabhi*.'

Sita looked at her giant brother-in-law, who suddenly seemed so vulnerable and alone.

'Lakshman, my sister listens to me. Trust me—'

'No, *Bhabhi*,' interrupted Lakshman, shaking his head. 'Forest life will not be easy. We will face death every day. You know that. You are tough, you can survive. But she is…' Tears welled up in his eyes. 'She wanted to come, *Bhabhi*, but I don't think she should. I convinced her not to… This is for the best.'

'Lakshman…'

'This is for the best, *Bhabhi*,' repeated Lakshman, almost as though he was convincing himself. 'This is for the best.'

Chapter 29

It had been an eventful six months since Ram, Lakshman and Sita had left Ayodhya. Word that Dashrath had passed away had made Ram repeatedly curse his fate for not being able to perform the duties of an eldest son and conduct the funeral rites of his father. It broke Ram's heart that he had discovered his father so late in his life. Returning to Ayodhya was not possible, but he had performed a *yagna* in the forests for the journey his father's soul had undertaken. Bharat had remained true to his word. He had placed Ram's slippers on the throne of Ayodhya, and had begun governing the empire as his brother's regent. It could be said that Ram was appointed emperor in absentia. It was an unorthodox move but Bharat's liberal and decentralising style of governance made the decision palatable to the kingdoms within the Sapt Sindhu.

Ram, Lakshman and Sita had travelled south, primarily walking by the banks of rivers, moving inland only when necessary. They had finally reached the borders of the Sapt Sindhu, near the kingdom of South Kosala, ruled by Ram's maternal grandfather.

Ram went down on both knees and touched the ground with his forehead; this was the land that had nurtured his mother. As he straightened, he looked at his wife and smiled, as if he knew her secret.

'What?' asked Sita.

'There are people who have been shadowing us for weeks,' said Ram. 'When do you plan to tell me who they are?'

Sita shrugged delicately and turned to the forest line in the distance, where she knew Jatayu and his soldiers walked stealthily. They had remained out of sight, though close enough to quickly move in if the need arose. Evidently, they were not as discreet as she would have liked them to be; more likely, she had underestimated her husband's abilities and keen awareness of his surroundings. 'I will tell you,' said Sita, with a broad smile, 'when the time is right. For now, know that they are here for our protection.'

Ram gave her a piercing look, but let it go for now.

'Lord Manu banned the crossing of the Narmada,' said Lakshman. 'If we cross, then we cannot return, according to the law.'

'There is a way,' said Sita. 'If we travel south along *Maa* Kaushalya's father's kingdom, we may not have to "cross" the Narmada. The entire kingdom of South Kosala lies to the east of the origin of the Narmada River. And the river itself flows west. If we simply keep travelling south, we will reach the *Dandakaranya* without "crossing" the Narmada. So, we would not be violating Lord Manu's ban, right?'

'That's a technicality, *Bhabhi*, and you know it. It may work for you and me, but it won't for Ram *Dada*.'

'Hmm, should we travel east and leave the Sapt Sindhu by boat then?' asked Ram.

'We can't do that,' said Sita. 'The seas are ruled by Raavan. He has dotted the Indian peninsula with port-forts. It is common knowledge that he dominates the western coast, but the fact is, he has outposts on the eastern coast as well. That rules out the sea routes. But Raavan doesn't hold sway in the hinterland. We will be safe south of the Narmada, in the forests of Dandak.'

'But *Bhabhi*,' argued Lakshman, 'Lord Manu's laws clearly state—'

'Which Lord Manu?'

Lakshman was shocked. *Didn't Bhabhi know who Lord Manu was?* 'The founder of the Vedic way of life, *Bhabhi*. Everyone knows…'

Sita smiled indulgently. 'There have been many Manus, Lakshman, not just one. Each age has its own Manu. So when you speak of the laws of Manu, you will have to also specify which Lord Manu.'

'I didn't know this…' said Lakshman.

Sita shook her head, as she teased the men affectionately. 'Did you boys learn anything at all in your *gurukul*? You know very little.'

'I knew that,' Ram protested. 'Lakshman never paid attention in class. Don't lump me with him.'

'Shatrughan was the one who knew everything, *Dada*,' said Lakshman. 'All of us depended on him.'

'You more than the others,' joked Ram, as he stretched his back.

Lakshman laughed as Ram turned to Sita. 'Okay, I concede your point. But it was the Manu of our age who decreed that we cannot cross the Narmada. And, that if we do, we cannot return. So…'

'It wasn't a law. It was an agreement.'

'An agreement?' asked Ram and Lakshman together, surprised.

Sita continued. 'I'm sure you're aware that Lord Manu was a prince from the kingdom of Sangamtamil, deep in the south of India. He led many of his own people, and those of

Dwarka, up north into the Sapt Sindhu, when their own lands were swallowed by the rising sea.'

'Yes, I'm aware of that,' said Ram.

'But all the people from these two lands did not leave with Lord Manu. The majority remained behind in Sangamtamil and Dwarka. Lord Manu had radical ideas about how a society should be organised, which many did not agree with. He had his share of enemies. He was allowed to leave with his followers, from both Sangamtamil and Dwarka, on the condition that he would never venture back. In those days, Narmada formed the upper boundary of Dwarka, with Sangamtamil of course being in the deep south. In effect, they promised to leave each other in peace and part ways. The Narmada was to be the natural boundary under the agreement. It was not a law, but an agreement.'

'But if we are his descendants, then we need to honour the agreement that he made,' said Ram.

'Valid point,' said Sita. 'But tell me, what does an agreement require at the very least?'

'It needs two parties to agree on something.'

'And, if one of the parties doesn't exist anymore, is the agreement still valid?'

Ram and Lakshman were stumped.

'Many parts of Sangamtamil were already submerged by the time Lord Manu left. The rest went underwater soon after. The seas rose rapidly. Dwarka survived for longer. Progressively though, as the seas rose, the large land mass of Dwarka that had been attached to India was reduced to a long, lonely island.'

'Dwaravati?' asked Ram, incredulously.

Dwaravati had been a long, narrow island off the coast of western India, running north to south for nearly five hundred kilometres. The island was swallowed by the sea over three thousand years ago. The survivors from Dwaravati dispersed all over the mainland, and frankly, no one took their claims of being the descendants of the original Dwarkans seriously. This was mainly because the Yadavs, belonging to a powerful kingdom based near the banks of the Yamuna, stridently claimed that they were the sole direct descendants of the Dwarkans. The truth was that the intermingling among the different tribes across India had been so widespread, everybody could claim descent from both the Sangamtamils and the Dwarkans.

Sita nodded. 'The island of Dwaravati was home to the true survivors of Dwarka. Today, they exist among us all.'

'Wow.'

'So the pure descendants of the Sangamtamils and Dwarkans are long gone. The only ones around are us, their common descendants. How will we breach an agreement we made with ourselves? There's no other party anymore!'

The logic was irrefutable.

'So, *Bhabhi*,' said Lakshman, 'should we be heading south and staying in the forests of Dandak?'

'Well, yes. It is the safest place for us.'

Ram, Lakshman and Sita stood on the southern banks of the Narmada River. Ram went down on one knee and reverentially picked up a fistful of soil. He smeared it across his forehead in three horizontal lines, like the followers of Lord Rudra did with the holy ashes consecrated by the Gods. He whispered, 'May the land of our ancestors … the soil that was witness to great karma … bless us.'

Sita and Lakshman followed Ram's example as they smeared a *tilak* across their foreheads.

Sita smiled at Ram. 'You do know what Lord Brahma said about this land, right?'

Ram nodded. 'Yes; more often than not, whenever India faces an existential crisis, our regeneration emerges from the Indian peninsula, from the land that is to the south of the Narmada.'

'Do you know why he said that?'

Ram shook his head.

'Our scriptures tell us that the south is the direction of death, right?'

'Yes.'

'Death is believed to be inauspicious in some foreign lands to the west of us; to them it signifies the end of everything. But nothing ever really dies. No material can ever truly escape the universe. It just changes form. In that sense, death is actually also the beginning of regeneration; the old form dies and a new form is born. If the south is the direction of death, then it is also the direction of regeneration.'

Ram was intrigued by this thought. 'The Sapt Sindhu is our *karmabhoomi*, the *land of our karma*. And the land to the south of the Narmada is our *pitrbhoomi*, the *land of our ancestors*. This is the land of our regeneration.'

'And, one day, we will return from the south to drive the regeneration of India.' Saying so, Sita held out two cups made of dried clay. They contained a bubbly milk-white liquid. She handed one to Lakshman and the other to Ram.

'What is it, *Bhabhi*?' asked Lakshman.

'It's for your regeneration,' said Sita. 'Drink it.'

Lakshman took a sip and grimaced. 'Yuck!'

'Just drink it, Lakshman,' ordered Sita.

He held his nose as he drained the liquid. He walked to the river and rinsed his mouth as well as the cup.

Ram looked at Sita. 'I know what this is. Where did you get it from?'

'From the people who protect us.'

'Sita…'

'You are important to India, Ram. You have to remain healthy. You have to stay alive. We have a lot to do when we return, fourteen years from now. You cannot be allowed to age. Please drink it.'

'Sita,' laughed Ram, 'one cup of Somras is not going to achieve much. We need to drink it regularly for years for it to be effective. And you know how difficult it is to procure Somras. There will never be enough.'

'Leave that to me.'

'I'm not drinking it without you. What's the point of my long life, if I don't have you to share it with?'

Sita smiled. 'I have already had mine, Ram. I had to, as one normally falls ill the first time one drinks the Somras.'

'Is that why you were ill last week?'

'Yes. If all three of us were to fall ill at the same time, it would be difficult to manage, right? You looked after me when I was unwell. And I will take care of Lakshman and you now.'

'I wonder why the Somras makes one fall ill the first time.'

Sita shrugged. 'I don't know. That is a question for Lord Brahma and the *Saptrishis*. But don't worry about the illness; I have enough medicines in my bag.'

Sita and Ram were both poised on one knee, staring intently at the wild boar. Ram held his bow with the arrow nocked, ready to fire.

'Sita,' whispered Ram, 'I have the animal in perfect sight. I can finish it immediately. Are you sure you want to do this?'

'Yes,' whispered Sita. 'Bows and arrows are your thing. Swords and spears are mine. I need the practice.'

Ram, Sita and Lakshman had been in exile for eighteen months now. Sita had finally introduced Jatayu to Ram some months back. Trusting Sita, Ram had accepted the Malayaputra and his fifteen soldiers as members of his team. Together they were one short of twenty now; more defendable than a group of three. Ram understood this, as well as the importance of allies in the situation they were in. But he remained wary of the Malayaputras.

Admittedly, Jatayu had given him no reason to be suspicious, but Ram could not ignore the fact that he and his people were followers of Guru Vishwamitra. Ram shared his guru Vashishtha's misgivings about the chief of the Malayaputras; he baulked at the ease with which Vishwamitra had been willing to use the *Asuraastra*, with little regard for the law.

The members of the party had settled into established routines as they moved deeper into the forests of Dandak. Still not having found a suitable enough permanent camp, they usually stayed in one place for around two to three weeks before moving on. Standard perimeter and security formations had been agreed upon. Cooking and cleaning duties were shared by rotation, as was the task of hunting. But since not everyone in the camp ate meat, hunting wasn't something that was required often.

'These beasts are dangerous when they charge,' warned Ram, looking at Sita with concern.

Sita smiled at her husband's protectiveness as she drew her sword. 'Which is why I want you to stay behind me once you fire the arrow,' she teased.

Ram smiled in return. He focused his attention on the wild boar as he took aim. He pulled the bowstring back and released the arrow. The missile flew in a neat arc, brushed past its head and landed to its left. The animal jerked its head in the direction of the intruders who had dared to disturb its peace. It grunted aggressively but did not move.

'Once more,' said Sita as she slowly rose, her knees slightly bent, her feet spread wide, the sword held to the side.

Ram quickly nocked another arrow and fired. It whizzed past the boar's ear and buried itself into the ground.

Another belligerent grunt was accompanied by a stomping of its feet, this time. It lowered its head threateningly as it stared in the direction that the arrow had come from. Its curved tusks projected from below the snout, like two long knives, ready to strike.

'Now, get behind me,' whispered Sita.

Ram dropped his bow, quickly slipped a few feet behind her, and drew his sword as well; he wouldn't lose a second if she needed his help.

Sita screamed loudly as she jumped into view. The beast immediately took up the challenge that was thrown. It charged towards her with fearsome speed, its head low, its tusks jutting out like menacing swords. Sita stood her ground, breathing steadily as the wild boar speedily moved towards her. At the last second, when it appeared that it was upon her and would gore her to death, Sita took a few quick steps and leapt high into the air; an exquisite leap with which she flew horizontally above the charging boar. As she did, she struck her sword vertically down, stabbing the animal's neck. Her suspended body-weight made the blade sink deep into the neck, shattering the cervical vertebrae. She superbly leveraged the sword hilt to flip forward and land on her feet, just as the boar collapsed, dead, in front of Ram.

Ram's eyes widened with wonder. Sita strode back to the boar, breathing hard. 'The sword needs to simply break the neck and the animal dies instantly. No pain.'

'Clearly,' said Ram, sheathing his sword.

Sita bent down, touched the boar's head, and whispered, 'Forgive me for killing you, O noble beast. May your soul find purpose again, while your body sustains my soul.'

Ram held the hilt of Sita's sword in a firm grip and attempted to prise the blade out of the beast's body. It was stuck. He looked at Sita. 'It has gone in deep!'

Sita smiled. 'Let me retrieve your arrows while you pull it out.'

Ram began the delicate operation of extracting Sita's sword from the boar's neck. He needed to make sure that the blade didn't get damaged by rubbing against the hard bone. After extricating it he sat on his haunches and wiped it clean with some leaves; he checked the edges; they remained sharp; there was no damage. He looked up to see Sita approaching him from the distance, with the arrows that he had fired in the beginning. He pointed at her sword and raised his thumb, signalling that it was still in fine fettle. Sita smiled. She was still some distance away from him.

'My Lady!'

A loud shout rang through the jungle. Ram's eyes flew towards Makrant, a Malayaputra, as he raced towards Sita. Ram looked in the direction that the man was pointing. His heart jumped into his mouth as he saw two wild boars emerge from the thick of the woods, charging straight at Sita. Her sword was with him. All she had was her knife. Ram sprang to his feet and sprinted towards his wife. 'Sita!'

Alerted by the panic in his voice, Sita whirled around. The boars were almost upon her. She drew her knife and faced the animals. It would have been suicidal to make a dash for it, away from them; she could not outrun them; better to look them in the eye. Sita stood steady, took quick deep breaths and waited.

'My Lady!' shouted Makrant, as he leapt in front of Sita just in time, swinging his sword as he successfully deflected the first attack. The first boar swerved away but the second charged in, even as Makrant struggled to regain his balance. Its tusk pierced his upper thigh.

'Sita!' screamed Ram, as he threw her sword to her, drawing his own as he rushed towards Makrant.

Sita caught the sword deftly and turned to the first beast, which had turned around now and was charging down at her again. Makrant, impaled momentarily on the other boar's tusk, had been flung into the air by its fearsome momentum. But the weight of his body had thrown the boar off balance as well, making him tip to the right, exposing its underbelly. Ram chose that moment to stab it viciously. The blade sank into the beast's chest, right through to its heart. It collapsed to the ground, dead.

Meanwhile, the first boar swung its head fiercely as it closed in on Sita. She jumped up high, tucking her feet up, neatly avoiding the boar. On her way down, she swung her sword, partially decapitating the beast. It wasn't clean, but was enough to incapacitate the animal; it fell to the ground. Sita yanked her sword out as she landed. She went down on one knee and struck hard again, beheading the beast completely, putting it out of its misery.

She turned around to see that Ram was rushing towards her, his sword held to the side.

'I'm all right!' she reassured him.

He nodded and headed towards Makrant as Sita also ran to the injured Malayaputra. Ram hastily tied the soldier's *angvastram* around the injury, barely staunching the blood that continued to gush out. He quickly came to his feet and picked up Makrant.

'We have to get back to the camp right away!' Ram said.

The wild boar's tusk had cut through his upper quadriceps, piercing the femoral artery. Fortunately, the tusk had come into contact with the hard pelvic bone, flinging him off as the beast's jangled nerves made it shake its head on impact. This had probably saved his life, for if the tusk had pushed through and penetrated deeper, it would have ruptured his intestines. The resultant infection would have been impossible to treat in the jungle; it would have meant certain death. The man had lost a lot of blood, though, and was not yet out of danger.

Ram, mindful that Makrant had unselfishly risked his life to save his wife, worked tirelessly to nurse the soldier back to health, ably assisted by Sita. For Ram, it was the most natural thing to do. But it surprised the Malayaputras to see a Sapt Sindhu royal willingly doing work that was not, customarily, his domain.

'He is a good man,' said Jatayu.

Jatayu and two Malayaputra soldiers were outside the camp's main tent, cooking the evening meal.

'I'm surprised that, despite being a prince, he is willing to do the work that mere soldiers and medical assistants should be doing,' said one of the Malayaputras, stirring the contents of a pot on a low flame.

'I have always found him impressive,' said the other soldier, chopping some herbs on a wooden block. 'He has absolutely no airs, unlike the other royal Sapt Sindhu brats.'

'Hmm,' said Jatayu. 'I have also heard how he effectively saved Makrant's life by acting quickly. If he had not killed the boar immediately, it could have gored Makrant again, possibly killing him, apart from harming Lady Sita as well.'

'He's always been a great warrior. We have seen and heard enough instances of that,' said the second soldier. 'But he is also a good man.'

'Yes, he treats his wife well. He is calm and clear-headed. He leads well. He is a good warrior. But most importantly, it is clear that he has a heart of gold,' said the first Malayaputra soldier, full of praise. 'I think Guru Vashishtha probably chose well.'

Jatayu glared at the soldier, almost daring him to say another word. The poor man knew that he had gone too far. He immediately fell silent as he shifted his attention to the task of stirring the pot.

Jatayu understood that he could not afford any doubts among his men regarding this issue. Their loyalty was to lie exclusively with the Malayaputra goal. 'No matter how trustworthy Prince Ram may appear, always remember, we are the followers of Guru Vishwamitra. We have to do what he has ordered us to do. He is our chief and he knows best.'

The two Malayaputra soldiers nodded.

'Of course, we can trust him,' said Jatayu. 'And it is good that he also appears to trust us now. But do not forget where our loyalties lie. Is that clear?'

'Yes, Captain,' said both the soldiers simultaneously.

Six years had lapsed since Ram, Sita and Lakshman had left Ayodhya.

The band of nineteen had finally settled along the western banks of the early course of the mighty Godavari River, at *Panchavati,* or the *place with five banyan trees.* The river provided natural protection to the small, rustic, yet comfortable camp. The main mud hut at the centre of the camp had two rooms— one for Ram and Sita, and the other for Lakshman—and an open clearing for exercise and assembly. A rudimentary alarm system had been set around the far perimeter as warning against wild animals.

The perimeter of this camp was made of two circular fences. The one on the outside was covered with poisonous creepers to keep animals out. The fence on the inside comprised nagavalli creepers, rigged with an alarm system consisting of a continuous string that ran all the way to a very large wooden cage, filled with birds. The birds were well looked after, and replaced every month with new ones that were caught, as the old ones were released. If anyone made it past the outer fence and attempted to enter the nagavalli hedge, the alarm system would trigger the opening of the birdcage roof. The noisy flutter of the escaping birds would offer a few precious minutes of warning to the inmates of the camp.

Another cluster of huts to the east housed Jatayu and his band of soldiers. Despite Ram's trust in Jatayu, Lakshman remained suspicious of the Malayaputra. Like most Indians, he held strong superstitions about the Nagas. He simply could not bring himself to trust the 'vulture-man', the name Lakshman had given to Jatayu behind his back.

They had faced dangers, no doubt, in these six years, but these had not been due to any human intervention. The occasional scars served as reminders of their adventures in the jungle, but the Somras had ensured that they looked and felt as young as the day they had left Ayodhya. Exposure to the harsh sun had darkened their skin. Ram had always been dark-skinned, but even the fair-skinned Sita and Lakshman had acquired a dusky appearance. Ram and Lakshman had grown beards and moustaches, making them look like warrior-sages.

Life had fallen into a predictable pattern. Ram and Sita liked to go to the Godavari River in the early morning hours, to bathe and spend some private time together. It was their favourite time of the day.

This was one such day. They washed their hair in the clear waters of the Godavari, and then sat on the banks of the river, indulging themselves with conversation over an array of fresh berries, as they dried their hair in the early morning breeze. Ram combed Sita's hair and braided it. Sita then moved behind her husband and ran her fingers through his half-dry hair, untangling the strands.

'Ouch!' protested Ram, as his head was jerked back.

'Sorry,' said Sita.

Ram smiled.

'What are you thinking?' asked Sita, as she gingerly untangled another knot.

'Well, they say the jungles are dangerous and it is the cities where you find comfort and security. It has been exactly the other way round for me. I have never been more relaxed and happy in my life than in the *Dandakaranya*.'

Sita murmured in agreement.

Ram turned his head to look at his wife. 'I know that you suffered, too, in the world of the "civilised"…'

'Yeah, well,' said Sita, shrugging. 'They say it takes immense pressure to create diamonds.'

Ram laughed softly. 'You know, Guru Vashishtha had said to me, when I was a child, that compassion is sometimes an overrated virtue. He told me the story of the butterfly emerging from the hard pupa. Its life begins as an "ugly" caterpillar. When the time is right, it forms a pupa and retreats behind its hard walls. Within its shell, it transforms into a butterfly, unseen, unheard. When ready, it uses its tiny, sharp claws at the base of its forewings to crack a small opening in the hard, protective outer shell. It squeezes through this tiny opening and struggles to make its way out. This is a difficult, painful and prolonged process. Misguided compassion may make us want to enlarge the hole in the pupa, imagining that it would ease the butterfly's task. But that struggle is necessary; as the butterfly squeezes its body out of the tiny hole, it secretes fluids within its swollen body. This fluid goes to its wings, strengthening them; once they've emerged, as the fluid dries, the delicate creatures are able to take flight. Making the hole bigger to "help" the butterfly and ease its struggle will only debilitate it. Without the struggle, its wings would never gain strength. It would never fly.'

Sita nodded and smiled. 'I was told a different story. Of small birds being pushed out of their nests by their parents so that they are forced to fly. But yes, the point was the same.'

Ram smiled. 'Well, wife! This struggle has made us stronger.'

Sita picked up the wooden comb and began running it through Ram's hair.

'Who told you about the little birds? Your guru?' asked Ram.

Since Ram was looking ahead, he didn't see the split-second of hesitation that flitted across her face. 'I've learnt from many people, Ram. But none was as great as your guru, Vashishtha*ji*.'

Ram smiled. 'I was lucky to have him as my guru.'

'Yes, you were. He has trained you well. You will be a good Vishnu.'

Ram felt a flush of embarrassment. While he was certainly willing to shoulder any responsibility for the sake of his people, the great title that Vashishtha felt certain Ram would achieve left him humbled. He doubted his capability, and wondered if he was even ready for it. He had shared these doubts with his wife.

'You will be ready,' said Sita, smiling, almost reading her husband's mind. 'Trust me. You don't know how rare a person you are.'

Ram turned to Sita and touched her cheek gently as he looked deep into her eyes. He smiled faintly as he turned his attention back to the river. She tied a knot on top of his head, the way he always liked it, then wrapped threaded beads around the knot to hold it in place. 'Done!'

Chapter 30

Ram and Sita had returned from a hunt with the body of a deer tied to a long wooden pole. They balanced the pole on their shoulders. Lakshman had stayed behind, it being his turn to cook. They had lived outside the Sapt Sindhu for thirteen years now.

'Just one more year, Ram,' said Sita, as the pair walked into the compound of their camp.

'Yes,' said Ram. They set down the pole. 'That's when our real battle begins.'

Lakshman walked up as he unsheathed a long knife from the scabbard tied horizontally across the small of his back. 'The two of you can begin your philosophy and strategy discussions while I attend to some womanly chores!'

Sita gently tapped Lakshman on his cheek. 'Men are also counted among the best chefs in India, so what's so womanly about cooking? Everyone should be able to cook!'

Lakshman bowed theatrically, laughing. 'Yeessss, *Bhabhi*!'

Ram and Sita laughed as well.

—— 衤 🐚 ☼ ——

'The sky is beautiful this evening, isn't it?' remarked Sita, admiring the handiwork of *Dhyauspita,* the *Sky Father.* Ram and Sita lay on the floor outside the main hut.

It was the fifth hour of the third *prahar*. The chariot of *Surya*, the Sun God, had left a trail of vivid colours behind as he blazed though the sky. A cool evening breeze blew in from the west, giving respite at the end of an unseasonal, oppressively hot day. The monsoon months had ended, heralding the beginning of winter.

'Yes,' smiled Ram, as he reached for her hand, pulled it close to his lips and kissed her fingers, gently.

Sita turned towards Ram and smiled. 'What's on your mind, husband?'

'Very husbandly things, wife…'

A loud clearing of the throat was heard. Sita and Ram looked up to find an amused Lakshman standing before them. They stared at him with mock irritation.

'What?' shrugged Lakshman. 'You're blocking the entry into the hut. I need my sword. I have to go for a practice session with Atulya.'

Ram shifted to the right and made room for Lakshman. Lakshman walked in. 'I'll be gone soon…'

No sooner had he stepped into the hut than he stopped in his tracks. The flock of birds in the cage linked to the alarm had suddenly fluttered noisily. Lakshman whirled around as Ram and Sita sprang to their feet.

'What was that?' asked Lakshman.

Ram's instincts told him that the intruders were not animals.

'Weapons,' ordered Ram calmly.

Sita and Lakshman tied their sword scabbards around their waist. Lakshman handed Ram his bow, before picking up his own. The brothers quickly strung their bows. Jatayu and his men rushed in, armed and ready, just as Ram and Lakshman tied quivers full of arrows to their backs. Sita picked up a long spear, as Ram tied his sword scabbard to his waist. They already wore a smaller knife scabbard, tied horizontally across the small of their backs; a weapon they kept on their person at all times.

'Who could they be?' asked Jatayu.

'I don't know,' said Ram.

'Lakshman's Wall?' asked Sita.

Lakshman's Wall was an ingenious defensive feature designed by him to the east of the main hut. It was five feet in height; it covered three sides of a small square completely, leaving the inner side facing the main hut partially open; like a cubicle. The entire structure gave the impression that it was an enclosed kitchen. In actual fact, the cubicle was bare, providing adequate mobility to warriors — though they would have to be on their knees — unseen by enemies on the other side of the wall. A small *tandoor,* a *cooking platform*, emerged on the outside from the south-facing wall. Half the enclosure was roof-covered, completing the camouflage of a cooking area; it afforded protection from enemy arrows. The south, east and north-facing walls were drilled with well-spaced holes. These holes were narrow on the inner side and broad on the outer side, giving the impression of ventilation required for cooking. Their actual purpose was to give those on the inside a good view of the approaching enemy, while preventing those on the outside from looking in. The holes could also be used to fire arrows.

Made from mud, it was not strong enough to withstand a sustained assault by a large force. Having said that, it was good enough for defence against small bands sent on assassination bids, which is what Lakshman suspected they would face. Designed by Lakshman, it had been built by everyone in the camp; Makrant had named it 'Lakshman's Wall'.

'Yes,' said Ram.

Everyone rushed to the wall and crouched low, keeping their weapons ready; they waited.

Lakshman hunched over and peeped through a hole in the south-facing wall. As he strained his eye, he detected a small band of ten people marching into the camp premises, led by a man and a woman.

The man in the lead was of average height and unusually fair-skinned. His reed-thin physique was that of a runner; this man was no warrior. Despite his frail shoulders and thin arms, he walked as if he had boils in his armpits, pretending to accommodate impressive biceps. Like most Indian men, he had long, jet black hair that was tied in a knot at the back of his head. His full beard was neatly-trimmed, interestingly coloured a deep brown. He wore a classic brown *dhoti* and an *angvastram* that was a shade lighter. His jewellery was rich but understated: pearl ear studs and a thin, copper bracelet. He looked dishevelled right now, as though he had been on the road for too long, without a change of clothes.

The woman beside him faintly resembled the man, but was bewitching; she was possibly his sister. Almost as short as Urmila, her skin was as white as snow; it should have made her look pale and sickly, instead, she was distractingly beautiful. Her sharp, slightly upturned nose and high cheekbones made her look like a Parihan. Unlike them, though, her hair was blonde, a most unusual colour; every strand of it was in place. Her eyes were magnetic. Perhaps she was the child of *Hiranyaloman Mlechchas; fair-skinned, light-eyed and light-haired foreigners who lived half a world away towards the north-west*; their violent ways and incomprehensible speech had led to the Indians calling them barbarians. But this lady was no barbarian. Quite the contrary, she was elegant, slim and petite, except for breasts that were disproportionately large for her body. She wore a classic, expensively-dyed purple *dhoti,* which shone like the waters of the Sarayu. Perhaps it was the legendary silk cloth from the east, one that only the richest could afford. The *dhoti* was tied fashionably low, exposing her flat tummy and slim, curvaceous waist. Her blouse, also made of silk, was a tiny sliver of cloth, affording a generous view of her cleavage. Her *angvastram* had deliberately been left hanging loose from a shoulder, instead of across the body. Extravagant jewellery completed the picture of excess. The only incongruity was the knife scabbard tied to her waist. She was a vision to behold.

Ram cast a quick glance at Sita. 'Who are they?'

Sita shrugged.

'Lankans,' whispered Jatayu.

Ram turned to Jatayu, crouching a few feet away. 'Are you sure?'

'Yes. The man is Raavan's younger half-brother Vibhishan, and the woman is his half-sister Shurpanakha.'

'What are they doing here?' asked Sita.

Atulya had been observing the approaching party through a hole in the wall. He turned towards Ram. 'I don't think they have come to make war. Look...' He gestured towards the hole.

Everyone looked through the peepholes. A soldier next to Vibhishan held aloft a white flag, the colour of peace. They obviously wanted to parley. The mystery was: what did they want to talk about?

'Why the hell would Raavan want to speak with us?' asked Lakshman, ever suspicious.

'According to my sources, Vibhishan and Shurpanakha don't always see eye to eye with Raavan,' said Jatayu. 'We shouldn't assume that Raavan has sent them.'

Atulya cut in. 'Apologies for disagreeing with you, Jatayu*ji*. But I cannot imagine Prince Vibhishan or Princess Shurpanakha having the courage to do something like this on their own. We must assume that they have been sent by Lord Raavan.'

'Time to stop wondering and start asking some questions,' said Lakshman. '*Dada?*'

Ram looked through the hole again, and then turned towards his people. 'We will all step out together. It will stop them from attempting something stupid.'

'That is wise,' said Jatayu.

'Come on,' said Ram, as he stepped out from behind the protective wall with his right hand raised, signifying that he meant no harm. Everyone else followed Ram's example and trooped out to meet the half-siblings of Raavan.

Vibhishan nervously stopped in his tracks the moment his eyes fell on Ram, Sita, Lakshman, and their soldiers. He looked sideways at his sister, as if uncertain as to the next course of action. But Shurpanakha had eyes only for Ram. She stared at him, unashamedly. A look of recognition flashed across a surprised Vibhishan's face when he saw Jatayu.

Ram, Lakshman and Sita walked in the lead, with Jatayu and his soldiers following close behind. As the forest-dwellers reached the Lankans, Vibhishan straightened his back, puffed up his chest, and spoke with an air of self-importance. 'We come in peace, King of Ayodhya.'

'We want peace as well,' said Ram, lowering his right hand. His people did the same. He made no comment on the 'King of Ayodhya' greeting. 'What brings you here, Prince of Lanka?'

Vibhishan preened at being recognised. 'It seems Sapt Sindhuans are not as ignorant of the world as many of us like to imagine.'

Ram smiled politely. Meanwhile, Shurpanakha pulled out a small violet kerchief and covered her nose delicately.

'Well, even I respect and understand the ways of the Sapt Sindhuans,' said Vibhishan.

Sita watched Shurpanakha, hawk-eyed, as the lady continued to stare at her husband unabashedly. Up close, it was clear that the magic of Shurpanakha's eyes lay in their startling colour: bright blue. She almost certainly had some *Hiranyaloman Mlechcha* blood. Practically nobody, east of Egypt, had blue eyes. She was bathed in fragrant perfume that overpowered the rustic, animal smell of the Panchavati camp; at least for those in her vicinity. Not overpowering enough for her, evidently. She continued to hold the stench of her surroundings at bay, with the kerchief pressed against her nose.

'Would you like to come inside, to our humble abode?' asked Ram, gesturing towards the hut.

'No, thank you, Your Highness,' said Vibhishan. 'I'm comfortable here.'

Jatayu's presence had thrown him off-guard. Vibhishan was unwilling to encounter other surprises that may lay in store for them, within the closed confines of the hut, before they had come to some negotiated terms. He *was* the brother of the enemy of the Sapt Sindhu, after all. It was safer here, out in the open; for now.

'All right then,' said Ram. 'To what do we owe the honour of a visit from the prince of golden Lanka?'

Shurpanakha spoke in a husky, alluring voice. 'Handsome one, we come to seek refuge.'

'I'm not sure I understand,' said Ram, momentarily flummoxed by the allusion to his good looks by a woman he did not know. 'I don't think we are capable of helping the relatives of…'

'Who else can we go to, O Great One?' asked Vibhishan. 'We will never be accepted in the Sapt Sindhu because we are Raavan's siblings. But we also know that there are many in the Sapt Sindhu who will not deny you. My sister and I have suffered Raavan's brutal oppression for too long. We needed to escape.'

Ram remained silent, contemplative.

'King of Ayodhya,' continued Vibhishan, 'I may be from Lanka but I am, in fact, like one of your own. I honour your ways, follow your path. I'm not like the other Lankans, blinded by Raavan's immense wealth into following his demonic path. And Shurpanakha is just like me. Don't you think you have a duty towards us, too?'

Sita cut in. 'An ancient poet once remarked, "When the axe entered the forest, the trees said to each other: do not worry, the handle in that axe is one of us".'

Shurpanakha sniggered. 'So the great descendant of Raghu lets his wife make decisions for him, is it?'

Vibhishan touched Shurpanakha's hand lightly and she fell silent. 'Queen Sita,' said Vibhishan, 'you will notice that only the handles have come here. The axe-head is in Lanka. We are truly like you. Please help us.'

Shurpanakha turned to Jatayu. It had not escaped her notice that, as usual, every man was gaping intently at her; every man, that is, except Ram and Lakshman. 'Great Malayaputra, don't you think it is in your interest to give us refuge? We could tell you more about Lanka than you already know. There will be more gold in it for you.'

Jatayu stiffened. 'We are the followers of Lord Parshu Ram! We are not interested in gold.'

'Right...' said Shurpanakha, sarcastically.

Vibhishan appealed to Lakshman. 'Wise Lakshman, please convince your brother. I'm sure you will agree with me when I say that we can be of use to you in your fight when you get back.'

'I could agree with you, Prince of Lanka,' said Lakshman, smiling, 'but then we would both be wrong.'

Vibhishan looked down and sighed.

'Prince Vibhishan,' said Ram, 'I am truly sorry but—'

Vibhishan interrupted Ram. 'Son of Dashrath, remember the battle of Mithila. My brother Raavan is your enemy. He is my enemy as well. Shouldn't that make you my friend?'

Ram kept quiet.

'Great King, we have put our lives at risk by escaping from Lanka. Can't you let us be your guests for a while? We will leave in a few days. Remember what the *Taittiriya Upanishad* says: *"Athithi Devo Bhava"*. Even the many *Smritis* say that the strong should protect the weak. All we are asking for is shelter for a few days. Please.'

Sita looked at Ram. A law had been invoked. She knew what was going to happen next. She knew Ram would not turn them away now.

'Just a few days,' pleaded Vibhishan. 'Please.'

Ram touched Vibhishan's shoulder. 'You can stay here for a few days; rest for a while, and then continue on your journey.'

Vibhishan folded his hands together into a namaste and said, 'Glory to the great clan of Raghu.'

'I think that spoilt princess fancies you,' said Sita.

Ram and Sita sat alone in their room in the second hour of the fourth *prahar*, having just finished their evening meal. Shurpanakha had complained bitterly about the food that Sita had cooked that day. Sita had told her to remain hungry if the food was not to her liking.

Ram shook his head, his eyes clearly conveying he thought this was silly. 'How can she, Sita? She knows I'm married. Why should she find me attractive?'

Sita lay down next to her husband on the bed of hay. 'You should know that you are more attractive than you realise.'

Ram frowned and laughed. 'Nonsense.'

Sita laughed as well and put her arms around him.

The guests had been staying in Panchavati with the forest-dwellers for a week now. They had not been troublesome at all, except for the Lankan princess. However, Lakshman and Jatayu remained suspicious of the Lankans. They had disarmed the visitors on the first day itself, and locked up their weapons in the camp armoury. They also maintained a strict but discreet and staggered twenty-four-hour vigil, keeping a constant watch on the guests.

Having stayed awake the previous night with his sword and warning conch shell ready by his side, a tired Lakshman had slept through the morning. He awoke in the afternoon to observe unusual activity in the camp.

As he stepped out of the hut, he came upon Jatayu and the Malayaputras emerging from the armoury with the Lankan weapons. Vibhishan and his party were ready to leave. Having collected their weaponry, they waited for Shurpanakha, who had gone to the Godavari to bathe and get ready. She had requested Sita to accompany her, for help with her clothes and hair. Sita was happy to finally be rid of the troublesome diva whose demands in this simple jungle camp were never-ending. She had readily agreed to this last request.

'Thank you for all your help, Prince Ram,' said Vibhishan.

'It was our pleasure.'

'And may I request you and your followers to not reveal to anyone where we are headed?'

'Of course.'

'Thank you,' said Vibhishan, folding his hands into a namaste.

Ram looked towards the dense forest line, beyond which lay the Godavari. He expected his wife Sita and Vibhishan's sister Shurpanakha to emerge from that direction any moment now.

Instead, a loud female scream emanated from the forest. Ram and Lakshman cast a quick glance at each other and then moved rapidly in the direction of the sound. They came to a standstill as Sita emerged from the woods, tall, regal but dripping wet and furious. She dragged a struggling Shurpanakha mercilessly by her arm. The Lankan princess' hands had been securely tied.

Lakshman immediately drew his sword, as did everyone else present. The younger prince of Ayodhya was the first to find his voice. Looking at Vibhishan accusingly, he demanded, 'What the hell is going on?'

Vibhishan couldn't take his eyes off the two women. He seemed genuinely shocked for a moment, but quickly gathered his wits and replied. 'What is your sister-in-law doing to my sister? She is the one who has clearly attacked Shurpanakha.'

'Stop this drama!' shouted Lakshman. '*Bhabhi* would not do this unless your sister attacked her first.'

Sita walked into the circle of people and let go of Shurpanakha. The Lankan princess was clearly livid and out of control. Vibhishan immediately rushed to his sister, drew a knife and cut the ropes that bound her. He whispered something into her ear. Lakshman couldn't be sure what Vibhishan said, but it sounded like 'Quiet'.

Sita turned to Ram and gestured towards Shurpanakha, as she held out some herbs in the palm of her hand. 'That pipsqueak Lankan stuffed this in my mouth as she pushed me into the river!'

Ram recognised the herbs. It was normally used to make people unconscious before conducting surgeries. He looked at Vibhishan, his piercing eyes red with anger. 'What is going on?'

Vibhishan stood up immediately, his manner placatory. 'There has obviously been some misunderstanding. My sister would never do something like that.'

'Are you suggesting that I imagined her pushing me into the water?' asked Sita, aggressively.

Vibhishan stared at Shurpanakha, who had also stood up by now. He seemed to be pleading with her to stay quiet. But the message was clearly lost on the intended recipient.

'That is a lie!' screeched Shurpanakha. 'I didn't do anything like that!'

'Are you calling me a liar?' growled Sita.

What happened next was so sudden that very few had the time to react. With frightening speed, Shurpanakha reached to her side and drew her knife. Lakshman, who was standing to the left of Sita, saw the quick movement and rushed forward, screaming, '*Bhabhi!*'

Sita quickly moved in the opposite direction to avoid the strike. In that split second, Lakshman lunged forward and banged into a charging Shurpanakha, seizing both her arms and pushing her back with all his force. The elfin princess of Lanka went flying backwards, her own hand, which held the knife, striking her face as she crashed into the Lankan soldiers who stood transfixed behind her. The knife struck her face horizontally, cutting deep into her nose. It fell from her hand as she lay sprawled on the ground, the shock having numbed any sensation of pain. As blood gushed out alarmingly, her conscious mind asserted control and the horror of it all reverberated through her being. She touched her face and looked at her blood-stained hands. She knew she would be left with deep scars on her face. And that painful surgeries would be required to remove them.

She screeched with savage hate and lunged forward again, this time going for Lakshman. Vibhishan rushed to her and caught hold of his maddened sister.

'Kill them!' screamed Shurpanakha in agony. 'Kill them all!'

'Wait!' pleaded Vibhishan, stricken with visceral fear. He knew they were outnumbered. He didn't want to die. And he feared something even worse than death. 'Wait!'

Ram held up his left hand, his fist closed tight, signalling his people to stop but be on guard. 'Leave now, prince. Or there will be hell to pay.'

'Forget what we were told!' screeched Shurpanakha. 'Kill them all!'

Ram spoke to a clearly stunned Vibhishan, who held on to a struggling Shurpanakha for all he was worth. 'Leave now, Prince Vibhishan.'

'Retreat,' whispered Vibhishan.

His soldiers began stepping back, their swords still pointed in the direction of the forest-dwellers.

'Kill them, you coward!' Shurpanakha lashed out at her brother. 'I am your sister! Avenge me!'

Vibhishan dragged a flailing Shurpanakha, his eye on Ram, mindful of any sudden movement.

'Kill them!' shouted Shurpanakha.

Vibhishan continued to pull his protesting sister away as the Lankans left the camp and escaped from Panchavati.

Ram, Lakshman and Sita stood rooted to their spot. What had happened was an unmitigated disaster.

'We cannot stay here anymore,' Jatayu stated the obvious. 'We don't have a choice. We need to flee, *now*.'

Ram looked at Jatayu.

'We have shed Lankan royal blood, even if it is that of the royal rebels,' said Jatayu. 'According to their customary law, Raavan has no choice but to respond. It would be the same among many Sapt Sindhu royals as well, isn't it? Raavan will come. Have no doubt about that. Vibhishan is a coward, but Raavan and Kumbhakarna aren't. They will come with thousands of soldiers. This will be worse than Mithila. There it was a battle between soldiers; a part and parcel of war; they understood that. But here it is personal. His sister, a member of his family, has been attacked. Blood was shed. His honour will demand retribution.'

Lakshman stiffened. 'But I didn't attack her. She—'

'That's not how Raavan will see it,' interrupted Jatayu. 'He will not quibble with you over the details, Prince Lakshman. We need to run. Right now.'

Around thirty warriors sat together in a small clearing in the forest, briskly shovelling food into their mouths. They appeared to be in a tearing hurry. All of them were dressed alike: a long brownish-black cloak covered their bodies, held together across the waist by a thick cord. The cloaks could not conceal the fact that each carried a sword. The men were all unnaturally fair-skinned, an unusual sight in the hot plains of India. Their hooked noses, neatly beaded full beards, sharp foreheads, lengthy locks emerging from under square white hats, and drooping moustaches made it clear who these people were: Parihans.

Pariha was a fabled land beyond the western borders of India. It was the land that was home to the previous Mahadev, Lord Rudra.

The most intriguing member of this motley group was its leader, clearly a Naga. He too was fair-skinned, just like the Parihans. But in every other respect, he stood apart from them. He was not dressed like them. He was, in fact, dressed like an Indian: in a *dhoti* and *angvastram*, both dyed saffron. An outgrowth jutted out from his lower back, almost like a tail. It flapped in constant rhythm, as though it had a mind of its own. The hirsute Naga leader of the Parihans was very tall. His massive build and sturdy musculature gave him an awe-inspiring presence and a godly aura. He could probably break an unfortunate's back with his bare hands. Unlike most Nagas, he did not cover his face with a mask or his body with a hooded robe.

'We have to move quickly,' said the leader.

His nose was flat, pressed against his face. His beard and facial hair surrounded the periphery of his face, encircling it with neat precision. Strangely though, the area above and below his mouth was silken smooth and hairless; it had a puffed appearance and was light pink in colour. His lips were a thin, barely noticeable line. Thick eyebrows drew a sharp curve above captivating eyes that radiated intelligence and a meditative calm; they also held a promise of brutal violence, if required. His furrowed brow gave him a naturally intellectual air. It almost seemed like the Almighty had taken the face of a monkey and placed it on a man's head.

'Yes, My Lord,' said a Parihan. 'If you could give us a few minutes more… The men have been marching continuously and some rest will…'

'There is no time for rest!' growled the leader. 'I have given my word to Guru Vashishtha! Raavan cannot be allowed to reach them before we do! We need to find them now! Tell the men to hurry!'

The Parihan rushed off to carry out the orders. Another Parihan, who had finished his meal, walked up to the Naga. 'My Lord, the men need to know: Who is the primary person?'

The leader didn't hesitate even for a second. 'Both. They are both vital. Princess Sita is important to the Malayaputras, and Prince Ram is to us.'

'Yes, Lord Hanuman.'

—— |抗| 🐟 ☼ ——

They had been on the run for thirty days. Racing east through the *Dandakaranya*, they had moved a reasonable distance parallel to the Godavari, so that they couldn't be easily spotted or tracked. But they couldn't afford to stray too far from the tributary rivers or other water bodies, for the best chance of hunting animals would be lost.

Ram and Lakshman had just hunted a deer and were making their way back to the temporary camp through the dense jungle. They carried a long staff between them, Ram in front, carrying one end on his shoulder, and Lakshman behind, balancing the other. The deer's body dangled from the wooden pole.

Lakshman was arguing with Ram. 'But why do you think it's irrational to think Bharat *Dada* could…'

'Shhh,' said Ram, holding his hand up to silence Lakshman. 'Listen.'

Lakshman strained his ears. A chill ran down his spine. Ram turned towards Lakshman with terror writ large on his face. They had both heard it. *A forceful scream!* It was Sita. The distance made faint her frantic struggle. But it was clearly Sita. She was calling out to her husband.

Ram and Lakshman dropped the deer and dashed forward desperately. They were still some distance away from their temporary camp.

Sita's voice could be heard above the din of the disturbed birds.

'… Raaam!'

They were close enough now to hear the sounds of battle as metal clashed with metal.

Ram screamed as he ran frantically through the forest. 'Sitaaaa!'

Lakshman drew his sword, ready for battle.

'… Raaaam!'

'Leave her alone!' shouted Ram, cutting through the dense foliage, racing ahead.

'… Raaam!'

Ram gripped his bow tight. They were just a few minutes from their camp. 'Sitaaa!'

'… Raa…'

Sita's voice stopped mid-syllable. Trying not to imagine the worst, Ram kept running, his heart pounding desperately, his mind clouded with worry.

They heard the loud whump, whump of rotor blades. It was Raavan's legendary *Pushpak Vimaan*, his *flying vehicle*.

'Nooo!' screamed Ram, wrenching his bow forward as he ran. Tears were streaming down his face.

The brothers broke through to the clearing that was their temporary camp. It stood completely destroyed. There was blood everywhere.

'Sitaaa!'

Ram looked up and shot an arrow at the *Pushpak Vimaan*, which was rapidly ascending into the sky. It was a shot of impotent rage, for the flying vehicle was already soaring high above.

'Sitaaa!'

Lakshman frantically searched the camp. Bodies of dead soldiers were strewn all over. But there was no Sita.

'Pri... nce... Ram...'

Ram recognised that feeble voice. He rushed forward to find the bloodied and mutilated body of the Naga.

'Jatayu!'

The badly wounded Jatayu struggled to speak. 'He's...'

'What?'

'Raavan's... kidnapped... her.'

Ram looked up enraged at the speck moving rapidly away from them. He screamed in anger, 'SITAAAA!'

'Prince...'

Jatayu could feel life slipping away. Using his last reserves of will, he raised his body, reached his hand out and pulled Ram towards him.

With his dying breaths, Jatayu whispered, 'Get ... her back ... I ... failed... She's important ... Lady Sita ... must be saved ... Lady Sita ... must be saved ... Vishnu ... Lady Sita ...'

... to be continued

Other Titles by Amish

The Shiva Trilogy

The fastest-selling book series in the history of Indian publishing

THE IMMORTALS OF MELUHA
(Book 1 of the Trilogy)

1900 BC. What modern Indians mistakenly call the Indus Valley Civilisation, the inhabitants of that period knew as the land of Meluha – a near perfect empire created many centuries earlier by Lord Ram. Now their primary river Saraswati is drying, and they face terrorist attacks from their enemies from the east. Will their prophesied hero, the Neelkanth, emerge to destroy evil?

THE SECRET OF THE NAGAS
(Book 2 of the Trilogy)

The sinister Naga warrior has killed his friend Brahaspati and now stalks his wife Sati. Shiva, who is the prophesied destroyer of evil, will not rest till he finds his demonic adversary. His thirst for revenge will lead him to the door of the Nagas, the serpent people. Fierce battles will be fought and unbelievable secrets revealed in the second part of the Shiva trilogy.

THE OATH OF THE VAYUPUTRAS
(Book 3 of the Trilogy)

Shiva reaches the Naga capital, Panchavati, and prepares for a holy war against his true enemy. The Neelkanth must not fail, no matter what the cost. In his desperation, he reaches out to the Vayuputras. Will he succeed? And what will be the real cost of battling Evil? Read the concluding part of this bestselling series to find out.

Ram Chandra Series

The second fastest-selling book series in the history of Indian publishing

SITA – WARRIOR OF MITHILA
(Book 2 of the Series)

An abandoned baby is found in a field. She is adopted by the ruler of Mithila, a powerless kingdom, ignored by all. Nobody believes this child will amount to much. But they are wrong. For she is no ordinary girl. She is Sita. Through an innovative multi-linear narrative, Amish takes you deeper into the epic world of the Ram Chandra Series.

RAAVAN – ENEMY OF ARYAVARTA
(Book 3 of the Series)

Raavan is determined to be a giant among men, to conquer, plunder, and seize the greatness that he thinks is his right. He is a man of contrasts, of brutal violence and scholarly knowledge. A man who will love without reward and kill without remorse. In this, the third book in the Ram Chandra Series, Amish sheds light on Raavan, the king of Lanka. Is he the greatest villain in history or just a man in a dark place, all the time?

Indic Chronicles
LEGEND OF SUHELDEV

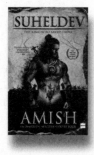

Repeated attacks by Mahmud of Ghazni have weakened India's northern regions. Then the Turks raid and destroy one of the holiest temples in the land: the magnificent Lord Shiva temple at Somnath. At this most desperate of times, a warrior rises to defend the nation. King Suheldev —fierce rebel, charismatic leader, inclusive patriot. Read this epic adventure of courage and heroism that recounts the story of that lionhearted warrior and the magnificent Battle of Bahraich.

Non-fiction

IMMORTAL INDIA

Explore India with the country's storyteller, Amish, who helps you understand it like never before, through a series of sharp articles, nuanced speeches and intelligent debates. In *Immortal India*, Amish lays out the vast landscape of an ancient culture with a fascinatingly modern outlook.

DHARMA – DECODING THE EPICS FOR A MEANINGFUL LIFE

In this genre-bending book, the first of a series, Amish and Bhavna dive into the priceless treasure trove of the ancient Indian epics, as well as the vast and complex universe of Amish's Meluha, to explore some of the key concepts of Indian philosophy. Within this book are answers to our many philosophical questions, offered through simple and wise interpretations of our favourite stories.

Sita

Amish is a 1974-born, IIM (Kolkata)-educated banker-turned-author. The success of his debut book, *The Immortals of Meluha* (Book 1 of the Shiva Trilogy), encouraged him to give up his career in financial services to focus on writing. Besides being an author, he is also an Indian-government diplomat, a host for TV documentaries, and a film producer.

Amish is passionate about history, mythology and philosophy, finding beauty and meaning in all world religions. His books have sold more than 6 million copies and have been translated into over 20 languages. His Shiva Trilogy is the fastest selling and his Ram Chandra Series the second fastest selling book series in Indian publishing history. You can connect with Amish here:

- www.facebook.com/authoramish
- www.instagram.com/authoramish
- www.twitter.com/authoramish

Other Titles by Amish

SHIVA TRILOGY

The fastest-selling book series in the history of Indian publishing

The Immortals of Meluha (Book 1 of the Trilogy)

The Secret of the Nagas (Book 2 of the Trilogy)

The Oath of the Vayuputras (Book 3 of the Trilogy)

RAM CHANDRA SERIES

The second fastest-selling book series in the history of Indian publishing

Ram – Scion of Ikshvaku (Book 1 of the Series)

Raavan – Enemy of Aryavarta (Book 3 of the Series)

War of Lanka (Book 4 in the Series)

INDIC CHRONICLES

Legend of Suheldev

NON-FICTION

Immortal India: Young Country, Timeless Civilisation

Dharma: Decoding the Epics for a Meaningful Life

'{Amish's} writings have generated immense curiosity about India's rich past and culture.'

– Narendra Modi
(Honourable Prime Minister, India)

'{Amish's} writing introduces the youth to ancient value systems while pricking and satisfying their curiosity…'

– Sri Sri Ravi Shankar
(Spiritual Leader & Founder, Art of Living Foundation)

'{Amish's writing is} riveting, absorbing and informative.'

– Amitabh Bachchan
(Actor & Living Legend)

'{Amish's writing is} a fine blend of history and myth…gripping and unputdownable.'

– BBC

'Thoughtful and deep, Amish, more than any author, represents the New India.'

– Vir Sanghvi
(Senior Journalist & Columnist)

'Amish's mythical imagination mines the past and taps into the possibilities of the future. His book series, archetypal and stirring, unfolds the deepest recesses of the soul as well as our collective consciousness.'

– Deepak Chopra
(World-renowned spiritual guru and bestselling author)

www.authoramish.com

'{Amish is} one of the most original thinkers of his generation.'
– Arnab Goswami
(Senior Journalist & MD, Republic TV)

'Amish has a fine eye for detail and a compelling narrative style.'
– Dr. Shashi Tharoor
(Member of Parliament & Author)

'{Amish has} a deeply thoughtful mind with an unusual, original, and fascinating view of the past.'
– Shekhar Gupta
(Senior Journalist & Columnist)

'To understand the New India, you need to read Amish.'
– Swapan Dasgupta
(Member of Parliament & Senior Journalist)

'Through all of Amish's books flows a current of liberal progressive ideology: about gender, about caste, about discrimination of any kind... He is the only Indian bestselling writer with true philosophical depth – his books are all backed by tremendous research and deep thought.'
– Sandipan Deb
(Senior Journalist & Editorial Director, Swarajya)

'Amish's influence goes beyond his books, his books go beyond literature, his literature is steeped in philosophy, which is anchored in bhakti, which powers his love for India.'
– Gautam Chikermane
(Senior Journalist & Author)

'Amish is a literary phenomenon.'

– Anil Dharker
(Senior Journalist & Author)

Sita
Warrior of Mithila

Book 2
of the
Ram Chandra Series

Amish

HarperCollins *Publishers* India

www.authoramish.com

First published in 2017

This edition published in India by HarperCollins *Publishers* 2022
4th Floor, Tower A, Building No. 10, Phase II, DLF Cyber City,
Gurugram, Haryana – 122002
www.harpercollins.co.in

2 4 6 8 10 9 7 5 3 1

P-ISBN: 978-93-5629-091-4
E-ISBN: 978-93-5629-094-5

This is a work of fiction and all characters and incidents described in this book are
the product of the author's imagination. Any resemblance to actual persons, living
or dead, is entirely coincidental.

Amish Tripathi asserts the moral right
to be identified as the author of this work.

Typeset by Sürya, New Delhi

Printed and bound at
Thomson Press (India) Ltd

MIX
Paper
FSC® C010615

This book is produced from independently certified FSC® paper
to ensure responsible forest management.

To Himanshu Roy
My brother-in-law,
A man who exemplifies the ancient Indian path of Balance,
A proud Lord Ganesh devotee who also respects
all other faiths,
A sincere Indian patriot,
A man with wisdom, courage, and honour.
A hero.

Om Namah Shivāya
The universe bows to Lord Shiva.
I bow to Lord Shiva.

From the Adbhuta Rāmāyana
(credited to Maharishi Valmikiji)

Yadā yadā hi dharmasya glanirbhavati suvrata |
Abhyutthānamadharmasya tadā prakṛtisambhavaḥ ||

O keeper of righteous vows, remember this,
Whenever dharma is in decline,
Or there is an upsurge of adharma;
The Sacred Feminine will incarnate.

She will defend dharma.
She will protect us.

List of Characters and Important Tribes
(In Alphabetic Order)

Arishtanemi: Military chief of the Malayaputras; right-hand man of Vishwamitra

Ashwapati: King of the northwestern kingdom of Kekaya; father of Kaikeyi and a loyal ally of Dashrath

Bharat: Ram's half-brother; son of Dashrath and Kaikeyi

Dashrath: Chakravarti king of Kosala and emperor of the Sapt Sindhu; husband of Kaushalya, Kaikeyi, and Sumitra; father of Ram, Bharat, Lakshman and Shatrughan

Hanuman: Radhika's cousin; son of Vayu Kesari; a Naga and a member of the Vayuputra tribe

Janak: King of Mithila; father of Sita and Urmila

Jatayu: A captain of the Malayaputra tribe; Naga friend of Sita and Ram

Kaikeyi: Daughter of King Ashwapati of Kekaya; the second and favourite wife of Dashrath; mother of Bharat

Kaushalya: Daughter of King Bhanuman of South Kosala and his wife Maheshwari; the eldest queen of Dashrath; mother of Ram

Kumbhakarna: Raavan's brother; also a Naga

Kushadhwaj: King of Sankashya; younger brother of Janak

Lakshman: One of the twin sons of Dashrath; born to Sumitra; faithful to Ram; later married to Urmila

Malayaputras: The tribe left behind by Lord Parshu Ram, the sixth Vishnu

Manthara: The richest merchant of the Sapt Sindhu

Mara: An independent assassin for hire

Naarad: A trader from Lothal; Hanuman's friend

Nagas: Human beings born with deformities

Raavan: King of Lanka; brother of Vibhishan, Shurpanakha and Kumbhakarna

Radhika: Sita's friend; Hanuman's cousin

Ram: Son of Emperor Dashrath of Ayodhya (capital city of Kosala) and his eldest wife Kaushalya; eldest of four brothers, later married to Sita

Samichi: Police and protocol chief of Mithila

Shatrughan: Twin brother of Lakshman; son of Dashrath and Sumitra

Shurpanakha: Half-sister of Raavan

Shvetaketu: Sita's teacher

Sita: Adopted daughter of King Janak and Queen Sunaina of Mithila; also the prime minister of Mithila; later married to Ram

Sumitra: Daughter of the king of Kashi; the third wife of Dashrath; mother of the twins Lakshman and Shatrughan

Sunaina: Queen of Mithila; mother of Sita and Urmila

Vali: The king of Kishkindha

Varun Ratnakar: Radhika's father; chief of the Valmikis

Vashishtha: Raj guru, the royal priest of Ayodhya; teacher of the four Ayodhya princes

Vayu Kesari: Hanuman's father; Radhika's uncle

Vayuputras: The tribe left behind by Lord Rudra, the previous Mahadev

Vibhishan: Half-brother of Raavan

Vishwamitra: Chief of the Malayaputras, the tribe left behind by Lord Parshu Ram, the sixth Vishnu; also temporary guru of Ram and Lakshman

Urmila: Younger sister of Sita; blood-daughter of Janak and Sunaina; later married to Lakshman

Note on the Narrative Structure

Thank you for picking up this book and giving me the most important thing you can share: your time.

I know this book has taken long to release, and for that I offer my apologies. But when I tell you the narrative structure of the Ram Chandra Series, perhaps you will understand why it took so long.

I have been inspired by a storytelling technique called hyperlink, which some call the multilinear narrative. In such a narrative, there are many characters; and a connection brings them all together. The three main characters in the Ram Chandra Series are Ram, Sita, and Raavan. Each character has life experiences which mould who they are and their stories converge with the kidnapping of Sita. And each has their own adventure and riveting back-story.

So, while the first book explored the tale of Ram, the second and third will offer a glimpse into the adventures of Sita and then Raavan respectively, before all three stories merge from the fourth book onwards into a single story.

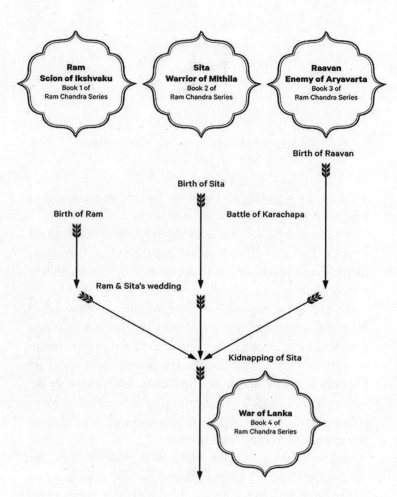

I knew it would be a complicated and time consuming affair, but I must confess, it was thoroughly exciting. I hope this will be as rewarding and thrilling an experience for you as it was for me. Understanding Sita and Raavan as characters helped me inhabit their worlds and explore the maze of plots and stories that make this epic come alive. I feel truly blessed for this.

Since this was the plan, I had left clues in the first book (**Ram – Scion of Ikshvaku**) which will tie up with the stories in the second and third books. Needless to say, there are surprises and twists in store for you in books 2 and 3 as well!

In fact, there was a very big clue in the last paragraph of **Ram – Scion of Ikshvaku**. Some had caught on to it. And for those who didn't, a big revelation awaits you in the first chapter of the second book, **Sita – Warrior of Mithila**.

I hope you like reading **Sita – Warrior of Mithila**. Do tell me what you think of it, by sending me messages on my Facebook, Instagram, or Twitter accounts given below.

Love,
Amish

www.facebook.com/authoramish
www.instagram.com/authoramish
www.twitter.com/authoramish

Acknowledgements

The acknowledgments written below were composed when the book was published in 2017. I must also acknowledge those that are publishing this edition of **Sita-Warrior of Mithila**. *The team at HarperCollins: Swati, Shabnam, Akriti, Gokul, Vikas, Rahul, and Udayan, led by the brilliant Ananth. Looking forward to this new journey with them.*

***

When one writes, one pours one's soul out on paper. They say it takes courage to do that. They also say that courage comes only when one knows that many stand with him. I'd like to acknowledge those who stand with me: Who give me courage: Who make me realise that I am not alone.

Neel, my 8-year-old son, my pride and joy. He reads a lot already. I can't wait for him to read my books!

Preeti, my wife; Bhavna, my sister; Himanshu, my brother-in-law; Anish and Ashish, my brothers, for all their inputs to the story. They read the first draft, usually as each chapter is written. And I discuss many of the philosophies with them in detail. I also wrote much of this book in Anish and Meeta's house in Delhi. I must have done something good in my previous life to be blessed with these relationships.

The rest of my family: Usha, Vinay, Meeta, Donetta, Shernaz, Smita, Anuj, Ruta. For their consistent faith and love.

Sharvani, my editor. She is as committed to my stories as I am. She is as stubborn as I am. She reads a lot, just like I do. She's as technologically-challenged as I am. We must have been siblings in a previous life!

Gautam, Krishnakumar, Neha, Deepthi, Satish, Sanghamitra, Jayanthi, Sudha, Vipin, Srivats, Shatrughan, Sarita, Arunima, Raju, Sanyog, Naveen, Jaisankar, Sateesh, Divya, Madhu, Sathya Sridhar, Christina, Preeti and the fantastic team at Westland, my publisher. In my humble opinion, they are the best publisher in India.

Anuj, my agent. A friend and a partner from the very beginning.

Abhijeet, an old friend and senior corporate executive, who worked with Westland to drive the marketing efforts for this book. The man is brilliant!

Mohan and Mehul, my personal managers, who manage everything so that I can have the time to write.

Abhijit, Sonali, Shruti, Roy, Kassandra, Joshua, Purva, Nalin, Nivedita, Neha, Nehal, and the team at Sideways, an exceptional company that applies creativity across all aspects of a business. Sideways helped formulate the business and marketing strategy for the book. They've also made most of the marketing material, including the cover. Which I think is one of the best covers I have ever seen. They were helped in the cover design by the Arthat team (Jitendra, Deval, Johnson) who are thoroughly outstanding designers.

Mayank, Priyanka Jain, Deepika, Naresh, Vishaal, Danish and the Moe's Art team, who have driven media relations and marketing alliances for the book. They have been strong partners and among the best agencies I have worked with.

Hemal, Neha and the Oktobuzz team, who have helped manage many of the social media activities for the book. Hardworking, super smart and intensely committed. They are an asset to any team.

Mrunalini and Vrushali, Sanskrit scholars, who work with me on research. My discussions with them are enlightening. What I learn from them helps me develop many theories which go into the books.

And last, but certainly not the least, you, the reader. It is only due to your support that I have been given the privilege of living the kind of life I do; where I can do what I love and actually earn my living from it. I can never thank you enough!

Chapter 1

3400 BCE, somewhere near the Godavari River, India

Sita cut quickly and efficiently, slicing through the thick leaf stems with her sharp knife. The dwarf banana trees were as tall as she was. She did not need to stretch. She stopped and looked at her handiwork. Then she cast a look at Makrant, the Malayaputra soldier, a short distance away. He had cut down perhaps half the number of leaves that Sita had.

The weather was calm. Just a little while ago, the wind had been howling through this part of the forest. Unseasonal rain had lashed the area. Sita and Makrant had stood under a thick canopy of trees to save themselves from the rain. The winds had been so loud that it had been almost impossible for them to talk to each other. And just as suddenly, calm had descended. The rain and winds had vanished. They'd quickly headed to a patch of the woods with an abundance of dwarf banana trees. For the entire purpose of the excursion was to find these leaves.

'That's enough, Makrant,' said Sita.

Makrant turned around. The wetness had made it hard to cut the leaf stems. Under the circumstances, he had thought that he had done a good job. Now, he looked at the stack of leaves by Sita's side. And then down at his own much smaller pile. He smiled sheepishly.

Sita smiled broadly in return. 'That's more than enough. Let's go back to the camp. Ram and Lakshman should be returning from their hunt soon. Hopefully, they would have found something.'

Sita, along with her husband Prince Ram of Ayodhya and her brother-in-law Lakshman, had been racing through the *Dandakaranya*, or forest of Dandak, to escape the expected vengeance of the demon-king of Lanka, Raavan. Captain Jatayu, leading a small company of the Malayaputra tribe, had sworn to protect the three Ayodhya royals. He had strongly advised that flight was the only available course of action. Raavan would certainly send troops to avenge his sister, Princess Shurpanakha, who had been injured by Lakshman.

Secrecy was essential. So, they were cooking their food in pits dug deep into the ground. For fire, they used a specific type of coal — anthracite. It let out smokeless flames. For abundant caution, the sunk cooking pot was covered with a thick layer of banana leaves. It ensured that no smoke escaped even by accident. For that could give their position away. It was for this reason that Sita and Makrant had been cutting down banana leaves. It was Sita's turn to cook.

Makrant insisted on carrying the larger pile, and she let him. It made the Malayaputra soldier feel like he was balancing his contribution. But it was this act that would eventually prove fatal for poor Makrant.

Sita heard it first. A sound that would have been inaudible a little while ago, with the howling winds. It was unmistakable now: the menacing creak of a bow being stretched. A common bow. Many of the more accomplished soldiers and senior officers used the more expensive composite bows. But the frontline soldiers used the common variety, made entirely of wood. These bows were usually more rigid. And, they made a distinct sound when stretched.

'Makrant, duck!' screamed Sita, dropping the leaves as she leapt to the ground.

Makrant responded quickly enough, but the heavier load made him trip. An arrow shot in quickly, slamming into his right shoulder as he fell forward. Before he could react, a second arrow struck his throat. A lucky shot.

Sita rolled as she fell to the ground and quickly steadied herself behind a tree. She stayed low, her back against the tree, protected for now. She looked to her right. The unfortunate Makrant lay on the ground, drowning rapidly in his own blood. The arrow point had exited through the back of his neck. He would soon be dead.

Sita cursed in anger. And then realised it was a waste of energy. She began to breathe deeply. Calming her heart down. Paying attention. She looked around carefully. Nobody ahead of her. The arrows had come from the other direction, obscured by the tree that protected her. She knew there had to be at least two enemies. There was no way a single archer could have shot two arrows in such rapid succession.

She looked at Makrant again. He had stopped moving. His soul had moved on. The jungle was eerily quiet. It was almost impossible to believe that just a few short moments ago, brutal violence had been unleashed.

Farewell, brave Makrant. May your soul find purpose once again.

She caught snatches of commands whispered in the distance. 'Go to ... Lord Kumbhakarna ... Tell ... she's ... here ...'

She heard the hurried footsteps of someone rushing away.

There was probably just one enemy now. She looked down at the earth and whispered, 'Help me, mother. Help me.'

She drew her knife from the scabbard tied horizontally to the small of her back. She closed her eyes. She couldn't afford to look around the tree and expose herself. She would probably be shot instantly. Her eyes were useless. She had to rely on her ears. There were great archers who could shoot arrows by relying on sound. But very few could throw knives at the source of a sound. Sita was one of those very few.

She heard a loud yet surprisingly gentle voice. 'Come out, Princess Sita. We don't want to hurt you. It's better if …'

The voice stopped mid-sentence. It would not be heard ever again. For there was a knife buried in the throat that had been the source of that voice. Sita had, without bringing herself into view, turned quickly and flung the knife with unerring and deadly accuracy. The Lankan soldier was momentarily surprised as the knife thumped into his throat. He died in no time. Just like Makrant had, drowning in his own blood.

Sita waited. She had to be sure there was no one else. She had no other weapon. But her enemies didn't know that. She listened intently. Hearing no sound, she threw herself to the ground, rolling rapidly behind low shrubs. Still no sign of anyone.

Move! Move! There's nobody else!

Sita quickly rose to her feet and sprinted to the slain Lankan, surprised that his bow was not nocked with an arrow. She tried to pull her knife out, but it was lodged too deep in the dead Lankan's vertebra. It refused to budge.

The camp is in trouble! Move!

Sita picked up the Lankan's quiver. It contained a few arrows. She quickly tied it around her back and shoulder. She lifted the bow. And ran. Ran hard! Towards the temporary camp. She had to kill the other Lankan soldier before he reached his team and warned them.

— ᚛ᚉ —

The temporary camp showed signs of a massive struggle. Most of the Malayaputra soldiers, except Jatayu and two others, were already dead. Lying in pools of blood. They had been ruthlessly massacred. Jatayu was also badly injured. Blood seeped out from numerous wounds that covered his body. Some made by blades, some by fists. His arms were tied tightly behind his back. Two Lankan soldiers held him up in a tight grip. A giant of a man loomed in front, questioning the great Naga.

Naga was the name given to people of the Sapt Sindhu born with deformities. Jatayu's malformation gave his face the appearance of a vulture.

The other two Malayaputras knelt on the ground, also bloodied. Their hands were similarly tied at the back. Three Lankan soldiers surrounded each one, while two more held them down. The Lankan swords were dripping with blood.

Raavan and his younger brother, Kumbhakarna, stood at a distance. Looking intently at the interrogation. Focused. Their hands clean of any blood.

'Answer me, Captain,' barked the Lankan. 'Where are they?'

Jatayu shook his head vehemently. His lips were sealed.

The Lankan leaned within an inch of the Naga's ear and whispered, 'You were one of us, Jatayu. You were loyal to Lord Raavan once.'

Jatayu cast a malevolent look at the Lankan. His smouldering eyes gave the reply.

The Lankan continued. 'We can forget the past. Tell us what we want to know. And come back to Lanka with honour. This is the word of a Lankan. This is the word of Captain Khara.'

Jatayu looked away and stared into the distance. Anger fading. A blank expression on his face. As if his mind was somewhere else.

The Lankan interrogator signalled one of his soldiers.

'As you command, Captain Khara,' said the soldier, wiping his sword clean on his forearm band and slipping it back into his scabbard. He walked up to an injured Malayaputra, and drew out his serrated knife. He positioned himself behind the youth, yanked his head back and placed the knife against his throat. Then he looked at Khara, awaiting the order.

Khara took hold of Jatayu's head such that his eyes stared directly at his fellow Malayaputra. The knife at his throat.

'You may not care for your own life, Captain Jatayu,' said Khara, 'but don't you want to save at least two of your soldiers?'

The Malayaputra looked at Jatayu and shouted, 'I am ready to die, my Captain! Don't say anything!'

The Lankan hit the young soldier's head with the knife hilt. His body slouched and then straightened again with courage. The blade swiftly returned to his throat.

Khara spoke with silky politeness, 'Come on, Captain. Save your soldier's life. Tell us where they are.'

'You will never catch them!' growled Jatayu. 'The three of them are long gone!'

Khara laughed. 'The two princes of Ayodhya can keep going, for all I care. We are only interested in the Vishnu.'

Jatayu was shocked. *How do they know?*

'Where is the Vishnu?' asked Khara. 'Where is she?'

Jatayu's lips began to move, but only in prayer. He was praying for the soul of his brave soldier.

Khara gave a curt nod.

Jatayu suddenly straightened and loudly rent the air with the Malayaputra cry. *'Jai Parshu Ram!'*

'Jai Parshu Ram!' shouted both the Malayaputras. The fear of death could not touch them.

The Lankan pressed the blade into the throat of the Malayaputra. Slowly. He slid the serrated knife to the side, inflicting maximum pain. Blood spurted out in a shower. As the youth collapsed to the ground, life slowly ebbing out of him, Jatayu whispered within the confines of his mind.

Farewell, my brave brother …

— ꛱꛰ —

Sita slowed as she approached the camp. She had already killed the other Lankan soldier. He lay some distance away. An arrow pierced in his heart. She had grabbed his arrows and added them to her quiver. She hid behind a tree and surveyed the camp. Lankan soldiers were everywhere. Probably more than a hundred.

All the Malayaputra soldiers were dead. All except Jatayu. Two lay close to him, their heads arched at odd angles. Surrounded by large pools of blood. Jatayu was on his knees, held by two Lankans. His hands were tied behind his back. Brutalised, injured and bleeding. But not broken. He was defiantly staring into the distance. Khara stood near him, his knife placed on Jatayu's upper arm. He ran his knife gently along the triceps, cutting into the flesh, drawing blood.

Sita looked at Khara and frowned. *I know him. Where have I seen him before?*

Khara smiled as he ran the knife back along the bloodied line he had just drawn, slicing deep into some sinew.

'Answer me,' said Khara, as he slid the knife along Jatayu's cheek this time, drawing some more blood. 'Where is she?'

Jatayu spat at him. 'Kill me quickly. Or kill me slowly. You will not get anything from me.'

Khara raised his knife in anger, about to strike and finish the job. It was not to be. An arrow whizzed in and struck his hand. The knife fell to the ground as he screamed aloud.

Raavan and his brother Kumbhakarna whirled around, startled. Many Lankan soldiers rushed in and formed a protective cordon around the two royals. Kumbhakarna grabbed Raavan's arm to restrain his impulsive elder brother.

Other soldiers raised their bows and pointed their arrows in the direction of Sita. A loud 'Don't shoot!' was heard from Kumbhakarna. The bows were swiftly lowered.

Khara broke the shaft, leaving the arrowhead buried in his hand. It would stem the blood for a while. He looked into the impenetrable line of trees the arrow had emerged from, and scoffed in disdain. 'Who shot that? The long-suffering prince? His oversized brother? Or the Vishnu herself?'

A stunned Sita stood rooted to the spot. *Vishnu?! How do the Lankans know? Who betrayed me?!*

She marshalled her mind into the present moment. This was not the time for distractions.

She moved quickly, without a sound, to another location. *They must not know that I'm alone.*

'Come out and fight like real warriors!' challenged Khara.

Sita was satisfied with her new position. It was some distance away from where she had shot her first arrow. She slowly pulled another arrow out of her quiver, nocked it on the bowstring and took aim. In the Lankan army, if the commander fell, the rest of the force was known to quickly retreat. But

Raavan was well protected by his soldiers, their shields raised high. She could not find an adequate line of sight.

Wish Ram was here. He would have gotten an arrow through somehow.

Sita decided to launch a rapid-fire attack on the soldiers to create an opening. She fired five arrows in quick succession. Five Lankans went down. But the others did not budge. The cordon around Raavan remained resolute. Ready to fall for their king.

Raavan remained protected.

Some soldiers began to run in her direction. She quickly moved to a new location.

As she took position, she checked the quiver. Three arrows left.

Damn!

Sita deliberately stepped on a twig. Some of the soldiers rushed towards the sound. She quickly moved again, hoping to find a breach in the protective circle of men around Raavan. But Khara was a lot smarter than she had suspected.

The Lankan stepped back and, using his uninjured left hand, pulled out a knife from the sole of his shoe. He moved behind Jatayu and held the knife to the Naga's throat.

With a maniacal smile playing on his lips, Khara taunted, 'You could have escaped. But you didn't. So I'm betting you are among those hiding behind the trees, *great* Vishnu.' Khara laid sarcastic emphasis on the word 'great'. 'And, you want to protect those who worship you. So inspiring... so touching ...'

Khara pretended to wipe away a tear.

Sita stared at the Lankan with unblinking eyes.

Khara continued, 'So I have an offer. Step forward. Tell your husband and that giant brother-in-law of yours to also step forward. And we will let this captain live. We will even let the two sorry Ayodhya princes leave unharmed. All we want is your surrender.'

Sita remained stationary. Silent.

Khara grazed the knife slowly along Jatayu's neck, leaving behind a thin red line. He spoke in a sing-song manner, 'I don't have all day ...'

Suddenly, Jatayu struck backwards with his head, hitting Khara in his groin. As the Lankan doubled up in pain, Jatayu screamed, 'Run! Run away, My Lady! I am not worth your life!'

Three Lankan soldiers moved in and pushed Jatayu to the ground. Khara cursed loudly as he got back on his feet, still bent over to ease the pain. After a few moments, he inched towards the Naga and kicked him hard. He surveyed the treeline, turning in every direction that the arrows had been fired from. All the while, he kept kicking Jatayu again and again. He bent and roughly pulled Jatayu to his feet. Sita could see the captive now. Clearly.

This time Khara held Jatayu's head firmly with his injured right hand, to prevent any headbutting. The sneer was back on his face. He held the knife with his other hand. He placed it at the Naga's throat. 'I can cut the jugular here and your precious captain will be dead in just a few moments, great Vishnu.' He moved the knife to the Malayaputra's abdomen. 'Or, he can bleed to death slowly. All of you have some time to think about it.'

Sita was still. She had just three arrows left. It would be foolhardy to try anything. But she could not let Jatayu die. He had been like a brother to her.

'All we want is the Vishnu,' yelled Khara. 'Let her surrender and the rest of you can leave. You have my word. You have the word of a Lankan!'

'Let him go!' screamed Sita, still hidden behind the trees.

'Step forward and surrender,' said Khara, holding the knife to Jatayu's abdomen. 'And we will let him go.'

Sita looked down and closed her eyes. Her shoulders slumped with helpless rage. And then, without giving herself any time for second thoughts, she stepped out. But not before her instincts made her nock an arrow on the bow, ready to fire.

'Great Vishnu,' sniggered Khara, letting go of Jatayu for a moment, and running his hand along an ancient scar at the back of his head. Stirring a not-so-forgotten memory. 'So kind of you to join us. Where is your husband and his giant brother?'

Sita didn't answer. Some Lankan soldiers began moving slowly towards her. She noticed that their swords were sheathed. They were carrying *lathis, long bamboo sticks*, which were good enough to injure but not to kill. She stepped forward and lowered the bow. 'I am surrendering. Let Captain Jatayu go.'

Khara laughed softly as he pushed the knife deep into Jatayu's abdomen. Gently. Slowly. He cut through the liver, a kidney, never stopping …

'Nooo!' screamed Sita. She raised her bow and shot an arrow deep into Khara's eye. It punctured the socket and lodged itself in his brain, killing him instantly.

'I want her alive!' screamed Kumbhakarna from behind the protective Lankan cordon.

More soldiers joined those already moving toward Sita, their bamboo *lathis* held high.

'Raaaam!' shouted Sita, as she pulled another arrow from her quiver, quickly nocked and shot it, bringing another Lankan down instantly.

It did not slow the pace of the others. They kept rushing forward.

Sita shot another arrow. Her last. One more Lankan sank to the ground. The others pressed on.

'Raaaam!'

The Lankans were almost upon her, their bamboo *lathis* raised.

'Raaam!' screamed Sita.

As a Lankan closed in, she lassoed her bow, entangling his *lathi* with the bowstring, snatching it from him. Sita hit back with the bamboo *lathi*, straight at the Lankan's head, knocking him off his feet. She swirled the *lathi* over her head, its menacing sound halting the suddenly wary soldiers. She stopped moving, holding her weapon steady. Conserving her energy. Ready and alert. One hand held the stick in the middle, the end of it tucked under her armpit. The other arm was stretched forward. Her feet spread wide, in balance. She was surrounded by at least fifty Lankan soldiers. But they kept their distance.

'Raaaam!' bellowed Sita, praying that her voice would somehow carry across the forest to her husband.

'We don't want to hurt you, Lady Vishnu,' said a Lankan, surprisingly polite. 'Please surrender. You will not be harmed.'

Sita cast a quick glance at Jatayu. *Is he still breathing?*

'We have the equipment in our *Pushpak Vimaan* to save him,' said the Lankan. 'Don't force us to hurt you. Please.'

Sita filled her lungs with air and screamed yet again, 'Raaaam!'

She thought she heard a faint voice from a long distance. 'Sitaaa ...'

A soldier moved suddenly from her left, swinging his *lathi* low. Aiming for her calves. Sita jumped high, tucking her feet in to avoid the blow. While in the air, she quickly released the right-hand grip on the *lathi* and swung it viciously with her left hand. The *lathi* hit the Lankan on the side of his head. Knocking him unconscious.

As she landed, she shouted again, 'Raaaam!'

She heard the same voice. The voice of her husband. Soft, from the distance. 'Leave … her … alone …'

As if electrified by the sound of his voice, ten Lankans charged in together. She swung her *lathi* ferociously on all sides, rapidly incapacitating many.

'Raaaam!'

She heard the voice again. Not so distant this time. 'Sitaaaa … .'

He's close. He's close.

The Lankan onslaught was steady and unrelenting now. Sita kept swinging rhythmically. Viciously. Alas, there were one too many enemies. A Lankan swung his *lathi* from behind. Into her back.

'Raaa …'

Sita's knees buckled under her as she collapsed to the ground. Before she could recover, the soldiers ran in and held her tight.

She struggled fiercely as a Lankan came forward, holding a neem leaf in his hand. It was smeared with a blue-coloured paste. He held the leaf tight against her nose.

As darkness began to envelop her, she sensed some ropes against her hands and feet.

Ram … Help me …

And the darkness took over.

Chapter 2

38 years earlier, North of Trikut Hills, Deoghar, India

'Wait a minute,' whispered Sunaina, as she pulled the reins on her horse.

Janak, the king of Mithila, and his wife, Sunaina, had travelled a long way to the Trikut Hills, nearly a hundred kilometres south of the Ganga River. They sought to meet the legendary *Kanyakumari*, the *Virgin Goddess*. A divine child. It was believed across the *Sapt Sindhu, land of the seven rivers*, that the blessings of the Living Goddess helped all who came to her with a clean heart. And the royal family of Mithila certainly needed Her blessings.

Mithila, founded by the great king Mithi, on the banks of the mighty Gandaki River, was once a thriving river-port town. Its wealth was built on agriculture, owing to its exceptionally fertile soil, as well as river trade with the rest of the Sapt Sindhu. Unfortunately, fifteen years ago, an earthquake and subsequent flood had changed the course of the Gandaki. It also changed the fortunes of Mithila. The river now flowed farther to the west, by the city of Sankashya. Ruled by Janak's younger brother Kushadhwaj, Sankashya was a nominally subsidiary kingdom of Mithila. To add to the woes of Mithila, the rains had failed repeatedly for a few years after the change of Gandaki's course. Mithila's loss was Sankashya's gain. Kushadhwaj rapidly rose in stature as the *de facto* representative of the clan of Mithi.

Many had suggested that King Janak should invest some of the old wealth of Mithila in an engineering project to redirect the Gandaki back to its old course. But Kushadhwaj had advised against it. He had argued that it made little sense to spend money on such a massive engineering project. After all, why waste money to take the river from Sankashya to Mithila, when the wealth of Sankashya was ultimately Mithila's.

Janak, a devout and spiritual man, had adopted a philosophical approach to his kingdom's decline in fortune. But the new queen, Sunaina, who had married Janak just two years earlier, was not the idle sort. She planned to restore Mithila to its old glory. And a big part of that plan was to restore the old course of the Gandaki. But after so many years, it had become difficult to find logical reasons to justify the costly and difficult engineering project.

When logic fails, faith can serve a purpose.

Sunaina had convinced Janak to accompany her to the temple of the *Kanyakumari* and seek her blessings. If the Child Goddess approved of the Gandaki project, even Kushadhwaj would find it difficult to argue against it. Not just the Mithilans, but many across the length and breadth of India believed the *Kanyakumari*'s word to be that of the Mother Goddess Herself. Unfortunately, the *Kanyakumari* had said no. 'Respect the judgement of nature,' she had said.

It was a disappointed Sunaina and a philosophical Janak, along with their royal guard, who were travelling north from the Trikut Hills now, on their way home to Mithila.

'Janak!' Sunaina raised her voice. Her husband had ridden ahead without slowing.

Janak pulled his horse's reins and looked back. His wife pointed wordlessly to a tree in the distance. Janak followed her direction. A few hundred metres away, a pack of wolves had surrounded a solitary vulture. They were trying to close in and were being pushed back repeatedly by the huge bird. The vulture was screaming and squawking. A vulture's squawk is naturally mournful; but this one sounded desperate.

Sunaina looked closely. It was an unfair fight. There were six wolves, weaving in and out, attacking the vulture in perfect coordination. But the brave bird stood its ground, pushing them back repeatedly. The aggressors were gradually drawing close. A wolf hit the vulture with its claws, drawing blood.

Why isn't it flying away?

Sunaina began to canter towards the fight, intrigued. Her bodyguards followed at a distance.

'Sunaina ...' cautioned her husband, staying where he was, holding his horse's reins tight.

Suddenly, using the distraction of the vulture with another attack from the left, a wolf struck with lethal effect. It charged in from the right and bit the bird's left wing brutally. Getting a good hold, the wolf pulled back hard, trying to drag the vulture away. The bird squawked frantically. Its voice sounding like a wail. But it held strong. It did not move, pulling back with all its strength. However, the wolf had strong jaws and a stronger grip. Blood burst forth like a fountain. The wolf let go, spitting parts of the severed wing as it stepped back.

Sunaina spurred her horse and began to gallop towards the scene. She had expected the vulture to escape through the opening the two wolves had provided. But, surprisingly, it stood in place, pushing another wolf back.

Use the opening! Get away!

Sunaina was speeding towards the animals now. The royal bodyguards drew their swords and raced after their queen. A few fell back with the king.

'Sunaina!' said Janak, worried about his wife's safety. He spurred his horse, but he was not the best of riders. His horse blithely continued its slow trot.

Sunaina was perhaps fifty metres away when she noticed the bundle for the first time. The vulture was protecting it from the pack of wolves. It was lodged in what looked like a little furrow in the dry mud.

The bundle moved.

'By the great *Lord Parshu Ram!*' exclaimed Sunaina. 'That's a baby!'

Sunaina pressed forward, rapidly goading her horse into a fierce gallop.

As she neared the pack of wolves, she heard the soft, frantic cries of a human baby, almost drowned out by the howling animals.

'*Hyaah!*' screamed Sunaina. Her bodyguards rode close behind.

The wolves turned tail and scampered into the woods as the mounted riders thundered towards the wounded bird. A guard raised his sword to strike the vulture.

'Wait!' ordered Sunaina, raising her right hand.

He stopped in his tracks as his fellow bodyguards reined their horses to a halt.

Sunaina was raised in a land to the east of Branga. Her father was from Assam, sometimes called by its ancient name, *Pragjyotisha*, the land of *Eastern Light*. And her mother belonged to *Mizoram*, the land of the *High People of Ram*. Devotees of the sixth Vishnu, Lord Parshu Ram, the Mizos were fierce warriors. But they were most well known for their instinctive understanding of animals and the rhythms of nature.

Sunaina intuitively knew that the 'bundle' was not food for the vulture, but a responsibility to be protected.

'Get me some water,' ordered Sunaina, as she dismounted her horse.

One of the guards spoke up as the group dismounted. 'My Lady, is it safe for you to …'

Sunaina cut him short with a withering look. The queen was short and petite. Her round, fair-complexioned face conveyed gentleness to the observer. But her small eyes betrayed the steely determination that was the core of her being. She repeated softly, 'Get me some water.'

'Yes, My Lady.'

A bowl filled with water appeared in an instant.

Sunaina locked her eyes with the vulture's. The bird was breathing heavily, exhausted by its battle with the wolves. It was covered in blood from the numerous wounds on its body. The wound on its wing was especially alarming, blood gushing out of it at a frightening rate. Loss of blood made it unsteady on its feet. But the vulture refused to move, its eyes fixed on Sunaina. It was squawking aggressively, thrusting its beak forward. Striking the air with its talons to keep the Queen of Mithila away.

Sunaina pointedly ignored the bundle behind the vulture. Focused on the massive bird, she began to hum a soft, calming tune. The vulture seemed to ease a bit. It withdrew its talons. The squawking reduced in volume and intensity.

Sunaina crept forward. Gently. Slowly. Once close, she bowed her head and submissively placed the bowl of water in front of the bird. Then she crept back just as slowly. She spoke in a mellifluous voice. 'I have come to help ... Trust me ...'

The dumb beast understood the tone of the human. It bent to sip some water, but instead, collapsed to the ground.

Sunaina rushed forward and cradled the head of the now prone bird, caressing it gently. The child, wrapped in a rich red cloth with black stripes, was crying desperately. She signalled a soldier to pick up the precious bundle as she continued to soothe the bird.

— ल्ॉ८ —

'What a beautiful baby,' cooed Janak, as he bent his tall, wiry frame and edged close to his wife, his normally wise but detached eyes full of love and attention.

Janak and Sunaina sat on temporarily set up chairs. The baby slept comfortably in Sunaina's arms, swaddled in a soft cotton cloth. A massive umbrella shaded them from the scorching sun. The royal doctor had examined the baby, and bandaged a wound on her right temple with some herbs and neem leaves. He had assured the royal couple that the scar would largely disappear with time. Along with the other physician, the doctor now tended to the vulture's wounds.

'She's probably just a few weeks old. She must be strong to have survived this ordeal,' said Sunaina, gently rocking the baby in her arms.

'Yes. Strong and beautiful. Just like you.'

Sunaina looked at her husband and smiled as she caressed the baby's head. 'How can anyone abandon a child like her?'

Janak sighed. 'Many people are not wise enough to count life's blessings. They keep focusing instead on what the world has denied them.'

Sunaina nodded at her husband and turned her attention back to the child. 'She sleeps like an angel.'

'That she does,' said Janak.

Sunaina pulled the baby up close and kissed her gently on the forehead, careful to avoid the injured area.

Janak patted his wife's back warmly. 'But are you sure, Sunaina?'

'Yes. This baby is ours. Devi *Kanyakumari* may not have given us what we wanted. But she has blessed us with something much better.'

'What will we call her?'

Sunaina looked up at the sky and drew in a deep breath. She had a name in mind already. She turned to Janak. 'We found her in a furrow in Mother Earth. It was like a mother's womb for her. We will call her Sita.'

— ᚱᚡ —

Sunaina rushed into Janak's private office. Reclining in an easy chair, the king of Mithila was reading the text of the *Jabali Upanishad*. It was a treatise on wisdom by the great Maharishi Satyakam Jabali. Shifting attention to his wife, he put down the text. 'So, has the Emperor won?'

It had been five years since Sita had entered their lives.

'No,' said a bewildered Sunaina, 'he lost.'

Janak sat up straight, stunned. 'Emperor Dashrath lost to a trader from Lanka?'

'Yes. Raavan has almost completely massacred the Sapt Sindhu Army at Karachapa. Emperor Dashrath barely escaped with his life.'

'Lord Rudra be merciful,' whispered Janak.

'There's more. Queen Kaushalya, the eldest wife of the Emperor, gave birth to a son on the day that he lost the Battle of Karachapa. And now, many are blaming the little boy for the defeat. Saying that he's an ill omen. For the Emperor had never lost a battle till this boy was born.'

'What nonsense!' said Janak. 'How can people be so stupid?'

'The little boy's name is Ram. Named after the sixth Vishnu, Lord Parshu Ram.'

'Let's hope it's lucky for him. Poor child.'

'I am more concerned about the fate of Mithila, Janak.'

Janak sighed helplessly. 'What do you think will happen?'

Sunaina had been governing the kingdom practically single-handedly, of late. Janak was spending more and more time lost in the world of philosophy. The queen had become increasingly popular in the kingdom. Many believed that she had been lucky for Mithila. For the rains had poured down in all their glory every year since she had come to the city as King Janak's wife.

'I am worried about security,' said Sunaina.

'And what about money?' asked Janak. 'Don't you think Raavan will enforce his trade demands on all the kingdoms? Money will flow out of the Sapt Sindhu into Lanka's coffers.'

'But we hardly trade these days. He cannot demand anything from us. The other kingdoms have a lot more to lose. I am more worried about the decimation of the armies of the Sapt Sindhu. Lawlessness will increase everywhere. How safe can we be if the entire land falls into chaos?'

'True.'

A thought crossed Janak's mind. *Who can prevent that which is written by Fate, be it of people or of countries? Our task is but to understand, not fight, what must be; and learn the lessons for our next life. Or prepare for moksha.*

But he knew Sunaina disliked 'helplessness'. So he remained silent.

The queen continued, 'I did not expect Raavan to win.'

Janak laughed. 'It's all very well to be a victor. But the vanquished get more love from their women!'

Sunaina narrowed her eyes and stared at Janak. Not impressed by her husband's attempt at wit. 'We must make some plans, Janak. We must be ready for the inevitable.'

Janak was tempted to respond with another humorous remark. Wisdom dictated restraint.

'I trust you completely. You'll think of something, I'm sure,' smiled Janak, as he turned his attention back to the *Jabali Upanishad*.

Chapter 3

While the rest of India was suffering the aftershocks of Dashrath's defeat to Raavan, Mithila itself was relatively unaffected. There was not much trade in any case to be negatively impacted. Sunaina had initiated some reforms that had worked well. For instance, local tax collection and administration had been devolved to the village level. It reduced the strain on the Mithila bureaucracy and improved efficiency.

Using the increased revenue from agriculture, she had retrained the excess bureaucracy and expanded the Mithila police force, thus improving security within the kingdom. Mithila had no standing army and did not need one; by treaty, the Sankashya Army of Kushadhwaj was supposed to fight the external enemies of Mithila, when necessary. These were not major changes and were implemented relatively smoothly, without disturbing the daily life of the Mithilans. There were mass disturbances in the other kingdoms though, which required gut-wrenching changes to comply with the treaties imposed by Raavan.

Sita's birthday had been established as a day of celebration by royal decree. They didn't know her actual date of birth. So they celebrated the day she had been found in the furrow. Today was her sixth birthday.

Gifts and alms were distributed to the poor in the city. Like it was done on every special day. With a difference. Until Sunaina had come and toned up the administration, much of the charity was grabbed by labourers who were not rich, but who were not exactly poor either. Sunaina's administrative reforms had ensured that the charity first went to those who were truly poor and needy; those who lived in the slums close to the southern gate of the inner, secondary fort wall.

After the public ceremonies, the royal couple had arrived at the massive temple of Lord Rudra.

The Lord Rudra temple was built of red sandstone. It was one of the tallest structures in Mithila, visible from most parts of the city. It had a massive garden around it — an area of peace in this crowded quarter of the city. Beyond the garden were the slums, spreading all the way to the fort walls. Inside the main *garba griha, the sanctum sanctorum* of the temple, a large idol of Lord Rudra and Lady Mohini had been consecrated. Seemingly in consonance with a city that had come to symbolise the love of knowledge, peace, and philosophy, the image of Lord Rudra was not in his normally fierce form. In this form, he looked kind, almost gentle. He held the hand of the beauteous Lady Mohini, who sat next to him.

After the prayers, the temple priest offered *prasad* to the royal family. Sunaina touched the priest's feet and then led Sita by the hand to a wall by the side of the *garba griha*. On the wall, a plaque had been put up in memory of the vulture that had valiantly died defending Sita from a pack of wolves. A death mask of its face had been made before the bird was cremated with honour. Cast in metal, the mask recorded the last expression of the vulture as it left its mortal body. It was a haunting look: determined and noble. Sita had made her mother relate the entire story on several occasions. Sunaina had been happy to oblige. She wanted her daughter to remember. To know that nobility came in many a form and face. Sita touched the death mask gently, reverentially. And as always, she shed a tear for the one who had also given her the gift of life.

'Thank you,' whispered Sita. She said a short prayer to the great God *Pashupati*, *Lord of the Animals*. She hoped the vulture's brave soul had found purpose again.

Janak discreetly signalled his wife, and the royal family slowly walked out of the Lord Rudra temple. The priests led the family down the flight of steps. The slums were clearly visible from the platform height.

'Why don't you ever let me go there, *Maa*?' asked Sita, pointing at the slums.

Sunaina smiled and patted her daughter's head. 'Soon.'

'You always say that,' Sita protested, a grumpy expression on her face.

'And, I mean it,' laughed Sunaina. 'Soon. I just didn't say how soon!'

— ॐ —

'Alright,' said Janak, ruffling Sita's hair. 'Run along now. I have to speak with Guru*ji*.'

The seven-year-old Sita had been playing with her father in his private office when Janak's chief guru, Ashtaavakra, had walked in. Janak had bowed to his guru, as was the tradition, and had requested him to sit on the throne assigned for him.

Mithila, not being a major player in the political arena of the Sapt Sindhu anymore, did not have a permanent *raj guru*. But Janak's court hosted the widest range of eminent seers, scholars, scientists and philosophers from India. Intellectuals loved the Mithilan air, wafting with the fragrance of knowledge and wisdom. And one of the most distinguished of these thinkers, Rishi Ashtaavakra, was Janak's chief guru. Even the great Maharishi Vishwamitra, Chief of the Malayaputra tribe, visited Mithila on occasion.

'We can speak later, if you so desire, Your Highness,' said Ashtaavakra.

'No, no. Of course not,' said Janak. 'I need your guidance on a question that has been troubling me, Guru*ji*.'

Ashtaavakra's body was deformed in eight places. His mother had met with an accident late in her pregnancy. But fate and karma had balanced the physical handicap with an extraordinary mind. Ashtaavakra had shown signs of utter brilliance from a very young age. As a youth, he had visited Janak's court and defeated the king's then chief guru, Rishi Bandi, in a scintillating debate. In doing so, he had redeemed his father, Rishi Kahola, who had lost a debate to Bandi earlier. Rishi Bandi had gracefully accepted defeat and retired to an ashram near the Eastern Sea to acquire more knowledge. Thus it was that the young Ashtaavakra became Janak's chief guru.

Ashtaavakra's deformities did not attract attention in the liberal atmosphere of Mithila, the kingdom of the pious king, Janak. For the sage's luminous mind was compelling.

'I will see you in the evening, *Baba*,' said Sita to her *father* as she touched his feet.

Janak blessed her. She also touched the feet of Rishi Ashtaavakra and walked out of the chamber. As she crossed the threshold, Sita stopped and hid behind the door. Out of Janak's eyesight, but within earshot. She wanted to hear what question had been troubling her father.

'How do we know what reality is, Guru*ji*?' asked Janak.

The young Sita stood nonplussed. Confused. She had heard whisperings in the corridors of the palace. That her father was becoming increasingly eccentric. That they were lucky to have a pragmatic queen in Sunaina to look after the kingdom.

What is reality?

She turned and ran towards her mother's chambers. '*Maa!*'

— ᛫ —

Sita had waited long enough. She was eight years old now. And her mother had still not taken her to the slums adjoining the fort walls. The last time she had asked, she had at least been offered an explanation. She had been told that it could be dangerous. That some people could get beaten up over there. Sita now believed that her mother was just making excuses.

Finally, curiosity had gotten the better of her. Disguised in the clothes of a maid's child, Sita slipped out of the palace. An oversized *angvastram* was wrapped around her shoulder and ears, serving as a hood. Her heart pounded with excitement and nervousness. She repeatedly looked behind to ensure that no one noticed her embark on her little adventure. No one did.

Late in the afternoon, Sita passed the Lord Rudra temple gardens and stole into the slums. All alone. Her mother's words ringing in her ears, she had armed herself with a large stick. She had been practising stick-fighting for over a year now.

As she entered the slum area, she screwed up her nose. Assaulted by the stench. She looked back at the temple garden, feeling the urge to turn back. But almost immediately, the excitement of doing something forbidden took over. She had waited a long time for this. She walked farther into the slum quarters. The houses were rickety structures made of bamboo sticks and haphazardly spread cloth awnings. The cramped space between the wobbly houses served as the 'streets' on which people walked through the slums. These streets also served as open drains, toilets, and open-air animal shelters. They were covered with garbage. There was muck and excreta everywhere. A thin film of animal and human urine made it difficult to walk. Sita pulled her *angvastram* over her nose and mouth, fascinated and appalled at the same time.

People actually live like this? Lord Rudra be merciful.

The palace staff had told her that things had improved in the slums after Queen Sunaina had come to Mithila.

How much worse could it have been for this to be called an improvement?

She soldiered on, gingerly side-stepping the muck on the muddy walkways. Till she saw something that made her stop.

A mother sat outside a slum house, feeding her child from a frugal plate. Her baby was perhaps two or three years old. He sat in his mother's lap, gurgling happily as he dodged the morsels from her hand. Every now and then, he obliged the mother and opened his mouth with theatrical concession, allowing her to stuff small morsels of food into his mouth. It would then be the mother's turn to coo in delight. Pleasing as it was, this wasn't what fascinated Sita. A crow sat next to the woman. And she fed every other morsel to the bird. The crow waited for its turn. Patiently. To it, this wasn't a game.

The woman fed them both. Turn by turn.

Sita smiled. She remembered something her mother had said to her a few days back: *Often the poor have more nobility in them than the actual nobility.*

She hadn't really understood the words then. She did now.

Sita turned around. She'd seen enough of the slums for her first trip. She promised herself that she would return soon. Time to go back to the palace.

There were four tiny lanes ahead. *Which one do I take?*

Uncertain, she took the left-most one and began to walk. She kept moving. But the slum border was nowhere in sight. Her heartbeat quickened as she nervously hastened her pace.

The light had begun to fade. Every chaotic lane seemed to end at a crossroads of several other paths. All haphazard, all disorganised. Confused, she blindly turned into a quiet lane. Beginning to feel the first traces of panic, she quickened her steps. But it only took her the wrong way, faster.

'Sorry!' cried Sita, as she banged into someone.

The dark-skinned girl looked like an adolescent; perhaps older. She had a dirty, unkempt look about her. The stench from her tattered clothes suggested that she had not changed them for a while. Lice crawled over the surface of her matted, unwashed hair. She was tall, lean, and surprisingly muscular. Her feline eyes and scarred body gave her a dangerous, edgy look.

She stared at Sita's face and then at her hands. There was a sudden flash of recognition in her eyes, as though sensing an opportunity. Sita, meanwhile, had darted into an adjacent lane. The Princess of Mithila picked up pace, almost breaking into a desperate run. Praying that this was the correct path out of the slum.

Sweat beads were breaking out on her forehead. She tried to steady her breath. She couldn't.

She kept running. Till she was forced to stop.

'Lord Rudra be merciful.'

She had screeched to a halt, confronted by a solid barrier

wall. She was now well and truly lost, finding herself at the other end of the slum which abutted the inner fort wall. The inner city of Mithila was as far as it could be. It was eerily quiet, with scarcely anyone around. The sun had almost set, and the faint snatches of twilight only emphasised the darkness. She did not know what to do.

'Who is this now?' A voice was heard from behind her.

Sita whirled around, ready to strike. She saw two adolescent boys moving towards her from the right. She turned left. And ran. But did not get far. A leg stuck out and tripped her, making her fall flat on her face. Into the muck. There were more of them. She got up quickly and grabbed her stick. Five boys had gathered around her. Casual menace on their faces.

Her mother had warned her about the crimes in the slums. Of people getting beaten up. But Sita had not believed those stories, thinking that the sweet people who came to collect charity from her mother would never hurt anyone.

I should have listened to Maa.

Sita looked around nervously. The five boys were now in front of her. The steep fort wall was behind her. There was no escape.

She brandished the stick at them, threateningly. The boys let out a merry laugh, amused by the antics of the little girl.

The one in the centre bit a fingernail in mock fear, and said in a sing-song voice, 'Ooh ... we're so scared ...'

Raucous laughter followed.

'That's a precious ring, noble girl,' said the boy, with theatrical politeness. 'I'm sure it's worth more than what the five of us will earn in our entire lives. Do you think that ...'

'Do you want the ring?' asked Sita, feeling a sense of relief as she reached for it. 'Take it. Just let me go.'

The boy sniggered. 'Of course we will let you go. First throw the ring over here.'

Sita gulped anxiously. She balanced her stick against her body, and quickly pulled the ring off her forefinger. Holding it in her closed fist, she pointed the stick at them with her left hand. 'I know how to use this.'

The boy looked at his friends, his eyebrows raised. He turned to the girl and smiled. 'We believe you. Just throw the ring here.'

Sita flung the ring forward. It fell a short distance from the boy.

'Your throwing arm could do with more strength, noble girl,' laughed the boy, as he bent down to pick it up. He looked at it carefully and whistled softly, before tucking it into his waistband. 'Now, what more do you have?'

Suddenly, the boy arched forward and fell to the ground. Behind him stood the tall, dark-skinned girl Sita had crashed into earlier. She held a big bamboo stick with both hands. The boys whirled around aggressively and looked at the girl; the bravado evaporated just as quickly. She was taller than they were. Lean and muscular.

More importantly, it appeared the boys knew her. And her reputation.

'You have nothing to do with this, Samichi …' said one of the boys, hesitantly. 'Leave.'

Samichi answered with her stick and struck his hand. Ferociously. The boy staggered back, clutching his arm.

'I'll break the other one too, if you don't get out of here,' growled Samichi.

And, the boy ran.

The other four delinquents, however, stood their ground.

The one that was felled earlier was back on his feet. They faced Samichi, their backs to Sita. The apparently harmless one. They didn't notice Sita gripping her stick, holding it high above her head and creeping up on the one who had her ring. Judging the distance perfectly, she swung her weapon viciously at the boy's head.

Thwack!

The boy collapsed in a heap, blood spurting from the crack on the back of his head. The three others turned around. Shocked. Paralysed.

'Come on! Quick!' screamed Samichi, as she rushed forward and grabbed Sita by the hand.

As the two girls ran around the corner, Samichi stole a glance back at the scene. The boy lay on the ground, unmoving. His friends had gathered around him, trying to rouse him.

'Quickly!' shouted Samichi, dragging Sita along.

Chapter 4

Sita stood, her hands locked behind her back. Her head bowed. Muck and refuse from the Mithila slums all over her clothes. Her face caked with mud. The very expensive ring on her finger missing. Shivering with fear. She had never seen her mother so angry.

Sunaina was staring at her daughter. No words were spoken. Just a look of utter disapproval. And worse, disappointment. Sita felt like she had failed her mother in the worst possible way.

'I'm so sorry, *Maa*,' wailed Sita, fresh tears flowing down her face.

She wished her mother would at least say something. Or, slap her. Or, scold her. This silence was terrifying.

'*Maa* ...'

Sunaina sat in stony silence. Staring hard at her daughter.

'My Lady!'

Sunaina looked towards the entrance to her chamber. A Mithila policeman was standing there. His head bowed.

'What is the news?' asked Sunaina, brusquely.

'The five boys are missing, My Lady,' said the policeman. 'They have probably escaped.'

'All five?'

'I don't have any new information on the injured boy, My Lady,' said the policeman, referring to the one hit on the head by Sita. 'Some witnesses have come forward. They say that he was carried away by the other boys. He was bleeding a lot.'

'A lot?'

'Well… one witness said he would be surprised if that boy …'

The policeman, wisely, left the words 'made it alive' unsaid.

'Leave us,' ordered Sunaina.

The policeman immediately saluted, turned, and marched out.

Sunaina turned her attention back to Sita. Her daughter cowered under the stern gaze. The queen then looked beyond Sita, at the filthy adolescent standing near the wall.

'What is your name, child?' asked Sunaina.

'Samichi, My Lady.'

'You are not going back to the slums, Samichi. You will stay in the palace from now on.'

Samichi smiled and folded her hands together into a *Namaste*. 'Of course, My Lady. It will be my honour to …'

Samichi stopped speaking as Sunaina raised her right hand. The queen turned towards Sita. 'Go to your chambers. Take a bath. Have the physician look at your wounds; and Samichi's wounds. We will speak tomorrow.'

'*Maa* …'

'Tomorrow.'

— ௫ —

Sita was standing next to Sunaina, who was seated on the ground. Both Sunaina and she were outside the private temple room in the queen's chambers. Sunaina was engrossed in making a fresh *rangoli* on the floor; *made of powdered colours, it was an ethereal mix of fractals, mathematics, philosophy, and spiritual symbolism.*

Sunaina made a new *rangoli* early every morning at the entrance of the temple. Within the temple, idols of the main Gods who Sunaina worshipped had been consecrated: Lord Parshu Ram, the previous Vishnu; Lord Rudra, the great Mahadev; Lord Brahma, the creator-scientist. But the pride of place at the centre was reserved for the Mother Goddess, Shakti *Maa.* The tradition of Mother Goddess worship was especially strong in the land of Sunaina's father, Assam; a vast, fertile and fabulously rich valley that embraced the upper reaches of the largest river of the Indian subcontinent, Brahmaputra.

Sita waited patiently. Too scared to talk.

'There is always a reason why I ask you to do or not do something, Sita,' said Sunaina. Not raising her eyes from the intricate *rangoli* that was emerging on the floor.

Sita sat still. Her eyes pinned on her mother's hands.

'There is an age to discover certain things in life. You need to be ready for it.'

Finishing the *rangoli*, Sunaina looked at her daughter. Sita relaxed as she saw her mother's eyes. They were full of love. As always. She wasn't angry anymore.

'There are bad people too, Sita. People who do criminal things. You find them among the rich in the inner city and the poor in the slums.'

'Yes *Maa*, I …'

'Shhh … don't talk, just listen,' said Sunaina firmly. Sita fell silent. Sunaina continued. 'The criminals among the rich are mostly driven by greed. One can negotiate with greed. But the criminals among the poor are driven by desperation and anger. Desperation can sometimes bring out the best in a human being. That's why the poor can often be noble. But desperation can also bring out the worst. They have nothing to lose. And they get angry when they see others with so much when they have so little. It's understandable. As rulers, our responsibility is to make efforts and change things for the better. But it cannot happen overnight. If we take too much from the rich to help the poor, the rich will rebel. That can cause chaos. And everyone will suffer. So we have to work slowly. We must help the truly poor. That is dharma. But we should not be blind and assume that all poor are noble. Not everyone has the spirit to keep their character strong when their stomachs are empty.'

Sunaina pulled Sita onto her lap. She sat comfortably. For the first time since her foolhardy foray into the slums, she breathed a little easier.

'You will help me govern Mithila someday,' said Sunaina. 'You will need to be mature and pragmatic. You must use your heart to decide the destination, but use your head to plot the journey. People who only listen to their hearts usually fail. On the other hand, people who only use their heads tend to be selfish. Only the heart can make you think of others before yourself. For the sake of dharma, you must aim for equality and balance in society. Perfect equality can never be achieved but we must try to reduce inequality as much as we can. But don't fall into the trap of stereotypes. Don't assume that the powerful are always bad or that the powerless are always good. There is good and bad in everyone.'

Sita nodded silently.

'You need to be liberal, of course. For that is the Indian way. But don't be a blind and stupid liberal.'

'Yes, *Maa*.'

'And do not wilfully put yourself in danger ever again.'

Sita hugged her mother, as tears flowed out of her eyes.

Sunaina pulled back and wiped her daughter's tears. 'You frightened me to death. What would I have done if something bad had happened to you?'

'Sorry, *Maa*.'

Sunaina smiled as she embraced Sita again. 'My impulsive little girl …'

Sita took a deep breath. Guilt had been gnawing away at her. She needed to know. '*Maa*, that boy I hit on the head … What …'

Sunaina interrupted her daughter. 'Don't worry about that.'

'But …'

'I said don't worry about that.'

— ᚱᚷ —

'Thank you, *chacha*!' Sita squealed, as she jumped into her *uncle* Kushadhwaj's arms.

Kushadhwaj, Janak's younger brother and the king of Sankashya, was on a visit to Mithila. He had brought a gift for his niece. A gift that had been a massive hit. It was an Arabian horse. Native Indian breeds were different from the Arab variety. The Indian ones usually had thirty-four ribs while the Arabian horses often had thirty-six. More importantly, an Arabian horse was much sought after as it was smaller, sleeker, and easier to train. And its endurance level was markedly superior. It was a prized possession. And expensive too.

Sita was understandably delighted.

Kushadhwaj handed her a customised saddle, suitable for

her size. Made of leather, it had a gold-plated horn on top of the pommel. The saddle, though small, was still heavy for the young Sita. But she refused the help of the Mithila royal staff in carrying it.

Sita dragged the saddle to the private courtyard of the royal chambers, where her young horse waited for her. It was held by one of Kushadhwaj's aides.

Sunaina smiled. 'Thank you so much. Sita will be lost in this project for the next few weeks. I don't think she will eat or sleep till she's learnt how to ride!'

'She's a good girl,' said Kushadhwaj.

'But it is an expensive gift, Kushadhwaj.'

'She's my only niece, *Bhabhi*,' said Kushadhwaj to his *sister-in-law*. 'If I won't spoil her, then who will?'

Sunaina smiled and gestured for them to join Janak in the veranda adjoining the courtyard. The king of Mithila set the *Brihadaranyak Upanishad* manuscript aside as his wife and brother joined him. Discreet aides placed some cups filled with buttermilk on the table. They also lit a silver lamp, placed at the centre of the table. Just as noiselessly, they withdrew.

Kushadhwaj cast a quizzical look at the lamp and frowned. It was daytime. But he remained quiet.

Sunaina waited till the aides were out of earshot. Then she looked at Janak. But her husband had picked up his manuscript again. Deeply engrossed. After her attempts to meet his eyes remained unsuccessful, she cleared her throat. Janak remained focused on the manuscript in his hands.

'What is it, *Bhabhi*?' asked Kushadhwaj.

Sunaina realised that she had no choice. She would have to be the one to speak up. She pulled a document out of the large pouch tied to her waist and placed it on the table. Kushadhwaj resolutely refused to look at it.

'Kushadhwaj, we have been discussing the road connecting Sankashya to Mithila for many years now,' said Sunaina. 'It was washed away in the Great Flood. But it has been more than two decades since. The absence of that road has caused immense hardship to the citizens and traders of Mithila.'

'What traders, *Bhabhi*?' said Kushadhwaj, laughing gently. 'Are there any in Mithila?'

Sunaina ignored the barb. 'You had agreed in principle to pay for two-thirds of the cost of the road, if Mithila financed the remaining one-third.'

Kushadhwaj remained silent.

'Mithila has raised its share of the money,' said Sunaina. She pointed to the document. 'Let's seal the agreement and let the construction begin.'

Kushadhwaj smiled. 'But *Bhabhi*, I don't see what the problem is. The road is not that bad. People use it every day. I myself took that road to Mithila yesterday.'

'But you are a king, Kushadhwaj,' said Sunaina pleasantly, her tone studiously polite. 'You are capable of many things that ordinary people are not. Ordinary people need a good road.'

Kushadhwaj smiled broadly. 'Yes, the ordinary people of Mithila are lucky to have a queen as committed to them as you are.'

Sunaina did not say anything.

'I have an idea, *Bhabhi*,' said Kushadhwaj. 'Let Mithila begin the construction of the road. Once your share of the one-third is done, Sankashya will complete the remaining two-third.'

'All right.'

Sunaina picked up the document and a quill from a side table and scribbled a line at the end. She then pulled out the royal seal from her pouch and marked the agreement.

She offered the document to Kushadhwaj. It was then that Kushadhwaj realised the significance of the lamp.

Lord Agni, the God of Fire, as witness.

Every Indian believed that *Agni* was the great purifier. It was not a coincidence that the first hymn of the first chapter of the holiest Indian scripture, the *Rig Veda*, celebrated Lord Agni. All promises that were sealed with the God of Fire as witness could never be broken; promises of marriage, of *yagnas*, of peace treaties ... and even a promise to build roads.

Kushadhwaj did not take the agreement from his sister-in-law. Instead, he reached into his pouch and pulled out his own royal seal. 'I trust you completely, *Bhabhi*. You can mark my agreement on the document.'

Sunaina took the seal from Kushadhwaj and was about to stamp the agreement, when he softly spoke, 'It's a new seal, *Bhabhi*. One that reflects Sankashya properly.'

Sunaina frowned. She turned the seal around and looked at its markings. Even though it was a mirror image of the symbol that would be marked on the agreement, the Queen of Mithila recognised it immediately. It was a single dolphin; the seal symbol of Mithila. Sankashya had historically been a subsidiary kingdom of Mithila, ruled by the younger members of the royal family. And it had a different seal: a single *hilsa* fish.

Sunaina stiffened in anger. But she knew that she had to control her temper. She slowly placed the document back on the table. The Sankashya seal had not been used.

'Why don't you give me your actual seal, Kushadhwaj?' said Sunaina.

'This is my kingdom's seal now, *Bhabhi*.'

'It can never be so unless Mithila accepts it. No kingdom will recognise this as your seal till Mithila publicly does so.

Every Sapt Sindhu kingdom knows that the single dolphin is the mark of the Mithila royal family's direct line.'

'True, *Bhabhi*. But you can change that. You can legitimise this seal across the land by using it on that document.'

Sunaina cast a look at her husband. The king of Mithila raised his head, looked briefly at his wife, and then went back to the *Brihadaranyak Upanishad*.

'This is not acceptable, Kushadhwaj,' said Sunaina, maintaining her calm expression and voice to hide the anger boiling within. 'This will not happen for as long as I'm alive.'

'I don't understand why you are getting so agitated, *Bhabhi*. You have married into the Mithila royal family. I was born into it. The royal blood of Mithila flows in *my* veins, not yours. Right, Janak *dada*?'

Janak looked up and finally spoke, though the tone was detached and devoid of anger. 'Kushadhwaj, whatever Sunaina says is my decision as well.'

Kushadhwaj stood up. 'This is a sad day. Blood has been insulted by blood. For the sake of …'

Sunaina too rose to her feet. Abruptly interrupting Kushadhwaj, though her tone remained unfailingly polite. 'Be careful what you say next, Kushadhwaj.'

Kushadhwaj laughed. He stepped forward and took the Sankashya seal from Sunaina's hand. 'This is mine.'

Sunaina remained silent.

'Don't pretend to be a custodian of the royal traditions of Mithila,' scoffed Kushadhwaj. 'You are not blood family. You are only an import.'

Sunaina was about to say something when she felt a small hand wrap itself around hers. She looked down. The young Sita stood by her side, shaking with fury. In her other hand was the saddle that Kushadhwaj had just gifted her. She threw the saddle at her uncle. It fell on his feet.

As Kushadhwaj doubled up in pain, the Sankashya seal fell from his hand.

Sita leapt forward, picked up the seal and smashed it to the ground, breaking it in two. The breaking of a royal seal was considered a very bad omen. This was a grievous insult.

'Sita!' shouted Janak.

Kushadhwaj's face contorted with fury. 'This is an outrage, *Dada!*'

Sita now stood in front of her mother. She faced her uncle, daring him with her eyes. Spreading her arms out to cover her mother protectively.

The king of Sankashya picked up the broken pieces of his royal seal and stormed out. 'You have not heard the last of this, *Dada!*'

As he left, Sunaina went down on her knees and turned Sita around. 'You should not have done that, Sita.'

Sita looked at her mother with smouldering eyes. Then turned to look at her father, defiant and accusing. There was not a trace of apology on her face.

'You should not have done that, Sita.'

— ᚱᚷ —

Sita held on to her mother, refusing to let go. She wept with wordless anguish. A smiling Janak came up to her and patted her head. The royal family had gathered in the king's private office. A few weeks had passed since the incident with Kushadhwaj. Sita, her parents had decided, was old enough to leave for *gurukul*, literally, the *Guru's family*, but in effect a residential school.

Janak and Sunaina had chosen Rishi Shvetaketu's *gurukul* for their daughter. Shvetaketu was the uncle of Janak's chief guru, Ashtaavakra. His *gurukul* offered lessons in the core subjects of Philosophy, Mathematics, Science, and Sanskrit. Sita would also receive education in other specialised subjects like Geography, History, Economics, and Royal Administration, among others.

One subject that Sunaina had insisted Sita be taught, overriding Janak's objections, was warfare and martial arts. Janak believed in non-violence. Sunaina believed in being practical.

Sita knew that she had to go. But she was a child. And the child was terrified of leaving home.

'You will come home regularly, my dear,' said Janak. 'And we will come and see you too. The *ashram* is on the banks of the Ganga River. It's not too far.'

Sita tightened her grip on her mother.

Sunaina prised Sita's arms and held her chin. She made her daughter look at her. 'You will do well there. It will prepare you for your life. I know that.'

'Are you sending me away because of what I did with *chacha*?' sobbed Sita.

Sunaina and Janak immediately went down on their knees and held her close.

'Of course not, my darling,' said Sunaina. 'This has nothing to do with your uncle. You have to study. You must get educated so that you can help run this kingdom someday.'

'Yes, Sita,' said Janak. 'Your mother is right. What happened with Kushadhwaj uncle has nothing to do with you. It is between him, and your mother and I.'

Sita burst into a fresh bout of tears. She clung to her parents like she'd never let them go.

Chapter 5

Two years had passed since Sita had arrived in Shvetaketu's *gurukul*. While the ten-year-old student had impressed her guru with her intelligence and sharpness, it was her enthusiasm for the outdoors that was truly extraordinary. Especially noteworthy was her skill in stick-fighting.

But her spirited temperament also created problems on occasion. Like the time when a fellow student had called her father an ineffectual king, more suited to being a teacher than a ruler. Sita's response had been to thrash the living daylights out of him. The boy had been confined to the *gurukul Ayuralay* for almost a month. He had limped for two months after that.

A worried Shvetaketu had arranged for extra classes on the subjects of non-violence and impulse control. The hot-headed girl had also been strictly reminded of the rules against physical violence on the *gurukul* premises. The art of warfare was taught to inculcate self-discipline and a code of conduct for future royal duties. Within the school, they were not allowed to hurt one another.

To ensure that the message went home, Sunaina had also been told of this incident on one of her visits to the *gurukul*. Her strong words had had the desired impact on Sita. She had refrained from beating other students since then, though her resolve was tested at times.

This was one such time.

'Aren't you adopted?' taunted Kaaml Raj, a fellow classmate.

Five students from the *gurukul* had gathered close to the pond on the campus. Three sat around Sita, who had drawn a geometric shape on the ground, using some ropes. Engrossed in explaining a theorem from the *Baudhayana Shulba Sutra*, she had been studiously ignoring Kaaml. As were the others. He was hovering around as usual, trying to distract everyone. Upon hearing his words, all eyes turned to Sita.

Radhika was Sita's best friend. She immediately tried to prevent a reaction. 'Let it be, Sita. He is a fool.'

Sita sat up straight and closed her eyes for a moment. She had often wondered about her birth mother. Why had she abandoned her? Was she as magnificent as her adoptive mother? But there was no doubt in her mind about one fact: She was Sunaina's daughter.

'I am my mother's daughter,' muttered Sita, looking defiantly at her tormentor as she pointedly ignored her friend's advice.

'Yes, yes, I know that. We are all our mothers' children. But aren't you adopted? What will happen to you when your mother has a real daughter?'

'Real daughter? I am not unreal, Kaaml. I am *very* real.'

'Yes, yes. But you are not …'

'Just get lost,' said Sita. She picked up the twig with which she had been explaining the *Baudhayana* theorem.

'No, no. You aren't understanding what I'm saying. If you are adopted, you can be thrown out at any time. What will you do then?'

Sita put the twig down and looked at Kaaml with cold eyes.

This would have been a good moment for the boy to shut up. Regrettably, he did not have too much sense.

'I can see that the teachers like you. Guru*ji* likes you a lot. You can come back here and teach all day when you get thrown out of your home!' Kaaml broke into maniacal laughter. No one else laughed. In fact, the tension in the air was crackling dangerously.

'Sita …' pleaded Radhika, again advising calm. 'Let it be …'

Sita ignored Radhika's advice yet again. She slowly got up and walked towards Kaaml. The boy swallowed hard, but he did not step back. Sita's hands were locked tightly behind her back. She stopped within an inch of her adversary. She looked at him and glared. Straight into his eyes. Kaaml's breath had quickened nervously, and the twitch in his temple showed that his courage was rapidly disappearing. But he stood his ground.

Sita took one more threatening step. Dangerously close to Kaaml. Her toe was now touching the boy's. The tip of her nose was less than a centimetre from his face. Her eyes flashed fire.

Sweat beads had formed on Kaaml's forehead. 'Listen … you are not allowed to hit anyone …'

Sita kept her eyes locked with his. She kept staring. Unblinking. Cold. Breathing heavily.

Kaaml's voice emerged in a squeak. 'Listen …'

Sita suddenly screamed loudly; an ear-splitting sound right in Kaaml's face. A forceful, strong, high-pitched bellow. A startled Kaaml fell back, flat on the ground and burst into tears.

And, the other children burst into laughter.

A teacher appeared seemingly from nowhere.

'I didn't hit him! I didn't hit him!'

'Sita …'

Sita allowed herself to be led away by the teacher. 'But I didn't hit him!'

— ௴ த —

'Hanu *bhaiya*!' cooed Radhika as she hugged her *elder brother*. Or more specifically, her elder *cousin* brother.

Radhika had asked Sita along to meet her favourite relative. The meeting place was around an hour's walk from the *gurukul*, deep in the jungles to the south, in a well-hidden clearing. This was where the cousins met. In secret. Her brother had good reasons to remain invisible to the *gurukul* authorities.

He was a Naga; a person born with deformities.

He was dressed in a dark-brown *dhoti* with a white *angvastram*. Fair-skinned. Tall and hirsute. An outgrowth jutted out from his lower back, almost like a tail. It flapped with rhythmic precision, as though it had a mind of its own. His massive build and sturdy musculature gave him an awe-inspiring presence. Almost a godly aura. His flat nose was pressed against his face, which in turn was outlined with facial hair, encircling it with neat precision. Strangely though, the skin above and below his mouth was hairless, silken smooth and light pink in colour; it had a puffed appearance. His lips were a thin, barely noticeable line. Thick eyebrows drew a sharp, artistic curve above captivating eyes that radiated intelligence and a meditative calm. It almost seemed like the Almighty had taken the face of a monkey and placed it on a man's head.

He looked at Radhika with almost paternal affection. 'How are you, my little sister?'

Radhika stuck her lower lip out in mock anger. 'How long has it been since I saw you last? Ever since father allowed that new *gurukul* to come up ...'

Radhika's father was the chief of a village along the river Shon. He had recently given permission for a *gurukul* to be set up close to the village. Four young boys had been enrolled. There were no other students. Sita had wondered why Radhika was still in Rishi Shvetaketu's *gurukul*, when another was now so close to home. Maybe a small, four-student *gurukul* was not as good as their Guru*ji*'s renowned school.

'Sorry Radhika, I've been very busy,' said the man. 'I've been given a new assignment and …'

'I don't care about your new assignment!'

Radhika's brother quickly changed the topic. 'Aren't you going to introduce me to your new friend?'

Radhika stared at him for a few more seconds, then smiled in surrender and turned to her friend. 'This is Sita, the princess of Mithila. And this is my elder brother, Hanu *bhaiya*.'

He gave his new acquaintance a broad smile as he folded his hands into a *Namaste*. 'Hanu *bhaiya* is what little Radhika calls me. My name is Hanuman.'

Sita folded her hands too, and looked up at the kindly face. 'I think I prefer Hanu *bhaiya*.'

Hanuman laughed warmly. 'Then Hanu *bhaiya* it is!'

— ᳯᱺ —

Sita had spent five years in the *gurukul*. She was thirteen years old now.

The *gurukul* was built on the southern banks of the holy Ganga, a short distance downriver from Magadh, where the feisty Sarayu merged into the sedate Ganga. Its location was so convenient that many *rishis* and *rishikas* from various *ashrams* used to drop into this *gurukul*. They, usually, even taught for a few months as visiting teachers.

Indeed, Maharishi Vishwamitra himself was on a visit to the *gurukul* right now. He and his followers entered the frugal *ashram,* home to almost twenty-five students.

'*Namaste*, great Malayaputra,' said Shvetaketu, folding his hands together and bowing to the legendary *rishi*, chief of the tribe left behind by the sixth Vishnu, Lord Parshu Ram. The Malayaputras were tasked with two missions: to help the next Mahadev, Destroyer of Evil, if and when he or she arose. And, to give rise to the next Vishnu, Propagator of Good, when the time was right.

The *gurukul* was electrified by the presence of the great Maharishi Vishwamitra; considered a *Saptrishi Uttradhikari, successor to the legendary seven rishis.* It was a singular honour, greater than receiving any of the men and women of knowledge who had visited before.

'*Namaste*, Shvetaketu,' said Vishwamitra imperiously, a hint of a smile playing on his face.

The staff at the *gurukul* had immediately set to work. Some helped the sage's followers with their luggage and horses, while others rushed to clean the already spick-and-span guest quarters. Arishtanemi, the military chief of the Malayaputras and the right-hand man of Vishwamitra, organised the efforts like the battle commander that he was.

'What brings you to these parts, Great One?' asked Shvetaketu.

'I had some work upriver,' said Vishwamitra, enigmatically, refusing to elaborate.

Shvetaketu knew better than to ask any more questions on this subject to the fearsome Malayaputra chief. But an attempt at conversation was warranted. 'Raavan's trade treaties are causing immense pain to the kingdoms of the Sapt Sindhu, noble Guru. People are suffering and being impoverished. Somebody has to fight him.'

Almost seven feet tall, the dark-skinned Vishwamitra was altogether of unreal proportions, both physically and in intellect. His large belly lay under a sturdy chest, muscular shoulders, and powerful arms. A flowing white beard grazed his chest. Brahminical, tuft of knotted hair on an otherwise shaven head. Large, limpid eyes. And the holy *janau, sacred thread*, tied over his shoulder. In startling contrast were the numerous battle scars that lined his face and body. He looked down at Shvetaketu from his great height.

'There are no kings today who can take on this task,' said Vishwamitra. 'They are all just survivors. Not leaders.'

'Perhaps this task is beyond that of mere kings, Illustrious One ...'

Vishwamitra's smile broadened mysteriously. But no words followed.

Shvetaketu would not let down his need for interaction with the great man. 'Forgive my impertinence, Maharishi*ji*, but how long do you expect to stay with us? It would be wonderful if my students could get the benefit of your guidance.'

'I will be here for only a few days, Shvetaketu. Teaching your children may not be possible.'

Shvetaketu was about to repeat his request, as politely as possible, when a loud sound was heard.

A speedy whoosh followed by a loud thwack!

Vishwamitra had once been a Kshatriya warrior prince. He recognised the sound immediately. Of a spear hitting a wooden target. Almost perfectly.

He turned in the direction that the sound had emerged from, his brows lifted slightly in admiration. 'Someone in your *gurukul* has a strong throwing arm, Shvetaketu.'

Shvetaketu smiled proudly. 'Let me show you, Guru*ji*.'

— ⸙ —

'Sita?' asked Vishwamitra, surprised beyond words. 'Janak's daughter, Sita?'

Vishwamitra and Shvetaketu were at one end of the sparse but well-equipped outdoor training arena, where students practised archery, spear-throwing and other *ananga* weapon techniques. At the other end was a separate area set aside for the practice of *anga* weapons like swords and maces. Sita, immersed in her practice, did not see the two *rishis* as they silently walked in and watched her get ready for the next throw.

'She has the wisdom of King Janak, great Malayaputra,' answered Shvetaketu. 'But she also has the pragmatism and fighting spirit of Queen Sunaina. And, dare I say, my *gurukul* teachers have moulded her spirit well.'

Vishwamitra observed Sita with a keen eye. Tall for a thirteen-year old, she was already beginning to build muscle. Her straight, jet-black hair was braided and rolled into a practical bun. She flicked a spear up with her foot, catching it expertly in her hand. Vishwamitra noticed the stylish flick. But he was more impressed by something else. She had caught the spear exactly at the balance point on the shaft. Which had not been marked, unlike in a normal training spear. She judged it, instinctively perhaps. Even from a distance, he could see that her grip was flawless. The spear shaft lay flat on the palm of her hand, between her index and middle finger. Her thumb pointed backwards while the rest of the fingers faced the other direction.

Sita turned to the target with her left foot facing it. It was a wooden board painted with concentric circles. She raised her left hand, again in the same direction. Her body twisted ever so slightly, to add power to the throw. She pulled her right hand back, parallel to the ground; poised as a work of art.

Perfect.

Shvetaketu smiled. Though he did not teach warfare to his students, he was personally proud of Sita's prowess. 'She doesn't take the traditional few steps before she throws. The twist in her body and strength in her shoulders give her all the power she needs.'

Vishwamitra looked dismissively at Shvetaketu. He turned his attention back to the impressive girl. Those few steps may add power, but could also make you miss the target. Especially if the target was small. He did not bother to explain that little detail to Shvetaketu.

Sita flung hard as she twisted her body leftward, putting the power of her shoulder and back into the throw. Whipping the spear forward with her wrist and finger. Giving the final thrust to the missile.

Whoosh and thwack!

The spear hit bang on target. Right at the centre of the board. It jostled for space with the earlier spear which had pierced the same small circle.

Vishwamitra smiled slightly. 'Not bad ... Not bad at all ...'

What her two spectators did not know was that Sita had been taking lessons from Hanuman, on his regular visits to see his two sisters. He had helped perfect her technique.

Shvetaketu smiled with the pride of a parent. 'She is exceptional.'

'What is her status in Mithila now?'

Shvetaketu took a deep breath. 'I can't be sure. She is their adopted daughter. And, King Janak and Queen Sunaina have always loved her dearly. But now that ...'

'I believe Sunaina was blessed with a daughter a few years back,' interrupted Vishwamitra.

'Yes. After more than a decade of marriage. They have their own natural-born daughter now.'

'Urmila, right?'

'Yes, that is her name. Queen Sunaina has said that she does not differentiate between the two girls. But she has not visited Sita for nine months. She used to come every six months earlier. Admittedly, Sita has been called to Mithila regularly. She last visited Mithila six months ago. But she didn't return very happy.'

Vishwamitra looked at Sita, his hand on his chin. Thoughtful. He could see her face now. It seemed strangely familiar. But he couldn't place it.

— ॥ॐ॥ —

It was lunchtime at the *gurukul*. Vishwamitra and his Malayaputras sat in the centre of the courtyard, surrounded by the simple mud huts that housed the students. It also served as an open-air classroom. Teaching was always done in the open. The small, austere huts for the teachers were a short distance away.

'Guru*ji*, shall we begin?' asked Arishtanemi, the Malayaputra military chief.

The students and the *gurukul* staff had served the honoured guests on banana leaf plates. Shvetaketu sat alongside

Vishwamitra, waiting for the Chief Malayaputra to commence the ceremony. Vishwamitra picked up his glass, poured some water into the palm of his right hand, and sprinkled it around his plate, thanking Goddess Annapurna for her blessings in the form of food and nourishment. He scooped the first morsel of food and placed it aside, as a symbolic offering to the Gods. Everyone repeated the action. At a signal from Vishwamitra, they began eating.

Vishwamitra, however, paused just as he was about to put the first morsel into his mouth. His eyes scanned the premises in search of a man. One of his soldiers was a Naga called Jatayu. The unfortunate man had been born with a condition that led to deformities on his face over time, classifying him as a Naga. His deformities were such that his face looked like that of a vulture. Many ostracised Jatayu. But not Vishwamitra. The Chief Malayaputra recognised the powerful warrior and noble soul that Jatayu was. Others, with prejudiced eyes, were blind to his qualities.

Vishwamitra knew the biases that existed in the times. He also knew that in this *ashram*, it was unlikely that anybody would have bothered to take care of Jatayu's meals. He looked around, trying to find him. He finally saw Jatayu, sitting alone in the distance, under a tree. Even as he was about to signal a student, he saw Sita heading towards the Naga, a banana-leaf plate in one hand, and a tray full of food in the other.

The *Maharishi* watched, as Jatayu stood up with coy amazement.

From the distance, Vishwamitra could not hear what was being said. But he read the body language. With utmost respect, Sita placed the banana-leaf plate in front of Jatayu, then served the food. As Jatayu sat down to eat with an embarrassed smile, she bowed low, folded her hands into a *Namaste* and walked away.

Vishwamitra watched Sita, lost in thought. *Where have I seen that face before?*

Arishtanemi, too, was observing the girl. He turned to Vishwamitra.

'She seems like a remarkable girl, Guru*ji*,' said Arishtanemi.

'Hmm,' said Vishwamitra, as he looked at his lieutenant very briefly. He turned his attention to his food.

Chapter 6

'Kaushik, this is not a good idea,' said Divodas. 'Trust me, my brother.'

Kaushik and Divodas sat on a large boulder outside their gurukul, on the banks of the Kaveri River. The two friends, both in their late thirties, were teachers at the Gurukul of Maharishi Kashyap, the celebrated Saptrishi Uttradhikari, successor to the seven legendary seers. Kaushik and Divodas had been students of the gurukul in their childhood. Upon graduation, they had gone their separate ways. Divodas had excelled as a teacher of great renown and Kaushik, as a fine Kshatriya royal. Two decades later, they had joined the prestigious institution again, this time as teachers. They had instantly rekindled their childhood friendship. In fact, they were like brothers now. In private, they still referred to each other by the gurukul names of their student days.

'Why is it not a good idea, Divodas?' asked Kaushik, his massive, muscular body bent forward aggressively, as usual. 'They are biased against the Vaanars. We need to challenge this prejudice for the good of India!'

Divodas shook his head. But realised that further conversation was pointless. He had long given up trying to challenge Kaushik's stubborn streak. It was like banging your head against an anthill. Not a good idea!

He picked up a clay cup kept by his side. It contained a bubbly, milky liquid. He held his nose and gulped it down. 'Yuck!'

Kaushik burst into laughter as he patted his friend heartily on his back. 'Even after all these years, it still tastes like horse's piss!'

Divodas wiped his mouth with the back of his hand and smiled. 'You need to come up with a new line! How do you know it tastes like horse's piss, anyway? Have you ever drunk horse's piss?!'

Kaushik laughed louder and held his friend by the shoulder. 'I have had the Somras *often. And I'm sure even horse's piss can't taste worse!'*

Divodas smiled broadly and put his arm around his friend's shoulder. They sat on the boulder in companionable silence, watching the sacred Kaveri as it flo ed gently by Mayuram, the small town that housed their gurukul. *The town was a short distance from the sea, and the perfect location for this massive* gurukul, *which taught hundreds of young students. More importantly, it also offered specialised courses in higher studies in different fields of knowledge. Being close to the sea, students from the Sapt Sindhu in the North could conveniently sail down the eastern coast of India to the* gurukul. *Thus, they did not need to cross the Narmada River from the north to south, and violate the superstitious belief that instructed against it. Furthermore, this* gurukul *was close to the submerged, prehistoric land of Sangamtamil, which along with the submerged ancient land of Dwarka in western India, was one of the two fatherlands of Vedic culture. This made its location uniquely holy to the students.*

Divodas braced his shoulders, as if gathering resolve.

Kaushik, knowing well the non-verbal cues of his friend, remarked, 'What?'

Divodas took a deep breath. He knew this would be a difficult conversation. But he decided to try one more time. 'Kaushik, listen to me. I know you want to help Trishanku. And, I agree with you. He needs help. He is a good man. Perhaps immature and naive, but a good man nonetheless. But he cannot become a Vayuputra. He failed their examination. He must accept that. It has nothing to do with how he looks or where he was born. It is about his capability.'

The Vayuputras were the tribe left behind by the previous Mahadev,

Lord Rudra. *They lived far beyond the western borders of India in a place called Pariha. The Vayuputras were tasked with supporting the next Vishnu, whenever he or she arose. And, of course, one of them would become the next Mahadev whenever Evil raised its dangerous head.*

Kaushik stiffened. 'The Vayuputras are intolerant towards the Vaanars *and you know it.'*

The Vaanars *were a large, powerful, and reclusive tribe living on the banks of the great Tungabhadra River, north of the Kaveri. The Tungabhadra was a tributary of the Krishna River farther to the north. The tribe had a distinctly different appearance: Mostly short, stocky and very muscular, some of them were giant-like too. Their faces were framed with fin , facial hair, which ballooned into a beard at the jaw. Their mouths protruded outwards, and the skin around it was silken smooth and hairless. Their hirsute bodies sported thick, almost furry hair. To some prejudiced people, the* Vaanars *appeared like monkeys and thus, somehow, less human. It was said that similar tribes lived farther to the west of Pariha. One of their biggest and most ancient settlements was a land called Neanderthal or the valley of Neander.*

'What intolerance are you talking about?' asked Divodas, his hand raised in question. 'They accepted young Maruti into their fold, didn't they? Maruti is a Vaanar *too. But he has merit. Trishanku doesn't!'*

Kaushik would not be dissuaded. 'Trishanku has been loyal to me. He asked for my help. I will help him!'

'But Kaushik, how can you create your own version of Pariha? This is not wise ...'

'I have given him my word, Divodas. Will you help me or not?'

'Kaushik, of course I will help! But, brother, listen ...'

Suddenly a loud, feminine voice was heard from a distance. 'Hey, Divodas!'

Kaushik and Divodas turned around. It was Nandini. Another teacher at the gurukul. *And a friend to both. Kaushik cast a dark, injured look at Divodas, gritting his teeth softly.*

'Guru*ji* …'

Vishwamitra's eyes. flew open, bringing him back to the present from an ancient, more-than-a-century-old memory.

'I am sorry to disturb you, Guru*ji*,' said Arishtanemi, his hands joined in a penitent *Namaste*. 'But you had asked me to wake you when the students assembled.'

Vishwamitra sat up and gathered his *angvastram*. 'Is Sita present?'

'Yes, Guru*ji*.'

— *ௐ* —

Shvetaketu sat on a chair placed in a discreet corner. He was clearly elated to see all the twenty-five students of his *gurukul* gathered in the open square. Vishwamitra sat on the round platform built around the trunk of the main *peepal* tree. It was the seat of the teacher. The great Chief Malayaputra would teach his students, if only for one class. This was a rare honour for Shvetaketu and his students.

The teachers of the *gurukul* and the Malayaputras stood in silence behind Shvetaketu.

'Have you learnt about our great ancient empires?' asked Vishwamitra. 'And the reasons for their rise and fall?'

All the students nodded in the affirmative.

'All right, then someone tell me, why did the empire of the descendants of the great Emperor Bharat decline? An empire that flourished for centuries, was annihilated within just two generations. Why?'

Kaaml Raj raised his hand. Shvetaketu groaned softly.

'Yes?' asked Vishwamitra.

'Guru*ji*,' answered Kaaml, 'they were attacked by foreigners and had internal rebellions at the same time. They were like the *kancha* marbles we play with. Everyone from everywhere was hitting them again and again. How could the empire survive?'

Saying this, Kaaml guffawed uncontrollably, laughing as if he had just cracked the funniest joke in human history. Everyone else remained silent. A few students at the back held their heads in shame. Vishwamitra stared at Kaaml with a frozen expression. The same expression was then directed towards Shvetaketu.

Not for the first time, Shvetaketu considered sending young Kaaml back to his parents. He really was a strange, untrainable child.

Vishwamitra did not deign to respond to Kaaml and repeated his question, this time looking directly at Sita. But the princess of Mithila did not answer.

'Bhoomi, why don't you answer?' asked Vishwamitra, using her *gurukul* name.

'Because I am not sure, Guru*ji*.'

Vishwamitra pointed to the front row. 'Come here, child.'

Since her last visit to Mithila, Sita had preferred to be alone. She mostly sat at the back of the class. Her friend Radhika patted her back, encouraging her to go. As Sita came forward, Vishwamitra gestured for her to sit. Then he stared at her eyes closely. Very few sages were adept at reading people's minds through their eyes. Vishwamitra was one such rare sage.

'Tell me,' said Vishwamitra, his eyes piercing through her mind. 'Why did the *Bhaaratas*, the descendants of the great Emperor Bharat, disintegrate so suddenly?'

Sita felt very uncomfortable. She felt an overpowering urge to get up and run. But she knew she could not insult the great *Maharishi*. She chose to answer. 'The *Bhaaratas* had a massive standing army. They could have easily fought on multiple battle fronts. But their warriors were …'

'They were useless,' said Vishwamitra, completing Sita's thought. 'And, why were they useless? They had no shortage of money, of training, of equipment, or of war weapons.'

Sita repeated something she had heard Samichi say. 'What matters is not the weapon, but the woman who wields that weapon.'

Vishwamitra smiled in approval. 'And why were their *warriors* incapable of wielding weapons? Do not forget, these were weapons of far superior technology than those of their enemies.'

Sita had not thought about this. She remained silent.

'Describe the *Bhaarat* society at the time of their downfall,' Vishwamitra demanded.

Sita knew this answer. 'It was peaceful. A liberal and polite society. It was a haven for arts, culture, music, conversations, debates… They not only practised but proudly celebrated non-violence. Both verbal and physical. It was a perfect society. Like heaven.'

'True. But there were some for whom it was hell.'

Sita did not say anything. But her mind wondered: *For whom?*

Vishwamitra read her mind as if she had spoken aloud. He answered, 'The warriors.'

'The warriors?'

'What are the chief qualities of warriors? What drives them? What motivates them? Yes, there are many who fight for honour, for the country, for a code. But equally, there are those who simply want a socially sanctioned way to kill. If not given an outlet, such people can easily turn to crime. Many great warriors, celebrated by humanity, narrowly escaped being remembered as social degenerates. What saved them from becoming criminals and instead, turned them into soldiers? The answer is the warrior code: The *right* reason to kill.'

It's difficult for a child to surrender certainties and understand nuances. Sita, after all just a thirteen-year-old, stiffened.

'Warriors thrive on admiration and hero worship. Without these, the warrior spirit, and with it, the warrior code, dies. Sadly, many in the latter-day *Bhaarat* society despised their soldiers and preferred to condemn them. Every action of the army was vehemently criticised. Any form of violence, even dharmic violence, was opposed. The warrior spirit itself was berated as a demonic impulse that had to be controlled. It didn't stop there. Freedom of speech was curtailed so that verbal violence could also be controlled. Disagreement was discouraged. This is how the *Bhaaratas* felt that heaven could be created on earth; by making strength powerless, and weakness powerful.'

Vishwamitra's voice became softer, almost as if he was speaking only to Sita. The assembly listened in rapt attention.

'Essentially, the *Bhaaratas* curbed their Kshatriya class drastically. Masculinity was emasculated. Great sages of yore who preached absolute non-violence and love were glorified and their messages amplified. But then, when barbaric invaders attacked from foreign lands, these pacifist, non-violent *Bhaarat* men and women were incapable of fighting back. These civilised people appeared like weak wimps to the brutal warriors from abroad.' With an ironic laugh, Vishwamitra continued, 'Unexpectedly, for the people of *Bhaarat* society, the *Hiranyaloman Mlechcha* warriors did not care for their message of love. Their answer to love was mass murder. They were barbarians, incapable of building their own empire. But they destroyed *Bhaarat* power and prestige. Internal rebels finished the job of destruction.'

'Guru*ji*, are you saying that to fight foreign monsters, you need your own monsters?'

'No. All I'm saying is that society must be wary of extremes. It must constantly strive towards attaining a balance among competing ideologies. Criminals must be removed from society, and meaningless violence must be stopped. But the warrior spirit must not be demonised. Do not create a society that demeans masculinity. Too much of anything creates an imbalance in life. This is true even of virtues such as non-violence. You never know when the winds of change strike; when violence may be required to protect your society, or to even survive.'

There was pin-drop silence.

It was time.

Vishwamitra asked the question he had steered the conversation towards. 'Is there an extremism that the Sapt Sindhu surrendered to which allowed Raavan to defeat them?'

Sita considered the question carefully. 'Yes, resentment and hatred towards the trading class.'

'Correct. In the past, because of a few monsters among their warriors, the *Bhaaratas* attacked the entire Kshatriya way of life. They became pathologically non-violent. There have been societies that have attacked the Brahmin way of life, becoming proudly anti-intellectual, because a few of their Brahmins became closed-minded, elitist and exclusivist. And the Sapt Sindhu in our age began to demean trading itself when a few of their Vaishyas became selfish, ostentatious, and money-grubbing. We gradually pushed trade out of the hands of the 'evil-moneyed capitalists' of our own society, and into the hands of others. Kubaer, and later Raavan, just gathered the money slowly, and economic power flowed naturally to them. The Battle of Karachapa was only a formality that sealed long historical trends. A society must always aim for balance. It needs intellectuals, it needs warriors, it needs traders, it needs artists, and it needs skilled workers. If it empowers one group too much or another too little, it is headed for chaos.'

Sita recalled something she had heard in one of the *dharma sabhas* of her father. 'The only "ism" I believe in, is pragmatism.'

It was said by a Charvak philosopher.

'Are you committed to Charvak philosophy?' asked Vishwamitra.

The Charvak School of philosophy was named after their ancient founder, an atheist who believed in materialism. He had lived near Gangotri, the source of the holy Ganga. The Charvaks only believed in what could be sensed by the physical senses. According to them, there was neither a soul, nor any Gods. The only reality was this body, a mix of the elements, which would return to the elements once it died. They lived for the day and enjoyed life. Their admirers saw them as liberal, individualistic and non-judgemental. On the other hand, their critics saw them as immoral, selfish and irresponsible.

'No, I am not committed to the Charvaks, Guru*ji*. If I am pragmatic, then I should be open to *every* school of philosophy. And accept only those parts that make sense to me, while rejecting other bits that don't. I should learn from any philosophy that can help me fulfil my karma.'

Vishwamitra smiled. *Smart, very smart for a thirteen-year-old.*

Chapter 7

Sita sat by the pond, reading *Nyayasutra*, the classic text which introduced a key school of Indian philosophy, *Nyaya Darshan*. A few months had passed since Vishwamitra had visited Rishi Shvetaketu's *gurukul*.

'Bhoomi,' said Radhika, using the *gurukul* name of Sita, 'someone from your home has come to meet you.'

Sita sighed with irritation. 'Can't they wait?'

She was compiling a list of questions she wanted to ask Rishi Shvetaketu. Now the exercise would be delayed.

— ༄ —

Samichi stood patiently, close to the jetty. Waiting for Sita.

A posse of ten men stood behind her. They were under her command.

Samichi was not the girl from the slums anymore. Having joined the police, she was a rapidly rising star there. It was common knowledge that the royal family liked her, indebted as they were to her for having saved Princess Sita in the Mithila slums. People were guarded in her presence. Nobody knew her exact age, including Samichi herself. Her appearance suggested that she was in her early twenties now. For a woman of her age, not born into nobility, to be commanding a posse in the police force was a rare honour. But then, she had saved the princess.

'Samichi!'

Samichi groaned as she recognised the voice. It was that ridiculous boy, Kaaml Raj. He was panting by the time he ran up to her. Excited.

'Someone told me you were here. I came as fast as I could.'

Samichi looked at the twelve-year-old. He held a red rose in his hands. She narrowed her eyes and resisted the temptation to shove him. 'I've told you …'

'I thought you'd like this rose,' said Kaaml shyly. 'I saw you enjoy the fragrance of the flowers the last time you were here.'

Samichi spoke in a cold whisper. 'I'm not interested in odours of any kind.'

Not to be deterred, Kaaml held out a hand, showing her his bleeding finger. A pathetic attempt to extract sympathy. He had pricked himself repeatedly with thorns before yanking the flower from the rose bush. Seeing that it wasn't working, he stepped closer. 'Do you have some medicine for my finger?'

Samichi stepped back to put some distance between them. In doing so, she stumbled on a stone. Just a little. Kaaml rushed forward to grab her. The poor boy genuinely wanted to help. What happened next was blinding in its speed. Samichi screamed in anger, twisted his arm, and viciously kicked him in the leg. As Kaaml fell forward, she brought her elbow up in a brutal jab. It cracked his nose. Instantly.

Kaaml clutched his bleeding nose, as Samichi shouted in anger, 'DO NOT TOUCH ME, EVER!'

Kaaml was crying desperately now. He lay on the ground in a frightened heap. Bloodied. Trembling. The policemen rushed forward and helped the boy to his feet. They cast a surreptitious, horror-filled glance at their leader. All of them had the same thought.

He's only a boy! What is wrong with her?

Samichi's stony face showed no trace of regret. She signalled a Mithila policeman with a dismissive wave of a hand. 'Get this idiot out of here.'

The policeman lifted the boy gingerly and walked away to find the *gurukul* doctor. The other policemen walked back to the jetty in a fearful procession. The air was thick with unspoken words about their captain.

Something is not right with Samichi.

'Samichi.'

All turned to see Princess Sita emerge from the trees. And, Samichi transformed like a chameleon. Smiling broadly, she rushed forward with warmth oozing from her eyes.

'How are you, Samichi?' asked Sita, as she embraced her friend.

Before Samichi could answer, Sita turned to the policemen standing at a distance and pulled her hands together into a *Namaste,* along with a warm smile. The policemen bowed low, also folding their hands into a *Namaste.*

'I wonder why your men always look so scared,' whispered Sita.

Samichi grinned and shook her head, holding Sita's hand, pulling her away, out of earshot of the policemen. 'Forget them, Princess,' said Samichi, her smile affectionate.

'I've told you before, Samichi,' said Sita, 'when we are alone, call me Sita. Not Princess. You are my friend. Anyway, it's not as if anyone thinks of me as a princess anymore.'

'Whatever anyone may think, I have no doubt that you are a princess of Mithila.'

Sita rolled her eyes. 'Yeah, right.'

'Princess, I have been sent to ...'

Sita interrupted Samichi. 'Sita. Not Princess.'

'Apologies, Sita, you must come home.'

Sita sighed. 'You know I can't, Samichi. I have caused enough trouble for *maa*.'

'Sita, don't do this to yourself.'

'Everyone knows about the incident with *chacha*. When I broke his royal seal,' Sita recalled her *uncle* Kushadhwaj's last visit to Mithila. 'He is endlessly troubling *maa* and Mithila. Everyone blames me for it. And rightly so. I should just stay away.'

'Sita, your father and mother miss you. Queen Sunaina is very sick. You really should ...'

'Nothing can happen to *maa*. She is a superwoman. You are just saying this to make me leave the *gurukul* and come home.'

'But ... it's the truth.'

'The truth is that *maa* should focus on Urmila and the kingdom. You know that *baba* is ... distracted. You yourself have told me what the people say about me. She doesn't need me to increase her problems.'

'Sita ...'

'Enough,' said Sita, raising her hand. 'I don't feel like talking about this anymore.'

'Sita ...'

'I feel like practising stick-fighting. Are you game?'

Anything to change the subject, thought Samichi.

'Come on,' said Sita, turning around.

Samichi followed.

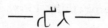

Vishwamitra sat in the lotus position in his austere hut at the Ganga *ashram* of the Malayaputras.

He was meditating. Trying to keep all thoughts out of his mind. But he was failing today.

He heard a whistling sound. And recognised it immediately. It was a common hill myna. A bird that has often been called the most amazing vocalist. It can whistle, warble, shriek, and even mimic.

What is it doing so far away from home? In the plains?

His mind wandered to an incident from the past. When he had heard the myna in a place he should not have.

Amazing how the mind wanders ... So flighty and unpredictable ...

The memory of that day, many decades ago, now came flooding back.

It was the day he had received the news of his former friend, Vashishtha, being appointed the *raj guru* of Ayodhya.

Vishwamitra felt his chest constrict. In anger. And pain.

That backstabber ... I did so much for him ...

His mind wandered to the exact moment he had heard the news. At the *ashram* of ...

Vishwamitra's eyes suddenly flew open.

By the great Lord Parshu Ram ...

He remembered where he had seen that face. Sita's face.

He smiled. This only reinforced his decision.

Thank you, Lord Parshu Ram. You made my mind wander only to help me find my path.

— ॐ —

'Guru*ji* ...' whispered Arishtanemi.

He stood next to Vishwamitra at the balustrade of the lead ship. They were in a five-vessel convoy that was sailing down the sacred Ganga, on their way to supervise a search being conducted by their miners for some special material. It would help them acquire a powerful weapon called the *Asuraastra*, leaving them less dependent on the Vayuputras.

Centuries ago, Lord Rudra, the previous Mahadev, had restricted the use of *daivi astras*. The approval of the Vayuputras, the living representatives of Lord Rudra, was mandatory for using the *divine weapons*. This was not to Vishwamitra's liking or comfort.

The great *Maharishi* had made elaborate plans. Plans which involved, perhaps, the use of the *Asuraastra*. He knew the Vayuputras did not like him. Not since the episode with Trishanku. They tolerated him because they had no choice. He was, after all, chief of the Malayaputras.

While the search was a slow and tedious process, Vishwamitra was confident that the material would be found, eventually.

It was time to move to the next phase of his plan. He had to select a Vishnu. He had just revealed his choice to Arishtanemi, his trusted lieutenant.

'You disagree?' asked Vishwamitra.

'She is exceptionally capable, Guru*ji*. No doubt about it. One can sense it, even at her tender age. But ...' Arishtanemi's voice trailed off.

Vishwamitra put his hand on Arishtanemi's shoulder. 'Speak freely. I am talking to you because I want to hear your views.'

'I spent some time watching her carefully, Guru*ji*. I think she is too rebellious. I am not sure the Malayaputras will be able to manage her. Or, control her.'

'We will. She has no one else. Her city has abandoned her. But she has the potential to be great. She *wants* to be great. We will be her route to realising it.'

'But can't we also keep searching for other candidates?'

'Your trusted aides gathered information on her in Mithila, right? Most of it was very encouraging.'

'But there was that case of her probably killing a boy in the Mithila slums when she was eight.'

'I see in that incident her ability to survive. Your investigators also said the boy was probably a criminal. She fought her way through, even as a small child. That's a positive. She has the fighting spirit. Would you rather she had died like a coward?'

'No, Guru*ji*,' said Arishtanemi. 'But I am wondering if there are possibly other candidates that we have not yet stumbled upon.'

'You personally know almost every royal family in India. Most of them are completely useless. Selfish, cowardly, and weak. And their next generation, the royal children, are even worse. They are nothing but genetic garbage.'

Arishtanemi laughed. 'Few countries have had the misfortune of being saddled with such a worthless elite.'

'We have had great leaders in the past. And we will have a great leader in the future too. One who will pull India out of its present morass.'

'Why not from the common folk?'

'We have been searching for a long time. Had that been Lord Parshu Ram's will, we would have found one by now. And don't forget, Sita is only an adopted royal. Her parentage is unknown.'

Vishwamitra did not feel the need to tell Arishtanemi what he suspected about Sita's birth.

Arishtanemi overcame his hesitation. 'I have heard that the Ayodhya princes ...'

The Malayaputra military chief stopped mid-sentence when

he saw Vishwamitra bristle. His famed courage vanished into thin air. Arishtanemi had indeed heard positive reports about the young princes of Ayodhya, particularly Ram and Bharat. Ram was a little less than nine years old. But Vashishtha was the *raj guru* of Ayodhya. And, Vashishtha was a subject Arishtanemi had learned to avoid.

'That snake has taken the Ayodhya princes to his *gurukul*,' said Vishwamitra, anger boiling within. 'I don't even know where his *ashram* is. He has kept it a secret. If *I* don't know then nobody knows. We only hear about the four brothers when they return to Ayodhya on holiday.'

Arishtanemi stood like a statue, barely breathing.

'I know how Vashishtha's mind works. I had made the mistake of considering him my friend once. He is up to something. Either with Ram or Bharat.'

'Sometimes, things don't work out as planned, Guru*ji*. Our work in Lanka inadvertently ended up helping ...'

'Raavan has his uses,' interrupted Vishwamitra. 'Don't ever forget that. And, he is moving in the direction we need him to. It will all work out.'

'But Guru*ji*, can the Vayuputras oppose the Malayaputras? It is our prerogative to choose the next Vishnu. Not that of the *raj guru* of Ayodhya.'

'For all their sham neutrality, the Vayuputras will do everything they can to help that rat. I know it. We do not have much time. We must start preparing now!'

'Yes, Guru*ji*.'

'And, if she is to be trained for her role, it too must begin now.'

'Yes, Guru*ji*.'

'Sita will be the Vishnu. The Vishnu will rise during my

reign. The time has come. This country needs a leader. We cannot allow our beloved India to suffer endlessly.'

'Yes, Guru*ji*,' said Arishtanemi. 'Should I tell the Captain to ...'

'Yes.'

— ꛳ —

'Where are you taking me, Radhika?' asked Sita, smiling, as her friend led her by the hand.

They were walking deep into the forest to the south of the *gurukul*.

'Hanu *bhaiya*!' screamed Sita in delight, as they entered a small clearing.

Hanuman stood next to his horse, rubbing the tired animal's neck. The horse was tied to a tree.

'My sisters!' said Hanuman affectionately.

The gentle giant walked up to them. He enclosed them together in a warm embrace. 'How are the two of you doing?'

'You have been away for far too long!' Radhika complained.

'I know,' sighed Hanuman. 'I'm sorry. I was abroad ...'

'Where do you keep going?' asked Sita, who found Hanuman's mysterious life very exciting. 'Who sends you on these missions?'

'I will tell you when the time is right, Sita ... But not now.'

Hanuman reached into the saddlebag tied to the horse and pulled out a delicate necklace made of gold, in a style that was obviously foreign.

Radhika squealed with delight.

'You guess correctly,' smiled Hanuman, as he handed it to her. 'This one is for you ...'

Radhika admired the necklace in detail, turning it around several times in her hands.

'And for you, my serious one,' said Hanuman to Sita. 'I've got what you've always wanted ...'

Sita's eyes widened. 'An *ekmukhi Rudraaksh*?!'

The word *Rudraaksh* literally meant the *teardrop of Rudra*. In reality, it was a brown elliptical seed. All who were loyal to the Mahadev, Lord Rudra, wore threaded *Rudraaksh* beads or kept one in their *puja* rooms. A common *Rudraaksh* seed had many grooves running across it. An *ekmukhi Rudraaksh* was rare, and had only one groove on its surface. Very difficult to find. Expensive too. Priceless for Sita, a staunch Lord Rudra devotee.

Hanuman smiled as he reached into the saddlebag.

Suddenly, the horse became fidgety and nervous, its ears flicking back and forth. Within moments its breathing was rapid and shallow. Conveying panic.

Hanuman looked around carefully. And he caught sight of the danger.

Very slowly, without any sign of alarm, he pulled Radhika and Sita behind him.

The girls knew better than to talk. They, too, could sense danger. Something was seriously wrong.

Hanuman suddenly made a loud, screeching sound; like that of an agitated monkey. The tiger hidden behind the tree immediately knew that its element of surprise was gone. It walked out slowly. Hanuman reached for the scabbard tied to his cummerbund and drew out his curved knife. Made in the style of the *khukuris* of the fierce Gorkhas, the blade of the knife was not straight. It thickened at mid-length, and then the thick section curved downwards. Like a sloping shoulder. At the hilt-end, the sharp side of the blade had a double-wave notch. Shaped like a cow's foot. It served a practical purpose. It allowed the blood from the blade to drip to the ground, instead of spreading to the hilt and making the knife-hold slippery. The cow's foot indentation also signified that the weapon could never be used to kill a holy cow. The handle was made of ivory. At the halfway mark, a protrusion emerged from all sides of the hilt. It served as a peg between the middle finger and the ring finger, making the grip secure. The *khukuri* had no cross-guard for a thrusting action. A less-skilled warrior's hand could slip forward onto the blade, in a thrust. It could cause serious injury to the knife-wielder.

But nobody in their right mind would call Hanuman less than supremely skilled.

'Stay behind me,' whispered Hanuman to the girls, as the tiger edged forward slowly.

Hanuman spread his legs apart and bent, maintaining his balance. Waiting. For what was to follow. Keeping his breathing steady.

With an ear-splitting roar, the tiger suddenly burst forward, going up on its hind legs, spreading its front legs out. Ready to hold the massive Hanuman in its grip. Its jaws opened wide, it headed straight for Hanuman's throat.

The tiger's tactic was sound: topple the human with its massive weight, pin him to the ground with its claws, and rely on its jaws to finish the job.

Against a lesser enemy, it would have prevailed. But, to its misfortune, it had attacked the mighty Hanuman.

The giant Naga was almost as big as the tiger. With one foot back, he arched his spine, flexed his powerful muscles; and, remained on his feet. Using his left hand, he held the tiger by its throat, and kept its fearsome jaws away. Hanuman allowed the tiger to claw his back. It would not cause much damage. He pulled his right hand back, flexed his shoulder muscles and brutally thrust the *khukuri* deep into the tiger's abdomen. Its outrageously sharp-edged blade sliced in smoothly. The beast roared in pain. Its eyes wide in shock.

Hanuman sucked in his breath and executed a draw-cut to the right, ripping deep into the beast's abdominal cavity. All the way from one end to the other. Vicious, but effective. Not only did most of the beast's abdominal organs get slashed, the knife even sliced through a bit of the backbone and the nerves protected inside.

The tiger's slippery intestines slid out of its cleaved abdomen, its hind legs locked in paralysis. Hanuman pushed the beast back. It fell to the ground, roaring in agony as its front legs lashed out in all directions.

Hanuman could have avoided further injury from its claws had he waited for the tiger to weaken. And let its front legs go down. But the animal was in agony. He wanted to end its suffering. Hanuman bent closer even as the tiger's claws dug deep into his shoulders. The Naga stabbed straight into the animal's chest. The blade cut right through, sliding deep into the beast's heart. It struggled for a few moments and then its soul escaped its body.

Hanuman pulled the blade out and whispered softly, 'May your soul find purpose once again, noble beast.'

— ᚱᚷᚷ —

'These things happen, Radhika,' said Hanuman. 'We're in the middle of a jungle. What do you expect?'

Radhika was still shaking with fear.

Sita had quickly pulled out the medical aid kit from the saddlebag and dressed Hanuman's injuries. They were not life-threatening but a few of them were deep. Sita stitched a couple of gaping wounds. She found some rejuvenating herbs around the clearing and made an infusion, using stones to grind the leaves with some water. She gave it to Hanuman to drink.

As Hanuman gulped the medicine down and wiped his mouth with the back of his hand, he watched Sita.

She is not nervous … She didn't get scared … This girl is special …

'I would not have imagined that a tiger could be brought down with such ease,' whispered Sita.

'It helps if you're my size!' laughed Hanuman.

'Are you sure that you can ride? Your wounds aren't serious, but …'

'I can't stay here either. I have to get back …'

'Another of your mysterious missions?'

'I have to go.'

'You have to do what you have to do, Hanu *bhaiya*.'

Hanuman smiled. 'Don't forget your *Rudraaksh*.'

Sita reached into the saddlebag and pulled out a silk pouch. She opened it slowly, carefully picking up the *ekmukhi Rudraaksh*. She stared at it in awe. Then she held it to her forehead with reverence before slipping it into the pouch tied to her waist.

Chapter 8

Shvetaketu could not believe his luck. The great Vishwamitra had arrived at his *gurukul* for the second time this year! He rushed to the gates of the *ashram* as the Malayaputras marched in.

'*Namaste*, Great One,' said Shvetaketu, smiling broadly, his hands joined together in respect.

'*Namaste*, Shvetaketu,' said Vishwamitra, smiling just enough to not intimidate his host.

'What an honour to have you call on our *gurukul* so soon after your last visit.'

'Yes,' said Vishwamitra, looking around.

'It is unfortunate that my students are not here to gain from your presence,' said Shvetaketu, his expression reflecting heartfelt regret. 'Most of them are away on vacation.'

'But I believe a few have stayed back.'

'Yes, Illustrious One. Sita is here ... And ...'

'I would like to meet Sita.'

'Of course.'

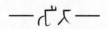

Sita stood with Maharishi Vishwamitra near the balustrade at the edge of the main deck of his anchored ship, facing the far bank of the Ganga. Vishwamitra had wanted privacy, away from the curious eyes of the teachers in the *gurukul*. A small brick-laid *yagna kund* was being readied by the Malayaputra *pandits* on the main deck of the ship, a little distance away from Sita and Vishwamitra.

Sita was confused. *Why does the* Maharishi *want to speak to me?*

'How old are you now, Sita?'

'I will turn fourteen soon, Guru*ji*.'

'That's not too old. We can begin, I think.'

'Begin what, Guru*ji*?'

Vishwamitra took a deep breath. 'Have you heard of the institution of the Vishnu?'

'Yes, Guru*ji*.'

'Tell me what you know.'

'It is a title given to the greatest of leaders, who are Propagators of Good. They lead their people into a new way of life. There have been six Vishnus in this present Vedic age that we live in. The previous Vishnu was the great Lord Parshu Ram.'

Jai Parshu Ram.'

Jai Parshu Ram.'

'What else do you know?'

'The Vishnus normally work in partnership with the Mahadevs, who are Destroyers of Evil. The Mahadevs assign a tribe as their representatives once their *karma* in a particular life is over. The tribe of the previous Mahadev, Lord Rudra, is the Vayuputras who live in faraway Pariha. The Vishnu of our age will work in close partnership with …'

'This partnership thing is not necessarily important,' interrupted Vishwamitra.

Sita fell silent. Surprised. This was not what she had learnt. 'What else do you know?'

'I know that the previous Vishnu, Lord Parshu Ram, left behind a tribe as well — the Malayaputras. And you, *Maharishiji,* are the chief of the Malayaputras. And if a Vishnu must rise in our age, to fight the darkness that envelops us, it must be you.'

'You are wrong.'

Sita frowned. Confused.

'The assumption you made in your last statement is wrong,' clarified Vishwamitra. 'Yes, I am the chief of the Malayaputras. But I cannot be the Vishnu. My task is to decide who the next Vishnu will be.'

Sita nodded silently.

'What do you think is the main problem corroding India today?'

'Most people will say Raavan, but I won't.'

Vishwamitra smiled. 'Why not?'

'Raavan is only a symptom. He is not the disease. If it hadn't been Raavan, it would have been someone else torturing us. The fault lies in us, that we allow ourselves to be dominated. Raavan may be powerful, but if we …'

'Raavan is not as powerful as the people of Sapt Sindhu think he is. But he revels in this image of the monster that he has created for himself. That image intimidates others. But that image is useful for us as well,' said Vishwamitra.

Sita didn't understand that last line. And, Vishwamitra chose not to explain.

'So, you say that Raavan is only a symptom. Then, what is the disease afflicting the Sapt Sindhu today?'

Sita paused to formulate her thoughts. 'I've been thinking about this since you spoke to us at the *gurukul* last year, Guru*ji*.

You said society needs balance. It needs intellectuals, warriors, traders, and skilled workers. And that ideally, the scale should not be tipped against any group. That there should be a fair balance between all.'

'And ...'

'So, why is it that society always moves towards imbalance? That's what I was thinking. It gets unbalanced when people are not free to live a life that is in alignment with their innate *guna*, their *attributes*. It can happen when a group is oppressed or belittled, like the *Vaishyas* in Sapt Sindhu today. It makes those with *Vaishya gunas* frustrated and angry. It can also happen when you're made to follow the occupation of your parents and clan, rather than what you may want to pursue. Raavan was born a Brahmin. But he clearly did not want to be a Brahmin. He is a Kshatriya by nature. It must have been the same with ...'

Sita stopped herself in time. But Vishwamitra was staring directly into her eyes, reading her thoughts. 'Yes, it happened with me too. I was born a Kshatriya but wanted to be a Brahmin.'

'People like you are rare, Guru*ji*. Most people surrender to the pressure of society and family. But it builds terrible frustration within. These are unhappy and angry people, living unbalanced, dissatisfied lives. Furthermore, society itself suffers. It may get stuck with Kshatriyas who do not possess valour, and cannot protect their society. It may get stuck with Brahmins who prefer to be skilled Shudras like medical surgeons or sculptors, and therefore will be terrible teachers. And ultimately, society will decline.'

'You have diagnosed the problem well. So, what is the solution?'

'I don't know. How does one change society? How do we break down this birth-based caste system that is destroying our noble land?'

'I have a solution in mind.'

Sita waited for an explanation.

'Not now,' said Vishwamitra. 'I will explain one day. When you are ready. For now, we have a ceremony to conduct.'

'Ceremony?'

'Yes,' said Vishwamitra, as he turned towards the *yagna kund,* which had been built at the centre of the main deck. Seven Malayaputra *pandits* waited at the other end of the deck. Upon a signal from Vishwamitra, they walked up to the *yagna kund.*

'Come,' said Vishwamitra, as he led her forward.

The *yagna* platform was built in an unorthodox manner, or at least one with which Sita was not familiar. It had a square, outer boundary, made of bricks. Encased within it was a circular inner boundary, made of metal.

'This *yagna kund* represents a type of *mandal,* a symbolic representation of spiritual reality,' Vishwamitra explained to Sita. 'The square boundary symbolises *Prithvi,* the earth that we live on. The four sides of the square represent the four directions. The space inside the square represents *Prakruti* or nature. It is uncultured and wild. The circle within represents the path of consciousness; of the *Parmatma.* The task of the Vishnu is to find the *Parmatma* within this earthly life. The Vishnu lights a path to God. Not through detachment from the world, but through profound and spiritual attachment to this great land of ours.'

'Yes, Guru*ji.*'

'You will sit on the southern side of the square.'

Sita sat in the seat indicated by Vishwamitra. The Chief

Malayaputra sat with his back to the north, facing Sita. A Malayaputra *pandit* lit the fire within the circular inner boundary of the *yagna* platform. He was chanting a hymn dedicated to Lord Agni, the God of Fire.

A *yagna* signifies a sacrificial exchange: you sacrifice something that you hold dear, and receive benediction in return. Lord Agni, the purifying fire, is witness to this exchange between humans and the divine.

Vishwamitra folded his hands together into a *Namaste*. So did Sita. He began chanting a hymn from the *Brihadaranyak Upanishad*. Sita and the seven Malayaputra *pandits* joined in.

Asato mā sadgamaya
Tamasomā jyotir gamaya
Mrityormāamritam gamaya
Om shāntishānti shāntih
Lead me from untruth to truth
Lead me from darkness to light
Lead me from death to immortality
For Me and the Universe, let there be peace, peace, peace

Vishwamitra reached into a pouch tied to his waist and withdrew a small scabbard. Holding it reverentially in the palm of his hand, he pulled out a tiny silver knife. He ran his finger over the edge, bringing it to rest on the tip of the blade. Sharp. He checked the markings on the handle. It was the correct one. He reached over the fire and handed the knife to Sita. It had to be passed from the northern to the southern direction.

'This *yagna* will be sealed in blood,' said Vishwamitra.

'Yes, Guru*ji*,' said Sita, accepting the knife with both hands as a mark of respect.

Vishwamitra reached into his pouch and retrieved another small scabbard. He pulled out the second knife and checked its blade. Perfectly sharp. He looked at Sita. 'The blood must only drop within the circular inner boundary of the *yagna kund*. Under no circumstances must it spill in the space between the metal and bricks. Is that clear?'

'Yes, Guru*ji*.'

Two Malayaputra *pandits* approached them silently and handed two pieces of cloth each to Vishwamitra and Sita. Each had been doused in neem-juice disinfectants. Without waiting for further instructions, Sita placed the sharp knife-edge on her left palm and folded her hand over the blade. Then, in a swift, clean motion, she pulled the knife back, cutting open the skin from edge to edge. Blood dribbled freely into the sacred fire. She did not flinch.

'*Arrey*, we needed just a drop of blood,' exclaimed Vishwamitra. 'A little nick would have been enough.'

Sita looked at Vishwamitra, unperturbed. She pressed the disinfectant cloth into her injured hand, careful not to spill any blood.

Vishwamitra quickly pricked his thumb with the knife edge.

He held his hand over the inner boundary of the *yagna kund*, and pressed his thumb to let a drop of blood fall into the flames. Sita also held out her left hand and removed the cloth, letting her blood drip into the fire.

Vishwamitra spoke in a clear voice. 'With the pure Lord Agni as my witness, I swear that I will honour my promise to Lord Parshu Ram. Always. To my last breath. And beyond.'

Sita repeated the words. Exactly.

'*Jai Parshu Ram*,' said Vishwamitra.

'*Jai Parshu Ram*,' repeated Sita.

The Malayaputra *pandits* around them chimed in. '*Jai Parshu Ram*.'

Vishwamitra smiled and withdrew his hand. Sita too pulled her hand back and covered it with the disinfectant cloth. A Malayaputra *pandit* walked up to her and tied the cloth tight around her hand, staunching the blood flow.

'It is done,' said Vishwamitra, looking at Sita.

'Am I a Malayaputra now?' asked Sita expectantly.

Vishwamitra looked amused. He pointed to Sita's knife. 'Look at the markings on your knife.'

Sita picked up the silver knife. Its blade-edge was stained with her blood. She examined the handle. It had three intricate letters engraved on it. Sages of yore, in their wisdom, had suggested that Old Sanskrit should not have a written script. They felt that the written word was inferior to the spoken; that it reduced the ability of the mind to understand concepts. Rishi Shvetaketu had had another explanation: the sages preferred that scriptures were not written down and remained oral so that as times changed, they could change easily as well. Writing things down brought rigidity into the scriptures. Whatever the reason, the fact was that writing was not valued in the Sapt Sindhu. As a result, there were many scripts that existed across the land. Scripts that changed from time to time and place to place. There was no serious attempt to develop a standard script.

The word on the handle was written in a common script from the upper reaches of the Saraswati River. Sita recognised it.

The symbols represented Parshu Ram.

'Not that side, Sita,' said Vishwamitra. 'Turn it around.'

Sita flipped the knife. Her eyes widened with shock.

The fish was the most common symbol across all scripts in India. A giant fish had helped Lord Manu and his band escape when the sea had devastated their land. Lord Manu had decreed that the great fish would be honoured with the title of Lord Matsya, the first Vishnu. The symbol of the fish represented a follower of the Vishnu. This was the symbol on Vishwamitra's knife handle.

But the symbol on Sita's handle was a modified version. It was a fish, no doubt, but it also had a crown on top.

The fish symbol minus the crown on it meant that you were a follower of the Vishnu. But if the fish symbol had a crown on top, it meant that you *were* the Vishnu.

Sita looked at Vishwamitra, bewildered.

'This knife is yours, Sita,' said Vishwamitra softly.

Chapter 9

The student quarters in Shvetaketu's *gurukul* were frugal. In
keeping with the general atmosphere of the place. Each student
occupied a small windowless mud hut, barely large enough to
accommodate a single bed, some clothes pegs and a place for
study materials. The huts had no doors, just doorways.

Sita was lying in bed, recalling the events of the previous
day on the Malayaputra ship.

She held the knife in her hand. She was in no danger of
getting cut since the blade was safely in the scabbard. Again
and again, her eyes were drawn to the knife handle. And the
beautiful symbol etched on its surface.

Vishnu?

Me?

Vishwamitra had said that her training would begin soon.
She would be old enough to leave the *gurukul* in a few months.
She would then take a trip to Agastyakootam, the capital of
the Malayaputras, deep in the south of India. After that, she
would travel across India, incognito. Vishwamitra wanted her
to understand the land that she would redeem and lead one day.
Along with his Malayaputras, he would guide her through this.
In the interim, she and Vishwamitra would prepare a blueprint
for the task ahead. For a new way of life.

It was all quite overwhelming.

'My Lady.'

Sita slipped out of bed and came to the doorway. Jatayu was standing at some distance.

'My Lady,' he repeated.

Sita folded her hands into a *Namaste*. 'I am like your younger sister, Jatayu*ji*. Please don't embarrass me. Just call me by my name.'

'No, I can't do that, My Lady. You are the ...'

Jatayu fell silent. Strict instructions had been given to the Malayaputras. Nobody was to speak of Sita as the next Vishnu. It would be announced at the right time. Even Sita had been prohibited from speaking about it with anyone. Not that she would have, in any case. She felt anxious, almost afraid, of what the title implied.

'Well then, you can call me your sister.'

Jatayu smiled. 'That is fair, my sister.'

'What did you want to talk about, Jatayu*ji*?'

'How is your hand now?'

Sita grinned as she touched the neem-leaf bandage with her other hand. 'I was a little too enthusiastic about drawing blood.'

'Yes.'

'I am all right now.'

'That is good to hear,' said Jatayu. He was a shy man. Taking a slow, long breath in, he softly continued, 'You are one of the very few people, besides the Malayaputras, who have shown kindness towards me. Even though Lord Vishwamitra had not ordered you to do so.'

All those months ago, Sita had served Jatayu some food simply because his face reminded her of the noble vulture who had saved her life. But she kept that to herself.

'You are probably unsure about this new situation,' said Jatayu. 'It's natural to feel overwhelmed.'

What he didn't tell her was that even some Malayaputras had their doubts about the choice of Sita as a Vishnu, but wouldn't dare openly challenge their formidable chief.

Sita nodded silently.

'It must be even more difficult because you cannot talk to anyone other than a Malayaputra about this.'

'Yes,' Sita smiled.

'If you ever need any advice, or even someone to talk to, you always have me. It is my duty to protect you from now onwards. My platoon and I will always be nearby,' said Jatayu, gesturing behind him.

Around fifteen men stood quietly at a distance.

'I will not embarrass you by revealing myself in public, in Mithila or anywhere else,' said Jatayu. 'I understand that I am a Naga. But I will never be more than a few hours' ride away. My people and I will always be your shadow from now on.'

'You could never embarrass me, Jatayu*ji*,' said Sita.

'Sita!'

The princess of Mithila looked to her left. It was Arishtanemi.

'Sita,' said Arishtanemi, 'Guru*ji* would like to have a word with you.'

'Excuse me, Jatayu*ji*,' said Sita, as she folded her hands into a polite *Namaste*.

Jatayu returned her salutation and Sita walked away, trailing Arishtanemi. As she faded into the distance, Jatayu bent down, picked up some dust from her footprint, and touched it respectfully to his forehead. He then turned in the direction that Sita had walked.

She is such a good soul …

I hope Lady Sita does not become a pawn in the battle between Guru Vishwamitra and Guru Vashishtha.

— ༃ —

Two months had passed. The Malayaputras had left for their capital, Agastyakootam. As instructed, Sita spent most of her free time reading texts that the chief of the Malayaputras had given her. They chronicled the lives of some of the previous Vishnus: Lord Narsimha, Lord Vaaman, Lord Parshu Ram, among others. He wanted her to learn from their lives, their challenges; and, how to overcome them and establish a new path that led to the Propagation of Good.

She took up this task with utmost seriousness and conducted it in privacy. Today, she sat by a tiny pond not frequented by other students. It was therefore with irritation that she reacted to the disturbance.

'Bhoomi, you need to come to the main *gurukul* clearing right away,' said Radhika, using Sita's *gurukul* name. 'Someone from your home is here.'

Sita waved her hand in annoyance. 'I'll be there, soon.'

'Sita!' said Radhika loudly.

Sita turned around. Her friend looked and sounded agitated. 'Your mother is here. You need to go. Now.'

— ༃ —

Sita walked slowly towards the main *gurukul* clearing. Her heart beating hard. She saw two elephants tied close to the walkway, which led to the *gurukul* jetty. She knew her mother liked bringing her elephants along. On Sunaina's visits, Sita and she would go on elephant rides deep into the jungle. Sunaina loved to educate her daughter on animals in their natural habitat.

Sunaina knew more about animals than anyone Sita had met. The trips into the jungle were among Sita's most cherished memories. For they involved the two most important entities in her life: Mother Earth and her own mother.

Pain shot through her heart.

Because of her, Kushadhwaj had imposed severe restrictions on Mithila trade. Her uncle's kingdom, Sankashya, was the main conduit for trade with her father's kingdom; and the prices of most commodities, even essentials, had shot through the roof. Most Mithilans blamed Sita for this. Everyone knew that she had broken Kushadhwaj's royal seal. And, that retaliation was inevitable. According to ancient tradition, the royal seal was the representation of the king; breaking it was comparable to regicide.

The blame had also seamlessly passed on to her mother, Sunaina. For everyone knew that it was Sunaina's decision to adopt Sita.

I have given her nothing but trouble. I have destroyed so much of what she spent her life building.

Maa *should forget me.*

Sita was even more convinced of her decision by the time she reached the clearing.

It was unusually crowded, even for a royal visit. Eight men were gathered around a heavy, empty palanquin. It was a palanquin she hadn't seen before: longer and broader. It appeared to be designed so that the person travelling in it could lie down. To the left, she saw eight women crowding around a low platform built around an *Ashok* tree. She looked all over for her mother, but did not see her anywhere.

She moved towards the women, about to ask where her mother was. Just then, a few of them moved aside, revealing Queen Sunaina.

It knocked the wind out of Sita.

Her mother was a shadow of her former self. She had been reduced to bare skin and bones. Her round, moon-shaped face had turned gaunt, with cheeks sunken in. She had always been short and petite, but had never looked unhealthy. Now, her muscles had wasted away, and her body was stripped of the little fat she had once had. Her eyes looked hollow. Her lustrous, rich black hair had turned sparse and a ghostly white. She could barely hold herself up. She needed her aides to support her.

As soon as Sunaina saw her precious daughter, her face lit up. It was the same warm smile where Sita had always found comfort and sanctuary.

'My child,' said Sunaina, in a barely audible voice.

The queen of Mithila held out her hands, her deathly pallor temporarily reduced by the abundance of a mother's love-filled heart.

Sita stood rooted to her spot. Hoping the earth would swallow her.

'Come here, my child,' said Sunaina. Her arms, too weak to be held up, fell on her sides.

Sunaina coughed. An aide rushed forward and wiped her mouth with a handkerchief. Specks of red appeared on the white cloth.

Sita stumbled towards her mother. Dazed. She fell to her knees and rested her head on Sunaina's lap. One that had always been soft, like Mother Earth immediately after the rains. It was bony and hard now, like the same earth after a series of devastating droughts.

Sunaina ran her fingers through Sita's hair.

Sita trembled in fear and sorrow, like a little sparrow about to see the fall of the mighty *Banyan* tree that had sheltered not just her body but also her soul.

Continuing to run her hand through Sita's hair, Sunaina bent down, kissed her head and whispered, 'My child …'

Sita burst out crying.

— ꯁꯥ —

The Mithila physician-in-attendance had vehemently opposed it. Even though severely weakened, Sunaina was still a formidable creature. She would not be denied the elephant ride into the jungle with her daughter.

The physician had played his final card. He had whispered into the queen's ear, 'This may well be your last elephant ride, Your Highness.'

And Sunaina had replied, 'That is precisely why I must go.'

The queen had rested in the palanquin while the two elephants were prepared for the ride. One would carry the physician and a few attendants, while the other would carry Sunaina and Sita.

When it was time, Sunaina was carried to the howdah of the seated elephant. A maid tried to clamber aboard, next to the queen.

'No!' a firm Sunaina decreed.

'But, My Lady …' pleaded the maid, holding up a handkerchief and a small bottle. The fumes from the dissolved herbal medicine helped boost her energy for short periods of time.

'My daughter is with me,' said Sunaina. 'I don't need anyone else.'

Sita immediately took the handkerchief and bottle from the maid and climbed aboard the howdah.

Sunaina signalled the mahout, who tenderly stroked the elephant behind its ears with his foot. The elephant rose very slowly, causing the least amount of discomfort to Sunaina.

'Let's go,' she ordered.

The two elephants ambled off into the jungle, accompanied by fifty armed Mithila policemen, on foot.

Chapter 10

The howdah swayed like a cradle with the animal's gentle walk. Sita held her mother's hand and huddled close. The mahout steered the elephants in the shade, under the trees. Nonetheless, it was dry and warm.

Sita, though, was shivering. With guilt. And fear.

Sunaina lifted her hand slightly. Sita instinctively knew what her mother wanted. She lifted Sunaina's arm higher, and snuggled in close. And wrapped her mother's arm around her shoulder. Sunaina smiled with satisfaction and kissed Sita on her forehead.

'Sorry that your father couldn't come, Sita,' said Sunaina. 'He had to stay back for some work.'

Sita knew her mother was lying. She did not wish to cause her daughter further pain.

Perhaps, it was just as well.

Sita had, in a fit of anger, told Janak the last time she had been in Mithila that he should stop wasting his time on spirituality and help Sunaina govern the kingdom. That it was his duty. Her outburst had angered Sunaina more than her father.

Also, little Urmila, Sita's four-year-old younger sister, was a sickly child. Janak had probably stayed behind with her, while their mother travelled to Shvetaketu's *gurukul*. In debilitating illness. To meet her troubled elder daughter. And, to make her come back home.

Sita closed her eyes, as another guilty tear rolled down her cheek.

Sunaina coughed. Sita immediately wiped her mother's mouth with the cloth. She looked at the red stains — signs that her mother's life was slowly slipping away.

Tears began to flow in a rush.

'Everyone has to die someday, my darling,' said Sunaina.

Sita continued crying.

'But the fortunate ones die with their loved ones around them.'

— ༌ ᚷ —

The two elephants were stationary, expertly stilled by their mahouts. The fifty Mithilan guards, too, were immobile, and silent. The slightest sound could prove dangerous.

Ten minutes back, Sunaina had spotted a scene rarely witnessed by human eyes: The death of the matriarch of a large elephant herd.

Sita remembered her mother's lessons on elephant herds. They tended to be matriarchal, led by the eldest female. Most herds comprised adult females with calves, both male and female, nurtured as common children. Male elephants were normally exiled from the herd when they came of age.

The matriarch was more than the leader of the herd. She was a mother to all.

The death of the matriarch, therefore, would be a devastating event for the herd. Or so one would imagine.

'I think it's the same herd that we saw a few years ago,' whispered Sunaina.

Sita nodded.

They watched from a safe distance, hidden by the trees.

The elephants stood in a circle around the corpse of the matriarch. Solemn. Motionless. Quiet. The gentle afternoon breeze struggled to provide relief as the sun shone harshly on the assembly. Two calves stood within the circle, near the body. One was tiny, the other slightly older.

'We saw that little one being born, Sita,' said Sunaina.

Sita nodded in the affirmative.

She remembered the birth of the matriarch's child. Her mother and she had witnessed it on another elephant ride a few years ago.

Today, that baby elephant, a male calf, was down on his knees next to his dead mother. His trunk was entwined with hers, his body shaking. Every few minutes, he would pull on the trunk of his mother's corpse, as though trying to wake her up.

The older calf, his sister, stood next to the baby. Calm. Still. Like the other members of the herd.

'Watch now …' whispered Sunaina.

An adult female, perhaps the new matriarch, slowly ambled up to the corpse. She stretched her trunk and touched the forehead of the dead body with utmost respect. Then she walked around the corpse solemnly, turned and simply walked away.

The other elephants in the circle followed her lead, one by one. Doing the exact same thing — touching the forehead of the dead former matriarch with their trunks, performing a circumambulation and then walking away.

With dignity. With respect.

None of them looked back. Not once. Not once.

The little male calf, however, refused to leave. He clung to his mother. Desperately. He pulled at her with helpless ferocity. His sister stood quietly by his side.

The rest of the herd came to a halt at a distance, not once turning around. Patiently, they waited.

After some time, the sister touched her little brother with her trunk.

The male calf pushed it away. With renewed energy, he stood on his feet and wrapped his trunk around his mother's. And pulled hard. He slipped. He got up again. Held his mother's trunk and pulled. Harder. He cast a beseeching look at his sister, begging for her help. With a gut-wrenching cry, he turned back to his mother, willing her to get up.

But his mother had succumbed to the long sleep now. She would wake up only in her next life.

The child refused to give up. Shifting from side to side, he pulled his mother's trunk. Repeatedly.

The sister finally walked up to her mother's corpse, and touched the forehead with her trunk, just like the others had. She then walked around the body of her mother. She came up to her brother, held his trunk and tried to pull him away.

The male calf began to screech heartbreakingly. He followed his sister. But he kept looking back. Again. And again. He offered no resistance, however, to his sister.

The sister, like every other elephant in the herd, walked steadily ahead. She did not look back. Not once. Not once.

Sita looked up at her mother, tears flowing down her cheeks.

'Society moves on, my child,' whispered Sunaina. 'Countries move on. Life moves on. As it should.'

Sita couldn't speak. She could not look at her mother. She held Sunaina close, burying her head in her mother's bosom.

'Clinging to painful memories is pointless, Sita,' said Sunaina. 'You must move on. You must live ...'

Sita listened. But the tears did not stop.

'There's no escape from problems and challenges. They're a part of life. Avoiding Mithila does not mean that your troubles will disappear. It only means that other challenges will appear.'

Sita tightened her grip on her mother.

'Running away is never the solution. Confront your problems. Manage them. That is the way of the warrior.' Sunaina lifted Sita's chin and looked into her eyes. 'And, you are a warrior. Don't ever forget that.'

Sita nodded.

'You know your sister was born weak. Urmila is no warrior. You must take care of her, Sita. And, you must look after Mithila.'

Sita made a promise to herself within the confines of her mind. *Yes. I will.*

Sunaina caressed Sita's face and smiled. 'Your father has always loved you. So does your younger sister. Remember that.'

I know.

'As for me, I don't just love you, Sita. I also have great expectations from you. Your karma will ensure our family's name survives for many millennia. You will go down in history.'

Sita uttered her first words since she had seen her mother at the *gurukul*. 'I am so sorry, *Maa*. I'm so sorry. I ...'

Sunaina smiled and held Sita tight.

'Sorry ...' sobbed Sita.

'I have faith in you. You will live a life that will make me proud.'

'But I can't live without you, *Maa*.'

Sunaina pulled back and held Sita's face up. 'You can and you will.'

'No ... I will not live without you ...'

Sunaina's expression became firm. 'Listen to me, Sita. You will not waste your life mourning me. You will live wisely and make me proud.'

Sita continued crying.

'Don't look back. Look to the future. Build your future, don't grieve for your past.'

Sita did not have the strength to speak.

'Promise me.'

Sita stared at her mother, her eyes brimming with misery.

'Promise me.'

'I promise, *Maa*. I promise.'

— ॐ —

It had been four weeks since Sunaina's visit to Shvetaketu's *gurukul*. Sita had returned home with her mother. Sunaina had manoeuvred for Sita to be appointed prime minister of Mithila, with all the executive powers necessary to administer the kingdom.

Sita now spent most of her time with Sunaina, looking after her mother's failing health. Sunaina guided Sita's meetings with the ministers of the kingdom in her private chambers, by her bedside.

Sita was aware that Sunaina was greatly concerned about her relationship with her younger sister. Thus, she made a concerted effort to bond with Urmila. The queen of Mithila wanted her daughters to build a strong relationship that would tide them over the difficult years ahead. She had spoken to them about the need for them to stand by each other. And the love and loyalty they must share.

One evening, after a long meeting in Sunaina's chambers, Sita entered Urmila's room, next to their mother's. She had asked an aide to arrange a plate of black grapes. Urmila loved black grapes. Dismissing the aide, she carried the plate into the chamber.

The room was dimly lit. The sun had set but only a few lamps were aglow.

'Urmila!'

She was not in bed. Sita began looking for her sister. She stepped into the large balcony overlooking the palace garden.

Where is she?

She came back into the room. Irritated with the minimal light, she was about to order for some more lamps to be lit, when she noticed a shaking figure bundled in a corner.

'Urmila?'

Sita walked over.

Urmila sat in the corner, her knees pulled against her chest. Her head down on her knees.

Sita immediately set the plate aside and sat down on the floor next to Urmila. She put her arm around her baby sister.

'Urmila ...' she said, gently.

Urmila looked up at her *elder sister*. Her tear-streaked face was lined with misery.

'*Didi* ...'

'Talk to me, my child,' said Sita.

'Is ...'

Sita squeezed Urmila's shoulders gently. 'Yes ...'

'Is *maa* leaving us and going to heaven?'

Sita swallowed hard. She wished *maa* was here to answer Urmila's questions. Almost immediately, she realised that Sunaina would soon not be here at all. Urmila was her responsibility. She had to be the one to answer her.

'No, Urmila. *Maa* will always be here.'

Urmila looked up. Confused. Hopeful. 'But everyone is telling me that *maa* is going away. That I have to learn to ...'

'Everyone doesn't know what you and I know, Urmila. *Maa* will just live in a different place. She won't live in her body anymore.' Sita pointed to Urmila's heart and then her own. '*Maa* will live in these two places. She will always be there in our hearts. And, whenever we are together, she will be complete.'

Urmila looked down at her chest, feeling her heart pick up pace. Then she looked at Sita. 'She will never leave us?'

'Urmila, close your eyes.'

Urmila did as her sister ordered.

'What do you see?'

She smiled. 'I see *maa*. She is holding me. She is caressing my face.'

Sita ran her fingers down Urmila's face. She opened her eyes, smiling even more broadly.

'She will always be with us.'

Urmila held Sita tightly. '*Didi* ...'

'The both of us, together, are now our mother.'

— ॐ —

'My journey in this life is drawing to an end,' said Sunaina.

Sita and Sunaina were alone in the queen's chambers. Sunaina lay in bed. Sita sat beside her, holding her hand.

'*Maa* ...'

'I'm aware of what people in Mithila say about me.'

'*Maa*, don't bother about what some idiots ...'

'Let me speak, my child,' said Sunaina, pressing Sita's hand. 'I know they think my achievements of the past have evaporated in the last few years. Ever since Kushadhwaj began to squeeze our kingdom dry.'

Sita felt the familiar guilt rise in her stomach.

'It is not your fault,' said Sunaina, emphatically. 'Kushadhwaj would have used any excuse to hurt us. He wants to take over Mithila.'

'What do you want me to do, *Maa*?'

Sunaina knew her daughter's aggressive nature. 'Nothing to Kushadhwaj ... He is your father's brother. But I want you to redeem my name.'

Sita kept quiet.

'It is said that we come with nothing into this world, and take nothing back. But that's not true. We carry our karma with us. And we leave behind our reputation, our name. I want my name redeemed, Sita. And I want *you* to do it. I want *you* to bring back prosperity to Mithila.'

'I will, *Maa*.'

Sunaina smiled. 'And, once you have done that ... you have my permission to leave Mithila.'

'*Maa*?'

'Mithila is too small a place for one such as you, Sita. You are meant for greater things. You need a bigger stage. Perhaps, a stage as big as India. Or, maybe history itself ...'

Sita considered telling Sunaina about the Malayaputras having recognised her as the next Vishnu.

It took her only a few moments to decide.

— ᳚ᚷ —

The head *pandit* walked up to Sita, holding a torch in his right hand. Other *pandits* were lined up at the back, chanting hymns from the *Garuda Purana*. 'It's time, My Lady.'

Sita nodded at him and looked down to her left. Urmila had not stopped crying since Sunaina's death. She held on to Sita's arm with both her hands. Sita tried to pry them open, but her sister clung on, even stronger. Sita looked at her father, who walked up, picked Urmila up in his arms and stood beside his elder daughter. Janak looked as devastated and lost as the young Urmila. He had lost the human shield that had guarded him, as he had soared the heights of philosophical wisdom. Reality had intruded rudely into his life.

Sita turned to the *pandit* and took the torch.

It had only been three months since Sunaina's visit to the *gurukul*.

Sita had thought she'd have more time with Sunaina. To learn. To live. To love.

But that was not to be.

She moved forward as she heard the *pandits* chant from the *Isha Vasya Upanishad*.

Vayur anilam amritam; Athedam bhasmantam shariram

Let this temporary body be burned to ashes. But the breath of life belongs elsewhere. May it find its way back to the Immortal Breath.

She walked up to the sandalwood logs that entombed her mother's body. She closed her eyes as she pictured her mother's face. She must not cry. Not here. Not in public. She knew that many Mithilans secretly blamed her for further weakening her mother in her illness, by making her travel to Shvetaketu's *gurukul*. She also knew that they blamed her for the troubles caused by Kushadhwaj.

She must be strong. For her mother. She looked to her friend, Samichi, who stood at a distance. Next to her stood Radhika, her friend from the *gurukul*. She drew strength from their support.

She stuck the burning log into the pyre. Washed with ghee, the wood caught fire immediately. The pyre burned bright and strong, as if honoured to be the purifying agent for one so noble.

Farewell, Maa.

Sita stepped back and looked at the sky, to the One God, *Brahman.*

If anyone ever deserved moksha, it is her, my mother.

Sita remembered her mother's words as they had witnessed the mourning of the elephant matriarch.

Don't look back. Look to the future.

Sita whispered softly to the cremation pyre. 'I *will* look back, *Maa.* How can I not? You are my life.'

She remembered her last coherent conversation with her mother. Sunaina had warned Sita to not trust either the Malayaputras or the Vayuputras completely if she were to fulfil her destiny as the Vishnu. Both tribes would have their own agenda. She needed partners.

Her mother's voice resonated in her mind. *Find partners you can trust; who are loyal to your cause. Personal loyalty is not important. But they must be loyal to your cause.*

She remembered her mother's last statement.

I will always be looking at you. Make me proud.

Sita took a deep breath and clenched her fists, making a vow. 'I will, *Maa.* I will.'

Chapter 11

Sita and Samichi sat on the edge of the outer fort wall. Sita moved forward and looked down at the moat that surrounded the city. It was a long way down. Not for the first time, she wondered what it would be like to fall, all the way to the ground. Would it hurt? Would she be released from her body instantly? Would she finally be free? What happens after death?

Why do these stupid thoughts enter my mind?

'Sita …' whispered Samichi, breaking the silence.

They had been seated together for some time. There were hardly any words exchanged between the two, as a distracted Sita kept looking beyond the wall. Samichi could understand Sita's pain. After all, it had just been a day since the princess had cremated her mother's dead body. Despite her recently reduced popularity, almost the entire kingdom was in mourning for their Queen Sunaina. Not just Sita, but all of Mithila had lost its mother.

Sita did not respond.

'Sita …'

Instinct kicked in. Samichi reached her arm out and held it in front of Sita. Attempting to prevent some unspoken fear from coming true. Samichi understood, only too well, the power of dark thoughts.

Sita shook her head. Pushing the unnecessary thoughts out of her head.

Samichi whispered again, 'Sita …'

Sita spoke distractedly. To herself. '*Maa*, as always, was right … I need partners … I will complete my karma … But I can't do it alone. I need a partner …'

Samichi held her breath, thinking that Sita had plans for her. Thinking that Sita was talking about what Sunaina had wanted for Mithila. And, the karma the dying queen had asked of her. But Sita was, in fact, dwelling on what the chief of the Malayaputras had tasked her with.

Sita touched the scar on her left palm, recalling the blood oath she had made with Vishwamitra. She whispered to herself, 'I swear by the great Lord Rudra and by the great Lord Parshu Ram.'

Samichi did not notice that Sita had, for the first time, taken an oath in the name of Lord Parshu Ram as well. Usually, the princess only invoked Lord Rudra's name. But how could she have registered the change? Her thoughts, too, had drifted; to her *True Lord,* the *Iraiva.*

Does Sita intend to make me her second-in-command in Mithila? Iraiva be praised … Iraiva will be happy …

— ௮௫ —

A year had passed since the death of Sunaina. The sixteen-year-old Sita had been administering the kingdom reasonably well. She had consolidated her rule by retaining the team that had advised Sunaina, careful to continue systems that her mother had instituted. The only major change she had made was to appoint her trusted aide, Samichi, as the Chief of Police. An appointment necessitated by the sudden death of the previous police chief, who had had an unexpected and fatal heart attack.

Jatayu, the Malayaputra captain, had been true to his word, and shadowed Sita along with his team of soldiers. They had been tasked with being her bodyguards. Sita did not feel the need for this extra protection. But who can shake off a shadow? In fact, she had had to give in to Jatayu's request and induct some Malayaputra soldiers into the Mithila police force. Their true identity was kept a secret from all, including Samichi. They followed Sita. Always.

Over the last year, Sita had grown to trust Jatayu. Almost like a brother. He was the senior most Malayaputra officer that she interacted with on a regular basis. And, the only person she could openly discuss her Vishnu responsibilities with.

'I'm sure you understand, don't you, Jatayu*ji*?' asked Sita.

Sita and Jatayu had rendezvoused an hour's ride away from Mithila, near an abandoned bangle-making factory. Her Malayaputra bodyguards had accompanied her, disguised as Mithila policemen. Jatayu had just told her that Vishwamitra expected her to come to Agastyakootam, the capital of the Malayaputras, a hidden city deep in the south of India. She was to be trained there for some months to prepare her for her role as the Vishnu. After that, for the next few years, she would remain in her hometown, Mithila, for half the year and spend the other half travelling around the Sapt Sindhu, understanding the land she had to save.

However, Sita had just told Jatayu that she was not ready to leave Mithila yet. There was a lot left to be done. Mithila had to be stabilised and made secure; not the least of all, from the threat posed by Kushadhwaj.

'Yes, my sister,' said Jatayu. 'I understand. You need a few more years in Mithila. I will convey this to Guru*ji*. I am sure he, too, will understand. In fact, even your work here is training, in a way, for your mission.'

'Thank you,' said Sita. She asked him something she had been meaning to for some time. 'By the way, I have heard that Agastyakootam is close to Raavan's Lanka. Is that true?'

'Yes, it is. But do not worry, you will be safe there. It's a hidden city. And, Raavan would not dare attack Agastyakootam even if he knew where it was.'

Sita was not worried about Agastyakootam's security. It was something else that troubled her. But she decided not to seek further clarification. At least for now.

'Have you decided what to do with the money?' asked Jatayu.

The Malayaputras had donated a grand sum of one hundred thousand gold coins to Mithila, to help Sita speedily establish her authority in the kingdom. It was a relatively small amount for the tribe; but for Mithila, it had been a windfall. The Malayaputras had officially called it an endowment to a city that had dedicated itself to knowledge and was the beloved of the *rishis*.

No one was surprised by this unprecedented generosity. Why wouldn't great *rishis* nurture the saintly king Janak's city of knowledge? In fact, Mithilans had gotten used to seeing many of the Malayaputras, and even the great *maharishi*, Vishwamitra, visit their city often.

There were two potential projects that needed investment. One was the road that connected Mithila to Sankashya. The other was cheap, permanent and liveable housing for the slum dwellers.

'The road will revive trade to a great extent,' said Jatayu. 'Which will bring in more wealth to the city. A big plus.'

'Yes, but that wealth will largely go to a small number of already rich people. Some of them may even leave, taking their wealth along with them to more trade-friendly cities. The road will not rid us of our dependency on the Sankashya port. Nor will it stymie my uncle's ability to freeze supplies to Mithila whenever he feels like. We must become independent and self-reliant.'

'True. The slum redevelopment project, on the other hand, will provide permanent homes to the poor. It will also remove an eyesore at one of the main city gates, making it accessible to traffic.'

'Hmm.'

'And, you will earn the loyalty of the poor. They are the vast majority in Mithila. Their loyalty will prove useful, my sister.'

Sita smiled. 'I am not sure if the poor are always loyal. Those who are capable of loyalty will be loyal. Those who are not will not, no matter what I may do for them. Be that as it may, we must help the poor. And we can generate so many jobs with this project, making many more people productive locally. That is a good thing.'

'True.'

'I have other ideas related to this project, which would increase our self-reliance. At least with regard to food and other essentials.'

'I have a feeling that you've made up your mind already!'

'I have. But it is good to listen to other wise opinions before taking the final decision. This is exactly what my mother would have done.'

'She was a remarkable woman.'

'Yes, she was,' smiled Sita. She hesitated a moment, took one more look at Jatayu, and then broached another sensitive topic. 'Jatayu*ji*, do you mind if I ask you a question?'

'Anytime you wish to, great Vishnu,' said Jatayu. 'How can I not answer?'

'What is the problem between Maharishi Vishwamitra and Maharishi Vashishtha?'

Jatayu smiled ruefully. 'You have a rare ability to discover things that you are not supposed to. Things that are meant to be a secret.'

Sita smiled with disarming candour. 'That is not an answer to my question, Jatayu*ji*.'

'No, it's not, my sister,' laughed Jatayu. 'To be honest, I don't know much about it. But I do know this: they hate each other viscerally. It is unwise to even mention the name of Maharishi Vashishtha in the presence of Maharishi Vishwamitra.'

— ᚱᚴ —

'Good progress,' whispered Sita. She was standing in the garden of the Lord Rudra temple in Mithila, looking at the ongoing work of rebuilding the city slums.

A few months ago, Sita had ordered that the slums at the southern gate of Mithila be demolished and new, permanent houses be built for the poor on the same land. These houses, built with the money given by the Malayaputras, would be given to the poor free of cost.

Samichi preened at the compliment from her prime minister. In an unorthodox move, Sita had assigned her, rather than the city engineer, with the task of implementing the project rapidly and within budget. Sita knew that her Police Chief was obsessively detail-oriented, with an ability to push her subordinates ruthlessly to get the job done. Also, having spent her early years in the slums, Samichi was uniquely qualified to understand the problems faced by the people living there.

Though the execution had been entrusted to Samichi, Sita had involved herself in the planning and design of the project after consulting the representatives of the slum dwellers. She had eventually worked out an innovative solution for not only their housing needs, but also providing them with sustainable livelihood.

The slum dwellers had been unwilling to vacate their land for even a few months. They had little faith in the administration. For one, they believed the project would be under construction for years, rendering them homeless for a long time. Also, many were superstitious and wanted their rebuilt homes to stand exactly where the old ones had been. This, however, would leave no excess space for neatly lined streets. The original slum had no streets to begin with, just small, haphazard pathways.

Sita had conceived a brilliant solution: building a honeycomb-like structure, with houses that shared walls on all sides. Residents would enter from the top, with steps descending into their homes. The 'ceilings' of all the homes would, from the outside, be a single, joint, level platform; a new 'ground level' above all the houses; an artificial ground that was four floors above the actual ground. It would be an open-to-sky space for the slum dwellers, with a grid of 'streets' marked in paint. The 'streets' would contain hatch doors serving as entries to their homes. This would address their superstitions; each one would get a house exactly at the same location as their original hovel. And, since the honeycomb structure would extend four floors below, each inhabitant would, in effect, have four rooms. A substantially bigger home than earlier.

Because of its honeycomb-like structure, Samichi had informally named the complex Bees Quarter. Sita had liked it so much that it had become the official name!

There was still the problem of temporary accommodation for the slum dwellers, while their new homes were being constructed. Sita had had another innovative idea. She converted the moat outside the fort wall into a lake, to store rain water and to aid agriculture. The uninhabited area between the outer fort wall and the inner fort wall was partly handed over to the slum dwellers. They built temporary houses for themselves there with bamboo and cloth. They used the remaining land to grow food crops, cotton and medicinal herbs. This newly allotted land would remain in their possession even after they moved back into the Bees Quarter, which would be ready in a few months.

This had multiple benefits. Firstly, the land between the outer fort wall and the inner fort wall, which had been left unoccupied as a security measure, was put to good use. Agricultural productivity improved. This provided additional income for the slum dwellers. Moving agriculture within the city wall would also provide food security during times of siege; unlikely though it seemed that impoverished Mithila would ever be attacked.

Most importantly, Mithilans became self-reliant in terms of food, medicines and other essentials. This reduced their dependence on the Sankashya river port.

Samichi had warned Sita that this might tempt Kushadhwaj to militarily attack them. But Sita doubted it. It would be politically difficult for her uncle to justify his army attacking the saintly king of Mithila. It would probably stoke rebellion even among the citizens of Sankashya. Notwithstanding this, it was wise to be prepared for even the most unlikely event.

Sita had always been uneasy about the outer moat being the city's main water supply. In the unlikely event of a siege, an enemy could poison the water outside and cause havoc. She decreed that a deep lake be constructed within the city as a precaution. In addition to this, she also strengthened the two protective walls of Mithila.

She organised the chaotic central market of the city. Permanent, uniform stalls were given to the vendors, ensuring cleanliness and orderliness. Sales increased, along with a reduction in pilferage and wastage. This led to a virtuous cycle of decrease in prices, further enhancing business.

All these moves also dramatically increased Sita's popularity. At least, among the poor. Their lives had improved considerably, and the young princess was responsible.

— ᘓ ᙭ —

'I must admit, I am surprised,' said Jatayu. 'I didn't expect a police chief to efficiently oversee the construction of your Bees Quarter so smoothly.'

Sita sat with Jatayu outside the city limits. The day had entered the third *prahar*. The sun still shone high in the sky.

She smiled. 'Samichi is talented. No doubt.'

'Yes. But …'

Sita looked at him and frowned. 'But what, Jatayu*ji*?'

'Please don't misunderstand me, great Vishnu. It is your kingdom. You are the prime minister. And, we Malayaputras concern ourselves with the whole country, not just Mithila …'

'What is it, Jatayu*ji*?' interrupted Sita. 'You know I trust you completely. Please speak openly.'

'My people in your police force talk to the other officers. It's about Samichi. About her …'

Sita sighed. 'I know … It's obvious that she has a problem with men …'

'It's more like hatred for men, rather than just a problem.'

'There has to be a reason for it. Some man must have ...'

'But hating all men because of one man's actions, whatever they may have been, is a sign of an unstable personality. Reverse-bias is also bias. Reverse-racism is also racism. Reverse-sexism is also sexism.'

'I agree.'

'If she kept her feelings to herself that would be fine. But her prejudice is impacting her work. Men are being targeted unfairly. You don't want to trigger a rebellion.'

'She does not allow me to help her in the personal space. But I will ensure that her hatred does not impact her work. I'll do something.'

'I am only concerned about your larger interest, great Vishnu. There is no doubt in my mind that she is personally very loyal to you.'

'I guess it helps that I am not a man!'

Jatayu burst out laughing.

— त्र —

'How are you, Naarad?' asked Hanuman.

Hanuman had just returned from a trip to Pariha. He had sailed into the port of Lothal in Gujarat, on his way eastward, deeper into the heart of India. He had been met at the port by his friend Naarad, a brilliant trader in Lothal who was also a lover of art, poetry and the latest gossip! Naarad had immediately escorted his friend, along with his companions, to the office behind his shop.

'I'm all right,' said Naarad heartily. 'Any better would be a sin.'

Hanuman smiled. 'I don't think you try too hard to stay away from sin, Naarad!'

Naarad laughed and changed the topic. 'The usual supplies, my friend? For you and your band?'

A small platoon of Parihans accompanied Hanuman on his travels.

'Yes, thank you.'

Naarad nodded and whispered some instructions to his aide.

'And, I thank you further,' continued Hanuman, 'for not asking where I am going.'

The statement was too obvious a bait, especially for Naarad. He swallowed it hook, line, and sinker.

'Why would I ask you? I already know you are going to meet Guru Vashishtha!'

Vashishtha was the royal guru of the kingdom of Ayodhya. It was well known that he had taken the four princes of Ayodhya — Ram, Bharat, Lakshman and Shatrughan— to his *gurukul* to train and educate them. The location of the *gurukul*, however, was a well-kept secret.

Hanuman stared at Naarad, not saying anything.

'Don't worry, my friend,' said Naarad, smiling. 'Almost nobody, besides me of course, knows who you are going to meet. And nobody, not even me, knows where the *gurukul* is.'

Hanuman smiled. He was about to retort when a loud feminine voice was heard.

'Hans!'

Hanuman closed his eyes for a moment, winced and turned around. It was Sursa, an employee of Naarad who was obsessed with him.

Hanuman folded his hands together into a *Namaste* and

spoke with extreme politeness, 'Madam, my name is Hanuman, not Hans.'

'I know that,' said Sursa, sashaying towards Hanuman. 'But I think Hans sounds so much better. Also, don't you think Sur is better than madam?'

Naarad giggled with mirth as Sursa came uncomfortably close to Hanuman. The Naga glared at his friend before taking a few steps back and distancing himself from his admirer. 'Madam, I was engaged in an important conversation with Naarad and …'

Sursa cut him short. 'And, I've decided to interrupt. Deal with it.'

'Madam …'

Sursa arched her eyebrows and swayed her hip seductively to the side. 'Hans, don't you understand the way I feel about you? The things I can do for you … And, to you …'

'Madam,' interrupted Hanuman, blushing beet-red, and stepping back farther. 'I have told you many times. I am sworn to celibacy. This is inappropriate. I am not trying to insult you. Please understand. I cannot …'

Naarad was leaning against the wall now, covering his mouth, shoulders shaking, laughing silently. Trying hard not to make a sound.

'Nobody needs to know, Hans. You can keep up the appearance of your vow. You don't have to marry me. I only want you. Not your name.' Sursa stepped forward and reached out for Hanuman's hand.

With surprising agility for a man his size, Hanuman sidestepped quickly, deftly avoiding Sursa's touch. He raised his voice in alarm, 'Madam! Please! I beg you! Stop!'

Sursa pouted and traced her torso with her fingers. 'Am I not attractive enough?'

Hanuman turned towards Naarad. 'In Lord Indra's name, Naarad. Do something!'

Naarad was barely able to control his laughter. He stepped in front of Hanuman and faced the woman. 'Listen Sursa, enough is enough. You know that …'

Sursa flared up. Suddenly aggressive. 'I don't need your advice, Naarad! You know I love Hans. You had said you would help me.'

'I am sorry, but I lied,' said Naarad. 'I was just having fun.'

'This is fun for you?! What is wrong with you?'

Naarad signalled a couple of his employees. Two women walked up and pulled an irate Sursa away.

'I will make sure you lose half your money in your next trade, you stupid oaf!' screamed Sursa, as the women dragged her out.

As soon as they were alone again, Hanuman glared at his friend. 'What *is* wrong with you, Naarad?'

'I was just having fun, my friend. Sorry.'

Hanuman held the diminutive Naarad by his shoulder, towering over him. 'This is not fun! You were insulting Sursa. And, harassing me. I should thrash you to your bones!'

Naarad held Hanuman's hands in mock remorse, his eyes twinkling mischievously. 'You won't feel like thrashing me when I tell you who the Malayaputras have appointed as the Vishnu.'

Hanuman let Naarad go. Shocked. '*Appointed?*

How can Guru Vishwamitra do that? Without the consent of the Vayuputras!'

Naarad smiled. 'You won't survive a day without the information I give you. That's why you won't thrash me!'

Hanuman shook his head, smiled wryly, hit Naarad playfully on his shoulder and said, 'Start talking, you stupid nut.'

Chapter 12

'Radhika!' Sita broke into a broad smile.

Sita's friend from her *gurukul* days had made a surprise visit. The sixteen-year-old Radhika, a year younger than Sita, had been led into the princess' private chambers by Samichi, the new protocol chief of Mithila. The protocol duties, a new addition to Samichi's responsibilities, kept her busy with non-police work of late. Sita had therefore appointed a Deputy Police Chief to assist Samichi. This deputy was male. A strong but fair-minded officer, he had ensured that Samichi's biases did not affect real policing.

Radhika had not travelled alone, this time. She was accompanied by her father, Varun Ratnakar, and her uncle, Vayu Kesari.

Sita had met Varun Ratnakar in the past, but this was her first meeting with Radhika's uncle and Ratnakar's cousin, Vayu Kesari. The uncle did not share any family resemblance with his kin. Substantially short, stocky and fair-complexioned, his muscular body was extraordinarily hairy.

Perhaps he is one of the Vaanars, thought Sita.

She was aware that Radhika's tribe, the Valmikis, were matrilineal. Their women did not marry outside the community.

Men, however, could marry non-Valmiki women; of course, on the condition that if they did, they would leave the tribe. Perhaps Vayu Kesari was the son of one such excommunicated Valmiki man and a Vaanar woman.

Sita bent down and touched the feet of the elderly men.

Both blessed Sita with a long life. Varun Ratnakar was a respected intellectual and thinker, revered by those who valued knowledge. Sita knew he would love to spend time with her father, who was, perhaps, the most intellectual king in the Sapt Sindhu. With the departure of his chief guru, Ashtaavakra, to the Himalayas, Janak missed philosophical conversations. He would be happy to spend some quality time in the company of fellow intellectuals.

The men soon departed for King Janak's chambers. Samichi, too, excused herself. Her busy schedule did not leave her with much time for social niceties. Sita and Radhika were soon alone in the Mithila princess' private study.

'How is life treating you, Radhika?' asked Sita, holding her friend's hands.

'I am not the one leading an exciting life, Sita,' smiled Radhika. 'You are!'

'Me?!' laughed Sita, rolling her eyes with exaggerated playfulness. 'Hardly. All I do is police a small kingdom, collect taxes and redevelop slums.'

'Only for now. You have so much more to do …'

Sita instantly became guarded. There seemed to be more to this conversation than was obvious at the surface level. She spoke carefully. 'Yes, I do have a lot to do as the prime minister of Mithila. But it's not unmanageable, you know. We truly are a small and insignificant kingdom.'

'But India is a big nation.'

Sita spoke even more carefully, 'What can this remote corner do for India, Radhika? Mithila is a powerless kingdom ignored by all.'

'That may be so,' smiled Radhika. 'But no Indian in his right mind will ignore Agastyakootam.'

Sita held her breath momentarily. She maintained her calm demeanour, but her heart was thumping like the town crier's drumbeat.

How does Radhika know? Who else does? I have not told anyone. Except Maa.

'I want to help you, Sita,' whispered Radhika. 'Trust me. You are a friend and I love you. And, I love India even more. You are important for India. *Jai Parshu Ram.*'

'*Jai Parshu Ram,*' whispered Sita, hesitating momentarily before asking, 'Are your father and you ...'

Radhika laughed. 'I'm a nobody, Sita. But my father... Let's just say that he's important. And, he wants to help you. I am just the conduit, because the universe conspired to make me your friend.'

'Is your father a Malayaputra?'

'No, he is not.'

'Vayuputra?'

'The Vayuputras do not live in India. The tribe of the Mahadev, as you know, can visit the sacred land of India anytime but cannot live here. So, how can my father be a Vayuputra?'

'Then, who is he?'

'All in good time ...' smiled Radhika. 'Right now, I have been tasked with checking a few things with you.'

— ॐ —

Vashishtha sat quietly on the ground, resting against a tree. He looked at his *ashram* from the distance, seeking solitude in the early morning hour. He looked towards the gently flowing stream. Leaves floated on the surface, strangely even-spaced, as if in a quiet procession. The tree, the water, the leaves ... nature seemed to reflect his deep satisfaction.

His wards, the four princes of Ayodhya — Ram, Bharat, Lakshman, and Shatrughan — were growing up well, moulding ideally into his plans. Twelve years had passed since the demon king of Lanka, Raavan, had catastrophically defeated Emperor Dashrath, changing the fortunes of the Sapt Sindhu in one fell blow.

It had convinced Vashishtha that the time for the rise of the Vishnu had arrived.

Vashishtha looked again at his modest *gurukul*. This was where the great Rishi Shukracharya had moulded a group of marginalised Indian royals into leaders of one of the greatest empires the world had ever seen: the *AsuraSavitr*, the Asura Sun.

A new great empire shall rise again from this holy ground. A new Vishnu shall rise from here.

Vashishtha had still not made up his mind. He wasn't sure which of the two — Ram or Bharat — he would push for as the next Vishnu. One thing was certain; the Vayuputras supported him. But there were limits to what the tribe of Lord Rudra could do. The Vayuputras and Malayaputras had their fields of responsibility; after all, the Vishnu was supposed to be officially recognised by the Malayaputras. And the chief of the Malayaputras ... His former friend ...

Well ...

I'll manage it.

'Guru*ji*.'

Vashishtha turned. Ram and Bharat had quietly approached him.

'Yes,' said Vashishtha. 'What did you find out?'

'They are not there, Guru*ji*,' said Ram.

'They?'

'Not only Chief Varun, but many of his advisers are also missing from their village.'

Varun was the chief of the tribe that managed and maintained this *ashram,* situated close to the westernmost point of the River Shon's course. His tribe, the Valmikis, rented out these premises to *gurus* from time to time. Vashishtha had hired this *ashram* to serve as his *gurukul* for the duration that the four Ayodhya princes were with him.

Vashishtha had hidden the true identity of his wards from the Valmikis. But of late he had begun to suspect that perhaps the tribe knew who the students were. It also seemed to him that the Valmikis had their own carefully kept secrets.

He had sent Ram and Bharat to check if Chief Varun was in the village. It was time to have a talk with him. Vashishtha would then decide whether to move his *gurukul* or not.

But Varun had left. Without informing Vashishtha. Which was unusual.

'Where have they gone?' asked Vashishtha.

'Apparently, Mithila.'

Vashishtha nodded. He knew that Varun was a lover and seeker of knowledge, especially the spiritual kind. Mithila was a natural place for such a person.

'All right, boys,' said Vashishtha. 'Get back to your studies.'

— ᚱᚷ —

'We heard that the Vishnu blood oath has been taken,' said Radhika.

'Yes,' answered Sita. 'In Guru Shvetaketu's *gurukul*. A few years ago.'

Radhika sighed.

Sita frowned. 'Is there a problem?'

'Well, Maharishi Vishwamitra is a little ... unorthodox.'

'Unorthodox? What do you mean?'

'Well, for starters, the Vayuputras should have been present.'

Sita raised her eyebrows. 'I didn't know that ...'

'The tribes of the Vishnu and the Mahadev are supposed to work in partnership.'

Sita looked up as she realised something. 'Guru Vashishtha?'

Radhika smiled. 'For someone who hasn't even begun training, you have picked up quite a lot already!'

Sita shrugged and smiled.

Radhika held her friend's hand. 'The Vayuputras do not like or trust Maharishi Vishwamitra. They have their reasons, I suppose. But they cannot oppose the Malayaputra chief openly. And yes, you guessed correctly, the Vayuputras support Maharishi Vashishtha.'

'Are you telling me that Guru Vashishtha has his own ideas about who the Vishnu should be?'

Radhika nodded. 'Yes.'

'Why do they hate each other so much?'

'Very few know for sure. But the enmity between Guru Vishwamitra and Guru Vashishtha is very old. And, very fierce ...'

Sita laughed ruefully. 'I feel like a blade of grass stuck between two warring elephants.'

'Then you wouldn't mind another species of grass next to you for company while being trampled upon, I suppose!'

Sita playfully hit Radhika on her shoulders. 'So, who is this other blade of grass?'

Radhika took a deep breath. 'There are two, actually.'

'Two?'

'Guru Vashishtha is training them.'

'Does he plan to create two Vishnus?'

'No. Father believes Guru Vashishtha will choose one of them.'

'Who are they?'

'The princes of Ayodhya. Ram and Bharat.'.

Sita raised her eyebrows. 'Guru Vashishtha has certainly aimed high. The family of the emperor himself!'

Radhika smiled.

'Who is better among the two?'

'My father prefers Ram.'

'And who do you prefer?'

'My opinion doesn't matter. Frankly, father's opinion doesn't count either. The Vayuputras will back whomsoever Guru Vashishtha chooses.'

'Is there no way Guru Vashishtha and Guru Vishwamitra can be made to work together? After all, they are both working for the greater good of India, right? I am willing to work in partnership with the Vishnu that Guru Vashishtha selects. Why can't they partner each other?'

Radhika shook her head. 'The worst enemy a man can ever have is the one who was once his best friend.'

Sita was shocked. 'Really? Were they friends once?'

'Maharishi Vashishtha and Maharishi Vishwamitra were childhood friends. Almost like brothers. Something happened to turn them into enemies.'

'What?'

'Very few people know. They don't speak about it even with their closest companions.'

'Interesting …'

Radhika remained silent.

Sita looked out of the window and then at her friend. 'How do you know so much about Guru Vashishtha?'

'You know that we host a *gurukul* close to our village, right? It is Guru Vashishtha's *gurukul*. He teaches the four princes in the *ashram* we have rented out.'

'Can I come and meet Ram and Bharat? I'm curious to know if they are as great as Guru Vashishtha thinks they are.'

'They are still young, Sita. Ram is five years younger than you. And, don't forget, the Malayaputras keep track of you. They follow you everywhere. We cannot risk revealing the location of Guru Vashishtha's *gurukul* to them …'

Sita was constrained to agree. 'Hmm.'

'I will keep you informed about what they are doing. I think father intends to have an honest conversation with Guru Vashishtha in any case. Perhaps, even offer his help.'

'Help Guru Vashishtha? Against me?'

Radhika smiled. 'Father hopes for the same partnership that you do.'

Sita bent forward. 'I have told you much of what I know. I think I deserve to know … Who is your father?'

Radhika seemed hesitant.

'You would not have spoken about the Ayodhya princes had your father not allowed you to do so,' said Sita. 'And, I am sure that he would have expected me to ask this question. So, he wouldn't have sent you to meet me unless he was prepared to reveal his true identity. Tell me, who is he?'

Radhika paused for a few moments. 'Have you heard of Lady Mohini?'

'Are you serious?' asked Sita. 'Who hasn't heard of her, the great Vishnu?'

Radhika smiled. 'Not everyone considers her a Vishnu. But the majority of Indians do. I know that the Malayaputras revere her as a Vishnu.'

'So do I.'

'And so do we. My father's tribe is the one Lady Mohini left behind. We are the Valmikis.'

Sita sat up straight. Shocked. 'Wow!' Just then another thought struck her. 'Is your uncle, Vayu Kesari, the father of Hanu *bhaiya*?'

Radhika nodded. 'Yes.'

Sita smiled. 'That's why ...'

Radhika interrupted her. 'You are right. That is one of the reasons. But it's not the only one.'

Chapter 13

'Chief Varun,' said Vashishtha, as he came to his feet and folded his hands into a respectful *Namaste*.

Varun had just returned from Mithila. And, Guru Vashishtha had been expecting a visit from him.

Vashishtha was much taller than Varun. But far thinner and leaner compared to the muscular and sturdy tribal chief.

'Guru Vashishtha,' said Varun, returning Vashishtha's greeting politely. 'We need to talk in private.'

Vashishtha was immediately wary. He led the chief out to a quieter spot.

Minutes later, they sat by the stream that flowed near the *ashram*, away from the four students, as well as others who might overhear them.

'What is it, Chief Varun?' asked Vashishtha, politely.

Varun smiled genially. 'You and your students have been here for many years, Guru*ji*. I think it's time we properly introduce ourselves to each other.'

Vashishtha stroked his flowing, snowy beard carefully, feigning a lack of understanding. 'What do you mean?'

'I mean … for example, the princes of Ayodhya do not have to pretend to be the children of some nobles or rich traders anymore.'

Vashishtha's thoughts immediately flew to the four boys. Where were they? Were they being rounded up by Varun's warriors? Chief Varun's tribe was not allowed, according to their traditional law, to help any Ayodhyan royals.

Perhaps, I wasn't so clever after all. I thought we would be safe if we just stayed away from the areas under Lankan or Malayaputra influ nce.

Vashishtha leaned forward. 'If you are concerned about your laws, you must also remember the one that states that you cannot harm the people you accept as your guests.'

Varun smiled. 'I intend no harm either to you or your students, Guru*ji*.'

Vashishtha breathed easy. 'My apologies, if I have offended you. But I needed a place that was ... safe. We will leave immediately.'

'There is no need to do that either,' said Varun, calm. 'I do not intend to kick you out. I intend to help you, Guru*ji*.'

Vashishtha was taken aback. 'Isn't it illegal for you to help the Ayodhya royalty?'

'Yes, it is. But there is a supreme law in our tribe that overrides every other. It is the primary purpose of our existence.'

Vashishtha nodded, pretending to understand, though he was confused.

'You must know our war cry: Victory at all costs ... When war is upon us, we ignore all the laws. And a war is coming, my friend ...'

Vashishtha stared at him, completely flummoxed.

Varun smiled. 'Please don't think I am unaware that my Vayuputra nephew steals into your *ashram* regularly, late at night, thinking we wouldn't notice. He thinks he can fool his uncle.'

Vashishtha leaned back, as a veil seemed to lift from his eyes. 'Hanuman?'

'Yes. His father is my cousin.'

Vashishtha was startled, but he asked in an even tone. 'Is Vayu Kesari your brother?'

'Yes.'

Varun was aware of the bond that Hanuman and Vashishtha shared. Many years ago, the guru had helped his nephew. He chose not to mention it. He knew the situation was complicated.

'Who are you?' Vashishtha finally asked.

'My full name is Varun Ratnakar.'

Suddenly, everything fell into place. Vashishtha knew the significance of that second name. He had found allies. Powerful allies. By pure chance.

There was only one thing left to do. Vashishtha clasped his right elbow with his left hand and touched his forehead with the clenched right fist, in the traditional salute of Varun's tribe. Respectfully, he uttered the ancient greeting. '*Jai Devi Mohini!*'

Varun held Vashishtha's forearm, like a brother, and replied, '*Jai Devi Mohini!*'

— ॐ —

Indians in the Sapt Sindhu have a strange relationship with the Sun God. Sometimes they want him, at other times, they don't. In summer, they put up with his rage. They plead with him, through prayers, to calm down and, if possible, hide behind the clouds. In winter, they urge him to appear with all his force and drive away the cold fury of the season.

It was on one such early winter day, made glorious by the energising sun, when Sita and Samichi rode out into the main palace garden. It had been refurbished recently on Sita's orders.

The two had decided on a private competition — a chariot race. It was a sport Sita truly enjoyed. The narrow lanes of the garden would serve as the racing track. They had not raced together in a long time. And, they had never done so in the royal garden before.

The garden paths were narrow, hemmed in with trees and foliage. It would require considerable skill to negotiate them in a chariot. The slightest mistake would mean crashing into trees at breakneck speed. Dangerous ... And, exhilarating.

The risk of it, the thrill, made the race worthwhile. It was a test of instinct and supreme hand-eye coordination.

The race began without any ceremony.

'*Hyaah*!' screamed Sita, whipping her horses, instantly urging them forward.

Faster. Faster.

Samichi kept pace, close behind. Sita looked back for an instant. She saw Samichi swerving her chariot to the right. Sita looked ahead and pulled her horses slightly to the right, blocking Samichi's attempt to sneak past her at the first bend.

'Dammit!' screamed Samichi.

Sita grinned and whipped her horses. 'Move!'

She swung into the next curve without reining her horses in. Speeding as her chariot swerved left. The carriage tilted to the right. Sita expertly balanced her feet, bending leftwards to counter the centrifugal forces working hard on the chariot at such fast speeds. The carriage balanced itself and sped ahead as the horses galloped on without slowing.

'*Hyaah*!' shouted Sita again, swinging her whip in the air.

It was a straight and narrow path now for some distance. Overtaking was almost impossible. It was the best time to generate some speed. Sita whipped her horses harder. Racing forward. With Samichi following close behind.

Another bend lay farther ahead. The path broadened before the curve, giving a possible opportunity for Samichi to forge ahead. Sita smoothly pulled the reins to the right, guiding the horses to the centre, leaving as little space as possible on either side. Samichi simply could not overtake.

'*Hyaah!*'

Sita heard Samichi's loud voice. Behind her. To the left. Her voice was much louder than normal. Like she was trying to announce her presence.

Sita read her friend correctly.

A few seconds later, Sita quickly swerved. But, unexpectedly, to the right, covering that side of the road. Samichi had feigned the leftward movement. She had actually intended to overtake from the right. As Sita cut in, that chance was lost.

Sita heard a loud curse from Samichi.

Grinning, Sita whipped her horses again. Taking the turn at top speed. Ahead of the curve, the path would straighten out. And become narrower. Again.

'*Hyaah!*'

'Sita!' screamed Samichi loudly.

There was something in her voice.

Panic.

As if on cue, Sita's chariot flipped.

Sita flew up with the momentum. High in the air. The horses did not stop. They kept galloping.

Instinctively, Sita tucked in her head and pulled her legs up, her knees close to her chest. She held her head with her hands. In brace position.

The entire world appeared to flow in slow motion for Sita.

Her senses alert. Everything going by in a blur.

Why is it taking so long to land?

Slam!

Sharp pain shot through her as she landed hard on her shoulder. Her body bounced forward, in the air again, hurled sickeningly with the impact.

'Princess!'

Sita kept her head tucked in. She had to protect her head.

She landed on her back. And was hurled forward, repeatedly rolling on the tough ground, brutally scraping her body.

A green blur zipped past her face.

Wham!

She slammed hard against a tree. Her back felt a sharp pain. Suddenly stationary.

But to her eyes, the world was still spinning.

Dazed, Sita struggled to focus on her surroundings.

Samichi brought her chariot to a halt, dismounted rapidly, and ran towards the princess. Sita's own chariot was being dragged ahead. Sparks flew in the air due to the intense friction generated by the chariot metal rubbing against the rough road. The disoriented horses kept galloping forward wildly.

Sita looked at Samichi. 'Get … my … chariot …'

And then, she lost consciousness.

— ᴦᴗ৲ —

It was dark when Sita awoke. Her eyelids felt heavy. A soft groan escaped her lips.

She heard a panic-stricken squeal. '*Didi* … Are you alright …? Talk to me …'

It was Urmila.

'I'm alright, Urmila …'

Her father gently scolded the little girl. 'Urmila, let your sister rest.'

Sita opened her eyes and blinked rapidly. The light from the various torches in the room flooded in. Blinding her. She let her eyelids droop. 'How long...have I been ...'

'The whole day, *Didi*.'

Just a day? It feels longer.

Her entire body was a mass of pain. Except her left shoulder. And her back. They were numb.

Painkillers. May the Ashwini Kumars bless the doctors.

Sita opened her eyes again. Slowly. Allowing the light to gently seep in. Allowing her pupils to adjust.

Urmila stood by the bedside, clutching the bedsheet with both hands. Her round eyes were tiny pools of water. Tears streamed down her face. Her father, Janak, stood behind his younger daughter. His normally serene face was haggard, lined with worry. He had just recovered from a serious illness. The last thing he needed was this additional stress.

'*Baba* ...' said Sita to her father. 'You should be resting...You are still weak ...'

Janak shook his head. 'You are my strength. Get well soon.'

'Go back to your room, *Baba* ...'

'I will. You rest. Don't talk.'

Sita looked beyond her family. Samichi was there. As was Arishtanemi. He was the only one who looked calm. Unruffled.

Sita took a deep breath. She could feel her anger rising. 'Samichi ...'

'Yes, princess,' said Samichi, as she quickly walked up to the bed.

'My chariot ...'

'Yes, princess.'

'I want to...see it ...'

'Yes, princess.'

Sita noticed Arishtanemi hanging back. There was a slight smile on his face now. A smile of admiration.

— ௬Χ —

'Who do you think tried to kill you?' asked Arishtanemi.

It had been five days since the chariot accident. Sita had recovered enough to be able to sit up in bed. Even walk around a bit. She ate like a soldier, quickly increasing her energy levels and boosting her alertness. A full recovery would take a few weeks.

Her left arm was in a sling. Her back was plastered with thick *neem* paste, mixed with tissue-repairing Ayurvedic medicines. Miniature bandages covered most parts of her body, protecting nicks and cuts to make them heal quickly.

'One doesn't need to be Vyomkesh to figure this out,' said Sita, referring to a popular fictional detective from folk stories.

Arishtanemi laughed softly.

The chariot had been brought to Sita's large chamber in the *Ayuralay*. Sita had examined it thoroughly. It had been very cleverly done.

Wood from another type of tree had been used to replace the two suspension beams. It was similar in appearance to the wood used in the rest of the carriage. It looked hardy. But was, in fact, weak. The nail marks that fixed the beams on the main shaft were fresh, despite care being taken to use old nails. One beam had cracked like a twig when strained by the speed of movement on uneven ground and the sharp turns. The beam had collapsed and jammed into the ground, seizing up the axle. This had brought the wheels to an abrupt halt when at a great speed. The chariot had levered up on the broken suspension beam as its front-end had rammed into the ground.

Very cleverly done.

Whoever had done this had the patience of a stargazer. It could have been done many months ago. It had been made to look like an old construction flaw, a genuine error. To make the death appear like an accident. And not an assassination. Sita had uncovered the conspiracy only through a close inspection of the nail marks.

The chariot was Sita's. The target obvious. She was the only one who stood between Mithila and its expansionary enemies. Urmila could simply be married off. And Janak ... Well. After Sita, it would only be a matter of time.

She had been extremely lucky. The accident had occurred when the last bend had almost been negotiated, making the chariot drag in a direction different from where Sita was flung due to the inertia of her bodily movement. Otherwise, she would have been crushed under the wheels and metal of her chariot. It would have been an almost certain death.

'What do you want to do?' asked Arishtanemi.

Sita had no doubt in her mind about who the perpetrator was behind her supposed accident. 'I was willing to consider an alliance. Frankly, he could have become the head of the royal family, too. After all, I have bigger plans. All I had asked for was that my father and sister be safe and treated well. And, my citizens be taken care of. That's it. Why did he do this?'

'People are greedy. They are stupid. They misread situations. Also, remember, outside of the Malayaputras, no one knows about your special destiny. Perhaps, he sees you as a future ruler and a threat.'

'When is Guru Vishwamitra coming back?'

Arishtanemi shrugged. 'I don't know.'

So we have to do this ourselves.

'What do you want to do?' repeated Arishtanemi.

'Guru Vishwamitra was right. He had told me once … Never wait. Get your retaliation in first.'

Arishtanemi smiled. 'A surgical strike?'

'I can't do it openly. Mithila cannot afford an open war.'

'What do you have in mind?'

'It must look like an accident, just like mine was meant to be.'

'Yes, it must.'

'And, it cannot be the main man.'

Arishtanemi frowned.

'The main man is just the strategist. In any case, I can't attack him directly … My mother had prohibited it … We must cut off his right hand. So that he loses the ability to execute such plans.'

'Sulochan.'

Sulochan was the prime minister of Sankashya. The right-hand man of Sita's uncle Kushadhwaj. The man who ran practically everything for his king. Kushadhwaj would be paralysed without Sulochan.

Sita nodded.

Arishtanemi's face was hard as stone. 'It will be done.'

Sita did not react.

Now, you are truly worthy of being a Vishnu, thought Arishtanemi. *A Vishnu who can't fight for herself would be incapable of fighting for her people.*

— ᴅᴜ ᴊ —

Mara had chosen his day and time well.

The boisterous *nine-day* festivities of the Winter *Navratra* always included the day that marked the *Uttarayan*, the beginning of the *northward movement* of the sun. This was the day the nurturer of the world, the sun, was farthest away from the northern hemisphere. It would now begin its six-month journey back to the north. *Uttarayan* was, in a sense, a harbinger of renewal. The death of the old. The birth of the new.

It was the first hour of the first *prahar*. Just after midnight. Except for the river port area, the city of Sankashya was asleep. The peaceful sleep of the tired and happy. Festivals manage to do that. The city guards, though, were among the few who were awake. Throughout the city, one could hear their loud calls on the hour, every hour: All is well.

Alas, not all the guards were as duty-conscious.

Twenty such men sat huddled in the guard room at Prime Minister Sulochan's palace; it was the hour of their midnight snack. They should not have left their posts. But this had been a severe winter. And, the snack was only an excuse. They had, in fact, gravitated to the warm fireplace in the room like fireflies. It was just a break, they knew. They would soon be back on guard.

Sulochan's palace was perched on a hill, skirting the royal garden of Sankashya at one end. At the other end was the generous River Gandaki. It was a truly picturesque spot, apt for the residence of the second-most powerful man in the city. But not very kind to the guards. The palace's elevation increased the severity of the frosty winds. It made standing at the posts a battle against the elements. So, the men truly cherished the warmth of the guard room.

Two guards lay on the palace rooftop, towards the royal garden end. Their breathing even and steady. Sleeping soundly. They would not remember anything. Actually, there was nothing to remember. An odourless gas had gently breezed in and nudged them into a sound sleep. They would wake up the next morning, guiltily aware that they had dozed off on duty. They wouldn't admit this to any investigator. The punishment for sleeping while on guard duty was death.

Mara was not a crass assassin. Any brute with a bludgeon could kill. He was an artist. One hired Mara only if one wanted to employ a shadow. A shadow that would emerge from the darkness, for only a little while, and then quickly retreat. Leaving not a trace. Leaving just a body behind. The right body; always, the right body. No witnesses. No loose ends. No other 'wrong' body. No unnecessary clues for the mind of a savvy investigator.

Mara, the artist, was in the process of crafting one of his finest creations.

Sulochan's wife and children were at her maternal home. The Winter *Navratra* was the period of her annual vacation with her family. Sulochan usually joined them after a few days, but had been held back this time by some urgent state business. The prime minister was home alone. Indeed, Mara had chosen the day and time well. For he had been told strictly: avoid collateral damage.

He looked at the obese form of Prime Minister Sulochan. Lying on the bed. His hands on his sides. Feet flopped outwards. As he would ordinarily sleep. He was wearing a beige *dhoti*. Bare-chested. He had placed his *angvastram* on the bedside cabinet. Folded neatly. As he ordinarily would have done before going to sleep. His rings and jewellery had been removed and placed inside the jewellery box, next to the *angvastram*. Again, as he ordinarily would.

But, he was not breathing as he ordinarily would. He was already dead. A herbal poison had been cleverly administered through his nose. No traces would be left behind. The poison had almost instantly paralysed the muscles in his body.

The heart is a muscle. So is the diaphragm, located below the lungs. The victim asphyxiated within minutes.

Perhaps, Sulochan had been conscious through it. Perhaps not. Nobody would know.

And Mara didn't care to know.

The assassination had been carried out.

Mara was now setting the scene.

He picked up a manuscript from a shelf. It chronicled the doomed love story of a courtesan and a peripatetic trader. The story was already a popular play throughout the Sapt Sindhu. It was well known that Sulochan liked reading. And that he especially loved a good romance. Mara walked over to Sulochan's corpse and placed the dog-eared manuscript on the bed, by the side of his chest.

Sulochan had fallen asleep while reading.

He picked up a glass-encased lamp, lit the wick, and placed it on the bedside cabinet.

His reading lamp ...

He picked up the decanter of wine lying on a table-top at the far end of the room and placed it on the cabinet, along with a glass. He poured some wine into the empty glass.

Prime Minister Sulochan had been drinking wine and reading a romantic novel at the end of a tiring day.

He placed a bowlful of an Ayurvedic paste on the bedside cabinet. He dipped a wooden tong in the paste, opened Sulochan's mouth and spread it evenly inside, taking care to include the back of his throat. A doctor would recognise this paste as a home remedy for stomach ache and gas.

The prime minister was quite fat. Stomach trouble would surely have been common. And he was also known to have enough Ayurvedic knowledge for home remedies for minor diseases and affliction .

He walked towards the window.

Open window. Windy night.

He retraced his steps and pulled the covering sheet up to Sulochan's neck.

Sulochan had covered himself up. He was feeling cold.

Mara touched the sheet and the *angvastram*. And cast a careful glance around the room. Everything was as it should be.

Perfect.

Sulochan had, it would be deduced, confused the beginnings of a heart attack for a stomach and gas problem. A regrettably common mistake. He had had some medicine for it. The medicine had relieved his discomfort. Somewhat. He had then picked up a book to read and poured himself some wine. He had begun to feel the chill, typical of a heart attack. He had pulled up his sheet to cover himself. And then the heart attack had struck with its full ferocity.

Unfortunate.

Perfectly unfortunate.

Mara smiled. He looked around the scene and took a final mental picture. As he always did.

He frowned.

Something's not right.

He looked around again. With animal alertness.

Damn! Bloody stupid!

Mara walked up to Sulochan and picked up his left arm. *Rigor mortis* was setting in and the body had already begun to stiffen. With some effort, Mara placed Sulochan's left hand on his chest. With strain, he spread the fingers apart. As if the man had died clutching his chest in pain.

I should have done this earlier. Stupid! Stupid!

Satisfied with his work now, Mara once again scanned the room. Perfect.

It looked like a simple heart attack.

He stood in silence, filled with admiration for his creation. He kissed the fingertips of his right hand.

No, he was not just a killer. He was an artist.

My work here is done.

He turned and briskly walked up to the window, leapt up and grabbed the parapet of the roof. Using the momentum, he somersaulted and landed on his feet above the parapet. Soon he was on the rooftop.

Mara was the invisible man. The dark, non-transferable polish that he had rubbed all over his skin, along with his black *dhoti*, ensured that he went unseen in the night.

The maestro sighed with satisfaction. He could hear the sounds of the night. The chirping crickets. The crackling fire from the guard room. The rustling wind. The soft snores of the guards asleep on the roof ... Everything was as it should be. Nothing was amiss.

He ran in the direction of the royal garden. Without any hesitation. Building up speed. As he neared the edge of the roof, he leapt like a cat and glided above the ground. His outstretched arms caught an overhanging branch of a tree. He swung onto the branch, balanced his way to the tree trunk and smoothly slid to the ground.

He began running. Soft feet. Silent breaths. No unnecessary sound.

Mara, the shadow, disappeared into the darkness. Lost to the light. Again.

Chapter 14

Mithila was more stable than it had been in years. The rebuilt slums, along with the ancillary opportunities it provided, had dramatically improved the lives of the poor. Cultivation in the land between the two fort walls had led to a spike in agricultural production. Inflation was down. And, the unfortunate death of the dynamic prime minister of Sankashya had neutralised Kushadhwaj substantially. No one grudged the now popular Sita her decision to carry out a spate of diplomatic visits across the country.

Of course, few knew that the first visit would be to the fabled capital of the Malayaputras: Agastyakootam.

The journey was a long and convoluted one. Jatayu, Sita, and a large Malayaputra company first travelled to Sankashya by the dirt road. Thereafter, they sailed on river boats down the Gandaki till its confluence with the mighty Ganga. Then, they sailed up the Ganga to its closest point to the Yamuna. They then marched over land to the banks of the Yamuna and sailed down the river till it met the Sutlej to form the Saraswati. From there, they sailed farther down the Saraswati till it merged into the Western Sea. Next, they boarded a seaworthy ship and were presently sailing down the western coast of India, towards the southwestern tip of the Indian subcontinent. Destination: Kerala. Some called it God's own country. And why not, for this was the land the previous Vishnu, Lord Parshu Ram, had called his own.

On an early summer morning, with a light wind in its sails, the ship moved smoothly over calm waters. Sita's first experience of the sea was pleasant and free of discomfort.

'Was Lord Parshu Ram born in Agastyakootam?' asked Sita.

Sita and Jatayu stood on the main deck, their hands resting lightly on the balustrade. Jatayu turned to her as he leaned against the bar. 'We believe so. Though I can't give you proof. But we can certainly say that Lord Parshu Ram belongs to Kerala and Kerala belongs to him.'

Sita smiled.

Jatayu pre-empted what he thought Sita would say. 'Of course, I am not denying that many others in India are as devoted to Lord Parshu Ram as we are.'

She was about to say something but was distracted as her eyes fell upon two ships in the distance. Lankan ships. They were moving smoothly, but at a startling speed.

Sita frowned. 'Those ships look the same as ours. They have as many sails as ours. How are they sailing so much faster?'

Jatayu sighed. 'I don't know. It's a mystery. But it's a huge maritime advantage for them. Their armies and traders travel to faraway regions faster than anyone else can.'

Raavan must have some technology that the others do not possess.

She looked at the mastheads of the two ships. Black-coloured Lankan flags, with the image of the head of a roaring lion emerging from a profusion of fiery flames, fluttered proudly in the wind.

Not for the first time, Sita wondered about the relationship between the Malayaputras and the Lankans.

— ᚱᚲ —

As they neared the Kerala coast, the travellers were transferred to a ship with a lesser draught, suitable for the shallower backwaters they would now sail into.

Sita had been informed in advance by Jatayu and knew what to expect as they approached the landmass. They sailed into the maze-like water bodies that began at the coast. A mix of streams, rivers, lakes and flooded marshes, they formed a navigable channel into the heart of God's own country. Charming at first glance, these waters could be treacherous; they constantly changed course in a land blessed with abundant water. As a result, new lakes came into being as old ones drained every few decades. Fortuitously, most of these backwaters were inter-connected. If one knew how, one could navigate this watery labyrinth into the hinterland. But if one was not guided well, it was easy to get lost or grounded. And, in this relatively uninhabited area, populated with all kinds of dangerous animals, that could be a death sentence.

Sita's ship sailed in this confusing mesh of waterways for over a week till it reached a nondescript channel. At first, she did not notice the three tall coconut trees at the entrance to the channel. The creepers that spread over the three trunks seemed fashioned into a jigsaw of axe-parts.

The channel led to a dead end, covered by a thick grove of trees. No sight of a dock where the ship could anchor. Sita frowned. She assumed that they would anchor mid-stream and meet some boats soon. Amazingly, the ship showed no signs of slowing down. In fact, the drumbeats of the pace-setters picked up a notch. As the rowers rowed to a faster beat, the vessel gathered speed, heading straight for the grove!

Sita was alone on the upper deck. She held the railings nervously and spoke aloud, 'Slow down. We are too close.'

But her voice did not carry to Jatayu, who was on the secondary deck with his staff, supervising some intricate operations.

How can he not see this! The grove is right in front of us!

'Jatayu*ji*!' screamed Sita in panic, sure now that the ship would soon run aground. She tightened her grip on the railing, bent low and braced herself. Ready for impact.

No impact. A mild jolt, a slight slowing, but the ship sailed on.

Sita raised her head. Confused.

The trees moved, effortlessly pushed aside by the ship! The vessel sailed deep into what should have been the grove. Sita bent over and looked into the water.

Her mouth fell open in awe.

By the great Lord Varun.

Floating trees were pushed aside as the ship moved into a hidden lagoon ahead. She looked back. The floating trees had moved back into position, hiding the secret lagoon as the ship sailed forward. Later, Jatayu would reveal to her that they were a special sub-species of the Sundari tree.

Sita smiled with wonder and shook her head. 'What mysteries abound in the land of Lord Parshu Ram!'

She faced the front again, her eyes aglow.

And then, she froze in horror.

Rivers of blood!

Bang in front of her, in the distance, where the lagoon

ended and the hills began, three streams of blood flowed in from different directions and merged into the cove.

It was believed that a long time ago, Lord Parshu Ram had massacred all the evil kings in India who were oppressing their people. Legend had it that when he finally stopped, his blood-drenched axe had spewed the tainted blood of those wicked kings in an act of self-purification. It had turned the river Malaprabha red.

But it's just a legend!

Yet here she was, on a ship, seeing not one, but three rapid streams of blood disgorging into the lagoon.

Sita clutched her *Rudraaksh* pendant in fear as her heart rate raced. *Lord Rudra, have mercy.*

— ↰⅄ —

'Sita is on her way, Guru*ji*,' said Arishtanemi, as he entered the Hall of Hundred Pillars. 'She should be in Agastyakootam in two or three weeks at most.'

Vishwamitra sat in the main *ParshuRamEshwar* temple in Agastyakootam. The temple was dedicated to the one that Lord Parshu Ram worshipped: Lord Rudra. He looked up from the manuscript he was reading.

'That's good news. Are all the preparations done?

'Yes, Guru*ji*,' said Arishtanemi. He extended his hand and held out a scroll. The seal had been broken. But it could still be recognised. It was the royal seal of the descendants of Anu. 'And King Ashwapati has sent a message.'

Vishwamitra smiled with satisfaction. Ashwapati, the king of Kekaya, was the father of Kaikeyi and Emperor Dashrath's father-in-law. That also made him the grandfather of Dashrath's second son, Bharat. 'So, he has seen the light and seeks to build new relationships.'

'Ambition has its uses, Guru*ji*,' said Arishtanemi. 'Whether the ambition is for oneself or one's progeny. I believe, an Ayodhya nobleman called General Mrigasya has shown ...'

'Guru*ji*!' A novice ran into the hall, panting with exertion.

Vishwamitra looked up, irritated.

'Guru*ji*, she is practising.'

Vishwamitra immediately rose to his feet. He quickly folded his hands together and paid his respects to the idols of Lord Rudra and Lord Parshu Ram. Then, he rushed out of the temple, followed closely by Arishtanemi and the novice.

They quickly mounted their horses and broke into a gallop. There was precious little time to lose.

Within a short while, they were exactly where they wanted to be. A small crowd had already gathered. On hallowed ground. Under a tower almost thirty metres in height, built of stone. Some heads were tilted upwards, towards a tiny wooden house built on top of the tower. Others sat on the ground, their eyes closed in bliss. Some were gently crying, rocking with emotions coursing through their being.

A glorious musical rendition wafted through the air. Divine fingers plucked the strings of an instrument seemingly fashioned by God himself. A woman, who had not stepped out of that house for years, was playing the *Rudra Veena*. An instrument named after the previous Mahadev. What was being performed was a *raga* that most Indian music aficionados would recognise. Some called it *Raga Hindolam*, others called it *Raga Malkauns*. A composition dedicated to the great Mahadev himself, Lord Rudra.

Vishwamitra rushed in as the others made way. He stopped

at the base of the staircase at the entrance to the tower. The sound was soft, filtered by the wooden walls of the house. It was heavenly. Vishwamitra felt his heart instantly settle into the harmonic rhythm. Tears welled up in his eyes.

'*Wah*, Annapoorna *devi, wah*,' mouthed Vishwamitra, as though not wanting to break the spell with any superfluous sound, even that of his own voice.

According to Vishwamitra, Annapoorna was undoubtedly the greatest stringed-instrument player alive. But if she heard any such words of praise, she might stop her practice.

Hundreds had gathered, as if risen from the ground. Arishtanemi looked at them uncomfortably. He had never been happy about this.

Offering refuge to the estranged wife of the chief court musician of Lanka? A former favourite of Raavan himself?

Arishtanemi possessed a military mind. Given to strategic thought. Not for him the emotional swings of those passionately in love with music.

But he knew that his Guru did not agree with him. So he waited, patiently.

The *raga* continued to weave its ethereal magic.

— ◁⊀ —

'It's not blood, my sister,' said Jatayu, looking at Sita.

Though Sita had not asked any question regarding the 'rivers of blood', the terror on her face made Jatayu want to ease her mind. She did not let go of her *Rudraaksh* pendant, but her face relaxed.

The Malayaputras, meanwhile, were anchoring the vessel to the floating jetty.

'It's not?' asked Sita.

'No. It's the effect of a unique riverweed which grows here. It lines the bottom of the stream and is reddish-violet in colour. These streams are shallow, so they appear red from a distance. As if it's a stream full of blood. But the 'blood' doesn't discolour the lagoon, don't you see? Because the riverweeds are too deep in the lagoon to be seen.'

Sita grinned in embarrassment.

'It can be alarming, the first time one sees it. For us, it marks Lord Parshu Ram's territory. The legendary river of blood.'

Sita nodded.

'But blood can flow by other means, in this region. There are dangerous wild animals in the dense jungles between here and Agastyakootam. And we have a two-week march ahead of us. We must stick together and move cautiously.'

'All right.'

Their conversation was cut short by the loud bang of the gangway plank crashing on the floating jetty.

— ૮ૅㅅ —

A little less than two weeks later, the company of five platoons neared their destination. They had cut through unmarked, dense forests along the way, where no clear pathway had been made. Sita realised that unless one was led by the Malayaputras, one would be hopelessly lost in these jungles.

Excitement coursed through her veins as they crested the final hill and beheld the valley that cradled Lord Parshu Ram's city.

'Wow ...' whispered Sita.

Standing on the shoulders of the valley, she admired

the grandiose beauty spread out below her. It was beyond imagination.

The Thamiravaruni river began to the west and crashed into this huge, egg-shaped valley in a series of massive waterfalls. The valley itself was carpeted with dense vegetation and an impenetrable tree cover. The river snaked its way through the vale and exited at the eastern, narrower end; flowing towards the land where the Tamil lived.

The valley was deep, descending almost eight hundred metres from the peaks in the west, from where the Thamiravaruni crashed into it. The sides of the valley fell sharply from its shoulders to its floor, giving it steep edges. The shoulders of the valley were coloured red; perhaps the effect of some metallic ore. The river picked up some of this ore as it began its descent down the waterfall. It lent a faint, red hue to the waters. The waterfalls looked eerily bloody. The river snaked through the valley like a lightly coloured red snake, slithering across an open, lush green egg.

Most of the valley had been eroded over the ages by the river waters, heavy rainfall, and fierce winds. All except for one giant monolith, a humongous tower-like mountain of a single rock. It stood at a proud height of eight hundred and fifty metres from the valley floor, towering well above the valley's shoulders. Massive in breadth as well, it covered almost six square kilometres. The monolith was coloured grey, signifying that it was made of granite, one of the hardest stones there is. Which explained why it stood tall, like a sentinel against the ravages of time, refusing to break even as Mother Nature constantly reshaped everything around it.

Early evening clouds obstructed her view, yet Sita was overwhelmed by its grandeur.

The sides of the monolith were almost a ninety-degree drop from the top to the valley floor. Though practically vertical, the sides were jagged and craggy. The crags sprouted shrubs and ferns. Some creepers clung on bravely to the sides of the monolith. Trees grew on the top, which was a massive space of six square kilometres in area. Besides the small amount of vegetation clinging desperately to the monolith's sides, it was a largely naked rock, standing in austere glory against the profusion of green vegetation that populated every other nook and cranny of the valley below.

The *ParshuRamEshwar* temple was at the top of the monolith. But Sita could not get a very clear view because it was hidden behind cloud cover.

The monolith was *Agastyakootam*; literally, the *hill of Agastya*.

The Malayaputras had eased the otherwise impossible access to Agastyakootam with a rope-and-metal bridge from the valley shoulders to the monolith.

'Shall we cross over to the other side?' asked Jatayu.

'Yes,' answered Sita, tearing her gaze away from the giant rock.

'Jai Parshu Ram.'

'Jai Parshu Ram.'

— ᚱ ᚷ —

Jatayu led his horse carefully over the long rope-and-metal bridge. Sita followed with her horse in tow. The rest of the company fell in line, one behind the other.

Sita was amazed by the stability of the rope bridge. Jatayu explained that this was due to the innovatively designed hollow metal planks that buttressed the bottom of the bridge. The foundations of these interconnected planks lay buried deep on both sides; one at the valley-shoulder end, the other at the granite monolith.

Intriguing as the bridge design was, it did not hold Sita's attention for long. She peered over the rope-railing at the Thamiravaruni, flowing some eight hundred metres below her. She steadied herself; it was a long and steep drop. The Thamiravaruni crashed head-on into the monolith that Sita was walking towards. The river then broke into two streams, which, like loving arms, embraced the sheer rock. They re-joined on the other side of the monolith; and then, the Thamiravaruni continued flowing east, out of the valley. The monolith of granite rock was thus, technically, a riverine island.

'What does the name Thamiravaruni mean, Jatayu*ji*?' asked Sita.

Jatayu answered without turning around. '*Varuni* is *that which comes from Lord Varun*, the God of Water and the Seas. In these parts, it is simply another word for *river*. And *Thamira*, in the local dialect, has two meanings. One is red.'

Sita smiled. 'Well, that's a no-brainer! The red river!'

Jatayu laughed. 'But *Thamira* has another meaning, too.'

'What?'

'Copper.'

— ௫ —

As Sita neared the other side, the clouds parted. She came to a sudden halt, making her horse falter. Her jaw dropped. In sheer amazement and awe.

'How in Lord Rudra's name did they build this?'

Jatayu smiled as he looked back at Sita and gestured that

she keep moving. He turned quickly and resumed his walk. He had been trained to be careful on the bridge.

A massive curvilinear cave had been carved into the monolith. Almost fifteen metres in height and probably around fifty metres deep, the cave ran all along the outer edge of the monolith, in a continuous line, its floor and ceiling rising gently as it spiralled its way to the top of the stone structure. It therefore served as a road, built into the monolith itself. The 'road' spiralled its way down to a lower height as well, till it reached the point of the monolith where it was two hundred metres above the valley floor. But this long continuous cave, which ran within the surface of the structure, with the internal monolith rock serving as its road and roof, did not just serve as a passage. On the inner side of this cave were constructions, again carved out of the monolith rock itself. These constructions served as houses, offices, shops and other buildings required for civilised living. This innovative construction, built deeper into the inner parts of the monolith itself, housed a large proportion of the ten thousand Malayaputras who lived in Agastyakootam. The rest lived on top of the monolith. There were another ninety thousand Malayaputras, stationed in camps across the great land of India.

'How can anyone carve something this gigantic into stone as hard as granite?' asked Sita. 'That too in a rock face that is almost completely vertical? This is the work of the Gods!'

'The Malayaputras represent the God, Lord Parshu Ram, himself,' said Jatayu. 'Nothing is beyond us.'

As he stepped off the bridge onto the landing area carved into the monolith, Jatayu mounted his horse again. The ceiling of the cave was high enough to comfortably allow a mounted soldier to ride along. He turned to see Sita climbing onto her horse as well. But she did not move. She was admiring the intricately engraved railings carved out at the edge of the cave, along the right side of the 'road'. The artistry imposed on it distracted one from the sheer fall into the valley that the railing prevented. The railing itself was around two metres high. Pillars had been carved into it, which also allowed open spaces in between for light. The 'fish' symbol was delicately carved into each pillar's centre.

'My sister,' whispered Jatayu.

Sita had steered her horse towards the four-floor houses on the left inner side of the cave road. She turned her attention back to Jatayu.

'Promise me, my sister,' said Jatayu, 'you will not shrink or turn back, no matter what lies ahead.'

'What?' frowned Sita.

'I think I understand you now. What you're about to walk into may overwhelm you. But you cannot imagine how important this day is for us Malayaputras. Don't pull back from anyone. Please.'

Before Sita could ask any further questions, Jatayu had moved ahead. Jatayu steered his horse to the right, where the road rose gently, spiralling its way to the top.

Sita too kicked her horse into action.

And then, the drumbeats began.

As the road opened ahead, she saw large numbers of people lined on both sides. None of them wore any *angvastrams*. The people of Kerala dressed this way, when they entered temples to worship their Gods and Goddesses. The absence of the *angvastram* symbolised that they were the servants of their Gods and Goddesses. And, they were dressed this way today, as their living Goddess had come home.

At regular intervals stood drummers with large drums hanging from cloth ropes around their shoulders. As Sita emerged, they began a rhythmic, evocative beat. Next to each drummer was a *veena* player, stringing melody to the rhythm of the drummers. The rest of the crowd was on their knees, heads bowed. And, they were chanting.

The words floated in the air. Clear and precise.

Om Namo Bhagavate Vishnudevaya
Tasmai Saakshine namo namah
Salutations to the great God Vishnu
Salutations, Salutations to the Witness

Sita looked on, unblinking. Unsure of what to do. Her horse, too, had stopped.

Jatayu pulled up his horse and fell behind Sita. He made a clicking sound and Sita's horse began to move. Forward, on a gentle gradient to the top.

And thus, led by Sita, the procession moved ahead.

Om Namo Bhagavate Vishnudevaya
Tasmai Matsyaaya namo namah
Salutations to the great God Vishnu
Salutations, Salutations to Lord Matsya

Sita's horse moved slowly, but unhesitatingly. Most of the faces in the crowd were filled with devotion. And many had tears flowing down their eyes.

Some people came forward, bearing rose petals in baskets. They flung them in the air. Showering roses on their Goddess, Sita.

Om Namo Bhagavate Vishnudevaya
Tasmai Kurmaaya namo namah
Salutations to the great God Vishnu
Salutations, Salutations to Lord Kurma

One woman rushed in, holding her infant son in her arms. She brought the baby close to the horse's stirrups and touched the child's forehead to Sita's foot.

A confused and troubled Sita tried her best to not shrink back.

The company, led by Sita, kept riding up the road, towards the summit of the monolith.

The drumbeats, the veenas, the chanting continued... ceaselessly.

Om Namo Bhagavate Vishnudevaya
Tasyai Vaaraahyai namo namah
Salutations to the great God Vishnu
Salutations, Salutations to Lady Varahi

Ahead of them, some people were down on their knees with their heads placed on the ground, their hands spread forward. Their bodies shook with the force of their emotions.

Om Namo Bhagavate Vishnudevaya
Tasmai Narasimhaaya namo namah
Salutations to the great God Vishnu
Salutations, Salutations to Lord Narsimha

The gently upward-sloping cave opened onto the top of the monolith. The railing continued to skirt the massive summit. People from the spiral cave road followed Sita in a procession.

The large area at the top of the monolith was well organised with grid-like roads and many low-rise buildings. The streets were bordered with dugouts on both sides that served as flower beds, the soil for which had been painstakingly transported from the fertile valley below. At regular intervals, the dugouts were deep, for they held the roots of larger trees. It was a carefully cultivated naturalness in this austere, rocky environment.

At the centre of the summit lay two massive temples, facing each other. Together, they formed the *ParshuRamEshwar* temple complex. One temple, red in colour, was dedicated to the great Mahadev, Lord Rudra. The other, in pristine white, was the temple of the sixth Vishnu, Lord Parshu Ram.

The other buildings in the area were uniformly low-rise, none built taller than the temples of *ParshuRamEshwar*. Some served as offices and others as houses. Maharishi Vishwamitra's house was at the edge of the summit, overlooking the verdant valley below.

Om Namo Bhagavate Vishnudevaya
Tasmai Vaamanaaya namo namah
Salutations to the great God Vishnu
Salutations, Salutations to Lord Vaaman
The chanting continued.

Jatayu held his breath as his eyes fell on a gaunt old lady. Her flowing white hair let loose in the wind, she sat on a platform in the distance. Her proud, ghostly eyes were fixed on Sita. With her felicitous fingers, she plucked at the strings of the *Rudra Veena*. Annapoorna *devi*. The last time she had been seen was the day that she had arrived at Agastyakootam, many years ago. She had stepped out of her home, today. She was playing the *Veena* in public, consciously breaking her oath. A terrible oath, compelled by a husband she had loved. But there was good reason to break the oath today. It was not every day that the great Vishnu came home.

Om Namo Bhagavate Vishnudevaya
Tasyai Mohinyai namo namah
Salutations to the great God Vishnu
Salutations, Salutations to Lady Mohini
Some purists believed that a Mahadev and a Vishnu could

not exist simultaneously. That at any given time, either the Mahadev exists with the tribe of the previous Vishnu, or the Vishnu exists with the tribe of the previous Mahadev. For how could the need for the destruction of Evil coincide with the propagation of Good? Therefore, some refused to believe that Lady Mohini was a Vishnu. Clearly, the Malayaputras sided with the majority that believed that the great Lady Mohini was a Vishnu.

The chanting continued.

Om Namo Bhagavate Vishnudevaya
Tasmai Parshuramaaya namo namah
Salutations to the great God Vishnu
Salutations, Salutations to Lord Parshu Ram

Sita pulled her horse's reins and stopped as she approached Maharishi Vishwamitra. Unlike the others, he was wearing his *angvastram*. All the Malayaputras in Agastyakootam were on top of the monolith now.

Sita dismounted, bent and touched Vishwamitra's feet with respect. She stood up straight and folded her hands together into a *Namaste*. Vishwamitra raised his right hand.

The music, the chanting, all movement stopped instantly.

A gentle breeze wafted across the summit. The soft sound it made was all that could be heard. But if one listened with the soul, perhaps the sound of ten thousand hearts beating as one would also have been heard. And, if one possessed the power of the divine, one would have also heard the cry of an overwhelmed woman's heart, as she silently called out to the beloved mother she had lost.

A Malayaputra *pandit* walked up to Vishwamitra, holding two bowls in his hands. One contained a thick red viscous liquid; and, the other, an equal amount of thick white liquid.

Vishwamitra dipped his index and ring finger into the white liquid and then the middle finger in the red liquid.

Then he placed his wrist on his chest and whispered, 'By the grace of the Mahadev, Lord Rudra, and the Vishnu, Lord Parshu Ram.'

He placed his three colour-stained fingers together in between Sita's eyebrows, then slid them up to her hairline, spreading the outer fingers gradually apart as they moved. A trident-shaped *tilak* emerged on Sita's forehead. The outer arms of the *tilak* were white, while the central line was red.

With a flick of his hand, Vishwamitra signalled for the chanting to resume. Ten thousand voices joined together in harmony. This time, though, the chant was different.

Om Namo Bhagavate Vishnudevaya
Tasyai Sitadevyai namo namah
Salutations to the great God Vishnu
Salutations, Salutations to Lady Sita

Chapter 15

Late in the evening, Sita sat quietly in the Lord Parshu Ram temple. She had been left alone. As she had requested.

The grand *ParshuRamEshwar* temple grounds spread over nearly one hundred and fifty acres on the summit of the granite monolith. At the centre was a man-made square-shaped lake, its bottom lined with the familiar reddish-violet riverweeds. It reminded her of the three apparently 'blood-filled' streams she had seen at the hidden lagoon. The riverweeds had been grafted here, so that they could survive in these still waters. The lake served as a store for water for the entire city built into this rock formation. The water was transported into the houses through pipes built parallel to the spiral pathway down the curvilinear cave structure.

The two temples of the *ParshuRamEshwar* complex were constructed on opposite sides of this lake. One was dedicated to Lord Rudra and the other to Lord Parshu Ram.

The Lord Rudra temple's granite inner structure had been covered with a single layer of red sandstone, transported in ships from a great distance. It had a solid base, almost ten metres in height, forming the pedestal on which the main temple structure had been built. The exterior face of the base was intricately carved with figures of *rishis* and *rishikas*. A broad staircase in the centre led to a massive veranda. The main temple was surrounded by delicate lattice, made from thin strips of a copper alloy; it was brown in colour, rather than the natural reddish-orange of the metal. The lattice comprised tiny square-shaped openings, each of them shaped into a metallic lamp at its base. With thousands of these lamps festively lit, it was as if a star-lit sky screened the main temple.

Ethereal.

Beyond the metallic screen holding thousands of lamps, was the Hall of Hundred Pillars. Each pillar was shaped to a near-perfect circular cross-section using elephant-powered lathes. These imposing pillars held the main temple spire, which itself shot up a massive fifty metres. The towering temple spire was carved on all sides with figures of great men and women of the ancient past. People from many groups such as the Sangamtamils, Dwarkans, Manaskul, Adityas, Daityas, Vasus, Asuras, Devas, Rakshasas, Gandharvas, Yakshas, Suryavanshis, Chandravanshis, Nagas and many more. The forefathers and foremothers of this noble Vedic nation of India.

At the centre of the Hall was the *sanctum sanctorum*. In it were life-size idols of Lord Rudra and the woman he had loved, Lady Mohini. Unlike their normal representations, these idols did not carry weapons. Their expressions were calm, gentle, and loving. Most fascinatingly, Lord Rudra and Lady Mohini held hands.

On the other side of the square lake, facing the Lord Rudra temple, was the temple dedicated to Lord Parshu Ram. Almost exactly similar to the Lord Rudra temple, there was one conspicuous difference: Lord Parshu Ram temple's granite inner structure was layered on top with white marble.

The *sanctum sanctorum* in the middle of the Hall of Hundred Pillars had life-sized idols of the great sixth Vishnu and his wife, Dharani. And, these idols were armed. Lord Parshu Ram held his fearsome battle axe and Lady Dharani sat with the long bow in her left hand and a single arrow in the other.

Had Sita paid close attention, she might have recognised the markings on the bow that Lady Dharani held. But she was lost in her own thoughts. Leaning against a pillar. Staring at the idols of Lord Parshu Ram and Lady Dharani.

She recalled the words of Maharishi Vishwamitra as he had welcomed her to Agastyakootam, earlier today. That they would wait for nine years. Till the stars aligned with the calculations of the Malayaputra astrologers. And then, her Vishnuhood would be announced to the world. She had been told that she had time till then to prepare. To train. To understand what she must do. And that the Malayaputras would guide her through it all.

Of course, until that auspicious moment, it was the sworn duty of every single Malayaputra to keep her identity secret. The risks were too high.

She looked back. Towards the entrance. Nobody had entered the temple. She had been left alone.

She looked at the idol of Lord Parshu Ram.

She knew that not every Malayaputra was convinced of her potential as the Vishnu. But none would dare oppose the formidable Vishwamitra.

Why is Guru Vishwamitra so sure about me? What does he know that I don't?

— ௐ —

A month had passed since Sita had arrived in Agastyakootam. Vishwamitra and she had had many extended conversations.

Some of these were purely educational; on science, astronomy and medicine. Others were subtle lessons designed to help her clearly define, question, confront or affirm her views on various topics like masculinity and femininity, equality and hierarchy, justice and freedom, liberalism and order, besides others. The debates were largely enlightening for Sita. But the ones on the caste system were the most animated.

Both teacher and student agreed that the form in which the caste system currently existed, deserved to be completely destroyed. That it corroded the vitals of India. In the past, one's caste was determined by one's attributes, qualities and deeds. It had been flexible. But over time, familial love distorted the foundations of this concept. Parents began to ensure that their children remained in the same caste as them. Also, an arbitrary hierarchy was accorded to the castes, based on a group's financial and political influence. Some castes became 'higher', others 'lower'. Gradually, the caste system became rigid and birth-based. Even Vishwamitra had faced many obstacles when, born a Kshatriya, he had decided to become a Brahmin; and, in fact, a *rishi*. This rigidity created divisions within society. Raavan had exploited these divisions to eventually dominate the Sapt Sindhu.

But what could be the solution for this? The *Maharishi* believed that it was not possible to create a society where all were completely and exactly equal. It may be desirable, but would remain a utopian idea, always. People differed in skills, both in degree and kind. So, their fields of activity and achievements also had to differ. Periodic efforts at imposing exact equality had invariably led to violence and chaos.

Vishwamitra laid emphasis on freedom. A person must be enabled to understand himself and pursue his dreams. In his scheme of things, if a child was born to Shudra parents, but with the skills of a Brahmin, he should be allowed to become a Brahmin. If the son of a Kshatriya father had trading skills, then he should train to become a Vaishya.

He believed that rather than trying to force-fit an artificial equality, one must remove the curse of birth determining one's life prospects. Societies would always have hierarchies. They existed even in nature. But they could be fluid. There would be times when Kshatriya soldiers comprised the elite, and then, there would be times when skilful Shudra creators would be the elite. The differences in society should be determined by merit. That's all. Not birth.

To achieve this, Vishwamitra proposed that families needed to be restructured. For it was inheritance that worked most strongly against merit and free movement in society.

He suggested that children must compulsorily be adopted by the state at the time of birth. The birth-parents would have to surrender their children to the kingdom. The state would feed, educate and nurture the in-born talents of these children. Then, at the age of fifteen, they would appear for an examination to test them on their physical, psychological and mental abilities. Based on the result, appropriate castes would be allocated to them. Subsequent training would further polish their natural skills. Eventually, they would be adopted by citizens of the same caste as the one assigned to the adolescents through the examination process. The children would not know their birth-parents, only their adoptive caste-parents. The birth-parents, too, would not know the fate of their birth-children.

Sita agreed that this would be a fair system. But she also felt that it was harsh and unrealistic. It was unimaginable to her that parents would willingly hand over their birth-children to the kingdom. Permanently. Or that they would ever stop trying to learn what happened to them. It was unnatural. In fact, times were such that it was impossible to make Indians follow even basic laws for the greater good. It was completely far-fetched to think that they would ever make such a big sacrifice in the larger interest of society.

Vishwamitra retorted that it was the Vishnu's task to radically transform society. To convince society. Sita responded that perhaps the Vishnu would need to be convinced, first. The guru assured her that he would. He laid a wager that over time, Sita would be so convinced that she would herself champion this 'breathtakingly fair and just organisation of society'.

As they ended another of their discussions on the caste system, Sita got up and walked towards the end of the garden, thinking further about it. The garden was at the edge of the monolith summit. She took a deep breath, trying to think of some more arguments that would challenge her guru's proposed system. She looked down at the valley, eight hundred and fifty metres below. Something about the Thamiravaruni startled her. She stopped thinking. And stared.

Why have I not noticed this before?

The river did not appear to flow out of the valley at all. At the eastern end of the egg-shaped valley, the Thamiravaruni disappeared underground.

What in Lord Rudra's name ...

'The river flows into a cave, Sita.' Vishwamitra had quietly walked up to his student.

— ɾ̃ᴋ —

Vishwamitra and Sita stood at the mouth of the natural cave, carved vertically into the rock face.

Intrigued by the flow of the Thamiravaruni, Sita had wished to see the place where it magically disappeared, at the eastern end of the valley. From a distance, it had seemed as if the river dropped into a hole in the ground. But, as she drew near, she had seen the narrow opening of the cave. A vertical cave. It was incredible that an entire river entered the small aperture. The thunderous roar of the river within the cave suggested that the shaft expanded underground.

'But where does all this water go?' asked Sita.

A company of Malayaputra soldiers stood behind Sita and Vishwamitra. Out of earshot. But close enough to move in quickly if needed.

'The river continues to flow east,' said Vishwamitra. 'It drains into the Gulf of Mannar which separates India from Lanka.'

'But how does it emerge from the hole it has dug itself into?'

'It bursts out of this underground cavern some ten kilometres downstream.'

Sita's eyes widened in surprise. 'Is this cave that long?'

Vishwamitra smiled. 'Come. I'll show you.'

Vishwamitra led Sita to the edge of the mouth of the cave. She hesitated. It was only around twenty-five metres across at the entry point. This forced constriction dramatically increased the speed of the river. It tore into the underground causeway with unreal ferocity.

Vishwamitra pointed to a flight of stairs to the left side of the cave mouth. It was obviously man-made. Steps had been carved into the sloping side wall. A railing thoughtfully provided on the right side, preventing a steep fall into the rapids.

Torrents of foam and spray from the rapidly descending river diminished vision. It also made the stairs dangerously slippery.

Vishwamitra pulled his *angvastram* over his head to shield himself from water droplets that fell from the ceiling. Sita followed suit.

'Be careful,' said Vishwamitra, as he approached the staircase. 'The steps are slippery.'

Sita nodded and followed her guru. The Malayaputra soldiers stayed close behind.

They wended their way in silence. Descending carefully. Deeper and deeper, into the cave. Sita huddled into her *angvastram*. Daylight filtered through. But she expected pitch darkness as they descended farther. The insistent spray of water made it impossible to light a torch.

Sita had always been afraid of the dark. Added to which was this confined, slippery space. The looming rock structure and the loud roar of the descending river combined altogether into a terrifying experience.

Her mother's voice called out to her. A memory buried deep in her psyche.

Don't be afraid of the dark, my child. Light has a source. It can be snuffed out. But darkness has no source. It just exists. This darkness is a path to That, which has no source: God.

Wise words. But words that didn't really provide much comfort to Sita at this point. Cold fear slowly tightened its grip on her heart. A childhood memory forced itself into her consciousness. Of being confined in a dark basement, the sounds of rats scurrying about, the frantic beat of her heart.

Barely able to breathe. She pulled her awareness into the present. An occasional glimpse of Vishwamitra's white robe disturbed the void they had settled into. Suddenly, she saw him turn left. She followed. Her hand not letting go of the railing.

Disoriented by sudden blinding light, her eyes gradually registered the looming figure of Vishwamitra standing before her. He held aloft a torch. He handed it to her. She saw a Malayaputra soldier hand another torch to Vishwamitra.

Vishwamitra started walking ahead again, continuing to descend. The steps were much broader now. Though the sound of the river reverberated against the wall and echoed all around.

Too loud for such a small cave.

But Sita could not see much since there were only two torches. Soon, all the Malayaputras held a torch each and light flooded into the space.

Sita held her breath.

By the great Lord Rudra!

The small cave had opened into a cavern. And it was huge. Bigger than any cave Sita had ever seen. Perhaps six hundred metres in width. The steps descended farther and farther while the ceiling remained at roughly the same height. When they reached the bottom of the cavern, the ceiling was a good two hundred metres above. A large palace, fit for a king, could have been built in this subterranean space. And still have room left over. The Thamiravaruni flowed on the right-hand side of this cavern, descending rapidly with great force.

'As you can see, the river has eroded this cave over the ages,' explained Vishwamitra. 'It is huge, isn't it?'

'The biggest I have ever seen!' said Sita in wonder.

There was a massive white hill on the left. The secret behind the well-lit interior. It reflected light from the numerous torches and spread it to all the corners of the cave.

'I wonder what material that hill is made up of, Guru*ji*,' said Sita.

Vishwamitra smiled. 'A lot of bats live here.'

Sita looked up instinctively.

'They are all asleep now,' said Vishwamitra. 'It's daytime. They will awaken at night. And that hill is made from the droppings of billions of bats over many millennia.'

Sita grimaced. 'Yuck!'

Vishwamitra's laughter echoed in the vastness.

It was then that Sita's eyes fell on something behind Vishwamitra. Many rope ladders hanging from the walls; so many that she gave up the attempt to count them. Hammered into place on top, they fell from the roof, all the way to the floor.

Sita pointed. 'What's that, Guru*ji*?'

Vishwamitra turned around. 'There are some white semi-circular bird nests in the nooks and crannies of these walls. Those nests are precious. The material they are made from is precious. These ladders allow us to access them.'

Sita was surprised. 'What could be so valuable about the material that a nest is made from? These ladders go really high. Falling from that height must mean instant death.'

'Indeed, some have died. But it is a worthy sacrifice.'

Sita frowned.

'We need some hold over Raavan. The material in those nests gives us that control.'

Sita froze. The thought that had been troubling her for some time made its reappearance: *What is the relationship between the Malayaputras and the Lankans?*

'I will explain it to you, someday,' said Vishwamitra, reading her thoughts as usual. 'For now, have faith in me.'

Sita remained silent. But her face showed that she was troubled.

'This land of ours,' continued Vishwamitra, 'is sacred. Bound by the Himalayas in the north, washed by the Indian Ocean at its feet and the Western and Eastern Seas at its arms, the soil in this great nation is hallowed. All those born in this land carry the sacred earth of Mother India in their body. This nation cannot be allowed to remain in this wretched state. It is an insult to our noble ancestors. We must make India great again. I will do anything, anything, to make this land worthy of our great ancestors. And, so shall the Vishnu.'

— ᘖᚎ —

Sita, Jatayu, and a company of Malayaputra soldiers were sailing back up the western coast towards the Sapt Sindhu. Sita was returning to Mithila. She had spent more than five months in Agastyakootam, educating herself on the principles of governance, philosophies, warfare and personal history of the earlier Vishnus. She had also acquired advanced training in other subjects. This was in preparation for her Vishnuhood. Vishwamitra had been personally involved in her training.

Jatayu and she sat on the main deck, sipping a hot cup of ginger *kadha*.

Sita set her cup down and looked at the Malayaputra. 'Jatayu*ji*, I hope you will answer my question.'

Jatayu turned towards Sita and bowed his head. 'How can I refuse, great Vishnu?'

'What is the relationship between the Malayaputras and the Lankans?'

'We trade with them. As does every kingdom in the Sapt

Sindhu. We export a very valuable material mined in the cavern of Thamiravaruni to Lanka. And they give us what we need.'

'I'm aware of that. But Raavan usually appoints sub-traders who are given the licence to trade with Lanka. No one else can conduct any business with him. But there is no such sub-trader in Agastyakootam. You trade directly with him. This is strange. I also know that he strictly controls the Western and Eastern Seas. And that no ship can set sail in these waters without paying him a cess. This is how he maintains a stranglehold over trade. But Malayaputra ships pay nothing and yet, pass unharmed. Why?'

'Like I said, we sell him something very valuable, great Vishnu.'

'Do you mean the bird's nest material?' asked Sita, incredulously. 'I am sure he gets many equally valuable things from other parts of the Sapt Sindhu ...'

'This material is *very, very* valuable. Far more than anything he gets from the Sapt Sindhu.'

'Then why doesn't he just attack Agastyakootam and seize it? It's not far from his kingdom.'

Jatayu remained silent, unsure of how much to reveal.

'I have also heard,' continued Sita, choosing her words carefully, 'that, apparently, there is a shared heritage.'

'That there may be. But every Malayaputra's primary loyalty is to you, Lady Vishnu.'

'I don't doubt that. But tell me, what is this common heritage?'

Jatayu took a deep breath. He had managed to sidestep the first question, but it seemed he would be unable to avoid this one. 'Maharishi Vishwamitra was a prince before he became a *Brahmin Rishi*.'

'I know that.'

'His father, King Gaadhi, ruled the kingdom of Kannauj. Guru Vishwamitra himself was the king there for a short span of time.'

'Yes, so I have heard.'

'Then he decided to renounce his throne and become a Brahmin. It wasn't an easy decision, but nothing is beyond our great Guru*ji.* Not only did he become a Brahmin, he also acquired the title of *Maharishi*. And, he scaled great heights to reach the peak by ultimately becoming the chief of the Malayaputras.'

Sita nodded. 'Nothing is beyond Guru Vishwamitra. He is one of the all-time greats.'

'True,' said Jatayu. Hesitantly, he continued. 'So, Guru Vishwamitra's roots are in Kannauj.'

'But what does that have to do with Raavan?'

Jatayu sighed. 'Most people don't know this. It is a well-kept secret, my sister. But Raavan is also from Kannauj. His family comes from there.'

Chapter 16

At twenty years of age, Sita may have had the energy and drive of a youngster, but her travels through much of India and the training she had received at Agastyakootam, had given her wisdom far beyond her years.

Samichi was initially intrigued by Sita's repeated trips around the country. She was told that they were for trade and diplomatic purposes. And, she believed it. Or, pretended to. As she practically governed Mithila with a free hand in the absence of the princess. But Sita was now back in Mithila and the reins of administration were back in the hands of the prime minister.

Radhika was on one of her frequent visits to Mithila.

'How are you doing, Samichi?' asked Radhika.

Sita, Radhika and Samichi were in the private chambers of the prime minister of Mithila.

'Doing very well!' smiled Samichi. 'Thank you for asking.'

'I love what you have done with the slums at the southern gate. A cesspool has transformed into a well-organised, permanent construction.'

'It would not have been possible without the guidance of the prime minister,' said Samichi with genuine humility. 'The idea and vision were hers. I just implemented it.'

'Not prime minister. Sita.'

'Sorry?'

'I have told you many times,' said Sita, 'when we are alone, you can call me by my name.'

Samichi looked at Radhika and then at Sita.

Sita rolled her eyes. 'Radhika is a friend, Samichi!'

Samichi smiled. 'Sorry. No offence meant.'

'None taken, Samichi!' said Radhika. 'You are my friend's right hand. How can I take offence at something you say?'

Samichi rose to her feet. 'If you will excuse me, Sita, I must go to the inner city. There is a gathering of the nobles that I need to attend.'

'I have heard,' said Sita, gesturing for Samichi to wait, 'that the rich are not too happy.'

'Yes,' said Samichi. 'They are richer than they used to be, since Mithila is doing well now. But the poor have improved their lot in life at a faster pace. It is no longer easy for the rich to find cheap labour or domestic help. But it's not just the rich who are unhappy. Ironically, even the poor aren't as happy as they used to be, before their lives improved. They complain even more now. They want to get richer, more quickly. With greater expectations, they have discovered higher dissatisfaction.'

'Change causes disruption ...' Sita said, thoughtfully.

'Yes.'

'Keep me informed of the early signs of any trouble.'

'Yes, Sita,' said Samichi, before saluting and walking out of the room.

As soon as they were alone, Sita asked Radhika, 'And what else has been happening with the other Vishnu candidates?'

'Ram is progressing very well. Bharat is a little headstrong. It's still a toss-up!'

— ᚱᚷ —

It was late in the evening at the gurukul of Maharishi Kashyap. Five friends, all of them eight years old, were playing a game with each other. A game suitable for the brilliant students who populated this great centre of learning. An intellectual game.

One of the students was asking questions and the others had to answer. The questioner had a stone in his hand. He tapped it on the ground once. Then he paused. Then he tapped once again. Pause. Then two times, quickly. Pause. Three times. Pause. Five times. Pause. Eight times. Pause. He looked at his friends and asked, 'Who am I?'

His friends looked at each other, confused.

A seven-year-old boy stepped up gingerly from the back. He was dressed in rags and clearly looked out of place. 'I think the stone taps represented 1, 1, 2, 3, 5, 8, right? That's the Pingala Series. Therefore, I am Rishi Pingala.'

The friends looked at the boy. He was an orphan who lived in the minuscule guard cabin of the local Mother Goddess temple. The boy was weak, suffering from malnutrition and poor health. But he was brilliant. A gurukul student named Vishwamitra had managed to convince the principal to enrol this poor orphan in the school. Vishwamitra had leveraged the power of the massive endowment that his father, the King of Kannauj, had given to the gurukul, to get this done.

The boys turned away from the orphan, even though his answer was correct.

'We're not interested in what you say, Vashishtha,' sneered the boy who had asked the question. 'Why don't you go and clean the guard's cabin?'

As the boys burst out laughing, Vashishtha's body shrank in shame. But he stood his ground. Refusing to leave.

The questioner turned to his friends again and tapped the earth once. Then drew a circle around the spot he had tapped. Then he drew the circle's diameter. Then, outside the circle, he tapped sharply once. Then, he placed the stone flat on the ground. Pause. Then he tapped the stone sharply again. Quickly. Eight times. 'Who am I?'

Vashishtha immediately blurted out, 'I know! You tapped the ground and drew a circle. That's Mother Earth. Then you drew the diameter. Then you tapped 1-0-8 outside. What is 108 times the diameter of the Earth? The diameter of the Sun. I am the Sun God!'

The friends did not even turn to look at Vashishtha. Nobody acknowledged his answer.

But Vashishtha refused to be denied. 'It's from the Surya Siddhanta ... *It's the correct answer ...'*

The questioner turned to face him in anger. 'Get lost, Vashishtha!'

A loud voice was heard. 'Hey!'

It was Vishwamitra. He may have been only eight years old, but he was already huge. Powerful enough to scare the five boys.

'Kaushik ...' said the boy questioner nervously, using the gurukul *name for Vishwamitra, 'this has nothing to do with you ...'*

Vishwamitra walked up to Vashishtha and held his hand. Then, he turned to the five boys. Glaring. 'He is a student of the gurukul *now. You will call him by his* gurukul *name. With respect.'*

The questioner swallowed. Shaking in fear.

'His gurukul *name is Divodas,' said Vishwamitra, holding Vashishtha's hand tighter. Divodas was the name of a great ancient king. It was Vishwamitra who had selected this* gurukul *name for Vashishtha and then convinced the principal to make it official. 'Say it.'*

The five friends remained paralysed.

Vishwamitra stepped closer, menace oozing from every pore of his body. He had already built a reputation with his fierce temper. 'Say my friend's gurukul *name. Say it. Divodas.'*

The questioner sputtered, as he whispered, 'Divo ... das.'

'Louder. With respect. Divodas.'

All five boys spoke together, 'Divodas.'

Vishwamitra pulled Vashishtha towards himself. 'Divodas is my friend. You mess with him, you mess with me.'

'Guru*ji*!'

Vashishtha was pulled back from the ancient, more than a hundred-and-forty-year-old memory. He quickly wiped his eyes. Tears are meant to be hidden.

He turned to look at Shatrughan, who was holding up a manuscript of the *Surya Siddhanta*.

Of all the books in the entire world ... What are the odds?

Vashishtha would have smiled at the irony. But he knew it was going to be a long discussion. The youngest prince of Ayodhya was by far the most intelligent of the four brothers. So, he looked with a serious expression at Shatrughan and said, 'Yes, my child. What is your question?'

$$— \, \maltese \, —$$

Sita and Radhika were meeting after a two-year gap.

Over this time, Sita had travelled through the western parts of India, all the way to Gandhar, at the base of the Hindukush mountains. While India's cultural footprints could be found beyond these mountains, it was believed that the Hindukush, peopled by the Hindushahi Pashtuns and the brave Baloch, defined the western borders of India. Beyond that was the land of the *Mlechchas*, the *foreigners*.

'What did you think of the lands of Anu?' asked Radhika.

Kekaya, ruled by Ashwapati, headed the kingdoms of the Anunnaki, descendants of the ancient warrior-king, Anu. Many of the kingdoms around Kekaya, bound by Anunnaki clan ties, pledged fealty to Ashwapati. And Ashwapati, in turn, was loyal to Dashrath. Or, at least so it was publicly believed. After all, Ashwapati's daughter, Kaikeyi, was Dashrath's favourite wife.

'Aggressive people,' said Sita. 'The Anunnaki don't do anything by half measures. Their fire, put to good use, can help the great land of India achieve new heights. But, when uncontrolled, it can also lead to chaos.'

'Agreed,' said Radhika. 'Isn't Rajagriha beautiful?'

Rajagriha, the capital of Kekaya, was on the banks of the river Jhelum, not far from where the Chenab River merged into it. Rajagriha extended on both sides of the river. The massive and ethereally beautiful palace of its king was on the eastern bank of the Jhelum.

'It is, indeed,' said Sita. 'They are talented builders.'

'And, fierce warriors. Quite mad, too!' Radhika giggled.

Sita laughed loudly. 'True ... There is a thin dividing line between fierceness and insanity!'

Sita noted that Radhika seemed happier than usual. 'Tell me about the princes of Ayodhya.'

'Ram is doing well. My father is quite certain that Guru Vashishtha will choose him.'

'And Bharat?'

Radhika blushed slightly. And, Sita's suspicions were confirmed.

'He's growing up well too,' whispered Radhika, a dreamy look on her face.

'That well?' joked Sita.

Her crimson face a giveaway, Radhika slapped her friend on her wrists. 'Shut up!'

Sita laughed in delight. 'By the great Lady Mohini, Radhika is in love!'

Radhika glared at Sita, but did not refute her friend.

'But what about the law ...'

Radhika's tribe was matrilineal. Women were strictly forbidden from marrying outside the tribe. Men could marry outside their tribe on condition that they would be excommunicated.

Radhika waved her hand in dismissal. 'All that is in the future. Right now, let me enjoy the company of Bharat, one of the most romantic and passionate young men that nature has ever produced.'

Sita smiled, then changed the subject. 'What about Ram?'

'Very stoic. Very, very serious.'

'Serious, is it?'

'Yes. Serious and purposeful. Relentlessly purposeful. Almost all the time. He has a strong sense of commitment and honour. Hard on others and on himself. Fiercely patriotic. In love with every corner of India. Law-abiding. Always! And not one romantic bone in his body. I am not sure he will make a good husband.'

Sita leaned back in her couch and rested her arms on the cushions. She narrowed her eyes and whispered to herself. *But he will probably make a good Vishnu.*

— ᘰᘏ —

A year had lapsed since the friends had last met. Her work having kept her busy, Sita had not travelled out of Mithila. She was delighted, therefore, when Radhika returned, unannounced.

Sita embraced her warmly. But pulled back as she noticed her friend's eyes.

'What's wrong?'

'Nothing,' said Radhika, shaking her head. Withdrawn.

Sita immediately guessed what must have happened. She held her friend's hands. 'Did he leave you?'

Radhika frowned and shook her head. 'Of course not. You don't know Bharat. He is an honourable man. In fact, he begged me not to leave him.'

She left him?!

'In the name of Lady Mohini, why? Forget about your tribe's silly law. If you want him then you have to fight for him ...'

'No. It's not about the laws ... I would have left the tribe if ... if I had wanted to marry him.'

'Then, what is the problem?' asked Sita.

'It wouldn't have worked out ... I know. I don't want to be a part of this "greatness project", Sita. I know Ram, Bharat, and you will do a lot for India. I also know that greatness usually comes at the cost of enormous personal suffering. That is the way it has always been. That is the way it will always be. I don't want that. I just want a simple life. I just want to be happy. I don't want to be great.'

'You are being too pessimistic, Radhika.'

'No, I am not. You can call me selfish but ...'

Sita cut in, 'I would never call you selfish. Realistic, maybe. But not selfish.'

'Then speaking realistically, I know what I am up against. I have observed my father all my life. There is a fire within him. I see it in his eyes, all the time. I see the same fire in you. And in Ram. A desire to serve Mother India. I didn't expect it initially, but now I see the same fire in Bharat's eyes. You are all the same. Even Bharat. And just like all of you, he is willing to sacrifice everything for India. I don't want to sacrifice anything. I just want to be happy. I just want to be normal ...'

'But can you be happy without him?'

Radhika's sad smile did not hide her pain. 'It would be even worse if I married him and all my hopes for happiness were tied to nagging him to give up his dreams for India and for himself. I'd eventually make him unhappy. I'd make myself unhappy as well.'

'But …'

'It hurts right now. But time always heals, Sita. Years from now, what will remain are the bittersweet memories. More sweet, less bitter. No one can take away the memories of passion and romance. Ever. That'll be enough.'

'You've really thought this through?'

'Happiness is not an accident. It is a choice. It is in our hands to be happy. Always in our hands. Who says that we can have only one soulmate? Sometimes, soulmates want such radically different things that they end up being the cause of unhappiness for each other. Someday I will find another soulmate, one who also wants what I want. He may not be as fascinating as Bharat. Or, even as great as Bharat will be. But he will bring me what I want. Simple happiness. I will find such a man. In my tribe. Or, outside of it.'

Sita gently placed a hand on her friend's shoulder.

Radhika took a deep breath and shook her head. Snapping out of her blues. She had been sent to Mithila with a purpose. 'By the way, Guru Vashishtha has made his decision. So have the Vayuputras.'

'And?'

'It's Ram.'

Sita took a long, satisfied breath. Then, she smiled.

Another year passed by. Sita was twenty-four years old now. She had visited the entire length of the western coast of India, the previous year. From the beaches of Balochistan all the way down to Kerala, which cradled Agastyakootam. She was finally back in Mithila, engaged in mounds of pending royal duties. Whatever little time she could spare, she spent with her younger sister, Urmila, and her father, Janak.

Kushadhwaj had not visited Mithila for a while. He wasn't in Sankashya either. Which was strange. Sita had tried to make inquiries about his whereabouts, but had not been successful so far. What she did know was that the Sankashya administration had lost much of its efficiency after Sulochan's death, universally believed to be the result of an unfortunate heart attack.

Sita was used to Radhika's unexpected visits, by now. Hence, she was delighted to receive her friend, whom she was meeting after a few months.

'How are things in your village, now that the excitement of hosting the princes of Ayodhya is gone?'

Radhika laughed. 'It's all right ...'

'Are *you* all right?'

'I'm getting there ...'

'And how is Ram doing in Ayodhya?'

'He has been made the chief of police. And Bharat the chief of diplomatic relations.'

'Hmm ... So Queen Kaikeyi still has her grip on Ayodhya. Bharat is better placed to catapult into the role of Crown Prince. The chief of police is a tough and thankless job.'

'So it would seem. But Ram is doing exceedingly well. He has managed to bring crime under visible control. This has made him popular among the people.'

'How did he manage that miracle?'

'He just followed the laws. Ha!'

Sita laughed, befuddled. 'How does Ram abiding by the law make any difference? The people also have to follow it. And, Indians will never do that. In fact, I think we enjoy breaking rules. Pointlessly. For the heck of it. One must be pragmatic when dealing with Indians. Laws must be enforced, yes. But this cannot be an end in itself. You may sometimes need to even misuse the law to achieve what you want.'

'I disagree. Ram has shown a new way. By simply ensuring that he, too, is accountable and subject to the law. No shortcuts are available to the Ayodhyan nobility anymore. This has electrified the common folk. If the law is above even a prince, then why not them?'

Sita leaned into her chair. 'Interesting ...'

'By the way,' asked Radhika, 'where is Guru Vishwamitra?'

Sita hesitated.

'I am only checking because we believe Guru Vashishtha has gone to Pariha to propose Ram's candidature as the Vishnu.'

Sita was shocked. 'Guru Vishwamitra is in Pariha as well.'

Radhika sighed. 'Things will soon come to a head. You better have a plan in mind to convince Guru Vishwamitra about Ram and you partnering as the Vishnus.'

Sita took a deep breath. 'Any idea what the Vayuputras will do?'

'I have told you already. They lean towards Guru Vashishtha. The only question is whether they will give in to Guru Vishwamitra. After all, he *is* the chief of the Malayaputras and the representative of the previous Vishnu.'

'I will speak with Hanu *bhaiya*.'

Chapter 17

'But, *Didi*,' pouted Urmila, keeping her voice low as she spoke to her *elder sister*, Sita, 'why have you agreed to a *swayamvar*? I don't want you to leave. What will I do without you?'

Urmila and Sita sat on a large, well-camouflaged wooden *machan* in a tree. Their feet dangled by the side. Sita's bow lay within hand's reach, next to a quiver full of arrows. The jungle was quiet and somnolent this hot afternoon. Most of the animals, it seemed, were taking a nap.

Sita smiled and pulled Urmila close. 'I have to get married sometime, Urmila. If this is what *baba* wants, then I have no choice but to honour it.'

Urmila did not know that it was Sita who had convinced her father to arrange the *swayamvar*. The *swayamvar* was an ancient tradition where the father of the bride organised a gathering of prospective bridegrooms; and the daughter selected her husband from among the gathered men. Or mandated a competition. Sita was actively managing the arrangements. She had convinced Vishwamitra to somehow get Ram to Mithila for the *swayamvar*. An official invitation from Mithila to Ayodhya would not have gotten a response. After all, why would Ayodhya ally with a small and relatively inconsequential kingdom like Mithila? But there was no way that Ayodhya would say no to the powerful Malayaputra chief's request just to attend the *swayamvar*. And, at the *swayamvar* itself, managed by her Guru, the great Malayaputra Vishwamitra, she could arrange to have Ram as her husband. Vishwamitra had also liked the idea. This way, he would displace Vashishtha and gain direct influence over Ram. Of course, he was unaware that Sita had other plans. Plans to work with Ram in partnership as the Vishnu.

God bless Hanu bhaiya! *What a fantastic idea.*

Urmila rested her head on Sita's shoulder. Although a young woman now, her sheltered upbringing had kept her dependent on her elder sister. She could not imagine life without her nurturer and protector. 'But ...'

Sita held Urmila tight. 'You too will be married. Soon.'

Urmila blushed and turned away.

Sita heard a faint sound. She looked deep into the forest.

Sita, Samichi, and a troop of twenty policemen had come to this jungle, a day's ride from Mithila, to kill a man-eating tiger that was tormenting villagers in the area. Urmila had insisted on accompanying Sita. Five *machans* had been built in a forest clearing. Each *machan* was manned by Mithila policemen. The bait, a goat, had been tied in the open. Keeping the weather in mind, a small waterhole had also been dug, lined with water-proofing bitumen. If not the meat, perhaps the water would entice the tiger.

'Listen, *Didi*,' whispered Urmila, 'I was thinking ...'

Urmila fell silent as Sita raised a finger to her lips. Then, Sita turned around. Two policemen sat at the other end of the *machan*. Using hand signals, she gave quick orders. Silently, they crawled up to her side. Urmila moved to the back.

Sita picked up her bow and noiselessly drew an arrow from the quiver.

'Did you see something, My Lady?' whispered a policeman.

Sita shook her head to signal no. And then, cupped her ear with her left hand.

The policemen strained their ears but could not hear anything. One of them spoke in a faint voice, 'I don't hear any sound.'

Sita nocked the arrow on the bowstring and whispered, 'It's the absence of sound. The goat has stopped bleating. It is scared stiff. I bet it's not an ordinary predator that the goat has sniffed.'

The policemen drew their bows forward and nocked arrows. Quickly and quietly.

Sita thought she caught a fleeting glimpse of stripes from behind the foliage. She took a long, hard look. Slowly, she began to discern alternating brownish-orange and black stripes in the dark, shaded area behind the tree line. She focused her eyes. The stripes moved.

Sita pointed towards the movement.

The policeman noticed it as well. 'It's well-camouflaged ...'

Sita raised her hands, signalling for quiet. She held the bowstring and pulled faintly, ready to shoot at the first opportunity.

After a few excruciatingly long moments, the tiger stepped into view, inching slowly towards the waterhole. It saw the goat, growled softly and turned its attention back to the water. The goat collapsed on the ground in absolute terror, urine escaping its bladder in a rush. It closed its eyes and surrendered itself to fate. The tiger, though, did not seem interested in the petrified bait. It kept lapping up the water.

Sita pulled the bowstring back, completely.

Suddenly, there was a very soft sound from one of the *machans* to the right.

The tiger looked up, instantly alert.

Sita cursed under her breath. The angle wasn't right. But she knew the tiger would turn and flee in moments. She released the arrow.

It whizzed through the clearing and slammed into the beast's shoulder. Enough to enrage, but not disable.

The tiger roared in fury. But its roar was cut short just as suddenly. An arrow shot into its mouth, lodging deep in the animal's throat. Within split seconds, eighteen arrows slammed into the big cat. Some hit an eye, others the abdomen. Three missiles thumped into its rear *bicep femoris* muscles, severing them. Its rear legs debilitated, the tiger collapsed to the ground. The Mithilans quickly reloaded their bows and shot again. Twenty more arrows pierced the severely injured beast. The tiger raised its head one last time. Sita felt the animal was staring directly at her with one uninjured eye.

My apologies, noble beast. But it was either you or the villagers under my protection.

The tiger's head dropped. Never to rise again.

May your soul find purpose, once again.

— ᗡᚷ —

Sita, Urmila, and Samichi rode at the head of the group. The policemen rode a short distance behind. The party was headed back to the capital city.

The tiger had been cremated with due respect. Sita had made it clear to all that she did not intend to keep the skin of the animal. She was aware that the opportunity to acquire the tiger skin, a mark of a brave hunter, would have made her policemen careful with their arrows. They would not have liked the pelt damaged. That may have led to the tiger merely being injured rather than killed.

Sita's objective was clear. She wanted to save the villagers from the tiger attacks. An injured animal would have only become more dangerous for humans. Sita had to ensure that all her policemen shot to kill. So, she had made it clear to all that the tiger would be cremated.

'I understand why you gave that order, Prime Minister,' said Samichi, 'but it's sad that we cannot take the tiger skin home. It would have been a great trophy, displaying your skill and bravery.'

Sita looked at Samichi, then turned to her sister. 'Urmila, fall back please.'

Urmila immediately pulled the reins of her horse and fell behind the other two, out of earshot.

Samichi pulled her horse close to Sita's. 'I had to say that, Sita. It will encourage Urmila to brag about your bravery and ...'

Sita shook her head and interrupted Samichi. 'Propaganda and myth-making are part and parcel of ruling. I understand that. But do not spread stories that will get debunked easily. I did not exhibit any skill or bravery in that hunt.'

'But ...'

'My shot was not good. Everyone present knows that.'

'But, Sita ...'

'Every single one knows that,' repeated Sita. 'Earlier too, you gave me all the credit for the hunt. Near the policemen.'

'But you deserved the ...'

'No, I did not.'

'But …'

'You believe you did me a service. No, Samichi, you did not. I lost respect among those men by receiving an undeserved compliment.'

'But …'

'Don't let your loyalty to me blind you. That is the worst thing you can do to me.'

Samichi stopped arguing. 'I'm sorry.'

Sita smiled. 'It's all right.' Then she turned to her younger sister and beckoned her. The three of them rode on, in silence.

— ᘉᙓ —

Sita had returned from the hunt just a few days earlier. Preparations for her *swayamvar* had begun in full swing. She personally supervised most of the work, ably assisted by Samichi and her younger sister, Urmila.

Sita sat in her chamber perusing some documents, when a messenger was announced.

'Bring him in.'

Two guards marched in with the messenger in tow. She recognised the man. He was from Radhika's tribe.

Saluting smartly, the messenger handed her a rolled parchment. Sita examined the seal. It was unbroken.

She dismissed the messenger, broke the seal and read Radhika's message.

Her anger rose even before she reached the last word. But even in her rage, she did not forget what she must do. She held the parchment to a flame till every inch of it was reduced to ashes.

Task done, she walked up to the balcony to cool her mind. *Ram … Don't fall into Guru*ji*'s trap.*

— ༼ ༡ —

Mithila was a few weeks away from Sita's *swayamvar*.

Sita's spirits had been uplifted by the news that Vishwamitra was on his way to Mithila. Along with the Malayaputras and the princes of Ayodhya. Her mind had been feverishly contemplating plausible excuses to cancel the *swayamvar*. In the absence of Ram, it would have been a pointless exercise.

'Sita,' said Samichi, saluting as she entered the princess' chamber.

Sita turned. 'Yes, Samichi?'

'I have some troubling news.'

'What's happened?'

'I have heard that your uncle Kushadhwaj has been invited to the *swayamvar*. In fact, he is inviting some of his friends as well. He's behaving like a joint host.'

Sita sighed. She should have guessed that her father would invite Kushadhwaj.

Such misplaced generosity.

On the other hand, Kushadhwaj had not visited Mithila in years. Perhaps, he had made his peace with his reduced circumstances.

'I am his niece, after all,' said Sita, shrugging her shoulders. '*Chacha* may want to demonstrate to the Sapt Sindhu royalty that he retains some influence in his elder brother's household and kingdom. Let him come.'

Samichi smiled. 'As long as the one you want also comes, right?'

'Ram is coming ... He is coming ...'

Samichi broke into a rare smile. Though she did not understand why Sita had suddenly developed an interest in Ram, and in allying with Ayodhya, she supported her princess wholeheartedly. Allying with Ayodhya, even in its weakened state, would only benefit Mithila in the long run. And, once Sita left for Ayodhya, Samichi expected to become even more powerful. Perhaps, even rule Mithila for all practical purposes.

After all, who else was there?

Chapter 18

A nervous Samichi stood in the small clearing. The ominous sounds of the jungle added to the dread of a dark, moonless night.

Memories from the past crashed into the present. It had been so long. So many years. She had thought that she had been forgotten. Left to her own devices. After all, Mithila was a minor, insignificant kingdom in the Sapt Sindhu. She hadn't expected this. A sense of gratification meshed with the unease of the moment to altogether overwhelm her mind.

Her left hand rested on the hilt of her sheathed sword.

'Samichi, did you understand what I said?' asked the man. His gravelly voice was distinctive. The result of years of tobacco and alcohol abuse. Accompanied by uncontrolled shouting.

The man was clearly a noble. Expensive clothes. All neatly pressed. Soft, well-coiffed and completely grey hair. An array of rings on all his fingers. Jewelled pommels decorated his knife and sword. Even his scabbard was gold-plated. A thick black line, a *tilak*, plastered the middle of his wrinkled forehead.

A platoon of twenty soldiers in black uniforms stood quietly in the shadows. Out of earshot. Their swords were securely sheathed. They knew they had nothing to fear from Samichi.

She was to receive Guru Vishwamitra at Sankashya the following day. She really couldn't afford this unexpected rendezvous. Not now. She mentioned the *True Lord*, hoping it would push Akampana back.

'But, Lord Akampana ...' said Samichi uneasily, '... *Iraiva*'s message ...'

'Forget everything you were told earlier,' said Akampana. 'Remember your oath.'

Samichi stiffened. 'I will never forget my oath, Lord Akampana.'

'See that you don't.' Akampana raised his hand and nonchalantly looked at his manicured nails. Perfectly cut, filed and polished. A light cream dye had been carefully painted on them. The nail on the slim pinkie finger though, had been painted black. 'So, Princess Sita's *swayamvar* will be ...'

'You don't have to repeat yourself,' interrupted Samichi. 'It will be done. It is in Princess Sita's interest as well.'

Akampana smiled. Perhaps something had gotten through Samichi's thick head after all. 'Yes, it is.'

— ॥ॐ॥ —

Sita sighed and lightly tapped her head. 'Silly me.'

She walked into her private *puja* room and picked up the knife. It was the day of the *astra puja*, an ancient ritual worship of weapons. And she had forgotten the knife in the *garbha griha*, at the feet of the deities, after the *puja*.

Fortunately, she had managed without the weapon today. She had always suspected that the wealthy merchant, Vijay, was more loyal to Sankashya than Mithila. Earlier that day, in the market place, he had tried to incite the crowd to attack her, when she had intervened to save a boy-thief from mob justice.

Fortunately, it had all ended well. No one had been injured. Except that stupid Vijay who would be nursing a broken rib for many weeks. She would visit the *Ayuralay* and check on him, probably in the evening or the next day. She didn't really care what happened to Vijay. But it was important to demonstrate that she cared equally for the well-being of the rich as well, and not just the poor. Even the irredeemably stupid ones among the rich.

Where is Samichi?

The Police and Protocol Chief was expected anytime now, escorting Guru Vishwamitra and his accompanying Malayaputras to Mithila. And, of course, Ram and Lakshman.

Suddenly, the doorman announced that Arishtanemi, the military chief of the Malayaputras, had arrived.

Sita answered loudly. 'Bring him in. With respect.'

Arishtanemi walked into the room. Sita folded her hands together in a respectful *Namaste* and bowed her head as she greeted the right-hand man of Maharishi Vishwamitra. 'Greetings, Arishtanemi*ji*. I hope that you are comfortable in Mithila.'

'One is always comfortable in the place one looks upon as home,' smiled Arishtanemi.

Sita was surprised to not find Samichi with him. This was unorthodox. Samichi should have escorted the senior officer, with respect, to her chambers.

'My apologies, Arishtanemi*ji*. Samichi should have led you to my chambers. I am sure that she meant no disrespect, but I will speak with her.'

'No, no,' said Arishtanemi, raising his hand reassuringly. 'I told her that I wanted to meet you alone.'

'Of course. I hope you are satisfied with the accommodation, especially for Guru Vishwamitra and the princes of Ayodhya.'

Arishtanemi smiled. Sita had come to the point quickly. 'Guru Vishwamitra is comfortable in his usual set of rooms at the palace. But Prince Ram and Prince Lakshman have been accommodated in the Bees Quarter.'

'Bees Quarter?!' Sita was aghast.

Has Samichi gone mad?

Almost as if he had heard her thought, Arishtanemi said, 'Actually, Guru*ji* himself wanted the princes to stay in there.'

Sita raised her hands in exasperation. 'Why? They are the princes of Ayodhya. Ram is the Crown Prince of the empire. Ayodhya will see this as a terrible insult. I do not want Mithila getting into any trouble because of …'

'Prince Ram does not see it as an insult,' interrupted Arishtanemi. 'He is a mature man of great understanding. We need to keep his presence in Mithila a secret, for now. And, even you must avoid meeting him for a few days.'

Sita was losing her patience. 'Secret? He has to participate in the *swayamvar*, Arishtanemi*ji*. That's why he is here, isn't he? How can we keep this a secret?'

'There is a problem, princess.'

'What problem?'

Arishtanemi sighed. He paused for a few seconds and whispered, 'Raavan.'

— ᚱᚷ —

'It is wise of you to have not met him till now,' said Samichi.

Sita and Samichi were in the royal section of the state armoury. A special room was reserved in this wing for the favourite personal weapons of the royalty. Sita sat on a chair, carefully oiling the *Pinaka*, the great bow of Lord Rudra.

Her conversation with Arishtanemi had upset her. Frankly, she had had her suspicions about what the Malayaputras were planning. She knew that they wouldn't go against her. She was crucial to their plans. But Ram was not.

If only I had someone to talk to. I wish Hanu bhaiya *or Radhika were here ...*

Sita looked up at Samichi and continued oiling the already gleaming *Pinaka*.

Samichi looked nervous. She seemed to be in a state of inner struggle. 'I have to tell you something. I don't care what the others say. But it is the truth, Sita. Prince Ram's life is in danger. You have to send him home, somehow.'

Sita stopped oiling the bow and looked up. 'His life has been in danger since the day he was born.'

Samichi shook her head. 'No. I mean real danger.'

'What exactly is unreal danger, Samichi? There is nothing that ...'

'Please, listen to me ...'

'What are you hiding, Samichi?'

Samichi straightened up. 'Nothing, princess.'

'You have been acting strange these past few days.'

'Forget about me. I am not important. Have I ever told you anything that is not in your interest? Please trust me. Send Prince Ram home, if you can.'

Sita stared at Samichi. 'That's not happening.'

'There are bigger forces at play, Sita. And, you are not in control. Trust me. Please. Send him home before he gets hurt.'

Sita didn't respond. She looked at the *Pinaka* and resumed oiling the bow.

Lord Rudra, tell me what to do …

— ॎ⅄ —

'My fellow Mithilans actually clapped?' asked Sita, eyes wide in incredulity.

Arishtanemi had just walked into Sita's private office. With disturbing, yet expected, news. Raavan had arrived in Mithila to participate in Sita's *swayamvar*. His *Pushpak Vimaan*, the *legendary flying vehicle*, had just landed outside the city. He was accompanied by his brother Kumbhakarna and a few key officers. His bodyguard corps of ten thousand Lankan soldiers had marched in separately and set up camp outside the city.

Sita was bemused by the news that the Mithilans had applauded the spectacle of the *Pushpak Vimaan* landing in the fields beyond the city moat.

'Most normal human beings applaud the first time they see the *Pushpak Vimaan*, Sita,' said Arishtanemi. 'But that is not important. What is important is that we stop Ram from leaving.'

'Is Ram leaving? Why? I thought he would want to prove a point to Raavan …'

'He hasn't made up his mind as yet. But I'm afraid Lakshman may talk his elder brother into leaving.'

'So, you would like me to speak with him in Lakshman's absence.'

'Yes.'

'Have you …'

'I've spoken to him already. But I don't think I had much of an impact …'

'Can you think of someone else who can speak to him?'

Arishtanemi shook his head. 'I don't think even Guru Vishwamitra will be able to convince Ram.'

'But …'

'It's up to you, Sita,' said Arishtanemi. 'If Ram leaves, we will have to cancel this *swayamvar*.'

'What in Lord Rudra's name can I tell him? He has never even met me. What do I tell him to convince him to stay?'

'I have no idea.'

Sita laughed and shook her head. 'Thank you.'

'Sita … I know it's …'

'It's okay. I'll do it.'

I must find a way. Some path will emerge.

Arishtanemi seemed unusually tense. 'There's more, Sita …'

'More?'

'The situation may be a little more complicated.'

'How so?'

'Ram was … in a way … tricked into coming here.'

'What?'

'He was made to understand that he was merely accompanying Guru Vishwamitra on an important mission in Mithila. Since Emperor Dashrath had commanded Ram to strictly follow Guru Vishwamitra's orders, he could not say no … He wasn't informed about the fact that he was expected to participate in this *swayamvar*. Till he arrived in Mithila, that is.'

Sita was shocked. 'You have got to be joking!'

'But he did agree to the *swayamvar* finally, a few days ago. On the same day that you had that fight in the marketplace to save that boy-thief …'

Sita held her head and closed her eyes. 'I can't believe that the Malayaputras have done this.'

'The ends justify the means, Sita.'

'Not when I'm expected to live with the consequences!'

'But he did agree to participate in the *swayamvar*, eventually.'

'That was before the arrival of Raavan, right?'

'Yes.'

Sita rolled her eyes. *Lord Rudra help me.*

Chapter 19

Sita and Samichi were headed for the Bees Quarter, accompanied by a bodyguard posse of ten policemen. The city was agog with the news of the appearance of Raavan, the king of Lanka and the tormentor of India; or at least, the tormentor of Indian kings. The most animated discussions were about his legendary flying vehicle, the *Pushpak Vimaan*. Even Sita's sister, Urmila, was not immune to reports about the Lankan technological marvel. She had insisted on accompanying her elder sister to see the *vimaan*.

They had marched to the end of the Bees Quarter, up to the fort walls. The *Pushpak Vimaan* was stationed beyond the city moat, just before the jungle. Even Sita was impressed by what she saw.

The *vimaan* was a giant conical craft, made of some strange unknown metal. Massive rotors were attached to the top of the vehicle, at its pointed end. Smaller rotors were attached near the base, on all sides.

'I believe,' said Samichi, 'the main rotor at the top gives the *vimaan* the ability to fly and the smaller rotors at the base are used to control the direction of flight.'

The main body of the craft had many portholes, each covered with circular metal screens.

Samichi continued. 'Apparently, the metal screens on the portholes are raised when the *vimaan* is airborne. The portholes also have a thick glass shield. The main door is concealed behind a section of the *vimaan*. Once that section swings open, the door slides sideward into the inner cabin. So the *vimaan* entrance is doubly sealed.'

Sita turned to Samichi. 'You know a lot about this *Lankan* craft.'

Samichi shook her head and smiled sheepishly. 'No, no. I just watched the *vimaan* land. That's all ...'

Thousands of Lankan soldiers were camped around the *vimaan*. Some were sleeping, others eating. But nearly a third had their weapons drawn, standing guard at strategic points in the camp. Keeping watch. Alive to any potential threats.

Sita knew this camp security strategy: The staggered one-third plan. One third of the soldiers, working in rotating four-hour shifts, always on guard. While the others rest and recuperate.

The Lankans don't take their security lightly.

'How many are there?' asked Sita.

'Probably ten thousand soldiers,' said Samichi.

'Lord Rudra have mercy ...'

Sita looked at Samichi. It was a rare sight. For her friend looked genuinely nervous.

Sita placed a hand on Samichi's shoulders. 'Don't worry. We can handle this.'

— ल̈ ⅄ —

Samichi bent down and banged the hatch door on the Bees Quarter roof. Ten policemen stood at the back. Sita cast Urmila a quiet, reassuring look.

Nobody opened the door.

Samichi looked at Sita.

'Knock again,' ordered Sita. 'And harder this time.'

Samichi did as ordered.

Urmila still wasn't sure what her sister was up to. '*Didi*, why are we …'

She stopped talking the moment the hatch door swung open. Upwards.

Samichi looked down.

Lakshman stood at the head of the staircase that descended into the room. Muscular with a towering height, his gigantic form seemed to fill up the space. He was fair-complexioned and handsome in a rakish, flamboyant way. A bull of a man. He wore the coarse white clothes of common soldiers when off-duty: a military style *dhoti* and an *angvastram* tied from his shoulder to the side of his waist. Threaded *Rudraaksh* beads around his neck proudly proclaimed his loyalty to Lord Rudra.

Lakshman held his sword, ready to strike should the need arise. He looked at the short-haired, dark-skinned and muscular woman peering down at him. '*Namaste*, Chief Samichi. To what do we owe this visit?' he asked gruffly.

Samichi grinned disarmingly. 'Put your sword back in the scabbard, young man.'

'Let me decide what I should or should not do. What is your business here?'

'The prime minister wants to meet your elder brother.'

Lakshman seemed taken aback. Like this was unexpected. He turned to the back of the room, where his elder brother Ram stood. Upon receiving a signal from him, he immediately slipped his sword in its scabbard and backed up against the wall, making room for the Mithilans to enter.

Samichi descended the stairs, followed by Sita. As Sita stepped in through the door hole, she gestured behind her. 'Stay there, Urmila.'

Lakshman instinctively looked up. To see Urmila. Ram stood up to receive the prime minister of Mithila. The two women climbed down swiftly but Lakshman remained rooted. Entranced by the vision above. Urmila had truly grown into a beautiful young lady. She was shorter than her elder sister, Sita. Also fairer. So fair that her skin was almost the colour of milk. Her round baby face was dominated by large eyes, which betrayed a sweet, childlike innocence. Her hair was arranged in a bun. Every strand neatly in place. The *kaajal* in her eyes accentuated their exquisiteness. Her lips were enhanced with some beet extract. Her clothes were fashionable, yet demure: a bright pink blouse complemented by a deep-red *dhoti* which was longer than usual — it reached below her knees. A neatly pressed *angvastram* hung from her shoulders. Anklets and toe-rings drew attention to her lovely feet, while rings and bracelets decorated her delicate hands. Lakshman was mesmerised. Urmila sensed it and smiled genially. Then looked away with shy confusion.

Sita turned and saw Lakshman looking at Urmila. Her eyes widened, just a bit.

Urmila and Lakshman? Hmm ...

'Shut the door, Lakshman,' said Ram.

Lakshman reluctantly did as ordered.

'How may I help you, princess?' asked Ram to Sita.

Sita turned and looked at the man she had chosen to be her husband. She had heard so much about him, for so long, that she felt like she practically knew him. So far all her thoughts about him had been based on reason and logic. She saw him as a worthy partner in the destiny of the Vishnu; someone she could work with for the good of her motherland, the country that she loved, this beautiful, matchless India.

But this was the first time she saw him as a flesh-and-blood reality. Emotion arose unasked, and occupied its seat next to reason. She had to admit the first impression was quite pleasing.

The Crown Prince of Ayodhya stood at the back of the room. Ram's coarse white *dhoti* and *angvastram,* provided a startling contrast to his dark, flawless complexion. His nobility lent grace to the crude garments he wore. He was tall, a little taller than Sita. His broad shoulders, strong arms and lean, muscular physique were testimony to his archery training. His long hair was tied neatly in an unassuming bun. He wore a string of *Rudraaksh* beads around his neck; a marker that he too was a fellow devotee of the great Mahadev, Lord Rudra. There was no jewellery on his person. No marker to signify that he was the scion of the powerful Suryavanshi clan, a noble descendant of the great emperor Ikshvaku. His persona exuded genuine humility and strength.

Sita smiled. *Not bad. Not bad at all.*

'Excuse me for a minute, prince,' said Sita. She looked at Samichi. 'I'd like to speak to the prince alone.'

'Of course,' said Samichi, immediately climbing out of the room.

Ram nodded at Lakshman, who also turned to leave the room. With alacrity.

Ram and Sita were alone in no time.

Sita smiled and indicated a chair in the room. 'Please sit, Prince Ram.'

'I'm all right.'

'I insist,' said Sita, as she sat down herself.

Ram sat on a chair facing Sita. A few seconds of awkward silence passed. Then Sita spoke up, 'I believe you were tricked into coming here.'

Ram did not say anything, but his eyes gave the answer away.

'Then why haven't you left?'

'Because it would be against the law.'

So, he has decided to stay for the swayamvar. *Lord Rudra and Lord Parshu Ram be praised.*

'And is it the law that will make you participate in the *swayamvar* day after tomorrow?' asked Sita.

Ram chose silence again. But Sita could tell that there was something on his mind.

'You are Ayodhya, the overlord of Sapt Sindhu. I am only Mithila, a small kingdom with little power. What purpose can possibly be served by this alliance?'

'Marriage has a higher purpose; it can be more than just a political alliance.'

Sita smiled. 'But the world seems to believe that royal marriages are meant only for political gain. What other purpose do you think they can serve?'

Ram didn't answer. He seemed to be lost in another world. His eyes had taken on a dreamy look.

I don't think he's listening to me.

Sita saw Ram's eyes scanning her face. Her hair. Her neck. She saw him smile. Ruefully. His face seemed to …

Is he blushing? What is going on? I was told that Ram was only interested in the affairs of the state.

'Prince Ram?' asked Sita loudly.

'Excuse me?' asked Ram. His attention returned to what she was saying.

'I asked, if marriage is not a political alliance, then what is it?'

'Well, to begin with, it is not a necessity; there should be no compulsion to get married. There's nothing worse than being married to the wrong person. You should only get married if you find someone you admire, who will help you understand and fulfil your life's purpose. And you, in turn, can help her fulfil her life's purpose. If you're able to find that one person, then marry her.'

Sita raised her eyebrows. 'Are you advocating just one wife? Not many? Most people think differently.'

'Even if all people think polygamy is right, it doesn't make it so.'

'But most men take many wives; especially the nobility.'

'I won't. You insult your wife by taking another.'

Sita raised her chin in contemplation. Her eyes softened. Admiringly. *Wow … This man is special.*

A charged silence filled the room. As Sita gazed at him, her expression changed with sudden recognition.

'Wasn't it you at the marketplace the other day?' she asked.

'Yes.'

Sita tried to remember the details. *Yes. Lakshman had been there too. Next to him. The giant who stood out. They were amongst the crowd on the other side. The onlookers. Not a part of the well-heeled mob that had wanted to lynch the poor boy-thief. I saw them as I dragged the boy away, after thrashing Vijay.* And then, she held her breath as she remembered another detail. *Hang on … Ram was … bowing his head to me … But why? Or am I remembering incorrectly?*

'Why didn't you step in to help me?' asked Sita.

'You had the situation under control.'

Sita smiled slightly. *He is getting better with every moment …*

It was Ram's turn to ask questions. 'What is Raavan doing here?'

'I don't know. But it makes the *swayamvar* more personal for me.'

Ram's muscles tightened. He was shocked. But his expression remained impassive. 'Has he come to participate in your *swayamvar*?'

'So I have been told.'

'And?'

'And, I have come here.' Sita kept the next sentence confined to her mind. *I have come for you.*

Ram waited for her to continue.

'How good are you with a bow and arrow?' asked Sita.

Ram allowed himself a faint smile.

Sita raised her eyebrows. 'That good?'

She arose from her chair. As did Ram. The prime minister of Mithila folded her hands into a *Namaste*. 'May Lord Rudra continue to bless you, prince.'

Ram returned Sita's *Namaste*. 'And may He bless you, princess.'

An idea struck Sita. 'Can I meet with your brother and you in the private royal garden tomorrow?'

Ram's eyes had glazed over once again. He was staring at Sita's hands in almost loving detail. Only the Almighty or Ram himself knew the thoughts that were running through his head. For probably the first time in her life, Sita felt self-conscious. She looked at her battle-scarred hands. The scar on her left hand was particularly prominent. Her hands weren't, in her own opinion, particularly pretty.

'Prince Ram,' said Sita, 'I asked—'

'I'm sorry, can you repeat that?' asked Ram, bringing his attention back to the present.

'Can I meet with you and your brother in the private royal garden tomorrow?'

'Yes, of course.'

'Good,' said Sita, as she turned to leave. She stopped as she remembered something. She reached into the pouch tied to her waistband and pulled out a red thread. 'It would be nice if you could wear this. It's for good luck. It is a representation of the blessings of the *Kanyakumari*. And I would like you to …'

Sita stopped speaking as she realised that Ram's attention had wandered again. He was staring at the red thread and mouthing a couplet. One that was normally a part of a wedding hymn.

Sita could lip-read the words that Ram was mouthing silently, for she knew the hymn well.

Maangalyatantunaanena bhava jeevanahetuh may. A line from old Sanskrit, it translated into: *With this holy thread that I offer you, please become the purpose of my life* …

She tried hard to suppress a giggle.

'Prince Ram …' said Sita, loudly.

Ram suddenly straightened as the wedding hymn playing in his mind went silent. 'I'm sorry. What?'

Sita smiled politely, 'I was saying …' She stopped suddenly. 'Never mind. I'll leave the thread here. Please wear it if it pleases you.'

Placing the thread on the table, Sita began to climb the stairs. As she reached the door, she turned around for a last look. Ram was holding the thread in the palm of his right hand. Gazing at it reverentially. As if it was the most sacred thing in the world.

Sita smiled once again. *This is completely unexpected* …

Chapter 20

Sita sat alone in her private chamber. Astonished. Pleasantly surprised.

Samichi had briefed her on the conversation between Lakshman and Urmila. Lakshman was clearly besotted with her sister. He was also, clearly, very proud of his elder brother. He simply wouldn't stop talking about Ram. Lakshman had told the duo about Ram's attitude towards marriage. It seemed that Ram did not want to marry an ordinary woman. He wanted a woman, in front of whom he would be compelled to bow his head in admiration.

Samichi had laughed, while relating this to Sita. 'Ram is like an earnest, conscientious school boy,' she had said. 'He has not grown up yet. There is not a trace of cynicism in him. Or, realism. Trust me, Sita. Send him back to Ayodhya before he gets hurt.'

Sita had listened to Samichi without reacting. But only one thing had reverberated in her mind — Ram wanted to marry a woman in front of whom he would be compelled to bow his head in admiration.

He bowed to me …

She giggled. Not something she did normally. It felt strange. Even girlish …

Sita rarely bothered about her appearance. But for some reason, she now walked to the polished copper mirror and looked at herself.

She was almost as tall as Ram. Lean. Muscular. Wheat-complexioned. Her round face a shade lighter than the rest of her body. She had high cheekbones and a sharp, small nose. Her lips were neither thin nor full. Her wide-set eyes were neither small nor large; strong brows were arched in a perfect curve above creaseless eyelids. Her straight, jet-black hair was braided and tied in a neat bun. As always.

She looked like the mountain people from the Himalayas.

Not for the first time, she wondered if the Himalayas were her original home.

She touched a battle scar on her forearm and winced. Her scars had been a source of pride. Once.

Do they make me look ugly?

She shook her head.

A man like Ram will respect my scars. It's a warrior's body.

She giggled again. She had always thought of herself as a warrior. As a princess. As a ruler. Of late, she had even gotten used to being treated by the Malayaputras as the Vishnu. But this feeling was new. She now felt like an *apsara*, a *celestial nymph* of unimaginable beauty. One who could halt *her* man in his tracks by just fluttering her eyelashes. It was a heady feeling.

She had always held these 'pretty women' in disdain and thought of them as non-serious. Not anymore.

Sita put a hand on her hip and looked at herself from the corner of her eyes.

She replayed the moments spent with Ram at the Bees Quarter.

Ram....

This was new. Special. She giggled once again.

She undid her hair and smiled at her reflection.

This is the beginning of a beautiful relationship.

— ᚱᚷ —

The royal garden in Mithila was modest in comparison to the one in Ayodhya. It only contained local trees, plants, and flower beds. Its beauty could safely be attributed more to the ministrations of talented gardeners than to an impressive infusion of funds. The layout was symmetrical, well-manicured. The thick, green carpet of grass thrown into visual relief by the profusion of flowers and trees of all shapes, sizes and colours. It was a celebration of Nature, expressed in ordered harmony.

Sita and Urmila waited in a clearing at the back of the garden. Sita had asked her younger sister to accompany her so that Urmila could spend more time with Lakshman. This would also give her some alone time with Ram, without the looming presence of Lakshman.

Samichi was at the gate, tasked with fetching the young princes of Ayodhya. She walked in shortly, followed by Ram and Lakshman.

The evening sky has increased his radiance... Sita quickly controlled her wandering mind and beating heart.

'*Namaste*, princess,' said Ram to Sita.

'*Namaste*, prince,' replied Sita, before turning to her sister. 'May I introduce my younger sister, Urmila?' Gesturing towards Ram and Lakshman, Sita continued, 'Urmila, meet Prince Ram and Prince Lakshman of Ayodhya.'

'I had occasion to meet her yesterday,' said Lakshman, grinning from ear to ear.

Urmila smiled politely at Lakshman, with her hands folded in a *Namaste*, then turned towards Ram and greeted him.

'I would like to speak with the prince privately, once again,' said Sita.

'Of course,' said Samichi immediately. 'May I have a private word before that?'

Samichi took Sita aside and whispered in her ear, 'Sita, please remember what I said. Ram is too simple. And, his life is in real danger. Please ask him to leave. This is our last chance.'

Sita smiled politely, fully intending to ignore Samichi's words.

Samichi cast a quick look at Ram before walking away, leading Urmila by the hand. Lakshman followed Urmila.

Ram moved towards Sita. 'Why did you want to meet me, princess?'

Sita checked that Samichi and the rest were beyond earshot. She was about to begin speaking when her eyes fell on the red thread tied around Ram's right wrist. She smiled.

He has worn it.

'Please give me a minute, prince,' said Sita.

She walked behind a tree, bent and picked up a long package covered in cloth. She walked back to Ram. He frowned, intrigued. Sita pulled the cloth back to reveal an intricately carved, and unusually long, bow. An exquisite piece of weaponry, it was a composite bow with recurved ends, which would give it a very long range. Ram carefully examined the carvings on the inside face of the limbs, both above and below the grip of the bow. It was the image of a flame, representative of Agni, the God of Fire. The first hymn of the first chapter of the *Rig Veda* was dedicated to the deeply revered deity. However, the shape of this flame was slightly different.

Sita pulled a flat wooden base platform from the cloth bag and placed it on the ground ceremonially. She looked at Ram. 'This bow cannot be allowed to touch the ground.'

Ram was clearly fascinated. He wondered why this bow was so important. Sita placed the lower limb of the bow on the platform, steadying it with her foot. She used her right hand to pull down the other end with force. Judging by the strain on her shoulder and biceps, Ram guessed that it was a very strong bow with tremendous resistance. With her left hand, Sita pulled the bowstring up and quickly strung it. She let the upper limb of the bow extend, and relaxed. She let out a long breath. The mighty bow adjusted to the constraints of the potent bowstring. She held the bow with her left hand and pulled the bowstring with her fingers, letting it go with a loud twang.

Ram knew from the sound that this bow was special. 'Wow. That's a good bow.'

'It's the best.'

'Is it yours?'

'I cannot own a bow like this. I am only its caretaker, for now. When I die, someone else will be deputed to take care of it.'

Ram narrowed his eyes as he closely examined the image of the flames around the grip of the bow. 'These flames look a little like —'

Sita interrupted him, impressed that he had figured it out so quickly. 'This bow once belonged to the one whom we both worship. It still belongs to him.'

Ram stared at the bow with a mixture of shock and awe, his suspicion confirmed.

Sita smiled. 'Yes, it is the *Pinaka*.'

The *Pinaka* was the legendary bow of the previous Mahadev, Lord Rudra. It was considered the strongest bow ever made. Believed to be a composite, it was a mix of many materials, which had been given a succession of specific treatments to arrest its degeneration. It was also believed that maintaining this bow was not an easy task. The grip, the limbs and the recurved ends needed regular lubrication with a special oil.

'How did Mithila come into the possession of the *Pinaka*?' asked Ram, unable to take his eyes off the beautiful weapon.

'It's a long story,' said Sita. She knew she couldn't give him the real reason. Not yet, at least. 'But I want you to practise with it. This is the bow which will be used for the *swayamvar* competition tomorrow.'

Ram took an involuntary step back. There were many ways in which a *swayamvar* was conducted. Sometimes the bride directly selected her groom. Or, she mandated a competition. The winner married the bride. However, it was unorthodox for a groom to be given advance information and help. In fact, it was against the rules.

Ram shook his head. 'It would be an honour to even touch the *Pinaka*, much less hold the bow that Lord Rudra himself graced with his touch. But I will only do so tomorrow. Not today.'

Sita frowned. *What? Doesn't he want to marry me?*

'I thought you intended to win my hand,' said Sita.

'I do. But I will win it the right way. I will win according to the rules.'

Sita smiled, shaking her head. *This man is truly special. Either he will go down in history as someone who was exploited by all. Or, he will be remembered as one of the greatest ever.*

Sita was happy that she had chosen to marry Ram. In a

tiny corner of her heart, though, she was worried. For she knew that this man would suffer. The world would make him suffer. And from what she knew about his life, he had suffered a lot already.

'Do you disagree?' asked Ram, seeming disappointed.

'No, I don't. I'm just impressed. You are a special man, Prince Ram.'

Ram blushed.

He's blushing again ...!

'I look forward to seeing you fire an arrow tomorrow morning,' said Sita, smiling.

— ᘓᘔ —

'He refused help? Really?' asked Jatayu, surprised.

Jatayu and Sita had met in the patch of the jungle that was now their regular meeting place. It lay towards the north of the city, as far away as possible from Raavan's temporary camp.

'Yes,' answered Sita.

Jatayu smiled and shook his head. 'He is no ordinary man.'

'No, he isn't. But I'm not sure whether the Malayaputras agree.'

Jatayu instinctively cast a glance around the woods, as if expecting to be heard by the formidable chief of the Malayaputras. He knew Vishwamitra did not like Ram. The Prince of Ayodhya was just a tool for the *Maharishi*; a means to an end.

'It's all right. The words will not carry to ...' Sita left the name unsaid. 'So, what do you think of Ram?'

'He is special in many ways, my sister,' whispered Jatayu, carefully. 'Perhaps, just what our country needs... His obsession with rules and honesty, his almighty love for this great land, his high expectations from everyone, including himself …'

Sita finally asked him the question that had been weighing on her mind. 'Is there anything I should know about the Malayaputras' plans regarding Ram tomorrow? At the *swayamvar*?'

Jatayu remained silent. He looked distinctly nervous.

'You have called me your sister, Jatayu*ji*. And this is regarding my future husband. I deserve to know.'

Jatayu looked down. Struggling between his loyalty to the Malayaputras and his devotion to Sita.

'Please, Jatayu*ji*. I need to know.'

Jatayu straightened his back and let out a sigh. 'You do know about the attack on a motley bunch of *Asuras* close to our Ganga *ashram*, right?'

Vishwamitra had gone to Ayodhya and asked for Ram and Lakshman's help in resolving a 'serious' military problem that he was facing. He had taken them to his *ashram* close to the Ganga River. He had then asked them to lead a contingent of his Malayaputra soldiers in an assault on a small tribe of Asuras, who were apparently, attacking his *ashram* repeatedly. It was only after the 'Asura problem' had been handled that they had left for Mithila, for Sita's *swayamvar*.

'Yes,' said Sita. 'Was Ram's life in danger?'

Jatayu shook his head dismissively. 'It was a pathetic tribe of a handful of people. They were imbeciles. Incapable warriors. Ram's life was never in danger.'

Sita frowned, confused. 'I don't understand …'

'The idea wasn't to get rid of Ram. It was to destroy his reputation with his most powerful supporters.'

Sita's eyes widened as she finally unravelled the conspiracy.

'The Malayaputras do not want him dead. They want him out of the reckoning as a potential Vishnu; and, under *their* control.'

'Are the Malayaputras intending to ally with Raavan?'

Jatayu was shocked. 'How can you even ask that, great Vishnu? They will never ally with Raavan. In fact, they will destroy him. But only when the time is right. Remember, the Malayaputras are loyal to one cause alone: the restoration of India's greatness. Nothing else matters. Raavan is just a tool for them.'

'As is Ram. As am I.'

'No. No ... How can you even think that the Malayaputras would use you as a ...'

Sita looked at Jatayu, silently. *Perhaps Samichi is right. There are forces far beyond my control. And Ram is ...*

Jatayu interrupted Sita's thoughts and unwittingly gave her a clue as to what she should do. 'Remember, great Vishnu. You are too crucial to the Malayaputras' plans. They cannot allow anything to happen to you. No harm can come to you.'

Sita smiled. Jatayu had given her the answer. She knew what she must do.

Chapter 21

'Do I know all there is to know about the Malayaputras' plans for the *swayamvar*, Arishtanemi*ji*?' asked Sita.

Arishtanemi was surprised by the question.

'I don't understand, Sita,' he said, carefully.

'How did Raavan get an invitation?'

'We are as clueless as you, Sita. You know that. We suspect it to be the handiwork of your uncle. But there is no proof.'

Sita looked sceptical. 'Right... No proof.'

Arishtanemi took a deep breath. 'Why don't you say what is on your mind, Sita ...'

Sita leaned forward, looked directly into Arishtanemi's eyes, and said, 'I know that Raavan's family has its roots in Kannauj.'

Arishtanemi winced. But recovered quickly. He shook his head, an injured expression on his face. 'In the name of the great Lord Parshu Ram, Sita. How can you think such thoughts?'

Sita was impassive.

'You think Guru Vishwamitra has any other identity now, besides being the chief of the Malayaputras? Seriously?'

Arishtanemi looked a little agitated. It was uncharacteristic of him. Sita knew she had hit a nerve. She could not have had a conversation like this with Vishwamitra. She needed to press home the advantage. Arishtanemi was one of the rare few who could convince Vishwamitra. She unnerved him further by choosing silence. For now.

'We can destroy Raavan at any time,' said Arishtanemi. 'We keep him alive because we plan to use his death to help you. To help you be recognised, by all Indians, as the Vishnu.'

'I believe you.'

Now, Arishtanemi fell silent. Confused.

'And I also know that you have plans for Ram.'

'Sita, listen to …'

Sita interrupted Arishtanemi. It was time to deliver the threat. 'I may not have Ram's life in my hands. But I do have my own life in my hands.'

A shocked Arishtanemi did not know what to say. All the plans would be reduced to dust without Sita. They had invested too much in her.

'I have chosen,' said Sita firmly. 'Now you need to decide what to do.'

'Sita …'

'I have nothing more to say, Arishtanemi*ji*.'

— ᚱᚷ —

The *swayamvar* was held in the Hall of Dharma instead of the royal court. This was simply because the royal court was not the biggest hall in Mithila. The main building in the palace complex, which housed the Hall of Dharma, had been donated by King Janak to the Mithila University. The hall hosted regular debates and discussions on various esoteric topics — the nature of dharma, karma's interaction with dharma, the nature of the divine, the purpose of the human journey …

The Hall of Dharma was in a circular building, built of stone and mortar, with a massive dome. The delicate elegance of the dome was believed to represent the feminine, while the typical temple spire represented the masculine. The hall was also circular. All *rishis* sat as equals, without a moderating 'head', debating issues openly and without fear; freedom of expression at its zenith.

However, today was different. The Hall of Dharma was set to host a *swayamvar*. Temporary three-tiered spectator stands stood near the entrance. At the other end, on a wooden platform, was placed the king's throne. A statue of the great King Mithi, the founder of Mithila, stood on a raised pedestal behind the throne. Two thrones, only marginally less grand, were placed to the left and right of the king's throne. A circle of comfortable seats lined the middle section of the great hall, where kings and princes, the potential suitors, would sit. The spectator stands were already packed when Ram and Lakshman were led in by Arishtanemi. Most contestants too had taken their seats. Few recognised the two princes of Ayodhya, dressed as hermits. A guard gestured for them to move towards the base platform of a three-tiered stand, occupied by the nobility and rich merchants of Mithila.

Arishtanemi informed the guard that he was accompanying a competitor. The guard was surprised. He had recognised Arishtanemi, the lieutenant of the great Vishwamitra, but not Ram and Lakshman. But he stepped aside to let them proceed. After all, it would not be unusual for the devout King Janak to invite even Brahmin *rishis*, not just Kshatriya kings, for his daughter's *swayamvar*.

Ram followed Arishtanemi to the allotted seat. He seated himself, as Lakshman and Arishtanemi stood behind him.

All eyes turned to them. Many contestants wondered who these simple mendicants were, who hoped to compete with them for Princess Sita's hand. A few, though, recognised the princes of Ayodhya. A conspiratorial buzz was heard from a section of the contestants.

'Ayodhya ...'

'Why does Ayodhya want an alliance with Mithila?'

Ram, however, was oblivious to the stares and whispers of the assembly.

He looked towards the centre of the hall; to the *Pinaka* bow placed on a table. The legendary bow was unstrung. An array of arrows placed by its side. Next to the table, at ground level, was a large copper-plated basin.

A competitor was first required to pick up the bow and string it. Itself no mean task. Then he would move to the copper-plated basin. It was filled with water, with additional drops trickling in steadily into the basin through a thin tube. Excess water was drained out by another thin tube, attached to the other side. This created subtle ripples within the bowl, spreading out from the centre towards the edge. Troublingly, the drops of water were released at irregular intervals, making the ripples unpredictable.

A *hilsa* fish was nailed to a wheel, fixed to an axle that was suspended from the top of the dome. A hundred metres above the ground. The wheel, thankfully, revolved at a constant speed.

The contestant was required to look at the reflection of the fish in the unstill water below, disturbed by ripples generated at irregular intervals, and use the *Pinaka* bow to fire an arrow into the eye of the fish, fixed on the revolving wheel high above. The first to succeed would win the hand of the bride.

Sita sat in a room on the second floor adjoining the Hall

of Dharma, directly above the royal Mithilan thrones, hidden behind a latticed window. She looked at Ram, seated in the circle of contestants.

The eldest prince of Ayodhya looked around. Sita felt as though he was seeking her out. She smiled. 'I'm here, Ram. I'm waiting for you. Waiting for you to win ...'

She noticed Samichi standing with a posse of policemen a short distance from the entrance. Samichi was staring at Ram. She looked up at the latticed window where Sita sat hidden from view. She had a look of utter disapproval.

Sita sighed with irritation. *Samichi needs to relax. I can handle the situation. Ram's life is not in danger.*

She turned her attention back to the princes of Ayodhya. She saw Lakshman bend close to his elder brother and whisper something. The expression on his face mischievous. Ram looked at his brother and glared. Lakshman grinned, said something more, and stepped back.

Sita smiled. *The brothers really love each other. Surprising, given the politics of their family.*

Her attention was drawn away by the court announcer.

'The Lord of the Mithi clan, the wisest of the wise, beloved of the *rishis*, King Janak!'

The court arose to welcome their host, Janak, the king of Mithila. He walked in from the far end of the hall. In a deviation from courtly tradition, he followed the great Malayaputra chief, Vishwamitra, who was in the lead. Janak had always honoured men and women of knowledge. He followed his own personal tradition on this special day as well. Behind Janak was his younger brother, Kushadhwaj, the king of Sankashya. Those aware of the strained relations between Janak and his younger brother, were impressed by the graciousness of the king of Mithila. He had let bygones be bygones and included the entire extended family in this celebration. Unfortunately, Kushadhwaj felt otherwise. He felt his brother had been naive as usual. Besides, Kushadhwaj had just played his own cards …

Janak requested Vishwamitra to occupy the main throne of Mithila, as he moved towards the smaller throne to the right. Kushadhwaj walked towards the seat on the left of the great *Maharishi*. This was exactly two floors below the room Sita was in, hidden behind a latticed window. A flurry of officials scuttled all over the place, for this was an unexpected breach of protocol. The king had offered his own throne to another.

A loud buzz ran through the hall at this unorthodox seating arrangement, but Sita was distracted by something else.

Where is Raavan?

She smiled.

So the Malayaputras have handled the king of Lanka. He won't be coming. Good.

The court crier banged his staff against the large bell at the entrance of the hall, signalling a call for silence.

Vishwamitra cleared his throat and spoke loudly. The superb acoustics of the Hall of Dharma carried his voice clearly to all those present. 'Welcome to this august gathering called by the wisest and most spiritual of rulers in India, King Janak.'

Janak smiled genially.

Vishwamitra continued. 'The princess of Mithila, Sita, has decided to make this a *gupt swayamvar*. She will not join us in the hall. The great kings and princes will, on her bidding, compete —'

The *Maharishi* was interrupted by the ear-splitting sounds of numerous conch shells; surprising, for conch shells were usually melodious and pleasant. Everyone turned to the source of the sound: the entrance of the great hall. Fifteen tall, muscular warriors strode into the room holding black flags, with the image of the head of a roaring lion emerging from a profusion of fiery flames. The warriors marched with splendid discipline.

Behind them were two formidable men. One was a giant, even taller than Lakshman. He was corpulent but muscular, with a massive potbelly that jiggled with every step. His whole body was unusually hirsute — he looked more like a giant bear than human. Most troubling for all those present, were the strange outgrowths on his ears and shoulders. He was a Naga. He was also Raavan's younger brother, Kumbhakarna.

Walking proudly beside him was Raavan, his head held high. He moved with a minor stoop; perhaps a sign of advancing age. Despite the stoop, Raavan's great height and rippling musculature were obvious. The muscles may have sagged a bit and the skin may have wrinkled, but the strength that remained in them was palpable. His battle-worn, swarthy skin was pock-marked, probably by a childhood disease. A thick beard, with an equal sprinkling of black and white hair, valiantly attempted to cover his ugly marks while a handlebar moustache set off his menacing features. He was wearing a violet-coloured *dhoti* and *angvastram*; only the most expensive colour-dye in the world. His headgear was intimidating, with two threatening six-inch-long horns reaching out from the top on either side.

Fifteen more warriors followed the two men.

Raavan's entourage moved to the centre and halted next to the bow of Lord Rudra. The lead bodyguard made a loud announcement. 'The king of kings, the emperor of emperors, the ruler of the three worlds, the beloved of the Gods, Lord Raavan!'

Raavan turned to a minor king who sat closest to the *Pinaka*. He made a soft grunting sound and flicked his head to the right, a casual gesture which clearly communicated what he expected. The king immediately rose and scurried away, coming to a standstill behind another competitor. Raavan walked to the chair, but did not sit. He placed his right foot on the seat and rested his hand on his knee. His bodyguards, including the giant bear-like Kumbhakarna, fell in line behind him.

Raavan finally cast a casual glance at Vishwamitra. 'Continue, great Malayaputra.'

Vishwamitra, the chief of the Malayaputras, was furious. He had never been treated so disrespectfully. 'Raavan ...' he growled.

Raavan stared at Vishwamitra with lazy arrogance.

The *Maharishi* managed to rein in his temper; he had an important task at hand. He would deal with Raavan later. 'Princess Sita has decreed the sequence in which the great kings and princes will compete.'

Raavan began to walk towards the *Pinaka* while Vishwamitra was still speaking. The chief of the Malayaputras completed his announcement just as Raavan was about to reach for the bow. 'The first man to compete is not you, Raavan. It is Ram, the prince of Ayodhya.'

Raavan's hand stopped a few inches from the bow. He looked at Vishwamitra, and then turned around to see who had responded to the sage. He saw a young man, dressed in the simple white clothes of a hermit. Behind him stood another young, though gigantic, man, next to whom was Arishtanemi.

Raavan glared first at Arishtanemi, and then at Ram. If looks could kill, Raavan would have certainly felled a few today. He turned towards Vishwamitra, Janak, and Kushadhwaj, his fingers wrapped around the macabre finger-bones pendant that hung around his neck. His body was shaking in utter fury. He growled in a loud and booming voice, 'I have been insulted! Why was I invited at all if you planned to make unskilled boys compete ahead of me?!'

Janak looked at Kushadhwaj before turning to Raavan and interjecting weakly, 'These are the rules of the *swayamvar*, Great King of Lanka …'

A voice that sounded more like the rumble of thunder was finally heard. The voice of Kumbhakarna. 'Enough of this nonsense!' He turned towards Raavan, his *elder brother*. '*Dada*, let's go.'

Raavan suddenly bent and picked up the *Pinaka*. Before anyone could react, he had strung it and nocked an arrow on the string. Everyone sat paralysed as he pointed the arrow directly at Vishwamitra.

Vishwamitra stood up, threw his *angvastram* aside, and banged his chest with his closed fist. 'Shoot, Raavan!' The sage's voice resounded in the great hall. 'Come on! Shoot, if you have the guts!'

The crowd gasped collectively. In horror.

Sita was shocked beyond words. *Guru*ji!

Raavan released the arrow. It slammed into the statue of Mithi behind Vishwamitra, breaking off the nose of the ancient king, the founder of Mithila. An unimaginable insult.

Sita was livid. *How dare he?*

'Raavan!' growled Sita, as she got up and whirled around, simultaneously reaching for her sword. She was stopped by her Mithilan maids, who held her back from rushing towards the stairs.

'No, Lady Sita!'

'Raavan is a monster …'

'You will die …'

'Look, he's leaving …' said another maid.

Sita rushed back to the latticed window. She saw Raavan throw the bow, the holy *Pinaka*, on the table and begin to walk towards the door. He was followed by his guards. In all this commotion, Kumbhakarna quickly stepped up to the table, unstrung the *Pinaka*, and reverentially brought it to his head. Holding it with both hands. Almost like he was apologising to the bow. Placing the *Pinaka* back on the table, he turned around and briskly walked out of the hall. Behind Raavan.

As the last of the Lankans exited, the people within the hall turned in unison from the doorway to those seated at the other end of the room: Vishwamitra, Janak and Kushadhwaj.

Vishwamitra spoke as if nothing had happened. 'Let the competition begin.'

The people in the room sat still, as if they had turned to stone. *En masse.* Vishwamitra spoke once again, louder this time. 'Let the competition begin. Prince Ram, please step up.'

Ram rose from his chair and walked up to the *Pinaka*. He bowed with reverence and folded his hands together into a *Namaste*. Sita thought she saw his lips move in a chant. But she couldn't be sure from the distance.

He raised his right wrist and touched both his eyes with the red thread tied around it.

Sita smiled. *May the* Kanyakumari *bless you, Ram. And, may she bless me with your hand in marriage.*

Ram touched the bow and tarried a while. He then brought his head down and placed it on the bow; as if asking to be blessed by the great weapon. He breathed steadily as he lifted the bow with ease. Sita looked at Ram intently. With bated breath.

Ram placed one arm of the bow on a wooden stand placed on the ground. His shoulders, back and arms strained visibly as he pulled down the upper limb of the *Pinaka*, simultaneously pulling up the bowstring. His body laboured at the task. But his face was serene. He bent the upper limb farther with a slight increase in effort, and tied the bowstring. His muscles relaxed as he let go of the upper limb and held the bow at the grip. He brought the bowstring close to his ear and plucked; his expression showed that the twang was right.

He picked up an arrow and walked to the copper-plated basin. Deliberate footsteps. Unhurried. He went down on one knee and held the bow horizontally above his head. He looked down at the water. At the reflection of the fish that moved in a circle above him. The rippling water in the basin danced as if to tantalise his mind. Ram focused on the image of the fish to the exclusion of all else. He nocked the arrow on the string of the bow and pulled slowly with his right hand. His back erect. The core muscles activated with ideal tension. His breathing steady and rhythmic.

Calmly, without any hint of nervousness or anxiety, he pulled the string all the way back and released the arrow. It shot up. As did the vision of each person in the room. The unmistakable sound of a furiously speeding arrow crashing into wood reverberated in the great hall. It had pierced the right eye of the fish, and lodged itself into the wooden wheel. The wheel swirled rhythmically as the shaft of the arrow drew circles in the air.

Sita smiled in relief. All the tension of the last few days was forgotten. The anger of the last few minutes, forgotten. Her eyes were pinned on Ram, who knelt near the basin with his head bowed, studying the rippling water; a calm smile on his face.

A part of Sita that had died years ago, when she had lost her mother, slowly sputtered to life once again.

I am not alone anymore.

She felt a bittersweet ache as she thought of her mother. That she wasn't around to see Sita find her man.

For the first time since her mother's death, she could think of her without crying.

Grief overwhelms you when you are alone. But when you find your soulmate, you can handle anything.

What was a painful, unbearable memory had now been transformed into bittersweet nostalgia. A source of sadness, yes. But also, a source of strength and happiness.

She pictured her mother standing before her. Smiling. Nurturing. Warm. Maternal. Like Mother Nature herself.

Sita was whole once again.

After a long, long time, she felt like whispering words that lay buried deep in her consciousness. Words that she thought she would have no use for once her mother had died.

She looked at Ram in the distance and whispered, 'I love you.'

Chapter 22

'Thank you, Arishtanemi*ji*,' said Sita. 'The Malayaputras stood by me. Guru*ji* put his own life at risk. I am grateful.'

It had been announced that the wedding of Ram and Sita would be carried out in a simple set of rituals that very afternoon. To Ram's surprise, Sita had suggested that Lakshman and Urmila get married in the same auspicious hour of the day. To Ram's further disbelief, Lakshman had enthusiastically agreed. It was decided that while both the couples would be wed in Mithila — to allow Sita and Urmila to travel with Ram and Lakshman to Ayodhya — a set of grand ceremonies would be held in Ayodhya as well. Befitting the descendants of the noble Ikshvaku.

In the midst of the preparations for the wedding ceremonies, Arishtanemi had sought a meeting with Sita.

'I hope this puts to rest any suspicions about where the Malayaputra loyalties lie,' said Arishtanemi. 'We have always been, and always will be, with the Vishnu.'

You will be with the Vishnu only as long as I do what you want me to do. Not when I do something that does not fit in with your plans.

Sita smiled. 'My apologies for having doubted you, Arishtanemi*ji*.'

Arishtanemi smiled. 'Misunderstandings can occur within the closest of families. All's well that ends well.'

'Where is Guru Vishwamitra?'

'Where do you think?'

Raavan.

'How is the demon king taking it?' asked Sita.

Vishwamitra had gone out on a limb to aggressively stop Raavan during the *swayamvar*. The King of Lanka had felt insulted. There could be consequences. Raavan's almighty ego was as legendary as his warrior spirit and cruelty. But would he take on the formidable Malayaputras?

Arishtanemi looked down thoughtfully before returning his gaze to Sita. 'Raavan is a cold and ruthless man, who makes decisions based on hard calculations. But his ego ... His ego gets in the way sometimes.'

'Cold and ruthless calculations would tell him not to take on the Malayaputras,' said Sita. 'He needs whatever it is we give him from the cavern of the Thamiravaruni.'

'That he does. But like I said, his ego may get in the way. I hope Guru Vishwamitra can handle it.'

Arishtanemi was astonished that Sita had not uncovered the entire secret of the aid that the Malayaputras provided Raavan. Perhaps, there were some things beyond even the redoubtable Sita's abilities. But he kept his surprise from showing on his face.

— ⟨⟩ —

The two weddings were simple sets of rituals, concluded quickly in the afternoon of the day of the *swayamvar*.

Sita and Ram were alone at last. They sat on floor cushions

in the dining hall, their dinner placed on a low stool. It was late in the evening, the sixth hour of the third *prahar*. Notwithstanding their relationship being sanctified by dharma a few hours earlier, an awkwardness underlined their ignorance of each other's personalities.

'Umm,' said Ram, staring at his plate.

'Yes, Ram?' asked Sita. 'Is there a problem?'

'I'm sorry, but … the food …'

'Is it not to your liking?'

'No, no, it's good. It's very good. But …'

Sita looked into Ram's eyes. *I am your wife. You can be honest with me. I haven't made the food in any case.*

But she kept these thoughts in her head and asked, 'Yes?'

'It needs a bit of salt.'

Sita was irritated with the Mithila royal cook. *Daya! I'd told him that the central Sapt Sindhuans eat more salt than us Easterners!*

She pushed her plate aside, rose and clapped her hands. An attendant rushed in. 'Get some salt for the prince, please.' As the attendant turned, Sita ordered, 'Quickly!'

The attendant broke into a run.

Ram cleaned his hand with a napkin as he waited for the salt. 'I'm sorry to trouble you.'

Sita frowned as she took her seat. 'I'm your wife, Ram. It's my duty to take care of you.'

He's so awkward … and cute …

Ram smiled. 'Umm, may I ask you something?'

'Of course.'

'Tell me something about your childhood.'

'You mean, before I was adopted? You do know that I was adopted, right?'

'Yes … I mean, you don't have to talk about it if it troubles you.'

Sita smiled. 'No, it doesn't trouble me, but I don't remember anything. I was too young when I was found by my adoptive parents.'

Ram nodded.

Will you also judge me by my birth?

Sita answered the question that she thought was on Ram's mind. 'So, if you ask me who my birth-parents are, the short answer is that I don't know. But the one I prefer is that I am a daughter of the earth.'

'Birth is completely unimportant. It is just a means of entry into this world of action, into this *karmabhoomi*. Karma is all that matters. And your karma is divine.'

Sita smiled. She was charmed by her husband's ability to constantly surprise her. Positively surprise her. *I can see what Maharishi Vashishtha sees in him. He is special ...*

Ram was about to say something when the attendant came rushing in with the salt. He added some to his food and resumed eating. The attendant retreated from the room.

'You were saying something,' said Sita.

'Yes,' said Ram, 'I think that ...'

Ram was interrupted again, this time by the doorkeeper announcing loudly, 'The chief of the Malayaputras, the *Saptrishi Uttradhikari*, the protector of the way of the Vishnus, Maharishi Vishwamitra.'

Sita was surprised. *Why is Guru*ji *here?*

She looked at Ram. He shrugged. He did not know what this visit was about. Ram and Sita rose as Vishwamitra entered the room, followed by Arishtanemi. Sita gestured to her attendant to get some washing bowls for Ram and herself.

'We have a problem,' said Vishwamitra, not feeling the need to exchange pleasantries.

Sita cursed under her breath. *Raavan …*

'What happened, Guru*ji*?' asked Ram.

'Raavan is mobilising for an attack.'

'But he doesn't have an army,' said Ram. 'What's he going to do with ten thousand bodyguards? He can't hold a city of even Mithila's size with that number. All he'll achieve is getting his men killed in battle.'

'Raavan is not a logical man,' said Vishwamitra. 'His ego is hurt. He may lose his bodyguard corps, but he will wreak havoc on Mithila.'

Ram looked at his wife.

Sita shook her head with irritation and addressed Vishwamitra. 'Who in Lord Rudra's name invited that demon for the *swayamvar*? I know it was not my father.'

Vishwamitra took a deep breath as his eyes softened. 'That's water under the bridge, Sita. The question is, what are we going to do now?'

'What is your plan, Guru*ji*?' asked Ram.

'I have with me some important material that was mined at my *ashram* by the Ganga. I needed it to conduct a few science experiments at Agastyakootam. This was why I had visited my *ashram*.'

'Science experiments?' asked Ram.

'Yes, experiments with the *daivi astras*.'

Sita drew a sharp breath. She knew the power and ferocity of the *divine weapons*. 'Guru*ji*, are you suggesting that we use *daivi astras*?'

Vishwamitra nodded in confirmation. Ram spoke up. 'But that will destroy Mithila as well.'

'No, it won't,' said Vishwamitra. 'This is not a traditional *daivi astra*. What I have is the *Asuraastra*.'

'Isn't that a biological weapon?' asked Ram. Deeply troubled now.

'Yes. Poisonous gas and a blast wave from the *Asuraastra* will incapacitate the Lankans, paralysing them for days on end. We can easily imprison them in that state and end this problem.'

'Just paralyse, Guru*ji*?' asked Ram. 'I have learnt that in large quantities, the *Asuraastra* can kill as well.'

Vishwamitra knew that only one man could have possibly taught this to Ram. His best friend-turned-foe, Vashishtha. The Chief of the Malayaputras was immediately irritated. 'Do you have any better ideas?'

Ram fell silent.

Sita looked at Ram and then at Vishwamitra. *I know exactly what Guru*ji *is trying to do.*

'But what about Lord Rudra's law?' asked Sita, a little aggressively.

It was well known that Lord Rudra, the previous Mahadev, had banned the unauthorised use of *daivi astras* many centuries ago. Those who broke the law would be punished with banishment for fourteen years, he had decreed. Breaking the law for the second time would be punishable by death.

The Vayuputras would be compelled to enforce the Mahadev's law.

'I don't think that law applies to the use of the *Asuraastra*,' said Vishwamitra. 'It is not a weapon of mass destruction, just mass incapacitation.'

Sita narrowed her eyes. Clearly, she wasn't convinced. 'I disagree. A *daivi astra* is a *daivi astra*. We cannot use it without the authorisation of the Vayuputras, Lord Rudra's tribe. I am a Lord Rudra devotee. I will not break his law.'

'Do you want to surrender, then?'

'Of course not! We will fight!'

Vishwamitra laughed derisively. 'Fight, is it? And who, please explain, will fight Raavan's hordes? The namby-pamby intellectuals of Mithila? What is the plan? Debate the Lankans to death?'

'We have our police force,' said Sita, annoyed at this disrespect shown to her force.

'They're not trained or equipped to fight the troops of Raavan.'

'We are not fighting his troops. We are fighting his bodyguard platoons. My police force is enough for them.'

'They are not. And you know that.'

'We will not use the *daivi astras*, Guru*ji*,' said Sita firmly, her face hardening.

Ram spoke up. 'Samichi's police force is not alone. Lakshman and I are here, and so are the Malayaputras. We're inside the fort, we have the double walls; we have the lake surrounding the city. We can hold Mithila. We can fight.'

Vishwamitra turned to Ram with a sneer. 'Nonsense! We are vastly outnumbered. The double walls …' He snorted with disgust. 'It seems clever. But how long do you think it will take a warrior of Raavan's calibre to figure out a strategy that works around that obstacle?'

'We will not use the *daivi astras*, Guru*ji*,' said Sita, raising her voice. 'Now, if you will excuse me, I have a battle to prepare for.'

— ᳚ᴛ —

'Where is Samichi?' asked Sita, surprised that the Mithila Chief of Police and Protocol was not in her office.

The sun had already set. Sita was marshalling her forces for an expected attack from Raavan. She did not think the demon king of Lanka would honour the rules of war. It was quite likely that he would attack at night. Time was of the essence.

'My Lady,' said an officer. 'We don't know where she has gone. She left immediately after your wedding ceremony.'

'Find her. Tell her to come to the fort walls. The Bees Quarter.'

'Yes, My Lady.'

'Right now!' ordered Sita, clapping her hands. As the officer hurried out, Sita turned to the others. 'Round up all the officers in the city. Get them to the Bees Quarter. To the inner wall.'

As the policemen rushed out, Sita walked out of her office to meet her personal bodyguards — the Malayaputras embedded in the Mithila police force. She checked to see if they were out of earshot. Then, she whispered to Makrant, a guard she had come to trust. 'Find Captain Jatayu. Tell him that I want all of you to protect the eastern secret tunnel on our inner wall. He knows where it is. Preferably, find a way to collapse that tunnel.'

'My Lady, do you expect Raavan to …'

'Yes, I do,' interrupted Sita. 'Block that tunnel. Block it within the hour.'

'Yes, My Lady.'

— 𝑟𝑥 —

'I cannot do that!' hissed Samichi, looking around to ascertain that nobody was near.

Akampana, unlike his usual well-groomed self, was dishevelled. The clothes, though expensive, were rumpled.

Some of the rings on his fingers were missing. The knife lay precariously in the scabbard, the blood-stained blade partly exposed. Samichi was shocked. This was an Akampana she did not know. Crazed and violent.

'You must do as ordered,' growled Akampana softly.

Samichi glared angrily at the ground. She knew she had no choice. Because of what had happened all those years ago …

'Princess Sita cannot be hurt.'

'You are in no position to make demands.'

'Princess Sita cannot be hurt!' snarled Samichi. 'Promise me!'

Akampana held his fists tight. His fury at breaking point.

'Promise me!'

Despite his anger, Akampana knew they needed Samichi if they were to succeed. He nodded.

Samichi turned and hurried off.

Chapter 23

It was late at night; the fourth hour of the fourth *prahar*. Ram and Sita had been joined by Lakshman and Samichi on top of the Bees Quarter, close to the inner wall edge. The entire Bees Quarter complex had been evacuated as a precautionary step. The pontoon bridge that spanned the moat-lake had been destroyed.

Mithila had a force of four thousand policemen and policewomen. Enough to maintain law and order for the hundred thousand citizens of the small kingdom. But against the Lankans, they were outnumbered five to two. Would they be able to thwart an attack from the Lankan bodyguards of Raavan?

Sita believed they could. A cornered animal fights back ferociously. The Mithilans were not fighting for conquest. Or wealth. Or ego. They were fighting for their lives. Fighting to save their city from annihilation. And this was not a traditional war being fought on open ground. The Mithilans were behind defensive walls; double walls in fact; a war-battlement innovation that had rarely been tried in other forts in the recent past. The Lankan generals were unlikely to have war-gamed this scenario. A lower ratio of soldiers was not such a huge disadvantage with this factor thrown in.

Ram and Sita had abandoned efforts to secure the outer wall. They wanted Raavan and his soldiers to scale it and launch an assault on the inner wall; the Lankans would, then, be trapped between the two walls, which the Mithilan arrows would convert into a killing field. They expected a volley of arrows from the other side too. In preparation for which the police had been asked to carry their wooden shields, normally used for crowd control within Mithila. Lakshman had quickly taught them some basic manoeuvres to protect themselves from the arrows.

'Where are the Malayaputras?' asked Lakshman.

Sita looked around, but did not answer. She knew the Malayaputras would not abandon her. She hoped they were carrying out last-minute parleys, laced with adequate threats and bribes, to convince the Lankans to back off.

Ram whispered to Lakshman, 'I think it's just us.'

Lakshman shook his head and spat, saying loudly, 'Cowards.'

Sita did not respond. She had learnt in the last few days that Lakshman was quite hot-headed. And she needed his short temper in the battle that was to follow.

'Look!' said Samichi.

Sita and Lakshman turned in the direction that Samichi had pointed.

Torches lined the other side of the moat-lake that surrounded the outer wall of Mithila. Raavan's bodyguards had worked feverishly through the evening, chopping down trees from the forest and building rowboats to carry them across the lake.

Even as they watched, the Lankans began to push their boats into the moat-lake. The assault on Mithila was being launched.

'It's time,' said Sita.

'Yes,' said Ram. 'We have maybe another half hour before they hit our outer wall.'

— ༬ —

Conch shells resounded through the night, by now recognised as the signature sound of Raavan and his men. As they watched in the light of the flickering flames of torches, the Lankans propped giant ladders against the outer walls of Mithila.

'They are here,' said Ram.

Sita turned to her messenger and nodded.

Messages were relayed quickly down the line to the Mithila police-soldiers. Sita expected a shower of arrows from Raavan's archers. The Lankans would fire their arrows only as long as their soldiers were outside the outer wall. The shooting would stop the moment the Lankans climbed over. The archers would not risk hitting their own men.

A loud whoosh heralded the release of the arrows.

'Shields!' shouted Sita.

The Mithilans immediately raised their shields. Ready for the Lankan arrows that were about to rain down on them.

Sita's instincts kicked in. *Something's wrong with the sound. It's too strong even for thousands of arrows. Something much larger has been fi ed.*

Hiding behind her shield, she looked at Ram. She sensed that he too was troubled.

Their instincts were right.

Huge missiles rammed through the Mithilan defences with massive force. Desperate cries of agony along with sickening thuds were heard as shields were ripped through. Many in the Mithilan ranks were brought down in a flash.

'What is that?' screamed Lakshman, hiding behind his shield.

Sita saw Ram's wooden shield snap into two pieces as a missile tore through it like a hot knife through butter. It missed him by a hair's breadth.

Spears!

Their wooden shields were a protection against arrows, not large spears.

How can spears be flung to this distance?!

The first volley was over. Sita knew they had but a few moments before the next one. She lowered her shield and looked around, just as Ram did.

She heard Ram exclaim, 'Lord Rudra, be merciful ...'

The destruction was severe. At least a quarter of the Mithilans were either dead or heavily injured, impaled on massive spears that had brutally ripped through their shields and bodies.

Ram looked at Sita. 'Another volley will be fired any moment! Into the houses!'

'Into the houses!' shouted Sita.

'Into the houses!' repeated the lieutenants, as everybody ran towards the doors, lifted them, and jumped in. It was a most disorganised retreat, but it was effective. In a few minutes, practically every surviving Mithilan police soldier had jumped to safety within the houses. As the doors closed, the volley of spears resumed on the roofs of the Bees Quarter. A few stragglers were killed as the rest made it to safety; for now.

As soon as they were secure within a house, Ram pulled Sita aside. Lakshman and Samichi followed. Samichi looked ashen-faced and nervous as she stood behind her princess, helplessly rubbing her forehead.

Sita was breathing hard, her eyes flitting like that of a cornered tigress, anger bursting through every pore.

'What now?' Ram asked Sita. 'Raavan's soldiers must be scaling the outer walls. They will be upon us soon. There's no one to stop them.'

Sita had run out of ideas. She felt helpless. And livid. *Dammit!*

'Sita?' prompted Ram.

Sita's eyes suddenly opened wide. 'The windows!'

'What?' asked Samichi, surprised by her prime minister.

Sita immediately gathered her lieutenants around her. She ordered that the wood-panel seals on the windows of the houses be broken open; the ones that shared the inner fort wall.

The Bees Quarter windows overlooked the ground between the two fort walls. Sita had found her vantage point. Arrows would be fired at the charging Lankans, after all.

'Brilliant!' shouted Lakshman, as he rushed to a barricaded window. He pulled back his arm, flexed his muscles, and punched hard at the wood. Smashing the barricade with one mighty blow.

All the houses in this section of the Bees Quarter were internally connected through corridors. The message travelled rapidly. Within moments, the Mithilans smashed open the sealed windows and began firing arrows. The Lankans were caught between the outer and inner wall. They had expected no resistance. Caught off guard, the arrows shredded through their lines. The losses were heavy.

The Mithilans fired arrows without respite, killing as many of the Lankans as they could. Slowing the charge dramatically. Suddenly, the conch shells sounded; this time it was a different tune. The Lankans immediately turned and ran, retreating as rapidly as they had arrived.

A loud cheer went up from the Mithilan quarters. They had beaten back the first attack.

— ᚛᚜ —

Ram, Sita, and Lakshman stood on the roof of the Bees Quarter as dawn broke through. The gentle rays of the sun fell on the harsh devastation of Lankan spears. The damage was heart-rending.

Sita stared at the mutilated Mithilan corpses strewn all around her; heads hanging by sinew to bodies, some with their guts spilled out. Many simply impaled on spears, having bled to death.

'At least a thousand of my soldiers …'

'We too have hit them hard, *Bhabhi*,' said Lakshman to his *sister-in-law*. 'There are at least a thousand dead Lankans lying between the inner and outer wall.'

Sita looked at Lakshman, her eyes brimming with tears. 'Yes, but they have nine thousand left. We have only three thousand.'

Ram surveyed the Lankan camp on the other side of the moat-lake. Sita's gaze followed his eyes. Hospital-tents had been set up to tend to the injured. Many Lankans, though, were furiously at work; hacking trees and pushing the forest line farther with mathematical precision.

Clearly, they did not intend to retreat to Lanka.

'They will be better prepared next time,' said Ram. 'If they manage to scale the inner wall … it's over.'

Sita placed her hand on Ram's shoulder and sighed as she stared at the ground. She seemed to gather strength from the simple touch. It was like she had a dependable ally now.

Sita turned around and looked towards her city. Her eyes

rested on the steeple of the massive temple dedicated to Lord Rudra, which loomed beyond the garden of the Bees Quarter. Fierce determination blazed from her eyes, resolve pouring steel into her veins.

'It's not over yet. I'll call upon the citizens to join me. Even if my people stand here with kitchen knives, we will outnumber the Lankan scum ten to one. We can fight them.'

Sita could feel Ram's shoulder muscles tensing under her touch. She looked at his eyes. She saw only confidence and trust.

He believes in me. He trusts me to handle this. I will handle this. I will not fail.

Sita nodded, like she had made up her mind. And rushed away, signalling some of her lieutenants to follow her.

Ram and Lakshman followed her too, trying to keep pace. She turned around. 'No. Please stay here. I need someone I can trust, someone who understands war, to stay here and rally the forces in case the Lankans launch a surprise attack.'

Lakshman tried to argue, but fell silent at a signal from Ram.

'We will stay here, Sita,' said Ram. 'No Lankan will enter the city as long as we are standing here. Rally the others quickly.'

Sita smiled and touched Ram's hand.

Then she turned and ran.

— ௴ 人 —

The third hour of the second *prahar* was almost ending. It was three hours before noon, in clear daylight. But this light had not blessed the city's residents with more wisdom. The news of the death of over one thousand courageous Mithilan policemen, and the devastation of the battle at the Bees Quarter, had not stirred the citizens to anger. Tales of the outnumbered and under-equipped Mithilan police, led by Prime Minister Sita, heroically fighting back the Lankans, had not inspired them. In fact, talks of surrender, compromise and negotiations were in the air.

Sita had gathered the local leaders in the market square in an effort to rally a citizen army to fight back the Lankans. This had been a few hours ago. That the rich would not think of risking their lives or property for their motherland wasn't surprising. It was shocking, though, that even the poor, who had benefited greatly from Sunaina's and then Sita's reforms, did not feel the need to fight for their kingdom.

Sita thought she would burst a capillary in utter fury, listening to the arguments being put forth by her fellow Mithilans; excuses to give a moral veneer to their cowardice.

'*We must be pragmatic* ...'

'*We haven't emerged from poverty, earned all this money, ensured good education for our children, built property, to just lose it all in one war* ...'

'*Seriously, has violence ever solved any problem? We should practise love, not war* ...'

'*War is just a patriarchal, upper-class conspiracy* ...'

'*The Lankans are also human beings like us. I am sure they will listen, if we talk to them* ...'

'*Really, is our conscience clean? We can say all we want about the Lankans, but didn't we insult Emperor Raavan at the* swayamvar ...'

'*What's the big deal if so many police officers died? It's their job to protect us. And die for us. It isn't as if they are doing this for free. What do we pay taxes for? Speaking of taxes, Lanka apparently has much lower tax rates* ...'

'*I think we should negotiate with the Lankans. Let's vote on that* ...'

At the end of her tether, Sita had even asked Janak and

Urmila to help her rouse the citizenry. Janak, respected as a saintly figure by the Mithilans, tried his best to urge them to fight. To no avail. Urmila, popular among the women, had no impact either.

Sita's fists were clenched tight. She was about to launch into an angry tirade against the cowardly citizenry when she felt a hand on her shoulder. She turned around to find Samichi standing there.

Sita quickly pulled her aside. 'Well, where are they?'

Samichi had been dispatched to find Vishwamitra or Arishtanemi. Sita refused to believe that the Malayaputras would abandon her at a time like this, especially when her city was threatened with annihilation. She was sure they knew she would die with her city. And she also knew that her survival mattered to them.

'I have searched everywhere, Sita,' said Samichi. 'I can't find them anywhere.'

Sita looked down and cursed under her breath.

Samichi swallowed hard. 'Sita ...'

Sita looked at her friend.

'I know you don't want to hear this, but we're left with no choice. We must negotiate with the Lankans. If we can get Lord Raavan to ...'

Sita's eyes flared up in anger. 'You will not say such things in my ...'

Sita stopped mid-sentence as a loud sound was heard from the Bees Quarter.

There were some explosions from a section of the roof of the Bees Quarter, hidden from where the battle with the Lankans had taken place just a few hours ago. A few seconds later, a small missile flew up from the same section. It sped off in a mighty arc, moving farther and farther away in a few short seconds. Towards the city moat, where Sita knew the Lankans were camped.

Everyone in the market square was transfixed, their eyes glued in the same direction. But none had any idea of what had just happened. None, except Sita.

She immediately understood what the Malayaputras had been up to all night. What they had been preparing. What they had done.

The Asuraastra.

As the missile flew high above the moat-lake, there was a flash of a minor detonation. The *Asuraastra* hovered for an instant above the Lankan camp. And then exploded dramatically.

The spectators in Mithila saw a bright green flash of light emerge from the splintered missile. It burst with furious intensity, like a flash of lightning. Fragments of the exploded missile were seen falling down.

As they witnessed this terrifying scene play out in the sky, the ear-shattering sound of the main explosion shook the very walls of Mithila. Right up to the market square where the citizens had been debating themselves to paralysis a few moments back.

The Mithilans covered their ears in shock. Some began to pray for mercy.

An eerie silence fell on the gathering. Many cowering Mithilans looked around in dazed confusion.

But Sita knew Mithila had been saved. She also knew what would follow. Devastation had fallen on Raavan and his fellow Lankans. They would be paralysed. In a deep state of coma. For days, if not weeks. Some of them would even die.

But her city was safe. It had been saved.

After the reversal at the battle of the Bees Quarter, perhaps this had been the only way to stop Raavan's hordes.

As relief coursed through her veins, she whispered softly, 'Lord Rudra, bless the Malayaputras and Guru Vishwamitra.'

Then, like a bolt from the blue, her elation suddenly evaporated. Raw panic entered her heart.

Who had fi ed the Asuraastra?

She knew that an *Asuraastra* had to be fired from a substantial distance. And only an extremely capable archer could do so successfully. There were just three people in Mithila right now who could shoot an arrow from the distance required to ignite and launch an *Asuraastra*. Vishwamitra, Arishtanemi and …

Ram … Please … No … Lord Rudra, have mercy.

Sita began sprinting towards the Bees Quarter. Followed by Samichi and her bodyguards.

Chapter 24

Sita bounded up the stairway of the Bees Quarter, three steps at a time. A grim-faced Samichi followed close behind. She was up on the roof in no time. Even from the distance, she could see the devastation in the Lankan camp. Thousands lay prone on the ground. Deathly silent. Demonic clouds of green viscous gas had spread like a shroud over the paralysed Lankans.

There was not a whisper in the air. The humans had fallen silent. So had the animals. The birds had stopped chirping. The trees did not stir. Even the wind had died down. All in sheer terror of the fiendish weapon that had just been unleashed.

The only sound was a steady, dreadful hiss, like the battle-cry of a gigantic snake. It was the sound of the thick viscous green gas that continued to be emitted from the fragments of the exploded *Asuraastra* missile that had fallen to the ground.

Sita held her *Rudraaksh* pendant in fear. *Lord Rudra, have mercy.*

She saw Arishtanemi and the Malayaputras standing in a huddle. She ran up to them.

'Who shot it?' demanded Sita.

Arishtanemi merely bowed his head and stepped aside; and, Ram came into Sita's view. Her husband was the only one holding a bow.

Vishwamitra had managed to pressure Ram into firing the *Asuraastra*. And thus, breaking Lord Rudra's law.

Sita cursed loudly as she ran towards Ram.

Vishwamitra smiled as he saw her approach. 'Sita, it is all taken care of! Raavan's forces are destroyed. Mithila is safe!'

Sita glared at Vishwamitra, too furious for words.

She ran to her husband and embraced him. A shocked Ram dropped his bow. They had never embraced. Until now.

She held him tight. She could feel his heartbeat pick up speed. But his hands remained by his side. He did not embrace her back.

She pulled her head back and saw a solitary tear trickle down her husband's face.

Guilt gnawed at her. She knew Ram had been forced to commit a sin. Forced due to his love for her. Forced due to his sense of duty, which compelled him to protect the innocent: The citizens of Mithila, even if they were selfish and cowardly.

She held Ram and looked deep into his empty eyes. Her face was creased with concern. 'I am with you, Ram.'

Ram remained silent. But his expression had changed. His eyes didn't have an empty look anymore. Instead they had a dreamy sparkle, as if he were lost in another world.

Oh Lord Rudra, give me the strength to help him. To help this magnificent man. Suffering because of me.

Sita continued to hold Ram in a tight embrace. 'I am with you, Ram. We will handle this together.'

Ram closed his eyes. He wrapped his arms around his wife. He rested his head on her shoulder. She could hear him release a deep, long breath. Like he had found his refuge. His sanctuary.

Sita looked over her husband's shoulder and glared at Vishwamitra. It was a fearsome look, like the wrathful fury of the Mother Goddess.

Vishwamitra glared right back, unrepentant.

A loud sound disturbed them all. They looked beyond the walls of Mithila. Raavan's *Pushpak Vimaan* was sputtering to life. Its giant rotor blades had begun to spin. The sound it made was like that of a giant monster cutting the air with his enormous sword. Within moments the rotors picked up speed and the conical flying vehicle rose from the earth. It hovered just a few feet above the ground; pushing against inertia, against the earth's immense pull of gravity. Then, with a great burst of sound and energy, it soared into the sky. Away from Mithila. And the devastation of the *Asuraastra*.

Raavan had survived. Raavan had escaped.

— ༪༫ —

The following day, a makeshift *Ayuralay* was set up outside the city. The Lankan soldiers were housed in large tents. The Malayaputras trained the Mithilan doctors to tend to those who had been rendered comatose by the lethal weapon. To keep them alive till they naturally emerged from the coma; a few days or maybe even a few weeks later. Some would never surface and pass away in their sleep.

Sita sat in her office, contemplating Mithila's governance after her impending departure to Ayodhya. There was too much to take care of and the conversation with Samichi was not helping.

The police and protocol chief stood before her, shaking like a leaf. Sita had never seen her friend so nervous. She was clearly petrified.

'Don't worry, Samichi. I'll save Ram. Nothing will happen to him. He won't be punished.'

Samichi shook her head. Something else was on her mind. She spoke in a quivering voice. 'Lord Raavan survived… the Lankans…will come back…Mithila, you, I…we're finished …'

'Don't be silly. Nothing will happen. The Lankans have been taught a lesson they will not forget in a hurry …'

'They will remember … They always remember… Ayodhya … Karachapa … Chilika …'

Sita held Samichi by her shoulders and said loudly, 'Pull yourself together. What's the matter with you? Nothing will happen!'

Samichi fell silent. She held her hands together in supplication. Praying. She knew what she had to do. She would appeal for mercy. To the True Lord.

Sita stared at Samichi and shook her head. Disappointed. She had decided to leave Samichi in charge of Mithila, under the titular rule of her father, Janak. Ensuring that there would be continuity in leadership. But now, she began to wonder whether Samichi was ready for additional responsibilities. She had never seen her friend so rattled before.

— ॐ —

'Arishtanemi*ji*, please don't make me do this,' pleaded Kushadhwaj.

Arishtanemi was in the section of the Mithila Palace allotted to Kushadhwaj, the king of Sankashya.

'You will have to,' said Arishtanemi, dangerously soft. The steel in his voice unmistakable. 'We know exactly what happened. How Raavan came here …'

Kushadhwaj swallowed nervously.

'Mithila is precious to all who love wisdom,' said Arishtanemi. 'We will not allow it to be destroyed. You will have to pay for what you did.'

'But if I sign this proclamation, Raavan's assassins will target me ...'

'And if you don't, *we* will target you,' said Arishtanemi, stepping uncomfortably close, menace dripping from his eyes. 'Trust me, we will make it far more painful.'

'Arishtanemi*ji* ...'

'Enough.' Arishtanemi grabbed the royal Sankashya seal and pressed it on the proclamation sheet, leaving its imprint. 'It's done ...'

Kushadhwaj sagged on his seat, sweating profusely.

'It will be issued in the name of King Janak *and* you, Your Majesty,' said Arishtanemi, as he bowed his head in mock servility.

Then he turned and walked out.

— ༃ —

King Janak and his brother, King Kushadhwaj, had authorised the imprisonment of the Lankan prisoners of war left behind by Raavan. Vishwamitra and his Malayaputras had promised that they would take the Lankan prisoners with them when they left for Agastyakootam. The sage intended to negotiate with Raavan on Mithila's behalf, guaranteeing the kingdom's safety in return for the release of the prisoners of war.

This news had been greeted with relief by the Mithilans, and not the least, Samichi. They were petrified of the demon king of Lanka, Raavan. But now, the people felt more at ease knowing that the Malayaputras would ensure that the Lankans backed off.

'We're leaving tomorrow, Sita,' said Arishtanemi.

The military chief of the Malayaputras had come to Sita's chamber to speak with her in private. Sita had refused to meet Vishwamitra since the day Ram had fired the *daivi astra*.

Sita folded her hands together into a respectful *Namaste* and bowed her head. 'May Lord Parshu Ram and Lord Rudra bless you with a safe journey.'

'Sita, I am sure you are aware that the time to make the announcement draws close ...'

Arishtanemi was referring to the declaration that would publicly announce Sita's status as the Vishnu. Once it was made, not just the Malayaputras, but the whole of India would recognise her as the saviour who would lead the people of this land to a new way of life.

'It cannot happen now.'

Arishtanemi tried to control his frustration. 'Sita, you can't be so stubborn. We had to do what we did.'

'*You* could have fired the *Asuraastra*, Arishtanemi*ji*. In fact, Guru*ji* could have fired it as well. The Vayuputras would have understood. They would have even seen it as a Malayaputra effort to protect themselves. But you set Ram up ...'

'He volunteered, Sita.'

'R-i-g-h-t ...' said Sita, sarcastically. She had already heard from Lakshman how Vishwamitra had emotionally blackmailed Ram into firing the divine weapon, exhorting him to protect his wife's city.

'Sita, have you forgotten what state Mithila was in? You are not appreciating the fact that we saved your city. You are not even appreciating the fact that Guru Vishwamitra will handle the crisis with Raavan, ensuring that you do not face any retaliation after what happened here. Seriously, what more do you expect?'

'I would have expected you to behave with ...'

Arishtanemi interrupted Sita, guessing what she would have said. '*Honour?* Behave with honour? Don't be childish, Sita. What I have always liked about you is the fact that you are practical. You are not taken by silly theoretical ideas. You know you can do a lot for India. You must agree to make the announcement of your Vishnuhood ...'

Sita raised an eyebrow. 'I wasn't talking about honour. I was talking about wisdom.'

'Sita ...' growled Arishtanemi, clenching his fists. He took a deep breath to control himself. 'Wisdom dictated that we not fire the *Asuraastra*. There are ... We have enough problems with the Vayuputras already. This would have further complicated our relationship. It had to be Ram.'

'Right,' said Sita. 'It *had* to be Ram ...'

Is she worried about Ram being punished for firing the Asuraastra?

'Ram will not be banished, Sita. The *Asuraastra* is not a weapon of mass destruction. Guru*ji* has already told you. We can manage the Vayuputras ...'

Arishtanemi knew the Vayuputras liked Ram and would probably agree to waive the punishment for the eldest prince of Ayodhya. And if they didn't ... Well, the Malayaputras wouldn't be too troubled by that. Their main concern was Sita. Only Sita.

'Ram believes that he should be punished,' said Sita. 'It is the law.'

'Then, tell him to grow up and not be silly.'

'Try and understand Ram, Arishtanemi*ji*. I am not sure you realise how important a man like that is for India. He can transform us into law-abiding citizens. He can lead by example. He can do a lot of good. I have travelled the length and breadth of this country. I don't think the ruling nobility, including yourselves, understand the simmering anger among the common folk against the elite. Ram, by subjecting himself to the same laws that apply to them, increases the credibility of the establishment. People will eventually listen to a message delivered by Ram.'

Arishtanemi shifted on his feet, impatiently. 'This is a pointless conversation, Sita. The Malayaputras, the only ones authorised to recognise a Vishnu, have chosen you. That's it.'

Sita smiled. 'Indians don't take kindly to choices imposed from above. This is a country of rebels. The people have to accept me as the Vishnu.'

Arishtanemi remained silent.

'Perhaps you didn't understand the point I was trying to make earlier about wisdom,' said Sita.

Arishtanemi frowned.

'I suppose the Malayaputras want to keep Raavan alive till, at some stage, I kill him and hence am accepted by all Sapt Sindhuans. Who would deny a leader who delivers them from their most hated enemy ... Raavan.'

Arishtanemi's eyes widened, as he understood what Sita was saying. The Malayaputras had just committed a major blunder. That too on a strategy that they had been planning for decades.

'Yes, Arishtanemi*ji*. You thought you were setting Ram up for punishment. But instead, you have made him into a hero for the common man. The entire Sapt Sindhu has suffered Raavan's economic squeeze. And they now see Ram as their saviour.'

Arishtanemi fell silent.

'Arishtanemi*ji*, sometimes, a too-clever-by-half plan can backfire,' said Sita.

— ɖ ⅄ —

Sita looked at her husband as he rode beside her. Lakshman and Urmila rode behind them. Lakshman was talking non-stop with his wife as she gazed at him earnestly. Urmila's thumb kept playing with the massive diamond ring on her left forefinger; an expensive gift from her husband. Behind them were a hundred Mithilan soldiers. Another hundred soldiers rode ahead of Ram and Sita. The convoy was on its way to Sankashya, from where it would sail to Ayodhya.

Ram, Sita, Lakshman, and Urmila had set off from Mithila two weeks after the *Asuraastra* laid waste the Lankan camp. True to their word, Vishwamitra and his Malayaputras had left for their capital, Agastyakootam, taking the Lankan prisoners with them. They would negotiate with Raavan on Mithila's behalf, guaranteeing the kingdom's safety in return for the release of the prisoners of war. The Malayaputras had also taken the bow of Lord Rudra, the *Pinaka*, which had been their treasure for centuries. It would be returned to Sita when she took on the role of the Vishnu.

Noting Samichi's improved state of mind, once the Lankan problem had been taken care of, Sita had made her friend Mithila's *de facto* prime minister. She would work in consultation with a council of five city elders established by Sita. Of course, all under the guidance of King Janak.

'Ram …'

Ram turned to his wife with a smile as he pulled his horse close to hers. 'Yes?'

'Are you sure about this?'

Ram nodded. There was no doubt in his mind.

Sita was impressed and worried at the same time. He truly did live by the law.

'But you are the first in a generation to defeat Raavan. And, it wasn't really a *daivi astra*. If you —'

Ram frowned. 'That's a technicality. And you know it.'

Sita paused for a few seconds and continued. 'Sometimes, to create a perfect world, a leader has to do what is necessary at the time; even if it may not appear to be the 'right' thing to do in the short term. In the long run, a leader who has the capacity to uplift the masses must not deny himself that opportunity. He has a duty to not make himself unavailable. A true leader will even take a sin upon his soul for the good of his people.'

Ram looked at Sita. He seemed disappointed. 'I have done that already, haven't I? The question is, should I be punished for it or not? Should I do penance for it? If I expect my people to follow the law, so must I. A leader is not just one who leads. He must also be a role model. He must practise what he preaches, Sita.'

Sita smiled. 'Well, Lord Rudra had said: "A leader is not just one who gives his people what they want. He must also be the one who teaches his people to be better than they imagined themselves to be."'

Ram smiled too. 'And I'm sure you will tell me Lady Mohini's response to this as well.'

Sita laughed. 'Yes. Lady Mohini said that people have their limitations. A leader should not expect more from them than what they are capable of. If you stretch them beyond their capacity, they will break.'

Ram shook his head. He did not agree with the great Lady Mohini. Ram expected people to rise above their limitations and better themselves; for only then was an ideal society possible. But he didn't voice his disagreement aloud. He knew that Sita passionately respected Lady Mohini.

'Are you sure? Fourteen years outside the boundaries of

the Sapt Sindhu?' Sita looked at Ram seriously, returning to the original discussion.

Ram nodded. 'I broke Lord Rudra's law. And this is his stated punishment. It doesn't matter whether the Vayuputras pass the order to punish me or not. It doesn't matter whether my people support me or not. I must serve my sentence.'

She smiled. *He will not stray. He is truly incredible. How did he survive in Ayodhya all these years?*

Sita leaned towards him and whispered, 'We... not I.'

Ram frowned.

Sita reached out and placed her palm on Ram's hand. 'You share my fate and I share yours. That is what a true marriage is.' She entwined her fingers through his. 'Ram, I am your wife. We will always be together; in good times and bad; through thick and thin.'

We will come back in fourteen years. Stronger. More powerful. The Vishnuhood can wait till then.

She had already decided that she would ask Jatayu for large quantities of the legendary *Somras*, the anti-ageing medicine created by the great Indian scientist, Brahma, many millennia ago. She would administer the medicine to Ram and herself to retain their vitality and youth in their fourteen years of exile. So that when they returned, they would be ready for the task ahead. Ready to change India.

She remembered a line she had read. A line supposedly spoken by Lady Varahi, the third Vishnu. *India will rise, but not for selfish reasons. It will rise for Dharma ... For the Good of all.*

She looked at Ram and smiled.

Ram squeezed her hand. His horse snorted and quickened its pace. Ram pulled back the reins gently, keeping it in step with his wife's steed.

Chapter 25

The two young couples sailed into the Ayodhya port to an overwhelming sight. It was as if all of Ayodhya had stepped out of their homes to greet them.

Sita had enjoyed her conversations with Ram during their journey. They had brainstormed on how best an empire can be organised for the good of the people. She had spoken about the concept that the state compulsorily adopt young children to break the evils of the birth-based caste system. Sita had not mentioned that she had grown to believe in the idea relatively recently; or that it was originally Vishwamitra's idea. Ram did not like or trust the Maharishi. Why taint a good idea with that dislike? They had also spoken about the *Somras* mass-manufacturing technology developed by Guru Vashishtha. Ram believed that the *Somras* should either be made available to all or none. Since taking away the *Somras* might be difficult, he suggested that Vashishtha's technology be used to make it available to all.

Enjoyable as those conversations had been, Sita knew they would probably not find the time to have more of them for a while. Ram had his work cut out in Ayodhya. To begin with, he had to ensure that he was not stopped from going on exile.

And, of course, he also had to explain his marriage to the adopted princess of the powerless kingdom of Mithila. Jatayu had quipped to Sita, that had the Ayodhyans known that she was the Vishnu, they would have realised that Ram had married up! Sita had simply smiled and dismissed his observation.

Standing at the ship's balustrade, Sita looked at the grand, yet crumbling, port of Ayodhya. It was several times larger than the Sankashya port. She observed the barricaded man-made channel that allowed the waters of the Sarayu River to flow into the massive Grand Canal that surrounded *Ayodhya*, the *unconquerable city*.

The canal had been built a few centuries ago, during the reign of Emperor Ayutayus, by drawing in the waters of the feisty Sarayu River. Its dimensions were almost celestial. Stretching over fifty kilometres, it circumnavigated the third and outermost wall of the city of Ayodhya. It was enormous in breadth as well, extending to about two-and-a-half kilometres across the banks. Its storage capacity was so massive that for the first few years of its construction, many kingdoms downriver had complained of water shortages. Their objections had been crushed with brute force by the powerful Ayodhyan warriors.

One of the main purposes of this canal was militaristic. It was, in a sense, a moat. To be fair, it could be called the Moat of Moats, protecting the city from all sides. Prospective attackers would have to row across a moat with river-like dimensions. The fools would be out in the open, vulnerable to a barrage of missiles from the high walls of the unconquerable city. Four bridges spanned the canal in the four cardinal directions. The roads that emerged from these bridges led into the city through four massive gates in the outermost wall: North Gate, East

Gate, South Gate and West Gate. Each bridge was divided into two sections. Each section had its own tower and drawbridge, thus offering two levels of defence at the canal itself.

Even so, to consider this Grand Canal a mere defensive structure was to do it a disservice. It also worked as an effective flood-control mechanism, as water from the tempestuous Sarayu could be led in through control-gates. Floods were a recurrent problem in India. Furthermore, its placid surface made drawing water relatively easy, as compared to taking it directly from the feisty Sarayu. Smaller canals radiated out of the Grand Canal into the hinterland of Ayodhya, increasing the productivity of farming dramatically. The increase in agricultural yield allowed many farmers to free themselves from the toil of tilling the land. Only a few were enough to feed the massive population of the entire kingdom of Kosala. This surplus labour transformed into a large army, trained by talented generals into a brilliant fighting unit. The army conquered more and more of the surrounding lands, till the great Lord Raghu, the grandfather of the present Emperor Dashrath, finally subjugated the entire Sapt Sindhu; thus, becoming the *Chakravarti Samrat* or *Universal Emperor*.

Dashrath too had built on this proud legacy, conquering far and wide to become a Chakravarti Samrat as well. That was until the demon of Lanka, Raavan, destroyed the combined might of the Sapt Sindhuan armies at Karachapa around twenty years ago.

The subsequent punitive trade levies that Raavan had imposed on all the kingdoms of the Sapt Sindhu, and mostly on Ayodhya, had sucked the treasury dry. It showed in the crumbling grandeur of the Grand Canal and its surrounding structures.

Despite its obviously fading glory, Ayodhya overwhelmed Sita. The city was bigger than any other in the Sapt Sindhu. Even in its decline, Ayodhya was many times grander than her Mithila. She had visited Ayodhya in the past, but incognito. This was the first time she was visible to all. Being gawked at. Being judged. She could see it in the eyes of the nobles and citizenry standing at a distance, held back by the Ayodhya royal bodyguards.

The gangplank hit the port deck with a loud bang, clearing her mind of the profusion of thoughts. A rakishly handsome man was bounding up the plank. He was shorter than Ram but far more muscular.

This must be Bharat.

He was closely followed by a diminutive, immaculately attired man with calm, intelligent eyes. He walked with slow, measured steps.

Shatrughan ...

'*Dada*!' hollered Bharat, as he ran up to Ram and embraced him.

Sita could see why Radhika had fallen for Bharat. He had obvious charisma.

'My brother,' smiled Ram, as he embraced Bharat.

As Bharat stepped back and embraced Lakshman, Shatrughan quietly embraced his eldest brother.

Within a flash, the four brothers were facing Sita and Urmila.

Ram held his hand out and said with simple pride, 'This is my wife, Sita, and next to her is Lakshman's wife, Urmila.'

Shatrughan smiled warmly and folded his hands together. '*Namaste*. It is an honour to meet both of you.'

Bharat smacked Shatrughan on his stomach. 'You are

too formal, Shatrughan.' He stepped forward and embraced Urmila. 'Welcome to the family.'

Urmila smiled, her nervousness dissipating a bit.

Then Bharat stepped towards his *elder sister-in-law,* Sita, and held her hands. 'I have heard a lot about you, *Bhabhi* ... I always thought it would be impossible for my brother to find a woman better than him.' He looked at Ram, grinned and turned his attention back to her. 'But my *dada* has always had the ability to manage the impossible.'

Sita laughed softly.

Bharat embraced his sister-in-law. 'Welcome to the family, *Bhabhi.*'

— ᘓ ᘔ —

The roads of Ayodhya were clogged with people waiting to receive their crown prince. A few had even extended their enthusiasm to welcome his bride. The procession inched forward at a snail's pace. The lead chariot had Ram and Sita. The prince was awkwardly acknowledging the wild cheering in the streets. Two chariots followed behind them. One had Bharat and Shatrughan, while Lakshman and his wife Urmila rode the second. Bharat flamboyantly acknowledged the multitude, waving his hands and blowing kisses with trademark flourish. Lakshman waved his trunk-like arms carefully, lest he hurt the petite Urmila, who stood demurely by his side. Shatrughan, as always, stood stoic, unmoved. Staring into the throngs. Almost like he was academically studying crowd behaviour.

The chanting of the crowd was loud and clear.

Ram!

Bharat!

Lakshman!
Shatrughan!

Their four beloved princes, the protectors of the kingdom, were finally together again. And most importantly, their crown prince had returned. *Victorious!* The defeater of the hated Raavan had returned!

Flowers were strewn, holy rice was showered, all were gay and happy. Though it was daytime, the massive stone lamp towers were lit up festively. Many had placed lamps on the parapets of their homes. Resplendent sunshine blazed with glory, as if in obeisance to the prince from the great clan of the Sun God himself. Ram of the Suryavanshis!

It took four hours for the chariots to traverse a distance that normally took less than thirty minutes. They finally reached the wing of the palace allocated to Ram.

A visibly weak Dashrath sat on his travelling throne, with Kaushalya standing next to him, waiting for his sons. A proper welcome ceremony had been laid out to receive the new brides. The eldest queen was a scrupulous upholder of tradition and rituals.

Kaikeyi had not deigned to reply to the invitation sent by Kaushalya, regarding the welcoming ceremony. Sumitra, of peace-loving Kashi, stood on the other side of Dashrath. Kaushalya leaned on her for support, always. Of course, Sumitra too was welcoming home a daughter-in-law!

Loud conch shells were heard as the *swagatam* ceremony began at the palace gate.

The four princes of Ayodhya and the two princesses of Mithila finally emerged from the melee. The Ayodhya royal guards, nervous as cats on a hot metal roof, heaved a visible sigh of relief as the royal youngsters entered the palace compound. Away from the multitude.

The royal procession moved along the elegant, marble-encrusted walkway in the compound. Verdant gardens were laid out on both sides. They slowed on reaching the entrance of Prince Ram's wing of the palace.

Sita hesitated as her eyes fell on Kaushalya. But she dismissed the thought that had struck her.

Kaushalya walked to the threshold holding the *puja thali* in her hands. It contained a lit lamp, a few grains of rice and some vermilion. She looped the *prayer plate* in small circles, seven times, around Sita's face. She picked up some rice and threw it in the air, above Sita's head. She took a pinch of vermilion and smeared it on Sita's parting on the hairline. Sita bent down to touch Kaushalya's feet in respect. Kaushalya handed the *thali* to an attendant, and placed her hands on Sita's head and blessed her. '*Ayushman bhav*, my child.'

As Sita straightened, Kaushalya indicated Dashrath. 'Accept your father-in-law's blessings.' Pointing towards Sumitra, she continued, 'And then, from your *chhoti maa*. We will then do the other ceremonies.'

Sita moved ahead to follow Kaushalya's instructions. Ram stepped forward and touched his mother's feet. She blessed him quickly and indicated that he seek his father's blessings.

Then she beckoned Urmila and Lakshman. Urmila, unlike Sita, did not dismiss the thought; the same one that had struck Sita earlier.

Kaushalya reminded her of her mother Sunaina. She had the same diminutive appearance and calm, gentle eyes. Kaushalya's skin was darker and her facial features were different, no doubt. Nobody could say that they were related. But there was something similar about them. The spiritually inclined would call it a soul connection.

Urmila waited for Kaushalya to finish the *aarti* ceremony, then bent down to touch her feet. Kaushalya blessed the younger princess of Mithila. As Urmila rose, she impulsively stepped forward and embraced Kaushalya. The Queen of Ayodhya was surprised at this unorthodox behaviour and failed to react.

Urmila pulled back, her eyes moist with emotion. She faintly voiced a word she had been unable to utter without crying, since Sunaina had died. '*Maa.*'

Kaushalya was moved by the innocence of sweet Urmila. Perhaps for the first time, the queen faced a woman shorter than herself. She looked at the round baby face, dominated by large child-like eyes. An image rose in her mind of a tiny sparrow that needed protection from the big, threatening birds around it. She smiled fondly, and pulled Urmila back into her arms. 'My child ... Welcome home.'

— ᳚᳚ᡃᡃ᳚Ꮬ —

A palace maid in the service of Queen Kaushalya stood, head bowed. Waiting for her instructions.

She was in the residential office of Manthara, the richest businesswoman in Ayodhya; arguably, the richest in the Sapt Sindhu. Rumours suggested that Manthara was even richer than Emperor Dashrath. Druhyu, her closest aide, could swear that there was substance to these rumours. Indeed. Very substantial substance.

'My Lady,' whispered the maid, 'what are my instructions?'

The maid fell silent, as Druhyu signalled her discreetly. She waited.

Druhyu stood submissively next to Manthara. Silent.

The disfigured Manthara sat on a specially designed chair that offered a measure of comfort to her hunched back. The scars on her face, remnants of a childhood affliction of small pox, gave her a forbidding appearance. At the age of eleven she had fallen ill with polio, leaving her right foot partially paralysed. Born to poverty, her physical disfiguration had added prejudice, not sympathy, to her formative years. She had, in fact, been teased mercilessly. Now that she was rich and powerful, no one dared say anything to her face. But she knew exactly what was said about her behind her back. For now, she was not only reviled for her deformed body, but also hated fiercely for being a Vaishya; for being a very rich businessperson.

Manthara looked out of the window to the large garden of her palatial estate.

The maid fidgeted impatiently on her feet. Her absence would be noticed in the palace before long. She had to return quickly. She cast a pleading look at Druhyu. He glared back.

Druhyu had begun to doubt the usefulness of remaining loyal to Manthara. The woman had lost her beloved daughter, Roshni, to a horrific gangrape and murder. The gang had been tried by the courts and executed. However, Dhenuka, the most vicious of them all, and the leader of the gang, had been let off on a legal technicality. He was a juvenile; and, according to Ayodhyan law, juveniles could not be awarded the death penalty. Ram, the prince of Ayodhya and chief of police, had insisted that the law be followed. *No matter what.* Manthara had sworn vengeance. Spending huge amounts of money, she had ferreted Dhenuka from jail and had had him killed in a slow, brutal manner. But her thirst for vengeance had not been quenched. Her target now was Ram. She had been patiently waiting for an opportunity. And one had just presented itself.

Druhyu stared at his mistress, his face devoid of expression.

The old bat has been wasting too much money on her revenge mission. It is affecting business. She has lost it completely. But what can I do? Nobody knows the condition of the True Lord. I am stuck with her for now ...

Manthara made up her mind. She looked at Druhyu and nodded.

Druhyu rocked back with shock, but controlled himself.

One thousand gold coins! That's more than this miserable palace maid will earn in ten years!

But he knew there was no point arguing. He quickly made a *hundi* in lieu of cash. The maid could encash it anywhere. After all, who would refuse a *credit document* with Manthara's seal?

'My Lady ...' whispered Druhyu.

Manthara leaned forward, pulled out her seal from the pouch tied to her *dhoti*, and pressed its impression on the document.

Druhyu handed the *hundi* to the maid, whose face could barely contain her ecstasy.

Druhyu quickly brought her down to earth. His cold eyes pinned on her, he whispered, 'Remember, if the information does not come on time or isn't true, we know where you live ...'

'I will not fail, sir,' said the maid.

As the maid turned to leave, Manthara said, 'I've been told that Prince Ram will soon be visiting Queen Kaushalya's wing of the palace to speak with Emperor Dashrath.'

'I will inform you about everything that is discussed, My Lady,' said the maid, bowing low.

Druhyu looked at Manthara and then the palace maid. He sighed inwardly. He knew that more money would be paid out soon.

— ॐ —

'*Didi*, just my section of the palace here is bigger than the entire Mithila palace,' said Urmila excitedly.

Urmila had carefully guided her maids in settling her belongings in her husband's chambers. Having put them to work, she had quickly rushed to meet Sita. Lakshman had been tempted to ask his wife to stay, but gave in to her desire to seek comfort in her sister's company. Her life had changed dramatically in a short span of time.

Sita smiled, as she patted her sister's hand. She still hadn't told Urmila that Ram and she would be leaving the palace shortly, to return only after fourteen years. Urmila would be left behind, without her beloved sister, here in this magnificent palace.

Why trouble her right now? Let her settle in first

'How are things with Lakshman?' asked Sita.

Urmila smiled dreamily. 'He is such a gentleman. He does not say no to anything that I ask for!'

Sita laughed, teasing her sister gently. 'That's exactly what you need. An indulgent husband, who treats you like a little princess!'

Urmila indicated her diminutive structure, straightened her back and retorted with mock seriousness, 'But I am a little princess!'

The sisters burst into peals of laughter. Sita embraced Urmila. 'I love you, my little princess.'

'I love you too, *Didi*,' said Urmila.

Just then, the doorman knocked and announced loudly, 'The Queen of Sapt Sindhu and Ayodhya, the Mother of the Crown Prince, Her Majesty Kaushalya. All rise in respect and love.'

Sita looked at Urmila, surprised. The sisters immediately came to their feet.

Kaushalya walked in briskly, followed by two maids bearing large golden bowls, the contents of which were covered with silk cloths.

Kaushalya looked at Sita and smiled politely, 'How are you, my child?'

'I am well, *Badi Maa*,' said Sita.

The sisters bent to touch Kaushalya's feet in respect. The Queen of Ayodhya blessed them both with a long life.

Kaushalya turned to Urmila with a warm smile. Sita noticed that it was warmer than the one she had received. This was a smile suffused with maternal love.

Sita smiled. Happy. *My little sister is safe here.*

'Urmila, my child,' said Kaushalya, 'I had gone to your chambers. I was told I would find you here.'

'Yes, *Maa*.'

'I believe you like black grapes.'

Urmila blinked in surprise. 'How did you know, *Maa*?'

Kaushalya laughed, with a conspiratorial look. 'I know everything!'

As Urmila laughed delicately, the queen pulled away the silk cloths with a flourish, to reveal two golden bowls filled to the brim with black grapes.

Urmila squealed in delight and clapped her hands. She opened her mouth. Sita was surprised. Urmila had always asked to be fed by their mother, Sunaina; but not once had she asked her sister.

Sita's eyes moistened in happiness. Her sister had found a mother once again.

Kaushalya picked a grape and dropped it into Urmila's open mouth.

'Mmm,' said Urmila, 'It is awesome, *Maa*!'

'And, grapes are good for your health too!' said Kaushalya. She looked at her elder daughter-in-law. 'Why don't you have some, Sita?'

'Of course, *Badi Maa*,' said Sita. 'Thank you.'

Chapter 26

A few days later, Sita sat in solitude in the royal garden.

It lay adjunct to the palace, within the compound walls. Laid out in the style of a botanical reserve, it was filled with flowering trees from not only the Sapt Sindhu but other great empires of the world. Its splendid diversity was also the source of its beauty, reflecting the composite character of the people of the Sapt Sindhu. Winding paths bordered what had once been a carefully laid out lush carpet of dense grass in geometric symmetry. Alas, like the main palace and the courts, the royal garden also had the appearance of diminishing grandeur and patchy upkeep. It was, literally, going to seed; a sorry reminder of Ayodhya's depleting resources.

But Sita was neither admiring the aching beauty nor mourning the slow deterioration that surrounded her.

Ram had gone to speak with Dashrath and his mother. He would insist that he be punished for the crime of using the *daivi astra* in Mithila without Vayuputra authorisation.

While that was Ram's conversation to handle, Sita was busy making plans to ensure that their lives would not be endangered in the jungle. She had asked Jatayu to meet her outside the city. She would ask him to shadow them during the exile, along with his team. She had no idea how the Malayaputras would react to her request. She knew that they were upset with her for refusing to be recognised publicly as the Vishnu. But she also knew that Jatayu was loyal to her and would not refuse.

'The revenue of a hundred villages for your thoughts, *Bhabhi* ...'

Sita turned to see Bharat standing behind her. She laughed. 'The revenue of a hundred villages from your wealthy Kosala or my poor Mithila?'

Bharat laughed and sat next to her.

'So, have you managed to talk some sense into *dada*?' asked Bharat. 'To make him drop his insistence on being exiled?'

'What makes you think that I don't agree with him?'

Bharat was surprised. 'Well, I thought ... Actually, I have done some background check on you, *Bhabhi* ... I was told that you are very ...'

'Pragmatic?' asked Sita, completing Bharat's statement.

He smiled. 'Yes ...'

'And, what makes you think that your brother's path is not pragmatic?'

Bharat was at a loss for words.

'I am not suggesting that your brother is being pragmatic consciously. Just that the path he has chosen — one of unbridled commitment to the law — may not *appear* pragmatic. But counter-intuitively, it may actually be the most pragmatic course for some sections of our society.'

'Really?' Bharat frowned. 'How so?'

'This is a time of vast change, Bharat. It can be exciting. Energising. But many are unsettled by change. The Sapt Sindhu society has foolishly decided to hate its Vaishyas. They see their businessmen as criminals and thieves. It is over-simplistic to assume that the only way a Vaishya makes money is through cheating and profiteering. It is also biased. Such radicalisation increases in times of change and uncertainty. The fact is that while a few businessmen may be crooks, most Vaishyas are hardworking, risk-taking, opportunity-seeking organisers. If they do not prosper, then society does not produce wealth. And if a society does not generate money, most people remain poor. Which leads to frustration and unrest.'

'I agree with ...'

'I am not finished.'

Bharat immediately folded his hands together into a *Namaste*. 'Sorry, *Bhabhi*.'

'People can adjust to poverty, if they have wisdom and knowledge. But even Brahmins command very little respect in India these days. They may not be resented like the Vaishyas, but it is true that the Brahmins, or even the path of knowledge, are not respected today. I know what people say about my knowledge-obsessed father, for instance.'

'No, I don't think ...'

'I'm still not finished,' said Sita, her eyes twinkling with amusement.

'Sorry!' Bharat surrendered, as he covered his mouth with his hand.

'As a result, people do not listen to the learned. They hate the Vaishyas and in the process, have ensured poverty for themselves. The people who are idealised the most today are the Kshatriyas, the warriors. "Battle-honour" is an end in itself! There's hatred for money, disdain for wisdom and love of violence. What can you expect in this atmosphere?'

Bharat remained silent.

'You can speak now,' said Sita.

Bharat removed the hand that covered his mouth and said, 'When you speak about the need to respect the Vaishya, Brahmin, or Kshatriya way of life, you obviously mean the characteristics and not the people born into that caste, right?'

Sita wrinkled her nose. 'Obviously. Do you really think I would support the evil birth-based caste system? Our present caste system must be destroyed ...'

'On that, I agree with you.'

'So, coming back to my question. In an atmosphere of hatred for money-makers, disdain for wisdom-givers, and love only for war and warriors, what would you expect?'

'Radicalisation. Especially among young men. Usually, they are the biggest fools.'

Sita laughed. 'They are not *all* foolish ...'

Bharat nodded. 'You're right, I suppose. I am a young man too!'

'So, you have a situation where young men, and frankly some women too, are radicalised. There is intelligence, but little wisdom. There is poverty. There is love of violence. They don't understand that the absence of balance in their society is at the root of their problems. They look for simplistic, quick solutions. And they hate anyone who doesn't think like them.'

'Yes.'

'Is it any surprise then that crime is so high in the Sapt Sindhu? Is it any surprise that there is so much crime against women? Women can be talented and competitive in the fields of knowledge, trading and labour. But when it comes to violence, the almighty has not blessed them with a natural advantage.'

'Yes.'

'These radicalised, disempowered, violence-loving youth,

looking for simplistic solutions, attack the weak. It makes them feel strong and powerful. They are especially vulnerable to the authoritarian message of the Masculine way of life, which can lead them astray. Thus, creating chaos in society.'

'And, you don't think *dada's* ideas are rooted in the Masculine way? Don't you think they're a little too simplistic? And, too top-down? Shouldn't the solution be the way of the Feminine? To allow freedom? To let people find balance on their own?'

'But Bharat, many are wary of the uncertainties of the Feminine way. They prefer the simple predictability of the Masculine way. Of following a uniform code without too much thought. Even if that code is made by others. Yes, Ram's obsession with the law is simplistic. Some may even call it authoritarian. But there is merit in it. He will give direction to those youth who need the certainties of the Masculine way of life. Radicalised young people can be misused by a demonic force in pursuit of endless violence and hatred. On the other hand, Ram's teachings can guide such people to a life of order, justice, and fairness. He can harness them for a greater good. I am not suggesting that your elder brother's path is for everyone. But he can provide leadership to those who seek order, certainty, compliance, and definite morals. To those who have a strong dislike of decadence and debauchery. He can save them from going down a path of hatred and violence and instead, build them into a force for the good of India.'

Bharat remained silent.

'Ram's true message can provide an answer, a solution, to the radicalisation that plagues so many young people today.'

Bharat leaned back. 'Wow ...'

'What's the matter?'

'I have argued with my brother all my life about his faith

in the Masculine way. I always thought that the Masculine way will inevitably lead to fanaticism and violence. But you have opened my mind in just one conversation.'

'Seriously, can you say that the Feminine way never degenerates? The only difference, Bharat, is that it deteriorates differently. The Masculine way is ordered, efficient and fair at its best, but fanatical and violent at its worst. The Feminine way is creative, passionate and caring at its best, but decadent and chaotic at its worst. No one way of life is better or worse. They both have their strengths and weaknesses.'

'Hmmm.'

'Freedom is good, but in moderation. Too much of it is a recipe for disaster. That's why the path I prefer is that of Balance. Balance between the Masculine and the Feminine.'

'I think differently.'

'Tell me.'

'I believe there is no such thing as too much freedom. For freedom has, within itself, the tools for self-correction.'

'Really?'

'Yes. In the Feminine way, when things get too debauched and decadent, many who are disgusted by it, use the same freedom available to them, to revolt and speak out loud. When society is made aware, and more importantly, is in agreement, reforms will begin. No problem remains hidden in a Feminine society for too long. But Masculine societies can remain in denial for ages because they simply do not have the freedom to question and confront their issues. The Masculine way is based on compliance and submission to the code, the law. The questioning spirit is killed; and with that, the ability to identify and solve their problems before they lead to chaos. Have you ever wondered why the Mahadevs, who had come to solve problems that nobody else could, usually had to fight whoever represented the Masculine force?'

Sita rocked back. She was startled into silence, as she considered what Bharat had said about the Mahadevs. *Oh yes ... He's right ...*

'Freedom is the ultimate answer. Despite all the uncertainties it creates, freedom allows regular readjustment. Which is why, very rarely does a problem with the Feminine way become so big that it needs a Mahadev to solve it. This magical solution is simply not available to the Masculine way. The first thing it suppresses is freedom. Everyone must comply ... Or, be kicked out.'

'You may have a point. But freedom without laws is chaos. I'm not sure ...'

Bharat interrupted his sister-in-law, 'I am telling you, *Bhabhi*. Freedom is the ultimate silver arrow; the answer to everything. It may appear chaotic and difficult to manage on the surface. I agree that laws can be flexibly used to ensure that there isn't *too much* chaos. But there is no problem that cannot ultimately be solved if you grant freedom to a sufficiently large number of argumentative and rebellious people. Which is why I think freedom is the most important attribute of life, *Bhabhi*.'

'More important than the law?'

'Yes. I believe there should be as few laws as possible; enough just to provide a framework within which human creativity can express itself in all its glory. Freedom is the natural way of life.'

Sita laughed softly. 'And what does your elder brother have to say about your views?'

Ram walked up to them from behind and placed his hands on his wife's shoulders. 'His elder brother thinks that Bharat is a dangerous influence!'

Ram had gone to his wing of the palace and had been told that his wife was in the royal gardens. He had found her deep in conversation with Bharat. They had not noticed him walk up to them.

Bharat burst out laughing as he rose to embrace his brother. '*Dada* …'

'Should I be thanking you for entertaining your *bhabhi* with your libertarian views?!'

Bharat smiled as he shrugged. 'At least I won't convert the citizens of Ayodhya into a bunch of bores!'

Ram laughed and said, tongue in cheek, 'That's good then!'

Bharat's expression instantly transformed and became sombre. 'Father is not going to let you go, *Dada*. Even you know that. You're not going anywhere.'

'Father doesn't have a choice. And neither do you. You will rule Ayodhya. And you will rule it well.'

'I will not ascend the throne this way,' said Bharat, shaking his head. 'No, I will not.'

Ram knew that there was nothing he could say that would ease Bharat's pain.

'*Dada*, why are you insisting on this?' asked Bharat.

'It's the law, Bharat,' said Ram. 'I fired a *daivi astra*.'

'The hell with the law, *Dada*! Do you actually think your leaving will be in the best interests of Ayodhya? Imagine what the two of us can achieve together; your emphasis on rules and mine on freedom and creativity. Do you think either you or I can be as effective alone?'

Ram shook his head. 'I'll be back in fourteen years, Bharat. Even you just conceded that rules have a significant place in a society. How can I convince others to follow the law if I don't do so myself? The law must apply equally and fairly to every single person. It is as simple as that.' Then Ram stared directly into Bharat's eyes. 'Even if it helps a heinous criminal escape death, the law should not be broken.'

Bharat stared right back, his expression inscrutable.

Sita sensed that the brothers were talking about a sensitive issue. Things were getting decidedly uncomfortable. She rose from the bench and said to Ram, 'You have a meeting with General Mrigasya.'

— ♃ —

Sita and her entourage were in the market. She didn't intend to buy anything. She had come out of the palace to give one of her guards the opportunity to slip away unnoticed. Had he left from the palace compound, his movements would have been tracked. But here, in the crowded marketplace, no one would miss one bodyguard from the large posse that guarded Sita.

From the corner of her eye, Sita saw him slip into a tiny lane that led out of the market. He had been ordered to arrange a meeting with Jatayu the following day.

Satisfied that her message would be delivered, Sita walked towards her palanquin to return to the palace. Her path was suddenly blocked by a grand palanquin that appeared out of nowhere. Covered with gold filigree, it was an ornate bronze litter with silk curtains covering the sides. It was obviously a very expensive and comfortable palanquin.

'Stop! Stop!' A feminine voice was heard from inside the curtained litter.

The bearers stopped immediately and placed the palanquin down. The strongest of the attendants walked to the entrance, drew aside the curtain and helped an old woman step out.

'*Namaste*, princess,' said Manthara, as she laboriously came to her feet. She folded her hands together and bowed her head with respect.

'*Namaste*, Lady Manthara,' said Sita, returning her greeting.

Sita had met the wealthy businesswoman the previous day. She had immediately felt sympathy for her. People did not speak kindly of Manthara behind her back. It did not seem right to Sita, especially keeping in mind that she had lost her beloved daughter, Roshni, in tragic circumstances.

One of Manthara's aides quickly placed a folded chair behind her, allowing her to sit. 'I am sorry, princess. I find it difficult to stand for too long.'

'No problem, Manthara*ji*,' said Sita. 'What brings you to the market?'

'I'm a businesswoman,' smiled Manthara. 'It's always wise to know what's happening in the market.'

Sita smiled and nodded.

'In fact, it's also wise to know what is happening everywhere else since the market is impacted by so many things.'

Sita groaned softly. She expected the usual question: Why was Ram insisting on being punished for the crime of firing a *daivi astra*?

'Manthara*ji*, I think it's best if we wait for …'

Manthara pulled Sita close and whispered, 'I've been told that the Emperor may choose to abdicate, making Ram the king. And that he may choose to undertake the banishment of fourteen years himself. Along with his wives.'

Sita had heard this too. She also knew that Ram would not allow it. But what troubled her was something else. *Where did Mantharaji hear this?*

Sita maintained a straight face. Something didn't feel right.

She noticed that Manthara's bodyguards were keeping other people in the market at bay. A chill ran down her spine.

This meeting wasn't an accident. It was planned.

Sita replied carefully, 'I have not heard this, Mantharaji.'

Manthara looked hard at Sita. After a few moments, she smiled, slightly. 'Really?'

Sita adopted nonchalance. 'Why would I lie?'

Manthara's smile broadened. 'I have heard interesting things about you, princess. That you are intelligent. That your husband confides in you. That he trusts you.'

'Oh, I am a nobody from a small city. I just happened to marry above myself and arrive in this big, bad metropolis where I don't understand much of what you people say. Why should my husband trust my advice?'

Manthara laughed. 'Big cities are complex. Here, often, the diffused light of the moon lends greater insight. Much is lost in the glare of the sun. Therefore, the wise have held that for real wisdom to rise, the sun must set.'

Is that a threat?

Sita feigned confusion.

Manthara continued, 'The city enjoys the moon and the night. The jungle always welcomes the sun.'

This is not about business. This is about something else.

'Yes, Mantharaji,' said Sita, pretending to be puzzled. 'Thank you for these words of wisdom.'

Manthara pulled Sita closer, staring directly into her eyes. 'Is Ram going to the jungle or not?'

'I don't know, Mantharaji,' said Sita, innocently. 'The Emperor will decide.'

Manthara narrowed her eyes till they were thin, malevolent slits. Then she released Sita and shook her head dismissively.

As if there was nothing more to be learnt here. 'Take care, princess.'

'You take care, Mantha*ji*.'

'Druhyu ...' said Manthara loudly.

Sita saw the right-hand man of Manthara shuffle up obsequiously. Though the look on his face was at odds with his manner.

Sita smiled innocently. *Something's not right. I need to find out more about Manthara.*

Chapter 27

Sita read the coded message quickly. It had come via Radhika. But the sender was someone else.

The message was terse, but clear: *I will speak to Guruji; it will be done.*

There was no name inscribed on the message. But Sita knew the sender.

She held the letter to a flame, letting it burn. She held on to it till it had reduced completely to ashes.

She smiled and whispered, 'Thank you, Hanu *bhaiya*.'

— ⟨⟩ —

Sita and Jatayu stood in the small clearing. It was their pre-determined meeting place in the jungle, an hour's ride from the city. Sita had made it in half that time. She had covered her face and body in a long *angvastram*, so that she wouldn't be identified. She had a lot to discuss with Jatayu. Not the least being her encounter with Manthara.

'Are you sure about this, great Vishnu?' asked Jatayu.

'Yes. I had initially thought that the city would be more dangerous for Ram. He has so many enemies here. But now I think the jungle may be where the true danger lies.'

'Then why not stay in the city?'

'Can't be done. My husband won't agree to it.'

'But ... Why not? Who cares about what others ...'

Sita interrupted Jatayu, 'Let me give you an insight into my husband's character. General Mrigasya, one of the most powerful men in Ayodhya, was willing to back Ram replacing Dashrath *babuji* as king. In fact, my father-in-law himself wants to abdicate in Ram's favour. But my husband refused. He said it's against the law.'

Jatayu shook his head and smiled. 'Your husband is a rare jewel among men.'

Sita smiled. 'That he is.'

'So, you think Manthara will ...'

'Yes. She is not interested in the game of thrones. She wants vengeance, especially against Ram for having followed the law; for not executing her daughter's juvenile rapist-murderer. It's personal.'

'Any idea what she is planning?'

'She will not do anything in Ayodhya. Assassinating a popular prince within the city is risky. I suspect she will try something in the jungle.'

'I have visited Ayodhya before. I know her and her cohort. I also know whom she depends on.'

'Druhyu?'

'Yes. I suspect he will be the one who will organise the assassination. I know whom he will try to hire. I can handle it.'

'I have a suspicion about Manthara and Druhyu. I suspect they are loyal to ...'

'Yes, great Vishnu,' interrupted Jatayu. 'Raavan is their true lord.'

Sita took a deep breath. Things were beginning to make sense.

'Do you want us to take care of Manthara as well?' asked Jatayu.

'No,' answered Sita. 'It's been difficult enough to stop Raavan from retaliating after what happened in Mithila. Manthara is his key person in Ayodhya, his main cash cow in the north. If we kill her, he may break his pact with the Malayaputras to not attack Mithila.'

'So … just Druhyu, then.'

Sita nodded.

'Let us meet tomorrow. I should know more by then.'

'Of course, Jatayu*ji,*' said Sita. 'Thank you. You are like a protective elder brother.'

'I am nothing but your devotee, great Vishnu.'

Sita smiled and folded her hands into a *Namaste.* 'Goodbye. Go with Lord Parshu Ram, my brother.'

'Go with Lord Rudra, my sister.'

Sita mounted her horse and rode away quickly. Jatayu picked up some dust from the ground where she had stood and brought it reverentially to his forehead. He whispered softly, *'Om Namo Bhagavate Vishnudevaya. Tasyai Sitadevyai namo namah.'*

He mounted his horse and rode away.

— ॐ —

Sita waited outside Vashishtha's private office. The guards had been surprised at the unannounced arrival of the wife of Prince Ram. They had asked her to wait since the *Raj Guru* of Ayodhya was in a meeting with a foreign visitor.

'I'll wait,' Sita had said.

The last few days had been action-packed. It had almost been decided by Dashrath that he would abdicate and install

Ram as king. Ram and Sita had decided that if that happened, Ram would abdicate in turn and banish himself, leaving Bharat to take over. Ideally, though, he didn't want to do that, as it would be a public repudiation of his father's orders. But it had not come to that.

On the day before the court ceremony to announce Emperor Dashrath's abdication, some dramatic developments had taken place. Queen Kaikeyi had lodged herself in the *kopa bhavan,* the *house of anger.* This was an institutionalised chamber created in royal palaces many centuries ago, once polygamy had become a common practice among the royalty. Having multiple wives, a king was naturally unable to spend enough time with all of them. A *kopa bhavan* was the assigned chamber a wife would go to if angry or upset with her husband. This would be a signal for the king that the queen needed redressal for a complaint. It was believed to be inauspicious for a husband to allow his wife to stay overnight in the *kopa bhavan.*

Dashrath had had no choice but to visit his aggrieved spouse. No one knew what had happened in the chamber, but the next day, Dashrath's announcement had been very different from what the rumours had suggested. Ram had been banished from the Sapt Sindhu for a period of fourteen years. Bharat had been named the crown prince in Ram's stead. Ram had publicly accepted the banishment with grace and humility, praising the wisdom of his father's decision. Sita and Ram were to leave for the jungle within a day.

Sita had little time left. She needed to tie up all the loops to ensure their security in the forest.

Vashishtha had not met Sita at all, since their arrival. Was the *Raj Guru* of Ayodhya avoiding her? Or had an opportunity not presented itself thus far? Anyway, she wanted to speak to him before she left.

She looked up as she saw a man emerge from Vashishtha's office. He was a tall, unusually fair-skinned man. He wore a white *dhoti* and an *angvastram*. But one could tell by the deliberate way he walked that he was distinctly uncomfortable in the *dhoti*. Perhaps, it wasn't his normal attire. His most distinguishing features were his hooked nose, beaded full beard and drooping moustache. His wizened face and large limpid eyes were an image of wisdom and calm.

He's a Parihan. Probably a Vayuputra.

The Parihan walked towards the main door, not noticing Sita and her maids in the sitting area.

'My Lady,' a guard came up to Sita, his head bowed in respect. 'My sincere apologies for the delay.'

Sita smiled. 'No, no. You were only doing your job. As you should.'

She stood up. Guided by the guard, she walked into Vashishtha's office.

— ᚱᚢᚱ —

'It must be done outside the boundaries of the Sapt Sindhu,' said Druhyu.

He was in a small clearing in the forest, having ridden east from the boundaries of the Grand Canal for around three hours. He waited for a response. There was none.

The assassin was seated in the distance, hidden by dark shadows. His *angvastram* was pulled close around his face and torso. He was sharpening his knife on a smooth stone.

Druhyu hated this part of his job. He had done it a few times, but there was something about Mara that spooked him.

'The Emperor has announced the banishment of Prince

Ram. His wife and he will be leaving tomorrow. You will have to track them till they are out of the empire.'

Mara did not respond. He kept sharpening his knife.

Druhyu held his breath in irritation. *How sharp does he need that damned knife to be!*

He placed one large bag of gold coins on the tree stump near him. Then he reached into his pouch and took out a *hundi*. It was stamped with a secret seal recognised only by one specific moneylender in Takshasheela, a city far in the northwestern corners of India.

'One thousand gold coins in cash,' said Druhyu, 'and a *hundi* for fifty thousand gold coins to be picked up at the usual place.'

Mara looked up. Then, he felt the tip and edges of his blade. He seemed satisfied. He got up and started walking towards Druhyu.

'Hey!' Druhyu gasped in panic as he turned quickly and ran back some distance. 'Don't show me your face. I'm not going to see your face.'

Druhyu knew no living person had seen Mara's face. He didn't want to risk his life.

Mara stopped at the tree stump, picked up the bag of gold coins and judged its weight. He set it down and picked up the *hundi*. He didn't open the document, but slipped it carefully into the pouch tied to his waistband.

Then, Mara looked at Druhyu. 'It doesn't matter now.'

It took a few moments for Druhyu to realise the import of what had been said. He shrieked in panic and ran towards his horse. But Mara, lean and fit, could move faster than Druhyu. Silent as a panther, fast as a cheetah. He was upon Druhyu in almost no time. He caught hold of Druhyu from the back, holding his neck in his left arm, pinioning him against his own body. As Druhyu struggled in terror, Mara hit him hard on a pressure point at the back of his neck with the knife hilt.

Druhyu was immediately paralysed from the neck down. Mara let the limp body slip slowly to the ground. Then he bent over Druhyu and asked, 'Who else has been contracted?'

'I can't feel anything!' screamed Druhyu in shock. 'I can't feel anything!'

Mara slapped Druhyu hard. 'You are only paralysed from the neck down. I can release the pressure point. But first, answer ...'

'I can't feel anything. Oh Lord Indra! I can't ...'

Mara slapped Druhyu hard, again.

'Answer me quickly and I will help you. Don't waste my time.'

Druhyu looked at Mara. His *angvastram* was tied across his face. Only the assassin's eyes were visible.

Druhyu hadn't seen his face. Maybe he could still come out of this alive.

'Please don't kill me ...' sobbed Druhyu, a flood of tears streaming down his face.

'Answer my question. Has anyone else been contracted? Is there any other assassin?'

'Nobody but you ... Nobody but you ... Please ... by the great Lord Indra ... Let me go ... please.'

'Is there anybody besides you who can find an assassin like me for Lady Manthara?'

'No. Only me. And you can keep the money. I will tell that old witch that you have taken the contract. You don't have to kill anyone. How will she know? She will probably be dead before Prince Ram returns ... Please ... Let me ...'

Druhyu stopped talking as Mara removed the *angvastram*

that veiled his face. Sheer terror gripped Druhyu's heart. He had seen Mara's face. He knew what would follow.

Mara smiled. 'Don't worry. You won't feel a thing.'

The assassin got down to work. Druhyu's body had to be left there. It had to be discovered by Manthara and the others in her employ. It was supposed to send a message.

— ⚔ —

Sita was sitting with her younger sister, Urmila, who had been crying almost incessantly.

Despite all that had been happening for the last few days, Sita had found time to come and meet Urmila repeatedly. Lakshman had insisted on coming along with Ram and Sita for the fourteen-year banishment. Initially, Lakshman had thought Urmila could also come along. He had later realised that the delicate Urmila would not be able to survive the rigours of the jungle. It was going to be a tough fourteen years. The forests could be survived only if you were sturdy and hard. Not if you were delicate and urbane. It had been tough for Lakshman, but he had spoken to Urmila and she had, reluctantly, agreed to not come along with the three of them. Though she was unhappy about it.

Sita too was constrained to admit that Lakshman was right. And she had come repeatedly to meet Urmila to help her younger sister make peace with the decision.

'First *maa* left me,' sobbed Urmila, 'Now you and Lakshman are also leaving me. What am I supposed to do?'

Sita held her sister warmly, 'Urmila, if you want to come, I will push for it. But before I do so, I need you to realise what jungle life means. We won't even have a proper shelter over our heads. We'll live off the land, including eating meat; and I know how you despise that. These are minor things and I know you will adapt to what needs to be done. But there is also constant danger in the jungle. Most of the coastline south of the Narmada River is in Raavan's control. So, we can't go there unless we intend to get tortured to death.'

Urmila cut in, 'Don't say such things, *Didi*.'

'We cannot go to the coast. So, we will have to remain deep inland. Usually, within the forests of *Dandakaranya*. The Almighty alone knows what dangers await us there. We will have to sleep lightly every night, with our weapons next to us, in case any wild animals attack. Night is their time for hunting. There are so many poisonous fruits and trees; we could die just by eating the wrong thing. I'm sure there will be other dangers we are not even aware of. All of us will need our wits about us at all times to survive. And in the midst of all this, if something were to happen to you, how would I face *maa* when I leave this mortal body? She had charged me with protecting you ... And, you are safe here ...'

Urmila kept sniffing, holding on to Sita.

'Did Kaushalya *maa* come today?'

Urmila looked up, smiling wanly through her tears. 'She is so wonderful. I feel like our *maa* has returned. I feel safe with her.'

Sita held Urmila tight again. 'Bharat is a good man. So is Shatrughan. They will help Kaushalya *maa*. But they have many powerful enemies, some even more powerful than the king. You need to be here and support Kaushalya *maa*.'

Urmila nodded. 'Yes, Lakshman told me the same thing.'

'Life is not only about what we want, but also about what we must do. We don't just have rights. We also have duties.'

'Yes, *Didi*,' said Urmila. 'I understand. But that doesn't mean it doesn't hurt.'

'I know, my little princess,' said Sita, holding Urmila tight, patting her back. 'I know …'

— द्ऊ —

Only a few hours were left for Ram, Sita, and Lakshman to leave for the jungle. They had changed into the garb of hermits, made from rough cotton and bark.

Sita had come to meet Guru Vashishtha.

'I've been thinking since our meeting yesterday, Sita,' said Vashishtha. 'I regret that we didn't meet earlier. Many of the issues that arose could have been avoided.'

'Everything has its own time and place, Guru*ji*.'

Vashishtha gave Sita a large pouch. 'As you had requested. I am sure the Malayaputras will also get you some of this. But you are right; it's good to have back-up.'

Sita opened the pouch and examined the white powder. 'This is much finer than the usual *Somras* powder I have seen.'

'Yes, it's made from the process I have developed.'

Sita smelt the powder and grinned. 'Hmmm … it becomes finer and smells even worse.'

Vashishtha laughed softly. 'But it's just as effective.'

Sita smiled and put the pouch in the canvas bag that she had slung around her shoulder. 'I am sure you have heard what Bharat has done.'

A tearful Bharat had come to Ram's chambers and taken his brother's royal slippers. If and when the time came for Bharat to ascend to kingship, he would place Ram's slippers on the throne. With this one gesture, Bharat had effectively declared that Ram would be the king of Ayodhya and he, Bharat, would function as a mere caretaker in his elder brother's absence.

This afforded a powerful shield of protection to Ram from assassination attempts. Any attempts to murder the future king of Ayodhya would invite the wrath of the Empire, as mandated by the treaties between the various kingdoms under the alliance. Added to the cold reality of treaty obligations was the superstition that it was bad karma to kill kings and crown princes, except in battle or open combat. While this afforded powerful protection to Ram, it would severely undercut Bharat's own authority and power.

Vashishtha nodded. 'Bharat is a noble soul.'

'All four of the brothers are good people. More importantly, they love each other. And this, despite being born in a very dysfunctional family and difficult times. I guess credit must be given where credit is due.'

Vashishtha knew this was a compliment to him, the *guru* of the four Ayodhya princes. He smiled politely and accepted the praise with grace.

Sita folded her hands together in respect and said, 'I've thought about it. I agree with your instructions, Guru*ji*. I will wait for the right time. I'll tell Ram only when I think we are both ready.'

'Ram is special in so many ways. But his strength, his obsession with the law, can also be his weakness. Help him find balance. Then, both of you will be the partners that India needs.'

'I have my weaknesses too, Guru*ji*. And he can balance me. There are so many situations in which he is much better than I am. That's why I admire him.'

'And, he admires you. It is a true partnership.'

Sita hesitated slightly before saying, 'I must ask you something.'

'Of course.'

'I guess you must also have been a Malayaputra once ... Why did you leave?'

Vashishtha began to laugh. 'Hanuman was right. You are very smart. Scarily smart.'

Sita laughed along. 'But you haven't answered my question, Guru*ji*.'

'Leave the subject of Vishwamitra and me aside. Please. It's too painful.'

Sita immediately became serious. 'I don't wish to cause you any pain, Guru*ji*.'

Vashishtha smiled. 'Thank you.'

'I must go, Guru*ji*.'

'Yes. It's time.'

'Before I go, I must say this. I mean it from the bottom of my heart, Guru*ji*. You are as great a guru as the one who taught me.'

'And I mean it from the bottom of my heart, Sita. You are as great a Vishnu as the one I taught.'

Sita bent and touched Vashishtha's feet.

Vashishtha placed his hands on Sita's head and said, 'May you have the greatest blessing of all: May you be of service to our great motherland, India.'

'Salutations, great *Rishi*.'

'Salutations, great Vishnu.'

Chapter 28

Eleven months had passed since Ram, Sita, and Lakshman had left Ayodhya on their fourteen-year exile in the forest. And a lot had happened.

Dashrath had passed away in Ayodhya. The three of them had received this heartbreaking news while still in the Sapt Sindhu. Sita knew it had hurt Ram that he had not been able to perform the duties of an eldest son and conduct the funeral rites of his father. For most of his life, Ram had had almost no relationship with his father. Most Ayodhyans, including Dashrath, had blamed the 'bad fate' of Ram's birth for the disastrous loss to Raavan at the Battle of Karachapa. It was only over the last few years that Ram and Dashrath had finally begun building a bond. But exile and death had forced them apart again. Returning to Ayodhya was not possible as that would break Lord Rudra's law, but Ram had performed a *yagna* in the forest for the journey his father's soul had undertaken.

Bharat had remained true to his word and placed Ram's slippers on the throne of Ayodhya. He had begun to govern the empire as his brother's regent. It could be said that Ram had been appointed emperor *in absentia*. An unorthodox move. But Bharat's liberal and decentralising style of governance had made the decision palatable to the kingdoms within the Sapt Sindhu.

Ram, Lakshman, and Sita had travelled south. Primarily walking by the banks of rivers, they moved inland only when necessary. They had finally crossed the borders of the Sapt Sindhu near the kingdom of South Kosala, ruled by Ram's maternal grandfather. Lakshman and Sita had suggested visiting South Kosala and resting there for a few months. But Ram believed that it was against the spirit of the punishment they were serving to exploit the comforts of the palace of royal relatives.

They had skirted South Kosala and travelled deeper south-west, approaching the forest lands of *Dandakaranya*. Lakshman and Ram had expressed some concern about travelling south of the Narmada. Lord Manu had banned the Sapt Sindhuans from crossing the Narmada to the South. If they did cross, they were not to return. Or, so it had been decreed. But Sita had pointed out that Indians had, for millennia, found creative ways to travel to the south of the Narmada without actually 'crossing' the river. She suggested that they follow the letter of Lord Manu's law, but not the spirit.

While Ram was uncomfortable with this, Sita had managed to prevail. Living close to the coast was dangerous; Raavan controlled the western and eastern coastlines of the subcontinent. The safest place was deep inland, within the *Dandakaranya*, even if that meant being south of the Narmada. They had travelled in a southwesterly direction, so that the source of the west-flowing Narmada remained to their north. They had, thus, reached land that was geographically to the south of the Narmada without technically 'crossing' the river. They were now at the outskirts of a very large village, almost a small town.

'What is this town called, Captain Jatayu?' asked Ram, turning to the Malayaputra. 'Do you know these people?'

Jatayu and fifteen of his soldiers had been trailing Ram, Sita, and Lakshman, ensuring their safety. As instructed by Sita, they had remained hidden. Ram and Lakshman did not know of their presence for a long time. However, despite their best efforts to stay hidden, Ram had begun to suspect that someone was shadowing them. Sita had not been sure how Ram would react to her seeking protection from some Malayaputras. So she had not told Ram about her decision to ask Jatayu to act as a bodyguard for them. However, as they crossed the borders of the Sapt Sindhu, the risks of assassination attempts had increased. Sita had finally been forced to introduce Jatayu to Ram. Trusting Sita, Ram had accepted the Malayaputra and his fifteen soldiers as members of his team. Together they were one short of twenty now; more defendable than a group of just three. Ram understood this.

'It's called Indrapur, Prince Ram,' said Jatayu. 'It is the biggest town in the area. I know Chief Shaktivel, its leader. I'm sure he will not mind our presence. It's a festive season for them.'

'Festivities are always good!' said Lakshman, laughing jovially.

Ram said to Jatayu, 'Do they celebrate *Uttarayan* as well?'

The *Uttarayan* marked the beginning of the *northward movement* of the sun across the horizon. This day marked the farthest that the nurturer of the world, the sun, moved away from those in the northern hemisphere. It would now begin its six-month journey back to the north. It was believed to be that part of the year which marked nature's renewal. The death of the old. The birth of the new. It was, therefore, celebrated across practically all of the Indian subcontinent.

Jatayu frowned. 'Of course they do, Prince Ram. Which Indian does not celebrate the *Uttarayan*? We are all aligned to the Sun God!'

'That we are,' said Sita. *'Om Suryaya Namah.'*

Everyone repeated the ancient chant, bowing to the Sun God. *'Om Suryaya Namah.'*

'Perhaps, we can participate in their festivities,' said Sita.

Jatayu smiled. 'The Indrapurans are a martial, aggressive people and their celebrations can be a little rough.'

'Rough?' asked Ram.

'Let's just say you need bulls among men to be able to participate.'

'Really? What's this celebration called?'

'It's called *Jallikattu.'*

— ᚴᚱ —

'By the great Lord Rudra,' whispered Ram. 'This sounds similar to our *Vrishbandhan* festival ... But very few play this game in the Sapt Sindhu anymore.'

Ram, Sita, Lakshman, Jatayu, and the bodyguards had just entered Indrapur. They had gone straight to the ground next to the town lake. It had been fenced in and prepared for the *Jallikattu* competition the next day. Crowds were milling around the fence, taking in the sights and sounds. Nobody was allowed to cross the fence into the ground. The bulls would be led there soon to acclimatise them for the competition the next day.

Jatayu had just explained the game of *Jallikattu* to them. It was, in its essence, a very simple game. The name literally meant a tied bag of coins. In this case, gold coins. The contestant had to yank this bag to be declared a winner. Simple? Not quite! The challenge lay in the place this bag of coins was tied. It was tied to the horns of a bull. Not any ordinary bull, mind you. It was a bull especially bred to be aggressive, strong and belligerent.

'Yes, it is similar to *Vrishbandhan, embracing the bull*,' explained Jatayu. 'The game itself has been around for a long time, as you know. In fact, some say that it comes down from our Dwarka and Sangamtamil ancestors.'

'Interesting,' said Sita. 'I didn't know it was so ancient.'

Many bulls, which would participate in the *Jallikattu*, were specially bred in the surrounding villages and within Indrapur itself. The owners took pride in finding the best bulls to breed with the local cows. And, they took even more pride in feeding, training and nurturing the beasts to become fierce fighters.

'There are lands far to the east, outside India's borders,' said Jatayu, 'where you find bull-fighting competitions as well. But in their case, the dice is loaded against the bulls. Those people keep the bulls hungry for a few days before the contest, to weaken them. Before the main bull-fighter gets into the ring, his team further weakens the beast considerably. They do this by making the poor bull run a long distance and stabbing it multiple times with long spears and blades. And despite weakening the bull so much, the bull-fighter still carries a weapon to fight the beast, and ultimately kill it.'

'Cowards,' said Lakshman. 'There is no *kshatriyahood* in fighting that way.'

'Exactly,' said Jatayu. 'In fact, even in the rare case that a bull survives that competition, it is never brought back into the arena again because it would have learnt how to fight. And that would tilt the scales in its favour instead of the bull-fighter. So, they always bring in a new, inexperienced bull.'

'And, of course, this is not done in *Jallikattu* ...' said Ram.

'Not at all. Here, the bull is well fed and kept strong and

healthy, all the way. Nobody is allowed to spear or weaken it. Experienced bulls, which have performed well in previous competitions, are allowed to participate as well.'

'That's the way to do it,' said Lakshman. 'That will make it a fair fight.'

'It gets even fairer,' continued Jatayu. 'None of the men competing against the bull are allowed to carry any weapons. Not even small knives. They only use their bare hands.'

Lakshman whistled softly. 'That takes real courage.'

'Yes, it does. In that other bull-fighting competition I told you about, the one outside India, the bulls almost always die and the men rarely suffer serious injury, let alone die. But in *Jallikattu*, the bulls never die. It's the men who risk serious injury, even death.'

A soft, childish voice was heard. 'That's the way real men fight.'

Ram, Sita, Lakshman, and Jatayu turned almost in unison. A small child, perhaps six or seven years of age, stood before them. He had fair skin and small animated eyes. For his young age, he was extraordinarily hairy. His chest was puffed with pride. His arms akimbo as he surveyed the ground beyond the wooden fence.

He's probably a Vaanar.

Sita went down on her knees and said, 'Are you participating in the competition tomorrow, young man?'

The child's body visibly deflated. His eyes downcast, he said, 'I wanted to. But they say I cannot. Children are not allowed. By the great Lord Rudra, if I could compete I am sure I would defeat everyone.'

Sita smiled broadly. 'I'm sure you would. What's your name, son?'

'My name is Angad.'

'A-N-G-A-D!'

A loud booming voice was heard from a distance.

Angad turned around rapidly. Fear in his eyes. 'My father's coming... I gotta go ...'

'Wait ...' said Sita, stretching her hand out.

But Angad wriggled out and ran away quickly.

Sita rose up and turned towards Jatayu. 'The name rang a bell, right?'

Jatayu nodded. 'I didn't recognise the face. But I know the name. That is Prince Angad. The son of King Vali of Kishkindha.'

Ram frowned. 'That kingdom is deep in the south of *Dandakaranya*, right? Isn't it aligned to ...'

Ram was interrupted by another booming voice. 'I'll be damned!'

The crowd made way as the chief of Indrapur, Shaktivel, walked up to them. His voice aggressive. 'You come to my town and nobody informs me?'

Shaktivel was a massive man. Swarthy. Tall. Muscled like an *auroch* bull, with a large belly, his arms and legs were like the trunks of a small tree. His most striking feature, however, was his extra-large moustache, which extended grandly down his cheeks. Despite his obvious strength, he was also getting on in age, as evidenced clearly by the many white hairs in his moustache and on his head. And, the wrinkles on his forehead.

Jatayu spoke calmly, 'We've just arrived, Shaktivel. No need to lose your temper.'

To everyone present, Shaktivel's eyes conveyed immense anger. Suddenly, he burst into loud laughter. 'Jata, you stupid bugger! Come into my arms!'

Jatayu laughed as he embraced Shaktivel. 'You will always be a ridiculous oaf, Shakti!'

Sita turned to Ram and arched an eyebrow. Amused at seeing two males express love for each other through expletives and curses. Ram smiled and shrugged his shoulders.

The crowds around began cheering loudly as the two friends held each other in a long and warm embrace. Clearly, the relationship meant a lot to them. Equally clearly, they were more brothers than friends. Finally, Shaktivel and Jatayu stepped back, still holding each other's hands.

'Who are your guests?' asked Shaktivel. 'Because they are my guests now!'

Jatayu smiled and held his friend's shoulder, as he said, 'Prince Ram, Princess Sita, and Prince Lakshman.'

Shaktivel's eyes suddenly widened. He folded his hands together into a *Namaste*. 'Wow ... the royal family of Ayodhya itself. It is my honour. You must spend the night in my palace. And, of course, come and see the *Jallikattu* tomorrow.'

Ram politely returned Shaktivel's *Namaste*. 'Thank you for your hospitality. But it's not correct for us to stay in your palace. We will stay in the forest close by. But we will certainly come for the competition tomorrow.'

Shaktivel had heard of Ram's punishment, so he didn't press the matter. 'You could at least give me the pleasure of having dinner with you.'

Ram hesitated.

'Nothing fashionable at my palace. Just a simple meal together in the forest.'

Ram smiled. 'That would be welcome.'

— ᚲᚷ —

'Look at that one,' whispered Lakshman to Sita and Ram.

It was just after noon the next day. Massive crowds had gathered at the lake-side ground, where the contest between man and beast was about to take place. The ground had a small entry on the eastern side, from where bulls would be led in, one by one. They had been trained to make a run for the exit at the western end, a good five hundred metres away. The men, essentially, had that distance to try and grab hold of the bull and pull out the bag of coins. If the contestant won, he would keep the bag of gold coins. More importantly, he would be called a *Vrishank*; a *bull warrior!* Of course, if any bull reached the western gate and escaped, without losing its bag, the owner of the bull would be declared winner. Needless to say, he would keep the bag of coins.

There were various breeds of bulls that were used in the *Jallikattu* competitions. Among the most popular was a type of zebu bulls that were specifically cross-bred for aggression, strength, and speed. They were extremely agile and could turn around completely at the same spot in a split second. More importantly, they also had a very pronounced hump; this was a requirement for any bull competing in the *Jallikattu*. Some believed that the humps were essentially fat deposits. They couldn't be more wrong. These humps were an enlargement of the *rhomboideus* muscle in the shoulder and back. The size of the hump, thus, was a marker of the quality of the bull. And, judging by the size of the humps on these bulls, they were, clearly, fierce competitors.

In keeping with tradition, proud owners were parading the bulls in the ground. This was so that human contestants could inspect the beasts. As tradition also dictated, the owners, one by one, began to brag about the strength and speed of their bulls; their genealogy, the diet they were fed, the training they had received, even the number of people they had gored! The greater the monstrosity of the bull, the louder and lustier the cheers of the crowd. And as the owner stood with his bull, many from the crowd would throw their *angvastrams* into the ring to signify their intention to compete with that beast.

But they all fell silent as a new bull was led in.

'By the great Lord Rudra …' whispered Lakshman, in awe.

Sita held Ram's hand. 'Which poor sod is going to grab the coins from that bull's horns?'

The owner of the bull was aware of the impact of the mere presence of his beast. Sometimes, silence speaks louder than words. He didn't say anything; nothing about its heredity, its awesome food habits, or fearsome training. He simply looked at the crowd, arrogance dripping from every pore of his body. In fact, he didn't expect any contestant to even try to compete against his bull.

The bull was massive, larger than all the others that had been paraded so far. The owner didn't clarify, but it seemed like a cross-breed between a wild gaur and the faster sub-breed of the domesticated zebu. Clearly though, the gaur genes had dominated in the making of this beast. It was gigantic, standing over seven feet tall at the shoulders with a length of nearly ten feet. It must have weighed in at one thousand five hundred kilograms. And practically all that one could see rippling under its skin was pure hard muscle. Its two horns were curved upwards, making a hollow cup on the upper part of the head, like a typical gaur bull. Zebu genes had prevailed in the make of the beast's skin. It was whitish grey and not dark brown like gaur skins usually are. Perhaps the only other place where the zebu genes had won was the hump. Normally, a gaur has an elongated ridge on its back; it's flat and long. But this bull had a prominent and very large hump on its upper shoulders and back. This was very, very important. For without that hump, this beastly bull would have been disqualified from the *Jallikattu*.

If a competitor managed to grab hold of the hump of a bull, his main task was to hold on tight, even as the bull bucked aggressively, trying to shake the human off. Through the tussle, the man had to somehow hold on; and if he held on long enough and pulled tight, the bull would finally slow down and the man could grab the bag.

The owner suddenly spoke. Loudly. Disconcertingly, considering the demonic animal he led, the voice of the man was soft and feminine. 'Some of you may think this bull is all about size. But speed matters as well!'

The owner let go of the rope and whistled softly. The bull charged out in a flash. Its speed blinding. It was faster than any other bull on this day.

Lakshman stared, awestruck. *Gaurs are not meant to be this fast!*

The bull turned rapidly in its spot, displaying its fearsome agility. As if that wasn't enough, it suddenly started bucking aggressively, and charging towards the fence. The crowd fell back in terror. Its dominance established, the bull sauntered back to its owner, lowered its head and snorted aggressively at the crowd.

Magnificent

Loud and spontaneous applause filled the air.

'Looks like the hump and skin colour are not the only things it inherited from its zebu ancestor,' whispered Sita.

'Yes, it has inherited its speed as well,' said Lakshman. 'With that massive size and speed … It's almost like me!'

Sita looked at Lakshman with a smile. It disappeared as she saw the look on her brother-in-law's face.

'Don't ...' whispered Sita.

'What a beast,' said Lakshman, admiringly. 'It will be a worthy competitor.'

Ram placed his hand on his brother's shoulder, holding him back. But before Lakshman could do anything, a loud voice was heard. 'I will compete with that bull!'

Everyone's eyes turned towards a violet-coloured, obviously expensive *angvastram* flying into the ring. Beyond the wooden fence stood a fair, ridiculously muscular and very hairy man of medium height. He wore a simple cream-coloured *dhoti* with one end of it sticking out like a tail. The clothes may have been simple, but the bearing was regal.

'That's Vali,' said Jatayu. 'The King of Kishkindha.'

— ᷍ᚷ —

Vali stood close to the barricaded entrance. The gaur-zebu bull was about to be let loose. It was a covered gate and the bull couldn't see who or what was waiting on the other side. Three bulls had already run. Two had been baited and their gold coins grabbed. But one bull had escaped with its package. It was a rapid game. Individual races rarely lasted more than a minute. There were at least a hundred more bulls to run. But everyone knew that this was the match to watch.

The priest of the local temple bellowed out loud. 'May the *Vrishank* above all *Vrishanks*, Lord Rudra, bless the man and the beast!'

This was the standard announcement before any *Jallikattu* match in Indrapur. And as usual, it was followed by the loud and reverberating sound of a conch shell.

After a moment's silence, the loud clanking of metal gates was heard.

'*Jai Shri Rudra!*' roared the crowd.

From the dark interiors of the covered gate, the beast emerged. Usually, bulls charged out, thundering past the press of humans who tried to lunge from the sides and grab the hump of the animal.

Getting in front of the bull was dangerous for it could gore you with its horns. Being at the back was equally dangerous for it could kick outwards with its formidable hind legs. Its side was the best place to be. Which is why, bulls were trained to dash across, giving men less time to try and grab from the two sides.

But this gaur-zebu bull simply sauntered out. Supremely sure of its abilities. Vali, who was waiting beside the gate, hidden from view, leapt up as soon as the bull emerged. Considering Vali was nearly one-and-a-half feet shorter than the bull, it was a tribute to his supreme physical fitness that he managed to get his arms around the bull's massive hump as he landed. The bull was startled. Someone had dared to hold its hump. It started bucking wildly. Bellowing loudly. Banging its hooves hard on the ground. Suddenly, showing awe-inspiring dexterity, it whirled almost a complete circle with monstrous speed. Vali lost his grip. He was flung away.

The bull suddenly calmed down. It stared at the prone Vali, snorted imperiously and began walking away. Slowly. Towards the exit. Staring into the crowds, nonchalantly.

Someone from the crowd shouted an encouragement to Vali. 'Come on! Get up!'

The bull looked at the crowd and stopped. It then turned towards the lake, presenting its backside to the crowd. It slowly raised its tail and urinated. Then, maintaining its blasé demeanour, it started walking again. Towards the exit. Just as leisurely.

Lakshman laughed softly, as he shook his head. 'Forget about baiting this bull. The bull is, in fact, baiting us!'

Ram tapped Lakshman on his shoulder. 'Look at Vali. He's getting up.'

Vali banged his fists hard on his chest and sprinted ahead. Light on his feet. His long hair flying in the wind. He came up from behind the bull.

'This man is a maniac!' said Lakshman, worried but animated. 'That bull can crush his chest with a single blow from its hind legs!'

As Vali came close to the bull, he jumped up, soaring high. He landed on top of the bull. The surprised beast, which hadn't seen Vali come up from behind, bellowed loudly and went up on its hind legs. Trying to shake the king off. But Vali held on firmly. Screaming at the top of his lungs!

The outraged bull roared. Louder than the man who clung to it. Letting its front legs fall to the ground, it lowered its head and bucked wildly. But Vali held on, screaming all the time.

The bull suddenly leapt into the air and shook its body. It still could not get rid of the man holding on desperately to its hump.

The entire crowd had fallen silent. In absolute awe. They had never seen a *Jallikattu* match last so long. The only sounds were the loud bellows of the bull and the roars of Vali.

The bull leapt up again and readied to fall to its side. Its weight would have crushed Vali to death. He quickly let go of the bull. But not fast enough.

The bull landed on its side. Vali escaped the bulk, but its front legs lashed Vali's left arm. Lakshman heard the bone crack from where he stood. To his admiration, Vali did not scream in pain. The bull was up on its feet in no time and trotted away.

From a distance, it looked at Vali. Anger blazing in its eyes. But it kept its distance.

'The bull is angry,' whispered Ram. 'I guess it has never had a human go so far.'

'Stay down,' said Sita, almost willing Vali to remain on the ground.

Lakshman stared at Vali silently.

If a man remained curled up on the ground, unmoving like a stone, a bull normally would not charge. But if he stood up …

'Fool!' hissed Sita, as she saw Vali rising once again, his bloodied and shattered left arm dangling uselessly by his side. 'Stay down!'

Lakshman's mouth fell open in awe. *What a man!*

The bull too seemed shocked and enraged that the man had risen once again. It snorted and shook its head.

Vali banged his chest repeatedly with his right fist and roared loudly, 'Vali! Vali!'

The crowd too began shouting.

'Vali!'

'Vali!'

The bull bellowed loudly, and banged its front hooves hard on the ground. A warning had been given.

Vali banged his chest again, his shattered left arm swinging uselessly by his side. 'Vali!'

The bull came up on its hind legs and bellowed once again. Much louder this time. Almost deafeningly loud.

And then, the beast charged.

Lakshman jumped over the fence, racing towards the bull at the same time.

'Lakshman!' screamed Ram, as he and Sita also leapt over and sprinted after Lakshman.

Lakshman ran diagonally, bisecting the path between Vali and the animal. Luckily for the prince of Ayodhya, the bull did not see this new threat.

Lakshman was much taller than Vali. He was also far more bulky and muscular. But even Lakshman knew that brute strength was useless against this gargantuan beast. He knew he would have only one chance. The bull's horns were unlike the pure zebu breed; pure zebu bulls had straight, sharp horns which worked like blunt knives while goring. The gaur-zebu bull's horns, on the other hand, were curved upwards, making a hollow in the upper part of the head.

The bull was focused on Vali. It had lowered its head and was thundering towards him. It didn't notice Lakshman come up suddenly from the side. Lakshman leapt forward, timing his jump to perfection, pulling his legs up. As he soared above the bull's head, he quickly reached out with his hand and yanked the bag off the horns. For that split second, the bull kept charging forward and Lakshman's feet came in line with the bull's head. He pushed out with his legs. Hard. Effectively using the bull's head as leverage, he bounced away. Lakshman's weight and size were enough to push the head of the bull down. As he bounded away, rolling on the field, the bull's head banged into the hard ground and it tripped, falling flat on its face.

Ram and Sita used the distraction to quickly pick up Vali and sprint towards the fence.

'Leave me!' screamed Vali, struggling against the two. 'Leave me!'

Vali's struggle led to more blood spilling out of his shattered arm. It increased the pain dramatically. But Ram and Sita did not stop.

Meanwhile, the bull quickly rose to its feet and bellowed

loudly. Lakshman raised his hand, showing the bag he held.

The bull should have charged. But it had been trained well. As soon as it saw the bag of coins, it lowered its head and snorted. It looked behind at its owner, who was standing close to the exit. The owner smiled and shrugged, mouthing the words, 'You win some. You lose some.'

The bull looked back at Lakshman, snorted, and lowered its head again. Almost as if it was accepting defeat gracefully. Lakshman pulled his hands together into a *Namaste* and bowed low to the magnificent beast.

The bull then turned around and started walking away. Towards its owner.

Vali, meanwhile, had lost consciousness, as Sita and Ram carried him over the fence.

Chapter 29

Late in the evening, Shaktivel came to the forest edge where Ram and his band were resting. A few men followed the Chief of Indrapur, bearing large bundles of weapons in their hands.

Ram stood up, folding his hands together in a *Namaste*. 'Greetings, brave Shaktivel.'

Shaktivel returned Ram's greeting. '*Namaste*, great Prince.' He pointed to the bundles being carefully laid on the ground by his men. 'As requested by you, all your weapons have been repaired, shone, polished, and sharpened.'

Ram picked up a sword, examined its edge and smiled. 'They are as good as new.'

Shaktivel's chest swelled with pride. 'Our metalsmiths are among the best in India.'

'They clearly are,' said Sita, examining a spear closely.

'Prince Ram,' said Shaktivel, coming close, 'a private word.'

Ram signalled Sita to follow him, as he was pulled aside by Shaktivel.

'You may need to leave in haste,' said Shaktivel.

'Why?' asked a surprised Sita.

'Vali.'

'Someone wanted him dead?' asked Ram. 'So, they're angry with us now?'

'No, no. Vali is the one who is angry with Princess Sita and you.'

'What?! We just saved his life.'

Shaktivel sighed. 'He doesn't see it that way. According to him, the two of you and Prince Lakshman made him lose his honour. He'd rather have died in the *Jallikattu* arena than be rescued by someone else.'

Ram looked at Sita, his eyes wide in surprise.

'It is not in my town's interest to have royal families fight each other here,' said Shaktivel, folding his hands together in apology. 'When two elephants fight, the grass is the first to get trampled.'

Sita smiled. 'I know that line.'

'It's a popular line,' said Shaktivel. 'Especially among those who are not from the elite.'

Ram placed his hand on Shaktivel's shoulder. 'You have been our host. You have been a friend. We do not want to cause you any trouble. We'll leave before daybreak. Thank you for your hospitality.'

— ᚱᚷ —

Ram, Sita, and Lakshman had been in exile for twenty-four months now. The fifteen Malayaputra soldiers accompanied them everywhere.

Each member of the small party had settled into an established routine, as they moved deeper into the forests of Dandak. They were headed in the westward direction, but had not been able to find a suitable enough permanent camp. They usually stayed in one place for a short while before moving on. Standard perimeter and security formations had been agreed upon. Cooking, cleaning, and hunting duties were shared by rotation. Since not everyone in the camp ate meat, hunting wasn't required often.

On one of these hunting trips, a Malayaputra called Makrant had been gored by a boar while trying to save Sita's life. The wild boar's tusk had cut upwards through the upper quadriceps muscles on his thigh, piercing the femoral artery. Fortunately, the other tusk of the boar had hit the hard pelvic bone; thus, it had not pushed through and penetrated deeper where it would have ruptured the intestines. That would have been fatal as the resultant infection would have been impossible to treat in their temporary camp. Makrant had survived, but his recovery had not been ideal. His quadriceps muscles were still weak and the artery had not healed completely, remaining partially collapsed. He still limped a great deal; a condition which could be dangerous for a soldier in the hazardous jungle.

Because of the injury it was impossible for Makrant to move easily through the forest. So, they had not moved camp for some time.

Makrant had been suffering for a few months. Jatayu knew something had to be done. And, he knew the cure as well. He simply had to steel himself for the journey …

'The waters of Walkeshwar?' asked Sita.

'Yes,' said Jatayu. 'The holy lake emerges from a natural spring bursting out from deep underground, which means it picks up specific minerals on its way to the surface. Those minerals infuse the waters with their divine goodness. That water will help Makrant's arteries recover quickly. We can also get some medicinal herbs from the island which will help his partly atrophied muscles to recover fully. He can have the full use of his legs again.'

'Where is Walkeshwar, Jatayu*ji*?'

'It's in a small island called Mumbadevi on the west coast. Specifically, the northern part of the Konkan coast.'

'Weren't we supposed to stop at an island close to it for supplies on our way to Agastyakootam? An island called Colaba?'

'Yes. Our captain had thought it would be a good idea to stop there. I had advised against it.'

'Yes. I remember.'

'Mumbadevi is the big island to the northwest of Colaba.'

'So, Mumbadevi is one of that group of seven islands?'

'Yes, great Vishnu.'

'You had advised against stopping there since it is a major sea base for Raavan's forces.'

'Yes, great Vishnu.'

Sita smiled. 'Then, it's probably not a good idea for Ram and me to accompany you.'

Jatayu didn't smile at Sita's wry humour. 'Yes, great Vishnu.'

'But the Lankans will not dare hurt a Malayaputra, right?'

Fear flashed momentarily in Jatayu's eyes, but his voice was even and calm. 'No, they won't …'

Sita frowned. 'Jatayu*ji*, is there something you need to tell me?'

Jatayu shook his head. 'Everything will be fine. I will take three men with me. The rest of you should stay here. I will be back in two months.'

Instinct kicked in. Sita knew something was wrong. 'Jatayu*ji*, is there a problem in Mumbadevi?'

Jatayu shook his head. 'I need to prepare to leave, great Vishnu. You and Prince Ram should remain encamped here.'

— ౮౸ —

It was dark when Jatayu and the three soldiers reached the shoreline of the mainland. Across a narrow strait, they saw the seven islands that abutted the south of the far larger Salsette Island. Torchlights on houses and tall lamp towers on streets and public structures had lit up the central and eastern side of Salsette Island. Clearly, the town had expanded on this, the largest island, in the area. It was ten times bigger than the seven islands to the south put together! It was logical that a fast-growing town had come up here. There were large freshwater lakes in the centre of the island. And enough open area to build a large town. Crossing into the mainland was easy since the creek that separated it was narrow and shallow.

There had been a time when the seven islands to the south of Salsette had been the centre of all civilisation in the area. The island of Mumbadevi had a wonderful harbour on its eastern shores, which worked well for larger ships. The port built at that harbour still existed. And clearly, it was still busy. Jatayu could also see lights on the other four smaller islands on the eastern side: Parel, Mazgaon, Little Colaba, and Colaba. But the western islands of Mahim and Worli were not clearly visible.

The hills at the western end of Mumbadevi, where Walkeshwar was, were tall enough to be seen from across the straits, during the day. In fact, the hills had once been visible at night as well. For that's where the main palaces, temples, and structures of the old city were. And they had always been well lit.

But Jatayu couldn't see a thing there. No torchlights. No lamp towers. No sign of habitation.

Walkeshwar remained abandoned. It remained in ruin.

Jatayu shivered as he remembered those terrible days. The time when he had been a young soldier. When Raavan's hordes had come ... He remembered only too well. For he had been one of the horde.

Lord Parshu Ram, forgive me ... Forgive me for my sins ...

'Captain,' said one of the Malayaputra soldiers. 'Should we cross now or ...'

Jatayu turned around. 'No. We'll cross in the morning. We'll rest here for the night.'

— ᚱᚺ —

Jatayu tossed and turned as he tried to sleep. Memories that he had buried deep within himself were bursting through to his consciousness. Nightmares from his long-hidden past.

Memories of when he was younger. Many, many years ago.

Raavan used our own people to conquer us.

Jatayu sat up. He could see the islands across the creek.

When he had been a teenager, Jatayu had carried the pain, the anger, of being ill-treated as a Naga. As someone who was deformed. But Nagas weren't the only ones ill-treated. Many communities had complaints against the rigid, supercilious, and chauvinistic elite of the Sapt Sindhu. And Raavan had seemed like a rebel-hero, a saviour of sorts to many of them. He took on the powers-that-be. And, the disenchanted flocked to him. Fought for him. Killed for him.

And, were used by him.

Jatayu had, at that time, enjoyed the feeling of vengeance. Of hitting out at the hated, self-absorbed elite. Until the time that his unit had been ordered to join an *AhiRaavan*.

Raavan's forces were divided into two groups. One group commanded the land territories, with commanders called *MahiRaavans* in charge. And the other group commanded the seas and the ports, with commanders called *AhiRaavans* in control.

It was with one such *AhiRaavan* called Prahast that Jatayu had been ordered to come to Mumbadevi and its seven islands.

These seven islands were peopled by the Devendrar community at the time, led by a kindly man called Indran. Mumbadevi and the other six islands were an entrepot, with goods stored for import and export with minimal custom duties. The liberal Devendrars provided supplies and refuge to any seafarer, without favour or discrimination. They treated everyone with kindness. They believed it was their sacred duty to do so. One such seafarer, who had been provided refuge for some time, was Jatayu, when he was very young. He remembered that kindness well. It was a rare place in India, where Jatayu had not been treated like the plague. He had been welcomed like a normal person. The shock of the compassion had been so overwhelming that he had cried himself to sleep that first night in Mumbadevi, unable to handle the flood of emotions.

And many years later, he had returned, as part of an army sent to conquer that very same Mumbadevi Island.

Raavan's strategic reasons were obvious. He wanted absolute control over all the sea trade in the Indian Ocean; the hub of global trade. Whoever dominated this Ocean, dominated the entire world. And only with absolute control could Raavan enforce his usurious customs duties. He had conquered or managed to gain control over most of the major ports across the Indian subcontinent and the coasts of Arabia, Africa, and South-east Asia. Those ports followed his rules.

But Mumbadevi stubbornly refused to charge high custom or turn away any sailor who sought refuge there. Its inhabitants believed this service was their duty. Their dharma. Raavan had to gain control over this important harbour on the sea route between the Indus-Saraswati coasts and Lanka.

AhiRaavan *Prahast had been sent to negotiate a solution. And, if needed, force a solution. The Lankan Army had been waiting, camped in their ships, anchored at the Mumbadevi harbour, off its eastern coast. For a week. Nothing had happened. Finally, they had been ordered to march to Walkeshwar, the western part of Mumbadevi, where the palace and a temple dedicated to Lord Rudra had been built, right next to a natural-spring-filled lake.*

Jatayu, being a junior soldier, was at the back of the line.

He knew the Devendrars couldn't fight. They were a peaceful community of seafarers, engineers, doctors, philosophers, and storytellers. There were very few warriors among them. Jatayu hoped desperately that a compromise had been reached.

The scene he saw at the main town square, outside of the palace, baffled him.

It was completely deserted. Not a soul in sight. All the shops were open. Goods displayed. But nobody to tend to, or even secure them.

At the centre of the square was a massive pile of corkwood, with some mixture of holy sandalwood. It was held in place by a metallic mesh. All drenched in fresh ghee. *It had clearly been built recently. Perhaps, the previous night itself.*

It was like a very large unlit cremation pyre. Humongous. Massive enough to potentially accommodate hundreds of bodies.

It had a walkway leading up to its top.

Prahast had come in expecting a ceremonial surrender, as he had demanded, and then the peaceful expulsion of the Devendrars. This was unexpected. He immediately made his troops fall into battle formations.

Sanskrit chants were emanating from behind the palace walls. Accompanied by the clanging of sacred bells and the beating of drums. It took some time for the Lankans to discern the words of the chants.

They were from the Garuda Purana. *Hymns usually sung during a death ceremony.*

What were the Devendrars thinking? Their palace walls

were not tough enough to withstand an assault. They did not have enough soldiers to take on the five-thousand-strong Lankan Army.

Suddenly, smoke began to plume out of the palace compound. Thick, acrid smoke. The wooden palace had been set on fi e.

And then, the gates were flung open.

Prahast's order was loud and clear. 'Draw! And hold!'

All the Lankans immediately drew their weapons. Holding their line. In military discipline. Expecting an attack ...

Indran, the king of the Devendrars, led his people out of the palace. All of them. His entire family. The priests, traders, workmen, intellectuals, doctors, artists. Men, women, children. All his citizens.

All the Devendrars.

They all wore saffron robes. The colour of fi e, of Lord Agni. The colour of the final journey.

Every single face was a picture of calm.

They were still chanting.

Every Devendrar carried gold coins and jewellery. Each one carried a fortune. And each one carried a small bottle.

Indran walked up the pathway to the stand that overhung the massive pile of wood. He nodded at his people.

They flung their gold coins and jewellery at the Lankan soldiers.

Indran's voice carried loud and clear. 'You can take all our money! You can take our lives! But you cannot force us to act against our dharma!'

The Lankan soldiers stood stunned. Not knowing how to react. They looked at their commander for instructions.

Prahast bellowed loudly. 'King Indran, think well before you act. Lord Raavan is the King of all three Worlds. Even the Gods fear him. Your soul will be cursed. Take your gold and leave. Surrender and you shall be shown mercy!'

Indran smiled kindly. 'We will never surrender our dharma.'

Then the king of the Devendrars looked at the Lankan soldiers. 'Save your souls. You alone carry the fruit of your karma. No one else. You cannot escape your karma by claiming that you were only following orders. Save your souls. Choose well.'

Some Lankan soldiers seemed to be wavering. The weapons in their hands shaking.

'Hold your weapons!' shouted Prahast. 'This is a trick!'

Indran nodded to his head priest. The priest stepped up to the pile of wood and stuck a burning torch deep into it. It caught fi e immediately. The pyre was ready.

Indran pulled out his small bottle and took a deep swig. Possibly a pain reliever.

'All I ask is that you not insult our Gods. That you not defile our temples.' Indran then stared at Prahast with pity. 'The rest is for you to do as you will.'

Prahast ordered his soldiers again. 'Steady. Nobody move!'

Indran pulled his hands together into a Namaste *and looked up at the sky. 'Jai Rudra! Jai Parshu Ram!'*

Saying this, Indran jumped into the pyre.

Jatayu screamed in agony. 'Noooo!'

The Lankan soldiers were too shocked to react.

'Don't move!' screamed Prahast at his soldiers again.

All the other Devendrars took their potions and started running up the walkway. Jumping into the mass pyre. Rapidly. In groups. Every single one. Men, women, children. Following their leader. Following their king.

There were one thousand Devendrars. It took some time for all of them to jump in.

No Lankan stepped up to stop them. A few officers close to Prahast, to the disgust of many, started picking through the gold jewellery thrown by the Devendrars. Selecting the best for themselves. Discussing the value of their loot with each other. Even as the Devendrars were committing mass suicide. But the majority of the Lankan soldiers just stood there. Too stunned to do anything.

As the last of the Devendrars fell to his fie y end, Prahast looked around. He could see the shocked expressions of many of his soldiers. He burst out laughing. 'Don't be sad, my soldiers. All the gold will be divided up equally among you. You will all make more money today than you have made in your entire lives! Smile! You are rich now!'

The words did not have the desired impact. Many had been jolted to their souls. Sickened by what they had witnessed. Within less than a week, more than half of Prahast's army had deserted. Jatayu was one of them.

They couldn't fight for Raavan anymore.

The loud sound of the waves crashing against hard rocks brought Jatayu back from that painful memory.

His body was shaking. Tears pouring from his eyes. He held his hands together in supplication, his head bowed. He gathered the courage to look across the straits at Mumbadevi. At the hills of Walkeshwar.

'Forgive me, King Indran ... Forgive me ...'

But there was no respite from the guilt.

— ௬ 人 —

It had been a few months since Jatayu's return from Mumbadevi.

The medicine from Walkeshwar had done wonders for Makrant. The limp had reduced dramatically. He could walk almost normally again. The atrophied muscles were slowly regaining strength. It was obvious that within a matter of months Makrant would regain the full use of his legs. Some Malayaputras were even planning hunts with him.

Sita had tried a few times to ask Jatayu why the mention

of Mumbadevi caused him such distress. But had given up over time.

Early today, she had stolen away from the group to meet Hanuman at a secret location.

'Prince Ram and you need to settle down at one place, princess,' said Hanuman. 'Your constant movement makes it difficult for me to keep track of you.'

'I know,' said Sita. 'But we haven't found a secure place yet.'

'I have a place in mind for you. It's close to water. It's defendable. You will be able to forage food easily. There is enough hunt available. And, it's close enough for me to track you.'

'Where is it?'

'It's near the source of the holy Godavari.'

'All right. I'll take the details from you. And, how's …'

'Radhika?'

Sita nodded.

Hanuman smiled apologetically. 'She's … She's moved on.'

'Moved on?'

'She's married now.'

Sita was shocked. 'Married?'

'Yes.'

Sita held her breath. 'Poor Bharat …'

'I have heard that Bharat still loves her.'

'I don't think he'll ever get over her …'

'I'd heard something once: Better to have loved and lost than never to have loved at all.'

Sita looked at Hanuman. 'Forgive me, Hanu *bhaiya*, I don't mean to be rude. But only someone who has never loved at all can say something like that.'

Hanuman shrugged his shoulders. 'Point taken. In any case, the location for the camp …'

Chapter 30

Six years had lapsed since Ram, Sita, and Lakshman had gone into exile.

The band of nineteen had finally settled along the western banks of the early course of the mighty Godavari, at *Panchavati*. Or the *place of the five banyan trees*. The site suggested by Hanuman. The river provided natural protection to the small, rustic, yet comfortable camp. The main mud hut at the centre of the camp had two rooms — one for Ram and Sita, and the other for Lakshman — and an open clearing for exercise and assembly.

Another cluster of huts to the east housed Jatayu and his band.

The perimeter of this camp had two circular fences. The one on the outside was covered with poisonous creepers to keep animals out. The fence on the inside comprised *nagavalli* creepers, rigged with an alarm system. It consisted of a continuous rope that ran all the way to a very large wooden cage, filled with birds. The birds were well looked after and replaced every month with new ones. If anyone made it past the outer fence and attempted to enter the *nagavalli* hedge, the alarm system would trigger the opening of the birdcage roof. The noisy flutter of escaping birds would offer precious minutes of warning to the inmates at the camp.

Ram, Sita, and Lakshman had faced dangers in these six years, but not due to any human intervention. The occasional scars served as reminders of their adventures in the jungle, but the *Somras* had ensured that they looked and felt as young as the day they had left Ayodhya. Exposure to the harsh sun had darkened their skin. Ram had always been dark-skinned, but even the fair-skinned Sita and Lakshman had acquired a bronze tone. Ram and Lakshman had grown beards and moustaches, making them look like warrior-sages.

Life had fallen into a predictable pattern. Ram and Sita liked to go to the Godavari banks in the early morning hours to bathe and share some private time together. Their favourite time of the day.

This was one such day. They had washed their hair the previous day. There was no need to wash it again. They had tied it up in a bun while bathing. After their bath in the clear waters of the river, they sat on the banks eating a repast of fresh berries and fruit.

Ram lay with his head on Sita's lap. She was playing with his hair. Her fingers got stuck in a knot. She gently tried to ease it out and untangle the hair. Ram protested mildly, but the hair came loose easily, without any need to yank it.

Sita smiled. 'See, I can do it gently as well.'

Ram laughed. 'Sometimes …'

Ram ran his hand through Sita's hair. It hung loose over her shoulder, down to where his head lay on her lap. 'I am bored with your ponytail.'

Sita shrugged. 'It's up to you to tie some other knot. It's open now …'

'I'll do that,' said Ram, holding Sita's hand and looking lazily towards the river. 'But later. When we get up.'

Sita smiled and continued to ruffle Ram's hair. 'Ram ...'

'Hmm?'

'I need to tell you something.'

'What?'

'About our conversation yesterday.'

Ram turned towards Sita. 'I was wondering when you would bring that up.'

Sita and Ram had spoken about many things the previous day. Most importantly, of Vashishtha's belief that Ram would be the next Vishnu. Ram had then asked who Sita's guru was. But Sita had sidestepped the answer.

'There should be no secrets in a marriage. I should tell you who my guru is. Or was.'

Ram looked directly into Sita's eyes. 'Guru Vishwamitra.'

Sita was shocked. Her eyes gave it away. Ram had guessed correctly.

Ram smiled. 'I'm not blind, you know. Only a favourite student could get away with saying the kind of things that you had said to Guru Vishwamitra in my presence that day in Mithila.'

'Then why didn't you say anything?'

'I was waiting for you to trust me enough to tell me.'

'I have always trusted you, Ram.'

'Yes, but only as a wife. Some secrets are too big even for a marriage. I know who the Malayaputras are. I know what your being Guru Vishwamitra's favourite disciple means.'

Sita sighed, 'It was silly of me to wait for so long. Passage of time makes a simple conversation more complicated than necessary. I probably should not have listened to ...'

'That's water under the bridge.' Ram sat up and moved close to Sita. He held her hands and said, 'Now, tell me.'

Sita took a deep breath. Nervous for some reason. 'The Malayaputras believe I am their Vishnu.'

Ram smiled and looked directly into Sita's eyes, with respect. 'I have known you for years. Heard so many of your ideas. You will make a great Vishnu. I will be proud to follow you.'

'Don't follow. Partner.'

Ram frowned.

'Why can't there be two Vishnus? If we work together, we can end this stupid fight between the Malayaputras and Vayuputras. We can all work together and set India on a new path.'

'I'm not sure it is allowed, Sita. A Vishnu cannot begin her journey by breaking the law. I will follow you.'

'There is no rule that dictates that there can be just one Vishnu.'

'Umm …'

'I know, Ram. There is no such rule. Trust me.'

'All right, assuming there isn't, you and I can certainly work together. I'm sure that even the Malayaputras and Vayuputras can learn to work together. But what about Guru Vashishtha and Guru Vishwamitra? Their enmity runs deep. And the Malayaputras will still have to acknowledge me. With things between our gurus being the way they are …'

'We'll handle that,' said Sita, as she inched close to Ram and embraced him. 'I'm sorry I didn't tell you for so long.'

'I thought you would tell me yesterday, when you were tying my hair. That's why I touched your cheeks and waited. But I guess you weren't ready …'

'You know, Guru Vashishtha believes …'

'Sita, Guru Vashishtha is just like Guru Vishwamitra. He is brilliant. But he is human. He can sometimes read situations incorrectly. I may be a devotee of the law, but I am not an idiot.'

Sita laughed. 'I'm sorry I didn't trust you earlier.'

Ram smiled. 'Yes. You should be. And remember, we are married. So, I can use this against you anytime in the future.'

Sita burst into peals of laughter and hit her husband's shoulder playfully. Ram held her hands, pulled her close and kissed her. They held each other in companionable silence. Looking at the Godavari.

'What do we do for now?' asked Sita.

'There's nothing to do till our exile is over. We can just prepare ...'

'Guru Vashishtha has accepted me. So, I don't think he will have a problem with our partnership.'

'But Guru Vishwamitra ... He'll not accept me.'

'You don't hold anything against him? For what he did in Mithila?'

'He was trying to save his Vishnu. His life's work. He was working for the good of our motherland. I'm not saying I condone his cavalier attitude towards the *daivi astras*. But I understand where he was coming from.'

'So, we don't tell the Malayaputras anything about what we have decided for now?'

'No. In fact, I'm not even sure we can tell the Vayuputras for now ... Let's wait.'

'There is one Vayuputra we can tell.'

'How do you know any Vayuputra? Guru Vashishtha had consistently refused to introduce me to any of them till I was accepted by all as a Vishnu. It could have caused problems.'

'I wasn't introduced to him by Guru Vashishtha either! I got to know him through sheer good fortune. I met him through a friend at my *gurukul*. I believe he can advise and help us.'

'Who is he?'

'He is Radhika's cousin.'

'Radhika! Bharat's Radhika?'

Sita smiled sadly. 'Yes ...'

'You know Bharat still loves her, right?'

'I have heard ... But ...'

'Yes, the law in her tribe ... I had told Bharat to not pursue her ...'

Sita knew Radhika's reasoning was different. But there was no point in revealing that to Ram. It was water under the bridge.

'What is her brother's name? The Vayuputra?'

'Hanu *bhaiya*.'

'Hanu *bhaiya*?'

'That's what I call him. The world knows him as Lord Hanuman.'

— ॐ —

Hanuman smiled, folded his hands together and bowed his head. 'I bow to the Vishnu, Lady Sita. I bow to the Vishnu, Lord Ram.'

Ram and Sita looked at each other, embarrassed.

Sita and Ram had told Lakshman and the Malayaputras that they were going on a hunt. They had, instead, stolen away to a clearing at least a half-day away. They had taken a boat ride downstream on the Godavari, where Hanuman was waiting for them. Sita had introduced Ram to Hanuman. And told him of their decision. Hanuman seemed to accept the decision very easily. Even welcoming it.

'But do you think Guru Vishwamitra and Guru Vashishtha will agree?' asked Sita.

'I don't know,' said Hanuman. Then looking at Ram, he continued, 'Guru Vishwamitra was very angry that Guru Vashishtha has told you that he expects you to be the Vishnu.'

Ram remained silent.

Hanuman continued. 'Your brother Lakshman is a brave and loyal man. He will die for you. But he can, sometimes, let out secrets that he shouldn't.'

Ram smiled apologetically. 'Yes, he said it in front of Arishtanemi*ji*. Lakshman doesn't mean any harm. He is …'

'Of course,' agreed Hanuman. 'He is very proud of you. He loves you a great deal. But because of that love, he sometimes makes mistakes. Please don't misunderstand. But I would suggest that you don't tell him about your little arrangement. Or, about me for that matter. At least for now.'

Ram nodded. Agreeing.

'What is the reason for the enmity between Guru Vashishtha and Guru Vishwamitra?' asked Sita. 'I have never been able to find out.'

'Yes,' said Ram. 'Even Guru Vashishtha refuses to speak about it.'

'I am not sure either,' said Hanuman. 'But I have heard that a woman called Nandini may have played a role.'

'Really?' asked Sita. 'A woman caused the rift between them? What a cliché.'

Hanuman smiled. 'Apparently, there were other problems as well. But nobody is sure. These are just speculations.'

'Anyway, what's more important is, do you think the Malayaputras and Vayuputras can come together on this?' asked Ram. 'Will they agree to the two of us being Vishnus?

I've been told by Sita that there is no law against it. But it is certainly against the standard protocol for Vishnus and Mahadevs, right?'

Hanuman laughed softly. 'Prince Ram, do you know how long the institutions of the Vishnu and Mahadev have been running?'

Ram shrugged. 'I don't know. Thousands of years? Since Lord Manu's times, I guess. If not earlier.'

'Right. And do you know exactly how many Vishnus and Mahadevs, in the many millennia, have actually emerged according to the plans and protocols laid down by the tribes left behind by the previous Vishnu or Mahadev?'

Ram looked at Sita. And then, back at Hanuman. 'I don't know.'

Hanuman's eyes were twinkling. 'Precisely zero.'

'Really?'

'Not once, not once has any Vishnu or Mahadev emerged exactly according to plan. The best laid plans always have a tendency to get spoilt. There have always been surprises.'

Ram laughed softly. 'We are a country that does not like order and plans.'

'That we are!' said Hanuman. 'The Mahadevs or the Vishnus didn't succeed in their missions because "plans were implemented exactly". They succeeded because they were willing to give their all for our great land. And they were followed by many who also felt exactly the same way. That is the secret. Passion. Not plans.'

'So, you think we will succeed in getting the Malayaputras and Vayuputras to agree?' asked Sita.

'Of course we will,' answered Hanuman. 'Don't they love India? But if you ask me how exactly we will succeed, my answer is: I don't know. No plans as of yet! But we have time. Nothing can be done till the both of you return to the Sapt Sindhu.'

— ௫ —

It had been more than thirteen years of exile now. In less than a year, Ram, Sita, and Lakshman would head back to the Sapt Sindhu and begin their life's greatest karma. Hanuman had, over time, managed to get the Vayuputras to accept Sita. And Arishtanemi, along with a few other Malayaputras, had begun to favour Ram. Vashishtha, of course, had no problem with Ram and Sita being the Vishnus together. But Vishwamitra ... well, he was another matter altogether. If he held out, the Malayaputras could not be counted on to be completely on board. After all, they were a relatively disciplined organisation that followed their leader.

But this was not occupying the minds of Ram and Sita right now. They lounged around in their section of the camp, watching the setting sun as it coloured the sky with glorious hues. Unexpectedly, the avian alarm system was triggered; the flock of birds in the cage had suddenly fluttered away noisily. Someone had breached their camp perimeter.

'What was that?' asked Lakshman.

Ram's instincts told him that the intruders were not animals.

'Weapons,' ordered Ram calmly.

Sita and Lakshman tied their sword scabbards around their waist. Lakshman handed Ram his bow, before picking up his own. The brothers quickly strung their bows. Jatayu and his men rushed in, armed and ready, just as Ram and Lakshman tied quivers full of arrows to their backs. Sita picked up a long spear, as Ram tied his sword scabbard to his waist. They already wore a smaller knife scabbard, tied horizontally across the small of their backs; a weapon they kept on their person at all times.

'Who could they be?' asked Jatayu.

'I don't know,' said Ram.

'Lakshman's Wall?' asked Sita.

Lakshman's Wall was an ingenious defensive feature designed by him to the east of the main hut. It was five feet in height; it covered three sides of a small square completely, leaving the inner side facing the main hut partially open; like a cubicle. The entire structure gave the impression that it was an enclosed kitchen. In fact, the cubicle was bare, providing adequate mobility to warriors. But unseen by enemies on the other side of the wall. They would have to be on their knees, though. A small *tandoor*, a *cooking platform*, emerged on the outside from the south-facing wall. Half the enclosure was roof-covered, completing the camouflage of a cooking area. It afforded protection from enemy arrows.

The south, east, and north-facing walls were drilled with well-spaced holes. These holes were narrow on the inner side and broad on the outer side, giving the impression of ventilation required for cooking. Their actual purpose was to give those on the inside a good view of the approaching enemy, while preventing those on the outside from looking in. The holes could also be used to shoot arrows. Made from mud, it was not strong enough to withstand a sustained assault by a large force. Having said that, it was good enough for defence against small bands sent on assassination bids. Which is what Lakshman suspected they would face.

Designed by Lakshman, it had been built by everyone in the camp; Makrant had named it 'Lakshman's Wall'.

'Yes,' said Ram.

Everyone rushed to the wall and crouched low, keeping their weapons ready. Waiting.

Lakshman hunched over and peeped through a hole in the south-facing wall. Straining his eye, he detected a small band of ten people marching into the camp premises. Led by a man and a woman.

The man in the lead was of average height. Unusually fair-skinned. His reed-thin physique was that of a runner; this man was no warrior. Despite his frail shoulders and thin arms, he walked as if he had boils in his armpits; pretending to accommodate impressive biceps. Like most Indian men, he had long, jet black hair that was tied in a knot at the back of his head. His full beard was neatly trimmed, and coloured a deep brown. He wore a classic brown *dhoti* and an *angvastram* that was a shade lighter. His jewellery was rich but understated: pearl ear studs and a thin copper bracelet. He looked dishevelled. As though he had been on the road for too long, without a change of clothes.

The woman beside him faintly resembled the man, possibly his sister. Bewitching. Almost as short as Urmila. Skin as white as snow. It should have made her look pale and sickly. Instead, she was distractingly beautiful. Sharp, slightly upturned nose. High cheekbones. She almost looked like a Parihan. Unlike them, though, her hair was blonde, a most unusual colour. Every strand of it was in place. Her eyes were magnetic. Perhaps she was the child of Hiranyaloman Mlechchas: fair-skinned, light-eyed, and light-haired foreigners who lived half a world away towards the north-west. Their violent ways and incomprehensible speech had led to the Indians calling them barbarians. But this lady was no barbarian. Quite the contrary, she was elegant, slim, and petite, except for breasts that were disproportionately large for her body. She wore a classic, expensively dyed purple *dhoti*, which shone like the waters of the Sarayu. Perhaps it was the legendary silk cloth from the far-eastern parts of India; one that only the richest could afford now. For Raavan had established a complete monopoly on it and had jacked up the prices. The *dhoti* was tied fashionably low, exposing her flat tummy and slim, curvaceous waist. Her silken blouse was a tiny sliver of cloth, affording a generous view of her cleavage. Her *angvastram* had deliberately been left hanging loose from a shoulder, instead of across the body. Extravagant jewellery completed the picture of excess. The only incongruity was the knife scabbard tied to her waist. She was a vision to behold.

Ram cast a quick glance at Sita. 'Who are they?'

Sita shrugged.

It was quickly clarified by the Malayaputras that the man was Raavan's younger half-brother Vibhishan, and the woman his half-sister Shurpanakha.

A soldier next to Vibhishan held aloft a white flag, the colour of peace. They obviously wanted to parley. The mystery was, what did they want to talk about?

And whether there was any subterfuge involved.

Ram looked through the hole again, and then turned towards his people. 'We will all step out together. It will stop them from attempting something stupid.'

'That is wise,' said Jatayu.

'Come on,' said Ram, as he stepped out from behind the protective wall with his right hand raised, signifying that he meant no harm. Everyone else followed Ram's example and trooped out to meet the half-siblings of Raavan.

Vibhishan nervously stopped in his tracks the moment his eyes fell on Ram, Sita, Lakshman, and their soldiers. He looked sideways at his sister, as if uncertain about the next course of action. But Shurpanakha had eyes only for Ram. She stared at him, unashamedly.

A look of recognition flashed across a surprised Vibhishan's face when he saw Jatayu.

Ram, Lakshman, and Sita walked in the lead, with Jatayu and his soldiers following close behind. As the forest-dwellers reached the Lankans, Vibhishan straightened his back, puffed up his chest and spoke with an air of self-importance. 'We come in peace, King of Ayodhya.'

'We want peace as well,' said Ram, lowering his right hand. His people did the same. He made no comment on the 'King of Ayodhya' greeting. 'What brings you here, Prince of Lanka?'

Vibhishan preened at being recognised. 'It seems Sapt Sindhuans are not as ignorant of the world as many of us like to imagine.'

Ram smiled politely. Meanwhile, Shurpanakha pulled out a small violet kerchief and covered her nose delicately. Lakshman noticed her fashionable and manicured finger nails, each one shaped like a winnowing basket. That was perhaps the root of her name. Shurpa was Old Sanskrit for a winnowing basket. And nakha meant nails.

'Well, even I respect and understand the ways of the Sapt Sindhuans,' said Vibhishan.

Sita watched Shurpanakha, hawk-eyed, as the lady continued to stare at her husband. Unabashedly. Up close, it was clear that the magic of Shurpanakha's eyes lay in their startling colour: bright blue. She almost certainly had some Hiranyaloman Mlechcha blood. Practically nobody east of Egypt had blue eyes. She was bathed in fragrant perfume that overpowered the rustic, animal smell of the Panchavati camp; at least for those in her vicinity. Not overpowering enough for her, evidently. She continued to hold the stench of her surroundings at bay, with the kerchief pressed against her nose.

'Would you like to come inside, to our humble abode?' asked Ram, gesturing towards the hut.

'No, thank you, Your Highness,' said Vibhishan. 'I'm comfortable here.'

Jatayu's presence had thrown him off-guard. Vibhishan was unwilling to encounter other surprises that may lie in store for them, within the closed confines of the hut. Before they came to some negotiated terms. He was the brother of the enemy of the Sapt Sindhu, after all. It was safer here, out in the open; for now.

'All right then,' said Ram. 'To what do we owe the honour of a visit from the prince of golden Lanka?'

Shurpanakha spoke in a husky, alluring voice. 'Handsome one, we come to seek refuge.'

'I'm not sure I understand,' said Ram, momentarily flummoxed by the allusion to his good looks by a woman he did not know. 'I don't think we are capable of helping the relatives of …'

'Who else can we go to, O Great One?' asked Vibhishan. 'We will never be accepted in the Sapt Sindhu because we are Raavan's siblings. But we also know that there are many in the Sapt Sindhu who will not deny you. My sister and I have suffered Raavan's brutal oppression for too long. We needed to escape.'

Ram remained silent.

'King of Ayodhya,' continued Vibhishan, 'I may be from

Lanka but I am, in fact, like one of your own. I honour your ways, follow your path. I'm not like the other Lankans, blinded by Raavan's immense wealth into following his demonic path. And Shurpanakha is just like me. Don't you think you have a duty towards us, too?'

Sita cut in. 'An ancient poet once remarked, "When the axe entered the forest, the trees said to each other: do not worry, the handle in that axe is one of us."'

Shurpanakha sniggered. 'So the great descendant of Raghu lets his wife make decisions for him, is it?'

Vibhishan touched Shurpanakha's hand lightly and she fell silent. 'Queen Sita,' said Vibhishan, 'you will notice that only the handles have come here. The axe-head is in Lanka. We are truly like you. Please help us.'

Shurpanakha turned to Jatayu. It had not escaped her notice that, as usual, every man was gaping intently at her; every man, that is, except Ram and Lakshman. 'Great Malayaputra, don't you think it is in your interest to give us refuge? We could tell you more about Lanka than you already know. There will be more gold in it for you.'

Jatayu stiffened. 'We are the followers of Lord Parshu Ram! We are not interested in gold.'

'Right ...' said Shurpanakha, sarcastically.

Vibhishan appealed to Lakshman. 'Wise Lakshman, please convince your brother. I'm sure you will agree with me when I say that we can be of use to you in your fight when you get back.'

'I could agree with you, Prince of Lanka,' said Lakshman, smiling, 'but then we would both be wrong.'

Vibhishan looked down and sighed.

'Prince Vibhishan,' said Ram, 'I am truly sorry but—'

Vibhishan interrupted Ram. 'Son of Dashrath, remember the battle of Mithila. My brother Raavan is your enemy. He is my enemy as well. Shouldn't that make you my friend?'

Ram kept quiet.

'Great King, we have put our lives at risk by escaping from Lanka. Can't you let us be your guests for a while? We will leave in a few days. Remember what the *Taittiriya Upanishad* says: "*Athithi Devo Bhava*". Even the many *Smritis* say that the strong should protect the weak. All we are asking for is shelter for a few days. Please.'

Sita looked at Ram. And sighed. A law had been invoked. She knew what was going to happen next. She knew Ram would not turn them away now.

'Just a few days,' pleaded Vibhishan. 'Please.'

Ram touched Vibhishan's shoulder. 'You can stay here for a few days; rest for a while, and then continue on your journey.'

Vibhishan folded his hands together into a *Namaste* and said, 'Glory to the great clan of Raghu.'

Chapter 31

'There is no salt in this food,' complained Shurpanakha.

It was the first hour of the fourth *prahar* and those in the Panchavati camp had settled down for their evening meal. It had been Sita's turn to cook. While Ram, Lakshman, and the rest were enjoying the food, Shurpanakha had found much to complain about. The lack of salt was just the latest in a litany of complaints.

'Because there is no salt in Panchavati, princess,' said Sita, trying very hard to be patient. 'We make do with what we have. This is not a palace. You can choose to stay hungry, if the food is not to your liking.'

'This food is worthy of dogs!' muttered Shurpanakha in disgust, as she threw the morsel of food she had in her hand back on the plate.

'Then it should be just right for you,' said Lakshman.

Everyone burst out laughing. Even Vibhishan. But Ram was not amused. He looked at Lakshman sternly. Lakshman looked at his brother in defiance, then shook his head and went back to eating.

Shurpanakha pushed her plate away and stormed out.

'Shurpa ...' said Vibhishan, as if in entreaty. Then he too got up and ran after his sister.

Ram looked at Sita. She shrugged her shoulders and continued eating.

— ༔༚ —

An hour later, Sita and Ram were in their hut. By themselves.

While no Lankan except Shurpanakha had been troublesome, Lakshman and Jatayu remained suspicious of them. They had disarmed the visitors and locked their weapons in the camp armoury. They also maintained a strict and staggered twenty-four-hour vigil, keeping a constant watch on the guests. It was Jatayu's and Makrant's turn to stay up all night and keep guard.

'That spoilt princess fancies you,' said Sita.

Ram shook his head, his eyes clearly conveying he thought this silly. 'How can she, Sita? She knows I'm married. Why should she find me attractive?'

Sita lay down next to her husband on the bed of hay. 'You should know that you are more attractive than you realise.'

Ram laughed. 'Nonsense.'

Sita laughed as well and put her arms around him. 'But you are mine. Only mine.'

'Yes, My Lady,' said Ram, smiling and putting his arms around his wife.

They kissed each other, languid and slow. The forest was gradually falling silent, as though settling in for the night.

— ༔༚ —

The guests had been in Panchavati with the forest-dwellers for a week now.

· Lakshman and Jatayu had insisted on continuing the staggered vigil, keeping a constant watch on the guests.

Vibhishan had announced that they would be leaving in a few hours. But Shurpanakha had insisted that she had to wash her hair before leaving. She had also demanded that Sita accompany her. To help her with her hair.

Sita had no interest in going with Shurpanakha. But she wanted to get rid of the spoilt Lankan princess as soon as possible. This had encouraged her to say yes.

Shurpanakha had insisted on taking the boat and going a long way downriver.

'Don't think I'm not aware that your disgusting camp-followers have been taking the opportunity to spy on me at my bath time!' Shurpanakha said with pretended outrage.

Sita grimaced and took a deep breath, not saying anything.

'Not your goody-goody husband, of course,' said Shurpanakha, coquettishly. 'He has eyes only for you.'

Sita, still silent, got into the boat, with Shurpanakha climbing in daintily. Sita waited for Shurpanakha to pick up one of the oars. But she just sat there, admiring her nails. Grunting angrily, Sita picked up both the oars and started rowing. It took a long time. Sita was irritated and tired before Shurpanakha directed her into a small hidden lagoon by the river, where she wanted to bathe.

'Go ahead,' said Sita. As she turned around and waited.

Shurpanakha disrobed slowly, put all her clothes into the cloth bag she had carried and dived into the water. Sita settled back, her head on the stern thwart, her body stretched out on the bottom boards, and waited. Feeling uncomfortable after some time, Sita pulled up some jute sacks, bundled them together into a pillow on the plank and rested her head again. The lazy daylight filtering through the dense foliage was calming her down slowly, lulling her to sleep.

She lost track of time as she fell into a short nap. A loud bird call woke her up.

She heard Shurpanakha frolicking in the water. She waited for what she thought was a reasonable time. Finally, Sita edged up on her elbows. 'Are you done? Do you want your hair untangled and tied?'

Shurpanakha stopped swimming for a bit and faced Sita with a look of utter contempt and disgust. 'I'm not letting you touch my hair!'

Sita's eyes flew open in anger. 'Then why the hell did you ask me to come h ...'

'I couldn't have come here alone now, could I,' interrupted Shurpanakha, like she was explaining the most obvious thing in the world. 'And, I wasn't about to bring one of the men along. Lord Indra alone knows what they would do if they saw me in this state.'

'They would drown you, hopefully,' muttered Sita, under her breath.

'What did you say?' snapped Shurpanakha.

'Nothing. Finish your bath quickly. Your brother wants to leave today.'

'My brother will leave when I tell him we can leave.'

Sita saw Shurpanakha looking into the forest beyond the banks of the lagoon. Sita followed Shurpanakha's gaze. Then she shook her head in irritation. 'Nobody has followed us here. No one can see you. In the name of all that is good and holy, finish your bath!'

Shurpanakha didn't bother to answer. Casting Sita a contemptuous look, she turned and swam away.

Sita held her fist to her forehead and repeated softly to herself. 'Breathe. Breathe. She's leaving today. Just breathe.'

Shurpanakha continued to steal glances at the forest. She couldn't see anyone. She muttered under her breath, 'None of these idiots are reliable. I have to do everything myself.'

— ᚴᚼ —

At the Panchavati camp, Vibhishan had come to speak to Ram.

'Great one,' said Vibhishan, 'you know we are leaving soon. Is it possible to return our weapons to us so that we may get going?'

'Of course,' said Ram.

Vibhishan looked at Jatayu and his Malayaputras a short distance away, then in the direction of the Godavari, the great river hidden by the dense foliage. His heart was beating fast.

I hope they have reached.

— ᚴᚼ —

'Enough!' said Sita, in irritation. 'You're as clean as you can be. Get out of the water now. We're leaving.'

Shurpanakha looked once again into the forests.

Sita picked the oars. 'I'm leaving. You can choose to stay or come along.'

Shurpanakha shrieked in anger, but surrendered.

— ᚴᚼ —

Sita rowed the boat back in short order. It was a ten-minute uphill walk thereafter to the camp. She waited for Shurpanakha to step out of the boat.

Sita didn't expect, nor get, any help from Shurpanakha to pull the boat onto the banks so that it could be tied securely to a tree with a hemp rope. Shurpanakha was behind Sita as she bent, wrapped the boat-rope around her right hand, held on to the gunwale of the boat, and began to tug.

Focused as she was on her task, as well as the physical strain of pulling a boat up the bank all by herself, she didn't notice Shurpanakha reach into her bag, pull out some herbs and creep up on her.

Shurpanakha used a specific kind of soap and perfume that she had carried with her for her bath. It had a distinctive fragrance. Very different from the feral smell of the jungle.

It was this smell that saved Sita.

She reacted almost immediately, letting go off the boat. Just as Shurpanakha jumped at her and tried to stuff the herbs into Sita's mouth, she turned and hit the Lankan princess hard with her elbow. Shurpanakha fell back, screaming in agony. Sita lunged forward towards the princess of Lanka but the rope wrapped around her wrist made her lose balance. Sensing an opportunity, Shurpanakha pushed Sita into the water. But as Sita fell, she elbowed the princess of Lanka again. Shurpanakha recovered quickly and jumped into the water after Sita, trying again to push the herbs into her mouth.

Sita was taller, tougher and more agile than the posh Shurpanakha. She pushed Shurpanakha hard, flinging her some distance away. She spat out the herbs, quickly pulled out her knife from the scabbard and cut the rope loose. She glanced at the herbs floating in the water, recognising them almost immediately. She pushed through the water to reach Shurpanakha.

Shurpanakha, meanwhile, had recovered. She swam towards Sita and tried to hit her with her fists. Sita grabbed and held both her wrists in her left hand; then yanked hard till the princess of Lanka was forced to turn around. Then Sita wrapped her arm around Shurpanakha's throat, holding her hard against her own body.

Then Sita brought the knife close to Shurpanakha's throat. 'One more move, you spoilt brat, and I will bleed you to death.'

Shurpanakha fell silent and stopped struggling. Sita pushed the knife back in its scabbard. Then used the remnants of the rope around her own wrist to restrain Shurpanakha's hands. She pulled Shurpanakha's *angvastram* and tied it across her mouth.

She reached into Shurpanakha's bag and found some more of the herbs.

'I'll push this into your mouth if you make any more trouble.'

Shurpanakha remained quiet.

Sita started dragging her towards the camp.

A short distance from the camp, the *angvastram* across Shurpanakha's mouth came loose and fell away. She immediately began screaming.

'Stay quiet!' shouted Sita, dragging her along.

Shurpanakha, though, kept screaming at the top of her voice.

A short while later, they emerged from the woods. Sita tall, regal but dripping wet and furious. Muscles rippling with the strain of dragging Shurpanakha along. The Lankan princess' hands remained securely tied.

Ram and Lakshman immediately drew their swords, as did everyone else present.

The younger prince of Ayodhya was the first to find his voice. Looking at Vibhishan accusingly, he demanded, 'What the hell is going on?'

Vibhishan couldn't take his eyes off the two women. He seemed genuinely shocked, but quickly gathered his wits and replied. 'What is your sister-in-law doing to my sister? She is the one who has clearly attacked Shurpanakha.'

'Stop this drama!' shouted Lakshman. *'Bhabhi* would not do this unless your sister attacked her first.'

Sita walked into the circle of people and let go of Shurpanakha. The Lankan princess was clearly livid and out of control.

Vibhishan immediately rushed to his sister, drew a knife and cut the ropes that bound her. He whispered into her ear. 'Let me handle this. Stay quiet.'

Shurpanakha glared at Vibhishan. Like this was all his fault.

Sita turned to Ram and gestured towards Shurpanakha. She held out some herbs in the palm of her hand. 'That pipsqueak Lankan stuffed this in my mouth as she pushed me into the river!'

Ram recognised the herbs. They were normally used to render people unconscious before surgeries. He looked at Vibhishan, his piercing eyes red with anger. 'What is going on?'

Vibhishan stood up immediately, his manner placatory. 'There has obviously been some misunderstanding. My sister would never do something like that.'

'Are you suggesting that I imagined her pushing me into the water?' asked Sita, aggressively.

Vibhishan stared at Shurpanakha, who had also stood up by now. He seemed to be pleading with her to be quiet. But the entreaty was clearly lost in transmission.

'That is a lie!' screeched Shurpanakha. 'I didn't do anything like that!'

'Are you calling me a liar?' growled Sita.

What happened next was so sudden that very few had the time to react. With frightening speed, Shurpanakha reached to her side and drew her knife. Lakshman, who was standing to the left of Sita, saw the quick movement and rushed forward, screaming, *'Bhabhi!'*

Sita moved quickly to get out of the way and avoid the strike. In that split second, Lakshman lunged forward and banged into a charging Shurpanakha, seizing both her arms and pushing her back with all his brute strength. The elfin princess of Lanka went flying back. Her own hand, which held the knife, struck her face as she crashed into the Lankan soldiers who stood transfixed behind her. The knife hit her face horizontally, cutting deep into her nose. It fell from her hand as she lay sprawled on the ground, the shock having numbed any sensation of pain.

As blood gushed out alarmingly, her conscious mind asserted control. She touched her face and looked at her blood-stained hands. The horror of it all reverberated through her being. She knew she would be left with deep scars on her face. Painful surgeries would be required to remove them.

She screeched with savage hate and lunged forward again, this time going for Lakshman. Vibhishan rushed to her and caught hold of his rage-maddened sister.

'Kill them!' screamed Shurpanakha. 'Kill them all!'

'Wait!' pleaded Vibhishan, stricken with visceral fear. He knew they were outnumbered. He didn't want to die. And he feared something even worse than death. 'Wait!'

Ram held up his left hand, his fist closed tight, signalling his people to stop but be on guard. 'Leave now, prince. Or there will be hell to pay.'

'Forget what we were told!' screeched Shurpanakha. 'Kill them all!'

Ram spoke to a clearly stunned Vibhishan, who held on to a struggling Shurpanakha for all he was worth. 'Leave now, Prince Vibhishan.'

'Retreat,' whispered Vibhishan.

His soldiers began to withdraw, their swords still pointed in the direction of the forest-dwellers.

'Kill them, you coward!' Shurpanakha lashed out. 'I am your sister! Avenge me!'

Vibhishan dragged a flailing Shurpanakha, his eye on Ram. Mindful of any sudden movement.

'Kill them!' shouted Shurpanakha.

Vibhishan continued to pull his protesting sister away as the Lankans left the camp and escaped from Panchavati.

Ram, Lakshman and Sita stood rooted to their spot. What had happened was an unmitigated disaster.

'We cannot stay here anymore,' Jatayu stated the obvious. 'We don't have a choice. We need to flee, now.'

Ram looked at Jatayu.

'We have shed Lankan royal blood, even if it is that of the royal rebels,' said Jatayu. 'According to their customary law, Raavan has no choice but to respond. It would be the same among many Sapt Sindhu royals as well, isn't it? Raavan will come. Have no doubt about that. Vibhishan is a coward, but Raavan and Kumbhakarna aren't. They will come with thousands of soldiers. This will be worse than Mithila. There it was a battle between soldiers; a part and parcel of war; they understood that. But here it is personal. His sister, a member of his family, has been attacked. Blood was shed. His honour will demand retribution.'

Lakshman stiffened. 'But I didn't attack her. She—'

'That's not how Raavan will see it,' interrupted Jatayu. 'He will not quibble with you over the details, Prince Lakshman. We need to run. Right now.'

Chapter 32

They had been on the run for thirty days. Racing east through the *Dandakaranya*, they had moved a reasonable distance parallel to the Godavari, so that they couldn't be easily spotted or tracked. But they couldn't afford to stray too far from the tributary rivers or other water bodies, for the best chance of hunting animals would be lost.

They had been surviving on dried meat and jungle berries or leaves, for long. Perhaps the Lankans had lost track of them, they thought. With the frugal food and constant marching, their bodies were weakening. So Ram and Lakshman had set out to hunt, while Sita and the Malayaputra soldier Makrant had gone to fetch banana leaves.

Secrecy was of the essence. So they were cooking their food in holes dug deep into the ground. For fire they used a very specific type of coal; anthracite, which let out smokeless flames. As added precaution, the buried cooking pot was also covered with a thick layer of banana leaves to ensure that even by chance, no smoke escaped, which could give their position away. It was for this that Sita and Makrant were cutting banana leaves. It was Sita's turn to cook.

Unknown to Sita, Raavan's *Pushpak Vimaan* had landed a short distance from the camp. Its ear-splitting noise drowned out by thunderous howling winds. Unseasonal rains had just lashed the area. A hundred Lankan soldiers had disgorged from the *Vimaan*, attacking the camp and killing most of the Malayaputras rapidly.

Some Lankans had fanned out to search for Sita, Ram, and Lakshman. Two of them had ambushed Sita and Makrant, who were on their way back to the camp. Makrant had died, hit by two arrows. One through his shoulder and the other through his neck. Sita had, through sheer skill, managed to kill these two Lankans, steal their weapons and reach the camp. There she had found that every single Malayaputra, except for Jatayu was dead. She had tried, heroically, to save Jatayu, but had failed. The Naga had been grievously injured trying to protect the one he worshipped as the Vishnu.

Kumbhakarna, the younger brother of Raavan, had ordered that Sita was to be captured alive. Many Lankan soldiers had charged at Sita at the same time. She had fought bravely, but was ultimately captured, incapacitated and rendered unconscious with a Lankan blue-coloured toxin.

They had quickly bundled her into the *Pushpak Vimaan* and taken off, just as Ram and Lakshman had reached the camp to find dead bodies strewn everywhere and the severely injured figure of Jatayu.

— ु॒र्ऽ —

Sita couldn't remember how long she had been unconscious. It must have been hours. She still felt a little groggy. Light was streaming in through the porthole windows on the walls of the *vimaan*. A constant, dull repetitive sound was causing her pain in her head. It took her some time to realise that it was the sound of the *vimaan's* rotors, muffled by the soundproof walls.

Not soundproofed enough.

Sita pressed her temples to ease the pain in her head. It worked only for a few moments. The pain was back soon.

Then she realised something odd.

My hands aren't tied.

She looked down at her legs. They weren't tied either.

She felt her hopes rise.

Almost immediately, it deflated and she laughed softly at her own stupidity.

Where am I planning to go? I'm thousands of feet up in the sky. That blue toxin has made me slow.

She shook her head slowly. Trying to clear it.

She was on a stretcher fastened onto a platform close to the wall.

She looked around. The *vimaan* was truly huge. She looked up. It was perfectly conical from the inside as well. Smooth metal all the way to the tapering top, high up. There was a painting at the summit. Her vision was a little clouded so she couldn't see what it was. At the exact centre of the *vimaan* was a tall, perfectly cylindrical pillar, stretching all the way to the top. It was solid metal, obviously sturdy. She felt like she was inside a giant temple spire. But the interiors, while spacious and comfortable, had frugal furnishing. None of the luxurious and expensive accoutrements of most royal vehicles; or at least the royal vehicles in the Sapt Sindhu. The *Pushpak Vimaan* was basic, sparse, and efficient. Clearly, more of a military vehicle than one for pomp and show.

Because it placed function over form, the *Pushpak Vimaan* was able to comfortably accommodate more than a hundred soldiers. They all sat silently, disciplined, in regular concentric arcs on the floor, right up to the *vimaan* walls.

She could see Raavan and Kumbhakarna seated on chairs that had been fastened to the floor. Their seating area had been screened partially. A curtain hung from an overhanging rod. They weren't too far. But they whispered. So, Sita could not hear much of what they were saying.

Still on the stretcher, she came up on her elbows. Making a heaving sound. She still felt weak.

Raavan and Kumbhakarna turned to look at her. They got up and started walking towards her. Raavan stumbled on his *dhoti*. Distracted.

Sita had managed to sit up by now. She sucked in her breath and looked defiantly at the two brothers.

'Kill me now,' growled Sita. 'Otherwise, you will regret it.'

All the Lankan soldiers stood up, drawing their weapons. But at a signal from Kumbhakarna, they held their positions.

Kumbhakarna spoke, surprisingly gently, 'We don't want to hurt you. You must be tired. You woke up very quickly. The toxin given to you was strong. Please rest.'

Sita didn't answer. Surprised by Kumbhakarna's kind tone.

'We didn't know,' said a hesitant Kumbhakarna. 'I ... I didn't know. We wouldn't have used that toxin otherwise ...'

Sita remained silent.

Then she turned towards Raavan. He was just staring at her. Unblinking. There was sadness on his face. Melancholy. And, his eyes appeared strange. Almost like there was love in them.

Sita shrank to the wall, pulling her *angvastram*, covering herself.

Suddenly, a hand appeared. A neem leaf. And, the blue-coloured paste. Her nose.

Sita felt darkness enveloping her vision. Slowly.

She saw Raavan looking to Sita's right, where the person

who had drugged her was standing. There was anger on his face.

And, darkness took over.

— ॐ —

Her eyes opened.

Diffused light streamed through the porthole windows. The sun was close to the horizon.

How long have I been unconscious?

Sita couldn't be sure. Was it a few hours? Or many *prahars?*

She edged up, again. Slowly. Weakly. She could see that most of the soldiers were asleep on the floor.

But there were no soldiers around the platform where she had been sleeping.

She had been left alone.

Raavan and Kumbhakarna were standing near their chairs. Stretching their legs. Whispering to each other.

Her vision cleared slowly. Allowing her to judge the distance. Raavan and Kumbhakarna were not more than fifteen or twenty feet from her. Their backs to Sita. They were in deep conversation.

Sita looked around. And smiled.

Someone has been careless.

There was a knife lying close by. On the platform where her stretcher was affixed. She edged over. Noiselessly. Carefully. Picked up the scabbard and unsheathed the blade. Slowly. Without making any sound.

She held the knife tight in her hand.

She took some deep breaths. Firing energy into her body.

She remembered what she had heard.

Kill the chief and the Lankans capitulate.

She tried to get up. The world spun around her.

She sat back on the platform. Breathing deeper. Firing more oxygen into her body.

Then, she focused. She got up stealthily and crept towards Raavan.

When she was just a few feet from Raavan's back, she raised her knife and lunged forward.

A loud scream was heard as someone grabbed Sita from behind. An arm around her neck. A knife pressed close to her throat. Sita could feel that her attacker was a woman.

Raavan and Kumbhakarna whirled around almost immediately. Most of the Lankan soldiers got up too.

Kumbhakarna raised his hands slowly. Carefully. He spoke in a calm but commanding voice. 'Drop the knife.'

Sita felt the arm around her throat tighten. She could see that by now, all the Lankan soldiers were on their feet. She surrendered and dropped her knife.

Kumbhakarna repeated. A little harsher this time. 'I said, drop the knife.'

Sita knit her brow. Confused. She looked down at the knife she had dropped. She was about to say that she had no other knife, when she felt a prick on her neck. The attacker, holding her from behind, had brought the knife in closer. Its tip drawing blood.

Kumbhakarna looked at Raavan before turning back to the attacker holding Sita. 'Khara is dead. This will not bring him back. Don't be silly. I am ordering you. Drop the knife.'

Sita could feel the arm clasped around her neck tremble. Her attacker was struggling with deep emotions.

Finally, Raavan stepped closer and spoke in a harsh, commanding, almost terrifying tone. 'Drop the knife. Now.'

Sita felt the arm clasped around her throat relax. It was suddenly pulled back. And a soft whisper was heard.

'As you command, Iraiva.'

Sita was stunned as she heard the voice. She spun around. Staggered. She fell back, holding the wall of the *vimaan* for support.

Willing breaths into her body, she looked again at the face of her attacker. The one who had wanted to kill her a few moments ago. The one who obviously had strong emotions for Khara. The one who obviously was under the complete control of Raavan.

The one who had saved her life once …

The one she had thought was her friend.

Samichi.

… *to be continued.*

Other Titles by Amish

The Shiva Trilogy

The fastest-selling book series in the history of Indian publishing

THE IMMORTALS OF MELUHA
(Book 1 of the Trilogy)

1900 BC. What modern Indians mistakenly call the Indus Valley Civilisation, the inhabitants of that period knew as the land of Meluha – a near perfect empire created many centuries earlier by Lord Ram. Now their primary river Saraswati is drying, and they face terrorist attacks from their enemies from the east. Will their prophesied hero, the Neelkanth, emerge to destroy evil?

THE SECRET OF THE NAGAS
(Book 2 of the Trilogy)

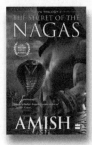

The sinister Naga warrior has killed his friend Brahaspati and now stalks his wife Sati. Shiva, who is the prophesied destroyer of evil, will not rest till he finds his demonic adversary. His thirst for revenge will lead him to the door of the Nagas, the serpent people. Fierce battles will be fought and unbelievable secrets revealed in the second part of the Shiva trilogy.

THE OATH OF THE VAYUPUTRAS
(Book 3 of the Trilogy)

Shiva reaches the Naga capital, Panchavati, and prepares for a holy war against his true enemy. The Neelkanth must not fail, no matter what the cost. In his desperation, he reaches out to the Vayuputras. Will he succeed? And what will be the real cost of battling Evil? Read the concluding part of this bestselling series to find out.

Ram Chandra Series

The second fastest-selling book series in the history of Indian publishing

RAM – SCION OF IKSHVAKU
(Book 1 of the Series)

He loves his country and he stands alone for the law. His band of brothers, his wife, Sita, and the fight against the darkness of chaos. He is Prince Ram. Will he rise above the taint that others heap on him? Will his love for Sita sustain him through his struggle? Will he defeat the demon Raavan who destroyed his childhood? Will he fulfil the destiny of the Vishnu? Begin an epic journey with Amish's latest: the Ram Chandra Series.

RAAVAN – ENEMY OF ARYAVARTA
(Book 3 of the Series)

Raavan is determined to be a giant among men, to conquer, plunder, and seize the greatness that he thinks is his right. He is a man of contrasts, of brutal violence and scholarly knowledge. A man who will love without reward and kill without remorse. In this, the third book in the Ram Chandra Series, Amish sheds light on Raavan, the king of Lanka. Is he the greatest villain in history or just a man in a dark place, all the time?

Indic Chronicles
LEGEND OF SUHELDEV

Repeated attacks by Mahmud of Ghazni have weakened India's northern regions. Then the Turks raid and destroy one of the holiest temples in the land: the magnificent Lord Shiva temple at Somnath. At this most desperate of times, a warrior rises to defend the nation. King Suheldev —fierce rebel, charismatic leader, inclusive patriot. Read this epic adventure of courage and heroism that recounts the story of that lionhearted warrior and the magnificent Battle of Bahraich.

Non-fiction

IMMORTAL INDIA

Explore India with the country's storyteller, Amish, who helps you understand it like never before, through a series of sharp articles, nuanced speeches and intelligent debates. In *Immortal India*, Amish lays out the vast landscape of an ancient culture with a fascinatingly modern outlook.

DHARMA – DECODING THE EPICS FOR A MEANINGFUL LIFE

In this genre-bending book, the first of a series, Amish and Bhavna dive into the priceless treasure trove of the ancient Indian epics, as well as the vast and complex universe of Amish's Meluha, to explore some of the key concepts of Indian philosophy. Within this book are answers to our many philosophical questions, offered through simple and wise interpretations of our favourite stories.

Raavan

Amish is a 1974-born, IIM (Kolkata)-educated banker-turned-author. The success of his debut book, *The Immortals of Meluha* (Book 1 of the Shiva Trilogy), encouraged him to give up his career in financial services to focus on writing. Besides being an author, he is also an Indian-government diplomat, a host for TV documentaries, and a film producer.

Amish is passionate about history, mythology and philosophy, finding beauty and meaning in all world religions. His books have sold more than 6 million copies and have been translated into over 20 languages. His Shiva Trilogy is the fastest selling and his Ram Chandra Series the second fastest selling book series in Indian publishing history. You can connect with Amish here:

- www.facebook.com/authoramish
- www.instagram.com/authoramish
- www.twitter.com/authoramish

Other Titles by Amish

SHIVA TRILOGY

The fastest-selling book series in the history of Indian publishing

The Immortals of Meluha (Book 1 of the Trilogy)

The Secret of the Nagas (Book 2 of the Trilogy)

The Oath of the Vayuputras (Book 3 of the Trilogy)

RAM CHANDRA SERIES

The second fastest-selling book series in the history of Indian publishing

Ram – Scion of Ikshvaku (Book 1 of the Series)

Sita – Warrior of Mithila (Book 2 of the Series)

War of Lanka (Book 4 in the Series)

INDIC CHRONICLES

Legend of Suheldev

NON-FICTION

Immortal India: Young Country, Timeless Civilisation

Dharma: Decoding the Epics for a Meaningful Life

www.authoramish.com

'{Amish's} writings have generated immense curiosity about India's rich past and culture.'

— **Narendra Modi**
(Honourable Prime Minister, India)

'{Amish's} writing introduces the youth to ancient value systems while pricking and satisfying their curiosity…'

— **Sri Sri Ravi Shankar**
(Spiritual Leader & Founder, Art of Living Foundation)

'{Amish's writing is} riveting, absorbing and informative.'

— **Amitabh Bachchan**
(Actor & Living Legend)

'{Amish's writing is} a fine blend of history and myth…gripping and unputdownable.'

— **BBC**

'Thoughtful and deep, Amish, more than any author, represents the New India.'

— **Vir Sanghvi**
(Senior Journalist & Columnist)

'Amish's mythical imagination mines the past and taps into the possibilities of the future. His book series, archetypal and stirring, unfolds the deepest recesses of the soul as well as our collective consciousness.'

— **Deepak Chopra**
(World-renowned spiritual guru and bestselling author)

'{Amish is} one of the most original thinkers of his generation.'
– Arnab Goswami
(Senior Journalist & MD, Republic TV)

'Amish has a fine eye for detail and a compelling narrative style.'
– Dr. Shashi Tharoor
(Member of Parliament & Author)

'{Amish has} a deeply thoughtful mind with an unusual, original, and fascinating view of the past.'
– Shekhar Gupta
(Senior Journalist & Columnist)

'To understand the New India, you need to read Amish.'
– Swapan Dasgupta
(Member of Parliament & Senior Journalist)

'Through all of Amish's books flows a current of liberal progressive ideology: about gender, about caste, about discrimination of any kind... He is the only Indian bestselling writer with true philosophical depth – his books are all backed by tremendous research and deep thought.'
– Sandipan Deb
(Senior Journalist & Editorial Director, Swarajya)

'Amish's influence goes beyond his books, his books go beyond literature, his literature is steeped in philosophy, which is anchored in bhakti, which powers his love for India.'
– Gautam Chikermane
(Senior Journalist & Author)

'Amish is a literary phenomenon.'

– Anil Dharker
(Senior Journalist & Author)

Raavan
Enemy of Aryavarta

Book 3
of the
Ram Chandra Series

Amish

HarperCollins *Publishers* India

www.authoramish.com

First published in 2019

This edition published in India by HarperCollins *Publishers* 2022
4th Floor, Tower A, Building No. 10, Phase II, DLF Cyber City,
Gurugram, Haryana – 122002
www.harpercollins.co.in

2 4 6 8 10 9 7 5 3 1

Copyright © Amish Tripathi 2019, 2022

P-ISBN: 978-93-5629-097-6
E-ISBN: 978-93-5629-098-3

Typeset by Jojy Philip, New Delhi 110 015

Printed and bound at
Thomson Press (India) Ltd

Om Namah Shivāya

The universe bows to Lord Shiva.

I bow to Lord Shiva.

To You,

I was drowning,
In Grief, in Anger, in Depression.
You have pulled me into the open air of Peace,
If only for a little while,
By merely listening to my words.

And it is not Mere Words when I say,
That you will always have my quiet gratitude,
You will always have my silent love.

'When extraordinary good fortune of overwhelming
Glory comes to a person,
Retreating misfortune increases the power
of its Sorrows.'

— Kalhana, in *Rajatarangini*

Who among you wants to be great?
Who among you wants to lose all chance at happiness?
Is this Glory even worth it?

I am Raavan.
I want it all.
I want fame. I want power. I want wealth.
I want complete triumph.
Even if my Glory walks side by side with my Sorrow.

List of Important Characters and Tribes

Akampana: A smuggler; one of Raavan's closest aides

Arishtanemi: Military chief of the Malayaputras; right-hand man of Vishwamitra

Ashwapati: King of the northwestern kingdom of Kekaya; father of Kaikeyi and a loyal ally of Dashrath

Bharat: Ram's half-brother; son of Dashrath and Kaikeyi

Dashrath: Chakravarti king of Kosala and emperor of the Sapt Sindhu; father of Ram, Bharat, Lakshman and Shatrughan

Hanuman: A Naga and a member of the Vayuputra tribe

Indrajit: Son of Raavan and Mandodari

Janak: King of Mithila; father of Sita

Jatayu: A captain of the Malayaputra tribe; Naga friend of Sita and Ram

Kaikesi: Rishi Vishrava's first wife; mother of Raavan and Kumbhakarna

Khara: A captain in the Lankan army; Samichi's lover

Krakachabahu: The governor of Chilika

Kubaer: The chief-trader of Lanka

Kumbhakarna: Raavan's brother; also a Naga

Kushadhwaj: King of Sankashya; younger brother of Janak

Lakshman: One of the twin sons of Dashrath; Ram's half-brother

Malayaputras: The tribe left behind by Lord Parshu Ram, the sixth Vishnu

Mandodari: Wife of Raavan

Mara: An independent assassin for hire

Mareech: Kaikesi's brother; Raavan and Kumbhakarna's uncle; one of Raavan's closest aides

Nagas: Human beings born with deformities

Prithvi: A businessman in the village of Todee

Raavan: Son of Rishi Vishrava; brother of Kumbhakarna; half-brother of Vibhishan and Shurpanakha

Ram: Son of Emperor Dashrath and his eldest wife Kaushalya; eldest of four brothers; later married to Sita

Samichi: Police and protocol chief of Mithila; Khara's lover

Shatrughan: Twin brother of Lakshman; son of Dashrath and Sumitra; Ram's half-brother

Shochikesh: The landlord of Todee village

Shurpanakha: Half-sister of Raavan

Sita: Daughter of King Janak and Queen Sunaina of Mithila; also the prime minister of Mithila; later married to Ram

Sukarman: A resident of Todee village; Shochikesh's son

Vali: The king of Kishkindha

Vashishtha: Raj guru, the royal priest of Ayodhya; teacher of the four Ayodhya princes

Vayuputras: The tribe left behind by Lord Rudra, the previous Mahadev

Vedavati: A resident of Todee village; Prithvi's wife

Vibhishan: Half-brother of Raavan

Vishrava: A revered rishi; the father of Raavan, Kumbhakarna, Vibhishan and Shurpanakha

Vishwamitra: Chief of the Malayaputras; also temporary guru of Ram and Lakshman

Note on the Narrative Structure

Thank you for picking up this book and giving me the most important thing you can share: your time.

I know many of you have been patiently waiting for the release of the third part of the Ram Chandra series. My sincere apologies for the delay, and I hope the book will live up to your expectations.

Some of you may wonder why I decided to change the name of the book from *Raavan – Orphan of Aryavarta* to *Raavan – Enemy of Aryavarta*. Let me explain. While writing Raavan's story, I realised a few things about the man. Right from when he was a child, Raavan raged against the circumstances he found himself in. He was very much a man in charge of his destiny. Initially, I felt Raavan had been cast aside by his motherland and was thus, in a sense, an orphan. But as the story unfolded in my mind, I felt the decisions that took him away from his motherland were deliberate. He *chose* to be the enemy rather than being cast into the role of the orphan.

As some of you know, I have been inspired by a storytelling technique called hyperlink, which some call the multilinear narrative. In such a narrative, there are many characters; and a connection brings them all together. The three main characters in the Ram Chandra series are Ram, Sita and Raavan. Each character has life experiences, which mould who they are, and each has their own adventure and riveting backstory. Finally, their stories converge with the kidnapping of Sita.

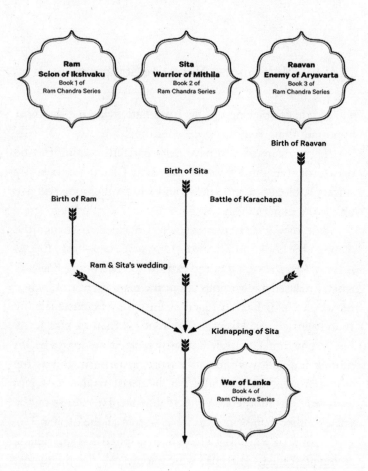

So while the first book explored the tale of Ram, the second the story of Sita, the third burrows into the life of Raavan, before all three stories merge from the fourth book onwards into a single story. It is important to remember that Raavan is much older than both Sita and Ram. In fact Ram is born on the day that Raavan fights a decisive battle—against Ram's father Emperor Dashrath! This book, therefore, goes further back in time, before the birth of the other principal characters—Sita and Ram.

I knew that writing three books, in a multilinear narrative, would be a complicated and time-consuming affair, but I must confess, it was thoroughly exciting. I hope it is as rewarding and thrilling an experience for you as it was for me. Understanding Ram, Sita and Raavan as characters helped me inhabit their worlds and explore the maze of plots and stories that illuminate this great epic. I feel truly blessed for this.

Since I was following a multilinear narrative, I left clues in the first book (*Ram – Scion of Ikshvaku*) as well as the second (*Sita – Warrior of Mithila*), which tie up with the stories in the third. There are surprises and twists in store for you here, and many to follow!

I hope you enjoy reading *Raavan – Enemy of Aryavarta*. Do tell me what you think of it, by sending me messages on my Facebook, Instagram, or Twitter accounts given below.

Love,
Amish

www.facebook.com/authoramish
www.instagram.com/authoramish
www.twitter.com/authoramish

Acknowledgements

The acknowledgements written below were composed when the book was published in 2019. I must also acknowledge those that are publishing this edition of **Raavan-Enemy of Aryavarta**. *The team at HarperCollins: Swati, Shabnam, Akriti, Gokul, Vikas, Rahul, and Udayan, led by the brilliant Ananth. Looking forward to this new journey with them.*

***

It has been a terrible two years. I have been cursed with more grief and suffering in this benighted period, than what I had experienced in my entire life before. Sometimes I felt that the structure of my entire life was collapsing. But it did not. I survived. The building still stands. This book worked like a keystone. And the ones I acknowledge below, have been my buttresses; for they have held me together.

My God, Lord Shiva. He has really tested me these last two years. I hope He will make it a little bit easier now.

The two men I have admired most in my life, men of old-world values, courage, and honour; my father-in-law Manoj Vyas and my brother-in-law Himanshu Roy. They are both up in heaven now, looking at me. I hope I can make them proud.

Neel, my 10-year-old son; and you will pardon this father's emotionality when I say, 'My boy is the best there ever was and ever will be!'

Bhavna, my sister; Anish and Ashish, my brothers, for all their inputs to the story. As always, they read the first draft. Their views, support, affection, and encouragement are invaluable.

The rest of my family: Usha, Vinay, Shernaz, Meeta, Preeti, Donetta, Smita, Anuj, Ruta for their consistent faith and love. And I must acknowledge the contribution of the next generation of my family towards my happiness: Mitansh, Daniel, Aiden, Keya, Anika and Ashna.

Gautam, the CEO of my publisher Westland, and Karthika and Sanghamitra, my editors. If there are people outside of my family, who are the closest to this project, it is this trio. They are an unbeatable mix of capability, politeness and grace. Here's hoping for a long innings together. The rest of the brilliant team at Westland: Anand, Abhijeet, Ankit, Arunima, Barani, Christina, Deepthi, Dhaval, Divya, Jaisankar, Jayanthi, Krishnakumar, Kuldeep, Madhu, Mustafa, Naveen, Neha, Nidhi, Preeti, Raju, Sanyog, Sateesh, Satish, Shatrughan, Srivats, Sudha, Vipin, Vishwajyoti and many others. They are the best team in the publishing business.

Aman, Vijay, Prerna, Seema, and the rest of my colleagues at my office. They take care of my business work which gives me enough free time to write.

Hemal, Neha, Candida, Hitesh, Parth, Vinit, Natashaa, Prakash, Anuj, and the rest of the Oktobuzz team, who have designed the cover for the book, and done a fantastic job at it. They have also made the trailer and helped manage many of the social media activities for the book. A brilliant, creative, and committed agency.

Mayank, Shreyaa, Sarojini, Deepika, Naresh, Marvi, Sneha, Simran, Kirti, Priyanka, Vishaal, Danish and the Moe's Art team, who have driven media relations and marketing alliances for the book. They are more than an agency, they are advisors.

Satya and his team who have shot the new author photos that have been used on the inside cover of this book. He made a rather ordinary subject look better.

Caleb, Kshitij, Sandeep, Rohini, Dharav, Heena and their respective teams who support my work with their business, legal and marketing advice.

Mrunalini, a brilliant Sanskrit scholar, who works with me on research. My discussions with her are enlightening. What I learn from her helps me develop many theories which go into the books.

Aditya, a passionate reader of my books, who has now become a friend and a fact-checker.

And last, but certainly not the least, you, the reader. I know this book has been delayed a lot. My sincere apologies for this. Life just took me away from writing. But it did bring me back. And I will not falter from here on. Thank you for your patience, love and support.

Chapter 1

3400 BCE, Salsette Island, west coast of India

The man screamed in agony. He knew his end was near. He wouldn't have to bear this pain much longer. But he had to hold on to the secret till then. He had to. Just a little longer.

He steeled himself and repeated the chant endlessly in his mind. A chant that held immense power. A chant sacred to all in his tribe: the tribe of the Malayaputras.

Jai Shri Rudra… Jai Parshu Ram… Jai Shri Rudra… Jai Parshu Ram.

Glory to Lord Rudra. Glory to Lord Parshu Ram.

He closed his eyes, focusing on the mantra. Trying to forget his present surroundings.

Give me strength, Lords. Give me strength.

His nemesis stood over him, preparing to inflict yet another wound. But before he could strike, he was pulled back roughly. By a woman.

She whispered in an angry, guttural voice, 'Khara, this is not working.'

Khara, a platoon commander in the Lankan armed forces, turned towards Samichi, his childhood love. Until a few years back, Samichi had been the acting prime minister of Mithila, a small kingdom in north India. But she had since abandoned her post and was focused on finding the whereabouts of the person who had appointed her. The princess she had once served: Sita.

'This Malayaputra is a tough nut,' Khara whispered. 'He won't break. We have to find the information some other way.'

'There is no time!'

Samichi's whisper was rough in its urgency. Khara knew she was right. The man on the rack was their best possible source of information for now. Only he could tell them where Sita, her husband Ram, his brother Lakshman, and the sixteen Malayaputra soldiers accompanying them were hiding. Khara also knew how important it was to extract this information. It was their chance to get back into the good books of Samichi's *true lord*. The one she called *Iraiva*—Raavan, the king of Lanka.

'I am trying, but he will not last much longer like this,' Khara said in a low voice, trying to mask his disappointment. 'I don't think he'll talk.'

'Let me try.'

Before Khara could respond, Samichi strode up to the table where the Malayaputra lay shackled. She yanked off his dhoti and threw it aside. She then wrenched his langot away, leaving the poor man completely exposed and moaning in shame.

Even Khara seemed horrified. 'Samichi, this is—'

Samichi shot him a sharp look and he fell silent. Even torturers had a code of conduct. At least in India. But clearly, Samichi had no qualms about flouting it.

The Malayaputra's eyes were wide open in panic. Almost as if he could anticipate the pain that was to follow.

Samichi picked up a sickle lying nearby. It was dangerously sharp on one side, serrated on the other. A cruel design crafted to inflict maximum pain. She moved towards the torture rack, the sickle in her hand. She held it up, felt its sharp edge, letting it prick her finger and draw blood. 'You will talk. Trust me. You will talk,' she snarled as she poised the sickle between the Malayaputra's legs. Dangerously close.

She moved the sickle slowly, deliberately. It sliced through the soft epidermis and cut deeper. Deeper into the scrotum. Inflicting the maximum pain possible at a point that had an almost sadistic concentration of nerve endings.

The Malayaputra screamed.

He cried, he pleaded for it to stop.

It wasn't his Gods he cried to. This was beyond them now. He was calling out to his mother.

Khara knew then. The Malayaputra would talk. It was only a matter of time. He would break. And he would talk.

—ॐ‌I—

Raavan and his younger brother Kumbhakarna sat comfortably inside the Pushpak Vimaan, the legendary flying vehicle, as it flew over the dense jungle.

The king of Lanka was quiet, his body tense. He clutched his pendant tightly—the pendant that always hung from a gold chain around his neck. It was made of the bones of two human fingers, the phalanges of which were carefully fastened with gold links.

Many Indians believed in the existence of tribes of demonic warriors that adorned themselves with relics from the bodies of their bravest adversaries. In doing so, they were said to transfer to themselves the strength of the dead men. The Lankan soldiers, thoroughly loyal to Raavan, believed and propagated the legend that the pendant around his neck was made from the remains of an archenemy's hand. Only Kumbhakarna knew the truth. Only he knew what it meant when Raavan held the pendant tight, the way he was gripping it now.

Leaving his elder brother to his silent ruminations, Kumbhakarna looked around the Pushpak Vimaan. The gargantuan flying vehicle was shaped like a cone that gently tapered upwards. Its many portholes, close to the base, were sealed with thick glass, but the metallic window shades had been drawn back. The diffused light of the early morning sun streamed in, lighting up the interiors. Though the vehicle was reasonably soundproof, the loud sound of the main rotor at the top of the vimaan could be heard. Added to that was the noise of the many smaller rotors, close to the base of the aircraft, which helped control the directional and lateral movements of the flying machine.

The craft's interiors, while spacious and comfortable, were done in a simple, minimalist style. As Kumbhakarna looked up, his eyes fell on the only embellishment inside the vimaan—a large painting of a single rudraaksh, near the inner summit of the vimaan. A brown, elliptical seed, the rudraaksh literally meant the 'teardrop of Rudra'. All those who were loyal to the *God of Gods*, the *Mahadev*, Lord Rudra, wore threaded rudraaksh seeds on their body or placed it in their puja rooms. The painting depicted a particular type of rudraaksh that had a single groove running across it. The original, much smaller seed, which was the model for the painting, was known as an *ekmukhi*. A rare kind of rudraaksh, it was difficult to find and extremely expensive. A specimen impaled on a gold thread was kept in Raavan's private temple in his palace.

Apart from the painting, the vimaan was mostly bare—more of a military vehicle than one designed for luxury. Because it placed function over form, it was able to accommodate more than a hundred passengers.

Kumbhakarna noticed with satisfaction that the soldiers sat silently, in disciplined arcs that fanned out across the vimaan. They had just finished eating. Fed and rested, they were ready for action. It was a matter of a few hours before they would descend on Salsette Island. There, Kumbhakarna had been told, Samichi awaited them with crucial information about the exiled Ayodhya royals—Ram, Sita, his wife, Lakshman, his younger brother—and their band of Malayaputra supporters.

The Lankan soldiers believed they were on their way to avenge the insult to their mighty king's sister, Shurpanakha, who had been injured by Prince Lakshman. While cosmetic surgery would take away the physical marks of the injury to her nose, the metaphorical loss of face could only be avenged with blood. The soldiers knew that. They understood that.

But few of them stopped to wonder exactly what Princess Shurpanakha and Prince Vibhishan, the younger half-siblings of Raavan, had been doing so far away, deep in the Dandakaranya, with the exiled and relatively powerless royals of Ayodhya.

'They are complete idiots,' said Raavan gruffly, keeping his voice low. A curtain draped on an overhanging rod partially screened Raavan's and Kumbhakarna's chairs from the rest. 'I should never have trusted them with this mission.'

After a botched encounter and the resultant skirmish with Ram and the others, Vibhishan had taken Shurpanakha and the Lankan soldiers on a quick march back to Salsette, on the west coast of India. From there, led by Raavan's son Indrajit, they had taken a ship back to Lanka. Upon hearing of their failed mission, Raavan had left his capital city immediately, with as many soldiers as could be accommodated in the Pushpak Vimaan.

Kumbhakarna took a deep breath and looked at his elder brother. 'It's in the past now, Dada,' he said.

'Such fools! Vibhishan and Shurpanakha have taken after their stupid barbarian mother. They can't even handle a simple job.'

Raavan and Kumbhakarna were the sons of Rishi Vishrava and his first wife, Kaikesi. Vibhishan and Shurpanakha were also the sage's children, but by his second wife, Crataeis, a Greek princess from the island of Knossos in the Mediterranean Sea. Raavan abhorred his half-siblings, but had been forced to accept them, by his mother, after their father's death.

'Every family has its idiots, Dada,' said Kumbhakarna with a smile, trying to calm his brother down. 'But they're still family.'

'I should have listened to you. I should never have sent them.'

'Forget it, Dada.'

'Sometimes I feel like—'

'We'll handle it, Dada,' Kumbhakarna interrupted him. 'We'll kidnap the Vishnu, and the Malayaputras will be left with no choice but to give us what we want. What we need.'

Raavan took his brother's hand. 'I've given you nothing but trouble, Kumbha. Thank you for always sticking by me.'

'No, Dada. I am the one who has given you nothing but trouble since my birth. I am alive because of you. And I will die for you,' Kumbhakarna said, his voice edged with emotion.

'Nonsense! You will not die anytime soon. Not for me. Not for anybody. You will die of old age, many many years from now, when you have bedded every woman you want to and drunk as much wine as your heart desires!'

Kumbhakarna, who had been celibate and a teetotaller for several years now, laughed. 'You do enough of that for both of us, Dada!'

—ऱॏ—

Strong winds buffeted the Pushpak Vimaan. The vehicle lurched and juddered, like a toy in the hands of a giant demonic child. The rain was coming down hard. They watched it fall in sheets, past the thick glass of the portholes.

'By the great Lord Rudra, it can't be my fate to die in a stupid air crash.'

Raavan double-checked the body grip that held him securely in his chair. As did Kumbhakarna. These grips had been specially designed to evenly distribute the force of restraint over the torso of the seated passengers. Even their thighs were restrained.

The Lankan soldiers, meanwhile, had attached themselves to the standard grips fixed to the floor and walls of the vimaan. Most of them were managing to keep calm, and the contents of their stomach within. Some of them, however, being first-time travellers in the vimaan, were vomiting copiously.

Kumbhakarna turned to Raavan. 'It's an unseasonal storm.'

'You think?' said Raavan, grinning. Nothing brought out his competitive spirit like adversity.

Kumbhakarna turned to look at the four pilots, who were struggling with the levers, trying to direct the craft against the wind with the sheer force of their bodies against the controls.

'Not too hard!' shouted Kumbhakarna, making his voice carry over the howling wind. 'If the levers break, we are done for.'

All four men turned towards Kumbhakarna, who was probably the best vimaan pilot alive.

'Don't fight the wind so hard that the controls break,' ordered Kumbhakarna. 'Let it flow. But not too loose either. Just keep the vimaan upright and we'll be fine.'

As the pilots gave the levers some slack, the vimaan lurched and swung even more vigorously.

'Are you trying to make me throw up?' asked Raavan, grimacing.

'Puking never killed anyone,' said Kumbhakarna. 'But an air crash would do the job most efficiently.'

Raavan scowled, took a deep breath, and closed his eyes. He gripped his hand brace even tighter.

'Plus, there is a positive side to this storm,' said Kumbhakarna. 'These loud winds will drown out the noise of the rotors. We'll have the element of surprise on our side when we attack them.'

Raavan opened his eyes and looked at Kumbhakarna, his eyebrows furrowed. 'Are you crazy? We outnumber them five to one. We don't need an element of surprise. We just need to land safely.'

The battle was short and decisive.

There were no Lankan casualties. All the Malayaputras, save their captain Jatayu, and two of his soldiers, were dead or critically injured. But Ram, Lakshman and Sita were missing.

While Kumbhakarna set about organising the efforts to find the trio, Raavan stood staring at a Malayaputra soldier who lay flat on his back on the ground. The man was still alive, but barely. Moving rapidly towards his death with every raspy breath.

Thick blood was pooling around his body, soaking into the wet mud and discolouring the green grass. The vastus muscles on his thighs had been slashed through. Almost down to the bone. Blood gushed out in torrents from the many severed arteries.

Raavan stared. As always, he was fascinated by the sight of a slow death.

He could hear Kumbhakarna.

'Jatayu is a traitor. He was one of us before he defected to the Malayaputras. I don't care what you do to him. Get the information, Khara.'

'Yes, Lord Kumbhakarna,' said Khara. He sounded relieved. Samichi and he had proven their worth, with information and muscle. He saluted and marched away towards his quarry.

Raavan focused on the dying Malayaputra. He was losing blood fast. It seemed to be spurting out from what appeared to be a small incision on his abdomen. But Raavan could see that the wound was deep. The kidneys, liver, stomach, had all been cut through. The man's body was twitching and shivering as the blood drained out of it.

Kumbhakarna's words pierced his consciousness again.

'I want seven teams. Two men in each team. Spread out. They can't have gone far. If you find the princes, or the princess, do not engage. One of you should come back and inform us while the other continues to track them.'

Raavan's attention was still on the Malayaputra. His left eye had been gouged out. Perhaps by a Lankan soldier wearing hidden tiger claws on his hand. The partially severed eyeball hung out of the eye socket, held tenuously by the optic nerve. Blood dripped weakly from the bloody, discoloured white ball.

The Malayaputra's mouth was open, his chest heaving. Trying to swallow air and pump oxygen through his body. Desperately trying to stay alive.

Why does the soul insist on hanging on to the body until the absolute last minute? Even when death is clearly the better alternative?

'Dada.' Kumbhakarna's voice broke his reverie. Raavan raised a hand for silence and his brother obeyed. Raavan looked on as the Malayaputra's life slowly ebbed away. His breathing grew more and more ragged. The harder he breathed, the more quickly the blood flowed out of his numerous wounds.

Let go …

Finally, there was a deep convulsion. The last, shallow breath escaped out of the dying man's mouth. For a moment, all was still. He lay with his eyes wide open, as if in panic. Both fists clenched tight. Toes bent at an ungainly angle. Body rigid.

And then, slowly, he went limp.

A few moments passed before Raavan turned away from the corpse in front of him. 'You were saying?' he asked Kumbhakarna.

'They can't have gone far,' said Kumbhakarna. 'Khara will get the information out of Jatayu soon. We'll find the Vishnu. We'll get her alive.'

'What about Ram and Lakshman?'

'We'll do our best not to hurt them. And make them think that this is revenge for what was done to Shurpanakha. Do you want to go back to the vimaan and wait?'

Raavan shook his head. *No.*

—੧੪੧—

'Let me see Sita,' said Raavan.

'Dada, there's no time. King Ram and Prince Lakshman are close by, they might reach soon. I don't want to be forced to kill them. This is perfect. We've got the Vishnu, and Ayodhya's so-called king has not been injured. Let's leave now. You can see her once we are back in the vimaan.'

The Lankans were in a small clearing where the Malayaputras had set up their temporary camp. They were surrounded by dense forest, with almost nothing visible beyond the tree line. Kumbhakarna was understandably eager to leave before the princes arrived on the spot.

Raavan nodded, and started walking towards the vimaan. His advance guard marched ahead, while Kumbhakarna strode alongside. The main body of soldiers followed, bearing the stretcher that carried a bound and unconscious Sita. The rear guard brought up the end.

Knowing that Ram and Lakshman were free and armed, the Lankans were on their guard. They did not want to be surprised by a hail of arrows.

Periodically, a voice sounded in the distance. Getting louder, and closer, with every repetition.

'Sitaaaaaaa!'

It was Ram, the eldest son of the late King Dashrath of Ayodhya. Since Ayodhya was the supreme power in the region, Dashrath was also the emperor of the *Sapt Sindhu*, the *Land of the Seven Rivers*. When Ram was banished for fourteen years for the unauthorised use of a *daivi astra*, a *divine weapon*, during the Battle of Mithila, Dashrath had nominated Bharat to be the crown prince instead. However, when it was time for Bharat to be crowned emperor after Dashrath's passing, he had, against all expectations, placed Ram's slippers on the throne and begun ruling the empire as his elder brother's representative.

Technically then, despite being in exile, Ram was the reigning king of Ayodhya and the emperor of the Sapt Sindhu. In absentia. Even though he had never formally been crowned king. Treaty obligations on other kingdoms within the Sapt Sindhu would be triggered if he was hurt or killed. These kingdoms would then be forced to mobilise for war against those who had harmed their emperor. And Raavan knew Lanka could not afford a war. Not right now.

But there was no such obligation with regard to the wife of the emperor.

The anguished voice was heard again. 'Sitaaaaaaa…'

Raavan turned towards Kumbhakarna. 'What do you think he'll do? Can he rally the armies of the Sapt Sindhu?'

Kumbhakarna, surprisingly sprightly despite his massive size, kept pace alongside Raavan. He said thoughtfully, 'It depends on how we play it. There are many who oppose Ram and his family in the Sapt Sindhu. If we can make it known that Sita was kidnapped to avenge the attack on Shurpanakha, it will give the kingdoms that don't want to go to war an excuse to back out. Also, there are no treaty obligations that refer to the eventuality of any Ayodhya royal, other than the emperor, being hurt. So they are not treaty-bound to march just because we've kidnapped the emperor's wife. Those who want to stay away can choose to stay away. I don't think he'll be able to rally a large army.'

'So those idiots, Shurpanakha and Vibhishan, have proved to be of some use after all.'

'Useful idiots,' offered Kumbhakarna, with a twinkle in his eye.

'Hey, I have the copyright on that term!' said Raavan, laughing and playfully slapping Kumbhakarna's massive belly.

The brothers had reached the Pushpak Vimaan and now quickly stepped in.

The soldiers followed and started taking their positions inside the craft. Raavan and Kumbhakarna were soon bracing themselves in preparation for take-off. The doors of the vimaan closed slowly with a hydraulic hiss.

'She's a fighter!' said Kumbhakarna with an appreciative grin, nodding in Sita's direction. The Lankan soldiers hovered around her, fastening straps around her unconscious body.

It had been a struggle to capture the brave warrior princess.

Thirty days had passed since the botched encounter between Shurpanakha and the princes, and the Ayodhyan royals had eased their guard, presuming that the Lankans had lost track of them. That day, they had decided to step out and get themselves a proper meal. Sita had gone to cut banana leaves with a Malayaputra soldier called Makrant. Ram and Lakshman had gone hunting in a separate direction.

The two Lankan soldiers who had discovered Sita had managed to kill Makrant, but were, in turn, killed by Sita. She had then stolen to the devastated Malayaputra camp and picked off several Lankans from behind the tree line, using a bow and a quiverful of arrows very effectively, moving quickly from one hiding place to another. But she had not been able to get to either Raavan or Kumbhakarna, who had been sealed off behind protective flanks of Lankan soldiers. Finally, she had been forced to come forward to save her loyal follower, Captain Jatayu. It was then that she was overpowered and rendered unconscious with a toxin, before being tied up and hauled to the vimaan.

'The Malayaputras believe she is the Vishnu,' said Raavan, laughing softly. 'She'd better be a good fighter!'

According to an ancient Indian tradition, towering leaders, the greatest among greats, who could become the propagators of goodness and harbingers of a new way of life, were recognised with the title 'Vishnu'. There had been six Vishnus till now, and the tribe of the Malayaputras had been founded by the sixth Vishnu, Lord Parshu Ram. Now the Malayaputras had recognised a seventh, one who would establish a new way of life in India: Sita. And Raavan had just kidnapped her.

The soldiers around Sita dispersed and returned to their positions.

She lay there, safely strapped onto the stretcher, some twenty feet away from Raavan. Her angvastram was drawn over her body, and the straps were tight across her torso and legs. Her eyes were closed. Saliva trickled out of the corner of her mouth. A large quantity of a very strong toxin had been used to render her unconscious.

For the first time in their lives, Raavan and Kumbhakarna saw Sita's face.

Raavan felt his breath stop. He sat immobile, heart paralysed. Eyes glued to her face.

To Sita's regal, strong, beautiful face.

Chapter 2

Fifty-six years earlier, the ashram of Guru Vishrava, close to Indraprastha, India

For a four-year-old, Raavan was quite sure and steady in his movements.

The precocious child was Rishi Vishrava's son. The celebrated rishi had married late, when he was over seventy years of age. Though you couldn't tell by looking at him: the magical anti-ageing Somras he drank regularly kept him looking youthful. In his long career spanning many decades, Rishi Vishrava had made a name for himself as a great scientist and spiritual guru. In fact, he was considered to be among the greatest intellectuals of his generation.

Being the son of such a distinguished rishi, the weight of expectations rested heavily on Raavan's young shoulders. But it appeared he would not disappoint. Even at this early age, he had a fearsome intellect. It seemed to all who met him that the child would someday surpass even the vast achievements of his illustrious father.

But the universe has a way of balancing things. With the positive comes the negative.

As the sun set on the far horizon, Raavan patiently tied the fragile legs of the hare he had trapped to two small wooden stumps sticking up from the ground. The creature struggled frantically as the boy pinned it down with his knee and pulled the ropes taut. It lay there with its limbs splayed, underside and chest exposed to the sky. The little boy was satisfied. He could begin work now.

Raavan had dissected another hare the previous day. Studied its muscles, ligaments and bones in detail, while it was still breathing. He had been keen to reach the beating heart. But the hare, having suffered enough already, died before he could cut through the sternal ribs. Its heart had stopped by the time Raavan got to it.

Today, he intended to go straight for the animal's heart.

The hare was still struggling, its long ears twitching ferociously. Normally, hares are quiet animals, but this one was clearly in a state of panic. For good reason.

Raavan checked the sharpness of his knife with the tip of his forefinger. It drew some blood. He sucked at his forefinger as he looked at the hare. He smiled.

The excitement he felt, the rapid beating of his heart, took away the dull ache in his navel. An ache that was perennial.

He used his left hand to steady his prey. Then he held the knife over the animal, the tip pointed at its chest.

Just as he was about to make the incision, he sensed a presence near him. He looked up.

The Kanyakumari.

In many parts of India, there was a tradition of venerating the *Kanyakumari*, literally the *Virgin Goddess*. It was believed that the Mother Goddess resided, temporarily, within the bodies of certain chosen young girls. These girls were worshipped as living Goddesses. People came to them for advice and prophecies—they counted even kings and queens among their followers—until they reached puberty, at which time, it was believed, the Goddess moved into the body of another pre-pubescent girl.

There were many Kanyakumari temples in India. This particular Kanyakumari who stood in front of Raavan was from Vaidyanath, in eastern India.

She was on her way back to Vaidyanath after a pilgrimage to the holy Amarnath cave in Kashmir, and had stopped at Rishi Vishrava's ashram. The holy cave, buried under snow for most of the year, housed a great lingam made of ice. It was believed that this cave was where the first Mahadev had unveiled the secrets of life and creation.

The Kanyakumari's entourage had returned from the pilgrimage with their souls energised but their bodies exhausted. The Goddess had decided to stay for a few weeks in Rishi Vishrava's ashram by the river Yamuna, before continuing on her journey to Vaidyanath.

The rishi had welcomed her visit as a blessed opportunity to speak to the Goddess and expand his understanding of the spiritual world. Despite his best efforts, however, the Kanyakumari had kept to herself and spent little time with him or the many inhabitants of his ashram.

But that had only added to the natural magnetism and aura of the living Goddess. Even Raavan, usually preoccupied in his own world, had stared at her every chance he got, fascinated.

He looked up at her now, transfixed, knife poised in mid-air.

The Kanyakumari stood in front of him, her expression tranquil. There was no trace of the anger or disgust that

Raavan was used to seeing whenever anyone from the ashram caught him at his 'scientific' experiments. Nor was there any sign of sorrow or pity in her eyes. There was nothing. No expression at all.

She just stood there, as if she were an idol made of stone—distant yet awe-inspiring. A girl no older than eight or nine. Wheat-complexioned, with high cheekbones and a small, sharp nose. Long black hair tied in a braid. Black eyes, wide-set, with almost creaseless eyelids. Dressed in a red dhoti, blouse and angvastram. She had the look of the mountain people from the Himalayas.

Raavan instinctively checked the cummerbund tied around his waist, on top of his dhoti. It was in place, covering his navel. His secret was safe. Then he remembered the hideous pockmarks on his face, the legacy of the pox he had suffered as a baby. Perhaps for the first time in his life, he felt self-conscious about his appearance.

He shook his head to get the thought out of his mind.

'*Devi* Ka… Kanyakumari,' he whispered, letting the knife drop to the ground. His eyes were fixed on the *Goddess*.

The Kanyakumari stepped forward without a word, her expression unchanged. She bent down and picked up the knife. With quick, efficient movements, she cut the restraints on the wretched hare.

She then picked it up and gently kissed it on the head. The hare was quiet in her hands, its panic forgotten. The voiceless animal seemed to know that it was safe again.

For a fleeting moment, Raavan thought he saw the Kanyakumari's eyes light up with love. Then the mask came back on.

She put the hare down and the animal bounded away.

The Kanyakumari looked again at Raavan and returned the knife to him.

Her face remained impassive.

Without saying a word, she turned and walked away.

Not for the first time since she had arrived at the ashram, Raavan wondered what the Kanyakumari's birth-name had been, before she was recognised as a living Goddess.

—ॐ—

Raavan had slipped out of the house as soon as his mother, Kaikesi, fell asleep. He moved quickly towards his destination.

He was seven years old now. And already renowned in many ashrams, besides that of his father's, as a brilliant child with a formidable intellect. He had started his training in the martial arts as well, and was already showing great promise. As if that wasn't enough, he had a keen ear for music too. His favourites were the stringed instruments, especially the magnificent Rudra Veena. It was only a few months since he had started learning to play the veena, but he was already in love with it.

The Rudra Veena was named after the previous Mahadev, Lord Rudra, whom Raavan worshipped with a passion. The instrument was considered to be among the most difficult to play. He had been told that to master it required years of practice—each time he heard this, he drove himself harder, for how could Raavan be any less than the best?

As he walked quickly through the darkness, Raavan's mind was on the contest that had been arranged for the following morning, against a musician called Dagar. A young and already well-known Rudra Veena player, Dagar was visiting Rishi Vishrava's ashram.

Though it was only a friendly competition, Raavan had no desire to lose.

He thought again of the first time he had beheld the instrument of his choice. He had felt a deep reverence as he touched the rounded teak-wood fingerboard fixed on two large resonators: they were made of dried and hollowed out gourds, he had been told. On both ends of the tubular body were woodcarvings of peacocks, known to be the favourite birds of Lord Rudra. Twenty-two straight wooden frets were fixed to the fingerboard with wax and there were three separate bridges.

This most dramatic of instruments had eight strings— four main and three drone strings on one side of the player and one drone string on the other. All the strings were wound around the eight friction pegs on the tuning head.

During that first lesson, Raavan had watched as the older students sat on the floor and settled the veena with one gourd over the shoulder. Some of them rested it on their left knee. That was when he had realised that the instrument was customised for the person who handled it; there was no question of one-size-fits-all.

Anyone who has observed the structure of the Rudra Veena knows that it is an extremely complex instrument to understand, let alone play. Wire plectrums worn on the index and middle fingers of the right hand are used to pluck the main strings, while the drone strings are played with the nail of the little finger. The strings have to be manipulated with the left hand from beneath the horizontal neck, made more difficult by the fact that the right hand ends up blocking the drone string on the side.

But what truly separates the Rudra Veena from other stringed instruments is the dramatically higher quality of resonance, which is due to the two large gourds attached to its ends. The frequency and strength of the resonance have a significant impact on the tonal quality and the music.

Damage the gourds. Damage the resonance. Damage the music.

Raavan quietly slipped into the small hut where he knew the musical instruments were kept. Dagar's veena was there too. Musicians were known to worship their instruments every night and morning. It seemed Dagar was no different. Puja flowers and burnt incense sticks lay at the base of his Rudra Veena.

Raavan sniggered to himself.

Dagar's prayers will not be answered tonight.

He worked quickly, without a sound. First, he slipped the cloth cover off the instrument. Then he unscrewed the gourd on the left and felt its insides. Polished and smooth. He took out a metallic wrench from the pouch tied to his waist and used it to begin scratching the insides of the gourd.

Dagar would not be immediately able to make out that the resonance was not right, not even while tuning his instrument the next day. He would realise it only when playing the raga during the competition. By which time, it would be too late.

Raavan kept glancing towards the door as he worked. He couldn't think of a single excuse to offer if someone were to walk in just now. But there was no time to worry about that. He focused his energies on the task at hand.

—१६१—

The morning of the competition dawned clear and blue-skied. Much to the surprise of the ashram's inhabitants, the Kanyakumari of Vaidyanath was back amongst them. It had been a good three years since her previous visit. This time, she was on her way to Takshasheela, the famed university-town in north-west India, along with her entourage. And Rishi Vishrava's peaceful ashram had proved to be an ideal resting point.

With the Kanyakumari as a witness, the two musicians began playing. The contest didn't last long. Dagar's damaged veena ensured that he gave up barely ten minutes into his performance, and his younger opponent was declared the winner.

But Vishrava knew his son well.

He dragged Raavan to their frugal hut immediately after the competition.

'What did you do?' he hissed, closing the door behind them so no one could overhear the conversation.

'Nothing!' said Raavan defiantly, his head barely reaching up to his father's chest, his eyes blazing. 'I was just better than that idiot whom you like to favour.'

'Mind your tongue,' said Vishrava, his fists clenched with anger. 'Dagar is one of the finest young Rudra Veena players of this modern age.'

'Not fine enough to beat me,' Raavan scoffed.

'The Kanyakumari is here. How can I allow any subterfuge in her presence?'

Raavan didn't know what the word meant. 'Subter*what*?'

Kaikesi, who was standing behind them, spoke up in a gentle voice. 'Vishrava, if you feel that Raavan is guilty of deceit, please publicly announce Dagar as the winner. Raavan will understand. Perhaps the Kanyakumari herself can—'

Raavan cut in. 'But your husband is guilty of deceit too. He has been lying since the time of my birth. Why doesn't he tell the Kanyakumari about that? Why doesn't he tell everyone the truth about me?'

The old sage raised his hand in anger.

'Please don't!' pleaded Kaikesi, rushing up and throwing her arms around her son. 'You have to stop hitting him. It's wrong... please...'

'Silence! This is all your fault. I am suffering due to your karma. Your bad karma has infected his navel! And his mind!' Vishrava's voice was bitter.

'Hey!' said Raavan angrily. 'Don't talk to her. Talk to me.'

Enraged, Vishrava pushed Kaikesi aside and lunged at Raavan. He slapped the boy hard on his cheek. The seven-year-old went flying across the room. Kaikesi shrieked and ran to shield her son.

Vishrava looked at the boy lying on the ground. Raavan's cummerbund had come undone, revealing a small purple outgrowth from his navel—his birth deformity. Proof that he was a Naga. All across India, people believed that birth deformities were the consequence of a cursed soul, of bad karma carrying over from the previous birth. And such blighted people were called Nagas.

Vishrava spoke with barely disguised disgust. 'Cover that thing!' He glared at his wife. 'Your son will destroy my name.'

Raavan pushed his mother's protective hand away. 'Yes, I will. Because everyone knows I am better than you in every way.'

'Arrogant brat! Lord Indra has bestowed his gifts on the wrong person,' growled Vishrava as he turned to leave.

'Yes, go away! Get lost! I don't need you!' Raavan shouted, struggling to keep his voice level despite the tears that threatened to well up.

The ever-present ache in his navel intensified. Growing in ferocity.

—१७१—

Raavan was sitting by the side of the mighty Yamuna River, not far from his father's ashram. His cheek still burned, though the tears had long dried up.

He was staring at the ground, a magnifying glass in his hand. With great care, he focused the rays of the sun into a powerful band of light, burning the little ants that scurried about. He was breathing hard, raw anger still pulsating in every vein. His navel throbbed, the centre of constant pain.

The fragrance reached him first. He felt his breath catch.

He turned his head and saw her.

The Kanyakumari.

His body froze, the magnifying glass still in his hand. Burnt and shrivelled ants lay near his feet. The sun's concentrated rays singed the grass.

The Kanyakumari's expression remained calm. No sign of disgust. Nor anger.

She stepped closer and took the glass from Raavan's hand.

'You can be better than this.'

Raavan did not say anything. His mouth was suddenly dry. The long-held breath escaped in a sigh.

The Kanyakumari smiled slightly. An ethereal smile. The smile of a living Goddess.

She pointed towards the ashram, where the music competition had taken place in the morning. 'You can be better than that too.'

Raavan felt his lips move. But no words came out. His mind was blank. Unable to construct even simple thoughts and words.

His heart had picked up pace. He noticed that the ache in his navel had magically disappeared. For a few moments.

'At least try,' said the Kanyakumari.

She turned and walked away.

—१७—

'You would have won anyway,' Dagar said, smiling.

It was past sunset. Most of the ashram's residents were back in their huts. Raavan had come to see Dagar, bringing with him the holy lotus garland he had won earlier in the day. Reluctantly, his eyes unable to meet Dagar's, he had mumbled a confession. The older contestant had responded graciously.

Dagar, like most others present at the event, had suspected that something was not right with his instrument. He had examined the veena after the competition and quickly identified the problem. But he couldn't bring himself to be angry. Raavan was a child, after all.

Raavan did not say anything. He stood with his head bowed. Thinking of the Kanyakumari. She was to leave the next morning.

The sixteen-year-old Dagar, standing head and shoulders over the younger boy, ruffled his hair. 'You have talent. Use that to win. You don't need to do anything underhand.'

Raavan nodded silently. He didn't like his hair being ruffled by anyone.

Except her… he would do anything to get her to ruffle his hair.

'And don't worry,' said Dagar, with a smile. 'My veena is being repaired. No permanent damage done.'

Raavan let out a long breath. He had expected the ache in his navel to disappear. But it hadn't.

'And you can keep this,' said Dagar, returning the lotus garland to him.

Raavan grabbed it. And ran back home.

Chapter 3

Two years passed. Raavan turned nine. Every day, he strove consciously to keep the Kanyakumari's words alive within him. *You can be better,* he often reminded himself. Very rarely did he do anything without considering what her reaction to it might be. And it appeared to be working. He got along more easily with the people in the ashram; some actually seemed to like him.

He had also started covering his navel with a cummerbund when he was at home. He knew it embarrassed his father that his son was a Naga, and he had been trying his best for the past two years to not aggravate the situation.

As a result, the fights with his father had reduced.

So had the pain. It was still there. But so mild that Raavan sometimes forgot about the growth on his navel.

Then, one day, Rishi Vishrava left the ashram for a long journey westward. To the island of Knossos in the Mediterranean Sea. The king of Knossos had expressed a desire to meet the eminent rishi, and Vishrava had decided to accept the invitation.

A few weeks after his departure, Kaikesi discovered that she was pregnant. She considered sending a messenger after the rishi, asking him to turn back. But then decided against it. She would surprise him on his return.

Also, truth be told, the thought weighed heavily on her mind: *What if the second child turned out to be a Naga too?*

Unaware of his mother's misgivings, Raavan was excited about the arrival of a younger sibling. He hung around his mother constantly, taking care of her and making sure she had everything she needed. Until, finally, the day arrived.

A wet nurse was attending to Kaikesi inside the house. Raavan waited outside, eagerly pacing up and down, almost like an anxious father-to-be. Waiting for news.

Many of the ashram's residents waited with him. But it was a long labour. Twelve hours had already passed. Slowly, people began returning to their huts, until only Raavan and Kaikesi's elder brother Mareech were left. Mareech had arrived several days earlier, to help his sister through her pregnancy in Rishi Vishrava's absence.

After some time, even Mareech decided to call it a night. 'I'm going to sleep, Raavan. So should you. The midwife will call us. I've given her strict instructions.'

Raavan shook his head. Wild horses couldn't drag him away.

'All right,' said Mareech, getting up. 'I'll be next door. You are to come and fetch me as soon as the midwife calls. Is that clear?'

'Yes.'

'As soon as you hear anything, call me immediately.'

'I heard you the first time, Uncle.'

Mareech laughed softly and ruffled Raavan's hair.

Raavan jerked his head back and looked at his uncle in irritation. Mareech laughed even louder and raised both hands in mock apology. 'Sorry... sorry!'

Chuckling to himself, he turned and walked away, and Raavan set his hair back in place. Neatly.

Now all alone, the young boy looked up at the starless sky. The tiny sliver of a new moon struggled to push the darkness away. Lamps had been lit around the open courtyard in front of the hut, creating tiny enclaves of light.

As he stared into the darkness, he thought he saw shadows lurking in the distance. The breeze picked up, the sound of it somehow eerie. Like ghost whispers. The nine-year-old shivered. The pain at the centre of his body returned. His navel throbbed in fear.

He folded his hands together in prayer and began chanting the *Maha Mrityunjay* mantra. *The great chant of the Conqueror of Death.* Dedicated to the Mahadev, the God of Gods. Lord Rudra.

As he repeated it, over and over again, he felt the fear disappear. Slowly. Leaving his muscles relaxed. His heartbeat slower.

The pain in his navel quietened once again.

He looked into the darkness with renewed confidence.

Who will fight me? Come on! Who will fight me?

Lord Rudra is with me.

Strangely, his navel began hurting again.

He began chanting even more fervently.

Suddenly, a loud scream resounded through the night. 'Raavan!'

It was Kaikesi.

Raavan sprang up and ran towards the hut.

'Raavan!'

He could hear the sound of a baby crying.

'Raavan!'

His mother's cry was more urgent this time.

Raavan flung the door open and rushed into the hut.

It was dark inside. Only a few lamps threw shadows across the floor. His mother was still on the bed. Weak. Struggling to get up. Tears pouring down her cheeks.

The midwife was holding the baby. Rather, she was dangling it by one leg. It was a boy. Raavan noticed that the baby was quite large for a new-born. As he took in the scene in front of him, he realised to his horror that she was about to smash the baby's head on the ground.

'Stop!' he screamed, dashing forward and drawing his short sword in one quick motion.

The midwife froze as she felt the blade against her abdomen.

'Hand over my brother, now!' Raavan said, his voice hoarse.

'You don't know what you are doing! I am saving your mother! I am saving you!' the midwife screeched.

It was only then that Raavan noticed the outgrowths on the baby's ears. The strange lumps made his ears look like pots. There were outgrowths on his shoulders too, like two tiny extra arms. The new-born was unusually hirsute. And he was howling.

Raavan pressed the sword against her skin, puncturing it. 'I said, hand him over.'

'You don't understand. He has to die. He is cursed. He is deformed. He is a Naga.'

'If he dies, so will you.'

The midwife hesitated, resisting the pressure of the sword that threatened to pierce her abdomen. She wondered if she could survive a stab wound if a physician attended to her immediately.

'You will not survive this,' snarled Raavan, as if reading her mind. 'My sword is long enough to cut through your abdomen and slice your spinal cord. I have practised on animals. Even human bodies. No doctor will be able to save you. Just give me my baby brother and I'll let you go.'

The midwife was in a dilemma. She had her orders, and she was expected to follow them. But she didn't want to die as a consequence. She knew of Raavan's experiments. She knew he was good with a blade. Everyone knew.

Raavan pushed closer. 'Give. Him. To. Me.'

The midwife looked at the furious expression on his face with a sense of foreboding. She had seen it before, this bloodlust. On the faces of warriors. People who killed. Sometimes, simply because they enjoyed it.

And then she noticed.

Raavan's cummerbund had come undone. His navel was visible, and the ugly outgrowth. Proof that he, too, was a Naga.

The shocked woman stood rooted to the spot.

She could hear people gathering outside. They would support her. They knew what they had to do.

There was no reason for her to die. She thrust the baby into Raavan's arms and rushed out.

—ॐ—

Raavan could hear the angry voices outside. Arguments. People screaming about order. Ethics. Morals.

The door of the hut was closed. But there was no lock on it. Anyone could barge in at any moment.

He tried to control his breathing, his body tense. He gripped his sword tightly. Ready to kill anyone who entered. He looked back at his baby brother. Safe in his mother's arms. Suckling at her breast contentedly. Unaware of the danger they were in.

His mother's face, though, was a picture of terror.

'What are we to do, Raavan?' asked Kaikesi.

Raavan didn't answer. His alert eyes were glued to the door, ready to attack anyone who dared to try and harm his loved ones.

Suddenly, the door swung open and Mareech rushed in. His sword was drawn. Blood dripped from its edge.

Kaikesi moaned in fear and hugged her baby to her chest. She pleaded with her *elder brother*, '*Dada*, please! Don't kill us!'

The baby pulled back from his mother and started crying again.

Raavan stepped in front of Mareech. Brandishing his sword. His voice surprisingly calm. 'You will have to fight me first.'

Mareech shot him an impatient look. 'Shut up, Raavan!' He turned to his sister. 'What's wrong with you, Kaikesi? I am your brother! Why would I kill you?'

Kaikesi looked at him, confused.

Without wasting any more time, Mareech yanked a cloth bag off a hook on the wall. And threw it towards Raavan. 'Two minutes. Pack whatever you need for your brother and mother.'

The boy stood unmoving. Baffled.

'Now!' shouted Mareech.

Raavan snapped back to reality. He pushed his sword back into its scabbard and picked up the bag, rushing to obey his uncle.

Mareech turned to Kaikesi. 'Get up! We have to leave!'

Within a few minutes, they were outside the hut. Raavan had the cloth bag slung over his shoulder. His baby brother was secure in his mother's arms, the palm of her right hand supporting the new-born's neck.

The residents of the ashram were gathered in front of the hut. Angry faces, torches in their hands.

Three bodies lay on the ground. Cut down by Mareech's sword.

Mareech himself stood in front of his sister and her children, brandishing his sword at the crowd. The ashram's residents mostly comprised intellectuals and artists. Good at social boycotts. Good at verbal violence. Good at mob violence as well. But unequipped to handle a trained warrior.

'Stay back,' Mareech growled.

Slowly, he edged towards the stables, sword aloft. His eyes still on the crowd. Quickly, he helped his sister mount a horse. Raavan was soon seated on another. In a flash, Mareech opened the gates wide and vaulted on to his own horse.

And they galloped out of the ashram.

—१७१—

The group had been riding for hours. Eastwards. The sun was already up, and rising higher and higher.

'Please, Dada,' pleaded Kaikesi. 'We have to stop. I can't carry on like this.'

'No' was the simple answer from a grim-looking Mareech.

'Please!'

Mareech bent and whipped Kaikesi's horse, sending it cantering again.

—ॐ—

It was almost noon by the time they sat down to rest.

Mareech didn't think much of the tracking and fighting skills of the ashram's residents. But better safe than sorry, he had said, each time Kaikesi begged him to slow down.

They were in the Gangetic plains, where the thick alluvial soil and low, rocky terrain made it easy for someone to track them. They had changed directions often. Riding through streams. Moving through flooded fields. Doing all that was necessary to avoid being hunted down.

The three horses were safely tethered and Kaikesi was resting against a tree, suckling her infant. Mareech had left Raavan on guard while he went foraging for food.

He was soon back with two rabbits. In the bag over his shoulder were some roots and berries.

They cooked and ate the food quickly.

'Twenty minutes of rest,' said Mareech. 'Then we ride out again.'

'Dada,' said a tired Kaikesi. 'I think we've left them far behind. Why don't we stay here for a little while?'

'No. It's safer to move on to Kannauj. Our family is there. They will protect us.'

Kaikesi nodded.

Mareech looked at Raavan, noticing he had not touched his food. 'Eat up, son.'

'I'm not hungry.'

'I don't care whether you are hungry or not. Do you want to protect your mother and brother? Then, you need to be strong. And for that, you have to eat.'

Raavan started to protest.

'Just eat, Raavan,' said Kaikesi.

Raavan looked at his mother, then turned back to his food and started eating.

'I don't understand how the ashram people can do this,' Kaikesi said. 'I am the wife of their preceptor. We are the family of their guru. How dare they!'

Mareech glared at his sister. 'Are you trying to play dumb, Kaikesi? Or are you in denial?'

'What do you mean?'

'Do you really think they made this decision on their own?'

'What are you insinuating, Dada?'

'It's clear as daylight. They were following instructions!'

Kaikesi shook her head in disbelief. 'No, it can't be. He left before learning of my pregnancy.'

'It was him. He suspected this might happen, so he left instructions. Those people were simply carrying out orders.'

'I refuse to believe it.'

'Refusing to believe the truth doesn't make it any less true. We had heard about it in Kannauj. Why do you think I came to stay with you at the ashram?'

Kaikesi kept shaking her head. 'No, no. It can't be true.'

Raavan spoke up. 'My father ordered them to kill us?'

Mareech looked at Raavan and then back at Kaikesi. He had forgotten the boy's presence in the exchange with his sister.

'I asked you something,' said Raavan.

'Kaikesi?' Mareech said helplessly.

'Uncle, did my father order our killing?' asked Raavan.

'Kaikesi…' Mareech repeated.

His sister remained silent. Still shaking her head. Tears rolled down her cheeks.

'Uncle…'

Mareech turned to Raavan. 'You have to take care of your family now. You may as well know the truth.'

Raavan kept quiet. His fists clenched tight. He knew the answer already. But he wanted to hear it.

'From what little I know, he didn't order your death or your mother's,' said Mareech. 'But he did order the killing of your brother, in case he turned out to be a Naga.'

Raavan drew in a sharp breath. Anger and grief clouded his mind. He looked at his brother, sleeping peacefully in his mother's lap. The two short extra limbs at the top of his shoulders moved slightly in his sleep. The rest of his body was motionless.

Raavan bent and picked up his infant brother. He cradled him in his arms, his eyes radiating love. 'Nothing will happen to you. Nobody will hurt you. Not as long as I am alive.'

Over his head, Mareech and Kaikesi looked at each other, nonplussed and, at the same time, overcome. Mareech touched the boy's shoulder sympathetically, but Raavan shrugged the comforting hand away and continued to croon to the baby.

Chapter 4

Two days had passed since Mareech had helped Kaikesi and her sons escape from Vishrava's ashram. They were camped in a clearing in the jungle for the night, the horses tied in a circle around the camp.

It was the third day of the waxing moon. With the dense jungle cover and the night-time fog, visibility was reduced to barely a few feet. So Mareech set about lighting a small fire. Not just for heat, but also for safety.

He sat hunched over a flat wooden board that had a notch cut into its surface. The fireboard. In his hands he held a long slender piece of wood, which spun when he rubbed his palms together. Patiently, he got the wooden spindle into the notch. Waiting for the glowing black dust, like smouldering coal, to collect. It was a primitive and time-consuming method, but their only option in the jungle.

As he waited, Mareech's eyes fell on the dark outlines of his sister and her infant son. They appeared to be sleeping, fatigued after the day's journey. The baby, only a few days old, had a name now: Kumbhakarna—the one with pot-shaped ears. It was Raavan who had suggested it and Kaikesi and Mareech had instantly agreed.

Mareech looked at Raavan, who sat close to him. The nine-year-old's knife was out of its scabbard. Mareech tried to get a look at Raavan's face.

Were his eyes closed?

He was about to scold Raavan and order him to help with the fire, when the boy brought down his knife in a flash. There was a loud screech. Mareech stared at him, stunned. It was too dark for him to be certain, but it appeared his nephew had just pinned down a hare with his knife.

Very few people could shoot arrows unguided by vision. Even fewer could throw knives based on sound alone. But to stab a fast-moving animal like a hare, based only on sound, was unheard of.

Mareech looked at Raavan in awe, his mouth slightly open. Then he turned his attention back to where the smouldering dust had started collecting on the fireboard. Quickly, he slid the dust onto the small pile of tinder he had collected. Then he blew on it gently, till the tinder caught fire. One by one, he transferred the flame to the logs he had arranged beside the burning tinder. Soon there was a roaring fire in the centre of the small clearing.

The fire taken care of, Mareech turned to Raavan. The boy had begun skinning the hare's hind legs. With a start, Mareech noticed the animal was still alive. Making frantic, yet weak sounds, like an agonised pleading. In the light of the fire, Mareech could also see Raavan's expression.

A chill ran up his spine.

He got up, and in one fluid move, pulled out his own knife, took the hare from Raavan and stabbed it in the heart. He held the blade there for a few moments, till the hare stopped moving. Then he handed it back to Raavan. 'This animal has done nothing to you.'

Raavan stared at Mareech, his face devoid of expression. After a long, still moment, he turned back to the hare and started skinning it again. Mareech walked over to where his bag lay and pulled out some dried meat. He began heating it over the flame, using a slim, sharpened rod as a skewer.

'Uncle.'

Mareech looked up.

'I didn't thank you,' said Raavan.

'There's no need for that.'

'Yes, there is. Thank you. I will remember your kindness. I will remember your loyalty.'

Mareech smiled at the nine-year-old who spoke like an adult. And went back to heating the meat.

If only the night would pass quickly, and the dawn arrive soon. For the next day, they would finally be home, in Kannauj.

—र६ई—

The ancient city of Kannauj had blessed many Indians with a great deal.

Situated on the banks of the holy Ganga, the city had been a great centre of manufacturing, especially of fine cloth, as far back as anyone could remember. It was known for its production of equally fine perfumes. It had also long been a centre of debate, research and shared knowledge, and was the heartland of the Kanyakubj Brahmins, a community of illustrious, if impoverished intellectuals. The joke among the Kanyakubjas was that Saraswati, the Goddess of Knowledge, was very kind towards them, while Lakshmi, the Goddess of Prosperity and Wealth, was wont to ignore them altogether.

As a seat of learning, the city was home to many of the finest thinkers and philosophers of the time, including the celebrated Rishi Vishwamitra, who had been born into the royal family of Kannauj. But it turned out to be not so understanding when it came to the weary band of runaways that showed up at its gates, seeking sanctuary.

Kaikesi and Mareech's parents, it transpired, had decided that it was best to excommunicate their daughter as soon as they heard that she had given birth to a Naga child. By this time, the well-kept secret of Raavan's identity had also been revealed. And, of course, everyone knew that it was Kaikesi's fault. After all, the revered Rishi Vishrava could not be responsible for the bad karma that gave birth to their Naga offspring.

Even those who sympathised with Kaikesi's plight had no inclination, or will, to take on their community or their elders.

Within a day of reaching Kannauj, the four of them found themselves outside the city once again, on the banks of the holy Ganga, wondering where they could go.

'What do we do now?' asked Kaikesi.

Mareech looked away at the river, his mind seething with anger. He couldn't believe that his family had turned its back on them. Even those who had initially supported his decision to go to Vishrava's ashram to protect his sister had changed their tune. They'd had the temerity to tell him, 'We didn't expect Kaikesi to actually give birth to a Naga! How could we have expected that?'

'Dada,' Kaikesi said again, 'what is to become of us?'

'I don't know, Kaikesi!' said Mareech. 'I don't know!'

Raavan had been using a smooth stone to sharpen the blade of his knife. He looked up and said, 'I do. Let's go further east. Let's go to Vaidyanath.'

'Vaidyanath?' asked Mareech, surprised. 'What's in Vaidyanath?'

The Kanyakumari, thought Raavan. But, for some reason, he didn't want to say it aloud. He started sharpening his knife again. 'I know who's not there: my father.'

Mareech kept quiet.

'Let's travel eastwards, towards the rising sun. Some light of wisdom may dawn on us as well.'

'You made that line up yourself?' Mareech asked, impressed.

Raavan glanced at him superciliously. 'No, I read it somewhere. You should try reading too, Uncle. It's a good habit.'

Mareech rolled his eyes and looked away. *Pesky kid.*

—ॐ—

They found lodgings in a charitable guesthouse in a small village, a short distance from the famous Vaidyanath temple. Vaidyanath was famed for its physicians, and Kaikesi lost no time in taking Kumbhakarna to one, to see if the outgrowths on his shoulders and ears could be removed. The doctor, however, advised against it. There was too much vascularity in the outgrowths, too many blood vessels, and removing them surgically could lead to the death of the child, he said. In any case, Kumbhakarna seemed like a happy baby whose outgrowths, unusually, did not cause him pain. It was best that he learn to live with them.

Kaikesi was deeply disappointed. So was Raavan. But the reason for his disappointment was different. Not that he spoke of it to anyone.

The next morning, at the crack of dawn, they left for the main Vaidyanath temple. It would soon be time for the morning aarti, the public offering of devotion to the Mahadev, Lord Rudra.

The Vaidyanath temple was, in effect, a huge complex of many temples, set in the middle of a dense jungle. There were temples dedicated to the previous Vishnus, to the many Goddesses who protected India, to Lord Indra, Lord Varun, Lord Agni, and others. Of course, the largest temple was dedicated to Lord Rudra. The Mahadev. The God of Gods.

The temple complex was separated from the flood-prone Mayurakshi by marshlands and flood-plains that sponged the excess waters of the tempestuous river during the monsoon season, thus keeping the temples safe. Several species of medicinal herbs and roots grew in the swamp, making the small temple-town a treasure trove of medicines for the treatment of most diseases. In fact, its name derived from this: Vaidyanath, the Lord of the Medicine Men.

The main temple of Vaidyanath was shaped like a giant lotus. It had an uncomplicated but enormous core, with a hall, the sanctum sanctorum, and a spire built of stone and mortar, following the standards prescribed in the Aagama architectural texts. The main spire shot up a massive fifty metres from a fifteen-metre base. On top of the base, a hundred and eight wooden 'petals' had been affixed—an architectural triumph. Each petal was four times the size of a full-grown man. Made from the wood of robust sal trees, among the best hardwoods anywhere in the world, each petal had been further hardened through a process of chemical treatment and painted with a pink dye. They were laid out on four levels, one above the other, to create a gargantuan lotus flower that encompassed the core of the temple. The main spire was painted yellow and grew out of the centre of this lotus like a giant pistil. The base was coloured green, to signify the stem of the lotus. The elongated base was hollow and functioned as a tunnel-shaped entry into the temple.

It was almost surreal. And deeply symbolic.

The lotus was a flower that retained its fragrance and beauty even while growing in slush and dirty water. It posed a silent challenge to the humans who visited the temple, to be true to their dharma even if those around them were not. The number of petals—one hundred and eight—was significant too. The people of India, the followers of the dharmic way, attached a huge significance to the number. They believed that it was a divine number repeated again and again in the structure of the universe. The diameter of the sun was a hundred and eight times the diameter of the earth. The average distance from the sun to the earth was a hundred and eight times the diameter of the sun. The average distance of the moon from the earth was a hundred and eight times the diameter of the moon. There were several other examples of this number appearing almost magically in the universe. Over time, it had been incorporated into many rituals. For instance, it was recommended that a mantra be chanted a hundred and eight times.

At the far end of the temple, in the sanctum sanctorum, was a life-size idol of Lord Rudra. The Lord sat cross-legged, like a yogi, his eyes closed in concentration. Right behind him was a massive three-metre high lingam-yoni—an ancient depiction of the One God. The lingam was in the shape of half an egg, and some ancients believed that it represented the Brahmanda, or the Cosmic Egg, which allowed creation to coalesce. Others believed that it was a representation of masculine energy and potential. At the base of the lingam was a yoni, often translated as 'womb', but literally the 'origin' or 'source'; a symbol of feminine energy and potential. The union of the lingam and the yoni represented creation, a result of the partnership between the masculine and the feminine, an alliance between passive Space and active Time from which all life, indeed all creation, originated.

Outside the sanctum sanctorum, in the centre of the lotus-shaped temple, was the main gathering hall for devotees.

By the time Raavan and his family reached the temple, they had little time to admire either its beauty or symbolism. The aarti had already begun in the main hall. And it was spectacular.

Thirty massive drums were placed sideways on large stands positioned throughout the hall. Big, burly men holding drumsticks the size of their own arms stood beside them, pounding the drums repeatedly.

Dhoom-Dhoom-danaa-Dhoom-Dhoom-danaa.

The beat and the rhythm pulsated through Raavan's body. He could feel the waves of sound in his bones. And like everyone else in this throng of Lord Rudra's devotees, he too was compelled to dance to the tune. Even Kumbhakarna, the little baby, shook his arms excitedly.

Dhoom-Dhoom-danaa-Dhoom-Dhoom-danaa.
Dhoom-Dhoom-danaa-Dhoom-Dhoom-danaa.

As the music gained in tempo, male and female devotees surged across the hall, towards the two-hundred-odd bells that hung from different points. They began ringing them now. In perfect harmony.

Then, in a low voice, the devout, in tune with each other, began chanting a simple disyllabic word. A word of immense power.

'Maha… dev!'

'Maha… dev!'

'Maha… dev!'

As the chanting gained momentum, the voices grew louder and louder. In ecstatic devotion to the Mahadev. The Greatest God. The God of Gods. Lord Rudra himself.

The drums kept pace with the chanting.

Dhoom-Dhoom-danaa-Dhoom-Dhoom-danaa.

Dhoom-Dhoom-danaa-Dhoom-Dhoom-danaa.

Raavan looked around him. For the first time in his life, he experienced the sheer joy of being a part of something bigger than himself. He was a devotee of Lord Rudra. They all were. And there was no differentiation here. None at all. Rich men danced next to their visibly poor compatriots. Students pirouetted next to their teachers. People with deformities chanted beside soldiers blessed with formidably fit bodies. Purist priests danced with hedonist aghoras. Women danced with men and transgender people. Children with their parents. People of all denominations and castes. Indians and non-Indians.

No differentiation.

Freedom.

Freedom from judgement. Freedom from expectations. Freedom from right and wrong. Freedom from Gods and Demons. Freedom to be oneself. And revel in the union with Lord Rudra.

Dhoom-Dhoom-danaa-Dhoom-Dhoom-danaa.

'Maha… dev!'

Dhoom-Dhoom-danaa-Dhoom-Dhoom-danaa.

'Maha… dev!'

The aarti ended on a high, with a wild, throaty cry that echoed through all of Vaidyanath.

'Jai Shri Rudra!'

Glory to Lord Rudra.

As though on cue, the drums and the bells fell silent. Only the echoes remained, lingering in the hushed silence of a deep and blissful devotion.

The aarti had lasted no more than five minutes. But it gave the joy of a lifetime to all those who were present there. Raavan glanced around him. There was ecstasy on every face. He looked at his uncle Mareech and his mother Kaikesi. Tears of joy were flowing down their cheeks. Raavan felt his own cheeks and was surprised to find them moist.

He whispered to himself, 'Jai Shri Rudra!'

Loud voices were suddenly heard from the crowd.

'Kanyakumari!'

'Kanyakumari!'

At the end of the aarti, it was customary for the Kanyakumari to perform the first traditional puja, the *Rudrabhishek* of the lingam-yoni. The Virgin Goddess had come forward to fulfil her duty.

Everybody looked up. Craning their necks. Balancing on their toes to look beyond those in front of them. All keen to catch a glimpse of their living Goddess.

But not Raavan. He kept his eyes on the ground. His fists clenched tight.

'Is this a new Kanyakumari?' asked Kaikesi.

Mareech glanced at his sister before turning back to look at the Kanyakumari, his hands held together in devotion. 'Yes. I am told the previous Kanyakumari got her first period a few months ago. She has moved on and a new Kanyakumari has been recognised.'

Kaikesi swayed gently, rocking baby Kumbhakarna back to sleep. 'I've always wondered what happens to them afterwards. Where do they go? What do they do?'

Mareech shrugged. 'I don't know. Maybe they go back to their villages once they are not Kanyakumaris anymore. But how can anyone find them? Very few even know their original birth-names.'

Raavan raised his head and stared at the new Kanyakumari. Hatred flashed in his eyes.

For a brief, insane moment, he considered lunging forward and striking her dead. That would get rid of her forever. But he banished the thought as quickly as it had occurred to him. It was pointless. They would simply recognise another girl-child as the Kanyakumari. *His* Kanyakumari was not coming back. He didn't know where she was. He didn't even know her real name.

He knew almost nothing. All he remembered were her words. Her voice. And her face.

Her angelic face was burnt into his mind. A face that made all the pain go away.

The thought he had been avoiding finally burst through to his consciousness. He was never going to see her again. She was gone from his life. Forever.

He felt his breath constricting. As though he was suffocating.

He took his mother's hand. 'We have to go.'.

'What? Why? The Kanyakumari—'

'You can ask for her blessings tomorrow. Let's go.'

Raavan turned and walked away.

Chapter 5

'Leave?' asked Mareech, surprised. 'Why?'

Mareech, Kaikesi, Raavan and Kumbhakarna were back in their small room in the guesthouse.

Raavan's voice was calm. 'I had hoped we could find a cure for Kumbhakarna here. But the doctors have told us there is not much they can do. So there's no point in hanging around anymore.'

'But we didn't come here only to find a cure for Kumbhakarna. It's a safe place, at least for some time.'

'I don't want to just be safe. I want to achieve something. I can't do that here.'

Mareech sighed, a little irritated with this precocious young boy. 'Raavan, you are nine years old. You are a child. Just take it easy and let the adults—'

'I am not a child,' said Raavan firmly, interrupting Mareech. 'I am the eldest male in my family. I have responsibilities.'

Mareech tried hard to supress a smile. 'All right, great elder, tell me, which place do you think would be better than Vaidyanath? There is a tradition of selfless charity here. Your mother and brother can live on the free food and lodging that's provided at this guesthouse. How will you feed them if we go elsewhere?'

'I have read of great ports to the east which trade with lands like Bali and Malay. We could go there. We could work there.'

'Raavan, don't assume that it will be easy to find—'

'I have already decided, Uncle,' said Raavan. 'I have spoken to maa as well. The question is, what do you want to do?'

Mareech looked at his sister in surprise. He didn't know that she had already acquiesced to Raavan's demand. The look on Kaikesi's face was a mixture of helplessness and resignation. Many years later, Mareech would remember this as the first of many surrenders. The moment when his relationship with Raavan changed. The moment Raavan went from being his young nephew to his future lord and commander.

'All right,' he said. 'Let's go further east.'

— ।।১।। —

It had been four years since Raavan and his family moved east, to a small town on the shore of the Chilika lake.

Chilika was a vast lagoon, among the largest in the world, extending over more than 1,000 sq km, north-east to south-west, on India's eastern coast. Some of the major distributaries of the mighty Mahanadi River, such as the Daya and Luna rivers, drained their waters into the lake. Fifty other minor rivers fed the Chilika besides. During the monsoon, the heavy downpour caused the lake to swell even more.

A first-time visitor to the kingdom of Kalinga, settled around the delta of the Mahanadi, could be forgiven for assuming that the fertile land, abundance of fresh water and a regular bountiful monsoon were responsible for its immense prosperity. In reality, while agriculture was indeed a munificent source of the kingdom's riches, its overflowing coffers were the result of brisk trade with other regions, near and far.

And the centre of this trade was the Chilika lake.

Given its dimensions, Chilika allowed for the construction of several ports along its shores. The deep draught of the lake meant even the biggest seafaring ships could sail into it comfortably. Several islands in the lake, most of them close to its seaward side, served as minor ports for smaller ships, thus dividing the heavy traffic of vessels. Most crucially, the lake's eastern boundaries, which separated it from the Eastern Sea, were marked by a series of sand flats. These worked as breakwaters to stop the stormy sea from intruding into Chilika, making the lake waters a calm refuge for ships. Two openings in these sand flats, the broader one at the northern end and a narrow one at the southern end, allowed ships to sail into the lake. Furthermore, from Chilika, one could sail up the Mahanadi to the kingdom of South Kosala and then travel northwards into the heartlands of the Sapt Sindhu.

Chilika provided a safe and secure harbour, and afforded easy access to a rich hinterland. In fact, the richest hinterland in the world.

At any point in time, there were at least a few hundred ships, large and small, anchored in the lake. And a smaller number of ships waiting to berth. Cargo was constantly being loaded or taken off vessels. Traders could be heard negotiating aggressively, while Customs officials tried to extract the tax revenues due to the state. Sailors were routinely spotted making their way to the shore, on their day off, looking for wine and women. Tavern owners and women tried their best to attract as many sailors as possible. Meanwhile, soldiers on duty worked to maintain some semblance of order amidst the chaos.

What made Chilika a favourite among traders was that, unlike in other parts of India, trading activities were not unduly restricted here.

Over the past few decades, in many parts of the Sapt Sindhu, ordinary people as well as the ruling families had turned against the trading caste of Vaishyas on account of what was perceived to be large-scale corruption. Severe restrictions had been placed on trading activities. Traders needed licenses at every stage, and these had to be procured from non-Vaishya administrators. As it turned out, far from ending corruption, an element of bribery—large amounts at that—was added to the process. On top of that, the administrators, in their arrogance, did not think they were doing anything wrong in leeching bribes from the traders. They looked at it as a way of punishing the 'thieves'.

Of course, any wise person would know that to blame an entire community for the faults of a few was to take an extremely myopic view of things. Every society needs entrepreneurs and merchants as much as it needs intellectuals, warriors and artisans. And an imbalance in the structure, favouring a particular class, ends up creating problems. Unfortunately, there was a shortage of wisdom in the ruling class in the Sapt Sindhu and the trading community continued to be persecuted.

Eventually, traders from across the Sapt Sindhu got together under the leadership of Kubaer, the wily businessman-ruler of Lanka. Kubaer struck a deal with the emperor of the Sapt Sindhu, and its subordinate kingdoms, by which he took over all their trading activities and paid the empire a large share of the profits. However, this did nothing to make the traders' lives easier. Kubaer's method of maximising his profits was to squeeze their margins. By allying with him, the traders, it turned out, had merely jumped from the frying pan into the fire.

The only kingdom in the Sapt Sindhu that had refused to join up with Kubaer so far was Kalinga. Therefore, while trading had become difficult in most parts of the country, it had intensified in Chilika. The port was under the control of the king of Kalinga, who ruled from his capital, Cuttack, over eighty kilometres north of the lake. 'Cuttack' literally meant military cantonment or royal camp, the name resonant of the warrior past of the Kalingans. But over many centuries, the people there had grown into a non-violent and peace-loving community, whose interests lay in trading and in cultural and intellectual pursuits. This also made the Kalinga kings relatively liberal in their approach to the vexed issue of state controls. As a result, several Vaishya families chose to settle in Kalinga and ply their trade there.

But things were slowly changing. The anti-Vaishya mood in the rest of the country had begun to seep through to Kalinga. Everyone wanted to ingratiate themselves with Dashrath, the powerful king of Ayodhya, who was also the emperor and overlord of the Sapt Sindhu. And it was well known that the mood in Ayodhya was anti-Vaishya. Furthermore, the mighty kingdom of South Kosala, in the upper parts of the Mahanadi, not far from Kalinga, had recently forged a strong alliance with Ayodhya through marriage. Princess Kaushalya had become the first wife of Emperor Dashrath.

Influenced by its powerful relatives, South Kosala too had started placing severe restrictions on trade. Kalinga, sensing the shift in its immediate neighbourhood, had started realigning itself too. A Naharin administrator from the lands to the north-west of Babylon, in Mesopotamia, was brought in as the governor of Chilika to 'discipline' the wayward traders. Nobody knew the man's original name, but he had taken on an Indian one: Krakachabahu, the one with 'arms like a saw'. Regrettably, his style of administration was as repugnant as his name. However, the Kalinga king, far away in his capital city, left Krakachabahu to run Chilika by himself.

Soon, traders in Kalinga began suffering the same tax terrorism and countless regulations that their fellow traders endured in the other kingdoms of the Sapt Sindhu. If they couldn't do business even in Chilika, where could they? Despondent, some decided to give up trading altogether, but the majority laboured on, for it was the only profession they had any experience in. However, the feeling was gathering strength that they had to look for ways to bypass Krakachabahu's oppressive restrictions.

It wasn't long, then, before smuggled goods began to find their way from the Sapt Sindhu to the outside world. There was very little that Indians required from foreign lands since they had plenty of home-grown produce to live on. Even if something was smuggled in, it could get confiscated in any of the kingdoms of the Sapt Sindhu if it lacked the customary permits. Understandably then, the smuggling market was geared more towards exports. The Sapt Sindhu produced many goods that the world wanted. Smuggling them out became a convenient way to avoid hefty export duties and make good profits.

A three-tier smuggling system evolved over time. The first tier involved transporting manufactured products from different kingdoms in the Sapt Sindhu to Chilika. This was relatively simple because many of these goods could easily be mixed with legal exports. It was also the least risky—and the least profitable—of the tiers. The second-tier operators used small cutter-boats to run the gauntlet of Krakachabahu's tax-boats in Chilika before escaping into the sea, either undetected or after bribing the Customs officers. The third tier came into effect in the Eastern Sea, where large seafaring ships, anchored many nautical miles south of Chilika and hidden among other ships waiting to sail into harbour, picked up goods from the cutter-boats and sailed off into distant foreign lands.

Now, the second tier clearly constituted the riskiest part of the operation. And yet, since it was mainly done by young smugglers in small boats, who were desperate to make ends meet, the cream of the profits was skimmed by the third tier: the owners of the large seafaring ships. They negotiated prices down by playing one against the other, while they themselves charged the full and legal, duty-paid price in foreign markets like Arabia, Malay or Cambodia.

When they had first moved here, Raavan and Mareech had taken up employment as dock workers. They survived the hard toil for some time, but eventually, encouraged by the opportunities on offer, Raavan had hired a small cutter-boat and progressed to second-tier smuggling. He had quickly made a name for himself as a smart lad and a talented sailor who was willing to take risks and sneak out goods in the most adverse conditions. It was not a surprise, therefore, when he was approached by a smuggler called Akampana, who specialised in the third tier.

Normally, smugglers in the third tier were capable seafarers, raking in huge profits. Akampana, however, was a bit of a misfit in that category. His was among the least profitable third-tier operations. He was notorious for delaying payments to his crew or not paying them at all. It had reached a point where men simply refused to work for him. But he did have a major asset—his own ship. A large one. One that was capable of sailing on the high seas.

The only way a smuggler in the second tier could graduate to the profitable third tier was by owning or working on a seafaring ship. Knowing this, Raavan agreed to meet Akampana.

The next day, Raavan and Mareech, along with their regular crew of five cutthroats, sailed out in their cutter-boat to a small, hidden lagoon south of Chilika, where Akampana's house was located.

Raavan ordered his crew to row the boat close to Akampana's ship, which was anchored not too far from the shore.

'By the great Lord Varun,' exclaimed Mareech, invoking the name of the God of Water and the Seas in his surprise. 'Does this Akampana not do any maintenance work on his ship at all?'

One of the ways to classify ships was by the number of masts they possessed. Most seafaring ships that came to Chilika had three masts. So did Akampana's. But the sorry state of the vessel was quite obvious. The rigging, including the sails, looked worn and incapable of drawing wind effectively. In fact, the sails hadn't even been furled up to prevent damage from sudden gusts of wind, which were quite common in the area. The masts were clearly in desperate need of fresh woodwork. The crow's nest on top of the main mast had most of its floorboards missing. The tar on the ship's hull, crucial for keeping the vessel waterproof and preventing leakages, needed recoating.

'I thought Akampana's ship had a reputation for speed,' Raavan said, equally surprised.

'So did I,' said Mareech. 'Are you sure you want to work with this man?'

Raavan stared at the ship, lost in thought. Then, abruptly, he threw his angvastram aside. 'Stay here.'

'What are you doing?' asked Mareech.

Before he could finish, Raavan had slipped into the water and was swimming towards the ship. When he got to it, he stopped and floated alongside, carefully examining the hull. He then dived underwater to look at the part just below water. He came back up and swam the length of the ship, this time not just looking at it but feeling it with his fingers, disappearing underwater and coming up every few minutes to take a breath before going back in again. On Mareech's orders, the cutter-boat followed, circling the ship and keeping abreast of Raavan.

When Raavan finally swam up to the surface and climbed onto the boat, Mareech looked at him questioningly.

'There's something odd about this ship,' said Raavan.

'What?'

'Not one barnacle. Not one mussel. No shipworms. The hull is as smooth as it must have been on the day it was made.'

Biofouling was a hazard as old as sailing itself. The wooden base of ships provided a ready breeding ground for barnacles and other sea creatures. They clung to the wet surface, multiplying and growing to cover much of the hull below water. Some ships were so badly infested that it was impossible to even see the wooden surface below the waterline.

These bumpy masses of barnacles drastically reduced the speed of a ship. Another peril was the infestation of shipworms, a type of clam that grew as long as two feet. These creatures bored holes into the wooden hull, causing slow, long-term damage. It was with good reason that they were called the termites of the sea. Raavan had never seen a seafaring ship, the hull of which was *not* infested with these creatures. But Akampana's ship was, strangely, completely devoid of them.

Raavan knew that the best way to clean the hull was in a dry dock where the ships were rested on a dry platform so that workers could scrape off the sea creatures and repair or replace the wood. But it was impossible for smugglers to get access to a dry dock. So what they usually did was careen the ship—essentially, ground it on a beach at high tide and turn it on its side. This allowed the hull to come up above the water so that it could be cleaned, and the old wood repaired or replaced.

As if on cue, Mareech spoke up. 'Maybe they careened the ship and cleaned the hull?'

Raavan shook his head. 'Uncle, if Akampana hasn't had the sense to tie up the sails to prevent accidental damage, do you think he would have gone to the trouble, and the expense, of careening the ship?'

Mareech nodded. 'Valid point.'

Raavan considered the facts before him. With no biofouling, Akampana's ship could travel at nearly twice the speed of other ships. A huge competitive advantage.

He made up his mind.

—१६१—

'I cannot pay all of you a salary,' said Akampana, 'but I can give you a small share of the profits that we make.'

Raavan and Mareech had left their motley team at a distance, out of earshot. It would make negotiation easier. The three men sat on wooden chairs in an unkempt garden that had clearly seen better days. In the same compound stood Akampana's large, crumbling mansion. The house was located not far from the shore, so Akampana's ship was clearly visible from where they were seated.

As soon as Mareech heard what Akampana was offering, he looked askance at Raavan, waiting for his nephew to refuse the ridiculous offer. But Raavan remained silent, his expression inscrutable.

Akampana, a slim man of average height, shifted uneasily. He touched his forehead, unknowingly smudging the *tilak,* the *long, black mark* drawn across it. Finally he broke the silence.

'Listen,' he said, 'we can work out something for living expenses but—'

An angry female voice interrupted him. 'What the hell is going on here?'

They turned to see a tall, sharp-featured woman marching towards them.

'Are you trying to hire a crew again, Akampana?' asked the woman, her exasperation evident to everyone.

Akampana was visibly nervous. 'We have to do some business to earn money, dear wife. These people—'

'Business? You don't know how to do business! You keep making losses. I am not giving you any more money. I am not selling any more of my jewellery. Just sell that damned ship!'

'No, but—'

'You are a moron!' shouted the woman. 'You will be better off if you realise that and stay within your limits.'

'But we need—'

'No buts! Just sell that cursed ship! I could have gone with Krakachabahu, you know that. He was interested in me. I rejected the affections of the governor of Chilika and stuck by you. But I have had enough of your foolishness. Just sell that ship!'

Akampana looked away in embarrassment. But his silence only appeared to infuriate his wife further. Her tone became even more aggressive. 'What is the matter with you? You know I am speaking the truth, right?'

'Of course,' simpered Akampana. 'How could I think otherwise, dear wife?'

The woman shook her head, glared at Raavan and Mareech, then turned and stomped off.

Akampana watched the retreating back of his wife, an expression of intense loathing on his face. Then he checked himself, conscious of being in company. He cleared his throat and turned to Mareech, a weak smile on his face. It was Mareech's turn to look away, embarrassed.

But Raavan didn't seem affected at all. 'Here's what we'll do,' he said, as if they hadn't been interrupted. 'We'll take the ship, repair it at our own cost, and start sailing it. You are welcome to join us if you wish. And the profits will be shared, ninety–ten.'

Akampana brightened. 'Ninety seems fair.'

Raavan regarded Akampana with lazy nonchalance. 'Ninety for me. Ten for you.'

'What? But… but it's my ship.'

Raavan got up. 'And it can continue to rot here.'

'Listen, I don't—'

'And I'll also take care of your wife for you.'

Even Mareech, who had got used to his thirteen-year-old nephew's ruthless ways over the last few years, looked at Raavan in shock.

Akampana glanced nervously in the direction his wife had gone, and then at Raavan. 'What… what do you mean?'

'I'll do what you are too scared to even think about.'

Akampana swallowed visibly. But it was obvious from his expression that he was interested.

'It's a deal,' said Raavan firmly.

Chapter 6

In the two years since Raavan, now fifteen, had taken over Akampana's ship, he had already turned it into a hugely profitable enterprise. After repairing the ship, he had run many successful smuggling missions, supplying goods far and wide, and raking in revenues.

Since the north Indian ports were becoming more and more resistant to free and easy trade, Lanka had emerged as one of the most dynamic entrepôts in the Indian Ocean rim. Raavan had made frequent trips to the island in the past twelve months. On one of these, he had discovered that Kubaer, the trader-king of Lanka, was his guru-brother—a disciple of his father, Vishrava. But this was not something Raavan mentioned to anyone in Lanka. He didn't want any help from his father—not from the person, not even from the name.

As his business grew, Raavan decided to make the main port of Lanka, Gokarna—literally, the cow's ear—his base. The city was conveniently located in the north-east of the island. It had a natural harbour, with a deep bay and land jutting out on the seaward side, acting as natural breakwaters. It was in a position, therefore, to receive and safely anchor ships during any season in the year. A crucial advantage.

The *Mahaweli* Ganga, the longest river in Lanka, flowed into the Gokarna bay at its southern end. This was useful, for it offered a navigable channel for ships to sail deep into the heartland of the island. The river had been named many years ago by Guru Vishwamitra—the chief of the Malayaputra tribe, which had been left behind by the previous Vishnu, Lord Parshu Ram. Perhaps the venerable rishi wished to honour the river that flowed beside his own hometown, Kannauj, by naming this one the *Great Sandy* Ganga.

Guru Vishwamitra was held in high esteem in Lanka, not only because he was a great rishi, but also because he had helped settle the island and turn it from a rural backwater into one of the powerhouses on the Indian Ocean trade routes. There was a time when Lanka was only known for being the surviving part of the great submerged land of Sangamtamil—one of the two antediluvian fatherlands of Vedic India. People used to travel from across the Indian subcontinent to pray at the ruins of the ancient temples built by their forefathers. But all that had changed. Now, they came here to grow rich. And most of those who had arrived recently were from Kalinga.

As things stood, most Lankans were happy with Kubaer's rule. And the trader-king and his people continued to accord the greatest respect to Vishwamitra. For it was he who had, more than a century ago, helped King Trishanku Kaashyap establish the great Lankan capital city of Sigiriya, and while very few mourned the deposition of the increasingly unpopular monarch some years later, Vishwamitra remained dear to them.

Raavan had never travelled inland to Sigiriya, which was a hundred kilometres south-west of Gokarna. He had, however, purchased a beautiful house in Gokarna, close to the great Koneshwaram temple, dedicated to Lord Rudra.

It had been built in ancient times, on a promontory off the northern part of the bay that jutted out into the Indian Ocean. Kaikesi visited the temple every day, with the six-year-old Kumbhakarna in tow. Raavan's little brother was still too young to be sailing with him.

On that particular day, Kaikesi was visiting the Koneshwaram temple with a sense of purpose. She knew that Vishwamitra was in the city, en route to Sigiriya. Many years ago, she had met both Vishwamitra and his right-hand man Arishtanemi, at Vishrava's ashram. While the meeting with Vishwamitra had been all too brief, she had spent considerable time with Arishtanemi and had even started thinking of him as her brother. She had used her influence with him to wrangle a meeting with Vishwamitra. The fact that Kaikesi's own family, especially her grandfather, had once been a close friend of Vishwamitra's father, King Gaadhi, was not mentioned. With good reason.

'Please don't tell anyone that I used my husband's name to arrange this meeting,' Kaikesi pleaded with Arishtanemi, as she led Kumbhakarna by the hand.

Arishtanemi nodded. He knew of the strained relationship between Vishrava and his first wife's children. Especially now that Vishrava had married again, bringing home a foreigner from Knossos as his wife. 'Don't worry. I won't.'

Kaikesi smiled. 'Thank you, brother.'

Arishtanemi led them into the guesthouse attached to the Koneshwaram temple, where Vishwamitra was staying. 'Wait here for a minute.'

Kaikesi was confused. 'But...'

'Just do as I tell you,' Arishtanemi said, before disappearing inside.

Standing outside the door, Kaikesi could hear snatches of the conversation.

'I don't have time to do all this, Arishtanemi. You should—'

Kaikesi walked in, pulling Kumbhakarna along.

A gigantic, barrel-chested man was sitting on the floor in the lotus position. Vishwamitra. He looked up as he heard Kaikesi walk in. He recognised her as Vishrava's wife. And the granddaughter of his father's closest advisor.

He made no attempt to hide his irritation. 'Listen Kaikesi, your grandfather caused enough trouble after my father's death and I am not—'

Vishwamitra stopped mid-sentence as he spotted the child standing next to Kaikesi, holding her hand. The six-year-old was big for his age and could easily pass off for a ten-year-old. He was also extraordinarily hairy. The rishi noticed the crude outgrowths from his shoulders and ears, which clearly established that he was a Naga. Only a doting mother would find a child as ugly as Kumbhakarna beautiful. But Vishwamitra had a big heart. Especially for those whom he perceived to be disadvantaged. His face creased in a smile. 'What a lovely child.'

Kaikesi looked at Kumbhakarna with pride in her eyes. 'He is.'

Vishwamitra beckoned to the boy. 'Come here, child.'

Kumbhakarna nervously slid behind his mother, clutching the end of her angvastram.

'His name is Kumbhakarna, noble Maharishi,' said Kaikesi respectfully.

Vishwamitra bent sideways to catch the child's eye. 'Come here, Kumbhakarna.'

Kumbhakarna took a quick peek at the rishi. Then retreated behind his mother.

Vishwamitra laughed softly. He turned to Arishtanemi and pointed at a plate. His previous visitors had left some homemade sweets for him. Arishtanemi brought the plate to the maharishi.

'I have some laddoos, Kumbhakarna,' said Vishwamitra with a smile, as he chose one and held it out.

At the mention of his favourite sweet, Kumbhakarna stepped forward hesitantly. He looked up at his mother. She smiled and nodded. He ran to the maharishi and grabbed the laddoo. Vishwamitra laughed and held Kumbhakarna affectionately, then made him sit by his side.

Kaikesi, not nervous any longer, went down on her knees before the seated Vishwamitra.

'Great Malayaputra,' said Kaikesi, 'I wanted to request… my son Kumbhakarna… He is…'

'Yes, I know. Sometimes the outgrowths bleed a lot. It's painful. And it can be fatal if not controlled,' Vishwamitra said, looking straight into Kaikesi's eyes. The great sages of yore had the power to read a person's thoughts merely by looking closely at their eyes. Vishwamitra, one of the greatest modern sages, also had this capability.

'You know everything, Guruji. Can you help him?'

'I can't cure it completely. That would be impossible. But I can reduce the bleeding. And I can certainly keep this adorable child alive.'

Tears of relief filled Kaikesi's eyes as she brought her head down to rest on Vishwamitra's feet. 'Thank you, thank you.'

Vishwamitra touched Kaikesi on the shoulder and bade her rise. 'But he has to take my medicines every day. He can never stop. Never. Or death will start closing in.'

'Yes, Guruji. I will never—'

'They are rare medicines. And difficult to obtain. Arishtanemi here will ensure that you get them regularly. Make sure you keep the medicines away from bright light and heat. And use them exactly as Arishtanemi tells you to.'

'Thank you. Thank you, Guruji. How can I ever repay you?'

'You can tell your grandfather to apologise to me for what he did all those years ago.'

Kaikesi didn't know what to say. Her grandfather was no more. She said nervously, 'Guruji, my grandfather… he…'

'He's dead?' asked Vishwamitra, surprised. 'Oh!'

'Guruji,' said Kaikesi, the tears flowing freely again.

'In the name of Lord Parshu Ram, stop crying and speak.'

'Noble Maharishiji …'

Vishwamitra looked into Kaikesi's eyes. 'Someone else has the same condition?'

Kaikesi wiped her tears and said, 'Nothing can be hidden from you, Guruji. My other son, Raavan… He is also a Naga.'

Vishwamitra exhaled softly. He smelt an opportunity here. *Raavan was a Naga too?*

'He's a… he's a…'

Vishwamitra cut in. 'I know he is a smuggler.'

Kaikesi looked at Arishtanemi anxiously and then back at Vishwamitra. Tears poured down her cheeks. 'We went through some very difficult times, Guruji. He… he did what he had to. He's my son, Guruji… I can ask him to stop the…'

Vishwamitra sat quietly, his mind racing.

From what I've heard, Raavan is already gaining a reputation. He is young, but able to acquire and inspire followers. Efficient. Intelligent. Cruel, too. A potential warrior. He could serve my purpose. He could serve the purpose of Mother India.

Kaikesi was still crying. 'The growth on his navel has started bleeding, great Malayaputra. He will die like this. Please help him. He is not a bad person. Circumstances have forced him to become what he is.'

If his outgrowths bleed, he will always need my medicines to stay alive. He will be under my control. Always.

'Please, Guruji.' Kaikesi prostrated herself at Vishwamitra's feet again. 'Please help us. We are both from Kannauj, you and I. Please. Help me. Help my son.'

Vishwamitra smiled. 'It has been difficult. I know.'

Kaikesi sobbed silently, still crouched at the maharishi's feet.

Vishwamitra placed a benevolent hand on her head. 'I will have medicines sent every month for the both of them. I will keep them alive. As long as I can and must,' he said.

—ॐ—

As soon as Kaikesi and Kumbhakarna left, Arishtanemi turned to Vishwamitra. He looked puzzled.

'Guruji,' he said carefully. 'I don't understand why you want to help Raavan. Kumbhakarna is a child. He needs your help. But Raavan? I have heard stories of his ruthlessness. His cruelty. And he is not even an adult yet. He will only get worse.'

Vishwamitra smiled. 'Yes, he is cruel. And you are right, he will only get worse.'

Arishtanemi looked even more confused. 'Then why do you want to help him, Guruji?'

'Arishtanemi, the Vishnu will rise during my tenure as Chief of the Malayaputras.'

The Malayaputras, the tribe left behind by the previous Vishnu, Lord Parshu Ram, had two missions to fulfil. The first was to help the next Mahadev, the Destroyer of Evil, whenever he or she arose. And the second was to identify from their midst the next Vishnu, the Propagator of Good, when the time was right.

Arishtanemi looked shocked. 'Guruji, umm... I don't mean to question your judgement, but I'm not sure Raavan... you know... the role of the Vishnu is very...'

'Are you crazy, Arishtanemi? Do you think I would ever consider Raavan for the role of Vishnu?'

Arishtanemi gave a short nervous laugh, clearly relieved. 'I knew it couldn't be that... I was just...'

'Listen to me carefully. If you take away all the traditions and the hoopla, then who, or what, is the Vishnu to an ordinary Indian?'

Arishtanemi remained silent. He had a feeling that whatever he said would be the wrong answer.

Vishwamitra explained, 'A Vishnu is basically a hero. A hero that others willingly follow. And they follow the Vishnu simply because they trust their hero.'

'But what does that have to do with Raavan, Guruji?'

'What does every hero need, Arishtanemi?'

'A mission?'

'Yes, that too. But besides a mission?'

Arishtanemi smiled, as he finally understood. 'A villain.'

'Exactly. We need the right villain to act as the foil for our hero. Only then will people see the hero as their saviour, as the Vishnu. And only then will they follow the Vishnu along the path that we have determined. A path that will revive the greatness of this land. That will allow it to take its rightful place once again in the world. That will remove poverty and hunger. End injustice. End the oppression of the lower castes, the poor and the disabled. That will make the present-day Indians worthy of their great ancestors.'

'I understand now, Guruji,' said Arishtanemi, bowing his head. 'If all I've heard of Raavan is correct, he has the potential to be a good villain.'

'A perfect villain. For not only will he be a believable villain, he will also always be under our control,' Vishwamitra said.

'Yes. Without our medicines from Agastyakootam, he will die.'

Agastyakootam was the secret capital of the Malayaputras, hidden deep in the hills, in the sacred land of Kerala.

Vishwamitra nodded, as if confirming the plans to himself. 'We will help Raavan rise. And when the time is right, we will destroy him. For the good of Mother India.'

'For the good of Mother India,' Arishtanemi echoed.

Vishwamitra's expression changed as his mind harked back to the past. When he spoke again, it was with barely suppressed rage. 'That... that man will not stop me from fulfilling my destiny.'

Arishtanemi knew who Vishwamitra was talking about: his childhood friend turned mortal enemy, Vashishtha. But he knew better than to respond. He stood quietly, waiting for the wave to pass.

—{i}—

'Dada!' Kumbhakarna screamed excitedly, running down the stairs. His elder brother was walking into the house accompanied by Akampana and Mareech.

The massive profits Raavan had made over the last few years had turned the seventeen-year-old into one of the wealthiest traders in Lanka. But his success had only made him hungry for more. He spent most of his time out at sea, working hard. As a result, visits to his lavish new mansion, perched on one of the hills that surrounded Gokarna, were rare. And these rare visits were a source of delight for his eight-year-old brother, Kumbhakarna.

'Dada!' yelled Kumbhakarna again, rushing into the large courtyard that formed the centre of the mansion, straight towards Raavan. His belly jiggled as he sprinted.

Raavan dropped the gifts he was carrying and spread his arms, laughing, 'Slow down, Kumbha! You are too big for these games now!'

But Kumbhakarna was too excited to listen. He may have been only eight but he was already as big as a fifteen-year-old. The two extra arms on top of his shoulders shook wildly, as they always did when he was excited. With his unusually hirsute body, he resembled a small bear.

As Kumbhakarna jumped into his brother's arms, the impact caused Raavan to stagger. Kumbhakarna giggled happily.

Raavan swung his brother around, laughing. For a few moments, the ever-present pain in his navel was gone.

Kaikesi emerged from the kitchen in the far corner of the ground floor. From her bloodshot eyes, it was clear that she had been crying. 'Raavan.'

Raavan set Kumbhakarna down and looked at her, his expression changing to one of resignation. The pain in his navel was back. 'What is it, Maa?'

'Nothing.'

Raavan rolled his eyes. 'Maa, what is it?'

'If you need to ask, then you are not a good son.'

'Well, then, I am not a good son,' said Raavan, always on edge with his compulsively gloomy mother. 'I'm only going to ask you one more time. What is the problem?'

'You have come home after four months, Raavan. Don't you want to spend time with your family? Why do I have to keep demanding this? Is money all that matters to you?'

'I can spend all my time with you and we can live in a hovel, dying of hunger. Or I can work and keep all of you in comfort. I have made my choice.'

Mareech and Akampana shuffled their feet uncomfortably. These testy exchanges between Kaikesi and Raavan were becoming more frequent.

Kaikesi was on the verge of reminding her ungrateful son that it was because of her, and the medicines she had obtained by pleading with Vishwamitra, that he was still alive. But she thought better of it. Raavan now had an independent relationship with Vishwamitra. He didn't really need her.

Despite his young age, Kumbhakarna had already begun to assume the role of peacemaker between his beloved mother and brother. Now, gauging the tension in the air, he spoke up. 'Dada, you promised to show me your secret chamber!'

Raavan looked at his younger brother with a smile. 'But what about your gifts?'

'I am not interested in the gifts!' said Kumbhakarna. 'I want to see your chamber. You promised!'

The room that Kumbhakarna was so eager to see was on the topmost floor of Raavan's mansion. Off limits to everyone else, the room remained perpetually locked, with Raavan possessing the only set of keys. Even the windows were barricaded. During his short trips to Gokarna, Raavan spent hours by himself in the secret chamber. Nobody else was allowed in. Nobody.

But the last time he had come home, Kumbhakarna had managed to exact a promise from Raavan that he would be allowed into the chamber. There was almost nothing Raavan could refuse his not-so-little brother.

Raavan smiled broadly as he took Kumbhakarna's hand in his own. 'Come, Kumbha. Let's go.' As he was walking away, he pointed to where he had dropped the packages. 'Maa, your gift is somewhere in there. Take it.'

—ॐ—

Raavan's secret chamber was much larger than Kumbhakarna had imagined. And darker. He coughed softly as the dust that had settled over the room in the past few months flew around, assaulting his nostrils.

'Wait here, Kumbha,' said Raavan, as he dropped the keys in a bowl placed on a side table. Torch in hand, he walked around, lighting all the other torches placed in the room. Large polished copper plates ran the length of the walls. They reflected the light of the torches, illuminating every corner of the room.

'Wow…' whispered Kumbhakarna, delighted that he was now privy to a part of his brother's life that nobody else was, not even their mother. He turned around and closed the door, pushing the latch in.

'Do you like it?' asked Raavan.

Kumbhakarna nodded, walking around in amazement, trying to soak it all in.

A majestic Rudra Veena was propped up against a wall. Kumbhakarna had heard the celestial sound of the instrument through closed doors, each time Raavan visited. Arranged in a row along the wall were other instruments—a tabla, dhol, damru, thavil, sitar, chikara, shehnai, flute, chenda and many others. Kumbhakarna had heard his brother play all of them.

'What's that, Dada?' asked Kumbhakarna, pointing at an instrument he had never seen before, or even read about.

The double-stringed musical instrument was kept on a gold-plated stand. Its bow was attached to a clip on the side.

'That is something I invented. I call it the Hatha.'

'Hatha?' asked Kumbhakarna. 'What does that mean?'

Raavan ruffled Kumbhakarna's hair and smiled before looking away. 'Hatha', in old Sanskrit, meant a man stricken with despair.

'I'll tell you some other time,' Raavan said, as the dull pain in his navel surged again.

'But if you have invented it, it should be named after you, Dada!' said Kumbhakarna.

Raavan looked thoughtful for a moment. His brother's suggestion was appropriate in more ways than one, considering the instrument's plaintive sound often reminded him of his own despair. 'Yes. You are right. I'll call it the Raavanhatha from now on.'

'Will you play it for me, Dada?'

'Some other time, Kumbha. I promise.'

Raavan had created the instrument in memory of the Kanyakumari. Playing it would only remind him of her.

Kumbhakarna squinted at the far wall. 'Are those paintings?'

Raavan reached for Kumbhakarna's hand. He wanted to lead him out of the chamber. He wasn't ready for this.

Not yet. But then, for some reason he couldn't understand, he restrained himself. He had held on to his pain for too long, all alone. He realised that, deep in his heart, he wanted Kumbhakarna to know. He wanted to share his pain with his brother. He wanted to share his hopes.

Tears welled up unbidden in Raavan's eyes.

Kumbhakarna ran towards the paintings.

Raavan walked slowly behind him, taking the opportunity to wipe his eyes. And take a deep breath. That always helped.

Kumbhakarna stared at the painting on the far left.

It was that of a girl. A girl no older than eleven or twelve. A round face. Fair-skinned. High cheekbones and a sharp, small nose. Long black hair, tied in a braid. Dark, piercing, wide-set eyes and almost creaseless eyelids. Her body was clad demurely in a long red dhoti, blouse and angvastram.

Divine. Distant. Awe-inspiring.

To Kumbhakarna, she looked like the Mother Goddess.

Kumbhakarna looked at his brother. 'Did you paint this, Dada?'

Raavan was too choked up to speak. He nodded.

'Who is she?'

Raavan took a deep breath. 'She is the Kan… Kan… Kanyakumari.'

Kumbhakarna observed the painting closely. Even to his young eyes, the display of devotion, of worship and love, was obvious in every brushstroke.

He glanced again at his brother's sad face, then turned back to the painting. That was when he noticed the other painting, to the right of the one he had been studying.

It was the same girl. Everything appeared to be the same. Except for the colour of her clothes. They were white.

He turned back to his brother. 'She looks older here.'

Raavan nodded. 'Yes. Exactly one year older.'

Slowly, Kumbhakarna walked along the wall, looking at the paintings. Each subsequent one depicted the same girl, only slightly older. Her breasts filled out. Her hips got curvier. She seemed to grow a little taller.

When he reached the tenth painting, Kumbhakarna stopped and stood quietly for a long time. It was the last in the series. The girl was now a woman. Perhaps twenty-one or twenty-two years old. Her clothes were a soft violet: the most expensive dye in the world and the colour favoured by royalty. She was tall. Striking. Long hair. Full, feminine body. Uncommonly attractive.

There was something otherworldly about her beauty. Her face. Her eyes. Her expression. She looked like a Goddess. The Mother Goddess.

'Does she pose for you every year?' asked Kumbhakarna, confused.

Raavan pointed to the first painting, of the adolescent girl. 'That was the last time I saw her.'

'So how did you paint these?'

'I see her growing older in my mind.'

'Why do you paint her, Dada?'

'Looking at her makes the pain go away, Kumbha...'

'What's her name?'

'I told you.' Raavan closed his eyes and took a deep breath to steady himself. 'Ka... Kanyakumari.'

'That's just a title, Dada. Even I know that. There are many Kanyakumaris. And she is probably not a Kanyakumari anymore if she is a grown woman. What's her real name?'

'I don't know.'

'Which tribe is she from?'

'I don't know.'

'Where is she now?'

'I don't know.'

Kumbhakarna's heart grew heavy. Tears welled up in his eyes. He walked up to Raavan and embraced him. 'We will find her, Dada.'

The tears were flowing down Raavan's cheeks now. There was no stopping them. He held his brother tight. The pain in his navel was excruciating.

'We will find her, Dada, we will! I promise.'

Chapter 7

'It's good to be home!' said Kumbhakarna, his extra arms shaking slightly, as they always did when he was excited. Though he was only ten, his voice had already begun to change.

Two years had passed since Raavan had allowed his younger brother into his secret chamber. They were now on their way back from a short trip to the Nicobar Islands, an important port en route to South-east Asia. It was Kumbhakarna's first trade voyage ever, and Raavan had wanted to ensure that it wasn't too long and uncomfortable.

Raavan sighed. 'I don't like coming home. I prefer the sea.'

'But home is home, Dada.'

'And maa is maa… I can't handle her constant crying. It's like she produces tears at will, just to irritate me. One of these days, I'll…'

Raavan stopped speaking as he saw Kumbhakarna's expression change. He knew that as much as his younger brother loved him, he did not appreciate these rants against their mother.

'All right, all right,' he said, patting Kumbhakarna's shoulder. 'You know I won't do anything drastic. But you handle her tears this time.'

The ship was slowing down gradually as it reached the mouth of the harbour. The brothers watched while the helmsman steered towards their allocated berth. As they passed other ships on their way in, heads turned to stare at the by now legendary ship as it prepared to dock. Its blinding speed on the high seas had given Raavan a huge competitive advantage in the cutthroat world of smuggling. With his fast growing profits, he had already built a fleet of five ships.

Raavan was conscious of being watched. He rather enjoyed the attention. But he continued to look straight ahead, pretending not to notice the admiring, and jealous, eyes gawking at him. He would not preen in front of others. That would be a sign of weakness. And nineteen-year-old Raavan did not believe in letting his weaknesses show.

The trader-prince, they called him. He liked that.

'Dada,' said Kumbhakarna, nudging Raavan to draw his attention.

Raavan turned. Akampana was standing at the port, waiting for them, clearly excited about something.

'Looks like the dandy has some news for us,' Raavan said, preparing to disembark.

—ॐ—

'Raavan, I've found the secret! I've found the…'

'Quiet!' Raavan said severely, tapping him on the head.

Akampana stopped speaking, looking suitably chastened.

They were still in the port area, surrounded by people. Raavan knew that the success of any trading operation depended on reliable information about the commodities and goods that various ships were carrying, and the destinations they were headed for. It was critical to hold on to one's trade secrets.

He continued walking, as his bodyguards pushed people out of the way, clearing his path. Akampana fell into step behind him, smoothing his hair down. A few strands of hair had escaped their coiffure earlier, when Raavan had tapped him on the head. He turned to his assistant, who was walking alongside, for a towel. Some of the perfumed hair oil had come off on his hands.

—ॐ—

'Now,' said Raavan. 'Start talking.'

They were in Raavan's private chamber in his well-appointed mansion. Raavan was leafing through the many messages that had arrived for him while he was away. Mareech and Akampana sat across from him, on the other side of a large desk. Kumbhakarna was sitting by the window, drinking lemon juice.

'I'm sorry, Raavan,' said Akampana nervously. 'I shouldn't have spoken up at the port and it—'

'Yeah, yeah,' Raavan interrupted, waving his hand dismissively without looking up. 'Get to the point. I don't have all day.'

Akampana leaned forward. The excitement in his voice was palpable. 'I've found it. I know what the secret is.'

Raavan put the papyrus scroll down and picked up a quill. He dipped it in the inkpot and started writing a note on the side of the message he was reading. 'You know I don't like riddles. Speak plainly. What have you found?'

'I've got the information we were looking for. From one of the descendants of King Trishanku Kaashyap.'

Raavan stopped writing. He replaced the quill in its hold, leaned back in his chair and said, 'Continue.'

'You do know that Trishanku Kaashyap's body was never found after—'

'I know Trishanku's entire story. Don't give me a history lesson. Get to the point,' Raavan snapped.

Trishanku Kaashyap was the first king of Lanka in the modern age. His kingdom had been established with the help of Vishwamitra. But over time, his subjects had wearied of Trishanku's violent and selfish ways, and he had been deposed. Even Vishwamitra, realising his mistake in supporting Trishanku, had helped the people's rebellion.

Mareech asked the question that was on everyone's mind. 'Have you found the secret?'

'Yes!' said Akampana triumphantly.

The secret in question related to Raavan's main ship, once owned by Akampana. Despite the remarkably inept way in which Akampana had handled it, the ship had never suffered any biofouling and had continued to travel at twice the speed of other ships. Akampana himself did not know what made his ship special. All he knew was that it had once belonged to a descendant of Trishanku Kaashyap.

'There is a special material that has to be ground and mixed with oil—an oil from Mesopotamia—and rubbed on the hull once every twenty years,' said Akampana. 'It keeps barnacles and other sea creatures away. It's as simple as that.'

Raavan leaned forward. 'And where does one find this special material, Akampana?'

'It's with your friends. The Malayaputras. They call it the cave material for some reason.'

'I guess that's because they found it in a cave,' said Raavan sarcastically.

'Perhaps you are right,' said Akampana, oblivious as usual.

Raavan rolled his eyes and turned to Mareech. 'Fix a meeting with them. Quickly.'

— ॐ —

'Why do you need the cave material, Raavan?' asked Vishwamitra.

By a strange coincidence, Vishwamitra and Arishtanemi had arrived in Gokarna that very week, en route to Sigiriya. Raavan had lost no time in going to meet them. But he had insisted on going alone. Without Akampana, or even Mareech.

'I have some plans for trading with it, Guruji,' answered Raavan, his head bowed. He was always polite and deferential with Vishwamitra.

'Are you planning to cut us out and sell directly to Kubaer? Are you planning to reduce our profits?'

Raavan knew that the Malayaputras sold the cave material directly to Kubaer. He had been told by Akampana that the material, whatever it was, was poisonous for humans. And that it was refined and used as a mixture in the fuel for the Pushpak Vimaan, the legendary flying vehicle owned by Kubaer. The other ingredients used for the fuel mixture were almost as costly. Which was one of the reasons the Pushpak Vimaan was used so rarely, and why similar vimaans had not been built. They were simply too expensive to run.

Raavan was prepared for the question. He looked up and folded his hands together in a namaste. 'No, Guruji. Would

I ever do that to the mighty Malayaputras? But having said that, Chief-Trader Kubaer isn't buying the material from you anymore because it's too expensive. As you know, he has even stopped using the Pushpak Vimaan.'

'So are you planning to buy the Pushpak Vimaan and use it yourself?'

Raavan had guessed that the Malayaputras were not aware that the cave material helped prevent biofouling on ships or they would have been using it on their own vessels. Listening to Vishwamitra now, he became certain of this. If all went well, he would be the only one with the competitive advantage of superfast ships.

'Leasing the Pushpak Vimaan is an option as well, Guruji. Chief-trader Kubaer never says no to an opportunity for making profits, does he?'

'And what are you going to do with the Pushpak Vimaan?'

'Oh, a little bit of this and a little bit of that.'

Although using the vimaan for trade would be a losing proposition because of the exorbitant running cost, Raavan did actually plan to use it. After all, he had to convince the ever-vigilant Malayaputras that he was buying the cave material only for the purpose of flying the vimaan. On prospecting trips maybe. Or even holidays!

Vishwamitra looked intently at Raavan, trying to read his mind. But he hit a blank wall. Raavan had by now learnt the technique of blocking even the most powerful rishi from reading his mind.

'All right,' said Vishwamitra. 'You will have to pay five hundred thousand gold coins per consignment. And you will have to take at least three consignments a year.'

It was a ridiculous price. Way beyond what Kubaer paid. And the insistence on a minimum purchase was unheard of.

But Raavan didn't flinch. He had done his calculations already. 'I agree to the price, Guruji. But I cannot agree to the minimum number of consignments. I don't know how often I will use the vimaan. I will try my best to buy three consignments every year. But there may be some years when I am unable to do so. I should not be penalised for that.'

Vishwamitra nodded. 'All right.'

Standing beside them, Arishtanemi could not believe his ears. Five hundred thousand gold coins per consignment! With that much money, the Malayaputras could begin the search for daivi astra material in earnest. The daivi astras were weapons of mass destruction, whose use had been severely restricted by the previous Mahadev, Lord Rudra. He had decreed that they could not be deployed without the permission of the Vayuputras, the tribe left behind by Lord Rudra. But Vishwamitra had plans of his own. He wanted the Vishnu to rise in his time. For that to happen, and to manage the course of events, he had to have independent control of the daivi astras. This deal with Raavan would give him the funds to seek out and quarry the material required for the manufacture of the divine weapons. Arishtanemi could not help but smile at the irony: it was the pirate Raavan who would free them from their dependency on the Vayuputras.

'Thank you so much, Guruji,' said Raavan, bending to touch the maharishi's feet.

'*Ayushman Bhava*,' said Vishwamitra, blessing Raavan with *a long life*.

'I wonder what he is planning to do, Guruji,' said Arishtanemi.

'I'm confused too,' said Vishwamitra. 'The only use for the cave material, other than as fuel for the Pushpak Vimaan, is as a poison.'

'Yes. But for all practical purposes, it's a pretty useless poison.'

Arishtanemi was right. The cave material was a very slow-acting poison. One would have to administer it regularly to the victim, for many weeks, for it to have any effect. And when it was refined into a potent poison, it emanated a distinctively foul smell, which rather defeated the purpose. The intended victim would smell it from miles away!

'Maybe he wants to be the only one in the world with a flying machine, even if it bankrupts him. I had thought Raavan would serve our purpose. That he could grow into a worthy villain. But it looks like he's surrendered to mere vanity,' Vishwamitra said, looking disappointed.

'He can still serve our purpose, Guruji. With that much gold at our disposal, we can begin our search for the daivi astra materials in earnest.'

'True. But getting the cave material is difficult.'

'Please don't worry about that, Guruji,' said Arishtanemi. 'I'll ensure that we get all the material we need.'

—१७१—

'Raavan, have you gone mad?' Mareech blurted. A steely look from his nephew forced him to control himself and check his tone. 'Listen to me, Raavan, we have worked hard… *you* have worked hard to build up all we have now. Five hundred thousand gold coins per consignment is too much. We can never—'

'My numbers are never wrong. I calculate that if we can build a fleet of two hundred ships as soon as possible, and run them continuously on the main trade routes—spice, cotton, ivory, metal and diamond—we will recover our investment in three years. After that, it's pure profit.'

'Two hundred ships? Raavan, I like your confidence, and I've always had faith in your vision. But this kind of scale is unimaginable. And unmanageable. The risks are too high.'

'On the contrary, scaling it up will reduce our risk.'

'But Raavan, no trader has ever owned a fleet of two hundred ships. It's unheard of!'

'That's because there has never been a trader called Raavan before this.'

Akampana tried to butt in. 'Are you sure we cannot negotiate further with the Malayaputras? Guru Vishwamitra and his followers live very frugal lives. I don't see what they need so much money for. Maybe there is still some room for negotiation...'

'I am not going back on a deal that I've signed already,' said Raavan firmly.

'Perhaps we can expand slowly, then? Start with say, twenty ships. One consignment of cave material is enough for that. We can see how it works and—'

Raavan cut in. 'No. We will begin with two hundred.'

'But, Raavan,' said Akampana, nervously fiddling with his many finger rings. 'Building two hundred ships means we will need ten consignments. That means we will need to pay five million gold coins.'

'That is correct.'

'Raavan, listen to me,' said Mareech. 'Five million gold coins is more than the annual revenue of most kingdoms in the Sapt Sindhu. We will have to mortgage everything we have to raise that kind of money.'

'Then we should do that.'

'Dada,' interrupted Kumbhakarna.

Raavan turned to his younger brother. 'Yes?'

'I have an idea.'

'What?'

'People talk freely in front of me because they think I am only a child and—'

'Please get to the point quickly, Kumbhakarna. You know Raavan does not like long-winded answers,' Akampana interjected. He looked at Raavan for confirmation, but withered on receiving an angry glare. Raavan had all the time in the world for Kumbhakarna.

'We may not need to borrow the money,' continued Kumbhakarna calmly. 'We can just steal it.'

Raavan shook his head. 'Not a good idea. We'll have to hit too many targets to raise five million. And each time we hit a place, the risk will increase.'

'Not really, Dada. All we need to do is hit one big target.'

'We can't target royal treasuries, Kumbha. The security is too tight.'

'I wasn't talking about a royal treasury.'

'There is someone in India, other than a king, who has five million gold coins?' Raavan raised an eyebrow, intrigued.

'Krakachabahu, the governor of Chilika.'

Mareech nearly choked on the cardamom-flavoured milk he was drinking. 'Krakachabahu? How can we steal from him? The entire Kalinga fleet will be after us. We will not have a safe harbour anywhere in the Indian Ocean.'

'But Uncle,' said Kumbhakarna politely, 'this is money that Krakachabahu has stolen from the king of Kalinga. He has been taking a cut from the Customs revenue for years. He keeps the money hidden in an underground vault in his palace. He will never be able to admit that he had it in the first place. That's the beauty of stealing from a thief; he cannot complain.'

'Hmm...' Raavan's eyes sparkled.

'I've also heard that a lot of his wealth is conveniently in the form of precious stones. Small, lightweight, and easy to steal. And they can be converted to gold at any port in the Indian Ocean.'

Raavan turned to Mareech and Akampana, a proud smile on his face. 'My brother!'

'But Raavan,' said Akampana, 'we can't just walk into Krakachabahu's palace. It's one of the best-guarded residences in India. And most of the guards are from his native land, Nahar.'

Mareech, who had begun to warm to the idea, countered Akampana. 'Yes, but the chief of the palace guards is Prahast.'

Raavan smiled as soon as he heard the name. 'He owes me one.'

'Exactly,' said Mareech. 'You saved his life once. And he has always wanted to work with you. The fact that he is greedy and ruthless makes him perfect for the job.'

'Let's start the preparations. We sail to Chilika in a month.'

Chapter 8

'The plan looks good, Dada,' said Kumbhakarna.

Two weeks had passed since Kumbhakarna had suggested looting Krakachabahu's treasure. The brothers were reviewing their strategy, late in the evening, in Raavan's wood-lined personal library, with its collection of thousands of manuscripts.

Knowledge was highly prized in India. Small manuscript collections were not uncommon in homes, though only universities and temples had large, well-stocked libraries. It was said, with reasonable confidence, that no individual had more manuscripts in his private collection than Raavan. What is more, he had actually read most of them.

'I came up with it,' said Raavan. 'Of course it's good!'

'Maybe, but I came up with our target!'

'Okay, okay,' Raavan said, laughing. 'You are the king of everything, Kumbha.'

Kumbhakarna bowed theatrically and laughed along. 'I want to read something interesting, Dada. Anything you'd recommend?'

Raavan looked around his huge library. He was extremely possessive about his manuscripts. He didn't allow anyone to borrow them. Except Kumbhakarna. There were very few things that he refused Kumbhakarna. 'How about I read you a poem instead?'

'A poem?'

'Yes.'

'Composed by whom?'

Raavan remained silent. He looked almost embarrassed.

Kumbhakarna raised his eyebrows. 'By you, Dada?'

'Yes.'

'By the great Goddess Saraswati, how did this miracle happen? I had no idea you composed poetry!'

'Will you keep quiet and listen?'

'Of course!'

Raavan picked up a scroll, looking nervous and excited at the same time. He cleared his throat, then said, 'It's called "The Ballad of the Sun and the Earth".'

'How eloquent! I like it already.'

'Shut up and listen, Kumbha.'

'Sorry, I'll try to be serious. Poetry is no joking matter after all.' Kumbhakarna smiled impishly.

'Well, it's a story as much as it's a poem. Now, listen:

'The Ballad of the Sun and the Earth

The Clouds rush to the Mountain…'

Kumbhakarna interrupted. 'What are the clouds and the mountain doing there? I thought this was about the sun and the earth.'

Raavan glared at Kumbhakarna, who immediately put his hands together contritely.

'No interruptions, I am warning you,' Raavan said. He took a deep breath and started again.

The Ballad of the Sun and the Earth

The Clouds rush to the Mountain,
they caress him gently,
they fight for his attention,
they rise to kiss his lips.
The Clouds believe the Mountain is smitten,
that he stands so high to not let them pass,
that he stands uncomfortably still, with rishi-like repose,
because he waits for their return every year.
There's no doubt in their mind:
The Mountain loves them.

It's sad that they'll never know
that the Mountain doesn't care for them,
he only wants the nourishing rain they carry,
he doesn't nudge them up to kiss them,
he does it to break them and get what he wants,
and by the time they understand,
it's too late.

It's sad that no Cloud survives to warn the others.

The River rushes to the Sea,
her instincts tell her this is her destiny.
She's grown up on stories of love,
on tales of blind and illogical passion,
and she's in too much of a hurry to
meet her lover, to stop and think.
But when she sees the Sea,
his immensity, depth, power,

she hesitates and meanders.
But her innate romanticism wins,
And she flows happily into his arms.

It's sad that she'll never know
that the Sea doesn't love her,
that the Sea is too lost in his own grandiosity
to even notice the River.
That her loving embrace doesn't change the Sea,
that the water she received as a gift from the Sea
was actually given to her by a philanthropic Sun.

It's sad that by the time the River realises the truth,
She's already lost her identity.

And then there's the Earth.
Unlike the others, she thinks more than feels,
Her mind is more powerful than her heart,
She sees the Sun,
Luminous and spirited, alone and magnificent,
Has so much and is so wasteful with it.
The Earth, being smart,
Uses the Sun's wasted energy,
Nourishes herself and grows,
in character, in mind, body and spirit.
She marvels at her own brilliance
and what she's done with her life.
She fears the Sun and his immense power,
and detests the way he lavishes his God-given gifts.

It's sad that she'll never know that the Sun could have
left,

Yet he stands there all alone, so that he can give to the Earth.
He burns himself, so she may benefit from it,
He wants to come closer, but he knows he can't,
He knows his passion is so strong that he'll hurt her,
So he stands apart and admires his Lady.

It's sad that no one's around to tell the Earth
Tell her just how much the Sun loves her.

Raavan put the scroll away and waited for his brother's response.

Kumbhakarna looked contemplative.

'Dada, that was powerful,' he said after a moment.

Raavan smiled. 'Do you really like it?'

'I love it! Trust me, Dada, there will come a time when even the Mahadevs and the Vishnus will quote this poem!'

Raavan laughed. 'You really do love me a lot, kid brother…'

'That I do! But seriously, Dada, you can play music, you sing, you write poetry, you are a warrior, you are wealthy, you are well-read, you are super-intelligent. There's no one like you in the whole wide world!'

Raavan puffed out his chest exaggeratedly. 'Quite right. There is nobody like me!'

They burst out laughing.

—— ॐ ——

A month had passed since the decision to rob Krakachabahu had been made. Raavan and his crew were to sail out of the Gokarna port the following day. Considering the speed at which the ship could sail, they expected to be in Chilika within a few days. Akampana, Mareech and a hundred soldiers would accompany him. Kumbhakarna had insisted on tagging along too, and after a few unconvincing attempts at dissuading him, Raavan had relented.

Mareech and Akampana had already struck a deal with Prahast. He would first help Raavan steal Krakachabahu's treasure, and then leave Chilika with them. Most opportunely, Krakachabahu had recently sailed out to his homeland Nahar, situated in between the Tigris and Euphrates rivers. Half a world away from Chilika.

The night before the proposed heist, Raavan decided to visit his favourite courtesan, Dadimikali, the most expensive courtesan in the most elite pleasure house in Gokarna. Only the best would do for him!

He lay on the bed now, a sheet pulled up to his waist. Dadimikali was lying on her stomach, her head resting on Raavan's thighs. Nude as the day she was born. She was lithe of body and slim, with curves in all the right places.

'I don't think I'll be able to walk properly tomorrow,' she giggled. She turned towards Raavan and felt her way up. 'But it looks like you are ready for more.'

Raavan stretched his arms and cracked his knuckles. 'I don't think you can take it.'

Dadimikali gazed at his face lovingly. 'You know I can take anything from you.'

Raavan looked away. Bored. Dadimikali's affection was becoming increasingly cloying. His mind wandered to the dog he had killed a few months back. The one that had kept following him around.

Mangy, pathetic-looking creature. Disgusting. It needed to be put out of its misery.

'Raavan?'

Raavan didn't answer. He focused on his breathing. A long-dormant animal was slowly beginning to stir inside him.

'Raavan,' whispered Dadimikali. 'I think I love you.'

Raavan could feel the animal inside him awaken.

Dadimikali edged up and pressed her naked breasts against him. Love poured out of her eyes. 'You don't have to tell me you love me. I understand. I just want you to know that I love you.'

'What are you staring at?' growled Raavan.

He knew his swarthy skin was attractive to most women. But the pockmarks on his face always made him feel self-conscious. He was growing a beard and a moustache to hide as many of the marks as he could.

Dadimikali kept gazing at him. 'I'm looking at your beautiful face…'

She moved closer, pouting her lips in readiness for a kiss. Raavan grabbed her by the hair and yanked her head back.

'Which part of my face are you staring at?' he demanded.

Dadimikali knew that Raavan sometimes liked things rough. She lay back on the bed with her hands clasped behind her head. Surrendering completely. 'I am your slave. Do what you want with me.'

Raavan was gripped by desire. The desire to know what it would feel like to peel the beautiful skin off Dadimikali's face and see the pink flesh underneath. To slice through it. Hacking at the tissue and arteries. Reaching the bone. Sawing through the bone. He felt his breath quicken with excitement. The animal inside him was roaring now.

Oblivious to the reason for Raavan's excitement, Dadimikali edged closer once again. She kissed Raavan gently. Offering herself to him. Submissively.

He bit down on her lips. Hard. Drawing blood. She didn't cry out. She remained still. Waiting for Raavan to do more.

Raavan's breath quickened. His body urged him to finish what he had started. He felt intoxicated. Then, from the deep recesses of his mind, he heard a soft voice.

Dada…

Kumbhakarna's voice. Filled with innocence. And fear.

No. Not her. I can't keep it quiet here. Kumbhakarna will find out…

But the animal inside growled louder.

I have the money to keep it quiet.

He looked into Dadimikali's trusting eyes. Her puckered lips. Her heaving chest.

She wants it. She's asking for it. She's pathetic. Disgusting. She needs to be put out of her misery.

He wrapped his arms tightly around her. Crushing her. She whimpered slightly. But did not complain.

'I am yours. Do what you will with me…'

Suddenly, Raavan heard the familiar, calm voice in his head. *You can be better than this.*

The voice of the Kanyakumari. The voice of a living Goddess.

His navel throbbed, the pain intensifying.

Raavan pushed Dadimikali away and leapt off the bed. She reached for him, trying to stop him from leaving. 'What happened? What did I say?'

'Get away from me!' he hissed.

Tears welled up in her eyes. 'Don't leave me… please…'

Raavan turned and slapped her across the face. Savagely. As she fell back on the bed, he picked up his clothes and stormed out of the room.

—१७१—

Raavan and Kumbhakarna stood on the upper deck of the ship, admiring the view. They had just sailed into Chilika lake. Mareech and Akampana were on the lower deck, supervising the progress of the vessel towards the small island of Nalaban, in the centre of the lake.

The entire island had been reserved for Krakachabahu's use. His palace was on the top of a hill, right in the middle of the island. The hill was man-made, created from the earth that had been dredged up from Chilika lake to increase the depth of the water so large ships could enter. Much of the land around the house had been left undisturbed. Wild and lush. Nalaban was also a bio hotspot, welcoming large numbers of varied species of birds during their winter migration.

Krakachabahu was perceived to be a simple man, dedicated to his job. His apparent respect for Mother Nature and the simple gubernatorial palace helped him maintain appearances with the king of Kalinga, and hide his thieving. The truth was that he planned to take his illicit skimming of the Kalinga revenues and leave soon. He had stashed away enough money, and he intended to use it to raise an army to conquer Nahar. His long-term plan was to rule his home country.

But he didn't know that his plan was about to be upended by an upstart trader from Lanka.

'You remember my instructions, right?' Raavan asked his brother.

'I do, Dada, but can't I come with you?'

'No, you can't. We've discussed this already. Now repeat my instructions.'

'We'll sail to the secondary wharf on the island and present our manifest as a trading ship from Thailand. All of you will go in carrying empty chests, which you will fill with Krakachabahu's gold and precious stones. Then you will carry them back to the ship.'

Raavan laughed and ruffled Kumbhakarna's hair. 'Kumbha, that's what I need to do. Tell me what you are supposed to do.'

'Oh that, yeah… So, I'll be waiting at the wharf for you. In case I see any sign of trouble, I'll sound the ship's horn and sail out. I'll wait for you at the main wharf on the other side of the island. And you'll meet me there.'

The main wharf had been damaged a few months ago, when a craft lost control of its steering and rudder mechanism, and crashed into it. It was under repair now and all traffic had been directed to the secondary wharf.

'That's correct. Now, I am leaving some men here with you. But you will not attempt to be unnecessarily brave if there is trouble. You will sail out and meet me at the main wharf, the damaged one.'

'Yes, Dada.'

Raavan bent closer to Kumbhakarna. 'Promise me that you will sail away and not do anything foolish.'

'Have I ever disobeyed your instructions, Dada?' asked Kumbhakarna, looking hurt.

'Often,' said Raavan sardonically. 'Go on, promise me. Swear in the name of Lord Rudra.'

'Dada! I can't take Lord Rudra's name so casually.'

'Swear!'

'Fine! I swear in the name of Lord Rudra. I'll sail away at the first sign of trouble and meet you at the main wharf.'

'Good.'

—ᚱᚦᛁ—

'By the great Lord Indra!' exclaimed Raavan, turning the flawless pink diamond around in his hand. 'It's hard to believe this little rock is worth four hundred thousand gold coins.'

The colour of a diamond significantly determined its value. If a white diamond exhibited a yellow hue, its price went down. If it exhibited a pink hue, a much rarer phenomenon, its price shot up.

Mareech stepped closer to admire the precious stone. 'It's not little by any stretch of the imagination, Raavan. It's the biggest diamond I have ever seen.'

Akampana stood to one side, looking around nervously.

'Doesn't it look like it's bleeding from the inside?' asked Raavan, enchanted. 'I wonder how it got this pink hue.'

Nobody knew how or why a diamond acquired its colour. Some said it was because of the pressure exerted on the stone over many millennia. Others opined that the enormous forces unleashed by earthquakes caused a diamond's colour to change. A few even considered a pink diamond to be unlucky. A carrier of bad karma.

'Would you know?' asked Raavan, showing the diamond to Akampana.

'Raavan, it doesn't matter how it became pink. As long as it is pink. Let's leave. Please.'

Raavan laughed softly. 'Always so nervous, Akampana.'

He stepped back from the tiny, secret chamber that had been artfully built into the thick wall. He looked at Prahast, standing at the far end of the room. Prahast's loyal soldiers were positioned alongside him, their swords drawn. Dripping with blood. In front of them were three eunuchs on their knees. Part of Governor Krakachabahu's Naharin security team. They bore the wounds of the gruesome torture they had been subjected to, until they revealed the location of the secret chamber where the precious stones were kept.

Raavan nodded at Prahast. The men immediately swung their swords and decapitated the three eunuchs. Raavan's instructions had been clear. No eye-witnesses were to be left behind to identify the perpetrators of the robbery. Everyone in the palace—the security staff, the maids, the cooks, the helpers—had been killed. In cold blood.

Prahast had managed to corrupt half the security force, with loyalty earned over many years and large amounts of gold promised over the previous week. His men had launched a surprise attack on the other Naharins in the palace. Swift and clean.

Nobody outside had an inkling of the massacre that had taken place within the palace. In an attempt to mislead Krakachabahu, dead bodies had been brought into the palace earlier. Their faces had been smashed in to prevent identification. To convince the Naharin governor of Chilika that Prahast and the others in his security force had also been killed during the robbery.

It was a brutal plan. But also efficient and practical. Like Raavan himself.

On Prahast's advice, Raavan had decided against killing the workers whom they had seen repairing the damaged wharf, at some distance from the governor's residence. To kill them in the open was to risk exposure. In any case, the workers were never allowed near the palace or the secondary wharf. So the chances of them identifying Raavan and his gang were next to none.

Raavan's men had already carried the gold out of the palace in large chests. These were being loaded on the ship right now. He had stayed behind, with Mareech, Akampana and a few others to gather the precious stones. For just these stones were worth a little over two million gold coins.

Raavan stepped forward and stared at the decapitated bodies of the three Naharin eunuchs. As the blood continued to leak out of their gaping necks, he stood still, almost hypnotised. Drawn to the bloody spectacle before him.

He bent forward. Trying to distinguish the different arteries through which the thick red fluid was gushing out. The bodies were lifeless. But their hearts didn't seem to know that yet. They were still pumping. Weakly. But still despatching blood to heads that weren't there anymore.

Akampana touched Raavan's arm. 'Raavan…'

Raavan snapped out of his reverie and slipped the stone in his hand into the pouch tied to his cummerbund, where it clinked against the others. He took a deep breath and looked at the others. 'Let's go.'

Just then, the ship's horn sounded. Loud. Insistent.

'Run!' shouted Raavan.

Everyone reacted immediately. They knew what they had to do. The plan was clear. They had to rush to their horses and ride like the wind to the main wharf. Kumbhakarna would be waiting for them there, in Raavan's ship.

'Hyaah!'

Raavan and his men rode their horses hard. Ten of them. Mareech in the lead. Raavan bringing up the rear-guard. They were riding downhill, fast and furious.

'To the right!' shouted Mareech, pointing.

A fork in the road was coming up. The road to the right led downhill to the damaged wharf. The other one went straight to the secondary wharf, which was visible in the far distance. Where Raavan's ship should have been. But it was missing. From high up on the hill, they could see another large ship moored there. It had just cruised in, for the sails were still up. So was the flag. It was Krakachabahu's vessel. He had returned early.

'Faster!' shouted Raavan.

He could see riders racing out of the secondary wharf. Riding up the main road. Up the hill. Towards them. Perhaps Krakachabahu had sensed something was wrong.

'To the other wharf!' screeched Akampana. He was riding in the middle of the group. Nervous as a cat on a hot metal roof.

The horses swerved onto the road to the right. It was about a five-minute ride downhill to the wharf. Raavan could see a forward scout rider galloping up the straight road, towards them. Krakachabahu's man.

Raavan pulled his knife out of its scabbard, took the reins of his horse in his mouth, and focused for a moment. Holding his breath, he flung the blade at the rider. It rammed into the man's throat. As he fell from his horse, Raavan swerved to the right, riding hard behind his men.

'Hyaah!'

As they thundered down the road towards the damaged wharf, through the dense forest vegetation, Raavan could see the road more clearly. It was now a straight ride to the wharf, which meant they would be easy targets for Krakachabahu's mounted archers. And he was right at the back of the line. The first target.

Damn!

Thinking quickly, he yanked the string that crisscrossed his shoulder and pulled the shield tied on his back upwards. He could survive an arrow in his back. Not one that pierced his throat.

The wharf was just a little way ahead. The road was getting narrower. Much of it was taken up by the scaffolding built for port repairs. A few men were on the scaffolding, while others stood around on the road.

The horsemen thundered ahead.

'Move!' screamed Mareech, as he hurtled past.

The workers rushed to get out of the way, in a sudden state of panic. One of the more unfortunate ones came under Akampana's horse. The riders didn't slow down. The man was run over repeatedly by the many horses that followed Akampana's. By the time Raavan passed, he had been pummelled to a pulp.

Since there were no posts to tie the ship to, Kumbhakarna had had the sailors drop anchor. Keeping the ship as close as he could to the edge of the wharf, with the help of grappling hooks. The strongest amongst the sailors hung close to the anchor line, a large axe in his hands, ready to strike and cut the thick rope as soon as Raavan and the others were on board.

There was a wide gap between the wharf's edge and the ship. But the Lankan horses had been trained to jump high and far. Precisely for scenarios where a quick escape was necessary. Such as now.

Mareech did not slow down as he galloped through the damaged wharf.

'Hyaah!'

He whipped his horse to a frenzy, causing it to gallop harder. Faster and faster. Right at the edge of the wharf, he screamed, 'DASHA!'

Dasha was the old Sanskrit word for the number ten. Nobody knew why Raavan had insisted on this particular word when the horses were being trained, but his men had obeyed him unquestioningly, as usual.

Mareech's horse knew the command well, and leapt forward. High and far. He landed neatly onto the ship's deck. Mareech thundered on for a few feet more, clearing the way for the others behind him.

One after the other, the riders leapt onto the ship. One of Prahast's Naharin soldiers timed his jump wrong. His horse fell short and dropped into the water. The man banged his head hard against the shipboards, breaking his neck. He died instantly. Nobody stopped to look at him. They had no time.

'Come on!' screamed Mareech. He was standing by the balustrade of the ship now, having dismounted from his horse. Prahast came speeding forward, timing his jump perfectly, and landed safely on the ship. Raavan was next. The last of them.

Krakachabahu and his men were closing in. Just two hundred metres away.

'Come on, Dada!' screamed Kumbhakarna.

One of Krakachabahu's archers took his horse's reins into his mouth, positioned his riding bow in front of his chest, and released an arrow.

It was a lucky shot. At a fast-moving target.

The arrow slammed into the horse's digital flexor tendons on the lower part of his right hind leg. Severing it cleanly. It didn't seem like a big wound. There was hardly any blood. But it was debilitating for the galloping beast. The right leg, useless and incapable of bearing weight, collapsed. And the horse, because of the fearsome speed it was moving at, fell hard, its head hitting the ground, its neck twisting at an unnatural angle.

Raavan, alert as ever, had already untangled himself from the stirrups. Smoothly dismounting as the horse fell to the ground, he rolled away from it and was back on his feet almost instantly. He ran forward in the same smooth motion.

'Dada!' Kumbhakarna's voice was filled with anxiety and fear.

Everyone around him had the same thought.

Raavan is not going to make it.

Mareech looked at Kumbhakarna and then back at Raavan. 'Lord Rudra be merciful...'

There was no way a man could jump over the gap that most of the horses had strained to bridge.

But this was no ordinary man. This was Raavan.

He sprinted down the wharf. Dashing ahead, towards the edge. Towards the port crane meant for loading cargo on ships. It hadn't been used in months. It was about to be put to use in an unexpected way.

Krakachabahu's men were still raining arrows at him. Some flew past Raavan. Others missed him by a whisker. But none hit their target.

As he neared the edge of the wharf, Raavan leapt high and grabbed the hook block of the crane. One leg scissored out to kick the winch. His timing was perfect. The winch wound out quickly, allowing the hoist rope to spool out. Holding on to the hook, Raavan soared over the water, towards the ship, as arrows flew around him.

Kumbhakarna and the rest of the crew stood rooted to their spots. Transfixed by this adrenaline-charged display of athleticism.

As soon as he was at a suitable height, Raavan gathered momentum, swung his body forward, and let go of the hook. He soared high in the air, then dropped easily onto the ship's deck. He rolled smoothly to break his fall and was back on his feet immediately.

His men stood around him, awestruck. Silent.

'Let's go!' Raavan shouted.

Kumbhakarna turned to the man at the anchor rope. 'Cut it!'

The sailor swung the axe, and in one mighty blow, severed the thick rope. The grappling hooks were rapidly released.

'Row now! Quickly!' ordered Kumbhakarna.

On command, the pace setters in the galley deck below started beating their drums. The men began rowing in tandem. The ship lumbered ahead. Pulling out of the wharf.

Krakachabahu's men continued to shoot arrows at them.

'Get down!' shouted Raavan.

The men went down on their knees, taking cover behind the balustrades.

'Faster!' ordered Kumbhakarna. The pace setters pounded up the beat and the rowers picked up their pace.

'Unfurl sails!'

One of the sailors, who had been hiding behind the tabernacle, started turning the winch. This was an engineering innovation that Raavan had perfected. It allowed one of the sails to be unfurled rapidly, with the guidance of a winch rigged on the deck. The sail started spreading out quickly. It would catch the wind soon.

As the ship pulled away, Raavan could hear the angry shouts of Krakachabahu's men in the distance. Safe behind the balustrade, he looked at Kumbhakarna and grinned.

Mareech clapped Raavan on the shoulder. 'We've done it, Raavan! We've done it!'

Raavan smiled. He rose to his feet and made an obscene gesture at Krakachabahu's men in the distance. One of the Naharins shot an arrow that whizzed past his face.

Mareech pulled his nephew down. 'What are you doing? We are not out of danger yet. Stay down!'

Raavan's face was pale, his body strangely still.

'Dada?' Kumbhakarna said worriedly, feeling Raavan's body for any wounds.

Raavan pushed Kumbhakarna aside and rose to his feet. His gaze was directed at the workers who were cowering near the scaffolding. Another arrow whizzed by. But Raavan didn't duck.

Mareech pulled him down again. 'What is wrong with you? Stay down!'

Raavan fell back on the deck unsteadily. He looked like he had seen a ghost. His breathing was ragged. He pushed Mareech away and rose again.

This time an arrow hit him on the shoulder, slamming into him with brutal force. But Raavan didn't flinch. His eyes were glued to the scaffolding.

'Dada!' Kumbhakarna screamed in panic, pulling him down again.

He noticed the sudden tears in his elder brother's eyes.

'Ka…' Raavan was crying. 'Kanya…'

This time, Kumbhakarna rose. He narrowed his eyes and looked towards the fast receding shore. At the scaffolding. At the workers there. At one person in particular, standing in the centre.

It was her.

He recognised her from the paintings.

While everyone else was cowering, she stood there unmoving. Upright. Like the living Goddess that she was. The signs of hard physical labour marked her and yet her face was luminous. She watched the ship go, her expression stately and calm. She radiated a quiet dignity. Almost like she was willing them to stop the violence. With her moral force.

There could be no doubt. It was her.

Mareech reached out and pulled Kumbhakarna down as another arrow whizzed by. He shouted angrily at his nephews, 'What has gotten into you both?'

Kumbhakarna looked at Raavan. He said what Raavan couldn't find the strength to say. 'The Kanyakumari…'

As if energised by the divine word, Raavan broke the shaft of the arrow buried in his shoulder. He stood up again and turned around. Ready to jump into the lake. Ready to swim to her.

'Raavan!' screamed Mareech, grabbing his nephew. 'Stop this madness!'

'Let me go!' Raavan cried hoarsely, struggling to free himself. 'Let me go!'

Everyone on the ship stared at their leader. Wondering what was going on.

Kumbhakarna held Raavan tight. 'Dada, you can't go back now! You will be killed!'

'Let me go!' Raavan tried to push the others away and get to his feet.

'Dada! Listen to me, please. You will die before you reach her!'

'Let me go!'

'I will come back for her, Dada! I will find her!'

'Let me go!' Raavan repeated in desperation.

Mareech was too stunned to react. He had never seen Raavan like this.

'Dada!' Kumbhakarna wouldn't let go of his brother. 'Please, trust me. I'll come back for her. I'll find her. I give you my word. But right now, you need to stay with us.'

'Let me go.' Raavan's voice was ragged. Broken.

'Dada, I will find her. I promise.'

'Let me go…'

The mast unfurled completely and caught the wind. The ship sailed out and away from the shore. Away from Krakachabahu's arrows.

Away from her.

Away from the Kanyakumari.

'Let me go…'

Chapter 9

In a little less than a month, Kumbhakarna was back in Kalinga. After the daring robbery on Nalaban Island, they had sailed to Lanka in a sombre mood. They had reached Gokarna in a day and a half, and the precious merchandise had been quickly unloaded and stored in the basement of Raavan's mansion, in a specially built and well-guarded chamber, with multiple locks for additional security. Kumbhakarna had immediately set about preparing for his journey back to the island. He had purchased a new ship, one that could not be traced back to Raavan in any way. He had also hired a small crew of young men from southern Africa. All of this had been accomplished in three weeks.

Then Kumbhakarna set off again, sailing up north. Towards Chilika lake. Towards the Kanyakumari.

By now, news had got around that a band of Naharins who had planned to follow the governor of Chilika into rebellion had double-crossed him and taken him prisoner. They had sailed out to Nahar with the captive Krakachabahu, intending to hand him over to the king. When a rebellion fails, it is pragmatic for the rebels to betray their leader to the incumbent ruler and save at least their own hides. Without the money that Krakachabahu had amassed over the years, the Nahar rebellion was as good as dead.

Nevertheless, sailing directly into the lake would have been risky, Kumbhakarna knew. He may be young, but he was not rash. There could still be some loyalists of Krakachabahu in Chilika.

So, Kumbhakarna sailed up north, beyond Chilika, intending to enter Kalinga via the mouth of the Mahanadi. But on the way, he decided to stop at the famous Jagannath temple in Puri, which lay between the lake in the south and the river to the north.

The Jagannath temple was considered to be one of the holiest spots in India. It was close to the coast and clearly visible from the sea. Kumbhakarna anchored his ship and then set out on a rowboat to the shore, accompanied by ten African guards.

The temple complex, consisting of thirty temples, was built on an enormous stone platform spread over ten acres. The central temple, one of the tallest and largest in India, was the *Jagannath* temple; a shrine dedicated to the *Lord of the Universe*. The Vishnu. The Vishnu before all other Vishnus. The Vishnu who was the *Witness*. The *Saakshin*.

Unlike most idols in temples, which were made of stone or metal, the Jagannath idol was made of wood. The wood of a neem tree, to be precise. Every twelve years, it was replaced with a freshly carved one.

The dark idol had a massive head, emerging directly from the chest, without a discernible neck. The arms were in line with the upper lip. The eyes were large and round. The waist was where the form ended. No legs. No hands.

The Saakshin Vishnu was, strictly speaking, a witness. The rich *black colour*, *krishna* in old Sanskrit, was testimony to its provenance, that this God hailed from before the beginning of time. Before even light was created. For before light was created, all was dark. All was black.

The absence of hands signified that He would not enact any karma of His own. The absence of legs showed that He would not move, either towards you or away from you. He was neutral. He would take no sides in petty human rivalries. He was beyond personal likes and dislikes.

Some believed that it was inaccurate to even assign a gender to the God. He was beyond such petty divisions. He was unity. The source.

Most importantly, He had no eyelids. His eyes were forever open. He was always watching.

According to the ancients, this was the highest form of divinity that humans were capable of understanding. For the Saakshin Vishnu was the Primal Being. Floating through time. Witnessing it all, as people lived their lives and the universe breathed its karma.

The prayers that were offered to Him were also unusual.

Devotees did not go to the Jagannath temple to merely ask for His blessings. They went with a larger purpose, when they were ready to carry out their paramount karma. To ensure that it was recorded in the memory of the Primal Being. The account of their karma in the Saakshin Vishnu's memory would decide whether the devotee would get freedom from the cycle of birth and rebirth.

Kumbhakarna believed that he was about to embark on the greatest karma of his life. He went down on his knees in front of the great idol. His back bent. His head touching the floor.

Chanting. At long last, he rose and said what every devotee of the Saakshin Vishnu said when facing Him: 'Witness me, My Lord.'

Witness me as I carry out the greatest karma of my life.

——१७१——

It had been three years since the Nalaban Island robbery. Twenty-two-year-old Raavan had become reclusive and rarely ventured out of Gokarna. While he was still involved in the business and made the decisions on all key strategic issues, he did not go out to sea or travel. He remained in Gokarna, watching the sea from the heights of his hilltop mansion. Waiting for Kumbhakarna.

All this time, Kumbhakarna had been sending regular updates from Kalinga. The dock-repair workers they had seen the Kanyakumari with had travelled westward, deeper into the heart of Kalinga. The next time Raavan heard from Kumbhakarna, it was with the news that they were encamped at Vaidyanath, close to the Mayurakshi River. It wasn't too far from Kalinga.

In the meantime, Mareech had started managing Raavan's vast business empire. He had used the money looted from Krakachabahu to commission the building of large new ships. The best ship-builders in Gokarna and across the land had their entire capacity blocked by Raavan's purchase orders. He was taking delivery of five or six ships every month; an unprecedented happening that shocked the trading community all across the Indian Ocean rim.

Gradually, Raavan built up a fleet of two hundred ships. An advance payment for the cave material had been made to the Malayaputras. Raavan's men took each new ship, as soon as it was delivered, to Unawatuna, a hidden alcove on the southern coast of Lanka. They careened the ships there. The cave material was then kneaded, mixed with other ingredients, and painstakingly rubbed on to each ship's hull. It was a long and laborious process. And done in secret by a small, loyal crew that was very well rewarded for its efforts.

As Raavan's fleet grew, so did its reputation for speedy travel. Manufacturers and artisans found it profitable to trade with him. They knew that their goods would be delivered and sold much faster if they went to Raavan, as compared to other traders. On Raavan's instructions, Mareech also began to use their vastly superior fleet to apprehend and loot other ships along the busy trade routes of the Indian Ocean. The pirate vessels would appear like the wind, plunder and kill the sailors on the target ships, and sink them to ensure that no trace was left of their crimes. Many of the ships they destroyed belonged to Kubaer. Because of the lack of witnesses, no one made the connection with Raavan. They believed the attacks to be the handiwork of pirates.

Of course, Raavan's plan did not end with merely raiding other ships for treasure. Exploiting the growing fear of pirate attacks at sea, he started building his own mini army under the leadership of Prahast. He claimed it was a protection force for his ships. Though it was unusual for a trader to have a standing corps of trained soldiers, many thought it was a logical way to protect profits. Some of the other traders started hiring the services of Raavan's protection force too. Not only did Raavan make profits from hiring out his force, his soldiers also became a source of information for him, about his rivals and their trading plans.

Profits flowed in at a tremendous pace. Raavan was already among the wealthiest traders in Gokarna. He would soon be one of the wealthiest traders in the world. Wealthy enough for even the richest man on the planet, Kubaer, to take notice.

Aware that they could not risk the Malayaputras finding out about the real use of the cave material, Mareech had gone about leasing the Pushpak Vimaan from Kubaer. He had negotiated very hard on the price so that it would seem like a credible deal. Kubaer, the ever-pragmatic trader, had readily agreed. The vimaan was so expensive to run that he had virtually stopped using it. And, like any machine not put to regular use, it was slowly rusting away. From his point of view, any deal was better than no deal.

When Mareech took over the Pushpak Vimaan, the first thing he did was to strip away all the luxuries that Kubaer had built into the flying craft. Out went the gold-plated bed with its soft mattress and the large, well-stocked kitchen for the preparation of exotic food. The vimaan was deprived of everything that smacked of ineffectual opulence without providing any practical value. Removing these luxuries vastly reduced the weight of the craft. The reduced payload meant that the quantities of cave material required to fly the aircraft came down drastically. This slashed the cost of running the craft.

Mareech also limited the use of the vimaan. It would now be used only for flights to distant lands. To seek information, and for trade in extremely valuable but light cargo, such as precious stones. Raavan sometimes accompanied him on these flights.

It was one such trip that Mareech had come to discuss with Raavan.

'Are you sure about this information?' asked Raavan gruffly, as he continued his workout.

Mareech and Raavan were on the first-floor balcony of his mansion. The house was situated on a tall hill that jutted into the sea. It afforded brilliant views of the Indian Ocean, which stretched as far as the eye could see. And beyond. Raavan came here every morning to perform the *Surya namaskar, salutations to the Sun God,* a perfect combination of exercise and spirituality.

'Yes, the sailor is from southern Africa,' said Mareech. 'It's first-hand news. He has seen the things he speaks of.'

The man in question was Lethabo, one of the African sailors who had travelled to Kalinga with Kumbhakarna. He had turned up a few months ago with a message for Raavan, but an injury had prevented him from returning to his post with Kumbhakarna, who was presently in Vaidyanath. Mareech had gone to visit the sailor at the Gokarna Ayuralay where he was being treated. And that's how he had learnt of the great mines full of precious stones, close to the southern tip of the African continent. Marked by a giant flat-topped mountain, which locals called the Table Mountain.

'Hmm…' Raavan remained non-committal as he finished his routine and did obeisance to the Sun God.

'Raavan, it may be worth taking the Pushpak Vimaan there. Even if we find just a few precious stones, it will cover the cost of the trip. And if we do find a mine… well, I leave it to your imagination.'

Raavan walked to the edge of the balcony and rested his hands on the railing. He looked towards the ocean, then away at the horizon.

'Raavan?'

Raavan remained silent.

'Raavan, what is your decision?'

There was no response.

Mareech sighed. He walked up to his nephew and touched him on the shoulder.

'Raavan...'

'Kumbha...'

'What?'

Raavan pointed to a ship at the edge of the horizon. Its sails raised high. A flag aflutter. The flag of Kumbhakarna.

'How can you make out the markings on the flag from this distance?' asked Mareech in disbelief.

'It's him. I know it is,' said Raavan, his face radiating delight.

He turned around and almost ran outside, hollering at his guards to follow. He would board a ship quickly and sail out to meet his younger brother. He was too impatient to wait.

He had to have news of her as soon as possible.

News of the Kanyakumari.

—रोI—

'Are you sure?'

Raavan had sailed out without delay, meeting his brother a few nautical miles from the Gokarna port. Kumbhakarna had been surprised by Raavan's sudden appearance, but he could understand his elder brother's anxiety. It had been three years.

After an emotional reunion, Raavan had taken Kumbhakarna aside, to one end of the upper deck. And fired his questions. Questions about the Kanyakumari.

'Yes, Dada, I am sure. I have seen her myself.'

Raavan's eyes lit up. 'You've seen her?'

Kumbhakarna smiled. 'Yes. Lucky me!'

Raavan smiled broadly. 'Indeed. But how far away is this place?'

'The village she stays in is quite far inland. In fact, it's close to the Vaidyanath temple.'

'Vaidyanath temple? Seriously? We stayed there for some time when you were a baby.'

'Yes, I know,' said Kumbhakarna. 'I've heard the entire tale from maa.'

'But the Vaidyanath temple is quite close to the local Kanyakumari temple, is it not? What is the name of the place? Trikut? Why would she go back to live as an ordinary woman in the land where she was once worshipped as a Goddess?'

'Apparently, it's quite common for former Kanyakumaris to settle down close to the temple where they once reigned as living Goddesses. It has been known to happen not just at the Trikut Kanyakumari temple, but at many other Kanyakumari temples across India. I guess with so many other former Kanyakumaris around, a support structure is available for them to rebuild their lives.'

'Hmm,' said Raavan, barely listening to what Kumbhakarna was saying.

I should have gone to Vaidyanath much earlier. It was the logical thing to do, to search for her there. How foolish I have been! I've wasted so many years.

'Dada…'

'What?' asked Raavan, bringing his mind back to the present.

'I just want to say that there is a slight problem.'

'What problem?'

'Umm…'

'Come on, out with it. There is nothing that your dada can't handle.'

'Dada, the Kanyakumari… She's… she's married.'

Raavan waved his hand in dismissal. 'Oh, that's no problem. We'll handle it.'

'Handle it? How?' Kumbhakarna looked anxious.

'Don't be stupid, Kumbha,' Raavan scoffed. 'We will not kill her husband. How can we? He's the Kanyakumari's husband. We'll buy him off.'

'But…'

'You leave that to me. How quickly can we leave for Vaidyanath?'

'We can leave in a few days.'

'Good!'

Kumbhakarna laughed and mock-saluted Raavan. 'At your command, Iraiva!'

Iraiva was a title that Akampana used for Raavan. It meant 'True Lord' in the dialect that was spoken in Akampana's homeland, far away in the Pashtun regions of north-western India. The title had caught on. Many of Raavan's sailors now called him Iraiva.

Raavan embraced his brother and ruffled his hair. Kumbhakarna, despite being nine years younger than Raavan, was nearly as tall as he was.

'But you haven't asked me the most obvious question, Dada,' said Kumbhakarna. 'I guess I've been away too long. And you're getting slower as time passes.'

Raavan pulled back from Kumbhakarna and frowned. 'What question is that?'

'Something you've wanted to know since forever. Ask me. I have the answer.'

Raavan's face brightened as he caught on. 'You know it? You know her name?'

Kumbhakarna nodded, laughing softly.

Raavan grabbed his brother by the shoulders. 'Tell me, you fool! What is her name?'

'Vedavati.'

Raavan held his breath. Letting the ethereal name echo in his ears. Through his body. Through his spirit.

Vedavati.

The embodiment of the Vedas.

Raavan looked away from his brother, towards the sea. He felt as if his heart would burst at the sound of that divine name. He dared not speak it out loud. His soul wouldn't be able to handle it. He let the name echo softly in the confines of his mind.

Vedavati...

Chapter 10

The brothers were to leave the next morning. The fastest ship in their fleet had been prepared for the journey ahead.

Surya, the Sun God, had called it a night. Fortunately, Som, the Moon God, had taken up the baton. It was a beautiful full-moon night. Some parts of the sea and the exquisite coastline of Gokarna were illuminated in the glimmer of the diffused moonlight. There were almost no clouds in the sky, and the star-studded night resembled a jewelled canopy. A cool, moist sea breeze soothed the senses. The discordant noises of the city had died down. Raavan looked up towards the sky.

Love was in the air. And the pirate-trader breathed it in.

'I can't wait till tomorrow!' he said, drinking some more wine.

Kumbhakarna smiled. He had begged off sharing the wine with his elder brother. Their mother was home.

Raavan savoured the elegant flavour of his drink, holding the glass up in appreciation. He glanced at the bottle. Then at Kumbhakarna's empty hands.

'Seriously?' asked Raavan. 'She actually told you not to pick up my bad habits? Sometimes I think I should just—'

Kumbhakarna interrupted his elder brother. 'Dada, does it really matter? She is our mother...'

Raavan sighed. He drank some more wine.

Though Kumbhakarna respected his mother's wishes, at least in her presence, Kaikesi's well-meaning warnings to her younger son went unheeded. Kumbhakarna idolised Raavan. His elder brother had always been his hero. Bad habits? He wanted to emulate *every* habit of Raavan's. The only thing he wished his brother wouldn't do was insult their mother.

'So, tell me more about her,' said Raavan. 'The Kanyakumari…'

Kumbhakarna had noticed that despite knowing her name, Raavan could not bring himself to say it. He wondered what else he could tell Raavan about Vedavati. He had already described her physical form. It was remarkable how closely she resembled the woman in Raavan's paintings.

'She truly is extraordinary, Dada,' said Kumbhakarna. 'You know how hard life is for most people, right? Taxes have gone up and jobs have been difficult to come by.'

The anti-trader policies of most of the Sapt Sindhu kingdoms had resulted in a dramatic decline in business activities. An equally dramatic decline in tax revenues had followed. At the same time, royal expenditure had gone up due to the imperial preoccupation with war. So tax rates had been increased. This had further diminished the prospects for business and impacted job opportunities. In this atmosphere of desperation, crime too had increased. And as usual, the common folk suffered the brunt of it all. Mini rebellions were breaking out all over the country, especially against the petty nobles and landlords who served the kingdoms' rulers. But Raavan was not interested in the condition of the people at this moment.

'Tell me about the Kanyakumari.'

'It's linked to that, Dada. The Kanyakumari's husband...'

Kumbhakarna stopped as he saw Raavan's jaw clench.

Raavan looked away for a moment and then back at his brother. 'Yes, what about him?'

Kumbhakarna continued, 'His name is Prithvi. He is, or was, a businessman from Balochistan, in the far western corner of India. He settled in Vaidyanath many years ago and tried his hand at some business. But he ended up making heavy losses.'

'Loser.'

Kumbhakarna decided to let Raavan's jealous remark pass without comment. He had been told that Prithvi was an honest, straightforward, decent man. Even if he wasn't the sharpest businessman going.

'These losses in business,' continued Kumbhakarna, 'left him heavily indebted to the local landlord. To repay his debt, he is now working for the man.'

'So the Kanyakumari is stuck doing some menial job because of her idiot husband?'

'It appears she is there by choice, Dada. She too works for the landlord. Everyone in the area knows that she was the Kanyakumari and they respect her. Therefore, she is able to broker peace between the common people and the landlord, whenever it becomes necessary. The landlord ensures that there is enough food for his people. He also gets them jobs wherever he can, on his farm, or at construction sites in and around Chilika. They are reasonably content because of this and have no reason to rebel. Theirs is one of the more peaceful villages you will find in the Sapt Sindhu. Which is an achievement in these times of penury and anger. And it is all underwritten by the moral authority of Vedavatiji.'

Raavan's takeaway from all this was just one thing. 'So, all we have to do is repay the debt to a petty village landlord and the Kanyakumari is free?'

'Umm… Dada, I don't know if it will be that simple.'

'It *is* that simple. There is so much you have to learn about life, Kumbha. You are still very young.'

—१७१—

Raavan's ship was sailing up the eastern coast of India, towards Branga. Towards the mouth of the holy Ganga. They intended to sail up the river, to the point where it came closest to Vaidyanath. The crew would then march overland to the sacred temple town. The river Mayurakshi began its journey close to Vaidyanath, and flowed east to empty itself into the westernmost distributary of the Ganga. An amateur sailor might make the mistake of thinking that sailing up the Mayurakshi would be the fastest way to reach Vaidyanath. But Raavan was not an amateur. He knew that the Mayurakshi was a flood-prone river with treacherous and fast-moving currents. Sailing on it would be hard work, and slow. Better to sail further up the Ganga, and then walk or ride the rest of the way.

'Are you sure you are fit enough to ride all the way to Vaidyanath?' asked Raavan, playfully patting Kumbhakarna's immense belly.

The brothers were on the upper deck of the ship, walking down the corridor, towards the captain's cabin. Raavan had just finished an hour of dance practice on the open deck, accompanied by his favourite musician, Surya. He had hired Surya at considerable expense some time ago, and persuaded him and his wife Annapoorna to accompany them on the voyage so he could continue to practice the dance form he was currently attempting to perfect.

'Don't worry about me, Dada. I am not the one who goes breathless at the mere mention of that "divine name",' said Kumbhakarna, a mock-devout expression on his face.

Raavan burst out laughing and Kumbhakarna thumped him on the back, laughing even more loudly. They entered the cabin and Kumbhakarna shut the door behind them. Raavan walked up to an ornate cabinet and fetched a glass decanter and goblet. He poured himself some wine.

'Maa is not here, Kumbha,' said Raavan, holding the glass high. 'You should try some.'

'I have tried some already, Dada!' Kumbhakarna grinned. 'But I don't like drinking at sea. It makes me feel like vomiting.'

'Yuck,' grimaced Raavan, 'I did not need to know that.' He flopped down on a chair placed near a porthole, across from his brother. 'Anyway, now that I know you have tried wine already, I have to get you to try women. There are some very good courtesan-houses on the way. We'll stop at one of them. Let you experience… shall we say, a woman's touch.'

Kumbhakarna giggled. Embarrassed and excited at the same time. He had heard stories. But he had no idea what he was supposed to do with a woman.

'The only problem with women is their mouth,' continued Raavan. 'They talk. And what is more, they talk utter nonsense. You do know that in some parts of the world, they believe that heaven is above and hell is below, right? Well, it's the exact opposite with women. With women, there is heaven below and hell above!'

Raavan laughed aloud at his own joke. Kumbhakarna joined in somewhat uncertainly.

'That is not true of all women, Dada,' he offered. 'When Vedavatiji speaks, one can sense the wisdom—'

Before he could complete the sentence, Raavan cut in. 'The Kanyakumari is not just a woman. She is a living Goddess.'

'Of course, Dada.'

Raavan looked out of the porthole, sipping his wine. Thinking of what he would tell her when he saw her. How he would woo her.

Why will she refuse me? Especially when she finds out how I feel about her. When she gets to know how rich and powerful I am… and worthy of her love.

'Dada, I just want to be honest about something. You should consider it seriously too.' Kumbhakarna's voice interrupted Raavan's thoughts.

Observing his younger brother's grave expression, Raavan became serious too. 'What is it?'

'It's just that…' Kumbhakarna hesitated.

'What happened, Kumbha? Out with it.'

'Dada… don't take this the wrong way… but honestly, I just don't think the Kanyakumari will be impressed by your dancing. So don't dance for her, please. I can guarantee that she will run away from you if you do.'

Raavan picked up a small cushion that lay nearby and threw it at Kumbhakarna, who collapsed in peals of laughter.

Raavan was laughing too. 'You are certainly not the good little boy who maa fears I will corrupt.'

Kumbhakarna grinned. 'Trying to follow your example, Dada!'

Raavan picked up another cushion that was at hand and threw it at Kumbhakarna. His younger brother caught it effortlessly, and put it behind his back. 'I think I'm comfortable enough now, thank you. I won't be needing any more!'

Laughter filled the cabin. As he wiped away the tears of mirth, Raavan looked at his younger brother with love. And pride. For these few light-hearted moments, even the ever-present pain in his navel seemed to have disappeared. Joy and hope filled his heart.

— ३७१ —

Kumbhakarna couldn't stop smiling as he walked unsteadily back to the ship.

Raavan put his arm around his little brother's shoulders, leaned in close and whispered, 'How was it?'

They were in Mahua Island and Kumbhakarna had just visited a courtesan-house for the very first time. The island was at the mouth of the western-most distributary of the Ganga, at the point where the great river, burdened with water and silt, sluggishly met the Eastern Sea. There was a courtesan-house here, owned by a woman called Vasantpala, which was renowned across the region. Raavan had decided it was the perfect place for his brother's initiation into the world of carnal pleasures.

He had taken Vasantpala's advice and chosen a famous courtesan called Zabibi for his younger brother. Zabibi was from Arabia, and had come to India only recently, to make her fortune. She was no less than an *apsara*, a *celestial nymph*. Long-limbed and supple, she was blessed with lustrous black hair. Though new to the land, she was already famed for her beauty and her impeccable taste in clothes and jewellery. And most importantly, she was experienced in the art of love.

Only the best would do for Kumbhakarna.

'I think I am in love,' whispered Kumbhakarna, looking stricken and intoxicated at the same time.

Raavan burst out laughing. He continued walking, then stopped when he realised his brother was not next to him.

Kumbhakarna was standing still. Looking dreamily at the early morning sky. The two extra arms on his shoulders drooped, as if they too were inebriated. 'I am not joking, Dada. I think I am in love.'

Raavan raised his eyebrows.

'I don't want to leave her here. Can't I have her forever? Can't I marry her?'

Raavan walked back to where Kumbhakarna stood, put his arm around his shoulders, and started walking his reluctant brother along.

'Dada, I am serious…'

'Kumbha, women like Zabibi are meant to be used, not loved.'

The flash of anger on Kumbhakarna's face gave Raavan pause.

'Dada! Don't speak of Zabibi that way!'

'It was a transaction, Kumbha. She gave you pleasure, you gave her money. She is not interested in you. She is interested in the money.'

'No, no! You don't know what she told me. She couldn't believe that I was just a boy. She said she had never been with a man like me.'

'I paid her, Kumbha. She is a professional. Of course she said things that you wanted to hear.'

'But she didn't lie to me and say things to make me feel good. She meant what she said. She didn't say that I was good looking. I know I am not. But she did say that I was intelligent. Which I am. And that I am strong. And...' Kumbhakarna smiled shyly, 'and good in bed.'

Raavan couldn't help laughing again. 'My naïve little Kumbha! This world is full of selfish people. They will tell you what you want to hear in order to get what they want from you. To protect yourself, you must know how to use them to get what you want. That's the way the world works.'

'But Dada, Zabibi is different. She is—'

'She is no different. She is just clearer about what she wants. She wants money. And she'll give you sex in return. It's simple. Some men want honour. Why? I don't know. But they do. So, give it to them. Give them an honourable way to die. And profit from it. Some women believe that flaunting their beauty is empowering. So, compliment them, have sex with them, and cast them away. Use people before they can use you. Most people in the world are contemptible. Many hide behind pretentions. The ones who succeed are the ones who are honest with themselves. Zabibi is honest. She doesn't care about you. She cares about herself. She's here for a few years to earn enough money, and then she'll go back to her husband in Arabia.'

Kumbhakarna was shocked. 'She's married? She lied to me!'

'Yes, she lied to you. But she didn't lie to the most important person in her life—herself! You should not be shocked. Instead, you should learn from her. Be clear about what you want. But hide it well. It will help you get what you want.'

Kumbhakarna was silent for some time, thinking over what his brother had said. Finally he said, 'That's why we are attacking Kubaer's ships, right? But we do it in such a way that everyone thinks it's the work of pirates.'

'Exactly. Now you are learning. Kubaer's strength is his wealth, and the more of it we take away, the more insecure he will get. In his desperation, he will turn to the only person in Lanka with a league of well-trained and armed men—me. He will seek my help to secure his wealth. I will obviously help the hapless man. And become the chief of the army of Lanka. From there, it will be a short distance to becoming the king.'

Kumbhakarna's chest puffed out with pride. 'My brother, the king of Lanka!'

Raavan smiled. 'Always remember why we are strong, why we are successful. Because we don't fool ourselves that we are honourable or good. We know who we are. We accept it. We embrace it. That's why we beat everyone. That's why we will continue to beat everyone.'

'Yes, Dada.'

Raavan walked on, with Kumbhakarna ambling along beside him.

Chapter 11

'We have to go back, Dada!'

'Kumbha, you are being silly. Go to your cabin.'

Their ship was to leave Mahua Island in a few hours. Kumbhakarna had just come rushing into Raavan's cabin with some news. Earlier, when he had been with Zabibi, enjoying the courtesan's attentions, he had barely noticed the very young girl, not more than eight years of age, who had served him alcohol and food. Before she left the room, he had seen her linger beside the chair on which he had casually flung his angvastram. He hadn't thought much of it then.

Back in his cabin, he had noticed a small knot tied to the end of the fabric. He had opened it to find a tiny piece of papyrus. With two words written on it, in a childish handwriting. He handed the note to Raavan.

Raavan read it aloud. 'Help me.'

'We have to.'

'Help whom?'

'The little girl in the courtesan-house.'

'How do you know it was her?'

'I just know, Dada. She looked troubled. Now that I think about it, there was fear in her eyes. She needs our help.'

'Kumbha, I gave you a long lecture only half an hour ago! We succeed because of our ability to exploit people. Not because we are do-gooders.'

'Dada, you were the one who once told me that if you find someone vulnerable and in serious trouble, help them—and then make them your slave for life. If she is being abused, and we help her, she will be loyal to us forever. She could be useful.'

'Nonsense, Kumbha. You just want to help her and you are trying to find a justification for it.'

'Maybe I am. It will cost us very little. How much does it take to buy the services of a young girl after all? She will be worth it. I saw fire in her eyes.'

'A moment ago, you said you saw fear in her eyes. Which was it? Fear or fire?'

'Dada, I am telling you. This girl could be useful.'

Raavan shook his head in dismay. Then he pointed a finger at Kumbhakarna. 'This is the last time I am helping some random person because of you.'

'It's not help, Dada. It's business. It will be profitable. Trust me.'

—१६१—

'Vasantpala, it is a good price and you know it,' said Raavan impatiently. 'Ten gold coins. Take it and be done with it. Don't waste my time.'

Raavan and Kumbhakarna had returned to Vasantpala's establishment, accompanied by twenty guards. Raavan had thought this would be a quick negotiation. But he was in for a surprise.

The little girl Kumbhakarna wanted to rescue was standing by the wall. Head bowed. Hands clasped together. She was shaking. Perhaps in fear. Perhaps in anticipation of freedom.

'It's not that simple, my lord,' said Vasantpala. 'Ten gold coins may not be enough for her.'

Raavan was irritated. 'You have made more than enough money from me over the years, Vasantpala. Don't be a fool. You can easily get another serving girl or boy. Who has jobs these days?'

'She is not just a serving girl.'

Raavan looked at the girl again. He noticed the ligature marks on her hands and feet; marks that indicated that she was often tied up. He knew that some men liked to have sex with very young girls and boys, even tie them up during the act. He had never understood it. It was disgusting. Abominable.

'How much, then?' he asked.

'Two hundred gold coins. She is profitable.'

Raavan held his right hand out. One of his aides stepped up and gave him a papyrus sheet and pen. Raavan wrote on it, marked it with his seal and threw it at Vasantpala. 'One hundred gold coins is my final offer. You can cash this *hundi* anywhere.'

Vasantpala picked up the sheet and read it carefully. She smiled. 'Thank you, my lord, but this will not be enough.'

'I am not haggling with you, Vasantpala. This is my final offer. Or we can tear up that hundi and—'

Vasantpala interrupted him. 'I wasn't asking for more money for myself, my lord. This is good enough for me. But you will need to pay somebody else too.'

Raavan frowned. 'Who?'

'Her father,' answered Vasantpala.

Raavan turned towards the little girl, shocked. But only for a moment. *All fathers are assholes. Just like mine.*

The little girl raised her head and looked at Vasantpala. Her eyes were burning with rage. And hatred. But almost immediately, her expression changed. She seemed stoic once more. Head bowed. Docile.

Woah! This girl may actually be worth it.

Raavan turned towards Vasantpala. 'Her father?'

'Who do you think sold her to us?'

—ॐ—

The little girl's father lived a short twenty-minute walk away from the courtesan-house. One of Vasantpala's aides led Raavan and his entourage there. On the way, he informed Raavan that the girl never spoke. They didn't know if she had been born dumb. Raavan had a feeling that the girl's loss of speech had more to do with the torture she had suffered at such a young age.

They reached the place to find a modest house in a relatively deserted locality. But it was in better shape than Raavan had expected, considering the state of the little girl. The area around the house was clean. The walls had been reinforced recently with fresh bricks. The roof looked new. There was a small garden outside, with a flower bed. All very tastefully done.

Vasantpala's aide knocked on the door and stepped aside. A middle-aged man answered the door. He was shorter than Raavan and thin, except for a small potbelly. He wore an expensive silk dhoti. A thick gold chain gleamed around his neck. His long hair was neatly oiled and tied.

'Is this your daughter?' asked Raavan, pointing at the little girl.

The man looked at her and then back at Raavan. He noticed the daunting musculature of the pirate-trader. His eyes took in the expensive clothes and jewellery. Obviously, a rich customer. 'Yes, she is.'

'I have something to ask. I want to know—'

The man cut in. 'One gold coin per hour. You can use a room in my house. If you want to do something different, like with her mouth or backside, the rates go up. However, if you want to tie her up, or beat her, we will have to negotiate. Because if you break any bones, she will not be able to earn anything for a few months at least.'

Raavan stepped closer to the man.

'So, what will it be?' asked the father, a little uncertainly.

In answer, Raavan swung his fist viciously at the man's face. Hitting him squarely on the nose. The sickening crunch confirmed that he had broken a bone. As the man fell to the ground, blood spurting from his nose, Raavan turned to look at the little girl. She was staring at her father. At her father's blood.

She didn't blink. She didn't look away.

Raavan turned to his men. 'Tie him to that tree. On his knees.'

The man was howling in pain.

Raavan's men dragged him to a tall coconut palm close by and tied him to it. On his knees. Hands behind the trunk. Both legs secured. Face towards Raavan. Utterly helpless. Still screaming at the top of his lungs.

'In the name of Lord Indra, cover this idiot's mouth,' said Raavan, his face screwed up in revulsion.

One of the guards immediately produced a piece of cloth and stuffed it into the man's mouth. They gagged him with another, longer piece of cloth which was then secured around the trunk of the tree. Not only could he not create a racket now, he could barely move his head. Only soft, muffled sounds escaped his mouth.

Raavan turned to look at Kumbhakarna. Communicating with his eyes. *Watch and learn.*

'You,' said Raavan to the little girl. 'What's your name?'

The girl didn't say anything. Kumbhakarna was about to remind Raavan that she couldn't speak, but his elder brother signalled for him to be quiet.

'Come here,' Raavan said to her.

She stepped closer. The tall and extravagantly muscled Raavan towered over her. She barely came up to his waist. Suddenly Raavan pulled out a knife. The girl stepped back in alarm.

'Don't be afraid. This knife is for you.' Saying this, Raavan flipped the knife around and handed it, hilt first, to the girl.

She studied it closely. It was long, with a firm, metal hilt and cross-guard. The blade was sharp on the outer side and serrated on the inner. The sharper side helped the blade slide smoothly into flesh. The serrated side caused maximum damage and pain while pulling the knife out. Manufactured by the talented metalsmiths of Gokarna, it had been designed by Raavan himself.

The little girl held the knife tightly. Her hands were trembling. Then she looked at her father. The man's eyes widened with fear. His muffled cries became more high-pitched.

I am your father…

Forgive me…

I am your father…

'Come with me,' said Raavan. He walked up to the pathetic figure tied to the tree. The little girl followed.

The man was now shaking, and in a state of utter panic. He struggled against the ropes that confined him. But he had been trussed up well. His muffled cries were the only sounds to be heard. Everyone else was silent.

Raavan slapped the man hard. 'Oh, shut up!'

Raavan turned to the girl and pointed to the place on her father's neck, at the base, where the jugular vein and carotid artery carried blood between the head and the heart. Almost as if imparting a lesson, he said to the little girl, making a slashing action with his hand, 'Make a large, deep cut here, and your father will die in a few minutes.' Then he pointed to the heart and pressed a hand on the man's chest. 'Stab here, and he will die much faster. But you have to make sure you get it right. You don't want the knife to get deflected by the ribs. That is hard bone. Sometimes, the knife can ricochet back from the ribs and you may end up hurting yourself. So, I wouldn't recommend trying it right now. You can train for it later.'

The little girl nodded. Like an eager student. A ferociously eager student.

'Or,' continued Raavan, pointing to the man's lower abdomen, 'you could stab him here. In the guts. No bones to deflect the knife. But the problem is that it will take time for him to bleed out. We may have to hear him scream for twenty, maybe even thirty minutes, as he bleeds to death. And if the wound is not deep enough, the blood flow will be very slow. It could take hours. And I don't have that much time to waste on your father. So, if you are going to stab him here, make sure it's a deep wound.'

The desperate man was struggling to free himself.

'It's up to you now,' said Raavan.

The little girl looked at her father. All her reserves of self-control seemed to have run out as she shook in fury. She gripped the knife hard in both hands. Her father's eyes were pleading for mercy. Tears mixed with sweat and blood.

Raavan stood aside, waiting for the girl to decide.

But even he was surprised by how quickly it happened.

The girl acted fast. No second thoughts. No hesitation. She stepped up and stabbed her father in the guts. Thrusting her shoulder forward as she did so. Choosing the slow, painful death for him. The man emitted a sound of sheer agony. His eyes were wide in panic and pain. His reactions only seemed to egg the girl on. She pushed the knife in harder, using both her hands. When she finally yanked it out, a fountain of blood spurted out. Dyeing her hands red. Her clothes. Her body. Everything.

She didn't flinch. She didn't step back. She stood there drenched in her father's warm blood.

Raavan smiled. 'Good girl.'

But the girl was not done. She stepped forward and stabbed her father again. And again. And again. And again. Always in the abdomen. Always in the guts.

She was silent through it all.

No sounds of anger. No screaming. No shouting.

Just pure, silent rage.

She kept stabbing her father until his abdomen was ruptured, and the intestines started spilling out.

Kumbhakarna said to Raavan, 'Dada, make her stop.'

Raavan shook his head. *No.*

His eyes were fixed on the girl.

She raised the knife and stabbed her father again.

When she finally stepped back, she had inflicted nearly twenty-five wounds on his flailing body. Her face, her hands, her body, her clothes, were slick with blood. It was almost like she had bathed in her father's blood.

She turned around and looked at Raavan. He was momentarily staggered.

She was smiling.

She walked up to Raavan, went down on her knees, and placed the bloodied knife at his feet.

Raavan placed his hands on her shoulders and pulled her to her feet.

'What is your name?' he asked.

The girl said nothing.

Raavan said, 'I am your master now. You will work for me. You will be loyal to me. And I will protect you.'

The girl remained silent.

Raavan repeated his question. 'What is your name?'

The little girl had heard what Raavan's followers called him. Iraiva. The True Lord.

She finally spoke. In a childish voice that was disconcertingly calm. 'Great Iraiva, my name is Samichi.'

Chapter 12

Raavan and his entourage had reached the bungalow in Vaidyanath that Kumbhakarna had rented for their stay. It was a nondescript building at a safe distance from the temple complex, and had none of the luxuries Raavan was now used to. But the brothers had decided to keep a low profile. With so many major temples in the region, many members of the royalty and nobility from across the Sapt Sindhu frequented the area. That meant high security. And a well-known smuggler would be a prize catch for the tax inspectors and the police in the Sapt Sindhu. The brothers had even chosen fake names for themselves: Jai and Vijay, rather than Raavan and Kumbhakarna.

Within an hour of reaching their place of stay, Raavan and Kumbhakarna set out to find Vedavati. She was an hour's ride away, in a village called Todee.

Historically, temples in India were not just centres of worship, but also hubs of social activity around which community life revolved. Most temple complexes had ponds for the use of the local population. Food was provided for the poor, in the form of prasad. Free primary education was made available for children who lived in the villages nearby. Temples in larger towns offered higher education as well. Villagers could access basic medical help at temples in their neighbourhood. In addition, most temples acted as storehouses where essential grains were kept, to provide for people when the rains failed. If they were exceptionally wealthy, they even paid for local building projects, such as houses for the poor and check dams on streams. All of this was made possible because of the donations that the temples received from people, rich and poor.

But like most things now, the system was fraying. As trade declined, so did the donations. Even at the major temples, funds were beginning to dry up. To make matters worse, the royal families were using some pretext or the other to take over temples—ostensibly, to 'run them better'. Soon, a significant portion of the temple donations was being siphoned off into royal treasuries.

Naturally, the charitable work that most community temples funded also began to suffer. Local infrastructure too was badly hit.

But this was not the case in Todee. Here, the local landlord, Shochikesh, was working with the villagers to create a check dam on a stream that flowed close by. It would help conserve water for the dry season. The landlord had supplied the material and the villagers provided the labour. Everyone would benefit.

This seemingly impossible collaboration had only been made possible because of Vedavati. For, while the villagers did not find it easy to trust the landlord, everyone trusted the Kanyakumari. Everyone.

And there she was, supervising the operation. Standing on a slightly raised platform, uncaring of the sweat gathering on her forehead and the dust flying all around.

Work on the check dam was progressing quickly. All the able-bodied men of the village were on the job, with hardly any breaks. The landlord stood on the same platform as Vedavati, observing the work. They were racing against time and he felt the pressure. He had even managed to convince his wayward son, Sukarman, to come and help out. The check dam had to be completed very soon. Not because the rainy season was upon them—there were still many months to go for that. The reason was Vedavati.

She was pregnant. Very obviously pregnant. Work on the dam had to be finished before she went away to the hospital attached to the nearby Vaidyanath temple, to give birth to her child. Neither the villagers nor the landlord's men were sure they could work together without her calm presence. She was the only one who was capable and trustworthy enough to resolve all their disputes satisfactorily.

Raavan and Kumbhakarna tethered their horses a few hundred metres away from the worksite, and cautiously made their way towards it on foot. Raavan had decided they would spend the first day observing the Kanyakumari, without showing themselves.

'Dada,' began Kumbhakarna.

'Softer!' shushed Raavan. 'Someone may hear us.'

Kumbhakarna looked around. There was no one to be seen. But he dutifully lowered his voice to a whisper. 'Dada, why are we hiding? Nobody knows us here. We can tell people that you are a trader visiting the Vaidyanath temple and that you stopped here on your way back to your rest house. You can then go and speak with the Kanyakumari. Only she will recognise you.'

Raavan shook his head.

Kumbhakarna wondered if he was the reason for Raavan's cautiousness. 'I have been here before, Dada. The people around here do not have any biases against Nagas. I'm safe here.'

Raavan looked at Kumbhakarna. 'I'll rip out any eyes that glare at you,' he said quietly. He was walking carefully. Avoiding dry leaves or twigs that might snap under his feet.

Kumbhakarna smiled to himself. His big brother was nervous.

'Do you know that we lived close to Todee for a few days when you were a baby?' asked Raavan, keeping his voice low.

'You've told me, Dada.' Kumbhakarna raised his hand and held up three fingers. 'Only three times in the last five minutes.'

'Oh, have I? I guess I must have…'

Kumbhakarna smiled broadly this time. He had never seen his brother so anxious.

—ৼৢI—

The brothers had found the perfect hiding spot, behind some dense vegetation. It had a clear view of the worksite at the stream. None of the workers had noticed their approach. Nobody had noticed them hiding. They were pirate-traders after all. Concealing themselves when required was a necessary professional attribute.

There were over fifty people at the worksite. But Raavan had eyes for only one of them.

He was transfixed. Practically paralysed. His gaze focused on Vedavati, as she walked among the villagers.

He couldn't help thinking that the muse had truly blessed him, for she looked uncannily like his own paintings of her. She was tall for a woman. Fair, round face, high cheekbones, and sharp, small nose. Black, wide-set eyes with creaseless eyelids. Her long, black hair flowed down her back in a tight braid. Her image was burned into his mind. He had painted her as a curvaceous woman, with a full feminine body. She looked even more voluptuous now. Her frayed, yet clean clothes did not detract from her magnetism.

Kumbhakarna whispered, 'I'm sorry, Dada. I didn't know that the Kanyakumari was pregnant. It didn't show earlier...'

But Raavan wasn't listening. He just kept looking at her, unable to believe that he was finally in her presence.

It took Kumbhakarna a while to realise why, despite the resemblance, Vedavati looked just that bit different from Raavan's paintings of her. It was not her baby bump. It was something else. On Raavan's walls, she appeared divine and awe-inspiring, but also quite aloof and distant. She was different in real life. She still looked divine, yes. Awe-inspiring, yes. But there was nothing distant about her. Warmth and kindness shone in her eyes as she moved among the villagers. Like a Mother Goddess.

'Dada,' whispered Kumbhakarna.

Raavan placed his hand on Kumbhakarna's shoulder. He didn't say anything, but the gesture was enough.

Stay quiet, little brother. Let me look... Let me finally live my life...

—१७३—

Kumbhakarna said softly, 'Dada, don't you think it's time we…'

He stopped speaking, as Raavan raised his hand to signal for silence.

A whole week had passed since their arrival in Vaidyanath. They had been coming to the worksite every day, changing their hiding place each time. Getting a different perspective of the worksite. Getting a different view of the people there. Getting a different darshan of the Kanyakumari.

What didn't change was the fact that they hadn't spoken to her yet. Not even made their presence known.

Kumbhakarna was at a loss. His mighty, indomitable brother simply couldn't muster up the courage to speak to Vedavati. His confidence and easy charm with women seemed to have abandoned him. Bereft of his usual bravado, he just stood in hiding and stared at the object of his devotion.

His Kanyakumari. His Goddess.

But Kumbhakarna could not keep staring at the Kanyakumari forever. So he observed the others at their work, and at rest. Over the past week, he had seen enough of the villagers, and their interactions, to start forming opinions of them. Shochikesh, the landlord, seemed like a genuinely good man. He wasn't attired as grandly as most landlords in Lanka, but he seemed to care for the villagers. The villagers appeared to respect him, even if they did not trust him. Shochikesh's son Sukarman, on the other hand, was a spoilt brat. Lazy. Selfish. Slacking off, and once, even stealing money when nobody was looking. But always on his best behaviour whenever the Kanyakumari or his father were close by.

Why am I wasting my time looking at these idiots?

Kumbhakarna turned to his brother. 'Dada…'

Raavan raised his hand again for silence.

Kumbhakarna refused to be silenced this time. He was at his wits' end, waiting for Raavan to make a move. He imagined spending the rest of his life hiding behind foliage and keeping an eye on the Kanyakumari. No, he had to do something. 'Dada, why don't we just kidnap her?'

Raavan glared at Kumbhakarna, horrified. 'What the hell is wrong with you? She's a Goddess! How can—'

Kumbhakarna interrupted his brother, laughing softly, 'Dada, I still remember your speech in Mahua Island. The Power-of-using-and-exploiting-people speech. I thought we were good at that! What are we doing hiding behind bushes and looking at villagers going about their business?'

Raavan looked outraged for a moment. Then he smiled and shook his head. '*Vaamah kaamo manushyaaNaam yasmin kila nibadhyate; jane tasmiMstvanukroshah snehashcha kila jaayate.*'

He was quoting the words of a brilliant philosopher, one of the great Valmikis, the tribe left behind by the Lady Vishnu, Mohini. The line in old Sanskrit, a statement of helplessness by a man in love, translated as: *It is ominous for a man to feel desire; for a man who is bound up in desire feels compassion and fondness.*

The unspoken truth: such a man would be weak.

Kumbhakarna's eyes twinkled with mischief as he smiled at his elder brother.

Raavan turned to look at Vedavati in the distance and whispered, 'Tomorrow… We'll go speak to her tomorrow.'

—१६१—

'Yes,' said Kumbhakarna, politely folding his hands together in a namaste. 'We are traders who came to visit the great

Mahadev temple in Vaidyanath. We were on our way to the rest house when we heard that there was a check-dam project going on here. So, we thought we would come and see it.'

As decided, Kumbhakarna and Raavan had finally emerged from their self-imposed hideout. Both the brothers had, wisely, come dressed in relatively simple clothes. In these impoverished times, amidst a community that was making the best of its constrained circumstances, it would have been impolite, even dangerous, to show off their wealth. Kumbhakarna was only thirteen years old, but he understood one of the most basic of human emotions: jealousy.

Of course, to the landlord and the villagers, Kumbhakarna looked like a grown man of at least twenty. And to his credit, Shochikesh did not even glance at the outgrowths that marked Kumbhakarna as a Naga.

'You are most welcome to share our lunch, noble travellers,' said Shochikesh. 'We may not be well-off, but we know our dharma. *Athithi devo bhava.*'

Kumbhakarna folded his hands and bowed his head in respect, acknowledging Shochikesh's recitation of an old Sanskrit line from the Taittiriya Upanishad. *Any guest is like God.* He nudged his elder brother, who followed suit. But Raavan's attention was focused elsewhere. On the woman who was walking towards them.

The Kanyakumari.

The Virgin Goddess.

Vedavati.

'What did you say your names are?' asked Shochikesh.

'My name is Vijay,' said Kumbhakarna. 'And my elder brother's name is Jai.'

Shochikesh smiled. 'Both your names mean victory. Your parents must have had high hopes!'

Kumbhakarna laughed genially. 'And we dashed those hopes!'

Shochikesh smiled. He pointed at his red hair. 'Well, my parents named me *Shochikesh*. One with *hair like fiery flames*, apparently! But there is nothing else about me that is fiery!'

'Maybe it is the duty of all children to disappoint their parents?' Kumbhakarna kept the banter going, hoping his brother would snap out of his reverie soon.

Shochikesh chuckled. On some unspoken instinct, he turned to look at his son, Sukarman, who was sitting not far away, watching the others at their work. And the smile was wiped off his face. *Sukarman* meant *One who did good deeds*. Harsh truths, even when garbed in humour, continue to inflict pain. 'In any case, you are most welcome to have lunch with us.'

Kumbhakarna did not get a chance to respond to Shochikesh. For Vedavati had made her way up to them. Her left hand was on her distended belly, supporting her unborn child. Kumbhakarna looked at her and smiled. Raavan, on the other hand, stood staring at the ground.

'Our noble landlord Shochikesh is right,' said Vedavati. 'You are most welcome to have lunch with us.'

Raavan lifted his head slightly and smiled. This was the voice he had ached to hear all these years. It was like a salve for his soul. He let it echo inside him, in his entire being. The words themselves were of little consequence.

He tried to say something. To respond. But his vocal chords seemed constricted. No sound escaped his mouth.

Kumbhakarna looked at his tongue-tied brother, and then at Vedavati. The painful truth was obvious to him. Vedavati had no idea who Raavan was. She didn't recognise him at all.

Kumbhakarna bowed and said politely, 'Great Kanyakumari, it is—'

'I am not the Kanyakumari anymore,' interjected Vedavati, smiling warmly.

Kumbhakarna nodded. 'Of course, noble Vedavatiji. But I don't know if we can stay for lunch. Because we have to—'

'We'll stay!'

If Kumbhakarna had not felt the firm hand of his elder brother squeezing his shoulder, he would probably not have recognised the voice. It was an alarmingly childish squeak. Not the usual baritone of the powerful Raavan.

'Wonderful!' Vedavati smiled at Raavan. Then she turned and walked away.

Kumbhakarna stared at his brother, who was now smiling absurdly at Vedavati's retreating form. He had a bizarre look on his face. Of ecstasy. He couldn't have been happier.

Kumbhakarna swallowed a lump in his throat. He had read somewhere that there was nothing worse than unrequited love. But they were wrong. There was something worse: Unrequited love that was not even aware of it being one-sided. He couldn't watch his brother, the man he admired above all, succumbing to such heart-break.

He looked away, his mind racing to find solutions to this strange new predicament.

Chapter 13

'It was quite shocking,' said Vedavati. 'We were going about our work as usual, when suddenly these people emerged out of nowhere and killed one of our colleagues. This is what the powerless are subjected to in our society.'

Raavan and Kumbhakarna were in Todee again. They had been coming back regularly for the last few days, under the pretext of wanting to learn the techniques of check dam construction.

On this particular day, they were having lunch with Shochikesh and Vedavati. Far enough from the work camp to be away from the dust.

Kumbhakarna had been curious to know more about safety measures at the work site. And they had got talking about past incidents and accidents that they had themselves encountered, or heard about. It was Shochikesh who had brought up the episode of a workman who had lost his life while working on a wharf three years ago. At Chilika Lake. Near Governor Krakachabahu's residence.

Kumbhakarna had stiffened at the mention of the incident, though he had controlled himself in time. Raavan, however, had remained unruffled as they listened to Shochikesh, and then Vedavati, talk about that day, about the cruel men whose horses had trampled over the hapless young worker.

Shochikesh had gone on to expound some sketchy details of the robbery at the governor's residence. Kumbhakarna had tried his best to pretend he was hearing it all for the first time. With appropriate expressions of shock and outrage.

'From what we found out later,' said Shochikesh, 'the attack may have been the work of Governor Krakachabahu's enemies from his native land, Nahar. When two elephants fight, the grass gets trampled. We were the grass.'

'But this is adharma,' said Vedavati. 'Whatever quarrels the Kshatriyas have with each other, they have to ensure that no innocents are harmed.'

Raavan nodded in agreement, his expression giving nothing away.

'That's true,' said Shochikesh. 'But who cares about dharma these days? We have forgotten our traditions and culture. We are an embarrassment to our ancestors.'

Kumbhakarna once again thanked his stars that he had been on the ship during the raid at Chilika, too far away for these people to recognise him. He assumed Raavan had ridden by so fast that nobody had got a good look at him, especially not Vedavati. Also, Raavan's beard was fuller than it had been three years ago. And his face looked very different with the handlebar moustache he now sported.

Maybe it's a blessing that she doesn't recognise him at all. Either from father's ashram or from Chilika.

—१६१—

Vedavati was in the last stages of her pregnancy by now, and judging by the kicks that often took her by surprise, she was carrying a strong baby. And a strong baby needed robust nutrition. Rice cooked in milk, with a dash of cardamom and ginger, was considered excellent for the mother and her unborn child. But the small village of Todee did not grow or have access to cardamom. Black cardamom was usually grown in the foothills of eastern Nepal, Sikkim and Bhutan. It was expensive and difficult to obtain.

But what was difficult for others was easy for Raavan. He had sent out his men and procured five sacks of the fragrant spice. It was a huge amount, considering how little was required for one meal. He presented the cardamom to Vedavati, telling her that it was for the use of the entire village. He had also got some tools which he knew would make the construction work easier.

It was a deeply grateful Vedavati who sat with Raavan over lunch the next day. Shochikesh was away in Vaidyanath. And Kumbhakarna had suddenly, and conveniently, remembered that he had some unfinished work in the village.

As the two sat eating quietly, Raavan retained his calm demeanour, despite the storm in his heart.

'Jai,' said Vedavati, using what she had been told was Raavan's name. 'Are you from the Indraprastha region? From your accent, it appears that you are.'

Raavan did not want to reveal his antecedents to Vedavati. Not yet. 'I have spent some time there. But not much.'

Vedavati looked uncertainly at him. 'Jai, we are grateful for your generosity, of course, but I do hope you haven't stretched yourself too much for us. If you don't mind my asking, what is it that you do? How can you afford to do so much charity?'

'Oh, I work in… trade. Importing things people here may need, and exporting items from here that people in other lands may fancy.'

'I see. And it's profitable?'

If I had misplaced that money spent on the cardamom and the tools, I wouldn't even have noticed it.

Raavan kept his thoughts to himself, and said, 'Yes. It's a little difficult with the new licenses and restrictions. But I can make ends meet.'

'That's good to know,' said Vedavati. People who are innately decent and straightforward tend to accept others at face value. 'Thank you, Jai. Your help means a lot to my village.'

Raavan shrugged. *It's nothing.*

'Not everyone who can help, does,' continued Vedavati. 'Not in these times.'

'Not everyone is… Jai,' Raavan said, laughing, and stopping himself just in time from giving away his real name.

Vedavati smiled, ignoring his conceit. 'These villagers have suffered greatly. They are the real victims of all that's going on these days. And most people don't care about helping those less fortunate than themselves. The tradition of charity is slowly being forgotten in India. We are forgetting our dharma.'

Raavan blanched but held his tongue.

'I don't mean someone like you,' said Vedavati, misinterpreting Raavan's expression. 'But across the land today, dharma has been reduced to just rituals and talk. The philosophy that underpins the rituals, and the reason why we follow them, is being forgotten.'

'Oh, I agree with you,' Raavan said. 'There is a great deal of uncalled out hypocrisy everywhere. But…'

'But what?' asked Vedavati.

'Well, I don't think these villagers should be thought of as victims.'

Vedavati stopped eating, surprised. 'You think they aren't?'

'Oh, they *are* victims.'

Vedavati smiled, shook her head and resumed eating. 'I don't understand what you are saying.'

'Of course they are victims,' Raavan said. 'Just like every other person in the world. All of us are victims in some way or the other. But that doesn't mean we should *think* of ourselves as victims.'

Vedavati looked up at Raavan, intrigued.

He continued, 'All of us have been through times when life seemed unfair. In such situations, we can choose to see ourselves as victims and blame the rest of the world. We can drown ourselves in the false comfort of knowing we are not responsible for our difficulties and expect others to change our lives. Or, we can pick ourselves up. Be strong. And fight the world.'

'It's true that all of us face adversity in life, Jai, but surely not everyone's troubles are the same. Some people are at a greater disadvantage than others. And they need our assistance. Of course, nobody should expect others to solve their problems entirely but the strong must help...'

'...help the "cult of victimhood"?' interrupted Raavan.

'What?'

'The lot who just want to whine and complain.' Raavan put his hands up and mimed in a high-pitched voice, 'Oh, poor me. Look at me. Look at how much I'm suffering. Somebody come and take care of me. I'm a victim of society.'

Vedavati bit her lip as though to stop a smile from forming, then frowned. 'Jai, we shouldn't indulge the weaknesses of others, but we shouldn't mock them either.'

'I'm… I'm not… Noble Kanyakumari, perhaps it was wrong of me to make fun of them. I'm sorry. But this is the way I see it: There is a lion and a deer within each of us. Only if we nurture the lion will we make something of ourselves. If we indulge the deer, we'll be running and hiding all our lives.'

'So… the hunter and the hunted.'

'Yes.'

'And we should always aim to be the hunter, I suppose? Because the hunted cannot possibly have any virtues to recommend them?'

'If we cannot fight for ourselves, how will we protect and provide for those who depend on us?'

'So that's how you see it? Every hunter is a magnificent warrior, and the hunted deserve no respect?'

'You don't agree, great Ve… Veda… Kanyakumari?'

Vedavati looked at him sympathetically. She thought Raavan had a stutter that became acute whenever he had to speak a name, especially one that began with a 'v'. So she had yielded to being called Kanyakumari by him.

'Jai, have you heard of the Panchatantra?'

Raavan nodded readily. 'Of course!'

Panchatantra, literally the five treatises, was a part of the primary learning of every child in India. It contained stories of talking animals, with a moral lesson embedded in each tale.

'Sometimes,' said Vedavati, 'we don't have to depend on animal fables to learn lessons in dharma. Sometimes, we can learn from real animals too.'

Raavan leaned forward, his curiosity aroused.

'This happened a long time ago,' said Vedavati. 'I was still a Kanyakumari. I had travelled a great deal, including to the wonderful lands of the brave Andhras. Close to the river port of Amaravati.'

'I've been there. It's stunningly beautiful. Truly a city worthy of its name.'

'Yes, there are people who believe that the modern city of Amaravati is located in exactly the same place where, sometime in the faraway past, Lord Indra, the king of the Devas, lived.'

'Yes, I have heard that too. For all you know, it could be true.'

'Anyway, while we were there, the local ruler wished to take us on a tour of the jungle that lies between the holy Krishna and Godavari rivers. Much of it was open grassland, and we travelled on elephant back. Sometime during the day, we saw an old lion, with his cubs.' Vedavati paused before asking, 'Do you know what happens to many lions in their old age?'

'Yes.' Raavan nodded. 'There is no sight more painful than that of a powerful hunter past its prime. I've seen it often enough: an old lion challenged by another, usually younger, lion. If he is defeated but lucky enough to survive, he has to flee the territory. The young challenger takes over the pride, and the lionesses switch their allegiance to him. This younger lion might even kill the cubs of the older lion. The mothers watch from the side lines, helpless. They probably see it as a command from their new master—new rules in the new pride.'

'The ways of the jungle can be cruel.'

'Now, if this older lion you saw had his cubs with him, he must have managed to save them somehow. Maybe he and his cubs together escaped the wrath of the young challenger.'

'Very possible,' Vedavati said. 'So, as you know, hunting is difficult for an old lion. And if you happen to be one with a few cubs to feed, life can become a huge struggle. This lion's cubs were starving. He was starving. They were weak. And desperate.'

'What happened next, noble Kanyakumari?'

'When we saw this lion, he was at the other end of the grassland, with his three cubs behind him. He had just spotted a few deer that had probably got separated from the main herd. A mother, with her babies. There were four fawns. One of them was clearly weaker than the others. The runt of the family.'

'Food for his cubs...'

Vedavati noticed that Raavan's first thought was for the lion and his hungry cubs. He seemed to identify with the hunter, even when the hunter was old and weak. 'Of course. But remember, the lion was old. A hunter past his best days. What do you think he did?'

'Why, he would have gone for the weakest fawn, of course. It would provide less meat, but at least he could be certain of catching it and feeding his cubs. A little food is better than no food. His cubs and he would survive another day. Become a little stronger.'

Vedavati smiled. 'You understand the hunter's mind-set well, Jai.'

Raavan returned her smile, though he wasn't entirely certain she meant it as a compliment.

'So, as you correctly guessed, the lion charged at the runt among the deer,' continued Vedavati. 'The doe, sensing danger, lifted her head up, her eyes searching for any movement. On spotting the lion, she moved instantly, alerting the fawns, and they fled towards the tree line, running and leaping over each other. They were swift. All except one. The lion increased his pace. He was weak, but he was still a lion. He began closing the distance to the tiny fawn. It was just a matter of time, a few seconds perhaps, before he would catch up with his prey. It seemed that the lion and his cubs would finally get their meal.'

'And then?'

'Then, much to our surprise, the doe slowed down. The bigger fawns had reached the edge of the clearing, and would vanish into the foliage any moment. Away from the lion. But the runt was still at risk. The mother stopped running, then came to a stop.'

Raavan found that he was holding his breath. 'Then?'

'The lion turned towards the doe. A full-grown deer would last him and his cubs much longer than the little one. He changed course. Since the mother deer was practically stationary, he was upon her in no time at all.'

'Didn't the doe bolt away at the last minute? Now that she had deflected attention from her baby?'

Vedavati shook her head. 'No. She just stood there, watching the little one get to safety.'

'What did the lion do?'

'The lion also came to a halt. Just a few metres from the doe. He seemed confused. The runt, meanwhile, had caught up with his siblings. They turned to look at their mother, bleating frantically, as if pleading with her to flee. But the doe remained where she was. She made a sound, just once. Like she was ordering her children to run away. Perhaps she did not want them to see what was to follow.'

Raavan remained silent. *What a mother…*

Vedavati said, 'The story doesn't end there.'

'So what happened next?'

'The lion looked at the fawns, way out of his reach now. Crying and bleating for their mother. Then he looked at the mother deer, standing just one short leap away. And he seemed paralysed. Like he couldn't bring himself to kill the splendid deer in front of him. And then, he turned to look at his own cubs in the distance. Hungry and waiting to be fed.'

Raavan watched the changing expressions on Vedavati's face as she relived those moments in the jungle.

'What should the lion do? What does dharma say? Should he be a good father and kill to feed his starving children? Or should he exercise his goodness and gift life to a magnificent mother?'

'I… I don't know,' answered Raavan.

'We assume that animals cannot think in terms of dharma. Perhaps they are not able to *express* dharma, since they cannot speak. But why should we assume that dharma does not touch them too? Dharma is universal. It touches everyone.'

Raavan remained silent, listening with his head and his heart.

Vedavati continued to speak. 'Dharma is complicated. It is often not about the *what*, but the *why*. If the lion had been hunting for pleasure—which most animals are not capable of—we might call it an exercise in adharma. Since he was hunting to feed his starving children, it's fair to say he was following his dharma. If the deer had allowed circumstances to overwhelm her and not attempted to save her children, it would have been adharma. But her sacrifice to save her children can only be thought of as dharma. In the field of dharma, intentions matter as much, if not more, than the act itself. But one thing is clear. *Only* if you put your duty above yourself do you even have a chance of attaining a life of dharma. Selfishness is the one thing that's guaranteed to take you away from it.'

'Life was unfair to both the lion and the deer,' Raavan remarked thoughtfully. 'Both were victims.'

'Life is unfair to everyone. As Sikhi Buddha said, the fundamental reality of life is *dukha*. There is no escaping the *grief* that permeates every corner of this illusory world. Accepting this basic truth is the first step towards trying to overcome it.'

'Everyone is struggling... I suppose we must try to understand and learn, rather than judge.'

'Precisely. If you don't judge, you can open the space in your heart to help others. And that will take you towards dharma.'

'But how did it all end, noble Kanyakumari? Did the lion kill the doe?'

'That's not the point of this story, Jai.'

Raavan smiled. And stopped asking questions.

— १७६ —

'This is taking too long, Dada,' said Kumbhakarna. They had been in the Vaidyanath area for nearly a month already. 'Mareech uncle had wanted us to return as soon as possible. There's that business in Africa— '

Raavan stopped him with a gesture. 'It's nothing that Mareech cannot handle on his own.'

'But Dada, what about our crew? And Samichi. They're all sitting around doing nothing, probably wondering why they are cooped up in this guesthouse with no—'

Raavan interrupted his brother. 'Just give them something to do, Kumbha. Send them on some short trade mission or something.'

Kumbhakarna fell silent. Raavan looked dreamily out of the window. It was late at night. All they could hear was the chirping of crickets. Occasionally, an owl hooted in the distance. Raavan had returned to the guesthouse in the evening after a long conversation with Vedavati. He stared at the moon and sighed.

'Isn't it beautiful today?'

Kumbhakarna turned and stared at the moon. It looked pretty ordinary to him. He exhaled softly and looked back at Raavan. 'Dada...'

'Shhh!' Raavan picked up the Raavanhatha lying next to him. 'Listen. I've composed something new.'

He strummed the instrument, as though testing its sound. And began.

From the first time he had heard it, Kumbhakarna had thought of the Raavanhatha as an instrument of grief. It tugged at your heart and brought tears to your eyes.

But tonight, Raavan's deep, attractive voice, the lilt of the melody he had composed, and the whisper of the wind, combined with the ethereal sound of the Raavanhatha to create an island of ecstasy and bliss. He managed to coax the musical instrument of grief to create a melodious tune of joy.

The possibility to turn negative into positive always exists. But it takes a Goddess to inspire the change.

Chapter 14

What do you do when a woman you love deeply, a woman you have dreamt of and worshipped, is lost to you forever? You steel your heart and reconcile yourself to life without her.

Then, by a twist of fate, you meet her again. And you find out that she is committed to someone else. You try to ignore this truth. Ignore the existence of another in her life. Suppress the instinctive hatred you feel.

But you cannot keep away from her. You get to know her better. Fall even more deeply in love with her—if that's possible. And then, you meet the other man. The… husband. And he is everything you did not expect. He is handsome. Honest. Kind. Generous. He is noble, in a way that you know you can never be.

And he loves her. Perhaps as much as you love her. He respects her. Perhaps more than you respect her.

And somewhere deep in your heart, a soft, monstrous, unwelcome voice is heard. You are forced to listen to the truth that you don't even want to acknowledge: that maybe, just maybe, he is better for her than you are.

What do you do then? What do you do?

The only logical thing to do is to hate and despise that man, even more than you did earlier.

It *was* logical. Raavan told himself that.

Prithvi, Vedavati's husband, had returned to the village. When he heard this, Raavan decided to stay away for a few days, pleading some personal work. Until, one day, he took the bit between his teeth and made his way to the worksite with Kumbhakarna.

It was late in the afternoon and a welcome breeze cooled the hot day. Shochikesh was away, ostensibly to make arrangements for some materials that were required for work to continue on the check dam. But Raavan knew better. Shochikesh's son, Sukarman, had been caught stealing from the temple donation-box again; he claimed he had gambling debts to pay off. Shochikesh was trying to get the money back quietly, before word got around. Raavan kept the news to himself. He didn't want to cause any distress to the pregnant Vedavati.

'Thank you once again, Jai,' said Prithvi, addressing Raavan. Like many people from the Baloch region in the far west of India, Prithvi was tall, with clean-cut features and a clear, fair complexion. Even Raavan had to admit that he was a handsome man. 'The tools you donated have really helped pick up the pace of work here. It's heartening to meet a businessman who believes in dharma and charity.'

Raavan smiled and waved his hand awkwardly, not sure how to react to compliments from a man he loathed.

'So how was your trip, Prithviji?' asked Kumbhakarna.

Prithvi glanced at Vedavati before replying. 'It went very well. I made a good profit this time. Around six hundred and fifty gold coins.'

Raavan found it hard not to snigger. *That's a good profit? I earn as much in an hour.*

'Finally, I have enough to take care of my wife and child,' said Prithvi, taking Vedavati's hand in his.

Vedavati rested her head on Prithvi's shoulder. Raavan looked away, focusing on some birds on the treetops close by.

'And you have returned just in time,' said Kumbhakarna.

'Yes!' said Prithvi proudly. 'Just a few more weeks now before our child enters the world.'

Kumbhakarna nodded in agreement. 'By the way, I was thinking that some more tools might help advance the work on the check dam. If you have some time, I could show you what I mean.'

Prithvi looked at Vedavati.

'I'd much rather rest, Prithvi,' said Vedavati. 'My back is killing me.'

Prithvi smiled and caressed Vedavati's face gently. 'I'll be back soon.'

After Prithvi had left with Kumbhakarna, Raavan relaxed a little. 'How bad is it? Should I send for some medicines from Vaidyanath?'

Vedavati shook her head. 'No, I don't think that's necessary. We'll be leaving for Vaidyanath in a week in any case.'

Raavan nodded, trying not to let his feelings show.

'He is a good man, you know,' said Vedavati.

Raavan looked at her, startled. 'Of course he is. I would never think otherwise.'

'And I love him. He is my husband.'

'I... of course... I mean...'

Vedavati held Raavan's gaze steadily. She was making sure her message carried without hurting his feelings.

'So where did we first meet?' she asked suddenly.

Raavan was taken aback. He wasn't sure what she meant.

'I asked Vijay one day, why it is that you both look at me like you know me from before. From my days as a Kanyakumari, perhaps. For some reason I can't be sure of, you seem familiar to me as well. Not Vijay, to be honest. I would certainly have remembered him.' Vedavati was too polite to state the obvious—Kumbhakarna's Naga features made it difficult for anyone to forget him. 'So, I am certain you and I have met before. But where did we meet?'

The lie came smoothly to Raavan's tongue. 'It could be when I came to Vaidyanath many years ago. I visited the Kanyakumari temple and you blessed me. It was so long ago, though. We were both children. It's amazing that you find anything even remotely familiar about me.'

Vedavati stared into Raavan's eyes. For a moment, he thought she was going to tell him that she knew he was lying. But she merely nodded.

'So you are a devotee of Lord Rudra?' Vedavati asked.

Raavan smiled and touched his ekmukhi rudraaksh pendant. 'Yes, I am. Jai Shri Rudra!'

'Jai Shri Rudra,' repeated Vedavati, smiling and clasping her own rudraaksh pendant. 'So, let me ask you: Are you a devotee of His actions or what He represents as the Mahadev?'

Raavan frowned. 'Is there a difference?'

'Of course there is.'

'How so? A person is defined by what he or she does. By his vocation or career. Karma defines the individual. A person without karma may as well be dead.'

Vedavati smiled. 'I didn't say that karma is not important. But it's not the *only* thing that's important. There are other things too.'

'And what are those other things?'

'*Swatatva*, in old Sanskrit. Literally, the e*ssence of your Self*. Or more simply, your Being.'

'Being?'

'Being is a complex word, and not easy to understand. Like dharma.'

'I understand dharma.'

'Do you?' Vedavati smiled.

'All right. I admit dharma is a complex concept. We could debate its nuances for many lifetimes. But surely, Being is not so complex.'

'It is. But to understand Being, you first need to understand karma. Your actions are your karma. It is what you do. Tell me, why do you perform any action that concerns others? Because you expect a reaction—hopefully, a reaction that will make you happy.'

'So, are you saying that karma is transactional and hence, selfish?'

Does she know that I donated things to this pathetic village only to be close to her?

Vedavati shook her head. 'Don't get into what is good or bad. It is what it is. That's all. Karma is most certainly transactional.'

'And Being isn't?'

'No, it isn't. That's what makes it so important. And powerful.'

'I don't understand.'

'I'm sure you've been told that the only way for the mind to find peace is by learning to be calm and centred.'

'Yes,' said Raavan, rolling his eyes.

'Why did you roll your eyes?'

'I didn't mean to. I'm sorry.'

Vedavati laughed. 'I didn't say it was wrong. I just asked why you did it.'

Raavan laughed softly. 'Because it's very easy to counsel people that they should be calm and centred. But no one tells you how to do it!'

'Exactly. That is the problem. People keep thinking that they have to do something to achieve that state. Be successful in their profession, perhaps, or go on a holiday, or make the right friends, or find a different spouse…. But even after they make that change, they find they are not calm. So then they think they have to do something more. Something different. It's a never-ending cycle. Basically, calmness and centeredness are always elusive because people assume they have to do something, gain good karma, to get there.'

'So, the problem is with our focus on karma?'

'Yes. It's very difficult to be calm and centred if your entire focus is on that. For karma is action in the hope of something in return. Like, if you give charity to someone, you expect at least respect in return. It's a transaction. And if the result of your actions is not what you expected, you feel let down and become unhappy. Even worse, if the karma you get in return for your actions *is*, in fact, what you expected, you discover that the happiness you derive from it is fleeting. If dissatisfaction is guaranteed, how can you find peace of mind?'

'How?'

'Simply by Being what you are meant to Be. By staying true to your *Swatatva*.'

Raavan leaned back. The beauty of the logic filled his mind.

Vedavati continued, 'I am not saying we shouldn't focus on action. Without our karma, we may as well be dead. But karma should not be the centre of our lives. If we truly discover our Being, our Swatatva, and live in consonance with what we are meant to be, then everything becomes easy. We don't have to try hard to carry out our karma. Because we will not do anything in the vain hope of something else. We will do it simply because it is in consonance with our Being. With what we were born to Be.'

Raavan had never felt as centred or calm as in these last few weeks with Vedavati. She had answers for him. Answers to questions that he didn't even know he had. 'And what do you think I am born to Be, great Kanyakumari? What is my Swatatva supposed to be?'

'A hero.'

Raavan burst out laughing. Vedavati remained silent, confident in the truth of her assertion.

Raavan controlled his mirth and said, 'I apologise, Kanyakumari. I am not a hero. You certainly are. But not me. I am as close as anyone can be to a...' Raavan stopped before the word 'villain' could escape his mouth.

Vedavati leaned forward. 'Your Swatatva is demanding it of you. You want to be a hero. You want to be an *arya*. You want to be *noble*. That's why, whatever your reasons for leaving the Sapt Sindhu, you came back here. I have been told that you live in Lanka. That's where all the rich people in the Sapt Sindhu are escaping to. But you keep coming back here. Why? Because you want the acceptance and respect of the aryas here. You will never have peace of mind till you accept who you are.'

Raavan remained silent. His eyes glazed over. He was a small child again. Desperately seeking the approval of Vedavati. Of the Kanyakumari. His heart picked up pace. He could smell her fragrance again. The scent from all those years ago. He could hear her commands, her young voice, in his mind.

You are better than this. At least try.

No, I am not.

Yes, you are. This is who you want to be.

I just want to hurt my father. I hate him.

Do you want to defeat him?

Yes.

Defeat your father, by all means. But don't do it by hurting him. Do it by being better than him.

'Jai?'

Vedavati's voice pulled Raavan out of his internal, tumultuous world. 'Sorry… what?'

'I am not suggesting that you desire the respect of the nobility in the Sapt Sindhu. There is nothing "arya" about them, no real nobility. But I can see you want the respect of the true aryas. Those who still remember our old ways. Those who are genuinely noble. Who may not be powerful today, but are dharmic. You want their acceptance. Jai, all you have to do is to accept who you are. And you will find peace.'

She looked at him intently. 'At least try.'

—ॐ—

'That didn't go as planned,' said Kumbhakarna.

He had just come back from Todee. Raavan had sent him to offer a job to Prithvi and had been waiting for him eagerly at the guesthouse. But the news was disappointing.

'Did you tell them everything?' asked Raavan. 'Including the bit about the money?'

'Yes I did, Dada. I know how important this is for you.'

'All that idiot will have to do is to be my personal secretary,' said Raavan. 'Write letters. I am sure even he can manage that. I am willing to pay him two thousand gold coins every year for it! Why did he say no?'

'Perhaps the offer was too kind for Vedavatiji.'

'The Kanyakumari? Why did she get involved in this?'

'Well, Prithviji was very enthusiastic about the offer. He said they could leave for Lanka a few months after the birth of their baby. Then he went to ask Vedavatiji about it. And she said no.'

'But why? I thought she wants me to…'

'Wants you to what?'

'Nothing. Why did she refuse?'

'She wouldn't say.'

'But did you ask her?'

'I did, Dada.'

Raavan looked away. Staring out of the window.

'And then she said the strangest thing.'

'What?'

'She told me to tell you that it took her some time, but she finally remembered.'

'Remembered what?'

'About the hare and the ants.'

Raavan turned to look at Kumbhakarna, stunned. He had been recognised. How much did she know? Did she know about the robbery too? She would hate him if she did. 'Did she say anything about Chilika? About Krakachabahu?'

'No. Why would she? I don't think she connects that with us.'

Raavan remained silent.

'But, Dada, what did she mean by the hare and the ants?'

Raavan did not respond.

Chapter 15

'I thought you wanted to encourage me to do good,' said Raavan.

Raavan had come to Todee by himself to meet Vedavati. He knew he could not prolong his stay much longer and would have to leave for Lanka soon. He had been away too long. But how could he leave without her? Raavan was desperate—he had to convince her, somehow.

'I can't travel,' said Vedavati.

'After your baby is born? Perhaps you can come then.'

Vedavati remained silent.

'Please... I am begging you.'

'You know you don't need me.'

'I do! Please... Nothing needs to change. You can remain married to him. To... Prithvi. I will not make any demands on you. I just need you to be in Lanka. Just be there... just let me look at you every day. That's all I ask for. Please... please... Veda... Ve... Please, great Kanyakumari.'

'You don't need me,' Vedavati repeated calmly.

There were tears in Raavan's eyes. 'I do... I know what I need.'

'No. You don't know what you need. For then you would know that you already have it.'

'But I don't!' Raavan couldn't conceal his agitation. 'I need you! I need you!'

'You don't need me. You need yourself.'

'What does that mean? I don't...'

'Think about it. What have I been to you so far? Only an image in your mind. It's you who wanted to be a better version of yourself. All you needed was an excuse. An excuse to motivate you, help you improve what you had become as a reaction to what your father did to you. You hung on to me as that excuse. What I am trying to tell you is that you don't need the excuse anymore. In fact, you should never need someone else to better yourself. That is dangerous. I could die tomorrow. Then what will you...'

Raavan clenched his fists. 'I will destroy anyone who hurts you. I will rip their—'

'Why do you assume someone will hurt me? I could die of an illness. There will be nobody to blame then, right?'

Raavan fell silent.

'When you start on the most important journey of your life, you cannot be dependent on anyone else. For you would be binding your *purpose*, your *swadharma*, to the fate of another person. That is dangerous. Especially for someone as important as you are.'

'I am not...' Raavan stopped himself from cursing. 'I am not important. I am not even a good person. You don't know the kinds of things I've done.'

'Don't be so hard on yourself. You've been taking care of your mother and your younger brother since you were a child. You have built a trading empire almost single-handedly. You have strength, you have courage, and you are a capable man.'

'I… I have done some terrible things to build my empire. I am…' Raavan was struggling to be completely honest for the first time in his life. 'I am a monster. I know I am a monster. I enjoy being a monster. I need you to save me. You are my chance. My only chance, if I am to make something… something noble of myself.'

'That's where you are wrong. I am not your chance. You are your own chance. You think you are a monster? Which great man does not have a monster inside him?'

Raavan stared at Vedavati. Silent.

'What you term a monster is the fire every successful man has within him,' continued Vedavati. 'A fire that will not let him rest. A fire that drives him to work hard. To be smart. To be relentless. Focused. Disciplined. For those are the ingredients of success. That fire is like a monster that will not allow you to lead an ordinary life. But there is one thing that differentiates a successful man from a great man. One key thing: Does the monster control you or do you control the monster? Without the monster, you would have been ordinary. With the monster, you have a chance to attain greatness. Not a guarantee, but a chance. To seize that chance, you need to control the monster and use your unique and enormous abilities, in the cause of dharma.'

'I can't do it without you.'

'Me? I'm nobody.'

'You are the Kanyakumari! You are a living Goddess! You are noble in a way I could never be. You are kind and generous. You are the purest person I have ever met. I am an impure, selfish bastard.'

Vedavati looked at him steadily without saying anything.

Raavan immediately turned contrite. 'I didn't mean to curse. I'm sorry.'

'There is no need to use an expletive to emphasise a point.'

'I'm sorry.'

Vedavati smiled. 'So, you think I'm pure? Have you noticed that there are no fish to be found in water that is too pure?'

Raavan was quiet. It took him a few moments to realise that Vedavati was right.

'I may be pure, but have I made any real difference in the lives of people? I may be noble in my actions, but I am not capable of commanding the attention of those outside my village. Only those who can reach millions of people can improve the lives of millions of people. Nobility without capability is limiting, it only results in good theory.'

'But…'

'Listen to me, Raavan. Truly great people, who have left a positive stamp on history and in the hearts of millions of followers, combined a cold, ruthless mind with a warm, dharmic heart.'

'I don't have it. I don't have a heart. I don't…'

Vedavati leaned forward and took Raavan's hand in hers. It was the first time she had touched him. His heartbeat seized for a moment.

'You *do* have a warm heart, Raavan. Don't use it just to pump blood through your body. Let it also propel dharma through your soul. Rise to do good. Do good for this land of ours, which is suffering in poverty, chaos and disease. Help the poor. Help the needy. Do good.'

Tears pooled in Raavan's eyes.

'Lead India back to greatness, make it truly *Aryavarta* once again. Make it a *noble land* once more. And then I will come and live in Lanka. Not as your Goddess. But as your devotee. My husband and I will worship you.'

Raavan didn't know what to say. He was surprised to see himself through Vedavati's eyes. Was he really as capable as all that?

'I have faith in you. You can do it. This long-suffering motherland of ours has enough villains already. It desperately needs a hero. Rise to become one.'

Raavan sat quietly, listening.

'You are a devout worshipper of Lord Rudra, aren't you?' asked Vedavati, her voice kind and gentle.

Raavan looked up and nodded. *Yes.*

'I am sure you know what the Lord's name means. Rudra is the "One who roars". The One who roars to protect good people. And what do you think Raavan means? What have you been told it means?'

Raavan didn't say anything.

'What did your father tell you? What does it mean?'

'He told me it means "One who scares people". Raavan is one who puts fear into people.'

'Your father was only half right. The root of the word "Raavan" is "Ru". So Raavan would be "the One who roars to frighten people".'

'Are you saying that the root of my name and that of Lord Rudra's is the same?'

'It is. But the question is, what will you roar for, Raavan? Will you roar to frighten people? Or will you, like Lord Rudra, roar to shield those who need protection?'

Vedavati's words sent a flood of positive energy and inspiration coursing through Raavan. More than ever, he felt connected to the Mahadev, the God of Gods.

'Roar, noble Raavan,' said Vedavati. 'But roar in favour of dharma. Roar to protect the innocent, the poor, the needy.

Be a true follower of the Mahadev. Be aggressive, but for the good of others. Be tough, but only to nurture the weak. Be fearsome, but only to fight for the virtuous. That is what Lord Rudra stood for. Follow the Lord's example.'

Raavan didn't say a word.

'Jai Shri Rudra,' said Vedavati.

'Jai Shri Rudra!'

Vedavati smiled and gently let go of Raavan's hand.

The first step on the path for all true followers of the Mahadev is a ritual sacrifice of the ego. Raavan knew what he had to do. He kneeled in front of the seated Vedavati. Taking a deep breath, he bent his hitherto unyielding back and brought his head down to the Kanyakumari's feet. For the first time in his life, he sought the blessings of another living person.

Vedavati put both her hands on Raavan's head and blessed him. 'May you always live in dharma. May dharma always live in you.'

Raavan drew himself up to his full six feet and three inches, and pulled out a sheet of papyrus from the pouch tied to his cummerbund. 'Please accept this, noble Vedavati. Don't say no.'

For the first time, Raavan's heart was in control as he spoke aloud that divine name. He didn't stutter.

'No to what?' she asked.

'My first act of genuine goodness.'

'Why do you run yourself down like that? You have done good before. You have done good for your brother. For this village. For…'

'Those were selfish acts. I protected those who were my own. Even the stuff I handed out here was meant to impress you. When I wrote and sealed this hundi, I had a selfish reason for it, but I don't anymore. I am giving it to you because I know you will do good with it.'

'Raavan, I cannot take money from you.'

'It's not for you, noble Vedavati. This is a hundi for fifty thousand gold coins, and it's for this entire region. I know you will use it well.'

'But…'

'Please don't refuse. Don't stop me in my first act of genuine kindness. I will consider it a blessing.'

Vedavati took the hundi from Raavan's hand, touched it to her forehead and said, 'It is my privilege, noble Raavan. I will use it for the good of the common people.'

'That means a lot to me. I intend to come back here as an arya and ask for what is due to me then.'

'And it will not be denied. Prithvi and I will be honoured.'

Raavan folded his hands together in a namaste. 'I will take your leave now, gentle Vedavati. My blessings for your unborn child. He or she is truly lucky to have a mother like you and a father like Prithvi.'

'Thank you, great Raavan.'

Every time Vedavati said his name out loud, a pleasurable current ran through Raavan's being. 'Till we meet again, Vedavati. Jai Shri Rudra.'

'Jai Shri Rudra.'

As Raavan walked away from her, he felt a lightness in his being that he had never felt before. Positive energy coursed through him. Even the pain in his navel had ceased to bother him. He walked with a spring in his step, the name of the Mahadev on his lips and the Kanyakumari in his heart.

A man with a purpose.

A man walking with dharma.

Neither he nor Vedavati noticed Sukarman, Shochikesh's son, hiding behind the bushes. He had been there the entire time and had heard everything. But only four words from the conversation reverberated in his mind. *Fifty thousand gold coins!*

—१६१—

'This is generous,' said Kumbhakarna, his eyebrows raised in surprise.

'This is only the beginning,' Raavan responded, a serene smile on his face.

Kumbhakarna had never seen his brother smile as much as he had over this past week. In the seven days since Raavan had last met Vedavati, he had transformed into a new person—full of hope and enthusiasm. He had been planning how to use his immense wealth to help India. He was contemplating the conquest of a small kingdom in the Sapt Sindhu, to be set up as a model dominion for the common people

He also wanted to build a large hospital attached to the Vaidyanath temple, which would treat poor people from across the Sapt Sindhu, free of cost. The amount he was thinking of donating was sizeable and had led to Kumbhakarna's comment on his generosity.

'Are you sure, Dada?' asked Kumbhakarna. 'This is a huge amount of money.'

'It's only a drop in my ocean of wealth, Kumbha. You know that. Now, take the hundi to the local moneylender and get the gold. We will donate it and then leave for Lanka. There is a lot to do and not enough time.'

Kumbhakarna smiled and nodded. 'Your word is my command, great devotee of the Ka... Ka... Kanyakumari.'

Raavan punched Kumbhakarna on his arm. 'Stop teasing me, will you!'

Kumbhakarna was still laughing as he left the room.

—ॐ—

'Wow,' said the moneylender. 'Two hundis from the great Raavan on the same day.'

Kumbhakarna took the receipt from the moneylender and put his seal on it. The moneylender would use this signed receipt and Raavan's original hundi to get the amount reimbursed through Raavan's closest trading office, in Magadh. And of course, earn a generous commission on the transaction.

'Eighty thousand gold coins,' continued the chatty moneylender, 'is a lot of money for our small Vaidyanath. And all in the same day!'

'And a good commission for you as well,' said Kumbhakarna, good-humouredly.

'Yes!' beamed the moneylender. 'I can finally buy the piece of land my wife and I have been eyeing for some time now.'

Kumbhakarna smiled as he handed the receipt over and took the outsized bags of coins. Two soldiers from his posse of armed men picked up the bags and moved towards their bullock cart. Kumbhakarna thanked the moneylender and turned to leave.

Then suddenly, he stopped. His sixth sense prickled.

'The woman who came earlier to redeem Raavan's other hundi,' said Kumbhakarna. 'Did she—'

'Not a woman,' interrupted the moneylender. 'It was a man. He was here just an hour ago.'

It was Prithviji then.

'A very young man he was too,' continued the moneylender.

Kumbhakarna felt a sense of foreboding enter his heart. 'Show me the receipt.'

The moneylender shook his head. 'I can't show you the receipt. It would…'

He stopped talking as Kumbhakarna dropped fifty gold coins on the counter and extended a hand commandingly. Without any further hesitation, the moneylender reached into the small cabinet below the counter and fished out the receipt. Kumbhakarna took one look at it, turned, and ran for his horse.

He was soon galloping through the streets to the main stables of Vaidyanath. That was where a man would go, to hire a horse or find a place on a departing cart, if he wished to travel beyond the city limits.

He knew he had to rush. There was little time.

For the name on the receipt had been clearly inked: Sukarman.

Chapter 16

Raavan slapped Sukarman viciously across the face. 'Did you actually think you would get away with this?'

Kumbhakarna had reached the horse stand just in time. Sukarman and his five associates were about to leave with their ill-gained wealth. Kumbhakarna and his guards had easily overpowered the six youths and confiscated the coins they were carrying. The thieves had then been presented before Raavan.

'You are lucky I am a changed man,' growled Raavan. 'Otherwise your tortured body would be lying here, half-dead by now.'

Sukarman strained against his captors, looking terrified.

Kumbhakarna gestured to the other five, who stood clustered around Sukarman. 'Who are these men, Sukarman? I don't recognise them. They are not from your village,' he said.

Sukarman was shivering now, too petrified to answer.

'Let's take him back to Todee, Dada,' said Kumbhakarna. 'We can let Vedavatiji decide what is to be done with him.'

Raavan continued to stare at Sukarman. Despite the show of anger, he was quite in control of his emotions. At the mention of Vedavati, he felt even calmer. 'We could, but I suspect she will forgive him. And this bastard does not deserve forgiveness.'

Sukarman suddenly lost control of his bladder and wet himself. Raavan's first reaction was to laugh, but then he stopped.

A thought too painful to consider mauled its way into his consciousness. For a few seconds, he was paralysed, afraid even to acknowledge it.

Oh Lord Rudra… No…

Stricken with horror, Raavan turned to look at his younger brother. His heart sank when he saw that Kumbhakarna's expression mirrored his own. He turned his gaze to Sukarman, as if in a trance. The colour had vanished from the man's face. He stood there, trembling, a wretched figure. Raavan felt his heart turn to ice. This wasn't just a robbery… This was…

Lord Rudra, have mercy!

It was Kumbhakarna who gathered his wits first. He moved swiftly, shouting as he ran, 'Guards! Everyone! We are riding out to Todee! Now!'

—१७३—

Less than an hour later, Raavan's entourage of over one hundred soldiers thundered into Todee. Only Samichi had been left behind on Kumbhakarna's orders. Sukarman had been tied to the back of a horse, whose reins were in the hand of one of Raavan's mounted warriors. His five companions were being hauled back to Todee in a similar manner.

As the horses galloped into the village, it became immediately obvious that something was amiss.

There was a deathly silence all around.

Raavan whipped his horse and continued to race ahead, leading the way to Vedavati's house at the centre of the village. There was a massive crowd in the open square right outside it. Almost the entire village seemed to have congregated there.

Raavan vaulted off his horse and ran towards the house, pushing people aside. His heart was pounding. His mouth felt dry with foreboding.

Kumbhakarna was close behind him.

As Raavan shoved a scrawny villager out of his way, he nearly tripped over something lying on the ground.

Without so much as a glance, he straightened up and stumbled on, towards the modest hut that belonged to Vedavati and Prithvi.

It was Kumbhakarna who realised what it was that Raavan had tripped over.

Prithvi's bloodied and mutilated body.

Oh Lord Rudra…

There had clearly been a struggle. Prithvi had been stabbed multiple times, and had probably bled to death. It was clear that he had died slowly. A trail of blood on the ground suggested that he had tried to drag himself towards his house, till his body gave way.

Kumbhakarna looked up. Towards Prithvi's house. Where the pregnant Vedavati would have been.

And then he heard a cry.

It was the sound of raw, unfathomable anguish. The broken voice of a soul struck down with unimaginable grief.

He ran towards Vedavati's hut, roughly pushing aside everyone in his path. He emerged through the crowd to see Raavan on his knees outside the open door. Sobbing uncontrollably.

Steeling his heart, Kumbhakarna looked through the open door into the one-room hut. The sight made his blood curdle. Vedavati lay on the floor, her right arm twisted at a strange angle. Her left hand was on her belly, as if she was protecting her unborn child. Or had died trying to protect it. For most of the stab wounds were on her belly. She had been knifed at least fifteen to twenty times. The blood had flowed and congealed around her, a macabre red shroud cradling her dead body. Her face, always so still and serene, had not been spared either. The attacker had jabbed the knife straight into her left eye. By the look of it, it was a deep wound. Perhaps the wound that had finally killed her. The blow that had snuffed out the light of the Living Goddess.

Kumbhakarna bent over, unable to believe what he was seeing. Blinded by tears, he stumbled towards his brother and reached out to touch his shoulder.

Raavan shrank back at the touch, as though seared by fire. He looked at his younger brother. Tears streaming down his face.

Kumbhakarna collapsed on his knees. 'Dada…'

Raavan looked up at the skies. To the cloud palaces where the Gods were supposed to live. 'YOU SONS OF BITCHES!! WHY?! WHY HER?! WHY?!!'

Kumbhakarna embraced Raavan, not knowing what else to do, or say.

They say tears can wash away grief. They lie.

There are some kinds of grief that even a million tears cannot wash away. Which haunt you for life. For all time.

They say time heals all wounds. They lie.

Sometimes, the grief one is cursed with is so immense that even time surrenders to it.

The brothers held each other. Crying inconsolably.

—१७१—

Raavan's men had slowly gathered around Raavan and Kumbhakarna. None of them truly understood what was going on. But they could see that their trader-prince was devastated.

The villagers, too stunned to do anything, stood around weeping.

Shochikesh slowly staggered up to Raavan. His eyes were swollen with tears and his body stooped with grief. 'I am so sorry, Jai... I...'

He still had no idea who Raavan was.

'Where the hell were all of you when this happened?' Raavan snarled. The rage of the entire universe seemed to sweep through him.

'Jai... There's nothing we could have done... We rushed here when we heard noises... but they were armed...'

Raavan felt the fury rise again within him. He looked around. There were at least two hundred villagers assembled near the hut. He looked at Sukarman and his five accomplices, each one securely tied to the trunk of a tree beside the hut.

Two hundred against six.

Raavan's voice dropped to a menacing whisper as he addressed Shochikesh. 'She was your Goddess. She held up this entire pathetic village. Cared for it like a mother. And all of you together could not protect her from six thugs?'

'I am so sorry… we… Many got scared and ran away…'

Raavan rose to his full height, towering over Shochikesh. 'Ran away? You sons of bitches ran away?'

Shochikesh looked at the Lankan trader's bloodshot eyes, his own panic rising. He tried to reason with Raavan. 'But… But what could we…'

The words remained frozen on Shochikesh's lips. His eyes widened as he looked down to see a knife buried deep in his body. He stood in shock for a moment, before he let out an agonised scream. Raavan had drawn his long knife in one smooth, rapid arc and thrust it into the other man's abdomen. The scream infuriated Raavan even more. He rammed the knife in further, twisting it viciously. The blade ripped through to the other side, the point bursting out of Shochikesh's back. Raavan yanked his weapon out and pushed Shochikesh back. The flame-haired man fell to the ground, bleeding copiously. It would be a slow, painful death.

The villagers stood rooted to their spots, paralysed with fear.

Raavan looked down at Shochikesh's body for a moment. Then the trader from Lanka hawked and spat on the Todee landlord.

Continuing to look down, Raavan ordered in a low growl, 'Kill them all.' Then he pointed to where Sukarman and his gang were tied up. 'Except them.'

The villagers scattered and ran screaming in all directions as Raavan's soldiers rushed to obey their lord's command. The residents of Todee did not stand a chance. Every one of them was killed.

—१८१—

Corpses littered the ground. Men. Women. Children. Cut down where they stood. It was all over in just a few minutes.

Raavan stood next to one of Sukarman's associates, while Kumbhakarna stood on his other side. The Lankan soldiers, holding their bloodied swords, were at the back. Sukarman's hands had been nailed to a door that faced the trees where his associates had been tied up. He could see exactly what was being done to them.

Raavan held a burning log to the man's arm, letting the fire incinerate the skin and roast the flesh. The sickening smell of burning flesh pervaded the atmosphere. The blood-curdling screams of the man being slowly burnt alive rent the air.

But Raavan wasn't even looking at the victim of his torture. His eyes were focused on Sukarman's face. 'Did you do this only for money? Or were you ordered by someone to kill her?'

The petrified Sukarman began to blabber. 'I... so sorry... forgive me... please... forgive me... take all the money...'

Pure, unadulterated rage flashed in Raavan's eyes. He raised the flaming log and held it closer to his agonised victim's face. Then he turned his attention back to Sukarman. 'You think this is about money?'

Kumbhakarna spoke up. 'Where is the Kanyakumari's baby?'

When Vedavati's body was examined, her womb had been found to be empty. Which meant that she had given birth to her child before she was killed.

However, there was no trace of the baby.

'Sukarman, I asked you a question. Where is the baby?' growled Kumbhakarna.

Sukarman remained silent, looking down at the ground. Fear had made him lose control of his bladder again.

'Sukarman.' Kumbhakarna's fists were clenched tight. 'You'd better talk.'

Suddenly, one of Sukarman's associates spoke up. 'He ordered me to do it. Sukarman did. I didn't want to.'

'What did you do?' snarled Kumbhakarna, glaring at the man.

'He ordered me to. It's his fault…'

'WHAT DID YOU DO?'

The man fell silent.

Kumbhakarna strode up and looked him fiercely in the eye.

'What did you do? Tell me. And you will have mercy.'

The man looked at Sukarman and then back at Kumbhakarna. 'He ordered me to… throw the baby into the wild. And let the animals… eat… I mean…' His words stumbled to a stop. Even his pathetic barbarian soul was ashamed of the terrible crime he had committed.

Indians believed that to kill a baby was a horrific sin, and it would pollute one's soul for many births. Sukarman's gang had thought they would get around this commandment by letting wild animals do the deed for them.

Kumbhakarna looked at Raavan, too shocked for words. He had not expected such an answer. Even for savages like these, this seemed abominably cruel.

A baby left in the wild for wild animals to feast on… Lord Rudra have mercy.

'Mercy,' pleaded the man. 'I told you the truth… Mercy…'

Kumbhakarna glanced at Raavan again. Raavan nodded. Kumbhakarna drew his sword and beheaded the man in one clean strike.

The decapitated head of the criminal flew in the air and hit the head of his associate tied up next to him. He screamed in panic, as a bloody fountain erupted through the gaping neck, on to him.

A loud flapping of wings made Raavan and Kumbhakarna look up. A kettle of vultures was descending on the village. They watched as one of the birds tentatively pecked at one of the dead bodies that lay scattered about on the ground. On discovering meat that was still warm, the bird squawked in delight and began feasting on it.

Raavan turned his attention back to the man burning beside him. Uncontrollable tears of rage flowed from his eyes as he looked at the now insensate, almost unrecognisable creature slumped against his bonds. He felt no pity, no remorse. Only fury.

—१७१—

Raavan and Kumbhakarna sat on the ground, their backs against the wall. The five dead men were still tied to the trees. Sukarman, barely alive, had been yanked away from the door to which he had been nailed, and tied to a tree. Some of his bloodied flesh still clung to the nails. He had fallen unconscious under the slow burning and torture. But Raavan was careful to ensure that Sukarman didn't die. He had to suffer as much pain as was humanly possible. Pain, the very memory of which would terrify his soul for several lifetimes.

Meanwhile, Raavan's soldiers had carried the lifeless bodies of Vedavati and Prithvi to the village landlord's house. They had to be washed and clothed before the cremation ceremonies.

By now, the vultures had been joined by other creatures of the wild. Crows. Wild dogs. Hyenas. There was enough meat for everyone. The animals ate quietly. They didn't fight with each other. They didn't make too much noise. They knew there was enough food to last them for several days.

It was an eerily macabre sight. Wild animals everywhere, feasting silently on dead human bodies. An unconscious man tied to a tree. Soldiers with bloodied swords standing to attention. And two brothers, braving their broken souls, sitting outside the house of the woman they admired. The person they loved. The Goddess they worshipped.

Raavan's eyes were bloodshot and swollen, his face drained of all expression. Kumbhakarna took his brother's bloodied hands in his own. The blood of the criminals who had killed Vedavati had soaked their limbs but it had done nothing to cleanse their grief. What words could alleviate anguish such as this?

At last, Raavan spoke. 'I hate this…' He stopped as tears began flowing down his cheeks again.

Kumbhakarna looked at his brother. Silent.

Raavan's voice emerged, raw with grief and anger.

'I hate this cursed land.'

Chapter 17

Each time Sukarman slipped into unconsciousness, a bucket of water drenched his face. He had to be kept conscious, to experience every moment of the torture. Though his body hung limp, the taut ropes kept him upright against the tree. He had been stripped bare except for his loincloth. Blood oozed from his numerous lesions and almost every inch of him was either scorched or slashed. Except his face.

When Sukarman finally managed to open his eyes, he saw the Lankan pirate-trader standing in front of him.

Raavan.

Among the richest men in the world. Certainly, the angriest man alive. A man with an intense craving for vengeance. 'Why didn't you just take the money?' Raavan's voice was a mixture of rage and desperate sadness. 'Why? Why did you have to kill her?'

Hope flickered in some corner of Sukarman's mind. He thought he might still have a chance to explain himself. And the thought fired some energy into him. 'I did try... I tried so hard... But she wouldn't... listen.'

Raavan looked at Kumbhakarna and then back at Sukarman.

'I told her that she'd never cared about money before... so why now? But she wouldn't agree... she was being... stubborn... Even that husband of hers suddenly grew a spine and snubbed me. She asked me to take everything else they owned... but she wouldn't give me... your hundi... But everything else they owned was worth nothing... and I needed to settle my gambling debts... My debtors would have killed me... I told her that... but she was being so... unreasonable,' he wheezed.

Raavan stared at Sukarman in disbelief.

Sukarman's voice was barely audible as he continued, 'I told her... that you would give her more... that you... are fabulously rich... wouldn't care... but she refused to listen... She said she would not part with the hundi... said the hundi was holy... it had been given by someone who had discovered dharma... that she would not surrender Raavan's chance to discover the God within him...'

A low moan escaped Kumbhakarna, as he clutched his hair in despair. But Raavan just kept staring at Sukarman, unable to respond.

Sukarman was not done. Misreading Raavan's silence, he mumbled, 'I was trying to reason with her, but one of the others lost his patience... I can't blame him... She was being... stubborn.'

Raavan had had enough. He lunged at Sukarman and unleashed a vicious upper cut that caught him on the chin. Sukarman's head snapped back and hit the trunk of the tree. Kumbhakarna stepped up and grabbed him by the hair, holding his head steady as he punched him squarely in the jaw, breaking it with an unmistakable crack. Then he pushed the broken jaw down, forcing Sukarman's mouth open.

Raavan picked up a small piece of half-burnt coal and pushed it into the slack mouth.

Sukarman's body convulsed as the red-hot coal singed the skin of his mouth before being pushed down his throat. Kumbhakarna held his mouth open, while some of the Lankan soldiers rushed forward with more pieces of burning coal. Raavan took them one by one and stuffed them down Sukarman's throat. He was using his bare hands, unheeding of the pain. As more and more pieces of burning coal found their way down Sukarman's oesophagus, his body flailed in agony.

He was being burnt alive, from the inside out.

But Raavan and Kumbhakarna would not stop. They kept forcing more coal pieces into Sukarman's digestive tract.

After some time, he stopped moving.

A pungent smell of burnt flesh permeated the air. Smoke was coming out of Sukarman's mouth. His stomach seemed aglow. As though his insides had caught fire. The wretched man was being cooked alive.

Still, the brothers did not stop.

Rage had taken over their souls completely.

They had lost everything.

Their Goddess. Their world. Their sanity.

They had lost it all.

—ૐ—

Preparations for the ceremony were complete. Two large pyres had been prepared. The bodies of Vedavati and Prithvi had been cleaned, bathed and dressed in fresh white clothes. Sacred Vedic chants had been whispered into their ears. It was believed that the power of the mantras would give the souls of the departed the strength to continue on their journey.

Once all this had been done, holy water was poured into their mouths and tulsi leaves placed on their lips. Some more tulsi leaves were bunched together and placed in their nostrils and ears. Vedavati's hands were arranged on her chest, with her thumbs tied together. The big toes of her feet had also been tied together. The same was done for Prithvi. It was believed that this helped conjoin the right and left energy channels, thus ensuring the movement of energy in a circle within the body. Earthen lamps were lit at the precise spots where Vedavati and Prithvi had been found dead, with the flame facing south, in honour of Lord Yama, the God of Death and Dharma.

Through all of this, Raavan and Kumbhakarna remained outwardly calm. There was no space here for undignified crying and indecorous mourning. Dignity. Respect. Honour. That was what the Goddess deserved. The great Kanyakumari would leave this earth in the same manner in which she had lived. With dignity, respect and honour.

The two brothers stood beside Vedavati's unlit pyre. She would be cremated first, and then Prithvi.

Holy ghee was brought in an earthen pot. Kumbhakarna held the vessel as Raavan scooped out dollops of ghee and poured it over Vedavati's body. As he did so, both the brothers chanted from the *Garuda Purana*. When Raavan wiped his hands clean, some of his men came up and placed more wooden logs on Vedavati's body. Soon, only her face was visible.

As Raavan stepped back, a wooden log was brought to him, lit with holy fire.

Kumbhakarna gathered the courage to look at Vedavati's face one final time. The punctures had been covered. A patch had been put over the hole where her left eye had been.

Her face—even now, after all that she had suffered—was calm and gentle. Like that of a Goddess. Kumbhakarna struggled to hold back his tears. He would not be undignified. Not in front of her. Not in front of his Goddess.

He had heard it said enough times, that the tears of loved ones made it difficult for the departed soul to leave the world. The living had to control and suppress their grief, for the good of the dead.

He looked at Vedavati's still body waiting to be engulfed in flames, and unexpectedly, all of a sudden, the rage left him.

He looked around in a daze, as though waking up from a long sleep. In the village beyond, he could see that wild animals were still feasting on the dead bodies of the villagers. Men and women who could be called cowards, but not criminals. He looked back at Vedavati's face and was ashamed. Of himself, and of what he had done.

He knew that she would be disappointed in him and his brother. He turned to look at him now.

Raavan was holding the log with the holy flame and walking up to the pyre.

Kumbhakarna stepped back.

Raavan pushed the log into the pyre, setting it ablaze. Letting *Lord Agni*, the all-purifying *God of Fire*, consume the body of the Goddess.

Someone handed Raavan an earthen pot filled with holy water. He punctured it and, following the sacred tradition, started walking anti-clockwise around the blazing pyre. Water trickled out of the small hole in the pot as he walked. He performed the circumambulation three times. In doing so, he was, in effect, stating to the world that he would assume the responsibility for repaying Vedavati's debts. Not monetary debts, for money was meaningless to the soul—he was promising to repay her unfinished karmic debt and ensuring that she would be free of all attachments and responsibilities in this world. Her soul could then, hopefully, travel towards *moksha*, and be *liberated from the cycle of births*.

Kumbhakarna looked at his brother as he circled the pyre, and then at the village they had destroyed.

There was much to do. Much to atone for.

He hoped they wouldn't let her down.

—— १८१ ——

It was late in the morning the next day, when Raavan and Kumbhakarna woke up. They had spent the night on the banks of a lake not far from the village. Despite the exhaustion of the day, they had managed barely a few hours of sleep.

Both the pyres were still smouldering, though the flames had died out. The physical bodies of the noble Kanyakumari and her gentle husband had been reduced, mostly, to ash. Twenty of Raavan's soldiers had been stationed at the cremation ground through the night, to keep away any wild animals that might choose to venture there. Their fears were unfounded, though. There was enough food to keep the animals in the village.

After their ritual bath, Raavan and Kumbhakarna went back to the cremation site. A few ceremonies still remained to be done. They began with Vedavati's pyre.

A bucket of holy water had been arranged. Tulsi leaves floated on its surface. Raavan took a coconut and smashed it on the ground. It broke vertically, from one narrow end to the other. This was rare and considered auspicious; the soul would certainly find moksha. The coconut water was added to the water in the bucket. The solution was stirred by hand as Sanskrit hymns were chanted. When this was done, Raavan ritually drizzled the holy water onto the smouldering pyre, extinguishing the last of the flames.

Four Lankan soldiers came up and removed the ashes from the platform. Kumbhakarna and Raavan bent over the pile and painstakingly sifted through it for the *asti*, the small pieces of bone that hadn't been reduced to ash in the pyre. Almost everything else that formed part of the body—flesh, organs, muscles—had been consumed. The ashes were to be returned to Mother Earth in an easily usable form. What remained of the bones would be immersed in the holy waters of the Ganga.

Raavan knew that *asti* was the root for the Sanskrit word *astitva,* which meant *existence.* These bones, which had tenaciously refused to be consumed by the holy fire, symbolised the remnants of existence. They had to go back to the source of it all, to the Mother Goddess, in the form of the flowing, nurturing river. They would merge with the water, in the bosom of the Mother Goddess, so that even the residual bits of existence could find peace.

Raavan and Kumbhakarna carefully washed each of the small bones, then placed them in an earthen pot. It was almost impossible to distinguish which part of the body they had been a part of. Then, to his utter surprise, Raavan came upon the bones of two fingers which seemed almost intact. The flesh, the muscles, the tendons, had all been burnt away. What survived were three bone phalanges from each of the two fingers. Six phalanges in all. Clearly distinguishable.

When most of the skull had not survived, what were the chances of these phalanges surviving?

As he held the fragile bones in his open palm, it struck Raavan—these were probably the vestiges of the hand with which Vedavati had held his hand. For the first time. Just a few days ago. She had never touched him again.

He would never see her again. But he could still hold her hand.

Raavan couldn't control himself anymore.

He wept as he touched the bones to his forehead, like they were hallowed relics of the most divine Goddess. And then he kissed them lightly.

She had left these for him.

He knew, then, that he would survive. That he would find a way to live the rest of his life. For he knew that he could hold her hand any time he wished to.

She had left these for him as a crutch. So that he could walk through the agony that he knew the rest of his life would be. With her hand as support.

With her hand to hold.

—ॐ—

Raavan turned the urn over and let Vedavati's remains slip into the holy river. Further down, Kumbhakarna did the same for Prithvi.

It had been three days since the cremation. The brothers had ridden out towards the river with all their soldiers, picking up young Samichi on the way. Despite Kumbhakarna's repeated pleas, Raavan had refused to conduct funeral ceremonies for the villagers of Todee and had left their dead bodies where they were. As rotting food for wild animals. He had no qualms about condemning their souls to suffering for all eternity.

Raavan watched closely as the earthly remains of Vedavati disappeared into the holy river. The asti were a part of the Mother now.

But he hadn't surrendered all of it. He had kept the finger phalanges, the remnants of Vedavati's hand. They hung around his neck now, bunched together to form an unlikely pendant.

He started up the steps of the river ghats, with the urn still in his hand.

'Dada,' said Kumbhakarna, stepping out of the water. 'You have to drop the urn into the river too.'

Raavan looked down at the urn—empty and bereft. As though it, too, was in mourning.

'Dada…'

Raavan did not respond. He looked around him. At the holy Ganga, the verdant banks, the dense forest cover… at the land of India. The land blessed by the Gods.

He closed his eyes. A feeling of disgust overcame him.

A country that cannot honour its heroes doesn't deserve to survive.

'Dada… the urn…' Kumbhakarna reminded him.

To Kumbhakarna's surprise, Raavan turned and started walking back towards the shore.

'Dada?'

Raavan reached the river bank, bent down, and picked up some soil—the earth of the Sapt Sindhu—and put it in the urn. Then he started walking back into the river, at a furious pace, like a man possessed.

'Dada, what are you doing?'

Raavan bent and dipped the urn in the water, so that the soil was washed away. Like he was immersing the asti of the land itself.

'Dada?' Kumbhakarna's voice conveyed his mounting anxiety.

Raavan filled the urn with water and poured it over his head. Like the ritual bath at the end of a funeral ceremony.

'No, Dada!' Kumbhakarna rushed forward, frantic to stop Raavan. But he was too late.

Raavan broke the urn on his arms and let the pieces fall into the river. Then he turned towards Kumbhakarna, eyes blazing and fists clenched tight. Rage poured out of every cell of his body. He gritted his teeth and said, 'This country is dead to me.'

'Dada, listen to me…'

'Control the monster, did she say?'

'Dada, what are you saying? Listen to me…'

'I will unleash the monster! I will destroy this land!'

Chapter 18

'Magnificent piece, Dada,' said Kumbhakarna.

Two long years had passed since Vedavati's death.

Twenty-four-year-old Raavan had been playing a raga dedicated to the *Devi*, the *Goddess*. Most of the ragas created in honour of the Goddess celebrated her motherly embodiment. There were others dedicated to her manifestation as a lover, a daughter, an artist and so on, but very few were dedicated to the warrior Goddess. The raga Raavan had composed captured the essence of this form—fierce, angry, and wild. Like nature in all its tempestuous and uncontrollable glory.

He called the Raga *Vaashi Santaapani*. The *roar of the furious Goddess*.

'I have yet to hear another piece that's as powerful,' said Kumbhakarna. 'In fact, I think it's the most beautiful raga I have heard in my life.'

Raavan nodded absentmindedly. He didn't seem to care too much for the compliment.

'Even the word Vaashi is so appropriate, Dada. The sound of a blazing flame—isn't that its original meaning? I doubt you can get more evocative than that.'

'Hmm.'

Kumbhakarna touched his brother on the shoulder almost tentatively. 'You know, they say grief and tragedy often bring out the best in an artist.'

Raavan looked at his brother in irritation. 'And who are these "they"? Whoever they may be, they are morons! Nobody goes looking for tragedy. Nobody wants to experience grief just to be able to create art.'

Kumbhakarna realised his brother was not in the mood for this conversation. He tried to change the subject. 'I am happy that work is consuming more and more of your time, Dada. Drowning oneself in work is the best way to push negative thoughts away.'

Raavan truly had been busy. Over the previous year and a half, he had leveraged his vast wealth and control over the only credible armed force in Lanka, to inveigle himself closer to the Lankan throne. Kubaer, the ruler of Lanka, had come to depend on him to provide security for his trading ships. Many other traders had taken to paying for the services of Raavan's security forces. And since, unknown to most, Raavan controlled both the pirates and the militia, whenever someone hired his men for protection, the pirate attacks on their ships stopped. Raavan's wealth and resources had grown exponentially, as had his clout and reputation. He was now on the verge of being formally appointed as the head of the Trading Security Force of Lanka. His plan was simple: to get his private militia appointed as the official Lankan Security Force. Not only would the cost of maintaining and arming his soldiers fall to the Lankan treasury, the soldiers would remain loyal to Raavan, even after their transfer. Over time, he would expand the force to make it as large and well-equipped as a regular army. An army trained to take on the Sapt Sindhu empire.

'Yes,' said Raavan. 'Work is a good distraction.'

Kumbhakarna smiled, glad to get a few words out of his brother. But he wasn't prepared for what came next.

'This silly female notion maa has, that talking about problems can help one come to terms with grief, is utter nonsense. The masculine way is better. Drown yourself in work. Suppress the grief. Don't think about it and don't let it come out. Let it remain trapped in some deep, dark dungeon of your heart, even if it festers there. And when you are old and tired, have a nice fatal heart-attack, and it's all over,' Raavan finished.

Kumbhakarna thought it wise to not say anything. It was obvious. Let alone suppress his grief, Raavan remained crushed by it. He had thrown himself into work with the single-minded ambition of bringing the Sapt Sindhu down, but nothing seemed to give him pleasure anymore. Kumbhakarna had thought he would tactfully broach the suggestion his mother had made, of an early marriage. But perhaps this was not the right time to speak of it.

—ॐ—

Kubaer looked extremely nervous. 'Raavan, I am not sure it's advisable to take on the most powerful empire in the world.'

Four years had passed since Vedavati's death.

Kubaer and Raavan were in the Lankan ruler's private office. Raavan and Kumbhakarna had moved to Sigiriya some time back, leaving their mother in Gokarna. As soon as he had been appointed head of Lanka's Trading Security Force, Raavan had started making preparations to move closer to the

Lankan throne. He had bought a huge mansion not far from Kubaer's palace.

Since moving to the Lankan capital, Raavan had also started working on his plan to trigger a war against the Sapt Sindhu. He needed a plausible reason to provoke the empire into attacking the small island kingdom, and he knew what it could be. As a first step, he proposed reducing the share of the profits that the Sapt Sindhuans appropriated from cross-border trade. After months of persuasion, he had finally managed to engage Kubaer in a discussion on the matter. Kubaer, a prudent sixty-nine-year-old compared to Raavan's impetuous twenty-six, was not a warrior; he was a businessman who valued pragmatism. He privileged profit over pride and thought caution was a necessary quality. His skill lay in charming and negotiating a beneficial deal, not inviting trouble.

'I've said it before and I'll say it again: Why should we give up nine-tenths of our profits to the Sapt Sindhu?' asked Raavan. 'Why should we do all the hard work and let them take most of our money?'

'We are not actually giving them ninety per cent, Raavan,' said Kubaer with a sly smile. 'Our accounts are creative. We overstate our costs. In actual fact, they don't get more than seventy per cent.'

Raavan had already anticipated Kubaer's comeback, but he decided to play along. He would not make the mistake of underestimating the chief-trader of Lanka, like the Sapt Sindhuans did, solely because of his physical appearance. Kubaer's round, cherubic face and smooth complexion belied his advanced age. But he was so obese that he waddled ponderously, like a duck. He usually wore brightly coloured clothes; today, it was a shocking blue dhoti and a yellow angvastram, and his body was bedecked with ornate jewellery. His effeminate mannerisms and life of excess had made him an object of ridicule for the warrior class. But Raavan knew the effete exterior hid a sharp, ruthless mind, devoted to one cause alone: profit.

'But even seventy per cent is too high!' he countered.

'Thirty per cent is good enough for me. I save a considerable part of it, while the Sapt Sindhu squanders away most of its share. So my wealth is greater than theirs. And do you know why they don't save anything?' Kubaer asked.

'Forget about their savings, Great One. Why should we care about how much money Ayodhya or its subordinate kingdoms have? We should care about our own wealth. If we reduce their commissions, we will have more profit for ourselves.'

'You didn't answer my question. I'll tell you why we have higher savings than they do, even though we earn less. It's because the Sapt Sindhu wastes a lot of money on unnecessary wars. We don't. War is bad for business, it's bad for profits and wealth. If we reduce the commissions, they will certainly attack us. We will then be forced to mobilise our army and spend money, no, *waste* money, on a silly war. And that's—'

Raavan interrupted Kubaer. 'What if I agree to fund our war effort?'

Kubaer frowned with suspicion. 'The entire war?'

'Everything. You won't have to spend a single coin. I'll pay for it all.'

Kubaer had the natural mistrust of an astute trader for a deal that sounded too good to be true. Raavan, he knew, was too shrewd to do something only for glory. 'And why, pray, would you help me at all?' he asked.

'Because you will then share half the increased commissions with me.'

Kubaer smiled. Any kind of selfish interest, he understood and respected. Experience had taught him that the best business deals were struck when both parties were honest about their own interests. 'So, let me make sure I understand this. You can't declare war without my approval. And you think this war will be profitable.'

'Yes to both.'

'But what guarantee is there of victory?'

'None. But is there any guarantee that our ships will not sink in the sea when we send them out to trade? We estimate the probabilities and take the best bet. A calculated bet. We are traders. That's what we do.'

'All that is very well, but what if we lose?'

'Then you should do the pragmatic thing.'

'If we lose the battle,' said Kubaer, choosing his words carefully, 'the pragmatic thing would be to tell the Sapt Sindhuans that this was all your idea.'

'You are right. That would indeed be the pragmatic thing to do. If we fail, let me take the blame. It's my idea, after all. Keep yourself, and the other traders of Lanka, safe. But if we win, I get half the increased commissions.'

Kubaer smiled. 'All right, Raavan. You will have your war. Just make sure I don't make a loss. Nothing spoils my day like an unanticipated loss.'

'Honourable One, have I ever let you down?' Raavan asked with a smile.

Kumbhakarna was worried. 'Dada, we may be over-reaching with this.... Are we biting off more than we can chew?'

The brothers were at home in Sigiriya, the capital of Lanka.

'We are not, Kumbha,' said Raavan. 'We'll bite it all. We'll chew it all. We'll digest it all.'

'Dada, the Sapt Sindhu rulers do nothing except fight wars. We are traders. Our soldiers are essentially pirates. They fight for money, and money alone. If there is no profit in sight, they will abandon the battle. But the Sapt Sindhu soldiers actually celebrate "martyrdom" in battle. They die for bizarre causes like honour and glory. How are we supposed to defeat such morons?'

'Through good tactics.'

'I think you...'

'No, I am not being overconfident.'

'But even if we can defeat them, how are we going to turn a profit from it? The cost of the campaign will be too high.'

'Don't worry. Once we win, we will start taking ninety per cent of the profits, if not more.'

Kumbhakarna nearly choked on the wine he was drinking. 'Ninety per cent! For us?'

Raavan frowned. 'Yes, of course.'

'Dada, I don't think we can enforce a treaty like that. It will be too much for the Sapt Sindhu kings to swallow. They will have no choice but to keep on fighting. The ensuing rebellions will destroy them, but they will wear us out too. And we simply don't have enough soldiers to control all the Sapt Sindhu kingdoms and their people in peacetime.'

'We'll break their spirit in one major battle. Destroy their entire army. I am not interested in imposing our rules on their citizens, so where is the need to control them? We'll only impose our trade conditions on them. And slowly suck them dry.'

'But, Dada,' said Kumbhakarna, 'a commission this big will destroy the Sapt Sindhu economy over time. We would end up killing the golden goose that feeds us.'

Raavan's expression gave little away as his eyes met Kumbhakarna's.

'Precisely,' he said.

—ૐ—

Burly soldiers rowed the large boat in quick strokes towards the shore. Raavan sat in front, his right hand on the gunwale. Kumbhakarna sat behind him, observing his flexed arms, the massive triceps that were visibly tense.

Dada is upset.

Raavan looked straight ahead, towards the *Sapt Sindhu*— the *Land of the Seven Rivers*.

Kumbhakarna looked to his left, at Kubaer's boat being rowed rhythmically towards the shore by ten sailors.

It had only been a year since Raavan had convinced Kubaer to wage war against the Sapt Sindhu. Events had proceeded rapidly after that.

Within a matter of months, Raavan had mobilised and trained his army. He had also brought in mercenaries from around the world, promising them a rich share of the spoils.

Once the Lankan army was ready, Kubaer had sent an official communication to the emperor of the Sapt Sindhu, Dashrath. When his message reached Ayodhya, the capital city from where Dashrath ruled all the northern parts of the Indian subcontinent, it immediately set teeth on edge.

The old-elite royal families of the Sapt Sindhu, with their disdain for the trader-class Vaishyas, considered the effete Kubaer an upstart. They just about tolerated his existence. To receive a 'royal communication' from the trader-ruler of Lanka was seen as an affront. Traders were not supposed to send royal communications to emperors of ancient imperial dynasties. They were supposed to send humble, grovelling petitions. And as if that wasn't outrageous enough, the demand to reduce the empire's commissions on profits was seen as an intolerable insult to Kshatriya pride. Such a dishonour could not be stomached.

Dashrath had immediately rallied all of his subordinate kings across the land and mobilised an army. The plan was for his troops to march to Karachapa, one of Kubaer's biggest trading hubs, on the west coast of the Sapt Sindhu. Dashrath planned to destroy the Karachapa fort and trading warehouses. He had assumed that this would be enough to bring Kubaer to his senses. If not, some of the other ports held by Kubaer would also be destroyed, and ultimately, Lanka itself would come under siege.

Raavan had anticipated that the Sapt Sindhuans would take exception to Kubaer's message and march out to war immediately. His own troops were in a state of readiness. His specially designed ships, buffed with the enigmatic cave material, were prepared for battle. As soon as he received intelligence of the Sapt Sindhu army mobilising, and the direction of their march, the ships set sail, moving quickly up the western coast of peninsular India, to arrive at Karachapa.

There were too many ships in Raavan's navy for even the massive Karachapa port to accommodate. Besides, Raavan knew the Sapt Sindhuans had spies within Karachapa and the last thing he wanted was to generate curiosity about the radically different designs of his ships. They were a part of his battle plan, his secret weapon. So most of the ships were anchored offshore.

Later in the day, Raavan and Kumbhakarna boarded a rowboat and headed up to the beach of Karachapa. The rowboat hit the sand with a lurch and four soldiers jumped off, into the shallow waters, and pulled the boat onto the beach. Raavan remained immobile. Looking straight ahead.

Kumbhakarna could feel his breath quickening. They were returning to the Sapt Sindhu after five years. The last time they were here, they had immersed Vedavati's ashes in the holy Ganga.

It is said, and rightly, that whatever the memories associated with the past, every person's heart beats faster when they return to the land of their roots. The pain of separation, and the joy of homecoming, are universal. And nothing can compare to the sheer relief of returning to the lap of your mother, the most comfortable place in the world.

Kumbhakarna jumped off as soon as the boat was out of the water. He bent down and picked up some wet sand, the soil of his motherland, and with great veneration, brought it to his forehead. He touched it to both his eyes and kissed it. As he placed the sand back on the ground with utmost respect, he whispered, 'Jai Maa.'

Glory to the Mother.

He saw Raavan, who had gone slightly ahead of him, bend down to pick up some sand too. Kumbhakarna smiled.

Perhaps returning to the motherland has finally thawed his heart.

Kumbhakarna watched as Raavan brought his hand closer to his face and stared at the sand in it for what seemed like an eternity. He hesitated to go closer. Perhaps he should let his brother have this moment to himself.

He felt a vast sense of relief that the past was finally behind them. His elder brother had been through so much, raged against the world for so long, but it seemed he was finally ready to welcome some peace within. This war would be fought, of course. It had to be done. For profit. But, at least, returning to the motherland had alleviated some of Raavan's deep-seated sorrow. Or so Kumbhakarna thought.

Raavan opened the palm that cradled the sand, bringing it closer to his mouth. Then, slowly, deliberately, he hawked and spat into it. His entire body seemed to convulse in rage as he flung the sand to the ground and crushed it under his foot.

'Fuck this land.'

Chapter 19

'Shouldn't we be going over to their camp?' asked Kubaer nervously.

Dashrath, the overlord of the Sapt Sindhu, had marched right across his sprawling empire, from Ayodhya, its capital, to Karachapa. Within just a few hours of his arrival, he had sent a terse message to Kubaer, summoning him for a discussion on the terms of ceasefire.

In the early years of his reign, Dashrath had built on the powerful legacy he had inherited from his father, Aja. Rulers in various parts of India had either been deposed or made to pay tribute and accept his suzerainty, thus making Dashrath the Chakravarti Samrat, or the Universal Emperor.

'We are not going to his camp, noble Chief-Trader,' replied Raavan, trying hard to keep his irritation in check. 'The Ayodhyan will see it as our weakness. If we have to meet, it has to be on neutral ground—neither their camp, nor ours.'

'But… '

'No buts. We have come to fight, not to surrender.'

Raavan's approach had been clear from the start. Over the last week, he had ordered his troops to destroy all the villages in a fifty-kilometre radius around Karachapa. Standing crops had been burnt down. Harvested grain and livestock had been confiscated and commandeered as food for the Lankan soldiers. Wells had been poisoned with the carcasses of dead animals.

A scorched earth policy.

The Lankan army would be well fed and rested within the Karachapa walls. However, the Sapt Sindhu army, camped outside the city, would find it difficult to feed their five hundred thousand soldiers, given the ravaged countryside. Their numerical advantage would turn into a liability.

'But what if Emperor Dashrath doesn't retreat despite the food shortage?' asked Kubaer, anxiously. 'What if he attacks immediately?'

Raavan smiled. 'I am counting on you, great Chief-Trader, to provoke Dashrath to do precisely that. I will take care of the rest.'

'*Emperor* Dashrath,' corrected Kubaer.

Raavan preferred to speak only the man's name. No unnecessary respect towards an enemy. 'Just Dashrath,' he said quietly.

—ॐ—

Dashrath was in no mood for extended parleys.

'I order you to restore our commission to the very fair nine-tenths of your profits and, in return, I assure you I will let you live,' he said firmly.

After exchanging some terse messages, the adversaries had finally decided to meet on neutral ground. The chosen site was a beach, midway between Dashrath's military camp and the Karachapa fort. The emperor was accompanied by his father-in-law King Ashwapati, his general Mrigasya and a bodyguard platoon of twenty soldiers. Kubaer had arrived with Raavan and twenty bodyguards.

The Sapt Sindhu warriors could scarcely conceal their contempt as the obese Kubaer waddled laboriously into the tent. The chief trader had disregarded Raavan's advice to wear sober clothes and had dressed, instead, in a bright green dhoti and a pink angvastram. The jewellery he wore was flashier than usual. He had reasoned that a display of his fine taste would earn him the appreciation of the Sapt Sindhu leaders. What it did was to convince his opponents that they were dealing with an effete Vaishya; a peacock who knew little of warfare.

'Your Highness…' said Kubaer timidly, 'I think it might be a little difficult to keep the commissions fixed at that level. Our costs have gone up and the trading margins are not what they—'

'Don't try your disgusting negotiating tactics with me!' shouted Dashrath as he banged his hand on the table for effect. 'I am not a trader! I am an emperor! Civilised people understand the difference.'

Raavan clenched his fists under the table. Kubaer was not following any part of his advice, either in demeanour or in speech.

Dashrath leaned forward and said with controlled vehemence, 'I can be merciful. I can forgive mistakes. But you need to stop this nonsense and do as I say.'

Kubaer shifted uneasily on his chair and glanced at the impassive Raavan, who sat to his right. Even seated, Raavan's height and rippling musculature were surprising to the Sapt Sindhuans. They had not expected to find a warrior like this amidst what they derisively called a trader's protection force.

Raavan's battle-worn, swarthy skin was pockmarked as a result of a childhood encounter with disease. His thick beard, accompanied by a handlebar moustache, only added to his menacing appearance. His attire was unremarkable and sober, consisting of a white dhoti and a cream angvastram. His headgear was designed to add to his intimidating presence, with two threatening six-inch-long horns reaching out from the top on either side. The message was clear: Raavan was no mere soldier; he was a bull among men.

The Sapt Sindhuans kept glancing at the well-built Lankan general sitting amongst them, expecting him to say something. But Raavan sat still, offering neither opinions nor objections.

Kubaer turned back to Dashrath. 'But, Your Highness, we are facing many problems, and our invested capital is—'

'You are trying my patience now, Kubaer!' Dashrath snapped. 'You are irritating the emperor of the Sapt Sindhu!'

'But, my lord…'

'Look, if you do not continue to pay our rightful commissions, believe me, you will all be dead by this time tomorrow. I will first defeat your miserable army, then travel all the way to that cursed island of yours and burn your city to the ground.'

'But there are problems with our ships, and labour costs have—'

'I don't care about your problems!' Dashrath was shouting now.

'You will, after tomorrow,' said Raavan softly.

The emperor had lost his temper. The time was right.

Dashrath swung around to look sharply at Raavan. 'How dare you speak out of—'

'How dare you, Dashrath?' asked Raavan, his voice clear and ringing.

Dashrath, Ashwapati and Mrigasya sat in stunned silence, shocked that this mere sidekick of a trader should have the temerity to address the emperor of the Sapt Sindhu by his name.

Raavan suppressed a smile. They were behaving exactly as he had expected. *These people are so easy to play. Their egos will be their undoing.*

The time had come to twist the knife.

'How dare you imagine that you can even come close to defeating an army that I lead?' asked Raavan with a half-sneer on his lips.

Dashrath stood up angrily, and his chair went flying back with a clatter. He thrust a finger in Raavan's direction. 'I'll be looking for you on the battlefield tomorrow, you upstart!'

Slowly and menacingly, Raavan rose from his chair, with his fist closed tight around the pendant that hung from a gold chain around his neck. Holding her hand gave him strength. It was also a constant reminder of why he was doing all this.

As Raavan's fist unclenched, Dashrath stared at the pendant. It was obvious that the emperor was horrified by what he saw. He probably thought the Lankan to be a monster who vandalised the bodies of his enemies.

Let Dashrath believe I am a cannibalistic beast. It will be a competitive advantage in battle.

'I assure you, I'll be waiting,' said Raavan, with a hint of amusement lacing his voice, as he watched Dashrath gape at him. 'I look forward to drinking your blood.'

That's enough. Let him stew in his anger.

Raavan turned around and strode out of the tent. Kubaer wobbled out hurriedly behind him, followed by the Lankan bodyguards.

—१६१—

'You weren't able to sleep either?' asked Kumbhakarna.

Raavan turned towards his brother and smiled, letting go of the pendant in his hand.

It was the fifth hour of the fourth prahar—just an hour before midnight. Raavan had been standing on the ramparts of the Karachapa fort, looking towards the Sapt Sindhu camp and the many fires lit there. The night was quiet, and the sounds of conversation and laughter carried all the way to the fort.

'Looks like the enemy isn't sleeping either,' said Raavan.

Kumbhakarna laughed. 'These Sapt Sindhu Kshatriyas think war is a party.'

Raavan took a deep breath. 'By this time tomorrow, we will own the Sapt Sindhu.'

'Technically, won't it be Kubaer who owns it?'

'And who the hell do you think owns that fat slob?'

Kumbhakarna burst out laughing, and a moment later, Raavan joined in. Kumbhakarna put an arm around his brother.

'You should laugh more, Dada,' he said. 'She would have liked that.'

Raavan's right hand instinctively sought the pendant again. 'The best way to honour her is to destroy the army that defends the filthy society that killed her.'

Kumbhakarna remained silent. He knew there was no point in saying anything to Raavan about this.

Raavan stared at the inky black sea. He couldn't see them, but he knew his ships were there, anchored more than two kilometres from shore. Those ships, with their unusually broad bow sections, were crucial to his battle plans.

'The ships are to remain where they are,' said Raavan. 'I don't even want the rowboats to be lowered.'

'Obviously,' said Kumbhakarna.

Raavan liked how his brother always seemed to read his mind. With the Lankan ships far away, and the rowboats still aboard, the Ayodhyans would assume that the vessels would have no role to play in the battle. Even if there was a reserve force on board those ships, it would not be possible to bring them into combat quickly enough.

And that's how the trap would be set.

'Do you think they will fall for it?' asked Kumbhakarna.

'They have taken every bait so far, haven't they? I have faith in their arrogance. Their assumption that we are stupid traders and incapable of battle is what will cause them to make mistakes tomorrow. Also, remember they have five hundred thousand soldiers. We have a little over fifty thousand in the city. The odds must look very good to them. And people do reckless things when they think the odds are in their favour.'

'But unless the emperor commits them to an attack formation on the beach, our ships will be useless.'

'Precisely,' said Raavan, turning to look at Kumbhakarna. 'That's what I wanted to talk to you about.'

'I'll do it, Dada. I'll lead some of the battalions outside the city walls and offer them—us—up as bait. And when the Ayodhyans charge at us, you can do the rest with the ships.'

'You know almost exactly how my mind works,' said Raavan, smiling.

Kumbhakarna grinned. 'Almost? I always know what you are thinking.'

'Not entirely. We'll follow the battle plan that you just laid out. Except, I'll be the bait. And you'll be leading the ships.'

Kumbhakarna was aghast. 'No, Dada!'

'Kumbha...'

'No!'

'You've said to me often enough, that you'll do anything for me.'

'Yes, I will. I'll put my life at risk. And you'll win the battle.'

'Kumbha, I'm asking you to do something far more difficult. I want you to allow me to put my own life at risk.'

'That's not possible, Dada.'

'Kumbha, listen to me...'

'No!'

'Kumbha, that arrogant fool Dashrath hates me. I am the one who can drive him to act rashly. I have to be here.'

'Then I'll stay with you. Let Uncle Mareech lead the ships.'

'My life will be at risk, Kumbha. You are the only one I can trust to have my back.'

'Dada...'

'You are the only one who will ensure that I don't die.'

Kumbhakarna raised his hand to cover Raavan's mouth. 'Shhh! Maa has told you not to speak of your own death. Just because the Almighty has given you a mouth doesn't mean you have to use it to say stupid things!'

'Then make sure that I don't have to speak of it again. Lead the ships.'

'Dada!' Kumbhakarna was exasperated.

'It's an order, Kumbha. I can trust only you. You have to do this for me. You have to ensure that the ships sail in on time.'

Kumbhakarna clasped Raavan's hands tightly, not saying anything.

'We will win tomorrow,' said Raavan. 'And then our era will begin. History will never forget the names of Raavan and Kumbhakarna.'

—१७१—

The next day, by the fourth hour of the second prahar, Raavan was battle-ready. Mounted on his warhorse, and waiting at the frontline.

Much to the shock of his enemies, and even some of his own followers, he had surrendered the immense defensive benefits of staying behind the well-designed fort walls. Instead, he had arranged about fifty thousand soldiers—most of his army—in standard chaturanga formation outside the fort walls, on the beach.

The Lankans now had their enemy to the front and the fort walls behind them. Presenting a seemingly soft target to Dashrath and his army.

A Lankan bait for the warriors of the Sapt Sindhu.

And the bait had been taken.

The emperor of Ayodhya had arranged his army along the beach, in a *suchi vyuha*, the *needle formation*. Dashrath knew that charging the fort from the landward side was not an option. Raavan's hordes had planted dense thorny bushes all around the fort, except along the wall that ran beside the beach. Dashrath's army could have cleared the bushes and created a path to reach the fort, but that would have taken weeks. With the Lankan army having scorched the land around Karachapa, and the resultant absence of food and water outside the fort, the option was simply not viable. The army had to attack before they ran out of rations.

Dashrath should have stopped to consider why Raavan had blocked all possible options of engagement except for the one along the beach. The king of Ayodhya had never lost a battle in his illustrious military career. His strategic instincts should have alerted him. But Raavan's insulting words the previous day still played on his mind, and he had let his pride get the better of his judgement.

The beach was wide by most standards, but it wasn't enough for a large army—hence Dashrath's tactical decision to form a suchi vyuha. The best of his troops would take position alongside him, at the front of the formation, while the rest of the army would fall into a long column behind them. They intended a rolling charge, whereby the first lines would strike the Lankan ranks, and after twenty minutes or so of battle, slip back, allowing the next line of warriors to charge in. It would be an unrelenting surge of battle-hardened soldiers aiming to scatter and decimate the enemy troops of Lanka.

Ashwapati, the king of Kekaya and Dashrath's father-in-law, had misgivings about this strategy. He had pointed out that only a few tens of thousands of their soldiers would be engaged in battle at any point of time, while most of the others waited at the back. By forcing the battle along the narrow beach rather than a large battleground, Raavan had negated the huge numerical advantage of the Sapt Sindhu army. But Ashwapati's concerns had been brushed aside by a confident Dashrath.

To Dashrath's mind, the Lankans were traders who were incapable of sophisticated battle tactics. The apparently stupid move of positioning the army outside the fort walls had only convinced him that Raavan and his troops had no understanding of what they were doing.

Far away, at the other end of the beach, Raavan looked to his right, to where his ships lay at anchor more than two kilometres out at sea. The rowboats were not visible. Kumbhakarna was following his instructions perfectly.

Raavan turned his gaze back to the Sapt Sindhuans.

His arrogant and overconfident enemies had not even sent spy boats out to investigate the broad bow sections of his ships. They really should have done that.

A smile played on his lips. *Bloody fools.*

Raavan flexed his shoulders and arms. The most irritating part of battle was the waiting. Waiting for the other side to charge. You couldn't allow yourself to be distracted and you couldn't waste energy either. He had warned his troops not to tire themselves out by screaming obscenities at the enemy or chanting war cries. They had been ordered to wait silently.

Clearly, Dashrath had given no such instructions to his soldiers. They were roaring their war cries, their voices rising and falling in a frenzy. Charging themselves on adrenaline. And tiring themselves out in the bargain.

Raavan had worn his trademark battle helmet with its six-inch horns sticking out threateningly from the sides. It was a challenge to his enemies; to Dashrath.

I am here. Come and get me.

Dashrath, meanwhile, was on his well-trained and imposing-looking war horse, surveying his amassed troops. He ran his eyes over them confidently. They were a rowdy, raucous bunch, with their swords already drawn, eager for battle. The horses, too, seemed to have succumbed to the excitement of the moment, making the soldiers pull hard at their reins, to hold them in check. Dashrath could almost smell the blood that would soon be shed; the massacre that would lead to victory!

He squinted as he observed the Lankans and their commander up ahead in the distance. He felt a jab of anger as he remembered Raavan's words from their last meeting. The upstart trader would soon feel his wrath. He drew his sword and held it aloft, and then bellowed the unmistakable war cry of his kingdom, Kosala, and its capital city, Ayodhya. '*Ayodhyatah Vijetaarah!*'

The conquerors from the unconquerable city!

Not everyone in his army was a citizen of Ayodhya, and yet they were proud to fight under the great Kosala banner. They echoed their emperor's war cry. 'Ayodhyatah Vijetaarah!'

Dashrath roared as he brought his sword down and spurred his horse. 'Kill them all! No mercy!'

'No mercy!' echoed the riders of the first charge, taking off behind their fearless lord.

Riding hard, riding fearlessly, riding to their own destruction.

As Dashrath and his finest warriors charged down the beach towards the Lankans, Raavan's troops remained immobile. When the enemy cavalry was just a few hundred metres away, Raavan unexpectedly turned his horse around and retreated from the frontlines, even as his soldiers held firm.

Raavan's strategy was clear—what was important was victory, not a display of manhood and courage. For Dashrath, however, brought up in the ways of the Kshatriyas, personal bravery was the most important trait of a general. Raavan's apparent cowardice infuriated him. He kicked his horse to a gallop, intending to mow down the Lankan frontline and quickly reach Raavan. And the Ayodhyans followed their lord, racing hard.

This was exactly what Raavan had hoped for. The Lankan frontline swung into action. The soldiers suddenly dropped their swords and picked up unnaturally long spears, almost twenty feet in length, which had been lying at their feet. Made of wood and metal, they were so heavy that it took two men to pick one up. The soldiers pointed these spears, tipped with sharp copper heads, directly at Dashrath's oncoming cavalry.

The mounted soldiers could not rein in their horses in time, and rode headlong into the spears, which tore into the unprepared beasts. Their riders were thrown forward while the horses collapsed under them. Even as the charge of Dashrath's cavalry was halted in its tracks, Lankan archers emerged, high on the walls of the Karachapa fort. They started shooting a continuous stream of arrows in a long arc from the heights of the fort ramparts, into the dense formation of Dashrath's troops at the back, shredding the Sapt Sindhu lines.

Many of Dashrath's warriors, who had been flung off their impaled horses, stumbled up to engage in fierce hand-to-hand battle with the enemy. Their king led the way as he swung his sword ferociously, killing all who dared to come in his path. But all around him, he could see the devastation being wrought upon his soldiers, who rapidly fell under the barrage of Lankan arrows and superbly trained swordsmen. Minutes later, Dashrath gestured to his flag bearer, who raised his flag high in response. It was the signal for the soldiers at the back to join the charge, in support of the first line.

This was the moment Raavan had been waiting for.

On Kumbhakarna's orders, the Lankan ships abruptly weighed anchor. Big ships always stay offshore, unless there is a proper harbour available. Naval warriors are transported to the beaches in small rowboats. But Kumbhakarna did not lower the rowboats. He ordered the ships themselves to speed to the beach! The sailors, who had been on full alert, extended oars and began to row rapidly to the shore. The ships' sails were up at full mast to help them catch the wind. Within minutes, arrows were being fired from the decks into the densely packed forces under Dashrath's command. The Lankan archers on the ships ripped through the massed ranks of the Sapt Sindhuans.

No one in Dashrath's army had factored in the possibility of the enemy ships beaching with speed; ordinarily, it would have cracked their hulls. What they didn't know was that these were amphibious crafts with specially constructed hulls that could absorb the shock of grounding. Even as the landing crafts stormed onto the beach with tremendous velocity, the broad bows of the hulls rolled out from the top. These were no ordinary bows of a standard hull. They were attached to the bottom of the hull by huge hinges, and they simply rolled out onto the sand like a landing ramp. This opened a gangway from the belly of the ships straight onto the beach. Cavalrymen mounted on disproportionately large horses imported from the West thundered out of the ships and straight onto the beach, mercilessly slicing through the men who blocked their path.

The Sapt Sindhuans were now battling at both ends—at the frontlines against Raavan's soldiers at the Karachapa fort walls, and at the rear, with the unexpected attackers from the ships, led by Kumbhakarna.

The trained instinct of a skilled warrior seemed to warn Dashrath that something terrible was ensuing at the rear guard.

As he strained to look beyond the sea of battling humanity, he detected a sudden movement to his left and raised his shield just in time to block a vicious blow from a Lankan soldier. With a ferocious roar, the king of Ayodhya swung brutally at his attacker, his sword slicing through a chink in the armour. The Lankan fell back, as his abdomen was ripped open and blood spurted out, accompanied by slick pink intestines that tumbled out in a rush. Dashrath turned away and looked behind him, to his troops in the rear formations.

'No!' he yelled.

A scenario he had never foreseen was playing out in front of his eyes. Caught in the vicious pincer attack of the archers and the foot soldiers at the fort walls in front, and the fierce Lankan cavalry from the beached ships at the back, the spirit of his all-conquering army was collapsing rapidly. Dashrath stared in disbelief as some of his men broke ranks and began to retreat.

'No!' he thundered. 'Fight! Fight! We are Ayodhya! The Unconquerables!'

Meanwhile, with everything going exactly as he had expected, Raavan kicked his horse into a canter and led some of his men down the beach on the left, skirting the sea. It was the only flank that was open to counter-attack by the Ayodhyans. Accompanied by his well-trained cavalry, Raavan hacked his way through the outer infantry lines before they could regroup. He had to hold his position at the fort walls while Kumbhakarna massacred the rear lines.

Raavan wasn't interested in killing Dashrath. That didn't matter at this point. His focus was on victory. And to achieve that, he had to break this last remaining holdout of the Ayodhyans.

Slowly but surely, hemmed in by the soldiers at the fort walls, the attackers led by Kumbhakarna at the rear, and the crushing attack by Raavan's men along the flanks, Dashrath's army fell into disarray. Panic set in among the ranks. And before long, a full disorderly retreat began.

This was not a battle anymore. It was a massacre.

But Raavan did not stop. He did not order a ceasefire. He did not allow his troops to show mercy.

His orders were clear and he shouted them aloud: 'Kill them all! No mercy! Kill them all!'

And his soldiers obeyed.

Chapter 20

Raavan tapped his empty wine goblet reflectively. An attendant at the other end of the chamber began making his way forward, but slowed as he noticed Kumbhakarna rising from his seat to attend to his brother.

Kumbhakarna refilled the goblet before pouring some wine for himself. Then he looked up and signalled to the attendant to leave. The man saluted and withdrew from the room.

It had been five months since the rout of the Sapt Sindhu army in the Battle of Karachapa. Dashrath had barely survived, saved by the bravery of his second wife, Kaikeyi, the daughter of the king of Kekaya, Ashwapati.

'Do you think we should have killed the emperor?' asked Kumbhakarna, taking a sip of wine and settling back in his comfortable chair.

'I did consider it,' said Raavan, shaking his head. 'But I think it's better this way. A quick death on the battlefield would have been a blessing for him. The humiliation of the defeat will extinguish his spirit little by little. The military failure, and the treaty we have imposed, will destroy his mental peace. With an unstable and insecure leader, the morale of the

Sapt Sindhu is unlikely to recover. They are not going to give us any trouble as we slowly squeeze the empire dry. If we had killed Dashrath, we would have turned him into a martyr. And martyrs can be dangerous. They can trigger rebellions.'

'So you think the bravery of Queen Kaikeyi has actually helped us.'

'She wasn't trying to help us, she was only trying to save her husband. But she is a brave woman. And I have no doubt she will be treated poorly by her ungrateful subjects. They don't know how to honour their heroes.'

'Apparently, Emperor Dashrath and his first queen Kaushalya were blessed with a son the day we defeated him in Karachapa. They call him Ram.'

'After the Vishnu?' asked Raavan, laughing softly in derision. Ram was the birth name of the sixth Vishnu, more commonly known as Parshu Ram. 'They must have high expectations of that baby!'

'The funny thing is, they blame the poor child for their defeat in Karachapa. Apparently, he brought them bad luck.'

'So our victory had nothing to do with my brilliant war strategies? It was all because some queen went into labour at the same time?!' Raavan laughed.

Kumbhakarna grinned back at him.

'You should laugh more often, Dada,' he said. 'Vedavatiji would have liked you to.'

'Stop telling me that again and again.'

'But it's the truth.'

'How do you know it's the truth? Did her soul come and inform you?'

Kumbhakarna shook his head. 'Dada, you will not be healed till you are able to think of her with a smile on your face. If you feel sadness and anger each time you remember her, you'll turn a beautiful memory into poison. It's been so many years. You have to learn to move on.'

'Are you saying I should forget how she died? That I should live in a state of foolish oblivion?' Raavan snapped.

Kumbhakarna remained calm. 'I did not say that. How is it possible for us to forget how she died? But that's not the only memory of her we have, right? It's one of the many memories she left behind. Spend time with those other memories too. The happy times you had with her. Then you will not drown in sadness whenever you think of her.'

'Maybe I like the sadness. It comforts me.'

'If you spend enough time with anything, you start liking it, even sadness.'

Raavan shook his head. Clearly, there was to be no more conversation on the subject.

Kumbhakarna fell silent.

'Anyway, when is the first instalment of the war reparations reaching Sigiriya?' asked Raavan.

'In a few weeks, Dada. In a few weeks, Lanka will go from merely rich to fantastically wealthy. Perhaps the wealthiest kingdom in the world.'

Before the Battle of Karachapa, Lanka was entitled to retain only ten per cent of the profits from its trade with the Sapt Sindhu. Ninety per cent belonged to Ayodhya, the representative of the empire. Ayodhya would, in turn, share this commission with its subordinate kingdoms. After the battle, Raavan had unilaterally slashed Ayodhya's commission to just nine per cent, keeping the rest for Lanka. In addition, he had drastically reduced the prices of all manufactured goods purchased from the Sapt Sindhu. If that wasn't enough, he had also ordered Ayodhya to return, with retrospective effect, the surplus amount that the kingdoms had been paid over the previous three years, going by the new calculation—as war reparations. Raavan knew that this sweeping reduction in commissions would pauperise the empire over time, while making Lanka extremely prosperous. Of course, since he was going to keep half the increased Lankan profits, he would soon be stupendously rich as well. And powerful.

'What next, Dada?' asked Kumbhakarna.

Raavan walked over to a large window in the chamber and looked out at the verdant gardens beyond. His mansion in Sigiriya was a short distance from the giant monolithic rock that housed the palace of Kubaer—chief-trader of Lanka and the richest man in the world.

Kubaer may not have known too much about warfare, but he did understand the need to protect his immense wealth. Over the last few decades, he had vastly improved the defensive systems of the city. Sigiriya was surrounded by rolling boulder-strewn hills. Each of the tall boulders had structures built on their flat tops, to house soldiers who could fight off any trespassers from an unassailable height. This was in addition to the sturdy walls and moats that surrounded the city.

But Kubaer did not concern himself only with security. Despite his garish taste in clothes and jewellery, he had a surprisingly fine eye for architecture. And he had turned what was already an achingly beautiful city into a truly exquisite symbol of grace and elegance.

The city, built on a large plateau, was adorned with stunning gardens and public walkways. Beautifully landscaped lawns, irrigated by waterways and underground channels, dotted the outskirts, while tall, evergreen trees spread their branches on either side of the main roads. Even the many boulders within the city had been incorporated into what the Sigiriyans called boulder gardens, with intricate fountains adding to their grace and beauty. There were tastefully designed halls for public functions, libraries, amphitheatres, lakes for boating, and everything else that was required for civilised living. Lanka was a part of the larger Vedic world and many temples to different Vedic Gods graced various parts of the city. The largest of the temples, of course, was dedicated to Lord Parshu Ram, the sixth Vishnu and the founder of the Malayaputra tribe. This temple had been built and consecrated by the great Rishi Vishwamitra himself.

Raavan, however, was not swayed by all of Sigiriya's fineries. His attention was focused on the monolith called Lion's Rock, which rose a sheer two hundred metres from the surrounding countryside. The city was named after this rock; Sigiriya harked back to the Sanskrit *Sinhagiri* or *Lion's Hill*. At the top of the monolith was the massive palace of Kubaer. It represented the triumph of human imagination over nature's bounty. Colossal, and yet delicately refined.

At the base of the monolith were roughly concentric terraced gardens that showcased the skilful use of water-proofed brick walls. Each of these gardens rose a little higher than the one next to it, and a winding road led up to the rock, through lush parks speckled with fountains. The pathway from the northern side led up to one of the most stunning architectural achievements of Sigiriya: The Lion Gate.

The Lion Gate was called so because there actually was a gargantuan lion's head carved high above the entrance. The gate stood between the lion's two front paws, each the height of an average man, while the massive head reared up, visible to all the citizens of Sigiriya from far and wide. The monolith itself was shaped like the body of a colossal lion, seated in regal splendour, its head surveying its territory from high above.

It was a magnificent sight.

On top of the monolith, across an area spread over two square kilometres, stood the massive palace complex of Kubaer, complete with pools, gardens, private chambers, courts, offices, and unimaginable luxuries designed to please the richest man in the world.

'What is next is that we take control of that,' said Raavan, pointing towards Lion's Rock.

'What!' Kumbhakarna couldn't conceal his shock. 'Isn't it too early to get rid of Kubaer, Dada? We are still not strong enough and…'

Raavan frowned. 'Not that,' he clarified. 'That.'

Kumbhakarna followed the pointing finger more closely this time. Raavan was pointing towards Lion's Rock, but not at Kubaer's palace. The steps going up from the Lion Gate led to a mid-level terrace, about one hundred metres lower than the top of the monolith. The pathway carved into the rock and leading to the terrace had a wall alongside it that was made of evenly cut bricks covered with polished white plaster. So highly polished that anyone walking by could see their reflection in it. It was called, rather unimaginatively, the Mirror Wall. Beyond the Mirror Wall, the rock was designed to look like a cloth saddle for the massive lion that the monolith represented. The saddle was covered with gorgeous frescoes depicting beautiful women. Nobody knew who these figures represented. They had been painted during Trishanku Kaashyap's time, and had been lovingly maintained. Beyond the frescoes, the pathway led to the lower-level palaces, behind lavish gardens, ponds, moats and ramparts which protected the upper-citadel, where Kubaer's personal palace stood.

It was these lower-level palaces that Raavan was pointing at.

'Meghdoot?' asked Kumbhakarna.

The lower-level palaces housed some of the concubines and younger wives of Kubaer. But one of these palaces was the home of Meghdoot, the prime minister, who was in charge of revenues, taxes, Customs and general administration. Raavan, being the general in command of the Lankan army and the police was, effectively, the head of all the muscle power. Meghdoot was head of all the money. Together, they ran the kingdom for Kubaer. If Raavan were to add Meghdoot's portfolio to his own, he would effectively have more power than the chief-trader. After that, replacing him would only be a matter of time. A soft coup.

Kumbhakarna was careful with his words, even though they were alone. 'You do realise that we would have to—'

'Yes, I do,' interrupted Raavan. 'But it must look like an accident. Otherwise it will be difficult for me to take over.'

'Hmm…'

'It's a difficult task. We can't have a thug do it. We need an artist.'

'I'll find someone,' Kumbhakarna said thoughtfully.

—ॐ—

It had been a month since Raavan had ordered the assassination of Meghdoot, the prime minister of Lanka, but Kumbhakarna had been unable to find a way forward. He had finally turned to their uncle for help. And today, Mareech had informed him that the man for the job had been found.

Eager to update his brother with this news, Kumbhakarna went looking for him, but he was nowhere to be found. Finally, he went down to the secret chamber hidden away in the deep interiors of the palace. No one apart from the two brothers was permitted entry here, just like in Raavan's private chamber in Gokarna.

As soon as he walked in, Kumbhakarna turned and locked the door behind him. A single torch had been lit. His brother was inside.

The first thing he saw in the semi-darkness was a gold-plated Raavanhatha. It lay on the ground, broken, its strings ripped apart. In the deathly quiet of the chamber, he thought he heard the sound of someone crying.

As his eyes adjusted to the darkness, Kumbhakarna saw Raavan slumped on a tall wooden stool, his back to the door. His head was in his hands and his entire body shook as he cried. Deep, anguished sobs wrenched from the depths of sorrow and despair.

In front of Raavan stood an easel. On it, a vaguely familiar image had been scratched out with rough, angry strokes that nearly concealed its outlines. It took a moment for Kumbhakarna to decode the drawing, but then he saw that it was an unfinished profile of Vedavati. Pregnant, her form full and voluptuous. The outlines sketched and ready for the colours to be filled in. The eyes were half drawn—and that's where Raavan seemed to have given up.

Kumbhakarna knew that Raavan had stopped painting Vedavati since that day of the gruesome killings. Until then, she had grown older in his imagination, gradually, year after year. And he had been able to see her in his mind's eye, in fine detail, almost as though she stood beside him while he painted. But after her death, the will to paint had died too, and now, when he sought to capture her on canvas again, it seemed that the blessing, the power of creative vision, had vanished.

Kumbhakarna was aware that even he couldn't fully comprehend the rage and resentment his brother felt. Only an artist can understand the despair of being abandoned by his muse, his lifelong inspiration. Only someone who has loved can know the immeasurable agony of losing the object of one's passion. Only a devout believer who has touched the Divine can know the soul-emptying misery of his Goddess being taken from him.

Kumbhakarna walked over to Raavan quietly.

He knelt beside his elder brother and put an arm around him. Raavan turned and buried his face in his brother's shoulder, weeping as though nothing could comfort him again, ever.

They held each other for a long while, not saying anything. Their shared grief drowned everything else out—all thoughts, all words.

It was Raavan who broke the silence. 'I need control… of Lanka… quickly.'

'Yes, Dada.'

'I need to destroy… I need to… those bastards… Sapt Sindhu… destroy completely…'

Kumbhakarna remained silent.

Raavan controlled himself with some effort, then said, 'Get me that assassin.'

'Yes, Dada.'

'Quickly.'

'Yes, I will.'

When you fill a clogged drain with more water than it can hold, it's bound to overflow and contaminate everything around it. When grief overwhelms someone, when they are enraged at what fate has done to them, their fury often overflows and is inflicted upon the world.

That's the only way in which they can cope with their own life—a life that holds no meaning anymore.

—१७६१—

'Are you sure?' asked Raavan, his expression quizzical.

Raavan and Kumbhakarna had travelled to Gokarna for this meeting. They didn't want to risk anyone in Sigiriya getting even a whiff of their plan.

Mareech and Akampana had just entered the house through a side entrance, hidden from view. They were accompanied by a young, wiry man.

Mareech said to Raavan, his voice soft but confident, 'Trust me. I have seen some of his work myself. He is exceptional. Right up there with the Vishkanyas.'

The *Vishkanyas*, or *poison-bearing women*, were renowned assassins. They were raised from a very young age to be killers, with small doses of poison being administered to them daily. Eventually they became immune to the poison. But even a kiss from them was known to be fatal. And if their poison didn't get you, their weapons would. They were the deadliest killers the world had ever known.

'Right up there with the Vishkanyas?' Kumbhakarna did not try to hide his scepticism, as he looked at the man who stood next to Akampana. 'Really, Uncle, there has to be some limit to exaggeration.'

Mareech looked at the potential assassin. He could see why they did not think much of him. Of small build, with long curly hair and dimples on both cheeks, he exuded a genial charm. There was not a scar in sight. More than a cold-blooded assassin, he looked like a no-good philanderer who knew only how to seduce women.

'Who's next on the list?' asked Raavan, irritated that he had come all the way to Gokarna to meet someone who was evidently unfit for the job.

Mareech didn't answer. He turned to the assassin and nodded.

The lithe body moved with lightning speed, reaching behind Akampana in a flash. Before the dandy trader could even react, a finger had jabbed him hard and precisely on a pressure point at the back of his neck. Instantly, Akampana was paralysed from the neck down. The attacker grabbed him by the shoulders and gently let him slide down to the ground.

Akampana was able to move his head, just about. His eyes swivelled left and right in panic. 'I can't feel anything! I can't feel anything! Help me! Oh Lord Indra!' He called out to Raavan. 'Iraiva! Iraiva! Please help!'

But his 'true lord' was laughing. Positively surprised by what he had seen. He turned to his brother. 'This chap isn't bad, Kumbha!'

Kumbhakarna wasn't amused, however. He said to Mareech, who was laughing along with Raavan, 'Uncle, tell him to let Akampanaji go at once. This is not right. He is one of us.'

Akampana was still jabbering in terror. 'Lord Raavan! Iraiva! Don't kill me! Please! I haven't done anything!'

Raavan controlled his mirth and asked Mareech, 'Uncle, this is reversible, right?'

'Yes, my lord.' The cause of all the anxiety answered Raavan directly. 'I can release the hold. But, if I have to, I can also kill him peacefully while he is still paralysed.'

Hearing this, Akampana moaned again in panic, 'Iraiva! Help!'

'Oh, shut up, Akampana!' said Raavan, before turning to the assassin with keen interest. 'So does the victim feel anything?'

'Not when I work this particular pressure point. There are others that will leave him paralysed but feeling the pain.'

Raavan didn't conceal the fact that he was impressed. 'What is this man's name, Uncle?'

'His very name means death,' said Mareech. 'Mara.'

Raavan turned back to the young man. 'All right, Mara. You are hired.'

'Iraiva!' screamed Akampana. 'Release me!'

Raavan looked at Akampana and then at Mara. 'Can you release his body but paralyse his tongue?'

Everyone burst out laughing. Even Akampana smiled weakly.

Kumbhakarna was still not amused. The two extra arms on top of his shoulders were stiff. He turned to his elder brother, disapproval writ large on his face. 'Dada…'

'All right, all right,' Raavan said.

He gestured to Mara. 'Release him.'

Chapter 21

'Not bad,' said Vishwamitra, clearly impressed. 'Not bad at all.'

Vishwamitra and Arishtanemi were in Agastyakootam, the hidden capital of the Malayaputras. It had been a year since the Battle of Karachapa.

'Yes, Raavan truly is turning out to be the perfect villain,' said Arishtanemi. 'There is no person more hated in the Sapt Sindhu than him. Not only did he defeat the empire comprehensively, he has imposed such an extortionate treaty on them that they will soon go from being the wealthiest land in the world to among the poorest.'

'When I heard of the conditions he had proposed, I assumed Raavan was asking for an outrageous cut so that when he finally settled for less, his magnanimity would be lauded. Clearly, that is not what he had in mind. He is actually ramming the terms of the treaty down their throats. Ayodhya has never been so weak. Which means that finally, that… that… spineless abomination of a man has been shown his place.' Vishwamitra couldn't bring himself to speak the name he despised above all.

Arishtanemi knew his guru was referring to Vashishtha, the *raj guru*, the *royal sage* of the Ayodhya court and chief adviser of the royal family. As always, the mere thought of Vashishtha was enough to agitate Vishwamitra.

Arishtanemi smoothly changed the subject. 'Yes, Ayodhya is weaker now than it has ever been. And the way Raavan forced Kubaer's hand was masterly, for the chief-trader himself would never have pushed the treaty and the war reparations to this extent. He may be greedy, but he is also a coward. And let's not forget, the assassination of Meghdoot was a deft touch, impeccably timed.'

'Are you sure about that?' asked Vishwamitra, forgetting about Vashishtha for the moment. 'Because I have heard conflicting reports. There are enough people who believe that his death was caused by drowning—accidental drowning.'

'I am sure, Guruji. He didn't drown. He *was* drowned.'

'But—'

'It was beautifully planned. Everyone knew that Meghdoot was rehearsing for his role as the doomed poet Kalidas, in his favourite play, *Jalsandesh*. And we all know how that famous lake scene played out.'

'But I heard a wine glass and a decanter were found next to the pool where he drowned.'

'Also a part of the setup. Meghdoot was a colourful character who liked his wine and women, so it made sense to place a glass of wine there. A red herring, if there ever was one. Besides, there was no sign of injury on Meghdoot. No signs of any struggle. The post-mortem showed there was water in his lungs. He died by drowning. Everything fits too well to be true, Guruji. There is no reason for anyone to suspect anything.'

'So, you think it was too perfect?'

'Exactly. Real life is messy. Nothing is ever perfect, but this death was. That's what got me suspicious, and I decided to investigate.'

'So, who is the person behind this?'

'Someone called Mara. That's obviously not his real name. Which mother would name her child "death"? I don't know anything about his background yet, but wherever he came from, he is a genius. I suspect he is young and still honing his craft. There are things he needs to work on.'

'Such as?'

'Well, for one, he is not secretive enough. He has shown his face to too many people. He is good, but he can be trained to improve.'

'Is that what you intend to do?'

'I do believe Mara could be a useful asset for us, Guruji.'

'I'll leave that to you. Do what you have to. I am more interested in what Raavan is going to do next. When do you think he will take Kubaer out?'

'I don't think he will, for now. With Meghdoot gone, he controls both the revenue department and the military directly—the first Lankan minister to do so. He has, in fact, already started excluding Kubaer from *sabhas*, saying that the voice of the chief-trader is too pure to be heard in these petty *administration meetings*. He is, for all practical purposes, already the king of Lanka. There is no need for him to upset the balance by overthrowing Kubaer.'

'Hmm... clever move. But I am a bit sceptical about the wisdom of enforcing such ridiculous terms on the Sapt Sindhu. He will end up killing the golden goose that feeds him.'

'Is that relevant, Guruji? We have him exactly where we need him. He is setting himself up to be the perfect villain. All of the Sapt Sindhu will grow to dread him. We should start searching for a Vishnu now.'

'Of course. But we can't lose sight of Raavan's motives either. We need to know what's going on in his mind so that we can control him better. It is important to understand exactly what is pushing him to take this position on Ayodhya. I don't think it's just his lust for money and power. He seems to be driven by a sort of unbridled, almost unhinged rage. Because his actions defy all logic—of business and politics.'

'I'll find out, Guruji.'

'Also, let's start charging him more for the cave material and the medicines.'

Arishtanemi chuckled. 'Yes, Guruji. I was thinking that too. We'll certainly put the money to better use than he will.'

—१७१—

Raavan flung open the door to the ship's cabin and walked briskly in, his face sweaty and flushed.

Kumbhakarna, looking similarly exhausted, followed his brother. There were two Lankan soldiers with him. As he entered the cabin, he stopped the soldiers outside. 'Keep your swords drawn and stay vigilant. Don't allow anyone else in.'

Raavan had already poured two goblets of wine for them. He handed one to his younger brother.

'Thanks, Dada,' said Kumbhakarna, regarding the bloodstained goblet for a moment before draining the wine in one gulp. There was nothing like good wine after the exertions of a battle.

Raavan downed his glass just as efficiently. He was still trying to catch his breath.

It had been two years since the Battle of Karachapa. With the Sapt Sindhu having capitulated completely, money was pouring into Lanka at a furious pace. Raavan was now the prime minister of the island kingdom and the general of the Lankan army, making him the most powerful man in the land. Kubaer had been reduced to a ruler in name only.

Mareech and Akampana ran the twenty-nine-year-old Raavan's business empire under Kumbhakarna's able supervision. Mareech had been tasked with expanding the business as far and wide as possible and dominating global trade. He had already appointed 'approved key traders' in every kingdom of the Sapt Sindhu. All trade with the empire was done only through these appointees. This was a strategic move—it gave the Lankans greater control over their trade with the Sapt Sindhu, and also allowed them to build loyal allies in each kingdom.

Akampana's task was to ensure that the accounting and financing of this vast enterprise—the biggest business corporation in history—was clean, with no scope for either employees or associates to drain money out through corruption.

All their plans had been executed smoothly so far. Raavan was now wealthier than Kubaer and had begun to focus more on enjoying his immense wealth. The richest man in the world wanted his lifestyle to reflect his newfound status—the finest wine and food, the most beautiful women, music and dance—only the best of everything would do for Raavan. He indulged in all that satiated his *desire*, his *kaama*.

The palaces situated on the lower levels of Lion's Rock had been taken over soon after the previous prime minister's unfortunate death. Raavan had evicted Meghdoot's family and Kubaer's junior wives and concubines, merging their palaces into a sweeping, opulent estate over which he presided with all the pomp of a ruler.

He had also begun to travel for pleasure—something he had rarely done before—accompanied by Kumbhakarna and a few of his chosen concubines. It was as they were sailing peacefully over calm seas towards the Arabian Peninsula that one of the ship's officers had burst into Raavan's cabin, with the news that a pirate vessel had been spotted speeding towards them. The brothers had just returned to the cabin after taking care of the unwanted diversion.

'Fools!' said Raavan. 'Attacking us! What were they thinking?'

Kumbhakarna rose from his chair, wine glass in hand, took Raavan's from him and walked over to the table. He put them down before cleaning his bloodied hands with a towel. Then he wiped the goblets clean. When he was done, he poured out some more wine and walked back to his brother, bearing the two goblets and the piece of cloth. 'Here, Dada. Use this to wipe your hands. Lord Indra alone knows whose blood that is.'

Raavan looked down at his bloodied hands. His clothes were stained red too. But not one speck of blood on his expensive clothes or his body was his own. There was not a cut on him. He sniffed the blood on his hand before sticking out his tongue and licking it.

'Yuck!' Kumbhakarna made a face.

'Hmmm,' said Raavan, thoughtfully. 'It's an interesting taste.'

Kumbhakarna, still looking nauseated, held the goblet away from Raavan. 'You need to clean your mouth first.'

'I'll just wash it down,' Raavan said, as he took the goblet from Kumbhakarna and gulped down the wine. He wiped his mouth with the back of his hand, smearing some more blood on his face. 'So, what were we talking about? Before those bonehead pirates attacked?'

Kumbhakarna shook his head, trying not to think about what he had just witnessed. 'We were talking about meeting Vibhishan and Shurpanakha. You promised maa you would, remember?'

After Vishrava and his second wife, Crataeis, had passed away, Kaikesi had decided to adopt their children, Vibhishan and Shurpanakha. The two children, accompanied by some others from the ashram of the great sage Vishrava, had found their way to their wealthy half-brother Raavan's abode in Lanka, seeking refuge. They had not anticipated the reception they would get there. Raavan, still angry with his father, had thrown his half-siblings out of his home and refused to shelter them. But Kaikesi had stood up to her son and insisted on bringing them back, saying she had responsibilities towards them.

Raavan did not approve of his mother's act of apparent altruism. 'Kumbha, you know what maa is really like. Her compassion is all fake. She's only taken them in to show the world how virtuous she is.'

'Dada, what's wrong with you? How can you say that about maa?'

'I haven't said anything untrue. Tell me, what has she done to deserve any of this? What sacrifices has she made for our happiness? I am the one who is working hard and paying for her comfortable life in that magnificent mansion. I am the one who pays for all the charity that she does—and publicises.

And I am the one who is paying for those useless half-siblings of ours whom she has decided to adopt and shower with attention. She just struts around exclaiming, "Oh, look! Look, how great I am."' Raavan opened his eyes wide and mimicked his mother's slightly high-pitched voice. 'She's a fraud. Let her try to build her own life by herself. Then she can prance around the world teaching lessons in morality, for all I care. I am tired of her virtue signalling.'

'Dada, I wish you wouldn't be so harsh on her. Besides, what do Vibhishan and Shurpanakha have to do with any of this? They are little children.'

The outgrowths on Kumbhakarna's shoulders were stiff and straight, a clear sign that he was upset.

Raavan sighed. 'You are too genuinely kind for your own good, Kumbha.'

Kumbhakarna remained silent.

Raavan threw his arms up in surrender. 'All right, all right! I'll meet them when I get back to Sigiriya.'

Kumbhakarna smiled. 'That's my boy.'

'Excuse me!' said Raavan, straightening up. 'What do you mean "boy"? Don't forget I am your elder brother.'

'Yeah, yeah,' said Kumbhakarna, laughing.

Raavan smiled at him. 'I let you get away with too much.'

'That's because you can't manage without me.'

'Well, my life manager, tell me, what have you done about Kubaer?'

'We've discussed this already, Dada. There's no need to try and remove him. He's practically your prisoner in any case. He can't step out of his upper citadel without passing through our lower terraces. His bodyguards are our men. We control his life.'

'But what is the point of having him around at all?'

'Listen to me, Dada. Kubaer's idea of doing away with taxes within Lanka was brilliant. We don't need tax revenues in any case, with the flood of money coming in from the Sapt Sindhu. And by proclaiming that all citizens are exempt from paying any taxes at all, he has bought the loyalty of his subjects for life.'

Raavan shook his hand. 'No. It's been too long. I want to be known as the king of Lanka.'

'Sounds to me like you already have a plan.'

'Obviously. That's why I am talking to you.'

'What do you want me to do?'

'I'll tell you… but only after we're finished with these guys.' Raavan drained his glass and threw it away, then he got up and strode briskly to the door.

Kumbhakarna followed in his brother's footsteps.

They were on the main deck of the ship in no time. It was a pleasure boat, so the deck was massive and grand. At the moment though, it resembled a battleground. The bodies of the pirates lay all over. Not one Lankan had been killed, though a few had suffered minor injuries. Next to the large ship, bobbing in the sea, was the much smaller pirate craft, attached to Raavan's vessel with grappling hooks. The pirates had assumed their target carried some rich, chicken-hearted businessman whose crew could be easily overpowered. They had chased down Raavan's ship and boarded it, screaming fierce battle cries. Regrettably for the pirates, that had been the extent of their fierceness. They had come face to face with soldiers who were amongst the finest warriors in the Indian Ocean. Most of the pirates were dead within the first few minutes of battle. The rest, many of them grievously injured, had been lined up at the far end of the deck, shackled and on their knees.

The brothers walked up to the prisoners, their loyal Lankan soldiers close behind them. They stopped in front of a stocky young man who was on his knees, blood flowing from a deep cut on his forehead.

'So, Dada, what do you want to do with these morons? Should we find out who they work for? Maybe we can sell them as slaves somewhere in the Mediterranean?'

By way of answer, Raavan simply flexed his shoulders, then drew his sword and in one swift, mighty blow, beheaded the man kneeling in front of him.

Kumbhakarna shrugged. 'Or we could do that.'

The Lankans followed the example of their lord and commander. They drew their swords and put every one of the pirates out of their misery.

Chapter 22

Three years had passed since the Battle of Karachapa. Raavan was now the sole ruler of Lanka, having got rid of Kubaer. It had been surprisingly easy.

The main contact for trade in Ayodhya for the Lankans was a woman called Manthara. Over the years, Kubaer had come to trust her implicitly. However, a message from Raavan asking her to choose between higher commissions for compliance on the one hand, and severe punishment in case of disobedience on the other, had made the pragmatic Manthara switch sides in a hurry. On Raavan's instructions, she had put the idea in Kubaer's head that Raavan had hired an assassin to get rid of him. This was not the truth, but Kubaer believed it. To nudge him further towards the edge, Manthara let him know that his former prime minister, Meghdoot, had not died by accidental drowning but had, in fact, been assassinated on Raavan's orders. This, of course, was the truth.

The terrified Kubaer had quickly abdicated the throne, publicly announcing that he had nothing more to achieve. He now wished to retire to Devabhoomi in the Himalayas, he said, and perhaps even go further, to Kailash. He was seen off in Lanka with the respect and honour due to someone who was on his way to taking *sanyas*. But *ascetism* was far from Kubaer's mind, especially since Raavan had allowed him to leave with most of his personal wealth, as well as his wives and favourite concubines. He had even allowed Kubaer the use of the Pushpak Vimaan to travel north—the flying vehicle was now officially Raavan's property. And Kubaer had been appropriately obsequious while publicly appreciating Raavan's generosity.

To ensure that there were no counterclaims or even grumbling about Raavan's right to the Lankan throne, Kumbhakarna had suggested that Kubaer himself crown the new king before he left. The ever-reasonable trader was only too willing to place the crown on Raavan's head. Once a ruler had publicly abdicated his throne in favour of another, there could be no earthly reason for the latter to assassinate him. It was only logical.

As soon as he became the undisputed king of Lanka, Raavan abandoned the rather tame title Kubaer had preferred, of chief-trader. Instead, he assumed far more grandiose ones, such as the King of Kings, Emperor of Emperors, Ruler of the Three Worlds, Beloved of the Gods, and a few others. When Kumbhakarna joked about the pompous new titles, he was told by his brother to shut up.

With everything going just the way he wanted it to, Raavan should have been happy and satisfied. However, right at this moment, he didn't look particularly pleased.

'I don't know why I let you talk me into this,' he said.

Raavan and Kumbhakarna were on their way to the lower-citadel palace that was now Kaikesi's abode. The brothers had moved into Kubaer's magnificent palace on top of Lion's Rock. To reach the lower citadel, they had to pass through the large, flat piece of ground that had been converted into a landing pad for the Pushpak Vimaan. They were followed by a phalanx of one hundred bodyguards, who maintained a discreet distance from the king and his brother.

'Dada, I know you are unhappy about this, but they moved into their palace a week ago. They have been delaying the *grahpravesh puja* just for you. You know delaying such a ceremony is inauspicious. We can't keep them waiting anymore,' Kumbhakarna replied.

'She has deliberately brought some priests from the Sapt Sindhu for the ceremony. She knows that will irritate me. When will you understand how devious our mother is?' Raavan snapped.

Kumbhakarna thought it best to ignore his elder brother's dark mood and continued walking.

As they neared the palace, they could see Kaikesi standing at the entrance, with the young Vibhishan and Shurpanakha hiding behind her. Both children were under ten years of age, and were terrified of Raavan. The priests Kaikesi had invited were standing next to her, issuing instructions in a low voice. At least a hundred maids stood behind them, responding to every demand. Kaikesi was enjoying the luxuries that came with her son's good fortune.

As soon as Raavan was within hearing distance, Kaikesi glanced at the sun and declared, 'You are late.'

'I can leave,' said Raavan.

His mother pursed her lips and muttered something under her breath. Then she took the puja thali from the priest standing next to her and looped it in small circles around Raavan's face. Three times. As Raavan stepped aside, she repeated the action for Kumbhakarna.

'Come in,' she said gruffly, waiting for Raavan and Kumbhakarna to enter before her. As Raavan was about to cross the threshold into the palace, she said loudly, 'Right foot first.'

Raavan stopped, glanced at his mother, then at the priests standing next to her, and put his left foot forward.

'Dada!' Kumbhakarna exhaled noisily in frustration, then conscientiously and carefully placed his right foot over the threshold. 'The palace looks beautiful, Maa,' he said. 'You have done a wonderful job, and in such little time.'

Kaikesi looked at her son and sighed, tears welling up in her eyes. 'Forgive me for being so emotional, my son. It's just that it's rare for me to receive compliments these days. I do so much for others, yet no one appreciates me.'

Raavan turned around abruptly and barked, 'I need to leave quickly, Maa. I have lots of work to do. Where is this stupid puja supposed to happen? Let's get it over with.'

Kaikesi raised her voice immediately. 'Mind your words, Raavan. It's not a stupid puja! It's the way in which we honour our ancestors and our culture. Don't be disrespectful!'

Raavan stepped closer to his mother. 'You're right. It's not a stupid puja. It's a *very* stupid puja.'

Kumbhakarna had had enough of this childishness. 'Stop it, both of you!' He looked around to see all the maids studiously examining the floor, while the priests seemed absorbed in setting out the materials for the puja. Only young Vibhishan and Shurpanakha looked visibly petrified. Kumbhakarna turned back to his mother and elder brother. 'Let's do the ceremonies quickly. Then you will not have to cause each other any more grief.'

'He doesn't need me to cause him any grief,' said Kaikesi bitingly. 'He's quite capable of doing it to himself.'

Raavan turned to her, fists clenched tight. 'What do you mean, Maa?'

'You know exactly what I mean.'

'I dare you to say it openly. What do you mean?'

Kumbhakarna tried to calm tempers once again. 'Listen, let's do this puja later. We'll come back. Let's...'

Kumbhakarna fell silent as Raavan raised his hand. He stepped closer to his mother, towering over her. The air between them bristled with hostility. 'Say it, Maa. What did you mean?'

Kaikesi didn't step back. The source of all her wealth and power was her eldest son, yet she had grown to despise him. She also knew that however angry he was, Raavan would never harm her. She could get away with saying almost anything. 'Don't forget that I am your mother. I know every little detail of what happens in your life. And you know who I am talking about.'

'Who are you talking about? Say it. Say it!'

Kumbhakarna pleaded with them again. 'Maa, please don't say anything.' He turned to Raavan. 'Dada, let's go. Come on.'

Raavan continued to glare at his mother, molten rage in his eyes. 'Say it!'

'It was all your fault! If you had honoured your mother and listened to her as a good son should, none of this would have happened! Understand that the Gods punished you. They punished someone innocent because of you. It was because of your lack of dharma that the Kanyakumari, the noble Vedavati, was killed!'

'MAA!' Raavan screamed as he reached for his knife.

'Stop!' Kumbhakarna rushed to stand between them, pushing Raavan back and away from their mother. 'Dada, no!'

Raavan was out of control now. He stabbed the knife in the air as he raged at his mother. 'You bitch! You can't survive a day without my protection! And you dare to take her name! You dare to insult the Kanyakumari! You dare to insult Ved…'

Raavan's voice continued to resonate through the corridors as Kumbhakarna almost dragged his brother out of the palace.

—१७६१—

'Love?' asked Vishwamitra, genuinely surprised.

Following the great maharishi's orders, Arishtanemi had investigated the likely cause of Raavan's attitude towards the Sapt Sindhu. And he had, by chance, stumbled on the truth.

'Yes. Apparently, he was in love with a Kanyakumari.'

'Which Kanyakumari?'

'Vedavati.'

Vishwamitra narrowed his eyes and looked at his lieutenant. 'Arishtanemi, how am I supposed to know which Kanyakumari that is? You think I know all their birth-names? Which temple? And for what period?'

'Sorry, Guruji. She was the Kanyakumari of Vaidyanath. And this was a long time ago. Probably two decades at least.'

'So he met her when he was a child?'

'Yes, I believe so.'

'But we never saw her with him, did we? Not since we began tracking him.'

'Apparently they met in his father's ashram and didn't see each other for many years after. Then they met again, perhaps eight or nine years ago. I'm not entirely sure of the time.'

'So you are saying he was in love with her all this time, through his childhood? Even though he didn't meet her for several years?'

'Apparently so.'

'What sense does that make?'

'It makes no sense, but that's what happened. In any case, when he found her again, with his brother's help, she was married to someone else.'

Vishwamitra leaned back as the realisation hit him. 'Lord Parshu Ram be merciful! Is this the former Kanyakumari who was killed in her own village? What was the name of that place… Todee?'

'Yes, Guruji.'

'Her husband was also killed, wasn't he?'

'Yes.'

'And the entire village was exterminated? Brutally?'

'Yes. Nobody really knows what happened, since there were no survivors. Some people from a neighbouring village discovered the bodies a few days later. They chased the wild animals away and performed the funeral ceremonies for all the dead villagers of Todee.'

'But I remember hearing that the corpses of the Kanyakumari and her husband had been cremated with full Vedic honours.'

'Yes. That's what I heard as well.'

'There's only one interpretation possible then,' Vishwamitra said.

Arishtanemi nodded. 'I was thinking the same thing, Guruji. Raavan was attracted to Vedavati, but by the time he found her, she was married to someone else. She must have refused to leave her husband for him, and enraged at her rejection, Raavan killed her and her husband. Perhaps he tried to rape her… we will never know the complete truth. To wipe out any evidence of his crime, he must have massacred the entire village.'

Vishwamitra was too appalled to speak. He'd had a long life—there were some who thought he was at least a hundred and fifty years old—and had seen some terrible things in his time. The world had never been a kind place, but savagery of this magnitude was beyond his imagination. Not since the reign of Trishanku Kaashyap could he remember hearing of anything like it.

'Well, Guruji,' said Arishtanemi, 'we wanted a villain, and we've got one. A monstrous one at that.'

'Kumbhakarna could not have been involved in this, surely,' Vishwamitra said. He had always had a soft spot for the little Naga boy who had come to see him with his mother many years ago.

'I cannot be sure, Guruji. But he is completely under Raavan's thumb.'

Vishwamitra clasped his hands under his chin, deep in thought. Then he took a deep breath and shook his head. 'I met that Kanyakumari once, the Kanyakumari from Vaidyanath… I remember her. She was still a child then. Joyous, and kind to everyone, even animals. How a person treats those weaker than them is a good indicator of their character. Yes, I remember her… She could mimic the sound of a hill myna almost accurately. And she mimicked me as well.' Vishwamitra smiled as he said this. 'A wonderful girl, pure of mind and heart… a truly noble soul. She did not deserve to die the way she did.'

'We have to create an India where such purity and nobility are respected once again, Guruji.'

There was a brief silence, then Vishwamitra said decisively, 'We have to find the Vishnu now. Yes, we have to... We have to revive our great land. We have to make it worthy of our ancestors once again.'

'We have the villain we were looking for,' said Arishtanemi. 'Now, we need to quickly identify the noble Vishnu who will take our plan to fruition.'

Master and disciple looked at each other, their eyes alive with a sense of mission.

—१७—

'Dada!' Kumbhakarna's voice was low and uneven. He seemed to be struggling with his emotions.

It had been five years since the Battle of Karachapa. Raavan had been the ruler of Lanka for more than two years now. The royal family's problems had spilled out into the open, with Kaikesi telling almost anyone who would listen to her that Raavan was not her son anymore, and she did not wish to be associated with him. Instead, she said, Vibhishan and Shurpanakha were to be treated like her own children.

It was obvious to everyone that Kaikesi's status in Lanka— all the luxuries she enjoyed, the charities she funded, the honour she was accorded, and the power she wielded—was founded on her identity as Raavan's mother. But no one had the courage to say this to her face. In fact, many fed her insecurities to get favours for themselves in return.

But of one thing there was no doubt: there was only one true power centre in Lanka, indeed in the entire Indian subcontinent, if not the world, and that was Raavan. And no one dared to confront Raavan. On the contrary, they rushed to obey his every command and followed every instruction unquestioningly. Some went a step further in the hope of winning his approval. It was one such excess that was tormenting Kumbhakarna greatly.

'What is it, Kumbha?' sighed Raavan. 'Just manage whatever needs to be managed.'

'There is nothing left to be managed, Dada.' Kumbhakarna's tone was unfailingly polite, as it always was when he spoke to his brother in public, but he was visibly distraught.

Raavan stared at Kumbhakarna for a moment, and then nodded to the dainty woman sitting on his lap. She got up, picked up her blouse in a single, languid movement, and left. The other dancers in the chamber followed suit.

'So what do you want me to do?'

'You must remove Prahast from the army.'

Raavan's forces were divided into two contingents. One of them, led by officers who had been given the title of MahiRaavan, were responsible for the territories on land. The other group, commanded by officers called AhiRaavan, managed the seas and the ports. Among the AhiRaavans was Prahast, who, since betraying the governor of Chilika, had become an officer in Raavan's army and was greatly feared for his brutality.

'Kumbha, if we need to control the seas, we need ruthless officers like Prahast. Are you forgetting that it's thanks to him that we captured Krakachabahu's wealth many years ago?'

'Dada, there is a difference between ruthlessness and adharma.'

'Don't be immature, Kumbha! There is nothing called dharma or adharma. There is only success and failure. And I refuse to be a failure, ever. I am Raavan.'

'And I am Kumbhakarna, Dada. Nobody in this world loves you as I do. And my job is to stop you from committing a great sin.'

'The only real sin is to be poor and powerless, as we once were. Do you remember how helpless we were in our childhood? We will never go back to those days.'

'Dada, how much more wealth and power do we need? You are the wealthiest man in the world. You are the most powerful man in the world. You don't need more.'

'Yes, I do. You say I am the wealthiest man in the world. Well, I cannot rest till I am the richest man in history. And once I achieve that, who knows, I may want to become wealthier and more powerful than the Gods! Maybe that's not a bad idea, actually. The citizens of Lanka should learn to worship me as a God.'

'Dada, if you want to be a God, then consider how a God would behave. Would he allow the kind of crimes that Prahast has committed?'

'Let me be the judge of how I should behave.'

'Dada, what Prahast has done in Mumbadevi is beyond evil!' said Kumbhakarna.

'Once again, let me be the judge of that. What did he do?'

The Mumbadevi port was situated on the western coast of India, at a strategic point on the sea route between the Indus–Saraswati coast and Lanka. Raavan wanted absolute control over trade in the Indian Ocean—the hub of global trade. Whoever dominated this ocean would dominate the world.

He had managed to gain control over most of the major ports across the Indian subcontinent and the coasts of Arabia, Africa and South-east Asia. In all of these places, he had managed to enforce his usurious Customs duties. He had also, through his ally, King Vali in Kishkindha, put restrictions on the land trade routes south of the Narmada River. He now had the most prosperous region in the world, the Sapt Sindhu, in a vice-like grip. And he squeezed it for riches for himself and for Lanka.

Mumbadevi alone stubbornly refused to charge high Customs duties or turn away any sailor who sought refuge there. The Devendrars, the ruling community of Mumbadevi, believed that commerce had to go hand-in-hand with service, and they would not veer from doing their duty, their dharma. Raavan had decided he had to stop this for the good of his business. There could be no challenge to his vice-like grip: not only would it mean a loss of revenue, it would also weaken his image as the all-powerful king of Lanka.

'He has taken control of the Mumbadevi port,' Kumbhakarna began.

'So? *I* ordered him to take control of the port. Are you questioning my orders?'

'No, Dada! I am not questioning your orders. I am questioning your subordinate's methods.'

'I don't care about the methods. He was supposed to deliver results. If he has, then that's good enough for me.'

'Dada, all of Mumbadevi is destroyed.'

'So what? We can use the Salsette Island close by as a port.'

Kumbhakarna was shocked. 'Dada, did you hear what I just said? Forget about Salsette. All of Mumbadevi is destroyed. Every single Devendrar is dead. Their palace has been burned to the ground, their houses lie demolished. No one has survived—men, women, children. Their bodies were piled high on a mass pyre. The half-charred body of the kindly King Indran was also found. It looks like they were all burned alive.'

Raavan did not react. It appeared that he was momentarily staggered by the news.

'They were all non-combatants,' continued Kumbhakarna. 'They were not warriors. Killing them like this is an act of adharma. I have heard that some of our soldiers were so disgusted by Prahast's actions that they have deserted the army. He has lost nearly a third of his five-thousand-strong brigade. Prahast has come back to Lanka with all the wealth of the Devendrars, hoping that mere gold will stop us from punishing him.'

Raavan looked down, deep in thought. His right hand instinctively reached for the pendant around his neck.

Kumbhakarna moved to kneel beside his brother. 'Dada, you have to punish Prahast. We cannot allow adharma like this. An example has to be set.'

Raavan remained silent for some time before looking up at Kumbhakarna.

'Dada?'

'Yes, an example has to be set,' Raavan said. 'So, here's what we will do. Prahast will be transferred. The wealth he looted from Mumbadevi will be confiscated and added to the Lankan treasury. And we will send out raiding parties after the deserters. A few of them will have to be publicly executed.'

Kumbhakarna looked at his brother in shock.

'Kumbhakarna, I agree with you. Prahast overdid it. But we cannot remove him from the army. We are hated by most of the world. We need his ruthlessness on our side. Also, we simply cannot allow desertions. It would destroy our army. We don't have to go after them all, that would take too much effort. We just need to find a reasonable number, maybe one or two hundred of the deserters. And execute them. That should serve as a warning for the rest.'

'Dada... but...'

'Do it, Kumbha,' said Raavan, the tone of his voice brooking no further disagreement.

The king of Lanka turned towards the door and clapped his hands. The dancers came rushing back in, some of them removing their blouses as they ran. Kumbhakarna knew that the meeting was over.

Chapter 23

Eleven years after the Battle of Karachapa, Lanka's domination of global trade was complete. Not only had Raavan's personal wealth grown beyond measure, but he had transformed the small island kingdom into a world power. The heavy taxes levied on the Sapt Sindhu were bleeding the Land of the Seven Rivers dry, but even in its vastly reduced state, it remained wealthy. There was plenty for Lanka to continue to extract from.

Lanka by now had absolute control over the trade routes and every major port in the Indian Ocean. Consequently, it dominated the flow of trade across the world. The kingdom glittered with riches and had come to be known as Golden Lanka—with zero taxes, heavily subsidised living, free healthcare and education, twenty-four-hour water supply to homes through lead pipes, sprawling public gardens, sports stadiums, concert halls, and so on. There were no poor people in Raavan's Lanka.

Raavan himself, now thirty-eight, had acquired a God-like status in the kingdom. People had begun to worship his likeness in a few temples that had come up over the past year. Only his mother Kaikesi dared to oppose this deification: she had publicly declared that Raavan was dishonouring the ancient Vedic ways by encouraging such worship while he was still alive.

On the personal front, too, things had changed for Raavan. He had finally given in to Kumbhakarna's persuasions and taken a bride. Mandodari was the pious and beautiful daughter of a minor noble called Maya, who was the landlord of two small but prosperous villages in central India. Unfortunately, it soon became clear to her and to others around them, that Raavan had only married her to spite the land he professed to hate. As though he wanted the great empire of the Sapt Sindhu to acknowledge that he had the power not only to defeat their armies and seize their wealth, but to take away their women too. The only positive consequence of the ill-fated union was the birth of a son, Indrajit, whom Raavan truly loved.

The twenty-nine-year-old Kumbhakarna, meanwhile, had become increasingly melancholic. He cherished his brother but was unhappy about some of the things that he was forced to do because of his unwavering loyalty to him. Torn between his love for his brother and a desire to follow his dharma, he had begun to look for excuses to escape Lanka as often as he could. He travelled far and wide, sometimes on trade missions and negotiations, and other times on military expeditions, to put down the menace of piracy on the high seas. He grasped at any legitimate reason to stay away from Sigiriya.

It was on one such trip that Kumbhakarna found himself in the Ethiopian kingdom of Damat, a long-standing ally of Lanka. For as long as anyone could remember, trade between the West and India had flourished via the Western Sea, access to which was through the narrow Mandab strait in the Red Sea or the strait of Hormuz in the Persian Gulf, also called Jam Zrayangh by the locals. Any Egyptian or Mesopotamian trading ship had to enter the Western Sea at either of these points before sailing on to India. In a master stroke, Raavan had conquered the ports of Djibouti and Dubai, which controlled the two straits. Now, ships from Damat and other kingdoms that lay further west had to pay heavy Customs duties at either of these two ports to enter the Western Sea and the main Indian Ocean trade routes.

Kumbhakarna was in the kingdom to meet its ruler and fix the trade quotas and Customs duties for the next year. After the meetings were done, he had decided to stroll around the markets of the city of Yaha-Aksum, the capital of Damat. With just a day to spare before he left for Lanka, there wasn't enough time to explore all the sights and sounds of this beautiful city he was visiting for the first time.

Suddenly, a familiar sound caught his attention—a drumbeat that he did not expect to hear so far from home.

Dhoom-Dhoom-danaa-Dhoom-Dhoom-danaa.

Dhoom-Dhoom-danaa-Dhoom-Dhoom-danaa.

He started walking in the direction of the sound, as if pulled by an invisible thread.

Dhoom-Dhoom-danaa-Dhoom-Dhoom-danaa.

A few minutes later, he found himself in front of a graceful stone structure that looked unexpectedly like an Indian temple—a large platform made of red sandstone at ground level and a spire shooting high up into the sky, like a namaste to the Gods. The outer walls were decorated with beautifully sculpted figures of celestial nymphs, rishis, rishikas, kings and queens, all of whom were dressed Indian-style. The only difference was that their faces were distinctly African.

Kumbhakarna had met a few people from the African continent who had settled in India. He also knew of some rishis and rishikas who were originally from Africa. However, nothing had prepared him for a temple dedicated to Lord Rudra in the heart of Yaha-Aksum.

As he entered the temple, the drumbeats grew louder.

Dhoom-Dhoom-danaa-Dhoom-Dhoom-danaa.

Large stands were placed at different points in the main temple hall, before the sanctum sanctorum. On each of these stands were placed three massive drums, in a row. Tall muscular men, holding long drumsticks, stood on the sides, beating the drums rhythmically. The temple compound was filled with people dancing. A dance of sheer, ecstatic abandon.

The mood was electric, and it instantly infected Kumbhakarna. His body began to move of its own volition, and soon he was dancing as well. The booming ecstasy of Lord Rudra's music filled his mind and soul.

As the beat picked up pace, the dancing grew frenzied. The temple compound was alive with the raw energy of Lord Rudra's devotees. Gradually, the tempo built up till it reached a crescendo and ended with a loud triumphant cry of 'Jai Shri Rudra!'

Kumbhakarna raised his voice in ecstasy to join the call to the Lord.

Glory to Lord Rudra!

'Jai Devi Ishtar!'

Glory to Goddess Ishtar!

Kumbhakarna looked around at the happy faces around him, sweaty from the exuberant dancing. Some had tears of happiness flowing down their cheeks. Some were still in a trance. Strangers hugged, wishing each other well. Kumbhakarna too was embraced. No one seemed to notice that he had deformities, that he was a Naga.

'What brings you here, Kumbhakarna?'

Kumbhakarna turned to see a tall, distinguished-looking man with unblemished chocolate-coloured skin. While his features made it plain that he was a local from Damat, he was dressed in a saffron dhoti and angvastram, the colour of detachment and monkhood. A knotted tuft of hair at the top of his shaven head announced that he was a Brahmin. A flowing salt-and-pepper beard softened his face, and despite his imposing physical presence, he conveyed an impression of tranquillity, with his calm, gentle eyes. He was clearly a man at peace with himself.

Kumbhakarna frowned. 'I've seen you before.'

The Brahmin smiled and nodded.

'Yesterday, at the court?'

'Right,' said the man. 'I was standing at the back. You are observant.'

'I tend to notice important people,' said Kumbhakarna, smiling politely and folding his hands in a respectful namaste. 'But I didn't know you are a fellow devotee of Lord Rudra. What is your name, my friend?'

The man smiled and responded with a namaste. 'You can call me M'Bakur, my friend.'

'M'Bakur?' Kumbhakarna was surprised. 'Do you know, there's an old Sanskrit word called Bakur—it means a war trumpet.'

'I do. And, in our language, when we add the sound *M* to it, it means a *great* war trumpet.'

Kumbhakarna smiled broadly. 'Great name. But you seem to be a man of peace.'

'I've had enough of war. And I have the scars to prove it.'

'So the mighty sword has been put down in favour of temple drums?'

M'Bakur laughed softly. 'Dancing is much more fun than fighting, wouldn't you agree?'

Kumbhakarna laughed too, and nodded.

'I had my reasons for becoming a temple priest,' said M'Bakur. 'What is your reason for being a trade negotiator when your heart is clearly not in it?'

'Excuse me? Are you telling me I am not good at it?' Kumbhakarna was not sure whether to take offense.

'I didn't say that. I just said your heart isn't in it. I watched the negotiations yesterday. I was surprised. You could have asked for better terms. You left too much on the table for us.'

Kumbhakarna remained silent.

'It seemed to me that you were compensating for something. Overcompensating, perhaps. Like helping us would take some load off your mind.'

Kumbhakarna looked around. The temple had largely cleared out. Most of the devotees had left. He looked back at M'Bakur. 'Who are you?'

'Sit with me, my friend,' said M'Bakur in a gentle voice.

They sat in the main temple hall, resting their backs against the pillars. Kumbhakarna looked towards the sanctum sanctorum in the distance. It housed a life-size idol of Lord Rudra: a tall, muscular figure with long, open hair and a flowing beard.

Lord Rudra, as he had been in real life—magnificent and fearsome.

Kumbhakarna folded his hands together and bowed in deep reverence, as did M'Bakur.

The idol of a Goddess placed to the right side of Lord Rudra was nearly as tall as the Lord himself. The serene face had African features, though the body was dressed in an Indian-style dhoti, blouse and angvastram. An egg in the left hand and a long sword in the right identified her as the Goddess of Love and War. Kumbhakarna and M'Bakur bowed to the idol of Lady Ishtar as well.

The Lankan asked once again, 'Who are you?'

'Someone who can help you,' answered M'Bakur.

'Who says I need help?'

'Not everything needs to be said. When you see someone attempting to harm themselves, it is evident that they need help. But I guess you're wondering if you can trust me…'

Kumbhakarna remained silent.

M'Bakur bowed forward and whispered, 'I am a friend of Hanuman.'

Kumbhakarna looked at him, startled. Hanuman was a member of the legendary Vayuputra tribe. A gentle giant with a heart of gold, he was always on hand to help anyone in need. He had saved Kumbhakarna's life once, a long time ago. But he had extracted a promise from him never to speak of it, and Kumbhakarna had honoured that promise. However, he had remained forever grateful to Hanuman, and had always looked for an opportunity to repay that debt.

Any friend of Hanuman's was a friend of his.

'Are you a Vayuputra?' asked Kumbhakarna.

M'Bakur nodded. *Yes.*

'And you don't hate me?'

M'Bakur laughed softly. 'Why should I hate you?'

'I mean…' Kumbhakarna sighed. 'I am…'

'Go on.'

'Look, you are from the divine Vayuputra tribe. The tribe left behind by Lord Rudra. You are tasked with protecting the holy land of India. And I am the brother of the man who is destroying India.'

'Destroying India! Really?' asked M'Bakur, his eyes widening in mirth. 'Do you think your brother is all that powerful?'

Kumbhakarna was nonplussed. He was used to people speaking of his brother in exalted tones. He had never heard someone question his power or the extent of his influence. 'What? I don't understand.'

M'Bakur smiled. 'Tell me, how do you feel about someone destroying India?'

'It's… it's my land. I love my motherland.'

'And is your motherland so weak that one man can destroy it? Or, let me put it another way. If a land is so fragile that a single man can destroy it, does it even deserve to survive?'

'What are you saying?'

'Have you heard of *Matsya Nyay*?'

'Who hasn't? The bigger fish will always eat the smaller fish. I suppose you could call it *the law of the fish.*'

'You do know the law does not just apply to fish, right?'

Kumbhakarna laughed. 'Yes, I do.'

'It's about the law of Mother Nature. The survival of the fittest.'

'Yes, and it's a cruel law. That's why we've moved away from it. We don't kill those who are weaker than us. We protect them.'

'That is the human code of conduct, but nature doesn't work that way. Cruelty and kindness are human concepts.

Nature prioritises balance. And balance sometimes calls for tough love.'

'Tough love?'

'There's love that weakens you, and then there's love that prepares you for what lies ahead. Sometimes that love may appear tough, but it's necessary. If you are a parent who is only concerned with the here and now, you will give your child whatever she wants, because you want to see a smile on her face. But if you are a parent thinking of your child's future, you will realise that spoiling your child is the worst thing you can do.'

'Yes, but if you are too tough, the child will break.'

M'Bakur smiled. 'And that is the difference between nature and us. Mother Nature doesn't keep track all the time, she lets the laws of survival take over. And yes, sometimes the weak break and go extinct. But human beings are different. We can think and… well, we can keep track. We can modulate the tough love to the right level; tough enough to strengthen, but not so tough as to break.'

'What does this have to do with my brother, or me?'

'Have you ever stopped to consider whether, like the play of Mother Nature, there are some larger forces controlling our lives too? That possibly, your brother is a puppet in the hands of such a force?'

Kumbhakarna was too surprised to answer.

M'Bakur changed tack suddenly. 'Have you ever seen forest fires?'

'I have.'

'Are they good or bad?'

'It depends.'

'Depends on what?'

'Depends on whether the fire is controlled or uncontrolled.'

'Exactly. A controlled forest fire removes all the deadwood; deadwood, beyond a point, can turn toxic and destroy the forest. If small, controlled forest fires are not used to clear the ground, the chances of a massive, uncontrolled fire breaking out would increase. And an uncontrolled forest fire could destroy everything. That's not good, right?'

'That's not good at all.'

'Exactly. So a small forest fire is like using a small poison to kill a bigger poison.'

Kumbhakarna stiffened. 'My brother is not a poison.'

M'Bakur smiled. He didn't answer. He didn't apologise either.

Kumbhakarna got up, ready to leave.

'We haven't finished,' said M'Bakur.

'What makes you think you are so much better than my brother?' Kumbhakarna asked, sitting down again. 'To me, your casual acceptance of people suffering for some apparent "long-term good" seems as wrong as what my brother does.'

'You know, from Mother Nature's perspective, the opposite of right is not wrong, it's left.'

'That's just sophistry. What the hell do you mean?'

'I mean that there is no one right way, no ideal solution. The world usually suffers most at the hands of those who believe in perfection, those who don't realise that there is no one ideal. The truly wise, however, realise that you can only look for an optimal solution, not an ideal solution. A solution that could help *most* people is worth pursuing. Because there can't be a solution that will help *all* people. India is suffering because the Kshatriyas have become all-powerful, and in their arrogance, they have been oppressing the Shudras and the Vaishyas. We need to break their stranglehold before society can be set right again. And that is the role that Raavan is playing. He can break the Kshatriyas.'

'Why are you telling me all this? I could go and tell my brother how you are using him.'

'And you expect him to listen to you?' asked M'Bakur. 'Do you think he will suddenly turn dharmic?'

'Do you expect me to believe that you people are dharmic?'

M'Bakur smiled. 'If only questions on dharma could be answered so simply.'

'Try me.'

'Dharma is complex. We could spend whole lifetimes discussing what it is and what adharma is. But what truly matters is whether our intentions are dharmic—the outcome is beyond our control and cannot therefore be a measure of dharma.'

'Intentions?'

'Someone may try to do good for others, like the Vayuputras, for instance, are trying to do. Will we actually succeed? Only time will tell. But we know that our intentions cannot be doubted. We are thinking of the good of others, and not just our own objectives. That is the first step towards dharma. When you ignore your own selfish interests for the sake of others.'

Kumbhakarna leaned forward. 'Once again, why are you telling me all this?'

'Because Raavan's demonic nature may well be used for the greater good. But we want his soul to be saved as well.'

Kumbhakarna frowned. 'And you think I am naïve enough to believe that the Vayuputras care about him?'

'Why not? We care about everyone. We may not be able to help everyone, but we care about everyone.'

'But what do you want from me?'

'We hope that you will help your brother.'

'And what do you think I have been doing?'

'Negotiating bad deals does not help your brother.'

'We have more money than we can ever use. I may as well spread it around a bit. At least some good will come of it. Every bit spent in charity is good for dharma.'

M'Bakur smiled. 'Have you heard of Lord Vidur?'

'Of course I have,' answered Kumbhakarna. 'Who has not heard of the great philosopher, one of the most brilliant men in history?'

'Lord Vidur said that there are two ways to waste money. One, by giving charity to the unworthy. Second, by not giving charity to the worthy.'

'I have been…'

'Your trade concessions help the rulers and traders in my kingdom. They don't need charity. It's the poor who need help. Not only in Damat, but everywhere. Find them and help them. Help them in the name of your brother. Earn some good karma for him. Don't give in to melancholy. Find purpose. I know your brother saved your life at birth. Now it is your duty to help his soul.'

Kumbhakarna looked thoughtful as he listened intently to M'Bakur's words.

'And don't give up on him,' continued M'Bakur. 'We live in a period of constant change. I am sure an opportunity to save Raavan's soul will come again. He may be too ignorant to see it, but he will need you to help him when the time comes.'

Kumbhakarna spoke softly, his eyes moist. 'I have lost my brother. I love him, but I have lost him. I have lost him to his anger. To his pain. I have lost him to his grief over…'

'Over the death of Vedavati,' said M'Bakur. 'I know.'

Kumbhakarna stared at M'Bakur. Shocked that he knew something about Raavan that was so personal. And a secret from most.

'Don't forget that he loves you too. You and his son Indrajit are probably the only people alive whom he truly loves.'

'Indrajit loves him in return. Perhaps even more than I do.'

M'Bakur smiled. 'I know. But he is a little child. He cannot help his father, at least not yet. So it becomes your responsibility to save Raavan. That is your swadharma in this life. Do it well.'

—ᎡᏮᏆ—

'Dada, this money makes no difference to us.' Kumbhakarna was upset and angry. The two extra arms on top of his shoulders stood stiff and straight.

It had been seventeen years since the Battle of Karachapa. Kumbhakarna was in Raavan's private chamber. As usual, there were some half-naked women dancing in the centre of the massive room. Raavan was on his reclining chair, his fingers idly playing with the hair of the woman on his lap. He had a marijuana-infused chillum in his free hand.

Kumbhakarna could have performed the act of charity by himself, with his own money. But he wanted this specific donation to go from Raavan's personal income. It had to be that way.

Raavan took a deep drag of the chillum and stared at Kumbhakarna, a lazy, inebriated smile on his lips. He spoke through the smoke rings. 'I will burn all my money, but I will not let any of it go to the Sapt Sindhu. Even if it is for a hospital in Vaidyanath.'

Kumbhakarna looked around the chamber. The women, the smoke, the alcohol, the marijuana, the excesses. 'You are burning your money already, Dada.'

'Well, I've earned it… I can do what I want with it.'

Kumbhakarna turned to the dancers and said sharply, 'Leave us.'

The women stopped dancing, but didn't leave the hall. They stood where they were, half defiant, half afraid, waiting for Raavan's order.

Kumbhakarna gestured to the woman on Raavan's lap. 'Get out.'

The woman tried to get up, but Raavan pulled her roughly back against his chest. 'Don't cross your limits, Kumbhakarna,' he snapped.

Kumbhakarna stepped forward and pointed at the pendant that hung around Raavan's neck. 'This hospital was a promise you made in the name of the Kanyakumari, Dada. We took on her karmic debts at her cremation ceremony. You may have forgotten it, but I have not. I am going to get that hospital built. It will treat patients free of cost and it will save lives. And you will stamp this hundi with your seal.'

Raavan was silent. There was no expression on his face, neither anger nor remorse, not even grief. He had sought refuge from his pain in drugs, alcohol and silly women. The price for that asylum was the surrender of his mind.

Kumbhakarna stepped forward, took hold of Raavan's hand and pressed the ring on his forefinger, with the royal seal, on the document. The charity was now authorised to spend Raavan's money.

Kumbhakarna glanced at the woman perched uncomfortably on his brother's lap and said, 'You have a wife, Dada. She should not be insulted like this.'

Raavan didn't answer.

Kumbhakarna turned and walked out of the chamber.

The woman on Raavan's lap edged closer to him and caressed his cheek. With an air of affected concern, she whispered, 'I don't like the way your brother speaks to you.'

Raavan's reaction was swift. His fist shot out and hit the woman hard on her face. Breaking her nose. As she tumbled to the ground, screaming in pain, he shouted at the dancers in the distance, 'Get out of here! All of you!' He pointed at the sobbing woman lying at his feet, her face red, her nose streaming blood. 'And take this bitch with you!'

As the women ran from his chamber, Raavan fell back in his chair and held Vedavati's fingers tightly. Tears forced their way through his closed eyes and ran down his cheeks.

You can be better than this. At least try.

Chapter 24

'I don't know if I am doing the right thing. I seem to be causing him a lot of stress,' said Kumbhakarna. 'He is very weak these days.'

It had been a few months since Kumbhakarna had forced Raavan's hand over building a charitable hospital in Vaidyanath. He was now in the temple-town, checking on all preparations before construction began. Money had been allocated. Doctors had been identified and hired. The building was to be ready in a few months. M'Bakur, who had remained in touch with Kumbhakarna over the years, was also in Vaidyanath to help wrap up work.

'Your brother may be many things,' said M'Bakur, 'but he is certainly not weak.'

'The truth is, it's depressing to see him these days. He has almost surrendered to drugs and alcohol. He's nearly forty-five years old, he can't keep abusing his body like this. And I am making it worse with all the stress I am causing him.'

'You're wrong. Stress is good.'

'Oh, come on, M'Bakurji. How can stress be good?'

M'Bakur gestured to a small stove on a platform behind them, on which was placed a vessel filled with water.

Cooking in this boiling water was a simple lunch of eggs and potatoes.

'You see this boiling water?' M'Bakur said.

'What does that have to do with stress?' asked Kumbhakarna.

'It will help you understand.'

Kumbhakarna sighed. 'Why can't you people not speak in riddles?'

'Because speaking in riddles is fun. And you will understand a thought better if you decode it through a riddle. As someone said: *Parokshpriyaa Vai Devaaha.*'

The saying in old Sanskrit roughly translated to, *the Gods like indirect speech.*

'So, philosophy can never be conveyed directly?' questioned Kumbhakarna.

'It can, of course. But it's much more interesting to have it conveyed in the form of a complex riddle. Deciphering the message keeps the fun of philosophy alive. Also, the understanding thus derived feels like an achievement. If there is no sense of achievement or wonder, even the most important message fails to find its target.'

'So, I am expected to understand the bigger point you're trying to make with this boiling water?' asked Kumbhakarna.

'Not only will you understand it, you will arrive at it yourself.'

Kumbhakarna threw up his hands in exasperation. 'All right, then. In answer to your question, yes, I see the boiling water.'

'Both, the eggs and the potatoes, are in the same water, right?'

'Yes, obviously. I can see that.'

'So, they are both being cooked in water boiled to the same temperature, in the same atmosphere, and in the same vessel that is on top of the same fire?'

'Yes.'

'What will happen to the egg in this boiling water?'

'It will become a boiled egg.'

M'Bakur laughed. 'That much is obvious. What I want to know is, how is the boiled egg different from the original egg?'

'It's harder.'

'Absolutely! Now, consider the potatoes. How will they fare in the water?'

Kumbhakarna smiled. 'They will become softer.'

'You see? The same boiling water, the same vessel, the same temperature, yet the eggs harden and the potatoes soften.'

'So the boiling water is like stress. Different people react to it differently. It hardens some and softens others. Is that your point?'

'That's the obvious point, but think about it a bit more. What is the egg like before the stress of the boiling water hits it?'

'It has a tough shell, but the inside is liquid.'

'So the egg is hard on the outside but soft inside. And the boiling water, the stress, makes it hard inside as well, does it not?'

'Yes.'

'Now consider the potato. How would you describe it?'

'It has a flimsy peel—so, soft on the outside and hard on the inside.'

'People respond to stress in much the same way. Those who are soft on the inside become harder with the right amount of stress, and those who are hard on the inside become softer. If you think about it this way, then the right amount of stress becomes necessary to balance your character. Too much stress is not good—it may break you. But no stress is not good either. You need the right amount of stress to balance your character and make you grow.'

'So, are you saying that the stress I'm causing my brother will toughen him up again?'

M'Bakur shook his head. 'I am not talking about your brother. I am talking about you.'

Kumbhakarna frowned, taken aback.

'There are people across the world with biases against your kind, the Nagas. You have a hard, scary exterior. But inside, you are gentle and sensitive. You are one of the finest men I have had the pleasure of knowing.'

Kumbhakarna didn't say anything, though he flushed with pleasure at the unexpected compliment.

M'Bakur continued, 'The truth is that you are the one who is feeling the stress of what's happening to your elder brother. The stress is toughening you up. It's preparing you to face what will come.'

'What will come?'

'The Vishnu.'

'The Vishnu?'

'The seventh Vishnu will come. It will be a tough time for those on the path of adharma. The responsibility of guiding and bringing your brother's soul on to the right path will be yours, Kumbhakarna. You will also have to save the innocents of Lanka. You will need to be tougher.'

'I have heard nothing about a Vishnu coming…'

M'Bakur smiled. 'Only fools react to a fire when it is upon them. The wise see it coming many years before it's even been lit.'

'But why will the Vishnu go after my brother?'

M'Bakur looked at Kumbhakarna, his eyebrows raised at the obviously stupid question.

Kumbhakarna retreated quickly, a little shamefaced. 'Who is this Vishnu? What is his or her name?'

M'Bakur hesitated for a split second before he replied, 'The answer is not clear.'

M'Bakur knew he could not tell Kumbhakarna the truth, but he wasn't lying either. At least, not technically.

— १७१ —

'You called for me, Dada?' asked Kumbhakarna loudly, standing at the door of the chamber.

Twenty years had passed since the Battle of Karachapa. The previous year had witnessed a change in Raavan's attitude. The forty-seven-year-old had worked consciously to subdue his addictions. He had started taking control of his business once again. He would even occasionally inquire about the hospital in Vaidyanath, though he had never visited it.

Kumbhakarna assumed his brother had been shaken out of his apathy and self-indulgence by the tragedy that had suddenly befallen Sigiriya a few years back. A mysterious plague had taken the city in a vice-like grip and all attempts to end it had failed. Strangely, its effects were most evident amongst children. Babies were being born prematurely, and many had died during childbirth. Those who survived were growing up with learning disabilities, loss of appetite, almost constant abdominal pain, sluggishness and fatigue. Some experienced hearing loss and had frequent convulsions or seizures. Adults weren't free of pain either. Many of them suffered debilitating joint and muscle pains and crushing headaches. Large numbers of pregnant women suffered miscarriages and stillbirths and many had died during labour.

While the physical symptoms caused widespread distress, even more harmful was the lowering of morale across the land. The finest doctors in Lanka were unable to understand the cause of the plague, let alone find a cure for it. With almost the entire population suffering in some way or the other, rumours had started up about some kind of a curse that had fallen on Sigiriya.

What worried Raavan the most about the plague was the weakening of his army. He could have strengthened the Lankan forces by recalling a few battalions from the various trading outposts across the Indian Ocean, but that would have left those ports defenceless. Also, it would have alerted Lanka's enemies to the fact that all was not well in the island kingdom, and that, in turn, would have stoked rebellions.

While Raavan applied himself to the task of supplementing the city's defences without word getting out to the Sapt Sindhu, Kumbhakarna's approach to the problem was to invest more money in research and the training of doctors and nurses. He was thinking about this now as he waited for his brother to respond.

Then he heard Raavan's voice. 'Yes, Kumbha. Come on in.'

Kumbhakarna entered Raavan's secret chamber, where many of his elder brother's favourite musical instruments and some of his most treasured manuscripts, numbering in the thousands, were stored. Most importantly, his precious paintings of the Kanyakumari were kept there.

'Why is the lighting so low?' He asked.

Raavan pointed to the torches on the wall. 'You can fire them up now. I needed soft diffused light to complete this last part.'

Kumbhakarna lit the torches and reached his brother's side to see what he had been working on. He gaped at the sight of the canvas.

Raavan asked, 'What do you think?'

Kumbhakarna stopped himself from saying the words that came to his mind. *Scary and magnificent at the same time.*

It was a painting of Vedavati, but not the Vedavati he had known. In the painting, she was the same age she had been when she died, but that was where the resemblance ended. This woman was strong and powerful, her body muscular and sinewy. She was much taller than she had been in real life. Though Raavan had not meddled with her proportions, her curves looked less pronounced because of the more athletic frame. The cumulative impact of all of Raavan's changes meant she looked less nurturing and more fierce, like a warrior princess. She was riding a magnificent horse, her open hair flying in all directions. One hand held a bloodied sword that was raised high, ready to strike again. In front of her, on the muddy ground, on their knees, were many of the kings of the Sapt Sindhu. They looked desperate and fearful. Some had their mouths open in a scream. A few had been beheaded already, while the others were clearly pleading for mercy. In the background, far in the distance, were the common people—the Indians—poor and worn out, but exuberantly cheering their Goddess as she massacred their oppressors.

Scary and magnificent at the same time.

'What do you think?' asked Raavan again.

'It's… it's spectacular, Dada! I don't know what to say,' Kumbhakarna stuttered.

'I am glad you think so,' said Raavan. 'This is how the world should remember her. This is how the world will remember her.'

But this is not how she was.

Kumbhakarna kept his thoughts to himself.

'Look at her face. I have painted her exactly as she was when we last met.'

'Yes, Dada. It's amazing that you still remember her so clearly, even after twenty years and more.'

'How can a soul forget the reason for its existence?'

Before Kumbhakarna could respond, Raavan turned and picked up a letter, his eyes sparkling with excitement. 'Look at this.'

Kumbhakarna took the letter and read it quickly. 'What does this mean?'

'What does it mean?' asked Raavan. 'Are you blind? Read it again. It's clear as crystal.'

'Yes, but…'

'But what?'

'It's an invitation from the kingdom of Mithila to attend Princess Sita's swayamvar.'

Mithila was a kingdom in the Sapt Sindhu whose best days were well behind it. It had been a wealthy river-port town once, settled near the Gandaki River. But the change in the course of the river many years ago, due to an earthquake, had vastly reduced the town's prosperity, and power. However, even in its diminished state, Mithila commanded respect across the Sapt Sindhu. It was a city loved by the rishis and rishikas, and at least in spiritual and intellectual terms, it remained one of the most venerated kingdoms in India.

'Exactly.'

'But why would…'

'Why would I go?'

'This is a trap, Dada. You know the Sapt Sindhu royals hate you. Why would they invite you? Please don't go.'

Raavan looked surprised. 'I thought you wanted me to try and make peace with the Sapt Sindhu.'

Kumbhakarna looked at the painting of Vedavati briefly before turning back to Raavan.

'I began that painting many months ago. I am willing to make a fresh start,' Raavan said. 'This invitation has made me think that maybe we can actually get along with the Sapt Sindhuans. Maybe our wealth can be used for some good too. The question is, are you with me?'

Kumbhakarna remembered M'Bakur's words from more than eight years ago. *I am sure an opportunity to save Raavan's soul will come again… he will need you to help him when the time comes.*

He stepped up to embrace Raavan. 'Of course I am with you, Dada!'

If we can walk away from adharma, the Vishnu will have no reason to attack us.

— १७१ —

Akampana was confused. 'But Iraiva, I don't understand. Mithila? They're… they're nobodies. They're only respected as intellectuals and philosophers. They have no real power.'

Akampana's true lord, Raavan, would normally have told him to shut up and do as he was told. But men of consequence, men who do big deeds, usually have a weakness: they like to speak of their big deeds. They like to hear how great they are, if not in words, then with a look of admiration in the eyes of their acolytes. Raavan was no different. He normally spoke of his plans only to Kumbhakarna. Indrajit was still too young, and Raavan had little respect for anyone else. But lately, communication between the brothers had been strained. Kumbhakarna's constant talk of dharma had begun to weary Raavan.

'You will swear to never speak of this to anyone,' said Raavan.

Akampana immediately made a pathetic attempt at the standard Lankan salute. 'Of course, Iraiva.'

'Not even to Kumbhakarna.'

Akampana's chest swelled with pride. At last, his true lord had realised his value. He was placing greater trust in him than in his own blood. 'Wouldn't dream of it, Iraiva. I swear. I swear on the great Lord Jagannath.'

'So here is what I am going to do. As soon as I win the swayamvar, I will take over Mithila and have King Janak follow my commands. I will force him, and his rishi council, to acknowledge me as a living God. Mithila may be powerless in temporal matters, but when it comes to spiritual matters, it is among the most respected, perhaps even rivalling Kashi. Only the land along the Saraswati River commands greater reverence. If Mithila starts worshipping me as a God, then many other Sapt Sindhu kingdoms will follow its example. They will build temples to me while I am still alive. Then, and only then, can I be assured of immortality.'

There was another aspect to the swayamvar that excited Raavan. His marriage to Princess Sita would be the ultimate humiliation for the Sapt Sindhuans; it would show them that he was capable of taking not only their ports and wealth, but also their women. He had married Mandodari for similar reasons. But Mandodari was the daughter of a mere landlord. Sita was the daughter of a king—a true princess. The thought of snubbing the royals by marrying one of them gave Raavan immense satisfaction. But he couldn't say this to Akampana. Loyal servant though he was, Raavan couldn't possibly discuss his personal life with him.

The loyal servant, meanwhile, was still reeling with shock. 'But Iraiva, do you think that they will...'

'They will.'

'Who am I to disagree with you, great Iraiva? But, I mean... the Sapt Sindhu people are stubborn. They are not as open-minded as we Lankans are. Even the Vishnus and the Mahadevs did not have temples built to them while they were alive.'

Raavan leaned forward, his face close to Akampana's. 'Are you saying that I am less than a Vishnu or a Mahadev?'

'I wouldn't dare suggest it, noble Iraiva! You are greater than them, of course. But I don't know if the Sapt Sindhuans will see this obvious truth. Sometimes people refuse to acknowledge that the Sun God has risen even though it is midday!' Akampana said with an unctuous smile.

'You don't need to worry about that. They will see the truth for what it is. Trust me.'

'I am sure you are right, Iraiva. Why else would they think of inviting you?'

'They didn't think of it. I got them to do it.'

'Really?' Akampana was impressed.

'Yes. Kushadhwaj, the king of Sankashya, is the brother of King Janak of Mithila. He is deep in debt to Lanka. His business affairs have been a mess since his prime minister, Sulochan, died suddenly of a heart attack some years ago. We forgave much of his debt and he arranged the invitation.'

'That was very well handled, great Iraiva.'

Raavan looked pleased with Akampana's compliment. 'Yes, I did handle it well.'

'By the way, we have someone in Mithila too, my lord.'

Raavan had official trade representatives in every kingdom of the Sapt Sindhu. But that was not all. He had also established a secret spy network throughout the kingdoms. These spies and loyalists worked for him undercover, quietly ensuring that his agendas were effectively pursued.

'I didn't think Mithila was important enough for us to have someone stationed there,' said Raavan. 'But I suppose it will serve us well. Who is it?'

'Well, we haven't been actively managing her for years. As you say, my lord, Mithila is not a very important kingdom, and we don't do much trade with it. But our spy is quite high up in the kingdom's administration—the chief of police and protocol in Mithila.'

'Who is he?'

'She, my lord. Her name is Samichi.'

Raavan froze at the mention of the girl. He had not wanted to associate with anyone, except Kumbhakarna, who had been with him when Vedavati was killed. Their presence only reminded him of that terrible day. All the Lankan soldiers who had accompanied him to Todee had been sent to nondescript posts where he would never have to see them again. Hearing

Samichi's name brought back memories and reminded him yet again of his failure to protect Vedavati.

'You speak to her and make sure everything is arranged in my favour,' he said.

'Of course, Iraiva.'

'Nothing must go wrong.'

'Absolutely, Iraiva.'

'And I don't want to see or meet Samichi when I am there. Is that clear?'

Akampana was confused, but he readily agreed. 'Whatever you say, Iraiva.'

—१७I—

The Pushpak Vimaan hovered in the air for some time, as its rotors decelerated slowly. Then, very gently, it descended to the ground. Raavan had excellent pilots working for him.

As the doors slid open, Raavan emerged from the innards of his legendary flying craft, followed by Kumbhakarna. Vali, the king of Kishkindha and scion of the legendary Vaanar dynasty, stood at a safe distance, his entire court in tow.

Raavan's corps of ten thousand soldiers had already left for Mithila, sailing up the east coast of India and then up the Ganga. They would march onward to Janak's kingdom after disembarking from their ships, and wait for Raavan to arrive. Since there were enough days in between, Raavan had decided to stop at Kishkindha on his way to Mithila.

Strewn with massive boulders and rocky hills, the terrain of Kishkindha resembled a moonscape. The mighty Tungabhadra, flowing north-east, meandered through this surreal land before merging with the Krishna River up north.

In consonance with the nature- and idol-worshipping ways of most of the Vedic people, great temples had been built in many parts of the city, venerating the sacred Tungabhadra, the land around it, and the ancient Gods. Each district of Kishkindha was built around a temple, which was surrounded by markets, amphitheatres, libraries, parks and houses. Vali was a wise and strong ruler. His land was prosperous and his people happy. And his reputation for bravery, honour and dignified conduct had spread far and wide.

'Something is wrong,' whispered Kumbhakarna, as they walked towards their waiting hosts.

There was no sign of the traditional Vedic welcome they had expected. No bedecked elephants, no ornamented cows, and no holy men holding ceremonial prayer plates. Not only that, the welcoming party was shrouded in an uncomfortable silence—there was no music or sounds of chanting.

Vali stood quietly at the head, his hands folded in a polite namaste. The king of Kishkindha was a fair, unusually hirsute and extraordinarily muscular man of medium height. He was dressed in full ceremonial attire, but he seemed distracted.

'I don't see Sugreev,' whispered Raavan to Kumbhakarna.

Sugreev was Vali's younger half-brother, and in Raavan's opinion, an effete moron. Most people agreed with Raavan's low opinion of the man, seeing in Sugreev the spoilt, indolent sibling of a great king, one who could not match the accomplishments of his over-achieving elder brother and managed his insecurities by drinking and gambling. Sugreev had committed enough indiscretions to deserve being kicked out of the kingdom, but the protection of their mother, Aruni, had ensured that Vali had not expelled his younger brother.

'Neither do I,' said Kumbhakarna softly.

Raavan smiled, sensing an opportunity.

—र७I—

Kishkindha had a matrilineal society. The ascendency to the throne did not pass from father to son, but from mother to daughter. The husband of the daughter succeeded the husband of the mother as king. But Lady Aruni, headstrong and powerful, had broken with tradition and made her capable elder son the king. She hadn't been blessed with a daughter, and rather than letting the royal line pass to her younger sister's female descendants as tradition dictated, she had decided to keep the throne within her immediate family.

Raavan was familiar with this history, but that was not what interested him right now, as he sat beside Vali in the guest wing of the Kishkindha royal palace. No one else, except Kumbhakarna, was around, not even Vali's bodyguards.

Raavan's expression was carefully calibrated to show concern. 'You look distracted, King Vali. I hope the share of Customs duties being given to you is not too low? My men can be a little greedy at times,' he said.

Vali smiled wanly. 'Your people know that I cannot be pushed around. I am Vali.'

Raavan laughed heartily. 'You're the man, my friend.'

Vali looked at Raavan, a sad expression on his face. Though he remained silent, his bereft eyes seemed to convey a message. *Man? Me?*

Raavan was now confident that the information he had received this morning from his spies was correct. But he had to be certain before he made his move.

'My friend,' he said. 'Where is Angad? I don't see him anywhere. I hope he is well?'

Angad was Vali's five-year-old son and the apple of his eye. The tough, stern and distant Vali, more respected than loved, was a different man when he was with his only son. He played and laughed with him, and indulged him any chance he got. Even occasionally becoming a horse for Angad to ride around on. Since Angad's birth, Kishkindha's citizens, and even the royal family, had come to see a casual, fun-loving side to Vali.

'Yes… Angad… he's…' Vali stopped speaking, his face a picture of agony, his voice choked.

Raavan was now certain his information was correct. He controlled his breathing. He couldn't allow his excitement to show.

Later. I'll take over Kishkindha later. After I've taken Mithila.

Kumbhakarna, on the other hand, was shocked at the distraught look on Vali's face. He had never seen the mighty Kishkindha king like this. 'Great king,' said Kumbhakarna, 'is everything all right?'

Vali suddenly got up and stood in front of them, his hands clasped together. 'Forgive me, my friends. I… I must go. I will come back in a while.'

Raavan and Kumbhakarna also rose immediately.

'Of course, Vali,' said Raavan, his face a picture of concern. 'Please let us know if there is anything we can do.'

'Thank you. We'll speak later.' Saying this, Vali rushed out of the chamber.

Kumbhakarna stared at Vali's retreating form and then turned to his elder brother in bewilderment. 'I didn't realise King Vali was so close to his mother.'

Vali's mother Aruni had passed away just a month ago, after a brief illness.

'It's not about his mother,' said Raavan.

Kumbhakarna looked surprised. 'Then what is it? He looks almost frail. I've never known him to bow down to any misfortune. Something is worrying him.'

Raavan cast a quick glance at the doorway, making sure that they were, indeed, alone. 'What we are speaking of will remain between us. Strictly between us.'

'Of course,' said Kumbhakarna immediately. 'What is this about?'

'It's about Angad.'

'Angad? Has something happened to that lovely child?'

'Nothing has happened to him yet. What matters is what happened before he was born.'

'Before he was born?'

'Yes. Are you familiar with the tradition of niyoga?'

Kumbhakarna was taken aback. Niyoga was an ancient tradition by which a woman, whose husband was incapable of producing a child, could request and appoint another man to impregnate her. For various reasons, this man was usually a rishi.

For one thing, most rishis were revered for their high intellectual prowess, a quality they would hopefully pass on to their offspring. More importantly, since most rishis were wandering mendicants, it was almost certain that they would not lay claim to the child. According to the law, any child produced as a result of a union sanctioned by niyoga would be considered the legitimate child of the woman and her husband; the biological father could not claim fatherhood and would have to remain anonymous.

'From what my spies tell me,' continued Raavan, 'Vali was once very seriously injured while trying to save Sugreev. This happened many years back, during a hunt. The side effect of the medicines that saved his life was that he couldn't have children. This was, for obvious reasons, kept secret.'

'That useless brother of his,' said Kumbhakarna in disgust. 'So, you mean King Vali's wife Tara decided to…'

'Not Tara,' Raavan interrupted him. 'It was apparently his mother. The Queen Mother decided that Vali's child should rule Kishkindha after him. And turned to niyoga for a solution.'

'So what?' asked Kumbhakarna. 'What difference does it make if Angad is not his biological son? The rules are clear. Since King Vali is Queen Tara's husband, he will be considered the father of her son, even if the child was sired by someone else. And Angad is a wonderful boy. He will make a great ruler one day. I can see, even at this young age, that he has his noble father's spirit, drive and intelligence.'

'Well, it's a little more complicated than that.'

'How so?'

'You know what Aruni was like.'

'I have heard stories, yes, of the Queen Mother's headstrong ways…'

'Yes, in any case, I think when people are close to death, they start thinking about their souls. They want to repent for their sins and "speak the truth".'

'What truth did she tell King Vali?'

'Apparently, when Aruni decided that a niyoga was necessary for the sake of an unbroken lineage, she didn't want to take Vali's wife to a rishi.'

'So what did she do?'

'She wanted to ensure that it was *her* bloodline that continued to rule. So she…'

'Oh my God!' Kumbhakarna exclaimed, as the truth hit home.

Sugreev.

Kumbhakarna held his head, feeling Vali's pain. 'I can't even imagine how distraught he must be. Angad is his pride and joy. And now… to know the truth… that it's Sugreev's cowardly blood that runs in Angad's veins…'

'Exactly,' said Raavan.

'Does Angad know?'

'As far as I know, he does not.'

'So the Queen Mother told King Vali this?'

'Yes. On her deathbed, apparently.'

'Why didn't she just remain quiet about it?'

'Guilt? She must have known that she did not do right by Vali and wanted to confess to him before her death.'

'How incredibly selfish! To cleanse her own soul of bad karma, she confessed to her son and gifted him a lifetime of trauma.'

'You know how selfish mothers can be…'

Kumbhakarna ignored the barb. 'Did King Vali confront that coward, Sugreev?'

'Yes, and he confessed to it, said he had no choice in the matter. That he had only complied with their mother's order.'

'Bullshit!' said Kumbhakarna. 'I am sure Sugreev was delighted at the prospect of his child ascending the throne someday.'

'Vali threw Sugreev out of the kingdom when he found out the truth,' said Raavan. 'I would have killed him!'

'Lord Rudra have mercy!' said Kumbhakarna. 'What a mess.'

Raavan sympathised with Vali, but he couldn't help feeling pleased about the good fortune that had fallen into his lap. He could now use the fight between Sugreev and Vali to wipe out the Vaanar dynasty and bring wealthy Kishkindha under the Lankan yoke. Vali's army would become his to command and could then be used for the defence of Lanka, if he so wished.

He breathed a sigh of relief. He might finally have found a solution to the problem he had been struggling with for so long: the depleting strength of his forces in Lanka.

But he didn't think Kumbhakarna would approve of his plan. He would have to handle this alone.

Chapter 25

The Pushpak Vimaan flew smoothly, thousands of feet above the holy land of India, travelling from Kishkindha to Mithila. Raavan and Kumbhakarna were seated in comfortable chairs, strapped in for safety. They would land in Mithila soon, in time for Raavan to attend Princess Sita's swayamvar.

At the moment, though, their minds were not on Mithila, or Sita.

'Celibacy, Kumbha?' sneered Raavan. 'Seriously? Women were created for one purpose alone. And you would deny them that purpose by turning celibate?'

'Seriously, Dada, why are you so disrespectful towards women?' asked Kumbhakarna. He knew he had annoyed his elder brother by announcing that he would undertake the forty-one-day oath that would allow him to travel to Shabarimala, the sacred Lord Ayyappa temple in the deep south of India. Raavan saw this as yet another sign that his brother was moving away from him and towards a strictly dharmic way of life.

'Would you rather I respect them, dear brother?' asked Raavan, laughing. 'Trust me, women are not looking for respect or honour. They want someone to pay their bills and to give them protection. In return, they are prepared to give love, or something resembling it!'

'Dada, you are about to get married for the second time. I really think you need to update your views on women.'

'Listen, Kumbha, I have more women in a fortnight than you have had in your entire life. I know how they think. They may say they like nice, sensitive men. But remember, women never say what they mean. In reality, they dismiss the gentle, domesticated sort of men as weak and unreliable. They want real men—tough, strong men.'

'Our dharma says that a real man is one who respects women.'

'So a real man is one who surrenders himself and becomes a doormat for women?'

'I never said that. A real man is one who respects himself and treats others with respect too.'

'Bullshit. I can tell you from personal experience, four women don't add up to the worth of one man. In fact, even four hundred women do not add up to the worth of one man.'

'What nonsense! Do you even hear yourself, Dada?'

'All the time. And I don't hear anything wrong!'

Kumbhakarna took a deep breath to control his irritation. 'Forget it. Your views cannot shake my beliefs or the vows that I will undertake for Lord Ayyappa.'

'How does your being celibate please a God?' sniggered Raavan, clearly trying to annoy Kumbhakarna.

'It's not only about celibacy, Dada,' Kumbhakarna explained patiently. 'By taking the *vow*, I am pledging my loyalty to Lord Ayyappa, the son of the previous Mahadev, Lord Rudra, and the Vishnu, Lady Mohini. Though Lord Ayyappa is worshipped across the land in thousands of temples, the *vratham* applies only to the temple of Shabarimala. A small forest-dwelling community in that region, led by Shabari, the Lady of the Forest, maintains the temple. And for all devotees, the rules are clearly laid out.'

Kumbhakarna ticked off the rules on his fingers: 'We will not eat meat or consume alcohol during the period of the forty-one-day vratham. We will sleep on the floor. We will not hurt anyone, either physically or with our words. We will stay away from all social functions. The point is to live simply and focus on high thinking.'

'All that sounds very noble. But tell me something, you keep talking about how much you respect women. You do know that women are not allowed into the Shabarimala temple? Isn't that disrespectful to them?'

'Women are allowed! Of course they are. Only women who are in the reproductive stage of their life are not allowed in this particular temple. Basically, women who are capable of menstruating are forbidden entry.'

'Aha! So you think reproduction is impure? And menstruating women will contaminate the temple? Do you know that in the Kamakhya temple in north-east India, menstrual blood is considered sacred and worshipped?'

'You are misunderstanding me on purpose, Dada. The ban on menstruating women has nothing to do with menstrual blood being impure. How can any Indian think that? It's about the path of *sanyas*, of *renunciation*.'

Kumbhakarna continued, 'As you know, practically all the temples in India follow the *gruhasta* route, the path of the *householder*. The rituals in these temples are built around the worldly life, celebrating relationships like that between a husband and wife, or a parent and child, or a lord and his subjects. The *renunciates* or *sanyasis* have temples too, many of them being rock-cut caves in remote mountainous regions; non-sanyasis are not allowed entry into these. The only way of entering a sanyasi temple is by giving up all worldly attachments, renouncing one's family and material belongings, and permanently joining a sanyasi order.'

Raavan pretended to be alarmed. 'Are you becoming a sanyasi? Are you going to leave me? What the hell!'

Kumbhakarna laughed. 'Dada, listen to me. The Shabarimala temple is not for those who have taken permanent sanyas. We just have to be sanyasis for the forty-one days of the vratham. It essentially gives us a short experience of the life of a sanyasi. If you understand this, then all the vows I mentioned earlier make sense. For these forty-one days, we have to stay away from all the pleasures and comforts of life, as well as extreme emotions. That's why the rule against consumption of intoxicants or meat, and sex. The temple is dedicated to the male sanyasi route, women in their reproductive phase are not allowed in, but young girls and older women are welcome. Similarly, there are temples dedicated to the female sanyasi path, where adult men are not allowed, like the Kumari Amman temple. There are temples for the sanyas of transgender people too. Misunderstandings arise because you worldly people don't know enough about our sanyasi ways.'

'Okay, okay, I give up,' said Raavan, holding his hands up in mock surrender. 'Go for your pilgrimage. When is it? In a few months?'

'Yes.' Kumbhakarna smiled and murmured, '*Swamiye Sharanam Ayyappa.*'

We find refuge at the feet of Lord Ayyappa.

While he may have been mocking his younger brother, Raavan was not about to disrespect Lord Ayyappa. The forest Lord was, after all, the son of Lord Rudra and Lady Mohini. He was considered to be one of the greatest warriors that ever lived.

He repeated after Kumbhakarna, 'Swamiye Sharanam Ayyappa.'

Before Raavan could say anything more, a loud announcement was heard. 'We are about to land. Please check your straps.'

Raavan and Kumbhakarna double-checked the straps with which they were secured to their chairs. The hundred soldiers within the Pushpak Vimaan did the same.

Raavan looked down at *Mithila*, the *city for the sons of the soil,* through the portholes. From up in the air, Mithila looked very different from the other large Indian cities, which were mostly located on the banks of rivers. Mithila had originally been a river-port town, but after the Gandaki River had changed course to flow westward a few decades ago, the fate of Mithila had altered dramatically. From being counted among the great cities of the Sapt Sindhu, it had witnessed a speedy decline. It was now far poorer than the other cities of the empire, which were themselves being rapidly impoverished by Raavan. So much so that Raavan had dismissed his appointed sub-traders in Mithila. There simply wasn't enough work for them.

'It's rare to see such a dense forest coming almost all the way up to the city,' said Raavan.

Being a fertile, marshy plain that received plentiful monsoonal rain, the land around Mithila was extremely productive. Since the farmers of Mithila had not cleared too much land, the forest had used the bounty of nature to create a dense border all around the city.

'Look at the moat,' said Kumbhakarna, surprised.

From the air, they could see a body of water around the fort that must have served as a defensive moat once, with crocodiles in it for preventive security. Now, it was a lake to draw water from.

The lake circumscribed the entire city within itself so effectively that Mithila was like an island. Giant wheels drew water from the lake, which was carried into the city through pipes. Steps had been built on the banks for easy access to the water.

'They don't have a proper defensive moat anymore!' said Raavan, astonished.

'I think it's a smart move. They don't need one. Why would anyone attack Mithila? There is no money to be looted here. And they freely distribute their only treasure: their knowledge.'

'Hmm… you're right.'

As the brothers looked at the moat around the fort, they observed an inner wall, about a kilometer inside the main fort wall. The area between the outer and the inner fort walls was neatly partitioned into plots of agricultural land. The food crops appeared ready for harvest.

Raavan was impressed. 'Good idea. At least someone in Mithila has military sense.'

Growing crops within the fort walls would secure the food supply during any siege. Also, since there was no human habitation there, this area would be a killing field for anyone who managed to breach the outer wall. An attacking force would lose too many men in the effort to reach the inner wall, without any hope of a quick retreat.

Kumbhakarna agreed with his elder brother. 'Yes, it's a brilliant military design; two fort walls with uninhabited land in between. We should try it too.'

As the Pushpak Vimaan hovered over the ground for a little while, they could see one of the main gates of Mithila. There were no coat of arms emblazoned across the gate, unlike in most forts in India.

Instead, an image of *Lady Saraswati*, the *Goddess of Knowledge*, had been carved into the top half of the gate.

There was a couplet inscribed below the image, but it was not readable from this distance.

'I wonder what the couplet says,' said Raavan.

'I remember Akampanaji telling me about it,' said Kumbhakarna.

> '*Swagruhe Pujyate Murkhaha;*
> *Swagraame Pujyate Prabhuhu;*
> *Swadeshe Pujyate Raja;*
> *Vidvaansarvatra Pujyate.*'
>
> *A fool is worshipped in his home.*
> *A chief is worshipped in his village.*
> *A king is worshipped in his kingdom.*
> *A knowledgeable person is worshipped everywhere.*

Raavan smiled. Truly, a city dedicated to knowledge. Truly, a city beloved of the rishis. Truly, a city that would serve his purpose well.

Small, circular metal screens descended over the portholes, blocking the view.

'We're landing,' said Kumbhakarna.

As the thunderous sound of its rotors dipped, the Pushpak Vimaan slowly descended to the ground. It touched down in the space earmarked for it, far outside the outer fort wall, in the clearing ahead of the forest line. Raavan's bodyguard corps of over ten thousand soldiers had already gathered there, in orderly formation.

Raavan took a deep breath. 'Time for action.'

— ₹б‍I —

'Something is not right, Dada,' said Kumbhakarna. 'Let's leave.'

Raavan had set up camp outside Mithila. Safer to be there, surrounded by his soldiers, than within the city walls of a Sapt Sindhu kingdom. A kingdom that he had, through his trade policies, impoverished.

'But King Kushadhwaj invited me himself!' said Raavan, outraged. He had been waiting for Kumbhakarna and his aides to return from their visit to the royal court in Mithila, where they had gone to announce his arrival.

'I know, but he was quiet throughout. So was King Janak.'

'Then who the hell was speaking?'

'Guru Vishwamitra.'

'What in Lord Indra's name is Guruji doing here? There is no debate during a swayamvar ceremony!'

'I don't know what he is doing here, but I can tell you that he seemed to be making all the decisions. And I was not even allowed to meet Princess Sita.'

'What does this mean?' Raavan was getting more and more agitated. 'I am Lanka. Ruler of the most powerful kingdom in the world. The richest land on earth. I have done Mithila a favour by agreeing to come here to win the hand of Sita. How can they treat me this way?'

'Dada, let's just leave. The Sapt Sindhuans will never accept us. You tried. You did it with a clean heart. You wanted to make a fresh start. But these people won't let that happen. To hell with this "Aryavarta". Let us be happy in Lanka, in our own corner of India. Let's leave.'

'And let the entire world know I was humiliated? So that any insignificant bastard can rebel against me tomorrow? Never. I will not leave!'

'Dada, listen to me. Guru Vishwamitra was trying to tell me, without actually saying so, that you would not be welcome at the swayamvar. Each time I looked at King Kushadhwaj, he was busy examining the floor. He didn't say a word. None of this bodes well.'

'Why didn't you tell them that we were invited by that fool Kushadhwaj?'

'What's the point, Dada? He did not want to acknowledge us. We are not welcome here. Let's just leave.'

'No, we will not!'

'Dada…'

'Raavan will not be insulted this way! Lanka will not be insulted this way! I don't care what they think. I will go to the swayamvar and I will win. I will leave with Sita, even if I just throw her into the dungeons of Sigiriya afterwards. I will win this swayamvar. I will redeem my honour!'

'Dada, I don't think that—'

'Kumbhakarna! My decision is final!'

—र७I—

On the day of the swayamvar, Raavan and Kumbhakarna left their camp, accompanied by thirty soldiers. Fifteen marched ahead of them and fifteen behind. The soldiers were dressed in their ceremonial best, as the representatives of the richest kingdom in the world ought to be. They carried the standard of Lanka: black flags, with the head of a roaring lion emerging from a background of fiery flames.

Given that they were not welcome at the swayamvar, Kumbhakarna had arranged for a battalion of a thousand soldiers, armed to the teeth, to follow Raavan and his bodyguards. They were to wait outside the venue of the swayamvar. Kumbhakarna wanted to play it safe, but without provoking the Malayaputras.

The Lankans crossed the pontoon bridge over the lake and marched through the open gates of the outer wall, and then past the inner wall. The soldiers behind Raavan and Kumbhakarna blew on their conch shells, attracting as much attention as they could.

Most of the citizens of Mithila were headed to the swayamvar, or had already got there. The few who remained in the city came out of their houses to stare at the procession. The procession of the richest and most powerful man in the world. Faced with the pomp and grandeur of the Lankan party, the peaceful inhabitants of Mithila withdrew. They did not want to offend or aggravate the Lankans in any way.

Raavan kept his eyes on the path ahead, his posture that of a king returning victorious from battle. He refused to even glance at the meek citizens of Mithila.

The swayamvar had been organised in the Hall of Dharma, inside the palace complex, instead of at the royal court. The building had been donated by King Janak to the Mithila University and the hall regularly hosted debates and discussions on various esoteric topics—the illusion of this physical world, the nature of the soul, the source of Creation, the value and beauty of idol-worship, 'the philosophical clarity of atheism… King Janak was a philosopher-king who focused all his kingdom's resources on matters of spiritual and intellectual interest.

The circular hall was crowned with a large, elegant dome. Its walls were decorated with portraits of the greatest rishis and rishikas from times past. In some ways, the circular design embodied King Janak's approach to governance: a respectful regard for all points of view. During debates, everyone sat at the same level, as equals, without a regulating 'head', deliberating issues openly and without fear.

For the purpose of the swayamvar, temporary three-tiered spectator stands had been erected near the entrance to the hall. At the other end, on a wooden platform, was placed the king's throne. A statue of the great King Mithi, the founder of Mithila, stood on a raised pedestal behind the throne. Two thrones, only marginally less grand, were placed to the left and right of the king's throne. A circle of comfortable seats lined the middle section of the great hall, where kings and princes – the potential suitors – were seated.

Accompanied by the loud cacophony of Lankan conch shells, Raavan and Kumbhakarna made their grand entry along with their entourage of thirty bodyguard. The battalion of one thousand soldiers waited outside the hall. Out of sight, but close at hand. Ready to charge to the aid of their king if summoned.

Raavan and Kumbhakarna walked ahead, looking around at the arrangements.

The upper levels of the three-tiered spectator stands were packed with ordinary citizens, while the nobility and the rich merchants occupied the first platform. The contestants sat in a circle, on comfortable chairs, in the middle section of the hall. Every seat was occupied. Princess Sita would be able to see all that was going on without being visible herself, as she had decided to make it a *gupt swayamvar.*

In the centre of the hall, placed ceremoniously on a table top, was an unstrung bow. The legendary Pinaka, the bow of Lord Rudra Himself. A number of arrows were placed beside it. Next to the table, at ground level, was a large copper-plated basin. Competitors were required to first pick up the bow and string it, which itself was no mean task. They would then have to move to the basin, which was filled with water, with more trickling in steadily from the top. This created gentle ripples within the bowl, spreading out from the centre towards the edge. To make things more difficult, and unpredictable, the drops of water were released at irregular intervals.

A hilsa fish was nailed to a wheel, which was fixed to an axle that was suspended from the top of the dome, a hundred metres above the ground. The wheel revolved at a constant speed. The contestants were required to look at the reflection of the fish in the unstill water below, and use the bow to fire an arrow into the eye of the fish. The first to succeed would win the hand of the bride.

Raavan did not pause to look at the task set for the potential suitors. Neither did he appear to notice that his entry into the hall had interrupted the speech of the great Malayaputra, Guru Vishwamitra. This was an unprecedented insult to the maharishi. But Raavan did not seem to care. For something else had caught his attention. Every seat in the competitors' circle was occupied.

They haven't reserved a place for me! The bloody bastards!

Raavan's entourage moved to the centre of the hall and halted next to Lord Rudra's bow. The lead bodyguard made a loud announcement. 'The King of Kings, the Emperor of Emperors, the Ruler of the Three Worlds, the Beloved of the Gods, Lord Raavan!'

Raavan turned towards a minor king who was sitting closest to the Pinaka, grunted softly, and gestured with his head. The terrified man rose without question and scurried away to stand behind another competitor. Raavan walked towards the chair, but did not sit. He planted his right foot on the seat and rested his hand on his knee. Kumbhakarna and his men fell in line behind him. Then, almost lazily, Raavan turned his gaze to the other end of the hall, where the thrones were placed.

Maharishi Vishwamitra was seated on the royal throne of Mithila, the one customarily reserved for the king. The present king of Mithila, Janak, sat on the smaller throne to the right of the great maharishi, while the king's younger brother, Kushadhwaj, sat to the left of Vishwamitra.

Raavan spoke loudly to Vishwamitra in the distance. 'Continue, great Malayaputra.'

Raavan did not even deem it fit to apologise for the great insult of interrupting the chief of the Malayaputras in the middle of his speech.

Vishwamitra was furious. He had never been treated so disrespectfully. 'Raavan…' he growled.

Raavan stared back at him with complete insouciance.

Vishwamitra managed to rein in his temper; he had an important task at hand. He would deal with Raavan later. 'Princess Sita has decreed the sequence in which the great kings and princes will compete.'

Raavan took his foot off the chair and began to walk towards the Pinaka while Vishwamitra was still speaking. The chief of the Malayaputras completed his announcement just as Raavan was about to reach for the bow. 'The first man to compete is not you, Raavan. It is Ram, the prince of Ayodhya.'

Raavan's hand stopped a few inches from the bow. He looked at Vishwamitra and then turned around to see who had responded to the sage. He saw a young man, around twenty years of age, dressed in the simple white clothes of a hermit. Behind him stood another young, though gigantic man, next to whom was Arishtanemi. Raavan glared first at Arishtanemi, and then at Ram. If looks could kill, Raavan would have certainly felled a few today.

This is that little kid born in Ayodhya on the day I defeated his father! And Vishwamitra has the gall to put this child up against me? Against the king of Lanka? Against the ruler of the world?

Raavan turned to face Vishwamitra, his fingers wrapped around Vedavati's finger-bone pendant that hung around his neck. He needed her. He needed her voice. But he couldn't hear anything. Even she had abandoned him during this great humiliation.

Raavan growled in a loud and booming voice, 'I have been insulted!'

Kumbhakarna, who stood behind Raavan's chair, was shaking his head imperceptibly. Clearly unhappy.

'Why was I invited at all if you planned to make unskilled boys compete ahead of me?!' Raavan's body was shaking with fury.

Janak looked at Kushadhwaj with irritation before turning to Raavan and interjecting weakly, 'These are the rules of the swayamvar, Great King of Lanka…'

A voice that sounded more like the rumble of thunder was finally heard. It was Kumbhakarna. 'Enough of this nonsense!' He turned towards Raavan. 'Dada, let's go.'

Raavan suddenly bent and picked up the Pinaka. Before anyone could react, he had strung it and nocked an arrow on the string. Most people could not even lift the mighty Pinaka easily. Yet Raavan, in a supreme display of strength and skill, had smoothly picked it up, strung the bow and nocked an arrow before anyone could react. The speed and dexterity with which he moved was mind-numbing. Even more remarkable was the target of his arrow.

Everyone sat paralysed as Raavan pointed the arrow directly at Vishwamitra, the great maharishi and the chief of the legendary Malayaputras.

The Malayaputras were the tribe left behind by the previous Vishnu. So their chief was, in a way, a representative of the Vishnu. For someone to even say a rude word against the chief Malayaputra was unprecedented. But for someone, even a man as powerful as Raavan, to point an arrow at Vishwamitra? It was unthinkable.

The crowd gasped collectively in horror as Vishwamitra stood up, threw his angvastram aside, and banged his chest with his closed fist. 'Shoot, Raavan!'

Everyone was stunned by the warrior-like behaviour of the great maharishi. Such raw courage in a man of knowledge was rare. But then, Vishwamitra had been a warrior once.

The sage's voice resounded in the great hall. 'Come on! Shoot, if you have the guts!'

I should shoot him. The pompous nutcase… But the medicines… For Kumbhakarna… For me…

Raavan shifted his aim ever so slightly and released the arrow. It slammed into the statue of King Mithi behind Vishwamitra, breaking off the nose of the ancient king.

The king of Lanka looked around. He had insulted the founder of the city. The ancient king was respected and idolised by all. His memory remained sacred even today. Raavan expected at least some Mithilans to respond with righteous rage.

Come on! Fight for King Mithi's honour. Give me an excuse to order all my soldiers in and massacre all of you!

But no Mithilan stood up. Shamefully, swallowing their pride, they remained seated even at the public insult to the memory of the founder of their kingdom.

Cowards!

Raavan dismissed Janak with a wave of his hand as he glared at Kushadhwaj. He threw the bow on the table and began to walk towards the door, followed by his guards.

In all this commotion, Kumbhakarna stepped up to the table, quickly unstrung the Pinaka, and reverentially brought the bow to his head with both hands.

My apologies, great Lord Rudra. My brother did not mean any insult to your sacred bow. He has surrendered to his emotions. Please don't hold this against him.

With utmost respect and dignity, Kumbhakarna placed Lord Rudra's bow, the Pinaka, back on the table. Then he turned around and briskly walked out of the hall, following a seething Raavan.

Chapter 26

'How dare they!' Raavan was pacing up and down inside the stationary Pushpak Vimaan. 'How dare they? I am Lanka! I am their lord! How dare they?'

Kumbhakarna tried to calm him. 'Let it be, Dada. I told you what to expect. Let's just leave.'

'Leave? Leave? Are you crazy, Kumbhakarna?'

Kumbhakarna knew that if his elder brother was calling him by his proper name instead of 'Kumbha', he was in no mood to listen to any brotherly advice about staying calm.

'These pathetic losers have insulted me,' Raavan hissed, his fists clenching and unclenching. 'They have humiliated me in public. They will pay the price!'

'Dada,' Kumbhakarna said, his tone even. 'What do you intend to do?'

Raavan pointed towards Mithila. 'I'll burn the city to the ground! I'll kill everyone in it! I'll grind this city of the sons of the soil into the soil!'

'Dada, why punish innocent civilians for the crimes of their leaders?'

'If civilians don't rebel against the crimes of their leaders, then they are criminals too!'

'But Dada—'

'No buts! I said they are criminals too!'

Kumbhakarna changed tack, trying to appeal to reason rather than compassion. 'Dada, the crown-prince of Ayodhya is in there. Apparently, he won the swayamvar for Princess Sita's hand. He will not abandon his wife and escape Mithila. My intel also tells me that, over the last few years, Prince Ram has become Emperor Dashrath's favourite son. If we end up killing him, the emperor will almost certainly declare war on us. And if the emperor calls for war, treaty obligations will force other kingdoms to join too. You know we cannot afford to fight a war right now. It's only our reputation that keeps us safe.'

Raavan cursed. Kumbhakarna was right. The plague had weakened the Lankan army. An all-out war was out of the question.

But Raavan's anger would not be pacified easily. 'Whatever it is, we are not leaving,' he said.

'Dada, I was told by Akampana, who had it from Samichi, that there are nearly four thousand policemen and policewomen in Mithila. They will be able to put up a fight.'

'But we have ten thousand Lankan warriors.'

'Even a five-to-two advantage will be negated by their defensive double walls. You know that.'

Raavan was not ready to give up. 'I've heard that there's a secret tunnel on the eastern side of that inner wall. We can send a small force to enter the city through the tunnel. Once our soldiers overpower the guards at the gateway and fling the main city gates open, the army can take over. We will massacre them!'

Kumbhakarna had also heard about the secret tunnel from Akampana, who had sourced the information from Samichi.

Akampana had told Kumbhakarna that while agreeing to lead them through the secret tunnel, Samichi had exacted a promise from the Lankan that Princess Sita would not be harmed during the attack. This was a bizarre demand from someone who had sworn loyalty to Raavan and Lanka. Maybe all the talk of a secret tunnel was a trap. Kumbhakarna doubted Samichi's loyalty. Clearly, Raavan did not.

'Prepare for an attack,' he said.

'Dada, I still think—'

'I said, prepare for an attack!'

Kumbhakarna took a deep breath, bowed his head and whispered unhappily, 'Yes, Dada.'

—ॐI—

It was late at night, the fourth hour of the fourth prahar. Torches lined the Lankan camp. Raavan's bodyguards had been working feverishly through the evening, chopping down trees in the forest and building rowboats to carry them across the moat. Simply marching across was out of the question since the Mithilans had destroyed the pontoon bridge.

Raavan was standing beside the lake, looking across the water to the fort walls. He wore armour that covered his torso. Two swords and three knives hung from his waist. Two smaller knives were hidden in his shoes. An arrow-filled quiver was tied to his shoulders, across his back. He held a bow in his left hand. Raavan was ready for battle.

Standing next to the king of Lanka was Kumbhakarna. He had even more weapons on his person than Raavan, since the extra arms on top of his shoulders were also capable of flinging knives.

Their soldiers were armed and ready too. Ten thousand Lankans stood at a distance, close to the boats—on full alert, and with a reputation to protect.

Raavan lowered the scope he was looking through. 'They have nobody on the outer walls.'

Kumbhakarna pulled up his own scope and looked through it, examining the walls thoroughly. 'Hmm. That makes sense. They want us to scale the outer wall. Most of their soldiers are on the ramparts of the inner walls. While we are rushing towards the inner walls, they will fire arrows on us and hope to kill as many of our soldiers as possible in that zone of death.'

Raavan sniggered. 'Somebody in that namby-pamby city of intellectuals has battle sense, but not enough to match ours. We won't be climbing over the inner walls. We'll be racing through the open gates.'

Kumbhakarna nodded.

'When are we likely to get news?' asked Raavan.

Kumbhakarna continued to stare at the fort as he replied, 'The fact that we haven't got news till now does not bode well.'

'I don't care. We are not retreating.'

Kumbhakarna turned to his elder brother. 'I know, Dada.'

Just then, Akampana came rushing towards them. 'Iraiva! Iraiva! It was a trap!'

'Softly, you fool!' hissed Raavan.

'What happened?' asked Kumbhakarna.

'The secret tunnel had already collapsed onto itself, great Iraiva. Even worse, that traitor Jatayu and his Malayaputras were on top of the wall, firing arrows at us. We lost half the platoon. Ten of the men escaped somehow to give me the news. Perhaps Samichi has been discovered and forced to reveal our battle strategy to them.'

'Or Samichi lied to us,' said Kumbhakarna.

'It doesn't matter,' said Raavan. 'We are still attacking.'

'Dada…'

'I have a backup plan.'

Kumbhakarna looked towards the boats. Large wooden contraptions were being loaded on to them. 'What's that?'

'My backup plan,' said Raavan. 'Let's go.'

The soldiers began to push their boats into the moat. It would take half an hour for all the ten thousand soldiers to cross the lake and assemble on the other side of the water, outside the fort.

The Battle of Mithila had begun.

—ॐ—

The Lankans organised themselves outside the outer walls with great efficiency.

Since there was no resistance—no Mithilan soldiers on the ramparts shooting arrows at them or pouring down boiling oil—they could move about freely.

Kumbhakarna, meanwhile, was staring in wonder at Raavan's innovation—his backup plan.

'This is brilliant, Dada. It just might work,' said Kumbhakarna.

'It *will* work!' said Raavan.

'You're the man! You still have it.'

'I never lost it!' said Raavan.

The object of Kumbhakarna's admiration, a device Raavan had invented, was simple in design and devastating in its potential to destroy. It consisted of a large stand with an enormous bow, almost the size of a man, fixed at the far end, horizontal to the ground. The bow was fastened to an axle at the centre, with an extremely thick bowstring attached to it. A rough seat had been built at the other end of the stand, where the archer would sit. The job of the archer was to load an enormous arrow, almost the size of a small spear, onto the bow, then pull the bowstring back with both hands and let it fly. A system of gears and pulleys allowed the stand to be adjusted so that the direction and angle of the arrow could be controlled.

There were a thousand of these stands, with one thousand bows mounted on them.

Essentially, Raavan had adopted the standard tactic of an attacking army firing arrows at soldiers on a fort wall and turbo-charged it.

They already knew, thanks to Samichi's information, that the 'soldiers' on the Mithila side were mere police personnel, not warriors. They would not have metallic shields, only wooden ones. Shields that were good enough to stop a hail of arrows but were certainly not sturdy enough to stop missiles the size of spears.

'They won't know what hit them,' Kumbhakarna said. 'They'll keep wondering how we are managing to reach them with spears thrown from outside the outer walls. They'll wonder if we have monsters and giants in our army!'

Raavan grinned, the bloodlust rising in him. Nothing got his heartbeat going like the heat of battle. 'They won't have time to wonder. They'll be too busy dying.'

'Should I order the attack?'

Raavan looked around. Long ladders had been set up against the outer walls of the fort. Spotters had been stationed on top of the ladders, each with a scope, to focus on the inner walls of Mithila and report the destruction that would follow shortly. Raavan expected the Mithilan soldiers to flee as soon as the attack of the spears began. But a good general trusts hard data more than his expectations. Unlikely though it was, there was still the chance that a few courageous Mithilans would put up a fight. Once he received confirmation that there were no Mithilan defenders in sight anywhere near the inner fort wall, the Lankan soldiers would scale the outer walls and charge.

Raavan looked at Kumbhakarna. 'Let's begin the massacre.'

Since this was a charge at night, orders could not be conveyed through flags. Kumbhakarna turned to his herald and nodded. The herald immediately raised a conch shell and blew into it. The signal rolled out, the length and the breaks in the sound conveying Raavan's message to the soldiers. The other heralds across the Lankan lines repeated the signal.

The archers began putting arrows to the massive bows. After a brief pause, the conch shells signalled again and a fusillade of Lankan spears was released. A thousand missiles flew together on their deadly journey towards a city built for knowledge and not war. The Mithilans cowered behind their wooden shields. Shields that were utterly inadequate for blocking the spears coming their way.

Raavan and Kumbhakarna waited for a sign from the lookouts. A moment later, each of them could be seen raising a closed fist, almost in unison.

A loud cheer went up from the Lankans on the ground below. '*Bharatadhipa Lanka*!'

Lanka, the Lord of India! Or more accurately, *Lanka, the ruler of India!*

'Direct hit!' roared Raavan. The spears had torn into the Mithilan ranks amassed at the inner fort wall. 'No time to waste! Fire one more volley.'

The archers bent to their task immediately. It would take a few minutes for all the bows to be ready.

'We cannot fire once our men scale the outer wall,' said Kumbhakarna. 'We may hit our own soldiers while they are running towards the inner wall.'

'That is why I want another round of spears fired,' said Raavan. 'I want the Mithilans in retreat before we charge.'

Kumbhakarna looked up at the lookouts. Almost all of them had both hands above their heads in a swinging motion.

'Look, Dada! We may not have to fire another round,' said Kumbhakarna. 'They are in retreat already.'

Raavan grunted in disgust. 'Bloody cowards. Can't even withstand one volley!'

'Should we charge?'

'No. Fire another round for safety's sake.'

The lookouts were now holding their arms over their heads, crossed together. The Mithilans were in full retreat.

Kumbhakarna looked at Raavan as another booming, ominous whoosh was heard. A thousand more spears sprang out of the bows and flew towards the inner ramparts, ripping into the stragglers among the fleeing Mithilans.

At least one thousand of the four thousand Mithilan warriors were downed in those devastating few minutes. Without a single Lankan life being lost.

The lookouts were now clapping their open palms together above their heads. The signal was clear. There were no Mithilans on top of the inner wall anymore. They were either dead or had run away.

'Charge!' roared Raavan.

The heralds announced the orders down the line, and the Lankans began scaling the outer wall, roaring their battle cries.

Weapons drawn. Ready to kill. Ready to destroy the hapless residents of Mithila.

They were in for a surprise.

Mithila was a poor city, and the little wealth it had was distributed unfairly. The rich were too rich. And the poor, too poor.

As a consequence of this, the rich lived in luxurious mansions in the heart of the city, while the poor lived in decrepit slums and hovels close to the walls of the fort. Sita, the princess of Mithila and its prime minister, had not been able to countenance such injustice. So she had raised money, through taxes and support from outsiders, to redevelop the slums. Since there wasn't enough land to construct large houses for all the slum-dwellers, she had come up with an ingenious solution—a four-storied honeycomb structure, which extended right up to the inner fort walls.

Because of its shape, this massive building that had replaced the slum was called the Bees Quarter. Many of the former slum-dwellers had punched windows through the walls of the fort, which were also now the walls of their homes. Sita had not stopped them. Considering the minor status of Mithila within the Sapt Sindhu power structure, security had never been as paramount for her as the upliftment of the poorer citizens.

The windows in the walls had been temporarily sealed for the swayamvar, with wood-panel barricades. But now, the Mithilans had quickly broken and removed these barricades, giving them a clear view of the empty grounds between the two fort walls—and an easy outlet for shooting arrows at the Lankans who came rushing from the outer fort wall towards them. Since the Mithilans were inside the Bees Quarter, the roof protected them from any further missile attacks.

Basically, a makeshift improvisation in urban engineering had turned into an immense strategic advantage during battle!

The Lankans, unaware of the danger that awaited them, were charging forward in a frenzy. They ran towards the inner wall, carrying ladders. Ready to scale the second wall, weapons in hand, and ravage the hapless citizens of Mithila. They expected no resistance.

'Kill them all!' thundered Raavan, running shoulder-to-shoulder with his soldiers, bloodlust in his eyes. 'No mercy! No mercy!'

In the tremendous din that the Lankans were making, Raavan didn't hear a loud command in the distance. From within the Bees Quarter. An order bellowed by Sita and her husband, Ram. 'Fire!'

To the shock of the charging Lankans, arrows suddenly came raining down on them. Raavan looked up at the inner ramparts before realising that the arrows were being shot from the windows lower down, within the wall. Windows they did not even know existed.

The Lankans were caught off-guard as the arrows cut through their lines. The losses were heavy, with almost every missile finding a mark, since the soldiers had been hurtling forward in dense formations. In the confusion, part of the charge stalled, with some of Raavan's men running helter-skelter to avoid the projectiles aimed at them, while others cowered behind their shields. The Mithilans shot their arrows without respite, killing as many of the enemy as they could.

The soldiers around Raavan and Kumbhakarna pulled their shields forward, protecting the brothers.

'Retreat, Dada!' shouted Kumbhakarna. 'We are in a death zone.'

'Never!' roared Raavan. 'All we need to do is scale the inner wall. Our army will finish them off! A few more minutes!'

'Dada! In a few more minutes, you will not have an army left!'

Kumbhakarna could see that Raavan was seething. He also knew he could not give the order to retreat without Raavan's permission. 'Dada, they are shooting us down like fish in a barrel! Give the order!'

Behind the protective barrier of shields, Raavan looked around. At his loyal soldiers falling all around him, cut down ruthlessly.

The king of Lanka nodded, the movement barely visible in the darkness.

Kumbhakarna turned to his herald. 'Retreat!'

The conch shells were sounded, and their tune was picked up by heralds across the Lankan line. But this time, they played a different strain. At the signal, the Lankans turned and ran, retreating as rapidly as they had arrived.

A loud cheer went up from the Mithilans in the Bees Quarter.

The first Lankan attack had been repelled.

Chapter 27

It was the fifth hour of the first prahar the following day.

The sense of shock in the Lankan camp was greater than the actual devastation. They had expected an easy victory against the apparently peace-loving Mithilans. What they had not expected was a strong counter-attack.

Raavan had initially been incensed at the previous night's outcome, but on reflection, he realised the odds were still in their favour. The Lankans had lost a thousand men the previous night. But so had the Mithilans, according to the intelligence from Samichi. The loss of a thousand soldiers weighed a lot more on the smaller Mithilan force. While Princess Sita's army was now made up of three thousand irregular soldiers drawn from the police force, the Lankans still had nine thousand battle-hardened veterans. Furthermore, they had received word from Samichi that the ordinary citizens of Mithila were horrified at the devastation wrought by the Lankans the previous night. Morale was at an all-time low and Princess Sita was trying hard to rally her citizens to fight, but it seemed unlikely that she would succeed.

The more he thought about it, the more Raavan was convinced that his forces still had the strength to conquer and destroy the city of King Mithi. And now, more than ever, it was a matter of prestige.

The Lankans had been hard at work all night. The injured were being treated inside makeshift hospital tents, while parts of the forest were being cleared at a rapid pace. By the morning, they had enough wood for their needs. Some of the soldiers worked in groups to saw and shape the hardwood into planks. Others linked these planks into giant rectangular shields with sturdy handles on the sides as well as at the base. Each shield was capable of protecting twenty men.

Raavan, accompanied by Kumbhakarna, walked up and down the lines, supervising the work.

'The tortoise shields are coming along well,' said Kumbhakarna. Though he had not been enthused at the prospect of battle at first, Kumbhakarna knew that leaving was out of the question. If they retreated after their unsuccessful first attempt, news would spread throughout the Sapt Sindhu that a tiny, powerless kingdom had managed to beat back the mighty Lankans in battle. This would electrify Raavan's enemies. If they had avoided battle in the first place, the effect would not have been as devastating. But it was too late now. They would have to fight and defeat Mithila to forestall other rebellions.

'Yes,' said Raavan. 'Tonight, we will charge again. We will break the outer walls, there's no need to scale them. In any case, no Mithilan will be out there. Once we are past the outer walls, protected by our tortoise shields, we'll breach the inner walls. These fools are not prepared for a siege. We underestimated them earlier. We will not make the same mistake again.'

Kumbhakarna nodded. But it continued to bother him that Guru Vishwamitra and some of his Malayaputras were still inside the fort. One never took the mighty Malayaputras lightly. Never.

Raavan's mind was still on the battle to come. 'Once we breach their walls, we will destroy them all. Nobody should be left alive, not even the animals.'

Kumbhakarna did not say anything.

'You continue checking the shields,' said Raavan. 'I want to read the spy reports.'

'Yes, Dada.'

Kumbhakarna walked away, deep in thought. He knew they had to fight this battle, but he couldn't shake off the sense of foreboding that gripped him.

He was moving among the men, checking the tortoise shields, when he heard the unmistakable sound of an arrow whizzing through the air. He ducked instinctively, only to see the arrow slam into a plank of wood at his feet. He looked up in surprise.

Who in Mithila can fire an arrow that travels this distance with such unerring accuracy?

He stared at the walls. All he could make out were two unusually tall men standing on the inner wall ramparts, and a third, who was a trifle shorter. The third man held a bow; he seemed to be looking directly at him.

Kumbhakarna stepped forward to examine the arrow that had buried itself in the wood. There was a piece of parchment tied to its shaft. He tugged it off, untied the note, and read it quickly.

Lord Rudra have mercy!

—ॐ—

'You actually believe they will do this, Kumbhakarna?' asked Raavan, snorting with disgust as he threw the note away.

Kumbhakarna had come running to Raavan and taken him aside to show him the note. It was from Ram, the crown-prince of Ayodhya and now the husband of Sita, the princess-prime minister of Mithila. The short note warned, very clearly, that the Malayaputras had set up an Asuraastra missile on the inner fort walls of Mithila, out of reach of the Lankan soldiers. And that if the Lankans did not demobilise their army and retreat, Ram would fire the Asuraastra. Raavan had one hour to decide.

'Dada,' said Kumbhakarna, 'if they fire an Asuraastra, it could be—'

'They don't have an Asuraastra,' interrupted Raavan. 'They're bluffing.'

The Asuraastra was considered by many to be a daivi astra, used as a weapon of mass destruction. Lord Rudra, the previous Mahadev, had banned the unauthorised use of daivi astras many centuries ago, and practically everyone obeyed his diktat. Anyone who broke the law, he had decreed, would be punished with exile for fourteen years. Breaking the law for the second time would be punishable by death. The tribe left behind by Lord Rudra, the Vayuputras, would enforce this punishment strictly.

However, there were those who insisted that the Asuraastra was not, strictly speaking, a weapon of mass destruction, only of mass incapacitation. And since it could not be termed a daivi astra, it could possibly escape Lord Rudra's ban. Raavan did not concern himself with whether the Asuraastra qualified as a daiva astra or not. He simply refused to believe that the Malayaputras had an Asuraastra at all. He knew it was extremely difficult to access the core material for building one—there was none to be got in India for sure. He did not see the point in worrying about a weapon that his enemy was unlikely to possess.

'But Dada, the Malayaputras do have—'

'Vishwamitra is bluffing, Kumbhakarna!'

Shocked to hear Raavan refer to Guru Vishwamitra by his name alone, Kumbhakarna fell silent.

—ॐ—

Nearly three hours had passed since the Lankans had received the warning. By now, even Kumbhakarna had begun to wonder if the note had been a bluff, though the vague sense of impending doom refused to leave him.

'Are you convinced now, Kumbha?' asked Raavan. 'You know I am never wrong.'

Kumbhakarna wished he could share his brother's conviction, but his own instincts said otherwise.

'You are aware of the punishment for firing a daivi astra, right?' asked Raavan. 'Do you expect the Malayaputras to break Lord Rudra's law? Guruji knows very well that even if we kill everyone else in Mithila, we would not dare touch them. They are safe.'

What Raavan didn't know was that the Malayaputras were out of options. Even though they were mindful of Lord Rudra's laws, they had to protect Sita at any cost.

Kumbhakarna's instincts were right.

'Can I please have your permission to step out now?' asked Raavan sarcastically.

On Kumbhakarna's insistence, Raavan had grudgingly remained within the parked Pushpak Vimaan. One of the metals used to build the fuselage of the vehicle was lead, and it was well-known that lead was an inhibitor of the effects of various daivi astras, including the Asuraastra. That's why it was sometimes called a magic metal. Kumbhakarna had been keeping an eye on the section of the Mithila fort from where the warning arrow had been fired. At the first sign of trouble, he intended to close the vimaan door, so that his brother would be safe.

Kumbhakarna shook his head. 'No, Dada. Please. It's my job to protect you.'

'And it's my job to protect you from your own stupidity! Step aside now. I need to go check if the boats are ready for the weight of the tortoise shields.'

'Dada, please listen to me.'

'In the name of Lord Rudra, have you gone insane, Kumbhakarna?' Raavan asked, exasperated.

'Please, Dada. Your safety is most important.'

'I am not a child who needs your protection!'

'Please stay here, Dada,' said Kumbhakarna. 'I will go and check the boats.'

'Dammit!'

'Dada, just think you are doing it to humour me. I have a bad feeling—'

'We can't make battle plans based on your "feelings"!'

'I beg of you. Stay in the vimaan. I'll go and check on the boats.'

Raavan sat back angrily. 'Fine!'

—१७६१—

Kumbhakarna was at the lake, instructing the Lankan soldiers to load the tortoise shields on the boats. He still had one wary eye on the fort, checking for any sign of the Asuraastra being fired.

He turned to look at the vimaan parked some distance behind him and was relieved to see a scowling Raavan standing just inside the flying craft.

Kumbhakarna gestured for Raavan to remain where he was, then turned back to watch the work on the boats.

All of a sudden, that sense of foreboding inside him seemed to strengthen. Painfully. Like someone had grabbed his guts and was squeezing them dry.

He looked towards the fort. Towards the section of the inner wall that had the Bees Quarter abutting it. His eyes widened in alarm.

What Kumbhakarna did not know was that the Malayaputras had finally found someone to trigger the Asuraastra. Someone to take the blame, and the punishment, for possibly breaking Lord Rudra's commandment. Someone whose desire to save the woman he loved was strong enough to make him break the law, something he would not normally consider—Sita's husband, Ram.

A flaming arrow shot by Ram was tearing through the air at a fearsome speed.

Lord Rudra have mercy.

Kumbhakarna turned around instantly, screaming, 'Dada!'

He charged towards the Pushpak Vimaan, running as hard as his legs would allow.

Meanwhile, at the top of the Bees Quarter, the flaming arrow slammed into a small red square on the Asuraastra missile tower, pushing it backwards. The fire from the arrow was captured in a receptacle behind the red square, and from there it spread rapidly to the fuel chamber that powered the missile. There was a flash of intense light, and a series of soft explosions. A few seconds later, heavy flames gathered near the base of the tower.

Kumbhakarna reached the vimaan and leapt for the entrance, throwing his weight on his elder brother, who went flying backwards into the vimaan. Kumbhakarna's momentum carried him inside as well.

But the door of the craft was still open.

The Asuraastra missile took off and flew in a high arc over the walls of Mithila, covering the distance in a few short seconds. The Lankan soldiers on the outer side of the moat-lake looked up in surprise and panic. The missile could mean only one thing.

A daivi astra.

They were doomed. They knew that.

There was no time to react. No time to run. And where would they run and hide?

They were out in the open. Easy prey for the Asuraastra.

Even while devastation sped towards them, none of the Lankans could tear their eyes away from the spectacle. As the missile flew high above the moat-lake, there was a small, almost inaudible explosion, like that of a firecracker meant for a child.

The terror in the soldiers' hearts was quickly replaced by hope.

Maybe the daivi astra had failed.

But the Malayaputras and the princes of Ayodhya, who stood at the top of the Bees Quarter, knew better. They had covered their ears, as instructed by Guru Vishwamitra.

The assault of the Asuraastra had not yet begun.

Kumbhakarna, meanwhile, had sprung to his feet, even as Raavan lay sprawled on the floor of the vimaan. He rushed to the door and hit the metallic button on the sidewall with the full weight of his body. The door of the vimaan began to slide shut slowly. Too slowly.

The door will not close in time.

Without a second thought, Kumbhakarna took up position. Just inside the vimaan. Just behind the doorway. As the sliding door moved into place, closing slowly, agonisingly slowly.

Kumbhakarna. Blocking the still open part of the doorway with his gigantic form.

So that the effects of the explosion would not travel beyond him.

Kumbhakarna. Ready to sacrifice himself. For the man he loved.

For his brother.

For his dada.

The Asuraastra hovered above the Lankan soldiers for a moment, and then exploded with an ear-shattering sound that shook even the walls of Mithila in the distance. The Lankans felt their eardrums burst painfully, the air sucked out from their lungs.

But this was only a prelude to the devastation that would follow.

An eerie silence followed the explosion. Then spectators on the Mithila rooftops saw a bright green flash of light emerge from where the missile had splintered. It burst with furious intensity and hit the Lankans below like a flash of lightning. They stayed rooted, stunned into a temporary paralysis. Fragments of the exploded missile showered down on them.

Kumbhakarna saw the flash of green light just as the door of the Pushpak Vimaan slid shut. Even as the door sealed and locked automatically, saving those inside the flying vehicle from any further injury, Kumbhakarna collapsed, unconscious.

'Kumbhaaaaaaa!' Raavan rushed to his younger brother, screaming.

Outside the vimaan, the Asuraastra was still not done. The real damage was yet to come.

A dreadful hissing sound radiated out, like the battle-cry of a gigantic snake. Simultaneously, the fragments of the missile that had fallen to the ground emitted demonic clouds of green gas, which spread like a shroud over the stupefied Lankans.

The gas was the actual heart of the Asuraastra. The real weapon. The explosions and the paralysing green light primed the victim. The thick green gas was the slayer.

In a few minutes, the deathly gas enveloped the Lankans, who lay paralysed in the clearing outside the Pushpak Vimaan. It would put them in a coma that would last for days, if not weeks. It would kill some of them. But at the moment, all was deceptively calm. There were no screams and no cries for mercy. No one made an attempt to escape. They simply lay on the ground, motionless, waiting for the fiendish astra to push them into oblivion. The only sound in the otherwise grim silence was the hiss of the gas spewing from the missile fragments.

Inside the vimaan, a devastated Raavan was on his knees, holding his younger brother in his arms. Tears streamed down his face as he shook the body of his paralysed brother repeatedly, trying to wake him up. 'Kumbha! Kumbha!'

Some thirty minutes had passed. The Asuraastra had completed its devastation of the Lankan troops.

A small, skeletal crew present inside the craft had escaped. One of them was a doctor. As standard operating procedure, the vimaan was always manned and ready for flight.

The doctor had managed, with the help of his emergency kit of medicines, to release Kumbhakarna from the paralytic effects of the missile. His body was still immobile and his breathing was ragged, but he could move his head a little. He lay on the floor of the vimaan. Blood seeped very slowly from his Naga outgrowths. His head was on his elder brother's lap.

He tried to say something, but his tongue was swollen and his speech was slurred and unintelligible.

'Be quiet,' whispered Raavan, his cheeks wet with tears. 'Rest. You will be fine. I won't let anything happen to you.'

'Thatha… thuuu… thokay?'

Raavan's tears flowed more strongly as he understood what his younger brother was saying. Even in this state, Kumbhakarna was more concerned about Raavan's wellbeing. The king of Lanka kissed his younger brother's forehead gently. 'I am okay. You rest, little brother, you rest.'

Kumbhakarna's partially paralysed face shaped itself into a crooked smile. 'Thuuu… thowe… thmee.'

Raavan smiled through his tears. 'Yes. Yes, I owe you, my brother. I owe you.'

Kumbhakarna shook his head slightly, the crooked smile still on his face. 'Thust… thoking…'

'Rest, Kumbha. Rest…'

Kumbhakarna closed his eyes.

Raavan held his brother's head close to his chest, crying. 'I am so sorry, Kumbha. I am so sorry. I should have listened to you.'

'My lord,' whispered one of the Lankan soldiers, looking through a porthole.

Raavan looked up.

'The gas is still visible,' the man said. 'It has wrapped itself around our men. What do we do?'

Raavan knew what that meant. All his soldiers who lay on the ground outside the Pushpak Vimaan would be paralysed for days, if not weeks. They would be in a coma, from which some of them would never awake. He couldn't step out either. For the effects of the gas could still be strong.

The Battle of Mithila had been lost. His bodyguard corps was destroyed. He had no soldiers left, besides the few within the vimaan. There was nothing he could do.

But that didn't seem to matter so much now.

He looked down at his brother. And pulled him closer.

All that mattered was his brother. He had to get Kumbhakarna back on his feet.

Raavan looked at the pilots of the Pushpak Vimaan. 'Fly us out of this cursed place.'

Chapter 28

Raavan breathed deeply. 'Finally, a chance to get back at the Malayaputras,' he said.

A little more than thirteen years had passed since the Battle of Mithila. Raavan and Kumbhakarna were in Sigiriya, in the king's private office in the royal palace. The memory of the battle had faded with time, but the wound was still raw for Raavan.

The humiliating defeat and the devastating destruction of Raavan's ten-thousand-strong bodyguard corps had not had as much of an impact across the Sapt Sindhu as he had feared. For a short period after the Battle of Mithila, others within the Sapt Sindhu had started dreaming of challenging Lankan authority. They had even begun to see Ram, the prince of Ayodhya, as the leader of the resistance. But before the movement could gather force, Ram had been banished for fourteen years from the Sapt Sindhu by King Dashrath, for the unauthorised use of the daivi astra, in accordance with the laws of the previous Mahadev. All dreams of a rebellion had died with his departure. The fact that Ram's wife Sita, the princess of Mithila, and his younger brother Lakshman had left with him had hit morale further.

Raavan had endured a loss of prestige too. His people had expected him to return to Mithila and destroy it to avenge the defeat he had suffered, but Raavan knew that the Lankan army was in no condition for an all-out war. Besides, the Malayaputras had left Mithila with the Lankan soldiers, who had been revived and then imprisoned. The price for returning them was Raavan's solemn oath, in Lord Rudra's name, that he would not attack Mithila or any other kingdom in the Sapt Sindhu.

To ensure that Raavan kept his word, Guru Vishwamitra had warned him that if he so much as thought of mobilising his army to attack the Sapt Sindhu, he would stop receiving the medicines that kept him and Kumbhakarna alive. To drive the point home, he had further raised the price of the medicines and the cave material. Though burning with humiliation, Raavan had had no choice but to accept these terms. But he had been waiting for a chance to get back at the Malayaputras, and it seemed now that an opportunity had finally presented itself.

'It's not about vengeance, Dada,' said Kumbhakarna. 'It's about getting what we want. We have to be careful. Very careful.'

'That may be true for you. For me, getting back at the Malayaputras is just as important. But I would never do anything silly, or in anger. I am not stupid.'

Kumbhakarna threw up his hands in acceptance. 'All right.'

'The important thing is, they have a Vishnu now. And an interesting choice of a Vishnu too,' Raavan said thoughtfully.

'Yes,' said Kumbhakarna. 'Suddenly a lot of things are making sense. For instance, I could never understand why the Malayaputras were so desperate to save Mithila. They used the Asuraastra, defying the ban by Lord Rudra and possibly damaging their relations with the Vayuputras permanently. An insignificant kingdom like Mithila was surely not worth such a risk. But it's apparent now that they were not trying to save their precious city of sages, but their Vishnu! They knew that you were so angry, you would have killed everyone there that day.'

Raavan nodded. 'True. They don't care for their own lives. They care only about their mission. And for their mission to succeed, they need the Vishnu.'

'Princess Sita.'

'Who would have thought they would select someone from tiny, powerless Mithila for a Vishnu,' said Raavan, flexing his right shoulder. He was close to sixty years old now, and aches and pains had become a constant part of his life. Also, the medicines that kept him alive were taking a toll on his strength. The mysterious plague ravaging Sigiriya was only causing further damage.

'She wasn't the only candidate,' said Kumbhakarna.

Raavan looked at his younger brother, surprised.

'The Vayuputras and Guru Vashishtha believe that Ram should be the next Vishnu,' said Kumbhakarna.

Vashishtha was the raj guru and chief adviser to the Ayodhya royal family. But his position within the Sapt Sindhu royalty wasn't the main reason he was held in such high esteem across the land. He was also a *maharishi*, a *great man of knowledge*, whose intellect was unmatched. His only equal, perhaps, was the chief of the Malayaputras, Maharishi Vishwamitra. It was also well known that Maharishi Vashishtha was very close to the Vayuputras, the tribe left behind by the previous Mahadev, Lord Rudra.

'Ram? Really?'

'Yes.'

'That's awkward,' said Raavan. 'What are the Vayuputras and Guru Vashishtha trying to do? Create marital discord between Ram and Sita?'

Kumbhakarna laughed. 'In any case, what the Vayuputras or Guru Vashishtha think about the Vishnu has no bearing on the final choice. The Vishnu is selected by the Malayaputras alone. And Guru Vishwamitra has made his choice. Sita will be the next Vishnu.'

Raavan leaned back in his chair and took a deep breath. 'What is the cause of this fight between Guru Vashishtha and Guru Vishwamitra? Weren't they friends once?'

'I don't know, Dada. That's something for another story, another book. It has nothing to do with us.'

'But you do know a lot about most things,' said Raavan. 'How did you find out so much about this Vishnu business?'

'It's best if you don't know.'

'Why?'

'Just trust me, Dada.'

Raavan stared at Kumbhakarna. 'Why do I get the feeling sometimes that we are pawns in a much bigger game?'

'Every human being is a pawn, Dada. But in chess, the pawn that breaches the other side suddenly becomes very powerful.'

Raavan raised his eyebrows and smiled. 'There is a difference between chess and real life, little brother.'

'Of course. But chess is a representation of real life. How you play chess says a lot about how you live as well.'

'Wise words,' said Raavan. 'In any case, I trust you completely, Kumbha. Any time I have not trusted you, I have suffered.'

Kumbhakarna laughed and stifled a yawn.

'Feeling sleepy again?' asked Raavan, a guilty look on his face.

The Asuraastra had had a debilitating effect on Kumbhakarna. Born a Naga, he had suffered aches and discomfort since his childhood. His outgrowths were painful at the joints, and would bleed profusely during his childhood. The Malayaputra medicines had helped keep the pain and bleeding in check. However, exposure to the noxious Asuraastra's green light had caused a massive deterioration in his condition. Furthermore, at fifty-one, he was not as strong as he had once been. The renewed bleeding and pain were almost unbearable now.

The Malayaputra physicians had visited Sigiriya and formulated some new medicines that helped manage the pain and the bleeding to some extent, but they also made Kumbhakarna extremely lethargic. He slept for most part of the day, every day. The only way he could get his focus back was by avoiding having the medicines for a few days. But the pain would return almost immediately, and the bleeding would restart if he skipped the medicines for more than five days. Anything beyond that, and his life itself would be at risk.

And all this because he had put himself in danger to save his brother's life during the Battle of Mithila.

Raavan had not been able to forgive himself. He had curtailed all his other plans over the last thirteen years— from the expansion of the Lankan empire to the takeover of Kishkindha. He focused instead on ensuring that his younger brother remained alive and as healthy as possible.

Kumbhakarna smiled at Raavan. 'I'm all right, Dada.'

Raavan smiled and patted his brother's shoulder.

'In any case,' Kumbhakarna continued, 'we have nothing to do with the Vayuputras or Guru Vashishtha. We only need the Malayaputras under our control. And that will happen when we take the Vishnu away. They will want to free her at any cost, and that's when we can really squeeze them dry. We'll demand the medicine supply we need for the next twenty years in one shot—without paying their ridiculous prices. Nothing stops us from demanding more from the Malayaputras as long as the Vishnu remains imprisoned in Lanka.'

Raavan nodded.

'Do we go ahead then?' asked Kumbhakarna.

'Yes, we have to kidnap Sita.'

'Remember, Dada, it's not about vengeance. We will only ask for what we want. We just need some leverage over the Malayaputras. We will not kill the Vishnu.'

Raavan nodded.

'She will be our prisoner.'

'Yes.'

'A political prisoner. She will be kept in one of the palaces in Lanka, not in the dungeons.'

'I get it, Kumbha! You don't have to go on about it!'

Kumbhakarna smiled and put his palms together in apology.

—१७१—

'Dada, I don't think this is a good idea,' whispered Kumbhakarna.

Raavan was in his private chamber in the royal palace of Sigiriya, with Kumbhakarna. Raavan's son, the twenty-seven-year-old Indrajit, was also present. Indrajit had the same intimidating physical presence as his father. He was tall and astonishingly muscular, with a voice that was deep and commanding. He had also inherited his mother's high cheekbones and thick brown hair, which he wore in a leonine mane, with two side partings and a long knot at the crown of his head. An oiled handlebar moustache sat well on his smooth-complexioned face. His clothes were sober—a fawn-coloured dhoti and a creamy white angvastram. He wore no jewellery, except for the ear studs that most warriors in India favoured. The plague that was ravaging Lanka had had no impact on Indrajit, which made Raavan proud.

The king of Lanka adored his son. He had picked the name himself: *Indrajit* meant *one who could defeat the king of the Gods, Indra.*

Indra was the legendary king of the Devas in the hoary past. The name had, over time, become a title for all who were considered the kings of the Gods. Raavan's high aspirations for his son were no secret.

'I agree with Kumbhakarna Uncle,' said Indrajit, speaking quietly so his voice wouldn't carry far. 'This is an important mission. I think we should be the ones to carry it out. We can't leave it to Uncle and Aunty, who are a hideous combination of arrogance and incompetence.'

Raavan regarded the man and the woman who stood at a respectful distance from him. Vibhishan and Shurpanakha—his half-siblings and Indrajit's 'uncle and aunty'. The two had volunteered for the job of kidnapping Sita. Raavan could barely keep his revulsion from showing on his face when he looked at them. They were born of a father he hated and a stepmother he despised, and if that wasn't enough, his rent-a-tear mother Kaikesi had adopted and nurtured them. She would go to any length to undermine him, he thought again.

'We'll take care of it, Dada,' said Vibhishan politely to his much older half-brother.

Vibhishan was of average height and unusually fair-skinned. His reed-thin physique was that of a runner. But he held his thin arms wide, as if to accommodate impressive biceps. His long, jet-black hair was tied in a knot at the back of his head. His full beard was neatly trimmed and dyed a deep brown. He wore a rich purple dhoti and a pink angvastram, with a lot of jewellery. He was a complete dandy and, according to Raavan, full of false politeness and humility.

'I am not your dada,' said Raavan firmly. 'I am your king.'

'Of course, my lord,' said Vibhishan, immediately correcting himself and holding his ears in respectful apology.

Raavan rolled his eyes.

'Our idea will work, my lord,' Vibhishan said.

Raavan's spies had informed him that Sita, Ram and Lakshman were camped in Panchavati, a peaceful spot along the Godavari River, with sixteen Malayaputra soldiers for their protection. Raavan was suspicious of the fact that only sixteen soldiers had been tasked with the security of someone as important as the Vishnu, but he was told that Sita was still angry with the Malayaputras for forcing Ram to fire the Asuraastra. She had refused their support. The soldiers with her were under the command of Jatayu, whom she considered her brother—which apparently was the only reason she had agreed to their presence.

Vibhishan proposed that they use Shurpanakha's beauty to distract Ram and Lakshman. An encounter with her would presumably lead to the two men letting their guard down. Shurpanakha would then find some pretext to lead Sita away from Ram and Lakshman, and kidnap her. The Ayodhya princes would be told that Sita had attacked Shurpanakha out of jealousy, and in the fight that ensued, she had accidentally drowned in the river. Since the Godavari was prone to swift currents, it was likely that her body would never be found.

This way, Vibhishan reasoned, they would be able to kidnap Sita without having the blame fall on Lanka.

'Why not just send in our soldiers and pick her up?' asked Kumbhakarna.

'What if Ram gets injured or hurt in the process?' Vibhishan responded with a question of his own.

What Vibhishan left unsaid was obvious to all. Ram was, technically, the king of Ayodhya, and the king of Ayodhya was considered to be the emperor of the Sapt Sindhu. If he died at the hands of a Lankan, treaty obligations would force all the kingdoms of the Sapt Sindhu to declare war on Lanka. And Lanka could not afford to fight a war right now. The army was too weak to go into a battle.

Kumbhakarna was still not convinced. 'I am sure we can find a better way to separate Ram and Sita without using our own sister as bait.'

'We fight with the weapons we have been blessed with, Dada,' said Vibhishan. 'And Shurpanakha has been blessed with extraordinary beauty.'

Shurpanakha smiled proudly, pleased with the compliment. She resembled Vibhishan, but unlike her sickly brother, she was bewitching in appearance. She had more of her Greek mother's genes than her Indian father's. Her skin was pearly white, and her eyes magnetic. She had a sharp, slightly upturned nose and high cheekbones. Her hair was blonde, a most unusual colour in India, and every strand of it was always in place. Everything about her petite frame was elegant.

She wore a classic, expensively dyed purple dhoti, which was tied fashionably low, exposing her slim, curvaceous waist. Her silken blouse was a tiny sliver of cloth, affording a generous view of her cleavage. Her angvastram, deliberately hanging loose from a shoulder, revealed more than it concealed. Extravagant jewellery completed the picture of excess.

Shurpanakha seemed convinced of her ability to pull off this plan. Kumbhakarna, however, was still sceptical. He turned to Indrajit for his opinion.

The confident young man spoke up immediately. 'Vibhishan Uncle, please don't think I am being rude, but I have honestly not heard a more stupid idea in my life. I don't see how this will work.'

Vibhishan tensed in anger, but controlled his tongue with superhuman effort. Being insulted by his elder brother was something he had learnt to live with. But to hear such words from this pup? It was intolerable!

'Do you think any man with a heart that beats can even think of resisting this?' asked Shurpanakha, pointing at herself.

'Good God, Shurpanakha! You are my sister. How can you say such things in my presence?' Kumbhakarna was appalled.

'You have turned celibate, Dada,' said Shurpanakha to Kumbhakarna, almost tauntingly. 'You will not understand.'

Kumbhakarna turned to Raavan. 'Dada, I don't approve of this. I say we go with our original plan.'

'Dada,' said Shurpanakha to Raavan—she had none of the diffidence that Vibhishan was saddled with—'I will handle this. You don't need to get your hands dirty. Allow us to earn your trust.'

Raavan thought about it. Kumbhakarna was already looking tired and sleepy. He would have to be given his medicines soon. Then there was Indrajit—his pride and joy. His heir. If there was a way to avoid putting these two at risk...

'Also, my lord,' said Vibhishan, 'many people believe that we are not close to you. So, even if we are caught out, in all likelihood, Sita's disappearance will not be linked to you. It will be like an independent act by relatives you don't like. Your hands will remain clean.'

Raavan narrowed his eyes. *That does make some kind of sense.*

'Dada,' Shurpanakha persisted, 'you have nothing to lose. If we fail, you can go to Panchavati with your soldiers in any case. What's the harm in giving us a chance?'

Yeah... What's the harm?

'All right,' said Raavan.

Shurpanakha whooped in delight, clapping her hands together.

Vibhishan went down on his knees ceremoniously and brought his head down to the floor, paying obeisance to Raavan. 'You will not regret this, my lord.'

Raavan looked at him. *Pretentious moron.*

Chapter 29

It had been many weeks since Vibhishan and Shurpanakha had sailed out of Lanka, to the port of Salsette, on the western coast of India. Located north of the ruined Mumbadevi port, the island was now the primary Lankan outpost in the area. It was also the port closest to Panchavati, where Ram, Sita and Lakshman were camped, along with sixteen Malayaputra soldiers.

Indrajit had accompanied his uncle and aunt to Salsette, but had been ordered to take no further part in the mission. Raavan did not want to put his son's life at risk. The brave young man had protested vociferously, but had finally submitted to his father's directive.

From Salsette, Vibhishan and Shurpanakha had marched with a company of soldiers to Panchavati, with the intention of kidnapping Sita.

But the mission had turned out to be a disaster.

'I am sorry,' Raavan said to Kumbhakarna. 'I should have listened to you.'

Raavan and Kumbhakarna were in the Pushpak Vimaan, accompanied by a hundred soldiers, flying towards Salsette.

Not only had Shurpanakha failed to kidnap Sita, she had been caught and bound by her. Sita had dragged the bleating

Lankan princess to the Panchavati camp, where the waiting Lankan soldiers had nearly come to blows with the followers of Ram and Sita. Worse, Shurpanakha had been accidentally injured on her nose by Lakshman.

Vibhishan had quickly ordered a retreat without offering a fight, thus keeping himself, his sister and their soldiers alive. They had rushed back to Salsette, and from there, led by Indrajit, had sailed back to Lanka, to appraise Raavan of their plight.

Raavan had responded by setting off from Lanka immediately, with as many soldiers as could be accommodated in the Pushpak Vimaan. While cosmetic surgeries would, over time, take away the physical marks of Shurpanakha's injury, the metaphorical loss of face could only be avenged with blood.

Raavan couldn't stop cursing his inept half-siblings all through the flight, but he also realised, with some prodding from Kumbhakarna, that he finally had a legitimate excuse to attack Ram's camp. After all, any outrage against a member of the Lankan royal family had to be responded to. It was a matter of honour, and any reasonable person would agree that it could not be construed as an act of war. And that would hopefully nullify the treaty obligations which bound other kingdoms within the Sapt Sindhu to come to Ayodhya's aid.

Kumbhakarna looked at his brother and smiled, waving the apology aside. 'It's all right, Dada. We've spoken about this already and cussed out our idiot half-siblings enough. Let's focus on what we have to do right now. We have to kidnap the Vishnu. That's it. Let's keep our minds clear.'

'True,' said Raavan, smiling. He stretched his arms over his head. 'You know what the most irritating part of an attack is?'

'What?'

'The waiting.'

'That is true.'

'It's excruciating to know we will be in the heat of battle soon, but till it starts, we have to sit around doing nothing. We have to talk and behave normally, keeping our heartrate in check and bloodlust high, but not so high that we lose control.'

Kumbhakarna laughed. 'But you will keep your bloodlust in check out there as well.'

Raavan glowered at Kumbhakarna.

'Dada, be realistic. You are not what you used to be. You are nearly sixty years old now. Your navel outgrowth and the continuous use of medicines have weakened you. You've fought enough battles. Let the soldiers do the fighting now.'

'Well, you're not exactly fighting fit either!' Raavan exclaimed petulantly.

Kumbhakarna glanced towards the pilots of the craft, who were within earshot.

'Which is why I will avoid fighting as well,' he said, keeping his voice low.

'They attacked our family. And you want us to not react?' Raavan spoke in an angry whisper.

'No, Dada. I want you to react intelligently.'

'I am not a coward!'

'I didn't say you are.'

'Then I must fight.'

'Absolutely not.'

'You don't have the right to order me around, Kumbhakarna.'

'You are right, I don't. But I do have the right to demand the first of the three boons you promised me.'

In a fit of guilt and remorse after the Battle of Mithila, where his mistake had caused permanent damage to Kumbhakarna's health, Raavan had told his younger brother that he could demand three boons from him, at any time in the course of their lives. And that those three demands would be met, come what may. Kumbhakarna had not asked for anything. Until now.

Raavan grunted angrily. He knew he had no choice. 'You are not playing fair, Kumbha!'

'We'll get the Vishnu, Dada. We'll kidnap her. But there is no need for you to put your life at risk.'

Raavan looked away, fuming.

Kumbhakarna laughed softly. 'Look at the bright side, Dada. I only have two boons left.'

—१७१—

Raavan looked out of the porthole at the land of Salsette below him.

They had stopped briefly at the port, to pick up Samichi and her lover, Khara, who was also a captain in the Lankan armed forces. The vimaan had taken off once again, with its course set towards the Godavari River.

Ram, Sita, Lakshman and the Malayaputras with them had abandoned Panchavati soon after the botched encounter with Shurpanakha and Vibhishan. Lankan intelligence had lost track of them. But Samichi had managed to find the exact location of the Vishnu and her companions by brutally torturing a captive Malayaputra. It turned out that they were still close to the river, though much further down from Panchavati. As soon as Kumbhakarna was informed of this, he had ordered them to join his raiding party.

Raavan looked at Samichi, and then at his younger brother. 'Why do we need to take this woman along? I don't like having her around!'

'I know it troubles you, Dada,' said Kumbhakarna calmly. 'But she knows their exact location.'

'So what? We have the information now. We can go by ourselves.'

'Samichi knows Princess Sita better than any of us. She was in the service of the Vishnu for many years. Her advice may prove useful.'

'You could have debriefed her thoroughly before we left Salsette. I still don't see why she has to travel with us.'

'It's better to have her with us.'

'She was there during the Battle of Mithila. A fat lot of good that did us. She was useless!'

'But she is trying to make herself useful now. Let's give her the opportunity. What do we have to lose?'

Raavan took a deep breath and did not answer.

'Dada, trust me, please. It's important that we get the Vishnu; that we capture her alive. Let's put our emotions aside and focus on that.'

'You can be really infuriating, Kumbha! I don't know why I even painted you,' Raavan burst out suddenly.

'You've made a painting of me?' Kumbhakarna was genuinely surprised. He knew that every painting created by Raavan had only one constant character in it. 'You painted me with the Kanyakumari?'

Raavan nodded in the affirmative.

'When do I get to see it?' asked Kumbhakarna.

Raavan picked up a cloth bag lying next to him and pulled out a rolled-up canvas.

'What? You have it with you?' Kumbhakarna was delighted.

Raavan handed over the canvas to his brother.

Kumbhakarna unrolled it, shifting a little to make sure nobody else in the vimaan could see it. 'Wow!'

Raavan's eternal muse, the Kanyakumari, was at the centre of the painting. She looked older. Her hair was almost completely grey and her face was finely lined. She had a slight stoop. She looked at least sixty years old, if not more. But her face still had that angelic splendour—of grace, beauty and kindness.

She was helping a small child who was trying to climb a wall.

Kumbhakarna smiled. 'This child looks familiar!'

Raavan laughed softly, for the child was Kumbhakarna. Hairy, almost bear-like, with pot-like ears and two extra arms sticking out on top of his shoulders. Despite his oddities, the child looked adorable. Happy and huggable.

'Where am I going?' asked Kumbhakarna, his eyes fixed on the painting.

Raavan pointed to the fencing on top of the wall. A circular symbol in the shape of a wheel was repeated several times, to form a railing. Kumbhakarna recognised it only too well.

'The wheel of dharma.'

'Yes,' said Raavan. 'You will rise to achieve your dharma.'

'I don't see you in this painting. Where are you?'

Raavan didn't answer.

'Where do you see yourself, Dada?'

Raavan remained silent.

Kumbhakarna examined the painting closely. He then turned towards his elder brother, clearly unhappy. 'Dada—'

On the wall, visible only if one looked closely, were ten faces. Nine of them exhibited the *navrasas*, or *nine major emotions*, as described in the *Natyashastra*: love, laughter, sorrow, anger, courage, fear, disgust, wonder and tranquillity. The tenth face, in the centre, had no expression at all. A blank slate.

Kumbhakarna could see what Raavan had attempted in the painting. The king of Lanka was sometimes addressed as *Dashanan* by his subjects, for they said that he had the knowledge and power of *ten heads*. Raavan had sought to play on this name, and the symbolism that attaches to emotions in the Indian artistic tradition, to convey a much deeper meaning. Traditional wisdom says that true spiritual awakening is possible only when one transcends the wall of emotions that keeps one imprisoned in this illusory world. In the painting, Raavan had made himself the wall that the child Kumbhakarna was trying to scale.

'Climb over the wall of emotions you have for me, my brother,' said Raavan. 'Leave me, and find dharma. I am too far gone. There is no hope for me. But you are a good man. Rediscover your childhood and your innocence. Leave me and start from the beginning once again. Walk the path of dharma, for I know that is what your soul desires.'

Kumbhakarna rolled up the canvas tightly without a word, and slipped it back into Raavan's cloth bag.

'Kumbha... listen to me.'

'I am carrying out my dharma, Dada,' he said.

'Kumbha—'

'Enough now.'

An unseasonal storm had buffeted the Pushpak Vimaan as the Lankans approached the temporary campsite of the exiles. The pilots had somehow managed to land the craft without any damage. Dangerous as the storm was for the flying vehicle, it had inadvertently helped the Lankans. The howling winds had drowned out the sound of the vimaan's massive rotors. They had managed to disembark without being noticed and had successfully maintained the element of surprise as they attacked the temporary camp.

The battle had been short and sharp.

The Malayaputras were heavily outnumbered, so it was no surprise that there were no Lankan casualties. All the Malayaputras, save Captain Jatayu and two of his soldiers, were dead or critically injured.

But Ram, Lakshman and Sita were missing. Kumbhakarna had organised seven teams, of two soldiers each, to spread out and search for the trio.

At the same time, Captain Khara had been tasked with extracting information from the surviving Malayaputras, especially Captain Jatayu.

Raavan and Kumbhakarna stood at a distance, where they wouldn't have to get their hands dirty. Thirty soldiers stood close to them, ready to protect their royals at the first sign of trouble.

'This is taking too long,' muttered Raavan to Kumbhakarna.

'Should we go back and wait inside the vimaan?' asked Kumbhakarna.

Raavan shook his head. *No.*

Khara was still working on Jatayu, who was now on his knees, held by two Lankan soldiers. The Malayaputra's hands were tied behind his back. Jatayu had been brutalised; he was severely injured and bleeding, but he was not broken.

'Answer me,' said Khara, as he slid the knife along Jatayu's cheek, drawing some more blood. 'Where is she?'

Jatayu spat at him. 'Kill me quickly. Or kill me slowly. You will not get anything from me.'

Khara raised his knife in anger, about to strike at Jatayu's throat. Suddenly, an arrow whizzed in from behind the forest line and struck his hand. The knife fell to the ground as he yelped in surprise and pain.

Raavan and Kumbhakarna whirled around, startled. The Lankan soldiers close to them rushed in and formed a protective cordon around them. Kumbhakarna grabbed Raavan's arm to restrain his impulsive elder brother from charging into battle.

Other Lankan soldiers raised their bows in the direction that the enemy arrow had been fired from. They couldn't see anything. Somebody had shot the arrow from deep behind the forest line, behind the visually impenetrable line of trees.

'Don't shoot!' ordered Kumbhakarna loudly. He wanted the Vishnu alive.

The Lankan bows were swiftly lowered.

Khara broke the shaft, leaving the arrowhead buried in his hand. It would stem the blood for a while. He looked into the impenetrable line of trees. Into the darkness. And scoffed in disdain. 'Who shot that? The long-suffering prince? His oversized brother? Or the Vishnu herself?'

There was no response.

'Come out and fight like real warriors!' Khara shouted

There was no response to that taunt either.

Raavan and Kumbhakarna remained well protected by their soldiers, their shields raised high.

'Send the soldiers in,' said Raavan, pointing towards the part of the forest that the arrow had been shot from.

'No,' said Kumbhakarna. 'We should not thin out our force any further. There are three of them. They could have spread out. They can pick you off if our soldiers aren't with us.'

'Kumbha, I am not that important. Get those—'

Kumbhakarna interrupted his elder brother. 'Dada, you are the entire reason for this raid. We are kidnapping the Vishnu to keep you alive with the Malayaputra medicines. I will not put your life at risk.'

Before Raavan could argue any more, five more arrows were shot in a rapid-fire attack. In quick succession. Right where Raavan and Kumbhakarna were. But this was from a different direction. Far from where the first arrow had been shot.

The arrows hit the soldiers surrounding the brothers. Five Lankans went down. But the others did not budge. The cordon around Raavan remained resolute. Ready to fall for their king.

The bodyguards were showing the mettle they were made of.

'It looks like there are two of them in the forest,' whispered Kumbhakarna. 'I hope the Vishnu hasn't escaped.'

Raavan didn't say anything. He was getting suspicious. There was too much of a time lag between the first attack on Khara and the second five-arrow attack directed at himself and Kumbhakarna.

Some of the Lankan soldiers took off in the direction that the latest attack had come from.

Then came the sound of someone stepping on a twig. From another direction. Three soldiers rushed towards the sound.

Raavan was sure now. 'There is just one person. He is moving around quickly behind the forest line to confuse us.'

'Are you sure?' asked Kumbhakarna.

Before Raavan could respond, Khara moved. He stepped behind Jatayu, and using his uninjured left hand, held a knife to his throat.

One can chase hidden attackers in all directions. Or, one can draw them out with a well-targeted threat. Khara was smart. He did the smart thing.

'You could have escaped,' he said tauntingly. 'But you didn't. So I'm betting you are among those hiding behind the trees, great Vishnu. And you want to protect those who worship you. So inspiring... so touching...' Khara pretended to wipe away a tear.

Raavan, far in the distance, his view of Khara blocked by the many Lankan soldiers surrounding him, smiled. He turned to Kumbhakarna. 'I like this Khara.'

Khara continued aloud, 'So I have an offer. Step forward. Tell your husband and that giant brother-in-law of yours to also step forward. And we will let this captain live. We will even let the two sorry Ayodhya princes leave unharmed. All we want is your surrender.'

No response.

Khara grazed the knife slowly along Jatayu's neck, leaving behind a thin red line. He said in a sing-song voice, 'I don't have all day...'

Suddenly, Jatayu struck backwards with his head, hitting Khara in the groin. As the Lankan doubled up in pain, Jatayu screamed, 'Run! Run away, my lady! I am not worth your life!'

Three Lankan soldiers moved in and pushed Jatayu to the ground. Khara cursed loudly as he got back on his feet, still bent over to ease the pain. After a few moments, he inched towards the Malayaputra and kicked him hard. He surveyed the treeline, turning in every direction that the arrows had been fired from. All the while, he kept kicking Jatayu again and again. He bent and roughly pulled Jatayu to his feet.

This time Khara held Jatayu's head firmly with his injured right hand, to prevent any head-butting. The sneer was back on his face. He held the knife to the Malayaputra's throat. 'I can cut the jugular here and your precious captain will be dead in just a few moments, great Vishnu,' he said. He moved the knife to the Malayaputra's abdomen. 'Or, he can bleed to death slowly. All of you have some time to think about it.'

There was still no response.

'All we want is the Vishnu,' yelled Khara. 'Let her surrender and the rest of you can leave. You have my word. You have the word of a Lankan!'

A feminine voice was heard from behind the trees. 'Let him go!'

Kumbhakarna whispered to Raavan, 'It's her. It's the Vishnu.'

Khara shouted, still holding the knife to Jatayu's abdomen, 'Step forward and surrender. And we will let him go.'

And Sita, the princess of Mithila, the one recognised as the Vishnu by the Malayaputras, stepped out from behind the forest line. Holding a bow, with an arrow nocked on it. A quiver tied across her back.

The Lankan royals could not see the Vishnu. Raavan tried to push through the cordon surrounding him, to catch a glimpse of her. But he was pulled back by Kumbhakarna.

'Dada,' said Kumbhakarna, 'her husband and brother-in-law could still be hidden in the trees. We cannot risk you being in the open.'

'Dammit!'

'You promised me, Dada.'

Raavan remained where he was. Angry. But compliant.

'Great Vishnu,' sniggered Khara, letting go of Jatayu for a moment, and running his hand along an ancient scar at the back of his head. Stirring a not-quite-forgotten memory. 'So kind of you to join us. Where is your husband and his giant brother?'

Sita didn't answer. Some Lankan soldiers began moving slowly towards her. Their swords were sheathed. They were carrying *lathis, long bamboo sticks*, which were good enough to injure but not to kill. Their instructions were clear. The Vishnu had to be captured alive.

Sita stepped forward and lowered the bow, an arrow still nocked on it. 'I am surrendering. Let Captain Jatayu go.'

Khara laughed softly as he pushed the knife deep into Jatayu's abdomen. Gently. Slowly. He cut through the liver, a kidney, never stopping…

'Nooo!' screamed Sita. She raised her bow and shot an arrow into Khara's eye. It punctured the socket and lodged itself in his brain, killing him instantly.

'I want her alive!' screamed Kumbhakarna from behind the protective Lankan cordon.

More soldiers joined those already moving toward Sita, their bamboo lathis held high.

'Raaaam!' shouted Sita, as she pulled another arrow from her quiver, quickly nocked and shot it, bringing another Lankan down instantly.

It did not slow the pace of the others. They kept rushing forward.

Sita shot another arrow. Her last. One more Lankan sank to the ground. The others pressed on.

'Raaaam!'

The Lankans were almost upon her, their bamboo lathis raised.

'Raaam!' screamed Sita.

As a Lankan closed in, she lassoed her bow, entangling his lathi with the bowstring, snatching it from him. Sita hit back with the bamboo lathi, straight at the Lankan's head, knocking him off his feet. She swirled the lathi over her head, its menacing sound halting the suddenly wary soldiers. She stopped moving, holding her weapon steady.

Conserving her energy. Ready and alert. One hand held the stick in the middle, the end of it tucked under her armpit. The other arm was stretched forward. Her feet spread wide, in balance. She was surrounded by at least fifty Lankan soldiers. But they kept their distance.

'Raaaam!' shouted Sita, praying that her voice would somehow carry across the forest to her husband.

'We don't want to hurt you, Lady Vishnu,' said a Lankan, politely. 'Please surrender. You will not be harmed.'

Sita cast a quick glance at Jatayu.

'We have the equipment in our Pushpak Vimaan to save him,' said the Lankan. 'Don't force us to hurt you. Please.'

Sita filled her lungs with air and screamed yet again, 'Raaaam!'

She thought she heard a faint voice from a long distance away. 'Sitaaa…'

A soldier moved suddenly from her left, swinging his lathi low. Aiming for Sita's calves. She jumped high, tucking her feet in to avoid the blow. While in the air, she quickly released her right-handed grip on the lathi and swung it viciously with her left. The lathi hit the Lankan on the side of his head. Knocking him unconscious.

As she landed, she shouted again, 'Raaaam!'

She heard the voice of her husband. Soft, from a distance. 'Leave... her... alone...'

Kumbhakarna heard the faint voice too. He looked towards Raavan. And then shouted his order to the soldiers. 'Capture her now! Now!'

Ten Lankans charged in together. Sita swung her lathi ferociously in all directions, incapacitating many.

'Raaaam!'

She heard the voice again. Not so distant this time. 'Sitaaaa...'

The Lankan onslaught was steady and unrelenting now. Sita kept swinging rhythmically. Viciously. Alas, her enemies were one too many. A Lankan swung his lathi at her, from behind. Into her back.

'Raaa...'

Sita's knees buckled under her as she collapsed to the ground. Before she could recover, the soldiers ran in and held her tight. She struggled fiercely as a Lankan came forward, holding a neem leaf in his hand. It was smeared with a blue-coloured paste. He held the leaf tight against her nose. And Sita keeled over into unconsciousness.

'Carry her to the vimaan! Quickly!'

Kumbhakarna turned to his elder brother. 'Let's go, Dada.'

'Let me see Sita.'

'Dada, there's no time. King Ram and Prince Lakshman are close by, they might get here soon. I don't want to be forced to kill them. This is perfect. We've got the Vishnu and the king of Ayodhya has not been injured. You can see her once we are all in the vimaan. Let's go.'

Raavan and Kumbhakarna started walking towards the craft, still surrounded by their bodyguards. The Lankan soldiers followed, carrying Sita, unconscious on a stretcher.

— ୧७I —

The Lankans began climbing in and taking their seats in the Pushpak Vimaan.

The last of the soldiers pressed a metallic button on the sidewall and the door began to slide shut with a hydraulic hiss.

As the brothers reached their seats, Kumbhakarna turned towards the pilots. 'Get us out of here quickly.'

While Raavan and Kumbhakarna braced for take-off, the unconscious Sita was being strapped on to a stretcher fixed on the floor of the Pushpak Vimaan.

'She's a fighter!' said Kumbhakarna, with an appreciative grin.

When the attack took place, Sita, accompanied by a Malayaputra soldier called Makrant, had gone to cut banana leaves for dinner. Ram and Lakshman were away hunting. They had all assumed that the Lankans had lost track of them.

The two Lankan soldiers who had discovered Sita had managed to kill Makrant but were, in turn, killed by Sita. She had then stolen to the devastated Malayaputra camp and had killed several Lankans from behind the tree line, using a bow and a quiver full of arrows very effectively from her hiding places. But her desire to save her loyal follower Jatayu had been her undoing.

'The Malayaputras believe she is the Vishnu,' said Raavan, laughing. 'She had better be a good fighter!'

Just then, the Lankans who were crowded around Sita left her and went to find their own seats in the vimaan.

Her unconscious body lay on a stretcher, some twenty feet away from where Raavan sat. She wore a cream dhoti and a white single-cloth blouse. Her saffron angvastram had been drawn over her entire body, with the straps of the stretcher tight across her. Her head was turned to the side, and her eyes were closed. Saliva drooled out of her mouth.

It was a large quantity of a very strong toxin that had been used to render her unconscious.

For the first time in their lives, Raavan and Kumbhakarna saw Sita.

The warrior princess of Mithila. The wife of Ram. The Vishnu.

Raavan stared at her.

Breath on hold. Heart immobile. Transfixed.

A shocked Kumbhakarna looked at his elder brother, and then at Sita. He couldn't believe his eyes.

The baby had survived. Thirty-eight years. She was a woman now.

Sita was unusually tall for a Mithilan woman. With her lean muscular physique, she looked like a warrior in the army of the Mother Goddess. There were proud battle-scars on her wheat-complexioned body.

But Raavan's eyes were glued to her face. One that he had seen before.

It was a shade lighter than the rest of her body, with high cheekbones and a sharp, small nose. Her lips were neither thin nor full. Her wide-set eyes were neither small nor large; strong brows arched in a perfect curve above creaseless eyelids. Her long, lustrous black hair had come undone and fell in a disorderly manner to the side of her face. She had the look of the mountain people from the Himalayas.

He knew this face well. It was a little thinner than the original. Tougher. Less tender. There was a faint birthmark on the right temple; perhaps a remnant of a childhood injury.

But there could be no doubt. Mother Nature had crafted this face from the same mould.

It was a face that Raavan could never forget. It was a face that he had seen grow old in his mind. It was a face that he loved.

The vimaan began to ascend as the mighty rotors roared to life, spinning powerfully.

Raavan could not breathe. He clutched his armrest tightly, trying to find a stable hold in a world spiralling out of control.

Perhaps the time had come, to finally settle an old karmic debt.

Ka,.. Ka…

The vimaan lurched, buffeted by a sudden gust of strong wind. But Raavan didn't notice.

He continued staring, wordlessly.

His breathing ragged.

His heart paralysed.

Time standing still.

It was obvious. It was obvious from her face.

Sita was the child of Prithvi.

Sita was the daughter of Vedavati.

—ॐ—

'Guruji! Guruji!'

Arishtanemi rushed into the modest private chamber of his guru in Agastyakootam, the hidden capital of the Malayaputras.

Vishwamitra opened his eyes slowly, roused from his deep, meditative state. Normally, no one would dare to interrupt him at such a time. But this was an exception. He was expecting some news and had ordered Arishtanemi to inform him the moment it was received.

'Yes?' he asked now in his distinctive voice.

'It has happened, Guruji.'

'Tell me everything.'

'Raavan and Kumbhakarna received intelligence from Samichi about the whereabouts of Sita, Ram and Lakshman. They flew there in the Pushpak Vimaan and carried out a surprise raid.'

'And?'

'They have kidnapped Sita. Everyone in the camp was killed. I have been told that Ram and Lakshman survived only because they were out hunting at the time.'

Vishwamitra leaned back, a slight smile on his face. *We're back in the game.*

'Guruji, I don't know why we delayed sending more Malayaputras to their aid. We knew Raavan would seek vengeance for what happened with Shurpanakha. We could have saved—'

'Saved whom?'

'Jatayu and the other Malayaputras with them. They were all killed in the raid.'

'They sacrificed themselves for the greater good of Mother India. They are true martyrs. We will honour them. We will build temples to Jatayu and his band.'

'But what about Sita, Guruji? The Lankans have our Vishnu. From what I have heard, they captured her alive. But I don't know if Raavan can be trusted to not hurt her. Or, even worse, kill her.'

'He will not hurt her. Trust me.'

'Guruji, you and I both know he is a monster. Who can predict how a monster will behave?'

Vishwamitra looked at Arishtanemi thoughtfully. The time had come to reveal the secret.

'A monster, you say? Let me ask you then, do you know of any person this monster has been good to?'

Arishtanemi frowned at the strange question. 'I can only think of his brother, Kumbhakarna. And even he has been ill-treated at times.'

'Only his brother? Really? Nobody else?'

'Well, obviously, he is kind to his son. Oh yes! Also, his long-dead love, Vedavati.'

'Vedavati is the reason he will not hurt Sita,' said Vishwamitra.

Vishwamitra had long suspected that their earlier interpretation of the events at Todee had been off the mark. Many years ago, he had sent Arishtanemi and a few others, once again, to unearth more details. Arishtanemi had spoken to the men who had discovered the corpses at Todee and learned that a few bodies had been found tied to the trees close to Vedavati's house. Each of them bore clear signs of extreme torture. The bodies of the others who had died had been found strewn all around the village, suggesting that they had been chased and struck down while trying to escape. The corpses had been left to be eaten by wild animals. Arishtanemi had also ascertained that the only bodies that had been treated with respect and cremated with full Vedic honours were those of Vedavati and her husband Prithvi.

All this had caused Vishwamitra to revise his opinion on what had transpired. Perhaps Raavan had behaved honourably, contrary to what they had thought. Perhaps the men who had been tied to the trees and tortured were the ones who had killed Vedavati and her husband.

The conclusion was clear: Raavan had loved Vedavati deeply and had treated her well, till the end. The massacre was a result of his anguish at losing her. He must have ordered the killing of the villagers in a rage, after her death.

Vishwamitra was fairly certain that the tribe of the Mahadev, the Vayuputras, had reached the same conclusion. But he suspected they were unaware of what had happened after the massacre. They had not made that last crucial connection. That Vedavati's child had survived. Or they would have behaved differently towards Sita.

Arishtanemi was still looking puzzled. 'What connection can there be between Vedavati and Sita, Guruji? Why will Raavan not hurt her?'

'He will not hurt her because Sita is Vedavati's daughter.'

Arishtanemi was stunned. 'What?'

Vishwamitra nodded, the hint of a smile on his face. *Yes, we're definitely back in the game.*

'How long have you known this, Guruji? When did you find out?'

'Just before my decision to appoint Sita as the Vishnu. When she was about thirteen years of age.'

'By the great Lord Parshu Ram! That's nearly twenty-five years ago!'

'Yes. And it was the sound of a hill myna that helped me make the connection.'

'A hill myna? Really?'

'Yes. When I realised the connection, I became even more certain that my choice was right. Sita will be the perfect Vishnu, the ideal hero. Because the villain will never be able to bring himself to kill this hero.'

Arishtanemi bowed to his chief, in awe. 'You are truly worthy of being Lord Parshu Ram's torch-bearer, my lord.'

Vishwamitra acknowledged the compliment with a smile and said, 'Jai Parshu Ram.'

'Jai Parshu Ram,' repeated Arishtanemi. 'What now, Guruji?'

'Now, we use all our resources, our soldiers, our money— and Hanuman—to attack Lanka. Sita will destroy Raavan. And all of India will accept her as the Vishnu.'

'Why Hanuman? Considering he is close to… ' Arishtanemi stopped himself just in time. He had been about to name his guru's arch-rival, Vashishtha.

'Many reasons,' said Vishwamitra. 'The most important one being that Hanuman loves Sita like a sister. And Sita trusts him like she would a brother.'

Arishtanemi smiled, shaking his head in wonder. 'There is nobody like you, Guruji. No one else could have planned this.'

'Wait and see. I have no doubt that Mother India will be saved. And she will be saved by our Vishnu. We will be remembered forever for this. Our ancestors will be proud of us,' Vishwamitra declared.

Arishtanemi put his hands together in respect and said, *Jai Shri Rudra. Jai Parshu Ram.*

Glory to Lord Rudra. Glory to Lord Parshu Ram.

Vishwamitra repeated the chant of the Malayaputras. 'Jai Shri Rudra. Jai Parshu Ram.'

—१७१—

'Divodas! Turn around and face me!'

Vashishtha, known as Divodas during his gurukul days, turned to face the man who had once been his closest friend: Vishwamitra.

'Kaushik…' said Vashishtha, through gritted teeth, using the gurukul name of Vishwamitra. 'This is all your fault.'

Vishwamitra looked at the cremation pyre and then back at Vashishtha. 'She's dead because of you. Because you simply couldn't do what had to be done! Sigiriya and Trishanku were supposed to be—'

Vashishtha stepped closer, interrupting Vishwamitra. 'Don't you dare! She died because of you, Kaushik! She died because you insisted on doing something that should never have been done. I told you! I warned you!'

Vashishtha was thin and lanky to a fault. His head was shaved bare but for a knotted tuft of hair at the top of his head, which announced that he was a Brahmin. His flowing black beard gave him the look of a philosopher. At the moment, though, he looked anything but gentle. He was shaking with fury, fists clenched tight. Rage poured out of his eyes.

As tall as Vashishtha was, he was dwarfed by the strapping Vishwamitra, who stood facing him. Almost seven feet in height, dark-skinned and barrel-chested, with a muscular torso and a rounded belly, Vishwamitra intimidated people just by his presence. His long black beard and knotted tuft of hair flew wild and free in the wind. He looked like he was fighting for control, to stop himself from wringing Vashishtha's neck.

'*Get out of here,*' *snarled Vishwamitra.* '*I will not kill you in front of her.*'

Vashishtha stepped even closer and stared coldly at Vishwamitra. Their friendship was long dead. Its remains burned in the pyre that was consuming the woman they had both loved. From that same seething fire, a new enmity was being born. An enmity that would last more than a hundred years.

'*You think I am scared of you? Bring it on! Let's battle! Say when!*' *Vashishtha proclaimed.*

Vishwamitra raised his hand, then with great effort, controlled himself and stepped back. '*I will fulfil her dream. I will show her that I am better, better than you are.*'

'*You are nobody to do anything for her! She was mine. I will—*'

'Guruji!'

Vashishtha opened his eyes, coming back to the present from the ancient, nearly-century-old memory.

He said a quick prayer in his mind and asked, 'What happened?' He had sent his friend Hanuman to save them, to save Sita and Ram. He could only hope Hanuman had reached in time.

'We received word from Lord Hanuman, Guruji. I am sorry, but Raavan has kidnapped Princess Sita.'

'And Ram?'

'The Lankans killed all the Malayaputras who were with Princess Sita. But from what we've been told, Prince Ram and Prince Lakshman are still alive. Our Vishnu is safe. The news is not as bad as it first seemed.'

The Vayuputras had supported Vashishtha's decision to recognise Ram as the Vishnu. They too believed that it would be good for India. Technically, though, as the tribe of the previous Mahadev, they only had the right to recognise the next Mahadev and not the next Vishnu.

'The news *is* bad, my friend,' said Vashishtha. 'The war has been triggered.'

'But… but I am not sure Raavan wants a war, Guruji. We know that Lanka is very weak.'

'It doesn't matter what Raavan wants. He's a mere puppet. He's not the one who is behind this.'

'Then who is?'

'Vishwamitra.'

'But—' The Vayuputra messenger held his tongue. He knew of the animus between Vashishtha and Vishwamitra. The worst enemy you can have is someone who was once a dear friend. He knew better than to get in the way of a battle as titanic and malignant as that between Vashishtha and Vishwamitra.

'What do we do now, Guruji?'

Vashishtha's fists were clenched tight, his muscles tense. His eyes, normally kind and gentle, burned with fury. His face was a picture of determination.

'Now… we fight!'

… *to be continued.*

Other Titles by Amish

The Shiva Trilogy

The fastest-selling book series in the history of Indian publishing

THE IMMORTALS OF MELUHA
(Book 1 of the Trilogy)

1900 BC. What modern Indians mistakenly call the Indus Valley Civilisation, the inhabitants of that period knew as the land of Meluha – a near perfect empire created many centuries earlier by Lord Ram. Now their primary river Saraswati is drying, and they face terrorist attacks from their enemies from the east. Will their prophesied hero, the Neelkanth, emerge to destroy evil?

THE SECRET OF THE NAGAS
(Book 2 of the Trilogy)

The sinister Naga warrior has killed his friend Brahaspati and now stalks his wife Sati. Shiva, who is the prophesied destroyer of evil, will not rest till he finds his demonic adversary. His thirst for revenge will lead him to the door of the Nagas, the serpent people. Fierce battles will be fought and unbelievable secrets revealed in the second part of the Shiva trilogy.

THE OATH OF THE VAYUPUTRAS
(Book 3 of the Trilogy)

Shiva reaches the Naga capital, Panchavati, and prepares for a holy war against his true enemy. The Neelkanth must not fail, no matter what the cost. In his desperation, he reaches out to the Vayuputras. Will he succeed? And what will be the real cost of battling Evil? Read the concluding part of this bestselling series to find out.

The Ram Chandra Series

The second fastest-selling book series in the history of Indian publishing

RAM – SCION OF IKSHVAKU
(Book 1 of the Series)

He loves his country and he stands alone for the law. His band of brothers, his wife, Sita and the fight against the darkness of chaos. He is Prince Ram. Will he rise above the taint that others heap on him? Will his love for Sita sustain him through his struggle? Will he defeat the demon Raavan who destroyed his childhood? Will he fulfil the destiny of the Vishnu? Begin an epic journey with Amish's latest: the Ram Chandra Series.

SITA – WARRIOR OF MITHILA
(Book 2 of the Series)

An abandoned baby is found in a field. She is adopted by the ruler of Mithila, a powerless kingdom, ignored by all. Nobody believes this child will amount to much. But they are wrong. For she is no ordinary girl. She is Sita. Through an innovative multi-linear narrative, Amish takes you deeper into the epic world of the Ram Chandra Series.

Indic Chronicles
LEGEND OF SUHELDEV

Repeated attacks by Mahmud of Ghazni have weakened India's northern regions. Then the Turks raid and destroy one of the holiest temples in the land: the magnificent Lord Shiva temple at Somnath. At this most desperate of times, a warrior rises to defend the nation. King Suheldev —fierce rebel, charismatic leader, inclusive patriot. Read this epic adventure of courage and heroism that recounts the story of that lionhearted warrior and the magnificent Battle of Bahraich.

Non-fiction

IMMORTAL INDIA

Explore India with the country's storyteller, Amish, who helps you understand it like never before, through a series of sharp articles, nuanced speeches and intelligent debates. In *Immortal India*, Amish lays out the vast landscape of an ancient culture with a fascinatingly modern outlook.

DHARMA – DECODING THE EPICS FOR A MEANINGFUL LIFE

In this genre-bending book, the first of a series, Amish and Bhavna dive into the priceless treasure trove of the ancient Indian epics, as well as the vast and complex universe of Amish's Meluha, to explore some of the key concepts of Indian philosophy. Within this book are answers to our many philosophical questions, offered through simple and wise interpretations of our favourite stories.